THE ROUTLEDGE HANDBOOK
OF GREEK MYTHOLOGY

THE ROUTLEDGE HANDBOOK OF GREEK MYTHOLOGY

Based on
H.J. Rose's *Handbook of
Greek Mythology*

Robin Hard

Routledge
Taylor & Francis Group

LONDON AND NEW YORK

First published 2004
by Routledge

First published in paperback 2008
by Routledge
2 Park Square, Milton Park, Abingdon, Oxon, OX14 4RN

Simultaneously published in the USA and Canada
by Routledge
270 Madison Ave, New York, NY 10016

Reprinted 2009, 2010

Routledge is an imprint of the Taylor & Francis, an informa business

© 2004, 2008 Robin Hard

Typeset in Garamond by
Florence Production Ltd, Stoodleigh, Devon
Printed and bound in Great Britain by
TJ International Ltd, Padstow, Cornwall

British Library Cataloguing in Publication Data
A catalogue record for this book is available from
the British Library

Library of Congress Cataloging in Publication Data
A catalog record has been requested for this title

ISBN10 0–415–18636–6 (hbk)
ISBN10 0–415–47890–1 (pbk)
ISBN10 0–203–44633–X (ebk)
ISBN13 978–0–415–18636–0 (hbk)
ISBN13 978–0–415–47890–8 (pbk)
ISBN13 978–0–203–44633–1 (ebk)

In Memory of
LAUNCELOT FREDERIC HARD
1916–2002

CONTENTS

— ·◆· —

— Contents —

— Contents —

ILLUSTRATIONS

———— ·◆· ————

MAPS

FIGURES

xi

PREFACE

—— •◆• ——

Although this is essentially a new book in its present form, I originally embarked on it with the intention of producing a revised version of H.J. Rose's classic *Handbook of Greek Mythology*, and the final product remains indebted to that work in many respects, incorporating some material from it and following its general plan in parts, especially in the chapters on divine mythology. Herbert Jennings Rose (1883–1961), who was professor of Greek at St Andrews from 1927 to 1953, wrote extensively on ancient religion and mythology, publishing an edition of Hyginus' mythological manual in 1928, and was also an accomplished translator who introduced works of notable continental scholars such as M.P. Nilsson and R. Pettazzoni to an English-speaking audience. He remarks in the preface to his mythological handbook that he felt impelled to write it because, as a teacher of Classics, he had often felt handicapped by the lack of book of moderate length containing an accurate account of Greek mythology in accordance with the results of modern research; and the resulting volume, which was first published in 1928, certainly fulfilled a need among students and others who were interested in the subject. It has continued to be of service, moreover, in more recent times, even though many books of a related kind have been published since it first appeared, including various dictionaries of classical mythology and the two-volume surveys of Robert Graves (which has proved very popular in spite of its eccentricities) and Carl Kerényi (the second volume of which, *The Heroes of the Greeks*, was translated into English by Rose himself). After it had remained in print for seventy years, however, its present publishers thought it desirable that it should be revised to take account of advances in knowledge and the changing needs of its readership. The book has inevitably come to seem old-fashioned or even unreliable in certain respects. To take only one example, advances in archaeology and other disciplines and the decipherment of Linear B (a Mycenaean script) have affected our understanding of the origins and earliest history of some of the major gods (see e.g. p. 170). As a guide to the canon of Greek myth, the book also had one notable shortcoming from the beginning, namely that the coverage of heroic myth is disproportionately brief, especially when it is considered that Greek myth as recorded in classical literature consists predominately of heroic legend (for surprisingly few stories are recorded about the actions of the gods among themselves). I therefore undertook to prepare a revised edition by extending the coverage of this area of myth fairly considerably, with the addition of new chapters, and by altering or augmenting the text to a more limited extent elsewhere to take account of changing knowledge and requirements. The outcome turned out to be thoroughly unsatisfactory, too much of a dog's dinner to be at all palatable. If the original book had been blander, such an approach might have proved practicable; but it is in fact too personal, too idiosyncratic, to be amenable to discreet emendation and augmentation. It was necessary that a few gentle alterations should suffice or else that the book should be substantially rewritten; and having already progressed some way along the latter path, I decided to follow it to the end. Although the final work owes more of a debt to Rose's handbook than may be apparent at first sight, and I value that continuity, it is substantially longer and so different in much of its approach and content that it cannot be regarded as a replacement or substitute. I hope, indeed, that Rose's book may be kept in print for a while yet and perhaps even attain its centenary.

•➤• The names of deities and heroes and heroines from Greek myth are given in their original Greek form, except in a very few cases where it would seem absurdly pedantic to do so. Please see the introduction to the index for remarks on the pronunciation of Greek names and on the relationship between Greek and Latinized forms of those names. In the case of geographical names and the names of mythical and historical peoples, Anglicized and Latinized forms have been used much more frequently when it was considered that such forms would be used in normal conversation (e.g. Boeotia rather than Boiotia). Since ancient Greek authors are almost always referred to under the Anglicized or Latinized form of their name in conversation and in non-technical literature and library-indexes, it seemed preferable to use such forms to accord with normal usage and avoid any danger of confusion.

•➤• When Greek tales from Roman sources are summarized in the text, the mythical figures who appear in them will naturally be referred to under their proper Greek names rather than their Latin names as in the Latin sources. It should be remembered in this connection that the Romans liked to identify Greek gods with equivalent deities from the Roman and Italian tradition, and would refer to Greek gods under their Latin names when narrating myths from the Greek tradition. In the works of Roman authors such as Ovid and Hyginus, the main Greek deities will thus appear as follows:

Aphrodite as Venus
Ares as Mars
Artemis as Diana
Athena as Minerva
Demeter as Ceres
Dionysos often as Liber (if not as Dionysus or Bacchus)
Hephaistos as Volcanus (Anglicized to Vulcan)
Hermes as Mercurius (Anglicized to Mercury)
Hestia as Vesta
Kronos as Saturnus (Anglicized to Saturn)
Poseidon as Neptunus (Anglicized to Neptune)
Zeus as Iuppiter (Anglicized to Jupiter)

The name of Persephone was corrupted to Proserpina in Latin, that of Herakles to Hercules, and that of Leto to Latona. Other names were translated, e.g. Eros to Cupido or Amor, Pluto to Dis (see p. 108), Helios to Sol.

•✦• I have made my own translations when citing passages from Greek literature; these are intended above all to be clear and literal, and do not pretend to offer an adequate impression of the literary qualities of the original.

•✦• When indicating the time of origin of Greek writings and legends, and so on, it is often convenient or indeed necessary to refer to broad eras of Greek history rather than to specific centuries or dates. The *Archaic* period can be regarded as having extended from 800 or 750 BC to 480, i.e. from the end of the dark ages to the time of the Persian Wars; the *Classical* period from 480 to the death of Alexander the Great in 323 BC (or more loosely as extending over the fifth and fourth centuries, which was generally speaking the period of the greatest cultural achievements of the Greeks); the *Hellenistic* period from the death of Alexander to the end of the first century BC; and the *Roman* period from the first century AD onward (or more precisely from 31 BC, when Augustus defeated the forces of Antony and Cleopatra at the battle of Actium).

•✦• The names of mythical characters are marked in capitals at the beginning of the main discussion of their mythology; bold type is used to indicate that a succession of mythical characters belong to a common group under discussion, for instance as children of the same parents (as on p. 519) or as participants in a joint enterprise (as on p. 317).

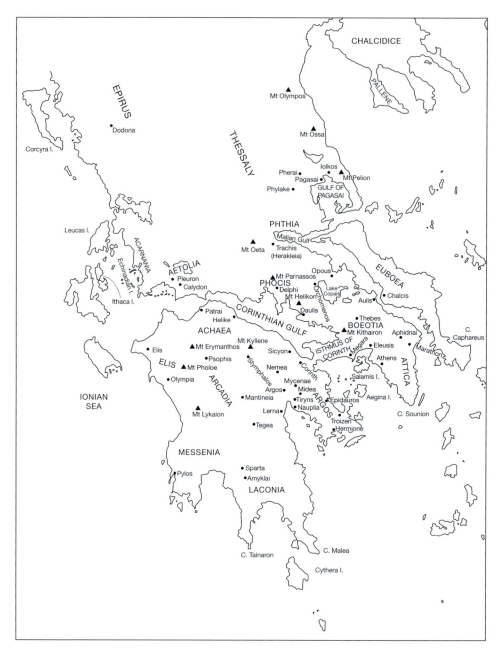

Map 1 Mainland Greece

Map 2 The Aegean area

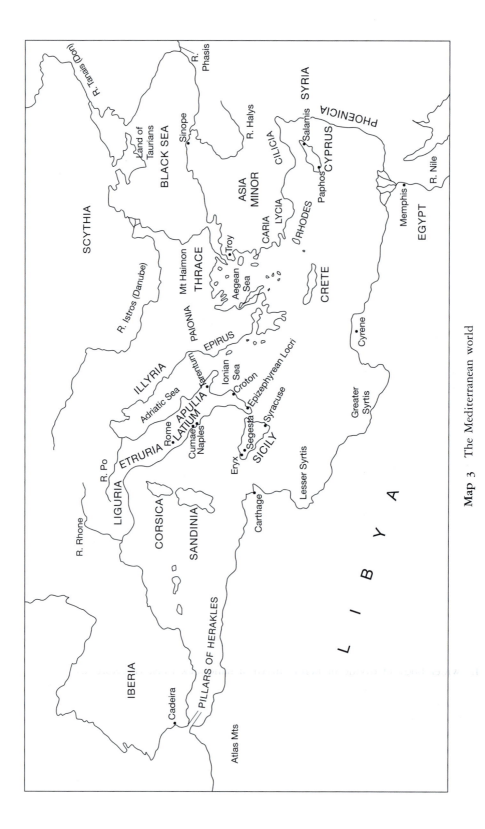

Map 3   The Mediterranean world

CHAPTER ONE

SOURCES FOR
GREEK MYTH

———— •◆• ————

The myths of the ancient Greeks, like the myths of most other cultures, were forever in a state of flux, undergoing constant change as they were passed on by word of mouth and retold in different ways by authors of successive ages. A handbook such as this must aim in the first place to provide a systematic account of the canon of early Greek myth, as initially established in archaic and classical poetic literature, especially early epic and tragedy, and then summarized and systematized in prose by the early mythographers. A good impression of the nature of the resulting vulgate or standard tradition, as conceived by mythographers of the Hellenistic or early Roman period, can be gained from the only general mythological handbook to survive from Greek antiquity, the *Library* of Apollodorus. The main myths and legends were organized into a pseudo-historical pattern to provide a remarkably coherent history of the universe and divine order and of the Greek world in the heroic era (which was conventionally thought to have ended in the period following the Trojan War); and this history was underpinned by rigorous systems of divine and heroic genealogy, which were essential if consistent chronologies were to be developed. The individual myths within this broad framework could be recorded in a variety of forms; even within the earlier literature, between the time, say, of Homer and that of Euripides, they could undergo a multitude of variations, and later developments could also leave their mark. Although powerful versions might tend to establish themselves in the general imagination at the expense of others, as in the case, for instance, of Aeschylus' account of the murder of Agamemnon (see p. 509), it is almost always misleading to talk as if there could be a standard version of a myth that was set in stone from some early time. Quite apart from merely narrating myths and placing them in their proper context within the wider body of divine or heroic myth, a handbook must therefore also attempt to trace the history of the more important myths, examining how they evolved over time and came to be narrated in differing ways by different authors in different genres. Since people who have an interest in Greek myth will not necessarily have any very extensive knowledge of ancient literature, and since some authors and writings that are important for myth are not widely familiar outside specialist circles, it was thought that it might thus be helpful to preface this handbook with a brief survey of the main literary sources for Greek myth. The relevant authors are listed separately in alphabetical order rather than discussed together in their historical setting to make it easier for readers to seek further information on authors or works of literature that are mentioned in the main text.

Cross-references to other authors are marked by an asterisk preceding the name of the author. For reasons indicated in the preface, ancient Greek authors are referred to under the Anglicized form of their name (which is often of Latin origin) even though figures from myth are referred to under the proper Greek form of their name. The authors who are named in the list were Greek (or at least wrote in Greek) unless otherwise stated. The history of Greece after the dark ages is conventionally divided into four main eras, the Archaic, Classical, Hellenistic and Roman; please see the preface for the significance of these terms.

ACUSILAUS of Argos (probably writing at the end of the sixth century BC), early mythographer who wrote about the legendary history of his native Argolid (see p. 230) and other regions, providing prose accounts of many legends from the epic tradition. Less is recorded about his writings than about those of his most important successors, *Pherecydes and *Hellanicus.

AELIAN (Claudius Aelianus, c. AD 172–235), prose author whose *Historical Miscellany* and anthology of animal stories contain some material of mythological interest. Translations of both are available in the Loeb series.

AESCHYLUS (525–456 BC), the earliest of the three great Athenian tragic poets whose works are not entirely lost. Of the eighty or ninety plays of Aeschylus, six of undoubted authenticity have survived. The three plays of the *Oresteia* trilogy, which portray a cycle of revenge within the Pelopid ruling family at Mycenae, are works of extraordinary profundity and resonance that can be ranked with the Homeric epics as the most imposing monuments of ancient literature. The first play in the trilogy, the *Agamemnon*, shows how the Mycenaean king of that name was murdered by his wife Klytaimnestra (Clytemnestra) after he arrived back from the Trojan War; and the next play, the *Libation-bearers* (*Choephoroi*), shows how Agamemnon's son Orestes, who was sent abroad before the murder and grew up in exile, returned to Mycenae to avenge his father's death by killing Klytaimnestra and her lover Aigisthos. The final play in the trilogy, the *Eumenides*, shows how Orestes was then persecuted by the Erinyes (Furies), even though Apollo had sanctioned the killings, until he was acquitted of matricide at Athens at a trial superintended by Athena (see p. 511). The other surviving plays are stiffer and less immediately engaging. The *Seven against Thebes*, the last play in a Theban trilogy, tells how seven champions from Argos confronted seven Theban defenders at the seven gates of Thebes during the first of the two Theban Wars (see p. 321); and the *Suppliants*, which was the last play in a trilogy devoted to the myth of the Danaids, tells how the fifty Danaids approached the Argives as suppliants after fleeing from Egypt to avoid marrying their cousins, the fifty sons of Aigyptos. There is very little direct action in either play; indeed, more than half of the latter is composed of choral lyrics. The *Persians* is one of the rare tragedies that dealt with historical subjects, in this case the defeat of Xerxes during the Persian Wars. As regards the *Prometheus*

Bound, the seventh play attributed to Aeschylus, there is disagreement on whether it is a genuine work of Aeschylus or was written at a slightly later period by another author (or at least heavily revised from a play by Aeschylus). It is remarkable in any case for its unusual portrayal of Zeus, who is presented as a newly established tyrant who exercises his power by the naked use of force. He has Prometheus nailed to a rock to punish him for having opposed his will by championing the interests of mortals; but Prometheus came to be released in a later play in the trilogy, and some sort of reconciliation must therefore have been achieved between Zeus and himself (see pp. 95–6).

ALCAEUS of Mytilene (born in the second half of the seventh century BC), an early lyric poet who was a contemporary and compatriot of Sappho.

ALCMAN (seventh century BC), early author of choral lyric who lived in Sparta.

ANTONINUS LIBERALIS (probably second century AD), mythographer, author of a surviving anthology of transformation myths, the *Collection of Metamorphoses*, which provides prose summaries of forty-nine stories of the kind. Most of the narratives are based on lost poetic accounts by two Hellenistic authors, *Nicander, who composed a poem in five books on mythical transformations, and a certain Boio or Boios (probably a pseudonym), who wrote a long poem called the *Ornithogonia* that contained rather artificial tales in which groups of people were turned into birds. There is an English translation by F. Celoria (London, 1992) and a French translation in the Budé series.

APOLLODORUS is the name traditionally ascribed to the author of the *Bibliotheke* or *Library*, the only comprehensive mythological handbook to have survived from classical antiquity. Although once regarded as a work of Apollodorus of Athens, a learned scholar of the second century BC who wrote about mythology and religion among other subjects, it is in fact a relatively late compilation of unpretentious character, probably written in the first or second century AD. The final sections of the book (dealing mainly with the Pelopids and the Trojan War) are preserved only in two prose epitomes discovered in the late nineteenth century; but the narrative is so concise throughout that most readers are unlikely to notice any change. The *Library* is in effect a mythical history of Greece, organized on a genealogical basis in accordance with the pattern established in the Hesiodic *Catalogue* (see under Hesiod) and followed by early prose mythographers such as *Pherecydes – the authority most frequently cited – and *Hellanicus; and since it is largely based on good early sources and very little has survived from the works of the early mythographers, it is extremely useful as a summary guide to the early vulgate tradition. Even if it may seem rather elementary in parts, it provides the best surviving accounts of many stories (hence the extensive use that has been made of it by compilers of mythological dictionaries and handbooks), and the stories are all placed in their proper context and accompanied by full genealogies. Translations are available in the Loeb series (in two volumes with useful references to other ancient sources) and Oxford World Classics.

APOLLONIUS of Rhodes (third century BC), a learned Hellenistic poet, author of the *Argonautica*, an epic in four books that recounts the story of Jason's quest for the golden fleece and his travels with the Argonauts. Since nothing has survived of early Argonautic epic, this is our main source for the legend along with the accompanying *scholia, which provide all manner of information on earlier versions of the story and local legends associated with the voyage and other relevant matters. From an artistic point of view, the poem is more impressive for its depiction of the changing feelings of Medeia and the love that develops between her and Jason than for its portrayals of heroic action. We also possess an incomplete *Argonautica* in Latin by a poet of the first century AD, Valerius Flaccus, and a curious late poem in Greek, the *Orphic Argonautica*, which is largely dependent on Apollonius (although it also borrows from other sources and offers a divergent account of the return journey of the Argonauts). A French translation of the latter poem may be found in the Budé series. The *Fourth Pythian Ode* of Pindar provides the fullest earlier account of the story of the Argonauts.

ARATUS (c. 315–240 BC), Hellenistic didactic poet, author of an extremely popular astronomical poem, the *Phaenomena*, which describes the constellations and their risings and settings on the basis of information provided by the great astronomer Eudoxus of Cnidus (active in the first half of the fourth century BC). Although Aratus lays no great emphasis on astral mythology, recounting or referring to such myths on only twelve occasions, his poem did much to encourage popular interest in the constellations and their myths. The standard collection of constellation myths was compiled somewhat later by *Eratosthenes in a prose treatise. The scholia to the *Phaenomena* have more to say about the matter, as do the Latin adaptations of the poem by Germanicus Caesar (15 BC–AD 19) and Avienus (fourth century AD).

ARISTOPHANES (born mid-fifth century BC), Athenian comic playwright, author of eleven surviving plays. Although not based directly on traditional myths as is usually the case with early tragedy, these are sometimes of value for what they reveal about particular myths or popular attitudes to myth and religion. The *Frogs*, in which Dionysos and his slave Xanthias make a visit to the land of the dead, may be singled out for what it reveals about the mythology and popular lore of the Underworld in the classical period.

ARISTOTLE (Aristoteles, 384–322 BC), philosopher with an encyclopaedic range of interest. His writings occasionally touch on mythological matters, and a spurious work in the Aristotelian corpus, *On Marvellous Things Heard*, records some curious mythological traditions relating to foreign parts. The remains of the pseudo-Aristotelian *Peplos* are of some interest for what they report about the fates of various warriors who fought at Troy.

ATHENAEUS (writing in about AD 200), author of the *Sophists' Banquet* (*Deipnosophistai*), an eccentric compilation in fifteen books that records more than anyone could possibly want to know about banquets and convivialities. Since Athenaeus draws on a wide range of sources and is never reluctant to provide a quotation, much of value that would otherwise have been lost, some of it relating to myth, is preserved among the dross. There is a translation with a full index in the Loeb series.

BACCHYLIDES (died mid-fifth century BC), lyric poet, a nephew of Simonides and contemporary of Pindar. Substantial remains of his epinician odes (choral odes written in honour of victors at the games) and six of his dithyrambs have been recovered from papyri discovered in the nineteenth century. The former poems are constructed in a similar manner to those of *Pindar, with a mythical narrative at their heart; and although Bacchylides lacks the dash and genius of his greater contemporary, he has distinctive gifts of his own as a storyteller. A good impression of this may be gained from the fifth of his epinician odes, which describes how Herakles met and conversed with the shade of Meleagros when he descended to the Underworld to fetch Kerberos, and was moved to tears by his account of his premature death. Another well-preserved ode describes how the daughters of Proitos, king of Tiryns, once offended Artemis and were stricken with madness until the goddess was appeased. The dithyrambs also contain attractive mythical narratives, describing for instance how Theseus proved to Minos that he was a son of Poseidon (see pp. 345–6) or first arrived in his ancestral homeland of Athens.

BION of Smyrna (late second century BC), a pastoral poet who is best known as the probable author of the *Lament for Adonis*.

CALLIMACHUS (c. 305–240 BC), Hellenistic poet and scholar who compiled the classified catalogue of the books in the library at Alexandria. His six *Hymns*, which are full of interesting mythological lore, have survived complete because some editor in late antiquity included them in a collection of hymns along with the *Homeric Hymns* and other poems of a comparable nature. Although modelled on the *Homeric Hymns*, they are altogether different in character, as would be expected, as highly sophisticated poems that are learnedly playful and often gently ironic in tone. The third hymn, addressed to Artemis, is particularly charming. The fifth tells how Teiresias came to be struck blind after seeing Athena naked (see p. 330), while the sixth describes how the Thessalian hero Erysichthon was punished with insatiable hunger after felling some trees in a grove of Demeter (see p. 133). Even if these poems may seem rather dry on first acquaintance, they can be very beguiling when one comes to appreciate their author's distinctive humour and tone of voice. The rest of his poetry is preserved in fragments alone, many recovered from papyri.

CICERO (106–43 BC), Roman politician, orator and prose writer, who sometimes refers to Greek legends and mythical matters in his religious and philosophical treatises.

COLLUTHUS (probably fifth century AD), author of the *Rape of Helen*, a mercifully short epic poem in 394 lines; translated in the Loeb series.

CONON (probably writing at the end of the first century BC or beginning of the next), mythographer, author a collection of fifty legends of varied nature in which foundation legends are especially prominent. It is preserved in an epitome prepared by the Byzantine scholar Photius (and a French translation is thus available in the Budé edition of Photius' *Library*).

DIODORUS SICULUS (i.e. of Sicily, first century BC), Greek Sicilian historian, author of a universal history in fourteen books. In contrast to historians of a more critical turn of mind, Diodorus did not exclude the period of legend from his survey, and the earlier books are thus of considerable value to the mythologist. As is understandable in a work with historical pretensions, he tended to favour rationalistic accounts from the Hellenistic period, but some of the material that he included as a consequence is of great interest in its own right, notably a report on *Euhemerus and extracts from two works of Dionysius Scytobrachion ('the Leather-armed', in reference to his prolific output) that offered novelistic versions of the myths of the Argonauts and the Amazons. The fourth book, however, which deals with the mythical history of the heartland of Greece, seems to have been largely based on a mythological handbook and includes more conventional material from the earlier vulgate. The biography of Herakles is worthy of special note since it provides a valuable supplement to that in *Apollodorus' handbook. There is an excellent translation in Loeb series.

DIONYSIUS of Halicarnassus (first century BC), Greek literary critic and historian. He lived at Rome for over twenty years, where he compiled the *Roman Antiquities* (*Romaikē Archaiologikē*), a long and indeed tiresomely prolix history of Rome from the earliest times up until the Punic Wars. The first book, which deals with the prehistory of the area and the origins and founding of the city, has much to say about Greek legend in so far as it relates to Rome and Italy.

EPIC CYCLE, and early epic in general (apart from the works of *Homer and *Hesiod). (i) The epic cycle was a collection of early epic poems that were ordered into a cycle to provide a chronological account of major episodes from Greek myth. Although there may well have been different collections that varied in their content, the poems that are described as cyclic in the surviving records are an obscure poem called the *Titanomachia*, which dealt with the earliest history of the world and the gods (presumably covering some of the same ground as the *Theogony*), and two series of heroic epics, a shorter series dealing with the family of Oedipus and the Theban Wars and a longer series dealing with the Trojan War and its origins and aftermath. (ii) Although very little is known about the *Titanomachia* and the Theban epics, we are better informed about the poems of the Trojan cycle, partly because more fragments and testimonies have been preserved, and partly because we possess short summaries of their contents that were compiled in the Roman period by a certain *Proclus. The first of the Trojan epics, the *Cypria*, explained the origins of the war and offered an account of its progress up until the period covered in the *Iliad*. The significance of its title is wholly uncertain. The *Aithiopis* picks up the story again where the *Iliad* leaves off, describing how the Amazon Penthesileia and the Ethiopian prince Memnon arrived to fight as allies of the Trojans (see pp. 446ff). It also described the death of Achilles, who was shot by Apollo and Paris as he was advancing toward the city after killing Memnon. The contents of the next two epics, the *Little Iliad* (*Ilias Mikra*) and the *Sack of Troy* (*Iliupersis*), seem to have overlapped to some extent. The former epic described the suicide of Aias (Ajax) and the events that immediately preceded the fall of Troy, and apparently went on to describe the sack itself, which was of course the subject of the latter poem. The *Returns* (*Nostoi*) provided a supplement to the *Odyssey* by describing the return journeys of the main Greek heroes other than Odysseus (see pp. 482ff), and the final epic in the series, a relatively late poem called the *Telegonia*, provided an eccentric account of the later life of Odysseus after his wanderings (see pp. 500–1). Proclus' summaries and fragments from the poems are translated in the Hesiod volume in the Loeb series. (iii) Although we know the names of many other archaic epic poems and epic poets, little or nothing is recorded about most of them. Various poets wrote epics about Herakles, for instance, including a Spartan called Cinaethon and a Rhodian called Peisander and, at a relatively late period, Herodotus' uncle Panyassis of Halicarnassus. Similar poems were written about Theseus, and the adventures of Jason and the Argonauts must also have been a popular subject; the *scholia to Apollonius tell us a certain amount about how the latter story was recounted in an early epic called the *Naupactia*. The legends of the Greek regions would also have been recounted in early epic; a poem called the *Phoronis* offered an account of the earliest history of the Argolid (see p. 227) and a Corinthian epic poet called Eumelus offered a distinctive account of the earliest history of his own land (see pp. 431–2). Since epic poems, oral and written, would have been the main literary medium for mythical narrative in the archaic period, it is salutary to remember how very little we know about these early epics. For a helpful guide to this area of Greek literature, with translations of relevant passages, see G.L. Huxley, *Greek Epic Poetry; Eumelos to Panyassis* (London, 1966).

ERATOSTHENES (c. 285–194 BC), versatile Alexandrian scholar who compiled the standard collection of constellation myths, the *Catasterisms* (*Katasterismoi*). The short book of that title that has been transmitted to us under his name is an epitome that was prepared by some later author; further information about the contents of the original work can be found in the *Astronomy* of *Hyginus and the scholia to *Aratus' *Phaenomena* and to Germanicus' Latin adaptation of that poem. A translation of the epitome and the relevant section of Hyginus' *Astronomy* can be found in Theony Condos, *Star Myths of the Greeks and Romans* (Grand Rapids, 1997).

EUHEMERUS of Messenia (writing in about 300 BC), author of the *Sacred Scriptures*, a book that explained the origin of the gods in rationalistic terms by suggesting that they had been great rulers and conquerors of the past who had come to be accorded divine honours. Although the original work is lost, much is known about it from what is recorded by *Diodorus (6.1, easily accessible in the Loeb translation) and Lactantius.

EURIPIDES (c. 485–406 BC), Athenian tragic poet, a slightly younger contemporary of Sophocles. Since two collections of his plays have survived, one an anthology put together in the Roman period and the other a section of an alphabetical edition of his complete works, we possess nineteen of his tragedies, far more than for Aeschylus and Sophocles. Seven relate to the Trojan War and its aftermath. The *Iphigeneia at Aulis* tells how that daughter of Agamemnon was brought to sacrifice to enable the Greek fleet to sail to Troy (see p. 447), while the *Iphigeneia in Tauris* tells how she was recovered from the distant land of the Taurians by her brother Orestes some years after the war (see pp. 512ff). The *Rhesus* (which may be wrongly ascribed to Euripides) dramatizes a tale from the *Iliad*, telling how the Thracian prince of that name was killed in his sleep by Odysseus and Diomedes after he arrived at Troy to fight as an ally of the Trojans. The *Trojan Women* (*Troades*) and the *Hecuba* (*Hekabe*) are poignant tragedies that portray the fate of leading women of Troy after the fall of the city. The *Helen* is a curious tragicomedy based on an unconventional version of Helen's legend in which a phantom of her accompanied Paris to Troy while she herself remained in Egypt during the years of the war (see p. 445). Hektor's widow Andromache was said to have become the concubine of Achilles' son Neoptolemos in Epirus after the war; Euripides' *Andromache* presents her as falling victim to the jealousy of Neoptolemos' childless wife Hermione, who plots unsuccessfully to kill her along with her young son (see p. 515). Three other tragedies of Euripides are devoted to Theban myth. The *Bacchae*, a very late work and perhaps the finest of the surviving plays, shows how Pentheus, king of Thebes, was visited with a gruesome punishment when he tried to outlaw the unbridled rites of Dionysos (see p. 173). The *Phoenician Women* is a very long play (apparently with a post-Euripidean ending) that deals with the quarrel between the sons of Oedipus and the resulting Theban War, while the *Suppliants* tells how the mothers of the Argive chieftains who were killed in the conflict sought the help of Theseus after the Thebans forbade the burial of the Argive dead. The plots of two tragedies that are devoted to stories from Athenian myth, the *Hippolytus* and the *Ion*, are summarized below on pp. 358–9 and 407–8. Three other plays deal with Herakles and his children. The *Alkestis* tells how Herakles saved Alkestis from death after she volunteered to die in place of her husband Admetos, while the *Madness of Herakles* tells how the hero rescued his family from a usurper at Thebes but then proceeded to slaughter his children in a fit of madness inspired by Hera. Soon after the death of Herakles, Eurystheus, king of Mycenae, tried to save himself from any future threat from the family by eliminating the hero's children; in the *Children of Herakles* (*Herakleidai*), Euripides shows how they appealed to the Athenians as suppliants and defeated and killed Eurystheus with their help. In the *Orestes*, the Mycenaean prince of that name narrowly escapes death after being brought to trial by the citizens of Argos for killing his mother Klytaimnestra and her lover Aigisthos; and the *Medea* (*Medeia*) shows how the Colchian heroine of that name exacted revenge on her husband Jason after he told her that he was planning to abandon her to marry a Corinthian princess (see p. 398). And finally, the *Cyclops* is the only complete satyr-play to survive from antiquity; it offers a comical version of the Homeric story of Odysseus and Polyphemos, in which Seilenos and his Satyrs are presented as having been taken prisoner by the ogre just before the arrival of Odysseus.

EUSTATHIUS (twelfth century AD), Byzantine scholar and churchman, author of long surviving commentaries on the *Iliad* and the *Odyssey*. These are of value in so far as they preserve material from the ancient scholarly tradition that would otherwise have been lost.

HELLANICUS of Lesbos (active in the second half of the fifth century BC), mythographer and author of writings on ethnography and chronology. More is recorded about his works than those of any other early mythographer apart from *Pherecydes. He compiled useful histories of various legendary families such as the Deukalionids and Atlantids, and left his mark on the subsequent tradition by refining and synchronizing the heroic genealogies. He was apparently an inelegant writer, however, whose narratives were less appealing than those of Pherecydes. Through his *Atthis*, a local history of Attica (which is mentioned by Thucydides, 1.97, though not with any great enthusiasm), he helped to inaugurate the distinctive genre of Atthidography (see p. 363).

HERODOTUS (fifth century BC), author of a long historical work in nine books, the *Histories* (*Historiai*, i.e. 'Investigations'), which provides an account of the conflict between Greece and Persia and its historical background. It is a very wide-ranging study that sets out to explain the growth of Persian power in relation to the histories of other lands outside Greece and developments within the Greek world itself. It is of great value as a source for legend and for matters relating to legend, all the more so since the author is always willing to digress and can never resist a good story.

HESIOD (c. 700 BC), Boeotian epic and didactic poet. (i) Two surviving poems, the *Theogony* and the *Works and Days*, can be regarded as genuine works of Hesiod (even if it is not universally agreed that they can be ascribed to the same poet). One further poem, the *Shield*, which was certainly not of his authorship, has been transmitted to us under his name, and a number of other poems are ascribed to him in ancient sources. Very little is known of most of these other poems, but one of them, the *Catalogue of Women*, which was again of post-Hesiodic origin, was a mythological poem of considerable importance that can be partially reconstructed from many surviving fragments and testimonies. (ii) The *Theogony* (*Theogonia*, i.e. birth or generation of the gods) provides a comprehensive genealogical history of the origins of the gods, explaining how the universe and the main gods and goddesses came into being, and how the present divine order came to be established under the third ruler of the universe, Zeus. Since this was not only a very ancient account of these matters but came to be accepted as the standard account, the poem is a mythological document of the first importance, and we will take it as our main guide in Chapter 2 and much of Chapter 3. It also describes how Zeus quelled a revolt by the fearsome monster Typhon. The end of the poem was altered when the *Catalogue of Women* was appended to it, but although it is accepted that part of the concluding section of the present text is post-Hesiodic, scholars have disagreed as to where exactly the genuine work of Hesiod breaks off. The most distinguished modern editor of the poem, M.L. West, has argued that the end comes at line 900, while others would place it later at line 929 or 962. (iii) As a poem that is mostly about farming and favourable and unfavourable days of the month, the *Works and Days* is less relevant to our subject, except in the two sections of the poem that narrate the story of the first woman Pandora (42–105) and the myth of the five races (106–201, see pp. 69–70). (iv) The only other complete poem to be preserved under Hesiod's name is the *Shield* (*Aspis*), a short work in 480 lines that describes how Herakles defeated the Thessalian villain Kyknos and his divine father Ares in two successive fights (see p. 282). The poem is known as the *Shield* because more than a third of it is devoted to a description of the images on Herakles' shield, in a passage that was evidently modelled on Homer's description of the shield of Achilles in the *Iliad*. It is prefaced with an *ehoie* (see below) from the *Catalogue* relating to Alkmene and was presumably written after that poem in the sixth century BC. A translation can be found in the Hesiod volume in the Loeb series; since the author was too incompetent to be able to organize his material properly or bring his subject to life, the poem cannot be said to be anything more than a historical curiosity. (v) Most of the other poems that were ascribed to Hesiod are little more than names to us. They include an astronomical poem known as the *Astronomia* and a book of moral precepts known as the *Maxims of Cheiron*, and mythological poems such as the *Melampodia*, which recounted the legends of Melampous and other seers (providing for instance an account of the contest in divination between Mopsos and Kalchas, see p. 488), and the *Aigimios*, which is named after a Dorian associate of Herakles but apparently recounted a variety of legends including that of Io. (v) The genealogical epic known as the *Catalogue of Women* – or simply the *Catalogue* – is the only pseudo-Hesiodic poem (apart of course from the *Shield*) of which we possess substantial remains. Well after the lifetime of Hesiod, probably in the early sixth century BC, some unknown author decided to write a continuation to the *Theogony* so as to provide a genealogical history of the main heroic families also. As was noted above, the end of the *Theogony* was altered quite radically to prepare for the transition to this new subject-matter, as can be appreciated from the present state of the text. Since the origin of each of the main heroic lines was traced to a mating between a god and a mortal woman, the new poem (or relevant portion of the combined poem) came to be known as the *Catalogue of Women*; it was also called the *Ehoiai* because the story of each of these women was introduced with the formulaic phrase *ē hoiē*, 'or like she who . . .'. From its semi-divine beginning, each heroic line would have been followed down to the period of the Trojan War or thereabouts, and the principal legends associated with the members of the line would have been narrated, usually quite briefly, as the successive heroes and heroines were introduced. It was a work of the first importance, comparable in its own way to the *Theogony*, because it established the panhellenic system of heroic genealogy that was adopted and refined by the early prose mythographers (such as *Pherecydes and *Hellanicus) and can still be recognized, though with many variations from the later tradition, in the mythological handbook of *Apollodorus. In tracing the histories of such families as the Inachids, Deukalionids and Atlantids in the second part of the present handbook, we will be following the lines that were laid down by the Catalogue-poet. Although no manuscripts of the poem have survived, a fair number of quotations and testimonies can be found in the works of ancient authors, and many additional fragments, some quite extensive, have been recovered from papyri. As a consequence, a surprising amount has come to be known about the structure of the poem, and parts of it can be reconstructed in some detail; for a full discussion, see M.L. West, *The Hesiodic Catalogue of Women* (Oxford, 1985). Many of the individual fragments are translated in the Hesiod volume in the Loeb series, but they lose much of their meaning when taken out of context. There is an Italian parallel translation of the standard edition of Merkelbach and West (from *Fragmenta Hesiodea*, Oxford, 1967) in the Hesiod volume in the French Pléiade series; it may be hoped that someone will publish a similar translation in English one day.

HOMER (probably late eighth century BC). (i) The *Iliad* and the *Odyssey*, the national epics of the Greeks, were traditionally ascribed to a poet called Homer (Homeros), on whom we have no trustworthy information. There is disagreement on whether the two poems can be ascribed to the same author (and indeed on whether each of them was basically the work of a single author, although scholars have been less inclined to attempt to trace different sections to different origins since greater understanding has been gained of the process of creation in oral poetry). There is good reason to suppose that they were composed in Ionia on the west coast of Asia Minor. They certainly contain some later interpolations, even if these cannot always be recognized with any assurance. (ii) In contrast to the usual pattern in epic, in which a succession of episodes would be described in simple chronological order and the traditional history of the war or adventure or whatever provided the principle of unity, the entire narrative of the *Iliad* is ordered around a single incident in the tenth year of the Trojan War – the anger and withdrawal of Achilles – and the time-span is comparatively restricted. The main action is concentrated in a period of only four days and nights, and the span of the whole story does not extend beyond fifty-one days; but the poem is artfully constructed so as to make it seem that it epitomizes the entire trajectory of the war. The articulating theme of the poem, as announced in the first line, is the wrath of Achilles, the mightiest of the Greek warriors, who withdraws from the fighting in anger at being deprived of his captive maiden Briseis by the Greek commander Agamemnon, giving the Trojans an opportunity to advance out of their city and place the Greek army under severe threat; but after his closest friend Patroklos is killed, he returns to the battlefield to seek vengeance and drives the Trojans back, killing many of them including their greatest warrior, Hektor. A full summary of the plot may be found on pp. 462ff. (iii) The poem makes many allusions to the preceding history of the war and to its conclusion and aftermath, and also refers to events from the earlier lives of the participants and to stories from other cycles of legend and from divine mythology. The loquacious Nestor likes to reminisce about his youthful adventures in the western Peloponnese, and Phoinix recounts the story of the Aetolian hero Meleagros while trying to persuade Achilles to return to the fight (see p. 417); but full narratives of stories that have no direct connection with the war are naturally infrequent. The long muster-list in the second book (the so-called 'catalogue of ships', 2.493–759) preserves a large amount of very ancient information about the geography of Greece in the legendary era and the heroic families that were supposed to have ruled in it. A useful summary of the mythical history of Troy is provided by Aineias in the twentieth book (208–40). The poem also has much to say about the lives and characters of the gods. It records two versions, for instance, of myth in which the young Hephaistos was said to have been hurled down from Olympos (see p. 165). (iv) The hero of the *Odyssey*, Odysseus, was a cunning and resourceful warrior who came from the island of Ithaca off the west coast of Greece. The epic describes how he wandered through distant seas for ten long years after being driven far off course while sailing home from Troy, and exacted vengeance on his return against a crowd of local noblemen who had been revelling in his palace during his absence, squandering his property and courting his wife. See pp. 492ff for a summary of his adventures. The epic falls into three main parts. The first four books (the so-called *Telemachia*) tell how Telemachos, the young son of Odysseus, visited Nestor at Pylos and Menelaos at Sparta to seek news of his missing father; the next eight books (5–12) describe the adventures of Odysseus in foreign seas, partly as narrated by Odysseus himself at a banquet in his last port of call (9–12); and the last twelve books tell how he arrived home in Ithaca, exacted vengeance against the suitors after due preparation, and was reunited with his faithful wife Penelope. In books 3 and 4, the poem reveals a fair amount about the events that immediately followed the sack of Troy, and about how other heroes, including Agamemnon, fared during their return voyages and after arriving home (see pp. 482ff).

HOMERIC HYMNS, a collection of thirty-three poems in epic metre addressed to various greater and lesser deities. Although widely ascribed to Homer in ancient times, they are in fact of varied authorship and were composed at widely differing times, ranging from the seventh or eighth century BC to the fifth century or even later. While many are no more than brief preludes (*prooimia*) that would be chanted by rhapsodes before epic recitations, a few are substantial narrative poems of considerable charm that describe important episodes in the lives of the gods. The *Hymn to Demeter* (no. 2) tells how the corn-goddess Demeter searched for her daughter Persephone after she was abducted by Hades, and finally forced Zeus to take action on her behalf by causing the earth to remain barren and so depriving the gods of their sacrifices (see pp. 126ff). The poem explains the origin of the Eleusinian Mysteries and alludes to various aspects of Eleusinian cult, and was presumably composed in the area of Eleusis, perhaps in the late seventh century BC. The *Hymn to Apollo* (3), which may well have been put together from two originally separate poems, describes how Leto came to give birth to her divine twins Apollo and Artemis on the island of Delos, and goes on to explain how Apollo came to establish his oracle and shrine at Delphi (see pp. 144 and 188). The *Hymn to Hermes* (4), which is broadly humorous in tone, describes how the infant Hermes set off to rustle the cattle of Hermes on the day of his birth, but reached an accommodation with Apollo soon afterwards and was assigned his main functions as a god (see pp. 161ff). The longer of the two hymns addressed to Aphrodite, the fifth, describes how the goddess seduced Anchises, a member of the Trojan royal family, on Mount Ida in the Troad and conceived Aineias to him (see pp. 200–1ff). The much shorter *Hymn to Dionysos* (7) describes how some pirates tried to abduct the god in his youth, provoking him to transform them into dolphins after first working some miracles as a manifestation of his power (see p. 177). The short *Hymn to Pan* (19) is also of some interest for its description of the nature and birth of the goat-footed god. Translations are available in the Hesiod volume in the Loeb series and elsewhere; they make delightful reading even in a plain prose translation.

HYGINUS (Gaius Julius Hyginus), a learned freedman of Augustus who became the librarian of the Palatine Library, the putative author of two works of mythological interest, the *Fabulae* (i.e. *Mythical Tales*, also known as the *Genealogiae*), a handbook of mythology, and the *Astronomia*, a popular treatise on astronomy. Both books were compiled from Greek sources. Since their author was a scholar of limited competence who could make elementary mistakes in translating from the Greek, it is generally agreed that these cannot be genuine works of Hyginus, and they were probably written after his time in the second century AD. The 220 chapters of the *Fabulae* consist either of brief mythological narratives or of catalogues (e.g. of mothers who killed their sons, persons who were suckled by animals, inventors and their inventions). Although the sources of the narratives are rarely indicated, the book seems to draw most heavily on tragic sources. The second book of the *Astronomia* contains the fullest surviving collection of constellation myths, derived mainly from *Eratosthenes. English translations of the *Fabulae* and this 'poetic astronomy' may be found in Hyginus, *The Myths*, ed. and trans. M. Grant (Lawrence, Kansas, 1960), and there are good French translations, with useful notes, in the Budé series.

LUCIAN (Loukianos, second century AD), orator and prose-writer of Syrian birth who quite often touches on mythological matters in his copious works. In some of his satirical dialogues, most notably the *Dialogues of the Gods* and *Dialogues of the Sea-gods*, he makes fun of the traditional portrayal of the gods and traditional themes from myth, while other works, such as the *Charon* and the *Dialogues of the Dead*, are of interest in relation to traditional ideas about the afterlife and Underworld.

LYCOPHRON (born c. 320 BC), Hellenistic poet, author of a mythological puzzle-poem, the *Alexandra*, in which the Trojan seer Kassandra delivers riddling prophecies about the fall of Troy and the subsequent fates of those who took part in the war. Although not exactly pleasurable reading, it is of great value as a source of mythological information if read in conjunction with the extensive ancient *scholia and the Byzantine commentary of John Tzetzes. Particular attention is devoted to the Italian West. Primarily on account of a seemingly anachronistic reference to Roman power (1227ff), some scholars have argued that the poem must have been written somewhat later by another author in the second century BC.

MIMNERMUS (second half of the sixth century BC), elegiac poet. The fragments of one of his poems, the *Nanno*, contain interesting mythical allusions to Jason's quest and to Helios' nightly journey to the place of his rising (see pp. 43–4).

MOSCHUS of Syracuse (second century BC), bucolic poet, author of an attractive epyllion or miniature epic, the *Europa*, which tells how Zeus assumed the form of a bull to abduct the heroine of that name from Phoenicia to Crete.

MUSAEUS (probably late fifth century AD), author of an attractive miniature epic that tells the tragic story of Hero and Leandros, two lovers who lived on opposite banks of the Hellespont (see p. 577); a translation may be found in the Loeb series (in the same volume as the fragments of Callimachus).

NICANDER of Colophon (second century BC), Hellenistic poet. Two of his didactic poems, the *Theriaka* and *Alexipharmaka* (which dealt with poisonous animals and antidotes to poisons respectively), have survived intact, but he was of greater importance from a mythological point of view for his lost *Heteroioumena* (i.e. *Metamorphoses*), a collection of transformation myths. *Ovid drew on the poem when writing his *Metamorphoses*, and *Antoninus Liberalis provides summaries of some of the stories recounted in it.

NONNUS (probably fifth century AD), of Panopolis in Egypt, author of the *Dionysiaca*, an interminable epic in forty-eight books that deals with Dionysos and his expedition to India; translated in the Loeb series.

OVID (Publius Ovidius Naso, 70–19 BC), Roman poet who had an extensive knowledge of Greek myth and Alexandrian poetry. His most ambitious poem, the *Metamorphoses*, is a collection of transformation legends in fifteen books. The poem begins with the origin of the universe and ends with the apotheosis of Romulus, and the intervening stories are skilfully woven together with regular alterations in tone to ensure that it forms a unified epic-style poem. Except in the last two books, which are devoted to Roman and Italian matters, the stories are drawn almost exclusively from Greek legend. Some were quite ancient while others originated in the more recent literature, for transformations were a popular theme among Hellenistic poets such as *Nicander. Most of the fictional letters in Ovid's *Heroides* are addressed from heroines of Greek legend to their lovers or husbands, and the poet also refers to Greek myths elsewhere in his poems.

PALAEPHATUS (probably fourth century BC), author of the *Incredible Tales* (*Peri Apiston*), a mythographical work that provides rationalistic (if highly implausible) explanations for the origins of seemingly impossible tales from heroic legend, for instance those that involve monsters. The author, who may have written under a pseudonym, was apparently an associate of Aristotle who was active in the latter part of the fourth century BC; if that is the case, the book provides the earliest evidence for a number of important legends. A translation and commentary is available, by J. Stern (Wauconda, Illinois, 1996). A similar work of later origin has been transmitted to us under the name of Heraclitus. In contrast to *Euhemerus and his followers, such authors did not attempt to rationalize divine myths.

PARTHENIUS of Nicaea (first century BC), late Hellenistic poet and mythographer, author of *Sufferings in Love* (*Erōtika Pathēmata*), a collection of prose summaries of thirty-six love-stories, mostly obscure and of relatively late origin. In relation to early myth, many are of interest for the way in which standard motifs from earlier myth are recycled in them. Translations are available in the Loeb series and in J.L.

Lightfoot's recent edition of the works of Parthenius (Oxford, 1999, with illuminating discussions and commentary).

PAUSANIAS (second century AD), author of a *Description of Greece* in ten books, covering the entire Peloponnese and much of Central Greece. Pausanias visited all the main towns and other sites of interest in these areas to investigate their traditions and topography, monuments and antiquities, and cults and local mythology. The resulting work is a source of the very highest value for the mythologist. It records local traditions about the ancient history of the cities and lands that he passed through, and many legends that were attached to local monuments and landmarks; and although it has to be remembered that he collected this local material at a relatively late period, he also preserves a large amount of information that relates unquestionably to the early mythical tradition, both in references to early literature (for he was widely read and was willing to extend his reading to seek answers to specific questions) and in descriptions of early works of art such as the mural paintings of Polygnotos (fifth century BC) or the chest of Kypselos (sixth century). For mythological purposes at least, the edition in the Loeb series is to be preferred to the Penguin translation, which omits some heroic genealogies without any immediate warning and translates some Greek names into English in a haphazard and confusing manner.

PHERECYDES of Athens (probably active in the first half of the fifth century BC), early mythographer, a prolific writer who compiled comprehensive accounts of the legendary history of Greece, drawing most of his material from early epic and organizing it on a genealogical basis in accordance with the procedure developed in the Hesiodic *Catalogue* (see under Hesiod). These works of Pherecydes, which were known as the *Historiai* or *Genealogiai*, were published by the Alexandrian scholars in an edition in ten books, and were very widely consulted by scholars and poets as a standard source for narratives from early legend. As we know from a few surviving passages, the stories were recounted with pleasing simplicity in a naïve paratactic style. Although no manuscripts of Pherecydes' writings have been transmitted to us, we know a fair amount about their contents, largely because the scholiasts refer to them with notable frequency. *Apollodorus cites Pherecydes by name thirteen times in his little manual, more than any other authority, and uses him as his main source in some sections of the book (for instance in his account of the life of Perseus).

PINDAR (c. 518–438 BC), author of choral lyric, perhaps the greatest lyric poet of ancient Greece. In addition to numerous fragments, four complete books of his poetry have survived, consisting of odes that he wrote in honour of victors at the four main athletic festivals, the Olympian, Pythian, Nemean and Isthmian Games. These epinician odes (i.e. 'odes of victory') are of greater value as sources of myth than might be supposed, for the poet rarely devotes many lines to the victory or victor but soon passes on to a mythical narrative after a short prelude, and devotes much of the poem to the myth before returning to praise the victor and his prowess or good fortune at the end. His victory is most effectively ennobled by being presented against this mythical background. The myth could be introduced on a variety of pretexts, typically in connection with the family history of the victor or with the traditions of his homeland or the place of his victory. Although the narratives may be quite long, they are rarely developed in a straightforward chronological manner as in epic poetry, for the poet tends to concentrate on particular aspects of the story that are relevant to his 'argument', and to start in the middle of the story and range backwards and forwards in time. Pindar recounts or refers to a great many myths in his poems, and provides the first surviving mention or proper account of many a story. Three full and relatively straightforward narratives may be singled out by way of example. In his *Seventh Olympian Ode*, Pindar explains how the Sun-god Helios came to win the island of Rhodes as his special domain (see p. 43); in his *Ninth Pythian Ode*, he tells how Apollo abducted the nymph Kyrene to North Africa as his mistress after seeing her wrestling with a lion in her native Thessaly (see p. 152); and in his *Sixth Olympian Ode*, he describes the birth, exposure and rescue of the seer Iamos (see p. 548). The oldest detailed account of the very ancient myth of the Argonauts may be found in the *Fourth Pythian Ode*.

PLATO (c. 429–347 BC), Athenian philosopher and author of philosophical dialogues. Although his writings cannot be said to be of any great value as a source for myth (except perhaps in relation to the mythology of the Underworld and afterlife), they are full of mythological allusions and contain distinctive philosophical myths of Plato's own invention.

PLINY the Elder (Gaius Plinius Secundus, AD 23/4–79), Roman writer, author of a *Natural History* in thirty-seven books, an encyclopaedia of the natural world that records a vast amount of miscellaneous information.

PLUTARCH (mid-first century AD until after 120), author of biographies and of essays and dialogues on moral, religious and other subjects. He quite often touches on mythological matters in the latter works (which are known collectively as the *Moralia*). The apocryphal myths in the pseudo-Plutarchean *Greek and Roman Parallel Stories* and *On Rivers* should not be taken too seriously. A very useful life of Theseus may be found among Plutarch's biographies, but his life of Herakles is lost (which would be more regrettable if we did not possess full accounts of that hero's life by Diodorus and Apollodorus).

PROCLUS, the author of some surviving summaries of the Trojan epics in the *epic cycle. It is not known whether the Proclus in question was the Neoplatonic philosopher of that name (fifth century AD) or a grammarian of the second century AD.

QUINTUS of Smyrna (probably fourth century AD), author of a late epic poem in fourteen books, the *Posthomerica*, which was written to provide a synoptic account of the final stages and conclusion of the Trojan War after the poems of the *epic cycle had ceased to be read (or at least fallen from favour). It describes all that took place after the period covered in the *Iliad*, ending with the sack of Troy and the perilous return voyage of the conquering army. Although Quintus would have drawn much of his material from fairly late sources, he was deliberately conservative in his choice of sources, taking care to avoid novelistic or revisionist accounts. A translation is available in the Loeb series; although there are some attractive passages, the poem as a whole is long-winded and artificial and does not often come to life.

SAPPHO of Lesbos (born late seventh century BC), author of lyric poetry, mainly of an intimate character.

SCHOLIA, ancient explanatory notes preserved in the margins of ancient writings. Since myth so often provided the subject-matter for Greek poetry and drama, many of these are inevitably devoted to mythological matters, narrating myths to account for allusions in the text in question, explaining specific points that arise from narratives in the text, citing parallels and variants from other sources (often from literature that is lost to us), and so on. Most of what we know of early mythographers such as *Pherecydes and *Hellanicus is derived from scholia. The scholia to the Homeric epics and to Pindar, Euripides, Apollonius and Lycophron are particularly valuable as sources of mythological information. Latin scholia can also be useful to the student of Greek mythology, notably the scholia to the poems of Vergil and the Theban epic of Statius.

SENECA (c. 40 BC–AD 65), Roman politician, philosopher and writer, author of nine melodramatic tragedies that were based on stories from Greek legend and modelled on plays of the Attic tragedians, especially Euripides, namely the *Hercules Furens*, *Hercules on Oeta*, *Medea*, *Phaedra*, *Oedipus*, *Thyestes*, *Agamemnon*, *Troades* and *Phoenissae*.

SERVIUS (fourth century AD), Roman scholar who is best remembered as the author of a commentary on the poems of *Vergil. The longer version of his commentary (known as *Servius auctus* or *Servius Danielis*) incorporates material from other authors. These and other ancient notes on Vergil's works contain valuable reports on Greek legend, preserving some stories that are recorded in no other source.

SIMONIDES (c. 556–468 BC), lyric poet. Far less of his poetry survives than is the case with his nephew Bacchylides and great successor Pindar, and little of what does survive has anything to do with myth. This is a shame because he seems to have had gifts of his own as a narrative poet who was capable of writing with great simplicity and pathos. These qualities are shown to the full in a wonderful little poem (543 *PMG*) in which Danae sings a sad lament to her sleeping baby Perseus as they are drifting through rough seas in a little chest (see p. 239). We have to rely in the main on scholiasts' reports for an idea of how Simonides recounted other myths.

SOPHOCLES (c. 496–406 BC), Athenian tragic poet, a contemporary of Euripides. The most widely familiar of his seven surviving plays are those that portray the sad fate of Oedipus and his daughter Antigone. In *Oedipus the King* (*Oidipous Tyrannos*), Sophocles shows how it finally came to be revealed that Oedipus had unknowingly killed his father and married his mother; and the *Oedipus at Colonus*, a very late work, portrays the last hours of the blind and exiled king of Thebes, describing how he died in mysterious circumstances at Colonus (Kolonos) in Attica after arriving there with Antigone as his guide. Antigone herself is the heroine of the *Antigone*, which tells how she provoked her own death by attending to the burial of her brother Polyneikes in contravention of a decree of Kreon, king of Thebes. Two of the other plays of Sophocles are set in the final period of the Trojan War, namely the *Ajax* (or *Aias* in Greek), which tells how the mighty warrior of that name came to commit suicide after being defeated in a contest for the arms of the dead Achilles (see p. 470), and the *Philoktetes*, which tells how the great archer of that name was finally recovered from the island of Lemnos after being marooned there by his comrades (see pp. 449–50). The *Women of Trachis* (*Trachiniai*) deals with the events that led up to the death of Herakles, while the *Elektra* portrays the predicament of Elektra, daughter of Agamemnon, at Mycenae after the murder of her father. The action of the latter play is set at the time when Elektra's brother Orestes returns to avenge the murder. Substantial remains of one of Sophocles' satyr-plays, the *Trackers* (*Ichneutai*), have been recovered from papyri; it tells how Seilenos and his crew of cowardly Satyrs tracked down the infant Hermes after his theft of Apollo's cattle.

STATIUS (Publius Papinius Statius, c. 45–96 AD), Roman poet, author of the *Thebais*, a Theban epic in twelve books that tells the story of the conflict between the two sons of Oedipus. He also embarked on an epic account of the life of Achilles, the *Achilleis*, of which only two books were completed.

STEPHANUS of Byzantium (c. sixth century AD), author of a large geographical lexicon, the *Ethnica*, which contained information on mythological and historical matters. Although we possess very little of the original text, its contents are partially preserved in a surviving epitome.

STESICHORUS (first half of the sixth century BC), Greek Sicilian lyric poet. Although classed as an author of choral lyric, Stesichorus wrote long narrative poems that seem to have had more in common with epic than with conventional lyric poetry. Among the many mythical subjects that are known to have been treated by him are the hunt for the Calydonian boar, Herakles' theft of the cattle of Geryon (probably providing the basis for Apollodorus' account of that episode, see p. 264), Eriphyle's betrayal of her husband, the sack of Troy, and the revenge of Orestes; but although his poems apparently exerted a considerable influence on the development of the mythical tradition, almost nothing is preserved of them. Stesichorus himself became a subject of legend, as we will see (p. 583), for he was said to have written a poem of recantation to win back his eyesight after he had been blinded by Helen for insulting her in one of his poems.

STRABO (c. 64 BC–AD 19), historian and geographer, author of a surviving geographical treatise in seventeen books. The bulk of the work is a descriptive regional geography of the known world, compiled chiefly from secondary sources.

Since Strabo is primarily interested in the world as a habitation for man and a setting for human activities and history, he quite often has occasion to refer to mythological matters in relation to the traditions and historical background of the areas that he surveys. His respect for Homer's authority encouraged him to include antiquarian material. A translation with a good index can be found in the Loeb series.

THEOCRITUS (active in the first half of the third century BC), a Hellenistic poet who is best remembered as the founder of the ancient genre of bucolic or pastoral poetry, although he was actually more versatile than this might suggest. His poems (apart from the epigrams) are traditionally known as *Idylls*, but it should not be inferred from this that all are idyllic in the modern sense since the term could originally be applied to poems that contained a wide range of subject-matter; one of the finest of Theocritus' idylls is a thus a portrayal of city-life in which two chattering women set off from home to attend a festival of Adonis, while others are mythical narratives in miniature epic form. *Idyll* 13, the *Hylas*, tells how Herakles' favourite of that name was snatched away by amorous spring-nymphs; *Idyll* 24, the *Herakliskos* (*Little Herakles*), tells how the infant Herakles strangled two snakes that were sent against him by Hera; *Idyll* 22, the *Hymn to the Dioskouroi*, tells how Polydeukes confronted the brutal Amykos in a lethal boxing-match (see p. 386), and then offers a rather unusual account of the conflict between the Dioskouroi and the sons of Leukippos (see p. 529). From among the spurious poems in the Theocritean corpus, *Idyll* 25, *Herakles the Lion-killer*, is worthy of mention, and others too, genuine and spurious, are of mythological interest; *Idyll* 6, for instance, is a pastoral poem in which two shepherds sing of the love of Polyphemos and Galateia. We possess poems by two of Theocritus' successors, *Moschus and *Bion, and there is an anonymous poem of related type, the *Megara*, in which the wife and mother of Herakles talk to one another of their sorrows. The poems of Theocritus are translated along with those of his successors in the volume in the Loeb series entitled *The Greek Bucolic Poets*, and other translations can be found elsewhere.

THEOGNIS (sixth century BC), elegiac poet of aristocratic temper; almost 1,400 lines of verse, evidently of varied origin, are preserved under his name, but only a handful are of mythological interest.

THUCYDIDES (died c. 400 BC), author of a history of the Peloponnesian War which is the most impressive exercise in historical analysis to have been attempted by any ancient author. The work starts with a short account of the earlier history of Greece extending back into the period of legend (chapters 2–19 of the first book, known as the *archaiologia*).

TRYPHIODORUS (probably fifth century AD), author of the *Capture of Troy*, a short epic in 691 lines; translated in the Loeb series.

VALERIUS FLACCUS (writing in the latter part of the first century BC), Roman poet, author of an incomplete Argonautic epic, the *Argonautica*.

VATICAN MYTHOGRAPHERS, the name ascribed to the authors of three medieval collections of mythical tales that are preserved in a manuscript in the Vatican Library; the narratives are drawn from Latin scholia and late Latin sources. French translations are available or in the course of preparation.

VERGIL (Publius Vergilius Maro, 70–19 BC), Roman poet, author of the *Eclogues*, a book of pastoral poems, the *Georgics*, a poem about farming and bee-keeping, and the *Aeneid*, an epic poem in twelve books that describes how the Trojan prince Aeneas (Aineias in Greek) wandered to Italy after the fall of Troy and established himself in Latium to become the ancestor of the founder of Rome (see pp. 588ff). Vergil often refers to persons or stories from Greek legend, or borrows from Greek legend or adapts it to suit his own purposes; and the surviving commentaries on his works by *Servius and other scholars often refer to such matters as a consequence, and can be a valuable source for the mythologist.

XENOPHON (c. 430–354 BC), historian and author of prose treatises, mainly on practical subjects; he rarely has occasion to refer to matters of mythological concern.

CHAPTER TWO

THE BEGINNINGS
OF THINGS

—— ·•· ——

FIRST BEGINNINGS

Although conflicting accounts were inevitably offered of the origins of the gods and the physical universe, Hesiod's *Theogony*, an epic history of the divine order composed in about 700 BC (see p. 9), came to be accepted by the Greeks as the standard mythical account of the earliest history of the world; and we will thus adopt it as our main guide in the first section of this book, while examining how the world and the lesser and higher deities were supposed to have come into existence, and how Zeus and the Olympian gods attained supreme authority.

Before considering Hesiod's cosmogony, it may be useful to picture how the world was visualized by the Greeks in early times. They began with the notion that early peoples generally seem to possess, namely that its real form corresponds to the form that it appears to have when as much of it as can be viewed at once is observed from their particular viewpoint. Now unless the observer is shut in between long lines of hills like an Egyptian, or confined to an island or archipelago like the inhabitants of the South Pacific, the world might appear to take the form of a circular disc, more or less level except where mountains or hills rise up from it, and capped by the immense roof or dome of the sky. On the one side the sun and stars can be seen rising above the horizon, while on the other they disappear at their setting; and as they always rise on the same side, in the east, they must presumably make their way back again, either under the ground or by some other hidden route. This and no other was the earliest Greek picture of the world, presupposed by the earliest legends and surviving inconsistently into later ones. More specifically, the Greeks supposed that the boundary of this disc of the earth was formed by the stream of Ocean (Okeanos), which was not an ocean in the modern sense but a great river flowing around in a circle. The sky was envisioned as a substantial roof or dome, sometimes said to be made of bronze or iron.[1] It rose a considerable height above the earth, but not an immeasurable distance. The residence of the gods was now imagined as being the sky itself, now the summit of Mt Olympos on the northeastern borders of Greece. If one could pile three large mountains one above another, as the gigantic Aloadai set out to do when they revolted against the gods (see p. 91), it would be sufficient to form a ladder to heaven.[2] The tale of Phaethon's ascent in the chariot of the Sun (see p. 45), to take but one instance, implies that if one could travel far enough to the east, one would reach the place where the sky touches the earth and the sun-god begins his ascent. Far to the west on the other hand, where the sun goes down, there was a place of darkness, near which an entrance to Hades could be found, as we will see in connection with Homer's account of Odysseus' visit to the world of the dead (see p. 109). Hades was commonly pictured, of course, as a murky realm that lay somewhere far beneath the earth, and might thus be reached through one of the many deep rifts in the strata of the Greek rocks, *katavóthra* as they are called in the native tongue, such as the famous one at Tainaron in the southern Peloponnese. This is amply witnessed in the myths of Orpheus, Herakles and other heroes who were said to have made incursions into Hades by such routes whilst still alive.

It may be noted that Homer and Hesiod can speak of a place as lying beneath the earth and at the edges of the earth as if there were no conflict between the two concepts. In stating, for instance, that some monsters were confined beneath the earth by their father Ouranos, Hesiod says that he 'made them live beneath the broad-path earth, where they suffered anguish, being set to dwell underground in the furthermost distance, at the bounds of the great earth'; or in a passage in the *Iliad*, Homer speaks in similar terms of the banished Titans.[3]

Of the actual geography of the world, a differing amount was known, as might be expected, in different ages. In the Homeric epics, Greece proper and part of the coast of Asia Minor are familiar ground for the most part, but beyond that, little enough is known. The more distant adventures of Odysseus are located in a fairy-tale realm, even if fabulous places on his itinerary came to be identified with real places in the seas around Italy in the later tradition. To Aeschylus, some two centuries later, southern Italy is familiar territory enough, but the interior of Asia Minor begins to fade into the unknown and marvellous;[4] and after the conquests of Alexander, those who wanted a land of wonders had to go further again, to India (see p. 579) or Northern Europe. Little was ever known about the regions of Africa that lay to the south of the lands that fringed its Mediterranean shores.

Having this conception of the world in which they lived, the Greeks from quite early times were interested in the question of its genesis; and it is natural that Hesiod's theogony, or account of the origins and successive generations of the gods, should start with a cosmogony, to explain how the many-layered universe that forms the seat of their rule came into being.

First of all, so Hesiod tells us, came CHAOS.[5] This word, which seems literally to mean 'gaping void', signifies something more than mere empty space; for Chaos is a primal feature of the universe, a murky reality which will be represented in the forthcoming genealogies as the source of much that is dark and negative in the world. It is worth noting that Hesiod imagines it as something that is solid enough to be affected by the heat of Zeus' thunderbolt.[6] When the universe is fully constructed, it will be situated between Earth and the lowest region of all, Tartaros.[7] Although *chaos* is a neuter noun in Greek, Chaos is treated as female in so far as it is personified as a deity. It should be remarked that the word Chaos carried no connotations of disorder or confusion in early usage.

If Chaos comes first, she is followed by three other entities, first broad-bosomed **Gaia** (Earth), the ever-sure seat of the gods, and then gloomy **Tartaros** in a recess of the broad-pathed earth, and finally **Eros**, the personification of love or, perhaps more accurately, of desire.[8] Although it is quite often assumed that all three are born out of Chaos as her offspring, this is not stated by Hesiod nor indeed implied, for the emergence of Chaos and her three successors is described in a single sentence governed by the same verb *geneto* ('came to be'). Gaia, Tartaros and Eros are best regarded as being primal realities like Chaos that came into existence independently of her. Chaos will form a distinctive family of her own, as we will see, through two children of hers who are explicitly stated to have been born *from* her.[9]

Of these four primal entities, two alone will be of genealogical significance, Chaos and, above all, Gaia. EROS is introduced at this early stage because he is the motor that will drive the process of mating and procreation that will bring everything else into being. As a mythical agent, he could be pictured in a variety of ways, whether as an ancient and all-powerful cosmic force as in the present context,[10] or as a potent force of nature who inspires all living beings with procreative desire, or as a mischievous boy-god (or even child-god) who pricks gods and mortals with his arrows to inflame them with desire. Broadly speaking, he grows younger and more frivolous as time progresses; he will be considered further in his nature as a god of love when we come to deal with Aphrodite (see p. 196). It is harder to say why Hesiod should have included TARTAROS among these first beings. He may perhaps have done so because Tartaros is set so much apart from everything else in the world; for it will be the nethermost region of the completed universe, lying far beneath the earth (or in its very deepest recesses), at a lower level even than Hades. It is stated in a subsequent passage in the *Theogony* that Tartaros lies as far beneath the earth as heaven rises above the earth, and that a bronze anvil cast down from the earth would fall down for nine days and nights before reaching Tartaros on the tenth.[11] Or according to a comparable but somewhat different reckoning in the *Iliad*, Tartaros lies as far beneath Hades as heaven rises above the earth.[12] As originally conceived, Tartaros served as a remote and secure prison for banished deities, and was wholly separate from Hades, which was a home for dead mortals. In the course of time, however, the distinction became increasingly blurred, and authors from Plato onward regularly use Tartaros as a convenient name for the region of Hades in which the undeserving dead suffer posthumous punishment (see p. 120).[13] The personified Tartaros was occasionally named as a father of sinister children, such as Typhon in the *Theogony*, or of Echidna and Thanatos (Death) in later sources.[14]

The next stage in the development of the universe commenced when Chaos and Gaia proceeded to generate further children from themselves without contact with any male partner.

Chaos produced a son and daughter by such means, EREBOS and black NIGHT (or NYX in Greek).[15] Night is far more important than her brother because she will found the main branch of the family of Chaos by generating a dismal brood of children from herself (see pp. 25ff); for the most part, the children and grandchildren of Night will not be mythical figures of any substance, but rather personifications of dark, destructive and negative forces. Erebos is a fitting brother for Night as a personification of darkness, especially of the darkness of the Underworld; his name was used quite often from the time of Homer onwards as a poetic name for the Underworld in its nature as a realm of gloom. He fathered two children by Night, a daughter, DAY (or HEMERA in Greek), and a corresponding brother, AITHER, who personifies brightness as manifested in the bright upper air.[16] Although it may seem odd at first sight that these radiant children should be born into this family of darkness, it is really perfectly logical since Night and Day, and the dark and the bright, are interrelated opposites that succeed one another. Brightness is bound to enter the world, moreover, at a later stage than darkness because its emergence marks a positive advance in the development of the universe. From the classical period onward, Hemera was quite often identified with Eos (Dawn), the goddess who brings the light of day.

If Chaos will become the progenitor of all manner of negative and harmful forces through her daughter Night, Gaia will be the progenitor of all that is positive and substantial in the world, including the features of the physical universe that have yet to emerge, and the deities who preside over every department of nature, and all the great gods and goddesses. Gaia's family will be built up in a different way from that of Chaos, for she will begin by generating two male partners from herself and then mate with them to found two separate lines of largely different character. As the first and greatest of her self-generated children, she brings forth 'starry OURANOS (Sky), equal to herself, to cover her over on every side'; and she then generates two prominent features of her own topography that could be regarded as being in some sense distinct from herself, the Mountains (*Ourea*) and the 'barren sea with its seething billows' as personified in PONTOS or Sea.[17] Gaia will take Ouranos as her consort to found the main divine family from which the Olympian gods and goddesses will spring; and she will found a smaller and more specialized family through a liaison with Pontos, consisting mainly of sea-gods and nymphs and beings of a monstrous or grotesque nature who needed to be set apart from deities of the Olympian order.

To summarize, there were four primal realities, Chaos, Gaia, Tartaros and Eros, which apparently entered existence independently of one another; and the two that were of genealogical significance, Chaos and Gaia, prepared for the foundation of the three great families of Hesiod's system by generating children from themselves, Chaos a daughter who would found a family through parthenogenesis, and Gaia two sons with whom she would mate to found two families by the normal processes of generation. Since the family of Chaos' daughter Night occupies a place apart in Hesiod's scheme, we will begin with that before passing on to survey the two families that were founded by Gaia, the greater through her union with Ouranos, and the lesser through her association with Pontos.

As was noted above, there were other mythical cosmogonies that followed a different pattern from that of Hesiod. Night (Nyx) was elevated to a higher position in some, figuring as the first being of all in one Orphic cosmogony, and as a member of the first couple with Tartaros or Aer in schemes ascribed to Mousaios and Epimenides respectively.[18] The *Iliad* refers, by contrast, to a tradition in which the first couple were Okeanos and Tethys, two deities of the waters (see further on pp. 36–7). Some of the most interesting and elaborate schemes are those preserved in the Orphic literature (i.e. in apocryphal writings ascribed to the legendary singer Orpheus from the late archaic period onwards). A characteristic feature of these was the world-egg from which a demiurge or creator-god – who was given various names such as Phanes, Protogonos or Eros – was supposed to have sprung. Aristophanes refers to the world-egg in a gentle parody of an Orphic cosmogony in one of his comedies, the *Birds*: Chaos, Night, Erebos and Tartaros existed first of all when there was neither earth, nor air, nor sky; and in the bosom of Erebos, black-winged Night brought forth a wind-egg from which golden-winged Eros (the demiurge) emerged.[19] According to one scheme from the Orphic literature, Chronos, unageing Time, existed first of all and gave birth to Aither, Chaos and Erebos; and Chaos created an egg from Aither, from which Phanes or Protogonos emerged, a bisexual being who then mated with himself to set the course of creation in train.[20] In the ensuing account of the successive generations of gods and their conflicts, traditional matter from Hesiod was drawn in where appropriate.

The rationalistic cosmogonies that were developed by the early philosophers from the sixth century BC onwards marked a new departure (though not an absolute break, since they would not have taken the form that they did if it had not been for the influence of early myth and of mythical patterns of thought). Starting from an undifferentiated *archē* or first principle, for instance water or air, such schemes set out to explain in purely rational terms how the various elements (aither, air, fire, water, earth) separated out and then how the fully differentiated universe came to be formed from these elements.[21] Features of the traditional Hesiodic cosmogony were sometimes reinterpreted in the light of such speculations in the later tradition. A good example of this can be found in the cosmogony at the beginning of Ovid's *Metamorphoses*, in which Chaos becomes a formless mixture of the elements or principles of matter, hot and cold, soft and hard, heavy and light. After this initial disorder was resolved, by some god or some process of nature, the different elements separated out and came to predominate at different levels in the universe, fiery aither in the vault of heaven, and air below it, and earth at the lowest level of all, embraced by the waters of the sea.[22] According to other reinterpretations, Chaos was identified with the primordial water or fire (an idea supported by false etymologies that derived its name from *cheisthai*, to flow, or *kaiō*, to burn), or was said to signify the empty space that must first exist if things are to have a place to exist in.[23] Much later, we still find traces of the classical cosmogony mingling with accounts derived from the Hebrew creation-myth; thus in a paraphrase of Genesis, falsely ascribed to St Cyprian and written in very indifferent Latin hexameters, the traditional chaos replaces the 'deep' of the original.[24]

THE FAMILY OF NIGHT

NIGHT (NYX) was a highly respected but rather vague figure in Greek myth. According to a tale in the *Iliad*, even Zeus held her in awe, for when Hypnos (Sleep) once sought refuge with her to escape the fury of Zeus (see p. 30), he let him go, angry though he was, 'for he shrank from doing anything that would displease swift-passing Night'.[25] If Hesiod could call her deadly (*oloē*)[26] with her noxious progeny in mind, she could also be regarded as kindly because she brings release from the cares of the day,[27] much like her son Hypnos. She could be pictured as an umbrageous goddess who flutters through the air on dark wings or perhaps rides through it in a chariot. In myth, she is above all a cosmogonical deity, making no appearance in mythical tales except in the above-mentioned story from the *Iliad* (and also an unusual version of the myth of Zeus' courtship of Thetis in which Night rather than Themis, see p. 52, is said to have warned him not to marry

Thetis).[28] She was credited with prophetic powers as the latter tale would indicate, and had some connection with oracles; Pausanias mentions that there was an oracle of Night at Megara.[29]

After bearing two children, Aither and Day, to her brother Erebos (see above), Night produced many more children on her own without recourse to a male partner.[30] The majority of them have no connection with myth, cult or the visible world, and could be described in modern terms as abstractions; but Hesiod and his contemporaries would have viewed them from a different perspective, regarding them as forces – here dark and negative forces – that exercise a real power in the world (as in a sense they do). They could be regarded accordingly as divinities of a kind, even if most of them are barely personified.

Since the worst of all negative forces is death, which annuls our very existence, it is no surprise that Hesiod's list of these children of Night should begin with hateful **Moros** (Fate, especially with regard to the time of our death), black **Ker** (Doom) and **Thanatos** (Death personified). Further down the list we find two groups of goddesses, the **Moirai** (Fates) and **Keres** (Dooms or death-spirits), who correspond to Moros and Ker respectively and yet are appreciably different. **Hypnos** (Sleep), who is named next after Thanatos and was traditionally regarded as the brother of death, is a privative force of a different but related kind who robs us of all awareness and animation at night, at least in so far as we are not troubled by **Oneiroi** (Dreams), the illusory night-visions that disturb our sleep. **Geras** (Old Age), who leads us toward death, occasionally appears with Herakles on vase-paintings as a bent and emaciated old man; Herakles, who finally overcame age and death to achieve immortality, keeps him at bay by threatening him with his club. Various negative features of human existence are represented in **Oizus** (Pain), **Apate** (Deceit), **Nemesis** (Retribution), and **Eris** (Strife). Eris will produce a series of children of her own who personify all that arises from strife (see pp. 30–1). Nemesis, the personification of retribution and righteous indignation, was a more substantial deity than many of her fellows, for she was honoured in cult at Rhamnous in Attica and at Smyrna and other Ionian cities, and appears in an ancient myth as a victim of the ardour of Zeus and the mother of Helen of Troy (see p. 438). **Philotes**, whose name means friendship or love, is listed along with Apate (deceit) and evidently represents pleasure of love or sex in the present context; she is included among the children of Night because she is associated with the dark and all too often with guile and deceit. The **Hesperides** (Daughters of Evening) are included here, even though they are lovely nymphs who cause no harm to anyone, because they live in the far west near the sunset and darkness (see below). And finally there is **Momos** (Blame or Censure), the personification of fault-finding, who appears in fables and the like as a sort of licensed jester who carps at the works and deeds of the gods.

MOMOS makes only a single appearance in serious myth, in connection with the origins of the Trojan War; when Earth once complained that she was overburdened by all the mortals who were swarming over her surface, Zeus proposed to destroy much of the human race by means of floods and thunderbolts, but Momos found fault with this plan and suggested that it would be better to contrive the origin of a mighty war (see further on p. 437).[31] His other main story is a fable in which Zeus, Prometheus and Athena invited him to judge their handiwork, a bull, a man, and a house respectively. He criticized the bull, saying that its eyes should have been placed on its horns to enable it to see what it was attacking, and criticized the man, saying that his mind should have been placed on the outside of his body to make his bad qualities visible to all, and criticized the house also, saying that it should have been mounted on wheels to enable people to move if they should acquire bad neighbours; but this was all too much for Zeus, who was so infuriated by his carping that he banished him from Olympos forever.[32] Momos' criticism of the bull is already mentioned by Aristotle, though in a somewhat different form.[33] According to another tale, Momos was dismayed to find that Aphrodite was so very beautiful that he could find nothing at all to criticize in her, and salved his honour as best he could by making fun of her sandals.[34]

A few of these children of Night are mythical figures of some significance who merit further consideration, especially the Moirai but also the Hesperides and Hypnos and Thanatos.

The MOIRAI, who may be more familiar under their Latin name of the Fata or FATES, are a group of goddesses who assign individual destinies to mortals at birth, particularly with regard to the timing of their death. They are initially classed as children of Night in the *Theogony* in accordance with their nature as appointers of death, but are reclassified later in the poem as daughters of Zeus and Themis (Law or Right Order) because they contribute to the proper ordering of the world under the authority of Zeus (see p. 78).[35] It would seem that they originated not as abstract powers of destiny but as birth-spirits, much like the ones who in the modern folklore of the area visit new-born children and determine what their portion in life shall be. The familiar myth in which the Moirai appear after the birth of Meleagros to foretell what his lot shall be, and also to specify a condition for his death (see p. 414), was surely rooted in very ancient folklore. In their capacity as goddesses who appoint the fate of mortals, they were objects of cult in many parts of the Greek world, as inscriptions and monuments abundantly testify. They do not appear at all frequently in myth however. Although one or all of them may be portrayed as attending the births of gods or mortals, they have little occasion to make any specific intervention in mythical tales unless they want to reveal some feature of a person's fate, as in the case of Meleagros, or else are required to take action when a person's fate needs to be altered in some way. One of the Moirai, Klotho, is thus presented by Pindar as superintending the revival of Pelops when he is brought to life again after being killed by his father[36] (see p. 503 for the circumstances); and in a tale from Aeschylus, Apollo is said to have made the sisters drunk in order to persuade them to allow a substitute to die in place of Admetos (see p. 151).[37] Apollodorus reports that they helped Zeus to quell two major revolts by tricking Typhon into eating some fruits that would gravely weaken him (see p. 85) and by clubbing two of the Giants to death with bronze cudgels.[38]

The Moirai are regularly represented as spinners from the earliest times. Although Homer makes only a single reference to the Moirai in the plural (in remarking that they have given an enduring heart to man), he speaks of the thread that is spun by Moira for Hektor at the time of his birth; and the *klōthes* (spinners) who are mentioned in the *Odyssey* as spinning people's fates at the time of their birth may surely be identified with the Moirai.[39] Hesiod and later authors report that there are three Moirai named Klotho (the Spinner), Lachesis (the Apportioner) and Atropos (the Inflexible);[40] in their rare appearances in art, they are shown as handsome women, in literature they may be imagined as very old. The thread that they spin is (or carries on it) the destiny of each individual in turn, and when it is broken, a life comes to an end.

Later poetical imagination elaborated this imagery in various ways, making the Fates spin a gold thread, for example, when spinning the fate of a particularly fortunate individual, or take up an abandoned task when someone is recalled to life.[41] Their Hesiodic names might already suggest a division of labour, with Klotho spinning the thread, Lachesis determining its allotted length, and Atropos cutting it off pitilessly at the time of a person's death. Or else Klotho may hold the distaff while Lachesis spins off the thread and Atropos cuts it short.[42] Or the inexorable Atropos may have the past as her province (for it is now unchangeable), while Lachesis is concerned with the future, and Klotho presides over the present, spinning each person's particular destiny.[43] Plato brings the Moirai into his great eschatological myth in the *Republic*, dividing their functions in a manner that is too complicated to be summarized here.[44] One or all of them may be represented in art as reading or writing the book of fate, hence presumably the quaint statement in Hyginus that they invented some letters of the Greek alphabet.[45] As might be expected, they are often associated on the one hand with Eileithuia, the goddess of childbirth, and on the other with Ananke (Necessity), Tyche (Fortune) and other personifications who have some connection with fate or destiny.

The word *moira* means 'portion' or 'allotment', and could be used accordingly as a term for a portion of land, or a person's portion at a meal, or the share that is allotted to a person when spoils are being divided. By a natural extension, the word could be applied to describe the lot or fate that is apportioned to a person in life; and the awesome power that apportions our fates could thence be personified as Moira, Fate or Necessity, or as a trio of Moirai or 'Apportioners'. In Latin, the plural Fata seems to be little more than an adaptation of the singular *fatum*, 'that which is spoken', 'the decree of the gods', to the plural number of the Greek goddesses, although it does occur once or twice without a mythological reference, meaning 'the decrees', much as we might say indifferently 'the commandments' or 'the commandments of God'. Later the neuter plural *Fata* gave rise to a feminine singular, quite foreign to classical Latin, which still exists in the Italian and French words for 'fairy' (*fata*, *fée*). A surer instinct led the Romans to identify their own spirits of birth, the Parcae (Paricae, from *parere*, to bring forth) with the Moirai, although the identification may have been encouraged by a false etymology in which Parca was derived from *pars*, a word equivalent to the Greek *meros* or *moira*.

The HESPERIDES were a group of nymphs who lived in the garden of the gods at the westernmost edges of the earth, where they guarded a wondrous tree (or trees) that bore golden apples. They were aided in their task by a formidable snake, a child of Phorkys and Keto sometimes named as Ladon (see p. 64), who coiled himself around the tree or trees.[46] Or in a less favoured account, the snake was stationed there to prevent the Hesperides themselves from pilfering the golden apples. In connection with this latter account, Pherecydes states that Gaia had presented the trees as a wedding-gift to Hera, who had been so impressed by their beauty that she had ordered that they should be planted in the garden of the gods.[47]

Figure 2.1 *Garden of the Hesperides*, by Frederick Lord Leighton (1830–1896). Courtesy of the Board of Trustees of the National Museums and Galleries on Merseyside (Lady Lever Art Gellery, Port Sunlight).

The Hesperides, who were famous for their beautiful voices, seem to have entertained themselves by singing and dancing in the usual manner of nymphs. Their duties were none too strenuous in any case, for the garden of the gods lay so far away that it attracted no thieves at all until Herakles was sent to steal some of the golden apples as one of his labours (see p. 269). In connection with that legend, as we will see, the Hesperides were sometimes relocated to the far north. There were usually thought to have been three of them, even if their number can vary from two to seven; and they are commonly named as Hespere (or Heperie, or Hesperathousa) and Erytheia (or Erytheis) and Aigle,[48] in reference to the evening, the red of the evening sky and the brightness of the day respectively.

HYPNOS (Sleep) and his brother THANATOS (Death) were always closely associated in the Greek mind, whether as personified agents or simply as concepts. They reappear in a subsequent passage in the *Theogony*, which states that they had neighbouring homes in a dark and gloomy place at the ends of the earth near the home of their mother Night.[49] Even if their actions have obvious similarities, the two brothers are of opposite character, for Hypnos 'roams peacefully over the earth and is kindly to mortals' while Thanatos 'has a heart of iron, a heart within his breast of pitiless bronze, and keeps a firm grip on any mortal once he catches hold of him; and he is hateful even to the immortal gods'.[50] In the *Iliad*, which describes the pair as twins without saying anything about their parentage, they raise the corpse of Sarpedon from the battlefield at Troy at the order of his father Zeus to carry it home to Lycia.[51] This episode inspired some memorable vase-paintings, which typically show the brothers as winged and dressed in full armour. Elsewhere in the *Iliad*, Hera visits Hypnos on Lemnos to ask him to lull her husband to sleep after she has made love with him, to distract him while some orders of his are being disobeyed; but the godling is initially reluctant, saying that Zeus had been furiously angry when he had performed this service for her on a previous occasion, and would have hurled him out of heaven into the sea if he had not taken refuge with Night. Hera wins him round, however, by promising to give him Pasithea, one of the Charites (Graces), as a bride.[52] Hypnos acquired no further myths in the subsequent tradition apart from one that linked him to Endymion, an Eleian hero who was famed for his eternal sleep (see p. 411); according to this tale, Hypnos fell in love with Endymion and caused him to sleep with his eyes open so as to be able to enjoy the sight of their beauty.[53] Some late authors, notably Ovid and Statius, diverted themselves by painting poetic pictures of his realm; Ovid presents him as sleeping on an ebony couch in a dark cave in the land of the Cimmerians, with his thousand sons, the Dreams, lying around him; the stream of Lethe (Oblivion) glides softly over pebbles into the cave inducing slumber, while poppies and countless soporific herbs bloom outside.[54]

As for Thanatos, there could be little role for him in serious myth because Hermes was thought to conduct the dead to the Underworld and Hades presided over them after their arrival. In the two memorable myths in which he does arrive to haul mortals away to the lower world only to meet with humiliation, he is very much a figure from folklore. When he arrived at Corinth to fetch Sisyphos, the cunning hero deferred his death by tying him up (see further on p. 431);[55] and in Euripides' version of the story of Alkestis, Herakles lay in wait for Thanatos when he was due to fetch her from her tomb, and wrestled her away from him to return her to her husband (see p. 152).[56]

We must conclude our survey of the family of Night by returning to ERIS (Strife), who was the only child of Night to produce a series of children of her own. She has only a single proper myth, though one of some importance, which tells how she stirred up the quarrel between Hera, Athena and Aphrodite that was settled through the judgement of Paris, and so helped to set in course the train of events that led to the outbreak of the Trojan War (see further on p. 437).[57] As in the case of the interrelated story of Momos mentioned above, and also the story of Zeus' pursuit of Nemesis (which resulted in the conception of Helen), this myth can be traced back to the *Cypria*, the first epic in the Trojan cycle; it would seem that the author of this poem liked to assign a more solid role to personifications of this kind than was usual in high literature. Homer refers to Eris in the *Iliad* along with other minor deities and personifications who stir up frenzy on the battlefield; at the beginning of the eleventh book, Zeus sends him down to inspire the Greeks with ardour for battle, which he achieves by standing in the middle of their camp and uttering a terrible piercing cry.[58]

The children of Eris represent the many harmful and destructive things that arise from discord and strife, namely Toil (Ponos), Oblivion (Lethe), Famine, Sorrows, Fights, Battles, Murders, Manslayings, Quarrels, Lies, Disputes, Lawlessness, Delusion (Ate) and Oath (Horkos).[59] This is allegory of the most obvious kind for the most part; the last two alone require further comment.

ATE represents the delusion or clouding of the mind that leads people to commit acts of ill-considered folly. There is a striking portrayal of her mode of action in the nineteenth book of the *Iliad*, in which Agamemnon tries to excuse himself for having robbed Achilles of his prize of war Briseis (see p. 463) by claiming that he had been deluded by Ate who blinds all men, an accursed being 'who has delicate feet, for it is not on the ground that she walks, no, she tramples over the heads of men, bringing harm to mankind and ensnaring one or another'.[60] Agamemnon goes on to say that even Zeus himself had once been deluded by Ate, when Hera had tricked him into swearing an oath that would enable her to ensure that the inheritance that he had intended for his son Herakles would go to another (see p. 248). Zeus was so angry to discover how he had been deluded that he had seized Ate by her hair and had hurled her down to the earth, where she now works her mischief on mortals.[61] According to Apollodorus, she fell to earth on the hill of Ate in the Troad, on the spot where Ilos would later found the city of Troy (see p. 523).[62]

HORKOS (Oath) is introduced into the list in connection with perjuries; he personifies the curse that will be activated if a person swears a false oath. Hesiod expresses the matter in allegorical terms in the *Works and Days*, by stating that the Erinyes (Furies) assisted at the birth of Horkos when Eris brought him to birth to bring trouble to those who perjure themselves.[63]

GAIA, OURANOS AND THE TITANS

We must now pass on to the two great families that were founded by GAIA (Earth) through her unions with her two self-generated partners, first Ouranos (Sky) and then Pontos (Sea). As has already been noted, the family that she founded with Ouranos was the nobler of the two, bringing into being all the greatest gods and goddesses, while the family that she founded with Pontos consisted mainly of sea-beings and monsters. Of her two partners, moreover, only Ouranos can be regarded as having been a true husband of hers, for she is linked to Pontos (who has no myths and is barely personified) for genealogical purposes alone. Ouranos and Gaia are in fact the primordial couple in Hesiod's account of the earliest history of the world, even if they are not the first beings of all or the progenitors of all subsequent beings; and the first proper myth in that history is the one that tells how Ouranos provoked the dissolution of his marriage and his own downfall by his mistreatment of his wife and children. Important though he may have been at this early stage, Ouranos makes no further appearance in myth after the end of his union with Gaia (except in so far as he is said to have delivered prophecies to children of his). There is no evidence that he was ever worshipped or played any part in Greek cult; at most, he might be invoked along with other deities in oaths.

Ouranos was sometimes called Akmonides, i.e. son of Akmon, probably in accordance with a very early usage. The Byzantine scholar Eustathius (who claims that Alcman, a poet of the late seventh century BC, already referred to Ouranos as son of Akmon) records an ancient etymological speculation on the matter, saying that the father of Ouranos was called Akmon because the movement of the heavens is 'unwearying' (*akamatos*).[64] It has been suggested in more recent times that the name may be connected with Old Persian and Sanskrit *acman*, in which case it would mean stone, in reference to the solid vault of heaven. Whatever the true meaning of the word, it may well have originated as a cultic title or epithet of Ouranos; in like manner, Hyperion is sometimes a title of the sun-god Helios, and sometimes the father of Helios. But the matter remains a mystery.

In contrast to her male partners, the earth-goddess GAIA or GE was honoured in cult in classical times, though not as a deity of any great significance. Shrines are recorded for her in various parts of Greece, including one on the south slope of the Athenian acropolis, where she was honoured as Ge Kourotrophos (rearer of children), and a joint temple with Zeus Agoraios in Sparta.[65] She had no festivals, however, and seems to have been honoured most frequently in conjunction with other deities. The Greeks liked to invoke her in oaths for much the same reason that they would invoke the sun-god Helios (see p. 43), because no one could break an oath in any part of the world without her being aware of it; in a scene in the *Iliad*, two lambs are fetched for sacrifice when a solemn oath is due to be sworn, a black female lamb for Gaia and a white male for Helios.[66] From as far back as our evidence extends, Gaia always represents the earth as a whole (even if she may once have been conceived more narrowly, rather like Tellus at Rome, as the power residing in the patches of earth with which her worshippers were immediately concerned and acquainted). It hardly needs repeating that the earth was not pictured as a globe in the earliest times, but as a plane or disk of indefinite expanse; but the true shape of the earth was discovered quite early, certainly by the late fifth century BC. Although Gaia acts as a personal being in her myths, and is sometimes shown rising up from the ground in human form in works of art (as when she delivers the earth-born Erichthonios to Athena, see p. 185), it cannot be said that she was really imagined as a fully anthropomorphic deity, for she remained too closely identified with the earth as a physical body. In a Homeric Hymn that is addressed to her, she is praised accordingly as the mother of all (*pammētēr*) and oldest being of all who nourishes all living creatures and brings prosperity to the human race through her harvests.[67]

Gaia bore three sets of children to Ouranos, first a group of primordial gods who were known as the **Titans** (properly Titanes in Greek), and then two sets of monsters, the one-eyed **Kyklopes** and the hundred-armed giants who came to be known as the **Hekatoncheires** or Hundred-Handers. Ouranos hated them all, however, and prevented them from emerging into the light, causing such anguish to Gaia that she finally urged them to take action against him. The youngest of the Titans, Kronos, who was the only one who had the courage to do so, laid an ambush for his father, armed with a sickle that his mother had prepared for the purpose; and he cut off the genitals of Ouranos as he approached his wife to make love, so bringing their union to a violent end and making it possible for Gaia to bring their children to the light at last. Kronos hurled the severed genitals into the sea, where sea-foam gathered around them to generate the goddess Aphrodite (see p. 194); and some blood dripped from them on to Gaia, causing her to conceive three further sets of children, the Erinyes, Giants and Meliai (see p. 38).[68]

This story of the mutilation of Ouranos and his separation from Gaia has obvious cosmological implications; since the sky now rises high above the earth, it is suggested in the myths of many cultures that Earth and Sky, as the first couple or at least a primordial couple, must somehow have been drawn apart at a very early stage in the history of the world. This is often achieved in a gentler fashion than in the present story. In an ancient Egyptian myth, for instance, Shu, the personification of the air, is said to have interposed himself between the earth-god Geb and the sky-goddess Nut to raise the latter's body high over that of her partner. Or in Maori myth from far away in New Zealand, the union between the first couple Rangi and Papa, the female Earth and male Sky, became the first source of life, but all that they brought forth remained imprisoned between them initially because they never relaxed from their embrace; so the first gods, who formed part of their offspring, consulted together and resolved that Tane, the god of forests and birds, should separate Rangi and Papa by using his body to hold them apart; and when he did so light appeared in the world for the first time.[69] Closer to home in the ancient Near East, the Hurro-Hittite myth of Ullikummi referred to the sundering of the earth and sky; and the upward flight of Anu in the Hurro-Hittite succession myth summarized below (see p. 34) implies the same. Hesiod makes no reference, however, to the raising up of the sky, and he may not even have been aware of this aspect of the story; he is concerned above all with the dynastic implications of the intrafamilial conflict.

By mutilating Ouranos and so bringing his union with Gaia to an end, Kronos displaced him as the main god, establishing himself as the new lord of the universe with his fellow Titans as his subordinates. This was not the final order of things, however, since Kronos maltreated his children like his father before him, and was destined to be overthrown by them in his turn. Having been warned by Gaia and Ouranos that he would be displaced by his own son, Kronos tried to remove the danger by swallowing each of his children at birth; but his plan was foiled because his wife Rhea hid his youngest son and gave him a stone to swallow instead; and Zeus duly caused the downfall of Kronos when he came of age, by compelling him to disgorge his other children and then banding together with them to banish him and his fellow Titans to Tartaros.[70] The initial story of the mutilation and displacement of Ouranos thus forms part of an overarching 'succession myth' which tells how the present divine order came to be established under Zeus in the third generation, after the fall of his father and grandfather. The Olympian gods, who replaced the Titans as the principal gods, were either brothers and sisters of Zeus or else children of his (with two possible exceptions, see p. 80). This succession myth will be examined in detail in the next chapter, when we come to deal with the rise of Zeus and origin of the Olympian order. Since the Kyklopes and Hekatoncheires, the monstrous children of Ouranos and Gaia, are mainly of interest for the part that they play in the succession myth, consideration of them will also be deferred until then (as will full treatment of the mythology of Kronos and Rhea). We will concentrate for the present on the TITANS, in their common nature as a collective body of former gods, and in their individual nature as the founders of the various lines that make up the family of Ouranos and Gaia in Hesiod's genealogical scheme.

Of all the Titans, only Kronos and Rhea are accorded distinctive roles of their own in the succession myth, while the others act solely as a collective body. In the *Theogony* (though not in all accounts, see p. 68) the latter make no contribution at all to the ousting of Ouranos, which is effected by Kronos alone; but they benefit from it to become the chief gods of the pre-Olympian order under the rule of Kronos. They subsequently take common action in the Titanomachy, the great war in which they attempt to quell the insurrection mounted by Zeus and his allies, but are defeated and banished from the upper world forever. So is it possible to say anything meaningful about their common nature, beyond the fact that they are the banished ruling gods of an earlier generation? This was once a question that gave rise to a considerable amount of speculation. A much-favoured theory suggested that the Titans were old prehellenic gods who had been displaced by the Olympian gods of the Greek invaders. If that were so, the myth of the great war between the Olympians and the Titans could be explained in historical terms, as reflecting the struggle of belief that the suppression of the older religion had entailed. It was often proposed, furthermore, that the old gods must have been nature-powers of a less advanced or less moral nature than the Olympian gods. Another theory appealed to late evidence of doubtful value to suggest that the Titans were phallic deities. The whole nature of the discussion altered, however, when it came to be realized that the Greek succession myth bears a marked resemblance to myths of a comparable nature from the ancient Near East. Although other eastern succession myths had been known at an earlier period, the crucial factor in this regard was the publication in 1946 of a Hurro-Hittite myth that provides a particularly close parallel to Hesiod's myth.[71]

The Hurrians, an ancient people who lived in northern Syria and adjoining areas, were subjugated in the fourteenth century BC by the Hittites, who were much influenced by their culture and have transmitted some of their myths to us on cuneiform tablets. One such myth tells of the sequence of events that led to the accession of the Hurrian equivalent of Zeus. Anu (Sky), who corresponds to the Greek Ouranos, seized power by deposing an obscure predecessor, Alalu, and reigned for nine years until his cupbearer, Kumarbi, engaged him in battle and defeated him. As Anu was trying to escape into the heavens, Kumarbi dragged him down by his feet, and bit off his genitals and swallowed them. As he was then rejoicing in his triumph, Anu warned him to think again, saying that his action had caused him to become impregnated with three terrible gods. Although Kumarbi immediately spat out the contents of his mouth, the Storm-god was already inside him, and eventually emerged from his body. The text is very defective from this point onwards, but it is clear enough that the Storm-god, who was the main god of the Hurrians and Hittites just as Zeus was the main god of the Greeks, finally displaced Kumarbi as ruler.[72] Hesiod's myth may also be compared with a very ancient Babylonian myth in the poem known as the *Enuma Elish*, and also with a Phoenician myth (of questionable status, but thought to be at least partially authentic) which is preserved in a Greek work of the early Roman period.[73] When the implications of these foreign parallels came to be appreciated, it came to be generally accepted that the Greek succession myth was not of native origin, but was based on a myth that had been introduced from the Near East.

If this was the case, a group of displaced earlier gods corresponding to the Titans must have been introduced as part of the imported myth. The Hurro-Hittite equivalents of the Titans were known as the former gods (Hesiod refers to the Titans or Kronos in corresponding terms on two occasions),[74] while their Babylonian equivalents were known as the dead gods. If the question of the origin of the Titans is viewed from this perspective, two possibilities arise. There may have been an early group of native gods of that name who were identified with the former gods of the imported myth; or else the name Titan was simply a title that was applied by the Greeks to the gods of eastern origin. There is no way of telling which alternative is true, and it makes little practical difference in any case, since we know nothing whatever of the original nature of the Titans if they had once enjoyed a separate existence in Greece. The essential point is that the Titans, as they are known to us as a collective body from the time of Hesiod onwards, are precisely what they are presented as being in the succession myth of eastern origin, the former ruling gods who were banished from the upper world when the present divine order was established. This is their 'nature', and nothing is served by enquiring any further; they have no other stories or functions as a collective body in conventional myth, and they had no place in Greek cult. The etymology of their name is uncertain; there is some ancient evidence to suggest that it may have meant 'princes' or the like. Hesiod offers an ingenious but obviously factitious double etymology, stating that Ouranos conferred this title on them in reproach, 'for he said that they strained (*titainontes*) and insolently performed a dreadful deed, for which vengeance (*tisin*) came to them afterwards'.[75]

To turn aside from the conventional mythology of the Titans for a moment, they figure prominently in an esoteric myth of unusual interest; for in a tale that originated in the Orphic literature, the human race is said to have sprung from the remains of the Titans after Zeus had destroyed them with a thunderbolt. This came about in the following circumstances. Zeus raped his mother Rhea, who is here identified with Demeter, to father Persephone; and he later had intercourse with Persephone in the form of a snake to father Dionysos, who is often given the title of Zagreus in this connection. Zeus intended to make Dionysos the ruler of the world, but the jealous Hera incited the Titans to attack him. Diverting his attention with toys of various sorts, notably a mirror, they pulled him from his throne and killed him; and they then tore him to pieces and devoured him. Athena contrived to save his heart, however, and took it to Zeus, so making it possible for Dionysos to be reborn from Semele. Zeus punished the Titans by destroying them with his thunderbolt, and the human race sprang up from the soot that was left from their bodies. Human beings have been of mixed nature ever since, being partly divine, since the Titans had eaten Dionysos Zagreus before they were destroyed, and partly wicked, owing to the wicked nature of the Titans. This extraordinary myth, which contradicts normal Greek tradition at every turn, was probably of quite early origin. Plato refers to the old Titanic nature of man in the *Laws*, and there is reason to suppose that Pindar already knew of the story.[76]

Hesiod assigns individual names to all the Titans, listing six male Titans and six females (known as the Titanides).[77] In view of Kronos' special role in the succession myth and his status as the second lord of the universe, he would surely have been identified as a Titan in the prior tradition. Confirmation of this can be found in Homer, since Kronos is mentioned on three occasions in the *Iliad* as one of the banished gods in Tartaros (who are named as Titans on one occasion).[78] The formulaic epithets Kronios and Kronides which are regularly applied to Zeus in the Homeric epics are indication enough that Kronos had been regarded as the father of Zeus from very ancient times; since such epithets are not applied to any other deity, Zeus may perhaps have been his only child in the original tradition. It is quite likely that Kronos was first brought into the succession myth, and thus enlisted as a Titan, because he was the acknowledged father of Zeus in the native tradition. Kronos' consort Rhea also has a special place in the succession myth as the 'mother of the gods' (i.e. of the first generation of Olympian gods) and by virtue of the crucial role that she plays in saving Zeus from being swallowed by Kronos. She is named as a Titan in the *Theogony*, and had presumably been long identified as such (unless the Titans were once thought to be exclusively male). Since Iapetos (the father of Atlas, Menoitios and Prometheus, see below) is mentioned along with Kronos in the *Iliad* as a god imprisoned in Tartaros, it would seem that he too had come to be classed as a Titan by the time of Homer and Hesiod, perhaps because he was a father of children who were enemies of Zeus.[79] There is no comparable evidence to show whether any other Titan in Hesiod's list was already known as such.

It is obvious from a casual glance that the deities in Hesiod's list of Titans are of such disparate nature and origin that they could not possibly have formed a common group from very early times. Some have Greek names, others foreign names; some are nature-gods, some are abstractions, some are nonentities who were probably never anything more than genealogical links. Some of them, moreover, for reasons that will be considered presently, could not have shared the common fate of the Titans as former gods who were banished forever. It is altogether probable that the Titans, with the possible exception of Kronos, were originally an anonymous collective body, and one may suspect that most of the deities in the standard list, as established in the *Theogony*, were first named as Titans by Hesiod himself (who may also may also have been the first to establish that they were specifically twelve in number). It was essential that he should provide them with a full set of names if he was to draw them into his genealogical system; and he liked to assign appropriate names to members of groups of deities in any case, even to the many Nereids and Ocean-nymphs.

We must now consider why the specific deities named by Hesiod should have been enrolled as Titans. **Kronos**, **Rhea** and **Iapetos** have already been discussed, as deities who were almost certainly named as Titans in the existing tradition. **Okeanos** was the god of the outer Ocean, the great river that supposedly encircled the earth and was the source of all other waters, salt and sweet alike.[80] It could obviously be assumed that the lord of these waters must have been a very ancient deity who had been at his post from the very earliest times. According to a passage in the *Iliad*, indeed, he and his consort **Tethys** were none other than the first couple from whom all the gods had sprung[81] (an idea that was apparently derived from a Babylonian myth in which Apsu and Tiamat, representing the sweet and salt waters respectively, were portrayed as the first couple). Even if they could not be regarded as the first gods of all in the context of the succession myth, Hesiod accords them only a slightly lower status by including them among the Titans, as would be fitting for venerable deities whose union could account for the origin of all the lesser streams of the world. Okeanos seems ill-fitted, on the other hand, to share in the collective actions and fate of the Titans, since his streams are a permanent feature of the world and one might suppose that he would be obliged to remain in them at the edges of the earth. The story in the latter part of the *Theogony* in which he tells his daughter Styx to assist Zeus against the Titans[82] (see p. 49) is consistent with the thought that he did not join with the other Titans in fighting against Zeus; and in Apollodorus' theogony, in which the Titans are presented as attacking Ouranos as a collective body, it is explicitly stated that Okeanos took no part in that enterprise.[83] **Themis**, the personification of law and right order, and **Mnemosyne**, the personification of memory, belong very appropriately among the Titans in so far as they represent ancient and fundamental forces in the world; but it can hardly be imagined, on the other hand, that they have been banished from the world since the fall of the Titans. Even in the *Theogony* itself (though in a part of the poem that may have been added after Hesiod's time), they reappear after the banishment of the Titans as early wives of Zeus. Themis figures, furthermore, as we will see, in a number of myths set in the Olympian era.

The other Titans in Hesiod's list are obscure deities who are of genealogical significance alone; none have any recorded myths, and they may well have had no stories even in Hesiod's time, being remembered only as parents or ancestors of more important deities (if they were not invented by the poet himself, as is possible in one or two cases). **Hyperion** is mentioned in the Homeric epics and other early poetry as the father of the sun-god Helios; and his name is also used on occasion as a title of Helios himself.[84] Since the sun and other main luminaries of the sky must have come into existence at an early stage in the development of the world, Hyperion could be fittingly enlisted as their Titan father. **Koios** also finds a natural place among the Titans as the father of Leto, who was the mother of two major Olympian deities, Artemis and Apollo. Hyperion and Koios have Titan consorts assigned to them, **Theia**, 'the Divine' and **Phoibe**, 'the Radiant', respectively; it required no great ingenuity, whether on the part of Hesiod or some predecessor, to invent figures such as these. And finally there is **Kreios** (or Krios), whose nature and origin are a mystery. As we will see, he served a useful if minor genealogical function by fathering husbands for some early goddesses. There was not always complete agreement on the identity of the Titans in the subsequent tradition; Apollodorus, for instance, omits Phoibe, replacing her with Dione[85] (the consort of Zeus at Dodona, and mother of Aphrodite in one account, see p. 80).

In addition to fathering children by Gaia through his marital relations, Ouranos caused her to conceive some further children in less conventional circumstances; for when Kronos severed his genitals and threw them away (see further on p. 67), some blood gushed out of them on to the ground, causing Gaia to become pregnant with three sets of children, the Erinyes, the Giants (Gigantes in Greek) and the Meliai.[86]

The **Giants** will be discussed in the next chapter in connection with their revolt against Zeus and the Olympian order (see pp. 86ff). It is likely that they had always been regarded as earth-born, as their Greek name would suggest; and since they were superhuman beings who were akin to the gods (though not fully divine), it could be appropriately added that the fertilizing power of the divine blood of Ouranos had caused the earth to bring them forth. This detail may well have been invented by Hesiod himself. It is likely that he would have regarded them as beings of relatively minor importance, since the myth of their revolt against Zeus probably originated after his time (see p. 86). The **Meliai** were a race of nymphs, ash-tree nymphs in the strict sense; but since Hesiod offers no separate account of the origin of others of their kind, he is presumably using the term in a general sense to cover all forms of tree-nymph. As one of the most important forms of nymph, tree-nymphs will be considered along with the other nymphs in Chapter 6. These nymphs resemble the Giants in being more than human and less than divine. The remaining set of children, the **Erinyes**, are the only ones that will require any detailed examination here.

The ERINYES or FURIES were avenging spirits who exacted terrible but just retribution against people who committed murder and other grave crimes, especially within the family. Since Hesiod says nothing at all about their activities, we must turn to Homer to gain an idea of the kinds of offence that they were thought to punish in early tradition. The *Iliad* tells how Amyntor cursed his son Phoinix to the Erinyes for having seduced his concubine (see p. 458); and when Althaia cursed her son Meleagros for having killed some brothers of hers, 'the Erinys who walks in darkness and is pitiless of heart heard her from Erebos'.[87] Or in the *Odyssey*, Telemachos suggests that his mother Penelope might curse him to the Erinyes if he should send her away, and Odysseus remarks that Oedipus has been sorely troubled by the Erinyes of his mother since she hanged herself[88] (after discovering that her husband Oedipus was also her son, see p. 311). In a fragment from another early epic, the *Thebais*, the Erinys is said to have paid due heed to Oedipus when he cursed his sons (see p. 315).[89] These sources and others of the kind indicate that the Erinyes were thought to take a special interest in offences committed by one member of a family against another (especially younger against older, child against parent), and were often spurred into action by a curse from the injured party. It is therefore fitting that Hesiod should present them as having been born as a consequence of an offence that had been committed by a son against his father.

Other allusions in the Homeric epics show that the Erinyes also had broader concerns. Homer remarks in the first place that anyone who swears a false oath will be punished by the Erinyes in the world below;[90] and Hesiod alludes to this function in figurative terms in the *Works and Days* when he says that the Erinyes assisted at the birth of Horkos (see further on p. 31).[91] They became the main agents of retribution in the Underworld in the late tradition, punishing the dead for sins of any kind. It is remarked in the *Odyssey*, though as a mere possibility, that even beggars may have their Erinyes[92] (for they have no one else to avenge them). Most interesting of all, however, is a passage in the *Iliad* which suggests that they may act to uphold the proper order of things even where no human offence is involved;

for after Xanthos, one of the divine chariot-horses of Achilles, had spoken aloud to address a prophecy to his master, the Erinyes cut off his voice (plainly because it is unnatural for horses to speak).[93] The aphoristic philosopher Heraclitus (mid-sixth century BC) writes correspondingly – though obviously in a more figurative vein – that 'the Sun will not overstep his measures, for if he does, the Erinyes, ministers of justice, will seek him out'.[94]

Their most celebrated stories in heroic mythology relate nonetheless to offences within the family, telling how they punished two Argive heroes, Orestes and Alkmaion, for having killed their mothers (see pp. 327 and 511). Although both young men took this drastic action to avenge the death of their father, and even gained the consent of Apollo at Delphi beforehand, the Erinyes knew no pity in such cases, and took no account of mitigating circumstances; the deed was their sole concern. They thus embody early ideas of justice from the time before it came to be appreciated that animus is a necessary part of every crime, and that a deed which is committed through mere accident or as a result of *force majeure* does not carry with it the full moral or legal responsibility of a deliberate act. Yet even so, they are a long way from representing the most primitive stages of moral consciousness, for they punish, not families or clans, but solely the individual who commits the deed. They may, however, be said to represent the moral ideas of the clan, for they are regularly on the side of the elders, not only of fathers or mothers but also of elder brothers.

In art and literature, they are regularly represented as formidable beings, stern of aspect, carrying torches and scourges, and generally wreathed with serpents, or having serpents in their hair or carrying them in their hands. They were presented in an especially loathsome form in Aeschylus' *Eumenides*, as dark vampire-like creatures who crawled around on all fours, with pus oozing from their eyes and sinister rasping breath;[95] it was said, indeed, that they were so horrifying at the first performance that women in the audience suffered miscarriages. But it is noteworthy, as an example of the Greek hatred for all that is monstrously hideous, that no artist makes the Erinyes ugly or misshapen; they are rather beautiful but fierce-looking women, known for what they are by their expression and the scourges and other implements which they carry, and in general as unlike Etruscan or medieval devils as possible.

The Erinyes have no individual names in the early tradition, and are of indeterminate number; it is not until the Roman period that the idea appears that there were three of them named Alekto, Tisiphone and Megaira.[96] Aeschylus and some later authors depart from Hesiod by classing them as daughters of Night, as seems appropriate enough, while Sophocles describes them as daughters of Skotos (Darkness personified) and Earth.[97] They were equated with the Eumenides (Kindly Ones) and Semnai (Venerable Ones), goddesses of gentler aspect and more propitious name who were honoured in cult at Athens and elsewhere. They had no equivalents in Roman belief, their Latin name, Furiae, being perhaps no more than an attempt at a translation (*furere*, to be raging mad, being taken as an equivalent to Greek *erineuein*); as the Furiae, they were sometimes identified with an obscure Roman goddess, Furrina.

DESCENDANTS OF THE TITANS

In considering the families of the Titans, we will exclude for the present the Titans who were the ancestors of the Olympian gods, and also those who became wives or mistresses of Zeus. If Kronos and Rhea, the founders of the main Olympian line, and Koios and Phoibe, the grandparents of Apollo and Artemis, are therefore put aside along with Themis and Mnemosyne, who will both enter into liaisons with Zeus, we are left with four Titan families whose members will consist mainly of deities who are connected with the natural world and its ordering. Two of these families are founded by Titan couples, namely **Okeanos** and **Tethys**, and **Hyperion** and **Theia**, while the two others are founded by male Titans who wed outside the circle of their sisters, namely **Iapetos**, who married his Okeanid niece Klymene, and **Kreios**, who married into the other family of Gaia by taking Eurybia, daughter of Pontos, as his wife. For a survey of the origins of the Olympian gods, see p. 80; and for the children of the Titans Themis and Mnemosyne, see p. 78.

Okeanos and Tethys and their children the Okeanids and rivers

OKEANOS was the god of the Ocean (Okeanos, a word of non-Greek origin), a great river that was thought to encircle the lands of the earth on every side. The goddess TETHYS was traditionally regarded as his wife; indeed in one tradition, as we have just seen, the pair were regarded as the first couple and the ancestors of the other gods. Hesiod, who has other ideas on that matter, acknowledges the venerable status of Okeanos, at least as the source of all the rivers and springs of the earth, by classing him as the eldest of the Titans.[98] Even if he was not a nonentity like some of his brothers and sisters, he lived too far away and was too closely identified with his streams to make many appearances in mythical narratives. The *Iliad* reports that Rhea entrusted her daughter Hera to Okeanos and Tethys to be reared in their palace in the Ocean while Zeus was confronting Kronos and the Titans; and Pherecydes recounts a tale in which Okeanos tried to intimidate Herakles by raising his waves while the hero was crossing his waters to fetch the cattle of Geryoneus (see p. 264).[99] The god appears on the stage in the *Prometheus Bound*, arriving on a griffin or some creature of the kind to offer sympathy and advice to the enchained Prometheus.[100] Tethys came to be identified with the sea in Hellenistic and later times; an astral myth suggests that she refuses to allow the Great Bear to set into the sea out of consideration for the feelings of her former foster-child Hera (for this polar constellation, which never sets below the horizon, was supposed to represent a former mistress of Zeus, Kallisto, who had been transformed into a bear, see p. 541).[101]

Okeanos and Tethys produced 3,000 (i.e. innumerable) sons, comprising all the RIVERS of the world (*Potamoi*, which are masculine in Greek), and 3,000 daughters, the Ocean-nymphs or OKEANIDS (Okeanidai, or Okeaninai). The functions of the latter were by no means confined to the water; Hesiod remarks that they are scattered everywhere, haunting the earth and deep waters alike, and observes in particular that they watch over the young.[102]

The *Theogony* offers a catalogue of forty-one Okeanids. Although the names of many of them are no more than poetic inventions as in the case of the Nereids, a few noteworthy figures may be found among them. **Metis**, the personification of cunning intelligence, was swallowed by Zeus after conceiving Athena to him, and reappears accordingly in a later section of the *Theogony* (see p. 77), as does the Okeanid **Eurynome**, who bore the Charites to him (see p. 78). **Peitho** (Persuasion), who presided over all forms of persuasion from the political to the amatory, was often regarded as an attendant of Aphrodite (see p. 198). **Tyche** (Fortune, equivalent to the Roman Fortuna) became a goddess of some importance in Hellenistic and later times when she came to be widely honoured in cult both as a universal power and in relation to the fortunes of particular places or potentates. **Dione**, who was sometimes regarded as a consort of Zeus, was the mother of Aphrodite in the Homeric account (see p. 80). Hesiod includes a **Kalypso** in the list, but it need not be assumed that he had the lover of Odysseus (see p. 497) in mind; although Odysseus' liaison with the goddess of that name is mentioned in the present text of the *Theogony*, the reference comes at the very end of the poem in a section that was added after Hesiod's time.[103] Homer describes her as a daughter of Atlas. **Doris** was the wife of Nereus and mother of the Nereids (see p. 51), **Klymene** the wife of the Titan Iapetos (see p. 49), **Kallirhoe** the wife of Chrysaor and mother of Geryoneus (see p. 62), **Perseis** the wife of Helios, and **Iduia** the wife of Aietes, king of Colchis. If Hesiod places **Styx**, the goddess of the infernal river of that name, at the end of the list, he indicates that he is doing so because he regards her as the most important of the Okeanids;[104] she will be considered below in connection with her husband (see p. 49). Most of the maidens who are named as attendants of Persephone in the *Homeric Hymn to Demeter* are Okeanids from Hesiod's list.[105] Apollodorus classes Amphitrite, the consort of Poseidon, as an Okeanid rather than as a Nereid as in the *Theogony*.[106] The chorus in the *Prometheus Bound* is formed from a group of Okeanids.

On the male side of the family, Hesiod names only a few of the most notable RIVERS by way of example; and we will narrow the range further by picking out the four that are of greatest interest from a mythological point of view, the Eridanos, Acheloos, Alpheios and Skamandros. Originally a mythical stream that lay somewhere in north-west Europe, the ERIDANOS came to be identified with the Po[107] (or sometimes with the Rhône, or with both rivers in a geographically impossible combination, see p. 393). Phaethon was supposed to have plunged into it when he fell from the chariot of the Sun (see p. 45), and the Argonauts were sometimes said to have sailed along it during their return journey, to pass from the head of the Adriatic to the western Mediterranean (see p. 394). Since amber was conveyed from the Baltic to the Mediterranean by way of the river-systems of western Europe (among other routes), it is understandable that the Eridanos should have come to be regarded as its source in Greek lore;[108] for the legend that was devised to explain why amber appears in the river, see p. 45. The Greeks applied the name of the river to the great river-like constellation in the southern sky that is still known as Eridanus.[109] The god of the Eridanos has no myths as a personal being. The ACHELOOS, which rose in Epirus in north-western Greece and flowed to the sea near the northern entrance to the Corinthian Gulf, was the largest river in Greece. The river and its god play a significant role in the legend of the Argive hero Alkmaion (see p. 327); and Herakles wrestled with him for the hand of Deianeira, who came from Calydon not far from his streams (see p. 280).

Acheloos also appears in two transformation myths recounted by Ovid. According to one, some naiad nymphs forgot to invite him to a local sacrifice and festival along with other deities of the area, causing him to swell with rage until his waters flooded over and washed them out to sea to become the Echinades, a group of islands just outside the Corinthian Gulf, not far from the mouth of the Acheloos.[110] The other tale tells how he once seduced a maiden called Perimele, whose father Hippodamas was so angry to learn of it that he hurled her over a cliff into the sea. Acheloos held her up in the water, however, and appealed for the help of Poseidon, who turned her into an island that was known by her name.[111]

The god of the ALPHEIOS, the longest river in the Peloponnese, was famous for his love of ARETHOUSA, a Syracusan spring-nymph. Although the idea of the river's journey through the sea to Sicily was certainly quite old since it was known to Ibycus and Pindar, the bucolic poet Moschus (second century BC) is the first author to state that Alpheios made the journey out of love. Emerging from his river-mouth, he dived into the depths of the sea, passing through it in such a way that his own waters never mingled with its salt-waters.[112] Ovid and Pausanias explain the origin of the Syracusan spring through transformation-stories. According to Ovid, Arethousa was originally a Peloponnesian nymph who was more interested in hunting than love, but inadvertently awakened the love of Alpheios by bathing naked in his waters after a hunting-trip. When he pursued her afterwards, Artemis tried to rescue her from him by first enveloping her in a mist and then transforming her into a stream; but since Alpheios simply resumed his original form to mingle his waters with those of the newly created stream, Artemis was obliged to take further action by opening up a cleft in the earth to enable Arethousa to escape to Sicily, where she formed the spring that bore her name.[113] Ovid does not state that Alpheios travelled to Syracuse thereafter to pursue his love, as in the traditional story; and we are presumably not meant to assume this, for Artemis arranged her removal to Sicily for the specific purpose of preventing Alpheios from mingling with her. In Pausanias' account, Alpheios also acquired his final form as the result of a transformation, for he was originally a Peloponnesian hunter who fell in love with a huntress called Arethousa. As is generally the case with huntresses in myth, she had no desire to marry him or anyone else, and therefore fled across the sea to Syracuse, where she was turned into a spring in unexplained circumstances; and Alpheios was then turned into a river 'out of love' (presumably to enable him to mingle with the spring).[114]

The SKAMANDROS (Scamander) is familiar from the *Iliad* as the main river of the Trojan plain. Homer reports that it sprang up from two adjoining springs, one steaming hot and the other ice-cold, and was known to the gods as Xanthos[115] (the Yellow River, evidently because it was coloured by the soil that was carried in its waters). Skamandros was highly honoured by the Trojans, who sacrificed many bulls to him and used to cast living horses into his streams.[116] While Achilles was advancing against Troy after the death of Patroklos, he gravely offended Skamandros by polluting his waters with a multitude of Trojan corpses; and on finding that his protests were greeted with contempt, the river-god overflowed his banks, casting the bodies ashore and almost drowning Achilles. When he then called on the assistance of Simoeis, the other main river of the Trojan plain, Achilles would surely have perished if Hera (an eager supporter of the Greeks) had not asked Hephaistos to force Skamandros to return to his courses by setting fire to his banks.[117] Later sources report that Teukros, the first king of Troy, was a son of Skamandros, and that two subsequent kings, Tros and Laomedon, were married to daughters of his (see p. 521ff).[118] This reflects a common pattern in which primordial rulers or their wives are classed as children of local river-gods, as is understandable since rivers are such prominent features of the untransformed landscape.

According to a tradition mentioned by Aristotle, the Skamandros was called the Xanthos because it turned sheep yellow if they drank from it. This idea inspired a late myth in which Hera, Athena and Aphrodite (or the latter alone) were said to have bathed in it to turn their hair gold before the judgement of Paris.[119]

The children and descendants of Hyperion and Theia

The Titan HYPERION and his wife and sister THEIA, who have no myths of their own, were the parents of three children who brought light to the heavens, Helios (the Sun, Sol in Latin), Selene (the Moon, Luna in Latin) and Eos (Dawn, Aurora in Latin).[120] These deities were little worshipped in Greece, although HELIOS was often invoked in oaths in his capacity as an all-seeing god who would be able to bear witness to any perjury. His most important cultic centre was Rhodes, where he was honoured as a god of the very first rank. Pindar recounts a legend that explains how he came to be lord of the island. Long ago, when the gods were dividing the earth among themselves, Helios was granted no land of his own because he happened to be absent (presumably on his daily journey through the sky). Although Zeus offered to make amends by ordering a recasting of the lot, Helios told him that he would be satisfied with a wonderful new land that he had seen rising up from the sea, the fertile island of Rhodes. So he took Rhodes as his bride and fathered seven sons by her, one of whom (named elsewhere as Kerkaphos) was destined to father the eponyms of the three greatest cities of the island, Ialsysos, Kameiros and Lindos.[121] On the mainland, Helios was most highly honoured at Corinth; see p. 103 for the story of how he competed with Poseidon for the city and land. From the classical period onwards, he was sometimes identified with Apollo, who was a radiant deity like himself.[122] The fact that both gods were archers (the Sun's rays being described as his arrows by a common and natural metaphor) may have encouraged the identification.

In art and literature Helios is normally represented as a charioteer who drives across the sky each day from east to west (although he is also imagined very occasionally as riding on horseback, or as flying on his own wings); in pictorial images, his head is often surrounded with a nimbus and rays of light. His chariot-team consists of four (or less commonly, two) gleaming horses, which are usually winged in earlier images. The poets liked to give them appropriate names such as Pyroeis (Fiery), Eoos (Orient), Aithon or Aithops (Blazing), Phlegon (Flaming) and the like.[123] Helios plunged into the stream of Ocean in the furthermost west after his daily journey, where he bathed and relaxed before travelling back to the east during the night. It was naïvely imagined that he made this journey by floating around the encircling Ocean in a huge golden cup which had been made for him by Hephaistos; he lent it to Herakles on one or two occasions as we shall see (pp. 264 and 271). His palace lay near the sunrise in the east (although we occasionally hear of a western palace in the late tradition). According to the early elegiac poet Mimnermus, he kept his sunbeams in a golden chamber in his palace.[124]

It is mentioned in the *Odyssey* that Helios owned seven herds of immortal cattle and seven flocks of sheep which were pastured by two of his daughters on Thrinacia, an island vaguely situated in the remote west (though later identified with Sicily). When detained on this island by bad weather, the followers of Odysseus killed some of the cattle to satisfy their hunger even though their leader had expressly ordered them not to, an act of sacrilege that was reported to Helios by his daughter Lampetie. Helios was so angry that he approached Zeus and the other gods with his grievance, threatening to desert the sky and shine among the dead in Hades if he was not adequately avenged; so Zeus took action on his behalf by striking Odysseus' ship with a thunderbolt, causing the death of everyone on it apart from Odysseus himself (see also on p. 497).[125] Helios also appears in a wholly different context in the *Odyssey*, as the all-seeing god who informed Hephaistos that his wife Aphrodite was engaging in an adulterous love affair with Ares (see p. 201). By virtue of his position in the sky, he is able to perform a comparable service for Demeter in the *Homeric Hymn to Demeter*, by telling her that her daughter has been carried away by Hades (see p. 127).[126]

Augeias, king of Elis, was sometimes said to have acquired his innumerable cattle (see p. 260) from his father Helios; according to Theocritus, twelve of them were special swan-white beasts that were sacred to Helios.[127] For the tales in which Helios was said to have reversed his course to provide a portent for Atreus or in horror at the cannibal meal served by Atreus, see p. 506.

The official consort of Helios, if one may so call her, was Perse or Perseis, daughter of Okeanos, who bore him two children in the earliest tradition, Aietes, king of Colchis, whose legend will be recounted in connection with the Argonauts, and the enchantress Kirke, whose remote island home was visited by Odysseus (see p. 494) and the Argonauts (see p. 395). Further children are credited to the couple in later sources, most notably Pasiphae, the wife of Minos, and Aloeus, a primordial king of Sicyonia (see p. 432).[128] Lampetie and Phaethousa, who tended the cattle of Helios on Thrinacia, are described in the *Odyssey* as daughters of his by a certain Neaira.[129]

The most notable of the illegitimate children of Helios was PHAETHON ('the Radiant'), who was borne to him by Klymene, the wife of Merops, king of the Ethiopians; this Klymene is said to have been a daughter of Okeanos like the wife of Helios (although she must obviously be distinguished from the Okeanid of that name who is the wife of Iapetos in the *Theogony*).[130] Although there is no very early evidence for the famous legend of Phaethon's misadventure with his father's chariot, the story was probably recounted in the Hesiodic literature[131] (whether the *Catalogue* or the *Astronomy*) and certainly in the lost *Heliades* of Aeschylus. The story takes the following form in the fullest narrative by Ovid. Phaethon was reared by Klymene in her husband's palace, which lay in the remote east no great distance from the palace of Helios. She told him that he was a son of Helios, and he bragged about his high descent until one of his comrades could stand it no longer and retorted that it was a lie. When he approached his mother for reassurance, she swore by Helios himself that she had spoken the truth and advised him to visit his father's palace if he wanted further confirmation. So he set off for the splendid palace of the sun-god, which had walls and pillars of gleaming metal and a roof of ivory; and he received a kindly welcome from Helios, who acknowledged him as his son and offered him the choice of whatever he most desired. When he responded by asking to drive the chariot of the sun across the sky on the following day, Helios tried to warn of the dangers, but was finally obliged to grant his consent in accordance with his promise. As Helios had foreseen, Phaethon was unable to control the spirited chariot-horses and drove an erratic course, sometimes soaring too high and sometimes descending too low, much to the alarm of Earth, who began to fear for her own survival as her surface caught fire and her waters dried up. So she appealed urgently to Zeus, who hurled a thunderbolt at Phaethon, causing him to fall from the chariot and plunge to his death in the river Eridanos (see p. 41) far below.[132] All the main features of this story can be found in earlier sources; there was also a slightly different version in which Phaethon mounted the chariot in secret without gaining his father's permission.[133]

Phaethon's sisters, the HELIADES, mourned for him so grievously after his death that Zeus or the gods took pity on them and transformed them into poplar-trees; they continue to weep for their brother in their new form, shedding resinous tears into the Eridanos, hence the origin of amber.[134] Or in a less favoured account, their father transformed them into trees to punish them for yoking his chariot for Phaethon without his consent.[135] The death of Phaethon was also lamented by KYKNOS, king of the Ligurians, a superb musician who had been a relative or friend of his, or indeed his lover. The gods (or Apollo specifically) pitied his sorrow and turned him into a swan (*kyknos* in Greek), a bird that shares his musical nature and sings mournfully before it dies.[136] Some accounts add that Kyknos was transferred to the sky to become the constellation of the Swan (Cygnus).[137]

When a myth was devised to explain the origin of the heliotrope, a plant that keeps its flowers constantly turned toward the sun, Helios was bound to play a central part in it. Ovid's account runs as follows. On beholding LEUKOTHOE, daughter of Orchamos, king of Persia, the most beautiful girl in the land of spices, Helios conceived a desperate passion for her, forgetting all his previous loves. So he made his way into her room in the guise of her mother and dismissed her attendants, and then resumed his proper form in order to seduce her. One of his former mistresses, a certain KLYTIE (who is described elsewhere as a sister of Leukothoe) was so jealous of Leukothoe that she caused it to become generally known that she had a lover. On hearing the rumour, her cruel father buried her alive, and she died before Helios could rescue her. Overcome by sorrow, he sprinkled nectar over her body and the surrounding soil, causing an incense-tree to grow up in place of her. As for Klytie, he would have nothing to do with her, and she pined away for love of him, refusing all food and drink, until she finally turned into a heliotrope; and she retains her love for Helios even in this new form, as is witnessed in the movement of the flowers of the heliotrope. In another account, the father of Leukothoe is called Orchomenos, which would imply that her story is now set in Boeotia in mainland Greece.[138]

The gently radiant SELENE (or Selenaia, or quite often Mene in poetic usage), the goddess of the moon, could be pictured as a charioteer like her brother; no one who has seen the Parthenon marbles is likely to forget the marvellous head of one of her chariot-horses that survives among them. Some authors specify that she drives a pair rather than a four like her brother, in accordance with the standard image in vase-paintings and other works of art. She is drawn by two snow-white horses or occasionally by oxen. Or in some portrayals, she rides through the heavens on a horse (or steer or mule, or even a ram), facing sideways with both legs on one flank of her mount.[139] There is an attractive literary account of her journey through the sky in the *Homeric Hymn to Selene*, which also reports that she once slept with Zeus and bore him a daughter called Pandeia (an obscure figure whose name may have been derived from a title of Selene).[140] The only notable legend recorded for the moon-goddess is the one that tells of her love for Endymion, a hero of Elis in the western Peloponnese; see further on p. 411. There is also an interesting but poorly attested legend in which Pan is said to have seduced her. Vergil mentions in passing in the *Georgics* that he won her over by offering her the snowy fleece of a sheep, and the scholia report that the Hellenistic poet Nicander offered an account in which Pan wrapped himself in a sheepskin to approach her.[141] The rusticity of the tale suggests that it may have originated as a local legend in Arcadia.

There is some disagreement about the descent of Selene. According to the *Homeric Hymn to Hermes*, her father was Pallas, son of Megamedes (otherwise unknown),[142] who may perhaps be identified with the Pallas who is classed as a son of the Titan Kreios in the *Theogony*. Or in the *Homeric Hymn to Helios*, Hyperion is said to have fathered her and her two siblings by Euryphaessa ('she who shines far and wide') rather than by Theia.[143] One or two passages in tragedy refer to her as a daughter of Helios (rather than as his sister), which seems appropriate enough in view of her borrowed light.[144] Herse (Dew), the goddess or personification of the dew, is described as a daughter of Zeus and Selene in a lyric fragment from Alcman,[145] but this is really no more than an allegorical fancy referring to the heavy dew-fall associated with clear moonlit nights. Selene was quite often equated with Artemis in post-classical times, just as Helios came to be equated with Apollo; this already seems to be implied in a fragment from Aeschylus which suggests that Selene was a daughter of Leto.[146] She was of importance in magic as a goddess who could be appealed to in the laying of spells, especially love-spells; in the second *Idyll* of Theocritus, she is invoked by a girl who is portrayed as laying a spell of this kind.[147]

The third child of the union between Hyperion and Theia was EOS (the Dawn, Latin Aurora). As a light-bringing goddess who ascends into the sky ahead of Helios, she represents something more than what we might ordinarily understand by the dawn, namely the light of the new day (and, to an increasing extent, even daylight without qualification). Hemera, Day personified, was often identified with Eos as a consequence, even if she is a separate being in the *Theogony* (see p. 24). Eos is usually shown as winged in works of art, unlike her brother and sister; but in her capacity as a light-bringer, she ascends in a chariot just as they do, commonly a two-horse chariot like that of Selene. In poetry from Homer onwards, she is described by picturesque epithets that refer to the colours of the sky at dawn, such as 'rosy-fingered' (*rhododaktylos*) or 'saffron-robed' (*krokopeplos*).[148]

Eos has a comparatively well-marked personality, being pictured as an amorous goddess who liked to abduct handsome young men. The most famous and best-recorded story of this kind is that which tells of her relationship with TITHONOS, a son of Laomedon, king of Troy, and a brother of Priam. The legend was plainly very ancient since both the *Iliad* and the *Odyssey* refer to Eos as rising 'from her bed beside lordly Tithonos' when she sets off to bring the light of day to gods and mortals.[149] Homer mentions that Tithonos was a son of Laomedon, and later sources indicate that he was a legitimate child of the king (by Strymo, daughter of Skamandros in most accounts).[150] The *Homeric Hymn to Aphrodite* provides the earliest full account of his story. Eos carried him off and asked Zeus to render him immortal, but never thought to ask in addition that he should retain his youth and so be exempted from the ravages of age. While he was still young, the two of them lived happily together by the streams of Ocean at the edges of the earth; but when the first grey hairs began to sprout on his head and chin, Eos abandoned his bed even though she continued to take care of him in her house, providing him with food and ambrosia and fine clothing; and when he became so feeble that he could no longer move his limbs, she laid him in a room behind closed doors, where he has babbled away helplessly ever since.[151] According to a familiar tale that first appears in the classical period, Eos finally transformed him into a musical insect, the cicada (*tettix*).[152] This idea was presumably inspired by the reference to the cease-less talking (*aspetos phēmē*) of the incapacitated Tithonos in the Homeric Hymn; the high-pitched talk of old men is compared to the singing of cicadas in a famous passage in the *Iliad*.[153] It may also be relevant that cicadas were supposed to survive on dew alone (for it would seem that Tithonos was no longer fed when he was shut up behind closed doors). It is stated in one late source that Eos transformed him so as to be able to enjoy his song.[154] In earlier and happier days, she bore him two children, namely Memnon, king of the Ethiopians, who fought as an ally of the Trojans in the last stages of the Trojan War (see p. 468), and Emathion, who was killed by Herakles in Ethiopia (see p. 271).[155] We should imagine that the couple lived somewhere in the remote east near the dawn. Their son Memnon was usually associated with the east accordingly, as we will see, rather than with the African Ethiopia.

The *Odyssey* refers to two other love affairs of Eos, stating in the first place that she abducted the hunter Orion, causing resentment among the gods, who tended to disapprove of liaisons between goddesses and mortals; so they incited Artemis to kill him in his new home of Ortygia (usually identified with Delos in later times).[156] This account of the death of Orion was displaced by other stories in the later tradi-tion (see pp. 563–4). The *Odyssey* also mentions that Eos was so attracted by the beauty of Kleitos, son of Mantios, a grandson of the great seer Melampous, that she carried him away to dwell with the immortals.[157] It is reported in the *Theogony* (in a section added after Hesiod's time) that Eos loved a certain Kephalos and bore him a son Phaethon (not to be confused with the son of Helios above), who was seized by Aphrodite to serve in her temple.[158] Although this Kephalos – who was appar-ently a son of Hermes – was properly a separate figure from the Kephalos, son of Deion who was the husband of Prokris in Attic legend, the two were sometimes identified in the later tradition, and Eos was occasionally introduced into the legend of Kephalos and Prokris as a consequence (see further on p. 372). To explain the over-susceptible nature of Eos, some claimed that Aphrodite caused her to be constantly falling in love to punish her for having slept with Ares (who was Aphrodite's lover or husband).[159]

In addition to her many lovers, Eos had an official consort, ASTRAIOS (Starry), a son of the Titan Kreios and the Okeanid Eurybia. Her children by this marriage were the stars of the heavens and the three main winds, Boreas (the North Wind), Zephyros (the West Wind) and Notos (the South Wind).[160]

Hesiod singles out the Morning Star, HEOSPHOROS, as the most notable of the starry children of Eos. It should be remembered in this connection that the planets or 'wandering stars' (*planētes asteres*) were not regarded as being essentially different from the fixed stars. The planet now known as Venus was called Heosphoros (Dawn-bringer) and Phosphoros (Light-bringer) in Greek in its nature as the Morning Star, or Hesperos as the Evening Star (*hesperos astēr*); it was recognized quite early, however, certainly before the classical period, that the two stars are one and the same. Even if Eos were not the mother of all the stars, it might naturally be assumed that Heosphoros would be a child of hers since he is the harbinger of the dawn. It was perhaps as a result of this initial thought, indeed, that Hesiod decided to make her the mother of all the stars and gave her a starry husband. Although Heosphoros has no surviving myths as a personal being, he makes some slight appearance in the heroic genealogies as the father of Keux, husband of Alkyone (see p. 410), and of Telauge, the mother of Autolykos.[161]

Eos was presumably regarded as a suitable mother for the winds because the wind often rises at dawn in Greece. Hesiod classes the three greatest winds as her children while all the harmful winds of inferior nature are described as offspring of the monstrous Typhon (see p. 84). Although ZEPHYROS (the West Wind) is characterized as a cleansing wind in the *Theogony* and tends to be stormy in Homer, he is customarily viewed as mild and gentle in the later tradition (an idea preserved in our English word 'zephyr'). The divine messenger Iris visits 'fierce-blowing Zephyros' in his home in the *Iliad*, while he is dining there with the other winds, to summon him and Boreas to blow on the funeral-pyre of Patroklos, for Achilles had prayed for their help after it had failed to kindle.[162] As we will see (p. 58), Homer states that Zephyros fathered the horses of Achilles by a Harpy. BOREAS, the violent North Wind, descended on Greece from his northern homeland of Thrace. His most important story is the Athenian legend that told how he abducted Oreithuia, a princess of that land, to make her his wife (see further on p. 371). She bore him twin sons, Zetes and Kalais, the Boreads (Boreadai), who shared something of their father's nature as winged beings who could fly swiftly through the air, and were famous for their pursuit of the Harpies (see p. 387). As a consequence of his marital connection with Athens, Boreas brought special help to the Athenians on more than one occasion (see p. 371). NOTOS, the god of the moist west wind (which was considered to be unhealthy) never developed into a mythical figure of any significance. The Winds were usually pictured as winged and bearded, and often as wild of aspect. According to differing conceptions that can both be found in Homer, the winds could be regarded either as independent agents or as being subject to the control of Aiolos, the lord of the winds (see p. 493).[163]

The children of Kreios and Eurybia

The Titan KREIOS (or Krios), a thoroughly obscure figure, married a daughter of Pontos (Sea) called Eurybia. They had three sons, Astraios, Pallas and Perses, who were of genealogical significance alone as the husbands of Eos, Styx and Asterie respectively, goddesses of greater individuality than themselves.[164] Astraios has already been considered in connection with Eos. PALLAS (genitive *Pallantis*, to be distinguished from Pallas, gen. *Pallados*, the well-known title of Athena) married STYX, the goddess of the infernal river of that name (see p. 109), who is classed by Hesiod as the eldest of the Okeanid nymphs. As her children by Pallas, she gave birth to four personifications, Zelos (Emulation or Glory), Nike (Victory), Kratos (Strength or Power) and Bia (Might or Force).[165] When the great war between the Titans and the younger gods was about to break out and Zeus was assembling his allies, Styx, at the urging of her father Okeanos, brought him her children, who all represented forces that would be invaluable in the forthcoming conflict. Zeus was duly grateful and paid high honour to Styx and her children, declaring that the solemn oaths of the gods would be sworn by her waters, and that her children would live with him forever (in so far as the qualities that they represent would become attributes of his own).[166] When serious disputes arose between the gods thereafter, Zeus would send Iris to the Underworld to fetch some water from Styx in a golden jug; and if any god swore falsely by it, he would be deprived of nectar and ambrosia for a year (and so rendered insensible), and would be banished from the company of the gods for nine years.[167] PERSES, the remaining son of Kreios and Eurybia, married Asteria, a daughter of the Titans Koios and Phoibe, and fathered the goddess Hekate by her (see p. 193).[168] Hesiod remarks that he was pre-eminent for his wisdom, but no myths are recorded to show how he displayed it. He should be distinguished from two mortal heroes of the same name, a brother of Aietes (see p. 400) and a son of Perseus (see p. 242).

The children of Iapetos and Klymene

The Titan IAPETOS married the Okeanid Klymene (or the Okeanid Asia) and fathered four sons by her, Prometheus and Epimetheus, whose interrelated myths will be considered in the next chapter (see pp. 92ff), and Atlas, who supported the heavens, and the comparatively obscure Menoitios.[169] Hesiod indicates that MENOITIOS clashed with Zeus like his more famous brother Prometheus, but offers no details, merely stating that Zeus struck him with a thunderbolt and hurled him down to Erebos (the nether darkness, presumably of Tartaros) on account of his folly and presumption.[170] It appears that later authors knew little more about him than we do. Apollodorus remarks, to be sure, that he was struck down by Zeus during the war between the Titans and the younger gods (evidently because he was supporting the Titans), but this may well be some mythographer's conjecture rather than a genuine early tradition.[171]

ATLAS performed the arduous but essential duty of holding up the sky. Much as in the case of Menoitios, it was suggested in later times that he had angered Zeus by supporting (or even leading) the Titans in their war with the younger gods, and was burdened with this duty as a consequence;[172] but there is no reason to assume that it was regarded as a punishment for some specific offence in the early tradition. According to the *Theogony*, he supports the sky on his head and hands, standing at the edges of the earth near the Hesperides (i.e. in the far west); or in a gentler account in

Figure 2.2 Herakles holds up the sky for Atlas. Drawing after a Greek vase-painting.

the *Odyssey*, he holds the tall pillars that keep the earth and sky apart, apparently standing somewhere in the sea.[173] In works of art he is usually shown holding up a globe that represents the sky (and sometimes has figures of the constellations marked on it accordingly). Although Pausanias states that he was shown holding up the earth and sky in images on the chest of Kypselos and the barriers around the statue of Zeus at Olympia,[174] the artists had presumably intended the globe to represent the sky alone. Herodotus is our earliest source for the rationalistic account in which sky was said to rest on Mt Atlas in the western reaches of North Africa.[175] Atlas lived so far away and was so constrained by his task that there was little occasion for him to appear in heroic myth; indeed, the story in which Herakles took over his burden while he went to fetch the apples of the Hesperides (see p. 272) is his only myth of that nature that is at all ancient. He was of genealogical importance nonetheless as the founder of one of the great heroic families, that of the Atlantids; see Chapter 15.

THE FAMILY OF PONTOS AND GAIA

Gaia founded another family of a rather different nature by mating with her son PONTOS (Sea). Most of its members were either nymphs of the waters, or else monstrous beings who could be fittingly imagined as having sprung from the form-less element. Pontos himself is barely personified, and has no myths or cult; the great god of the seas in the Greek tradition was Poseidon, an Olympian deity. Gaia bore five children to Pontos, one of whom, **Eurybia**, has already been mentioned as the wife of the Titan Kreios. **Nereus** was a sea-god who fathered a great many sea-nymphs, the Nereids, and **Thaumas** was the father of the Harpies and of Iris, goddess of the rainbow. Nereus and Thaumas took Okeanids from Gaia's other family as their wives, while **Phorkys**, who was a sea-god like Nereus, married his sister **Keto** to found an alarming family of monsters.[176]

Nereus and Doris and their daughters the Nereids

NEREUS, the eldest son of Pontos and Gaia, was a sea-god who lived in a shining cave in the depths of the sea with his many daughters, the Nereids. He was of limited significance in myth and of virtually none in cult, at least by classical times. Hesiod describes him as truthful and never-deceiving, evidently because he was gifted with prophetic powers (as was so often the case with sea-deities), and states that he is called 'the old one' (*gēron*, a title suggestive of the wisdom of old age) because he is unerring and gentle and ever mindful of what is right.[177] This name of the 'old one' or 'old man of the sea' was a collective title which could also be applied to other sea-gods who were of subordinate rank to Poseidon, such as Phorkys (see p. 58) and Proteus (see p. 484), who are both called by that title in the *Odyssey*.[178] As Hesiod's description would imply, Nereus seems to have been viewed as a kindly, wise and helpful deity who was hardly ever formidable as sea-gods were inclined to be. Nereus has only a single myth of any real note, the quite ancient story in which Herakles wrestled with him to force him to reveal the route to the Hesperides (see p. 269). Although he tried to escape by transforming himself into water and fire and all manner of different beasts, the hero kept a firm grip on him until he was finally willing to speak;[179] the struggle is depicted on vase-paintings from the sixth and fifth centuries BC, which show Nereus with a fish-tail initially but later in fully human form. In another quite early tale, he delivered the cup of the sun to Herakles after Helios had offered to lend it (see p. 264);[180] and in one of Horace's odes, he imposes a calm to halt the ship of Paris after his abduction of Helen and rises up from the sea to warn him of all the evil consequences that will follow from his action.[181] It is sometimes suggested in late sources that he reared Aphrodite in his home under the sea.[182]

Nereus married the Okeanid Doris and fathered a large family of sea-nymphs, the NEREIDS (Nereides), who lived with their parents under the sea.[183] They were of

Figure 2.3   A Nereid riding a cuttlefish. Drawing after a Greek vase-painting.

considerable significance in popular belief and cult, far more so than Nereus himself. Herodotus reports, for instance, that the Persians offered sacrifice to them in accordance with Greek practice when their fleet was once struck by a persistent storm off the coast of Greece. With very few exceptions, they remained together as virgins, emerging from their home only to sport with the sea-beasts in the waves above or to dance on the shore.[184] If Nereids were a form of mermaid in ancient belief (although it should be noted that they were not fish-tailed), their name has come to be applied to land-nymphs and fairies in modern Greece, quite displacing the Dryads, Meliai and so forth. By another shift of meaning, the name Gorgon has come to be applied to mermaids.

Poets exercised their ingenuity in devising pretty names for the Nereids, mostly referring to the sea and seafaring, such as Neso or Nesaie, 'island-girl', Eulimine, 'good-harbour-woman', Kymatolege, 'wave-stiller', and Pontoporeia, 'sea-farer'. Hesiod provides a catalogue of fifty names, and other lists which vary to differing extents may be found in the *Iliad*, Apollodorus and Hyginus.[185] The Nereids are rarely accorded any specific role as a group in mythical narratives, although Homer reports that they went ashore with their sister Thetis to mourn the deaths of Patroklos and Achilles (see pp. 464 and 468), and it is stated in later epic that they helped the Argonauts through the Wandering Rocks at the bidding of Hera (see p. 395).[186] Three emerge as separate personalities with stories of their own, namely Amphitrite, the queen of the seas, who will be considered later in connection with her husband Poseidon (see p. 104), and Thetis, the mother of Achilles, who was forced into an unhappy marriage with a mortal, and Galateia, who was courted by the Kyklops Polyphemos in a relatively late myth set in Sicily. Mention should also be made of a lesser Nereid, Psamathe, who was caught by surprise by Aiakos, king of Aegina, and bore him a son Phokos (see p. 531).

The Nereid Thetis and her brief marriage to Peleus

THETIS was a beautiful Nereid who was once courted by both Poseidon and Zeus. It was fated, however, that she would give birth to a son who would be more powerful than his father; and the Titan Themis, who shared the prophetic powers of her mother Gaia, alerted the two gods to this danger, adding that if either of them should father this son by her, he would wield a weapon mightier than either the thunderbolt or trident. Having gained power by deposing his own father just as his father Kronos had before him, Zeus needed no second warning and agreed with his brother that it would be safer to marry her off to a mortal. At the suggestion of Themis, the Thessalian hero Peleus (see pp. 533ff) was selected for this honour because of his exceptional piety. Such is the account offered by Pindar,[187] who writes elsewhere that Zeus assigned Thetis to Peleus to reward him for his righteousness in spurning the advances of the wife of Akastos (see p. 534).[188]

An idiosyncratic version of this story was offered in the Prometheus trilogy ascribed to Aeschylus. We are told in the surviving *Prometheus Bound* that Prometheus has learned from Gaia (who is here described as his mother and is equated with Themis[189]) that Zeus is fated to father a son mightier than himself and meet his downfall if he marries a certain bride;

Figure 2.4   Peleus wrestles with Thetis. Red-figure vase-painting.

but because he has quarrelled with Zeus and been persecuted by him as a consequence, he refuses to disclose the identity of this bride, even though he is warned by Hermes that Zeus will inflict even worse sufferings on him if he persists in his refusal.[190] It would seem, however, that in the next play in the trilogy, the *Prometheus Unbound*, he revealed that Thetis was the fateful bride, and so won his release.[191] This account of the story was presumably invented by the playwright himself for his own immediate purposes. On the course of events in the trilogy, see further on p. 95.

In a wholly different version from the *Cypria*, the first epic in the Trojan cycle, it was Thetis herself who rejected the idea of a union between herself and Zeus, out of respect for the feelings of Hera; for according to an ancient tradition that can be traced back to the *Iliad*, Thetis had been fostered and reared by Hera. Zeus was so angered by the rebuff that he swore that she would have a mortal for a husband. This version was apparently recounted in the Hesiodic *Catalogue* too.[192]

However it came to be decided that Thetis should be married to a mortal, this was not a prospect that she would willingly accept, and Peleus was therefore obliged to capture her by force in the first place, which was by no means easy considering that she was a sea-goddess who could transform herself at will. He lay in wait for her by the Thessalian coast and caught her by surprise as she emerged from the sea, and then kept a firm grip on her even though she tried to escape from him by assuming all manner of different forms. Pindar is the first author to allude to the story in the surviving literature, remarking that the goddess turned herself into fire and a lion with sharp claws and fearsome teeth; but Peleus' capture of Thetis can be traced back to the seventh century BC in the visual arts, and her transformations are regularly indicated from the second half of the sixth century onwards.[193] It is clear from both the literary and artistic evidence that she was thought to have turned herself into a lion and snake in particular; we know from Pausanias that the chest of Kypselos already showed her with a snake emerging threateningly from her hand (as an indication of the respective transformation).[194] Authors from Herodotus and Euripides onward often locate the incident at Cape Sepia in Thessaly, at the southern end of the eastern coastal district of Magnesia. In connection with the great storm that destroyed part of Xerxes' fleet in the area in 480 BC, Herodotus reports that part of the coast was sacred to Thetis, and that the Persians offered sacrifice to her and the Nereids.[195] Later sources claim that Cape Sepia acquired its name because Thetis turned herself into a cuttlefish (*sēpia*) during her struggle with Peleus, and was at last overpowered by him while in that form.[196] Peleus was sometimes said to have been acting on the advice of the wise Centaur Cheiron when he ambushed Thetis and seized her as his bride.[197] It is likely that this story in which he wins her by his own exertions was of separate origin to that in which she is granted to him by Zeus, even if the two accounts do not necessarily conflict and came to be combined in the later tradition.

This picturesque tale was bound to appeal to Ovid; in his version, Peleus met with failure when he first tried to make love to the goddess. She liked to ride in from the sea naked on a dolphin to lie down in a cave by the shore, and Peleus happened to discover her there one day while she was asleep. When his words failed to move her, he resorted to action instead and wrapped his arms round her neck; but she proceeded to transform herself, first into a bird, then into a tree and lastly into a fearsome tigress, giving him such a fright that he allowed her to escape. He then sought the help of the gods of the sea, offering libations and sacrifices to them by the shore, until Proteus rose up and told him how his prospective bride could be captured, advising him to bind her fast while she was asleep and then hold her tight however often she transformed herself until she returned to her original shape. On finding herself vanquished by these means, she recognized that he had benefited from divine aid and yielded to his will, revealing that she was Thetis.[198]

After Peleus had won Thetis through this rough courtship, their marriage was formally celebrated on Mt Pelion in the presence of the gods.[199] Homer already mentions that they all attended the wedding, including Apollo with his lyre in hand;[200] and their procession as they approach Peleus' house, some on foot and some riding in chariots, is portrayed on some handsome vases from the sixth century onwards, notably the François Krater. This wedding is cited by Pindar along with that of Kadmos (who married the goddess Harmonia, see p. 297) as an illustration of the highest happiness that could be attained by a mortal man;[201] but the happiness of Peleus was destined to be short-lived since Thetis continued to feel that the union was unworthy of her, and abandoned her mortal husband soon after the birth of their only child (or only surviving child) Achilles. It is explained in many accounts that she was determined to have an immortal child and left home forever when her hopes were frustrated. In the earliest tale of the kind, from a lost Hesiodic poem, the *Aigimios*, she bore a series of children to Peleus and threw each of them into a cauldron of boiling water at birth to test whether they were immortal; but after many had perished as a consequence, Peleus stopped her from doing the same with Achilles, provoking her to desert him in a fury.[202] The Hellenistic poet Lycophron offers a similar story, saying that she killed six sons in succession by hurling them into a fire (presumably for the same reason as above) before Peleus intervened to rescue the seventh, Achilles.[203] Or according to another tradition, she took active measures to render Achilles immortal, just as Demeter had with her nursling Demophoon (see p. 128), by dipping him into a fire at night to burn away his mortal flesh, and rubbing his body with ambrosia by day to make it immortal and ageless; but Peleus saw the child writhing in the flames one night and cried out in horror, causing Thetis to abandon the enterprise and leave home forever.[204] It was commonly agreed that she left in any case, and that Peleus entrusted the young Achilles to the Centaur Cheiron to be reared and educated; see further on p. 458. For the late story in which Thetis is said to have rendered Achilles partly invulnerable at least by dipping him into the river Styx, see pp. 456–7.

The Nereid Galateia and her admirer Polyphemos

According to a relatively late and none too serious legend, the Nereid GALATEIA (Milk-white), aroused the love of a most improbable suitor, the Kyklops Polyphemos, who is familiar from the *Odyssey* as a one-eyed ogre who captured Odysseus and ate some of his men (see p. 492). In so far as his character was softened by the effects of love, he is represented as being a less formidable and savage creature than in the Homeric story, as he set out to win the favour of the sea-nymph with such untutored love-songs and other modes of courtship as his not very abundant wits could suggest. There could be no question, of course, of her yielding to her uncouth admirer, and she was able to keep at a safe distance from him by remaining in her own element. The story of this one-sided love affair, which is set in Sicily, can be traced back to a lost dithyramb, the *Kyklops* of Philoxenus of Cythera (c. 436–380 BC), of which only a few brief fragments survive. It told how Polyphemos took up the lyre to sing the praises of Galateia, and of how Odysseus tried to win his release from the ogre by offering to put his ingenuity to work to help him to gain his desire.[205] This poem became very celebrated, not least because it was supposed that the depiction of Polyphemos was intended as a satirical portrait of Dionysios I of Syracuse. The theme, which offered scope for both pathos and comedy, proved appealing to subsequent poets; a sample of the lovesick ogre's singing can be found in the eleventh *Idyll* of Theocritus. He is sadly aware that his single eye and squat nose have not advanced his cause with the nymph; and yet all the same, if she would only come up from the sea, he could offer her an abundance of milk and cheese, and fawns and bear-cubs as pets, and a snug cave to share with him in the mountain-side.[206]

Polyphemos has a rival in Ovid's account, a handsome youth called ACIS, who is a son of Faunus (a rustic Italian god comparable to Pan) by a local water-nymph, Symaethis. One day, after addressing his customary appeals and plaints to Galateia from a hill beside the sea, Polyphemos suddenly noticed that she was lying with Acis behind a rock, and reverted to his former ogreish ways in his jealousy; for he tore a huge rock out of the side of Mt Etna and hurled it at his rival, crushing him beneath it. Galateia turned his blood into water as it trickled from under the rock, so creating the stream on Etna that bore his name; and she turned Acis himself into the horned god of the stream. He retained his original features except that he was larger and his face was now a deep blue. This transformation story, which reappears in a few Latin sources without any great variation, may have been devised by Ovid himself.[207]

If Polyphemos was sometimes presented as having succeeded in his desire, it was simply because Galateia seemed a suitable mother for Galates (or Galas), the eponym of the Galatians (i.e. Celts of Gaul; the province of Galatia in Asia Minor acquired that name because Celtic immigrants settled there in the third century BC). The Hellenistic historian Timaeus, who was of Sicilian birth, described Galates as a son of Polyphemos and Galateia, while a conflicting story, also of Hellenistic origin, claimed that Herakles had fathered him by a Celtic princess as he was travelling through Gaul with the cattle of Geryon.[208] According to a tale of a very similar kind, Herakles fathered Keltos, the eponym of the Celts, in Gaul by Kelto or Keltine, daughter of Bretannos;[209] eponyms of this kind and their accompanying birth-stories could be invented as necessity demanded.

According to a tale from the late tradition, Nereus had an only son called NERITES who became the special favourite of Aphrodite while she was still living in the sea (for it is assumed here that she lived there for some time after being born from the sea-foam that surrounded the severed genitals of Ouranos). When she set off to Olympos to join the other gods, she wanted to take Nerites with her and offered him a pair of wings (evidently to equip him for the journey); but he preferred to remain beneath the waves with his parents and many sisters. Angered by the rejection, the goddess turned him into a sea-snail (*nēritēs*) and bestowed the wings on Eros instead, making him her constant companion from that time onward. There is also mention of another story in which Nerites was a favourite of Poseidon and was transformed by Helios, who was angered for some reason by the speed at which he drove his chariot across the waves.[210]

Thaumas and Elektra and their daughters Iris and the Harpies

THAUMAS, the next son of Pontos, is an obscure figure with no legends or cult; perhaps he was another old man of the sea. His name could be interpreted as meaning 'the wondrous' in Greek, even if it is not necessarily of Greek origin. He married Elektra, daughter of Okeanos, who bore him some swift-moving winged daughters, Iris and the Harpies.[211]

IRIS was the goddess or spirit of the rainbow, the Greek name of which, *iris*, still finds a place in modern European languages as the name for the coloured membrane around the pupil of the eye and in words such as iridescent. Her chief role, where she is not simply a personification of the rainbow itself, is to act as a messenger for the gods. Although she monopolises this role in the *Iliad*, Hermes tends to displace her in later literature (see p. 158). From the classical period onwards, she is regarded increasingly as the particular servant of Hera, as Hermes is of Zeus; Callimachus even portrays her as crouching like a dog under the throne of the great goddess, ready to run errands at her call at any moment.[212] In works of art, which generally depict her as winged and often in a short tunic with a herald's staff, she appears quite frequently in a subordinate role, acting as escort to the greater deities (as when she conducts them to the marriage of Peleus and Thetis) or sometimes as their cupbearer. 'Golden-winged Iris', as Homer calls her, makes many appearances in the *Iliad*, carrying messages from Zeus (or on one occasion, Hera) to mortals or other gods, or sometimes acting on her own initiative, as when she summons the Winds to kindle the pyre of Patroklos (see p. 48).[213] She is rarely to be found, however, in mythical narratives in the subsequent literature, making only two interventions of any real note. In the *Cypria*, the first epic in the Trojan cycle, it was she who informed Menelaos of Helen's abduction[214] (for he was absent in Crete at the time, see pp. 445–6); and in Argonautic myth, she was said to have intervened to restrain the Boreads from killing her sisters, the Harpies (see p. 387).[215] According to Hesiod, Zeus would send her to fetch water from the Styx if any god should need to swear a solemn oath (see p. 49).[216] Presumably because the rainbow was regarded as a sign of approaching rain, Iris is represented here and there as the wife of the rainy West Wind, Zephyros; according to Alcaeus at least, she bore Eros to him.[217] That she had a place in cult is asserted by a single witness, the obscure Hellenistic author Samos of Delos, who says that she was worshipped on Hekate's island near Delos.[218]

The earliest accounts represent the HARPIES as being exactly what their name implies in Greek, 'Snatchers', as female death-spirits who snatch people away causing them to disappear suddenly and without trace. Although Hesiod says nothing about their activities, merely observing that they keep pace with the winds, they are mentioned on three occasions in the *Odyssey* as female death-spirits who snatch people away, causing them to disappear in this mysterious fashion. In speaking of the long and unexplained absence of his father Odysseus, Telemachos remarks in that epic that he would not grieve as much if he knew that he had met with a glorious death in battle, 'but as it is, the Harpies have spirited him away leaving no report behind; he has gone out of sight, out of knowledge, and has left me nothing but anguish and tears'.[219] As when the swineherd Eumaios uses comparable language in reference to Odysseus later in the poem,[220] this is simply a manner of speaking; but it is revealing nonetheless about the way in which the Harpies were imagined. They appear in similar guise in a more strictly mythical context in Penelope's account of the strange history of the daughters of Pandareos. Having been left as orphans after their parents were killed by the gods, the girls benefited from the favour of four great goddesses, for Aphrodite nurtured them on cheese, honey and wine, while Hera made them lovely and wise beyond all other women, and Artemis increased their stature and Athena taught them handicrafts; but as Aphrodite was travelling to Olympos to ask Zeus to arrange suitable marriages for them, the Harpies snatched them away and handed them over to the Erinyes (Furies) as servants.[221] Although no explanation is offered for this sad turn in their fortunes, Penelope's narrative tells us a great deal about how the Harpies were viewed in

Homer's time, for she states initially that the girls were carried away by storm-winds (*thuellai*) and then that they were snatched away by *Harpuiai* as if this meant much the same. The Harpies are evidently visualized, then, as wind-spirits who can sweep people away, an idea reflected in their Hesiodic names, Aello (Stormwind) and Okypete (Swiftfoot). Later authors add a third Harpy, Kelaino (the Dark).[222] They are portrayed in works of art either as winged women or as large bird-like creatures with women's heads resembling the Sirens (as on the famous Harpy tomb from Xanthos in Lydia, now in the British Museum).

If the Harpies simply functioned as 'snatchers' who removed people from the company of the living and disappeared with them, they could hardly acquire any proper myths of their own; but in one story at least, they also appear as persecutors of the living. For in a well-known myth associated with the voyage of the Argonauts, they are said to have persecuted the Thracian seer-king Phineus by swooping down to snatch his food whenever he tried to eat, and by causing even the little that was left to reek of decay.[223] This feature of their activity is mentioned in tragedy[224] and was probably portrayed in the Hesiodic *Catalogue*. They seem to be pictured in a rather different way in this connection, for while they are terrible enough as death-spirits, there is nothing disgusting about them, but the Harpies that plague Phineus are repellent creatures which seem to be modelled on carrion-eating birds. They are not only hideous and ravenous, but so disgustingly filthy that they leave an intolerable stench behind and taint any food if they come into contact with it. For the various stories that were offered to explain why Phineus came to be persecuted by them, and the story of how they were put to flight and perhaps even killed by two winged Argonauts, the Boreads, see pp. 386–7. This is their only story of the kind, apart from that of their brief persecution of Aeneas' crew in the *Aeneid* (see p. 588), which was clearly invented by Vergil himself on the basis of the Argonautic legend.[225]

According to the *Iliad*, Achilles' immortal horses Xanthos and Balios (Chestnut and Dapple) were conceived by the Harpy Podarge (Swiftfoot) to Zephyros, the West Wind, as she was grazing on a meadow by the streams of Ocean, presumably in the form of a mare.[226] Two ideas seem to be at work here: a male wind-god and female wind-spirit would make excellent parents for wind-swift horses, and an ancient folk-belief belief suggested that mares could be impregnated by the wind, which is not unlike Homer's story. The early lyric poet Stesichorus reports that Phlogeos and Harpagos (Flame-bright and Snatcher), two horses owned by the Dioskouroi, were further children of Podarge (and some very late sources claim that Adrastos' wonder-horse Areion was fathered on a Harpy by Zephyros or Poseidon, although the older traditions were quite different, see p. 101).[227]

The monstrous children and descendants of Phorkys and Keto

PHORKYS, the last of the three sons of Pontos, was an old man of the sea like his brother Nereus. He married his sister KETO (Sea-monster woman) and founded a remarkable family of monsters,[228] which in Hesiod's account seems to have taken the form represented in Table 3 (if two ambiguities in the text are rightly interpreted).

The first children of Phorkys and Keto were the Graiai and Gorgons, two groups of sisters whose myths are intertwined. The name of the GRAIAI simply means

Figure 2.5 Running Medusa (Gorgon). Amphora, Munich.

'old women'. After initially describing them as 'fair-cheeked', which would imply that they were young and attractive, Hesiod explains their name by saying that they were grey-haired from birth.[229] There is no suggestion as yet that the sisters were old and decrepit as is usually (though not always) the case in later accounts and portrayals. There are two of them here, the beautifully clad Pemphredo and saffron-robed Enyo; but a third sister, Deino or Perso, is commonly added to the group in subsequent accounts.[230] It came to be believed that they not only resembled very old women, but that the three of them possessed only a single eye and tooth between them, which they would pass from one to another so as to be able to see and eat. This feature of their legend is first reported by Pherecydes, who presumably found it in early epic.[231] Pherecydes is also the first author to mention that Perseus visited them setting off to fetch the head of their sister, the Gorgon Medusa; in the usual account, he had been told that they could reveal the way to some nymphs who would provide him with some equipment that he needed for his quest, and he forced the Graiai to disclose this information by stealing their eye and tooth and refusing to hand them back until they spoke (see further on pp. 239–40). Or in an exceptional account by Aeschylus, the Graiai acted as sentries for the Gorgons, and Perseus hurled their single eye into Lake Tritonis in Libya to prevent them from warning their sisters of his approach.[232]

The GORGONS (Gorgones or Gorgous in Greek), who were three in number, were named Stheno, Euryale and Medusa. According to Hesiod, they lived beyond the outer Ocean toward the night in the vicinity of the Hesperides (i.e. near the sunset in the far west);[233] or in another early epic account from the *Cypria*, they lived in the midst of the Ocean on a rocky island called Sarpedon.[234] It is commonly agreed in subsequent sources that they lived in or beyond the Ocean, though not always in the west.[235] Aeschylus places them close to the Graiai, however, as we have seen, and indicates that both sets of sisters lived in the east in a place that was accessible by land.[236] Although Hesiod does not trouble to describe the Gorgons, they are consistently pictured as monsters of hideous aspect, so very hideous that the mere sight of them was sufficient to turn the beholder to stone. Their grinning heads were wreathed with snakes, and they had fearsome teeth, or even tusks like wild boars.

As Hesiod already mentions, Medusa was distinguished from her sisters by the fact that she alone was mortal; and it was for that reason that Perseus chose her as his victim when he was sent to fetch a Gorgon's head (see p. 240).[237] Hesiod has occasion to refer to this episode in the *Theogony* because, in the oddest of ways, it is of genealogical significance. For Medusa was pregnant at the time of her death, having previously slept with Poseidon in a soft meadow among spring flowers, and her unborn children, CHRYSAOR and PEGASOS, sprang from her neck when Perseus cut off her head.[238] The poet remarks that Chrysaor bore that name because he held a golden sword (*chryseion aor*) in his hands, but reveals nothing further about him except that he was the father of Geryoneus (see below);[239]

Figure 2.6 Perseus slaying the Gorgon. Ivory relief, sixth century BC. Samos Museum. Photo: Richard Stoneman.

and later sources are no more informative. The visual evidence, which is also very limited, suggests that Chrysaor was not monstrous in form like so many members of this family. The winged horse Pegasos, by contrast, is prominent in myth as the auxiliary of Bellerophon (see p. 434).

Although Homer makes no reference to the story of Perseus and Medusa, he does mention that 'the head of that terrible monster, the Gorgon, a thing of fright and terror' was attached to the aigis (see p. 74) of Athena;[240] and it is at least possible that it was already accepted in Homer's time that she had acquired it from Perseus, as is reported by later authors from Pherecydes onwards (see p. 242).[241] Homer also refers to the Gorgon's head as an ornament on human armour; the crowning feature of Agamemnon's shield, for instance, is a Gorgon's head which glares from it in a horrifying manner, with representations of Deimos and Phobos (Terror and Fear) on either side.[242] As images that were not only fearsome to behold but might also be credited with magical powers (i.e. for the repelling of harm), such images were carved on breastplates and shields in historical times, and also on walls and gates. Portrayals from early Greek art tally well with the Homeric passages, showing a horrible grinning head with a flat nose, lolling tongue and staring eyes. It seems likely that the Gorgon's head or *gorgoneion* originated as an apotropaic image, existing independently as such before it was turned into a complete monster and thence into a trio of monsters.

According to a strange story in Euripides' *Ion*, Athena acquired her *gorgoneion* by killing the Gorgon (here unnamed) during the battle between the gods and the Giants, after Gaia had brought the monster to birth to provide a fearsome ally for the Giants (who were sons of hers).[243] This was probably a tale of fairly late origin, perhaps invented by Euripides himself; there is no sign of it anywhere else, whether in the literary or artistic record.

To explain why Poseidon should have wished to sleep with Medusa, it was sometimes suggested that she had been exceptionally beautiful until she came to be transformed into the familiar monster. According to Ovid, she had been lovely in every respect and especially for her hair until Poseidon had seduced her in a temple of Athena, greatly angering the virgin goddess, who had transformed her hair into coils of snakes.[244] Or in another story of the kind, Athena apparently took this action after Medusa had angered her by claiming to rival her in beauty. It is appropriate in any case that Athena should have been the deity who transformed her since she wore Medusa's head on her aigis.[245] Irrespective of such stories, the Gorgon's head came to be portrayed in less monstrous form in artistic images from the fifth century BC onwards, in which she is often depicted as calmly and coldly beautiful, or, from about 300 BC, in pathetic mode with a look of horror or pain about her eyes.

The head of Medusa, or even her hair and blood, retained an extraordinary potency after her death. There are various tales in which Perseus is said to have made use of the Gorgon's head to turn his enemies to stone (see p. 242); Herakles gave a lock of her hair to Sterope, daughter of Kepheus, to protect the Arcadian city of Tegea (see p. 547); Athena collected some of her blood and gave it to Asklepios, who used blood from the left side of her body to put people to death, and blood from the right side to cure people or even raise them from the dead; or in Euripides' *Ion*, Athena is said to have given Erichthonios, king of Athens, a phial containing two drops of the Gorgon's blood, one of which was a deadly poison and the other a cure for disease.[246] The people of Argos claimed that the Gorgon's head was buried under a mound in their marketplace, where it doubtless served a useful function in averting harm.[247]

Chrysaor, the strangely born son of Medusa, mated with the Okeanid Kallirhoe to father a son of his own, GERYONEUS (or Geryones, or Geryon).[248] Although Hesiod merely describes him as three-headed, later accounts and images present him as being triple-bodied, with three upper bodies joined together at the waist, and either one pair of legs or three. It was sometimes supposed that he was winged also.[249] He lived in the outer Ocean in the remote west on the mythical island of Erytheia ('the Red Island', a suitable name for a place that lay close to the sunset); and he owned large herds of cattle which were tended by a herdsman called Eurytion, and guarded by the dog Orthos or Orthros (see below). When the Greeks came to know of Iberia, they came to suppose that Erytheia lay somewhere off its coast, sometimes identifying it with Gadeira (Cadiz, then not attached to the mainland) or another island of the area.[250] Or Geryoneus' home was located somewhere in Ambracia in north-western Greece according to an alternative account[251] (possibly of ancient origin if it dates back to the days when this could have been viewed as a remote area that lay somewhere near the sunset). Geryoneus lived too far away to be troubled by strangers until Herakles arrived to steal some of the monster's cattle as one of his labours; triple-bodied though he was, he proved to be no match for that hero, who killed him before departing with his plunder (see further on p. 265).

The next child of Phorkys and Keto was ECHIDNA ('Snake-woman'), who was formed like a beautiful woman in the upper half of her body, and otherwise like a terrible snake with speckled skin. The gods granted her a cave for a home, deep under the earth in the land of the Arimoi (probably somewhere in Asia Minor, see p. 85), where she lived far away from gods and mortals alike, feeding on raw meat.[252] As might be inferred from Hesiod's account of her, she had little occasion to appear in mythical tales.

Apollodorus records a strange tale from the Argolid in which Argos Panoptes (see p. 230) is said to have killed her in her sleep; she is described here as a daughter of Tartaros and Gaia who used to prey on passers-by.[253] The Scythian Echidna or snake-woman who forced Herakles to make love with her (see p. 267) was plainly a different creature.

By mating with Typhon, a monster no less terrible than herself, Echidna founded a family of monstrous beasts. The three who were certainly children of her own (for there are ambiguities in Hesiod's text) are Orthos, Kerberos and the Lernaian hydra.[254] **Orthos** (or Orthros) was the watchdog of Geryoneus who was finally shot or clubbed to death by Herakles (see p. 264). Although Hesiod says nothing about his appearance, he was evidently no ordinary dog; in artistic images, he is quite often shown with two heads. His brother **Kerberos**, the hound of Hades, is often said to have had many more, fifty in Hesiod's account, or no less than a hundred according to Pindar and some later authors.[255] In works of art, however, for practical reasons, he is typically shown with three (or less commonly two), and many authors from the Attic tragedians onwards describe him as three-headed accordingly.[256] He usually has a snake for a tail, and may have serpents springing from other parts of his body also. The *Iliad* and *Odyssey* both allude to him, though not by name and without a description, mentioning that Herakles once fetched him up from the Underworld (as his penultimate or final labour, see p. 268).[257] In contrast

Figure 2.7 Bellerophon slaying the Chimaira.

to the other monsters in this group, he made a valuable contribution to the ordering of the world by ensuring that the dead remained enclosed in the Underworld (see p. 112), and Herakles was therefore obliged to set him free afterwards to allow him to return to his duties. The third child of Echidna and Typhon was the **Lernaian hydra**, which was reared by Hera in the marshes of Lerna in the Argolid to be a danger to Herakles.[258] Although Hesiod says nothing about its appearance, it was a huge snake (*hydra* simply means water-snake in Greek) which was especially dangerous in the usual tradition because of its many heads. Herakles killed it nonetheless as one of his labours, with a little help from his nephew Iolaos (see p. 258).

The next monster in the family of Echidna is the **Chimaira**. It is not clear from Hesiod's language whether she was another child of Echidna or, as is perhaps more likely, the offspring of the hydra. She was a composite being of improbable design who was formed like a huge lion with the head of a goat (*chimaira*) springing from her back, and with a snake for a tail.[259] Since her tail was tipped with a snake's head, she had three heads overall. She lived in Lycia in Asia Minor until she was killed by Bellerophon (see p. 434). The dog Orthos mated with the Chimaira (or conceivably with his mother Echidna) to produce the last two members of the family, the Theban Phix, or **Sphinx** as she is more commonly known, and the **Nemean lion**.[260] The Sphinx was a monster of a familiar Near Eastern type with the body of a lion, the head of a woman, and wings. She persecuted the people of Thebes until Oedipus killed her or caused her take her own life (see further on pp. 309ff).

The Nemean lion was raised by Hera in the Argolid to be a danger to Herakles, who killed him as his first labour (see p. 256). Although he was doubtless very large and fierce, his only really exceptional feature was his impenetrable hide, which is first mentioned by Pindar and Bacchylides.[261] Echidna's branch of the family was thus devised to account for the origin of some well-known monstrous beasts that were killed by Herakles and other monster-slaying heroes. In the form of some of these monsters, we may recognize the influence of non-Greek, chiefly Near Eastern, fancy on the Greek mind.

The last of the offspring of Phorkys and Keto, after Echidna, was the huge snake that guarded the golden apples of the Hesperides (see p. 28). Although nameless in the early tradition, it was sometimes called Ladon in Hellenistic and later times.[262] In some accounts, though apparently not most, Herakles killed it when he stole some of the apples of the Hesperides as one of his labours (see p. 272).

Phorkys is mentioned in the *Odyssey* as the father of another child, the nymph Thoosa who was the mother of the Kyklops Polyphemos;[263] and from the classical period onwards the sea-monster Skylla, who presented such a danger to the Argonauts and Odysseus (see pp. 395 and 496), was usually classed as a daughter of Phorkys, whether by Hekate or a certain Krataiis (who is named as the mother of Skylla in the *Odyssey*).[264] According to a Hellenistic tale, Phorkys brought Skylla back to life again after she was killed by Herakles for stealing some of the cattle of Geryoneus; he revived her by applying burning torches to her body.[265]

CHAPTER THREE

THE RISE OF ZEUS
AND REVOLTS AGAINST
HIS RULE

—— .•. ——

O ur central concern in the present chapter will be the mythology of Zeus, the great king of the gods. As we have seen, he did not always occupy that position, but rose to power in the third generation by displacing his father Kronos, who had won power for himself and his fellow Titans by displacing his own father, Ouranos (Sky). The first part of the chapter will be devoted to an examination of the 'succession myth' (see p. 33) which tells of the family conflicts that provoked the fall of the previous ruling gods. Various side-issues will also be considered in this connection, including other aspects of the mythology of Kronos and his wife Rhea. After Zeus had established himself as the new ruler of the universe with the help of his brothers and sisters and other allies, the Olympian order remained to be completed. All the younger Olympian deities were fathered by Zeus himself (with the possible exception of Hephaistos if he was born to Hera alone, see p. 79);[1] and Zeus also fathered some lesser goddesses who represented aspects of the new order. Although Hera was commonly thought to have been his only wife, the *Theogony* formalizes his principal liaisons with other goddesses by classing them as a series of early marriages that preceded his final union with Hera; we will consider these liaisons and their issue in the order in which they are described in the *Theogony*, before concluding with a general survey of the origins of the Olympian gods. As a sovereign who had established his own power by revolting against the former ruling powers, Zeus had to quell various insurrections on his own account to prevent the cycle from being repeated. The main subject of the latter part of the chapter will be the three great revolts that were launched against Zeus and the Olympian order by the fearsome monster Typhon, by the earthborn race of Giants, and finally by two gigantic brothers, the Aloadai. We will conclude by examining the conflict of a rather different kind that arose between Zeus and a cousin of his, Prometheus, who provoked his anger by championing the interests of the human race.

THE GREEK SUCCESSION MYTH

In the standard version of the succession myth, as recounted by Hesiod, the Titans were the first-born children of the primordial couple Gaia (Earth) and Ouranos (Sky), who then generated two sets of monsters, the Kyklopes and the Hekatoncheires (Hundred-Handers).[2] The Titans have already been discussed in the previous chapter; although Hesiod assigns individual names to all of them (see pp. 36–7) and draws them into his genealogical scheme, two alone stand out from the collective body of the Titans in the succession myth, Kronos, the second ruler of the universe, and his wife Rhea. Before we pass on to consider how Kronos entered into conflict with his father, something must be said about the monstrous children of Ouranos and Gaia, who will have their own part to play in the succession myth.

The three KYKLOPES (Round-eyes), who were giants with a single eye in the middle of their forehead, would help Zeus to victory in his war against the Titans by providing him with his thunder-weapon (see p. 74). Their connection with thunder and lightning as the manufacturers of the thunderbolt is reflected in the names that Hesiod assigns to them, Brontes (Thunder-man), Steropes (Lightning-man) and Arges (Vividly bright, an epithet applied to Zeus's thunderbolt in early epic).[3] Since they must evidently have been skilled and powerful craftsmen, it came to be imagined in the Hellenistic tradition that they assisted the smith-god Hephaistos in his labours, toiling at his side in a huge forge under Mt Etna or elsewhere (see p. 166).[4] Although one would expect the Kyklopes to be immortal in view of their divine birth, Apollo was sometimes said to have killed them for having made the thunderbolt that killed his son Asklepios[5] (see p. 151); or according to a fragment from Pindar, Zeus killed them to ensure that nobody would be able to acquire arms from them in the future.[6]

In an astral myth of Hellenistic origin, it was said that the Kyklopes fashioned the altar on which Zeus and his allies swore their allegiance before making war against the Titans, and that this altar was later transferred to the heavens, presumably by Zeus himself, to become the constellation of the Altar (Ara) in the southern sky.[7] Pausanias reports that sacrifices were offered to the Kyklopes at an ancient altar at the Isthmus of Corinth,[8] but there is no indication otherwise that they were honoured in cult.

As ancient mythographers already remark,[9] these primordial Kyklopes should be distinguished from some mythical giants of two other kinds who were called by the same name, the Homeric Kyklopes and the master-builders of popular lore. The Kyklopes of the *Odyssey* lived a primitive pastoral life without government or law on a mythical island somewhere in the furthermost reaches of the sea; if all were like Polyphemos, the ogre who captured Odysseus (see p. 492), they were savage sons of Poseidon with a single eye.[10] The Kyklopes of the other race were giants of folklore who were supposed to have erected the walls of Mycenae and Tiryns (see pp. 237 and 243) and other Mycenaean structures whose 'Cyclopean' masonry seemed to lie beyond the capacity of ordinary human workmanship.[11] They may be compared with the giants of modern folklore who are credited with the erection of megaliths or are said to have thrown down massive stones of that kind while playing at quoits.

The second group of monstrous sons of Ouranos and Gaia consisted of three gigantic beings who each had fifty heads and a hundred arms; although Hesiod refers to them by their individual names alone, Kottos, Briareos and Gyges, mythographers in later times devised a convenient name for them, calling them the HEKATON-CHEIRES or HUNDRED-HANDERS[12] (the corresponding adjective is already applied to Briareos in the *Iliad*[13]). As hundred-handed giants of irresistible strength, they would be invaluable allies for Zeus in the struggle against the Titans. Since they were sent down to Tartaros afterwards to act as guards to the defeated Titans, they make no further appearance in myth, at least as a group.

One of the brothers, BRIAREOS (the Mighty One, also called Ombriareos), has independent stories nonetheless which are set during the period of Olympian rule. He is marked out from his brothers even in the *Theogony*, for it is stated there that Poseidon made him his son-in-law at some point after the fall of the Titans by offering him his daughter Kymopoleia (Wave-walker, otherwise unknown) as a wife.[14] The *Iliad* reports that he was once summoned to Olympos by Thetis to save Zeus from a threatened revolt by Hera, Poseidon and Athena[15] (see p. 82); since Thetis was a sea-nymph, this would suggest that he lived in the sea, as might also be inferred from his relationship with Poseidon in the *Theogony*. Homer also remarks that he was called Briareos by the gods but was known to mortals as Aigaion.[16] In the *Titanomachy*, an early epic now lost, Aigaion was apparently described as a son of Gaia and Pontos (Sea) who lived in the sea and fought as an ally of the Titans.[17] If this Aigaion can be identified with Briareos, as seems likely, this account of him clearly differed in crucial respects from that in the *Theogony*. A Corinthian tradition suggested that Briareos had acted as arbitrator when Helios and Poseidon had competed for possession of the land in early times (see p. 103).[18] He was honoured in cult on Euboea under two different names, as Briareos at Karystos and as Aigaion at Chalkis.[19] All in all, he is a most intriguing figure, and one would like to know more of him than can be gathered from these surviving scraps.

Trouble soon arose within the newly generated family of Ouranos because he hated his offspring and prevented them from coming to the light. Although Hesiod is vague about the cause of his hatred, it would seem that he took a dislike to them because they were terrible to behold, especially the monsters who were born first of all. He hid them deep away inside the earth as each was born, apparently blocking their emergence by engaging in ceaseless intercourse with his consort (although Hesiod is vague on this matter too); and he took delight in his wicked works. Gaia groaned under the strain and thought up a crafty plan. After first creating adamant (a mythical metal of extreme hardness), she used it to make a large jagged sickle, and then tried to persuade her children to take action against their father. All were frightened to respond except for Kronos, the youngest and most terrible of the Titans, who took the sickle from his mother and waited in ambush for his father in accordance with her instructions. As Ouranos was engaging in intercourse with his wife at nightfall, Kronos cut off his genitals with the sickle and cast them into the sea. Aphrodite, the goddess of love, sprang up from the foam that gathered around them in the waters (see p. 194); and three other groups of children, the Giants, Meliai and Erinyes, sprang up from the earth after it was fertilised by drops of blood that fell from them (see p. 38). The Titans were now able to emerge into the light, and to assume power as the lords of the universe under the sovereignty of Kronos. It would seem, however, that in Hesiod's version (unlike that of Apollodorus, see below) the Kyklopes and Hundred-Handers remained imprisoned beneath the earth until they were later rescued by Zeus.[20]

After his rise to power, Kronos married his sister Rhea, who bore him six splendid children, Hestia, Demeter, Hera, Hades, Poseidon and Zeus; but since he was warned by his parents that he was destined to be overpowered by his own son, he swallowed each of his children at birth, causing endless grief to his wife.[21] When Zeus was due to be born, Rhea finally consulted Ouranos and Gaia on her own account, asking them to devise a plan to enable her to save her forthcoming child and bring retribution on Kronos. On their advice, she secretly entrusted the new-born Zeus to Gaia in Crete (see further on pp. 74–5) and gave Kronos a large stone wrapped in swaddling-clothes, which he swallowed in the usual manner in place of his child.[22] Hesiod offers little detail on what happened next, merely stating that Zeus grew up quickly in his Cretan hiding-place, and then forced Kronos to vomit up his children in accordance with a plan that was suggested to his mother by Gaia. After first spewing up the stone, which Zeus installed at Delphi to be a sign and wonder to mortals (see p. 145), Kronos vomited up the five brothers and sisters of Zeus in the reverse order to that in which he had swallowed them. Zeus also released the Kyklopes, who had apparently remained imprisoned beneath the earth since they had been confined there by their father Ouranos; and they showed their gratitude by arming Zeus with his all-powerful weapon, the thunderbolt.[23]

Zeus now joined together with his brothers and sisters to wrest control of the universe from Kronos and the Titans, confronting them in the greatest war ever fought, the Titanomachy (*Titanomachia*). The Titans chose Mt Othrys in southern Thessaly as their stronghold, while Zeus and his allies fought from Mt Olympos on the northern borders of the province. The battle raged on for ten long years without either side gaining a clear advantage, until Gaia revealed to Zeus and the Olympians that they would be victorious if they recruited the Hundred-Handers as their allies. So Zeus released the monsters from their confinement (for they had remained imprisoned beneath the earth like the Kyklopes), and revived their strength and spirits with nectar and ambrosia. They were then quite happy to respond to Zeus's appeal for help. The struggle now reached its decisive phase as Zeus unleashed his full fury against the Titans, dazing them with his thunderbolts, while the Hundred-Handers pelted them with huge rocks in successive salvoes. The entire universe resounded to the battle, from the high heavens to murky Tartaros. Kronos and the Titans were finally overpowered by the many-handed monsters, who hurled them down to Tartaros to be imprisoned there for evermore. To ensure that they would be securely detained, Zeus appointed the Hundred-Handers as their warders. After their hard-won victory, Zeus and the younger gods assumed power as the new rulers of the universe in the third generation.[24]

Such is the standard account of the succession myth as provided by Hesiod; Apollodorus offers an account of uncertain origin (perhaps derived from the lost *Titanomachia*, or from the Orphic literature) which differs from the Hesiodic version in some important respects. The Hundred-Handers and Kyklopes are born before the Titans in this account, and are hurled down to Tartaros by their father while the Titans are apparently left unharmed. Distressed by the loss of her children who had been cast below, Gaia incited the Titans to attack their father, giving an adamantine sickle to Kronos; and all of them took part in the assault with the sole exception of Okeanos (see p. 37 for the significance of this). Kronos struck the decisive blow, however, as in Hesiod's version, by severing the genitals of Ouranos. After the dethronement of Ouranos, the Titans rescued their brothers from Tartaros and entrusted the sovereignty to Kronos. But Kronos imprisoned the two sets of monsters once again, and then swallowed his own children with the exception of Zeus, as in the usual story. When Zeus came of age, he sought the help of Metis (the personification of cunning wisdom, see p. 77), who tricked Kronos into swallowing an emetic drug to force him to disgorge his swallowed children. With the aid of his brothers and sisters, Zeus fought against Kronos and the Titans for ten years, but was unable to defeat them until Gaia prophesied that he would be able to do so if he enlisted the help of the monsters who had been banished to Tartaros by Kronos. So he killed their warder, a certain Kampe, and set them free. The Kyklopes armed him with his thunderbolt as usual, and also gave Poseidon his trident and provided Hades with a cap of invisibility. With the aid of these devices, and presumably the assistance of the Hundred-Handers too, Zeus and his allies now defeated the Titans and imprisoned them in Tartaros with the Hundred-Handers as their guards.[25]

Fitting though it may be that Kronos and the Titans, as a race of 'former gods', should be banished from the upper world forever, this is not always the case in post-Hesiodic accounts. Pindar states explicitly, for instance, in one of his odes, that the Titans were eventually released by Zeus; and in the *Prometheus Unbound*, a lost Aeschylean play, they appeared on the stage as the chorus along with Prometheus after he was released from Tartaros (see p. 96), which would imply that they had been set free by Zeus.[26] As has already been remarked, some individuals who are named as Titans in Hesiod's list could not have been removed from the upper world at this early stage in any case. Okeanos could not have deserted his streams (see p. 37), nor Tethys perhaps the sea; Themis and Mnemosyne are said to have engaged in liaisons with Zeus even in the *Theogony*, and they were permanent forces in the world as the personifications of memory and right order; and Kronos and Rhea were themselves thought to be active in the world in so far as they were honoured in cult.

THE FURTHER MYTHOLOGY OF KRONOS AND RHEA

Greek legend offers contrasting visions of KRONOS and his regime. If the succession myth presents him as a brutal tyrant who swallowed his own children, another tradition also to be found in Hesiod presents his reign as a time of innocent happiness when mortals lived long and virtuous lives under his benevolent rule. In this view, his mortal subjects lived lives of blissful ease, much like the inhabitants of the Isles of the Blessed (see p. 116), without toil or strife or need of law, owning all things in common and enjoying abundant fruits and crops that were brought forth by the earth of its own accord; and when they finally died, it was as though they were overcome by a gentle sleep. In short, it was the Golden Age, ὁ ἐπὶ Κρόνου βίος, *Saturnia regna*.[27] This peasant's daydream of a lost age of happiness was evidently rooted in folklore; and it is by no means difficult to understand why it came to be identified with the age of Kronos. Since everything in that age was quite the opposite of what could be witnessed in the harsh present under the rule of Zeus, it could be concluded that this must be an account of the conditions that had prevailed under the rule of Kronos, not because he was presented as being in any way benevolent in myth, but simply because he had presided over the previous divine order before things came to be as they now are.

In the celebrated myth of progressive decline in Hesiod's *Works and Days*,[28] these fortunate people who lived under the rule of Kronos are presented as being the first of five successive races, four of which are named after metals of decreasing value, namely gold, silver, bronze and iron. We belong to the fifth and worst race, that of iron. The gods created a golden race of mortals first of all, who lived an ideal life under Kronos in accordance with the usual legend; and when these first people came to die, as though falling asleep, without ever having suffered the ravages of age, they became beneficent spirits (*daimones*) who roam the earth delivering mortals from harm and watching over their deeds. The gods replaced them with a silver race which was inferior in both body and mind. The people of this race took a hundred years to reach maturity, remaining all the while at their mother's side, but lived only a brief and wretched life when they finally grew up, for they were foolish beings who were unable to refrain from wrongdoing and violence and failed to honour the immortal gods. Their impiety aroused the anger of Zeus, who eventually removed them from the earth to become blessed spirits in the Underworld.[29] Zeus then brought a bronze race into being, consisting of people who sprang from ash-trees (*meliai*, which might also be interpreted as meaning ash-tree nymphs). Their armour, their weapons and even their houses were made of bronze. Powerful, aggressive and flinty-hearted, they devoted themselves to war and slaughter until they were all destroyed as a result of their own violence, and passed to the dank house of Hades leaving no name behind.[30]

Before passing on to the last of his 'metallic' races, to which he himself belongs, Hesiod interposes the 'god-like race of heroes' who fought with honour in the Theban and Trojan Wars, and showed themselves to be nobler and juster than their predecessors in the bronze race; since it was agreed that the great heroes of epic lived just before the beginning of ordinary human history, the poet evidently felt obliged to include them at this point and so interrupt his scheme of decline. Hesiod's text is ambiguous on the matter of their ultimate fate, failing to make clear whether all were transferred to the Isles of the Blessed, or else only a portion of them while others were consigned to Hades.[31] As to the present age, Hesiod regrets that he was ever born into it, for the people of the race of iron have no respite from toil and sorrow by day, or from wasting away and perishing by night. Although not wholly bad, they will grow progressively worse until Zeus destroys them in their turn.[32] It should be noted that Hesiod does not refer to golden and other *ages*, even if modern authors often find it convenient to use these terms when referring to his myth; the 'golden age' is an expression of Latin origin (from *saeculum aureum*, an ambiguous phrase which can mean both golden race and golden age).

Although Kronos was not much honoured in cult, he had a most interesting festival, the Kronia, which was celebrated at Athens and other Ionian cities in particular, and also at Thebes in conjunction with a musical contest. On the day of the festival, the normal social distinctions were overturned, and slaves would be feasted by their masters and allowed to rampage through the town creating as much noise as they wished. This could be regarded as a temporary return to the life without toil or subordination that had prevailed during the reign of Kronos. Although the Kronia has often been viewed as a harvest-festival, this is now disputed. It was celebrated well after harvest-time at Athens (though not all places), in the month of Hekatombeion, which is said to have been known as Kronion in early times; and Kronos' customary attribute of the sickle does not necessarily have agricultural connotations, for it is associated with him in connection with his attack on his father in the succession myth, and sickles are used for similar purposes by other mythical figures who have nothing to do with agriculture (e.g. by Perseus against the Gorgon, p. 240, or by Herakles against the Hydra, p. 258). The rare representations of Kronos in art show him as a majestic but sorrowful old man holding a sickle. The Greeks frequently identified him with unlovely foreign deities such as Moloch, a Semitic god who was offered human sacrifices. The Romans identified him with Saturn (Saturnus or Saeturnus), an old Italian deity whose functions are obscure; Saturn's annual festival of the Saturnalia, at which slaves were granted exceptional liberties, resembled the Kronia in some notable respects, as was recognized in ancient times.

Later authors have a fair amount to say about Kronos after his defeat. Evidently because conditions on the Isles of the Blessed (see pp. 114ff) resembled those that were supposed to have prevailed under the rule of Kronos, some authors make him the lord of those islands; Pindar already presents him in this role, with Rhadamanthys as his assistant (*paredros*).[33] Some verses that purport to come from Hesiod's *Works and Days*, but are almost certainly a later interpolation, explain that Zeus released him from his banishment to enable him to assume this function.[34] Plutarch records a picturesque tale in which he sleeps forever in an island beyond Britain (i.e. at the extremities of the known world) with many followers around him and Briareos as his guard.[35] In rationalistic accounts of a Euhemeristic nature which represent Kronos and Zeus as early kings, Kronos is often said to have sought refuge in Italy after he was deposed, hiding from Zeus in Latium, hence its name (as though it were derived from the Latin word *latere*, to hide). Vergil alludes to this tradition in the *Aeneid*, saying that Saturnus (i.e. Kronos) had ruled at the future site of Rome during his exile, where he had unified the local people and ushered in a golden age.[36]

RHEA or RHEIA, the consort of Kronos, is a grandiose but somewhat vague figure who had little place in Greek cult (except in so far as she came to be identified with Kybele, see below). She was honoured to some extent, however, in conjunction with her husband, as at Athens, where she shared a temple with him in the precinct of Olympian Zeus, and at Olympia, where one of the six altars of the Twelve Gods (see p. 81) was dedicated to the two of them;[37] and she had a sacred cave on Mt Thaumasion in Arcadia which was closed to everyone except her own priestess.[38] Since it was commonly believed that Zeus was born in Crete, it is understandable that this should sometimes have been regarded as Rhea's home in the later tradition;[39] but there is no early evidence to suggest that she was actually a goddess of Cretan origin. As the mother of the gods (i.e. of the Olympian gods of the first generation), Rhea could easily be identified with that very old and widely worshipped power, the Mother, who was honoured under all manner of names in Greece, the Aegean islands and the Asian mainland, sometimes in conjunction with a male partner, sometimes alone. Although deeply rooted in the native tradition, the Greek cult of the Great Mother (Meter) came to be strongly influenced by the cult of the Phrygian mother-goddess Kybele, which entered the Greek world from Asia Minor. The Great Mother was identified with both Rhea and Demeter; and Rhea was often equated with Kybele, whose cult finally spread through much of the Roman Empire. This had implications for myth, above all because the Cretan Kouretes, who were associated with Rhea in connection with the rearing of Zeus

Figure 3.1   Rhea-Kybele. Marble statue, Roman period. Ny Carlsberg Glyptothek.

(see below), came to be confused or equated with the Korybantes, attendants of Kybele in Asia Minor (see p. 219).

Much of the mythology of Rhea, orthodox and unorthodox alike, has to do with her relationship with Kronos and her rescue of the new-born Zeus. Since there were legends that claimed that Zeus was born and reared in other places apart from Crete, local versions of the latter story take Rhea to many corners of the Greek world (especially in the Peloponnese, see p. 76 for examples) and of Asia Minor. For an Arcadian legend of a comparable nature in which she is said to have hidden the new-born Poseidon in Arcadia, giving Kronos a foal to swallow in place of him, see

p. 102. In the *Homeric Hymn to Demeter*, Zeus sends Rhea as his envoy when he wants to inform Demeter of his decision with regard to the fate of Persephone;[40] and in one quite early version of the story of the slaughter and revival of Pelops (see p. 503), it is Rhea who restores him to life again after he has been served as a meal to the gods.[41]

Rhea was not the only mate of Kronos, even if she alone is regarded as his wife, for an old tradition claimed that he fathered the Centaur Cheiron by an Okeanid nymph called PHILYRA. To account for the semi-equine nature of their offspring, it is explained in one version of the story that Kronos turned himself into a stallion to mate with her after she tried to escape from him by turning into a mare.[42] Or in the version recorded by Apollonius, he was caught *in flagrante* by Rhea as he was having intercourse with Philyra on an island of the same name in the Black Sea, and leapt up in the form of a horse (presumably by way of disguise), while Philyra fled the area in shame to settle in Thessaly, the traditional homeland of Cheiron.[43] Or according to Hyginus, Kronos had intercourse with Philyra in the form of a stallion while he was roaming the world in search of the infant Zeus, and Philyra was so shocked by the hybrid appearance of her child that she prayed to Zeus to be transformed, and was turned into a lime-tree (*philyra* in Greek).[44] This extra transformation was evidently a late fancy inspired by the etymology. Though already called Philyrides at the end of the *Theogony*, Cheiron is first described as a son of Kronos and Philyra in Pindar's odes.[45] In accordance with his divine origin, he was a wise and noble being, in marked contrast to most of the Centaurs (who were of very different birth, see p. 554).

ZEUS AND HIS EARLIER LIFE

To attempt anything more than the briefest of sketches of Zeus is obviously impossible. Many Indo-European peoples have a divine figure who more or less corresponds to him, such as Dyaus in India, Iuppiter (i.e. Dyaus pita, the addition meaning 'father') in Italy, or Tiwaz among the Germanic peoples. The root meaning of his name is apparently 'bright', and he is the god of the sky, or rather of the phenomena of the sky or, more accurately, those of the atmosphere. His primary functions appear to be connected with rain and the return of fine weather, and also, very characteristically, with thunder and lightning. Hence he is associated also with what depends so largely upon the weather, the fertility of the soil, although this is never a very prominent aspect of his cult or nature. To all this a long string of titles bear witness, such as Ombrios and Hyettios (Rainer), Ourios (Sender of favourable winds), Astrapaios (Sender of lightning), Bronton (Thunderer), Epikarpios (Producer of fruits), Georgos (Farmer), and so forth. But he is so widely worshipped that there is hardly a department of nature or of human activity with which he is not connected in some way. He is the protector of the household and social order, and all sovereignty and law proceeds from him; he is represented as having moral concerns from an early period, particularly as a guardian of suppliants and strangers and an overseer of oaths and justice. From the time of Homer onwards, he was so firmly established as the supreme god that we feel no surprise at finding his name used by thinkers of a monotheistic tendency as practically equivalent to 'God'. Although his myths include many that are early and grotesque, or late and frivolous, he never quite loses his majesty, and is consistently represented in art as a stately figure, a vigorous man in the prime of life, standing or sitting in a dignified attitude, usually draped from the waist down, bearing a sceptre or thunderbolt, or both, and attended by his familiar, the eagle.

Zeus is often represented, in art and literature alike, as associated with the oak, a tree marked out as appropriate not only by its beauty and majesty and its long life, but also by two conspicuous facts, namely that it grew very widely in ancient Greece and is struck very frequently by lightning (as the ancients noticed and modern forestry has proved statistically).

Two important attributes of Zeus are the thunderbolt and aigis. Of the former it need only be said that before the true character of electrical phenomena came to be understood, the destructive power of lightning encouraged the thought that some heavy and pointed missile came down from the sky with the lightning-flash; and what could be more natural than to assume that it was the special weapon of the sky-god? In Greek art, Zeus' thunderbolt was shown as a biconical object, often having conventionalized lightning-flashes attached, and sometimes wings also. It was fashioned for him, as we have seen, by the Kyklopes.

The aigis (or aegis in Latin form) is described, by various authors from Homer onwards, as a fringed garment or piece of armour that could be worn as a corselet or serve as a sort of shield; as worn or held by a god, it was not only a potent defence, but a magically powerful weapon that would inspire terror in an enemy if it were held out in the hand and shaken. Aigiochos, the Aigis-bearer, is a regular title of Zeus. According to the *Iliad*, Hephaistos gave it to him as a fearsome object that would cause terror in men, and it was bright to behold and shaggy-fringed, with a hundred golden tassels;[46] although Zeus shakes it at one point to induce panic in the Greeks, and it is suggested that he will shake it over Troy on the day that the city falls,[47] it is used more often by his favourite daughter Athena (and also by Apollo on two occasions).[48] In the subsequent tradition it is primarily an attribute of Athena, who can often be seen wearing it in vase-paintings. It is frequently fringed with snake-heads in such images. According to a Hesiodic fragment, it was fashioned by Metis for Athena.[49] As something that was worn or wielded by the god of thunder, it was once argued that it can be interpreted as a thunder-cloud, but the plain meaning of the word puts this out of court; *aigis* simply means a goat-skin, just as *nebris* means a fawn-skin. In its origin, this mysterious object is nothing more than a goat's hide with the hair on, forming a fringe. Just such a garment has been worn into modern times by Greek peasants, and it doubtless clothed many ancient wooden or stone cult-objects representing Zeus, for the clothing of statues was quite common in Greece. As it was of rough hide, it would serve its wearer as a defence, not only against the weather but also against an enemy's blow; and a divine aegis as worn or brandished by an immensely powerful deity might be imagined as a formidable protection and awe-inspiring object.

Something has already been said about the circumstances of Zeus' birth in connection with the succession myth (see p. 68), in which Rhea hid him away in Crete to save him from being swallowed by Kronos and tricked her husband by giving him a stone to swallow instead. According to Hesiod, she went to the Cretan town of Lyktos (to the west of Knossos) when she was due to give birth to Zeus, and entrusted him to her mother Gaia to nourish and rear; so Gaia hid him away deep inside herself in a remote cave on Mt Aigaion (otherwise unknown, but presumably to be identified with one of the various mountains near Lyktos that contain Minoan holy caves).[50] This account is peculiar to the *Theogony*, for in the subsequent tradition the cave is either located in Mt Ida in the centre of Crete or, less commonly, on Mt Dikte to the east.[51]

Zeus was reared during his infancy by a local nymph or nymphs. In what was perhaps the most favoured tradition, he was tended by the nymph Amaltheia, who fed him on milk from a she-goat that she owned;[52] or in another version which first appears in Callimachus, Amaltheia was the name of the goat itself, and the nymph Adrasteia fed Zeus on its milk along with sweet honeycomb; or else his nurses were Adrasteia and Ida, or the Idaian nymphs Helike and Kynosura, or others of their kind.[53] There were also various picturesque tales in which he was said to have been fed by bees or suckled by a sow or the like.[54] To prevent Kronos from being able to hear the infant's cries, some minor Cretan divinities, the Kouretes (see p. 219), danced a noisy war-dance near the entrance to the cave, clashing their spears against their shields.[55] Or in a slightly different account, Amaltheia hung the infant in a cradle from a tree so that he could be found neither in heaven nor on earth nor in the sea, and the Kouretes danced around the tree.[56] Much of this is connected with ritual, and Cretan ritual at that; excavations have shown that a fair number of cave-sanctuaries in Crete were very ancient holy places dating back to the Minoan period; the dances of the Kouretes can be related to similar dances performed by Cretan youths in initiation rituals and the like (see p. 219); and it seems that a divine child who was born (and probably died) every year was a prominent object of Cretan worship.

A curious tale about Zeus' cave in Crete is recorded by Antoninus Liberalis in his anthology of transformation myths. The cave (of unspecified location) was inhabited by sacred bees that had tended the infant Zeus, but was otherwise forbidden ground to gods and mortals alike. At one time four thieves had entered the cave nonetheless to steal some of the honey, wearing full armour (to protect themselves against the bees, and probably on account of its apotropaic value also). When they saw the swaddling-clothes of Zeus, however, and the blood that had been shed at his birth, their armour fractured and fell from their bodies; and Zeus would have killed them with a thunderbolt as punishment for their sacrilege if the Moirai (Fates) and Themis (as guardian of divine law) had not restrained him by reminding him that no one could be allowed to die in a place of such sanctity. So he transformed them into various birds that bore the same names as themselves (Laios, Kerkeos, Kerberos and Aigolios). The author remarks that the blood inside the cave used to boil up at a particular time every year, presumably on the anniversary of Zeus' birth, causing a mass of flame to issue from the cave.[57]

The astronomical literature also provides some odd tales about Zeus's childhood. In one such story, the nanny-goat that nursed the infant Zeus is said to have been a wondrous child of the sun-god Helios that so alarmed the Titans, apparently because of its radiant brightness, that they asked Earth to conceal it from their view in one of her caves in Crete. When Zeus came of age and was preparing for his war against the Titans, he learned that he would be victorious if he used the hide of the goat as a shield (i.e. as his aigis); and after he duly won his victory, he covered the bones of the goat with another skin, revived it and made it immortal, and placed it in the heavens as Capella (the Goat), a bright star in the constellation of the Charioteer (Auriga).[58] Or in another tale of the kind, Kronos set off in search of Zeus and arrived in Crete, but was deceived by his son, who concealed his presence by transforming himself into a snake and his two nurses into bears. Zeus later commemorated the incident by placing images of the three animals in the sky as the constellations of the Dragon and the Greater and Lesser Bear (Draco and Ursa Major and Minor).[59] Some said that he was removed to the island of Naxos when his father came in search of him, and was raised there from that time onwards.[60]

There were also numerous local traditions in which Zeus was said to have been reared in mainland Greece (especially the Peloponnese) or Asia Minor. According to Arcadian tradition, for instance, Rhea brought him to birth on Mt Lykaion (an important centre for his cult, see p. 538), and three local nymphs, Neda, Theisoa and Hagno, reared him on an area of the mountain that was known as Kretea. Neda was the nymph of the river Neda that rose on Lykaion and flowed westwards into Messenia; it was claimed that Earth had caused it to spring forth at the request of Rhea to enable her to wash the new-born Zeus. And the other two nymphs were eponyms of springs on the mountain.[61] The Messenians claim for their part that the Kouretes had conveyed the infant Zeus to their own territory, where he had been reared by Neda and Ithome (the eponym of the Messenian mountain of that name). In reporting this Messenian tale, Pausanias remarks that it would be impossible, even if one should wish it, to number all the peoples who insisted that Zeus had been born and reared in their land.[62]

When Zeus came of age, he returned to confront Kronos and the Titans as recounted above. After the defeat of the Titans, he had two important affairs to settle, to divide the conquered universe between himself and his brothers, and to provide himself with a consort; and he was subsequently obliged to quell various revolts against the new divine order.

According to a familiar tale which is recounted by Homer but not by Hesiod, the first of these matters was briefly and amicably arranged: Zeus, Poseidon, and Hades, the three male children of Kronos, cast lots for the three main divisions of the ancestral estate, the sky, the sea and the Underworld, agreeing to hold the earth and high Olympos in common. As the outcome of the lot, Zeus won the broad sky, and Poseidon the grey sea to be his home forever, and Hades the murky nether regions.[63] After descending to his infernal realm, Hades lived a life apart and had little contact with the Olympian gods.

THE BRIDES OF ZEUS AND THE ORIGINS OF THE OLYMPIAN GODS

In Hesiod's account at least, the marital affairs of Zeus were a much more complicated matter; for although Hera is the only goddess with whom Zeus could be said to have had a marital relationship in any proper sense, Hesiod presents his main liaisons with other goddesses as a series of previous marriages. As everyone knows, Zeus was a prodigiously amorous god who was associated with a great many other women, mortal and divine, and was credited with a multitude of children. In a richly humorous passage in the *Iliad*,[64] he recites a list of his conquests to his wife as he is about to make love with her, saying that he never felt such desire for any of them as he feels for her at present, not even for the wife of Ixion, or for Danae, Europa, Semele or Alkmene, or – among goddesses – Demeter or Leto (and he could have cited many more). There were of course good reasons, religious and mythological, why he should have come to be credited with many mistresses and children. With regard to his divine children, for instance, he was thought to be the only suitable father for great Olympian deities who were not his brothers or sisters; and lesser deities too who contributed to the divine order in some way could be fittingly regarded as his children. Or with regard to his love affairs with goddesses, he evidently came to be linked to some at least for cultic and religious reasons. Since he was the male sky-god, for example, it is understandable that he should have been paired with earth-goddesses like Demeter and Semele (who was originally a Thracian goddess of this kind, even if she was later classed as a mortal heroine, see p. 170). But once he was paired with several such goddesses in the legends of different areas, or linked to a variety of goddesses as the father of different children, problems arose as soon as attempts were made to correlate all the various legends (and such attempts were clearly made very early). He must either be represented as polygynous, or be supposed to have been gravely unfaithful to his legitimate queen. The former solution was impossible, for the Greeks themselves were always monogamous and naturally represented their gods as following the same practice; the latter was more in accordance with their own ideas, which tolerated such irregularities and gave children arising from them a recognized though subordinate place in the family. It was thus accepted that Zeus had a single wife, Hera, but fathered many illegitimate children, who, with certain exceptions, would acquire divine status if their mothers were goddesses, or be mortal if they were born to mortal mothers. In the *Theogony*, however, his main divine mistresses are presented as six wives whom he had taken before his final and definitive marriage to Hera; and even though this scheme seems to have left little mark on the subsequent tradition, it will be convenient to consider the various unions in the order in which they are presented in that poem.

Zeus took the Okeanid **Metis**, the personification of cunning wisdom, as his first wife, but this was a dangerous union because she was fated to bear two exceptional children, first a daughter, Athena, who would be almost as wise and strong as her father, and then a son who would displace him as ruler of gods and mortals. On being alerted of this peril by Gaia and Ouranos, he swallowed Metis in accordance with their advice while she was pregnant with the first child. So Athena was born in due time from his own body, emerging from his head (see further on p. 181), and the threatening son was never conceived.[65] Or in a rather different version from another poem in the Hesiodic corpus (possibly the *Melampodeia*), Zeus was so angry when Hera brought Hephaistos to birth as a fatherless child (see p. 79) that he set out to perform an equivalent action, and succeeded in some sense at least by having intercourse with Metis and then swallowing her so as to bring their child to birth from within himself.[66]

The various elements in this myth can be disentangled without any great difficulty. The savage motif of the swallowing was evidently recycled from the succession myth. Knowing that he was in danger of being displaced by one of his children (just as he had displaced his own father), Kronos swallowed his children at birth, but was foiled because Zeus was saved from being swallowed; since the cycle of displacement came to an end with Zeus, what could be more natural than to imagine a story in which Zeus came to know likewise that a son of his would displace him, but removed the danger by a similar ruse to that attempted by his father? In this case, of course, he swallows the prospective mother of the child rather than the child itself. In the second place, the swallowing of Metis can be seen as a sort of allegory; for by ingesting her, Zeus takes possession of the cunning wisdom that she represents, as is fitting for the chief god. In all probability, the story of the birth of Athena from the head of Zeus originated in very ancient times as an independent myth; but it could be drawn into the present story with good effect. For Athena bears an obvious affinity to Metis as a goddess who is noted for her practical wisdom (*metis*) and presides over all manner of crafts; and if it is assumed that Metis was pregnant with this appropriate child at the time when she was swallowed, it can be explained how Zeus himself came to be 'pregnant' with Athena.

After swallowing his first wife, Zeus married the Titan **Themis**, who represents another aspect of his rule as the personification of law and right order. She bore him two sets of children who contributed in their different ways to the ordering of the world, the Horai (Seasons, see further on p. 208), and the Moirai or Fates, whom we have encountered already as daughters of Night along with other sinister powers (see p. 27), but are now reclassified in so far as they apportion good and ill to mortals in accordance with the authority of Zeus.[67]

A fragment from Pindar describes Themis as the first wife of Zeus, saying that she was brought up to Olympos by the Moirai to become his bride and bore the Horai to him; the Moirai are clearly not children of hers in this account.[68] She is usually presented as an associate of Zeus rather than a consort, an adviser who warns him not to court Thetis (see p. 52) and helps him to plot the outbreak of the Trojan War in an early epic account; in one of the later Homeric Hymns, she sits beside him as his confidante, leaning toward him to listen to his words of wisdom.[69] She is gifted with prophetic powers like her mother Gaia, whom she is sometimes said to have succeeded as presiding deity at Delphi before the arrival of Apollo.[70] The Homeric epics credit her with a special role as a goddess who presides over the gatherings of gods and mortals.[71]

Zeus' third wife, **Eurynome**, was an Okeanid like his first; she bore him a single set of daughters, the Charites or Graces (see further on p. 208).[72] Rather more important was his next union with the corn-goddess **Demeter**, which led to the birth of Kore (the Maiden), otherwise known as Persephone (see pp. 125ff).[73] His next consort after Demeter was the Titan **Mnemosyne**, the personification of Memory, who bore him a set of nine daughters, the Muses, who will be considered in Chapter 6 (see pp. 204ff).[74] Since the Muses were originally goddesses of music and poetry above all, Mnemosyne was an obvious mother for them, not only because poetry preserves the memory of the past but also because the poet himself had to place special reliance on memory before the invention of writing. The sixth and last of these preliminary wives of Zeus was his cousin **Leto**, a daughter of the Titans Koios and Phoibe. She bore two great Olympian gods to him, Artemis and Apollo.[75] Since most subsequent accounts of their birth present their mother as a victim of the jealousy of Hera (see p. 188), it was more commonly assumed that Zeus was already married to Hera at the time of their conception. The divine twins were born on the holy island of Delos.

As his seventh and last wife in Hesiod's account, or as his only wife in the usual tradition, Zeus married his sister **Hera**.[76] It is indicated plainly enough in the *Iliad* that she was his first choice rather than his last, and it is even implied in one passage that the pair first made love before the banishment of Kronos.[77] As the great goddess of Argos since time immemorial, Hera was perhaps the most august of all the Greek goddesses, and it is thus understandable that she should have come to be linked to Zeus as his legitimate spouse, even though she would originally have had no connection with him. In matters of cult, indeed, she remained largely independent of him. She was primarily the goddess of marriage and married women; her nature, functions and myths will be examined in Chapter 5.

Hera bore three children to Zeus as the offspring of their marriage, namely **Hebe**, **Ares** and **Eileithuia**; and as a counter-miracle to the birth of Athena from the head of Zeus, she brought forth **Hephaistos** as a son of her very own without prior intercourse with her husband.[78] Such is the account in the *Theogony* at least; but in other sources, including the Homeric epics, Hephaistos is often regarded as an ordinary child of Zeus and Hera.[79] The character and myths of this god of fire and metal-working will be considered in Chapter 6, as will those of his murderous brother or half-brother, Ares, the god of war. Hebe and Eileithuia, two deities of relatively minor significance, are very appropriate children for a goddess who was intimately connected with the life of women, being respectively the goddess who personified the bloom of youth and the goddess of childbirth. Both goddesses appear in cult, though only to a very limited extent in the case of Hebe; neither of them makes much appearance in myth. Only a single story of any note is recorded for HEBE, namely that she married Herakles after he was raised to Olympos as a god and so came to share in the eternal youth of the immortals (see p. 286). She was otherwise available to perform minor services for her fellow Olympians, for instance as a cupbearer;[80] and according to a tale from Euripides, she once rejuvenated Iolaos, a nephew of Herakles, to enable him to kill a hated enemy of his family (see p. 288). Although EILEITHUIA is mentioned quite often in connection with her positive function in easing childbirth, she makes her most significant appearances in myth in two stories in which Hera sets out to hinder the birth of illegitimate children of Zeus; for Hera was said to have detained Eileithuia on Olympos when Leto was due to give birth to Apollo and Artemis (see pp. 188–9), and to have instructed her or the Eileithuiai to retard the birth of Herakles (see p. 248).

At Olympia in the province of Elis, Eileithuia was honoured in conjunction with a divine child called Sosipolis. The origin of this cult was explained by the following legend. On a certain occasion long ago, as the Eleians were expecting a counter-attack from an invading army of Arcadians, a local woman approached the Eleian commanders with a baby, and told them that he was her own son and that a dream had ordered her to hand him over to fight for Elis. Taking her at her word, the authorities laid him naked in front of the army; and when the Arcadians advanced, he changed into a snake, causing them such alarm that they turned and fled. After their victory, the Eleians raised a temple to the child at the spot where they thought that the snake had disappeared into the ground. They called the new god-child Sosipolis (Saviour of the State), and decided to worship Eileithuia in conjunction with him because 'she had brought him into the world' (a lame explanation by any standards).[81] There seems little doubt that Eileithuia, with her non-Greek name and Cretan origin, appears here as the divine mother of a divine child, quite on the Cretan model.

Homer and subsequent authors sometimes refer to Eileithuiai in the plural.[82] The name Eileithuia also appears as a title of Hera and Artemis, two major goddesses who concerned themselves with childbirth. The Romans equated Eileithuia with Lucina or Iuno Lucina, their goddess of childbirth.

There is one consort of Zeus, possibly the oldest of all, who is not to be found in Hesiod's list, namely DIONE. Although she is mentioned twice in the *Theogony*, first among the deities who are praised in the processional songs of the Muses (which would imply that she was a goddess of some eminence), and then among the daughters of Okeanos,[83] it is nowhere suggested that she has any special connection with Zeus. But Homer refers to her as the mother of Aphrodite, who is indubitably a daughter of Zeus in his poems, and he must therefore have known of the union between Zeus and Dione; she comforts and consoles Aphrodite in the *Iliad* when she arrives on Olympos after being wounded in battle by Diomedes (see p. 461).[84] There are various indications that suggest than she was once of greater importance than might be inferred from the scant mention of her in the works of the main poets. The *Homeric Hymn to Apollo* includes her, for instance, among the foremost goddesses who attended Leto's childbearing;[85] and it is itself significant that her name seems to be no more than a feminine equivalent of that of Zeus (which takes the form of Dios in the genitive). In classical times, she was a major goddess only at Dodona in Epirus, the site of an ancient oracle of Zeus, where she was honoured as the consort of Zeus Naios (of the running water).[86] Pherecydes describes Dione as a nymph of Dodona for understandable reasons, while Apollodorus makes her a far grander figure by numbering her among the Titans.[87] Hesiod's account of the origin of Aphrodite (see p. 67) largely supplanted the account in the *Iliad* that made her a daughter of Dione; this latter relationship is never reflected in cult, although poets in the later tradition sometimes refer to Aphrodite as Dionaie (i.e. daughter of Dione) or even call her Dione.

At this point, it may be useful to take stock of the origins of the main Olympian gods. As was remarked above, these were either brothers and sisters of Zeus or else children of his, with the possible exception of Aphrodite, if she was born from the sea-foam that surrounded the severed genitals of Ouranos (as in Hesiod's account, see p. 67), and Hephaistos, if he was a child of Hera alone. If Aphrodite is left aside for the present, the major Olympians can be divided into three groups. Those who belonged to the first generation as children of Kronos and Rhea were **Zeus**, **Hera**, **Poseidon**, and **Hestia**. Although Hades also belonged to this generation, he lived far away from Olympos in his underground realm. Four major gods were born as children of Zeus in the next generation, namely **Athena**, who was born from his head, and **Apollo** and **Artemis**, his twin children by Leto, and **Ares**, who was born to him as one of his children by Hera. **Hephaistos** also belongs to this generation, whether he was a son of Zeus and Hera or a son of Hera alone. And finally, during the heroic era, Zeus fathered **Dionysos** and **Hermes** by two mortal women, Semele, daughter of Kadmos, and Maia, daughter of Atlas, respectively. As for **Aphrodite**, she was the first-born of the Olympians if she was born in the manner described above, as was commonly assumed; or she belonged to the second generation if she was the daughter of Zeus and Dione as in the Homeric account. The genealogies of the Olympian gods are summarized in Table 1.

From the classical period onwards, it was commonly believed that there were twelve principal gods, an idea that was derived from cultic rather than strictly mythological considerations. The cult of the Twelve Gods originated in Asia Minor during the archaic period and was firmly established on the Greek mainland by the fifth century BC; Pindar refers to the cult of the Twelve Gods at Olympia, where they were honoured at six altars, and Herodotus and Thucydides both mention an altar that was raised to them in the Athenian agora by the younger Peisistratos.[88] The canonic list of the Twelve, as established at Athens and later transferred to Rome, ran as follows: Zeus, Hera, Poseidon, Demeter, Apollo, Artemis, Ares, Aphrodite, Hermes, Athena, Hephaistos and Hestia.[89] It will be noted that Hestia, who enjoyed a certain precedence in cult but was of no importance in myth (see p. 139), is included in the list while Dionysos is absent; but those who are named in it are otherwise the deities who would be regarded as the principal Olympians from a mythological point of view. A variety of other gods were listed among the Twelve in connection with the cult of the Twelve Gods in other localities. The following gods were honoured, for instance, at the six altars at Olympia: Zeus Olympios, Poseidon, Hera, Athena, Hermes, Apollo, the Charites (Graces), Dionysos, Athena, Alpheios (a river-god of the area, see p. 42), Kronos and Rhea.[90]

The great gods of the Greeks were fully anthropomorphic, even if some lesser divinities and nature-spirits had animal features (and some thoroughgoing monsters are included in the divine genealogies, mostly as descendants of Pontos). Like their counterparts in the Near East, making due exception for Egypt, they were imagined as glorious beings who were human in their outward appearance and broadly comparable to human beings in their emotions and desires and their family and social life. They differed from mortals, however, in two respects above all, that their bodies were immortal and unageing (though not immune to temporary harm), and that they enjoyed a form of bodily existence that imposed lesser restraints by far on their capacities than does our own. They were born as a result of sexual activity and had to grow up (even if they were sometimes wonderfully precocious, see for instance pp. 144 and 162), but they developed and grew no further after reaching their proper maturity; some were imagined as being youthful in appearance, others as more mature and majestic. The image of a god was not always fixed; Dionysos became more youthful as the tradition evolved, and a lesser god, Eros, even regressed into infancy. Although they needed food and drink to sustain their bodies, they were nourished by special divine food, nectar and ambrosia, which can be pictured as bearing some resemblance to honey and a honey-drink respectively; and a divine fluid, ichor, therefore ran through their veins rather than ordinary human blood, and they were immune to age and decay. This aspect of their physiology is summed up by Homer in connection with a wound suffered by Aphrodite, which caused the 'divine blood of the goddess' to flow out, 'ichor, such as runs through the veins of the blessed gods, for they eat no bread nor do they drink shining wine, and are therefore bloodless and are called immortals'.[91] Since they were immortal, there could be no question of their dying if they should be deprived of their proper nourishment; according to Hesiod, a god would sink into a coma if he should be deprived of it for a year for breaking his solemn oath (see p. 49), and so lose his vitality and power of speech. Nor could they die from wounds suffered in fights or battles, but they could suffer pain and benefit from the attention of a healer (as does Ares on one occasion in the *Iliad*), and they could be rendered insensible. And more broadly, their powers, though finite and corporeal, were much less limited than those of mortals; they could go immense distances in very little time, transform themselves at will and alter the appearance of persons or objects, see things from very far off, hear in heaven prayers made on earth, or even help or harm without actually being present.

THE REVOLT OF TYPHON

After winning power by revolting against Kronos, Zeus had to suppress a few revolts against his own rule. Since he was so much stronger than the other Olympian gods, threats would usually suffice to deter them from opposing his will, let alone from rebelling against his rule. In a striking passage in the *Iliad*, he boasts that if all the other gods and goddesses grasped one end of a golden cord and he the other, they would be unable to drag him down from Olympos, whereas he, if he set his mind to it, could haul them all up along with the earth and sea besides; and he could then tie the cord around a peak of Olympos, leaving everything dangling in mid-air.[92] Homer does report, however, that Hera, Athena and Poseidon had once planned to overpower Zeus and tie him up, but were foiled by the prompt action of Thetis, who summoned the hundred-handed Briareos (see p. 67) up from the sea to intimidate them.[93] There is no way of telling whether the poet drew this story from the prior tradition or simply invented it. Since the deities in question were ardent supporters of the Greek cause in the Trojan War, and often clash with Zeus on that account within the *Iliad* itself, it is certainly possible that there may have been an ancient tale in which they attempted to force their will on Zeus at some stage in the conflict. It was commonly agreed, however, that all the serious revolts against Zeus came from outside the Olympian circle, and were directed against the Olympian order as a whole. In the first place, Gaia brought forth beings of enormous size and power on two successive occasions, the monstrous Typhon and the race of the Giants, to make war against Zeus and the new ruling gods; and a further

Figure 3.2 Typhoeus. Bronze relief: shield band panel from Olympia.

revolt was mounted thereafter by the Aloadai, two gigantic sons of Poseidon who attempted to storm Olympos.

The myth of Typhon was almost certainly of earlier origin than that of the war between the gods and the Giants, which is not mentioned in Hesiod's *Theogony*. TYPHON (Typhaon in epic) or TYPHOEUS was the most terrible of these adversaries of Zeus, for he was so immensely strong that he could threaten the divine order single-handedly. According to Hesiod (who uses both forms of his name), Gaia bore him to Tartaros as the last of her primordial children, and he was such a formidable monster that he might well have succeeded in his revolt if Zeus had not been quick to respond to the threat.

> Strength lay in his hands, and the feet of the mighty god were untiring; and from his shoulders sprang a hundred serpent's heads, terrible dragon's heads with dark flickering tongues, and the eyes beneath the brows of these wondrous heads flashed fire, and fire blazed from every head as he glared around. In all his dreadful heads there were voices that sent forth every kind of unspeakable sound, for at one time they uttered words that would be comprehensible to the gods, and at other times sounds like those of a bellowing bull, proud in its untamed fury, and sometimes like those of a lion, relentless in its valour, and sometimes like those of yelping puppies, a wonder to hear, and sometimes he would hiss like a snake until the high mountains echoed.[94]

Although eloquent in its clumsy fashion, this earliest description of Typhon is neither complete nor precise. In the next literary portrait of him, from a prose summary of a poem by Nicander (second century BC), he has a great many arms in addition to his many heads, and he is also equipped with wings and has enormous dragon's coils springing from his thighs.[95] The wings can be found at an earlier period in vase-paintings, which generally depict Typhon as a composite being with a human head and torso and a lower body formed from two or more serpent's tails. Since snakes are chthonic beings that emerge from crevices in earth, earth-born men or monsters are quite often imagined as being serpent-tailed (as in the case of Kekrops, see p. 364, or the Giants in later portrayals). In Apollodorus' description of Typhon, which is full and memorable if muddled in places, there seems to be some confusion between these serpent's tails, as found in artistic images, and the serpent's heads that spring from Typhon's shoulders in the *Theogony*; for we are told that a hundred dragon's heads sprang from his arms, and that the serpent's coils from beneath his thighs reached up to his head when fully extended and emitted violent hisses. He was of such monstrous size (so the mythographer states) that he rose higher than any mountain, and could reach out to the east and the west with his outstretched arms; and he had wings all over his body, and foul hair sprang from his head and cheeks, and fire flashed from his eyes.[96]

In the early account by Hesiod, the issue is settled by single combat between Zeus and Typhon. Rising up against the monster in all his strength, Zeus thundered mightily as Typhon poured forth flame, until the earth, sea and sky began to boil, and the world to shake, causing even Hades to tremble in the subterranean land of the dead, and the Titans far below in Tartaros. Zeus leapt down from Olympos after these initial exchanges, and struck at Typhon and lashed him and burned his many heads, forcing him down to the ground as a maimed and helpless wreck; and he then completed his victory by hurling him down to Tartaros.[97] Nothing was left of him in the world above apart from his progeny, namely his offspring by Echidna (see p. 62) and all the fierce and harmful winds that bring danger to sailors and damage the crops.[98] These noxious winds of Typhoean origin are distinguished from the divine and beneficial winds that were brought forth by Eos (see p. 48). Hesiod does not explain why Gaia, who was otherwise well-disposed toward Zeus, should have wished to give birth to this threatening monster, nor does he state that she did so with hostile intent. According to Apollodorus, Gaia brought forth the Giants first of all in anger at the fate of the Titans, and brought forth Typhon as a further danger to the gods after the Giants were defeated by them (see further on p. 90).[99]

The *Homeric Hymn to Apollo* offers a different account of Typhon's origin in which Hera is said to have brought him to birth as a fatherless child because she was furious that her husband should have brought Athena to birth without her involvement (i.e. from his head). In her anger, she struck the ground with her hand and prayed to Earth, Sky and the Titans that she should bear a child on her own that would be as much stronger than Zeus as Zeus was stronger than Kronos. She gave birth in due time to Typhon, a being who resembled neither the gods nor mortal men, and she entrusted him to the Delphian she-dragon to be reared. The poet tells us very little about the subsequent life of the monster, merely observing twice that it was a danger to mortals.[100] According to a strange account from the Homeric scholia, Gaia complained to Hera after the slaughter of the Giants, prompting her to approach Kronos, who gave her two eggs smeared with his own semen and told her to bury them in the ground, saying that they would generate a being who would deprive Zeus of his power. Hera buried them as instructed, in Cilicia in Asia Minor, and the monstrous Typhon was born from them; but she then had second thoughts and informed Zeus, who struck Typhon down with a thunderbolt.[101]

In post-Hesiodic accounts of Typhon's career, many new features are introduced into his story, mainly from the east. Since Apollodorus provides a composite account that includes most of these new elements, it will be convenient to summarize his narrative before considering certain elements in further detail. When Typhon launched an attack against heaven itself, hurling flaming rocks and emitting fearsome hisses and screams, the gods were so terrified that they fled to Egypt, where they concealed themselves by transforming themselves into animals of various kinds. So Zeus was obliged to confront Typhon on his own, first pelting him with thunderbolts from a distance, and then striking at him with an adamantine sickle (*harpē*). After pursuing the wounded monster to Mt Kasion in Syria, he grappled with him face to face; but Typhon enveloped Zeus in his coils, wrested the sickle from him, and used it to cut the tendons from his hands and feet. He then carried him through the sea to Cilicia and deposited him in a cave there (the Corycian cave), hiding the severed tendons inside in a bear's skin; and he appointed a fellow-monster as guard, the she-dragon Delphyne, who was formed half like a snake and half like a beautiful maiden. Hermes and Aigipan (Goat-Pan) managed to steal tendons, however, and fitted them back into Zeus, who soon recovered his vigour and returned to the fray. Descending from heaven in a chariot, he hurled thunderbolts at Typhon and pursued him to Mt Nysa (of uncertain location, see p. 172), where the Moirai (Fates) deceived him into eating the 'ephemeral fruits' (otherwise unknown), which robbed him of some of his strength. When pursued onward to Haimon, a mountain-range in Thrace (or now Bulgaria), he was still strong enough to hurl entire mountains at Zeus; but Zeus hurled them back at him by means of a thunderbolt, causing him to shed so much blood (*haima*) that the range below was known as Haimon from that time forth. He then fled overseas to Sicily, where Zeus completed his victory by burying him under Mt Etna.[102]

The ignominious tale of the flight and transformation of the gods was of earlier origin than one might suppose if Pindar did indeed recount it in one of his processional odes, as is reported.[103] It was inspired by an Egyptian myth in which the god Seth and his followers were said to have transformed themselves into animals when pursued by Horus. Since the Greeks identified Typhon with Seth rather than the pursuer Horus and had no interest in the original significance of the transformations, the myth was naturally much altered when they adapted it for their own purposes, to provide a mythical explanation for the theriomorphic nature of the Egyptian gods. In the earliest version to have survived, as ascribed to Nicander, all the gods fled in a panic apart from Zeus, and they turned themselves into animals on their arrival in Egypt, Apollo into a hawk, Hermes into an ibis, Artemis into a cat, Hephaistos into an ox, and so forth.[104] The basic pattern is obvious enough: the Greek gods are identified with specific Egyptian gods in accordance with accepted tradition, and are said to have transformed themselves into the animal form associated with that Egyptian god. If the animal in question has some connection with the respective Greek god in native myth or cult, so much the better, but that is not the essential point. So Apollo, for instance, who happens to be compared to a hawk in the *Iliad* and elsewhere,[105] turns himself into a falcon in the present myth because he was identified with the Egyptian god Horus,[106] who was represented as a falcon or with a falcon's head. Ovid neglects the point in his later version by saying that Apollo turned himself into a crow, the bird that was most closely associated with him in Greek myth.[107]

A further detail is added to the story in astral mythology to provide a mythical explanation for the origin of Capricorn, a constellation representing a 'goat-fish', a Mesopotamian monster that had no counterpart in Greek myth. After fleeing to Egypt along with the other god, goat-footed Pan threw himself into the Nile, turning his hindquarters into those of a fish and his forequarters into those of a goat; and Zeus was so impressed by his ingenious disguise that he placed an image of the resulting goat-fish among the stars.[108]

Although Apollodorus' narrative takes Typhon into other areas besides, he was most closely associated with Asia Minor, especially the south-eastern province of Cilicia, which may well have been his original homeland. In a passing reference in the *Iliad*, Homer states that he lay in the land of the Arimoi (*ein Arimois*, a phrase that was also interpreted as referring to some mountains called the Arima);[109] and Hesiod states correspondingly that Echidna, a monster who bore children to Typhon in his account (see p. 62), lived in a cave beneath the earth *ein Arimoisin*.[110] Most scholars of Hellenistic and later times believed that the Arimoi were a people who lived somewhere in Asia Minor;[111] but even if they were right, as is likely enough, their ideas were apparently based on conjecture rather than direct evidence from the early tradition. It seems to have been well-established by Pindar's time in any case that Cilicia was Typhon's homeland, for the poet refers to him as 'Cilician Typhoeus', and remarks that he was reared in the 'renowned Cilician cave' that plays such an important part in Apollodorus' narrative.[112] Apollodorus' story of the stolen sinews was surely taken over from Near Eastern mythology; it has been observed that there is a parallel in the Hittite tale of the struggle between the Storm-god and the dragon Illuyanka. In that myth, the Storm-god was initially defeated by Illuyanka, who robbed him of his heart and eyes; but he went on to father a son who married the dragon's daughter and recovered the stolen heart and eyes with his wife's aid. When the Storm-god was then restored to his original condition, he set out against the dragon for a second time and killed him.[113]

Typhon's connection with Etna was fairly old even if it could not have been a very ancient feature of his legend. Pindar and the *Prometheus Bound* already mention that he is buried under the volcano and causes its eruptions by breathing forth streams of fire.[114] Apollodorus seems to be exceptional in ascribing the eruptions to the after-effects of the thunderbolts that were hurled against him by Zeus. According to an alternative tradition first recorded by Pherecydes, Zeus buried Typhon under the island of Pythekousai (i.e. Ischia, off Naples, which contains hot springs and a volcano which was still active in antiquity).[115] Other mythical explanations were also offered for the flame and smoke of Etna, for some claimed that the Giant Enkelados was buried under it (see p. 86), or that the forge of Hephaistos was located in it (see p. 166).

THE REVOLT OF THE GIANTS

The other major revolt against Zeus and the Olympian order was launched by the GIANTS (Gigantes), who were defeated by the gods with the aid of Herakles in the mighty conflict known as Gigantomachy (*Gigantomachia*). The Giants were earth-born as their Greek name implies; according to the *Theogony*, they were conceived by Gaia in the very earliest times from drops of blood that fell to the ground from the severed genitals of Ouranos.[116] Hesiod describes them as powerful warriors who wore gleaming armour and carried long spears in their hands, an account that conforms with the usual portrayal of them in archaic works of art. It is not clear whether the poet meant to suggest that they sprang up from the ground fully armed (like the Spartoi at Thebes, see p. 296); Claudian, a Roman poet of the fourth century AD, is the first author to state this explicitly.[117] Even though the Giants are presented as martial beings, there is no indication in the *Theogony* that they ever revolted against the gods (except perhaps in a late section of the poem probably added after Hesiod's time, which seems to refer to the contribution that Herakles was supposed to have made in helping to defeat the Giants).[118] There is indeed no proper evidence at all for the revolt until the first artistic representations appear in the second half of the sixth century BC.

Figure 3.3   The Battle of the Gods and Giants. A detail of the Great Altar of Pergamon.
Pergamon-Museum, Berlin.

Homer alludes to Gigantes on three occasions in the *Odyssey*. The Laistrygonians, some adversaries of Odysseus in the remote seas who seem to have been very large and were certainly very violent (see p. 494), are described as being 'not like men, but like Giants'; in another passage, 'the wild tribes of the Giants' are bracketed with the Phaeacians and Kyklopes as beings who are akin to the gods; and third, we are told that a certain Eurymedon once ruled the overbearing Giants but brought destruction on himself and his people (in unstated circumstances).[119] There is no reason to suppose that the latter story has anything to do with a revolt against the gods; nor can we assume that these Giants, who seem to have lived far away over the sea, were necessarily the same as Hesiod's (any more than in the case of the Kyklopes, see p. 66). According to a tale ascribed to the Hellenistic poet Euphorion, Hera was raped by the Giant Eurymedon while she was still living at home with her parents, and bore Prometheus to him as a son. When Zeus came to learn of this after marrying her, he hurled Eurymedon down to Tartaros and ordered that Prometheus should be thrown into chains, using his theft of fire as a pretext.[120] The obscure reference to Erymedon in the *Odyssey* must have inspired the invention of this revisionist myth.

It seems likely that the main features of the story of the Giants' revolt was established in an early epic account which was widely familiar by the early sixth century BC and came to be accepted as canonic. The richness and consistency of the artistic record from the sixth and fifth centuries would otherwise be hard to explain; and the popularity of the story in this period is also indicated in a disapproving remark by Xenophanes (born c.570), who mentions the Gigantomachy along with the Titanomachy as a violent subject best avoided in after-dinner recitations.[121] The earliest literary allusions reveal nothing about the content of the legend apart from the location of the battle and its most surprising feature, namely that the gods had to call on the assistance of Herakles (during the period of his earthly life when he was no more than a mortal hero). Pindar mentions that he brought the Giants to the ground with his arrows, including their king, Porphyrion, as they were confronting the gods on the plain of Phlegrai; and the Hesiodic *Catalogue* reports likewise that he brought destruction to the Giants at Phlegrai as he was returning from his campaign against Troy.[122] On maps of the Aegean, the most striking feature of its northern shoreline is the Chalkidike with its three 'prongs', the peninsulas of Pallene, Sithonia and Athos. Phlegra or Phlegrai, the traditional home of the Giants, was usually identified with the westernmost peninsula, Pallene (although the adjoining peninsula of Sithonia and some of the hinterland of the Chalkidike were sometimes also reckoned to be part of it). Although the Giants seem to have confronted the gods on their home ground of Phlegrai in the original story, accounts were developed in which they took the battle to the enemy by trying to storm Olympos; and specific duels were said to have ranged further abroad, as we will see, to the southern Aegean and as far away as Sicily. Some Hellenistic and later accounts transfer the entire conflict to other regions, such as Arcadia or the Phlegraean (Fiery) plain in the neighbourhood of Mt Vesuvius in Italy.[123]

Apollodorus is the first author to provide a full surviving account of the progress of the conflict. If the individual motifs from his narrative are checked against the earliest artistic and literary record, it soon becomes evident that this is a composite version which was constructed mainly from early material but also contains a few stories (or variants) from the later tradition. An element that was certainly old is the involvement of Herakles. The gods knew from an oracle that none of the Giants could be killed by them unless a mortal ally was present to finish them off; so Athena summoned the aid of the greatest of mortal heroes, Herakles, who was on the island of Cos at the time, having been driven there by storm-winds as he was sailing back from Troy (see p. 276). Now Gaia too was aware of this oracle, and tried to circumvent it by searching for a herb that would prevent her sons from being killed even by this mortal helper; but Zeus spoiled her plan by ordering Dawn and the Sun and Moon not to shine until he had plucked the herb himself. From that moment, the fate of the Giants was sealed.[124] This motif of the essential helper in which gods (or kings) have to depend on an inferior to achieve their victories can be found in the myths and folklore of many lands; we have already seen that Zeus had to rely on the Hundred-Handers to defeat the Titans. In an alternative account which was probably of Hellenistic origin, the gods had to seek the help of two 'demi-gods' and summoned Herakles and Dionysos,[125] who had both been fathered by Zeus on mortal mothers (and could thus be said to have earned their divine status by their services to the gods on this occasion).

The most dangerous of the Giants were Porphyrion (who is already singled out by Pindar and Aristophanes[126]), and Alkyoneus, who was immortal as long as he fought on his native soil. In Apollodorus' narrative, Alkyoneus is the first victim of Herakles, who kills him without any immediate divine assistance at the beginning of the battle. Although the Giant began to recover his strength when he was brought to the god by the hero's arrows in his native Pallene, Herakles dragged him beyond the frontiers of the land on the advice of Athena, and was then able to put him to death.[127]

There was a tradition that claimed that Alkyoneus provoked the entire conflict by rustling the cattle of the sun-god Helios.[128] Herakles' encounter with him was sometimes presented as a separate incident which had nothing to do with the Gigantomachy. According to Pindar, Alkyoneus confronted Herakles at Phlegrai as the hero was returning from his Trojan campaign with Telamon and other allies. Herakles shot him down, though not before he had destroyed twelve chariots by hurling a huge rock at them. Since the episode is placed in the homeland of the Giants and is associated with Herakles' Trojan expedition as usual, this was presumably a secondary version in which the incident was detached from the general conflict. Pindar describes Alkyoneus as a herdsman who was as huge as a mountain without specifying that he was a *Gigas*.[129] The scholia to the passage record another version in which Alkyoneus attacked Herakles and his companions at the Isthmus of Corinth as the hero was driving the cattle of Geryoneus to Argos.[130] In a version that is known only from vase-paintings, Herakles catches Alkyoneus by surprise while he is lying asleep on the ground, creeping up on him with his club or sword in his hand.

We must now trace the story to its conclusion as recounted in Apollodorus' version. After the death of Alkyoneus, Porphyrion launched an attack against Herakles and Hera, but Zeus distracted him by inspiring him with a lust for Hera and then struck him with a thunderbolt as he was tearing at the goddess's robes. Although this would surely have sufficed to kill the Giant in ordinary circumstances, Herakles in his role as special helper of the gods was obliged to finish him off with one of his arrows; and likewise in every succeeding case, gods would bring Giants to the ground in their various ways, leaving it for Herakles to deal the death-blow with his arrows. Since Apollo was a consummate archer like Herakles, the two of them attacked the Giant Ephialtes in conjunction, Apollo shooting him in the left eye and Herakles in the right; Dionysos and Hekate used their cultic emblems, the thyrsos and flaming torches respectively, against two other Giants, Eurytos and Klytios; Hephaistos, the divine blacksmith, pelted Mimas with missiles of red-hot iron; Athena killed the fleeing Enkelados by hurling the island of Sicily on top of him, and flayed another Giant, Pallas, to use his skin as a shield; while pursuing the Giant Polybotes through the Aegean, Poseidon broke a corner off the island of Cos and hurled it down on him, so creating the little island of Nisyros not far to the south; Hades, who wore the cap of invisibility (see p. 240) to hide himself from sight, felled another Giant, as did Artemis; the Moirai (Fates) brought two opponents down with bronze cudgels; and Zeus attacked others with thunderbolts, while Herakles shot every one of them as they lay close to death on the ground.[131] Although Ares is omitted from this narrative, he appears as an adversary of the Giants, especially Mimas, in vase-paintings and literary sources.[132] Of the two stories in which Giants have islands deposited on them, that in which Polybotes is buried under Nisyros probably originated in epic since it can be found in sixth-century vase-paintings, while the story of Enkelados with its more distant setting in the west was apparently of Hellenistic origin.[133]

The Giants were pictured in different ways at different periods. In the earliest images from the sixth century BC, they are generally portrayed as handsome hoplite warriors who wear armour and a helmet and fight with a lance or sword (or occasionally wield rocks when necessity demands, as do Homeric warriors). Although they must obviously have been very large and powerful if they were to match themselves against the gods, they were not originally imagined as giants in the full modern sense of the word. It is significant in this respect that when an ordinary mortal is called a *gigas* in early Greek literature, as is the brutal Kapaneus (see p. 320) in Aeschylus' *Seven against Thebes*, the word is suggestive of reckless or impious violence rather than exceptional size.[134] In the fifth century, an alternative representation appears in which the Giants are depicted as wild and primitive beings who dress in animal skins or simple tunics (or are even naked) and use rocks and boulders as their usual weapons. And finally, from the Hellenistic period onwards, the Giants are often depicted with serpent's coils for legs, as would be appropriate for earth-born beings, and as wholly gigantic in stature.[135]

In Apollodorus' account of the earliest history of the world, Earth is said to have brought the Giants to birth because she was angered by the fate of the Titans (who were children of hers); and when the Giants were defeated by Zeus and the Olympian gods just as the Titans had been before them, Earth's rage grew all the greater and she brought Typhon to birth to provide a further threat to the Olympian order.[136] Although this narrative orders the various conflicts into a tidy pattern, it presents certain difficulties because, in the first place, Earth had previously assisted Zeus against Kronos and the Titans (in Apollodorus' account as in Hesiod's, through her advice on more than one occasion), and, in the second place, Herakles' presence at the Gigantomachy would imply that it took place in the heroic era soon before the Trojan War rather than in the earliest times soon after the Titanomachy.

The *Theogony*, which makes no reference of course to a revolt of the Giants, dates the revolt of Typhon to the period immediately following the Titanomachy, after the Titans have been banished from the upper world but before the gods have formally invited Zeus to become the new ruler. Although one might infer from Hesiod's narrative that Gaia brought Typhon to birth in anger at the fate of the Titans (as Apollodorus says of the Giants), nothing is actually stated on the matter.[137]

THE ALOADAI AND THEIR REVOLT

Two gigantic sons of Poseidon called the ALOADAI (or Aloads in Anglicized form) were the last beings to mount a major revolt against the Olympian order, or at least threaten to do so. Although they were named after their putative father Aloeus, a Thessalian hero of Aiolid descent (see p. 410), they were really the product of an extramarital liaison between his wife Iphimedeia and the great god of the seas.[138] According to Apollodorus, whose account may well have been drawn from the early tradition, Iphimedeia fell in love with Poseidon and used to make repeated visits to the sea-shore, where she would scoop water from the sea with her hands and pour it into her lap, until the sea-god emerged from his realm one day and had intercourse with her.[139] She would presumably have become pregnant through contact with the seawater alone in the original story. There is also an alternative account of Hellenistic origin in which the Aloadai are described as earth-born, like the Giants and Typhon before them.[140] Their individual names were Otos and Ephialtes.

Their legend may best be approached through the earliest account in the *Odyssey*, which tells how Odysseus met the shade of Iphimedeia in the Underworld and learned from her that she had

> slept with Poseidon and so given birth to two sons, who were but short-lived, god-like Otos and far-famed Ephialtes, the tallest men who were ever nurtured by the grain-giving earth, and the most handsome by far after famous Orion. At nine years of age they were nine cubits [i.e. about fourteen feet] across, and nine fathoms [over fifty feet] in height; and the two of them threatened to raise the din of furious battle against the very gods on Olympos. They desired to pile Ossa on to Olympos and Pelion with its waving forests on to Ossa to enable them to scale the heavens; and they would have accomplished it if they had reached the full measure of their growth; but the son of Zeus whom Leto of the beautiful tresses brought forth [i.e. Apollo] destroyed them both before the down blossomed beneath their temples and their cheeks were clothed with the bloom of a young beard.[141]

Pelion and Ossa were the two greatest mountains of Magnesia, the coastal district of northern Thessaly, and Olympos was the next great mountain to the north. It is suggested in later accounts that the Aloadai actually piled up the mountains before they were stopped.[142]

Homer's narrative tells us less than we might want to know. How did Apollo kill the Aloadai, for instance, and did he take that action specifically to prevent them from storming heaven? Later authors link their death to misguided actions of theirs in the amatory sphere. According to the usual story, Ephialtes made unwelcome advances to Hera, and Otos to Artemis, provoking Artemis to cause their death on Naxos by means of a deception. For she turned herself into a deer and ran between them while they were out hunting, causing them to kill one another with their hunting-spears as they tried to hit the deer.[143] In some form at least, this story may well have been quite ancient, since Pindar already mentions that they met their death on Naxos.[144] Hyginus offers a rather different version, stating that Apollo sent a deer between them, with the same consequence, to divert them while they were attempting to rape Artemis. An interesting detail is added here, namely that they were punished for their misbehaviour in Hades, by being tied back-to-back by snakes to a column on which a screech-owl was seated.[145] It may be relevant to this latter tale that Otos shares his name with a species of owl in Greek; perhaps the brothers were tormented forever by the screeching of the owl.

Another fragment of the legend of the Aloadai can be traced back as far as the *Iliad*, which tells how they once tied up Ares, the god of war, and imprisoned him in a bronze jar for thirteen months; 'and there Ares, insatiate of war, would even have perished, if their stepmother, the all-beautiful Eereboia, had not brought news of the matter to Hermes; he then stole Ares away when he was already greatly weakened, for his cruel imprisonment was wearing him down'.[146] It would be interesting to know whether the Aloadai took this action to remove the war-god from the scene before launching their attack on heaven, or whether this was a wholly separate incident. For what it is worth, Homer's ancient commentators explain that Ares had angered the Aloadai by killing the young Adonis (see p. 199) after Aphrodite had asked them to watch over him;[147] but it seems most unlikely that this would have had anything to do with the original story of Ares' imprisonment.

The Aloadai were also credited with more constructive achievements. They were said to have founded Askra, the home-town of Hesiod in Boeotia, and to have inaugurated the cult of the Muses on Mt Helikon.[148] After their mother and sister Pankratis (or Pankrato) were abducted to Naxos, they sailed in search of them at the bidding of their father, and seized control of the island; they eventually quarrelled, however, and killed one another in battle in their island-kingdom.[149] It was stated in this connection that they were buried on Naxos, where they were honoured in hero-cult in historical times; but their graves could also be seen at Anthedon on the Boeotian coast, and Otos had yet another grave on Crete.[150] Iphimedeia for her part was worshipped at Mylasa in Caria.[151]

ZEUS AND PROMETHEUS

PROMETHEUS, a son of the Titan Iapetos (see p. 49), revolted against the authority of his cousin Zeus not in the hope of gaining power on his own account, after the manner of Typhon and the Giants, but to bring benefits and justice to the human race; and by resorting to subterfuge rather than the use of force, he achieved a considerable measure of success, even if he had to pay a heavy penalty afterwards. The myth of Prometheus was altered and developed significantly as time progressed. In the Hesiodic poems, he advanced the interests of mortals in two specific respects alone and suffered for his actions ever afterwards, while in the later tradition from Aeschylus onwards, he was the general benefactor (and sometimes even the creator and saviour) of the human race, and was eventually freed from his punishment and reconciled with Zeus. We will start with Hesiod's account of his story in the *Theogony*.

When gods and mortals ceased to meet directly and eat together, a new relationship was established in which mortals would sacrifice animals to the gods and share the victim with them without meeting face to face. According to Greek custom, the flesh and offal of the victims would be eaten after the sacrifice while their bones would be wrapped in fat and burned on the altar for the gods. To explain this arrangement, which seems to work to the disadvantage of the gods, Hesiod offers the following story. When the gods and mortals had quarrelled over the matter in the earliest times at Mekone (later Sicyon), Prometheus, for some unexplained reason, settled the dispute to the advantage of mortals by working a deception on Zeus. He killed an ox, cut it up, and separated the flesh and entrails from the bones; and he then covered the flesh and entrails with the ox's stomach to make that portion look unappetizing, and concealed the bones under a layer of shining fat. Although the poet tries to safeguard the wisdom of Zeus by saying that he was not really fooled, we are told that Zeus reached for the more appealing portion in any case, condemning the gods to receive the worse share at animal sacrifices ever afterwards.[152]

Zeus was so angered by the deception that he withheld the gift of fire from the race of mortals. But Prometheus came to their aid once again by stealing some fire from heaven in the dry, pithy stalk of a fennel-plant (*narthex*, i.e. *ferula communis*, a relative of the British cow-parsley whose stems contain a slow-burning white pith). Zeus responded to this second provocation by imposing a second punishment on mortal men (for there were no women as yet) and by consigning Prometheus to everlasting torment. As man's price for the stolen fire, Zeus arranged for the creation of a 'beautiful evil' (*kalon kakon*), the first woman. Hephaistos fashioned her from moistened earth at Zeus' order, and Athena clothed her in silvery robes and an embroidered veil, and adorned her with garlands and a golden crown of Hephaistos' workmanship. She was then brought before an assembly of men and gods, who wondered at the sight of her, realizing that she would be an irresistible snare for men. In the present account from the *Theogony*, in which the first woman is left unnamed, Hesiod says nothing about her subsequent life, but simply expatiates with some ardour on the miseries that women and marriage have brought to men ever since. To avoid marriage brings no benefit either, since Zeus has also ensured that men who do so will face a miserable old age.[153] As for Prometheus, Zeus had him bound to a pillar with unbreakable bonds, and sent an eagle against him each day to gnaw at his liver, which grew afresh each night. Although he was eventually released from this specific torment when Herakles shot the eagle (see p. 271), an exploit that was permitted by Zeus because it would bring glory to his son, there is no suggestion that Prometheus was freed from his bonds as in most later accounts.[154]

Hesiod offers a more detailed account of the myth of the first woman in his *Works and Days*. The centre of interest in this version is rather different, since the poet is

Figure 3.4 *Pandora*, by Harry Bates (1891). Marble, ivory and bronze.
© Tate, London 2003.

primarily concerned to explain why men live a life of toil after the life of ease that they were supposed to have enjoyed in the earliest times (see p. 69), when a day's work would have been sufficient to provide for a whole year. Prometheus and his benefactions were to blame as in the *Theogony*, for he angered Zeus by deceiving him (presumably over the sacrifices, although this is not stated), provoking him to hide away fire; and when he then stole some fire for the benefit of mortals, Zeus sent the first woman to bring trouble to men.[155] At the bidding of Zeus, Hephaistos mixed some earth and water together to fashion a young woman who was as beautiful as the immortal goddesses. Athena dressed and adorned her, and taught her needle-work and weaving; Aphrodite bestowed grace and allure on her; the Charites (Graces) and Peitho (as the personification of amorous persuasion) decked her with jewellery; the Horai (Seasons) crowned her with spring flowers; and Hermes finally taught her all manner of guile and deceit, and granted her the gift of speech. He named her PANDORA (*pan*, all, *dōra*, gifts) because all the Olympians were presenting her to men as a gift and affliction.[156] Zeus now ordered Hermes to take her to Epimetheus (Afterthought), the foolish brother of Prometheus, who accepted her as a wife even though he had been warned by Prometheus never to accept a gift from Zeus lest it should bring harm to men. Only afterwards, when it was too late, did he understand what he had done.[157] Rather strangely in view of the divine status of Epimetheus, this marriage is the means by which Pandora is introduced into the human race. The *Theogony* states likewise that Epimetheus brought harm to men by accepting the woman from Zeus.[158] It is stated in the later tradition that Pandora bore him a daughter, Pyrrha, the first woman to be born by natural process, who married her cousin Deukalion (see p. 402).

After arriving among mortals, Pandora opened the lid of a great jar that she had with her, causing a host of evils and diseases to be released among mortals for the first time; for until that moment, men had lived on the earth free from toil and sickness and other ills. Hesiod says nothing about the origin of the jar; presumably she had brought it with her from the gods. Through the will of Zeus, she replaced the lid of the jar before Elpis (Hope) could fly out. Even if the narrative is not entirely logical at this point (for Hope should properly have been allowed out with all the evils if she was to live among mortals), this surely means that hope is to be reserved for mortals as a palliative.[159] This motif of the jar of evils was presumably borrowed from fable or folklore; a related notion can be found in the *Iliad*, which states that Zeus possesses two urns from which he can dispense ills or blessings to mortals.[160]

For significant developments in the mythology of Prometheus, we have to wait until the *Prometheus Bound*, a tragedy of the fifth century BC that is ascribed to Aeschylus (but may have been wholly or partially of different authorship). The drama begins as Kratos and Bia (Might and Force), two ruthless agents of Zeus, bring Prometheus forward to be chained to a rock at some unspecified place in the far north (apparently not the Caucasus). Hephaistos has accompanied them to provide his services as a blacksmith, although he is far from enthusiastic about the task or about Zeus's manner of rule.[161] The immediate cause of Prometheus' punishment is his theft of fire as in Hesiod's version,[162] but we learn in the course of the play (which contains very little action) that he has brought many other benefits to mortals, and that at one time he has even saved them from being destroyed by a tyrannical Zeus who grudges their very existence. For although Prometheus (who is here described as a son of Gaia) had helped Zeus to power by advising him on how to defeat the Titans, he later fell out with him when Zeus not only ignored the interests of human beings after his rise to power, but wanted to eliminate them to replace them with a new race.[163] By daring to oppose his intent and champion the interests of mortals, Prometheus won the enduring hostility of Zeus, and subsequently compounded the offence by conferring all kinds of benefits on human beings.

He taught them how to make houses from bricks and wood, to submit animals to the yoke and bridle, to cross the seas on sailing ships, and to read the heavens so as to be able to reap and sow at the right seasons; he invented the art of number for them, moreover, and writing and medicine, and the interpretation of dreams and omens, and the mining of the treasures of the earth; in short, he introduced or invented all the arts that raise human beings from a state of nature.[164] Hesiod's story of his deception over the sacrifices is conspicuously absent. Although Zeus had the power to exact a cruel revenge, Prometheus had the advantage over Zeus in one crucial respect, that his mother had told him that if Zeus fathered a child by a certain mother (i.e. Thetis, see p. 52), she would bear him a son who would be more powerful than his father.[165] Knowing that Prometheus was in possession of such a secret, Zeus sent Hermes to him after he was enchained to force him to reveal it; but he remained defiant in the face of every threat, and the *Prometheus Bound* ends with him being hurled down to Tartaros.[166]

This play was apparently the first in a trilogy of which the second and third plays were the *Prometheus Unbound* and *Prometheus the Fire-bringer* (unless the latter was the first in the series). The action of the *Prometheus Unbound* was set in the mountains of the Caucasus, where Prometheus was now tied down and was suffering the painful attentions of the above-mentioned eagle; and since the chorus was formed from his fellow Titans (who are mentioned in the *Prometheus Bound* as being in Tartaros), it would seem that they had been released from Tartaros along with Prometheus himself. Herakles arrived at some stage and shot the eagle, as in the old account by Hesiod; and he then proceeded to release Prometheus from his chains, as is indicated in the title of the play. Prometheus must have appeased Zeus in the course of the play by revealing that Thetis was the goddess who was fated to bear a son who would surpass his father; but since he had been so stubborn in refusing to reveal the secret in the previous play, his change of heart was presumably motivated by something more than self-interest alone. It could well be that Zeus, who is a brutal tyrant in the *Prometheus Bound*, agreed to change his ways.[167] It was commonly accepted in the subsequent tradition that Prometheus was set free by Herakles, and also that the Caucasus was the site of his punishment.[168]

It was often said that Prometheus was not merely the benefactor of the human race, but the ancestor of part or all of it, or even its creator. According to a genealogy which first appears in the Hesiodic *Catalogue*, he and his brother Epimetheus fathered Deukalion and Pyrrha respectively, who formed the first couple in the Central Greek tradition (see p. 403).[169] Since both of the relevant sources are corrupt, we cannot tell who was named as Deukalion's mother in the *Catalogue*. The *Prometheus Bound* and Acusilaus agree that Prometheus was married to an Okeanid called Hesione (although Herodotus identifies his wife as Asia, who is his mother in the *Theogony*, and various other names are suggested in later sources).[170] The idea that Prometheus created the first human beings by moulding them from clay first appears in the Hellenistic period;[171] this would at least explain why he should have wished to act as their champion. According to a local tradition at Panopeus in Phocis, two clay-coloured rocks that could be seen there were formed from the clay that was left over when Prometheus had created the human race, hence their remarkable smell, which resembled that of human flesh.[172]

It has been plausibly suggested that Prometheus originated as a trickster figure of non-moral character who liked to pit his wits against those of Zeus, and that because he was sometimes represented as tricking Zeus to the advantage of human beings, he came to acquire a new and distinctive moral role as their benefactor and defender.

Prometheus was honoured in cult at Athens in particular, as a patron of the arts of fire that were so important to that city; he was thought to preside over pottery above all, while Hephaistos (another god who was especially honoured at Athens, see p. 165) presided over metal-work. Torch races were held in his honour at his Athenian festival of the Prometheia, and there was an altar to him as Fire-bringer (Pyrphoros) at the Academy.[173]

CHAPTER FOUR

THE BROTHERS AND SISTERS OF ZEUS

——— •◆• ———

Zeus had two brothers, Poseidon and Hades, who exercised supreme power within their own realms, and three sisters, his wife and queen Hera, and Demeter and Hestia. These other children of Kronos and Rhea will form the subject of the present chapter, along with the mythology of the Underworld and afterlife. When the world was divided between Zeus and his brothers after the defeat of the Titans (see p. 76), **Poseidon** and **Hades** were allotted realms of their own, the seas and the Underworld respectively, and so acquired sovereign status within their specific domains, even if Zeus retained ultimate power as the king of the gods. Zeus also had his special domain, of course, as the lord of the heavens. Through the possession of these separate kingdoms, the gods of this older generation are set apart from the younger Olympian gods, who have no comparable domains. Since Hades withdrew to his subterranean realm after receiving it in the draw and rarely left it thereafter, he led an isolated existence, having little to do with his fellow gods or the world of the living. The activities of Poseidon, by contrast, were by no means confined to the sea, nor did his functions as the god of that realm set him apart from the common world of gods and mortals. In their images, Poseidon and Hades bear a considerable resemblance to Zeus himself, as mature bearded men of severe and majestic aspect. As regards the sisters of Zeus, we have already encountered **Hera** as his consort, and **Demeter** as an early wife or mistress of his who bore Persephone to him. Most of the major myths of Hera, the goddess of marriage, relate to her marriage to Zeus in one way or another, while the main myth of the corn-goddess Demeter brings her into conflict with her brother Hades when he abducts her beloved daughter to provide himself with a wife. The least conspicuous member of the family, **Hestia**, was the virgin goddess of the hearth; although honoured quite highly in cult, she was too homebound to have any memorable adventures.

POSEIDON, THE LORD OF THE SEAS AND THE EARTHQUAKE

In accordance with the above-mentioned division of authority, POSEIDON shared power with Zeus in the upper world as the lord of the seas; and he was also the god of earthquakes and horses. A formidable deity who presided over violent forces of nature, he was a simpler figure than his brother, and one who was much less open to change and development as moral and theological ideas advanced. Perhaps the most likely etymology of his name is the one that presents it as meaning 'Husband of Earth', on the assumption that the second element in it, -*da*- , is an ancient name of the earth-goddess; this is far from certain, however, and other etymologies have been proposed that would link Poseidon's name to the seas or waters. Whatever the origin of his name, he was a very ancient Hellenic deity whose name appears on Mycenaean tablets from Pylos and Knossos; at Pylos indeed, on the Messenian coast, he was apparently the principal god, of greater importance even than Zeus. Although he is represented above all as the great god of the seas in Homeric epic and the subsequent tradition, this can hardly reflect his original nature if he was brought to Greece by the Hellenes, since they came from far inland and had no acquaintance with the sea until they arrived in their final home. It would seem that his character must have undergone considerable change in early times as he was developed into a sea-god and then specialized in that function; but the course of that process is now impossible to trace, unless by way of speculation. Accounts of him from the literary record follow the pattern set by Homer, who portrays him in his familiar guise as the majestic and intimidating monarch of the sea, repeatedly rising from, plunging into or journeying over his allotted realm, and stirring its waters to wreck his enemy Odysseus. In art, he is shown as a tall, mature and stately figure, not unlike Zeus in general appearance, but distinguished by his emblem, the trident, and by his wilder and more uncouth appearance, a feature that is emphasised in Hellenistic art especially. The Romans, for want of a better equivalent (for they originally had no maritime gods whatsoever), equated him with a rather obscure water-deity, Neptunus, anglicized into Neptune.

If Hades was sometimes described as 'another Zeus', the same could be said of Poseidon, who was the Zeus of the sea. He lived in a golden palace under the sea at Aigai,[1] off the island of Samothrace. His main attribute was his long-handled three-pronged trident, which served both as a sceptre and as a weapon; originally a humble fisherman's harpoon, it became a fearsome implement in his hands. He could use it to stir up the sea and calm it down again, or to split rocks, as when he caused the lesser Aias to be cast into the sea (see p. 485), or to reorder the topography of the earth, as when he created the Vale of Tempe in Thessaly.[2] Pindar and Aeschylus liken it to the thunderbolt of Zeus.[3] When he passed in procession through the sea, he would be attended by sea-nymphs and the beasts and monsters of the deep. In the Hellenistic and Roman periods, his sea-passage and marriage-procession became a favourite subject with artists, who liked to portray him in the company of Tritons (see p. 106), dolphins and Hippocamps (Hippokampoi, monsters with the fore parts of a horse and the hind parts of a fish); the latter sometimes draw Poseidon's chariot or even carry him on their back. The splendour of his progress is vividly evoked in the *Iliad*, in a famous passage which describes how he set off through the sea after descending from the highest peak of Samothrace:

> thrice he strode forward, and with the fourth stride reached his goal, Aigai, where his glorious palace was built in the depths of the sea, golden and

resplendent, imperishable forever; there he went, and harnessed a pair of bronze-hooved horses to his chariot ... and drove out over the waves. The monsters of the sea gambolled beneath him on every side; and the sea parted before him in joy as his horses flew swiftly onward, and the bronze chariot-axle below was not even wetted.[4]

The main features of Poseidon's activity are summarized succinctly in the little *Homeric Hymn to Poseidon*. After referring to him as the great god of the deep who is 'the stirrer of the earth and of the barren sea', the poem goes on to say that the gods have allotted a twofold office to the Earthshaker, to be a tamer of horses and saviour of ships.[5] As this would indicate, the might of Poseidon, whether to protect or destroy, was manifested above all in the power that he exercised over the elemental forces of nature. In his main sphere as a sea-god, he was far more a god of the stormy waters than of the sea at rest; and on land, he was the god of the earthquake, as the Homeric epics already acknowledge by referring to him as the Earthshaker[6] (Enosichthon; his titles of Seisichthon and Ennosigaios carry the same meaning). Any violent storm at sea could be attributed to his work. This is another aspect of Poseidon that is vividly portrayed by Homer, in his account of the god's persecution of Odysseus in the *Odyssey*. On one notable occasion, when Poseidon saw the hero at sea on a self-constructed raft (after leaving Kalypso's island see p. 497), he 'marshalled the clouds and, grasping his trident in his hands, stirred up the sea; and he roused the storm-blasts of every kind of wind, and enveloped the land and sea alike in cloud; darkness came rushing down from the sky, and the East Wind and the South and the tempestuous West Wind and heaven-born North Wind all dashed together as one, causing a great wave to come rolling forward; and then the knees of Odysseus quivered, and his heart within him'.[7] If he could send storms, he could also protect sailors and fishermen from the perils of the sea if properly propitiated; it would be wise to invoke his aid before setting out on a voyage. He could also stir up the sea to the benefit of his worshippers, as when a sea-storm destroyed a substantial portion of the Persian fleet off Thessaly in 480 BC. On hearing of this event, the Greeks paid credit where it was due by pouring libations to Poseidon and founding the new cult of Poseidon Soter (the Saviour) in his honour.[8] Just as he would stir the sea to its depths if he so willed, he would also stir the earth to its depths as lord of the earthquake. In such circumstances, the Greeks would know who to blame or appease. When Sparta, which was particularly prone to earthquakes, was struck by a severe earthquake in 464 BC, the Spartans interpreted this as Poseidon's retribution for an act of sacrilege that they had committed not long before, by expelling and killing some helots (serfs) who had sought sanctuary in a temple of Poseidon.[9] He might be appeased in time of earthquake if sacrifices were vowed to him as Poseidon Asphaleios, in the hope that he would hold the ground firm (*asphalos*), or hymns were addressed to him.[10] As a chthonian deity, he also performed a gentler and more useful function by causing springs to rise up from the earth. He is sometimes presented as creating them with a blow of his trident, as in the case of the salt-spring on the Athenian Acropolis (see below) or the spring of Amymone in Argos (see p. 235).

Poseidon as god of horses

Another feature of Poseidon that is singled out for mention in the Homeric Hymn cited above is his function as god of horses.[11] Although he was also connected with bulls to some extent, receiving them in sacrifice and sometimes sending them up from the sea in myth (as for Minos, see p. 338), his connection with horses was especially close in both myth and cult. This seems appropriate for a variety of reasons, whether because the horse represented one of the most powerful forces of nature that human beings could dominate, or because horses had chthonic associations, or because they were often credited with the creation of springs in Greek folklore. It is worth noting, however, that the Greeks did not use horse metaphors (as in the case of our 'white horses') to describe the waves and roaring of the sea; Poseidon's connection with horses was probably very ancient, perhaps even more ancient than his connection with the sea. He was widely worshipped as Poseidon Hippios (the Lord of Horses), horses played a prominent part in his cult, and legend even presented him as the father of the first horse. Horses were sacrificed to him and kept at his sanctuaries, and chariot races were held in his honour at some of his festivals; and charioteers would invoke his aid before a race, much like sailors at sea. The *Homeric Hymn to Apollo* refers to an unusual rite at Onchestos in which charioteers would jump from their chariot after whipping up their horses, and pray for protection from Poseidon in the future if the chariot was wrecked in an adjoining grove (which would have been sacred to the god).[12] But our main concern must be the myths that connect Poseidon with horses and the origin of the equine race.

In heroic myth, his sons Pelias and Neleus (see p. 380) and Hippothoon (see p. 344) are said to have been suckled by mares, and he is said to have given winged or wondrous horses to Idas and to his favourite Pelops to help them win their brides (see pp. 153 and 503). His most interesting horse-myths, however, are legends of a more primitive nature which tell how he was supposed to have fathered notable wonder-horses or indeed the first horse of all. According to Hesiod, as we have seen (see p. 60), he once slept with the monstrous Medusa, causing her to conceive the winged horse Pegasos, who sprang out of her body (along with Chrysaor) after Perseus cut off her head; and a legend that is no less extraordinary tells how he came to father Areion, the divine horse of Adrastos, by mating with Demeter while the pair of them were in horse-form. As recounted at Thelpousa in Arcadia, where the goddess was honoured as Demeter Erinys, the myth ran as follows. While Demeter was wandering through the world in search of her lost daughter (see pp. 126ff), Poseidon stalked her in the hope of making love to her; and when she tried to escape him by turning herself into a mare and mingling with some horses outside Thelpousa, he assumed the form of a stallion and had intercourse with her. The products of this union were the divine horse Areion or Arion (whose name probably meant 'very swift') and a daughter whose name could be revealed to initiates alone. It was claimed that Demeter had acquired her local title of Erinys (Fury) because she 'had been enraged' at Poseidon's treatment of her (for the verb *erineuein* could carry that meaning, i.e. to rage like a Fury). To explain why she was also honoured there as Demeter Lousia (Washing Demeter), it was added that she had washed in the river Ladon after the encounter.[13]

Areion was famous in legend from early epic onwards as the horse that carried Adrastos, king of Argos, to safety after his disastrous attack on Thebes (see p. 321). Some claimed that Areion was previously owned by Herakles, who had acquired him from Onkos, king of Thelpousa (or from Kopreus, king of Haliartos near Tilphousa), and later passed him on to Adrastos.[14] There were alternative accounts in which Poseidon fathered Areion by an Erinys near the spring of Tilphousa (see p. 144) in Boeotia, or by a Harpy.[15] The myth of Poseidon's horse-mating with Demeter was also recounted at Phigaleia in Arcadia, where Demeter was represented as horse-headed and black in colour; but the only child of the union in the Phigaleian tradition was the unnameable daughter mentioned above, whose public title among the Arcadians was Despoina (the Mistress, also a title of Kore/Persephone).[16] The cult of Poseidon Hippios (Lord of Horses) was especially prominent in Arcadia. According to an Arcadian tradition, Rhea saved Poseidon from being swallowed at birth by Kronos by hiding him in a sheepfold near Mantineia (hence the name of a local spring called Arne or 'Lamb-spring'), and giving her husband a foal to swallow instead, on the pretext that their son had been born as a horse.[17]

A legend from Thessaly in the north-east, which was a centre for the breeding of horses, represented Poseidon as the progenitor of the entire equine race. For when he had once been lying asleep in that land (where he was honoured under the title of Petraios, 'he of the rock'), he had shed some of his semen on to the rocky ground, fertilizing the earth and causing it to bring forth the first horse, Skyphios. Or in some later accounts, he caused that earth to bring forth Skyphios (and Areion too in one version) by striking the ground with his trident.[18] Or in secondary versions that were developed at Athens, Poseidon fertilized the ground at Kolonos just outside the city to produce the first horse, here called Skeironites, or else caused it to spring from the ground with a blow of his trident while competing with Athena for possession of Attica.[19]

Myths in which Poseidon competes with other deities for possession of Greek lands

Some of the most interesting and distinctive of Poseidon's stories are the local legends that tell how he competed with other deities to gain possession of various lands (i.e. to be adopted as the patron-deity of those lands). In the most famous by far, he competed with Athena for the possession of Attica in a contest that was judged by the Twelve Gods, or by the king of Athens, or its citizens. On arriving first in the land, Poseidon tried to establish his priority by striking the Acropolis with his trident to create a salt-water well, the so-called 'sea' of the Erechtheion (which lay inside the temple, and is said to have produced a sound resembling that of waves whenever the wind blew from the south). Athena arrived next and staked her claim by planting the first of Attica's many olive-trees, calling on Kekrops, the first king of Athens, to act as her witness. When Zeus referred the dispute to the Twelve Gods for arbitration, they judged in favour of Athena after hearing the testimony of Kekrops, apparently reaching this decision because they set greater store on the value of Athena's gift (which would be a mainstay of the economy) than on the question of priority. Poseidon was so enraged that he flooded the Thriasian Plain to the north-west of Athens, for a time at least; or else he planned to flood the entire land until Hermes arrived with a message from Zeus ordering him to desist.[20] The details of the story differ considerably in different accounts. Poseidon stakes his claim in one version, for instance, by causing the first horse to spring forth;[21] or Athena caused the olive-tree to spring up by striking the ground with her spear,[22] just as Poseidon created the 'sea' by striking the Acropolis with his trident; or with regard to the arbitration, Zeus himself acted as judge, or else Kekrops himself, or his son Erysichthon.[23] In a curious rationalistic account recorded by Varro, the Delphic oracle advised the people of Athens to decide between the two deities after an olive and some water had sprung forth as their symbols, and the male citizens (who all voted for the male god) were outvoted by the female citizens (who all voted for the goddess) because the women outnumbered the men by one.[24] Although Athena became the main god of Athens, a reconciliation could be said to have been reached since Poseidon was much worshipped there under various titles, enjoying a cult on the Acropolis itself as Poseidon Erechtheus (a title that links him to the mythical king Erechtheus, see p. 369). As we know from Pausanias, the 'sea' that he had created could still be seen in the time of Hadrian, as could Athena's olive-tree, which had miraculously regrown, sending up a long shoot within a single day, after the Persians had destroyed it while burning the sanctuaries on the Acropolis in 480 BC.[25]

Hera was said to have established her position as the great goddess of Argos through another such contest, which was judged by Phoroneus, the first king of the land (see p. 227), with the aid of three local river-gods, Inachos, Kephisos and Asterion; Phoroneus awarded the land to Hera, much to the anger of Poseidon, who retaliated by causing the rivers of the Argolid to run dry for much of the year.[26] He made partial amends later, however, by creating an ever-running spring at Lerna for one of the daughters of Danaos (see p. 235). According to an Argive cultic legend, Poseidon drowned much of the land in his wrath until Hera interceded to cause him to withdraw the flood, hence the origin of the sanctuary of Poseidon Proklystios ('he who dashes with waves', i.e. the Flooder) in Argos, which had supposedly been raised at the place from where the sea-flood had receded.[27] In similar contests set in the Greek islands, Poseidon had lost Naxos to Dionysos and Aegina to Zeus.[28] On two other occasions, however, compromises were proposed. When Poseidon competed with Athena to become the lord of Troizen, Zeus ordered the two of them to share the land, and they presided over it jointly ever afterwards, Poseidon under the title of Basileus (King) and Athena as Polias (Protector of the City) and Sthenias (the Mighty).[29] The Troizenians had a flood-story which bears some resemblance to that at Argos (although there is no indication that it was connected with a contest for the land), for it was said that Poseidon had once flooded the land, making it unfruitful with his salt-waters, until he had yielded to the prayers and sacrifices of the Troizenians, who worshipped him thereafter outside the city walls under the further title of Phytalmios (Fosterer of Growth).[30] In another contest set at Corinth, a compromise was proposed by the arbitrator, Briareos (one of the Hundred-Handers, see p. 67), who decided to award the Isthmus of Corinth to Poseidon but the acropolis of the city to Helios.[31] As to the significance of these various stories, it would certainly be wrong to attempt to interpret them in a simple historical sense, as if they reflected cultic conflicts in the distant past; it would seem, rather, that they express something about Poseidon himself and his place in the city, as an awesome and threatening deity who is highly honoured though not as a patron god.

Poseidon is quite prominent in the *Iliad*, which depicts him as a violent partisan who does everything possible from first to last to help the Greeks and harm the Trojans. He had reason enough to be hostile to Troy, since Laomedon, the father of Priam, had employed him and Apollo to build the walls of the city, but had insulted them and refused to pay them when they had completed the task (see p. 523).[32] When the Greeks built a wall to protect their ships, he complained at the assembly of the gods, saying that the fame of this new wall would overshadow that of the wall that he and Apollo had built;[33] but he intervened to rally the Greeks when the Trojans broke through to attack the ships, helping to turn the tide of the battle until Zeus ordered him to desist.[34] Although Poseidon plays a more restricted role in the *Odyssey*, his hostility to the main hero is a central motif of the poem. He was so angry with Odysseus for having blinded the Kyklops Polyphemos, who was a son of his, that he delayed the hero's return for many years and finally caused him to be cast adrift in the sea by means of the great storm described above[35] (although he survived to be washed ashore on the island of the Phaeacians, see p. 497); and Poseidon also punished the Phaeacians for sending Odysseus home in one of their magical ships.[36] In a later epic in the Trojan cycle, he caused part of the Greek fleet to be wrecked during its return voyage (to help Athena to avenge a grave act of sacrilege, see p. 485). He makes fewer appearances than one might expect in heroic mythology from later sources, being mentioned mainly in connection with his mortal children and the stories of their conception. Other characteristic tales tell how he sent bulls or monsters up from the sea as a bane or benefit to mortals. He sent up a bull as a favour for Minos, though with disastrous consequences in the long run (see pp. 338ff), and another at the request of Theseus to cause the death of Hippolytos (see p. 358); and to punish the presumption of Laomedon and of the mother of Andromeda, he sent sea-monsters against their lands (see pp. 240 and 523).

Poseidon's consort Amphitrite and his children by her and other mothers

AMPHITRITE, the consort of Poseidon, was generally thought to have been a daughter of Nereus (although an alternative tradition presented her as a daughter of Okeanos, and it is stated in one source that she was the mother of the Nereids).[37] She was a reluctant bride as was commonly the case with the Nereids, who preferred to live a carefree life as virgins in the company of their parents and many sisters. According to one account, Poseidon abducted her from the island of Naxos after she had emerged from the sea to dance on the shore with her sisters;[38] or else she fled from him when he tried to court her, and hid herself in the depths of the Ocean near Atlas (i.e. in the far west). In the latter case, Poseidon sent many envoys in search of her, including his special beast the dolphin, who discovered her in the outer Ocean and carried her to Poseidon on its back (or at least let him know where she was hiding). The god was so grateful that he declared the dolphin sacred and placed an image of it among the stars (as the northern constellation Delphinus).[39] After finally becoming the wife of Poseidon, Amphitrite lived at his side in his golden palace beneath the sea, enjoying high honour as the queen of the seas. Although she is depicted quite frequently in works of art as a goddess of noble aspect, often enthroned

Figure 4.1 Theseus under the sea. G. 104, Attic red-figure cup by Onesimos. Louvre.

beside her husband, she rarely appears in mythical tales. According to a fairly ancient legend, she offered a gracious reception to Theseus (here regarded as a son of Poseidon) when he threw himself off a ship to prove to Minos that he was a son of the god of the sea (see pp. 345–6); and a story of later origin claimed that she caused Skylla to be turned into a monster after discovering that her husband had embarked on a love affair with her (see p. 497). Poseidon and Amphitrite are credited with only a single child in the *Theogony*, the sea-god Triton, 'who holds the depths of the sea and lives with his mother and the lord his father, a fearsome god'.[40]

Apollodorus adds two daughters, Benthesikyme (Wave of the Deep) and Rhode, the nymph or personification of the island of Rhodes.[41] Rhode or Rhodos became the consort of the sun-god Helios, whose cult was especially prominent on Rhodes (see p. 43); conflicting accounts were offered of her birth. Benthesikyme is remembered solely as the foster-mother of Eumolpos (see p. 370).[42]

Nothing is known for certain about the meaning and origin of the names of Amphitrite and Triton, although it is possible that the common *trito* element (which is also to be found in Athena's ancient title of Tritogeneia, see p. 182) may have had something to do with water or the sea. TRITON was pictured as a merman with a human head and upper body and a fishtail. Greek sea-beings of this type probably originated in the native tradition as products of the popular imagination, even if representations of them may sometimes have been influenced by images of biform deities from the east. Although Triton is presented as a sea-god of some dignity in the passage quoted from the *Theogony*, he makes no significant appearance in conventional mythology except in his specific role as the god of Lake Tritonis in Libya. According to a tale of quite early origin which was known to Pindar and Herodotus,[43] he appeared to the Argonauts when they became trapped in the lake during their return voyage, and not only showed them the way to the open sea, but gave one of them a clod of earth from which the island of Thera would grow (see further on pp. 396–7). To explain Athena's title of Tritogeneia, some claimed that the goddess had been reared by Triton in Libya (see p. 182). This god of the lake was presumably a local deity who came to be identified with the Greek god. In vase-paintings from the sixth century BC, Herakles can be seen wrestling with Triton (rather than Nereus in all surviving literary accounts) to force him to reveal the way to the Hesperides (see p. 269; or perhaps to the island of Geryoneus). There are otherwise various tales from Latin sources that refer to Triton's favourite pastime of blowing on the conch-shell horn, an instrument that is his familiar attribute in works of art. Vergil tells how Misenus, a skilled trumpeter who accompanied Aeneas to Italy, was drowned by Triton for his presumption in challenging the gods to compete with him in blowing the conch-shell horn;[44] and in other tales, he is said to have induced panic in the Giants during their battle with the gods by blowing on his horn, and to have blown his horn after the great flood at the bidding of Zeus to recall the waters to their proper courses.[45]

Although there was apparently only a single Triton in the earliest tradition, his name came to be applied in a more general sense to an entire race of fishtailed sea-beings who accompanied Poseidon through the sea and sported with the Nereids. These became a favourite subject with artists in Hellenistic Greece and eventually in Italy too, especially for the decorative detail of sea-pieces; and female Tritons and Triton families came to be depicted, an idea foreign to early Greek tradition. As nature-spirits of no very high status, the Tritons entered into folklore in much the same way as mermaids in more recent times, and many stories would surely have been transmitted about them among sailors and people of coastal communities. As so often, we can refer to Pausanias for one or two local tales. Having seen two Tritons that were preserved at Rome and at Tanagra on the Boeotian coast, Pausanias was able to offer a precise description of their appearance, writing that they had green hair on their head, gills behind their ears, greenish-grey eyes, a finely scaled body, and a dolphin's tail instead of legs and feet.[46] There were two conflicting legends about the Tanagran Triton, who was the larger of the two. In one account, he had attacked some local women while they were bathing in the sea to purify themselves for the secret rites of Dionysos, who immediately came to their aid and overcame their would-be ravisher after a sharp fight. Or in another version, the Triton had been causing such trouble to the Tanagrans by seizing their cattle when they drove them down to the sea, or even attacking small boats, that they set a trap for him by leaving a large bowl of wine by the shore; and when he duly emerged from the sea, drained the wine, and fell asleep in a drunken stupor, one of the Tanagrans was able to creep forward and chop off his head with an axe. As proof of this latter detail, they could point to the headless state of the Triton in their temple of Dionysos.[47]

After Zeus who fathered innumerable children by mortal mothers, Poseidon was the god who is credited with the largest number of non-divine children. These can be divided into two main groups. As a god who was notoriously wild and unpredictable, Poseidon was naturally regarded as a suitable father for heroes or giants of a violent and uncouth nature; but as a great god who ranked second only to Zeus, he was also introduced into heroic genealogies for much the same reasons as his brother, to be enrolled as the divine founder of local royal lines, or as the divine father of notable heroes without adverse judgement as to their character. His greatest son in the latter group was Theseus (at least in the tradition of his birthplace, see p. 342); Pelias and Neleus may also be cited (see p. 380 for the story of their conception), and Belos and Agenor, the founders of the two main branches of the Inachid family (see p. 232). Others will be mentioned as they arise. Among his wild children in the other group, we find colourful and disreputable figures such as the Kyklops Polyphemos (see p. 492), the giant hunter Orion (in one account at least, see p. 561), the Aloadai who tried to storm heaven (see p. 91), Amykos who killed passing strangers in boxing-matches (see p. 386), the Athenian rapist Halirrhothios (see p. 365), and many of the ruffians who confronted Herakles (e.g. Antaios, see p. 270) and Theseus (e.g. Skeiron and Sinis, see pp. 342ff) during their travels.

HADES AND THE MYTHOLOGY OF THE UNDERWORLD

The grim lord of the Underworld

After winning the Underworld as his special domain when the world was divided between him and his two brothers, HADES lived apart from the other gods and had little to do with the affairs of the living. As the ruler of the dead, he was grim and mournful in his character and functions alike, and severely just, and inexorable in the performance of his duties. He acted in the manner of a jailer, ensuring that dead mortals who entered his dark kingdom never escaped back to the light of the sun; and his realm contained a place of punishment where some few who had gravely offended the gods, or indeed the wicked in general according to later ideas, would be subjected to torment or correction in the afterlife. But Hades was no enemy of the human race, nor was he radically different in nature from his more fortunate brothers; he was a terrible not a malevolent god.

The name of the lord of the Underworld appears in various different forms, as Hades in its familiar Attic guise, or as Aïdes or Aïdoneus (or as Aidos and Aidi in the genitive and dative only, probably from *Ais) in epic usage. The Greeks assumed that Aïdes simply means 'the Unseen' or 'Invisible'[48] (*a-ides*; the *a* is privative like 'un-' in English), and they may well have been correct, although this remains an open question; for some would argue, for instance, that the name is related to *aia*, earth, instead. In classical usage, the name of Hades was not applied directly to his realm, which was properly the abode or 'house' *of* Hades; in Greek, as an inflected language, the distinction could be indicated by use of the genitive form of his name without need of an accompanying noun. Since wealth comes from the depths of the ground in the form of crops and minerals, the Greeks often referred to Hades under the title of Plouton (the Wealthy or Wealth-giver), at least from the fifth century BC onwards. He acquired quite a variety of euphemistic titles, such as Polydegmon, Polydektes or Polyxeinos (all meaning the receiver or host of many, and hence the Hospitable), or Eubouleus (Wise in Counsel) or Klymenos (the Renowned), for the Greeks generally preferred not to speak directly of death in connection with themselves or their friends, whether to avoid ill-omened remarks or to pass over unpleasant realities. They would refer to Hades by such titles for much the same reasons as they would say that someone had 'departed' (*bēbēken*) or refer to the dead person as the 'blessed one' (*ho makaristēs*), or even begin such matter-of-fact documents as wills with the formula 'All will go well; but if anything should happen, I make the following dispositions'.[49] As the absolute ruler of a realm that was set apart from the rest of the world, Hades could also be called Zeus Katachthonios (Zeus of the Underworld) or simply 'the Other Zeus'.

Since the Romans had no death-god of their own, or had forgotten him if they ever did have one, they took over the Greek name Plouton (Latinized to Pluto) as their title for that deity, or else translated it by Dis, the contracted form of the Latin word *dives* (wealth). The name of his consort was corrupted into Proserpina, and nothing was added to the existing mythology of either. Hades was worshipped almost nowhere in Greece; in connection with his precinct and temple at Elis, which were opened on a single day in the year and were closed to all but the priest even then, Pausanias remarks that he knows of no one else who worships him.[50] There is mention, however, of a precinct of Hades at Triphylian Pylos (and it has been argued that the Klymenos who had a temple at Hermione can be identified with Hades).[51] Dis and Proserpina were honoured in cult at Rome from the time the Romans first became acquainted with the Greek deities. Hades is represented comparatively seldom in Greek art. When he is, he often carries a sceptre or key as a sign of his authority (or else a cornucopia in his nature as Plouton), and his form and features differ very little from those of Zeus, save in expression; Seneca describes the difference epigrammatically when he says of him *vultus est illi Iouis, sed fulminantis*, 'he has the look of Jove himself, but of Jove when he thunders'.[52]

The gloomy land of the dead

It was commonly assumed, of course, that Hades' kingdom lay somewhere far underground. In such matters, however, consistency is not to be looked for in the traditions of any people, and the Greeks were also inclined to place the abode of the dead in the far west (as already noted, see p. 22), where the sun and other heavenly bodies make their descent. Although both ideas can be found in the Homeric epics, they are already fully reconciled, for Odysseus' westward journey to the land of the dead[53] is no more than a special means of approach to an underground realm. Except in a passage in the final book of the *Odyssey* which is almost certainly part of a later interpolation,[54] there is no suggestion in Homer that the shades of the dead have to travel to the Underworld by such a route (or indeed have to seek any opening in the ground). When the shade of the dead Patroklos departs after speaking to Achilles in the *Iliad*, it vanishes away under the earth like smoke; and similarly, when Patroklos and Hektor die, their soul simply flits from their body and is gone to Hades without more ado.[55]

The belief that the shades of the dead were able to pass directly below, or the common belief of a somewhat later period that they were conducted below by Hermes, did not preclude the development of local traditions in which people claimed to have a cave, chasm or lake in their area which communicated with the Underworld (much like the hellmouths of modern folklore). Since living mortals who wanted to descend below as fully embodied beings would necessarily have to seek an opening of this kind, these local hellmouths were drawn into myth as the routes that were taken by great heroes of the past who visited Hades while still alive, such as Herakles, Theseus and Orpheus. Herakles, for example, was supposed to have found his way below through a bottomless cave at Tainaron in the southern Peloponnese (see p. 268). Or in divine myth, Dionysos was said to have descended through a bottomless lake at Lerna in the Argolid when he went to fetch his dead mother (see p. 171). Odysseus' journey in the *Odyssey* took him into more exotic regions. After sailing west over the outer Ocean toward the sunset, he arrived at the mist-enshrouded land of the Kimmerians, a people who never see the light of the sun. He beached his ship there and made his way to the boundary of the Underworld, at a place where two infernal rivers met.[56] Rather than venturing inside the world of the dead, as did the heroes mentioned above, Odysseus encouraged the dead to come to him by pouring libations to them and by sacrificing a lamb and ewe over a pit to provide blood for them to drink. As the fluttering shades drank from the blood, they recovered a measure of bodily consistency and sufficient understanding to be able to converse with their visitor.[57] Although Homer does not attempt to describe the topography of the lower world, he alludes to its most distinctive feature, the famous meadows of asphodel; for Odysseus sees the ghost of Achilles striding off through an asphodel meadow, and sees the dead hunter Orion herding ghostly beasts across it.[58] Romantic though its name may sound in English, asphodel is a dingy and unprepossessing plant which grows on barren ground, and we should imagine this accordingly as a bleak monochrome landscape that provides a suitable setting for the colourless half-life of the shades.

The abode of the dead is usually pictured as a gloomy subterranean land which contains these meadows of asphodel and also, in many subsequent accounts, groves and hills and other features of a conventional landscape. It is separated from the world of the living by a boundary-river, the Styx in the *Iliad*, but usually the Acheron in later sources.[59] Four infernal rivers are mentioned in the Odyssey, namely the **Styx, Acheron, Kokytos** (here described as a branch of the Styx) and **Pyriphlegethon** (also known as Phlegethon);[60] and a fifth river, **Lethe,** is added in the subsequent tradition.[61] Their names are significant in every case, meaning respectively the Abhorrent, the Woeful (if the name of Acheron can be rightly derived from *achos*, woe, distress), the River of Lamentation, the Fiery, and the River of Forgetfulness. The name of Pyriphlegethon had nothing to do originally with fires of punishment (although it is mentioned as a place of torment in occasional late passages), but simply referred to the flames of the funeral pyre. Acheron was sometimes said to have issued into a swampy lake or mere (Acherousia or the Acherousian lake);[62] its name was also used, by extension, as a poetic name for the Underworld. Hesiod mentions the Styx alone, stating that it flows down from the Ocean taking a tenth of its water, and that the gods swear their solemn oaths by it (see further on p. 49).[63]

The Styx, Kokytos and Acheron had counterparts in the upper world, the Styx in Arcadia, the Kokytos in Thesprotia in north-western Greece, and the Acheron in Thesprotia and elsewhere. There was a Styx in northern Arcadia that plunged several hundred feet down a sheer cliff-face near Nonakris (at the falls now known as Mavronero), much as the infernal river is said to flow down from a tall precipice in Hesiod's account. In the earliest surviving reference to the Arcadian Styx, Herodotus mentions that the Arcadians swore oaths by it and believed that waters from the infernal river issued into it.[64] There is no way of telling whether the traditional conception of the infernal river was influenced by knowledge of the Arcadian Styx and its falls, or whether, conversely, the Arcadian Styx was first given that name because its chilly falls resembled those of the Styx in Hesiod's description. It is no surprise that the waters of the Arcadian river should have been credited with sinister qualities. Pausanias reports, for instance, that they were reputed to bring death to animals and human beings who drank from them, and to have the power to dissolve or corrupt almost everything, including glass, crystal and agate, and even pottery; and a tradition claimed that Alexander the Great was poisoned with some Styx-water that was sent over to Asia in a horse's hoof, the only substance unaffected by its powers.[65] The Thesprotian Acheron was also rendered impressive by its setting, for it flowed through deep gorges in a wild landscape, occasionally disappearing underground, and passed through a marshy lake before emerging into the Ionian Sea; it had an oracle of the dead beside it, as did another Acheron near Heracleia Pontica in Asia Minor. There was also an Acheron is southern Elis.[66]

An allusion in Plato's *Republic* provides the earliest evidence for Lethe as a river of the Underworld. It is fitting that waters of Forgetfulness should flow through the Underworld since it is a realm of oblivion where the shades of the dead can expect to forget all or most of their earthly experiences. A poem by Theognis observes accordingly that Persephone brings *lēthē*, forgetfulness, to mortals by impairing their wits, and Aristophanes refers to an infernal plain of Lethe (which probably figured in Eleusinian eschatology).[67] Once the idea had arisen that waters of Lethe flowed through the Underworld, it could easily be imagined that the newly arrived dead would be deprived of their memory by drinking from them; and for those who believed in reincarnation, a subsequent draught of Lethe could explain why souls that have been reborn into earthly bodies remember nothing of the other world or of their previous incarnations. It is in the latter connection that Plato refers to a river of Forgetfulness (*Ameleta potamon*).[68] As a further thought, it might be imagined that newly departed persons who possessed the requisite knowledge might be able to abstain from drinking from the waters of Lethe and so retain their full memory and understanding. Instructions on this very matter are provided on gold leaves that have been excavated from the tombs of Bacchic initiates in southern Italy and elsewhere; on one such leaf from Hipponion on the heel of Italy, dating to about 400 BC, the initiate is told to avoid a spring on the right-hand side beneath a white cypress on entering Hades, but to drink instead from the cool waters that flow from the lake of Mnemosyne (Memory).[69] Although the spring that is to be avoided is not explicitly named, it is evidently a spring of *lēthē*, forgetfulness. In ordinary life, people who wanted to consult the oracle of Trophonios at Lebadeia (see p. 559) would drink from two neighbouring springs, first from that of Lethe to clear their mind of all previous thoughts, and then from that of Mnemosyne so as to be able to remember what the oracle would reveal.[70]

From the time of Homer onwards, the gates of Hades are a regular feature of Underworld imagery. In a battle-scene in the *Iliad*, for instance, Tlepolemos boasts that he will kill Sarpedon and cause him to 'pass through the gates of Hades'; and the lord of the Underworld is described in that epic as the 'warder of the gates' (*pulartēs*).[71] These gates could be pictured as forming the entrance to the 'house

Figure 4.2   Charon and Hermes. Attic white ground lekythos 2777, c. 440 BC. Staatliche Antikensammlungen und Glyptothek, München.

of Hades' as the home of the dead was often called;[72] and this body of imagery was well-suited to express how entry into the world of the dead was controlled and escape prevented. On the latter point, it will be sufficient to quote some lines from Hesiod:

> There [i.e. in the nether regions] stand the echoing halls of mighty Hades, god of the lower world, and of dread Persephone. A fearsome dog keeps pitiless guard in front, and has a nasty trick: he fawns on all who enter with wagging tail and both ears down, but he will not allow them to go out again, no, he keeps a careful guard and devours anyone whom he catches trying to go out through the gates of mighty Hades and dread Persephone.[73]

If the hell-hound Kerberos (see p. 62) guards the gates in this savage fashion, the ever-righteous Aiakos (see p. 53) was sometimes said to act as door-keeper or keeper of the keys.

How the dead passed below; their guide Hermes and ferryman Charon

We must now consider how the dead were supposed to make their way from this world to the other. There is no mention of any ferryman of the dead in the Homeric epics, and Hermes appears as escort of the shades in a single passage alone in the final book of the *Odyssey*. This passage describes him as guiding the shades of the dead suitors of Penelope to the other world by much the same route as was followed by Odysseus:

> past the streams of Ocean they went, and past the White Rock, past the gates of the Sun and the land of dreams, and quickly reached the meadows of asphodel, where is the dwelling-place of the shades, the phantoms of the departed.[74]

Hermes is not mentioned in this role again until the classical period when Aeschylus speaks of him coming to fetch a dead heroine, Skylla, at the time of her death;[75] and the earliest evidence from the visual arts takes us only a little further back, to the end of the sixth century BC. There is in fact good reason to suppose that the relevant passage in the *Odyssey* forms part of a later addition to the epic (as was already argued by some scholars in antiquity); and if that is indeed the case, a consistent pattern can be recognized in the Homeric epics in which the dead pass to Hades of their own accord without need for a guide or ferryman. Since the shades (*psychai*) are pictured as flimsy beings who flutter around like ghosts, it could easily be imagined that they would be able to vanish beneath the earth 'like smoke' (as does the shade of Patroklos after his visit to Achilles),[76] and to flit across the boundary-river and any other barrier without any difficulty. The soul flies off like a dream and is gone, or it flits out of the dead man's body and departs to Hades without more ado, bewailing its fate.[77]

In the Homeric account, however, the newly departed dead face one notable restriction with regard to their passage, namely that they cannot join the society of the dead until their earthly remains have been buried. When the shade of Patroklos appears to Achilles, he begs him to bury me as quickly as possible, so that I may pass through the gates of Hades; the shades, the phantoms of the dead, are keeping me at bay, nor do they allow me to join them beyond the river, but I must wander in vain along the outside of the broad-gated house of Hades.[78]

And when Odysseus visits the borders of the Underworld in the *Odyssey*, the first shade to approach him is that of his dead comrade Elpenor, who complains that he has been left unburied and appeals to his friend to rectify the matter, doubtless for the same reason as Patroklos.[79] The evidence from tragedy and other sources suggests that burial was no longer regarded as a precondition for entry to Hades by the classical period; this change may well have come about because Hermes and Charon were now thought to preside over the process by which the departed were integrated into the world of the dead.

Charon, the ferryman of the dead, is first mentioned in a fragment from the *Minyas*,[80] an early epic of uncertain date (probably sixth century BC or slightly earlier), and is depicted in vase-paintings from the end of the sixth century onwards. There are differing views on his origin, some arguing that he was a very old figure from popular belief, and others that he was a literary invention from the archaic period, as is perhaps more likely. It is also difficult to tell exactly when Hermes first acquired his role as conductor of the dead (*psychopompos*). By the fifth century in any case, the Homeric account of the passing of the dead had been displaced by another in which Hermes guided the shades of the dead to the nether regions, and Charon then ferried them across the boundary-river (usually Acheron, occasionally Styx) into the world of the dead. As we have seen, Hermes is portrayed as conductor of the dead in the present text of the *Odyssey*; but if it can be accepted that the relevant passage forms part of a later addition to the epic (perhaps dating to the early sixth century), it is reasonable to assume that this function was first assigned to the god at some stage in the archaic period. Although the immortals generally shunned all contact with death and the dead, Hermes, as a god who was especially associated with boundaries and their transgression (see p. 158), could be fittingly imagined as a god who would not shrink from crossing this most forbidding of boundaries, whether as *psychopompos* or in his more ancient function as a messenger. In the *Homeric Hymn to Demeter*, for instance, Zeus sends him below to ask Hades to return Persephone to the upper world.[81] On the exceptional occasions on which the dead were permitted to make visits to the upper world, it was the duty of Hermes to escort them (as in the case of Protesilaos for instance[82]). While acting as guide to the shades, Hermes did not lead them into their ultimate home (except in the unusual account in the final book of the *Odyssey*), but took them down to the border of the land of the dead, leaving it for Charon to convey them across the final frontier.

CHARON is consistently represented as a formidable old man of unexceptional appearance in the earliest images, but increasingly as ugly and squalid; for characteristic literary portraits, Aristophanes' *Frogs*, Vergil's *Aeneid* and Lucian's *Dialogues of the Dead* may be consulted.[83] Vergil describes him as foul and repulsive, with a tangle of unkempt white hair on his chin, and fiery eyes, and a filthy cloak as his garment. Except in a doubtful reference that makes him a son of Akmon (a being who was sometimes named as the father of Ouranos, see p. 32), no genealogy is recorded for him; he should presumably be regarded as a daimon or minor divinity. It is his duty to ensure that only those who are properly qualified are allowed to pass into the world of the dead; his only proper myth states accordingly that he was once thrown into chains for a year for ferrying over the living Herakles (when the hero travelled below to fetch Kerberos, see p. 268).[84] He never displaces Kerberos, who will be encountered on the far side of the river, where mortals who cross over while still alive might be able to pacify him by tossing him a honey-cake (i.e. giving him a share of the food of the dead, for such cakes were a very common form of offering). Since the ferryman of the dead could expect to be rewarded for his services, the dead were buried with a small coin in their mouth, Charon's obol. In Etruscan tradition, Charun, as he is called in the local language, is a demon of grim enough character who carries a heavy hammer to dispatch his victims; and Charon survived into modern Greek folklore as a figure called Charos, who is generally represented as riding a horse and carrying off young and old.

The ghosts who throng the Underworld are the merest shadows of living men and women, lacking the essentials of real vigorous life. All that survives from the living person is the tenuous *psychē* or 'breath-soul', which departs from the body at the time of death and finds its way into the company of the dead. The *psychē*, the name of which is related to the Greek word for breathing (*psychein*), was not originally regarded as a centre of consciousness, let alone a soul in the Socratic-Platonic and modern religious understanding; Homer never uses the term in connection with the mental functions of the living, referring instead to an array of 'faculties' that depend on the living body for their activity (such as the *thymos*, a sort of life-soul or affective centre, the *noos* or understanding, and the *phrenes*, literally the midriff). The *psychē* by contrast is the departing breath and the wraith that takes over as a continuation of the dead person's self. It is as insubstantial as breath or smoke; but it resembles the dead person in its outward appearance, and may thus be called an *eidōlon* or double. On the question of the level of consciousness of the departed *psychai*, the Homeric epics are by no means consistent, for it is suggested at times that they are wholly witless, while at other times they seem to possess some form of conscious life, and thus to be capable of acting spontaneously (as would be necessary if they were to prevent the unburied Patroklos from entering their company, or to approach Odysseus to drink the blood that he had poured for them).[85] This is not of course an area in which perfect logic and consistency can be expected; the discrepancy may perhaps be interpreted in terms of differing perspectives, for the shades may be regarded as witless by comparison with embodied mortals, while they yet must be supposed to possess some form of attenuated consciousness if they are to be capable of forming a society of their own and communicating with one another. It has also been argued that these are conflicting ideas of separate origin, and that the inconsistency thus arises because different strata of belief are preserved side by side in the Homeric epics.

Dead heroes and heroines who met with exceptional fates; the privileged few in Elysion or the Isles of the Blessed

Since the dead are not subjected to any form of posthumous judgement in the Homeric account, the mass of them share a common fate in the Underworld, living together as gibbering shades, rather like bats in a cave. Although this would certainly be a dispiriting prospect, the dying would have nothing positively dreadful to fear, however they might have behaved in their previous life. Pindar and Aeschylus are the first authors to refer to a general judgement of the dead that might assign individuals to a happier or worse fate in accordance with their merits. Aeschylus states that sentence will be passed by 'another Zeus', that is to say Hades himself (as we may also be supposed to infer from Pindar's vague reference to an anonymous 'somebody');[86] but in the subsequent tradition from the time of Plato onwards, the task was usually assigned to Minos and other dead heroes who had been renowned for their justice during their earthly lives (see further on p. 122). Although Minos is already portrayed in the *Odyssey* as dispensing justice to the shades with his golden sceptre in hand,[87] Homer clearly does not mean us to suppose that he is judging them for actions committed during their earthly lives; as a king among the dead, he is merely continuing his characteristic activity in the afterlife, much as the dead hunter Orion conducts a ghostly hunt (see p. 561). Only in a single connection, that of perjured oaths, does Homer ever suggest the ordinary dead might be punished below for deeds committed on this side of the grave. When Agamemnon is swearing an oath on one occasion, he invokes Zeus and the Earth and Sun as his witnesses along with 'the Erinyes [Furies] who exact vengeance on men beneath the earth when any has sworn a false oath'; and there is a similar passage elsewhere in the *Iliad* which refers to the punishment of dead perjurers without naming the punishers.[88]

If some few of the dead in Homer's account are assigned a better or worse fate than is reserved for most of their fellows, these are not ordinary mortals but great figures from the mythical past who are either specially favoured by the gods or, conversely, have incurred their everlasting hatred. A highly favoured few are spirited away body and soul together to Elysion, a far-off paradise at the end of the earth, while a few who have greatly offended the gods are subjected to perpetual torment in the world below. We will consider the exceptional fates of these heroes and heroines from legend, as presented by Homer and subsequent authors too, before passing on to consider post-Homeric eschatologies in which every dead mortal is assigned a better or worse fate on the basis of a posthumous judgement.

Elysion (or Elysium in Latin form) is first mentioned in a passage in the *Odyssey* in which Proteus, the old man of the sea, prophesies to Menelaos that he is destined not to die but to be conveyed by the immortals to the Elysian plain at the ends of the earth,

> where fair-haired Rhadamanthys dwells and life is easiest for men; for no snow falls there, nor do strong storms blow, nor is there ever any rain, but the Ocean constantly sends up gusts of the shrill-blowing West Wind to bring coolness to its people.[89]

The presence of Rhadamanthys, who has a name of prehellenic origin and was associated with Crete (see p. 351), has encouraged some to argue that Elysion was a survival from Minoan belief, but this is by no means certain. Whatever its origin, it is a land in which all is perfect happiness, materially but not grossly conceived, and no one ever dies. Since this corresponds to the state of affairs in the golden age when Kronos reigned (see p. 69), Kronos is sometimes said to rule Elysion in post-Homeric accounts, perhaps with Rhadamanthys as his subordinate.[90] In Homer's narrative and the early tradition in general, this abode of bliss lies some where far away on the earth's surface rather than in the world below, as is indeed the logical way to conceive of it, since Hades is a place for disembodied shades rather than for living persons who have been made immortal. Entrance to Elysion – or to the Isles of the Blessed (*makarōn nēsoi*) as this paradise is often called – is gained purely through divine favour, especially by heroes and heroines who are related to the gods; in the above-mentioned passage in the *Odyssey*, Menelaos is told that he will be granted this privilege because he is the husband of Helen and thus a son-in-law of Zeus. Those who are named as inhabitants of Elysion or the Isles of the Blessed in subsequent sources are mostly familiar heroes and heroines from early epic, such as Achilles (sometimes with Medeia as his consort), Diomedes, Peleus, Alkmene and Kadmos.[91]

Lyrical descriptions of life in the Isles of the Blessed can be found in two poems by Pindar, his second *Olympian Ode* and a fragment from one of his dirges, from which the following passages are worth citing:

> There the breezes of Ocean blow gently around the Isles of the Blessed, and flowers of gold blaze forth, some from the shore on radiant trees while others are nourished by the waters; and with garlands of these, they [the inhabitants] entwine their hands and crown their brows . . . in meadows red with roses, the land outside their city is shaded with incense-trees and is heavy-laden with golden fruits; some take their pleasure in horses and wrestling, and some in draughts, and some in lyres, while the flower of perfect bliss blooms amongst them; and a sweet fragrance wafts forever over that lovely land as they mingle every kind of incense into the far-shining fire on the altars of the gods.[92]

Those who were fortunate enough to be transferred to this realm would enjoy, in other words, for all time and in ideal surroundings, the kind of life that the Greeks of the leisured class would enjoy when they could, active and joyous, even strenuous, but with no compulsion to labour, 'for they trouble not the earth with the strength of their hands, nor the waters of the sea either, to gain a bare livelihood' (as Pindar states elsewhere when describing a sort of half-way house to this paradise).[93]

Another home for the privileged dead was Leuke (the White Island), which served as a retire-ment home for great heroes of the Trojan War. Originally a purely mythical place like the Isles of the Blessed, it was later identified with a small island in the Black Sea near the mouth of the Istros (Danube). In the *Aithiopis*, a lost epic in the Trojan cycle, Achilles was said to have been transferred there after his death by his mother, the goddess Thetis (see p. 469); and in the subsequent tradition, Patroklos, Antilochos and the greater and lesser Aias are mentioned among its inhabitants, as is Helen (or Medeia) as the consort of Achilles.[94] For the story of how a Greek from lower Italy was supposed to have visited the island and met some of its ghostly inhabitants in historical times, see p. 583.

In his myth of the five races, Hesiod states that the some or all of the members of his fifth race (i.e. that to which the great heroes of legend belonged) were transferred to the Isles of the Blessed by Zeus (see p. 70).

Elysion was located in the upper world in the original tradition because continuance of bodily life was thought to be essential to a vigorous and enjoyable existence; but when the idea developed that ordinary people might win a better fate for themselves in the afterlife by living well or receiving certain initiations, the imagery that was traditionally associated with this earthly paradise was borrowed to describe the part of the Underworld in which the virtuous dead could expect to live. In the late tradition, Elysion or Elysium could be used as a name for that special region of the Underworld, as in Vergil's *Aeneid*.[95] It hardly needs saying that the whole conception is transformed as a consequence.

Dead heroes and heroines who suffered cruel punishments in world below

If some who were especially dear to the gods were transferred to an earthly paradise as an alternative to death, some who had especially offended the gods were subjected to cruel and ingenious tortures in the Underworld after their death. Here again the earliest ideas are not strictly ethical, since those who are singled out for these punishments are not the worst evil-doers let alone the wicked in general, but simply certain persons who have excited the particular hatred of the gods. Odysseus sees three offenders suffering such treatment during his visit to the Underworld in the *Odyssey*. He first sees the gigantic **Tityos** lying stretched out on the ground, bound fast so that he is unable to fend off two vultures which peck at his liver, one on either side. His offence was that he had tried to rape Leto, the mother of Apollo and Artemis (see p. 147).[96] Next comes **Tantalos**, a wealthy Lydian king (see p. 502), who is subjected to everlasting hunger and thirst in cruelly frustrating circumstances. For he stands in a pool of water that splashes against his chin but vanishes away leaving nothing behind whenever he tries to drink from it; and heavily-laden fruit-trees of every kind spread their boughs above his head, but they are always tossed out of his reach by a gust of wind whenever he tries to pluck their fruit.[97] Odysseus offers no account of his crime; and since later authors disagree on the matter, and even about the nature of his punishment, we will return to the matter after considering the last of the Homeric sinners. This is **Sisyphos**, a former king of Corinth, who is condemned to roll a huge stone up a hill without any prospect of rest or release; for whenever he is about to reach the top of the hill, he is pushed back by the weight of the stone, and it rolls right down to the bottom. Once again the *Odyssey* neglects to explain his crime. According to Pherecydes, this task was imposed on him by Hades because he had escaped back to the upper world by means of a deception when he had died on the first occasion (see p. 431); in that case, his punishment also serves a practical function, since he can hardly attempt another escape if he is forever rolling his stone. Or in another account, this task was imposed on him by Zeus because he had told the river-god Asopos that Zeus had abducted his daughter Aigina (see p. 530).[98]

In the *Returns*, a lost epic in the Trojan cycle, Tantalos was said to have suffered a slightly different punishment from that described in the *Odyssey*, for a stone was suspended above his head by Zeus so that it threatened to crash down on him if he reached out toward the good things that were set in front of him.[99] In later accounts and in the visual arts too, this version is quite often combined with that found in

Homer.[100] It was explained in the *Returns* that Tantalos had been invited to live with the gods, and had been permitted to ask for whatever he most desired; but when he had presumptuously asked to enjoy the same life as the gods, Zeus had been so annoyed that he had fulfilled his promise in a purely formal manner, by granting him good things of every kind but in such circumstances that he would never be able to enjoy them. Or in a darker tale, which must have been quite ancient since it was known to Pindar, he tried to test the omniscience of the gods by serving the flesh of his child Pelops to them at a feast. They recognized the nature of the meal, however, and brought Pelops back to life again (see further on p. 503), and the author of the crime was made to suffer for it in the world below.[101] Pindar refers to the tale only to reject it, for he is unwilling to believe that the gods could ever have become involved in such unsavoury proceedings. He proposes instead that Tantalos suffers his punishment because he stole some nectar and ambrosia (the divine food of the gods, see p. 81) to share it with his fellow mortals.[102] Or in another account, which is first mentioned by Euripides, he betrayed the fellowship of the gods by revealing their secrets to mortals.[103] Or finally, in versions which are all too obviously of late origin, he incurred his punishment by abducting Ganymedes (an action normally ascribed to Zeus see p. 522), or by denying that the sun was a god, claiming instead that it was a mass of incandescent matter (a heresy first ascribed to Anaxagoras, a philosopher of the fifth century BC).[104]

It must now be asked whether the punishment that was assigned to each of these offenders was intended to reflect the particular nature of his offence. This certainly seems to have been the case with Tityos, since the liver was often regarded as the seat of the desires in ancient times; and if this notion was already current in Homer's age, it could have been appreciated that Tityos was made to suffer in the part of him with which he had lusted after Leto. Tantalos for his part had been admitted to the table of the gods and had abused the privilege, and it is therefore wholly fitting that he should not merely be made to suffer hunger and thirst, but to suffer it in such a way that he is kept permanently and painfully aware of his reversal of fortune. This is clearly the moral that was supposed to be drawn from his punishment in the *Returns*, and it is reasonable to assume that Homer's audience would have interpreted it in a similar way. The significance of Sisyphos' punishment is less immediately obvious. Of the various explanations that have been suggested, the most plausible relates it to the special nature of his crime as in the preceding cases: since he suffered this penalty (in one version at least) because he had cheated death by escaping back to the upper world, a symbolic meaning might be detected in the process by which he is perpetually checked and forced back again as he tries to make his way upwards.

Comparable punishments were assigned to other villains in the post-Homeric tradition, but none became as celebrated for their sufferings as the Homeric trio, apart perhaps from **Ixion**. Although the legend of his crime may have been quite ancient, no definite evidence has survived of it until the fifth century BC, when we learn that he tried to seduce Hera and was therefore tied to a wheel and whirled through the air on it (see further on p. 554). Although he would have been whirled through the upper air in the original story, his punishment was transferred to the Underworld at some stage in the Hellenistic period, and it must be admitted that

Figure 4.3 Ixion bound on his wheel. Lucanian cup, 400–380 BC.
Museum of Tübingen University.

he belongs very appropriately in the company of Tantalos and Tityos.[105] According
to an older tradition which is attested for an early epic, the *Minyas*, **Amphion** was
punished in Hades in some unspecified way for having mocked Leto and her children[106] (an offence ascribed to his wife Niobe alone in most accounts, see p. 157).
Salmoneus first appears in this company in the *Aeneid*.[107] As a mythical ruler who
tried to usurp the functions and privileges of Zeus (see p. 422), he belongs there
as fittingly as Ixion. Other heroes who are named among the tormented dead in
Roman sources, though not in any surviving Greek source, are **Phlegyas**, who dared
to attack Apollo's temple at Delphi,[108] and the **Aloadai**, who launched an assault
against heaven (see p. 91).[109]

In the later tradition, the **Danaids**, a group of former princesses from the Argolid, are often
added to the number of those who are made to perform futile tasks in the Underworld. As a
penalty for having murdered their husbands (see p. 234), they must constantly attempt to
fetch water in leaky pitchers, or to fill a large water-jar as the water runs out again through
a hole at the bottom of it. The pseudo-Platonic *Axiochos* (probably first century BC) provides
the earliest definite evidence for this punishment, mentioning it along with the punishments
imposed on Tantalos, Tityos and Sisyphos.[110] Futile water-carrying is recorded as a task for
the dead at a much earlier period than this, for vase-paintings from the end of the sixth century
BC onwards occasionally show little winged figures struggling to fill a leaky urn; but it can be
safely assumed that these images have nothing to do with the Danaids, especially since male

figures are shown in addition to female. In describing Polygnotos' painting of the Underworld from the fifth century BC, Pausanias mentions that it showed two women carrying water in broken pots, and that they were identified by an inscription as women who had failed to have themselves initiated into the mysteries.[111] This was presumably the original meaning of the motif; such an initiation would have assured these women or others like them of a better lot in the afterlife, but it is now too late for them to receive it however great their wish. The imagery is not hard to interpret if it is remembered that prospective initiates would have to take a purificatory bath before their initiation. When transferred to the Danaids in the later tradition, their futile task comes to symbolize their unavailing effort to procure water to purify themselves from their blood-guilt.

Oknos is another person who performs a futile task in the Underworld, constantly plaiting a rope as it is constantly devoured by a donkey which stands behind him (or beside him). Since his name means 'hesitation' or 'vacillation', his posthumous activity should doubtless be interpreted in the same way as that of the anonymous water-carriers, as illustrating the predicament of those who have put off their initiation until it is too late. He was shown with his donkey in Polygnotos' painting; in Pausanias' time, some explained the image in terms of a fable, saying that it referred to Oknos' fate during his lifetime as an industrious man with an extravagant wife who had spent all his earnings as quickly as he had brought them in.[112]

The significance of these mythical punishments changes as the tradition evolves. In the Homeric account, the fate of the tormented (as of the people who are transferred to Elysion) is wholly exceptional, and cannot be interpreted as providing a warning for ordinary people, who could expect to share a common fate in the afterlife. When the notion developed, however, that there might be an overarching order of justice in which the ordinary dead could be expected to be judged in another world for crimes committed in this, the suffering of dead sinners from myth naturally acquired an exemplary significance. In Vergil's depiction of the infernal place of punishment, Phlegyas is portrayed accordingly as shouting words of warning through the gloom, calling on others to learn from his example to behave righteously and scorn no god.[113] It is worth noting, furthermore, that there was not originally any separate place of punishment that could be described as a hell; in the *Odyssey*, Odysseus sees Tantalos, Tityos and Sisyphos suffering their pains among the shades in the common home of the dead. In subsequent eschatological schemes, however, which involve a judgement of the dead, it came to be imagined that the deserving and undeserving dead would be consigned to different regions of the Underworld, which would be bright and blissful in the one case and dismal and dolorous in the other. From the time of Plato onwards, the place of punishment or correction (or the worst part of it) is quite often called Tartaros. This usage entails a shift of meaning, as when the abode of the virtuous dead is called Elysion, since Tartaros was originally a wholly separate place that served as a prison for banished deities (see p. 23).

Developments in eschatological belief, and the idea of a universal judgement of the dead

The evolution of Underworld mythology over the centuries was inevitably much affected by developments in eschatological belief, whether in Greek society in general or in narrower circles within it. Although it would take us far out of our way to attempt to trace these developments in any detail, something must be said about the broader trends. With regard to the fate of the dead in the afterlife, two conceptions subsisted side by side in the classical period, the old one that suggested that most of the dead would share a common fate, and a newer one that suggested that the dead would meet with differing fates in accordance with their merits. In the ancient belief found in Homer, as outlined above, the dead would live together in the same surroundings in the nether gloom as witless or semi-witless shades. Even if a person fated to this half-life could have nothing horrific to fear, the prospect would be thoroughly dismal; Achilles declares in the *Odyssey* that he would rather be the meanest serf alive than the king of all the dead.[114] By the classical era, however, another view had also developed in which it was supposed that the departed might be rewarded or punished in accordance with their behaviour during their earthly lives, or that people might assure themselves of a better lot in the afterlife by receiving certain initiations. In that case, a pattern of light and shade is introduced into the picture, for some must be consigned to a brighter destiny, presumably in a brighter region of the Underworld, and others to a darker destiny. The mysteries, especially those at Eleusis, certainly exercised a considerable influence in this connection; most Athenians and many Greeks from elsewhere were initiated at Eleusis, and the rites seem to have been effective in enduing initiates with the subjective assurance that they would fare well in the afterlife. In Eleusinian eschatological belief, however, strictly ethical considerations remained very much in the background. In considering how it came to be imagined that the good might be rewarded and the evil punished in the afterlife, some allowance should be made for the simple evolution of moral sentiment; since evil is often rewarded in this world and the good often suffer, it came to be surmised that the accounts must be balanced in the afterlife if there is indeed any order of justice. As we will see, such ideas were certainly current in popular belief in the classical period; and they marked an advance on the cruder idea that the crimes of individuals might be punished in their children or descendants. Also of significance were various eschatological beliefs of an unorthodox nature that developed in relatively narrow circles, Pythagorean, Orphic and Bacchic, from the late archaic period onwards. Although ritual factors were important here also, members of such circles usually believed that it was necessary to lead a good and pure life if one was to meet with good fortune in the afterlife.

Among Pythagoreans and others who accepted the idea of the transmigration of the soul, elaborate eschatological schemes were devised in which the soul was thought to undergo successive rebirths, living alternately in an earthly body and in the other world, and to pass to equivalents of hell, purgatory and paradise after each earthly incarnation. These ideas found their way into high literature and general culture through the writings of such authors as Pindar and, above all, Plato. Thus in the second *Olympian Ode* of Pindar, which has already been partially quoted above, those who have lived a just and pious life in this world will enjoy a life of ease below in a region where the sun shines forever, while wrongdoers will be subjected to punishment; the soul then returns to the upper world, and whosoever keeps his soul free from all wrong on either side of the grave for three successive cycles will pass to the paradisal place described in the quotation above.[115] This account reflects a pattern of belief in which man is thought to have fallen from a divine origin to enter into a cycle of reincarnation, from which he can finally escape by virtuous conduct combined with certain ritual obligations, and so hope to achieve a condition of entire and eternal happiness. Plato again owes much to Orphico-Pythagorean teachings for the imagery and pattern of his great eschatological myths; while later, other religious and quasi-religious beliefs added their contribution. As the traditional Homeric ideas were interblended with subsequent ideas of diverse origin, authors from the time of Plato onwards came to offer curiously mixed descriptions of the afterlife, accompanied by increasingly elaborate and definite accounts of the topography of Hades.

As has already been mentioned, Pindar and Aeschylus are the first authors to make any definite reference to a judgement of the dead (see p. 115), and it was generally agreed by subsequent authors that the judgement was performed by dead mortals who had been exceptionally just during their earthly lives rather than by Hades himself. The three mythical heroes who are most often credited with this honour, namely Minos, Rhadamanthys and Aiakos, are first identified as infernal judges in the writings of Plato (died 347 BC).[116] It can be inferred from the language that he uses in this context that these were traditional names for the judges, probably derived from the mythology associated with the Eleusinian Mysteries. In conventional mythology, Minos and Rhadamanthys were two early members of the Cretan royal family who were celebrated for their justice and their wisdom as lawmakers (see pp. 338 and 351), while Aiakos was a king of Aegina who was a paragon of righteousness and often arbitrated in disputes (see p. 531). Plato adds the Eleusinian hero Triptolemos (see p. 131) to the list in his *Apology*, along with 'other demigods who have lived just lives',[117] but Triptolemos rarely figures in this role thereafter. Some authors apportion separate functions to the different judges as the fancy takes them; Plato suggests in the *Gorgias*, for instance, that Rhadamanthys judges the Asiatic dead and Aiakos the Europeans, while Minos has the last word if their judgement should need revision; or in Vergil's *Aeneid*, Minos presides over an infernal court which examines the cases of those who have been condemned to death on false charges, while Rhadamanthys judges the faults of the wicked in another region of the Underworld.[118] Aiakos was sometimes said to have been appointed to duties of another kind as the doorkeeper of Hades (or keeper of the keys, which comes to much the same thing);[119] and some authors continued to follow Homer in believing that Rhadamanthys spent his posthumous life in Elysion or the Isles of the Blessed (see p. 115).[120]

The dead are consigned by these judges to a better or worse region of the Underworld in accordance with their deserts, and so to a better or worse fate in the afterlife. Broadly speaking, the abode and manner of life of the favoured dead are pictured in terms of the imagery that was traditionally associated with Elysion or the Isles of the Blessed, while the unrighteous dead are condemned to the dismal half-life that was the common lot of the dead in the Homeric account, and perhaps to hard labour also and some form of correction or punishment. If due exception is made for the cruel fates that were traditionally assigned to a few notable figures from myth, Greek accounts of the punishment of the dead are very restrained by comparison that those that were once current in the Christian tradition. There is little direct reference to the infliction of physical torment, up until the Roman period at least. Such punishments as are recorded in connection with Eleusis are of a symbolic nature; the impure will lie in mud,[121] the uninitiated will strive in vain to carry purifying water in leaky vessels (see above). The picture darkens, however, as the Hellenistic period advances. In vase-paintings from lower Italy, the Erinyes (Furies) or the Poinai (Avengers), who are much the same, can be seen inflicting punishment on the dead with scourges or flaming torches; and the pseudo-Platonic *Axiochos* (probably first century BC) remarks that the wicked will pay for their sins everlastingly in Tartaros where they are 'licked by beasts, constantly burned by the torches of the Poinai, and subjected to all manner of torment'.[122] In literature from the Roman period, mythical monsters are sometimes presented as agents of retribution; in Lucian's *Dialogues of the Dead*, for instance, the dead Minos sees a temple-robber being torn apart by the Chimaira.[123]

That is not to say that popular fears about cruel punishments in the Underworld are unattested in the earlier literature. On the contrary, there is good reason to suppose that such apprehensions were fairly widespread in classical times. In Plato's *Republic*, for instance, the aged merchant Kephalos remarks to Socrates that many old people like himself feel disquiet in the face of death, for they begin to worry that the stories that are told of the world below, and of punishments that are inflicted there for wrongs committed here, may in fact be true.[124] One of the sayings of Democritus points in the same direction: 'Some people, who know nothing of the dissolution of mortal nature but are well acquainted with evil-doing in life, afflict the period of their life with worries and fears by inventing false tales about the period that will follow the end of their life'.[125] Pausanias' description of Polygnotos' painting of the Underworld gives an idea of how punishments for very grave offences would have been imagined by such people; in one scene, a man who had been wicked to his father was shown as being strangled by him when he arrived among the dead, and in another, a temple-robber received punishment from a woman, perhaps an Erinys, who (so Pausanias tells us) knew all about drugs and especially those that cause suffering to men.[126] Popular fears about the beasts, bogies and daimones of the Underworld also find little reflection in high literature. We would know nothing, for instance, about the repulsive Eurynomos if Pausanias had not referred to him in connection with Polygnotos' painting; this daimon of the Underworld, who devoured the flesh of the dead leaving only their bones behind, was blue-black in colour like a carrion-fly, had grinning teeth, and used a vulture's hide as his seat.[127] In Aristophanes' *Frogs*, which is a rich source for lore of the Underworld, Dionysos and his slave Xanthias fear that they will meet horrible monsters after rowing across into Hades, and are alarmed to encounter Empousa, a female bogey with a luminous face and a copper leg.[128]

Vergil's account of Aeneas' journey into the Underworld

Having begun with Homer's account of the Underworld, we may conclude with an epic account from the Roman period which reflects intervening developments, namely that offered by Vergil in the sixth book of the *Aeneid*; for in describing how Aeneas passes through the different regions of the Underworld in the company of the Cumaean Sibyl, Vergil provides the clearest and most elaborate and consistent account to be found in any classical writer after Plato. To gain entry into the Underworld, Aeneas plucks a golden bough on the advice of the Sibyl from a special tree in a grove near Cumae, and brings it with him as an offering for Proserpina

(Persephone); it is suggested in later sources that he took the bough from Diana's grove at Aricia, plucking it from the famous tree that was guarded by the 'king' of the grove.[129] After making their way below through a cave near Lake Avernus, Aeneas and the Sibyl encounter two alarming groups of beings at the threshold of Hades, the first consisting of personifications of all that is most terrible in life (such as Fear, Hunger, Death, War, and others who are described as members of the family of Night in Hesiod's *Theogony*), and the second consisting of traditional monsters of hybrid form such as the Hydra and Chimaira and the Centaurs, Harpies and Gorgons, or at least the shades of them. Temporary inhabitants of that region are the shades of the unburied dead, who have to remain on the near side of the infernal river for a hundred years until they can be ferried across to the world of the dead.[130]

After making their passage across the boundary-river (here the Styx) in Charon's boat, Aeneas and his companion are confronted by the three-headed Kerberos, but the Sibyl soon puts him to sleep by tossing him a drugged honey-cake. They then follow a path which runs through the various regions or zones that harbour those of the dead who are neither in Elysion nor in Tartaros. All are people who have died before their proper time for one reason or another. First, at the very entrance-way, the souls of dead infants can be heard bewailing their fate; in the next zone come those who have been condemned to death on false charges, but are now receiving true justice at a court convened by Minos; next come those who have died by their own hand (even though they would now be willing to endure any suffering under the light of the day, if only it were possible for them to find their way back again across the encircling coils of Styx); the fourth zone is formed by the Fields of Mourning (*Campi Lugentes*), the sorrowful home of those who have pined away for love or perished through its consequences; and finally, in the innermost zone, come warriors who have died a glorious death in battle. Aeneas and his companion now arrive at a place where the road divides, leading to Tartaros on one side and Elysion on the other.[131]

The two of them skirt the borders of Tartaros, which is separated from them by rings of battlements and by Pyriphlegethon, the flaming river of hell. The groans of the damned can be heard through the gates of Tartaros, and Tisiphone, the guardian of the gate, can be seen sitting in an iron tower beside the gates, clad in a bloodied robe. The Sibyl explains that Tisiphone, with some help from her sister-Furies, whips the most wicked of the dead through the gates with her scourge after Rhadamanthys has passed sentence on them; and she then tells Aeneas of the suffer-ings that are imposed there on various mythical heroes such as Tantalos, Ixion and Phlegyas (see above), and also on the Titans (who are now to be found in the same place since Tartaros has come to be regarded as a part of the Underworld). Vergil summarizes that character of the inmates of Tartaros most succinctly in the words *ausi omnes immane nefas ausoque potiti* – 'all had dared a monstrous and unspeakable deed, and had accomplished that which they had dared'.[132] He specifies violation of the closest ties of blood-relationship and social obligation, treason against one's native land, gross abuse of power, and direct offences against the gods.[133] With this account few in antiquity would have disagreed. At the end of their journey, Aeneas and the Sibyl arrive at Elysion, the bright and happy home of the righteous dead. Here Vergil places, among others, great and successful patriots, renowned warriors, priests and poets of more than common inspiration.[134] At this point we can take our leave of Aeneas, before he is accorded his preview of the future history of Rome (see p. 591).

HADES, PERSEPHONE AND DEMETER

To return to the god Hades himself, he had only a single myth of the first importance, the one that told how he ventured into the upper world to abduct Persephone as his bride. He rarely left his kingdom otherwise, if at all. Probably as the result of a misinterpretation of a passage in the *Iliad*, it came to be believed that he was wounded by Herakles at Pylos while he was assisting the king of that city against the hero[135] (see further on p. 278); and according to a minor myth from a very late source, he once abducted an Ocean-nymph called LEUKE from the upper world to make her his mistress, and was so distressed when she subsequently died that he caused the white poplar (*leukē*) to grow up in her memory in the Elysian Fields (here regarded as part of the Underworld).[136] If Hades was disinclined to venture above, his fellow gods, who shunned all contact with death and the dead, were no more willing to visit him in his own realm, with the exception of Hermes, who ventured into the Underworld when his duties as a messenger demanded it (and conducted the dead to the boundary-river at least, see above). Hades had little or nothing to do with the affairs of living mortals; at the most, it is suggested in two passages in the *Iliad* that he and Persephone might respond through the agency of the Erinyes (Furies) if mortals prayed to them to fulfil curses (see p. 38).[137] The few heroes who dared to descend into his realm while still alive placed themselves under his dominion by that very action, and he sometimes proved gracious, as in the case of Herakles and Orpheus (see pp. 268 and 552), and sometimes less so, as in the case of Theseus and Peirithoos (see p. 361). Hades also makes some appearance in heroic myth in stories in which he grants temporary leave of absence to heroes such as Protesilaos (see p. 450) and Sisyphos (who abused the privilege, see p. 431).

How Hades abducted Persephone as his bride, but was finally obliged to share her with her mother

Hades chose to marry PERSEPHONE, the only daughter of his sister DEMETER, who was the goddess of corn and agriculture generally, and the patroness of the Eleusinian Mysteries. Since he stole Persephone from the upper world in secret from her mother, who was greatly distressed by her disappearance and was determined to recover her, the ancient legend that tells of the abduction and its consequences is the main myth of Demeter as well as of Hades and the maiden herself. In the end, a compromise was imposed in which Persephone spent part of the year below with Hades and part in the upper world with her mother. Persephone was a goddess of twofold character accordingly, being at once the awesome queen of the dead and a goddess of the fertility of the earth in conjunction with Demeter. She was often

Figure 4.4   Rape of Persephone. Fresco from Tomb II at Vergina, 350–25 BC.

closely associated with her mother in cult, so much so that the pair could be referred to simply as the Two Goddesses (*tō Theō*) or the two Demeters or two Thesmophoriai. Persephone was also known as Kore (the Girl) in cult. Although the latter part of Demeter's name certainly means mother, the meaning of the first syllable is a matter for conjecture; the once-popular idea, already current in antiquity, that the name means 'Earth Mother' has come to be regarded as ill-founded.

The story of the abduction of Persephone is recounted as follows in the *Homeric Hymn to Demeter*, which provides the earliest and fullest account. While the maiden was once gathering flowers with her companions, Earth caused a wonderful flower to spring up in her path on behalf of Hades, a bloom of unparalleled size and beauty; and when Persephone reached out to pluck it, the ground opened up and Hades emerged in his golden chariot to seize her and carry her down to the Underworld. Although the Hymn names a purely mythical place, the Nysian plain, as the site of the abduction, the incident was usually placed in Sicily in the later tradition. Persephone's cries were heard by Hekate and Helios alone. Her mother soon grew anxious and hurried off in search of her, but could find no news of her, whether from gods or mortals or birds of omen. So lighting two torches (from the flames of Etna according to a later tradition), Demeter wandered the world for nine days, fasting all the while, until she met Hekate, who told her that she had heard her daughter crying out; and the two goddesses went off to consult the sun-god Helios,

Figure 4.5 Demeter and Kore. The Eleusis relief, fifth century BC. Eleusis Museum. Photo: Richard Stoneman.

who can see everything from his vantage-point in the sky. When Helios disclosed that Hades had abducted Persephone with the connivance of Zeus, Demeter was so upset and angry that she abandoned the company of the gods and hid herself among mortals in the guise of an old woman.[138]

After long wanderings, she arrived at Eleusis (to the north-west of Athens), and sat down by a well called Parthenion (the Maiden Well). When the daughters of Keleos, the king of the town, saw her there while fetching water and addressed her courteously, saying that she could be sure of a welcome from the women of the town, she led them to believe that she was an old woman who had been abducted from Crete by pirates, and asked them to help her to find some work. So they went off to consult their mother, Metaneira, who told them to invite the old woman home to act as nursemaid to her infant son Demophoon. After entering the palace, Demeter sat in disconsolate silence until her spirits were lifted by the jokes of a certain Iambe, who caused her to laugh for the first time since the loss of her daughter; and when Metaneira then offered her some wine, she asked for *kykeōn* instead, a drink containing barley-meal and pennyroyal. Coarse humour and raillery had their place in the Eleusinian Mysteries, as did the use of *kykeōn* as a ritual drink; in accounts from the later tradition, a woman called Baubo awoke the laughter of the goddess by raising her skirts to expose herself.[139]

To repay Metaneira for her kindness, the goddess set out to confer immortality on her nursling, by rubbing him with ambrosia each day and by immersing him in a fire each night to burn away all that was mortal in his body. Her plan succeeded satisfactorily until Metaneira saw her burying the infant in the fire one night and cried out in dismay. Enraged by this unexpected interference, the goddess threw the child to the ground and rebuked the queen, telling her that she was Demeter and would have rendered her child immortal if it had not been for her meddling. She now resumed her proper form and commanded that rites should be instituted in her honour at Eleusis, and she foretold furthermore that in the future a mock-fight would be mounted each year by the young men of the city in honour of her nursling. She promised that when her demands had been obeyed and a great temple had been raised to her, she would instruct the Eleusinians in her secret rites, which would be celebrated there in future days as the famous Eleusinian Mysteries.[140]

As long as Demeter was absent from Olympos and in mourning, the earth was infertile and famine-stricken, for without her influence nothing could grow or reach maturity. After the completion of her temple at Eleusis, she remained there grieving for a year, until the gods came to fear that the human race would die of hunger and that they would be deprived of their sacrifices as a consequence. So Zeus sent the divine messenger Iris to Demeter to instruct her to return to Olympos, but she refused to obey; and when he then sent all the other gods to her one after another to offer her handsome gifts and whatever she might desire, she still refused to change her mind, declaring that she would never set foot on Olympos nor allow the crops to spring forth until she had seen her daughter with her own eyes. Faced with this ultimatum, Zeus was obliged to send Hermes to the lord of the Underworld to ask him to release Persephone. Hades acceded to his brother's request, but secretly invited Persephone to eat a pomegranate seed (or seeds in some accounts) before she left, and so ensured that she would remain bound to his realm forever. When Demeter learned of this from her daughter after they were reunited, she realized that she would have to accept a compromise, and agreed to Zeus' proposal that Persephone should spend a third of the year in the world below as the consort of Hades, and the other two-thirds with her mother and the Olympian gods. Or in some late accounts, it was agreed that Persephone should spend half of the year below and half in the upper world.[141] Now that a settlement had been reached, Demeter restored fertility to the ground, and fulfilled her promise to the Eleusinians by instructing Keleos and other leading men of the city in her rites and mysteries.[142]

In the original version of the story, the mere action of eating from the pomegranate in the world below sufficed to bind Persephone to that world forever; but it is suggested in some later accounts that this fate came to be imposed on her because an inhabitant of the Underworld bore witness to the fact that she had eaten there. The fateful secret was disclosed by a certain ASKALAPHOS, who was a son of Acheron by the Underworld nymph Gorgyra or Orphne. Persephone was so enraged that she sprinkled him with water from an infernal river, the Phlegethon, causing him to be transformed into an ill-omened bird of the dark, the screech-owl.[143] Or in another version, Demeter punished him by confining him under a heavy rock, and transformed him into an owl later when Herakles rolled the rock aside during his visit to the Underworld (see p. 268).[144]

Another minor transformation story is recorded in connection with the abduction. When Persephone was brought below by Hades, MINTHE (or Menthe), a nymph of the Underworld who had previously been his mistress, boasted that she was more beautiful than the goddess and would soon win her lover back. Demeter was so angered by her presumption that she trampled her into the ground, and a mint-plant (*minthē*) sprang up in place of her; or else she was transformed into the herb by Persephone herself.[145]

In contradiction to the *Homeric Hymn to Demeter*, which assumes that the use of grain was already known at the time of Persephone's abduction, but intelligibly enough in a legend of this sort which has clearly grown out of the cult of the corn-goddess, it was often claimed in later times that Demeter first bestowed the gift of grain after she was reunited with her daughter; the Athenians liked to boast that they had been the first recipients of the gift (i.e. at Eleusis), and had been generous enough to pass it on to others.[146]

All manner of local legends came to be attached to this great myth of Demeter and Persephone. Two stories in particular are worth mentioning in connection with Demeter's visit to Attica. While she was once thirsty from the heat, a woman called Misme invited her into her cottage and offered her some *kykeōn* (the drink mentioned above which contained herbs and barley). The goddess drank it down so eagerly that the woman's impertinent son, ASKALABOS, laughed at her greed; and in her anger, she threw the remains of her drink into his face and transformed him into a spotted gecko (*askalabos*). The marks of the incident can still be seen on the body of the little house-lizard, for it is blotched with the little spots that were left by the barley-meal from the *kykeōn*.[147] This Hellenistic tale was clearly inspired by the episode in the Homeric Hymn in which Demeter broke her fast by drinking *kykeōn* that was brought to her by Metaneira.[148] In another Attic legend, Demeter once received hospitality from a man called PHYTALOS who lived on the sacred road between Athens and Eleusis, and rewarded him by giving him the first fig-tree.[149]

At Pheneos in Arcadia, which was one of the many locations at which Hades was supposed to have descended beneath the earth with Persephone, the local people pointed Demeter to the place of her disappearance, a chasm on Mt Kyllene above their city, and she rewarded them by granting them a special favour, that they should never lose more than a hundred men in any war.[150]

The Argives liked to believe that Persephone had been carried below at a site in their own land near Lerna.[151] When Demeter arrived in Argos in the course of her search, she was informed of the matter by Chrysanthis, the wife of a primordial ruler of the land, Pelasgos (see p. 538). Local tradition claimed that the goddess revealed her rites and mysteries on this occasion, and that her mysteries were introduced to Eleusis secondarily and at a later period, when the Argive hierophant (initiatory priest) quarrelled with the current ruler and fled to Attica.[152] Demeter was reputed to have worked a special miracle for the Argives as late as the third century BC; for when Pyrrhos, the warlike king of Epirus, attacked Argos after being frustrated in his ambitions in Italy and Sicily, the goddess struck him down in the streets of the city with a well-aimed tile from the roof-tops. Such at least was the local belief; sceptics would have it that the tile was thrown by an Argive woman who saw her son in confrontation with the king.[153]

In Hellenistic and later times, Persephone's abduction was usually located in Sicily, which was noted for its rich cornlands. According to one account, Hades opened up a chasm in the region of Syracuse to take her below, and caused the spring of Cyane (the Azure Spring) to gush forth at the spot.[154] In Ovid's version of this story, the spring was already in existence, and its nymph, CYANE, tried to block the path of Hades as he was making off with Persephone; but the god directed his chariot straight into her pool, hurling his sceptre into the bottom of it to open up a breach in the earth. Cyane was so upset by the fate of Persephone and her own humiliation that she wasted away with weeping, finally melting into the waters that she had presided over.[155] Others said that Kore had been abducted from the meadows around Enna or Henna at the very centre of the island, and that Hades had emerged from a grotto nearby that communicated with the Underworld. The people of Enna claimed that Demeter and her daughter had been born there, and that Demeter had first discovered corn there.[156] It seems likely enough that in this very fertile region a corn-goddess of some kind would have been honoured in local cult before any Greek had settled there.

The above-mentioned arrangement that obliged Persephone to spend a third of the year below the ground and two-thirds above evidently relates to the rotation of the seasons in connection with the growth of crops and vegetation. The Homeric Hymn indicates this directly enough by stating that Persephone emerges from the realm of darkness each year 'when the earth blossoms with fragrant spring flowers of every kind'.[157] Although the myth has quite often been interpreted as an allegory for the sowing of the seed-corn and its subsequent rise in the spring, it has been noted that this hardly accords with conditions in Greece, where the seed does not rest in the ground over the winter after the autumn sowing, but germinates after a brief delay and grows throughout the winter. It has been suggested accordingly that Persephone's stay in the Underworld corresponds to the period in the summer when the grain is kept in underground stores; but even if this provides a neat solution to the problem, there is no evidence that the Greeks themselves ever interpreted the myth in such a way.

Persephone appears quite frequently in myth as the awesome queen of the Underworld. It is assumed from the time of Homer onwards that she wields considerable authority in that realm, joining with her husband in making decisions with regard to the dead or to living heroes who venture below, and even acting on her own initiative on occasion. The *Iliad* suggests that she can be invoked in curses and act upon them in conjunction with Hades (see p. 125); and in the *Odyssey*, Odysseus prays to her along with Hades on approaching the Underworld, and she sends shades of the female dead to him and subsequently disperses them. Odysseus worries, furthermore, at the end of his visit that she may send some horrible bogey against him.[158] Most intriguingly, it is stated that it was she who had granted Teiresias his special privilege of retaining his wits after death (see p. 329), apparently on her own authority.[159] She is occasionally presented in subsequent sources as making independent decisions with regard to mortals in the Underworld, whether in allowing the dead Sisyphos to return to the upper world, or in allowing Herakles to depart with Kerberos or Orpheus with Eurydike.[160] As we shall see (p. 360), Theseus and Peirithoos entered the Underworld with the specific purpose of abducting her. She is hardly mentioned at all in connection with events in the upper world; the only tale worth citing is the one in which she competes with Aphrodite for custody of the young Adonis (see p. 199).

How Triptolemos spread the gift of Demeter; the other myths of Demeter, and her associate Iakchos

According to Attic tradition, Demeter's gift of grain was spread through the world by a young Eleusinian called TRIPTOLEMOS, an interesting figure who probably originated as a local deity, but is first mentioned in the *Homeric Hymn to Demeter* as one of the Eleusinian princes who received instruction from Demeter in her rites and mysteries.[161] Although many different accounts are offered of his birth, he is perhaps most frequently described as a son of the king who was reigning at Eleusis at the time of Demeter's visit (whether that king is named as Keleos, Eleusis or Eleusinos), and he is sometimes identified with the nursling who was tended by Demeter. Or else he was a son of Okeanos, or of Raros, whose meadow outside Eleusis was the first site to have been sown or harvested, or of Dysaules, another local hero with agricultural connections.[162] Vase-painters liked to show him as he might be pictured when setting off on his mission, seated in a two-wheeled chariot (which is apparently self-propelled and may be winged) with ears of corn in his hands. Or in literary accounts, he travels through the air in a chariot drawn by winged dragons as he sows the inhabited earth with grain and spreads knowledge of its cultivation. He was sent off on his mission by Demeter herself, who provided him with the necessary transport.[163]

Three specific tales are recorded of his adventures during his travels. When he arrived in Scythia, a local ruler called LYNKOS tried to murder him in his sleep so as to usurp the honour of spreading the gift of grain; but as the king was directing his sword for the blow, Demeter foiled his plan by transforming him into a lynx.[164]

Figure 4.6 Triptolemos in his chariot, surrounded by the gods

In the same region, CHARNABON, king of the Getai, plotted the destruction of Triptolemos, and arranged for one of his dragons to be killed to prevent him from escaping. On this occasion too, however, Demeter came to the rescue of her favourite, by hitching a new dragon to his chariot and returning it to him. As a lesson to others, she placed Charnabon in the sky with a dragon entwined around him, as the constellation Ophiouchos (the Serpent-holder).[165] And finally, at Patrai in Achaea, the ruler's son ANTHEAS yoked the dragon-chariot while Triptolemos was asleep and tried to sow some grain from it; but he was unable to control it (much as in the legend of Phaethon) and plunged to his death. Together with Eumelos, the father of dead youth, Triptolemos founded the Achaean city of Antheia in his memory.[166]

Of the other notable legends of Demeter, one has already been recounted in connection with Poseidon (see p. 101), while two remain to be considered here, one very old and very simple that tells of her love affair with a mortal, and another that tells how she punished an act of impiety that was committed against her in Thessaly. The former was already known to Homer, who states in the *Odyssey* that Demeter yielded to her passion for IASION and lay with him in a thrice-ploughed field.[167] The story also appears in the present text of the *Theogony*, which adds that the field was located in Crete and that the offspring of the union was a child called PLOUTOS, i.e. Wealth, representing above all the wealth yielded by the ground in the harvest.[168] Homer cites Iasion's story along with others to show how the gods resented love affairs between goddesses and mortals, and states accordingly that Zeus struck Iasion with a thunderbolt after learning of his liaison with Demeter. In some later accounts, he committed the grave offence of trying to rape the goddess (or, in a partially rationalized version, of desecrating her cultic image) and was struck down for gross impiety instead. Ovid remarks, by contrast, that Demeter came to lament his grey hairs, which would imply that he lived to a good old age.[169] There was disagreement about the place of his birth. If the *Theogony* implies that he was a Cretan (and he is described correspondingly as a grandson of Minos in some late sources),[170] some authorities from Hellanicus onwards say that he was a Samothracian, a son of Zeus by the Atlantid Elektra (see p. 521) and the brother of Dardanos. In this connection, his death is sometimes said to have prompted Dardanos' departure to the Troad (see p. 521).[171] It has long been recognized that the story of the mating on the ploughfield is a mythical reflection of a common fertility rite in which couples would have intercourse on the fields to encourage the growth of the crops.

In Hellanicus, and apparently the Hesiodic *Catalogue* too although the relevant part of the text is poorly preserved, the son of Elektra who became involved with Demeter was called Eetion rather than Iasion.[172] Iasion's name also appears as Iasios. According to a late tale preserved in the astronomical literature, Demeter bore two sons, Ploutos and Philomelos, to Iasion in Crete, and the two of them subsequently quarrelled because Ploutos, who was the richer as his name would suggest, refused to share any of his wealth with his brother. Under force of circumstances, Philomelos bought two oxen and invented the plough to scratch a living from the land; and his divine mother was so impressed by his ingenuity that she placed him in the heavens as the constellation Boötes (the Oxherd).[173]

The second of these myths tells how Demeter afflicted the Thessalian hero ERY-SICHTHON with perpetual hunger for cutting down a sacred grove of hers. Erysichthon, son of Triopas or Myrmidon, wanted wood to build a new hall or palace and, in an evil hour, chose to acquire the necessary timber by felling trees in a grove of Demeter. In the first full account of the story by Callimachus, he set out to perform the task with twenty of his servants, and when the goddess herself tried to warn him off in the guise of her priestess Nikippe, he merely threatened her with his axe. Angered beyond telling by his behaviour, she told him to continue with the work, for he would soon have real need of a banqueting-hall; and from that time onward, he was afflicted with a ravenous and insatiable hunger. The more he ate, the hungrier he grew and the thinner he became. He ate continuously throughout the day, consuming all his livestock, and his mules and horses and even the cat, until nothing at all was left and he was reduced to begging at the cross-roads.[174] It is stated in later accounts that he acquired money for food by repeatedly selling his daughter MESTRA into slavery; for her lover Poseidon had granted her the power to transform herself at will, and she was therefore able to escape on each occasion by turning into an animal of one kind or another.[175]

This myth was probably fairly ancient since a surviving passage from the Hesiodic *Catalogue* mentions that Erysichthon was called Aithon on account of his burning (*aithōn*) hunger. Hellanicus apparently said the same. The fact that Palaephatus thought it necessary to provide a rationalistic explanation for Mestra's powers would suggest that this aspect of her mythology was familiar by the early Hellenistic period. Mestra was mentioned as the daughter of Erysichthon in the *Catalogue*; Lycophron is the first author to state that she used her powers to provide food for her father.[176]

In Ovid's account, Erysichthon cut down the largest and oldest oak in the grove of Demeter, ignoring the warnings of the tree-nymph who lived in it; and after its destruction and the consequent death of the nymph, her sister Dryads approached Demeter in mourning to beg her to inflict due punishment on Erysichthon. The poet was doubtless inspired here by a passage in Callimachus' account in which Erysichthon began by cutting down an exceptionally large poplar-tree, causing it to utter a cry that alerted Demeter to the sacrilege. It is stated in both accounts that the nymphs of the grove used to dance under the tree in question. To return to Ovid's narrative, Demeter punished Erysichthon in the usual fashion, and he finally sold his daughter to raise money for food. She prayed for help from Poseidon, who transformed her into a fisherman to enable her to escape; and when her father sold her on subsequent occasions, she escaped in animal form each time (apparently as the result of separate interventions by Poseidon, for it is not stated that he gave her the power to transform herself).[177]

According to an alternative tradition, the fateful sacrilege was committed by TRIOPAS, the father of Erysichthon (or a brother of his) rather than by Erysichthon himself. In a version from the astronomical literature, Triopas offended Demeter by destroying a temple of hers (*sic*, possibly an error) to acquire material for the roof of his palace. She punished him initially by afflicting him with insatiable hunger, and added to his sorrows at the end of his life by sending a huge serpent against him. After his death, he was placed among the stars at her will as the constellation Ophiouchos (the Serpent-holder), in which the serpent can be seen tormenting him forever.[178]

This Thessalian Erysichthon should be distinguished from the Athenian of the same name (see p. 366).

Of some importance for cult, though of almost none for mythology, is IAKCHOS, a minor god who was associated with Demeter and Persephone at Eleusis. He seems to have originated as the personification of a refrain in much that same way as Hymenaios (see p. 223), in this case of the ritual cry of *Iakch' o Iakche* that was chanted by the initiates as they passed in procession from Athens to Eleusis. Although he was often equated with Dionysos, apparently for no better reason than that his name sounds like that of Bakchos, he was also described as a son of Dionysos, or of Demeter or Persephone (or indeed as the husband of Demeter).[179] He presided over the great procession of the initiates as they marched along the Sacred Way to Eleusis; his image was drawn in front of them on a cart and was accompanied by his priest, the Iakchagogos. The chorus of initiates in Aristophanes' *Frogs* appeals to Iakchos to shine on them as their leader.[180] He is connected with one notable miracle recounted by Herodotus. Just before the battle of Salamis, certain Greek allies of the invading Persians saw a supernatural cloud of dust (for there was no one left in Attica to make one) moving from Eleusis, and heard the Iakchos-hymn of the mysteries rising up from it; and as it moved towards the Greek camp at Salamis, the eye-witnesses knew that disaster was imminent for the Persian fleet.[181]

HERA

The wife of Zeus and goddess of marriage

HERA became the consort of her brother Zeus, and bore him three children of no exceptional stature, Ares, Hebe and Eileithuia; the smith-god Hephaistos was sometimes regarded as a further child of the union, or else as a son who was produced by Hera alone without prior intercourse with her husband (see p. 79). Although the cult of Hera had little to do with that of Zeus, her legends are mainly concerned with her marriage to him and all that followed from it, and she came to be viewed above all as the goddess of marriage and married women. It was inevitable that a goddess, as opposed to a god, should have been cast as the divine guardian of that all-important institution, and none could have been more suitable for the role than the wife of Zeus himself. The greatest centres of her cult were the ancient Heraion between Argos and Mycenae and her splendid temple on the island of Samos. Her connection with the Argolid was particularly close, as is acknowledged in Greek literature from the earliest times; Homer and Hesiod refer to her as Argive Hera (Hera Argeie) and Pindar praises Argos as the home of Hera.[182] It seems that she originated as the great goddess of Argos and that her association with Zeus is secondary. Her cult spread far and wide, however, flourishing in the Peloponnese and the Aegean islands in particular, and latterly the Greek colonies of the Italian west. Although her name may simply mean Lady or Mistress (as a feminine form of the word *herōs*), other etymologies have also been proposed.

Hera was pictured as a mature and even matronly woman whose noble and severe beauty was very different from that of Aphrodite. In art, she is shown as a tall and stately figure, usually fully draped, crowned with a sort of diadem (*polos*, sometimes with accompanying veil) or wearing a wreath, and carrying a sceptre. Homer refers to her as 'cow-eyed' (*boōpis*), an epithet that doubtless reflects her special connection with cattle in her native Argos; herds of cows were kept at the Argive Heraion, many votive images of cows have been discovered there, and it is known that Argive Hera particularly appreciated sacrifices of white cows. Her status as a marriage-goddess is indicated in many of her cultic titles. As the goddess who presides over the solemnization (*telos*) of marriage, she was widely honoured as Hera Teleia; and she could also be invoked as Zygia or Syzygia (she who unites in marriage), Gamostoles (she who prepares the wedding), and Gamelia (she who presides over marriage). Since the bride approaches legitimate marriage as a virgin, Hera can also be addressed and honoured as such, whether as Pais (the Girl) or Parthenos (the Maiden, as in her cult at Hermione, see below) or Nymphe (the Bride). According to a local tradition in the Argolid, she bathed in the spring of Kanathos near Nauplion every year to renew her virginity[183] (an idea that was probably suggested by a rite in which her cultic image was bathed in the spring). At Stymphalos in Arcadia, she was worshipped at three separate temples as Girl, Wife and Widow (*Pais, Teleia, Chērē*). Local legend explained the origin of the sanctuaries by saying that Temenos, son of Pelasgos, an early hero of the city, had reared the goddess and had erected three successive temples to her under these titles, the first when she was still a young virgin, the second at the time of her marriage to Zeus, and the third when she came back to Stymphalos for a while because she had quarrelled with her husband.[184] The real explanation of these epithets is, of course, that she was worshipped by all women, whatever their condition, and represented them at every stage in the usual course of their life.

As a goddess of married women, she would bring help to women in childbirth; she was honoured as Hera Eileithuia at Argos and Athens, and is presented in myth as taking direct action to ease the birth of Eurystheus (see p. 248). It is thus understandable that Eileithuia, the goddess of child-birth, a very ancient deity who can be traced back to the Mycenaean period, should have come to be classed as her daughter. Such emphasis was laid on Hera's function as a wife and patroness of married women that she was hardly conceived at all as a mother. She was never invoked or portrayed as such, and she had no very close or ancient connection with the children who came to be ascribed to her. These are of diverse origin, and it will be noted that they were not deities of the very highest dignity. Hera was not at all kind to her malformed son Hephaistos; for her unmotherly treatment of him, and his ingenious act of revenge, see pp. 165–6.

Local myths and cultic traditions relating to Hera's marriage or first union with Zeus

The most distinctive myths of Hera fall into two groups, those that tell how she was supposed to have married Zeus or first been seduced by him in various parts of the Greek world, and those of a more negative nature that tell how she persecuted mistresses and illegitimate children of Zeus. Since the tales in the latter category relate to heroic mythology for the most part, those in the first group will be our main concern in the present chapter.

According to a Cretan legend, Zeus wedded Hera with due ceremony on the island near the river Theren in the territory of Knossos. Diodorus reports that a temple stood on the very spot in his own day, and that the local people would offer annual sacrifices there 'and imitate the wedding-ceremony, just as tradition presents it as having been originally performed'.[185] Whether these rites went beyond the outward ceremonial of the marriage to end with a ritual re-enactment of the sacred union (*hieros gamos*, hierogamy) is impossible to say; although such rites are well attested for the ancient Near East, the Greek evidence is far less definite. The myth of Demeter recounted above in which she had intercourse with Iasion on a ploughfield (usually in Crete, see p. 132) certainly seems to point to a rite in which intercourse was performed to encourage the fertility of the crops. The whole of nature is brought into play in the famous scene in the *Iliad* in which Zeus encloses Hera in a cloud to make love with her on Mt Ida:

> then the son of Kronos clasped his wife in his arms, and beneath them the holy earth caused fresh-grown grass to spring forth, and dewy clover and meadow-saffron, and hyacinth thick and soft, that raised them off the ground; there the two of them lay down together, and were covered all around with a beautiful golden cloud, from which there fell glistening drops of dew.[186]

One of the main rites at Hera's festival of the Tonaia on Samos also seems to have referred to her wedding to Zeus (even if that did not necessarily exhaust the meaning of the ritual). Each year at that festival, her statue was brought out of her temple and carried down to the sea-shore, where it was purified and concealed under willow-twigs, with cakes set out in front of it; the celebrants would then withdraw, and make a show of searching for the statue and discovering it. The statue can be seen on Samian coins with the withies hanging down from it; the vegetation in question (that of *lygos*, or *agnus castus*, 'chaste lamb' in Latin) was symbolic of chastity, here presumably of Hera as a bride. The Roman antiquarian Varro states explicitly that the statue was draped with bridal robes, and that the festival was celebrated with rites imitative of marriage.[187]

A cultic legend explained the various procedures by saying that pirates had once tried to steal the statue, but had found that their ship would not sail with it on board and had therefore left it behind on the shore, where the Samians had found it and had tied it down with willow-twigs to put an end to its wanderings; but as is commonly the case with such stories, this reveals nothing about the proper meaning of the rites.[188] Another legend claimed that Hera's sanctuary on Samos had been founded by the Argonauts, who had brought her ancient cultic image from Argos.[189]

Most of the local legends and rites that are recorded in connection with the divine union refer to the first prenuptial intercourse between Zeus and Hera rather than to their wedding. It was claimed, indeed, on Samos that the pair had first slept together on that island in utter secrecy for three hundred years.[190] The *Iliad* already mentions that they first went to bed together without their parents knowing, but says nothing about the circumstances or place of the encounter.[191] It seems that Naxos also claimed to be the place of this prenuptial union, since the behaviour of

Zeus and Hera was cited in explanation of a local marriage-custom in which the bride would share her bed with a young boy on the night before her wedding.[192] Since Euboea was sacred to Hera and local tradition asserted that she had been reared there by a nymph called Makris,[193] it is no surprise that similar claims should have been put forward on that island too. No less than three places were pointed out as the actual site where the union had been consummated, two caves on the island itself and one on an islet nearby.[194]

Another local tradition located the first union at the south-eastern tip of the Argolid near the coastal town of Hermione. On seeing Hera there on her own before the time of her marriage, Zeus set out to seduce her. He assumed the form of a cuckoo and settled on the mountain that was known thenceforth as Cuckoo Mountain (Kokkyx or Kokkygion); and after stirring up a violent thunderstorm, he flew over to Hera as she was sitting on the mountain of Pron (the Headland) opposite, and alighted on her lap. Feeling pity for the wet and bedraggled bird, she sheltered it under her robe, at which point Zeus returned to his original form and proceeded to make love to her. Although she resisted him at first because they were children of the same mother, she yielded to him as soon as he promised to make her his wife. A temple of Hera Teleia (the Fulfilled, i.e. as wife) could be seen at the supposed site of the incident, and there was a temple of Zeus on the summit of Cuckoo Mountain nearby.[195] The great effigy of Hera at the Argive Heraion showed her holding a sceptre surmounted by a cuckoo, evidently in reference to the preceding legend, as Pausanias remarks;[196] this huge gold and ivory statue by Polykleitos, a distinguished Argive sculptor of the fifth century BC, was thought to rival Pheidias' statue of Athena in the Parthenon at Athens.

A Boeotian legend placed the prenuptial union on Mt Kithairon on the southern borders of the province. After Hera had been brought up on the island of Euboea, Zeus abducted her to Boeotia on the mainland opposite, and they took refuge on Kithairon, which, in the words of Plutarch, 'provided them with a shady cave, forming a natural bridal-chamber'. When Makris, the Euboean nymph who had reared Hera, came to look for her missing ward, she was warned off by Kithairon (i.e. the tutelary deity of the mountain), who assured her that Zeus was taking his pleasure there with Leto.[197]

Kithairon was the site of a remarkable fire-festival, the Daidala, which was celebrated by the Plataians on the summit of the mountain. In the usual ceremony, as mounted by the Plataians in every seventh year, a wooden idol (*daidalon*) would be dressed in bridal robes and dragged on an ox-cart from Plataia to the top of the mountain, where it would be burned after appropriate rituals. Or in the Great Daidala, which were celebrated every fifty-nine years, fourteen *daidala* from different Boeotian towns would be burned on a large wooden pyre heaped with brushwood, together with a bull and cow that were sacrificed to Zeus and Hera. This huge pyre on the mountain-top must have provided a most impressive spectacle; Pausanias remarks that he knew of no other flame that rose as high or could be seen from so far.[198] The cultic legend that was offered to account for the festival ran as follows. When Hera had once quarrelled with Zeus, as she so often did, she had withdrawn to her childhood home of Euboea and had refused every attempt at reconciliation. So Zeus sought the advice of the wisest man on earth, Kithairon, the eponym of the mountain (rather than the god of it as in the story above), who ruled at Plataia below in the very earliest times. Kithairon advised him to make a wooden image of a woman, to veil it in the manner of a bride, and then to have it drawn along in an ox-cart after spreading the rumour that he was planning to marry Plataia, a daughter of the river-god Asopos. When Hera rushed to the scene and tore away the veils, she was so relieved to find a wooden effigy rather than the expected bride that she at last consented to be reconciled with Zeus.[199] Or in another version of the story, Zeus sought advice on his marital problem from Alalkomeneus, the earth-born first man of Alalkomenai in western Boeotia, who helped him to cut and adorn the wooden effigy, which was known as Daidale (the Cunningly Wrought); Hera hurried down from Kithairon, where she had hidden herself, with all the women of Plataia at her heels; but as soon as she discovered the trick, the whole affair ended in laughter and good humour. Alalkomeneus was introduced into the story in this account because the Plataians collected the wood for the *daidala* from a grove of oak-trees near Alalkomenai. To pick out the appropriate tree, they would use a process of divination that depended on the behaviour of the crows of the area; for they would lay out some meat for the birds, wait until one of them flew off with a portion, and then observe which tree was chosen by it as a landing-place.[200]

Hera's myths of revenge

Although Hera was highly revered as a cultic deity, it was perhaps inevitable in view of Zeus' countless infidelities that she should have been condemned to an undignified role in many of her myths, which frequently present her as a wronged and vindictive wife who is constantly wrangling with her husband and persecuting his mistresses and their children. The main features of this portrait are already laid down in the *Iliad*, in which she sometimes comes close to being a comic figure, but is nonetheless a goddess of strong character and will who is a worthy match for her husband (even if she is bound to fail in the long run when she tries to oppose him). She risks his anger by intervening on behalf of the Greeks in the Trojan War after he has warned the gods not to interfere, achieving her aim at one point by seducing him on Mt Ida so as to distract him while Poseidon is spurring the Greeks to success.[201] Although Homer has little occasion to mention tales in which she fell out with her husband over his love affairs, he refers more than once to the hatred that she bore against his son Herakles, reporting that she had once caused such anger to Zeus by sending storm winds against the hero (see p. 276) that he had strung her up with a heavy weight attached to her feet (a form of torture that was inflicted on slaves in classical times).[202] The various tales from later sources in which she is said to have harried Zeus' lovers and children (for she could hardly take action against Zeus himself) are considered elsewhere in connection with her victims. These are not actually as numerous as one might suppose; she is not reported to have taken any action at all with regard to most of Zeus' innumerable love affairs. There are in fact only four notable bodies of myth of early origin in which she was said to have taken action in such circumstances, namely those in which she persecuted Leto while she was pregnant with divine twins by Zeus (see p. 189), and Semele and her son Dionysos and his nurses (see p. 172 etc.), and Io, an Argive mistress of Zeus (see pp. 228ff), and Herakles during his earthly life. She also caused the death of Kallisto in some versions of that heroine's legend (see p. 541).

As the guardian of marriage and wife of the supreme god, Hera could not conceivably have had any lovers herself; nor would any god or man normally have dared to lay hands on her. There is only a single myth of any note that tells of an attempt on her virtue, the quite early tale in which Ixion, a mortal protégé of her husband's, was foolish enough to try to seduce her. She merely informed her husband, who laid a trap for Ixion by fashioning a cloud-image of her (see p. 554). Endymion was sometimes said to have been condemned to his eternal sleep (or hurled down to Hades) for a similar offence (see p. 411). As a ruse of war, Zeus himself inspired one of the Giants with lust for her during the conflict between the Giants and the gods (see p. 89).

Like all the great goddesses, Hera could be ruthless towards mortals who offended her. To avenge the impieties of Pelias, who committed a murder in her sanctuary and scorned her rites thereafter, she set in course the train of events that led to his death (see p. 380); after she was passed over in the judgement of Paris, she became an enemy of Paris (sending storms against him while he was sailing off with Helen, see p. 445) and an ardent supporter of the Greeks during the Trojan War; in what was probably the original version of the myth of the Proitides, she sent them mad for mocking the poverty of one of her sanctuaries (see p. 428). For her blinding of Teiresias, see pp. 329–30. In lesser stories, she sent Orion's wife to Hades for claiming to rival her in beauty (see p. 562), and turned Antigone, a daughter of Laomedon, king of Troy, into a stork for the same offence. Or in another version of the latter story, she turned Antigone's hair into snakes to punish her for boasting that it was more beautiful than her own, but the gods pitied her plight and turned her into a stork, a bird that preys on snakes.[203]

HESTIA, THE VIRGIN GODDESS OF THE HEARTH

HESTIA was the first-born child of Kronos and Rhea and also the last-born, since she was the first to be swallowed at birth by her father and the last to be disgorged.[204] As the goddess of the hearth (*hestia*) and hearth-fire, she presided at the centre of the household and also at the communal hearth of the city. In other words, she was the Holy Hearth, as worshipped by many peoples because it is a natural centre of family cult, because an intimate connection is commonly sensed between fire and life, and because the hearth of a king or chief is of great importance in a primitive community, and a perpetual fire is often kept burning there, both for practical reasons to provide a light where needed, and also for ritual and magico-religious purposes. Although Hestia was highly honoured in Greek cult, even enjoying a certain precedence, she was never really conceived as a fully anthropomorphic being, and she has very little in the way of myth. At sacrifices, she would normally receive the first offering or a preliminary libation; in prayers she would usually be invoked before any other god; and at feasts, the first and final libations would normally be dedicated to her.[205] These practices inspired the proverbial phrase 'beginning with Hestia' (*aph'Hestias archesthai*), meaning to make a proper start or sound beginning.[206] When the fire crackled, it could be said that 'Hestia's laughing'.[207] The Romans identified her with their own hearth-goddess Vesta, whose name was probably of the same derivation and whose functions were virtually identical. Vesta was far more important, however, than her Greek counterpart in her public cult as a guardian of the state.

As a goddess who was closely identified with the hearth-fire and could be imagined as being confined to her place at the centre of the home, Hestia had little opportunity to appear in mythical tales. Plato alludes to her predicament (which was also, in a sense, her privilege) in his great myth in the *Phaedrus*, by stating that when the other gods pass in procession through the sky under the leadership of Zeus, 'Hestia remains in the house of the gods, all alone'. She is excluded from the ordinary activities of the gods and yet remains forever at the centre.[208] Since fire is naturally felt to be a pure (and purifying) element, Hestia was considered to be a virgin goddess, and her hearth was tended by the unmarried girls of the household. Thoughts of this nature are reflected in ancient taboos connected with the hearth-fire; Hesiod warns people not to expose their naked genitals to it after making love.[209] Myths of a very elementary kind were devised to explain how Hestia's choice of virginity came to be irrevocably established. According to the *Homeric Hymn to Aphrodite*, both Apollo and Poseidon had sought to marry her at one time, but she had stubbornly refused and had vowed to remain a virgin instead, placing her hand on the head of Zeus to swear a solemn oath to that effect; and Zeus had then granted her high honours in place of marriage, declaring that she should reside at the centre of the house and receive the choicest portion at sacrifices.[210] Or after the defeat of the Titans, she had begged Zeus to grant her everlasting virginity and the first portion of all sacrifices.[211] Vase-paintings sometimes show her outside the confines of the home, accompanying the other gods on festal occasions, such as the marriage of Peleus and Thetis. Ovid recounts a tale with a purely Roman aetiology in which her counterpart Vesta is saved from rape by the timely braying of an ass (see p. 222).

CHAPTER FIVE

THE YOUNGER OLYMPIAN
GODS AND GODDESSES

—— •◆• ——

The great Olympian deities who remain to be considered were all of younger birth than Zeus and the other children of Kronos, with the possible exception of Aphrodite. Zeus fathered three divine sons soon after his rise to power, **Hephaistos** and **Ares** by his wife Hera (unless she brought Hephaistos to birth without his involvement, see p. 79), and **Apollo** by his cousin Leto as the twin brother of Artemis; and he completed the Olympian family during the heroic era by fathering **Hermes** and **Dionysos** through liaisons with mortal women. As a radiant god of prophecy, music and healing, Apollo was the most exalted of these younger Olympian gods, and we will start with him accordingly before passing on to the children of Zeus' marriage. The deities who came to be classed as children of Zeus and Hera were of diverse origin and not of the very highest status; their daughters Hebe and Eileithuia cannot even be included in the present company as Olympian deities of the first rank. Of their sons, Hephaistos was something of an outsider among the Olympians, not only because he laboured as a manual worker in his function as the divine blacksmith, but also because he was partially deformed; and even if war, which was the special concern of his brother Ares, was not regarded as being ignoble in itself, Ares was a vicious and bloodthirsty god who delighted in mayhem and slaughter for their own sake, and was consequently not viewed with much respect by either gods or mortals. The two late-born Olympians, Hermes and Dionysos, were gods of idiosyncratic character, Hermes a divine trickster and messenger who was much concerned with boundaries and their transgression, and Dionysos a god of wine and ecstasy.

Zeus brought his dearest child, **Athena**, to birth from his own head after swallowing her mother Metis; and he fathered **Artemis** by the goddess Leto as the twin brother of Apollo. Both were virgin goddesses who enjoyed active pursuits, Athena as a warrior-goddess and city-goddess who was a patroness of arts and manufactures, and Artemis as a divine huntress who had no love for armies and cities but preferred to roam through the untamed countryside with her attendant nymphs. If **Aphrodite** was born from the sea-foam that surrounded the severed genitals of Ouranos as in the standard account derived from Hesiod (see p. 194), she was the first-born of the Olympian gods; or if she was of more conventional birth as the daughter of Zeus and Dione, as is suggested by Homer, she belonged to the same generation as Athena and Artemis. It makes no practical difference, however, whether she was of more ancient or more recent origin, since she was imagined as young and supremely beautiful, as the goddess of love and sexual allure.

APOLLO

Whatever his origin, APOLLO (Apollon) is the most characteristically Greek of all the gods in his developed form; and on account of the picturesque beauty with which Hellenic art and literature surrounded him, he is still widely familiar today, perhaps more than any other Olympian deity, as an embodiment of the Hellenic spirit. He embodies the Hellenic values of reason, harmony, lucidity and moderation; he is the unerring prophet who knows the true and the right and the will of his father Zeus, revealing them to mortals, though often in enigmatic fashion, through his many oracles; he is a god of purification and healing, but also the archer-god 'who strikes from afar' and inflicts plague and death with his arrows; he is the leader of the Muses (Mousagetes) and a patron of poetry and music, particularly that of the lyre; and although agriculture is not one of his main concerns, he acts as a protector of flocks and herds, and preserves grain and crops from bad weather, blight and vermin. His developed type in art is well known; his is the ideal male figure which has reached its full growth, but still has all the suppleness and vigour of youth. While all Greece worshipped him, and references to him are almost as numerous as to Zeus himself, his most famous shrines in Greece proper were Delphi on the mainland and the holy island of Delos; and he had many shrines in Asia Minor too, the best known being Klaros, Branchidai and Patara. His cult was introduced to Rome at an early period by way of Etruria and the Greek colonies of Magna Graecia, the first temple being erected to him in 432 BC; he was honoured there under his Greek name, having no proper Italian equivalent or parallel.

There is no general agreement on the derivation of Apollo's name. The most interesting of the various etymologies that have been proposed is the one that links the name, in its early Dorian form Apellon, to the word *apella*, a Dorian expression for a sheepfold and thence for annual assemblies that were held by the Dorian peoples. It has been suggested that Apollo may have been worshipped by the Dorians from an early period as a god who watched over flocks and herds, and that he may have been the god who presided over the *apellai*, and perhaps especially over young men's initiations that would have taken place at them (for Apollo represents the ideal of the *ephebos*, the adolescent arriving at manhood). No other Greek etymology seems very convincing. The fitting suggestion, for instance, that Apollo could mean 'he who drives away' (i.e. plague, disease) rests on the doubtful assumption that there was a word in Greek corresponding to *pellere* in Latin. It is also possible that his name was of non-Greek origin.

From the time of Homer onwards, Apollo is often called Phoibos Apollo or Phoibos; this title is frequently interpreted as meaning 'Bright' or 'Radiant', but its etymology is by no means certain. As a god who was undoubtedly associated with the idea of luminosity and radiance, Apollo was quite often identified with the sun-god Helios from the fifth century BC onwards (see p. 43). Another notable title of

Apollo of very ancient origin is that of Lykios or Lykeios, which was interpreted in three different ways in antiquity, as meaning either 'Lycian' or else 'Wolf-god' (*lykos* being a wolf in Greek) or, less plausibly, as signifying that Apollo was a god of light (cf. *lux* in Latin). If the second interpretation is correct, it would refer to the god's activities in warding away wolves from flocks and herds; it has had its proponents, especially among those who set great store on Apollo's Dorian connections. But the first interpretation seems most attractive in view of Apollo's early connections with Asia Minor, and with Lycia in the south-west specifically. The Homeric evidence is of particular importance here. In the *Iliad*, which presents Apollo as supporting the Trojans of Asia Minor against the Greeks, Athena urges Pandaros, a Lycian ally of the Trojans, to vow a sacrifice to Apollo Lykegenes (surely meaning 'the Lycian-born') for his safe return home.[1] All the shrines of Apollo mentioned by Homer are set in Asia Minor, and many of his most notable oracles were located at various points on its coast (including Patara in Lycia). Lycia was also linked in various ways to Apollo's cultic centre of Delos; the mysterious poet Olen, for instance, who was supposed to have written certain ancient hymns that were sung on Delos, was described as a Lycian.

Because of Apollo's many connections with Asia Minor, it was once widely argued that he and his cult were imported into Greece from that area. In further support of this view, it was suggested (for instance) that his mother Leto could be identified with the Lycian goddess Lada, and that it is significant that the Greeks should often have referred to him as Letoides, 'son of Leto', since this accorded with the Lycian custom, as attested by Herodotus,[2] of using matronymics (rather than patronymics as was normal in Greece). The main rival theory, which was of long standing but was rather eclipsed by the Asian theory, proposed instead that Apollo had been imported into Greece from the north. His Dorian connections might be interpreted as favouring such a view, and its advocates also pointed to certain features of his cult, notably the offerings that used to be sent to his shrine on Delos each year by a circuitous route from the north, supposedly from the Hyperboreans (see p. 148), and the great procession of the Stepteria that proceeded north from Delphi (see p. 145), perhaps following in reverse direction the route by which the god had first come to his Delphian shrine. If such theories about the god's origin have rather fallen into discredit in recent times, it is only partly because specific arguments advanced in favour of one view or another have been felt to be unsatisfactory, even if that has often been the case. It is doubtful, for instance, whether the cultic features that were cited in favour of the northern theory can bear the weight that was placed on them, or, on the other side, that Apollo's epithet of Letoides is really of any significance, since other sons of Zeus are regularly referred to as sons of their mother (e.g. Hermes as son of Maia). Even if it can be accepted, however, that Apollo had ancient and definite connections with Asia Minor, as was certainly the case, or with the Dorians and the north, it has come increasingly to be felt that it is pointless to seek for a single 'origin' for a god who was as complex as the classical Apollo, as if he had simply been imported from abroad with his name and cult and major aspects of his mythology. It would seem, rather, that he was a many-faceted figure who absorbed features from a variety of deities and from the cults and myths of different areas. If some features associate him with the west coast of Asia Minor or with the Dorians and the north, there are also features that associate him with other areas; in so far as he was a plague-god, for instance, who inflicts pestilence and death with his arrows, he was apparently modelled on the Semitic plague-god Reshep, who caused disease by shooting firebrands. Reshep was worshipped by the Phoenicians in Cyprus, where he was equated with Apollo. Notable features of Apollonian religion such as ecstatic prophecy and purification also associate him with the Near East, while his cultic hymn, the paean, seems to have originated in Crete.

How Apollo established his oracle at Delphi; the omphalos and tripod

Apollo was the son of Zeus and Leto, and the twin brother of Artemis.[3] After being turned away from many places owing to the jealousy of Hera, Leto brought her children to birth on the holy island of Delos, as will be described below in connection with Artemis (see p. 188). Like the wonder-child that he was, Apollo began his adventures immediately, and his first act, or nearly so, was to establish his oracular shrine at Delphi. According to the *Homeric Hymn to Apollo*, which provides the earliest account of his precocious adventures, he was never suckled at all by his mother, but received some nectar and ambrosia from Themis and burst free of his swaddling-clothes as soon as he tasted it. Declaring that the lyre would always be dear to him, and that he would announce the unfailing will of Zeus to mortals, he set off at once to seek a place for his oracle.[4] After travelling through much of northern and central Greece, he stopped at an attractive site by the spring of Telphousa (or Tilphousa) near Haliartos in western Boeotia; but Telphousa, the nymph of the spring, was reluctant to share the site with a deity who would far outshine her, and urged him to pass on to Mt Parnassos instead, saying that he would otherwise be constantly irritated by the noise of horses and mules as they watered at the springs.[5] Although he discovered an ideal spot for his shrine at the site of Delphi under Parnassos, he came to realize that Telphousa must have had ulterior motives in recommending it when he found that it was guarded by a fearsome dragon. Although this monster had previously killed all who had approached it, Apollo shot it dead with one of his arrows, and then returned to settle his score with Telphousa. He punished her by hiding her streams under a cliff (for they had previously risen in open ground); and he subordinated her cult to his own by erecting an altar to himself in a neighbouring grove, where he was honoured thenceforth as Telphousian Apollo.[6] The spring of Telphousa was otherwise noted in myth for its association with the Theban seer Teiresias, who was supposed to have died while drinking from its waters (see p. 331) and to have been buried nearby.

Apollo had now to consider how he could find suitable priests for his oracular shrine. As he was pondering the matter, he noticed that a fine ship was sailing from Crete to trade at Pylos on the west coast of the Peloponnese. So he intercepted it on the open sea, leaping on to its deck in the form of a huge and awesome dolphin. As the crew quivered with fear, he caused it to be blown swiftly along the west coast of the Peloponnese and into the Corinthian Gulf. After bringing it to shore at Crisa, on the southern shore of the Greek mainland near Delphi, he manifested himself in his true divine form and revealed his name. He ordered the Cretans to establish a cult to him as Apollo Delphinios and then accompany him to Delphi, where they and their descendants would serve as the keepers of his temple, receiving a share from the sacrifices; and with their arrival in Delphi, the Homeric Hymn draws to an end.[7]

It is stated in the Hymn that the region of Delphi acquired its old name of Pytho, and Apollo his corresponding title of Pythian Apollo, because the corpse of the dragon 'rotted' there (as though the name Pytho were derived from *pythein*, to rot).[8] The dragon is female in this account; see p. 84 for the story of its origin. In Hellenistic and later accounts, however, the Delphian dragon is usually a male creature called PYTHON, and is itself the eponym of the region (although there are also accounts in which the beast is named Delphyne or Delphynes or the like after Delphi[9]). Some said that the young Apollo was carried to Delphi by his mother and shot the dragon from her arms, either on his own or with the help of his sister.[10] As will be considered in further detail below (see p. 189), a tale from Hyginus claims that Python had tried to kill Leto during her pregnancy to prevent her from giving birth to her divine twins; in that case, Apollo travelled to the site of Delphi four days after his birth to kill the dragon by way of revenge.[11] The earth-goddess Gaia was often regarded as the original owner of the oracle. Aeschylus points to a peaceful transfer of power in which Gaia passed it on to her daughter Themis, and Themis to Apollo's grandmother Phoibe (a Titan, see p. 37), and Phoibe to Apollo.[12]

Since the oracle was presented in Delphian tradition as having formerly been the property of Earth, and since snakes are chthonian creatures, we may connect the dragon-slaying, whatever the precise details of the story, with the taking over of the shrine. Certain it is that Python was closely interwoven with the traditions and ritual of the place in historical times. At the great festival of the Stepteria (Festival of Wreathes), for example, the central figure, a well-born Delphian youth, would be led to a lightly constructed house known as 'Python's palace', which would be set on fire. The youth, apparently impersonating Apollo, would then make a show of going into exile, and actually set off on a long journey with attendants and much ceremony, passing by the sacred Pythian way northward through Thessaly to the Vale of Tempe, where he would be purified; and he would come back afterwards crowned with laurel, Apollo's special plant. Whatever the true meaning of all this curious ritual, there is no doubt that the ancients connected it with the slaying of Python, claiming in the usual account that Apollo had travelled to Tempe to be purified from the killing before he could take over the oracle. Or else the dragon had fled northwards in a badly wounded state, with the young god in close pursuit, until it finally expired.[13] At the Pythian Games, which were second only to those at Olympia, one of the leading events was a contest in flute-playing in which the subject was a descriptive piece representing the combat between the god and the monster.[14]

The other great features of Delphi, setting aside many of lesser note, were the omphalos and the tripod. The omphalos or navel-stone was supposed to mark the middle point of the earth's surface. It was conical in form, shaped like an old-fashioned beehive, and was covered with fillets of wool. On a striking ancient copy that can be seen by visitors at Delphi, the woollen meshes are sculpted on to the surface of the stone. Zeus was said to have discovered the central position of Delphi by sending out two eagles from opposite ends of the earth at the same moment, and then looking out to see where they met.[15] Golden images of the birds were set up by the omphalos, where they remained until they were carried off by Philomelos, a Phocian general who plundered Delphi in 356 BC. Some claimed, however, that

Figure 5.1   Apollo and Herakles struggle for the tripod at Delphi.
Red-figure vase, c. 525 BC. Antikensammlungen, Berlin.

the birds of the legend were not eagles at all (which were birds of Zeus) but swans or ravens (which were birds of Apollo).[16] Numerous representations of the omphalos are preserved in the visual arts, often showing the eagles too, and it is frequently referred to as the seat of Apollo. Occasionally we find Python coiled around it.

In practice, the tripod was the seat of prophecy; it was set up in a sunken area at the end of the temple of Apollo. His priestess, the Pythia, would sit on it as she delivered the oracles in a trance-like state. The idea seems to have been that the holy influence of the god could come beneath and enter her when she was thus lifted clear of the ground; Hellenistic authors suggest that her ecstasy was induced by vapours that rose up from a cleft in the ground, but this semi-rationalizing notion finds no support in the archaeological or geological evidence.[17] The Pythia was a virgin of Delphian birth who entered the service of the god for life, and always dressed like a girl. Her responses were rendered into verse-form (hexameters) by the priests before they were passed on to the enquirer.

The SIBYL (Sibylla), who was the supposed source of many oracles that circulated in writing, was said to deliver her prophecies in a state of inspired frenzy just as in the case of the Pythia,[18] and was sometimes linked to Delphi. In the oldest form of her legend, there was apparently a single prophetic woman called Sibylla who uttered her prophecies somewhere in Asia Minor. The village of Marpessos on Mt Ida in the Troad, an obscure place that is remembered for nothing else, claimed the Sibyl as its own, as did the more important town of Erythrai on the Lydian coast, and there was much controversy on the subject in antiquity. This Asian Sibyl won the favour of Apollo, to whose service she was much devoted, and he inspired her to give marvellous and infallible, if rather riddling, prophecies; some said that she wandered off to Delphi (among other places) at some stage and delivered prophecies there.[19] The meaning of her name, which may be of eastern origin, is wholly obscure. These oracles, of which an ever-increasing number entered circulation, were very popular. They were extant in many places, and consequently many towns claimed to be the birthplace of their author. In the end, as Sibylla came to be regarded as a generic term, a whole series of Sibyls sprang up, some with personal names of their own such as Herophile or Phyto, and the tradition became bewilderingly complex. Although estimates of their number vary, and there is much confusion because the same figures often reappear under different names, we may refer to a convenient list compiled by the Roman antiquary Varro, who distinguishes ten Sibyls:[20] the Persian, the Libyan, the Delphian (who is sometimes described as a sister or daughter of Apollo, or even as his wife), the Kimmerian (who, being located in Italy, seems to be the same as the Cumaean), the Erythraian (Herophile), the Samian (Phemonoe), the Cumaean (Amalthaia, the author of the celebrated Sibylline oracles of Rome), the Hellespontine (i.e. the Erythraian or Marpessian over again), the Phrygian (again the Marpessian), and finally the Tiburtine (the result of an attempt to find a Greek equivalent of the local goddess Albunea; hence the name 'Sibyl's Temple' quite unjustifiably given to one of the most famous ruins in Tivoli). On the Cumaean Sibyl, see also pp. 123 and 154. Mention should also be made of the Jewish and Babylonian Sibyl, usually identified with the Marpessian-Erythraian one, who is in some ways the most famous of all since the Sibylline oracles in the surviving collection – obviously late forgeries for the most part, containing Jewish and Christian propaganda disguised as ancient revelations – are in her name. Behind these shadowy figures there lurk, in all probability, a certain number of real women. The centuries intervening between the Dorian invasion and the time of full classical civilization were a time of great religious upheavals. From those times a variety of names survive not only of prophetesses like Sibylla but also of prophets such as Bakis, whose oracles were very popular during the Peloponnesian War, and Epimenides of Crete.

There is no reason why we should suppose either the Sibyl or the Delphic prophetess to have been frauds. The modern practice of spiritualism has made everyone familiar with the fact that certain persons can, voluntarily or otherwise, pass into an abnormal condition in which they speak, or even write, more or less intelligibly, without being conscious of it at the time or remembering it afterwards. Apollo, like many African deities who speak through prophets or 'mediums', no doubt found many of these abnormal persons to serve him in all sincerity, even if the priests at Delphi may often have altered or developed the Pythia's responses to a greater or lesser extent when preparing the edited official record, which was generally rendered in indifferent hexameters, couched for the most part in very riddling and obscure language, so that if the apparent sense of the prophecy proved false, the god could always take refuge behind another interpretation.

The killing of Tityos; Apollo's association with the Hyperboreans

Another early adventure of Apollo was his confrontation with TITYOS, a giant who tried to rape Leto soon after the birth of her children. Tityos is described as a son of Gaia (Earth) in the *Odyssey*, or as a son of Elara (a Boeotian heroine who was a daughter of Minyas or Orchomenos) in a Hesiodic fragment;[21] or in Pherecydes' account, which was devised to reconcile the preceding traditions, Tityos was fathered by Zeus on Elara, but was also earthborn, in a manner of speaking at least, because his mother brought him to birth from beneath the earth after Zeus had thrust her there for fear of Hera's jealousy.[22] Homer makes a brief reference to the crime of Tityos to explain why he was subjected to everlasting torment in Hades (see p. 117), saying that he had assaulted Leto as she was passing through Panopeus on her way to Pytho (Delphi). Panopeus lay to the east of Delphi in the same province of Phocis; a large mound in the neighbourhood was identified as the burial-place of Tityos.[23] Subsequent authors add that the two children of Leto (or one or the other alone) rushed to the scene to save their mother from him and shot him dead.[24] In less orthodox accounts, Tityos was punished in Hades because he had tried to lay hands on Artemis, or was struck dead by a thunderbolt from Zeus when he tried to attack Leto at the order of Hera.[25]

Apollo was closely associated in both myth and cult with the HYPERBOREANS, a mythical people who lived at the edges of the earth in the remote north. Their name was interpreted, rightly or wrongly, as indicating that they dwelt 'beyond the North Wind' (for Boreas was the name of that wind in Greek, see p. 48). As we will see later in the chapter (p. 190), their connection with Apollo was established even before his birth, for they sent envoys to Delos with offerings that they had vowed to ensure an easy childbirth for Leto. As often with the inhabitants of mythical realms at the edges of the earth, they were pictured as a just and pious people who lived a life free from all toil and conflict, diverting themselves with songs, dances and feasts; and their company was therefore much loved by Apollo, who was said to leave Delphi during the winter each year to spend some time in their land. According to the early lyric poet Alcaeus, he first visited their land soon after his birth, travelling there in a swan-drawn chariot which had been given to him by Zeus for his journey to Delphi; after directing the swans to fly north instead, he remained with the Hyperboreans for a full year, laying down laws for them, until he finally set off for Delphi in the middle of the following summer.[26] According to a further story, he later took refuge with the Hyperboreans for a while to escape the anger of Zeus after killing the Kyklopes (see below), and amber, a precious substance which came from the north, was formed from the tears that were shed by him during his exile.[27] For a conflicting account of the origin of amber, see p. 45. Although the land of the Hyperboreans was hardly accessible to ordinary human travellers, Pindar reports that Perseus found his way there in days of old and saw the Hyperboreans sacrificing hecatombs of asses to Apollo, who takes a special delight in their feasts and praises.[28]

In historical times, sacred offerings that were supposed to have come from the Hyperboreans used to arrive at Apollo's shrine at Delos. Wrapped in wheat-straw and of unspecified nature, they were sent by relay from some unknown location in the north. Herodotus provides a summary of their route, so far as it was known, saying that they were sent to Scythia initially and then passed on by a circuitous route until they first entered Greek hands at Dodona (in Epirus in the north-west); from there they were relayed in a south-easterly direction to the Malian Gulf and across to Euboea, and then down to the southern tip of the island and thence by sea to Tenos and Delos. They cannot be traced beyond Scythia, however, and their true origin remains a mystery. According to legend, the Hyperboreans had adopted a more conventional procedure on the first occasion, sending two envoys to

Delos with the offerings; but when the envoys (Hyperoche and Laodike, see further on p. 190) failed to return, they had decided that it would be safer to transmit the offerings by relay in the future.[29]

Apollo and Koronis, and their son the great healer Asklepios

A healer himself, Apollo was the father of the main god of healing and medicine, ASKLEPIOS (whose name was corrupted into Aesculapius in Latin). Although Asklepios was honoured both as a god and as a hero in cult, it seems likely that he originated as a hero and was raised to full divine status at a secondary stage. According to the standard tradition, Apollo fathered him by KORONIS, daughter of Phlegyas, a Thessalian heroine of Lapith descent (see p. 560). He was said to have fallen in love with her after catching sight of her as she was washing her feet in Lake Boibias in north-eastern Thessaly.[30] She became his mistress and conceived a child to him, but agreed to marry a mortal, Ischys, son of Elatos, during the time of her pregnancy. Or else she engaged in a secret love affair with Ischys, who was a Lapith like herself. It is explained in one account that she consented to the marriage because she was afraid that Apollo might not want to remain with her as a mere mortal[31] (much as in the legend of Marpessa). Although the *Homeric Hymn to Apollo* already refers to the antagonism between Apollo and Ischys, Pindar provides the first surviving account of the events that followed from it. When Koronis slept with Ischys in secret from her father, Apollo came to know of it through his own prophetic powers, and sent Artemis to Koronis' home-town to exact vengeance on his behalf. Artemis duly killed her along with many of her unfortunate neighbours; but as the flame was playing around her corpse on the funeral-pyre, Apollo could not bear to see his child destroyed together with its mother, and stepped forward to snatch it from her womb. Or in some accounts, he asked Hermes to recover the child, or shot Koronis himself.[32] Apollo was often said to have been informed of her infidelity by his faithful messenger the crow.[33] It could then be explained that crows have black plumage because Apollo turned his messenger black (from its original white) in anger at the unwelcome news. Although this familiar detail does not surface in the surviving literature until the Hellenistic period, it has a popular ring and may have been quite old since it can be traced back to the mid-fifth century BC in the visual arts.[34]

It is reported in late sources that Koronis' mortal lover was shot by Apollo or struck with a thunderbolt by Zeus.[35] An alternative tradition from the Peloponnese suggested that the mother of Asklepios was a Messenian princess, Arsinoe, daughter of Leukippos (see further on p. 424).[36] Or according to the local tradition at Epidauros on the east coast of the Argolid, the greatest centre of Asklepios' cult, Koronis brought him to birth in that region of the Peloponnese in the following circumstances. When her father Phlegyas, who was a notorious brigand (see p. 560), once visited the Peloponnese to spy out the land, he brought her with him without realizing that she was pregnant, and she exposed the new-born Asklepios on a mountain near Epidauros after giving birth to him during the journey.[37]

Apollo entrusted his new-born son to the wise Centaur Cheiron, who reared him in his cave on Mt Pelion in Thessaly. Under Cheiron's able tuition, Asklepios learned

Figure 5.2 Apollo and the Crow. White ground kylix, fifth century BC. Delphi museum.

much that was valuable including the art of medicine, which he developed to the highest state of perfection.[38] He makes no appearance in heroic saga (except in one or two late reports that suggest that he sailed with the Argonauts or joined the hunt for the Calydonian boar[39]). By a wife who is variously named though always called Epione in connection with his cult, he fathered a family of dual nature in accordance with his own mixed nature as an ancient hero and a healing-god. As Homer already records, he was the father of two sturdy epic heroes, Podaleirios and Machaon, who sailed to Troy as joint leaders of a contingent from north-western Thessaly. Since they had inherited their father's medical skills, they were able to help their comrades as healers and surgeons as well as taking part in the fighting;[40] the healing of Philoktetes in particular (see p. 471) was ascribed to one or other of them.[41] In the second place, Asklepios came to be credited with some children of another kind in connection with his healing-cult, a series of pale and shadowy figures without any myths who personify various concepts associated with the art of healing. Among them we find Hygeia (Health personified), who may often be seen in works of art either on her own or standing by her seated father, and Iaso (Healing), Panakeia (Cure-all, cf. panacea in Latin and English) and the little hooded child-god Telesphoros (Accomplisher).[42]

Asklepios' zeal as a healer carried him too far when he set out to revive the dead. According to varying accounts, he revived Hippolytos at the request of Artemis (see p. 359), or Lykourgos, son of Pronax, and Kapaneus, two Argives who died during the first Theban War, or Tyndareos, or Glaukos, son of Minos; or in some late accounts, he even revived so many mortals that Hades was impelled to complain. In any case, this interference with the established order of nature was too much for Zeus, who promptly dispatched Asklepios to the Underworld with a thunderbolt.[43]

Apollo's servitude to Admetos, and the story of Alkestis

Apollo was enraged by the death of his son, but he could hardly exact vengeance on his mighty father even if he had dared to attempt it, and therefore consoled himself by killing the Kyklopes who had made the thunderbolt. Since he had thus become guilty of bloodshed within his own divine clan, Zeus ordered that he should atone for his crime by serving a mortal master as a serf for a year.[44] It is claimed in one account that Zeus would even have hurled him down to Tartaros if his mother Leto had not intervened to save him.[45] In an alternative version which was presumably developed because the Kyklopes might be expected to be immortal as brothers of the Titans, Apollo is said to have killed the sons of the Kyklopes rather than the Kyklopes themselves.[46]

Since he was placed under an eminently just and considerate master, ADMETOS, son of Pheres, the king of Pherai in Thessaly (see p. 425), his sentence proved to be less humiliating than it might have been; and he repaid Admetos for his kindness by performing various services for him. While tending his cattle, he greatly increased their number by causing them to produce twins at every birth;[47] and he helped him to win his chosen bride, Alkestis, daughter of Pelias. Since her father had announced that he would give her to the suitor who could yoke a lion and a boar to a chariot, Apollo brought the chariot ready-yoked to Admetos, who then drove it off to Iolkos to display it to Pelias.[48] Although the king handed his daughter over in accordance with his promise, Admetos soon had occasion to call on the help of Apollo once again, for he forgot to honour Artemis while offering the wedding-sacrifices, so angering the goddess that she filled his wedding-chamber with coils of snakes as a portent of early death. Not only did Apollo explain the cause of the trouble and advise Admetos on how to propitiate the goddess, but he also visited the Moirai (Fates) and persuaded them to agree that Admetos should be granted a reprieve from death if another person would consent to die in his place. According to Aeschylus, he won this concession from these inexorable deities by softening their hearts with wine.[49]

When some years had passed and the time came for Admetos to die, he sought for someone to take his place, but no one, not even his aged father or mother, would agree to do so until his wife volunteered. So when the fatal day arrived, it was Alkestis who was summoned to the shades. Although Admetos' acceptance of his wife's self-sacrifice might strike us as ignoble and cowardly, few would have felt any discomfort over the matter when the legend was developed, for a woman's life was not regarded as being of proportionate value to that of a man. Alkestis was acclaimed accordingly as an exemplar of wifely devotion. All the same, it hardly seemed fair that she should actually have to fulfil her offer, and the tradition ensured that she was rescued in one way or another. In the earliest surviving account by Euripides, she found a saviour in Herakles as we will see; but there was also another version, first mentioned by Plato but quite possibly of ancient origin, in which the infernal gods (or Persephone specifically) sent her home again because they so admired her self-sacrifice.[50]

In Euripides' *Alkestis*, Herakles calls in on Admetos while travelling north to fetch the mares of Diomedes of Thrace (see p. 262), arriving at his home by sheer mischance just as he and his household are beginning their period of mourning. Even in this extremity, however, the claims of hospitality cannot be ignored; so Admetos tactfully pretends that no member of his family is dead, but merely an outsider who had been staying under his roof, and welcomes the hero as a guest, ordering his servants to see to his comfort.[51] But Herakles soon discovers the true state of affairs from a servant, and takes measures to put things right. According to popular belief, Thanatos, Death personified (see pp. 29–30), could be imagined as literally carrying off the dead, much as Charos is represented as doing in modern Greek folklore; so Herakles goes to the tomb of Alkestis to await the coming of this envoy from the lower world, and wrestles with him on his arrival to compel him to give up his prey.[52] Alkestis recovers her life as a consequence and is brought safely home. This play is very interesting for the way in which Admetos is presented as reacting when he comes to appreciate the full implications of his behaviour after his wife's departure. He comes to feel that his life is hardly worth living now that he has bought his survival at her expense; but it is never quite suggested that it was actually wrong for him to have accepted her self-sacrifice. Euripides was not the first author to introduce Thanatos into the story, for it is known that Thanatos came to fetch Alkestis in a play by an earlier tragedian, Phrynichos.[53] This story, with its somewhat primitive morality, its Moirai who can be made drunk, and its Death who is so solid and material that a valiant man can overcome him by sheer force of muscle, is full of folkloric elements.

Apollo and Kyrene, and their son the rustic god Aristaios

Apollo fathered the rustic god ARISTAIOS by KYRENE, a daughter of the Lapith king Hypseus, who was a son of the Thessalian river-god Peneios. Kyrene had no taste for handiwork or the company of maidens of her own age, but preferred to roam the uplands of Thessaly hunting wild beasts, as a sort of local Artemis. Pindar tells how Apollo caught sight of her as she was wrestling with a powerful lion, all on her own, without any weapons. His admiration for her courage turned to passionate love, and he consulted with the ever-wise Cheiron, who advised him to carry her across the sea to Libya, and to establish her as the queen of a flourishing city (for she was the eponym of Cyrene, the most important Greek colony in North Africa). So he abducted her from the windswept vales of Mt Pelion in his golden chariot and seduced her in her new homeland, causing her to conceive a splendid son, Aristaios. Hermes took the new-born infant to Greece and entrusted him to the care of the Horai (Seasons) and Earth, who reared him on nectar and ambrosia, the food of the gods.[54] Or else Apollo entrusted him to Cheiron to be reared in his cave on Mt Pelion; and when he grew up, the Muses taught him the arts of healing and prophecy, and appointed him to watch over their Thessalian flocks.[55] Or he was reared by nymphs who taught him rural arts which he later passed on to mortals.[56]

Aristaios was an unpretentious rustic god who was said to have invented many of the crafts, labours and pastimes of the countryside, such as bee-keeping, olive-growing, the preparation of wool, and hunting in general or some of its varieties.[57] He married Autonoe, a daughter of Kadmos, king of Thebes, and fathered a single son by her, the great hunter Aktaion, who met a premature death in tragic circumstances (see further on p. 298). According to Diodorus' neat little biography of him, he left mainland Greece forever after this calamity, first travelling to the island of Keos at his father's order, where he established rituals to relieve Greece from excessive heat in summer (see p. 177), and later wandering further abroad to Sardinia and Sicily, introducing his agricultural arts to these new areas.[58]

Vergil and other authors in the later tradition blame Aristaios for the death of Eurydike, the wife of Orpheus (see p. 552), saying that he conceived a passion for her and chased after her, and that she stepped on a poisonous snake and suffered a fatal bite as she was running away from him. Since Eurydike was a dryad nymph, her fellow nymphs took revenge on Aristaios by causing all his bees to die. As Vergil narrates in his fourth *Georgic*, he then sought the advice of his mother Kyrene, who referred him in turn to Proteus, the old man of the sea. By seizing Proteus as he lay asleep and maintaining his grip on him as he repeatedly changed shape, Aristaios forced him to reveal who was responsible for the trouble, and then reported back to his mother. Kyrene advised him to sacrifice four bulls and four heifers to appease the nymphs, and to leave their carcasses in a grove and return to the site nine days afterwards to offer poppies and a black ewe to Orpheus and a female calf to Eurydike. When he returned to the grove after that delay, bees poured out of the decaying carcasses of the cattle and gathered in a tree nearby, providing him with a new swarm for his hives.[59] The belief that bees arise from rotting meat was apparently widespread, and not confined to the Greeks; the fact lying behind it is the existence of a fly, *Eristalis tenax*, which closely resembles a bee and lays its eggs in carrion.

How Apollo met with frustration in his love for Marpessa, Kassandra and Daphne, and accidentally killed Hyakinthos

Apollo was generally more or less unhappy in his loves. We have already seen one example of this in the story of Koronis; and in another early tale in which a mortal rival got the better of him, MARPESSA, daughter of Euenos, a beautiful Aetolian princess (see p. 413), preferred to marry Idas, son of Lynkeus, an Aetolian prince (see p. 422), instead of him. Homer alludes briefly to the conflict between her two suitors, saying that Idas dared to raise his bow against Apollo for her sake; although no further details are offered, Idas evidently won his way because we are told that Marpessa lived with him and bore him a daughter Kleopatra (who became the wife of Meleagros).[60] According to the standard later version, which can be traced back to Simonides, Idas abducted Marpessa from her home in Aetolia, making use of some swift chariot-horses that he had acquired from Poseidon. Although her father

Euenos set off in pursuit, his mortal horses soon grew exhausted, and he gave up the chase at the river Lykormas in eastern Aetolia; he then slaughtered his horses in despair and drowned himself in the river, which was known as the Euenos ever afterwards. Idas continued on his way to Arene in his native Messenia, where he was confronted by Apollo, who had also taken a fancy to Marpessa. When the god tried to seize her, Idas raised his bow and threatened to attack him (or even began to fight with him); but Zeus intervened to separate the rivals, and allowed Marpessa to make her own choice. Fearing that Apollo would abandon her when she grew old, she chose in favour of her mortal suitor.[61] Or in another version, which was probably based on the famous myth of Oinomaos and Hippodameia (see p. 503), Euenos forced Marpessa's suitors to set off ahead of him in a chariot-race, on the agreement that he would hand over his daughter if the suitor escaped, but would kill him if he caught up with him. After he had killed many suitors as a consequence, and had fixed their heads to the walls of his house, Idas escaped with Marpessa by use of his special chariot-horses, and the story then proceeds as above.[62]

Another of Apollo's ill-fated passions was directed towards KASSANDRA (or Alexandra), one of the daughters of Priam, king of Troy. According to a story which first appears in Aeschylus' *Agamemnon*, the love-stricken god promised to grant her the gift of prophecy in return for her favours; but after acquiring the gift, she broke her promise and refused to yield to him. Now no god can recall his gifts; but Apollo could take measures nonetheless to render her powers a curse rather than a blessing, by ensuring that she would always be disbelieved even though her prophecies would always be true.[63] So when she tried to warn Paris of all the evils that would follow from his abduction of Helen, or to warn the Trojans against bringing the Wooden Horse into their city, her words fell on deaf ears. She remained a virgin until she was captured at the fall of Troy; for her sufferings on that occasion and her subsequent fate, see pp. 477–8.

Although Pindar is the first author in the surviving literature to mention explicitly that Kassandra was a seer (and an ecstatic seer moreover whose 'divinely inspired heart' moved her to predict the consequences of Paris' behaviour), it is likely that this was an old feature of her legend since she is reported to have delivered prophecies to Paris in the *Cypria*, an early epic in the Trojan cycle.[64] This need not imply, of course, that she was said to have acquired her powers by deceiving Apollo in earliest tradition.

According to an alternative account, she gained her powers when she and her brother Helenos were left overnight in the shrine of Thymbraian Apollo during their infancy, and snakes crept up to them and licked their ears.[65] Snakes were said to have conferred divinatory powers on the Peloponnesian seer Melampous by the same means (see p. 426). Unlike Kassandra, who delivered her prophecies in a state of inspired abandon, Helenos was a 'technical' seer who worked by interpreting bird-flights and other signs.

The relatively late story of Apollo and the Cumaean Sibyl, as recounted in Ovid's *Metamorphoses*, seems to have been modelled partly on the legend of Kassandra and partly on that of Tithonos (see p. 47). On meeting the Sibyl when she was a beautiful young girl, Apollo fell in love with her and offered her the choice of whatever she desired in the hope of winning her favours. So she pointed to a pile of dust-sweepings on the floor and asked to be granted as many birthdays as there were grains of dust in the pile. Only when it was too late did she realize that she had forgotten to ask for perpetual youth; and since she refused to allow Apollo the liberties that he had been hoping for, he withheld this additional favour from her, and she grew ever older and ever more shrivelled. She was destined to shrink into a tiny creature until she died at last after a thousand years (in accordance with the number of the grains of dust).[66] According to Petronius, she was finally hung up in a bottle at Cumae; and when children asked her, 'Sibyl, what do you want?', she would answer, 'I want to die'.[67]

According to a famous if not very early tale, Apollo's sacred plant, the *daphnē* or laurel, was brought into existence through the transformation of a girl of that name who had aroused the passion of Apollo. In the earliest surviving account of the transformation, DAPHNE was a daughter of Amyklas (an early king of Sparta, see p. 500) who used to roam through the Peloponnese as a huntress with a group of female companions. As a true follower of Artemis, she wanted to have nothing to do with love, but Leukippos, a son of Oinomaos, king of Pisa, conceived a passion for her and managed to win her friendship by disguising himself as a girl and joining her hunting-party. As misfortune would have it, Apollo was also in love with her, and he exposed Leukippos' ruse by inspiring Artemis and her companions with a desire to bathe in the river Ladon. They duly discovered the deception when Leukippos was obliged to undress, and they tore the unfortunate youth to pieces; but when Apollo tried to seize Daphne for himself, she took to flight and prayed to Zeus to be removed from human company, and was transformed accordingly into the plant that bore her name.[68] In all subsequent accounts, Apollo has no mortal rival. According to Ovid, who describes Daphne as a daughter of the river Peneios in Thessaly, she prayed to her father to transform her as she was fleeing the unwelcome advances of Apollo.[69] She was presumably brought into connection with the Peneios because Apollo was said to have brought the laurel from the Vale of Tempe, which was the outlet of the river. Or else she was a daughter of the river Ladon in Arcadia, and prayed to Mother Earth to save her in the corresponding circumstances; so Earth swallowed her up in a chasm, and sent up a laurel in place of her as a consolation to Apollo.[70]

Apollo proved to be no more fortunate when he turned his affections towards boys; the most celebrated of these was HYAKINTHOS of Amyklai near Sparta. He makes his first literary appearance in a poorly preserved fragment from the Hesiodic *Catalogue*, as a son of Amyklas, an early king of Sparta who was the eponym of the town of Amyklai (see p. 524); since a discus is mentioned at the end of the fragment, it can be inferred that Apollo killed him accidentally with a discus as in the standard later tradition. Euripides alludes to such a story in his *Helen*, saying that the Spartans performed nocturnal rites in honour of Hyakinthos who was killed by Apollo as they were competing in the discus. According to Ovid, Hyakinthos was struck on the rebound as he reached out to take the discus for his own throw.[71] Or in a more elaborate version, Zephyros (the West Wind; or else Boreas, the North Wind) competed with Apollo for the love of Hyakinthos, and was so jealous when the boy chose in favour of Apollo that he caused the god's discus to swerve aside as he was exercising with his favourite; but this is obviously a secondary version, suggested by an account in which Apollo's discus was blown off course by a gust of wind (as Perseus' discus was sometimes said to have been when he killed his grandfather with it, see p. 243).[72] To explain the origin of the hyacinth,

Figure 5.3 Dying Niobid. Roman marble sculpture.
Palazzo Massimo, Rome. Photo: Richard Stoneman.

a transformation myth was devised in which a red flower marked with the letters AI AI (meaning alas, alas) sprang from Hyakinthos' blood (or ashes) and bore his name ever afterwards.[73] Evidently a different plant from the modern hyacinth, this seems to have been a form of iris. The name of Hyakinthos is marked by the -*nth*-component as non-Indo-European. He originated as a pre-Hellenic deity who was especially honoured at Amyklai and gave his name to the ancient Dorian festival of the Hyakinthia. Whether his main myth was intended to account for his cultic subordination to Apollo, or owed anything at all to his cult at Amyklai, is a matter for dispute. Pausanias visited his tomb at Amyklai, and reports that the Amyklaian throne represented him as a bearded man rather than a beautiful boy.[74] For the story of Kyparissos, another favourite of Apollo who met an early death, see p. 571.

The killing of the Niobids, and Apollo's contest with Marsyas

If Apollo was a fervent lover, he was no less vigorous in exacting vengeance, although it was by no means always on his own account that he exercised his terrible powers. As has already been described, he killed the gigantic Tityos, perhaps with some help from his sister, to save his mother from being raped (see p. 147); and he joined together with his sister to massacre the NIOBIDS, the many children of NIOBE, to punish her for making a boast at Leto's expense. Niobe, daughter of Tantalos, had married a Theban ruler, Amphion (see p. 306), and had borne him a great many children, seven sons and seven daughters (or six of either sex, or ten, the numbers vary); and in an evil moment, she boasted that she was superior to Leto, who had only two children in all. So Apollo and Artemis drew their bows to avenge the insult, the former slaying all the sons of Niobe and the latter all the daughters. In her sorrow at the loss, Niobe withdrew to the land of her birth in Asia Minor, where she continued to weep for her children until Zeus relieved her from her distress by turning her to stone.[75] The pillar of rock into which she was supposed to be transformed could be seen by the curious in later times on Mt Sipylos in Lydia; according to Pausanias, who came from that area, it resembled a weeping woman when viewed from a distance.[76] Apollo also killed Phlegyas for attempting to plunder his sanctuary at Delphi (see p. 560), fought against Herakles when that hero tried to steal the sacred tripod from the Delphic oracle (see p. 273), and sent a plague against Troy when the king of that city, Laomedon, refused to pay the reward that he had promised to him and Poseidon for building the walls of Troy (see p. 523).

Another story, from outside the realm of heroic mythology, tells how Apollo imposed a gruesome punishment on the Phrygian Satyr MARSYAS for daring to challenge him to a musical contest. On finding the double flute (*aulos*) that had been discarded by its inventor Athena (see p. 183), Marsyas had picked it up and had taught himself to play it, eventually becoming so proficient that he thought that he could rival Apollo himself. The god agreed to compete with him on the agreement that the victor should do what he wished with the loser, and the Muses were invited to act as judges. When the contest began (or when his opponent seemed to be gaining the upper hand), Apollo turned his lyre upside down, played on it with consummate skill, and then challenged Marsyas to do the same; and when the Satyr was unable to (for a wind instrument must be blown from the proper end), Apollo was adjudged to be the victor. By way of a punishment, he suspended Marsyas from a pine-tree and flayed him alive. His shaggy hide could be seen in historical times at Kelainai, a city in southern Phrygia near the source of the river Marsyas.[77] The river was said to have sprung from the Satyr's blood, or from the tears that were shed for him by the local nymphs and Satyrs and shepherds.[78]

In another tale of this kind, also set in Asia Minor, Apollo engaged in a musical contest with the rustic deity Pan. Tmolos, the god of the Lydian mountain of that name, acted as judge, and the competitors played in turn, first Pan on his rustic reed-pipes and then Apollo on his lyre; and when Tmolos judged in favour of Apollo, his decision was approved by all who were present with the sole exception of Midas, king of Phrygia, who had been strangely moved by the wild music of Pan. Apollo showed what he thought of Midas' taste in music by transforming his ears into those of an ass. The king was exceedingly ashamed, and wore his turban over his ears to conceal the deformity. His barber was bound to observe the secret, however, and since he was incurably garrulous (for this was the professional vice of barbers even then) and yet could never dare to pass on the secret, he was soon ready to burst. So he finally relieved himself by digging a hole and whispering the secret into the ground. As misfortune would have it, some reeds grew up at that very spot, and whenever they were rustled by the wind, they betrayed the secret to all the world by whispering 'Midas has ass's ears'.[79] In another version of the story, Midas suffered this punishment for judging against Apollo when the god competed against Marsyas.[80]

HERMES

HERMES, the divine herald, was an ancient god who is mentioned on Linear B tablets. His name was almost certainly derived from the Greek word *herma*, meaning a cairn or heap of stones. Such cairns were a common sight by the Greek wayside, where they served as landmarks and boundary-markers; and as in the popular lore of other regions and ages, they became a focus for all kinds of superstitions. It would seem, then, that Hermes originated as a relatively humble being, as 'he of the stone-heap', the power that was supposed to reside in cairns. An aetiological myth was devised to account for this association, doubtless at a fairly late period: when he was brought to trial by the gods for having killed Argos Panoptes (see p. 229), they caused a heap of stones to pile up around him as they all cast their voting-pebbles to acquit him.[81] From the late archaic period onwards, boundary-markers were often erected in the form of a rectangular stone pillar with a bearded head on the top and a phallus on the side, usually erect; such an object, which is called a herm in English (from Latin *herma*), was known to the Greeks as a Hermes. Athens was particularly noted for the many herms that could be seen in its streets and squares.

When imagined in fully anthropomorphic form, Hermes is pictured above all as a herald and wayfarer. In this capacity, he is characteristically represented as wearing the broad-brimmed felt hat (*petasos*) that Greek travellers would wear to keep the sun out of their eyes, and carrying a herald's staff (*kerykeion*, or *caduceus* in Latin). He is of course far swifter and less earthbound than any human traveller, as is indicated in many images through his winged sandals or hat. His most important role by far in legend is to act as a messenger for the gods, and for Zeus in particular. He is sometimes merely dispatched to communicate the will of Zeus, as when he speeds above the waves like a bird to the remote island of Kalypso to order her to release Odysseus (see p. 497); or he may take direct action to put the will of Zeus or of the gods into effect, as when he guides Priam to the Greek camp at night to seek the return of Hektor's body, putting the guards to sleep as the two of them approach Achilles' hut.[82] The whole episode is very characteristic of Hermes, who tends to be discreet or even furtive in his approach and actions but is almost always benevolent to mortals. He performs numerous other missions, as we will see, for Zeus and the other gods, and acts as a special protector to Perseus (see pp. 239ff) and also to Herakles during that hero's incursion into the Underworld. As would

Figure 5.4 Hermes. Roman marble sculpture. Cos museum. Photo: Richard Stoneman.

be expected of a herald, he rarely takes the lead in any course of action, and he holds no very high place among the Olympians, but is rather the younger son of the family, running errands for the rest. Mortal heralds could naturally call on his protection, and he also presides over the arts that are required for effective communication, such as oratory and persuasive speech or interpretation in dealing with foreigners. An interpreter was known as a *hermeneus* accordingly (hence the modern term of hermeneutics).

Figure 5.5 A herm-maker. Red-figure cup, c. 510 BC. National museum, Copenhagen.

In accordance with his original nature as the spirit of the stone-pile, most of the functions of Hermes are related in one way or another to the wayside and wayfaring and to boundaries and the transgression of boundaries. Under such titles as Hodios (God of the Road) and Hegemenos or Agetor (Leader, Guide), he is the god of the road and the protector of all who travel on it, whether openly on legitimate business or more covertly for nefarious purposes. If he is the patron god of merchants and traders, he is also the patron of tricksters and thieves, a conferrer of fortune whether honestly or dishonestly gained. Brigandage and cattle-raiding, especially where undetected, were quite respectable sources of fortune in early days, and Hermes was supposed to have begun his career by rustling the cattle of Apollo. He was a god of luck, moreover, in the widest sense, and windfalls and strokes of good fortune of every kind lay within his gift. A lucky find or treasure-trove was known as a *hermaion* or *hermaia dosis* (i.e. gift of Hermes) accordingly. Like Apollo

Nomios, he was also a god whose influence extended over the traditional ancient forms of wealth, namely flocks and herds and their increase. In this connection in particular, he had a special association with Arcadia. He was concerned likewise with human fertility, and one of his oldest cultic emblems was the phallus, which always remained a prominent feature of his cult.

As a god who was concerned with boundaries and their transgression, he was able to cross over and so help others to cross over the most formidable boundary of all, that which separates the world of the living from the world of the dead. He was exceptional in this respect among the Olympian deities, who generally avoided all contact with death and the dead; no other god passed over this frontier, apart from Persephone of course (and perhaps one or two others in exceptional circumstances). In classical and later times at least, it was supposed that one of his most important offices was to serve as the *psychopompos* or 'conductor of souls' who guided the shades of the newly dead to their future home in the sunless realm. As was noted above in connection with the mythology of the Underworld, it seems likely that this was not a very ancient conception, and that this duty was first assigned to him well after the time of Homer and Hesiod (even if he is once presented as performing it in the present text of the *Odyssey*, see pp. 112–13). Associated though he may have come to be with death and the journey below, he was never pictured as a grim or formidable god, as in the case of Hades and Thanatos, but always as courteous and kindly, as befitted a herald.

In his earlier images from archaic art, Hermes was typically represented as a mature figure with a beard, as continued to be the case when his head was portrayed on herms. He appears with great frequency in Attic vase-paintings, whether as a leading figure in exploits of his own or as an attendant figure, usually clad in the traveller's garb described above. From the latter part of the fifth century BC onwards, his artistic type changes in accordance with developments in sculpture, and he comes to be represented as a beardless and naked youth (*ephēbos*), not unlike his half-brother Apollo, but younger and less muscular. It is thus that he is shown in the marvellous statue by Praxiteles (born c. 390 BC) that is the chief glory of the museum at Olympia. Such images of him were very often set up in the gymnasia and wrestling-schools (*palaistrai*), and he came increasingly to be regarded as a special patron of adolescent youths and their exercises. Hermes could also be portrayed in rustic guise as Kriophoros (the Ram-bearer), carrying a ram in his arm or on his shoulders.

The legend of his birth is recounted in the *Homeric Hymn to Hermes*, which handles the subject with the good-natured humour that befits it; for few Greek gods mind a harmless joke or two, and Hermes least of all. Zeus fathered him by Maia, a nymph or daughter of Atlas (see p. 519), who lived in a remote cave on Mt Kyllene in north-eastern Arcadia.[83] At dawn he was born, so the Hymn tells us, by noon he was playing on the lyre, and on that same evening he stole the cattle of Apollo.[84] The details of the story may be a little obscure here and there, but the outlines are clear. Hermes leapt out of his cradle soon after he was born and walked out of his mother's cave. On meeting a tortoise just outside, he was struck by a sudden inspiration, and picked it up and took it into the cave to convert it into a musical instrument. After killing it and scooping its flesh out of its shell, he inserted two curved horns into the leg-holes at one end of the shell, fitted a cross-piece between them, and stretched seven strings of sheep-gut back over the shell to create the first lyre. After singing an extempore song to its accompaniment, he returned to his main purpose by setting off to steal the cattle of Apollo.[85]

Making his way to Pieria to the north of Mt Olympos – a very tolerable walk for a baby – he stole fifty cows from a herd belonging to Apollo, and drove them off, making them walk backwards to confuse anyone who tried to search for them. He walked forwards for his own part, but concealed his tracks by wearing some improvised sandals woven from twigs of myrtle and tamarisk.[86] Later authors suggest that he disguised the trail of the cattle by tying branches to their tails to act as brushes, or by fixing little boots over their hooves.[87] He hurried south with the cattle through Thessaly and Central Greece, and then across the Isthmus to the Peloponnese. When an old man who was tending his vineyard happened to see him on the way at Onchestos in Boeotia, the god warned him that it was in his best interest to keep silent on the matter.[88] On reaching the river Alpheios in the western Peloponnese on the same night, Hermes called a halt and kindled a fire, inventing fire-sticks for the purpose; and he then slaughtered two of the cattle and divided their flesh into twelve portions to offer them in sacrifice to the Twelve Gods. As dawn was breaking, he finally returned to his mother's cave at Kyllene, slipping in through the keyhole, and tucked himself up in his cradle, the very picture of baby innocence.[89]

Although Maia was not deceived and did her best to scold him, he retorted that he merely wanted what was due to him as a divine son of Zeus, and would steal it as best he may if it were not granted to him.[90] Apollo arrived at the cave in a great fury on the next day, having been put on the track by the old man at Onchestos, and having recognized the identity of the thief through a bird-omen.[91] Brushing aside the bland assurances of Hermes, who claimed that he was too young even to know what cattle were let alone to steal them, Apollo hauled him off to Zeus to answer for his crime. After listening to a speech of consummate impudence from the infant god, who swore that had never done anything wrong and was incapable of telling a lie, Zeus laughed at his effrontery and ordered him to guide Apollo to the stolen cattle forthwith.[92] So he took Apollo to the cave where they were hidden, in the region of Triphylian Pylos, and soon mollified him by singing a song to the accompaniment of the wonderful music of his lyre. Apollo was so entranced by the sound of the newly invented instrument that he agreed to surrender his cattle in exchange for it; and after returning the cattle to their proper pastures, the two gods went up to Olympos together.[93] To console himself for the loss of his lyre, Hermes invented a new and humbler instrument for himself, the shepherd's pipes. After demanding that Hermes should swear never to steal from him again, Apollo swore to become his dearest friend and presented him with a three-branched golden staff (possibly though not necessarily to be identified with the caduceus of Hermes). Although Hermes also wanted to be taught the art of prophecy, Apollo explained that the highest forms of the art were reserved for himself alone, and recommended that he should consult three virgins called the Thriai who would be able to instruct him in a subordinate form of divination, evidently the use of *thriai* or divining pebbles. Zeus ordered for his part that Hermes should have dominion over trade, and beasts and flocks, and be appointed his messenger to Hades.[94]

Since the Thriai are described in the Hymn as winged sisters who flew hither and thither, fed on honeycomb, and were inspired to speak the truth through the eating of honey, it seems that they may have been imagined as being partly bee-like in form. They lived under a ridge of Mt Parnassos.[95] Later sources have nothing of substance to add except that Pherecydes described them as daughters of Zeus.[96]

The early lyric poet Alcaeus offered an account of the juvenile exploits of Hermes, but little is recorded of it beyond the fact that Hermes contrived to steal the quiver of Apollo while that god was trying to scare him into returning the stolen cattle.[97] A substantial portion of Sophocles' *Trackers* (*Ichneutai*), a Satyr-play based on the same body of legend, has been recovered from papyri; this is a burlesque in which Seilenos leads a chorus of Satyrs in pursuit of the infant cattle-thief on Apollo's behalf. Apollodorus' summary of the young god's adventures conflicts with the Homeric Hymn in certain details. Hermes' invention of the lyre is delayed, for instance, until after his theft of the cattle, and he is thus able to use gut from the two slaughtered cattle to make the strings. In this account, furthermore, Apollo covets Hermes' second musical invention, the shepherd's pipes, and offers him the golden staff in exchange for it; but Hermes demands to receive the art of divination in addition, and Apollo teaches him the use of divining-pebbles for that reason.[98]

The old man who saw Hermes passing with the cattle was sometimes named as BATTOS (Chatterbox) and was said to have been turned to stone as a punishment for his chattering. The story is recounted in the following way by Antoninus Liberalis, whose main source was probably the Hellenistic poet Nicander (although he also cites other authors including Hesiod). Apollo was distracted at the time of the cattle-theft because he had fallen in love with Hymenaios (see p. 223, here described as a son of Magnes) and was never out of his home for long. Hermes took advantage of his absence to drive away a hundred of his cows along with twelve heifers and a bull, after first putting the guard-dogs to sleep (presumably with his wand). Battos, who lived on a crag in Arcadia, noticed the cattle passing and demanded a reward for his silence. Although Battos swore to keep his side of the bargain, Hermes mistrusted him and came back in disguise to test him as soon as he had hidden the cattle; and Battos duly betrayed the secret in return for a woollen cloak. To punish his perfidy, the god turned him to stone with a touch of his wand. This story provides an explanation for the name of some crags in Arcadia known as the *Battou Skopiai* (the peaks or look-out-points of Battos).[99] Ovid offers a comparable story, stating that Battos was an old man who tended the mares of Neleus (the king of Pylos in Messenia, see p. 424). After receiving a cow from Hermes as the price for his silence, Battos betrayed the secret when the god returned in disguise and bribed him to talk by promising him a bull and a cow. In this case, Hermes turned him to flint.[100]

Although Hermes engaged in love affairs with some mortal women, notably Philonis (see p. 435) and Herse (see p. 366), and was said to have fathered various children by such liaisons, he never married, nor is he linked to any goddess in early myth.

It was doubtless inevitable that the bisexual godling HERMAPHRODITOS should have come to be described as a son of Hermes and Aphrodite. The cult of this strange being was probably derived from the Cypriot cult of Aphroditos, the bearded male Aphrodite; the earliest definite evidence for his cult in mainland Greece is provided by an Attic dedication from the early fourth century BC. Diodorus, the first author to refer to him as a son of Hermes, seems to consider that he was a hermaphrodite from the time of his birth.[101] Ovid recounts a legend, however, which explains his distinctive form by saying that he had been a handsome young man who had fused with an amorous water-nymph. Hermaphroditos, as he was called after his parents, was reared by naiad nymphs in the caves of Mt Ida in the Troad, but left home at the age of fifteen to wander through Asia Minor. When he reached Caria in the south-west, Salmakis, the nymph of a spring in that area, fell violently in love with him when she saw him approaching her pool. Although the ignorant youth was simply embarrassed when she made direct advances to him, she gained her opportunity when he jumped into her waters to bathe. Seizing him in a tight embrace, she prayed that the two of them should be united forever, and they were fused into a single being who shared the characteristics of both sexes. On observing the change that he had undergone, Hermaphroditos prayed to his divine parents, asking that any man who bathed there in the future should be robbed of his virility.[102] The spring of Salmakis, which lay at Halicarnassus, was credited with these enervating powers in historical times. Although this is Hermaphroditos' only proper myth, he appears quite often in art. During the Hellenistic era, when Greek artists came to be increasingly attracted to anomalous and pathetic subjects, this ambiguous figure was in high favour, and numerous representations, many having a morbid beauty, have survived. He has the genitals of a man but the breasts and general build of a woman.

Pan was commonly classed as a son of Hermes (see p. 215), as is understandable since he resembled Pan in certain respects, as a pastoral god who had special connections with Arcadia. According to a minor aetiological tale, Hermes once seized Hekate while he was out hunting and tried to rape her, but was deterred when she shrieked out in rage (*enebrimēsato*), hence the goddess's title of Brimo.[103]

The Italians identified Hermes with Mercurius (Mercury), whose name indicates in Latin that he was a god of merchants and their wares; Mercurius was often represented with similar attributes to those of Hermes, and apparently originated as a Roman offshoot of the Greek god.

HEPHAISTOS

It has been shown pretty convincingly that HEPHAISTOS, who has a non-Greek name, was a god of foreign and probably Asiatic origin. Although he was little worshipped on the Greek mainland except at Athens, his cult was of some importance in Asia Minor and the adjoining islands, and also the Greek colonies in the volcanic regions of Italy and Sicily. In Asia Minor, he was particularly associated with Lycia in the south-west, and above all the region of the Lycian Olympos, which was remarkable for the presence of large quantities of natural gas; he appears to have been the principal god of Phaselis, the main coastal city of that region. It has been suggested that he may have originated as a fire-god among the native peoples of Lycia, and that his cult may have spread from this original centre not only to other areas of the Anatolian mainland, but also to adjacent islands, especially Lemnos,

Figure 5.6   The return of Hephaistos to Olympos.

whose mountain, Moschylos, is volcanic though long extinct. The city of Hephaistias
on the north coast of the island was named after Hephaistos, and an ancient myth
that was already known to Homer presented him as having fallen to earth on the
island (see below). As a deity who was associated with fire, he was pictured as a
divine blacksmith from a very early period, and various places came to be identified as the site of his underground forge, wherever its presence could be inferred
from extensive emissions of fire and smoke. When his cult was transferred to the
volcanic regions of the west, the Aeolian (Lipari) islands near Sicily came to be
connected with him, and also to some extent Sicily itself and southern Campania.
In mainland Greece, Hephaistos was worshipped with considerable zeal in Attica,
which was home to many craftsmen whose trades depended on the use of fire, but
hardly at all anywhere else even if he was universally familiar as a god of myth.

In Homer, he is a fully accredited Olympian, a son of Hera. Although she apparently bore him as a child of her marriage in the Homeric view,[104] Hesiod and most
later authors agree that she brought him to birth without prior intercourse with
Zeus, by way of a counter-miracle because she was angry with Zeus for having
brought Athena to birth from his head.[105] According to two conflicting tales that
are recounted in different parts of the *Iliad*, he was thrown out of heaven during
his younger days, either by his mother or by Zeus. In one account, he was lame
from birth and Hera threw him out because she was ashamed of his deformity;
and when he landed in the sea below, he was rescued by Thetis and the Okeanid

Eurynome, who sheltered him in their cave beneath the Ocean for nine years. He repaid them for their care and protection by fashioning all manner of fine jewellery as the Ocean roared around outside.[106] Or in the other Homeric account, Zeus cast him out when he tried to intervene on his mother's behalf during one of his parents' many quarrels. On this occasion he alighted on Lemnos after falling all day, and was kindly received by the Sintians (*Sinties*), as the inhabitants are called in the *Iliad*. Although Homer says nothing definite on the matter, he was presumably lamed by his fall in this version (as is explicitly stated in some later accounts of the story).[107] According to a tale that can be traced well back into the archaic period, Hephaistos avenged his mother's action by sending her a golden throne that tied her fast by means of invisible cords when she sat on it. Although Ares and a succession of other gods tried to persuade him to return home to set her free, he refused to do so until Dionysos managed to bring him back in a drunken state after plying him with wine.[108] He can be seen in vase-paintings riding back to Olympos on an ithyphallic ass in the company of nymphs and Seilenoi.

As a limping god who toiled at a grimy craft, the Hephaistos of myth was not a figure of the highest dignity. Even in Homer, he is rather a figure of fun, at whose clumsy activities the gods laugh unquenchably (hence the proverbial phrase 'Homeric laughter') as he serves them at table.[109] His usual workshop in the early tradition lay neither on Lemnos nor anywhere else on the earth below, but in his house of bronze on Olympos where he fashioned marvellous objects of every kind,[110] some that were magical and some that were merely intricate and beautiful, ranging from the golden automata that helped him as servants in his house to armour of unparalleled splendour for the gods or specially favoured mortals. From the classical period onwards, his forge is located at various places in the everyday world. It was sometimes placed on Lemnos, where the blinded Orion was supposed to have visited it and to have received assistance from the god (see p. 563);[111] but since Lemnos had no active volcano, most authors preferred to imagine that the divine forge lay in the west, either under Mt Etna in Sicily[112] or under a volcano in the Aeolian islands to the north,[113] hence the flames and smoke that arose from them. In contrast to Homer, who presents Hephaistos as working on his own (with some help from his automata and a semi-automatic bellows), authors from Callimachus onwards provide him with assistants in the form of the Kyklopes, the primordial beings who had armed Zeus with his thunderbolt (see p. 66).[114] This furnished a pleasing theme for poets and artists, who loved to portray Hephaistos in his underground forge with his soot-blackened workmen around him, endlessly busy with divine tasks – preparing thunderbolts for Zeus, arrows for Artemis, arms for some favoured hero.

The creations of Hephaistos fall into three main classes. In the first place, he was a master-architect who created splendid homes for himself and all the other gods on Olympos.[115] It should be remembered in this connection that imperishable divine buildings were thought to be made of bronze, in part or in whole. The *Iliad* indicates, however, that his skills extended to masonry by referring to porticoes of polished stone that that he erected at the palace of Zeus.[116] He had an eye for detail too, for he made tightly closing doors for Hera's bedroom with a secret bolt which could be opened by no other god.[117] Down on earth, he erected a bronze temple of Apollo at Delphi, which was supposed to have stood there before the first stone temple was erected by the legendary builders Trophonios and Agamedes (see p. 558). There was disagreement on whether this bronze temple had burned down or been swallowed up in a chasm (which would surely be more plausible).[118]

In the second place, Hephaistos was a craftsman with superhuman capacities who could create automata that acted of their own accord. We are told in the *Iliad* that he was assisted in his house by maidens of gold who possessed understanding, speech and strength; and he also made tripods that were fitted with ears and wheels, and could make their way to and from the gatherings of the gods at his command.[119] The *Odyssey* adds that he fashioned dogs of gold and silver to guard the palace of Alkinoos.[120] Later sources refer to further automata, such as Talos, a bronze giant who was guarded the coast of Crete (see p. 396), and a golden dog that guarded a shrine of Zeus on the island (see p. 502), and golden singing figures that stood on the pediment of the Delphian temple mentioned above.

And third, Hephaistos made splendid arms and armour, and jewellery and other fine artefacts, which sometimes remained in the possession of the gods but are generally more important in myth if they enter the possession of mortals. The armour of Achilles (see p. 464), the breast-plate of Diomedes, and the sceptre of Agamemnon (see p. 396) may be mentioned from the *Iliad*,[121] and the necklace of Harmonia (see p. 297), the crown of Ariadne (see p. 397), and the sword of Peleus (see p. 534) from later sources. In a looser sense, any strange or wonderful object that makes an appearance in heroic legend, from the underground house of Oinopion (see p. 563) to the bronze-hooved cattle of Aietes, could be described as 'Hephaistos-made' (*Hephaistoteuktos*).

A particularly useful creation of Hephaistos was the golden cup that he made for the sungod Helios to carry him around the streams of Ocean from the place of his setting to that of his rising (see p. 44); in an early account by the lyric poet Mimnermus, this hollow golden bowl (or 'bed' as it is called here) is fitted with wings and presumably has some power of self-motion.[122]

Various myths, all recounted elsewhere, present Hephaistos as putting his powers of craftsmanship to good use in various ways. Zeus charged him with the creation of the first woman, Pandora, whom he moulded from moistened clay (see p. 94). He split the head of Zeus with an axe to ease the birth of Athena (see p. 181). In a famous story from the *Odyssey* in which Aphrodite is considered to be his wife, he catches her in adultery with Ares by laying a fine-woven net across his bed (see p. 201). There is no indication otherwise in early literature or art that he was thought to be married to Aphrodite; the *Theogony* points to another union of opposites, stating that he was married to Aglaia, the youngest of the Graces, and the *Iliad* suggests similarly that he was married to Charis (Grace personified).[123] For the story of his attempted rape of Athena, which resulted in the birth of Erichthonios, see p. 184. His other mortal children are minor figures who are identified as sons of his either on account of their lameness, as in the case of Periphetes (see p. 342) and the Argonaut Palaimonios,[124] or of their manual skills, as in the case of Ardalos, a legendary builder and musician of Troizen.[125]

In Rome, Hephaistos was identified with Volcanus (Vulcan), though not very appropriately, since Hephaistos became a smith-god and is hardly remembered in any other capacity, whereas Volcanus was the god of destroying fire, which he remained in his native cult, and had nothing to do with its productive applications.

ARES

ARES, the god of war, was a god of lesser stature than one might expect, above all because he represented the more brutal aspects of warfare – battle-frenzy and slaughter and strife as enjoyed for their own sakes. His name seems to have originated as an ancient word for war or battle, and he can virtually be regarded as bellicosity personified. Disciplined courage and chivalry were not his concern. He is portrayed in a most unflattering light from the time of Homer onwards, as a god who is disdained by other members of the Olympian circle; when he complains to his father in the *Iliad* after Diomedes has wounded him in battle, Zeus tells him not to sit and whine at his feet, saying that he finds him the most hateful of all the gods who inhabit Olympos, for he delights in nothing other than strife, war and slaughter.[126] Ares never developed into a god of social, moral or theological importance, in this respect contrasting sharply not only with Apollo but with the Italian Mars, with whom he was identified in Graeco-Roman cult and legend; for Mars had agricultural as well as warlike functions, however he came by them, and, at least in the Augustan cult of Mars Ultor, he was capable of embodying the idea of righteous vengeance, while his Greek counterpart was no more than a divine swashbuckler. This wild god lived in a suitably wild territory, the northern land of Thrace, which was noted for its savage, warlike peoples; in the *Iliad*, he sets out from Thrace when he comes to join battle, and he hurries off to Thrace in the *Odyssey* after he is caught in adultery by Hephaistos.[127] It is far from certain, however, that he was actually a god of Thracian origin as has often been supposed.

Doubtless because he is pictured as a butcher and berserker rather than a brave and self-controlled warrior, Ares quite often gets the worst of it in his martial encounters. Diomedes wounds him in the *Iliad*, as has been mentioned, with a little help from Athena, causing him to scream as loudly as nine or ten thousand men in battle and then flee up to heaven.[128] Athena herself treats him with some contempt in the battle of the gods later in the poem, felling him with a huge stone in a single blow, and mocking him for having presumed to match his strength against hers.[129] He engages more directly with mortals in battle than is usual for gods, and is even presented as stripping the armour from a fallen Greek warrior on one occasion.[130] According to the Hesiodic *Shield*, Herakles defeated him twice over, first bringing him to the ground with a thigh-wound during the fighting at Pylos (see p. 278), and later doing so again in single combat when he was attacked by Ares after killing his son Kyknos (see p. 283).[131] A humiliation of a rather different kind was imposed on him by the Aloadai, who imprisoned him in a bronze jar for thirteen months, and might even have caused his destruction if Hermes had not come to his rescue (see p. 92); this too is an ancient legend, for it is mentioned in the *Iliad*.[132]

Ares has a number of associates who accompany him into battle in the *Iliad*, including the female war-deity **Enyo** (sacker of cities) who is sometimes described as his mother or daughter.[133] Although **Enyalios** is no more than an epithet of Ares in Homer, he is sometimes distinguished as a separate god in later sources. He was certainly a very ancient figure since his name already appears on Mycenaean tablets. He was honoured in cult at various places, notably at Sparta, where his statue was kept enchained to ensure that the Spartans would never be deserted by him, and the boys used to sacrifice puppies to him before the ritual fight at the Platanistas.[134] At Rome, he was commonly identified with Quirinus, an ancient god who had martial functions, while Enyo was identified with Bellona. Various personifications also accompany Ares in the *Iliad*, his 'comrade and sister' **Eris**[135] (Strife, who is a daughter of Night and the mother of many unappealing children in the *Theogony*, see pp. 30–1), and **Deimos** and **Phobos** (Panic and Fear), and **Kydoimos**, who personifies the din and confusion of battle,[136] and the **Ker** or Death-spirit, whose cloak is red with human blood.[137]

According to the *Theogony*, Ares fathered three children by Aphrodite, the above-mentioned Deimos and Phobos, 'terrible gods who strike confusion into the close-packed ranks of men in numbing war', and a goddess of very different character, the gracious Harmonia, who became the wife of Kadmos, king of Thebes (see p. 297).[138] Ares was associated with Aphrodite from early times as a lover and cult-partner (see p. 201); for Homer's story of how Hephaistos, here exceptionally described as her husband, humiliated the pair by trapping them together during an assignation, see p. 201. Simonides and some later authors suggest that Aphrodite also bore Eros to Ares[139] (which would be appropriate enough, seeing that Ares loved the goddess and Eros waited upon her; but there were many other accounts of Eros' origin). As often with Poseidon, Ares was thought to be a suitable father for heroes of a savage or bellicose nature, such as Diomedes of Thrace and Kyknos, two notable adversaries of Herakles (see pp. 262 and 282), and Tereus of Thrace who raped and mutilated his sister-in-law (see p. 368), and others who will be mentioned later. In a looser sense, any warlike hero could be described as a scion of Ares.

Although Homer has a fair amount to say about Ares, especially in the fifth book of the *Iliad*, he rarely appears in mythical narratives thereafter, even where war and carnage are involved. The one major story in which he does play an important part

Figure 5.7 Herakles and a *kēr*. Drawing after an Attic vase.

is the Theban foundation-myth, since the founder, Kadmos, kills his sacred dragon (which is even described as his son in some accounts) and has to appease him before he can found the city (see pp. 295ff). After they are reconciled, the god offers his daughter Harmonia to Kadmos in marriage; but in some accounts his anger is long-lasting (see p. 330 for instance). He was otherwise closely associated with the Amazons, as their main god and as the father of prominent Amazons (or even of the entire race), and was said to have given his name to the Athenian high court of the Areiopagos after he was brought before it to be tried for murder in the first trial ever to be held there (see pp. 365–6).

DIONYSOS

Although it was once assumed that it had been settled almost beyond question that DIONYSOS, the god of wine and ecstasy, was a deity of foreign origin who arrived in Greece at a relatively late period, this can no longer be taken for granted. According to the traditional argument, he was introduced into Greece from Thrace after perhaps originating in Asia Minor, and his late irruption into the Greek scene is reflected in some of his most characteristic myths that tell how he had to overcome determined resistance in various parts of Greece. It has often been thought significant, furthermore, that he is barely mentioned by Homer (even if the poet knows something of his wild rites and his conflict with Lykourgos of Thrace). Some of the more recent archaeological evidence seems to point in another direction, however, suggesting that the name and cult of Dionysos could be of Mycenaean origin. His name has been found on Linear B tablets from Pylos in the Peloponnese; and he was apparently honoured without break at the sanctuary of Ayia Irini on Keos (an Aegean island to the south-east of Attica) from the early Mycenaean period into Greek times. It has also been pointed out that the Dionysian festival of the Anthesteria must have originated before the Ionian migration (c. 1000 BC), and that there is reason to suppose that the Dionysian festival of the Lenaia was of very ancient origin too.[140] As regards the name of Dionysos, its first syllable evidently refers to the sky-god (Zeus, genitive *Dios*), but the meaning of the rest is uncertain. It has been suggested that there may have been a word *nysos* (akin to Latin *nurus* or Greek νύος) meaning 'child' or 'son', or else that this component of the name was connected with the legendary Nysa where the god was said to have been reared.

Zeus and Semele, and the birth and infancy of their son Dionysos

There is no doubt about the origin of the name of Dionysos' mother SEMELE, for it is nothing but a Greek modification of that of the Thraco-Phrygian earth-goddess Zemelo. In Greek myth, however, she is fully mortal, as one of the four daughters of Kadmos, king of Thebes (see p. 298). Zeus fell in love with her and used to visit her in secret at night, exciting the jealousy of Hera, who plotted her rival's destruction. Appearing to her in the form of her aged nurse Beroe, Hera congratulated her

Figure 5.8 Dionysos. Hellenistic marble sculpture.
Thasos Museum. Photo: Richard Stoneman.

on the exalted rank of her lover, but advised her to impose a test on him to prove
that he was Zeus and truly loved her: let him appear to her in all the splendour of
his divinity, just as he would appear to his lawful divine consort.[141] Or in another
version, Hera suggested that this was the only way in which she could come to
experience the full pleasure of intercourse with a god.[142] So Semele persuaded Zeus
to promise her any favour she chose (or took advantage of a promise that he had
already made to that effect) and demanded that he should come to her just as he
came to Hera. He reluctantly agreed, and swept into her bedroom in a chariot to
the accompaniment of thunder and lightning; but her human frailty could not
endure his Olympian glory, and she died of fright and was burned to ashes. Before
her body was fully consumed, however, Zeus snatched her sixth- or seventh-month
child from her womb, and sewed it into his own thigh, from where it was subsequently brought to birth at the fulfilment of the normal time of gestation. Some
claimed that the child was already deified by contact with the divine fire. As for
the unfortunate Semele, she was later rescued from the Underworld by her son and
taken up to Olympos to become the goddess Thyone.[143]

After his extraordinary birth, which may be compared to that of Athena from
Zeus's head, Dionysos had to be provided with a nurse or nurses. The *Homeric Hymn*
(1) *to Dionysos* observes that there were conflicting traditions about the place of his

birth, which was located at his mother's home-city of Thebes, or on Naxos (an island that was specially associated with the god), or by the river Alpheios in the Peloponnese, or at other places besides; but there is no truth in any of this, so the poet asserts, for Zeus brought him to birth far away from men and in secret from Hera on Nysa, a lofty mountain in Phoenicia. The *Homeric Hymn* (26) *to Dionysos* states similarly that Zeus entrusted his son to the nymphs of Nysa, who reared him in a sweet-smelling cave on the mountain.[144] In some accounts, Zeus asked Hermes to convey the child to the nymphs of Nysa.[145] This mysterious place is already mentioned in connection with Dionysos in the *Iliad*, which states that Lykourgos (see below) chased 'the nurses of mad Dionysos down over the sacred mountain of Nysa'.[146] Ancient scholars offered all manner of conjectures about the location of this legendary mountain; the lexicographer Hesychius writes that it is 'not confined to any one place; we find it in Arabia, Ethiopia, Egypt, Babylon, Erythra (the Red Sea?), Thrace, Thessaly, Cilicia, India, Libya, Lydia, Macedonia, Naxos, the neighbourhood of Mt Pangaion, and at a place in Syria'.[147] Wherever the nymphs of Nysa may have lived and whoever they were, they nursed Dionysos faithfully and became his companions and followers. According to Ovid, he repaid their kindness by renewing their youth when they grew old; or else he rewarded them by placing them in the heavens as the star-cluster of the Hyades.[148]

One of Semele's sisters, Ino, the wife of the Boeotian ruler Athamas (see p. 420), is also named as a nurse of the infant Dionysos. The mythographers reconciled the two accounts by suggesting that the nymphs reared him initially but later passed him on to Ino for fear of Hera's anger, or, conversely, that Ino reared him initially until she and her husband were driven mad by Hera.[149] According to Apollodorus, who offers the latter version, Hermes brought the new-born Dionysos to Ino and Athamas and persuaded them to rear him as a girl; but when the couple were subsequently driven mad by Hera, Zeus rescued him from the goddess's anger by transforming him into a kid, and the divine messenger then passed him on to the Nysaian nymphs. The couple paid a heavy price for their services to Dionysos in any case, since the maddened Ino threw their younger son into a boiling cauldron and jumped into the sea with him, while Athamas hunted down their eldest son in the delusion that he was a deer; see further on p. 421.

The people of Brasiai or Prasiai, a town on the eastern seaboard of Laconia, offered their own distinctive account of the birth and childhood of Dionysos. In contrast to the other Greeks, they claimed that Semele had survived to give birth to him in the normal way, and that her father had enclosed her in a chest with her new-born child and had cast it into the sea. When the chest drifted ashore at Brasiai, Semele was found to be dead, but Dionysos was safe and sound. By a convenient chance, Ino happened to pass by and asked to take care of her nephew; she reared him there in a grotto which was shown to visitors as the scene of his childhood. A patch of level ground known as the garden of Dionysos stretched in front of it. The setting adrift of an erring daughter and her child is a standard motif in Greek myth, as can be seen in the story of Danae and Perseus (see p. 239) or Rhoio and Anios (see p. 569). A child who survives such an ordeal is marked out for a special destiny. The present tale diverges from others of the kind in one significant respect, that the mother fails to survive; for it was so firmly established that Semele had died leaving Dionysos an orphan that the framers of the local myth accepted this into their story.[150]

Myths in which Dionysos exacts terrible vengeance on mortals who reject him and his rites

Some of the most characteristic myths of the mature Dionysos are those in which he suffers persecution from mortals who refuse to acknowledge his divinity and try to suppress his rites when he first introduces them into their land. It hardly needs saying that those who venture to oppose him soon come to a bad end. One such myth is already recounted by Homer, who tells how LYKOURGOS, son of Dryas, once chased the nurses of Dionysos down from the sacred mountain of Nysa, striking them with an ox-goad and causing the god himself to plunge beneath the sea in terror. Dionysos was consoled, however, by the goddess Thetis, and Lykourgos paid a heavy price for his impious behaviour, for he was struck blind by Zeus 'and lived not long thereafter, for he had become hateful to the deathless gods'.[151] In subsequent accounts of this story, and in other myths of this kind, Dionysos is quite capable of looking after himself. According to Apollodorus, Dionysos took refuge beneath the sea when Lykourgos tried to expel him, and the Bacchants and Satyrs of his retinue were taken captive by his persecutor; but his followers were suddenly released thereafter (evidently through his miraculous intervention), and he drove Lykourgos mad. In his frenzy, Lykourgos killed his son Dryas in the belief that he was pruning a vine; and when his land was subsequently struck by a famine, his people caused his death at the bidding of an oracle by tying him up and exposing him on Mt Pangaion, where he was destroyed by horses. It is stated that this was the first occasion on which Dionysos was insulted and expelled by a mortal.[152]

Post-Homeric sources report that Lykourgos was the king of the Edonians in the northern land of Thrace.[153] His story varies considerably in different accounts; in that of Hyginus, for instance, he raped his mother in a fit of drunkenness after denying the divinity of Dionysos; and during his madness, he killed not only his son but his wife too, and cut off one of his feet in the delusion that it was a vine. He then met his own death at the hand of Dionysos himself, who threw him to his panthers on Mt Rhodope in Thrace.[154] Hyginus also refers to a version in which Lykourgos took his own life while in the grip of his madness.[155] In a chorus from Sophocles' *Antigone*, by contrast, it is suggested that he was merely imprisoned in a cave until his madness subsided.[156] The early epic poet Eumelus apparently offered a similar account to that of Homer, except that he stated that Lykourgos was acting at the incitation of Hera.[157] According to Stesichorus, Dionysos had once received a golden urn from Hephaistos after entertaining him on Naxos; and when Thetis offered him a kindly welcome under the sea after he was pursued by Lykourgos, he repaid her by giving her this urn, which would later hold the ashes of her son Achilles.[158]

The most famous of these opposition myths, and one of the most violent, is the Theban tale of PENTHEUS, which forms the subject of one of Euripides' finest plays, the *Bacchae*. Dionysos visited Thebes in anger because the three sisters of his mother Semele had denied that he was truly a son of Zeus; for they claimed that Semele had invented the story to conceal a love affair with a mortal, and that Zeus had struck her dead to punish her for her lie.[159] On his arrival, Dionysos manifested his powers by driving the three sisters mad along with the other women of the city, and causing them all to roam over Mt Kithairon as Bacchants. Thebes was now under the rule of Pentheus, who was the son of Agave, one of the princesses who had caused the trouble, and a grandson of the founder Kadmos. Believing that the new god was an impostor, Pentheus vigorously opposed his rites, paying no heed to the warnings of the seer Teiresias or of Kadmos (who was still living at the Theban court in his old age). When his guards brought in Dionysos, who was pretending for the moment to be no more than a votary of the god, he cross-examined him and ordered that he should be imprisoned in the stables of the palace.[160] But Dionysos escaped with ease, provoked an earthquake as a demonstration of his powers, and then appeared once again in front of his supposed captor. Impressed and yet still hostile, Pentheus allowed his extraordinary visitor to persuade him to disguise himself as a woman and to set off for the mountain to see with his own eyes what the followers of Dionysos were doing.[161] As he was spying on the women from high up in a pine-tree, Dionysos incited them to attack him, and they surrounded the tree, pushed it over, and tore him to pieces. His mother Agave, who took a leading part in the assault, ran back to the palace with his severed head in the delusion that he had been a mountain lion.[162] Not until later, when her frenzy subsided, did she realize what she had done. The play ends as she and her sisters depart into exile at the order of Dionysos, whose revenge is now complete.[163]

In another Boeotian tale of this kind, the MINYADES, the three daughters of Minyas, king of Orchomenos (see p. 558), also suffered a grim punishment for holding out against the new cult. When the other women of the city left their homes to roam the mountains as Bacchants, the three industrious princesses, who are named as Leukippe, Alkathoe (or Alkithoe) and Arsippe (or Arsinoe), disapproved of their unruly behaviour and preferred to sit at home at their looms. Although Dionysos himself appeared to them in the form of a young girl to urge them not to neglect his rites and mysteries, they spurned his advice. Angered by their obduracy, the god demonstrated his powers by transforming himself successively into a bull, a lion and a leopard, and by causing milk and nectar to drip from the frames of their looms. Overcome by terror at the sight of these prodigies, the three girls cast lots to see who should offer sacrifice to the god; and when the lot fell on Leukippe, the three of them joined together to tear her young son Hippasos to pieces. They then ran out to join the Bacchants on the mountainside, where Hermes touched them with his wand to transform them into a bat and two different forms of owl.[164] Or in another version in which Dionysos offered them no direct warning, the god caused ivy and vines to envelop their looms, and snakes to appear in their wool-baskets, and wine and milk to drip from the ceiling. When he then proceeded to send them mad, they tore the son of Leukippe to pieces as though he were a young fawn, and rushed off to join the other women who had been under the god's power from the beginning; but the women chased them away because they were polluted by their crime, and they were transformed into a crow, a bat and an owl.[165] Ovid alters the story significantly, transferring the sisters to Thebes, omitting the rending of Hippasos, and having them transformed into bats inside the house.[166]

There were also notable myths in the Argolid in which Dionysos either afflicted all the women of the land with madness or else just the Proitides, the three daughters of Proitos, king of Tiryns. The tradition is rather complicated in this case since the Proitides were also said to have suffered this fate because they had offended Hera, and it would seem that two tales of separate origin regarding the princesses and the Argive women respectively came to be confused (and also combined). It is likely that only the more general outbreak was associated with Dionysos in the first place. Since the madness of the Argive women and of the Proitides too in most accounts was said to have been cured by the great seer Melampous, this myth will be examined in connection with the history of his family in Chapter 12 (see pp. 428–9).

Some lesser tales of resistance are worthy of passing mention. One is a cultic legend that was offered to explain the origin of the cult of Dionysos Melanaigis (of the black goat-skin) at Eleutherai on the borders of Attica and Boeotia. When the daughters of Eleuther, the eponymous founder of the town, were granted a vision of Dionysos in a black goat-skin, they greeted it with scorn, causing such anger to the god that he drove them mad. At the order of an oracle, their father then founded the above-mentioned cult so as to appease the god and bring an end to their madness.[167] Ovid states in passing that Akrisios, the grandfather of Perseus, once shut the god out of his city of Argos and suffered as a consequence;[168] and it was said that Dionysos caused Telephos to trip over a vine-branch as he was being pursued by Achilles, and so suffer a grievous wound (see p. 446), because he had refused to pay the god the honours that were due to him.[169]

According to a very strange Argive legend, Dionysos attacked Argos in the time of Perseus with a force of women from the Aegean islands known as the Sea-women; but Perseus defeated them in battle, killing most of the women, whose common grave could be seen in Argos in historical times.[170] In some accounts, Perseus even killed Dionysos himself, either during the fighting or by hurling him into the bottomless lake at Lerna;[171] or else Perseus and the Argives established good relations with Dionysos after the war and offered him high honour.[172]

In the preceding myths that tell of the coming of Dionysos, people are regularly sent mad by the god, and some are even torn to pieces by women under his influence. The god himself was commonly imagined as roaming at the head of a revel-rout of followers, some semi-divine and some human, Satyrs, Seilenoi and nymphs, and as his human votaries, women known as Maenads (Mainades, literally 'mad-women'), Bacchantes (Bakchai in Greek, Bacchae in Latin) or Thuiades (i.e. women possessed, inspired). The women were also known as Bassarides, probably 'wearers of fox-skins' after one form of their ritual costume, another being the skin of a fawn. They regularly perform curious miracles, making fountains of milk or wine spring up from the ground; they are madly strong, able to tear goats, bulls and human beings to pieces with their bare hands; fire will not burn them nor weapons harm them; and despite their violence to various animals, they have a deep sympathy with them, often suckling kids, fawns and so forth. All this, wild as it sounds, is but an idealization of the enthusiastic ritual of the god. His worshippers sought, by ecstatic dancing and perhaps also the use of wine, to become possessed by their god; they were then called after one of his numerous names,[173] Bakchai, from Bakchos. Tales in which they rend and devour an animal (or even human) victim were also founded in fact; these wild sacrifices were due to a desire to assimilate the god himself, who was conceived sometimes as human in form, sometimes as bestial, his most common manifestations being the bull and the goat, although he often appears as a serpent. He was in fact a god of the fertility of nature; and even if he tended to become a wine-god and god of ecstasy principally, he was never restricted to that sphere. The nature-spirits who belonged to his retinue will be discussed along with the nymphs in the next chapter (see pp. 212ff). Although it is certainly possible that the rites of Dionysos may have met with real opposition here and there, it would be unwise to interpret the opposition myths in any simple historical sense; they express something essential about his permanent nature as a god whose epiphany subverts the norms of everyday morality and civic society.[174]

The myth of Ikarios and Erigone

Of stories in which Dionysos is shown as peacefully spreading his gifts, the most famous is the Attic legend of IKARIOS, which is set in the days of Pandion I, an early mythical king of Athens (see p. 368). Even here the god's advent has baneful consequences for those whom he visits. Ikarios was a humble farmer who lived in the country outside Athens with his unmarried daughter ERIGONE. One day, he received a visit from Dionysos, who gave him a vine-cutting and instructed him in the art of wine-making. After growing some vines from the cutting and preparing the first vintage of wine, Ikarios loaded some wine-skins on to a cart and set off to spread the gift of Dionysos to the people of Attica; or in a simpler version of the story, the god simply gave him some wine and he set off with it immediately.[175] On reaching Marathon in the north-east of the province (or Hymettos to the south of Athens), Ikarios distributed some wine to the local peasants, who were delighted with it at first and drank down quantities of it without thinking to water it. When they became intoxicated, however, they thought that Ikarios had poisoned or bewitched them and clubbed him to death; or when some of them fell to the ground in a drunken stupor, their companions suspected the worst and killed Ikarios. They threw his body into a ditch, or buried it under a tree. It so happened that he had been accompanied by the family dog, Maira, which rushed home in distress and guided Erigone to the site, pulling at her dress. On discovering that her father was dead, Erigone was so grief-stricken that she hanged herself; and the dog met its own death soon afterwards, either because it hurled itself into a well in its grief, or because it died of starvation while guarding Erigone's body.[176]

Dionysos was naturally enraged by these events, and responded in familiar manner by driving the girls of Attica mad, so that they proceeded to hang themselves just as Erigone had done. Some said that Erigone had prayed before her death that the daughters of the Athenians should perish just as she had until the murderers were punished. It is also stated in some accounts that Athens was struck by a plague, either as the sole disaster or in addition to the epidemic of suicides. When the Athenians consulted the Delphic oracle, they were told that they would find relief from their trouble if they captured and killed the murderers of Ikarios, and if they founded a new festival, the Aiora (Feast of Swings), in honour of Erigone.[177] In the course of this women's festival, a song would be sung to Erigone under the title of Aletis (the Wanderer, ostensibly because she had wandered in search of her father), and girls would be swung from the branches of trees on swings with wooden boards. It hardly needs saying that the rites would have preceded the aetiological tale; swinging rituals of this kind were by no means peculiar to the Aiora.

Figure 5.9   Ikarios receives the gift of wine from Dionysos. Marble relief.
Izmir Museum. Photo: Richard Stoneman.

In a further story that was attached to this myth, the murderers of Ikarios were said to have
fled to Keos, an island to the south-east of Attica. To punish the Keans for sheltering
them, the dog Maira, who had been turned into the dog-star (Seirios, or Canicula in Latin)
after his death, scorched the land with his heat causing famine and disease. The island was
ruled at that time by Aristaios, son of Apollo (see p. 153), who had settled there after the
tragic death of his son Aktaion; and he sought the advice of his father's oracle, which
instructed him to offer sacrifices to expiate for the death of Ikarios, and to pray to Zeus to
send cooling winds to moderate the heat of the dog-star. So he founded the cult of Zeus
Ikmaios ('of moisture') on Keos together with the annual rites that supposedly elicited the
Etesian winds, cooling northerly winds that blew in the Aegean for some forty days after
the rising of the dog-star.[178]
    It was said that Zeus (or Dionysos) so pitied the fate of Ikarios, Erigone and the dog
Maira that he transferred them to the heavens as the constellations Bootes, Virgo and Canis
Major respectively[179] (unless the dog became the dog-star).

Dionysos and the pirates; his journey to India, and wife and loves

One of the most charming myths of Dionysos is the story of his encounter with a
crew of pirates. As first recounted in the *Homeric Hymn* (7) *to Dionysos*, it runs as
follows. Some Tyrrhenian pirates caught sight of the god when 'he appeared by the
shore of the barren sea, in the likeness of a young man in the first flower of his
youth; beautiful were the dark locks of hair that waved about him, and on his sturdy

Figure 5.10 Dionysos transforms the mast of a ship into a vine, and the sailors into dolphins. Attic cup by Exekias, c. 530 BC. Staatliche Antikensammlungen und Glyptothek, München.

shoulders he wore a purple cloak'.[180] Ignoring the warnings of their helmsman, who recognized that he was no ordinary mortal, the pirates seized him and hauled him on to their ship, imagining that he was a young man of royal birth who would fetch a valuable ransom. They were not deterred even though the bonds fell off of their own accord when they tried to tie him up. When they sailed out to sea with him, strange miracles began to occur. First the ship streamed with wine and a divine fragrance arose from it; and then a vine spread along the top of the sail, and an ivy-plant twined around the mast, and garlands appeared on the rowlocks; and finally and most fearsomely, the god turned himself into a lion and caused a towering bear to appear. Overcome by terror when the lion seized the captain, the pirates jumped overboard into the sea, where they were turned into dolphins. The helmsman alone survived because he was held back by the god, who now revealed his identity to him.[181] Ovid, who recounts the same story with many variations of detail, names the helmsman as a certain Acoetes (presumably Akoites in the origin Greek) from Maeonia (Lydia), and reports that he became an enthusiastic member of the god's retinue thereafter.[182]

The Homeric Hymn does not mention where the pirates found Dionysos or where they were planning to take him; it is stated in subsequent accounts that he asked the sailors to take him to the island of Naxos, but they intended to sell him in Asia instead.[183] He is picked up on Ikaria in Apollodorus' account, or on Chios in that of Ovid. The miracles are generally elaborated in these later accounts. Apollodorus suggests, for instance, that Dionysos turned the mast and the oars of the ship into snakes.[184] The whole story is rather different in a version from the astronomical literature. As Dionysos was being carried on the ship together with some companions of his, he ordered them all to sing; the pirates were so enchanted by the sound that they began to dance around, and finally leapt unwittingly into the sea, where they were transformed into dolphins as usual; and the god commemorated the incident by placing an image of one of the dolphins in the sky, hence the origin of the constellation of the Dolphin (Delphinus). This version would explain why dolphins are fond of music (a belief that is also reflected in the legend of Arion and the dolphin, see p. 582).[185]

The god's triumphs were not limited to a handful of pirates. According to a fairly early body of myth (Euripides knew of it), he penetrated as a conqueror far into the interior of Asia; after Alexander's real conquests, Dionysos' fabled ones were extended and he was represented as having reached India. Here, however, the mythologist need not follow him; for we are leaving the realm of genuine myth and saga for a strange world in which pseudo-history and politics are blended together. On the one hand it was obviously desirable, from the point of view of Alexander and his successors, that they should be treading in the footsteps of a god, especially one who was readily identified with all manner of oriental deities; on the other, Dionysos was equated with Osiris, and Osiris Euhemerized into an early king of Egypt who went about spreading culture, by force if necessary. So this Indian Dionysos, as we find him in the long and very dull Dionysian epic of Nonnus (fifth century AD) for example, is no Greek god but a hodge-podge of the mythology of several nations, stirred together by Hellenistic princes and Hellenistic theories. The result does not lack interest, but is outside our present scope.[186]

Dionysos' conduct in the amorous sphere is rather exceptional for an Olympian god; he took a mortal, Ariadne, as his consort (see p. 347) and had little or no interest in passing dalliances. She was granted immortality in some accounts, as in the *Theogony*, which reports that Zeus made her deathless and immortal on behalf of Dionysos.[187] The couple were credited with various children, notably Oinopion (Wine-face), who ruled in Chios and was remembered for his encounter with Orion (see p. 562), and Staphylos (Grape-bunch), who was the father of Rhoio and grandfather of Anios, the seer-king of Delos (see p. 569).[188]

There are only a few minor tales that tell of other liaisons, and none that involve sexual violence. Ampelos, who is mentioned by Ovid and Nonnus as having been loved by Dionysos, is no more than a personification of the vine (*ampelos*). As a token of his favour, Dionysos presented him with a vine, which was trailed over an elm-tree; and when the youth fell to his death one day as he was culling some grapes from it, the god transferred him to the sky as the star Vindemiator (the Vintager, in the constellation Virgo), whose early rising marked the start of the grape-harvest. Or else Dionysos transformed him into a vine after he fell from a bull.[189]

Some said that Dionysos seduced Althaia with the tacit approval of her husband Oineus (see p. 414), and so became the father of Deianeira, the second wife of Herakles (see

p. 279);[190] according to Ovid he seduced Erigone when he introduced the vine to Attica (see above), winning her favours by offering her a bunch of grapes;[191] in the Hellespontine tradition, Priapos was his son by Aphrodite (see p. 222); and Nonnus tells of his unrequited love for the Amazon Nikaia.[192] Women play a major part in his myths, of course, but generally in other roles, as his nurses and companions or as participants in his rites or opponents of his cult.

In earlier artistic representations, until the second half of the fifth century BC, Dionysos is portrayed as a mature bearded man dressed in long robes. Vase-paintings often show him wreathed in ivy or vine, and holding a cup (*kantharos*) or drinking-horn in his hand. He may wear a panther-skin or deer-skin. From the latter part of the fifth century onwards, he is usually portrayed as a youthful figure, without a beard, who is lightly dressed if at all. His special emblem, which may be carried by himself or by his attendants or worshippers, is the *thyrsos*, a staff that is tipped with an ornament resembling a pine-cone, and often entwined with ivy or vine. His cultic hymn is the dithyramb (*dithyrambos*, probably a word of foreign origin).

ATHENA

The wise virgin goddess ATHENA was a war-goddess, a protector of cities, and a divine patroness of arts and crafts. The fuller form of her name, Athenaia or Athenaie, was shortened to Athene in epic and to Athena in later Attic usage. She was scarcely less important that Hera herself, and of greater importance in Athens where she was worshipped as the city's patron goddess. Although scholars have long disagreed as to whether she gave her name to her favourite city or derived her name from it, the latter alternative seems more probable. She appears on a Linear B tablet from Knossos as Atana Potinija (i.e. the Mistress of Atana or Athana), and it has been argued that she may have originated as a Mycenaean palace-goddess who protected the households and citadels of early kings. This would plausibly account for two main aspects of her nature that might seem inconsistent at first sight; her martial character and her connection with peaceful handicrafts, notably weaving and spinning, that were usually practised by women within the household. If she was once a divine protectress of the fortress-palaces of Mycenaean princes, she would presumably have assumed a martial aspect, and would thus have been well-fitted to become the city-goddess of later times, Athena Polias or Poliouchos (of the city, protector of the city), the armed maiden who acted as a guardian of the city, often from her temple on its fortress-hill. Her temple of the Parthenon on the Athenian Acropolis, which had once been the site of a Mycenaean palace, is still the crowning monument of Athens. In her other main aspect as a goddess of handicrafts (Athena Ergane), her patronage was wide-ranging, even if her original concern may have been the domestic crafts that were exercised in palace households. Her interests were by no means confined to women's crafts, for she could also serve as a patroness to craftsmen such as carpenters, potters and jewellery-makers; in this connection, her cult at Athens was closely linked with that of Hephaistos (see p. 165). From this beginning, she developed increasingly into a goddess of wisdom in general, until late

Figure 5.11 Birth of Athena. Drawing from a bronze relief, shield band panel from Olympia, c. 550 BC.

mythographers could consider her a personification of Wisdom in the abstract. She was represented as a moral and righteous deity of whom few, if any, unworthy tales were told. At Rome, she was identified with the important Italian goddess Minerva, who was a patroness of arts and crafts like herself.

The birth of Athena

Athena entered the world in most remarkable circumstances, as explained in Chapter 3; for her father Zeus swallowed her mother Metis while that goddess was pregnant with her, and then brought her to birth from his own head (see p. 77). According to the *Homeric Hymn* (28) *to Athena*, she sprang from his head in full armour, presenting such a fearsome sight that the gods were seized with awe, and Olympos reeled, and the earth cried out, and the sea tossed and foamed; the sun-god Helios stayed his horses until she had removed the heavenly armour from her shoulders, and Zeus was delighted with her, then as ever.[193] Pindar refers likewise to the awesome nature of her advent, stating that she leapt forth with a mighty cry, causing Ouranos and mother Gaia to tremble before her; and he adds a further detail which appears more than a century earlier in the visual arts, namely that Hephaistos eased her delivery by cleaving Zeus's head with an axe. Although others are sometimes named as having performed this service, whether Prometheus or Hermes, or an obscure daimon called Palaimon, the divine blacksmith always remains the favourite choice.[194]

A further development in the story of Athena's birth was suggested by her ancient title of Tritogeneia (which is of uncertain origin and meaning). This was often interpreted to imply that she was born (*egeneto*) by one of the various rivers or other waters that bore the name of Triton. According to the best-known story of the kind, she emerged from her father's head by the river Triton or Lake Tritonis in Libya (and was then reared there by Triton, the god of the river or lake, see p. 106, in some accounts). Aeschylus remarks in the *Eumenides* that the Libyan river saw her birth, and Euripides indicates the same of Lake Tritonis in his *Ion*.[195] Or according to local legends set in Greece itself, she was reared by the god of the river Triton in Boeotia, or was born and reared at Aliphera in Arcadia after Zeus brought her to birth by a spring there called the Tritonis.[196] It is quite possible that her title of Tritogeneia implies some connection with water, since the stem *trito* also appears in the names of the sea-deities Amphitrite and Triton.

According to a Rhodian legend, the first men to pay honour to the goddess after her birth were the Heliadai, the sons of the sun-god Helios on Rhodes, who were advised by their father that the people who first offered sacrifice to her would enjoy her presence forever. They acted in such haste, however, that they forgot to light a fire beneath the sacrificial victims, hence (it was claimed) the distinctive Rhodian practice of offering fireless sacrifices to the goddess. She was apparently well pleased by their good intentions, for she granted them skill in all manner of crafts, enabling them to make statues that were so lifelike that they seemed to be alive. This must have been a fairly ancient myth since it is already recounted by Pindar.[197]

Athena as a martial goddess and patroness of handicrafts; her title of Pallas

As might be expected in the case of so important and popular a goddess, a clear idea of Athena's personal appearance was formed at an early stage. She is represented in art and literature as a stately virgin, with a beautiful but severe face, grey eyes, and a powerful yet graceful build. She is normally shown fully armed with an elaborately crested helmet, wearing the aigis which serves her as a cuirass and cloak (see p. 74), and holding a long spear; the Gorgon's head (see p. 242) may be set on her aigis or shield, and her special bird, the owl, may be seated on her shoulder. In representations of the battle between the gods and the Giants, she is always prominent, and is shown striking down some of the most formidable of the enemy. Her titles constantly bear witness to her warlike character; in various places she is called Promachos (Champion), Sthenias (Mighty), Areia (Warlike, or companion of Ares), and so forth. The other side of her character, as the peaceful protector of her worshippers and their leader in all manner of skilled occupations, is brought out likewise by a series of titles. She is Polias (Goddess of the City), Bouleia (She of the Council), Ergane (Worker), Kourotrophos (Nurturer of Children, a title shared by several other goddesses). From Macedonia to Sparta, her importance was second only to that of Zeus himself, whose favourite daughter she was; in Homer, he has his special pet-name for her, 'dear grey-eyes',[198] and pays special heed to her even to the extent of arousing jealousy among the other gods.

Pallas was one of the commonest titles of Athena. This was seldom if ever a cult-title, but rather a poetic appellation of the goddess; although it is always used in conjunction with her proper name in the Homeric epics, which often refer to her as Pallas Athenaie, it is also used on its own in the subsequent tradition, until it virtually becomes an alternative name for the goddess. Its meaning and origin are uncertain. According to the most favoured explanation, it means 'Girl' or 'Maiden' (cf. *pallakē*, a concubine); but it was also suggested in antiquity that it was derived from *pallein*, to brandish, for Athena was often represented as brandishing a lance.[199] A fragment from Philodemos (first century BC) refers to a story that explained the title by saying that she had once had a companion of that name, a daughter of Palamaon, whom she had accidentally killed.[200] Apollodorus recounts a similar story in which Athena was reared by Triton in the company of his daughter Pallas. The two girls used to practise warlike exercises, but one day they quarrelled, and as Pallas was about to strike Athena with the weapon that she was holding, Zeus intervened on his daughter's behalf by stretching out his aigis. As Pallas looked up in surprise, Athena fatally wounded her, but was afterwards sorry for her playfellow's death, and therefore made an image of her which she clad in the aigis.[201] This was the famous Palladion (properly a cultic image of Athena herself), which fell to the earth in the land of Troy and served as a protective talisman for the city (see p. 523). Another story stated that one of the Giants had been called Pallas and that Athena had killed him during the war between the gods and the Giants, and had flayed him to use his skin as a shield.[202]

It is but natural that a war-goddess should be interested in the instruments of war, and we find accordingly that Athena is credited with having invented the war-chariot and the art of horse-taming. There is a very interesting myth that tells how she came to the assistance of the hero Bellerophon in the latter connection. His endeavours to catch and tame the immortal winged horse Pegasos had proved unavailing, since no earthly bridle could control the beast. One night, however, as he was sleeping in Athena's shrine on the advice of a seer, the goddess appeared to him and placed a celestial bridle in his hand, telling him that he should use it to tame his divine mount. He awoke to find that the wondrous bridle was actually lying at his side, and he put it to good effect (see further on p. 434).[203] Warships were also of interest to Athena (which may well be the reason why the sports at her great festival of the Panathenaia included a regatta, which is unusual in ancient games), and we shall see that she supervised the building of the *Argo*, the mythical precursor of the fifty-oared ships (pentekonters) that were used as war-galleys in historical times. On the borderline between her peaceful and her warlike occupations we may place her connection with music. She was actually worshipped under the title of Salpinx (Trumpet) at Argos,[204] and the flute (*aulos*, Latin *tibia*; really more like the oboe than the flute of today) was her invention. According to Pindar, she was inspired to invent the flute and its distinctive music on hearing the wild lamentations that were poured forth by the two surviving Gorgons after the death of their sister Medusa.[205] Later sources report that she came to dislike her invention because it distorted her face unbecomingly when she played on it, and that she therefore discarded her flutes (they were generally played in pairs).[206] Marsyas the Satyr picked them up, to her great annoyance and ultimately to his own detriment (see further on p. 157).

As patroness of peaceful handicrafts, Athena presided over arts and crafts practised by men and women alike, but especially over the distinctively feminine accomplishments of spinning and weaving, which were usually exercised in the home by the housewife with the aid of her daughters and servant-women. Homer refers to the goddess's concern for these 'works of Athena',[207] and mentions her as having fashioned richly embroidered robes for herself and Hera.[208] She was extensively worshipped in this connection, and is occasionally shown with a spindle in artistic images, even if such representations are far less common than those that show her in martial guise. At the festival of the Panathenaia at Athens, she would be presented with a robe (*peplos*) that was woven by the women of the city to clothe her great statue in the Parthenon.

A memorable if not particularly early myth is recorded for Athena in connection with her interests as a weaver; for it was said that she once came into conflict with a mortal craftswoman, ARACHNE, and treated her most unfairly if Ovid is to be believed. This Arachne was the most skilful weaver in Lydia, and boasted that she could even outdo Athena herself. The goddess appeared to her in the form of an old woman and warned her against presumption; but when Arachne refused to hear reason, she threw off her disguise and agreed to accept the challenge that the girl had offered. Athena wove into her web the story of her contest with Poseidon for Athens, and, as due warning to Arachne, the stories of various mortals who had aroused the wrath of the gods and been signally punished. Arachne chose for her subject-matter a collection of scandalous tales of the loves of the gods. Although Arachne's tapestry was flawlessly executed, her choice of subject proved too much for Athena's temper, which was never of the mildest, and she tore the offending fabric to pieces and beat Arachne with her shuttle. In her distress at this treatment, Arachne tried to hang herself, but Athena saved her and turned her into a spider; she continues to weave most skilfully in her new form, and has incidentally provided modern zoologists with a name for the spider-kind.[209]

Athena and her Athenian foster-son Erichthonios

It is only to be expected that special legends should have been developed to account for Athena's close relationship with Athens. According to a familiar tale which has already been recounted (see p. 102), she initially established herself as the patron goddess of Attica by defeating Poseidon in a contest for the land. As we saw above, this particular legend follows a fairly common pattern, for Poseidon was said to have met with failure (or limited success) in contests for a variety of lands, including Argos, where he was defeated by Hera. The Athenians had a further legend, however, of a wholly distinctive nature, which told how Athena established an even closer connection with Athens by becoming the 'mother' (so far as this was possible for a virgin goddess) of Erichthonios, the autochthonous ancestor of the Athenian people. Although the remarkable myth of his conception is recorded in differing forms, the basic story is always the same: Hephaistos tried to make love to Athena, but she repelled him in such circumstances that he emitted some semen on to the ground, causing it to become fertilized. Even if she could not be the mother of the child, she was thus involved in his conception; and she claimed him as her own by adopting and rearing him after he was brought to birth.

In one account, Hephaistos fell in love with Athena and tried to court her, but she sought to escape him by hiding in Attica at a place called Hephaistion, which supposedly owed its name to this incident; and when he caught and embraced her in a state of high excitement, she thrust him away with her spear, causing him to ejaculate on to the ground.[210] Or when Hephaistos returned to Olympos after being hurled down to the earth by his mother, Zeus allowed him the choice of whatever he most desired, and he asked to marry Athena; but Athena had no intention of allowing any such thing, and defended her virginity by force when he came to claim her, with the same consequences as above.[211] Or in yet another version, Hephaistos once chased after her with amorous intent when she visited him to acquire some weaponry, for he was feeling frustrated after he had been abandoned by Aphrodite. She resisted him with such vigour, however, that he ejaculated over her leg; and she wiped the semen away in disgust with a piece of wool and hurled it to the ground.[212]

The latter detail was inserted to provide an explanation for the name of Erichthonios, who could therefore be said to have been born from the ground, *chthōn*, because it had been fertilized through contact with the piece of wool, *erion*. Even without the benefit of this refinement, it could be explained that the child was called Erichthonios because he had been born from the ground as a result of the struggle, *eris*, between Hephaistos and Athena.[213]

When the time came for Gaia to bring the child to birth, she rose up from the ground to hand him to Athena, who thus became his adoptive mother. Although Athena initially placed him in a chest and entrusted it to the daughters of Kekrops, king of Athens, this proved to be a short-lived experiment for reasons that will be considered later (see p. 365), and she soon received him back again. From then onwards she reared him herself on the Acropolis; and when he grew up, he won the

Figure 5.12 Artemis. Roman marble sculpture.
Cos museum. Photo: Richard Stoneman.

throne of Athens and established the royal line from which the subsequent kings would be descended. He honoured his divine foster-mother by founding her greatest Athenian festival, the Panathenaia (see further on p. 368), and he was buried in her precinct after his death.[214]

This is a most intriguing and ingenious story. The Athenians prided themselves on their autochthony, and Erichthonios is pictured accordingly as earthborn, after the manner of his predecessor Kekrops (and two other primordial rulers in the Hellenistic king-lists, see p. 367). On the other hand, he is no ordinary earthborn 'first man' like Kekrops, Pelasgos (see p. 537) and others of their kind who sprang up from the ground without need for a father; for he is conceived to Hephaistos, a god who was worshipped at Athens along with Athena as a patron of handicrafts, and he is brought into a quasi-filial relationship with the virgin goddess herself.

Athena was usually benevolent in her dealings with mortals. She would offer technical assistance in enterprises such as the construction of the *Argo* or the Wooden Horse, and was always ready to offer support and advice to favoured heroes such as Perseus and Herakles. She supported the Greeks in the Trojan War, as might be expected after her defeat in the judgement of Paris, and plays a prominent role in the *Odyssey*, providing invaluable assistance to Odysseus and his son Telemachos. In her one notable revenge-story from the early tradition, she sent a violent storm against the Greek fleet after the Trojan War to avenge an act of sacrilege committed during the sack of Troy (see p. 481). In one account of the blinding of Teiresias, Athena caused his blindness because he saw her naked; but she compensated him at his mother's request by granting him the gift of prophecy (see p. 330).

ARTEMIS AND HER COUSIN HEKATE

Artemis the virgin huntress

We must now pass on to another virgin goddess, ARTEMIS, whose essential characteristics are immediately evident in the conventional portrayal of her in works of art, which commonly represent her as a young, tall and vigorous maiden who wears a short tunic reaching to her knees, carries a bow and quiver, and is often accompanied by a stag or doe. In all accounts, she is a virgin who devotes herself to hunting, and loves wild, untamed lands and their wildlife (hence her title of Agrotera, 'She of the Wild', an epithet already applied to her in Homer[215]). Her favourite hunting-ground is Arcadia, the mountainous heartland of the Peloponnese, and she likes nothing better than to roam through the wilds in the company of her attendant nymphs, who are vowed to virginity like herself. The *Homeric Hymn to Aphrodite* remarks that she never falls under the sway of the goddess of love, 'for archery is her delight, and the slaying of wild beasts in the mountains, and lyres too, and dancing, and piercing cries and shady woods, and' – the poet adds – 'the cities of just men'.[216] The *Odyssey* speaks of her in similar terms, telling how Artemis the archer roams over the mountains of Arcadia, rejoicing in the pursuit of boars and swift deer in the company of her nymphs.[217] A gentler side of her nature is shown in her concern for the young of all living things, whether of wild beasts, as an aspect of her nature as the protectress of wild animals, or of human beings.

According to a chorus from Aeschylus, she is kind to the helpless cubs of ravening lions and delights in the tender sucklings of all beasts that wander the wild.[218] Hence her role as a goddess of childbirth who is appealed to by women in labour, and her titles of Locheia (she of the childbed) and Kourotrophos (nurse of the young). She is also a goddess who presides over the initiation of young girls. Although kindly on occasion, she is a formidable goddess who acts as an agent of death, especially with regard to women, and is ruthless in avenging any slight. This side of her nature is much to the fore in her mythical tales, which frequently show her inflicting death and disaster on mortals.

As is understandable for a goddess who was connected with the life of women, Artemis came to be associated (or indeed equated) with the moon, to an even greater extent than Hera. The Stoic allegorists in particular liked to identify her with the moon; if she is presented as fighting against Hera in the battle of the gods in the *Iliad*, for example, it is because the moon cuts through the air (*aēr*, as symbolized by Hera) in its circuits, an idea that is confirmed by the name of Artemis – if it can be interpreted as meaning *aēro-temis* or air-cutter![219] Plutarch suggests at one point that Artemis is associated with childbirth by virtue of her nature as a moon-goddess.[220] This is a comparatively late development, however; neither the earliest references to Artemis in literature nor the earliest forms of her cult hint in any way that she was a lunar goddess.

Artemis also came to be identified with the infernal goddess Hekate (see p. 193). The Hesiodic *Catalogue* already seems to connect the two goddesses by stating that Iphigeneia was transformed into Artemis Einodia (a regular title of Hekate) after she was rescued from sacrifice by Artemis (see p. 513).[221] The identification is certainly quite early if Aeschylus has it in mind when he refers to Artemis Hekate[222] (but it is possible that this is no more than an epithet meaning 'far-darting', corresponding to Apollo's epithet of Hekatos).

Artemis' connection with wild animals connects her, not with any Greek goddess, but with the old deity who is often called the Mistress of Wild Animals (a title suggested by the Homeric phrase *potnia thērōn*, as applied to Artemis in the *Iliad*[223]), a great goddess of very ancient origin who was honoured under various names by the people of Minoan Crete, prehellenic Greece and Asia Minor. As we will see, Artemis was equated with two Cretan goddesses of that type, Britomartis and Diktynna. The etymology of her name is too uncertain to provide any evidence on her origin; it seems to appear in Linear B, although this is not entirely certain. We can be sure, however, that she was originally independent of Apollo and Leto. If she originated as a Mistress of the Animals, it must be acknowledged that she has undergone a considerable change, since the Aegean and Eastern goddesses of that type were mature mother-goddesses while Artemis is young and virginal (except in her cult at Ephesus, where she was represented as a many-breasted fertility-goddess).

The main features of the classical Artemis are already in evidence in the Homeric epics. Even if she was pictured as brave and skilful in the hunting-field and frequently fierce in her character, she was never regarded as a martial goddess; and although she is described in the *Iliad* as a supporter of the Trojans, she makes no appearance in the battle-scenes. On the one occasion in which she engages in hostilities of a kind, in the so-called battle of the gods in the twenty-first book, her contribution is none too impressive, for when she ventures to oppose Hera, the senior goddess beats her around the ears with her own bow and quiver, causing her to run off to her father Zeus in a flood of tears.[224] It would naturally be wrong to conclude too much about her contemporary status from a burlesque of this kind. Although she is clearly out of place in the military world of the *Iliad*, Homer portrays her in her preferred environment in a passage in the *Odyssey*, in which he illustrates the standing of Nausikaa among her handmaidens by comparing it to that of Artemis among her attendant nymphs:

> Even as Artemis the archer roams over the mountains, along the ridges of lofty Taygetos or Erymanthos, taking delight in the pursuit of wild beasts and swift-running deer, and the nymphs of the countryside, daughters of aigis-bearing Zeus, join in the sport, and Leto is glad of heart, while Artemis rises head and shoulders above them all and may be recognized with ease though all are beautiful – so did the unmarried maiden [i.e. the princess Nausikaa, see p. 498] stand out among her attendants'.[225]

She was evidently regarded as being of some significance in her own sphere in Homer's time since she is mentioned quite often in both epics as a goddess of wild things and killer of women, and for the part that she played in legends such as the hunt for the Calydonian boar. Homer places a particular emphasis on her function as an agent of death. She sometimes acts on behalf of another god or of the gods in general, as when she is said to have killed Ariadne because of witness that was brought against her by Dionysos (see p. 348), or Orion because the gods disapproved of his love affair with the goddess Eos (see p. 561).[226] Or in a more general sense, any sudden or unaccountable death of a woman could be attributed to the arrows of Artemis; when Odysseus meets his mother in the Underworld, he asks her accordingly whether she had died from a long illness or whether Artemis had killed her with her kindly arrow (for death can be a merciful release); and a woman who dies by falling into the hold of a ship is said to have fallen victim to the archer Artemis.[227] Homer is less concerned with killings in which the goddess acts to avenge personal grievances, although he does mention that she killed Laodameia, daughter of Bellerophon, in anger.[228]

How Leto came to give birth to Artemis and Apollo on Delos

In considering the legends of Artemis, we must return to the beginning to examine the circumstances in which she and her brother Apollo were born. According to the earliest full account in the *Homeric Hymn to Apollo*, LETO (a daughter of the Titans Koios and Phoibe, see p. 37) conceived the divine twins to Zeus but had difficulty in finding a place to give birth when her pregnancy reached its full term; for although she visited any number of lands, from Crete and Athens to Lemnos and Naxos, all turned her away for fear of becoming the birthplace of her son Apollo, who might be expected to be a formidable god who would lord it over gods and mortals alike. In the end, however, she persuaded the island of Delos to accept her by promising that Apollo would establish his main sanctuary there, and that he would honour Delos above all other places.[229] All the foremost goddesses came to attend the birth, with the exception of Hera who remained on Olympos, keeping

Eileithuia, the goddess of childbirth, with her. As a consequence, Leto suffered the pains of travail for nine days and nights without relief, until the other goddesses sent the divine messenger Iris to summon Eileithuia. Encouraged by the promise of a splendid necklace strung with golden threads, Eileithuia soon arrived on the scene, and Leto was at last able to give birth to her children. She gave birth to Apollo on Delos, clasping a palm-tree as she did so, and to Artemis on Ortygia, presumably as her second-born.[230] Ortygia seems to have been a separate place at this stage, although it was usually identified with Delos itself in the later tradition.

In subsequent accounts, Leto's difficulties in finding a place for the birth are explained by the hostility of Hera, which seems more natural and makes a better story. According to Callimachus, Hera sent her son Ares and the goddess Iris (who often acts as a special envoy of Hera in later literature) to warn every place in the Greek world not to receive her husband's mistress; but poor rocky Delos, then called Asterie, dared to resist the goddess's threats and invited Leto to come and give birth there.[231] Or in Apollodorus' version, Leto was chased all over the earth by Hera until she arrived at Delos, where she gave birth to her twin children, beginning with Artemis, who immediately helped with the delivery of Apollo.[232] The latter detail was suggested, of course, by Artemis' function as a goddess who brought help to women in childbirth. This account of the order of the two births is consistent with the tradition on Delos, where the birthday of Artemis was celebrated a day before that of her brother. Hyginus offers yet another version, in which Hera decreed that Leto should not give birth in any place that was lit by the light of the sun. The pregnant Leto was pursued, furthermore, by the Delphian dragon Python, who knew by his own prophetic powers that she would give birth to a son who would kill him; but Zeus came to the aid of his mistress by ordering Boreas (the North Wind) to carry her off to Poseidon; and to enable her to give birth without contravening Hera's decree, Poseidon took her to Delos and covered it over with waves for a period to cut it off from the light of the sun. Four days after his birth, so the story tells, Apollo avenged Python's treatment of his mother by travelling to Central Greece to shoot him dead with one of his arrows (see p. 145).[233]

Leto's sister ASTERIE was sometimes drawn into the legend of the birth of Apollo and Artemis. The first traces of her story appear in an imperfectly preserved poem by Pindar, which states that Asterie was once pursued by Zeus but tried to escape him and dropped into the sea to become the island of Ortygia. Later sources confirm what these remains would suggest, namely that Zeus set out to seduce Asterie after rendering her sister pregnant, but she sought to escape him and finally turned into the island of Asterie or Ortygia, later known as Delos, on which her sister gave birth to the divine twins soon afterwards. Some sources add that she transformed herself (or less satisfactorily, was transformed by Zeus) into a quail – *ortyx* – in the course of her flight, hence the name of Ortygia (Quail Island).[234]

According to a picturesque tale of Hellenistic origin, Leto took her children to Lycia in the south-western corner of Asia Minor after giving birth to them on Delos, and tried to wash them in a local spring called Melita; but she was chased away by some herdsmen who wanted to water their cattle there. A band of wolves (*lykoi*) came to her aid, however, by showing her the way to the river Xanthos; and after quenching her thirst and bathing her children in the river, she dedicated it to Apollo and named the land Lycia (Wolf-land) in honour of her guides. She then retraced her steps to punish the uncharitable herdsmen.

On finding that they were still by the spring, she transformed them into frogs and cast them into its waters, hence the semi-aquatic life that frogs have lived ever since.[235] Or in Ovid's version, some malicious peasants obstructed Leto and muddied the waters when she tried to quench her thirst at a pool in Lycia, and she punish them immediately by turning them into frogs.[236] Apollo has Lycian connections as we have seen (p. 143), and Leto herself seems to have originated in Asia Minor.

According to Delian legend, two maidens called Hyperoche and Laodike arrived from the land of the Hyperboreans (a mythical people of the remote north, see p. 148) soon after the birth of Artemis and Apollo, bringing thank-offerings that their people had vowed to the goddess of childbirth to ensure Leto of an easy delivery. They died on Delos and were buried near the temple of Artemis, where their supposed tomb could be seen in historical times; the young people of the island would cut off a lock of their hair and lay it on the tomb before their marriage. These were not the only Hyperboreans who were said to have been buried on the island, for two other maidens, Arge and Opis (or Oupis) were said to have arrived from the north somewhat earlier, at the time of the birth of the twins, and to have been buried behind the temple of Artemis. The ashes from the thigh-bones of animals that were burnt on the altar of Artemis would be scattered on their joint tomb.[237]

The extreme holiness of Delos made it no place for a burial in ordinary circumstances. Excavations have revealed that the cults of both pairs of maidens were centred on Bronze Age tombs, whose original significance would have been long forgotten by the time when the cults were developed. The name of Opis was derived from a cultic title of Artemis herself. In one account of the death of Orion, Artemis shot him for trying to rape Opis (see p. 563). Callimachus diverges from Herodotus by stating that the first Hyperborean offerings went brought by Oupis along with two companions, Loxo and Hekaerge[238] (cf. Loxias as a title of Apollo, and Hekaergos and Hekaerge as titles of Apollo and Artemis respectively). Hekaerge may have been an alternative name for Arge. When Delphi was attacked by the Gauls in 279 BC, two ghostly Hyperboreans, Hyperochos and Laodokos (whose names were evidently based of those of the first pair of Hyperborean maidens mentioned above) were supposed to have fought in its defence.[239]

There was a curious tale in which the pregnant Leto was said to have turned herself into a wolf to escape the persecutions of Hera, and to have travelled in that form from the land of the Hyperboreans to Delos; ever since that time, so the story would have us believe, wolves have given birth to their young only on the twelve days of the year that correspond to those on which the goddess made her long journey.[240]

Early deeds of Artemis; the goddess and her attendants

If Artemis assisted her brother in some of his earlier exploits, as was often claimed, her adventures began soon after her birth; it was sometimes said that she helped Apollo to shoot Python,[241] the Delphian dragon (see p. 145), and it was often said that she helped in the killing of Tityos, or indeed killed him on her own (see p. 148). She later joined together with her brother to kill all the Niobids (see p. 157), and shot Koronis, an unfaithful mistress of Apollo, on her brother's behalf (see p. 149). Although she usually had nothing to do with war, she played her part in the battle between the gods and the Giants, making good use of her bow (see p. 90).

Some of the most distinctive myths of the virgin goddess tell of her actions with regard to nymphs or maidens who accompanied her on the hunt. By becoming her companions and attendants, they bound themselves to the same way of life as their divine mistress, and she was merciless towards those who lost their virginity or ceased to join her on the hunting-field. The most famous of her erring associates (if that is proper term for a victim of rape) was the Arcadian heroine KALLISTO, who was likewise an ancient figure, and may well have originated as a by-form of the goddess herself (who had a cult in Arcadia, and in Athens too, as Artemis Kalliste, 'the most beautiful'). Kallisto was raped by Zeus and became pregnant with a son, Arkas, who was destined to give his name to Arcadia (see p. 540). Some months afterwards, when Artemis ordered her companions to undress to bathe with her in the midday heat, she noticed that Kallisto was pregnant and drove her away in a fury, and even transformed her into a bear by way of punishment in some accounts.[242] The myth is preserved in many different versions; see pp. 541–2 for a more detailed discussion. According to another tale of the kind, a certain MAIRA, daughter of Proitos, was shot by Artemis for ceasing to attend the hunt after she was seduced by Zeus. She was evidently not killed immediately since she survived to give birth to her child, a son Lokros who helped Zethos and Amphion in the building of Thebes. Such is her story as imperfectly transmitted in a brief summary of an account by Pherecydes; it may have been very ancient since Homer includes a Maira among the famous women who were seen by Odysseus in the Underworld.[243]

In one account of the myth of HIPPE, daughter of Cheiron, she was transformed into a horse by Artemis because she had ceased to honour the goddess and to accompany her on the hunt;[244] but there were many versions of her story, and it was more commonly said that she prayed to the gods to transform her to prevent her father from discovering that she was about to give birth to a child (see further on p. 409). Euripides makes a passing reference to a story in which Artemis drove an unnamed daughter of Merops from her company 'on account of her beauty', and turned her into a hind with horns of gold (perhaps the Cerynitian hind, see p. 259); she was presumably another companion who was raped or seduced on account of her beauty.[245]

BRITOMARTIS was a faithful Cretan companion of Artemis who attracted the lust of Minos. We have Solinus' word for it that her name is Cretan and meant 'sweet maid'; and she was properly a goddess, a Cretan deity who came to be identified with Artemis herself. In the earliest surviving account by Callimachus, her myth runs as follows. Minos, king of Crete, conceived a desperate passion for her, and pursued her over the hills of the island for nine months as she tried to hide from him as best she could, now under lofty oaks, now in the water-meadows; but finally, when she was all but caught, she was obliged to leap over a cliff into the sea. She survived unharmed, however, because she fell into the nets (*diktya*) of some fishermen; and she was therefore known from that time onwards as Diktynna (the Lady of the Nets).[246] This was the name of a Cretan goddess who was very like Britomartis, and was fully identified with her outside Crete itself; by means of a false etymology, this myth explains Diktynna's name (which was probably derived from that of Mt Dikte in Crete) as a title of Britomartis. To explain why myrtle was never used in connection with the cult of Britomartis/Diktynna, it was added that a myrtle branch had become entangled in Britomartis' clothing during her flight, and that she had therefore hated the plant ever since.[247]

A supplement to Britomartis' usual tale is provided in an anthology of Hellenistic transformation myths. To escape from Minos, she sought refuge with some fishermen who hid her in their nets; and she then sailed across to Aegina with a fisherman called Andromedes. At the end of the voyage, this fisherman added to her travails by trying to rape her, but she managed to escape by jumping overboard and hiding in a wood on the island. She then vanished without trace; and since a statue appeared in place of her in the sanctuary of Artemis, the Aiginetans founded a cult to her at the place where she had become invisible (*aphanēs*), under the name of Apheia.[248] It is difficult to tell when this ancient but obscure goddess first came to be identified with Britomartis/Diktynna; it is quite possible that the identification was relatively late, perhaps originating in the learned poetry of the Hellenistic era.

Tales of vengeance

If Artemis was harsh toward erring companions, she naturally showed no pity to those who offended against her own person. In one account at least, she killed her only male hunting-companion, Orion, because he tried to court or rape her (see pp. 563–4). She was often said to have contrived the death of the Aloadai for a similar reason (see p. 92), and she shot Bouphagos (Ox-eater), an obscure hero of her favourite land of Arcadia, when he tried to rape her.[249] When Aktaion happened to catch sight of her as she was bathing in a spring, she contrived a gruesome death for him by transforming him into a stag and causing him to be hunted down by his own hounds (see p. 298); but in a lesser-known story, she was comparatively lenient towards a certain Siproites who saw her naked in Crete, for she merely turned him into a woman.[250] According to a tale of a rather different kind, a cultic legend associated with the shrine of Alpheian Artemis at Letrinoi in Elis, the Peloponnesian river-god Alpheios (who was of an amorous disposition, see p. 42) once planned to rape her at Letrinoi while she was celebrating a night festival with her nymphs, but she caught wind of his intent and covered her own face and the faces of her companions with mud, so making it impossible for him to pick her out.[251]

Artemis also took appropriate action if she were denied her proper honours in cult or slighted in any respect. She sent a huge boar to ravage the lands of Oineus, king of Calydon, to punish him for forgetting her while he was offering sacrifices to all the gods (see p. 416); and she filled the marriage-chamber of Admetos with coils of snakes as an omen of early death to avenge a similar offence (see p. 151). Or in a less familiar legend, she shot a Phocian heroine, Chione, daughter of Daidalion, for criticizing her during a hunt or for claiming to be more beautiful than her.[252] The most interesting of these revenge myths is that in which Artemis demanded the sacrifice of Iphigeneia to punish an offence committed by her father Agamemnon. In many accounts, including the oldest of all, Iphigeneia turns out to be far from a victim, for she is often said to have been rescued by the goddess at the last moment and brought into close association with her; see further on pp. 447 and 513.

The Romans identified Artemis with the Italian woodland goddess Diana, who was not unlike her in many respects. The Italian goddess had no native statues of course, so in art the familiar figure of the huntress Artemis (Diane chasseresse) was used for both alike. As has been mentioned, the goddess is typically portrayed as a young and beautiful woman, with her chiton girt up to the knee, generally armed with a bow and quiver, and regularly accompanied by a stag or other beast. She is also shown in long robes, however. In so far as she came to be identified with the moon, her head may be surmounted by a crescent. Her emblems, besides attendant beasts and weapons, include the torch, which is a common attribute of goddesses of fertility because light is very commonly associated with life and birth. This is a point in which she resembled the goddess Hekate, who also aided women in child-birth and carried torches as a regular attribute.

Hekate as a high goddess and as queen of the ghosts

HEKATE is a cousin of Artemis in the standard Hesiodic genealogy, as the daughter of Leto's sister Asterie;[253] and the two goddesses, though certainly of separate origin, were quite frequently identified, probably from the classical period or even earlier. As commonly pictured in classical and later times, however, Hekate was very different from Artemis in most respects, as a grim and fantastic goddess who was queen of the ghosts, and therefore of all magic, the blacker the better.

To judge by the spread of related place-names and other evidence, Hekate originated in Caria in the south-western corner of Asia Minor, where she would have been worshipped as a principal goddess; but she was introduced to Greece quite early, certainly by the seventh century BC, as a goddess who was honoured in private cult. Although Homer makes no mention of her (as is understandable in view of the private nature of her worship), Hesiod praises her at some length and with evident personal enthusiasm, as a universal goddess. He declares that she bestows all manner of gifts on worshippers who enjoy her favour, such as wealth, success at the games, skill in horsemanship, victory in war, and good counsel; and he states that Zeus granted her exceptional privileges in spite of her Titan birth, both in heaven and on earth and at sea. The only realm to be left out of account is the Under-world, the very realm that is most closely associated with her in the later tradition. Precisely because the poet makes her the special focus of his religious ardour, his 'hymn to Hekate', as it has been called, throws little light on the individual character of the goddess.[254] Although we have no definite evidence on the subject, she was presumably worshipped in her original homeland as a great goddess who was not primarily concerned with the uncanny and magical. If she had no concern at all for such matters, however, it is hard to understand why she should have developed into the goddess who is familiar to us from classical and later accounts in Greece. The *Homeric Hymn to Demeter* (probably late seventh century BC) links her to Persephone in a way that suggests that she already had Underworld connections at the time of its composition. For the poem recounts that she heard Persephone cry out as she was being abducted by Hades and told Demeter of this, and that when Persephone later returned to visit her mother, Hekate embraced her and became her attendant and companion from that time onward.[255] It is clear from references in tragedy that Hekate was associated with spooks and the pathways of the night by the classical period at any rate.[256]

In her capacity as queen of ghosts, Hekate was also the goddess of pathways (Enodios) and of cross-roads (hence her title of Trioditios, 'she of the three ways'), for crossroads were regarded as great centres of ghostly and magical activity as in modern folklore. It is apparently for that reason that Hekate's statues often represent her in triple form, so that she may look simultaneously down all the roads that meet at the point where she is standing. She would send spooks up into the world at night, or would appear in her own right, especially at crossroads under the dim light of the moon, to roam the pathways at the head of a crew of ghosts. Her retinue, the host of Hekate, was made up of shades of the restless dead who had died prematurely or violently, or had received no proper burial. Since she would also be accompanied by loud-barking daimonic dogs, her passage bears a resemblance to the 'Wild Hunt' of Western European folklore. The goddess and her night-wandering companions might inflict madness or epilepsy on mortals who encountered them, and was certainly a source of night-terrors and bad dreams. To propitiate Hekate and her host, and so keep them at a safe distance, the Greeks would leave offerings for them at crossroads at the turn of the month; known as 'Hekate's suppers' (*deipna Hekatēs*; or simply *Hekateia*), these consisted of cakes, eggs, cheeses and the like.[257] Dogs were also sacrificed to Hekate, and the remains of purificatory sacrifices might be offered to the goddess and her crew with averted gaze. Magicians and sorcerers, on the other hand, would summon her aid for their own nefarious purposes, or even try to summon her up in person. The sorceress Medeia invokes her as her mistress and helper in Euripides' *Medeia*; and in Theocritus' second Idyll, a young woman is shown as praying for her help in some love-magic:

> Shine brightly for me, o Moon, for it is to you that I shall chant, silent goddess, and to infernal Hekate, who causes the very dogs to tremble before her as she passes over the graves of the dead and the dark blood. Hail grim Hekate, and remain with me to the end, so that these drugs of my making may prove as powerful as any of Kirke's, or of Medeia's, or of golden-haired Perimede's.[258]

On curse-tablets (*defixiones*) likewise, the writer often calls on Hekate to put a curse into action.

APHRODITE

The goddess of love

The one great goddess who remains to be considered is APHRODITE, who presided over sexual attraction and the pleasures of love (*ta Aphrodisia*) and all that is associated with them. In the standard account of her birth, as recounted by Hesiod, she grew from the foam (*aphros*) that gathered around the severed genitals of Ouranos (Sky) after they were thrown into the sea by his son Kronos (see p. 67). This would mean that she was born at an earlier stage than any other Olympian god. Homer offers a different account, however, which may well be of earlier origin, describing her as the daughter of Zeus and Dione (see p. 80), and thus as an Olympian god of the second generation like Apollo and Artemis.[259] As to her historical origin, it may be safely said that she owed a great deal, and probably almost all, to oriental influences. From the *Iliad* onwards, she is often called Kypris, 'Lady of Cyprus', where her cult was certainly very old and as certainly of non-Greek origin;[260] and she also had an ancient association with Cythera off the south-eastern corner of the Peloponnese, as is acknowledged by Hesiod, who states that she drifted past the island after her birth, hence her title of Kytheria, before stepping ashore on Cyprus which was destined to be her main home. Her shrine on Cythera, which contained an armed wooden idol of the goddess, was thought to be the earliest in Greece; Herodotus regarded it as being of Phoenician foundation.[261] It is in fact more than likely that she was a goddess of Semitic origin, as an adaptation of the great Semitic love-goddess who was known to the Phoenicians as Astarte and to the Babylonians as Ishtar. Aphrodite's title of Ourania, the Heavenly, corresponds to Astarte's as Queen of Heaven, and various aspects of her cult, such as the use of incense-altars and dove-sacrifices, and the occasional practice of temple-prostitution as at Corinth, can be related to cultic practices associated with Astarte/Ishtar.

Aphrodite was the goddess of love, beauty and fertility, and also of married love to some extent, although Hera tended to dominate in that area. She had marine associations as a goddess who was naturally associated with water and moisture, and was said to have risen up from the sea in the usual myth of her birth (hence her title of Anadyomene, 'she who rises up from the sea'); she was often shown with a shell as her attribute, or with a dolphin, and was widely honoured as a protector of sailors who could bring calm to the sea or victory in sea-battles. She had various titles in this connection, such as Pontia, Thalassia and Einalia (all meaning 'of the sea') or Euploia (as a goddess who can ensure 'a good voyage'). Her martial aspect, which may seem more surprising, can be explained by a similar trait in her Semitic equivalent; she was worshipped as an armed war-goddess at Cythera and Sparta especially, and as Nikephoros, the Bringer of Victory, at Argos. This is no doubt the real reason why she was commonly united with Ares, who was her cult-partner here and there, and her lover or husband in mythology (see p. 201). It was doubtless because of her connection with fertility that she was often associated with Hermes in cult. Although the Greeks followed Hesiod in relating her name to the *aphros*, sea-foam, from which she had supposedly sprung, its true origin and meaning are wholly uncertain; no Indo-European etymology has been proposed that is at all convincing.

Plato and Xenophon draw a sharp distinction between Aphrodite Ourania on the one hand, as the 'heavenly' goddess who presides over the highest form of love that is directed primarily towards the soul of the beloved, and Aphrodite Pandemos (of all the people) on the other hand, as the goddess who concerns herself with vulgar or mercenary love that is purely carnal in nature.[262] This is a literary conceit of a moralistic character that deliberately reinterprets the meaning of these cultic titles. Aphrodite was no less a goddess of sexual desire under her title of Ourania, which was derived, as we have seen, from her Semitic counterpart, who was not noted for her high-mindedness; and far from bearing immoral connotations, Aphrodite's title of Pandemos represents her as a civic goddess whose worship unites the whole people.

At Athens, Aphrodite Pandemos was a quiet and staid marriage-goddess, in whose worship nothing untoward seems to have taken place; according to local legend, Theseus founded the cult after he had united the people of Attica into a single state.[263] Plato's reinterpretation of these titles (if it was indeed his own) left its mark on the subsequent tradition nonetheless. Theocritus, for instance, opposes Aphrodite Ourania to Aphrodite Pandemos in one of his epigrams; and Pausanias reports a Theban tradition which claimed that Harmonia (the divine wife of the first king of the city, see p. 297) had given Aphrodite her title of Ourania in relation to love that was free from the lust of the body, and of Pandemos in relation to carnal love.[264] If exception is made for certain local exoticisms, such as the temple-prostitutes at Corinth, the public cult of Aphrodite in Greece was eminently respectable for the most part.

In 464 BC, a Corinthian athlete called Xenophon vowed to dedicate a hundred prostitutes to the service of Aphrodite in his native city if he won an Olympian victory. When the vow was due to be fulfilled after he won a double victory in the foot-race and pankration (all-in wrestling), Pindar was commissioned to write an ode to be sung in Aphrodite's temple, and responded with his customary panache by writing a poem that began,

> Guest-loving girls, servants of Persuasion [Peitho, see below] in wealthy Corinth, who burn the golden tears of fresh incense, often soaring upward in your minds to Aphrodite, the heavenly mother of loves, she who has granted you to pluck without reproach, girls, on lovely couches the fruit of gentle beauty . . .[265]

Eros and other associates of Aphrodite

As the goddess of love, Aphrodite is regularly attended by EROS, the personification of amorous desire, who fulfils his purposes by inspiring love in gods and mortals alike. After initially presenting him as a primordial cosmogonic power (see p. 23), the *Theogony* later reports that he attended Aphrodite from the time of her birth, and that he accompanied her to Olympos when she ascended to join the other gods.[266] In the subsequent literature, he is often tied to her even more closely, as being not merely her attendant but her son; the idea first appears in a fragment from Simonides, which describes him as being the merciless child whom she bore to Ares.[267] On this matter of his birth, however, all manner of conflicting suggestions were offered by the poets and inventors of cosmogonies. The early lyric poets have much to say about Eros and about the irresistible power that he exerts on his victims. Bitter-sweet, a loosener of limbs, he shakes the poet's heart like a wind descending on the mountain oaks; he is also a weaver of tales, an enchanter, who uses his magical arts to cast his victim into the nets of Aphrodite.[268] Euripides is the first author to suggest that he works this compulsion by means of his arrows.[269] In addition to being a god of the poets and cosmogonists, he was honoured quite extensively in cult. Some of his cults were certainly very old, notably that at Thespiai, where he was represented by an aniconic stone image which was doubtless of venerable antiquity.[270] His cult and images in the gymnasia reflect his concern with homosexual love, as awakened by the bodily attractions of young men and boys. In the Hellenistic period, as the idea of romantic love came increasingly to the fore in literature, Eros came to be imagined above all as a capricious and playful child-god; rather than being shown as a handsome young athlete, or as a young boy as in classical art, he was now generally shown as a pretty child, a little winged archer who was ever ready to work mischief on gods or mortals with his arrows. This is the form in which he has usually been imagined since the Renaissance, as innocuous Cupid rather than the old Greek Eros.

Although Eros can quite often be seen fluttering around in seduction-scenes or abduction-scenes on Attic vases, he is seldom introduced into mythical narratives, appearing for the most part in later writings and in a subordinate role, as part of the divine machinery for making one person fall in love with another. In Apollonius' Hellenistic epic, for instance, Aphrodite approaches her naughty and disobedient son to ask him to cause Medeia to fall in love with Jason; and she wins his compliance by promising to give him a beautiful ball, all golden except where it was overlaid with a spiral of dark blue, a marvel that had been made for the infant Zeus by his nurse Adrasteia.[271] Or in Ovid's *Metamorphoses*, Apollo rebukes the child-god for presuming to employ his own favourite weapon, the bow, so annoying the boy that he pays Apollo back by shooting a sharp golden arrow into him to cause him to fall in love with the nymph Daphne (see p. 155), and a blunt lead-tipped arrow into Daphne to cause her to take an aversion to her new admirer.[272]

As a fairy-tale with a considerable allegorical content, the story of Cupid (i.e. Eros) and Psyche (the soul personified) in Apuleius' *Golden Ass* stands apart from the ordinary mythology of Eros. It was probably based on a Hellenistic original. According to this tale, Psyche was a young princess who became so celebrated for her beauty that Aphrodite grew jealous and sent Cupid to wreak vengeance on her, telling him to make her fall in love with some utterly worthless man; but the plan went wrong because Cupid himself fell in love with the girl. Now Psyche was so extremely beautiful that no man dared to court her; and when her parents consulted an oracle of Apollo about the matter, they were told to expose her in bridal robes on a mountain, where some apparently fearsome bridegroom would come to claim her. When they did so, she was carried away by the wind to a deep valley, and found her way into a wondrously beautiful palace nearby. This turned out to be a magical palace where she was tended by invisible servants; and Cupid visited her there in her bedroom each night, and made love to her in the dark without revealing his identity. In the mean time, her two elder sisters had set out in search of her, and Cupid allowed them to see her, though against his better judgement, warning her to ignore them if they tried to persuade her to discover what he looked like. Such was their envy at her good fortune that they cast her into a panic by suggesting that her mysterious husband was an enormous snake who would finally swallow her alive. At their urging, she hid a knife and a lamp in her bedroom so as to kill him while he was asleep; but when she shone the lamp on him to do so, she saw that he was a winged youth of surpassing beauty and fell more in love with him than ever. All might have been well if some scalding oil from the lamp had not dripped on to his shoulder, causing him to wake with a start and then abandon her in anger at her disobedience. Overcome by regret and longing, the unfortunate Psyche, who was pregnant by now, roamed the world in search of him until she finally fell into the hands of Aphrodite, who forced her to undertake four seemingly impossible tasks. She was to separate a large heap of seeds and grains into its different components in a single day; but the ants of the neighbourhood took pity on her and she achieved the task with their aid. She was to fetch some wool from a flock of homicidal sheep; but a reed was stirred by some divine wind to tell her to wait until they were asleep, and then collect the wool that had become snagged on the thorns of the surrounding plants. She was sent to fetch a jar of water from the sacred streams of the Styx; but the eagle of Zeus remembered a debt that he owed to Cupid (who had helped him to carry off Ganymedes) and fetched the water on her behalf. And finally, she was to fetch Persephone's beauty-casket from the Underworld. She succeeded once again, with some supernatural aid, but disaster struck when she allowed her curiosity to get the better of her and opened the casket, for she was immediately overcome by a death-like sleep. Cupid had recovered from his wound in the meantime, and had come to miss Psyche so greatly that he had flown off to find her. On his arrival, he shut the cloud of sleep back into the chest and awakened Psyche by pricking her with one of his arrows. He then sought the permission of Zeus to take her up to heaven, where she lived with him as his immortal wife, bearing him a child called Voluptas (Pleasure).[273]

Two lesser figures who are mentioned as companions of Aphrodite (and sometimes of other gracious female deities such as the Charites and Horai) are HIMEROS and POTHOS, two personifications of amorous yearning. Hesiod states that Himeros – whose name means much the same as that of Eros – attended Aphrodite from her birth along with Eros, and that his house lay on Olympos close to those of the Muses and Charites.[274] Pothos (Desire, Yearning) enters the literary record somewhat later, but then appears much more frequently. Aeschylus is the first author to refer to him unequivocally as a personified being, mentioning him together with Peitho (the personification of amatory persuasion) as a child and assistant of Aphrodite.[275] A purely decorative and allegorical being, he has no myths at all.

Eros had a counterpart or double in ANTEROS (Counter-love, Love Returned); the altar of Anteros near the Acropolis at Athens had the following tale attached to it. An Athenian boy called Meles spurned the love of a metic (resident alien) called Timagoras, and told him to jump off the Acropolis if he really wanted to prove his love. But when the despairing Timagoras took him at his word and actually did so, Meles felt such remorse that he threw himself down from the same spot. In commemoration, the metics set up the altar of Anteros.[276] Pausanias mentions that there was a relief at the youths' training-ground at Elis that showed Anteros trying to wrest a palm-branch from Eros.[277]

Aphrodite and Adonis

In considering the myths of Aphrodite herself, we will do well to begin with the most easterly stories, of which the best known is that of her love for ADONIS; for here we have, without a doubt, the familiar oriental tale of the Great Mother and her divine lover. The name Adonis is probably derived from the Semitic ꜥadon, lord, and he is quite often identified with Tammuz, as for instance in the vulgate of Ezekiel.[278] To begin with the story of his birth, Myrrha (or Smyrna), the daughter of Theias, king of Assyria (or of Kinyras, see below), refused to honour Aphrodite, provoking the goddess to inspire her with an incestuous passion for her own father. With the connivance of her nurse, she slipped into his bed under cover of darkness, and he slept with her for twelve nights without realizing who she was; but when he discovered at last, he was horrified and chased after her sword in hand. As he was about to catch up with her, she prayed to the gods to be removed from human sight, and they responded by turning her into the tree that bears her name, the myrrh-tree (*myrrha* or *smyrna* in Greek). After the usual time of gestation for a human child, the bark of the tree broke open and Adonis was brought to birth.[279]

In Antoninus' version, which may have been derived from Nicander, Theias became curious about the identity of his mistress after she had become pregnant, and shone a light on her one night. In the anguish of the moment, she gave birth to her child prematurely, and prayed to be removed from the company of both the living and the dead; and Zeus responded by turning her into a myrrh-tree, which weeps resinous tears every year. Her father committed suicide for his own part.[280] Adonis was usually said to have been born from the tree, however, as in the version above. His mother is often described as a daughter of Kinyras (properly a king of Cyprus, see p. 573, although Hyginus refers to him as a king of Assyria by confusion with Theias),[281] and Aphrodite is often said to have performed the transformation.[282] In the lengthy narrative by Ovid, Myrrha took to flight after her father Kinyras discovered her identity by shining a lamp on her. She wandered for nine months until she arrived at the land of the Sabaeans in south-western Arabia (which was the main source of myrrh and frankincense in ancient times, and thus a suitable place for her transformation). She was turned into a tree there when she prayed to be removed from the living and the dead, and gave birth to her child in that form.[283]

The earliest evidence for Adonis is contained in reports on the Hesiodic corpus (probably the *Catalogue* in this case); he was apparently described there as a son of Phoinix, son of Agenor, and there may have been no exceptional story associated with his birth.[284]

When Aphrodite caught sight of the infant Adonis, she was so entranced by his beauty that she shut him up in a chest to conceal him from the other gods, and entrusted him to Persephone; but Persephone was equally impressed by his beauty and wanted to keep him for herself. The dispute was referred to Zeus, who decided that Adonis should spend a third of each year with each goddess and the rest of the year by himself. Since Adonis preferred to spend his own share of the year with Aphrodite, he spent the greater part of his time with her until she was robbed of his company by his early death; for as soon as he was old enough, he began to go out hunting, and was gored to death by a wild boar.[285] His death was sometimes regarded as having been more than an accident, for some accounts state that the war-god Ares, as the lover or husband of Aphrodite, sent the boar against him out of jealousy, or transformed himself into a boar to attack him;[286] or else Artemis sent the boar against him[287] (presumably to punish Aphrodite for having caused the death of her own favourite, Hippolytos, see p. 358).

In a less orthodox account of the arbitration between Aphrodite and Persephone, Zeus delegated the decision to the Muse Kalliope, who ordered that Adonis should spend half of the year with each goddess; and Aphrodite was so enraged by her judgement that she incited the women of Thrace to dismember Orpheus (here described as a son of Kalliope).[288]

Ovid offers a divergent account of Adonis' story, saying that he was brought up by local nymphs after he was born from the myrrh-tree in Arabia, and first attracted the attention and love of Aphrodite when he grew up to become an exceptionally handsome young man. Since hunting was his main enthusiasm, she abandoned her usual habits and haunts to follow him through the wilds on his hunting-trips, tucking her clothes up to her knees just as though she were Artemis. She kept well clear of the fiercest beasts, however, such as lions, wolves and boars, and urged her young favourite to do the same, warning that his youthful beauty was no defence against their teeth and claws. Her worst fears were realized when he was carried away by his zeal one day and tried to kill a wild boar, for it leapt up and fatally wounded him with a bite in the groin.[289]

According to Ovid, the grief-stricken Aphrodite sprinkled Adonis' blood with nectar, causing a fragile blood-red flower, the anemone, to spring up from it.[290] Or in another account, the first rose sprang up from the blood of Adonis, while the anemone sprang from Aphrodite's tears; or the anemone, which had previously been white, was stained red by the blood of Adonis, and the rose was turned red likewise when Aphrodite pricked herself on a thorn as she was wandering around bare-footed in her grief; or Adonis was transformed into the rose.[291]

Under the prettiness of this legend, we can see the outlines of an oriental myth of the Great Mother and of her lover who dies as the vegetation dies, but always comes to life again. This is most obvious in the story in which he spends part of the year – evidently the dead season – with Persephone, queen of the Underworld, but returns for the rest of the year to the arms of Aphrodite. This is simply a repetition, of course in a rather different context, of the myth in which Persephone herself spends part of the year below with Hades and part above with her mother, the corn-goddess Demeter (see p. 128). The death of the youthful favourite at the time of the dying of nature is also figured in the story of his premature death in the hunting-field. His cult as a dying god is already in evidence in the poetry of Sappho (late seventh century BC) and was popular in Greece from the fifth century. From Sappho we have the following two lines: 'Tender Adonis is dying, Kytherea [i.e. Aphrodite]; what are we to do?', 'Beat your breasts, girls, and rend your robes'; and a complete, if more artificial, lament for Adonis is preserved among the bucolic poetry of the Hellenistic period.[292] Besides the ceremonial singing and wailing of dirges, which were sometimes conducted over an effigy of the dead boy, the cult of Adonis, which was a women's cult for the most part, involved the preparation of 'gardens of Adonis', in which plants were germinated in very shallow soil in pots or potsherds, and so grew up with unnatural speed and withered just as quickly.[293]

How Aphrodite came to conceive Aineias to Anchises; Aphrodite, Ares and Hephaistos

The story of Aphrodite and ANCHISES follows a similar pattern in so far as the goddess, who here assumes the traits of the Great Mother of Ida, becomes involved in a liaison with a younger male partner in one of the lands that were associated with the Asianic mother-goddess. In its setting in Greek myth, however, the tale is woven into heroic mythology to account for the origin of a notable hero. Anchises is described in the *Iliad* and subsequent tradition as a grandson of Tros, the eponym of the land of Troy, and a member of the junior branch of the royal family, whose members lived outside the city on Mt Ida (see p. 522).[294] Either through the machinations of Zeus, who wanted to be avenged on Aphrodite for the trouble that she had caused to him and the other gods by inspiring them with love for mortals,[295] or else out of sheer wantonness of desire, she conceived a passion for Anchises when he was a handsome young man, and visited him one day as he was tending his cattle on Ida. As the story is recounted in the *Homeric Hymn to Aphrodite*, she went to her precinct at Paphos on Cyprus beforehand to be bathed and bedecked by the Graces, and then appeared to Anchises in the guise of a Phrygian princess.

She told him that Hermes had carried her off to Mt Ida to become his wife, and proposed that they should consummate their union without delay. Under the influence of the desire that she inspired in him, he took her by the hand and led her to his bed, which was covered with soft pelts of bears and lions that he had killed in the high mountains. She put him to sleep for a while after their love-making and finally revealed her true identity when he awoke.[296] He was much alarmed, fearing that he would become 'strengthless' (i.e. impotent) after sleeping with such a goddess; but she reassured him and told him that she would bear him a son, Aineias, who would be reared by the mountain nymphs until she brought the child to him in his fifth year. Before departing, she ordered him to say nothing of their encounter and to pass off Aineias as a child of his by a local nymph, warning him that Zeus would strike him with a thunderbolt if he was foolish enough to boast of having slept with her.[297] According to some later sources, he was indeed struck by a thunderbolt after revealing the secret (while drunk in one account), and was crippled or blinded as a consequence. This feature of the story was probably familiar by the classical period since a fragment from Sophocles' *Laokoon* refers to Anchises' 'thunder-stricken back'.[298]

So far, we have been dealing with legends that represent the goddess, not as married, but as forming more or less temporary unions with someone much inferior to herself – a proceeding quite characteristic of eastern goddesses, who are essentially mothers, not wives, and beside whom their lovers or husbands sink into comparative insignificance, even if some of them are not unimportant gods. Within the Olympian circle, she is linked to two gods, the fire-god Hephaistos, who was of eastern origin like herself, and the war-god Ares. In a famous tale in the *Odyssey*, Hephaistos is presented as her husband, and he catches her out when she secretly engages in an adulterous love affair with Ares. He learned of this from the sun-god Helios, who can see everything as he travels across the sky and came to tell him that Ares had been sleeping with his wife in his own home. Not daring to confront Ares on equal terms, he fashioned a subtle net which was immensely strong but so finely spun as to be invisible, and spread it around his bed, causing the guilty couple to be caught up in it when they lay down to make love; and he then summoned the other gods to witness the sight. The goddesses stayed in their homes for shame, but all the gods hurried to the scene, and unquenchable laughter arose among them when they saw the effects of Hephaistos' ingenuity. Hephaistos was very angry at first and talked of a divorce, threatening to reclaim the bride-price that he had paid to Zeus for his faithless daughter; but Poseidon pacified him by promising to stand surety for the compensation that was due to a wronged husband. So he released the captives from the net, allowing Ares to depart to his home in Thrace and Aphrodite to set off for her temple at Paphos in Cyprus, where she was bathed and adorned by the Graces.[299] This tale is obviously not meant to be taken too seriously; indeed, Hephaistos is not a very serious figure in mythology, as we have seen.

Although it is often stated on the basis of this story that Aphrodite was married to Hephaistos, as though that were the regular tradition in antiquity, this Homeric passage is in fact rather exceptional in that regard. Hephaistos has another wife in the *Theogony* and indeed in the *Iliad* (see p. 167), and it is clear from visual images from the archaic period onwards – and literary references from the classical period onwards – that Ares was generally regarded as the husband of Aphrodite, or at least as her accredited lover. On the François vase, for instance, from the early sixth century BC, she is shown arriving at the marriage of Peleus in the same chariot as Ares (just as Zeus arrives with Hera, and Poseidon with Amphitrite), while Pindar and Aeschylus refer to him directly as her husband.[300] For the children who are credited to the couple in the *Theogony* and elsewhere, see p. 169. The two deities were connected in cult to some extent, sharing a temple for example on the road between Argos and Mantineia.[301] Aphrodite could sometimes be a martial goddess, as in her Spartan cult as Aphrodite Areia,[302] but it is hard to say whether this had anything to do with her mythical union with Ares. Their union could be viewed in any case as a piquant union of opposites, which resulted most appropriately in the birth of a daughter called Harmonia.[303]

Although Aphrodite was sometimes credited with various other children, including Hermaphroditos (see p. 164), Priapos (see p. 222) and Eryx (see p. 395), no love-stories are recorded for her beyond those already mentioned. In her myths, the love-goddess is by no means promiscuous. She occasionally intervened to help mortal lovers, notably Paris after he judged her to be more beautiful than Hera and Athena (see p. 443), and the suitor of Atalanta (see p. 546); and conversely, she occasionally acted against mortals who refused to honour her or scorned the gift of love, as we have just seen with Smyrna, or in the story of Hippolytos (see p. 358).

In two striking tales from the islands, Aphrodite brought a statue of a beautiful woman to life for Pygmalion, king of Cyprus (see p. 574), and rejuvenated PHAON, a virtuous ferryman of Mytilene in Lesbos. When she appeared to Phaon in the guise of an old woman, he showed her every consideration and ferried her across to the mainland without demanding a fee; and by way of a reward, she gave him an alabaster pot containing a marvellous ointment that would make him young and handsome when he rubbed it into his skin. The women of Mytilene were much attracted to him thereafter, ultimately to his own detriment since he was finally caught in adultery and executed.[304] He may originally have been a figure like Adonis (or possibly even Adonis himself under another name), since Aphrodite is also reported to have fallen in love with him and to have hidden him in a lettuce-bed.[305] A strange story suggested that the Lesbian poetess Sappho fell hopelessly in love with him, and committed suicide as a consequence by hurling herself from the Leucadian Rock (a celebrated 'lover's leap' on the island of Leukas in the Ionian Sea).[306] The idea would probably have been inspired by a passage in one of her poems in which she wrote about Phaon as a legendary figure. One of Ovid's fictional letters in the *Heroides* is addressed from Sappho to Phaon.[307]

As in mythology, so in art, Aphrodite wavers between several types. Her oriental figures, as in the archaic idols found in Cyprus, show her in crudely naked form, typically with one or both hands up by her breasts and with her genitals frankly emphasized. In her earlier Greek statues, however, from the archaic and classical periods, she is decorously draped in long robes for the most part, and possesses a certain stiff dignity such as would not be inappropriate to Aphrodite Pandemos. From the mid-fourth century onwards, sculptures regularly portray her in graciously naked or semi-naked form, in images that vary with the skill of the artist from meritorious studies of the body of a healthy and well-proportioned woman to monuments that convey a suggestion of an ideal beauty. The Cnidian Aphrodite of Praxiteles (c. 350 BC, now lost, but familiar from copies), which showed her laying her clothing aside as she was about to enter her bath, became her most celebrated image in Graeco-Roman antiquity. The most popular of her surviving statues, the Venus de Milo (i.e. Aphrodite of Melos) in the Louvre, is an original work from the second century BC.

CHAPTER SIX

LESSER DEITIES AND NATURE-SPIRITS

— ·◆· —

Before we pass on from divine to heroic mythology, there are various lesser divinities who remain to be considered. From among the children who were fathered by Zeus on goddesses other than Hera (see pp. 76ff), three gracious groups of sister-deities, the Muses, Charites (Graces) and Horai (Seasons), have yet to be discussed. Ranking somewhere between deities such as these and the mortal race were the countless nature-spirits who haunted the waters, countryside and wilderness. Of most importance in everyday belief were the female spirits, the nymphs, familiar presences who were very popular in rural cult; their main male equivalents, the Satyrs and Seilenoi, belonged more to the world of art and literature, as mythical attendants of Dionysos. These male nature-spirits had animal features and ill-controlled appetites, as did the rustic god Pan, who originated in Arcadia as a god of shepherds and herdsmen, and figures in characteristic myths as a frustrated lover. The Phrygian myth of Attis and Kybele strikes a more exotic note in so far as it finds a place in the corpus of Greek mythology. We will conclude by examining various minor gods and daimones who are not included in Hesiod's genealogies, ranging from the Kouretes and Korybantes to the lustful Priapos and the wedding-god Hymenaios.

The Muses

In Hesiod's account, as we have seen, the MUSES (Mousai) were born to Zeus by Mnemosyne, the personification of Memory;[1] but a rival genealogy, which may have originated in a cosmological poem by Alcman (seventh century BC), claimed that they were born in the very earliest times as daughters of Ouranos and Gaia.[2] Some authors reconciled the two accounts by suggesting that there were two generations of Muses, the ancient Muses who were daughters of Heaven and their later-born companions who were daughters of Zeus.[3]

The Muses first appear in the works of Homer and Hesiod as goddesses on whom the epic poet relies for his inspiration, his memory and aspects of his knowledge. In the introductory section of the *Theogony*, Hesiod tells how the Muses of Mt Helikon once approached him as he was shepherding his flocks under the mountain and granted him his gift of song, breathing a divine voice into him to enable him to celebrate things that will be and things that have been in times gone by.[4] Scholars have been unable to agree on whether the poet was describing a genuine vision or dream of some kind or was merely following a literary convention. Hesiod goes on to say that the Muses delight the heart of their father Zeus on Olympos by singing of things past, present and future, and of the race of the gods, and of mortals and giants.[5] In contrast to poets of more recent times, who have tended to appeal to their Muse as a source of poetic afflatus, ancient poets place more emphasis on the wisdom and knowledge of the Muses, as deities who know all that is worth telling and can give the poet the ability to tell it, and also to remember it (a point that was especially important to oral poets of early times). Homer not only invokes the Muse as an unnamed goddess at the beginning of the *Iliad*, but appeals to the Muses at greater length in the second book of the epic before providing his long muster-role of the Greek commanders and their forces;[6] although this might not seem the most poetic part of the poem, it contains quantities of detailed and irreplaceable information about the heroic past that needed to be remembered if it was to be passed on to future generations. It is still invaluable to the modern mythologist. Homer tells the Muses that he needs their aid at this point because they are 'deities and are present at all things, and know all things, while we hear no more than a rumour and have no knowledge'.[7] As time passed, these wise and helpful goddesses came to be enrolled as the patrons of other forms of literature as they developed, and, by a natural extension, of other arts and intellectual pursuits also, such as philosophy and astronomy.

According to the standard tradition, as established by Hesiod, there were nine Muses named Kleio, Euterpe, Thaleia, Melpomene, Terpsichore, Erato, Polhymnia, Ourania and Kalliope.[8] In local cult and tradition, however, they were sometimes represented as being fewer in number and of different name (see below). They are mentioned as being nine in number in a passage in the *Odyssey*,[9] but in a part of the poem that may well have been added after Homer's time. Their pretty 'speaking names', which were probably invented by Hesiod himself, would originally have been devised to reflect aspects of their common nature and shared activities; since they liked to dance and sing, for instance, 'delighting in their beautiful voice (*opi kalēi*)',[10] four of them were called Kalliope, Polhymnia (Many Songs), Melpomene (she who sings) and Terpsichore (Delighting in the Dance). It was not until a considerably later period that authors tried to assign individual functions to each of the Muses in accordance with the specific meaning of her name. *Kalliope* of the beautiful voice could then be regarded as the Muse of epic poetry specifically, and *Polhymnia* as the Muse who concerned herself with hymns to the gods (or later, pantomime), and *Terpsichore* as the Muse of choral lyric and dancing. *Kleio* (or Clio in Latin form) is still familiar as the Muse of history, a responsibility that she acquired because her name might suggest that she celebrates (*kleiei*) the glorious deeds (*kleia*) of heroes and heroines of the past. *Thaleia* (Good Cheer) could be fittingly enlisted as the Muse of comedy, *Ourania* (the Heavenly) as the Muse of astronomy, *Erato* (the Lovely or Desirable) as the Muse of lyric poetry, which is so often erotic in content, and *Euterpe* (she that gladdens) as the Muse of flute-playing. *Melpomene* for her part commonly presided over tragedy. These are merely examples, since individual Muses are credited with different functions in different sources.[11] This division of labours should not be taken too seriously, however, for it was simply a game at the best and an exercise in pedantry at the worst.

Although the name of the Muses is apparently of Indo-European origin, its etymology remains a matter for conjecture. The principal centres of their cult in early times were the areas of Mt Olympos in the north-east (including Pieria) and of Mt Helikon in Boeotia, but they had lesser cults throughout the Greek world. Homer refers to them as the Olympian Muses, stating that they had their homes on Mt Olympos, while Hesiod, as a Boeotian, received his call from them in their main southern haunts, and tells how they would sing and dance on Helikon after first bathing in a spring on that mountain.[12] At the beginning of the *Works and Days*, however, Hesiod refers to them as 'Muses from Pieria', and he reports correspondingly in the *Theogony* that they were born there.[13] In relation to their different haunts, they could be called the Helikonian or Olympian Muses (both titles are applied by Hesiod) or the Pierian Muses (a title that first appears in Solon and the Hesiodic *Shield*[14]); but the use of such titles in no way implies that there was more than one group of Muses. They are known as goddesses of song and dance from the time of our earliest records; although it has often been suggested that they may have originated as water-spirits or spring-nymphs, the idea is not confirmed by any definite evidence from the early tradition. The Romans identified them with some obscure deities of their own, the Camenae, who had a sacred grove and spring outside the Porta Capena at Rome.

The name and number of the Muses show some variation in local cult and tradition. At Sicyon, for instance, three Muses were honoured, and there are also accounts in which they were five, seven or eight in number. Pausanias claims that the Helikonian Muses were originally three in number, but the names that he cites for them – Melete, Mneme and Aoide, i.e. Study, Memory and Song – are of such a nature that it is unlikely that he is referring to a genuinely ancient tradition.[15]

Like other deities, the Muses were jealous of their honour. Their only myths of any real significance tell how they punished mortals who dared to challenge them as singers. The Thracian bard THAMYRIS (or Thamyras), who was a son of the mythical musician Philammon (see p. 435), became so skilled at singing to the lyre (*kithara*) that he boasted that he could outsing even the Muses themselves. As the story is recounted by Homer, they encountered him at Dorion, a town in Nestor's kingdom in the western Peloponnese, and were so angered by his presumptuous boast that 'they maimed him, and took away his wondrous gift of song and caused him to forget his lyre-playing'.[16] Later sources specify that they blinded him (as may in fact have been Homer's meaning, even if his language is vague). The next full account is provided by the Hellenistic mythographer Asclepiades, who probably relied on a tragic source. Thamyris is now said to have engaged in a contest with the Muses in his homeland in Thrace, on the agreement that he would be able to sleep with all of them if he won (in accordance with the polygynous customs of the land), but that they would be able to treat him just as they wished if he should lose. When he was defeated, as was inevitably the case, they proceeded to rob him of his eyes.[17] Apollodorus provides a very similar account, saying that they deprived him of his eyes and also of his skills as a minstrel.[18] His stage-mask in tragedy showed his right eye as black and his left eye as white,[19] presumably to illustrate his condition before and after his defeat; Sophocles wrote a play about him, as perhaps did Aeschylus too.

In a later story of this kind, probably of Hellenistic origin, the Muses met with a challenge from the PIERIDES or EMATHIDES, the daughters of Pieros, king of Emathia or Pella in Macedonia. In the version ascribed to Nicander, Pieros, an earth-born king of Emathia, fathered a family of nine daughters at much the same time as the Muses were fathered by Zeus. These daughters, the Emathides, formed a choir to rival that of the Muses, and the two groups put their skills to the test in a singing-contest on Mt Helikon. When the Emathides raised their voices, the whole of nature darkened and nothing paid heed to their chorus; but when the Muses sang, the sky and stars and the sea and rivers ceased from their motions, and Mt Helikon swelled with pleasure, rising up into the sky until Pegasos, at the order of Poseidon, halted it by striking its summit with his hoof. To punish the Emathides for having presumed to challenge them, the Muses transformed them into birds of various different kinds.[20] Or in Ovid's account, the contest was judged by a jury of nymphs, who voted unanimously in favour of the Muses; and when the Pierides reacted to their defeat by abusing the victors, the Muses transformed them into magpies, harsh-voiced birds that can imitate human speech.[21] Since Pierides was a title that could be applied to the Muses in connection with their cult in Pieria, it is not hard to see how the idea could have arisen of a contest between them and the daughters of the eponym of Pieria. According to a strange legend of a comparable nature, Hera once persuaded the Sirens to match their voices against those of the Muses, but the Muses won and plucked out the feathers of the Sirens (who had bird-like bodies, see p. 496) to make crowns for themselves.[22]

There is otherwise little to record about the Muses as mythical figures. It would naturally be supposed that they would sing and dance at the gatherings of the gods, perhaps with Apollo, another great patron of music, as their companion and leader (hence his title of Mousagetes, or Leader of the Muses); and on special occasions, they might sing in the presence of mortals on the earth below, as when they led the wedding-songs at the marriages of Kadmos and Peleus (see. pp. 54 and 297), or arrived with Thetis and the Nereids to sing dirges for the dead Achilles (see p. 468). Although they might be best imagined as a group of virgin goddesses, children are quite often ascribed to one or another of them, above all because they seemed to be appropriate mothers for mythical musicians. Singers or dancers such as Orpheus and Linos or the Sirens and Korybantes are therefore regularly identified as offspring of a Muse.[23]

According to a curious tale recorded by Ovid alone, Pyreneus, king of Daulis in Central Greece, once offered shelter to the Muses when they were caught by a rainstorm as they were travelling to their temple on Mt Parnassos. Although he recognized who they were and assumed a humble and reverent tone when inviting them into his palace, he barred his doors to prevent them from leaving and then tried to rape them. They simply flew away, however, and when Pyreneus tried to chase after them by launching himself from the battlements, he plunged headlong to the ground below and was killed. This Pyreneus is otherwise unknown; one may suspect that his story had become distorted in the transmission.[24]

The Charites (Graces) and Horai (Seasons)

The CHARITES were lovely daughters of Zeus, usually thought to be three in number, who were born to him by the Okeanid Eurynome (see p. 78).[25] They are known as the GRACES in English in accordance with Latin usage (for their name was translated into Gratiae in Latin). As gracious goddesses who embody all that is beautiful and charming, and can lend grace and allure (*charis*) to works of art and nature and every area of life, they appear regularly as associates of the Muses and of Aphrodite. In the *Iliad*, the goddess of love wears an immortal robe which had been woven for her by the Charites, and in Demodokos' minstrel-song in the *Odyssey*, she is bathed, anointed and dressed by them in her sanctuary in Cyprus after being caught in adultery by Ares (see p. 201).[26] Or in the *Homeric Hymn to Aphrodite*, she is bathed and dressed by them in happier circumstances before she sets off to seduce Anchises.[27] Hesiod remarks that their home on Olympos lies beside that of the Muses,[28] who were often imagined as singing and dancing in their company. Sappho invokes them in three of her surviving poems, twice in conjunction with the Muses; and Pindar refers to them with notable frequency as deities who shed grace on poetry and festal occasions and many areas of life.[29]

Although their number varies, they are generally represented as a triad on the authority of Hesiod, who calls them Aglaia (Splendour), Euphrosyne (Joy) and Thaleia (Good Cheer).[30] As these names might suggest, they were particularly associated with the grace and delight of social gatherings and festivities. Pindar remarks that 'not even the gods can order dances and feasts without the aid of the holy Charites';[31] and they often appear in art and literature accordingly as goddesses who dance at the gatherings of the gods.[32] There is little doubt, however, that they were originally nature-goddesses who caused the crops and vegetation to flourish delightfully. This aspect of their nature is reflected in their names in Athenian cult, in which there were two Charites known as Auxo (i.e. fosterer of growth) and Hegemone (she who leads, sc. brings the plants forth from the earth).[33] They are common enough in art, where their three attractive and maidenly figures, initially draped, often naked in later times, were a favourite subject. The portrayal familiar from Renaissance art, in which they are shown as a naked and interlaced group, one viewed from the back and two from the front, is derived from a standard Hellenistic type. Two individual Charites are mentioned in the early tradition as marriage-partners; in the *Theogony*, Hephaistos is said to have married Aglaia, the youngest of the sisters, and in the *Iliad*, Hera promises Pasithea, 'one of the younger Charites' (here apparently more than three in number), to Hypnos for lulling Zeus to sleep on her behalf (see p. 30).[34] The most ancient centre of the cult of the Charites was thought to have been Orchomenos in Boeotia, where they were honoured in the form of stones that were said to have fallen from the heavens in the heroic era.[35]

The HORAI or SEASONS, another gracious set of sister-goddesses, bear some resemblance to the Charites but maintain a closer connection with the fruits of the earth. Although they are sometimes known as the Hours, their name does not really mean hour in the English or Latin sense, but simply time or season, and they represent the seasons of the year. This accounts in part for their varying numbers, for the ancients recognized anything from two seasons (i.e. summer and winter) up to the four that are usually acknowledged in temperate zones nowadays. They were most commonly imagined as being three in number (representing spring, summer and winter); and as well as being concerned with growth and fertility in connection with the turning year, they also acquired moral and social concerns as goddesses who protected the good order that is essential for the flourishing of agriculture and prosperity in general. This is reflected in their names in the *Theogony*, which calls them Eunomia, Dike and Eirene, in other words, Good Order, Justice and Peace.[36] Their agricultural concerns remained primary, however, in what little cult they had, as might be inferred from their cultic titles at Athens, where they were known as Thallo and Karpo (i.e. she who causes to sprout and to fruit respectively).[37] Like the Charites, they have no proper stories of their own, but appear in an accompanying role as charming minor deities who attend on the greater ones, especially Aphrodite, and dance at the gatherings of the gods. In the *Homeric Hymn* (6) *to Aphrodite*, they are said to have clothed the new-born Aphrodite when she emerged from the sea at Cyprus, and to have adorned her with gold and jewels before conducting her up to Olympos to join the other gods.[38] They are credited with a special duty in the *Iliad* as the gate-keepers of Olympos who are responsible for opening and closing the cloud-barriers, an idea that may have arisen because they were associated with the changing weather.[39] Hesiod classes them as daughters of Zeus and Themis (see p. 78).

The Nymphs

Some of the most appealing figures in ancient mythology and folklore are the multitude of NYMPHS (Nymphai) who were thought to inhabit nature in many of its aspects as spirits of the meadows and mountains, of trees and groves, of springs, streams and the sea. Their name literally means 'young marriageable women' or the like. Although some who were classed as nymphs could be quite important goddesses, as in the case of some of the Okeanids and Nereids (e.g. Amphitrite, Thetis), the mass of the nymphs were semi-divinities of comparatively minor status. They were of considerable significance in popular cult, however, precisely because they could be regarded as more accessible than the grander deities of public cult, and as beings who were more likely to be sympathetic to the everyday worries of mortals, especially those of women. They appear very frequently in myth, though often in a supporting or purely decorative role. For Hesiod's account of the origin of the Meliai (strictly ash-tree nymphs, but probably meaning tree-nymphs in general here), see p. 33. Homer refers to the nymphs as daughters of Zeus;[40] Odysseus invokes them as such on two occasions when offering sacrifice and appealing for their aid, and they help him to acquire food at one point by driving wild goats towards him and his men.[41] They live on the fringes of divine society; when Zeus orders Themis to summon a general assembly of the gods in the *Iliad*, they attend, as do the river-gods, 'for none of the rivers failed to come, apart from Okeanos, and none of the nymphs who haunt the lovely groves and the springs of rivers and the grassy water-meadows'.[42] Nymphs attended Artemis on her hunting-trips (as already mentioned by Homer, see p. 188) and Dionysos on his revels; they were available to act as nurses to infant gods, such as Zeus and Dionysos (see pp. 75 and 172), and indeed to mortals on occasion, as in the case of Aineias (see p. 201); they can often be found in the upper reaches of heroic genealogies as the wives of earthborn first men and primordial rulers; and as figures of greater individuality, they regularly appear in transformation myths, especially in those that were devised (mostly at a fairly late period) to account for the origin of plants and springs. They are represented one and all as beautiful and youthful, and fond of music and dancing, and very often as amorous, for they appear again and again as the partners in love not only of Satyrs but of gods and mortals too. They have prophetic powers, and can exert a strange spell on mortals, causing them to become *nympholēptai*, or filled with divine madness. Like the fairies of later folklore, whom they greatly resemble in some respects, they could become formidable when crossed (as we will see).

Nymphs were divided into different categories according to the provinces of nature that they inhabited or animated. There were nymphs of the hills, dales, pastures and mountains, nymphs of springs, rivers, lakes and the sea, and wood-nymphs and tree-nymphs. Apart from the Okeanids and Nereids, who have already been discussed, the only nymphs who are likely to be encountered in translated literature under their Greek titles are the **Dryads** and **Hamadryads** (Dryades, Hamadryades), who were tree-nymphs, the **Naiads** (Naiades), who were water-nymphs, whether of springs, rivers or lakes, and perhaps also the **Oreads** (Oreiades), who were mountain-nymphs.

There is no end to the number of different names that could be applied to nymphs; the Naiads, for instance, could be divided into Potamiads (river-nymphs), Kreneids (spring-nymphs), Limniads (nymphs of pools and lakes), and so on. The fact is that these were hardly proper names at all, but feminine adjectives that could be assigned to the noun *nymphē* at will. Beyond a certain point, this simply became an exercise in pedantry. No orthodox or exhaustive classification of such beings was ever attempted, and ancient authors were often careless or arbitrary in the application of such titles.

The Dryads, or tree-nymphs, derived their name from the word *drus*, which strictly meant an oak, but could be used in a looser sense as a term for large trees in general. Hamadryads were much the same; although ancient mythographers sometimes drew a distinction between Hamadryads, as nymphs who lived *in* specific trees and perished with them, and Dryads, as nymphs who simply lived *among* trees, it is most unlikely that this distinction was observed in ordinary usage or commonly intended in mythical narratives.

Although nymphs were certainly long-lived by comparison to human beings, they were not usually regarded as immortal. In a striking Hesiodic fragment, a naiad nymph indicates that beings of her kind have a life-span that corresponds to almost 10,000 human generations (9,720 to be precise!), for they live ten times as long as a phoenix, which lives nine times as long as a raven, which lives three times as long as a stag, which lives four times as long as a crow, which sees nine generations of men grow old.[43] It was commonly supposed that tree-nymphs died when their trees decayed or were cut down. A passage from the *Homeric Hymn to Aphrodite*, which states this of mountain-nymphs in general, deserves to be quoted in full:

the deep-breasted mountain-nymphs ... rank neither with mortals nor with immortals; they live a long life, to be sure, eating divine food and joining in lovely dances with the immortals, and with them the Seilenoi and keen-sighted Argeiphontes [i.e. Hermes] mingle in love in the depths of delightful caves; but at the time of their birth, pines or high-crowned oaks spring up with them on the nourishing earth ... and when their fated death approaches them, first these beautiful trees wither on the earth and their bark shrivels around them and their branches fall away, and then along with the trees, the souls of the nymphs leave the light of the sun.[44]

As we have already seen in the case of Erysichthon (see p. 133), a man could earn the hatred or gratitude of a tree-nymph by harming or saving her tree. According to one tradition, Arkas, the hero who gave his name to Arcadia (see p. 542), fathered his family by a hamadryad nymph whose tree he had once saved. For while he was out hunting one day, the nymph Chrysopeleia appealed to him to save her tree, which was in danger of being destroyed by a flooding stream, and he diverted the stream and secured the earth at the foot of the tree; and she therefore agreed to enter into a union with him and to bear him his heirs.[45] In another tale of the same kind, a certain Rhoikos, a young man of Knidos on the west coast of Asia Minor, came across an oak-tree that was in danger of falling over and told his servants to prop it up. The grateful tree-nymph, who had thus been saved from perishing along with her tree, offered him the choice of whatever he most desired, and he asked to become her lover. Appointing a bee to act as their go-between, she granted his request on condition that he should have nothing to do with other women. One day, however, when the bee came to summon him while he was engaged in a game of draughts, he responded brusquely to it, causing such anger to the nymph that she turned him blind. Such at least is the story as it has come down to us; but one may suspect that the bee would have informed her of some infidelity in the original version.[46] And finally, Apollonius tells how a certain Paraibios (a friend of the Thracian seer Phineus) brought a curse on himself and his children by ignoring the tears and pleas of a hamadryad nymph when she begged him not to cut down her oak-tree.[47]

For a further example of how a nymph would react when crossed in love, we may turn to the legend of the Sicilian herdsman Daphnis (who was himself the son of a nymph in accounts that describe him as a son of Hermes). As he was tending his flocks in Sicily, a local nymph fell in love with him and took him as her lover, telling him that he would lose his sight if he should ever be unfaithful to her; and when the daughter of a local ruler subsequently took a fancy to him and plied him with wine to lure him into her bed, the angry nymph blinded him just as she had warned. He found consolation for his misfortune in singing sorrowful songs, hence the origin of pastoral verse.[48] There were many versions of this story; according to Ovid, for instance, the nymph turned him to stone; or else he was blinded as usual but prayed for help to his father Hermes, who raised him up to heaven and caused a spring to gush forth in his name at the place where he had vanished.[49] In his fourth Idyll, Theocritus offers a wholly different account in which Daphnis is said to have boasted that he was more than a match for Eros, causing Aphrodite to afflict him with an all-consuming passion that apparently caused his death.[50] For other notable legends in which nymphs were presented as falling in love with mortals, see pp. 385 and 444.

The Satyrs and Seilenoi

It is a peculiarity of ancient Greek folklore that female nature-spirits, whether of land or sea, were imagined as being fully human in form while male nature-spirits were imagined as having animal features. The principal male nature-spirits were the SATYRS (Satyroi) and SEILENOI, lustful creatures of the wild who formed part of the retinue of Dionysos, and diverted themselves with wine-drinking, music and the pursuit of nymphs. As spirits of the wild life of the woods and hills, and particularly of their unrestrained and unguided fertility, they would have originated as creations of the popular imagination, in much the same way as the nymphs; but they became specialized in their role as attendants of Dionysos and had no place in cult. The Satyrs and their counterparts the Seilenoi, who are not easily distinguished from one another in earlier depictions at least, were consistently portrayed as quasi-human, but as more or less grotesque in their build and features, always male, always lustful and often visibly excited, and with some part of them definitely bestial. In the earlier tradition, as in Attic vase-paintings of the sixth to fifth century BC, Satyrs are usually shown with horse's tails and ears, and sometimes with legs resembling the hind legs of horses. They also have distinctive snub-nosed facial features; the traditional portrayal of Socrates shows him as looking much like a Satyr in that respect. From the Hellenistic period onward, they often have something of the goat about them, being shown with little horns, prick-ears, and often goat's legs. This, the type familiar from the famous Satyr of Praxiteles and other well-known works of art, clearly resembles Pan. In this later period, the Seilenoi are typically distinguished from the Satyrs as being older (and also retaining their equine ears). We sometimes hear of Papposeilenoi (i.e. daddy Seilenoi), and while the Satyrs are often merry with wine, the Seilenoi are apt to be heavily drunk; a not uncommon subject in art is a Satyr supporting a Seilenos who has drunk to excess. In Italy, the Satyrs were identified with some native wood-spirits, the Fauni.

There is no mention of Satyrs or Seilenoi in Homer or the genuine works of Hesiod. The earliest reference to Satyrs in the surviving literature can be found in a fragment from the Hesiodic *Catalogue*, which classes 'the worthless good-for-nothing Satyrs' with the mountain-nymphs and Kouretes as children of the daughters of Doros (see p. 219).[51] The Seilenoi make their first literary appearance in the passage from the *Homeric Hymn to Aphrodite* quoted above, as lovers of the mountain-nymphs. In the subsequent literature, and in artistic images too, the Satyrs and Seilenoi are a disreputable and rather comical crowd who are fond of sex and wine and dancing and revelry, and are usually utter cowards except in so far as the Dionysiac frenzy lends them a measure of courage. At the Athenian dramatic festivals of the classical period, each set of three tragedies would be followed by a comical Satyr-play composed by the same author; the chorus consisted of a group of Satyrs with Seilenos at their head, and the plot was a burlesque of a story from myth (usually relating to the subject matter of the preceding trilogy). An idea of the

Figure 6.1   Satyrs in action. Attic red-figure cup, British Museum.

nature of this curious genre of literature can be gained from the extensive remains of Sophocles' *Trackers* (*Ichneutai*) and the surviving *Cyclops* of Euripides, in which Seilenos and his Satyrs are introduced into the story of Odysseus and Polyphemos (see p. 492).

The one Satyr who stands out from the mass as an individual with a story of his own is Marsyas, who came to a bad end because he presumed to challenge Apollo to a musical contest (see p. 157). SEILENOS, the archetype or leader of the Seilenoi, is represented as a swaggering Falstaffian figure in his role as leader of the chorus in Satyr-plays, but also appears in more serious myth as the possessor of such wisdom as is to be found among beings of his kind. He was sometimes said to have acted as tutor to the young Dionysos, and he is presented as quite a philosopher in a fragment from Pindar that shows him preaching to the mythical flautist Olympos (a son of Marsyas and the eponym of Mt Olympos in Mysia) on the vanity of worldly wealth.[52] His best-known story, which probably originated as a folk-tale, tells how Midas, king of Phrygia, sought to benefit from his wisdom. Taking advantage of Seilenos' fondness for wine, Midas ordered some servants to mix wine into his favourite spring in Macedonia (or Phrygia), and to capture him and tie him up while he was incapacitated by the liquor. When Midas questioned the captive nature-spirit, asking him what is best and most desirable for human beings, he initially refused to say anything at all; and when he was finally compelled to speak, he rebuked Midas for insisting that he should be told what it was better for him not to know, namely that the best fate for mortals is not to be born at all, and the next best to meet their death as early as possible.[53] Seilenos emerged into cult in a minor way, for Pausanias found a temple in Elis that was dedicated to him (and to him alone, without Dionysos). Less impressive was his memorial at Athens, a stone of no great size on the Acropolis, just big enough for a small man to sit on, which had once served Seilenos as a seat when he had visited Attica in the train of Dionysos.[54]

Another legend in which Seilenos appears in the company of Midas is the famous tale of Midas' golden touch. When Seilenos once became heavily drunk as he was travelling through Phrygia in the train of Dionysos, some local peasants bound him in chains of flowers and took him to their king. Having been instructed in the mysteries of Dionysos by Orpheus and Eumolpos, Midas knew something about the god and recognized at once that this strange captive was a companion of his. So he entertained him liberally for ten days and nights, presumably making him drunker than ever, and then restored him to his young master. Delighted to have his tutor back again, Dionysos rewarded Midas by granting him a wish, and the king asked that whatever he touched should be turned at once to gold. Although initially entranced by his good fortune, Midas soon discovered that his new-found powers brought unexpected difficulties, for his food and drink turned to gold before he could consume them. When his thirst grew insupportable and he was threatened with starvation, he prayed to Dionysos to relieve him from the sufferings that he had incurred by his limitless greed, and the god ordered him to travel to the uplands of Lydia to wash himself in the source of the river Pactolus. As soon as he did so, his strange power passed from his body into the waters of the river, whose sands and banks have gleamed with gold ever since.[55]

Other male nature-spirits who were imagined as being part-animal or wholly animal in form were the river-gods and the Centaurs. If springs had nymphs as their presiding spirits, each river had its god, who was usually pictured in the form of a bull, or of a bull with a human head. River-gods were honoured in cult, and those of major rivers could be of some importance in myth, either for their legends or as progenitors of early heroes or heroines; some of the more notable river-gods have already been considered, as sons of Okeanos (see pp. 41–3). Although the semi-equine Centaurs surely originated as creatures of folklore, as wild spirits of the mountains and forests, they appear as beings of the mythical past alone in the recorded tradition, and will therefore be considered in connection with heroic mythology. They were associated with two areas in particular, the region of Mt Pelion in Thessaly, where they became embroiled in a conflict with the neighbouring Lapiths (see p. 555), and north-western Arcadia, where they provoked a fight with Herakles (see p. 258). The sea harboured comparable beings of mixed form, such as the fish-tailed Tritons (see p. 106).

Pan and his loves

Very similar to the Satyrs in many respects was the rustic deity PAN, an Arcadian god of shepherds and goatherds and their flocks and herds. He was usually pictured as being part-human in form and part-goat, with the horns, ears and legs of the latter; and he was goatish in character too, for he was lustful and sportive, a vigorous and fertile nature-spirit who could also be short-tempered, especially if disturbed in his noontide rest.[56] A characteristic power of his which has left its mark on ancient and modern speech is that of causing 'panic', a wild, groundless fear that strikes groups of people and causes them to behave like frightened and stampeded animals.[57] As a god of the wild uplands and of goatherds and shepherds, he especially liked to haunt their summer pastures in the mountains. Like them, he would divert himself with music by playing on the reed-pipe that is named after him and by singing and dancing with the nymphs.[58] It is therefore no wonder that he is prominent above all

Figure 6.2   Pan. Detail from a Roman marble sculptural group.
Cos museum. Photo: Richard Stoneman.

in pastoral poetry, and that although his cult spread far beyond his native Arcadia, he remained chiefly Arcadian. Of higher social and moral developments he knew nothing, apart from the fancy of some theologians that his name meant 'All' (as *pan* can mean in Greek) and that he could be viewed accordingly as a universal god.[59] The etymology itself is quite old, since Plato already plays with the thought, and the *Homeric Hymn to Pan* explains that he was given this name by the gods because he delighted the hearts of 'all' of them.[60] A more plausible etymology would suggest that his name comes from the same root as Latin *pa-sco* and means 'the Feeder', i.e. the pasturer of flocks. From the fifth century BC onwards, though the notion itself may be more ancient, there is also mention of Pans (Panes, Paniskoi) as a generic group.

Although Pan was commonly regarded as a son of Hermes, accounts of his parentage vary greatly, as is hardly surprising for a god of this kind who has no very close relation to any of the great Olympians. According to the *Homeric Hymn to Pan*, Hermes fathered him by the (unnamed) daughter of an Arcadian hero, Dryops; and when he was born with goat's feet, two horns and a full beard, his nurse was so shocked that she ran off and deserted him; but Hermes was delighted with his uncouth son, and carried him up to Olympos wrapped in the skins of mountain hares to show him off to the other gods.[61] In later sources, Hermes is often said to have fathered him by a most improbable mother, none other than Penelope, the faithful wife of Odysseus; indeed, Herodotus describes this as the common view of the Greeks.[62] The whole idea is so odd that it is tempting to suppose that this Penelope was not originally the wife of Odysseus, but an entirely different figure, perhaps an Arcadian nymph or the above-mentioned daughter of Dryops. If she did not bear Pan to Hermes, Penelope bore him to Apollo, or to her husband, or to one of her suitors or indeed all of them (a bizarre idea which was apparently inspired by the fact that the god's name can mean 'all').[63] Among other fancies, we find the suggestion that Zeus fathered him on Hybris (i.e. Wantonness) or that a shepherd called Krathis fathered him by one of his goats;[64] but that is quite enough on this matter.

Pan was forever pursuing the nymphs of the countryside, much like the Satyrs (although he did not share their other vice of heavy drinking, which was developed as a result of their association with Dionysos). He appears accordingly in various love-stories, in which he usually meets with nothing but frustration; the previously mentioned tale of his seduction of the moon-goddess Selene (see p. 46) is something of an exception. The picturesque story of SYRINX (Pan-pipes) explains the origin of his favourite musical instrument. Syrinx was a beautiful hamadryad nymph who rejected the approaches of the Satyrs and other nature-spirits, preferring to live as a virgin huntress. On catching sight of her one day, Pan conceived a passionate desire for her; and when he found that she would have nothing to do with him, he chased her through the countryside until she arrived at the river Ladon, where she prayed to the nymph of the stream (or to Earth) to save her, and was instantly transformed into a clump of reeds. So when Pan arrived at the spot and tried to seize her, he found that he was clasping nothing more than an armful of reeds. On hearing the wind blowing through the reed-bed, he was strangely moved by the desolate sound, and proceeded to create the first Pan-pipes (*syrinx*) by cutting some reeds of unequal length and joining them together with wax. Or in a rationalistic version, Syrinx was no more than a rustic maiden, and she merely vanished from view among the reeds as she plunged into them.[65]

Pan could be associated with pine-trees as a god of the high hills, and it was said that he liked to crown himself with pine-wreaths. It is therefore no surprise to hear that he should have fallen in love with a nymph called PITYS (Pine), a figure who is first mentioned in Theocritus' *Syrinx*. As in the case of Syrinx, his love was not reciprocated, and Pitys was turned into a pine-tree as she fled. In another version, Boreas (the North Wind) competed with Pan for her love, and was so angry when she preferred Pan that he killed her by blowing her over a cliff; but Earth took pity on her and transformed her into a pine-tree. Pines have made a mournful sound ever since whenever the North Wind blows through them.[66] This latter version was evidently inspired by the tale in which Apollo and Boreas were said to have competed for the love of Hyakinthos (see p. 155), just as the former version was inspired by the myth of Apollo and Daphne (see p. 155).

Pan fared no better when he fell in love with another nymph, ECHO, since she spurned him in favour of a Satyr. The outcome was more tragic on this occasion, for on finding that he could neither win her over nor run her down, he sent some shepherds mad, causing them to tear her to pieces so that only her voice survived.[67]

Ovid offers a different version of Echo's story. To save her fellow nymphs from being caught by Hera while they were dallying with Zeus in the mountains, Echo used to distract her with a constant flow of talk until they could escape. When Hera came to realize that she had been tricked, she curtailed Echo's powers of speech, declaring that the nymph would no longer be able to express any thought of her own, but merely to repeat the last words that she heard from others. While subject to this handicap, she fell in love with a youth called Narkissos (Narcissus in Latin form), a son of the river-god Kephisos by the nymph Leiriope. She followed him around in secret and finally contrived a meeting, but he repelled her when she tried to embrace him, for he was cold by nature, and she lived all alone in the woods from that time onwards. As she pined for her love, she gradually wasted away until nothing was left apart from her bones and her voice; and when her bones turned to stone, she was nothing more than an answering voice.

After Narkissos had rejected many admirers in this way, male and female alike, one of them prayed that he should suffer an unrequited passion on his own part. So one day, as he was leaning over a woodland pool to drink, he fell in love with his own reflection and remained forever at that spot, unable to tear himself away, until he died from exhaustion and unsatisfied desire. His hopeless passion was witnessed by Echo, who re-echoed his sighs and laments. Even in the Underworld, so Ovid tells us, he continues to stare at his reflection in the Styx. He was mourned by the woodland nymphs in the world above, but when his body was due to be cremated, it was nowhere to be seen, and a narcissus-flower was found to have grown up in place of it.[68] Other sources state that the flower sprang from his blood or that he was transformed into it.[69] Pausanias records a rationalized version of this story, saying that he had a twin sister of almost identical appearance, and that he tried to relieve his sorrow after she died by staring at his own reflection and imagining that it was her.[70]

Perhaps the most famous exploit of Pan was the help that he brought to the Athenians at the battle of Marathon (490 BC), by inducing fear in the Persian invaders. On the eve of the great struggle, the Athenians sent the runner Philippides (sometimes wrongly named as Pheidippides) to ask help from the Spartans, who were unable to respond in time because their laws prevented them from marching out before the full moon. Philippides was able to report, however, that he had been accosted by Pan as he was passing through Arcadia, and that the god had told him to 'take a message to the Athenians, asking them why they did not pay him any respect, seeing that he was their friend and had often helped them before, and would do so again'. So after Pan kept his promise by helping them in the battle, they founded a cult to him, with a shrine under the brow of the Acropolis.[71]

Stranger still is a later story that tells of the death of Pan. In the days of Tiberius, a ship that was sailing from Italy to Greece was becalmed near the islands of Paxos and Propaxos off north-western Greece. Suddenly a voice from the shore cried 'Thamuz!'. This was the name of the ship's pilot, an Egyptian, who made no reply at first but finally answered when summoned in this way for the third time. The voice then told him, 'When you draw opposite Palodes, tell them that great Pan is dead.' After some discussion, Thamuz decided that he would sail past without saying anything if a breeze blew up, but would obey the voice if the calm persisted. When they drifted near Palodes in the continuing calm, he shouted out, 'Great Pan is dead!', and was answered by innumerable voices crying out all at once in lamentation and amazement. It has been suggested that the sounds from the shore may have been ritual laments for Thamuz-Adonis; in that case, the cry 'Thamuz the all-great (*pammegas*) is dead' could have been misinterpreted as referring to great Pan (*Pan megas*). It is quite possible on the other hand that the story is simply a fiction.[72]

Attis and Kybele; the Kouretes and Korybantes

Just on the frontiers of classical belief and cult was the great Asiatic goddess KYBELE (or Kybebe), with her cult-partner ATTIS. According to the cultic legend from Pessinous, a main centre of her cult in Galatia (a central province of Asia Minor), she acquired her partner in the following circumstances. Agdistis, a doublet of Kybele, sprang up from the ground in that region after Zeus shed some semen on to it in his sleep (or as he was vainly attempting to make love to Kybele). Although the new-born being had both male and female genital organs, the gods (or Dionysos specifically) cut off its male organs to turn it into a female; and an almond-tree of marvellous beauty grew up from them with its nuts already ripe. When Nana, a daughter of the local river Sangarios, placed some of these nuts (or a blossom from the tree) inside her dress, they (or the blossom) disappeared and she found that she was pregnant with a child. She exposed the child at birth, but a he-goat somehow contrived to attend to him, and he survived to grow up into a wonderfully handsome youth called Attis (or Attes). Agdistis fell in love with him and grew frantically jealous when he was due to marry the daughter of the king of Pessinous. So she appeared at his wedding and drove him mad, and he cut off his genitals in his frenzy with fatal effect. The goddess was overcome by remorse afterwards, and persuaded Zeus to grant that the body of Attis should never decay, and that his little finger should continue to move and his hair to grow. This extraordinary tale purported to explain, among other things, why the priests of Kybele were eunuchs.[73]

In another version of the story of Attis, Kybele fell in love with him after seeing him by the river Gallos in Phrygia, and installed him as her temple-servant, warning him that he should remain chaste and always be faithful to her; but he abandoned her after falling in love with a tree-nymph called Sagaritis, and the angry goddess drove him mad, causing him to cut off his genitals.[74] Or in a rationalized version, Kybele was a Phrygian priestess who was exposed at birth by her father, but survived and later engaged in a secret love affair with a local youth called Attis, becoming pregnant as a consequence. Her parents recalled her to their home at this time, under the belief that she was still a virgin; but her father came to learn of her seduction, and killed Attis along with his nurses and cast them out unburied. Kybele went mad in her grief and roamed through the countryside in a frenzied state, beating on a kettle-drum (*tympanon*, as in the rites of the goddess). And at some later time, when the Phrygians were struck by a plague and famine, they received an oracle ordering them to bury Attis and to honour Kybele as a goddess. Since the youth's body had disappeared by this time, they fashioned an image of him and performed propitiatory rites, hence the origin of his cult.[75]

Both in cult and in legend, Kybele was frequently identified with Rhea (see p. 71); and for that reason, her attendants, the Korybantes, were frequently confused with the Kouretes, who, as already mentioned, attended the infant Zeus. Although these two groups of young male figures were certainly alike in many ways, it will be well to disentangle their traditions. The KOURETES (Kouretai) first appear in a rather surprising context, in a fragment from the Hesiodic *Catalogue* already mentioned in connection with the Satyrs, in which the Satyrs, the mountain-nymphs and 'the divine Kouretes, playful dancers' are all described as sharing a common origin, apparently as children of the daughters of Doros.[76] For this author then, as usually in later belief, they are superhuman beings of a lower order than the gods. They were famous in myth as the Cretan daimones who drowned out the cries of the infant Zeus by performing noisy war-dances in front of the cave where he was hidden (see p. 75). Although Callimachus in the Hellenistic era is the first author to make explicit mention of this story, Euripides seems to allude to it in the *Bacchae*, and it was presumably quite ancient.[77] As beings who were proverbial for their prophetic powers, they also appear in a tale from heroic mythology in which they advise Minos, king of Crete, on how to find his lost son Glaukos (see p. 353). Apollodorus records a curious tale in which Zeus is said to have killed them for abducting his son Epaphos from Egypt (see p. 232); but since they are presumably standing in for a group of foreign divinities, this cannot be regarded as part of their conventional mythology. The name of the Kouretes simply means young men or young warriors, and it has long been suspected that their main story is a mythical reflection of annual rites in which choruses of Cretan youths would perform ritual dances in honour of Zeus probably to promote fertility. In the hymn to Zeus from Palaikastro in Crete, which probably dates to the fourth century BC, such a chorus invites the son of Kronos with music and song (and by implication, dances too) to return to his birthplace of Dikte for the coming year, and to 'leap' to bring fertility to the island's animals and crops, and also bring benefit to its cities and ships, and so on. It is significant that Zeus should be invoked in this poem as the great Kouros who had once stepped out at the head of his daimones (i.e. the Kouretes, whose mythical dance is now imitated by the young men of the chorus).[78]

The KORYBANTES (Whirlers?), so far as the jumbled condition of our evidence (mostly from late sources) enables us to distinguish them from the Kouretes at all, were Asianic rather than Cretan, as daimones who attended on Kybele the Anatolian goddess. There were so many conflicting speculations about their parentage that it is hard to find any two authorities in agreement; they are most often described as sons of Rhea or Apollo by one parent or another, or as sons of a certain Korybas (who was himself a son of Kybele or a fatherless son of Kore).[79] They are constantly associated with ritual dancing, and with mysteries and magical cures; it would seem that the latter were taught only to women. Plato makes several interesting allusions to the Korybantic rites, above all in a passage in the *Laws* in which he explains how they provided a cure for mental disturbances;[80] the cure was homeopathic in character, for it was supposed that the patients could recover their mental equilibrium if their human madness could be displaced by divine madness induced by ecstatic music and dancing. The Korybantes have no proper myths except in so far as they came to be identified with the Kouretes (as was doubtless inevitable after Kybele came to be identified with Rhea). Euripides already mentions them along with the Kouretes (who are perhaps to be regarded as the same here) in connection with the infancy of Zeus, stating that they invented Rhea's drum at that time, evidently to be beaten while the dances were performed for the protection of Zeus.[81]

Some groups of minor divinities associated with the Greek islands

The KABEIROI were more important, even if the Greek world was hardly acquainted with them until the time of Athenian greatness. They were worshipped primarily in the northern Aegean region, especially on Lemnos, but also had notable Boeotian cults at Thebes and at Anthedon on the eastern coast. Their name is of uncertain meaning and origin; although it has long been argued that it may have been derived from a Semitic word, *qabir*, meaning mighty (which accords very well with their Greek titles as the *theoi megaloi* or *dunatai*, the great or mighty gods), there is nothing provably Semitic about their ritual or the history of their cult. It may perhaps have originated in Asia Minor. Be that as it may, they presided over an ancient mystery-cult whose content and rituals are largely unrecorded. They were often identified with another group of gods who presided over a mystery-cult in the northern Aegean, the GODS OF SAMOTHRACE (who were left unnamed in connection with their cult). These latter gods were supposed to protect initiates from all manner of dangers, especially those of the sea. Their effectiveness in this regard was attested by the many votive offerings that were set up at Samothrace by seafarers who had escaped disaster (although Diogenes observed that there would have been many more of them if they were also set up by the people who were *not* saved[82]). In myth, the Argonauts were initiated at Samothrace before sailing into unknown waters (see p. 384); and in historical times, the Samothracian mysteries became widely favoured during the Hellenistic and Roman periods, coming to be regarded as second only to those at Eleusis. There is no indication that the Samothracian mysteries and those of the Kabeiroi provided initiates with better expectations for the afterlife as did those at Eleusis.

It is no surprise that the mythology of beings such as the Kabeiroi should be inconsistent. There are three Kabeiroi in the earliest literary accounts; according to Pherecydes, they were born to Hephaistos by Kabeiro, daughter of Proteus (an old man of the sea), along with three sisters, while Acusilaus prefers to believe that they were the sons of a certain Kamillos who was himself a son of Hephaistos and Kabeiro.[83] It is understandable that they should have been connected with Hephaistos since he had a special association with Lemnos (see pp. 164–5), which was a main centre of their cult. In their cultic legend at Thebes, there were apparently only two of them, a young one and an old one.[84] Or else there were four of them, three male and one female, named Axieros, Kasmilos, Axiokersos and Axiokersa.[85]

Other strange groups of daimones who were associated with the Greek islands were the Dactyls (Fingers) and Telchines, who were pictured as smiths and sorcerers. Although the surviving record with regard to the IDAIAN DAKTYLOI is complex, inconsistent and fragmentary, it seems to have been generally agreed that they were blacksmith-magicians who were somehow connected with Rhea. As that goddess was about to give birth to Zeus on Mt Ida in Crete, she clutched the ground with her hands, and the mountain instantly brought the Daktyloi to birth, one for each of her fingers;[86] or when she brought Zeus to birth in the Diktaian cave in Crete, an attendant nymph, Anchiale, strewed some dust behind her, and the Daktyloi sprang up from it.[87] Since Rhea came to be identified with Kybele, the birth of the Daktyloi was sometimes placed in Kybele's homeland in Asia Minor, on Mt Ida in the Troad. Although it would be logical for there to be ten Daktyloi as in the preceding story, their numbers vary to an eccentric degree. There were five or six male Daktyloi who acted as metal-workers, on their own or with the help of their five sisters;[88] or there were a hundred overall, or twenty-six; or in an account ascribed to Pherecydes, there were thirty-two left-hand Daktyloi, who acted as sorcerers, and twenty right-hand Daktyloi who worked counter-magic.[89] Or according to a fragment from an early epic called the *Phoronis*, there were three Daktyloi named Akmon (Anvil), Damnameneus (effectively Hammer) and Kelmis (Smelter?) who first discovered the art of metal-working.[90] It was also said that the art was taught to them by Rhea.[91] Ovid mentions in passing that Kelmis was once a friend of the infant Zeus but was later turned into adamant (a mythical metal); and it is reported elsewhere that he suffered this fate because he behaved insolently towards Mother Rhea.[92] Some claimed that the Herakles who founded the Olympian Games was not the well-known hero but a dwarfish Dactyl of the same name.[93] These scraps are just enough to tantalize the researcher, and give an idea of what a world of folklore was contained in the mass of Greek literature now lost to us.

The TELCHINES were generally thought to have been primordial inhabitants of Rhodes, although they were also associated with other places such as Cyprus, Ceos and Sicyon. According to Diodorus, they lived at Rhodes until the great flood caused them the scatter in the age of Deukalion. Looking back from the Byzantine era, the lexicon of the Souda is uncertain whether they were malicious daimones or malicious men who had the evil eye.[94] The former interpretation is of course the correct one; some have compared them to the gnomes and Kobolds of northern European folklore. They were skilled in many arts, especially those of metal-working, which was indeed discovered by them according to some accounts; it was said that they fashioned the first statues of the gods.[95] Some traced their activities back to the very earliest times, claiming that they forged Poseidon's trident (a deed also ascribed to the Kyklopes, see p. 69) or even the sickle of Kronos.[96] They were so clever as magicians that they could alter their form and change the weather at will.[97] They were also proverbial for their malice, and were said to have sprinkled Rhodes with water from the Styx (an infernal river, see p. 109) to render it infertile.[98] It was often said that Zeus or some other god finally killed them on account of their malice and presumption.[99] According to a Rhodian tradition, Rhea entrusted the infant Poseidon to the Telchines and the Okeanid Kapheiro to be reared by them on Rhodes.[100]

Glaukos, Priapos and Hymenaios

GLAUKOS (Sea-Green; sometimes distinguished as Glaukos Pontios, 'of the sea') was a minor sea-god who had originated as a mortal. Before eating some magical grass which had rendered him immortal, he had been a humble fisherman who had lived at Anthedon on the Boeotian coast. One day, as he was sorting his catch, he had noticed that the fish from his nets and lines revived if he laid them down on a particular patch of grass; and when he plucked and chewed some of the grass to test its properties, he was immediately transformed into a fish-tailed sea-god with a green beard and body.[101] Although Aeschylus wrote a play about Glaukos, only a few scattered fragments survive, one of them telling how he was transformed after eating the 'immortal, everlasting grass'. Aeschylus located the incident in northern Euboea.[102] He was gifted with prophetic powers, as was so often the case with sea-deities, and rose up from the waves (so Apollonius recounts, see p. 383) to advise the Argonauts after they had been accidentally abandoned by two of their ship-mates.[103] In Euripides' *Orestes*, he is said to have appeared to Menelaos off Cape Malea to inform him of the murder of Agamemnon[104] (so taking over, in part at least, the function that is performed by Proteus in the *Odyssey*, see p. 484). For Ovid's story of his frustrated love for Skylla, see p. 497.

Although the cult of PRIAPOS arrived rather late in Greece, hardly spreading beyond its area of origin by the Hellespont until the end of the fourth century BC, it eventually became widely familiar and spread to Italy too. A preposterous little god who was represented as a more or less grotesquely misshapen man with an erect phallus of disproportionate size, he never seems to have been regarded as a very serious deity outside his original homeland. He watched over flocks, herds and bees, and brought help to herdsmen and fishermen; in later times, he was viewed above all as a guardian of vineyards, orchards and gardens, part scarecrow, part warning to human thieves, part luck-bringer; and in his capacity as a luck-bringer, he was often to be found at the doors of houses. Elegantly obscene Priapic verses were composed in his honour in both Greek and Latin. Such is the Priapos who is most familiar to us from his later career. In his region of origin, however, at Lampsakos and the surrounding area on the Asian shore of the Hellespont, he was a fertility-god of the first importance who was honoured on a level with the Olympian gods. Donkeys were sacrificed to him at Lampsakos, doubtless because they were credited with a lustful nature and exceptional progenitive powers.

The myths of Priapos are late and artificial; some are birth-legends from his native Helles-pontine region while others are tales that link him to his special animal, the donkey. He came to be described as a son of Dionysos and Aphrodite, as is understandable since he was associated with abandonment and sex; or perhaps Aphrodite conceived him to her favourite Adonis while Dionysos was away on his campaign in India. According to a local legend which sets his birth in Aparnis (later Abarnis) near Lampsakos, the jealous Hera touched the body of his pregnant mother to cause him to be born deformed, and Aphrodite was so horrified when she gave birth to a misshapen son with outsized genitals that she renounced him (*aparneito*, hence the name of Aparnis), abandoning him to be reared by shepherds.[105] This story was probably inspired by the similar story that was told about the birth of Pan (see p. 215).

Ovid recounts no less than three stories in which Priapos is frustrated by the untimely braying of a donkey as he is about to attempt a rape. According to one such tale in the *Fasti*, he crept up on the nymph Lotis while she was lying asleep in the open air after a feast of the gods; but at the critical moment, the ass of Seilenos brayed aloud, causing the nymph to awake with a start and Priapos to be exposed to general ridicule. He was so angry that he killed the donkey and welcomed sacrifices of donkeys ever afterwards.[106] Later in the same poem, Ovid tells the same story about Vesta (the Roman equivalent of Hestia see p. 139) to explain why donkeys were rested and garlanded on her feast-day at Rome.[107] Although there is no record of the preceding version in surviving Greek sources, it is reasonable to assume that it originated in Greece as a cultic aetiology, and that Ovid adapted it to provide a mythical explanation for this purely Roman practice associated with the Vestalia. He would doubtless have excluded one of the versions if he had lived to complete the *Fasti*. This is not quite the end of the matter since Ovid offers a different account of Priapos' attempted rape of Lotis in the *Metamorphoses*, stating that she was turned into a lotus-tree (presumably in response to a prayer of her own) as she was fleeing from him.[108] This story is evidently modelled on the famous transformation myth in which Daphne was turned into a laurel-tree (*daphnē*) as she was fleeing from Apollo (see p. 155). Ovid probably invented it to accord with the general theme of the poem (although it is of course possible that this was the original Greek version of the story of the attempted rape).

According to another donkey-story, Dionysos once came up against an impassable swamp as he was travelling to his father's oracle at Dodona to seek a cure for a fit of madness that had been inflicted on him by Hera. He found a way across, however, by riding through the marshes on a donkey that he encountered there; and after achieving his cure at Dodona, he rewarded the beast by granting it the power of human speech. It used its new-found powers to challenge Priapos to a contest over the size of their genital organs; but the god proved to be better-endowed and killed the beast to punish it for its impertinence.[109] This story is preserved in the astral myth that was devised to explain the origin of the two stars in the constellation Cancer that were (and still are) known as the Asses, or Aselli in Latin. Since there were two such stars, complications were introduced into the tale when it was adapted into a star-myth, but these need not concern us here.

To pass on to a more respectable god, HYMENAIOS was the deity who presided over weddings. His name was derived from the traditional wedding-cry of *Hymen of Hymenaie* (or the like), which could be interpreted as an invocation to a deity called Hymenaios (or Hymen). He was commonly pictured as a handsome young man, tall and rather epicene, carrying a bridal torch and wreath as his attributes. It is understandable that he should usually be classed as a son of one or other of the Muses,[110] since these were the deities who led the wedding-song (*hymenaios*) at marriages of the gods; or else he is described in some Latin sources as a son of Dionysos by Aphrodite or some unnamed mother.[111] Or else he had been a fine singer of mortal birth who had died on his wedding-day, or before his proper time, or as he was singing at the wedding-feast of Dionysos.[112] Or in a fully rationalized account, he was an ordinary Athenian when had died long ago and had come to be commemorated in the wedding-song as a result of the following course of events.

Though exceptionally handsome (so this story relates), Hymenaios was of modest birth, and when he fell in love with an Athenian girl of noble family, all he could do was follow her around to admire her at a distance. One day, as she and her friends were participating in the rites of Demeter at Eleusis, they were snatched away by some pirates, who also seized Hymenaios because he had been trailing his beloved. After the voyage, however, he managed to kill the pirates in their sleep, and made his way back to Athens on his own. On his arrival, he told the citizens about the fate of their missing daughters, and offered to fetch them back again if he were allowed to marry the one whom he loved. So he fulfilled his pledge and married her; and since the marriage proved to be exceptionally happy, it became the custom to invoke his name at weddings.[113] There is mention of a tradition in which an evidently mortal Hymenaios was restored to life by Asklepios, though nothing is recorded of the circumstances;[114] and some said that he was loved by Apollo, or Hesperos (the Evening Star), or Thamyris, or an obscure hero called Argynnos.[115] Argos is the only place that is ever mentioned as having a cult of Hymenaios.[116]

We may pass over, as not germane to a book of this kind, some legends of foreign deities which had no very wide currency among the Greeks, such as that of Isis, which in its late form, as known to Plutarch,[117] had patently been influenced by the story of Demeter. Deserving of passing mention, however, by way of a post-script, are two curiosities from Latin sources. Roman authors from Ovid onwards sometimes refer to the maiden in the sky – the constellation Virgo – as ASTRAIA (the Starry Woman), and state that she had abandoned the earth because she had been so appalled by human wickedness.[118] Although there is no indication that this name was ever applied to her in Greek literature, the tale of her departure origi-nated in an allegorical star-legend recounted by the Hellenistic poet Aratus, who wrote a well-known didactic poem on the phenomena of the heavens. Aratus tells how the star-maiden (here simply called Parthenos, the Maiden, the Greek equiva-lent of Virgo) had lived among human beings under the name of Dike (Justice) in the time of the golden race (see p. 224), but had withdrawn to the hills when morals had declined in the time of the silver race, now satisfying herself with reproaching human wickedness from a distance, and finally, in horror at the violence and injus-tice of the bronze race, had fled to the heavens, where her figure may still be seen as a silent reproach.[119] The idea that she could be called Astraia was evidently prompted by a remark at the beginning of the relevant section of Aratus' poem, in which he suggests that she may have been a daughter of Astraios[120] (who was the father of all the stars in Hesiod's *Theogony*, see p. 48). And lastly, something should be said of DEMOGORGON, whose 'dread name' appealed to the imagination of Spenser, Milton and, above all, Shelley. It is rather a shame that such a fine-sounding deity should be no more than a figment that was created by a copyist's blunder. In his Latin epic on the Theban War, Statius makes his Teiresias mention with awe 'the most High One of the triple universe, whom it is not lawful to know';[121] and an ancient commentator reports in a note on this passage, as presently preserved, that the poet meant Demogorgon.[122] But since there is no sign of this improbable name in any other ancient source, it is now agreed that the note originally referred to Demiurgus, the Demiurge or Creator-god.

CHAPTER SEVEN

THE EARLY HISTORY
OF THE INACHIDS

——— .•. ———

The first four chapters of our survey of heroic mythology will be devoted to the Inachid family, which ruled in Argos, Thebes and Crete and produced the greatest of all Greek heroes, Herakles. Since it was supposed that most of the main heroes and heroines of legend would have belonged to the royal family of their native area, the mythical history of each city and land was in all essentials the history of its ruling family, as organized on a genealogical basis. Once a consistent account had been developed of the succession within each kingdom, all the mythical figures and legendary events associated with that area could be assigned to a specific point in time in relation to the reigns of the various kings; and since the heroes and heroines of each kingdom often interacted with those of others, through wars and marriages, for instance, or participation in joint adventures, it was necessary that the genealogies of the separate royal families should be synchronized with one another (even if this was not always perfectly achieved, see e.g. p. 337). On this basis, a remarkably coherent pseudo-history came to be developed for much of legendary Greece. The process was initiated in epic, most notably in the *Catalogue of Women* (a genealogical poem of the early sixth century BC traditionally ascribed to Hesiod, see pp. 10–12), and was brought to a high degree of development thereafter by early prose mythographers such as Pherecydes and Hellanicus (see pp. 9 and 15). According to the simplest pattern, a single ruling family would provide the ruling line in a single centre, as in the case of the royal families of Athens and Arcadia, which were both descended from indigenous earthborn ancestors. In general, however, the heroic genealogies tended to be more sophisticated and economical than this, since the mythographers liked to unite different ruling lines within a single family by tracing them back to common ancestors. The present family of the Inachids offers a striking example of this, as does that of the Atlantids, in which the family of Helen at Sparta is drawn into the same genealogical system as that of her abductor Paris at Troy.

As may be appreciated from this, nothing could be less true of Greek heroic legend than to suppose that it tells of events that were situated in some vague and indeterminate mythical antiquity. Most significant heroes and heroines and their adventures could be dated to a specific point in time within the heroic era, and the heroic era itself could be placed in a datable relation to the era of conventional history, which was supposed to have begun in the generations immediately following the Trojan War. This mightiest of wars, in which leading heroes from all parts of Greece were said to have joined together in a common enterprise of unparalleled magnitude, was the culminating event of the heroic era, and a relatively short span of time was thought to have elapsed — usually no more than six or seven generations or so — between the time of origin of the various Greek royal lines and the outbreak of the war. The three other great panhellenic enterprises, the voyage of the Argonauts, the hunt for the Calydonian boar, and the Theban Wars, were supposed to have taken place in the generation preceding the Trojan War. We will begin with two great heroic families that were only marginally connected with the Trojan War, the Inachids and Deukalionids, and then consider the war itself before passing on to the families that were most closely connected with it. The three panhellenic adventures that preceded it will be discussed in relation to the first two families, as will the lives of Herakles and Theseus.

The Inachid family was descended from **Inachos**, the god of the greatest river of the Argolid, and was thus of Argive origin; but although Argos was long a main centre of Inachid rule, Inachid dynasties of comparable importance came to be established in Thebes and Crete as a result of the following course of events. An early Argive princess, **Io**, wandered off to Egypt for reasons that will be explained shortly and married the king of the land, who bequeathed his throne to a son whom she had borne to Zeus. This son of hers, Epaphos, was succeeded by one of his two grandsons, **Belos**, while his other grandson **Agenor**, the twin brother of Belos, went away to found a kingdom of his own in Phoenicia. Since descendants of Belos would come to rule in their ancestral homeland in Argos while two children of Agenor would found new Inachid lines in Thebes and Crete, Belos and Agenor were destined to become the ancestors of separate branches of the family within the Greek world. To start with the latter, Agenor had a beautiful daughter **Europa** who was removed to Crete at the will of Zeus, where she bore him three sons including Minos, the island's greatest mythical ruler; and when Agenor sent his sons in search of her, they all failed to find her and settled abroad as a consequence, including **Kadmos**, who founded the great city of Thebes in Central Greece at the bidding of the Delphic oracle. Belos for his part had two sons, **Aigyptos** and **Danaos**, who ruled in adjoining kingdoms and fathered a great many children, Aigyptos fifty sons and Danaos fifty daughters. Aigyptos was eager to marry his sons to his nieces and put pressure on his brother to agree, but Danaos was unwilling to see his family absorbed into that of his brother and tried to escape that predicament by fleeing to Argos with his daughters, the **Danaids**.

When the sons of Aigyptos subsequently arrived in pursuit, Danaos adopted a more ruthless stratagem by pretending to agree to the marriages but ordering his daughters to kill their husbands on their wedding night. He was disobeyed, however, by one of his daughters, **Hypermnestra**, who spared her husband **Lynkeus** and helped him to safety. Danaos, who had established himself as king of Argos, eventually consented to their marriage and was succeeded by their son Abas, who was succeeded in his turn by his twin sons **Proitos** and **Akrisios**. The twins had fought one another even in their mother's womb and now embarked on a war that resulted in the partition of the kingdom. The Argolid would not be reunited into a single kingdom until well after the Trojan War. The two foremost heroes in the family, Perseus and Herakles, were both descended from Akrisios, who ruled his half of the land from the city of Argos. After being warned by an oracle that his daughter would bear a son who would kill him, Akrisios tried to avert the danger by enclosing his daughter **Danae** in an underground chamber, but Zeus slipped through the roof in the form of a shower of gold and caused her to conceive the mighty **Perseus**. On learning of his birth, Akrisios enclosed him in a chest along with his mother and set it adrift in the sea. He and his mother were carried unharmed, however, to the rocky Aegean island of Seriphos, where they were offered shelter by a brother of the king. After growing up on the island and establishing his heroic credentials by fetching the head of the Gorgon Medusa and rescuing his prospective bride, **Andromeda**, from a sea-monster, Perseus sailed back to Argos to seek a reconciliation with his grandfather; but he came to kill him just as the oracle had predicted as the result of a tragic accident. After exchanging his grandfather's kingdom for that of Megapenthes, the son of his great-uncle Proitos, Perseus ruled in the Argolid thereafter, founding the stronghold of Mycenae as his seat of rule. The affairs of his immediate descendants are primarily of interest in relation to the origin of the most distinguished of them, **Herakles**, a great-grandson of his who came to be born in exile at Thebes.

The history of the early Inachids in Argos and Egypt, as summarized in the preceding paragraphs, will form the subject of the present chapter. Since Herakles spent most of his life outside his ancestral land and his mythology is so exceptionally rich, taking him to many different areas, his career will be examined separately in the next chapter along with the history of his descendants, the Heraklids. As for the other main branches of the family that were descended from Agenor, king of Phoenicia, the Kadmeian ruling line at Thebes will be considered in Chapter 9 and Europa's descendants in Crete in Chapter 10.

Phoroneus, the first ruler of Argos, and his immediate descendants

The first man of Argos, and perhaps the first man of all, was PHORONEUS, who was fathered by Inachos on an Okeanid nymph called Melia or Argia.[1] He was described as the first of mortal men in the *Phoronis*,[2] an archaic epic that would have recorded the local traditions about Phoroneus and the ancient history of the Argolid. He was more a culture-hero, however, than an epic hero in the conventional sense, as the primordial ruler of Argos who was supposed to have introduced the first elements of civilization and to have established the main cults of the land. In that respect, he may be compared to Pelasgos in Arcadia (see p. 537) or Kekrops at Athens (see p. 364). Just as Athens was noted for its association with Athena, Argos was marked out from other lands by its special association with Hera, who had been the great goddess of Argos from time immemorial, or, in mythical terms, ever since the reign of its first king. As in the case of Athena at Athens, Hera was said to have established her position as patron deity by defeating Poseidon in a contest for the land. Phoroneus was appointed as arbitrator, and he chose in favour of Hera after consulting with his father Inachos and two other river-gods of the area,

Kephisos and Asterion. Poseidon was so angry that he reduced most of the land to aridity by causing its rivers to run dry for much of the year, so turning it into the 'thirsty Argos' of proverb.[3] After inviting Hera into Argos in this way, Phoroneus established her cult by honouring her with the first sacrifices ever offered to her.[4] In his function as ruler, he gathered his people (one should not enquire too anxiously about their origin) into the first settled community, the 'town of Phoroneus', *astu Phoronikon*, which would later develop into the great city of Argos.[5] The Argives went so far as to claim that Phoroneus (rather than Prometheus) had first introduced fire to the human race, hence an eternal flame that was burned in his honour in the temple of Apollo Lykaios in Argos.[6]

Phoroneus married a nymph who is variously named as Teledike, Kerdo or Peitho,[7] and fathered a daughter NIOBE, who was the first mortal woman to bear a child to Zeus. This marked the opening of an era in mythological time that would be brought to an end when Alkmene, a descendant of Niobe in the sixteenth generation, gave birth to Herakles, the last child borne to Zeus by a mortal woman. As the child of her liaison with Zeus, Niobe gave birth to ARGOS, the eponym of the city and land. His tomb and sacred grove could be seen near the city of Argos.[8]

Argos, who has no myths at all, was succeeded by one of his sons, PEIREN (or Peiras, or Peirasos, or Peiranthos), who was the father of IO in the earliest tradition.[9] In some later accounts, however, the Argive king-list was lengthened slightly, and Io came to be described as a descendant of Argos in the third or fourth generation, as the daughter of a certain Iasos.[10] Or conversely, authors such as the Attic tragedians and Ovid, who were not concerned about the niceties of the local tradition or questions of mythical chronology, ignored all the intervening kings and simply described Io as a daughter of the river-god Inachos.[11] This latter genealogy became so familiar, indeed, that authors of the Hellenistic and Roman periods could refer to her as 'the daughter of Inachos' without needing to specify her name.

Io is seduced by Zeus, transformed into a cow, and placed under the guard of Argos Panoptes

The father of Io (whoever he may have been) appointed her to be the virgin priestess of Argive Hera, but she was so very beautiful that Zeus seduced her, and she came to be transformed into a cow as a consequence, temporarily at least. In Apollodorus' account, which may have been largely based on that offered in the Hesiodic *Catalogue*, Zeus turned her into a white cow with a touch of his hand when Hera came to learn of their relationship, and then swore to his wife that he had never had intercourse with the girl. As a result of this divine precedent, so 'Hesiod' remarks, perjuries committed for the sake of love have never attracted anger or punishment from the gods. Hera was not deceived, however, by Zeus's action in transforming Io or his protestations, and demanded that the cow should be handed over to her. She then placed it under the guard of ARGOS PANOPTES (the All-Seeing), who was well equipped to serve as a watchman because he never slept and had eyes all over his body, or at least one or two additional eyes in the back of his neck.[12]

Figure 7.1 Hermes killing Argos Panoptes. Io, on the right, is oddly represented as a bull. Attic red-figure amphora, c. 480 BC. Museum für Kunst und Gerwerbe, Hamburg.

In another account of Io's transformation, Hera performed it herself to put an end to the love affair; but Zeus continued to consort with Io in her new form by assuming the form of a bull, and Hera was then obliged to place the cow under the guard of the many-eyed Argos.[13]

Zeus was determined to gain possession of the cow and ordered Hermes, the patron god of thieves, to steal it away from under the eyes of its guard. It was tethered to an olive-tree in a sacred grove between Argos and Mycenae (or else by the Heraion near Mycenae). Although Hermes initially planned to remove it by stealth, his intentions were betrayed by a certain Hierax (Hawk, who may perhaps have been turned into a bird of that kind as a punishment for his indiscretion). So the god resorted to force instead, and killed Argos Panoptes with a well-aimed stone before untying the cow.[14] Or in Ovid's account, he lulled Argos to sleep by playing on his reed-pipes and by passing his magic wand over the monster's eyes, and then cut off his head with a sickle.[15] This story of the slaying of Argos was evidently devised to provide an explanation for Hermes' ancient title of Argeiphontes (of uncertain origin and meaning, but here interpreted as meaning Argos-slayer).[16]

Although it is unlikely that a local monster like Argos Panoptes would have been credited with any specific parentage in the earliest tradition, he is usually fitted into the Argive royal family at some point in surviving accounts, as a son or descendant of Argos, son of Niobe. Some followed Acusilaus, on the other hand, in describing him as earthborn. According to Pherecydes, who describes him as a son of Arestor and thus a great-grandson of the first Argos, Hera prepared him for his guard-duties by placing an extra eye in the back of his neck and rendering him sleepless; or in the Hesiodic *Aigimios*, in which he was also rendered sleepless by Hera, he had four eyes overall, two in the usual position and two on the back of his neck.[17] In the standard later tradition, however, he had numerous eyes all over his body, giving him a most striking appearance, as can be appreciated from portrayals of him in fifth-century vase-paintings. He was very large besides and liked to wear a bull's hide as a cape.[18] Apollodorus explains the origin of the cape by saying that Argos took it from a bull which had been causing havoc in neighbouring Arcadia; and he also reports that Argos once killed a Satyr who had been robbing the Arcadians of their cattle, and even killed the monstrous Echidna (see p. 62).[19] According to Moschus, a Hellenistic bucolic poet, the peacock with its many-eyed tail sprang up from the blood of the dead Argos; or in later accounts, Hera is said to have transferred his eyes into the tail of the peacock, or to have transformed Argos himself into a peacock.[20] The peacock was the special bird of Hera, just as the owl was the bird of Athena. The name of this Argos remains familiar in modern usage as a title for newspapers (which are supposed to let nothing escape their view) and in the expression 'Argos-eyed'. Apollonius attributes the building of the *Argo* to an Argos who wore a bull's hide cape; although this Argos, who is described as a son of Arestor, was evidently modelled on the present Argos, he can hardly be identified with him because the Argonauts lived many generations later; and the poet presumably intended that he should be regarded as a descendant of his.[21]

Apollodorus may be consulted for an account of the early history of the Argolid that was probably derived from the Argive mythographer Acusilaus (late sixth century BC) for the most part; Pelasgos, the earthborn first man of Arcadia (see p. 537), is here annexed to the Argive royal line as a son of Niobe and brother of Argos.[22] Acusilaus also provided Sparta with an Argive eponym in the form of a brother of Niobe called Sparton (although any Spartan would have been astonished to hear of this, as Pausanias remarks).[23] Peiren, the traditional father of Io, was an ancient figure with cultic associations; he was said to have erected the first cultic image of Hera, a pear-wood statue which was set up by him at Tiryns but later transferred to the great Heraion near Mycenae.[24]

The *Prometheus Bound* offers a singular account of Io's troubles. While asleep in her father's palace, she was visited by beguiling dreams that urged her to go out to the meadows of Lerna (to the south of Argos) to allow Zeus to make love to her. She took no action, however, and finally summoned up the courage to report her troubles to her father Inachos, who sent envoys to the oracles at Delphi and Dodona to ask what he should do; and when he at last received a clear answer, he was told that he should turn Io out of his house or else suffer the destruction of his race. When he took this action under force of necessity, Io was immediately transformed into a cow; and she was goaded by a gadfly to proceed to Lerna and then from land to land. Aeschylus' account of the events that followed Io's expulsion from the palace, as presented in her own narrative, is wilfully obscure; we are not told who transformed her, or when Zeus caused her to become pregnant. It is perhaps reasonable to assume that Hera transformed her and sent her on her wanderings in order to frustrate her husband's desire, and that Zeus had no physical relations with her until he made her pregnant in Egypt (her ultimate home, see below) with a touch of his hand.[25]

Ovid's account is picturesque and unproblematic. Hera realized that her husband was up to mischief on observing a patch of darkness that he had spread over Argos to conceal his dalliance; and as she was hurrying to the spot, Zeus turned Io into a cow to hide her presence. Hera then asked to be given the beast and placed it under guard, as in the early version summarized above. Ovid adds an attractive detail to the story at this point: to reassure her father Inachos, who had no idea where she was and feared that she was dead, the transformed Io revealed her identity and fate to him by tracing letters in the dust with her hoof.[26]

Io wanders to Egypt, where she is returned to human form and gives birth to Epaphos

On finding that Hermes had foiled her plan to confine the cow in one place, Hera sent a gadfly against it to ensure that it would now be constantly on the move without a moment's rest. In the final form of the myth, Io wandered all the way to Egypt before finding any relief. Although it is impossible to trace the earlier evolution of the myth in any detail or with much certainty, her wanderings would surely have been confined to the Argolid in the earliest tradition; and it has been plausibly suggested that she would have roamed from the city of Argos to the great Heraion near Mycenae, which was located on a hill known as Euboia. A subsequent version of the story, perhaps originating in Euboea itself, suggested that she travelled considerably further, to the island of Euboea (properly Euboia) off Central Greece; a fragment from the Hesiodic *Aigimios* indicates that she was once there and that Zeus named the island Euboea (interpreted as meaning 'Good Cow Land') in her honour; and in the later tradition at least, Io was sometimes said to have settled on Euboea and to have given birth to Zeus's son in a cave on the island.[27] By the classical period, a more extravagant version had established itself in which the transformed Io went all the way to Egypt, where Zeus restored her to her original form and so enabled her to give birth to her child. We should imagine her as travelling northwards through Greece, doubtless calling in at Euboea on the way, and then through Thrace and across the Bosporos (i.e. Cow's Strait) into Asia Minor, before passing down through Syria and Phoenicia to her ultimate destination. In the *Prometheus Bound*, her itinerary is more extravagant still, taking her to the Caucasus, where she meets the enchained Prometheus, who predicts that her journey will take her across the Cimmerian Bosporos and past the Graiai and Gorgons, and the Arimaspians and Griffins (see p. 580).[28] Some claimed that the Ionian Sea (between Greece and lower Italy) was named after her because she had visited its shores during her wanderings.[29]

When Io arrived in Egypt, Zeus returned her to her proper form, and she gave birth to a son, EPAPHOS, beside the banks of the Nile. It could be explained that he was given this name because Zeus had delivered his mother from her animal form with a touch (*epaphē*) of his hand, or had rendered her pregnant with a touch.[30] Io came to be identified with the Egyptian goddess Isis, although there is no definite evidence for this until the Hellenistic period, and her son Epaphos was identified with Apis, the bull-god who was worshipped at Memphis, as Herodotus already records.[31] In a relatively late myth which was obviously inspired by the Egyptian myth of Isis' search for the lost Osiris, the Kouretes are said to have stolen the infant Epaphos at the bidding of Hera, causing the unfortunate Io to set off on her travels once again; she roamed northward through Syria in search of him until she finally discovered him at Byblos, a coastal city to the north of Sidon, where she was being tended by the wife of the king. The Kouretes, who seem ill-suited to this role as former protectors of the infant Zeus (see p. 75), were presumably inserted in place of some Egyptian deities. We are told that Zeus killed them by way of punishment. After recovering her son, Io returned to Egypt, where she married Telegonos, the king of the Egyptians who adopted Epaphos as his successor.[32]

The immediate descendants of Io, and the dividing of the Inachid line

In the Greek tradition, Epaphos was the great city-founder of early Egypt. He is already mentioned in this connection by Pindar, who refers to 'the numerous cities founded in Egypt by the hand of Epaphos'; and Hyginus reports correspondingly that Zeus ordered him to fortify the cities in Egypt and reign there, and that he founded Memphis and many other towns.[33] Although Hyginus names his wife as Kassiepeia, it was commonly thought that he married Memphis, a daughter of the Nile, and founded the great city of Memphis in Lower Egypt in her name.[34] Memphis bore him a daughter who was of still greater significance as an eponym, namely LIBYE, who gave her name to the African territories to the west of Egypt (a much broader area than the modern Libya).[35] Poseidon abducted Libye and fathered twin sons by her, BELOS, who remained in Egypt and succeeded Epaphos as king, and AGENOR, who departed to Phoenicia to found a kingdom of his own.[36]

It is at this point that the Inachid family divides into its two main branches, for the Argive royal family will be formed from descendants of Belos, while two children of Agenor will found new Inachid ruling lines in Crete and Thebes; see Table 4. We will concentrate on Belos' branch of the family in the present chapter, examining in the first place how one of his sons and all of his grandchildren came to return to their ancestral homeland in Argos. The history of the Agenorids will be traced in Chapters 8 and 9. As was noted above, the immediate family of Agenor was scattered after his daughter Europa was abducted to Crete by Zeus; for he sent his sons in search of her, telling them to stay away until they had found her, and they all settled abroad after failing in their quest (see p. 294). His most important son, Kadmos, founded a royal line in Central Greece after founding the city of Thebes at the order of the Delphic oracle (see pp. 295ff), while Europa bore Minos and other children to Zeus on Crete, and so became the founder of the ruling family of the island (see pp. 337ff).[37]

The Danaids flee to Argos in the hope of escaping their suitors, the sons of Aigyptos

BELOS is of genealogical significance alone. His name is simply a Hellenized form of the Semitic word Baal (meaning Lord), a title that was applied to local presiding gods in the Near East. He succeeded to the Egyptian throne and married Anchinoe, daughter of the Nile, who bore him twin sons, DANAOS and AIGYPTOS.[38] Kepheus and Phineus, the father and uncle of Andromeda (see pp. 240 and 242), are also classed as sons of Belos in some accounts[39] (but see also on p. 295); and according to the Hesiodic *Catalogue*, he had a daughter Thronie who bore Arabos, the eponym of the Arabs, to Hermes.[40]

Aigyptos was of course the eponym of the Egyptians (Aigyptoi in Greek). According to Apollodorus, he was installed in Arabia by his father while Danaos was installed in Libya, but he later conquered the land of the Melampodes (Blackfeet, presumably Egyptians who were not already under the rule of his father) and named it Egypt after himself. He and Danaos fathered large families by many different women in a manner that was more oriental than Greek, Aigyptos fathering fifty sons, and Danaos fifty daughters who were known as the DANAIDS (DANAIDES). The two brothers eventually quarrelled because Aigyptos was determined to marry his sons to the Danaids, a scheme that was repugnant to Danaos since it would mean that his family would be absorbed into that of his brother, and his own position would be greatly weakened as a consequence. According to a surviving fragment from the *Danais*, an early epic that was devoted to the legend of Danaos, the Danaids went so far as to arm themselves by the banks of the Nile, evidently with the intention of resisting their cousins by force.[41] In accordance with a suggestion from Athena, Danaos tried to escape the problem by building a large fifty-oared ship and fleeing to Argos with his daughters. Some claimed that this was the first large seagoing ship ever to be constructed; and although this honour was more commonly credited to the *Argo* (see p. 382), the legend of Danaos is certainly set at an earlier period in mythical history.[42] In further explanation of his flight, it was sometimes stated that he had received an oracle warning him that he would be killed by one of the sons of Aigyptos if they should marry his daughters.[43]

After stopping off at Lindos on Rhodes, where the Danaids founded the temple of Athena and their father dedicated a statue to the goddess,[44] they arrived at Argos, which was now under the rule of GELANOR, son of Sthenelas. As the leading member of another branch of the Inachid ruling family, Gelanor had a legitimate claim to the throne, but he agreed to abdicate in favour of Danaos either of his own free will or in obedience to a sign from the gods. A local version of the story is recorded in the cultic legend that was devised to explain the origin of the shrine of Apollo Lykaios at Argos. When Danaos arrived to claim the kingdom, the citizens of Argos listened patiently to his arguments and those of Gelanor but found that the issue seemed so evenly balanced (as it might well have been on the crucial matter of descent) that they deferred their decision until the next day. The matter was resolved on their behalf, however, by a sign from the gods; for at dawn on the following morning, a wolf suddenly broke into a herd of cattle that was grazing just outside the city walls, and killed the leading bull; and the Argives interpreted this as a portent that indicated that the newcomer (as represented in the wolf) should displace the present ruler (as represented in the bull). Believing that Apollo had sent the wolf (*lykos*), Danaos expressed his gratitude by founding the cult of Apollo Lykaios (here interpreted as meaning Apollo of the Wolves). He also founded Larisa, the citadel of Argos, and gave his name to his subjects, who were known thenceforth as Danaans rather than Pelasgians as previously.[45]

Danaos incites his daughters to murder the sons of Aigyptos on their wedding-night

Refusing to be deterred by the flight of their cousins, the sons of Aigyptos soon arrived in Argos to press their suit. They assumed a conciliatory tone, inviting Danaos to abandon his enmity and consent to a union between the two families; but he mistrusted their intentions, and bore them a grudge in addition because he had been forced to flee from his original kingdom. So he mollified them by pretending to agree to the marriages, and cast lots to assign each of his daughters to a specific bridegroom; when the time came for the wedding, however, he secretly provided his daughters with daggers and instructed them to kill their husbands while they were asleep on their wedding-night. They all obeyed him with the sole exception of Hypermnestra (or Hypermestra), who spared her husband Lynkeus (see below).[46]

According to Apollodorus, Athena and Hermes purified the Danaids from their crime at the order of Zeus, and Danaos subsequently married them off by awarding them to the victors of an athletic contest.[47] This story of the contest must have been a fairly ancient story since it was known to Pindar, and the detail about the divine purification was probably at least as old, since something of the kind would have been necessary if the Danaids were to be marriageable after committing such a crime. As Pindar tells the story, Danaos found new husbands for forty-eight of his daughters (i.e. all except Hypermnestra and Amymone, see below) before noon on a single day by lining them up at the finishing-line of a race-track and causing their suitors to race for them. The suitors evidently made their choice (perhaps by touching their chosen bride) in the order in which they completed the race.[48] In a later version recorded by Pausanias, in which the story has lost its naivety and even acquired a comical edge, the young men of the time were unwilling to marry the Danaids on account of their guilt until Danaos offered to give them away without receiving a bride-price. When some suitors arrived, though not very many, he organized a foot-race to determine their order of choice; and the girls who were left over had to await the arrival of further suitors and another race.[49] According to a well-known story from the later tradition, the Danaids were punished forever in the world below by being forced to attempt the impossible task of fetching water in leaky jars, or filling a leaky cistern. As has already been observed, this motif of futile water-carrying was originally devised to illustrate the posthumous predicament of those who had failed to have themselves initiated into the mysteries, and the task was transferred to the Danaids at some stage in the Hellenistic period (see p. 119).[50]

It seems to have been firmly established in the local tradition that the massacre was committed at Lerna to the south of Argos, where the sons of Aigyptos had set up their camp. According to Pausanias, who based his report on direct knowledge of the local memorials, the bodies of the sons of Aigyptos were buried separately from their heads since the Danaids took the heads to their father in Argos as proof of their deed.[51] The proverbial phrase 'a Lerna of evils' referred to this tradition that claimed that the sons of Aigyptos had been buried there.[52] It is worth noting, incidentally, that if exception is made for one Byzantine account,[53] the bodies are always said to have been buried rather than thrown into the swamps or lakes of the area (an action that would have tainted the waters). Apollodorus is exceptional in suggesting that the Danaids buried the heads at Lerna and the bodies with proper funeral rites in front of Danaos; one may suspect that the proper locations have been inverted by error.[54]

Aigyptos was usually said to have remained behind in Egypt when his sons pursued the Danaids to Argos; but the early Attic tragedian Phrynichos represented him as travelling to Greece with his sons, and Pausanias records a story from Patrai that carries the same implication. For according to the local tradition at that city, which lay on the northern coast of the Peloponnese, he had fled to Patrai (then called Aroe) in horror at the murder of his children, and was buried there in a tomb that could be seen in historical times.[55]

The Danaid Amymone is seduced by Poseidon, and bears him a son, Nauplios

Two of the Danaids alone escaped the guilt of murder, Hypermnestra because she spared her husband and AMYMONE because she was unable to marry, having become pregnant beforehand in the following circumstances. On arriving in Argos, Danaos had found that there was a shortage of water and had sent his daughters in search of further supplies; and Amymone had wandered to the district of Lerna, on the shores of the Argolic Gulf a few miles south of the city of Argos. In contrast to most of the Argolid, which was notoriously dry, this was a well-watered region with permanent springs, streams and swamps; and it was said that it owed its abundant water to Amymone (in part at least) because she had encountered Poseidon there and he had rewarded her for her favours by creating a spring or springs with a blow of his trident. The fullest accounts all involve a Satyr, following a version developed by Aeschylus, who wrote a Satyr-play about Amymone to complement his Danaid trilogy. In the course of her journey, Amymone threw her hunting-spear at a deer, but happened to hit a sleeping Satyr instead; he leapt up and tried to rape her, but she was saved by the intervention of Poseidon, who scared the Satyr away and proceeded to seduce her, and rewarded her afterwards by revealing or creating the springs of Lerna.[56] Or in a slightly different version, the Satyr set out to rape her when she fell asleep from exhaustion, but Poseidon scared him off by hurling his trident, which became embedded in a rock; after winning her favours, he told her that she would gain her reward if she pulled the trident out of the rock, and three springs of water gushed forth when she did so (one for each prong).[57] This legend explained the origin of the spring of Amymone at Lerna, which gave rise to a sizeable stream of the same name.

By creating this new source of water, Poseidon made partial amends for having deprived Argos of most of its water long ago after he was defeated by Hera in a contest for the land (see p. 103). Lerna was richly provided with water because its springs were fed by underground channels from Arcadia; there were marshes there too which were significant in myth as the home of the Lernaian hydra (see p. 258), and a bottomless lake which communicated with the Underworld (see p. 109).[58] Amymone was supposed to have discovered a well at the city of Argos too, as were three of her sisters; the services that were performed by the Danaids in this regard were already noted in the Hesiodic *Catalogue*.[59]

As the result of her liaison with Poseidon, Amymone gave birth to a son, NAUPLIOS (Seafarer), who founded the city of Nauplia (later Nauplion) in the north-eastern corner of the Argolic Gulf.[60] He used this city, which was the sea-port of Tiryns, as his home-port during his long career as a seafarer. His legends fall into two groups, those in which rulers asked him to dispose of their daughters for different reasons (see pp. 355 and 543), and those in which he took action against the Greeks who had fought at Troy (see pp. 485 and 487) to avenge the murder of his son Palamedes at Troy (see p. 460). Ancient authors ascribe all these stories to the same person even though this would mean that he must have lived for many generations; Apollodorus notes the point by remarking that he was long-lived (*makrobios*, perhaps as a privilege granted to him by his divine father, as in the case of Sarpedon, see p. 350). Apollonius and some subsequent authors mention a later Nauplios who was a descendant of the original in the fifth generation, but only as a skilled seaman who sailed with the Argonauts;[61] there is no indication in surviving sources that the Nauplios who acted against the Greeks after the Trojan War was ever identified with this other Nauplios, son of Klytoneos, rather than the earlier son of Poseidon and Amymone.

In the *Returns*, an early epic in the Trojan cycle, the wife of Nauplios was apparently a certain Philyra, but in tragedy and later sources she is always Klymene, a daughter of Katreus, king of Crete;[62] for the story of how he came to marry her, see p. 355. The couple had one son of major importance, Palamedes, an ingenious inventor who met an ignominious death at Troy through the machinations of Odysseus (see pp. 459–60), and two other sons of lesser note, Oiax (see p. 460) and Nausimedon.[63]

The Danaid Hypermnestra saves her husband Lynkeus, and bears him a son, Abas

The only Danaid marriage to last beyond the wedding-day was that of HYPERM-NESTRA, who spared her husband LYNKEUS because she was grateful to him for not forcing himself on her during their wedding-night, or because she conceived an immediate love for him.[64] On learning from her of Danaos' plot, he took flight to Lyrkeia, a settlement high on a hillside a few miles to the north-west of Argos, and lit a beacon to let Hypermnestra know that he had escaped unharmed; and she lit one in response on Larisa, the acropolis of the city of Argos, to show that she too was safe. This legend furnished an explanation for the origin of an annual festival of beacons that was celebrated in Argos.[65] Danaos was so angered by Hypermnestra's disobedience that he had her imprisoned, or even went so far as to bring her to trial, alleging that she had placed his own life in danger by allowing Lynkeus to escape, and had made the disgrace all the worse for her sisters and himself by taking no part in the crime; but she was acquitted by the citizens of Argos, and commemorated her victory by dedicating a statue of Aphrodite Nikephoros (Bringer of Victory) in the city and by founding a sanctuary of Artemis Peitho (of Persuasion).[66] Danaos finally relented as time passed by and his anger subsided, and agreed to accept Lynkeus as his son-in-law and heir.[67] Or in a less favoured version, Lynkeus took matters into his own hands and seized power by killing Danaos.[68] He succeeded Danaos as king in any case, and was succeeded in his turn by his son ABAS, who shared equally in the blood of Danaos and Aigyptos.[69]

It was said that Lynkeus happened to be in the temple of Hera in Argos when Abas arrived with the news of Danaos' death. When he looked around for a gift to give to his son in memory of the occasion, his eyes fell on a shield that Danaos had carried during his youth and had later dedicated in the temple; so he took it down and gave it to Abas, and also founded the quinquennial games known as the Shield of Argos, at which the victors were awarded a shield.[70] Shields were something of an Argive speciality, but the mythographers disagree on whether the distinctive round shields of the land were invented by Danaos himself, or by his grandson Abas, or his great-grandsons Proitos and Akrisios.[71] The tomb of Danaos could be seen in the marketplace at Argos, not far from the joint tomb of Lynkeus and Hypermnestra.[72] Abas married Aglaia, daughter of Mantineus, who bore him twin sons, Proitos and Akrisios.[73] Some authors identified this Abas with the Euboean ruler of the same name (see p. 520), explaining that this son of Lynkeus finally left Argos to conquer Euboea.[74]

Proitos and Akrisios, the warring twin sons of Abas, divide the kingdom

In myth and folklore, twins tend to be presented either as the closest of friends or as the fiercest of enemies. PROITOS and AKRISIOS fought with one another even while they were still inside their mother's womb, and quarrelled over the kingdom after their father's death, resorting to arms to settle the issue.[75] According to the local tradition in the Argolid, they met in battle a few miles east of Argos by the road to Epidaurus, but their two armies proved to be so evenly matched that they were obliged to negotiate a compromise. So Akrisios, as the first-born, took power at the ancestral capital of Argos, while Proitos founded a new centre of rule at Tiryns, on a rocky hill in the Argive plain a few miles to the south-east of Argos. The reputed site of the battle was marked in historical times by a pyramidal monument with relief sculptures of Argive shields on the side; it was often said that the brothers invented these distinctive round shields during the conflict, making them either from wood or from bronze. The fight was commemorated in an annual Argive festival known as the Daulis.[76]

In a more elaborate account of the feud, as recorded by Apollodorus, Proitos was initially defeated and expelled by Akrisios, who agreed to the above-mentioned compromise only after Proitos had evened the odds by acquiring support from abroad. For when he was forced into exile, he sought refuge with Iobates, king of Lycia, in the south-western corner of Asia Minor; and Iobates not only gave him his daughter Stheneboia in marriage, but helped to restore him to his own land by providing him with a force of Lycian troops. With the aid of these new-found allies, Proitos established a foothold in the Argolid by occupying the hilltop at Tiryns, and compelled his brother to share the land with him. So Proitos ruled at Tiryns, which was fortified for him by the Kyklopes (see p. 66), while Akrisios ruled at Argos.[77] Proitos had Lycian connections from a very early period since the *Iliad* already mentions that his wife (here called Anteia) was the daughter of a Lycian king.[78] A choral ode by Bacchylides provides the earliest surviving account of his conflict with Akrisios, telling how the relentless feud between the two brothers, 'which sprang up from a small beginning', caused such misery to the people of Argos that they finally lost patience and appealed to the pair to divide the land into two.[79]

Proitos fathered a single son, Megapenthes, by his wife Stheneboia, and three daughters, Lysippe, Iphinoe and Iphianassa.[80] During his reign at Tiryns, he became involved in two unhappy episodes that will be considered in further detail elsewhere. In the first place, he offered refuge to Bellerophon, an exile from Corinth, but was provoked into dishonourable action when his wife falsely accused the young hero of having tried to rape her after he rejected her advances. Although Proitos sent him away to his father-in-law in Lycia with a secret message asking that he should be put to death, he was spared after surviving various perilous ordeals (see further on pp. 433–4).[81] It was sometimes said that he returned to Tiryns to wreak vengeance on Stheneboia (see p. 434). On another occasion, the three daughters of Proitos went mad (along with other women of the land in one version of the legend), and the king had to call on the aid of the great seer Melampous, who demanded a share of the kingdom for himself and his brother Bias as his fee for the cure (see pp. 428–9). This episode was of lasting significance because Melampous and Bias established new royal lines, introducing further complications into the pattern of rule in the Argolid. Proitos named his son Megapenthes (Great Sorrow) in commemoration of the anguish that was caused to him by the madness of his daughters.[82] Megapenthes succeeded to his father's kingdom, but later agreed to exchange it for that of Perseus, the grandson of Akrisios (see p. 243). We will consider the subsequent history of the descendants of Proitos, and also of the new royal lines descended from Melampous and Bias, in connection with the Theban Wars in Chapter 9 (see pp. 316ff and 332ff).

Danae bears Perseus to Zeus, and is set adrift with him by her father Akrisios

The other twin, Akrisios, married Eurydike, the daughter of Lakedaimon, king of Sparta, who bore him a daughter, DANAE, but failed to produce any male children. When he consulted the Delphic oracle about his lack of an heir, he was told that he would never father a male child, but that his daughter would give birth to a son who would kill him. In the hope of preventing her from ever coming into contact with men, he built an underground chamber of bronze in the courtyard of his palace and imprisoned her in it along with her nurse.[83] Or in an alternative version which first appears in Horace and Ovid, he imprisoned her in a tower of bronze.[84] His precautions achieved nothing, however, since Zeus fell in love with Danae and slipped down through the roof into her lap in the form of a shower of gold, causing her to conceive a mighty son, PERSEUS.[85]

On hearing the sound of Perseus' voice as he was playing in the underground chamber at the age of three or four, Danaos sent his servants to investigate, and they brought Danae up to the light together with her infant son and nurse. The king put the nurse to death and dragged Danae to the altar of Zeus Herkeios (of the Courtyard) to question her about the origin of her child. When she replied that

Zeus was to blame, he refused to believe her, and packed her into a chest along with her son and hurled it into the sea.[86] Or in a less favoured version, which may have been quite ancient if it is correctly ascribed to Pindar, Danae gave birth to Perseus after being seduced by her uncle Proitos (a tale that was evidently devised to explain why the two brothers came to be estranged).[87]

The chest drifted eastward across the Aegean to Seriphos, an island in the Cyclades; in some touching verses by Simonides, Danae sings a sad lament to her infant son as they are blown through the sea in the dark in their little brass-ribbed vessel.[88] They fell into kindly hands on their arrival, however, since DIKTYS, the brother of the king of Seriphos, took them into his home after the chest became entangled in his fishing-nets or was washed ashore on the beach. Diktys and his brother (or half-brother) POLYDEKTES were usually classed as sons of Magnes, son of Aiolos (see p. 436), although Pherecydes refers to them as sons of a certain Peristhenes who was descended from Nauplios. Perseus was reared by Diktys, who treated him and his mother as members of his own family, and all went well until the king caught sight of Danae and conceived a passion for her.[89]

The king of Seriphos sends Perseus to fetch the Gorgon's head

Being a man of very different character from his noble-minded brother, Polydektes was determined to gain her favours by fair means or foul, but realized that this would be difficult to achieve while her formidable son, who had now grown of age, was there to protect her; so he sent Perseus away on a dangerous mission under the following circumstances. Letting it be known that he was planning to marry Hippodameia, daughter of Oinomaos, and wanted to collect contributions for the bride-price that he would be obliged to pay to her father, he invited the leading men of the island, including Perseus, to an *eranos* (a form of feast at which those who attended were expected to make a contribution). When Perseus asked him what sort of contribution he was expecting, he replied 'a horse' (a very valuable item in those days), and the young man exclaimed that he would grudge him nothing, not even the Gorgon's head; so on the next day, when all the contributors arrived with their horses, Polydektes refused to accept a horse from Perseus, but pretended to take his purely rhetorical offer seriously and demanded that he should actually fetch the Gorgon's head. For the king was aware that the Gorgon was so ugly that anyone who saw her would be turned to stone, and he could thus expect to be rid of Perseus once and for all.[90] It is characteristic of such tales that the hero should propose his own ordeal, as we will see with Jason (p. 381). Although it is quite often stated in modern accounts that Perseus (who might be expected to have been poor) was unable to provide a horse, there is no indication of this in ancient sources; the idea seems to have arisen from a misreading of Apollodorus' narrative.[91]

Filled with despair at his seemingly hopeless predicament, Perseus withdrew to the remotest part of the island to brood on the matter; but his distress was observed by Hermes, who urged him take courage after hearing his story, and joined together with Athena to guide him to the sisters of the Gorgons, the Graiai (Old Women), who would be able to provide him with some invaluable information. By seizing the single eye and tooth that the three sisters shared between them (see p. 59), Perseus forced them to reveal the way to some nymphs who would be able to furnish him with the tools that would enable him to fulfil his task, namely some winged sandals to carry him through the air to the lair of the Gorgons at the ends of the earth, the cap of Hades to render him invisible as he seized the Gorgon's head, and a metallic satchel (*kibisis*, a word that appears in no other context) to hold the head after he had cut it off. After acquiring these objects from the nymphs, and also receiving an adamantine sickle (*harpē*) from Hermes, Perseus flew beyond the outer Ocean with Hermes and Athena, and crept up on the Gorgons as they lay asleep. For their origin and nature, see pp. 58–61.

The two deities advised him to avert his gaze as he cut off the Gorgon's head, and pointed to MEDUSA as the one whom he should attack since her two sisters were immortal. So he went up to Medusa, severed her head, placed it in the *kibisis*, and fled with all speed, successfully escaping the other two Gorgons, who tried to pursue him but were unable to find him because he was wearing the cap of invisibility. Such is Pherecydes' version, which originated in early epic; it is reported in subsequent accounts that Athena guided his hand as he cut off the head, and that he assisted himself in the process by observing the Gorgon's reflection in the polished surface of his bronze shield. Since Medusa was pregnant with Pegasos and Chrysaor, two children whom she had conceived to Poseidon (see p. 60), they sprang from her neck when her head was removed.[92] In a wholly different account from the lost *Phorkides* of Aeschylus, the Graiai acted as guards to their sisters, but Perseus prevented them from fulfilling their task by hurling their single eye into the Tritonian lake.[93]

Perseus rescues Andromeda from a sea-monster, and exacts revenge on the king of Seriphos

As Perseus was flying home with his trophy, he passed the kingdom of Kepheus, son of Belos or Phoinix, in Ethiopia (or Phoenicia), and noticed that a girl of wonderful beauty had been chained to a rock by the seashore. This was ANDROMEDA, a princess of the land, who had been exposed there as prey to a sea-monster as the result of an indiscretion that had been committed by her mother KASSIEPEIA. For the queen had foolishly boasted that she was lovelier than the Nereids, angering not only the sea-nymphs themselves but Poseidon too, who responded by sending a flood and a sea-monster against the land; and when the oracle of Ammon (at the oasis of Siwa in the Libyan desert) had declared that the calamity would not be brought to an end until Kassiepeia's daughter were offered up to the monster, the king had bound her to a rock by the shore at the insistence of his people. Perseus fell in love with her at first sight, however, and undertook to slay the monster if she would promise to marry him; or in a slightly different version, he approached her father Kepheus and won an equivalent promise from him. He then proceeded to kill the monster with his sword or sickle (or else turned it to stone by showing it the Gorgon's head).[94]

When he came to claim his bride, he met with some difficulty nonetheless, either because her parents were reluctant to hand her over to a stranger with uncertain

Figure 7.2 *Perseus and Andromeda*, by Frederick Lord Leighton (1830–1896). Courtesy of the Board of Trustees of the National Museums and Galleries on Merseyside (Walker Art Gallery).

prospects,[95] or because she was already betrothed to Phineus (or Agenor), a brother of Kepheus. But he overcame the scruples of her parents; or in the latter case, he turned Phineus (or Agenor) and his friends to stone with the Gorgon's head after discovering that they were plotting against him,[96] or defeated them by force of arms when they tried to seize Andromeda from him during the wedding-feast.[97] After spending a year or so at the court of his father-in-law, Perseus finally set off for Seriphos with his wife. Since Kepheus had no heir of his own, the departing couple allowed him to adopt their first-born child, Perses, who was destined to give his name to the Persians.[98]

In the Hellenistic and later tradition, Perseus was sometimes said to have brought Mt Atlas into being as he was passing through North Africa with the Gorgon's head. According to a version ascribed to Polyidos, a lyric poet of the fourth century BC, a Libyan shepherd called Atlas tried to block his passage, provoking the hero to petrify him by showing him the Gorgon's head. Or in Ovid's account, in which Atlas is a local ruler of exceptional size who owns large flocks of sheep, Perseus asked to rest for the night in his land, telling him that he was a son of Zeus; but Atlas turned him away with the same result, because he had been warned by a prophecy that a wonderful tree that he owned would be robbed of its golden fruit by a son of Zeus.[99] This prophecy referred of course to the apples of the Hesperides, which would be robbed by a different son of Zeus, namely Herakles (see p. 269). According to another tale, the poisonous snakes of Libya were born from drops of blood that dripped from the Gorgon's head as Perseus was flying overhead.[100]

On arriving back in Seriphos, Perseus found that his mother and his benefactor Diktys had sought refuge at the altars to escape the violence of the king. So he entered the palace and invited Polydektes to assemble his friends (or the islanders in general); and when they had gathered together, he showed them the Gorgon's head, causing all of them to be turned to stone in the attitude that they happened to have assumed at the time.[101] The island was notorious ever afterwards for its many rocks. Or in another account, Perseus displayed the head to Polydektes when the king accused him of having lied about killing Medusa.[102] Now that his mother was safe, Perseus installed Diktys on the throne in place of the dead tyrant, and returned the satchel, winged sandals and cap of Hades to Hermes (or Athena) to be taken back to the nymphs. As for the Gorgon's head, he gave it to his divine helper Athena, who fixed it to the centre of her aigis (see p. 74).[103]

Pindar alludes to an account in which Polydektes actually forced Danae into marriage before her son returned to rescue her.[104] Hyginus records a very odd version of the legend of Perseus and Danae in which Polydektes becomes their benefactor rather than their enemy and the quest for the Gorgon's head is eliminated. On discovering Danae and her infant in the chest, Diktys took them immediately to his brother, who married Danae and arranged for her son to be reared in the temple of Artemis; and when Akrisios learned of their where-abouts and came in search of them, apparently many years later, Polydektes interceded with him on their behalf, and Perseus swore for his own part that he would never cause his grand-father any harm. While Akrisios was detained on Seriphos by a storm, however, Polydektes died and Perseus killed his grandfather with a discus by accident (as in the usual story, see below) during the funeral games for the dead king. He then sailed on to Argos to claim his inheritance.[105]

Perseus accidentally kills his grandfather Akrisios, and founds Mycenae

After his adventures in Seriphos and the wider world beyond, Perseus wanted nothing more than to settle down in his ancestral homeland. So he sailed for Argos with his wife and mother, hoping to be reunited with his grandfather on his arrival. Akrisios heard that he was coming, however, and fled to Larisa in Thessaly, fearing that Perseus might kill him as the oracle had predicted if they should ever meet. When Perseus learned of this, he entrusted his wife and mother to his grandmother Eurydike and set off for Thessaly to convince his grandfather that he intended him no harm. While the two of them were still in Larisa, however, Teutamides, the king of the city, held some funeral games in honour of his father, and Perseus took the opportunity to demonstrate his skill with the discus (which was supposed to have been invented by him); and while making one of his throws, he accidentally struck his grandfather on the foot, inflicting a fatal wound on him.[106] Or in another version, he encountered his grandfather at Larisa by chance when he came to compete in the games.[107] The oracle was fulfilled as a result of this sporting accident in any case, and Akrisios was buried just outside Larisa, where his heroic shrine could be seen in historical times.[108]

Feeling ashamed to inherit his grandfather's kingdom after causing his death, Perseus approached Megapenthes, son of Proitos, who was now ruling at Tiryns, and asked him to exchange his kingdom for the former kingdom of Akrisios, which had been ruled from the city of Argos. Instead of ruling at Tiryns, however, or at Midea which also lay in the territory that he acquired through this exchange, Perseus founded a new stronghold further to the north at Mycenae (properly Mykenai).[109] According to one tale, he gave this name to the city because the cap from the end of his scabbard (*mykos* in Greek) had fallen off when he first arrived at the site, and this had been the sign that had prompted him to found the city there; or else he chose this name because he had been thirsty when he arrived there, and a refreshing spring had gushed forth when he had pulled up a mushroom (*mykos* again!).[110] With regard to the latter story, it may be relevant that a spring known as the Perseia could be seen at the city ruins in historical times.[111] Perseus invited the Kyklopes to construct the massive 'Cyclopean' walls that can still be seen at Mycenae, and also to fortify Midea for him.[112] The only adventure recorded for Perseus during his subsequent years in the Argolid is the strange story of his conflict with Dionysos and the women from the sea (see p. 175).

The children of Perseus and Andromeda; the exile of Amphitryon and Alkmene

Andromeda bore five sons to Perseus during their years in Mycenae, namely Elektryon, Sthenelos, Alkaios, Mestor and Heleios, and also a daughter who was named Gorgophone (Gorgon-slayer) in memory of her father's greatest deed.[113] Gorgophone first married Perieres, king of Messenia (see p. 422) and then Oibalos, king of Sparta; it was said that she was the first woman ever to remarry after her husband's death.[114]

The sons and immediate descendants of Perseus are of interest in relation to the origins and life of the greatest of his descendants, Herakles. **Elektryon**, who was initially the most powerful of his sons, succeeded him as king of Mycenae, and ruled there until he was killed in a freakish accident by his nephew **Amphitryon**, the son of his brother **Alkaios**. Recognizing that this would give him an opportunity to advance his own position, another son of Perseus, **Sthenelos**, seized power at Mycenae and banished Amphitryon from the land on an accusation of murder. So Amphitryon went off to Thebes, where he settled with **Alkmene**, the daughter of Elektryon. After sleeping with Zeus and Amphitryon on the same night, Alkmene gave birth to twin sons, bearing Herakles to Zeus and an inferior child to her husband. **Herakles** was thus born and brought up in exile while lesser men, initially Sthenelos and then his son **Eurystheus**, ruled over the former kingdom of Perseus (or at least the richest part of it). Zeus had intended, to be sure, that his son should become the great ruler in Argos, but Hera tricked him to ensure that Eurystheus (who was born at much the same time as Herakles) should gain that inheritance instead.

This sequence of events was first set in course when ELEKTRYON met with trouble from some descendants of his brother **Mestor** and called on the assistance of his nephew Amphitryon. Mestor and his wife, Lysidike, daughter of Pelops, had a single child, Hippothoe, who was abducted by Poseidon to the Echinadian islands, just to the north of the entrance to the Corinthian Gulf. She bore him a son there, Taphios (or Taphos), the eponym of the island of Taphos, who founded the royal family that would rule the islands thereafter. His people were called the Taphians or Teleboans; the mythographers explained the latter name by a false etymology, saying that Taphos conferred it on the islanders because he had 'gone far' (*tēlou ebē*) from his ancestral land of Argos. Pterelaos, the son and heir of Taphos, had six sons of his own who sailed to the Argolid in the time of Elektryon and laid claim to the throne of Mycenae, alleging that it properly belonged to them as descendants of the Perseid Mestor.[115]

It hardly needs saying that this story makes no sense at all in terms of any rational chronology, suggesting as it does that great-great-great-grandsons of Perseus could become involved in a dispute with a son of Perseus! In all likelihood, the Teleboan line was originally independent of the Perseids, and this chronological inconsistency was introduced when it came to be classed as a branch of Perseus' family. In another account which reduces the Teleboan line by one generation at least, Pterelaos was the son who was borne by Hippothoe after her abduction, and he in turn was the father of two sons, Taphios and Teleboas, who laid claim to Elektryon's kingdom.[116]

When Elektryon refused to acknowledge that the sons of Pterelaos had any claim to his kingdom, they proceeded to steal his cattle. A fierce fight developed as a consequence between the sons of Elektryon, who were all killed (apart from Likymnios, who was too young to take part), and the sons of Pterelaos, who were all killed likewise, apart from the one who was guarding the ships. Their surviving followers escaped with the cattle, however, and entrusted them to Polyxenos, the king of the Eleians in the western Peloponnese.[117] On learning of the fate of his sons, Elektryon made preparations for a punitive expedition against the Teleboans and invited AMPHITRYON to administer his kingdom during his absence. He placed his daughter Alkmene in the care of his nephew, making him swear that he would not touch her until his return. As it turned out, however, Elektryon never left his native shore. For Amphitryon soon secured the return of the stolen cattle by ransoming them from Polyxenos; and when one charged forward as he was receiving them back, he hurled his club at it to try to restrain it, and the club rebounded off its horns and struck Elektryon, killing him instantly. Or in a conflicting version from the Hesiodic *Shield*, he quarrelled with his uncle over cattle for some reason and killed him in anger. Whatever the exact circumstances of the killing, STHENELOS seized it as a pretext to banish Amphitryon and take control of Mycenae, Tiryns and Midea, the main strongholds in Perseus' former realm.[118] He ruled at Mycenae without incident from that time onwards and bequeathed the throne to his son EURYSTHEUS, who passed an uneventful existence until Herakles was instructed by the Delphic oracle to travel to the Argolid to perform twelve labours at his command.

Even if there was some initial division of power between the sons of Perseus, Sthenelos seems to have gained control of all or most of the territories and cities that had formerly been ruled by Perseus, including Tiryns and Midea. His son and heir Eurystheus is of importance in myth only in relation to his great half-cousin Herakles, whose life-history will be traced in the next chapter. Although Herakles was born abroad and spent most of his life in exile, he was obliged to perform twelve labours at the command of Eurystheus and came to be based in the Argolid for a time as a consequence (see pp. 253ff). It was commonly agreed that Eurystheus was as mean-minded and cowardly (see e.g. p. 257) as Herakles was noble and brave. After the death of Herakles, Eurystheus tried to rid himself of any future threat from the hero's sons and descendants, the Heraklids, by attacking the children of Herakles while they were at their most vulnerable (see p. 287); but he was defeated and killed, and the Heraklids invaded the Peloponnese soon afterwards to try to seize control of his kingdom and other territories too. It was the will of the gods, however, that the Heraklids should not succeed in their aim until well after the Trojan War, and they were either obliged to withdraw after an initial invasion or were checked at the Isthmus of Corinth (see p. 288). The Mycenaeans for their part were advised by an oracle that they should choose a member of a wholly different family, the Pelopids, as their new ruler. So the kingdom passed to Atreus, son of Pelops, and remained under Pelopid rule until his great-grandson Teisamenos was ousted by the Heraklids when they finally made their successful invasion (see pp. 505ff). The interlude of Pelopid rule at Mycenae will be considered along with other aspects of the history of that family in Chapter 14.

CHAPTER EIGHT

THE LIFE OF HERAKLES AND RETURN OF THE HERAKLIDS

— •◆• —

THE BIRTH OF HERAKLES AND HIS EARLY LIFE AT THEBES

Alkmene arrives in Thebes with Alkmene, and mounts a campaign against the Teleboans

Although Herakles was an Argive of Perseid stock by descent, he was born abroad in Thebes after his putative father AMPHITRYON departed into exile with his mother ALKMENE. As was described at the end of the last chapter, Amphitryon was exiled by his uncle Sthenelos for having killed another uncle, Elektryon, king of Mycenae (by accident in the usual account); and Alkmene, the daughter of Elektryon, who was already betrothed to him, accompanied him to his new home, as did Likymnios, her only surviving brother. Her other brothers had all been killed by Teleboan raiders shortly before the death of her father (see p. 244 for the circumstances). Kreon, the current ruler of Thebes, purified Amphitryon of the manslaughter and welcomed him to his city. Although Amphitryon now pressed Alkmene to marry him (or to consummate their marriage if they were already married), she declared that she would not accept him into her bed until he had exacted vengeance on the Teleboans for the death of her brothers.[1] So he made immediate preparations for a campaign against the Teleboans, who lived in a group of islands just outside the entrance of the Corinthian Gulf; and his forthcoming absence would provide Zeus with an ideal opportunity to approach Alkmene to father his great son Herakles.

When Amphitryon asked Kreon to assist him on the expedition, the king promised to fight as his ally if he would first rescue the Thebans from the depredations of the TEUMESSIAN FOX, a large and ferocious vixen which had established its lair on Mt Teumessos, about five miles north-east of Thebes; it had been sent by the gods to ravage the land and presented an exceptionally difficult problem because it was fated never to be caught. Knowing that Kephalos, son of Deion, owned a dog that was fated always to catch its prey (see p. 372 for its origin), Amphitryon visited him at his home in Attica, and asked him to allow it to be used against the fox in return for a share of the spoils from the forthcoming war. Or in another version, Kephalos was already in Thebes, having come there to be purified after accidentally killing his wife Prokris, and had brought the dog with him. He agreed to Amphitryon's request in any case, and a paradoxical situation arose when a beast that was fated to catch its prey was set in pursuit of another that was fated never to be caught. Zeus was obliged to intervene, and resolved the problem very neatly by turning both animals to stone, so that the dog never fails in the hunt and the fox is never caught.[2] Or in a later version from the astronomical literature that rather spoils the story, he turned the fox to stone but transferred the dog to the sky to become the constellation of the Great Dog (Canis Major).[3]

After winning Kreon's support by this means, Amphitryon collected together further allies, including Kephalos, Panopeus (from Phocis, see p. 565) and Heleios, the youngest son of Perseus,[4] and sailed away with them to attack the Teleboans. Although he ravaged most of their islands with little difficulty, he was initially unable to capture Taphos, the island of PTERELAOS, the king of the Teleboans, because Poseidon had implanted a golden hair in his head which rendered him immortal as long as it remained in place. As we saw in the last chapter (see p. 244), Pterelaos was descended from Poseidon, as his grandson in the usual account. The assailants finally received help from an unexpected quarter when KOMAITHO, the daughter of the king, fell in love with Amphitryon (or Kephalos in one account) after seeing him at a distance, and tried to win his favour by pulling the magical hair from her father's head. When Pterelaos died as a consequence, Amphitryon was able to complete his conquest; but instead of repaying Komaitho as she would have wished, he killed her in horror at her unfilial act of treachery.[5] For a very similar story set in Megara, see p. 340.

The conception and birth of Herakles

As soon as the spoils had been gathered together, Amphitryon set sail for Boeotia, eager to prove his success to his beloved and win his way into her bed. Shortly before he arrived, however, Zeus forestalled him by assuming his guise to seduce Alkmene. On being assured that vengeance had been executed against the Teleboans as she had demanded, and receiving a magnificent cup from the spoils by way of proof, Alkmene welcomed the disguised god into her arms; and he extended the time of their love-making by lengthening the night to three times its usual length. Later in the same night or on the next night, her true husband arrived home to report his triumph and so claim his promised reward. Surprised and disappointed to find that her welcome was none too passionate, he questioned her about the matter; and when she protested that she had received him warmly enough a very short time before, he consulted the seer Teiresias, who informed him of Zeus's deception. He made love with her on that night all the same, and she became pregnant with twin sons of contrasting nature, HERAKLES, a mighty hero and future god as her child by Zeus, and IPHIKLES (or Iphiklos), a hero of no very exceptional stature as her child by Amphitryon.[6]

It was not only on account of her beauty that Zeus set out to seduce Alkmene, but also because he wanted to father a very great hero by her who would bring benefit to the human race, and even to the gods themselves by helping them in their war against the Giants. He originally intended, furthermore, that this son of his should be a mighty ruler in Argos, but this part of his plan was foiled by Hera. As the story is recounted in the *Iliad*, Zeus boasted of his intentions to the other gods, telling them that Eileithuia, the goddess of childbirth, would bring a man to birth on that day who would be king over all who lived around him (i.e. in Argos), and would be born from the race of those who came from Zeus's blood (i.e. from the Perseids, who were descended from Perseus, son of Zeus). By making this ill-advised declaration, he alerted Hera, who resented all her husband's illegitimate children and immediately plotted to rob this one of his intended inheritance. She happened to know that Alkmene was not the only woman who was expecting a child of Perseid descent since the wife of Sthenelos, king of Mycenae, was also heavily pregnant. So she persuaded Zeus to swear formally that the son of his stock who would be born on that day would enjoy the destiny that he had announced; and she then instructed the Eileithuiai (goddesses of childbirth) to delay Alkmene's delivery, while she herself hurried down from Olympos to ensure that the wife of Sthenelos should bring her child to birth at once in the seventh month of her pregnancy. As a consequence, Eurystheus, the son of Sthenelos, was born on that day instead of Herakles, and Zeus was therefore obliged by his oath to grant him the inheritance that he had been planning to grant to Herakles.[7] This meant that Eurystheus became the great king of Mycenae (in succession to his father, see p. 245), while Herakles never had a kingdom of his own. Herakles was therefore destined to spend most of his life outside his ancestral homeland, and to be subordinate to Eurystheus even while he was there.

According to a tale first recorded in the Hellenistic era, the birth of Herakles was finally expedited through the ingenuity of a servant or friend of Alkmene. In the familiar version by Ovid, the goddess of childbirth, here appearing under her Latin name of Lucina, delayed the hero's birth by seven days and nights by sitting outside Alkmene's bedroom door with her legs crossed and her fingers intertwined (gestures of enclosure that would achieve their effect by a form of sympathetic magic). Alkmene had a clever servant-maid, however, who noticed the attitude of the goddess and recognized why she had adopted it. So this maid, GALANTHIS, suddenly ran out to her and cried, 'You must congratulate my mistress because she has given birth to a child!', prompting the goddess to leap up in astonishment and unlock her fingers and uncross her legs. The charm was undone as a consequence, and Herakles could be born at last. Angered by the girl's deception and by her subsequent laughter, the goddess turned her into a weasel, a beast that runs around the house much as Galanthis had done as a busy maidservant (for weasels – or more strictly, ferrets, i.e. domesticated polecats – were kept in the house in antiquity to keep down pests, much like cats in modern times).[8]

Or in a Greek version ascribed to the Hellenistic poet Nicander, Galinthias, as she is called here, was of high birth as a daughter of Proitos (a prominent Theban who gave his name to the Proitidian gates of the city), and was thus a friend and former playmate of Alkmene rather than a servant of hers. The story is much the same as in Ovid, except that the Moirai (Fates) assisted the goddess of childbirth in her task, and it was they who turned Galinthias into a weasel. This Greek account refers to an important matter, however, which is passed over by Ovid, the cultic implications of the myth. For we are told that Hekate made the weasel her attendant out of pity for Galinthias, and that Herakles later commemorated her services to him by erecting an altar to her outside his house at Thebes and offering sacrifices on it, hence the sacrifices that the Thebans used to offer to Galinthias before their festival of Herakles. It would seem that Galinthias was a heroine who had been honoured at Thebes from an early period and that someone was inspired to devise this transformation myth as an aetiology for the cult because her name was reminiscent of that of a weasel (*galeē* in Greek).[9] Pausanias records another version of the deception story in which the Pharmakides (Witches), the beings who were sent by Hera to delay the birth, were tricked by Historis, a daughter of Teiresias; there is no mention here of any transformation.[10]

The childhood and education of Herakles, and his murder of Linos

When Herakles was eight or ten months old, or even newly born, two huge snakes were sent by Hera to attack him and his half-brother in their cradle; but the infant hero seized them by their necks, one in each hand, and choked them to death. In the two fullest accounts of the episode by Pindar and Theocritus, the seer Teiresias was summoned to comment on the marvel, and took this as an opportunity to foretell the extraordinary destiny that lay in wait for Herakles, predicting that he would finally be received among the gods after overcoming many such dangers.[11] In an alternative version, the snakes were not sent by the goddess but by Amphitryon, who introduced them into the children's cradle to enable him to discover which of them was his son; when Herakles stayed to confront the snakes while Iphikles tried to escape, he recognized at once that Herakles was the child with divine blood in him.[12]

A further tale of the hero's infancy tells how Hera was deceived into suckling him. In the most familiar version of the story, Hermes took the baby Herakles up to Olympos and applied him to Hera's breast while she was asleep (or without revealing his true identity to her); and when she awoke (or learned who he was),

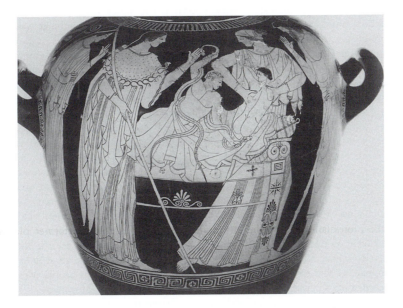

Figure 8.1 The baby Herakles strangles the serpents sent by Hera. Red-figure column krater. Perugia, Museo Nazionale; mus nat 73.

she pushed him away in such violent haste that some milk spilled out of her breast to form the Milky Way. She conferred immortality on him by her involuntary action, or the episode prefigured his future apotheosis at least.[13]

As would be expected, the hero's education was traditionally said to have been entrusted to the most celebrated experts. He learned the art of bowmanship from Eurytos of Oichalia, who was a grandson of Apollo (see p. 412) and a skilled archer like his divine ancestor, as were all the male members of his family. In one form of his legend, indeed, Eurytos was eventually killed by Apollo because he dared to challenge the god to an archery contest; but it was more commonly said that he died at the hand of his greatest pupil, Herakles himself (see p. 283). Autolykos instructed Herakles in the art of wrestling; so great a trickster (see p. 431) was presumably a past master of all the wiles of the ring. Herakles learned the art of chariot-driving from his father, and the art of war from Kastor.[14] Music was less to his taste, however, and less suited to his natural abilities. His music-teacher, LINOS, became so exasperated by his slowness that he eventually lost patience and struck him, to the great indignation of his young pupil, who struck back in anger with his lyre or plectrum, with fatal effect. Although Herakles escaped prosecution by citing a law of the great Cretan law-maker Rhadamanthys (see p. 351) that justified retaliation in self-defence, his father decided that it would be prudent to cut his education short at this point, and sent him out into the countryside to tend the family herds.[15]

There are three separate bodies of myth associated with musicians called Linos, the other two relating to figures of that name who would have lived at an earlier period in mythical history. The idea on which all these stories are founded, namely that there had once been a young musician called Linos who had met a premature and pitiable death, was inspired by the existence of an ancient reaping-song known as the 'Linos-song', which had a refrain of *ailinon* which could be interpreted as meaning 'alas for Linos!' (although it was in fact a word of foreign origin).

According to Argive tradition, Apollo fathered a son Linos by a princess of that land, Psamathe, who was the daughter of an early Argive ruler called Krotopos. She sent the child out to be exposed for fear of her father's anger, but the shepherd who was supposed to perform the task reared him as his own son instead, until the child happened to be torn apart by his dogs. On hearing of this, Psamathe was so distressed that she told the whole story to her father, who refused to believe that she had really borne the child to a god and ordered that she should be put to death. When Argos was struck by a plague as a consequence through the anger of Apollo, the citizens were advised by an oracle to appease the dead mother and child, and achieved this by means of prayers and laments (hence the origin of the Linos-song). Or in a rather different version, the infant Linos was torn apart by the king's sheep-dogs after he was exposed, and Apollo reacted by sending Poine (Vengeance personified) against Argos. Poine snatched the children of the city from their mothers until she was killed by a hero called Koroibos. When a plague broke out afterwards, Koroibos visited the oracle of Apollo at Delphi to discover how he could atone for the killing, and was instructed to take a tripod from the sanctuary and raise a temple to Apollo wherever he first dropped it. The tripod slipped from his hands on Mt Gerania in the Megarid; and the tomb of Koroibos could be seen nearby at the market-place at Megara.[16]

A Boeotian tradition suggested that Linos was borne to a certain Amphimaros, son of Poseidon, by the Muse Ourania. As befitted the child of a Muse, he grew up to become the finest of musicians, but soon provoked his own death at the hand of Apollo by claiming to rival the god as a singer. When grief for his death then spread through the world, the Linos-song was devised as a lament for him. This Linos, who is also described as a son of Apollo himself, was said to have been buried at Thebes.[17] As in the case of legendary musicians such as Orpheus and Mousaios, Linos' name came to be attached to apocryphal poems in historical times.

The lion of Kithairon, the daughters of Thespios, and a first campaign

When Herakles reached the age of eighteen, he embarked on his first adventure, setting off to confront the lion of Kithairon, a ferocious beast that haunted the mountain-range of that name on the southern borders of Boeotia. Since it was preying not only on Amphitryon's cattle but also on those of THESPIOS, the eponymous ruler of Thespiai in south-western Boeotia, Herakles stayed at his court for fifty nights while trying to track the beast. Now the king had fifty daughters, and he was so impressed by the young hero's strength that he wanted to ensure that each of his daughters should conceive a child to him. He achieved this in one account by introducing a different daughter into his bed each night, so that Herakles slept with each in turn in the fond belief that he was sleeping with the same girl on each occasion.[18] Or in versions which savour more of folklore, Herakles enjoyed the favours of all fifty in seven nights, or of forty-nine of them in a single night.[19] In the latter account, one of them refused to have anything to do with him, and he paid her back by forcing her to serve as his virgin priestess (a story that explained why the temple of Herakles at Thespiai was served by a virgin priestess who remained in that post until her death). This episode of the daughters of Thespios, which has its comical side as so often with Herakles, has no inherent connection with that of the lion-hunt. Diodorus tells it, indeed, as a separate story, stating that Thespios invited the young Herakles to a sacrifice and feast for the specific purpose of ensuring that all his daughters would bear children to him.[20] Each of his daughters bore a son to Herakles in any case, apart from the eldest (and the youngest too in one account) who bore him twins instead. The children were known as the THESPIADES after their grandfather. Herakles sent most of them to Sardinia when they grew up to found a colony under the leadership of his nephew Iolaos, except for a few who remained behind, seven at Thespiai and one or two at Thebes, to become founders of noble families in the province of their birth.[21] As for the myth of the lion-hunt, it was cast wholly into the shade by the more diverting story of the daughters of Thespios, and nothing is recorded of it beyond the fact that Herakles eventually killed the beast.[22]

Apollodorus is exceptional in suggesting that Herakles took his lionskin cloak from this lion; in other accounts, he took it from the Nemean lion (see p. 257), which was invulnerable and would therefore have an impenetrable hide. According to a conflicting legend, the lion of Kithairon was killed by Alkathoos, son of Pelops, rather than by Herakles (see further on p. 567).[23]

As Herakles was travelling back from the hunt, he happened to run across some heralds who had been sent by ERGINOS, king of Orchomenos, to collect an annual tribute that the Thebans were obliged to pay to him. This tribute had come to be imposed on them in the following circumstances. Some years earlier, Klymenos, the father of Erginos, had visited Onchestos, a town that lay between Orchomenos (a powerful city in north-eastern Boeotia, see p. 558) and Thebes, to attend a festival of Poseidon; and in the course of the celebrations, he had been murdered by some Thebans as the result of some trivial quarrel, or had been fatally wounded by a stone hurled by the charioteer of Kreon's father Menoikeus. After hearing of his father's death (or after receiving a direct order from his dying father), Erginos had waged a successful campaign against the Thebans, and had forced them to agree to send him an annual tribute of a hundred cattle for twenty years. Herakles was so angered by this imposition and by the arrogant behaviour of the heralds that he cut off their noses, ears and hands, and hung them around their necks on cords, telling them to take these to their king by way of tribute. Erginos responded by launching a second expedition against Thebes; but Herakles was available to command the Thebans on this occasion, and he soon killed Erginos and put his followers to flight. He then forced the Orchomenians to pay tribute to the Thebans, demanding that they should send twice as much as they had been receiving.[24]

In a Hellenistic account recorded by Diodorus, Erginos had taken precautions against a future revolt by depriving the Thebans of their weapons. So when he demanded that Herakles should be surrendered for having assaulted his heralds, Kreon was ready to yield to his superior power. Herakles procured arms for the Thebans, however, by stripping their temples of all the weapons that had been dedicated in them, and persuaded the young men of the city to strike for their freedom. On hearing that Erginos was advancing against the city, Herakles attacked him and his troops on narrow ground to deprive him of the advantage of his superior numbers, and killed him along with much of his army. He was then able to attack Orchomenos unexpectedly and burn it to the ground.[25] Some said that he destroyed the power of Orchomenos forever (see further on p. 558)

Herakles founds a family in Thebes with Megara, but kills their children in a fit of madness

Kreon rewarded Herakles for his services in the war by granting him his daughter MEGARA as a wife. He lived happily with her at Thebes for some years, fathering several children by her (from two to eight in varying accounts), until Hera finally intervened by inspiring him with a fit of homicidal madness. While in this state, he murdered his children, either by throwing them into a fire or by shooting them down with his arrows; and in some accounts, he also killed some or all of the children of his half-brother Iphikles. Apollodorus follows Pherecydes in stating that he threw his children into a fire, and adds that he inflicted the same fate on two children of Iphikles.[26] Or in Diodorus' version, he first tried to kill his nephew Iolaos, but shot his own children when Iolaos managed to escape.[27] Or in another account by Nicolaus of Damascus (a writer associated with the court of Herod the Great), Herakles killed two of the children of Iphikles and then his own children, tearing the last from his mother's breast; and he would have killed Megara too if she had not been rescued by Iphikles, who also saved his own eldest son Iolaos.[28] According to a local tradition at Thebes, Herakles would have killed his aged father too, an even graver crime in Greek eyes, if it had not been for the prompt action of Athena, who stunned him by hurling a stone at him; this stone, which was known as the *sōphronistēr* (i.e. stone of wisdom or restraint), could be seen in the city in historical times.[29]

Megara is mentioned in the *Odyssey* among the famous women of earlier times who were seen by Odysseus in the Underworld; the poet tells us nothing about her except that she was a daughter of Kreon and the wife of Herakles.[30] This story of the murder of her children was recounted by Stesichorus in the first half of the sixth century BC.[31] In referring to the cult of the eight dead sons of Herakles at the Elektran gates of Thebes, Pindar calls them bronze-armoured (or -armed, *chalkoarai*),[32] which would imply that they were grown up at the time of their death. The poet or his source may have altered the story to make it less shameful for Herakles, by representing his victims as having been more than defenceless children.

According to Apollodorus, Kreon offered his younger daughter to Iphikles at the same time as he offered Megara to Herakles; but Iphikles had already fathered his only significant son, Iolaos, by a previous wife, Automedousa, daughter of Alkathoos.[33]

In his surviving play on the episode, the *Madness of Herakles*, Euripides provides a peculiar account apparently of his own devising. While Herakles was away fetching Kerberos from Hades as his final labour, a certain Lykos (who was descended from the famous Lykos whose Theban career will be described in Chapter 9) killed Kreon to seize power at Thebes; and Megara found herself under threat, and sought refuge at the altar of Zeus with her children. On returning to find that Lykos had been planning to burn them to death, Herakles came to their rescue and killed the usurper; but was then driven mad by Hera, who sent Lyssa (Manic Fury personified) against him, causing him to slaughter his wife and children. Having heard rumours that Herakles was under threat from Lykos, Theseus arrived at Thebes after the hero had returned to his senses, and invited him back to Athens to be purified.

Herakles is instructed to perform twelve labours for Eurystheus

When Herakles recovered his sanity and realized what he had done, he went into voluntary exile, first visiting his former host Thespios, who agreed to purify him in accordance with the formal demands of Greek religion; and he then went to Delphi to ask where he should settle in the future. The Pythian priestess told him to go to Tiryns in the Argolid, where he was to live for ten years while he performed a series of labours that would be imposed on him by Eurystheus, king of Mycenae; and at the same time, she was able to give him the more welcome message that he would win immortality as the fruit of his toils and humiliations.[34] Or in the version offered by Nicolaus of Damascus, Eurystheus invited him to come to Tiryns when he went into exile, and he accepted the offer, remembering that Amphitryon had once received an oracle saying that Herakles would have to serve Eurystheus and would win glory as a result.[35] Or in Diodorus' account, Eurystheus had summoned him to perform the labours before his madness, but he had paid no attention until Zeus had let him know by some means that he would have to do so; he had then consulted the Delphic oracle, which gave him the same message as in the initial account above; and while he was still pondering on the matter (for he was understandably depressed at the thought that he would be subjected to a man who was much inferior to him), Hera sent him mad, causing him to kill his children, and he finally embarked on his labours after a long period of mourning.[36]

It was sometimes claimed that the priestess at Delphi first gave the hero his name of Herakles when telling him of his forthcoming labours, and that he had originally been named Alkaios (or Alkeides) after his putative grandfather; in that case, Apollo is supposed to have given him the name Herakles because he would win imperishable glory, *kleos*, by doing favours, *era*, to men, i.e. through his labours (ἦρα γὰρ ἀνθρώποισι φέρων κλέος ἄφθιτον ἕξεις).[37] It is certainly true that his name, which really means 'Glory of Hera', seems inappropriate for a hero who received nothing but hostility from Hera (at least until his apotheosis). Other mythographers devised varied explanations, suggesting, for instance, that the Argives conferred the name on him after his first exploit in strangling the pair of snakes as a baby, to indicate that he had gained glory, *kleos*, through *Hera* (who had sent the snakes with the intention of killing him!).[38]

THE LABOURS OF HERAKLES

The cycle of labours

At some stage in the development of the mythology of Herakles, perhaps as late as the fifth century BC, a canonic list came to be established of the tasks that he was supposed to have performed for Eurystheus. These were known to the Greeks as the *athloi*, a term generally rendered as *labores* in Latin, hence our modern expression, 'the labours', although neither of these translations quite catches the flavour of the original; an *athlos* was literally a contest, especially for a prize, and by extension a struggle or ordeal that involves toil and trouble. The term could therefore be applied most appropriately to describe the arduous tasks that were performed by Herakles for Eurystheus, all the more so since he was thought to have won immortality as the ultimate reward for his labours. Homer already uses the word (though not as yet with the latter suggestion) when referring to the harsh labours, *chalepous aethlous*, that were imposed on the hero by Eurystheus.[39] There is no reason to suppose, however, that Homer knew of any ordered cycle of labours. Although some of the exploits that were later included in the canonic cycle are recorded as early as the eighth century BC in works of art, and all but one – the clearing of the Augeian stables – are attested by the sixth century, it is not known when they came to be classed together as the cycle of labours that he performed for Eurystheus. The full canonic sequence first appears in a series of carvings for the metopes for the temple of Zeus at Olympia, which can be dated to c. 460 BC. Some have argued that these sculptures played a decisive role in establishing the canonic list, and that the standard number was thus determined by architectural considerations; or else the sequence may have imposed itself through an earlier epic account, perhaps in the *Herakleia* of Herodotus' uncle Panyasis; but this remains a matter for conjecture.

According to a classification that was devised by the early Greek mythographers, the exploits of Herakles could be divided into three main classes. These *athloi*, or labours, were distinguished on the one hand from the *parerga*, or incidentals, the chance adventures that befell the hero while he was performing his labours, and on the other hand from the *praxeis* or deeds, the major exploits that he performed of his own accord without orders from another. Artificial though it may have been, this scheme proved most convenient in enabling the mythographers to bring some sort of order into the mass of Herakleian myth. Legends that were located in areas associated with the labours could be bracketed with the appropriate labour as *parerga*, even if they had no original connection with them; and the other main deeds of the hero (apart from one or two youthful deeds set in Boeotia) could be relegated to the period after his labours as his various *praxeis*. We will now follow the labours with their associated *parerga* before passing on to the other adventures that were relegated in this way to the latter part of Herakles' life.

While performing his labours, Herakles received his orders from Eurystheus at Mycenae but lived elsewhere, basing himself at the ancient citadel of Tiryns to the south. He was accompanied to the Argolid by his nephew Iolaos, who assisted him in his labours as his charioteer, and also his half-brother Iphikles; but Megara remained at Thebes until Herakles visited her after his labours to settle his marital affairs (see p. 272).

Convenient summaries of the labours are provided by Diodorus and Apollodorus.[40] In the following account, we will consider them in the order in which they are narrated by Diodorus, although other lists or narratives show some slight variation in this respect; in particular, Herakles' journey to the Underworld to fetch Kerberos, which could certainly be regarded as his most daunting enterprise, was sometimes classed as his final labour rather than as his penultimate labour as below. The labours fall neatly into two groups of six, for the first six are set in the northern Peloponnese no great distance from Mycenae, while the final six take the hero further abroad, initially to Crete, Thrace and Asia Minor, and ultimately to the edges of the earth and the world below.

According to a tradition mentioned by Apollodorus alone, the priestess at Delphi originally told the hero that he would have to perform ten labours over twelve years, but he was obliged to perform twelve labours in the end because Eurystheus refused to acknowledge two of them, objecting that Iolaos had helped him to kill the hydra (see below) and that he had sought a fee from Augeias for clearing the Augeian stables.[41]

Amphitryon was usually thought to have died before the time of Herakles' labours; Apollodorus states that he was killed while fighting bravely alongside Herakles in the war against Orchomenos.[42] He was sometimes introduced into the story of Herakles' madness, however, as in the local tradition mentioned above in which he was saved by Athena, or in Euripides' surviving play on the matter (in which he came under threat from Lykos along with Herakles' wife and children).[43] Only a single exploit is recorded for him from his latter years at Thebes, his defeat of Chalkodon of Euboea (see p. 520), who was killed by him in a battle near Thebes when he tried to exact a tribute from the Thebans.[44]

Alkmene was sometimes said to have married the Cretan hero Rhadamanthys after Amphitryon's death (see p. 352); she lived to a great age, surviving to share the troubles of the Heraklids after her son's death (see p. 287). As for her brother Likymnios, when he had accompanied her to Thebes, he married Amphitryon's sister Perimede, who bore him three sons, first Oionos, whose subsequent murder would cause Herakles to conduct a campaign against Sparta (see p. 279), and then Argeias and Melas, who would be killed during Herakles' final campaign (see p. 283). The only significant tale recorded for Likymnios himself is the story of his death (see p. 293).

First labour: the Nemean Lion

As his first labour, Herakles was ordered to kill the monstrous Nemean lion that lived in the mountains near Nemea in the north-western corner of the Argolid. According to Hesiod, it was the offspring of Orthos and Chimaira (or possibly Echidna, see p. 63), and was reared by Hera, who caused it to roam the hills of Nemea, evidently with the intention of providing an ordeal for Herakles.[45] Or in another tradition, it was a child of the moon-goddess Selene (or was at least born on the moon), and lived on the moon until Selene cast it down to the earth with a fearsome shudder at the request of Hera.[46] It was especially formidable because it was invulnerable (except perhaps in the earliest tradition, for images from the visual arts suggest that there may once have been a version in which it could be killed with a sword). Although Herakles soon discovered that its hide was impenetrable to his arrows and sword, he was able to use his club and indeed his bare hands to greater advantage. In the standard later version, he struck fear into it by threatening it with his club, causing it to flee back to its lair, a two-mouthed cave on Mt Tretos (Perforated Mountain) near Nemea; and he then blocked up one mouth of the cave before entering through the other to seize it by its neck and strangle it.[47] Or in another account, he stunned the lion by battering it with his club at their first meeting, and then strangled it in the open air.[48]

Figure 8.2 Herakles strangles the Nemean lion. Attic amphora, circle of Exekias. Staatliche Antikensammlungen, Kassel.

After killing the lion, Herakles stripped it of its hide to provide himself with his familiar costume, which offered him excellent protection because it was impenetrable to any weapon. According to Theocritus, he was at a loss as to how he could cut it until some god inspired him with the thought that it might at least be penetrable to the lion's own claws.[49] Although Apollodorus states that he was merely ordered to fetch the animal's skin, he is usually said to have carried the lion itself to Eurystheus as proof of its death (as Apollodorus indeed describes him as doing later in his own narrative).[50] Eurystheus was so alarmed by the sight of it that he refused to allow Herakles into Mycenae from that time onwards, telling him to exhibit his trophies at the city gates. For further security, the cowardly king ordered that a bronze jar should be buried in the earth for him to hide in when Herakles arrived with his more fearsome trophies, such as Kerberos or the Erymanthian boar; and he issued his orders through an intermediary henceforth, the herald Kopreus (Dung-man), who is already mentioned in this connection in the *Iliad*.[51]

In the earliest tradition, Herakles wore metallic armour like any other warrior. He is first shown wearing a lionskin in works of art dating from the latter part of the seventh century BC, and it is not until the second half of the sixth century that the lionskin becomes his standard form of dress in Attic vase-painting.[52] Pindar and Bacchylides in the following century are the first authors to indicate that the hide was impenetrable.[53] By looking out through the jaw-space, the hero could use the beast's scalp as a sort of helmet. Apollodorus alone suggests that he cut his lionskin from the lion of Kithairon (see p. 251).[54]

Herakles was said to have cut his club from a wild olive-tree at Nemea or on the east coast of the Argolid before setting out against the lion;[55] or according to Theocritus, he acquired it on Mt Helikon in Boeotia by pulling up an entire olive-tree.[56] We hear elsewhere of a bronze or bronze-tipped club; this may have been the club that he was said to have received from Hephaistos.[57] His more conventional arms and armour were presented to him by various gods as a rewards for his prowess, either after he first demonstrated it by defeating the Orchomenians or after he completed the first five of his labours; according to Apollodorus, Hermes gave him a sword, Apollo a bow and arrow, Hephaistos a golden cuirass, and Athena a mantle.[58]

Before confronting the Nemean lion, Herakles called in at Kleonai, a town not far from Nemea, and stayed with a poor labourer called MOLORCHOS, whose son had been killed by the lion. Molorchos wanted to sacrifice a ram in honour of his guest, but Herakles told him to wait for thirty days and then make a sacrifice, offering it to Zeus the Saviour if he had returned safely from the hunt or else to himself as a hero if he were killed during the hunt. Gods and dead heroes were both honoured in Greek cult, the latter with distinctive chthonic rites. After pursuing the lion for twenty-eight days, Herakles killed it on the twenty-ninth day, but promptly fell asleep from exhaustion; on awakening, he hoisted the lion onto his shoulders and hurried back with it to Molorchos, hastily plucking some wild parsley (*selinon*) to make a crown for the sacrifice. He arrived back just in time to prevent Molorchos from making the sacrifice to him as a dead hero. Before departing on his way, Herakles reorganized the Nemean Games (which had been founded by Adrastos and the Seven, see p. 318) as a festival in honour of Zeus; it was claimed that the victors were awarded a crown of wild parsley because the hero had worn one at the above-mentioned sacrifice to Zeus. A version of this tale was recounted by Callimachus, who is the earliest author who is known to have mentioned it.[59] In astral mythology, Hera was said to have rewarded the lion by transferring it to the heavens to become the constellation of the Lion (Leo).[60]

Second labour: the Lernaian Hydra

This was a huge many-headed snake that lived in the swamps of Lerna some miles to the south of Argos. According to the *Theogony*, it was the offspring of Typhon and Echidna, and it was reared by Hera to become a danger to Herakles;[61] although Hesiod offers no description, it is regularly described as many-headed in subsequent accounts and is shown as such in visual images from the eighth century BC onwards. As for the number of its heads, estimates vary from just a few to as many as fifty or a hundred.[62] For obvious practical reasons, artists tend to portray it with relatively few heads. It was often said to have been exceptionally difficult to kill because as soon as one head was cut off, a new head, or more commonly two, would grow up in its place.[63] Hydra, which simply means water-snake, is not a proper name in Greek and does not necessarily carry any connotation of monstrosity.

After travelling to Lerna in his chariot with Iolaos, Herakles engaged with this formidable adversary, but soon found himself in difficulties because its heads regrew as quickly as he cut them off (or knocked them off with his club). To make matters worse, Hera provided it with an ally by sending an enormous crab to bite Herakles on the foot. He managed to kill the crab, however, by crushing it underfoot, and now felt that he was justified in calling on the help of Iolaos as an ally of his own. So Iolaos prepared some firebrands, and whenever Herakles cut off one of the hydra's heads, he would assist him by cauterizing the stump to prevent a new head (or heads) from growing. After removing its heads in this manner and killing it, Herakles dipped his arrows into its blood or gall, making them so poisonous from that time onward that the merest scratch would prove fatal. According to Apollodorus at least, one of its heads (here nine in number) was immortal, and the hero was therefore obliged to bury it under a heavy rock.[64] Some said that Herakles called on the help of Iolaos while under joint attack from the hydra and the crab, hence the origin of the proverb 'Even Herakles cannot fight against two'.[65] In astral mythology, Hera is said to have honoured the crab by transferring it to the heavens to become the constellation of the Crab (Cancer).[66]

Third labour: the Erymanthian Boar

This is perhaps the least interesting of all the adventures, even if it inspired some memorable images from Attic vase-painters, who liked to show Eurystheus cowering in his bronze jar as Herakles displays the boar to him. This beast, which was neither of divine origin nor gifted with any special powers, lived on Mt Erymanthos in north-western Arcadia and used to venture down to ravage the lands beneath. Having been ordered to capture it alive, Herakles frightened it out of its lair with loud shouts (or well-aimed stones) and chased it into deep snow, where he was able to net it. He then carried it back to Mycenae on his shoulders, which was quite a feat in itself.[67]

While seeking the boar, he visited the Centaur PHOLOS, who lived in a cave on Mt Pholoe to the south of Mt Erymanthos. Pholos set roast meat before him while eating his own meat raw (an indication of his semi-animal status); but he hesitated to offer any wine to his guest because the wine-jar in his cave belonged to all the Centaurs in common. Herakles insisted nevertheless and opened it up, to the anger of the other Centaurs, who soon detected the smell of the wine and arrived at the cave armed with rocks and fir-trees. In another account, Dionysos had left the jar with a Centaur four generations earlier, ordering that it should not be opened until Herakles arrived there as a visitor; and when it was duly opened for Herakles by Pholos, the Centaurs of the area were thrown into such a frenzy by the scent of the ancient wine that they attacked the cave. A fight developed in any case between the Centaurs and the hero, who shot some of them on the spot and put the others to flight. They sought refuge with Cheiron, who was then living at Cape Malea at the south-eastern tip of the Peloponnese, having been expelled from Mt Pelion by the Lapiths. As they were cowering around the noble Centaur, Herakles, who had pursued them all the way, shot an arrow at them and accidentally struck Cheiron in the knee. Since the painful wound was rendered incurable by the virulent poison on Herakles' arrow (which had come from the hydra's venom), Cheiron was later happy to surrender his immortality as the price for Prometheus' release (see p. 271). Herakles returned to Mt Pholoe to find that his host Pholos had met his death in the mean time. For while he had been examining one of Herakles' poisoned arrows, he had accidentally dropped it onto his own foot; or else he had cut himself with an arrow as he was drawing it from the body of a fallen Centaur to prepare him for burial.[68]

The Centaurs were primarily associated with northern Thessaly; it was said that they took refuge in Arcadia after they were driven out of their original homeland by Peirithoos and the Lapiths (see p. 555). Of those who survived the present confrontation with Herakles, Nessos settled on the river Euenos in Aetolia (see p. 281) while others were received at Eleusis by Poseidon, who hid them under a mountain. Herakles killed another Centaur, Eurytion, while visiting Dexamenos (the Hospitable), king of Olenos in Achaea, after clearing the Augeian stables; for Eurytion had forced the king to allow him to marry his daughter, and Herakles shot him when he arrived to claim her. Or in another version, Herakles killed him when he tried to rape the king's daughter at her wedding-feast (see p. 549).[69] Cheiron and Pholos were of nobler character than the other Centaurs, and of higher birth (see p. 555).

Fourth labour: the Cerynitian Hind

The golden-horned Cerynitian (or Ceryneian) hind, which was sacred to Artemis, lived by the river Kerynites (or on Mt Keryneia) in north-eastern Arcadia. Herakles was ordered to capture it alive; and since it was a sacred beast, it would be improper for him to cause it even the slightest harm. According to Apollodorus, he chased it through Arcadia for an entire year until he finally brought it to the ground with a skilful arrow-shot (evidently without injuring it) as it was about to cross the river Ladon. As he was carrying it to Mycenae on his shoulders, he ran across Artemis and her brother Apollo. She reproached him for having tried to kill her sacred beast, and wanted to take it away from him, but was appeased by his explanations and allowed him to pass on his way.[70] After showing the hind to Eurystheus, he set it free unharmed. Diodorus records various other ways in which he was said to have captured it, whether by the use of nets, or by tracking it down until he was able to surprise it in its sleep, or by running it down until it grew exhausted.[71] Although the chase was confined to the central Peloponnese in the usual account, Pindar offers a more extravagant version in which Herakles pursued the beast from Arcadia to the banks of the Istros (Danube) and thence to the mythical northern land of the Hyperboreans.[72]

Pindar remarks that Taygete (the eponym of Mt Taygetos on the western borders of Laconia, named elsewhere as a daughter of Atlas) had dedicated the hind to Artemis, and had inscribed it with the name of the goddess. According to the poet's ancient commentators, Artemis had once turned Taygete into a hind to save her from being raped by Zeus, and Taygete had shown her gratitude afterwards by dedicating the present hind to her rescuer.[73] There is no way of telling, however, whether this was a genuinely ancient story or simply a tale that was invented by some mythographer to account for Pindar's allusion. Whatever its origin, it is not easily reconciled with the commonly accepted tradition in which Taygete bore the founder of the Spartan royal line to Zeus (see p. 524). Callimachus offers a different account of the origin of the hind, saying that five such beasts, as large as bulls, had once lived at Parrhasia in southern Arcadia, where they had been seen by Artemis, who had captured four of them to draw her chariot; but Hera ensured that the fifth should escape to Mt Keryneia to provide a labour for Herakles in the future.[74] Although Euripides claims that it was a dangerous beast that caused trouble to the local people, this formed no part of the original tradition; as Diodorus observes, this was a labour that was to be achieved by ingenuity, without involving danger or the use of force.[75]

Fifth labour: the Stymphalian Birds

The thickly wooded shores of the Stymphalian Lake in north-eastern Arcadia provided a perfect habitat for huge flocks of birds. As his next labour, Herakles was ordered to drive them all away. The birds were not dangerous in the original story; they look rather like geese in vase-paintings, with short bodies and long necks. They could be expected to present a problem to Herakles simply because there were so many of them. In literary accounts, the hero frightened the birds out of their coverts by creating a din with a bronze rattle or castanets, and then shot them down with his arrows as they rose up into the air. Or in an early version by the epic poet Pisander of Rhodes, he merely frightened them away without killing them. There was disagreement on whether he made the bird-scarer himself or received it as a gift from Athena, who had acquired it from Hephaistos. It makes no appearance in vase-paintings and other visual images, which simply show the hero shooting the birds with his arrows, or attacking them with his club, or a sling, or indeed his bare hands.[76] By mentioning the Stymphalian birds in connection with the birds of the island of Ares in the Black Sea, which could shoot out their feathers like arrows (see p. 389), Apollonius was indirectly responsible for some late reports which attribute this capacity to the Arcadian birds.[77] Pausanias is certainly following a late tradition when he describes them as man-eaters, and compares them to some alarming Arabian birds that could peck through armour of bronze or iron.[78]

Sixth labour: the Augeian Stables

AUGEIAS, son of Helios (the Sun), who ruled at Elis in the north-western Peloponnese, was the proud owner of vast herds of cattle (which had been presented by his divine father in some accounts). Since their stables, or more accurately, enclosures, had been left uncleared, an enormous quantity of dung had accumulated, and Herakles was now ordered to clear it away in a single day. Before setting to work, he negotiated a fee of a tenth of the land with Augeias, who was happy to promise it because he believed that Herakles would not be able to complete the task in full. Rather than attempting to achieve it by hand, however, which would doubtless have been as impractical as it was humiliating, Herakles resorted to his wits and washed the dung away by diverting a river (or rivers) through the enclosures. In differing accounts, he rechannelled the Peneios and Alpheios, the two main rivers of the area, for this purpose, or else the Alpheios alone, or the Manios, a tributary of the Alpheios that ran through the city of Elis. Herakles returned to Augeias in triumph to claim his fee, only to find that the king had discovered that he was acting under orders from Eurystheus, and was unwilling to pay him for work that he would have had to perform in any case. According to Apollodorus, Augeias even denied that he had ever promised him a reward, and declared that he would be ready to submit to arbitration on the point; but when the matter was brought before the tribunal, Augeias' own son, Phyleus, offered evidence on behalf of Herakles, attesting that a reward had indeed been offered. Augeias was so furious that he expelled Herakles from the kingdom along with Phyleus before the votes could be counted. Homer may have been acquainted with this story, in some form at least, since he mentions that Phyleus went into exile after quarrelling with his father. When Herakles later returned to Elis to avenge the slight, he killed Augeias and invited Phyleus to take over the kingdom (see pp. 277–8).[79]

A comical tale of an eating-contest came to be attached to this labour. When Herakles tried to claim his reward for clearing the stables, a certain LEPREOS (the eponym of Eleian town of Lepreon or Lepreos) advised Augeias to throw him into chains. Herakles was aggrieved by the insult and later visited the home of Lepreos to confront him, but agreed to make friends with him at the urging of his mother, and then competed with him in a series of contests, in throwing the discus, in bailing out water, and in seeing who could consume a whole ox in the shortest time. Lepreos was inevitably defeated every time, and when he was defeated once again in a drinking-contest, he lost his temper and provoked his own death by challenging Herakles to single combat.[80] Or in another version, Lepreos was able to match Herakles in gluttony in an ox-eating contest, and became over-confident as a result and dared to challenge him to a duel.[81]

Seventh labour: the Cretan Bull

According to the usual tradition, this was the bull that had been sent up from the sea by Poseidon in response to the prayers of Minos, but had later been turned wild by the god after Minos had failed to sacrifice it to him (see p. 338); in that case, it should certainly have been exceptionally difficult to capture. Or in a divergent account by the early Argive mythographer Acusilaus,[82] it was the bull that had carried Europa to Crete (see p. 337; usually regarded as having been Zeus himself in animal form). Herakles was ordered to bring it back alive. Although Diodorus states that he was helped in the enterprise by Minos, Apollodorus says quite the opposite, stating that he sought the help of Minos but was told to tackle the beast on his own. For information on how he was supposed to have achieved this, we have to rely on vase-paintings, which indicate that he wrestled the bull to its knees and hobbled it. Diodorus reports that he rode through the sea to the Peloponnese on its back. He showed it to Eurystheus and then let it go; it wandered about for some time, finally taking up residence at Marathon in northern Attica, where it was subsequently killed by Theseus (see p. 344).[83] Or in some Latin accounts, Herakles killed it, or Eurystheus was tactless enough to dedicate it to Hera, who drove it away to Attica because it witnessed to the glory of Herakles.[84]

Eighth labour: the Horses of Diomedes

As his next labour, Herakles was sent north to fetch the savage horses of DIO-MEDES, son of Ares, the king of the Bistones in Thrace. The four horses in question, which would have formed Diomedes' chariot-team, were fed on human flesh; they are commonly described as mares (even if Hyginus, the only author to name them, happens to give them masculine names, Podargos, Lampon, Xanthos and Dinos).[85] In what was probably the oldest form of the story, as attested by Pindar and Euripides, the hero achieved the task on his own. Although the relevant fragment from Pindar is poorly preserved, it would seem that Herakles threw some unfortunate person to the horses to distract them while he was harnessing them; and Diomedes was apparently killed while trying to oppose him. Euripides refers to the blood-caked stables of the horses, and mentions that Herakles tamed them and drove them back to Mycenae in a four-horse chariot.[86] Herakles seems to have been unaccompanied in Diodorus' account also. After reporting that the horses' feeding-troughs were made from bronze and that the animals were fastened to them by iron chains, Diodorus explains that Herakles tamed them by throwing their own master to them; for he rendered them docile by feeding them on the flesh of the man who had taught them their unnatural practices.[87]

In the other main version of the story, as recounted by Apollodorus, Herakles sailed to Thrace with a company of volunteers, also taking his young favourite ABDEROS, who was a son of Hermes from Opous in Eastern Locris. After over-powering the men who were in charge of the stables, Herakles seized the mares and led them down towards the sea; but Diomedes and his followers came to recover them before he could sail away, and he left them in the charge of Abderos while he was confronting the enemy force. He soon killed Diomedes and put the Bistonians to flight, but returned to find that Abderos had been killed by the horses in the mean time. So he buried him at the spot and founded the city of Abdera in his memory (on the northern coast of the Aegean about halfway between the Chalcidice and the Hellespont). He then took the horses to Eurystheus, who set them free.[88] They wandered north toward their homeland until they arrived at Mt Olympos where they were torn apart by wild beasts; or according to Diodorus, Eurystheus dedicated them to Hera and their breed persisted until the time of Alexander the Great.[89] Ovid and Hyginus state that Herakles slaughtered them,[90] but this was evidently a late development. It was during his journey to Thrace that Herakles rescued Alkestis from death in Euripides' account of her story (see p. 152).

Ninth labour: the Belt of Hippolyte

As his next labour, Herakles went to the land of the Amazons to fetch the belt or 'girdle' of their queen, HIPPOLYTE. This was a heavy warrior's belt (*zōstēr*) rather than the light girdle that would have formed part of the ordinary clothing of women; Apollodorus calls it the belt of Ares and indicates that it was a symbol of Hippolyte's sovereignty.[91] Although the same author goes on to explain that Eurystheus sent for it because his daughter Admete wanted to acquire it, such an object would have been desirable in itself and well-suited to serve as a token of success, and it need not be assumed that any such explanation would have been offered or required in the early tradition. According to Euripides, the belt was deposited at Mycenae, presumably at the Heraion, along with a gold-spangled robe that had belonged to the queen.[92]

The land of the Amazons was usually thought to lie on the southern shores of the Black Sea, in the north-eastern corner of Asia Minor; after having undertaken labours in the south and north, Herakles now set out for the east. In the simplest version of the story, as found in Apollonius, he gained the belt on his own and without bloodshed, by capturing the queen's sister MELANIPPE in an ambush and then ransoming her in exchange for the belt. It seems to have been commonly believed, however, that he sailed to the area with a force of allies, and engaged the Amazons in a battle at which he either seized the belt or captured the enemy commander, Melanippe, to ransom her for the belt.[93] The battle is a very popular

C. Normand sculp

Figure 8.3 Herakles and Amazon. Drawing after a vase-painting.

subject in vase-paintings from the first half of the sixth century BC onwards (although there is no indication that a belt plays any special part in the story, and the specific opponent of Herakles is generally a certain Andromache, if any name is marked). Theseus was sometimes said to have accompanied Herakles as one of his allies (see p. 357).[94]

Apollodorus offers a distinctive account of this labour, saying that Hippolyte visited Herakles' ship to enquire about the reason for his visit after he called in at Themiskyra, the main city of the Amazons on the river Thermodon. She promised to give him the belt, and the matter might have been settled amicably if it had not been for the machinations of Hera, who mingled with Hippolyte's followers in the guise of an Amazon and told them that their queen was being abducted. They rode down to the ship fully armed as a consequence, causing Herakles to believe that treachery was afoot. So he killed Hippolyte, stripped her of the belt, and confronted the Amazons in battle before sailing off with his trophy.[95]

While sailing to (or from) this labour, Herakles saved Hesione, the daughter of the king of Troy, from being devoured by a sea-monster; but her father Laomedon refused to pay him the promised reward, and he returned to Troy after the completion of his labours to exact a devastating revenge (see p. 275). Apollodorus may be consulted for various minor episodes that came to be associated with Herakles' voyage.

Tenth labour: the Cattle of Geryon

The monstrous GERYON (or Geryoneus, or Geryones), who was three men joined into one, has already been mentioned as a child of Chrysaor (see p. 62); Herakles was ordered to fetch his cattle from his home-island of Erytheia (Red Island), which lay in the outer Ocean toward the sunset in the far west. The hero travelled out through North Africa, killing many wild beasts on the way to prepare the area for human settlement. As he was approaching the western bounds of Africa, he became exasperated by the heat of the sun and aimed his bow threateningly at the sun-god Helios, who was so impressed by his audacity that he offered him the use of his golden cup to take him across the Ocean to Erytheia.[96] This was the remarkable vessel in which Helios used to travel around the Ocean each night from the place of his setting to that of his rising (see p. 43). So Herakles took the cup from Okeanos or from the sea-god Nereus,[97] evidently during the daytime while Helios was not using it, and reached Erytheia with greater ease than he might have expected. According to Pherecydes, Okeanos tried to test his nerve by raising a heavy swell, but gave up in alarm when the hero threatened him with his bow.[98]

On reaching Erytheia (which originally lay in a purely fabulous realm, but was later thought to lie somewhere off the coast of southern Spain), Herakles set up camp on a mountain and awaited an opportunity to steal the cattle, which were purple in colour and were guarded by the herdsman Eurytion and the monstrous dog Orthos or Orthros (see p. 62), which had two or more heads. The dog soon detected the presence of the stranger and rushed to the attack, but was clubbed to death by Herakles, who also killed Eurytion when he came to the aid of the beast.

On learning of the disturbance from Menoitios, who was pasturing the cattle of Hades on the island, Geryon set off in search of Herakles and found him driving the cattle away along the side of a river; and a fierce fight ensued in which Geryon was shot dead. Making use of the cup of Helios once again, Herakles ferried the stolen cattle across to the Iberian coast, and then drove them across the Pyrenees and through southern Europe to Greece, visiting Italy and Sicily on the way.[99]

We must now consider some of the many adventures that befell Herakles as he was travelling to the far west and back again. His outward journey was comparatively uneventful (unless he was confronted Antaios and Bousiris at this time, as Diodorus suggests, rather than during his journey to the Hesperides, see p. 270). On reaching the western end of the Libyan (i.e. North African) coast, he raised the Pillars of Herakles to mark the western boundaries of the inhabited world. These were usually identified with the Rock of Gibraltar (Mt Calpe) and the mountain above Ceuta (Mt Abile) on either side of the Straits of Gibraltar;[100] and some claimed that Herakles also opened up the straits on this occasion to provide an outlet to the Ocean, or else narrowed the existing straits to make them impassable to the monsters of the Ocean.[101] In another account, the pillar-rocks were raised in the very earliest times by Briareos (one of the Hundred-Handers, see p. 67) and were later dedicated to Herakles in recognition of his services;[102] or else the pillars of Herakles were ordinary pillars that stood in the temple of Melkart, a Phoenician god who was identified with Herakles, at Gadeira (Cadiz) in southern Iberia.[103]

Herakles met with trouble quite frequently during his return journey because people were tempted to steal from the herd that he was driving through their lands. The Ligurians of southern France, for instance, attacked him for that reason not far from the city of Arles (which he was said to have founded, naming it Alesia in memory of his wandering, *alē*). Although he tried to repel them by use of his bow, he ran out of arrows and prayed for help to his father Zeus, who rained vast quantities of pebbles from the sky, enabling him to pelt his attackers with them until they withdrew. The area now known as the Plaine de la Crau, which is covered by masses of pebbles that reduce it to barrenness, was pointed out as the very spot where this wonder took place.[104]

Most interesting of all are the stories associated with Herakles' wanderings through Italy and Sicily; although they are neglected by Apollodorus, a conveniently accessible anthology is provided by Diodorus, who, as a Greek Sicilian, was naturally intrigued by this aspect of Herakles' mythology.[105] Leaving aside the other records and traces of his passage (his very footprints could be seen in Apulia, preserved like the tracks of a dinosaur[106]), we will concentrate on two interrelated stories from the southernmost stage of his journey. At Rhegion (Rhegium) on the Italian shore of the Straits of Messina, a bull broke free from the herd and swam across to Sicily; and since Herakles wandered around the area asking the local people whether they had seen a missing bull-calf (*italos*, or *vitulus* under the corresponding Latin name), the land came to be known as Italy from that time forth. It was also explained that Rhegion came to be called by that name because the bull 'broke away' there (as though the name were derived from the Greek verb *rhēgnumi* or *aporhēgnumi*).[107] Finding no sign of the bull in Italy, the hero crossed over to Sicily, where he discovered that ERYX, a local ruler in the west of the island, had gained possession of the beast and had mixed it among his own cattle. This Eryx was the eponym of the Sicilian mountain of that name (now Mt San Giuliano), which was the site of an important sanctuary of Aphrodite; he was a son of Aphrodite by Boutes (an Argonaut whom she had rescued, see p. 395) or by Poseidon. When he refused to surrender the bull unless Herakles could defeat him in a wrestling-match, the hero forced him to the ground three times (the usual condition for a victory) before proceeding to kill him.[108] Or in another account, Herakles was challenged to a wrestling-match by Eryx as he was making a circuit of the island with the cattle, and fought with him on the agreement that he would gain the kingdom if he won, but would surrender the cattle if he lost. After defeating Eryx, he entrusted the kingdom to the local people on condition that they would hand it over if any of his descendants should arrive in the area in the future to claim it. Dorieus, a member of the Spartan royal family (which was supposedly of Heraklid descent, see p. 291), came to Sicily toward the end of the sixth century BC and actually laid claim to the territory on these grounds (but was soon killed by enemies within the island).[109] For two minor adventures of Herakles in the toe of Italy, see p. 581.

The cult of Herakles (or Hercules as he was known in Latin) was introduced to Rome at a relatively early period, and a number of aetiological legends came to be developed by Roman authors in which he was said to have introduced cultic innovations while visiting the site of the city with the cattle of Geryon. The most interesting and by far the most famous is the one that was devised to account for the origin of his oldest cult at Rome, at the Ara Maxima (Greatest Altar) in the Forum Boarium. Originally a private cult administered by two old patrician families, the Potitii and the Pinarii, it was deemed to be of venerable antiquity (even if it cannot really have been so very ancient since Greek rites were practised at it). So what could be more natural than to imagine that it might have been founded by Herakles/Hercules himself in the very earliest times while he was in Italy, before he was a god and before the city yet existed? As he was resting by the Tiber with the cattle, so the story goes, a monster or brigand of the area called CACUS caught sight of the beasts from his lair on the Palatine hill (or the Aventine in one version), and stole some of them while the hero was lying asleep. Dragging them tail-foremost to his cave, he blocked up the entrance with a huge boulder and awaited the departure of their owner; and although Hercules noticed their absence and tried to find them, he failed in his efforts because all the tracks seemed to lead away from the cave, and he was finally obliged set off without them. As he was driving the remaining beasts away, however, some of them began to low and their fellows within the cave (or just one of them) bellowed in reply. Hastily seizing his club, Hercules rushed up the hillside toward the source of the noise, forced his way into the cave, and cudgelled or throttled Cacus to death to recover the cattle. In the traditional version, Cacus was a fire-breathing monster of semi-human appearance who tried to defend himself by spewing out blasts of flame; or in rationalistic accounts, he was simply a ruffian of exceptional size. On hearing of the death of Cacus, Evander (Euandros in Greek), an Arcadian who was said to have ruled at the site in the time, approached Hercules to express his gratitude, and reported that his mother (who was a prophetic nymph) had foretold that he was destined to be raised to the heavens as a god. Wanting to be the first to pay him divine honours, Evander raised the Ara Maxima to him as his first altar and sacrificed a calf to him; or in another version, Hercules, who was never noted for his modesty, raised the altar in his own honour in response to the prophecy.[110] To explain why the cult was originally controlled by the Potitii and Pinarii (until it was taken over by the state toward the end of the fourth century BC), some authors added that Hercules instructed members of these two families in the Greek rites that were to be practised at it.[111]

Although it was once widely argued that this tale of cattle-thievery was an ancient myth that was developed independently at Rome in accordance with a common Indo-European pattern, it is far more likely that it was an antiquarian legend of fairly late invention that was modelled on the various Greek tales (some quite old) in which people of a number of regions were said to have tried to rob the hero of his cattle during his long journey. Cacus himself was of Italian origin as would be expected. Although he appears as a seer in Etruscan images, he was apparently honoured as a fire-deity in early Rome in conjunction with a female counterpart called Caca. He was associated with the Palatine hill in particular (even if Vergil transfers his cave to the Aventine); a flight of steps known as the Scala Caci or 'Steps of Cacus' was cut into southern flank of the hill, leading up from the Circus Maximus. As a godling who was associated with fire, Cacus could easily be transformed into a fire-breathing monster who could serve as a worthy opponent for Hercules; and the fact that his name could be equated with *kakos*, the Greek adjective for bad or evil, may have encouraged this reinterpretation of his nature. The most imaginative detail in the resulting story, the monster's ruse in making the cattle walk backwards to his cave, was surely recycled from the famous episode in early Greek myth in which Hermes tried to conceal his theft of Apollo's cattle by that means (see p. 162).

After his Italian detour, Herakles drove the cattle around the top of the Adriatic and down toward Greece. But as he was doing so, Hera tried to frustrate him by sending a gadfly against the cattle, causing them to disperse among the foothills of the mountains of Thrace. With much difficulty, Herakles collected most of them together again, even if a few were left behind to become the ancestors of the wild cattle of Thrace. When he finally arrived in Mycenae, he delivered the cattle to Eurystheus, who sacrificed them to Hera.[112]

According to a picturesque tale recounted by Herodotus, Herakles' travels took him to Scythia, where a viper-woman stole his chariot-horses and demanded that he should sleep with her as a condition for their return. She was formed like an ordinary woman from the buttocks upwards, but otherwise like a snake. She managed to detain him in Scythia for some time, bearing him three sons, Agathyrsos, Gelanos and Skythes; and when the time came for him to depart, he left one of his bows and a sword-belt behind, telling her that the kingdom should go to the son who could draw the bow and put on the sword-belt in the proper way. When it later turned out that only the youngest, Skythes, was able to do so, she drove the other two away in obedience to their father's orders. The three brothers were the eponymous mythical ancestors of the Scythians and two neighbouring peoples, the Agathyrsoi and Gelanoi; and the story explained the origin of the distinctive Scythian bow, which resembled the bow that was supposed to have been used by Herakles.[113]

Eleventh labour: the Fetching of Kerberos

The most daunting of the labours of Herakles is also the one that can be traced to the earliest period, since the *Iliad* already mentions how 'Eurystheus sent him down to the house of Hades, keeper of the gates, to fetch the hound of hateful Hades from Erebos'. The Homeric epics also report that he received invaluable assistance from Athena and Hermes.[114] He descended to the nether regions through the route that was most commonly favoured by mythical adventurers, the bottomless cave at Cape Tainaron in the southern Peloponnese.[115] According to late Latin sources, the ferryman Charon was so alarmed to see him that he agreed to take him across to the land of the dead even though he was still alive, and was punished for this breach of his duties by being thrown into chains for a year.[116] Apollodorus remarks that the shades all fled at the sight of the hero, with the exception of Meleagros and the Gorgon Medusa. The story of his encounter with Meleagros is recounted in full in an ode of Bacchylides, who describes how Meleagros told him the sad story of his premature death, causing him to weep for the only time in his life, and recommended his sister Deianeira to him as a wife (counsel that the hero would eventually follow, see p. 279).[117] As for the Gorgon, Herakles drew his sword as if to fend her off until Hermes advised him that she was merely a harmless phantom. As he advanced further into the land of the dead, he came across Theseus and Peirithoos, who had been imprisoned there ever since they had entered Hades alive with the crazy intent of abducting Persephone (see p. 361); and he raised Theseus up from his seat to set him free (along with Peirithoos in some accounts). He also tried to help Askalaphos, an inhabitant of the Underworld who had been buried under a stone by Demeter (see further on p. 129). Wanting to procure blood for the shades (to restore their wits, see p. 109), he slaughtered some of the cattle of Hades, to the anger of their herdsman Menoitios, who challenged him to a wrestling-match; Herakles seized Menoitios in a firm grip and broke his ribs, but was obliged to let go of him when Persephone intervened.[118]

Kerberos would not allow himself to be captured without a struggle, and he was a formidable opponent even for the greatest of heroes, for he was not only large and powerful but had three heads (in the usual tradition at least) and a snake in his tail. The literary accounts of this episode are all relatively late. According to Apollodorus, Herakles asked Hades for permission to remove him, and was told that he could take him if he could overpower him without using any weapons; trusting to the protection of his breastplate and lionskin (which was of course impenetrable), he seized Kerberos' head in his arms and gripped him tightly, ignoring the bites that he was receiving from the snake in his tail, until the beast submitted.[119] Or in a slightly different version in which Herakles was ordered to overpower him without using his shield or metallic weapons, he used his lionskin for a shield and intimidated him by hurling sharp stones at him (or perhaps shooting stone-tipped arrows); and when Hades tried to obstruct him after he had seized the beast, he was understandably annoyed and threatened the god with his bow.[120] Diodorus is exceptional in suggesting that Persephone delivered Kerberos to him ready-chained.[121] The visual record takes us back to the sixth century BC, for vase-paintings from that period show Herakles confronting or pacifying the dog, often with Hermes or Athena (or both) standing by or even assisting. Other images show the hero approaching Persephone or Hades beforehand; since one or the other of them is sometimes shown watching as he pacifies Kerberos, it would seem that he was thought to have gained their permission beforehand as in the preceding literary accounts.

After successfully intimidating or mollifying Kerberos, Herakles brought him up to the world above to show him to Eurystheus, ascending at Tainaron (or through the temple of Artemis at Troizen, or through a cleft in the earth at Hermione nearby, or through a bottomless cave at Herakleia by the Black Sea[122]). As soon as he had proved the success of his mission, causing Eurystheus a considerable fright as he did so, he returned Kerberos to the gates of Hades to allow him to resume his normal duties.

Various minor tales came to be attached to this myth, originating either in local traditions or in the imagination of later poets. It was claimed, for instance, that the aconite, a notoriously poisonous plant, first sprang from gall that was spewed up by Kerberos on his arrival in the upper world (at Herakleia Pontica in this account).[123] Or according to an Argive legend, Kerberos escaped from Herakles by the spring of Kynadra on the road between Mycenae and the great sanctuary of Hera nearby, and that the water of the spring was therefore known as the Water of Freedom (*eleutherion hydōr*) ever afterwards; ex-slaves would drink from it after gaining their release.[124] Another story stated that the terrible aspect of the hell-hound caused a man who saw him to turn to stone.[125] It was said that Herakles had prepared himself for the journey to Hades by having himself initiated into the Eleusinian mysteries (which would seem a good idea since initiates were supposed to be assured of a better fate in the Underworld, though normally after their death of course). Since strangers from outside Attica were not yet allowed to be initiated, he had to be adopted beforehand by a local man, a certain Pylios; and since he was polluted because of his slaughter of the Centaurs, Demeter founded the lesser mysteries (preliminary rites celebrated at Agriai just outside Athens) to purify him from the bloodshed. He was then initiated by Eumolpos (see p. 370) or Mousaios. In future times, anyone who spoke Greek could be initiated unless polluted by murder.[126]

Twelfth labour: the Apples of the Hesperides

As his final labour (or his penultimate labour in some accounts, before his descent to Hades), Herakles was ordered to fetch some of the golden apples of the Hesperides. These grew on a wondrous tree (or trees) in the garden of the gods at the edges of the earth, where they were guarded by a group of beautiful nymphs, the HESPERIDES (see p. 28), and protected by a huge snake, sometimes named as Ladon[127] in the later tradition. To discover the way to this remote and mysterious place, Herakles consulted the nymphs of the Eridanos (a mythical river, later identified with the Po, see p. 41), who advised him to question Nereus, the old man of the sea; so he seized Nereus while he was asleep and kept him tied up as he repeatedly transformed himself, refusing to release him until he revealed the proper route.[128]

The Hesperides would traditionally have lived in the far west, as is indicated in their name (daughters of the evening), their proximity to Atlas (see below) and various other factors. In that case, Herakles would have had to make his way to the north-western corner of Africa. In the accounts offered by Pherecydes and Apollodorus,[129] however, he travels to the northern fringes of the world by a strangely circuitous route: starting near the Ocean in the west, he travels across the whole breadth of Africa until he reaches the encircling Ocean again on the opposite side of the world, and sails around it to the Caucasus, where he meets Prometheus, and then proceeds on foot toward Atlas and the Hesperides, here located in the remote north near the Hyperboreans. This relocation was evidently thought necessary because of the role that Prometheus, as a prisoner in the Caucasus, was supposed to have played in this version of the story (see below).

We will begin by tracing in greater detail the outward journey as it is described in this latter version. The curious route makes some sort of sense if it is remembered that the present starting-point would originally have been the goal of the journey, and that Herakles would originally have travelled *west* through Africa to reach it. Here too, of course, he must initially have passed west by some route after questioning Nereus. Setting off from Tartessos in southern Iberia, Herakles first travelled through North Africa to Egypt, encountering the Libyan giant ANTAIOS on the way. Antaios used to force passing strangers to wrestle with him, and killed every one of them until Herakles arrived; Pindar adds that he would take their skulls to roof the temple of Poseidon[130] (who was commonly regarded as his father). According to a familiar story that first appears in Roman sources, he was unconquerable by any ordinary wrestler because his strength increased whenever he came into contact with the ground.[131] Reversing the normal procedure in a wrestling-match, in which victory would be achieved by forcing the loser to the ground, Herakles therefore heaved him up from the ground and crushed him in his arms until he was dead.[132] Although this feature of Antaios' legend presumably originated in Greece, perhaps in the Hellenistic period, nothing is known for certain about its time of origin; there is no unequivocal evidence for it in the arts prior to its appearance in literary accounts by Ovid and Lucan. It was explained that Antaios was a son of the Earth and gained added strength through her touch, as is already stated by Ovid.[133]

Pindar and Pherecydes locate Antaios at Irasa near Cyrene, in the region of North Africa adjoining Egypt; according to the latter author, Herakles slept with Antaios' wife Iphinoe after his death, fathering a son by her, Palaimon or 'Wrestler' (also a title of the hero himself).[134] According to a late tradition, the wife of Antaios was Tinge (the eponym of Tingis, now Tangier, at the north-western corner of Africa), and Herakles' son by her was Sophax, the mythical ancestor of the kings of Mauretania, the westernmost province of North Africa.[135] The story has been shifted to the west in this version to enable Mauretanian royal family to claim descent from the great hero. Sophax was presumably named after Syphax, a great Numidian potentate of the third century BC. The supposed tomb of Tinge could be seen near Tangier. According to a none too serious tale, Herakles was tied down by Pygmies while he was lying asleep after his encounter with Antaios (see p. 580).

After arriving in Egypt, Herakles had another perilous encounter, now with the fictional pharaoh BOUSIRIS (whose name was derived from the name of a town in the Nile delta, Per-Usire or House of Osiris). He seized and imprisoned Herakles with the intention of bringing him to sacrifice, as was his usual practice with strangers. For when his kingdom had once remained barren for nine years, a seer from Cyprus, a certain Phrasios, had revealed that fertility would be restored if a male visitor from abroad were sacrificed to Zeus every year; and after initiating the process by slaughtering the seer himself, Bousiris had continued to sacrifice foreigners ever since. Herakles broke his shackles, however, as he was being brought to the altar, and killed Bousiris along with his son.[136] Bousiris was described as a son of Poseidon by Lysianassa, daughter of Epaphos, even though Epaphos as a child of Io (see p. 231) must have lived many generations earlier.[137] In his paradoxical defence of Bousiris, the Athenian orator Isocrates uses this chronological inconsistency as a pretext to discredit the whole story.[138]

The geography of Herakles' journey becomes somewhat confused at that point. According to Pherecydes (if the surviving summary can be trusted) he now made his way to Thebes (i.e. up the Nile to Upper Egypt) and across some mountains to 'outer Libya', which he cleared of wild beasts by use of his bow.[139] Diodorus states quite similarly that he travelled up the Nile to Ethiopia, where he killed the local ruler EMATHION, son of Eos, when subjected to an unprovoked attack from him.[140] In the rather muddled account by Apollodorus (who also mentions a journey to Rhodes), he killed Emathion after passing by Arabia, and then journeyed through Libya to the outer sea.[141] Taking these reports together, it makes some sense to imagine him travelling south through Egypt to the edge of the unknown, and then across to some ill-defined imaginary East Africa (or Outer Libya) adjoining the outer Ocean. He arrived somewhere on the eastern shores of Africa in any case, and borrowed the cup of Helios once again to sail north around the outer Ocean until he arrived at the Caucasus. Prometheus had been chained to a cliff in the Caucasus ever since he had incurred the anger of Zeus by stealing fire for mortals (see p. 96); and he was subjected to ever-renewed torment, for an eagle would peck each day at his liver, which grew anew each night. Herakles took pity on him and shot the eagle, and then sought the permission of Zeus to set him free entirely.[142]

According to Apollodorus, he achieved this by presenting Cheiron to Zeus as an immortal being who was willing to die in place of Prometheus. Now Cheiron, as we have seen just above (see p. 259), had been suffering unendurable pain ever since Herakles had accidentally wounded him with one of his poisoned arrows; and Apollodorus writes in this connection that 'he wanted to die, but was unable to because he was immortal – only when Prometheus offered himself to Zeus to become immortal in his place was he able to die'.[143] Since Prometheus was of divine birth, this cannot be literally interpreted as meaning that Cheiron exchanged his immortality for the mortality of Prometheus; nor could it easily be explained in that case why Zeus should have agreed to the release of Prometheus as a consequence. We are surely intended to suppose that by accepting death as a immortal being, Cheiron is in some sense taking over the punishment of Prometheus, who is therefore permitted to resume his normal existence as a god. Confirmation for this idea can be found in some lines from the *Prometheus Bound*, in which Hermes tells Prometheus that he can have no hope of release 'until some god reveals himself ready to take on your sufferings and descend of his own free will to sunless Hades'.[144] Although it might have seemed almost impossible that any immortal being would agree to sacrifice himself in this way, Cheiron was willing to accept death as the price that he would have to pay if he was to be released from the intolerable pain of his wound.

Prometheus repaid Herakles for his services by advising him on how he could best achieve his quest. He suggested that the hero should not attempt to fetch the apples himself, but should ask Atlas to do so on his behalf, offering to take over the burden of the sky in the mean time. Happy to be released from his exertions for a while, Atlas set off on his way, procured three apples from the Hesperides, and brought them back to Herakles; but he was understandably reluctant to return to his arduous duty, and asked Herakles to continue to hold the sky for the present, saying that he himself would take the apples to Eurystheus. Prometheus had foreseen that this might happen, however, and had suggested an appropriate ruse to Herakles, who tricked Atlas into taking the sky back by asking him to hold it for a moment while he prepared a pad for his head. The artistic evidence indicates that this version of the story, which is first recounted by Pherecydes, was familiar by the middle of the sixth century BC.[145]

In the other main version, which first appears in tragedy but can again be traced further back in the visual arts, Herakles plucked the apples himself after killing the dragon that guarded them.[146] This would almost certainly have been the original version of the legend. Although the literary sources offer no details on the killing, we can imagine it clearly enough from depictions in vase-paintings, which show the hero raising his club against the snake as it entwines itself around the apple-tree. In astral mythology, Zeus is said to have placed an image of the confrontation among the stars, representing Herakles as the constellation Engonasin (the Kneeler, now known as Hercules), in which he can be seen kneeling on one leg as he aims his club at the serpent as represented in the neighbouring constellation Draco.[147] Considering that the snake was no harmful monster but a servant of the gods which was protecting divine property, it might be thought that it would be improper for Herakles to kill it; and in a version which is recorded in vase-paintings and other images from the fifth century onwards, the killing is indeed suppressed, and Herakles acquires the apples in a peaceable manner from the Hesperid nymphs. This was the manner, incidentally, in which Atlas was said to have procured them.

After gaining the apples, whether by direct means or indirect, Herakles took them back to Mycenae and presented them to Eurystheus. As soon as Eurystheus was assured that the labour had been fulfilled, he returned the apples to Herakles; and the hero handed them on to Athena to be taken back to the garden of the gods, for they were too holy to be left anywhere else.[148] By the completion of his final labour (whether the fetching of the apples, as here, or the fetching of Kerberos as in the other tradition), Herakles freed himself forever from his servitude to the ignoble Eurystheus.

HERAKLES' SERVITUDE TO OMPHALE AND MAJOR CAMPAIGNS

Herakles tries to win Iole as his wife, murders her brother Iphitos, and is enslaved to Omphale

Now that Herakles was able to turn his thoughts to personal matters, he decided that the time had come for him to seek a new wife and found a new family. Since there could be no question of him returning to his original wife after killing the children of their union, he first travelled to Thebes to settle his affairs with Megara by arranging for her to marry his nephew Iolaos;[149] and having heard that EURYTOS, king of Oichalia, was offering his daughter IOLE to anyone who could defeat him and his sons in at archery, he travelled on to Oichalia (apparently in Euboea, see p. 283) to take up the challenge. We have already encountered Eurytos as the man who instructed the young Herakles in archery (see p. 250); his father Melaneus was a son of the archer-god Apollo. Although Herakles defeated Eurytos and his sons in the contest, the king refused to surrender his daughter to him, saying that he feared that the hero might kill her children if she should bear any to him, just as he had killed the children of his previous marriage. Eurytos was supported in his decision by all his sons apart from the eldest, IPHITOS, who argued that Iole should be handed over in accordance with the terms of the contest. Angry though he was, Herakles was obliged to depart without her, but vowed to return to seek revenge when circumstances permitted.[150] As events turned out, his return would be delayed for many years, until long after he had taken another woman, Deianeira, as his new wife; and by sacking Oichalia and seizing Iole, he would bring disaster to himself as well as to Eurytos (see pp. 283–4).

Shortly after Herakles' unhappy visit to Oichalia, some mares were stolen from the herds of Eurytos (or of his son Iphitos). Our sources disagree on the identity of the thief. Herakles may have stolen them as a first act of revenge, or else this was simply another theft by that prince of thieves Autolykos; and in the latter case, Herakles may have acquired the mares at second hand by buying them from Autolykos.[151] Suspicion fell on Herakles in any case, and Iphitos went to Tiryns to investigate. This led to the most discreditable episode in the hero's career, in which he murdered Iphitos after receiving him into his home as a guest. According to Diodorus, he took him to a lofty tower of the citadel and asked whether he could see the mares grazing below; and when Iphitos replied that he could not (for they had been hidden away beforehand), Herakles hurled him down to his death, saying that he had been falsely accused.[152] Although it was commonly accepted that this was a deliberate murder, an exculpatory version was also developed in which the hero was said to have killed Iphitos during a temporary fit of madness, as when he had killed his children.[153]

Herakles was struck by a terrible disease as a result of his crime and set off to seek purification. After meeting with a refusal from Nestor, king of Pylos, who was unwilling to purify him because of his friendship with Eurytos, he travelled on to Amyklai in Laconia, where the rites were performed by a certain Deiphobos, son of Hippolytos, who is otherwise unknown.[154] When the disease persisted nonetheless, Herakles visited Delphi to consult the oracle. The Pythian priestess refused to grant him a response, however, because he was polluted by the murder, and he was so angry that he started to plunder the temple, and carried off the Pythia's tripod (see p. 166) with the intention of founding an oracle of his own. Apollo had no intention of allowing any such thing and tried to seize the tripod back; but violence was averted by the intervention of Zeus, who separated his two sons by hurling a thunderbolt between them. It was now agreed that Herakles should receive a response, and he was told that he would be delivered from his affliction if he were sold into slavery and paid the purchase-price to Eurytos as compensation.[155] So he was put up for auction by Hermes, and was bought by OMPHALE, queen of Lydia, who offered three talents for him (perhaps a hundred times more than the average price for a slave in classical Athens). The money was duly offered to Eurytos, but he regarded it as tainted and refused to accept it.[156]

The confrontation between Herakles and Apollo over the tripod was a very popular subject in vase-paintings from the mid-sixth to fifth centuries BC, and can be traced back to the late eighth century in the visual arts. A passing observation by Pausanias would suggest that it was also a popular theme with early poets, even if there is little sign of it in the surviving literature.[157] The local tradition at Gytheion in Laconia claimed that Herakles and Apollo joined together to found the city after settling their quarrel over the tripod.[158]

Omphale, daughter of Iardanos (or Iardanes), was a widow who had assumed power in Lydia on the west coast of Asia Minor after the death of her husband Tmolos. Authors and artists of the Hellenistic and Roman periods liked to divert themselves by imagining how she behaved toward her improbable bondsman; a popular idea suggested that she forced him to dress in her delicate saffron robes and to assist the women of the court in their spinning, while she dressed in his lionskin and took possession of his club.[159] It could be supposed, furthermore, that he willingly consented to this treatment because he had fallen in love with her, and he was some-times said to have fathered a child or some children by her, either during the period of his servitude or after she had granted him an early release.

There were also more serious tales in which he performed proper heroic tasks to the benefit of the local people. One notable villain of the area was LITYERSES, an illegitimate son of Midas, who used to challenge passers-by to a harvesting contest (or simply forced them to help him in his fields) and then cut off their heads with his scythe at the end of the day, binding their bodies into the corn-stooks. When he was foolish enough to try this with Herakles, the hero beheaded him with the scythe that was provided for the work.[160] Or in another version, Herakles killed him to save Daphnis (see p. 211), who had wandered to the region from his native Sicily and had been put to work by Lityerses.[161] The name of Lityerses was derived from an ancient Phrygian reaping song, the Lityerses-song. Another local villain was SYLEUS, who used to force passing strangers to hoe his vineyards; Herakles killed him with his own hoe along with his daughter Xenodike, and burned his vines to their roots.[162] In a comical version from a Satyr-play by Euripides, Herakles was sold to Syleus (who presumably took the place of Omphale for the purposes of the play), and soon gave his purchaser reason to regret his temerity in buying him; for the clumsy hero caused havoc in his vineyard, and slaughtered one of his oxen and ransacked his cellars to satisfy his enormous appetites.[163] There was also a version of the story in which Herakles married Xenodike after killing her father, but stayed away from her so long that she died of a broken heart.[164] During this period, Herakles also ran across the KERKOPES, a pair of small ape-like men who were notorious for their thievery. They tried to steal his weapons as he lay asleep, but he woke up and caught them in the act, and then hung them upside down from either end of a pole to carry them off (just as game would be carried off after a hunt). Now their mother had warned them to beware of 'the black-bottomed man', and when they observed from their inverted position that the buttocks of Herakles were dark and hairy where they were not covered by his lionskin, they recognized that the warning had been fulfilled and laughed and joked about the matter, causing such amusement to Herakles that he decided to set them free. They came to a bad end nonetheless, for they were ultimately turned to stone for attempting to cheat Zeus himself.[165] In lesser-known tales, Herakles also defeated the Itones, some predatory neighbours of Omphale, and killed a huge snake by the Sagaris, a river of that area.[166]

Herakles launches a series of campaigns, starting with an attack on Troy

After expiating for the murder of Iphitos, Herakles returned to Tiryns to assemble an army for an expedition against Laomedon, king of Troy, who had offended him during the period of his labours. This campaign marks the beginning of the period of his greatest deeds (*praxeis*, as opposed to his *athloi* or labours, see pp. 254–5); for after bringing his Trojan campaign to a successful conclusion, he also became involved in a conflict with the Coans during his return, and went on to conduct three major campaigns within the Peloponnese itself. Since his war against Troy and subsequent campaign against Augeias in the Peloponnese were launched to avenge grievances that he had incurred during his labours, and since his three Peloponnesian campaigns fall into a natural group, these 'deeds' of Herakles could be plausibly assigned to a common period while he was still living in the Peloponnese after his labours. The fourth and final period of his life could be said to have begun when he left the Peloponnese to marry the Aetolian princess Deianeira. According to the biographies of Diodorus and Apollodorus, he lived in central Greece thereafter, first at Deianeira's home-city of Calydon and later at Trachis; and such adventures as were recorded for him in central and northern Greece (apart from the early episodes while he was based at Thebes) came to be assigned to this last period of his life.

During the third and penultimate period of his life with which we are presently concerned, Herakles either continued to live at Tiryns as he had during his labours, or else was forced out by Eurystheus after a time and moved to Pheneos in northern Arcadia, the home-city of his grandmother Laonome. According to the latter tradition, Eurystheus ordered him to leave after his first and unsuccessful assault against Augeias (see p. 277) on the allegation that he was plotting to seize power in Argos. Herakles benefited the people of Pheneos by digging potholes (which can still be seen) to drain the excess water from the plain outside the city.[167]

We will now trace the history of Herakles' major campaigns in the order in which they were said to have been conducted. As he had been travelling to the land of the Amazons to fetch the belt of Hippolyte (see pp. 263–4), he had sailed past Troy and had been struck by the plight of a maiden who had been tied to a rock by the shore. This was HESIONE, the daughter of the king, who had been exposed there at the order of an oracle, to serve as prey to a sea-monster that had been sent against the land by Poseidon (see further on p. 523). Feeling pity for the princess and seeing an opportunity for gain, Herakles had approached her father LAOMEDON and had offered to kill the monster in return for a specific reward, the divine horses that had been presented to Tros as compensation for the abduction of Ganymedes (see p. 522); but after he had fulfilled the task, Laomedon had refused to hand over the promised reward (or had tried to substitute ordinary horses for the divine ones).

The hero had been obliged to continue on his way, but had vowed to return at a future date to exact vengeance.[168]

According to an alternative tradition from the Hellenistic period, Herakles confronted the monster as he was sailing to Colchis with the Argonauts.[169] Herakles took no part in any of the great panhellenic adventures in the earlier tradition, and even when he was introduced into the story of the Argonauts in this way, he was usually said to have been left behind at an early stage in the voyage (see p. 385), for no specific tales were recorded for him in this connection and he might have tended to cast the colourless Jason into the shade. Some authors who were more interested in spinning a good yarn than observing the tradition acknowledged this latter point by making Herakles the leader of the expedition. If he did join the Argonauts, he sailed with them during the period of his labours or shortly after completing them.

Herakles assembled a sizeable army for the assault on Troy, recruiting the aid of some formidable heroes including Telamon, the father of Aias (see p. 533), and Oikles, the father of Amphiaraos, and led them across the Aegean in eighteen ships (or only eight according to the *Iliad*[170]). After arriving at the Troad, he left Oikles behind to guard the ships while he advanced against the city with the main force. Having been caught by surprise and finding himself outnumbered as a consequence, Laomedon tried to weaken the position of the invaders by advancing against their ships with the intention of setting fire to them; but although Oikles was killed in the ensuing confrontation, his followers escaped back to their ships and rowed away from the shore. Laomedon then withdrew toward the city and was killed along with most of his followers when he engaged with Herakles and the main force just outside the walls.[171] Or else he was killed during the storming of the city. Telamon was the first to break through the city walls, entering Troy ahead of Herakles, who was so angry at being outdone that he threatened Telamon with his sword. Thinking swiftly, Telamon piled some stones together and pacified the hero by telling him that he was building an altar to Herakles the Noble Victor (Kallinikos, a cultic title of Herakles).[172] All the sons of Laomedon apart from Priam were killed in the fighting. After his victory, Herakles made amends to Telamon by offering the king's daughter Hesione to him as a prize of war; and he allowed Hesione to pick out a single person to be freed from among the captives. When she picked her only surviving brother, he said that she must offer something in ransom for him, and she paid for him with her veil. For this reason, so it was said, Laomedon's son and successor, who had originally been called Podarkes, came to be known as Priam (as though his name were derived from *priamai*, to buy).[173] Since Telamon was already married, he took Hesione as a concubine rather than as his wife, and she bore him a son Teukros, who would later fight at Troy alongside his legitimate son Aias.[174]

Seeing an opportunity to cause harm to Herakles, Hera sent storm-winds against his ships as he was sailing home from Troy, causing him to be driven to the island of Cos in the south-eastern Aegean. Imagining that the strangers must be pirates, the Coans tried to repel them by pelting them with stones, but they forced a landing after nightfall and captured the main city. Herakles killed the king of the Coans, a certain Eurypylos, son of Poseidon and Astypalaia.[175] The island would subsequently be ruled by descendants of the hero, for he fathered a son Thessalos by

Astyoche, the daughter of the dead king. The Coans would be commanded at Troy by two sons of this Thessalos.[176] It was after this episode that Athena fetched Herakles to help the gods in their battle against the Giants (see further on p. 89).

In another account, Herakles lost five of his six ships in the storm and was wrecked on Cos in the last of them. After coming ashore, he met Antagoras, a son of the king who was tending the royal flocks, and asked him for a sheep to still his hunger; but Antagoras challenged him to a fight, and a general battle ensued when the Coans came to the help of Antagoras and Herakles too received support from his followers. On finding that the tide of battle was turning against him, Herakles sought refuge in a cottage which was inhabited by an old Thracian woman, who disguised him by dressing him in women's clothing. He subsequently returned to battle, defeated the Coans, and slept with the king's daughter as above, fathering Thessalos. This was a local version of the legend which was devised to explain why the priest of Herakles at Antimacheia on Cos used to wear women's clothing while offering sacrifice to him.[177]

Three Peloponnesian campaigns, against Augeias at Elis, Neleus at Pylos and Hippokoon at Sparta

After arriving back at Tiryns, Herakles made preparations for his first campaign in the Peloponnese, which was directed against AUGEIAS, king of Elis, in the northwest of the peninsula. Augeias had angered him in much the same way as Laomedon, by refusing to pay him the promised reward for a valuable service that he had performed, in this case the clearing of the Augeian stables (see p. 261). On hearing of Herakles' intentions, Augeias assembled an army of his own, placing it under the command of Eurytos and Kteatos, the MOLIONIDES (or Moliones), who would prove to be a match even for Herakles himself because they were two men joined into one. In the usual account, they were joined together at the waist (or shared a single torso) but had separate limbs and heads, so forming a single being with four legs, four arms and two heads.[178] Poseidon had fathered them by a certain Molione who was married to Augeias' brother Aktor.[179] Homer refers to them in the *Iliad* (calling them the Moliones on one occasion and the Aktoriones on another) without specifically stating that they were Siamese twins.[180] A fragment from Ibycus, a lyric poet of the sixth century BC, states that they were born as a united being from a silver egg.[181]

The Moliones demonstrated the military advantages of their combined form by inflicting a rare defeat on Herakles when he first advanced against Elis. They caused havoc to his army, killing his half-brother Iphikles, and forced him to withdraw to the Argolid.[182] Or in another version, which was obviously devised to spare Herakles the shame of defeat, he negotiated a truce with the Molionides after falling ill, but was attacked by them nonetheless when they learned of his condition and was forced to retreat after suffering heavy losses.[183] Herakles resorted to sharp practice to rid himself of these troublesome opponents, by ambushing them at Kleonai in the northwestern corner of the Argolid as they were travelling to the Isthmian Games as envoys of the Eleians, and were therefore supposed to be under the protection of a religious truce.[184] The Eleians demanded compensation from the Argives as a consequence, and stayed away from the Isthmian Games in perpetuity after it was denied to them.[185] With the Molionides out of the way, Herakles seized the city of Elis with little difficulty, killing Augeias and all his sons apart from Phyleus, who had been living in Doulichion ever since he had been banished by his father for testifying in favour of Herakles (see p. 261). In gratitude for his previous support, he summoned Phyleus back to rule the kingdom; and he also founded the Olympian festival and games, which were held in the province of Elis every four years.[186]

Herakles directed his next campaign against, NELEUS, the king of Pylos in Messenia (see p. 424), for having refused to purify him after the murder of Iphitos (see p. 273), or for having tried to rob him of the cattle of Geryon.[187] Nestor, a son of Neleus, refers to the episode in the *Iliad*, remarking that his father was killed along with his eleven brothers.[188] The most formidable of the sons of Neleus was the eldest, PERIKLYMENOS, because his grandfather Poseidon had granted him the power to change his shape at will.[189] This brought him no advantage, however, on the present occasion, since he was betrayed in the course of the fighting by Athena, who pointed out to Herakles that he had settled on the yoke of his chariot in the form of a bee, enabling the hero to shoot him dead with a well-aimed arrow. Such is the early account offered in the Hesiodic *Catalogue*; Apollodorus adds that Periklymenos had taken the form of a lion and snake beforehand.[190] In other versions, he was clubbed to death as a fly or shot as an eagle; or conversely, he escaped death by flying off as an eagle.[191] After engaging in a fierce battle with the remaining troops (and perhaps even with some gods, see below), Herakles finally prevailed and conquered the city, killing Neleus and all his sons apart from Nestor, who was below military age and absent at the time because he was being reared at Gerenia, a neighbouring town. As at Troy, Herakles allowed Nestor to take over the throne as the only surviving heir; and he continued to rule at Pylos until well after the Trojan War (see p. 424).[192]

Various reports suggest that Herakles confronted one or another of the gods in the course of the fighting. According to a passage in the *Iliad*, he shot Hades *en Pylō* among the dead, but it is far from certain that he is referring to sandy Pylos. As a scholion suggests, he may have had the gates (*pylos* or *pylē*, usually in the plural as *pylai*) of Hades in mind, and in that case the incident could have occurred while Herakles was fetching Kerberos. Hades went up to Olympos in any case to seek a cure from the healing-god Paion. In his ninth Olympian Ode, Pindar states that Herakles confronted Poseidon with his club while the god was helping to defend Pylos (as is understandable since Neleus was a son of his), and then goes on to say that the hero also confronted the archer Apollo, and Hades as he was assembling the dead with his wand. It is not entirely clear whether we are to understand that these latter confrontations also took place at Pylos; the scholiast asserts that these were properly separate incidents, relating to Herakles' theft of the Delphian tripod and seizing of Kerberos respectively. Some later authors certainly assume, however, that Herakles wounded Hades at Pylos, where he might well have come to assemble the many dead if not actually to fight as an ally of the Pylians.[193] It is stated in the Hesiodic *Shield*, furthermore, that Ares was wounded by the hero at Pylos, as was Hera in an account by the epic poet Panyasis.[194]

After his campaign against Neleus, Herakles attacked HIPPOKOON, king of Sparta (see p. 525), and his twelve or twenty sons to punish them for having fought as allies of Neleus (or for having refused to purify him after the murder of Iphitos).[195]

He was also angered by the death of his cousin OIONOS, son of Likymnios, who had been killed at Sparta in the following circumstances. While gazing at the palace of Hippokoon during a visit to Sparta, Oionos had been alarmed by a fierce watch-dog that had rushed out toward him, and had struck it with a well-aimed stone; and the sons of Hippokoon had reacted by rushing out in their turn with cudgels and clubbing him to death.[196] Oionos was otherwise remembered as the victor in the foot-race at the first Olympian Games.[197]

Since Hippokoon could call on the support of his many sons, Herakles visited Kepheus, king of Tegea, as he was passing through Arcadia, and invited him and his twenty sons to fight as his allies. Although Kepheus was reluctant to leave his city undefended, the hero persuaded him by providing his daughter with a lock of the Gorgon's hair that would put any attackers to flight if held up from the city walls (see further on p. 574).[198] With the support of these and other allies, Herakles killed Hippokoon and his sons in battle near Sparta and captured the city. The victory proved expensive, however, since Kepheus was killed along with all his sons (or all but three of them), as was Herakles' half-brother Iphikles (in one tradition at least, for it was also said that he was killed by the Molionides).[199] In one account of the story, Herakles was so enraged to hear of the fate of Oionos that he launched an immediate attack without proper support, but was seriously wounded in the thigh on this first occasion and was obliged to withdraw to Therapne (on the Eurotas to the south-west of Sparta), where his wound was cured by Asklepios.[200] This tale accounted for the origin of the local cult of Asklepios Kotyleus, which was said to have been founded by Herakles; it was explained that Herakles gave him this title of Kotyleus because his hip-joint (*kotylē*) had been healed by him there. After recovering from his wound, Herakles raised an army and launched a successful attack as above. Since Tyndareos, the rightful king of Sparta, had been expelled by Hippokoon and his sons (see p. 525), Herakles summoned him back to take over the throne.[201]

THE LATER LIFE OF HERAKLES IN CENTRAL AND NORTHERN GREECE

Herakles marries Deianeira and lives with her at Calydon until he accidentally kills a page-boy

After his campaign against Hippokoon, which would be the last of his wars in the Peloponnese, Herakles decided to leave the peninsula altogether to settle in Aetolia in the south-west corner of the mainland; for he wanted to marry DEIANEIRA, a daughter of Oineus, king of Calydon, and to found a new family in her homeland. As further explanation for his departure from the Peloponnese, some authors add that he also wanted to make a new start because he was so distressed by the death of his cousin Oionos and half-brother Iphikles.[202]

It was no easy matter for Herakles to win Deianeira as his bride since she was also being courted by Acheloos, the god of the great river of that name that flowed along the western borders of Aetolia. Sophocles tells how he had been visiting her father's palace to seek her hand, causing her great alarm, for he was a fearsome being who would manifest himself now as a bull, now as a man, and now as a man with the head of a bull. Herakles visited Acheloos by his own waters to wrestle with him for Deianeira, who watched anxiously from the bank. Although the river-god transformed himself into a bull and perhaps into other forms too, Herakles kept a firm grip on him and finally forced him to submit by breaking off one of his horns.[203]

Acheloos recovered his horn from Herakles by offering to exchange it for the horn of Amaltheia, a magical horn that had the power to provide as much food and drink as anyone could desire.[204] This horn had originally been a gift from Zeus to the nymph (or nymphs) who had reared him as an infant. In one account at least (see further on p. 75), he had been reared by a nymph called Amaltheia, who had fed him on the milk of a she-goat; and when he grew up, he broke a horn from the goat to turn it into a horn of plenty as a gift for his nurse. Or else Amaltheia was the name of the goat itself.[205] Apollodorus states the Amaltheia's horn of plenty was a bull's horn (evidently a misapprehension that arose because it was exchanged for the taurine horn of Acheloos). In the Roman world, the magical horn was known as the *cornu copias* (i.e. horn of plenty), or in later Latin *cornucopia*; and it could be regarded as an attribute of Copia, the personification of Plenty (and also of Ceres, the harvest-goddess, as a goddess of plenty). Ovid combines Greek and Roman motifs by suggesting that naiad nymphs filled the broken horn of Acheloos with fruits and flowers, and that Copia came to possess it as her horn of plenty. Hyginus records a similar story in which Herakles is said to have given the broken horn to the Hesperides, who created the horn of plenty by filling it with fruit.[206] Ovid says much the same about the horn of Amaltheia elsewhere, saying that her goat broke a horn off on a tree, and that she filled it with fruit and took it to the infant Zeus.[207]

Herakles lived at Calydon for some years with his new wife, who bore him several children, including Hyllos, whom we shall encounter again as the first leader of the Heraklids, and Ktesippos, the grandfather of Deiphontes (see p. 292), and a rare daughter, Makaria (see p. 287).[208] The hero was able to repay his hosts at some stage by assisting them in a war against the Thesprotians, who lived to the north of them in southern Epirus; after capturing their main city of Ephyra, he fathered a notable son, Tlepolemos (see p. 293), by Astyoche, the daughter of its ruler Phylas.[209]

As the result of an unfortunate accident, Herakles was finally obliged to seek a new home. For as he was feasting in the palace one day, a page-boy angered him in some way while pouring water to clean his hands, and he struck out at him with unintended force, causing his death (much as he had done with Linos long before, see p. 250). It was explained that the boy provoked this reaction by using water from a foot-bath, or simply by his clumsiness. The unfortunate page, who was given a variety of names such as Eunomos (Good Behaviour) or Kyathos (Wine-ladle), was of noble birth or even a relation of the king; and although his father was willing to forgive Herakles because he recognized that the killing had been an accident, the hero insisted on departing into exile to be purified and make a new start.[210] He decided to travel to southern Thessaly to seek refuge with his old friend Keux, who was king of Trachis (later Herakleia) at the head of the Malian Gulf. He was accompanied on the journey by his wife and young son Hyllos, and perhaps other children too.

Herakles confronts the Centaur Nessos and the Dryopians while travelling to his final home

The journey was not without its risks and adventures. Herakles and his wife had an unpleasant encounter with a Centaur first of all on reaching the river Euenos in eastern Aetolia. This Centaur, NESSOS, used to carry people across the river in return for a fee and offered to do the same on this occasion, alleging that the gods had appointed him to his post of ferryman on account of his excellent character. Although Herakles was quite capable of crossing on his own, he willingly paid Nessos to carry Deianeira; but the Centaur was really of no better character than most of his kind, and he attempted to rape Deianeira on reaching the opposite bank (or else in mid-stream). She alerted her husband by her loud screams, however, and he brought Nessos to the ground with one of his poisoned arrows. As the life ebbed from his body, Nessos told Deianeira that if she wanted to acquire a powerful love-potion to use on her husband, she should collect some of the semen that he had shed on to the ground and mix it with some blood from his wound. She took him at his word and did so, little realizing that the mixture would be a virulent poison because the blood was tainted with the poison (i.e. hydra's venom, see p. 284) from Herakles' arrow.[211] As we will see (p. 258), Deianeira later applied this unsavoury potion to some of her husband's clothing with terrible effect, just as Nessos would have hoped.

Later in the journey, Herakles and his family passed through the land of the Dryopians (Dryopes), who lived in the area between Mt Parnassos and southern Thessaly. On running across a Dryopian called THEIODAMAS who was driving a pair of bullocks, Herakles asked him for a little food for his young son Hyllos; and when this was refused to him, he secured a handsome supply of food by seizing and slaughtering one of the bullocks. Theiodamas rushed back to his city to rouse his fellow-Dryopians against the aggressor, and Herakles was hard-pressed in the fight that developed, falling into such danger that he had to arm his wife, who suffered a wound in the breast.[212] Or in a rather different version, Herakles met with no immediate trouble after seizing the bullock, but returned to campaign against the Dryopians after settling in Trachis.[213]

In the other main version of the story of Herakles' conflict with the Dryopians, he expelled them from their original homeland to punish them for a grave act of sacrilege, namely of plundering the temple of Apollo at Delphi under the leadership of their ruler Phylas. With the help of an army of Malians (i.e. men from Trachis and the surrounding area), Herakles defeated them in battle, killing their king, and then took them to Delphi as an offering to Apollo. The oracle ordered that they should be transferred abroad to the Peloponnese, and they settled in the Argolid at Asine, a coastal town to the east of Nauplion; but they were later expelled by the Argives and settled in a Messenian town of the same name.[214] The Asinaians of Messenia, who were proud to believe that they were of Dryopian descent, had their own ideas about their history, preferring to suppose that their ancestors had abandoned the city on Mt Parnassos before Herakles could capture them, and had later sailed over to the Argolid of their own accord, where Eurystheus had been happy to give them a new home at Asine because of his hatred for Herakles.[215] People who were also thought to be of Dryopian origin could be found in parts of Thessaly, Epirus, Euboea and Cyprus in historical times.[216]

Since the Dryopians were regarded as the original inhabitants of the province of Doris in the local tradition, while the Dorians of the Peloponnese (who rightly believed that they had come from the north) regarded Doris as their ancestral homeland, this story of the expulsion of the Dryopians resolved a contradiction in the mythology of Central Greece. For if the Dryopians had been driven out by Herakles, it could be explained that the Dorians had taken their place, moving down from further north in Thessaly to occupy the vacant land, and lived there until they invaded the Peloponnese under the leadership of the Heraklids (see below). This pattern of events is first attested by Herodotus, who alleges that the Dorians had moved from Thessaly to Doris (which had previously been known as Dryopis) and thence to the Peloponnese.[217]

Apollodorus mentions in passing that Herakles killed Laogoras, king of the Dryopians, a man of violence and ally of the Lapiths, as he was feasting in the sanctuary of Apollo. The latter detail would suggest that Laogoras was an alternative name for the Dryopian king who was supposed to have plundered Delphi.[218]

After the perils of the journey, Herakles brought his family safely to Trachis, which would be his home for the rest of his life.[219] Little is recorded of his host KEUX beyond the fact that was a good friend of Herakles (even if he was not powerful enough to protect his family after his death, see p. 287). This Keux, who is of unknown descent, should be distinguished from the Keux who was turned into a bird (see p. 410). He figured prominently in a lost Hesiodic poem, the *Marriage of Keux*, in which Herakles also appeared. Two children are recorded for him, a son Hippasos who was killed during Herakles' final campaign (see p. 283), and a daughter Themistonoe who became the wife of Kyknos, a violent opponent of Herakles whom we shall encounter shortly.[220]

Final campaigns and confrontations

While Herakles was living at Trachis, AIGIMIOS, son of Doros, the king of the Dorians, invited him to assist the Dorians in a border-war against a neighbouring people, the Lapiths (see p. 554), promising him a share of the kingdom as a reward. As their proximity to the Lapiths would indicate, the Dorians were living in northern Thessaly at this time prior to their arrival in Doris (see above). After marching north with some Arcadian followers, Herakles helped to defeat the Lapiths, killing their leader, Koronos, son of Kaineus, with his own hand. He refused to take the promised reward, however, asking instead that it should be kept in trust for his descendants. An enduring bond was established as a consequence between the Dorians and the hero's sons and descendants, the Heraklids, who would ultimately lead the Dorians to their final home in the Peloponnese.[221]

During his return journey, Herakles became involved in two individual confrontations. His first opponent, KYKNOS, was a brutal son of Ares who used to challenge passing strangers to single combat, and, in some accounts at least, would cut off their heads to use their skulls to construct a temple of Ares (or Apollo).[222] In the earliest surviving account in the Hesiodic *Shield*, Kyknos confronted Herakles and his charioteer Iolaos at the grove of Apollo at Pagasai (the port of Iolkos on the northern tip of the Gulf of Pagasai) with the intention of robbing them of their splendid armour;[223] but Herakles, whose ardour was fired up by Apollo, felled him in the resulting duel with a spear-throw to the neck.[224] When Ares then tried to avenge the death of his son, Athena turned his spear aside as it was flying through the air, and Herakles forced him to the ground in the single combat that followed, with a spear-thrust to the thigh.[225] Keux saw to the burial of Kyknos (here described as his son-in-law), but Apollo caused his grave and memorial to be washed away by the river Anauros because he had plundered the god's offerings during his lifetime.[226] Some later accounts locate the episode at Itonos in south-eastern Thessaly;[227] and Zeus is sometimes said to have put a stop to the fight between Ares and Herakles by hurling a thunderbolt between them.[228] In a version ascribed to Stesichorus, Herakles fled from the initial confrontation because Kyknos was aided by his father, but later caught Kyknos on his own and killed him.[229]

The second of these stories, which tells of Herakles' confrontation with the king of Ormenion (near Mt Pelion), is of lesser interest and probably of later origin. According to Diodorus, who names the king as Ormenios and is the first author to report the story, Herakles asked to marry his daughter, Astydameia, but was turned down on the wholly reasonable ground that he already had a legitimate wife in Deianeira; so the hero took matters into his own hands by killing the king, capturing his city and seizing his daughter. Or in Apollodorus' version, in which the king is named Amyntor, Herakles killed him when he was rash enough to try to prevent the hero from passing through his territory.[230]

Herakles now decided that the time had come for him to exact his long-delayed revenge on Eurytos, who had refused to surrender his daughter Iole to him after he had won her in an archery-contest (see p. 273). As has been mentioned, there was no settled tradition on the location of Eurytos' city of Oichalia, for it was variously identified with places in Arcadia, Messenia, north-western Thessaly and Euboea. Since it apparently lay no great distance by sea from Trachis, and Herakles stopped off at the north-western cape of Euboea during his return voyage, the Euboean site seems most plausible in connection with the present story. In that case, the city would have been situated near Eretria in the east-central region of the island, opposite southern Boeotia. The early epic poet Creophylus placed Eurytos' city in Euboea in his lost poem the *Sack of Oichalia*, as does Sophocles in the *Trachinian Women*.[231] Herakles assembled a large force for the enterprise, consisting of his own Arcadian followers and men from the surrounding area (i.e. Malians from the region of Trachis and Eastern Locrians). On arriving in Euboea, he soon captured Oichalia, killing Eurytos and all his surviving sons. The most notable losses on his own side were Argeios and Melas, two sons of his uncle Likymnios, and Hippasos, a son of Keux. After seeing to their burial and plundering the city, he set off for Trachis, taking Iole, the daughter of the dead king with him on his ship.[232]

Hyginus records an unsavoury tale in which Herakles tried to force Iole to marry him by threatening to kill her relations; but she continued to refuse him even though he proceeded to kill them one after another in front of her.[233] According to another tale, Likymnios was initially unwilling to allow his young son Argeios to join the expedition, but relented when Herakles swore to bring him home again; and he fulfilled the letter of his promise at least by cremating the body of the young man after his death and bringing his ashes home in an urn.[234]

The death and apotheosis of Herakles

In the course of his return voyage, Herakles called in at Cape Kenaion at the south-western tip of Euboea to offer a sacrifice to his father Zeus. He was unable to proceed with it at once, however, because he lacked the proper clothing, and he sent his herald LICHAS ahead to Trachis to fetch some ceremonial robes. While fulfilling his task, Lichas happened to mention to Deianeira that her husband was bringing Iole home with him as a captive; or he even told her that Herakles was in love with the princess. Alarmed by this unwelcome news, Deianeira called to mind the supposed love-potion that she had acquired by collecting blood and semen of the dying Centaur Nessos (see p. 281). As we saw above, Nessos had told her that this mixture would ensure the fidelity of her husband, but it was in fact a virulent poison because the Centaur's blood had been contaminated with hydra's venom from Herakles' arrow. Taking Nessos at his word, however, Deianeira rubbed some of it into her husband's robes before passing them on to Lichas. When Herakles put on the robes and approached the fire to make his intended sacrifice, the poison was activated by the heat of the flames and began to burn into his skin, causing him unendurable pain.[235]

In the rather different account in Sophocles' *Trachinian Women*, Lichas travelled to Trachis ahead of his master, bringing Iole with him along with other female captives from Oichalia; and Deianeira sent the robes to Herakles on her own initiative rather than in response to a message from her husband.[236] It is stated in this play that Herakles and his family had been exiled from Tiryns to Trachis as a result of the murder of Iphitos.[237] Bacchylides relates in one of his odes that Herakles stopped at Kenaion to sacrifice some of his spoils after burning Oichalia, intending to offer nine bulls to Zeus Kenaios, two to Poseidon, and an unyoked heifer to Athena; on hearing that Herakles was sending Iole to his house to become his wife, Deianeira sent the poisoned robe to him as usual.[238]

Supposing that Lichas was to blame for his sufferings, Herakles lifted him up by his feet and hurled him over the cliffs into the sea below;[239] as he was falling through the air, Lichas became petrified with fear, and turned into a rock that could be seen off the coast ever afterwards. Sailors took care not to step on it, as if it would be pained by their tread.[240] This story may have been inspired by the presence of some small islands off the coast called the Lichades.[241] Herakles tried to relieve himself of his pain by tearing off the poisoned tunic (or 'shirt of Nessos' as it is sometimes called), but this merely increased his agony since the fabric had become stuck to his skin and he pulled strips of his flesh along with it. As the poison burned down to his bones, he was carried into the ship and conveyed back to Trachis; and when Deianeira saw the effect of her action, she hanged herself (or stabbed herself) in remorse.[242]

Now believing that death was the only remedy available to him, Herakles made his way – or had himself carried – west from Trachis to the summit of Mt Oeta, where he constructed a pyre and climbed on to it.[243] Or else the pyre was constructed by Hyllos at his father's order, either on his own or with the help of his brothers.[244] Or in Diodorus' account, Likymnios and Iolaos travelled to Delphi at Herakles' order to enquire about a cure, but were told instead that they should build a pyre for him on the mountain and arrange for him to be carried there with his arms and armour.[245] When Herakles climbed on to the pyre and asked the bystanders to set light to it, no one dared to do so until Poias, the father of the great archer Philoktetes, happened to pass by while searching for his flocks and agreed to apply a torch to the wood. Herakles rewarded him by giving him his bow and arrows, which would later be used by Philoktetes at Troy; or in other accounts, Philoktetes lit the pyre and so received the bow and arrows from the hero himself.[246]

In the earliest tradition, Herakles died and departed to Hades just like any other mortal. Achilles remarks accordingly in the *Iliad* that he is willing to accept death whenever the gods bring it on him, 'for not even the mighty Herakles could escape death, very dear though he was to lord Zeus, son of Kronos, but fate overcame him and the dreadful anger of Hera';[247] and Odysseus sees him among the shades of the dead in the *Odyssey*, causing all the other shades to scatter like birds as he advances with an arrow in his bow, glaring fiercely around him as if about to shoot. Three lines are inserted, indeed, into the text of the *Odyssey* to explain that this was simply a phantom since the true Herakles was up above with the gods, but this is clearly an interpolation that was added to reconcile the Homeric account with later

Figure 8.4   Herakles and Athena. Interior of cup by Duris, c. 470 BC.
Staatliche Antikensammlungen, Kassel.

belief.[248] The lines in the *Theogony* that refer to Herakles' presence on Olympos can be regarded as being of later origin likewise, belonging as they do to a section of the poem that was almost certainly added after Hesiod's time.[249] Although it is hard to tell exactly when Herakles was first thought to have become a god, the evidence from the visual arts suggests that the idea of his ascent to heaven had established itself by the beginning of the sixth century BC. In Attic vase-paintings from that and the following century, he can regularly be seen climbing into a chariot, driven by Athena, Hermes or some other deity, to make his ascent to the home of the gods, or else rising into the air in a chariot as the pyre blazes below, or walking into the presence of the gods at the end of his journey. In literary accounts, he is said to have been raised up to heaven to the accompaniment of thunder by a cloud that passed under him as he sat on his pyre, or to have been carried up to heaven by Zeus in a four-horse chariot.[250] According to a notion that is first attested in the Hellenistic period, all that was mortal in him was burned away by the flames, leaving only the divine part that he had inherited from his father Zeus.[251] Diodorus reports no definite wonder, merely stating that the pyre was wholly consumed as the result of a lightning-strike, and that it was assumed that Herakles had entered the company of the gods because his bones were nowhere to be found.[252]

After Herakles was welcomed into the company of the gods on Olympos, Hera agreed to be reconciled with him at last, and allowed him to marry her daughter Hebe, the goddess of youth, in a union that symbolized his overcoming of age and death.[253] It is reported in one source that Hebe bore two sons to him, Alexiares and Aniketos,[254] but these are insubstantial figures whose names are based on cultic titles of Herakles. Some claimed that Hera formally adopted him as her son through a ceremonial re-enactment of his birth, by lying on a bed, drawing him close to her body, and allowing him to fall through her robes to the ground. Or in another story of the kind, she adopted him by offering him her breast.[255] After his eventful life as a hero, he now enjoyed the timeless existence of a god, which was doubtless very pleasant for him but leaves little for his biographer to report.

THE RETURN OF THE HERAKLIDS

Eurystheus meets his own death while trying to eliminate the Heraklids

The subsequent adventures of the sons and descendants of Herakles and Deianeira form an important saga, that of the return of the Heraklids (Herakleidai), which provided a mythological account of the Dorian invasion of the Peloponnese. Although Eurystheus tried to destroy the family of Herakles after the hero's death, he and his sons were killed during the ensuing conflict, and the Heraklids then assumed the offensive by trying to invade the Peloponnese. With Eurystheus and his sons out of the way, they could lay claim to Mycenae and the Perseid lands of the Argolid by virtue of Herakles' Perseid descent; and since Herakles had settled the succession at the other main centre in the Peloponnese, at Sparta (see p. 279) and at Pylos (see p. 278), which was then the ruling city of Messenia, they could seek to establish themselves as the overlords of much of the peninsula. Their initial hopes were frustrated, however, and their final conquest of the Peloponnese was delayed until well after the Trojan War (fifty years after in most accounts). As a result of the alliance that Herakles had established with the Dorians (see p. 282), the Heraklids were supported in the enterprise by a mainly Dorian invasion force; and since the Dorians, who were known to have lived in the north in the earliest times, could have had no prior claim to any territory in the Peloponnese, this legend, which presents them as having been led by Heraklids who founded the royal lines in the conquered lands, provided a mythical justification for their occupation of this new territory.

We should not expect to discover anything of value about the historical movement of peoples from this body of legend (any more than from the legendary account of the Ionian settlement of Asia Minor, see p. 408). The saga of the Heraklids seems to have been no more than a mythical construction, and there is good reason to suppose, furthermore, that the story of the Dorian invasion was first brought into connection with the myth of the return of the Heraklids at a secondary stage. It should be remembered, moreover, that the migration of the Dorians to the Dorian areas of the Peloponnese would not have been an invasion at all in the strict sense, but a very gradual process.

Although all the children and descendants of Herakles could be described as Heraklids (just as descendants of Inachos were Inachids), the name was generally used in reference to the descendants of Herakles and Deianeira who entered the Peloponnese. The Greek name for their 'return', *kathodos*, was doubly suitable, since it could mean both a return and a descent; by descending from Central Greece into the Peloponnese, the Heraklids were returning to the land of their forebears.

When Herakles was no longer available to protect his sons, Eurystheus attempted to eliminate them so as to ensure that his own branch of the family would maintain its dominance in the Perseid lands of the Argolid. The Heraklids initially sought refuge with Keux at Trachis, but he was not sufficiently powerful to protect them in the face of threats from Eurystheus,[256] and they were obliged to flee southward to Athens, where they claimed sanctuary by seating themselves on the altar of Eleos (Pity or Mercy personified). The Athenians, who were ruled at this time by Theseus (or his son Demophon), not only refused to deliver them to Eurystheus when he arrived in pursuit, but offered to fight at their side in the conflict that ensued.[257] When an oracle then declared that Athens would be assured of victory if a daughter of Herakles (or simply a high-born maiden) volunteered to be sacrificed, Makaria, the only daughter of Herakles and Deianeira, offered herself for sacrifice or took her own life.[258] Eurystheus was duly defeated in the fierce battle that followed, losing all his sons; but he escaped in his chariot and tried to flee home by way of the Isthmus of Corinth. He was overtaken, however, in the Megarid by Hyllos or Iolaos, and was captured or immediately killed. In one version of the story, Hyllos, the eldest son of Herakles and Deianeira, decapitated him and took his head back to Alkmene, who gouged out his eyes with weaving-pins;[259] or according to Euripides' surviving play on the matter, the *Heraklids*, Eurystheus was captured by Iolaos, the ageing nephew of Herakles, who returned him in chains to Attica, where Alkmene ordered his death. Euripides reports that Iolaos had prayed to Zeus and Hebe to be rejuvenated for a day to enable him to exact revenge on Eurystheus.[260] A tradition at Thebes suggested, indeed, that Iolaos was dead by this time and was allowed to rise from his grave for the purpose.[261]

The return of the Heraklids is delayed until well after the Trojan War

Although the Heraklids could now believe that they were in a position to return to their ancestral homeland in the Peloponnese, it was the will of the gods that their return should be delayed for many decades. This could hardly have been otherwise, since Herakles was known to have died before the Trojan War and it was equally well-established that Mycenae and Sparta were under Pelopid rule at the time of the war and for some time afterwards. Two main stories were offered to explain how the return of the Heraklids came to be delayed for such a long period. In the simpler account, which is already mentioned by Herodotus, Hyllos, son of Herakles, fought in single combat against a Peloponnesian champion when the Heraklids first tried to invade the Peloponnese, and the Heraklids stayed away for fifty or a hundred years (i.e. the full period of the delay) after his defeat in accordance with the terms of the duel; or in a more elaborate account which is best recorded by Apollodorus, an oracle ordered their withdrawal after they first entered the Peloponnese, and they met with defeat in successive generations thereafter when their misinterpretation of subsequent oracles encouraged them to invade before the proper time. The latter version indicates most clearly that the delay was no mere accident but was providentially ordained.

To start with the simpler version of the story, the Heraklids tried to force their way into the Peloponnese soon after the death of Eurystheus, but were confronted by a Peloponnesian army at the Isthmus of Corinth. To avoid unnecessary bloodshed, the leader of the expedition, HYLLOS, proposed that the issue should be settled by single combat between himself and a champion from the opposing army. As the sworn conditions of the duel, it was agreed that the Heraklids would be allowed to reclaim their ancestral rights in the Peloponnese if Hyllos won, but would attempt no further invasion of the Peloponnese for a hundred years (or fifty years) if he were defeated. ECHEMOS, the king of Tegea in Arcadia, volunteered to fight on behalf of the Peloponnesians and killed Hyllos in the ensuing fight. So the Heraklids were obliged to withdraw, and stayed away until the agreed period had elapsed. Most of the Heraklids in the intervening generations lived as guests of the Dorians in Doris in Central Greece.[262]

In the other main version of the legend, the Heraklids were successful in their first invasion of the Peloponnese and captured most of its main cities; but a plague broke out a year afterwards, and an oracle declared that this had come about because the Heraklids had returned before the proper time. So they withdrew to Attica and settled at Marathon for the present. Whether by the same or a different oracle, the former subjects of Eurystheus at Mycenae were instructed to choose a Pelopid as their new ruler. It happened that Atreus and Thyestes, two sons of Pelops, were living in the area after being exiled by their father, and Atreus won the throne after a bitter contest with his brother (see further on pp. 505ff). His accession marked the beginning of a period of Pelopid rule in the two greatest cities of the Peloponnese, initially at Mycenae and later at Sparta; see Chapter 14. After leading the Heraklids back out of the Peloponnese, Hyllos consulted the Delphic oracle, which stated that they should wait 'until the third harvest' before returning. Naturally assuming that this meant three years, Hyllos waited for that period and invaded the Peloponnese once again, only to be killed, apparently by Echemos at the Isthmus of Corinth as above. In this version, however, the Heraklids could not have sworn to stay away for a hundred years if he were killed, for the descendants of Hyllos led invasions in each successive generation until they finally succeeded.

After a short gap owing to the defective nature of our sources, we can pick up the story again as Hyllos' grandson, ARISTOMACHOS, son of Kleodaios, was consulting the Delphic oracle about a fresh invasion. On being told that the invasion would succeed if the Heraklids approached the Peloponnese 'by the narrow route', Aristomachos led them across the narrow Isthmus of Corinth, but was defeated and killed nonetheless. When Aristomachos' eldest son, TEMENOS, came of age, he consulted the Delphic oracle once again (in the company of his two brothers in one account), and was surprised to receive the same advice as before. On further questioning, the god explained that the Heraklids had brought their previous misfortunes on themselves by misinterpreting his oracles. For when he had spoken of the third harvest, he had meant the third generation of men rather than the third harvest of the earth; and when he had spoken of the narrow route, he had meant the short sea-route across the narrow Gulf of Corinth rather than the land-route across the narrow Isthmus. Since Temenos and his brother belonged to the third generation after Hyllos and were now aware of the proper route, they could make preparations in the confident belief that success lay within their grasp.[263]

The Heraklids invade the Peloponnese with their Dorian allies and draw lots for the three main kingdoms

Temenos assembled an army at Naupaktos on the northern shores of the Corinthian Gulf, and constructed a fleet of ships to ferry them across to the Peloponnesian coast.[264] The force consisted of Dorians for the most part. While it was still at Naupaktos, a priest of Apollo, Karnos by name, arrived there and wandered among the troops delivering oracles in an inspired frenzy. Although he meant no harm, they took him for a sorcerer who had been sent by the enemy to cause their destruction. So Hippotes, son of Phylas, one of the Heraklids, killed him with his spear, provoking Apollo to afflict the army with a famine and cause the destruction of the fleet. When Temenos sought the advice of the Delphic oracle, he was told that the murderer should be banished for ten years and that the Heraklids should take 'the three-eyed one' as their guide.[265] The meaning of the latter words remained a mystery to them until they came across a man riding on a one-eyed horse (or driving a one-eyed mule). This was OXYLOS, son of Andraimon, a member of the Aetolian royal family who had been exiled for killing his brother or some other person and was now returning home after spending a year in Elis; his horse had only a single eye because it had been struck in the other by an arrow. He agreed to act as guide to the Heraklids and their Dorian allies, and advised that they should make their crossing further to the west, starting at Molykrion.[266] After they arrived in the Peloponnese, he conducted them through Arcadia to attack TEISAMENOS, son of Orestes, the last Pelopid ruler of Argos and Sparta. The Peloponnesians were defeated as the oracle had foretold, and Teisamenos himself was either killed in battle or escaped to Aigialos (Achaea) on the north coast, where he was killed soon afterwards nonetheless (see p. 407). The Heraklids were then able to take possession of the main centres in the Peloponnese.[267]

As a reward for his services, Oxylos asked to be granted the throne of Elis in the north-western Peloponnese; since the Aetolian royal family had originally come from Elis (see pp. 411–12), his rule had a certain legitimacy.[268] Another region of the Peloponnese that never came under Heraklid rule was Arcadia, because its ruler, Kypselos, reached an accommodation with the Heraklids by means of a marriage-alliance (see p. 549).

The important city of Corinth, which was still ruled by descendants of its Deukalionid founder Sisyphos (see p. 430), acquired a Heraklid ruler and a Dorian population within a generation of the return of the Heraklids. Hippotes, son of Phylas, the Heraklid who was banished for killing the seer at Naupaktos (see above), fathered a son ALETES (Wanderer) during his subsequent wanderings; and when Aletes came of age, he attacked Corinth with a force of Dorians and put the Corinthians to flight after worsting them in battle. The Sisyphid rulers, Doridas and Hyanthidas, then submitted to him and were allowed to remain in the city. Aletes and his descendants ruled at Corinth for five generations until the monarchy was displaced by the Bacchiad oligarchy (in 747 BC according to the traditional reckoning).[269] After seizing control of Corinth, Aletes also tried to conquer Attica, but was foiled by the self-sacrifice of Kodros, the last king of Athens (see p. 376). Sicyon, Corinth's neighbour to the west, was also said to have been conquered by a Heraklid, in this case Phalkes, son of Temenos; since the king of Sicyon, a certain Lakestades, was descended from a son of Herakles, Phalkes allowed him to share the throne.[270]

After completing their conquest of the Peloponnese, the Heraklid leader cast lots to determine who should win the three main kingdoms of Sparta, Argos and Messenia. The senior Heraklids of this generation were **Temenos, Kresphontes** and **Aristodemos**, the three great-grandsons of Hyllos, son of Herakles (see Table 6); but Aristodemos was usually said to have been killed before the final invasion. Apollodorus states without further detail that he was killed by a thunderbolt while the army was at Naupaktos; or else he was murdered at Delphi by Medon and Strophios, sons of Pylades and Elektra, two cousins of Teisamenos whose family had good reason to fear the ambitions of the Heraklids.[271] Whatever the exact circumstances of his death, he was represented at the draw by his twin sons Prokles and Eurysthenes. This was the usual story at least; but the Spartans had their own ideas on the matter, as we shall see. Kresphontes was so anxious to gain possession of Messenia, the fertile south-western region of the Peloponnese, that he rigged the draw in his own favour. For after it had been agreed that the three parties should cast their lots into a water-jug, Kresphontes proposed that the first lots should be drawn for Sparta and Argos, leaving Messenia for the one whose lot remained in the jug; and he tossed a ball of compacted earth into the jug as his own lot rather than a pebble, so ensuring that the other lots would be drawn because his own would dissolve in the water.[272] This tale was devised to justify (or at least account for) the division of power in the Peloponnese from the seventh century BC onwards when Messenia fell under Spartan control; for it could be claimed in terms of the myth that the Heraklid rulers of Messenia eventually lost their ill-gotten gains to legitimate claimants.

In another account of the ruse of Kresphontes, the Dorians awarded Argos to Temenos (apparently on the ground that the best kingdom should go to the eldest brother), and Kresphontes asked that he should be allowed to choose Messenia since he too was of elder birth than Aristodemos. His wish was opposed, however, by Theras (see p. 329), who was representing the young sons of the dead Aristodemos, and he therefore resorted to a ruse to achieve his desire. After first persuading Temenos to collude with him, he proposed that the issue should be settled by a draw. Temenos then put two lots into a water-jug, one for the sons of Aristodemos and one for Kresphontes, on the agreement that the party whose lot was picked out should choose between the remaining kingdoms. Now Temenos had made both lots out of clay, but he had baked that of Kresphontes in a fire while he had merely dried the other in the sun; so when they were put into the water, the latter dissolved, and Kresphontes' lot was certain to be picked out. This version also provides a mythical explanation for the long-lasting hostility between Sparta and Argos, which could be said to have taken its start from Temenos' deception.[273]

The Heraklid rulers of Sparta, Messenia and Argos; the exile of Tlepolemos

As a result of the draw, however unsatisfactory it may have been, Temenos became the first Heraklid king of Argos, and Kresphontes that of Messenia, while Sparta was allotted to Prokles and Eurysthenes, the infant sons of Aristodemos. As the brother of Aristodemos' wife, Theras, son of Autesion, who was descended from the kings of Thebes, ruled Sparta as regent until the sons of Aristodemos came of age (see p. 571). The Spartans differed from most other Greeks in believing that Aristodemos had survived to become the first Heraklid king of their land. In that case, he fathered Prokles and Eurysthenes in Sparta shortly before his death; and when he died, it was decided that the twins should become the joint rulers of the land because they were indistinguishable and there was no way of telling which was the elder.[274] Whether they inherited the throne in these circumstances or it was allotted to them after their father's death as in the usual tradition, their joint assumption of the throne provided a mythical explanation for the peculiar institution of the dual monarchy at Sparta. As seems fitting, they married twin sisters, Lathria and Anaxandra, daughters of the Heraklid Thersandros, son of Agamedides.[275] The Agiad royal house, which was accorded a certain precedence in ceremonial matters at least, traced its descent to Eurysthenes through his son Agis, while the Eurypontid royal house traced its descent to the other twin Prokles, through his grandson Eurypon, son of Soas. In accordance with the common pattern in which mythical twins are either the best of friends or worst of enemies, Prokles and Eurysthenes were said to have quarrelled throughout their lives, hence the discord that often prevailed between the two royal houses in historical times.[276]

The first Heraklid rulers of Messenia and Argos both met violent ends. KRES-PHONTES married Merope, the daughter of Kypselos, king of Arcadia, who bore him three sons; but he was killed along with two of his sons when another Heraklid, Polyphontes, mounted a revolt against him and seized the Messenian throne. His younger son Aipytos (or Kresphontes) survived, however, either because he was being reared in Arcadia by Kypselos or because his mother sent him away to Kypselos in secret at the time of the revolt. In the early account from Euripides' *Kresphontes*, so far as it can be reconstructed from fragments and other records, Polyphontes was aware that the child, here called Kresphontes, had survived, and promised a reward of gold to anyone who would kill him; but he grew up unharmed and later returned to Messenia to avenge his father's death. He approached Polyphontes under a false name and told him that he had come to claim the reward for having killed the prince. While he was sleeping as a guest in the palace, his mother Merope, who had been forced into marriage with Polyphontes in the mean time, entered his room with an axe to kill him in the belief that he had murdered her son; but an old servant who was aware of his true identity warned her just in time. She then made a show of friendliness to Polyphontes and suggested that their guest should be invited to assist at a sacrifice; and when the young man was given a sword for that purpose, he plunged it into Polyphontes and so recovered his father's kingdom.[277] Or in another version, the son of the murdered king, here called Aipytos, as is usual in the later tradition, returned openly to Messenia and recovered the throne by force with the help of some Arcadian allies and other Peloponnesian kings.[278] Aipytos gained such a reputation among rich and poor alike for his just rule that the Messenian kings were known as Aipytids rather than Heraklids from that time onward.[279] The line was destined to be extinguished, however, at a relatively early period when the Spartans established their domination over the land.

In his kingdom at Argos, TEMENOS provoked trouble within his own family by favouring Deiphontes, the Heraklid husband of his daughter Hyrnetho, above his three sons. Fearing for their inheritance, the sons of Temenos plotted the murder of their father. This achieved nothing for them in one version of the story, since the Argives were so shocked by their crime that they drove them out and assigned the kingdom to Hyrnetho and her husband;[280] or in another version, Keisos, the eldest son of Temenos, took over the throne, and Deiphontes withdrew to Epidauros with many Argive followers.[281] As a matter of historical fact, the monarchy at Argos was not a long-lasting institution like the dual monarchy at Sparta. According to Pausanias' account of the legendary tradition, the Argives reduced the authority of the monarchy at such an early period that even Medon, the son and successor of the above-mentioned Keisos, was a monarch in no more than name, and the monarchy itself was abolished nine generations later.[282]

The kings of Macedonia claimed to be Heraklids of Temenid descent. According to a tale from Hyginus which was probably based on the lost *Archelaos* of Euripides, Archelaos, a son of Temenos, was driven out of Argos by his brothers and travelled to the court of Kisseus, a Macedonian king. Being under attack from neighbouring enemies at the time, Kisseus, promised him his daughter and the kingdom if he would put his enemies to flight. As he was coming for his reward, however, after achieving this, Kisseus told his servants to prepare a fire-pit and cover it over with light branches so that Archelaos would fall into it and be killed. In a more ancient myth, Ixion was said to have caused the death of his father-in-law by such means (see p. 554); but in the present story the prospective victim received a warning from a slave. On learning of the plot in this way, Archelaos lured the king to a private meeting and hurled him into his own fire-pit. On the advice of an oracle, he left afterwards taking a she-goat (*aiga*) as a guide and followed it to the site of Aigai, where he founded the royal capital of Macedonia.[283] This story may well have been invented by Euripides himself, who spent the final period of his life in Macedonia at the court of a historical Archelaos (reigned c. 413–399 BC). Other tales which credit the founding of the monarchy to more distant descendants of Temenos can be found in Herodotus and Diodorus.[284]

One further story is worthy of mention in connection with the Heraklids, the ancient legend of the exile of the Heraklid TLEPOLEMOS, who was a son of Herakles by the Epirote princess Astyoche (see p. 280), or by Astydameia, daughter of Amyntor.[285] Homer already reports that he killed Likymnios, the maternal uncle of Herakles, and was therefore obliged to depart into exile and built a fleet of ships, gathered together many followers, and sailed away to the island of Rhodes.[286] Subsequent authors add more details on the murder. According to Pindar, who locates the incident at Tiryns, Tlepolemos struck Likymnios with an olive-wood staff as the latter was emerging from the room of his mother Midea. This action was apparently committed in anger, but the exact circumstances are not explained.[287] In later accounts, Tlepolemos is said to have struck his great-uncle accidentally, either while aiming a blow at a slave who was leading the aged Likymnios along in a negligent manner, or because Likymnios happened to get in the way while he was beating a slave.[288] Apollodorus (who offers the latter version) states that the incident occurred when the Heraklids first invaded the Peloponnese shortly after the death of Eurystheus; or in another account, the citizens of Argos invited Tlepolemos and Likymnios to their city while the other Heraklids were excluded after the death of Hyllos, and the accidental killing took place in Argos after they had settled there.[289] Tlepolemos sailed away to Rhodes after the killing at the order of the Delphic oracle,[290] accompanied by many Dorian followers, and founded the island's three great Dorian cities, Lindos, Ialysos and Kameiros.[291] He amassed wealth and power in his new homeland, and later led the Rhodian contingent to the Trojan War in nine ships. The *Iliad* describes how he was killed in battle by the Lycian hero Sarpedon.[292]

CHAPTER NINE

THE MYTHICAL HISTORY
OF THEBES

THE FOUNDATION AND EARLY HISTORY
OF THEBES

The great city of Thebes in southern Boeotia, which ranked with Argos as the most important centre in mythical Greece, was ruled by the second main branch of the Inachid family. As was explained above (see p. 231), an early Argive princess, Io, a descendant (or even daughter) of the Argive river-god Inachos, wandered far away from her native Argos to settle in Egypt; and in that land, her granddaughter **Libye** subsequently bore twin sons to Poseidon called **Belos** and **Agenor**, who were the founders of the two principal branches of the family. **Danaos**, a son of Belos, returned to his ancestral homeland of Argos to found its Belid ruling line (see p. 233), while **Kadmos** and **Europa**, two children of Agenor who were born in Phoenicia where their father had settled, were destined to found the Agenorid ruling lines at Thebes and Crete respectively. We will follow the history of Kadmos' Theban line in the present chapter before returning to Europa and her descendants on Crete in the next.

Agenor sends Kadmos and his other sons in search
of Europa

To pick up the story of AGENOR where we left off in Chapter 7, he emigrated from Egypt to Phoenicia on the easternmost shore of the Mediterranean, where he founded a kingdom of his own and married Telephassa (of unrecorded parentage) or Argiope, daughter of the Nile. She bore him a daughter, Europa, and various sons including Kadmos, Phoinix, Kilix and Thasos.[1] **Europa** grew up to be so beautiful that she attracted the love of Zeus, who assumed the form of a bull to carry her across the sea to Crete, where he fathered Minos and other sons by her (see pp. 337ff). Mystified by her sudden disappearance, Agenor ordered his sons to set off in search of her, telling them that they were not to return in any circumstances until they had found her. They all failed in their search, however, and were therefore obliged to settle abroad.[2] **Kilix**, who is little more than an eponym, made his home in the south-eastern province of Asia Minor that was known as Cilicia (Kilikia) thereafter, while

Phoinix settled in Phoenicia not far from where he had set off; or else he settled in North Africa, which was a main centre of Phoenician colonization.[3] We will be primarily concerned with the travels of **Kadmos**, who set off with his mother Telephassa and brother **Thasos**. They searched through much of the Aegean until they arrived at Thrace on its northern shores, where Telephassa died; Thasos decided to give up at this point, and settled on the island off the Thracian coast that would bear his name ever afterwards. According to Herodotus, the famous gold-mines on the island were first discovered by Phoenician followers of Thasos.[4] During the preceding search, Kadmos had already established a Phoenician colony in the southern Aegean on the island of Thera (see p. 571). After seeing to the funeral of his mother and saying farewell to his brother, Kadmos decided to travel to Greece to consult the Delphic oracle about the location of his sister.[5]

Conflicting genealogies are recorded for most members of this family. Europa is quite often described as a child of Phoinix rather than of Agenor, as is Kadmos too on occasion. The *Iliad* refers to Europa as such, and the same is reported of the Hesiodic *Catalogue*, which specified that Phoinix was a son of Agenor and the father of Phineus.[6] We cannot be sure from the surviving evidence whether Kadmos was also a child of Phoinix in the *Catalogue*, or else a son of Agenor and thus an uncle of Europa (as is perhaps more likely). In connection with the search myth, Kadmos and Europa are always regarded as brother of and sister, and customarily as children of Agenor.[7] Thasos is variously described as a son of Agenor, Phoinix, Kilix or Poseidon. Kepheus, king of Ethiopia, the father of Andromeda (see p. 240), was fitted into this family somewhere (as is understandable in view of the location of his kingdom), being variously described as a son of Agenor, Phoinix or Belos; and the same is true of Phineus, the uncle of Andromeda (see p. 242, not to be confused with the Thracian Phineus).[8]

Kadmos follows a cow to the site of Thebes, where he kills a dragon and sows its teeth

Kadmos was told by the oracle that he should trouble himself no further about Europa, but should take a cow as his guide, follow it until it sank down exhausted on its right flank (i.e. on the side of good omen), and then found a new city at that spot. He discovered the special cow among the herds of a certain Pelagon, who lived in Phocis somewhere to the east of Delphi. In one version of the story he was left to discover it by his own devices as he was travelling away from Delphi, and picked out a cow that was walking along on its own among the herds of Pelagon;[9] or else the oracle was more precise, telling him to seek the herds of Pelagon and then look out for a particular cow that had a white mark resembling a full moon on each of its flanks.[10] After finding it by whatever means, he followed it as it ambled eastwards through Phocis and southern Boeotia until it finally sank to the ground at the site of Thebes.

After discovering the location of his city by this means, Kadmos decided to offer the cow in sacrifice to Athena (so inaugurating the Theban cult of Pallas Onka); or else he had been instructed by the oracle to sacrifice the cow to the Earth after reaching his goal.[11] Before he could proceed with the ritual, he needed some lustral water, and sent some of his companions to fetch it from a spring nearby. The spring was sacred to the war-god Ares, however, and it was guarded by a fearsome dragon that killed all or most of the men. As was usual with Greek dragons, which lacked the legs and wings of our modern dragons (which are of medieval design), this Theban dragon was pictured as large serpent; it was a son of Ares in one account rather than merely his servant, a child borne to him by Erinys Tilphousa.[12] On learning of the fate of his companions, Kadmos set off to confront the dragon and soon killed it, either by stabbing it with his sword or by striking it on the head with a massive stone or by both means.[13]

On the advice of Athena, he collected the dragon's teeth and sowed them in the ground. A host of armed men, known as the SPARTOI or 'Sown Men', sprang up from the teeth and proceeded to fight among themselves until only five were left.[14] They seem to have attacked one another of their own accord in the original story, as a result of their innate aggressiveness; but there was also a quite early version in which Kadmos threw stones at them out of fear, causing them to fight among themselves in the belief that they were being pelted by one another.[15] Be that as it may, there were five Spartoi in the end named Echion, Oudaios, Chthonios, Hyperenor and Peloros[16] (i.e. Snake-man, Ground-man, Earth-man, Overweening and Monstrous), who went on to found the noble families that would form the military caste of the new city. Before founding the city, Kadmos had to serve Ares for a year (or a great year, equivalent to eight ordinary years) to atone for having killed the dragon.[17]

In other versions of the story of the dragon's teeth, Athena sowed them with her own hands, or Ares ordered their sowing or actually sowed them.[18] Hellanicus offered an account in which only five Spartoi sprang from the teeth in the first place, and the initial battle was thus eliminated;[19] and he apparently stated that Ares would have killed Kadmos for slaying the dragon if Zeus had not restrained him.[20]

The story of the sowing of the dragon's teeth was recycled in Argonautic myth to provide an ordeal for Jason (see p. 390). To account for the origin of the teeth that were sowed by Jason (an event that must have occurred several generations after the lifetime of Kadmos), it was explained that Kadmos sowed some of the teeth from the Theban dragon while the rest were held back to be given to Aietes, who later handed them on to Jason to be sown. Pherecydes stated, for instance, that Ares and Athena gave half of the teeth to Kadmos, keeping the rest in reserve for Aietes; or else Aietes received a share of the teeth from Athena.[21] Misapprehensions can easily arise if one fails to keep in mind that Jason and Kadmos were ordered to sow the teeth for entirely different reasons; for Aietes ordered Jason to sow them to confront him with the perilous ordeal of killing the warriors who would spring up from them, while Athena (or Ares) ordered Kadmos to do so to provide him with useful citizens for his city. It was not in Kadmos' interest to kill them; and even in the variant mentioned above in which he provoked them to attack one another by throwing stones at them, he threw the stones in panic rather with the conscious intention of provoking a fight. Jason, on the other hand, adopted this as a deliberate stratagem on the advice of Medeia, to ensure that the armed men would be reduced in number before he attacked them directly. This motif of the stone-throwing would have originated in the Argonautic myth.

Although Apollodorus' summary of the foundation legend is drawn from good early sources for the most part, it is misleading in so far as it suggests that Kadmos underwent his servitude to Ares for having killed the Spartoi (rather than the Theban dragon);[22] this unhappy idea can be put aside as an error. Even if Ares' anger at the killing of the dragon would have been fully allayed by Kadmos' servitude in the original legend, the theme was too useful not to be reapplied in other connections, whether to account for Kadmos' subsequent trans-formation into a snake (see p. 300), or the sending of the Sphinx, or the need for an act of self-sacrifice if Thebes was to be defended from the Seven (see p. 330).

Kadmos marries the goddess Harmonia and founds Thebes

Ares was reconciled with Kadmos after his servitude was completed, and Zeus granted him a goddess as a wife, namely HARMONIA, the daughter of Ares and Aphrodite. All the Olympian gods descended from heaven to attend the wedding, which was celebrated on the Kadmeia, the acropolis of the new city; and the Muses themselves sang the marriage-hymns, accompanied by Apollo or the Charites (Graces) in some accounts.[23] Many splendid gifts were presented to the bride, most notably a divine necklace and robe (*peplos*) which would be much coveted in future times and become a source of sorrow to their owners. The robe was usually said to have been a gift from Athena, while the necklace, which had naturally been made by Hephaistos, was presented either by her or by Aphrodite. Or else the necklace was a gift from the bridegroom, who had acquired it either from its maker or from Europa (who had originally received it as a present from Zeus (see p. 337); this latter version, from Pherecydes, departs from the usual tradition by suggesting that Kadmos did meet his sister at some stage after her abduction to Crete).[24] Pindar cites this marriage along with that of Peleus – who married another goddess, Thetis (see p. 52) – as an illustration of the highest blessing that could be attained by a mortal man; but the poet refers to this peak of their good fortune to make a deeper point, that no mortal can expect to live a life that is free from reverses, for Kadmos and Peleus were both destined to meet with their full share of misfortune.[25] The sorrows of Kadmos arose mainly from the tribulations of his children, as we will see shortly, while Peleus was soon deserted by his wife, who thought it shameful to be yoked to a mortal, and lost his only son prematurely. In his marriage at least, however, Kadmos was indeed supremely fortunate, for Harmonia's attitude was very different from that of Thetis and the union proved to be happy and long-lasting.

Kadmos founded Thebes by building the upper city with the help of the Spartoi on the Theban acropolis, which was known as the Kadmeia. Thebes had two separate foundation-legends since it was sometimes said to have been founded by Zethos and Amphion, who belonged to another family; but the two legends were reconciled in the usual tradition by means of a division of labour, in which Kadmos was said to have built the upper city while Zethos and Amphion built or fortified the lower city at a later time (see further on p. 305). The house of Kadmos and bridal-chamber of Harmonia could be seen on the acropolis in historical times, as could the spot where the Muses were supposed to have sung during their wedding-feast.[26]

According to some Hellenistic accounts, Harmonia was mortal rather than divine, as a daughter of Zeus by a mortal mother, Elektra, daughter of Atlas. In that case, she was the sister of Iasion and Dardanos (see p. 521) and was brought up with them on the island of Samothrace in the northern Aegean, where Kadmos happened to come across her during his search for Europa. According to Ephorus, a historian of the fourth century BC, he abducted her as he was sailing by, hence the origin of a local ceremony in which the islanders conducted a ritual search for Elektra; or in Diodorus' account, he married her at a formal wedding on Samothrace, in the presence of the gods as in the traditional story of his marriage to the goddess at Thebes.[27] If it was accepted that Harmonia was a child of Elektra, it could be explained that the Elektran gates at Thebes were named after her mother (although another story suggested that they were named after a sister of Kadmos).[28]

The Greeks commonly explained the origin of their alphabet by saying that Kadmos had introduced it from Phoenicia. There were rival legends, however, as is so often the case with inventions, and some authors were naturally inclined to ascribe a purely Greek origin to the art of writing. An ancient tradition, already found in Stesichorus and perhaps originating in early Trojan epic, claimed this as one of the many inventions of the ingenious Palamedes (see p. 459); in the *Prometheus Bound*, writing is listed among the arts that were invented by Prometheus for the benefit of the human race; or in another account, doubtless of Hellenistic origin, the alphabet was invented by Aktaios, a primordial king of Athens, who named the letters in honour of his daughter Phoinike. This Aktaion or Aktaios was the father-in-law of Kekrops (see p. 365), who is also named as the inventor of the alphabet.[29]

The children of Kadmos and Harmonia; the death of Aktaion

The founder of Thebes and his divine consort had a son, Polydoros, and four daughters of far greater importance, Ino, Semele, Agave and Autonoe.[30] **Polydoros** was of genealogical significance alone as a male heir who could serve to link the founder of the city to the Labdakid dynasty (the family of Oedipus and Polyneikes), which would originally have had no connection with Kadmos. It is reported that he was sometimes known as Pinakos (Writing-tablet-man), evidently in reference to his father's service in introducing writing to Greece.[31] As we shall see (p. 300), Kadmos and Harmonia produced a further son, Illyrios, during their later years of exile.

The disasters that befell the daughters of Kadmos are mostly considered elsewhere. **Semele** provoked her own destruction by making her lover Zeus promise to visit her in his true divine form (see p. 171); she was pregnant at the time with his son Dionysos, who was snatched from her womb and sewn into the thigh of Zeus until it was time for him to be born. **Ino** and her husband Athamas reared the infant Dionysos for a while, much to the anger of Hera, who punished them by sending them mad and so caused the destruction of Ino and her two children (see pp. 172 and 421). **Agave** married Echion, one of the five Spartoi, and bore him a son Pentheus, who ruled Thebes for a short period as the successor of Kadmos. She and her son were destined to suffer at the hand of Dionysos, who incited her and other Theban women to tear Pentheus to pieces to punish him for having failed to acknowledge his divinity (see p. 173). **Autonoe** for her part married a minor rustic god, Aristaios (see p. 152), and bore him a single child, Aktaion, who died early in horrifying circumstances, as must now be recounted.

AKTAION had a passion for hunting, liking nothing better than to roam through the uplands of Boeotia with a pack of fifty hounds. One day, however, while still in the flower of his youth, he caused great offence to Artemis, who turned him into a stag and caused him to be hunted down by his own dogs. The most familiar version of the story, both in modern times and in the later classical tradition, is that which first appears in Callimachus' fifth *Hymn*, in which the goddess is said to have inflicted this punishment on him because he stumbled across her while she was naked. For as he was hunting one day on Mt Kithairon in southern Boeotia, he entered the thickly wooded Gargaphian valley to seek some relief from the midday heat; and it happened that Artemis had entered this valley, which was sacred to her, with similar intent, and Aktaion came across her as she was bathing with her attendant nymphs in a shady spring. The angry goddess threw some water into his face, saying that he could now tell everyone that he had seen her naked, if he was able to. The meaning of her words became clear when horns began to sprout from his head where the water had struck him and he gradually turned into a stag. He retained his wits, however, and was fully aware of what he was about to suffer as his dogs proceeded to hunt him down. Such is the story as recounted in the earliest full narrative by Ovid; Callimachus offers no details.[32] On the northern slopes of Kithairon, travellers could see a rock known as Aktaion's Couch (*koitē Aktaiōnos*) on which the hero used to sleep when wearied by the hunt, and from where he gained a fatal glimpse of Artemis as she was washing in a spring nearby.[33] Some late authors suggest that the goddess had ample reason to punish Aktaion because he was deliberately spying on her or even tried to rape her;[34] Diodorus already records a story of this kind, saying that he tried to make love to the goddess at her temple after dedicating the first fruits of his hunting to her.[35]

Aktaion incurred divine retribution for an entirely different reason in the earliest accounts, by seeking to marry his aunt Semele even though she was loved by Zeus. The early mythographer Acusilaus cited this as the reason for her transformation, and the Hesiodic *Catalogue* can be presumed to have said the same (in spite of a gap in the relevant papyrus, which preserves no more than the last two letters of Semele's name).[36] Pausanias ascribes a similar version to Stesichorus, reporting rather ambiguously that Artemis 'threw a deerskin' around Aktaion in the poem in question to cause him to be hunted by his dogs, and so prevented from taking Semele as his wife;[37] it is not clear whether the disputable phrase should be interpreted literally or as referring to a conventional transformation (as is surely more probable). In the surviving literature, Euripides is the first author to state that Artemis took action against Aktaion for an offence committed against herself, in this case boasting that he was a better hunter than her;[38] the legend of Aktaion was dramatized in early tragedy by Aeschylus and other authors, but virtually nothing is known about how the story was presented by them.

The dogs of Aktaion attracted considerable attention in their own right; catalogues were compiled of their names, and some authors liked to imagine how they would have reacted on realizing that their master was missing (or indeed that they had killed him). Apollodorus tells how they searched high and low for him, howling all the while, until their search brought them to the cave of the Centaur Cheiron, who allayed their grief by fashioning an image of their dead master; or according to a verse fragment which may have come from the Hesiodic *Catalogue*, they were in a divinely inspired frenzy when they killed him, but howled in distress when they became aware that he was dead, and shed warm tears for him. Several authors report that Artemis inspired them with madness to cause them to kill their master (even though this hardly seems necessary if he had already been turned into a stag).[39] As for his mother Autonoe, she left Thebes forever in grief at his death and settled in the Megarian village of Erenea, where her tomb could be seen in historical times.[40] Her husband Aristaios was said to have departed to Keos (see p. 177).

The exile and ultimate fate of Kadmos and Harmonia

Toward the end of their life, Kadmos and Harmonia left Thebes to live in exile in Illyria, a wild region adjoining the Adriatic in the north-west.[41] Whatever the original significance of this feature of their legend, it could easily be explained that their departure was prompted by the many troubles of their family.[42] It was commonly said that Kadmos abdicated in his old age in favour of his grandson Pentheus, the son of Agave, but remained in Thebes until his successor brought further disaster on the family by opposing Dionysos and his orgiastic rites (see p. 173);[43] after Pentheus met a grisly death as a consequence, Kadmos and Harmonia departed in despair (or at the bidding of Dionysos), leaving the kingdom in the hands of Polydoros, their only son. They travelled to Illyria in a cart drawn by two yoked oxen (hence the name of the town of Bouthoe in Illyria, which was supposedly founded by Kadmos and named as such because he and his wife had been drawn there swiftly, *thoōs*, by oxen, *bous*).[44] Two stories were put forward to explain how Kadmos came to win a kingdom for himself in his new homeland. According to Apollodorus, a war was in progress at the time between the Illyrians and the neighbouring Encheleans or 'Eel-people', who were advised by an oracle that they would defeat the Illyrians if they took Kadmos and Harmonia as their leaders; and after the Illyrians were duly vanquished, Kadmos was able to establish himself as their ruler.[45] Or in a less creditable tale that is briefly reported by Hyginus, Kadmos was accompanied to Illyria by his daughter Agave, who married Lykotherses, king of the Illyrians, and murdered him soon afterwards to secure the throne for her father.[46] Kadmos and Harmonia produced a late-born son, ILLYRIOS, who gave his name to the land and became the ancestor of its ruling family.[47]

In spite of her divine status, Harmonia was thought to have shared a common end with her husband. There were two separate traditions on this matter which were often combined, one suggesting that they were transferred to Elysion or the Isles of the Blessed (homes for the privileged dead in the upper world, see p. 114), and the other that they were transformed into snakes. Pindar mentions Kadmos together with Peleus and Achilles among those who have been granted the privilege of living in the Isles of the Blessed, as would be a fitting end for a notable hero who was married to a goddess; Menelaos is told correspondingly in the *Odyssey* that he will be transferred to Elysion by the gods because he is a son-in-law of Zeus.[48] In a report that is vaguely ascribed to 'the poets and mythographers', a Pindaric scholion states that Kadmos and Harmonia were conveyed to the Elysian Fields on a chariot drawn by winged dragons.[49] The story of their metamorphosis first appears in Euripides' *Bacchae* and resurfaces in Hellenistic sources. Nicander states that they lived in reptilian form ever after in the Illyrian province of Drileos, creeping around as a pair of fearsome snakes, while Euripides offers a combined version in which Ares transferred them to the Isles of the Blessed in their snake form. Apollodorus states similarly that they were turned into snakes and sent to the Elysian Fields by Zeus.[50] It has long been recognized that the two motifs have much the same significance since the heroized dead were often thought to manifest themselves in snake-form. It would be interesting to know whether Kadmos and Harmonia were ever thought to have lived on in snake-form as beneficent deities on the Kadmeia at Thebes; in the surviving tradition, however, the metamorphosis is always associated with their exile. Another theory suggests that Kadmos may have been identified with some Illyrian snake-hero. Whatever the original significance of the transformation, it came to be explained either as a punishment or as a deliverance from sorrow. Hyginus reports, for instance, that the pair were transformed at the will of Ares because he was still angry at the loss of his Theban dragon.[51] In the fullest surviving narrative, Ovid sets the stage for the transformation by telling how the couple once came to reflect on their many misfortunes during their disconsolate old age in Illyria. Both are described as being bowed down by age even though Harmonia was a goddess. Kadmos suggests Ares may have visited them with their sufferings to avenge his killing of the sacred serpent at Thebes, and prays that he himself may become a serpent if that is indeed the case. Even while he is speaking, his body begins to lengthen, and his skin to harden and darken and to grow a covering of scales; and as his familiar form and features disappear, Harmonia prays to share his fate. They are now a pair of harmless reptiles that neither fear nor injure human beings because they remember what they once were.[52]

Dionysos informs Kadmos of his future fate in Euripides' *Bacchae*, foretelling that he and his wife will be transformed into snakes (apparently as part of the punishment that the god inflicts on the family to avenge Pentheus' rejection of his rites). Although there is no direct reference to the couple's Illyrian exile – perhaps because there is a gap in the relevant section of the play – Dionysos goes on to say that they will drive into Greece in an ox-cart at the head of an army of foreigners, and will sack many cities until the invaders meet with disaster on attacking the oracle of Loxias (i.e. of Apollo at Delphi); but they themselves will be saved by Ares, who will transfer them to eternal life among the blessed. As we know from Herodotus, there was a tradition that some Encheleans and Illyrians had once met with destruction when they had attacked Apollo's temple at Delphi, but it seems that the original story had nothing to do with Kadmos; the present version was probably invented by Euripides himself. Quite the oddest feature in this account is the suggestion that the couple will already be in snake-form while leading the barbarian army, a notion that might be hard to credit if it were not clearly indicated in Kadmos' response that this is exactly what Dionysos had meant.[53]

The early Labdakids, and the Theban careers of Lykos and Nykteus

POLYDOROS, son of Kadmos, who succeeded to the throne after the brief and unfortunate reign of Pentheus, is hardly more than a name; for as was noted above, he was of genealogical significance alone as the link who served to tie the Theban dynasty of the Labdakids to the founder Kadmos. According to the unified genealogical scheme that was developed through this linkage, Polydoros was the father of Labdakos, the eponymous founder of the dynasty, which includes Oedipus and his warring sons Polyneikes and Eteokles among its members. Polydoros is mentioned as the son of Kadmos in the *Theogony* (though not in a part of the poem that can be ascribed to Hesiod himself), and then in Herodotus and tragedy.[54]

From what is reported by Apollodorus and Pausanias, the family history of Polydoros and his immediate descendants can be reconstructed as follows. Polydoros married Nykteis, daughter of Nykteus, and fathered a single child, LABDAKOS, who was still an infant when his father fell fatally ill; so Labdakos entrusted his son and throne to his brother-in-law Nykteus, inviting him to rule as regent. When Labdakos assumed power in his own right, he became embroiled in a border-war with his southern neighbour, Pandion, king of Athens, who defeated him with the aid of a Thracian ally, Tereus (see p. 368); but he met an early death like his father before him, and no further adventures are recorded for him. Apollodorus states elliptically that he perished because he was of like mind to Pentheus, which would suggest that he died prematurely because he tried to oppose Dionysos. His son LAIOS was only a year old at the time of his death, and power in Thebes passed to Lykos, the brother of Nykteus, who either ruled on Laios' behalf as regent or took advantage of the situation to seize power for himself. Lykos presided over the city for many years until he was killed (or driven out) by his great-nephews Zethos and Amphion, who established themselves as joint kings and forced Laios to depart into exile. Laios took refuge at the court of Pelops in the western Peloponnese, where he remained until he was finally able to secure his rightful throne after the death of the usurpers; and with the story of the birth and exposure of his son Oedipus, we enter on to familiar territory.[55]

As might be inferred from this summary, the major actors during this period of the mythical history of Thebes were not the Labdakids themselves but the regents and usurpers who ruled in their stead for so much of the time. So what was the origin of Lykos and Nykteus, and how did they attain such authority in the city? And why did Zethos and Amphion come to revolt against their great-uncle?

According to the usual tradition, LYKOS and NYKTEUS were born outside Thebes as sons of a minor Boeotian ruler, Hyrieus, the eponymous founder of the city of Hyria near the east coast of the province. Hyrieus himself was of Atlantid birth, a son of Poseidon by Alkyone, daughter of Atlas (see p. 520). His sons would have grown up at Hyria, but decided to seek their fortune at Thebes. Although Apollodorus offered an account of their movements, his text is poorly preserved at this point; it seems that they may have sought refuge at Thebes after killing Phlegyas, the king of the rapacious Phlegyans of north-western Boeotia (see p. 560). They arrived at Thebes during the reign of Pentheus in any case, and established close relations with the royal family. As a result of their friendship with the king, they were readily accepted as honoured citizens, and Lykos was eventually elected to a position of considerable power as the polemarch (military commander) of the city. Nykteus had two daughters, Nykteis, who married Polydoros as we have seen, and Antiope, who bore Zethos and Amphion to Zeus. Lykos married a woman called Dirke, whom we will meet below as the cruel stepmother of Antiope, but he is not reported to have fathered any children by her.[56]

Apollodorus refers to an alternative genealogy that represented Lykos and Nykteus as sons of Chthonios, one of the Spartoi (Sown Men); this was presumably a relatively late genealogy that was devised at Thebes itself to provide the interlopers with a proper Theban ancestry. The alteration makes no difference otherwise since Antiope and her children could be regarded as descendants of Nykteus as before. In the earliest tradition, however, Antiope was a daughter of the river-god Asopos and had no connection with Nykteus or Lykos by birth or otherwise.[57]

The Asopos in question was properly the small Boeotian river of that name rather than the Peloponnesian river; see also on p. 537. If this genealogy is accepted, Antiope's family history cannot follow the course that will be described below. Thus in the *Odyssey*, which classes her as an Asopid, her sons are presented as the original founders of Thebes (see p. 306) rather than as interlopers who seized power as a result of conflicts within their own family. We cannot tell for sure when Antiope first came to be described as a daughter of Nykteus of Atlantid descent; although such a descent is not explicitly attested for her by any author earlier than Euripides, it seems more likely than not that the Hesiodic *Catalogue* classed her as an Atlantid rather than an Asopid.[58] She was not always classed as an Asopid in archaic literature in any case since the *Cypria*, an early epic in the Trojan cycle, is known to have referred to her as a daughter of Lykourgos.[59]

Antiope, daughter of Nykteus, and her twin sons Zethos and Amphion

While Nykteus was ruling at Thebes, presumably during the childhood of Labdakos, Zeus seduced or raped his daughter ANTIOPE, causing her to become pregnant with twin sons. To escape her father's anger and threats of punishment, Antiope fled to Sicyon on the far side of the Isthmus of Corinth where she received a kind reception from the ruler, Epopeus, who asked her to become his wife. Or in a slightly different account, he ran across her at her hiding-place and took her to Sicyon to become his wife. Nykteus was so upset by this course of events that he soon died or committed suicide; but before his life came to an end, he charged his brother Lykos on oath to take action against Epopeus and Antiope. So Lykos marched against Sicyon, defeated and killed Epopeus, and brought Antiope back to Thebes as a captive. In the course of the journey, when they reached Eleutherai in southern Boeotia, Antiope gave birth to Zethos and Amphion, her twin sons by Zeus, and exposed them on Mt Kithairon. This version of the story was ultimately derived from the lost *Antiope* of Euripides; in that play, Zeus was said to have approached the unfortunate Antiope in the form of a Satyr.[60]

Pausanias records a different version of these events derived from the Sicyonian tradition. While Nykteus was acting as regent for Labdakos, Epopeus abducted Antiope from Thebes (perhaps after being rejected when he had asked to marry her), provoking her father to march against Sicyon. Epopeus gained the upper hand even though he was wounded in battle, inflicting a fatal injury on Nykteus and forcing the Thebans to withdraw. As Nykteus was lying on his deathbed after being carried back to Thebes, he transferred the regency to his brother and asked him to launch an even larger expedition against Sicyon to exact vengeance on Epopeus; and for less obvious reasons, he also asked him to punish Antiope if he could catch her (perhaps because she had colluded in her own abduction). As events turned out, Lykos had no occasion to resort to force, since Epopeus had died in the mean time and his successor was willing to surrender Antiope. She gave birth to her sons at Eleutherai during the return journey as above; it would seem that she had been seduced and rendered pregnant by Zeus before the time of her abduction.[61]

After being recovered from Sicyon, in whatever circumstances, Antiope was held in close confinement by Lykos and his wife DIRKE, and was cruelly mistreated by them for many long years. As for her twin children, ZETHOS and AMPHION, they had been rescued by a herdsman and were being reared by him in his cottage on the slopes of Mt Kithairon. When they were grown up, Antiope finally escaped from her imprisonment, either through the opportunity of the moment or because her fetters miraculously broke apart of their own accord; but although she managed to find her way to the cottage where her sons were living, Zethos mistook her for a runaway slave and turned her away. As chance would have it, Dirke happened to pass by while roaming the hills as a Bacchant and caught sight of Antiope; but although she dragged her away with the intention of killing her, Zethos and Amphion had set off in search of her after learning from their foster-father that she was their mother, and they managed to track her down before Dirke could cause her any serious harm. To avenge Dirke's ill-treatment of their mother, they tied her to a bull by her long hair, causing her to be trampled to death by it; and they then travelled to Thebes to exact vengeance on Lykos too by putting him to death or at least driving him out of the city. Or in another version of the legend, they enticed him out of the city by promising to deliver Antiope to him, intending to put him to death on his arrival; but Hermes restrained them and ordered Lykos to depart into exile. After seizing power in this way by killing or exiling the current ruler of Thebes, Zethos and Amphion consolidated their position by banishing Laios, the legitimate heir in the Kadmeian line.[62]

In addition to a more orthodox account, Hyginus records an odd version of Antiope's story in which she was initially married to her uncle Lykos. He cast her aside, however, after she was raped by Epopeus (in unspecified circumstances), and married Dirke instead. During her new life on her own, Antiope was seduced by Zeus. Presumably after observing the resulting pregnancy, Dirke came to suspect that she had been sleeping with her husband in secret, and ordered her servants to keep her chained up in the dark; but Zeus contrived that she should escape from her chains when her pregnancy reached full term, and she fled to Mt Kithairon, where she gave birth to her twin sons by a crossroads. They survived to take revenge on Dirke as in the usual tradition.[63] In his two accounts of the story, Hyginus talks as though the ruler of Sicyon were called Epaphos rather than Epopeus, but this is plainly an error.

A fragment by Asios, a Spartan epic poet of the archaic period, states that Antiope gave birth to Zethos and Amphion after conceiving them to Zeus and Epopeus. It would seem that the poet considered one child to have been divinely fathered while the other was of purely human birth, as was often believed of the Dioskouroi (or it is conceivable that the poet was merely indicating that Epopeus was their putative father).[64]

The name Dirke was attached to a well-known spring at Thebes and also to a stream that issued from it; a chorus in Euripides' *Bacchae* addresses Dirke, the nymph of these waters, in most flattering terms as a revered daughter of Acheloos.[65] It was surely not a Theban who took the step of applying this honoured name to the evil stepmother of Antiope's legend. Once it was accepted that the sons of Antiope had killed a mortal woman of this name, she came to be regarded as the eponym of the stream; and it came to be suggested accordingly that her body was thrown into the stream after her death, or that her ashes were scattered into it, or indeed that her blood or body was transformed into its waters.[66]

Pausanias offers a brief account of the subsequent life of Antiope. Since Dirke had honoured Dionysos above all other gods, he was greatly angered by her death and drove Antiope mad, causing her to wander through Greece in a state of frenzy. She was eventually rescued from this fate, however, by Phokos, son of Ornytion, who cured her of her madness (presumably by means of purificatory rites), married her and settled down with her at Tithorea in northern Phokis (some ten miles north-east of Delphi). Along with Phokos, son of Aiakos, this present Phokos, who was a grandson of Sisyphos from Corinth, was one of the two eponyms of the province of Phocis; see further on p. 565. The joint grave of Phokos and Antiope could be seen at Tithorea in historical times. Each year, when the sun was in the constellation of the Bull (Taurus), the Tithoreans would attempt to steal some earth from the burial-mound of Zethos and Amphion at Thebes to place it on that of Antiope; for a prophecy had revealed that their crops would thrive if they could do so, while those of the Thebans would fail.[67]

The reign of Zethos and Amphion, and the massacre of the Niobids

After establishing themselves as the joint rulers of Thebes, Zethos and Amphion fortified the city by erecting magnificent walls with seven gates; and in some accounts, they also constructed the lower city on the land beneath the citadel or Kadmeia, which had been settled by Kadmos.[68] These celebrated walls, which figure so prominently in the legend of the Seven against Thebes, may be regarded as products of the mythical imagination, for it is most unlikely that any Mycenaean fortification would have had as many as seven gates; such an extravagant provision would merely weaken the defences, and there is nothing in the topography of the site to indicate any reason for it. Each of the brothers contributed as best he could to the building-work, Zethos relying on his practical skills and brute strength while Amphion exploited his skills as a musician by singing so enchantingly to his lyre that the stones followed him to their proper positions of their own accord. The musical powers of Amphion are described in similar terms to those of Orpheus (see p. 551). This was probably a fairly ancient feature of his legend (even if Homer makes no mention of it when referring to Zethos and Amphion) since the *Europeia*, an early epic ascribed to the Corinthian poet Eumelos, stated that Hermes taught Amphion to play the lyre before any other mortal, and that animals and stones would follow after him when he sang to it. The Hesiodic *Catalogue* apparently mentioned that he made use of this power during the building of the walls, as is stated unequivocally in a fragment from Euripides. Most subsequent authors agree that he acquired his lyre from Hermes (although Pherecydes stated that it was presented to him by the Muses, and some later sources suggest that it was given to him by Apollo or Zeus); some explained that he earned this privilege by raising the first altar to the gods.[69] Zethos was traditionally presented as being of opposite character to his brother, as a bluff and practical man who devoted himself to cattle-breeding and virile pursuits. Euripides developed the contrast in a lost play of his, the *Antiope*, by portraying the brothers as proponents of two opposing ways of life, the practical and the contemplative, and by having them debate the value of each in a more or less philosophical manner.[70]

According to the standard tradition in classical and later times, as followed in the preceding narrative, Kadmos founded Thebes in the first place by building the upper city on the acropolis, while Zethos and Amphion became its second founders by fortifying (and perhaps constructing) the lower city while the legitimate Kadmeian heir was temporarily excluded. A pattern of this kind might seem to suggest that there were two separate foundation myths that needed to be reconciled; and it is in fact the case that there are accounts from the early tradition in which Zethos and Amphion are presented as the original founders. Odysseus states in the *Odyssey* that Antiope told him in the Underworld that 'she had slept in the arms of Zeus himself, and had given birth to two sons, Zethos and Amphion, who first founded the seat of seven-gated Thebes and fortified it with walls, for they could not live in spacious Thebes without the defence of walls, mighty though they were'. The early mythographer Pherecydes expands on the latter point by saying that the brothers built the walls to protect themselves against some specific enemies, the Phlegyans (a mythical people of Central Greece who were notorious for their violence and rapacity, see p. 560); the city was conquered nonetheless after their death by Eurymachos, king of the Phlegyans, who laid waste to it, leaving it deserted until Kadmos arrived at a later period and refounded it. It will be noted that this account reconciles the two foundation myths, but by adopting the opposite strategy to that generally adopted in the later tradition, by making Kadmos the second founder.[71] The *Odyssey* classes Antiope as a daughter of Asopos rather than of Lykos (as would probably have been the case with Pherecydes also); on this genealogical point and its implications, see further on pp. 302–3.

Amphion married NIOBE, the daughter of Tantalos from Asia Minor, who bore him numerous sons and daughters, from seven to ten of each in most accounts. As has already been mentioned (see p. 307), Niobe was so proud of her large family that she boasted that she had many more children than the goddess Leto, who had two alone, Artemis and Apollo. Leto was so offended that she called on her children to exact vengeance, and they proceeded to kill all the Niobids, Artemis shooting the female children and Apollo the males. In her grief at their death, Niobe left her husband and returned to her original homeland in Lydia, where she was turned to stone (see pp. 307 and 502).[72] Amphion was also said to have met his death as a consequence of these events, either because he was killed in the course of the massacre, or because he stabbed himself in his sorrow, or because he was shot by Apollo while he was trying to storm the god's temple (evidently in anger at the fate of his children).[73]

According to one tradition, Zethos married Thebe, a daughter of the river-god Asopos (see p. 536) and the eponym of Thebes;[74] or in another account of more ancient origin, he was married to AEDON (Nightingale), daughter of Pandareos. Pherecydes tells how Aedon grew jealous of Amphion for having so many children while she had only two, Itylos and Nais, and accidentally killed her son Itylos one night while trying to kill Alalkomeneus, a son of Amphion. When Zeus sent Poine (Vengeance personified) against her, she prayed to be transformed into a bird, and Zeus turned her into a nightingale. This story is cited in explanation of a passage in the *Odyssey* that remarks that the daughter of Pandareos, the nightingale of the greenwood (*chlōreis aēdōn*), sings sweetly in the springtime as she laments for her child Itylos, son of Zethos, whom she had killed accidentally with a sword. The origin of the nightingale and its sorrowful song was commonly explained in the subsequent tradition by the Attic legend of Tereus and Prokne (see p. 368). Pausanias reports that Zethos died of grief after hearing that his son had been murdered by his wife.[75]

Two of the children of Niobe and Amphion, a son Amyklas and daughter Meliboia, were sometimes said to have survived the massacre. This tradition is first reported by Telesilla, an Argive poetess of the fifth century BC; according to Pausanias, they were spared because they prayed to Leto for mercy, and they settled in Argos afterwards, founding the city's sanctuary of Leto in gratitude for their escape. Meliboia had been so frightened that she had turned pale (*chlōris*) from fear, and she remained so ever afterwards and therefore came to be known as CHLORIS; a statue of her could be seen beside that of Leto in the goddess' sanctuary in Argos.[76] Under her new name of Chloris, she won the foot-race at the first Heraian Games (the women's games at Olympia) after they were founded by Hippodameia as a thank-offering for her marriage to Pelops.[77] This Chloris should not be confused (as she occasionally was in antiquity) with the Chloris, daughter of Amphion, who married Neleus at Pylos; as the *Odyssey* and a fragment from the Hesiodic *Catalogue* make clear, the wife of Neleus was fathered by a different Amphion, a son of Iasos or Iasios who ruled at Orchomenos rather than at Thebes.[78]

Laios recovers his rightful throne, and exposes his son Oedipus

After the death of Zethos and Amphion, the legitimate ruler, LAIOS, son of Labdakos, was able to return to Thebes to reclaim his inheritance. He had been living in Elis in the north-western Peloponnese in the mean time, as a guest of Pelops, king of Pisa. A single story is recorded in connection with his exile. While teaching the art of chariot-driving to CHRYSIPPOS, a young illegitimate son of Pelops, he conceived a passion for him and carried him off with the intention of seducing him; but Chrysippos repulsed him and killed himself with his sword out of shame.[79] Some explained the subsequent misfortunes of the Labdakids by saying that Pelops cursed the entire family on hearing of the fate of Chrysippos; and in one account at least, the Sphinx was said to have been sent against Thebes by the marriage-goddess Hera to punish the Thebans for failing to take action against Laios.[80] This tale of the abduction of Chrysippos was recounted in some form in the lost *Chrysippos* of Euripides; but there was also a conflicting tale which was at least as old, and probably more so, in which Chrysippos was said to have been murdered by two of his half-brothers (see p. 505). Some authors tried to reconcile the two traditions by suggesting that Pelops recovered his lost son by force and brought him back to Pisa, where he was subsequently murdered by members of his own family.[81]

Laios married IOKASTE (Jocasta in Latinized form), who belonged to a side-branch of the Theban royal family as a daughter of Menoikeus and sister of Kreon. She was destined to become both the mother and the wife of Oedipus. The *Odyssey* diverges from the usual tradition, however, by naming Oedipus' mother as Epikaste.[82] When Iokaste initially failed to produce any children, Laios consulted the Delphic oracle, which warned him to abandon any thought of fathering a child since he would be killed by his son if he should have one. Although he kept out of his wife's bed for a time, he had intercourse with her one night while he was flushed with wine, causing her to conceive the fateful son. Soon after the child was born, Laios handed him over to a shepherd to be exposed, first thrusting a spike through his feet to ensure that he would not be recovered and reared, hence his name of OEDIPUS (properly OIDIPOUS in Greek) or 'Swell-foot'. In the most familiar account of these events, the shepherd (sometimes named as Euphorbos or Phorbos) was told to place him out to die on Mt Kithairon on the southern borders of Boeotia. Kithairon was also used as summer pasture by the Corinthians, and the shepherd felt such pity for the child that he handed him over to one of his Corinthian colleagues, who took him away to his master Polybos, the king of Corinth. Since Polybos and his wife Merope (or Periboia, or Medousa) had no children of their own, they decided to raise Oedipus as their own son. Or in a slightly different version, Oedipus was exposed on the mountain as Laios had ordered, but was discovered and rescued by some Corinthians, who took him to their king.[83] According to a less favoured tradition, Laios sent the child out to sea in a chest, but he was washed ashore safely at Corinth, or else at Sicyon, the next main city to the west. Oedipus was then reared in the royal household as usual; according to Hyginus, who does not specify the location, the queen, Periboia, discovered the child while she was washing clothes by the shore.[84]

There were also versions in which Oedipus was conveyed to Sicyon by a herdsman or shepherd after being exposed on Kithairon.[85] The king who reared him is named as Polybos whether he ruled at Corinth or Sicyon. The Sicyonian Polybos is described as a son of Hermes by Chthonophyle, daughter of Sikyon,[86] and is also known in another connection as the king of Sikyon who offered a home to Adrastos, king of Argos, during the period of his exile (see p. 332). It seems likely that the foster-father of Oedipus was this Sicyonian in the original tradition, and that the Corinthian version is secondary; for no genealogy is offered for the Corinthian Polybos, nor can any proper place be found for him in the early Corinthian royal line (which was descended from Sisyphos, see pp. 430ff). The name of Oedipus' foster-mother is more variable; Sophocles calls her Merope, Apollodorus and Hyginus call her Periboia, and other sources Medousa or Antiochis.[87] Although Polybos is fully aware that the child is a foundling in Sophocles' account, the queen sometimes passes him off as a child of her own marriage without her husband being aware of his true origin.[88]

Oedipus kills his father and wins the Theban throne by solving the riddle of the Sphinx

When Oedipus came of age, he set off for Delphi to enquire about his origins. According to Sophocles in *Oedipus the King*, he became concerned about the matter after he was taunted at a banquet by a drunken guest who accused him of not being a true son of Polybos. Although the king and queen tried to reassure him, the rumours persisted and the matter continued to trouble him until he decided to consult the Delphic oracle without the knowledge of his putative parents. The god at Delphi offered no response to him on the point in question, but revealed instead that he was destined to kill his father, and then to marry his own mother and father children by her. Assuming that the oracle was referring to Polybos and Merope, he resolved to stay away from his former home forever, and set off in the direction of Thebes. As he was approaching a point on his route where three roads ran together, he happened to meet an old man who was travelling by cart in the opposite direction accompanied by five attendants. When the herald who was proceeding at the head of the party tried to force him off the road, Oedipus struck back at him and continued on his way; but as he was passing the cart, the old man hit him on the head with his ox-goad. Not realizing that the stranger was his own father, Oedipus reacted by dealing him a fatal blow with his staff, and then set out to kill the other members of the group (although one of them escaped undetected). Without discovering anything further about his victims, he then resumed his journey and travelled on to Thebes.[89]

In the rather different account in Euripides' *Phoenician Women*, Oedipus encountered Laios at a point where their paths ran together as both of them were heading for Delphi, Oedipus to enquire about his parentage and Laios to ask whether his exposed son was truly dead. Laios' charioteer ordered Oedipus to stand out of the way of the king, but the proud youth ignored him and killed the old man when his feet were trampled by the advancing chariot-horses. He then seized the chariot and drove it back to Corinth to present it to Polybos, apparently without ever reaching Delphi.[90] This version in which both parties were travelling in the same direction may well have been the earlier form of the story, for it would explain why the confrontation took place at a place where roads ran together. The incident was supposed to have occurred at a site in Phocis called the Cleft Way (*schistē hodos*), where the road from Lebadeia (and thence from Thebes) was joined by a more northerly road from Daulis before ascending through a mountain-valley to Delphi.[91]

Since Laios had no children apart from the son whom he had exposed, the throne passed to the senior member of another branch of the royal family, KREON, son of Menoikeus. The Thebans began to be troubled soon afterwards by a fearsome monster, the SPHINX (Throttler), a winged creature with the body of a lion and the head of a woman, of a type familiar enough in Near Eastern art. Hesiod classes her as a child of Orthos and Chimaira (see p. 63), and refers to her as 'the deadly Phix that brought destruction to the Kadmeians'; in view of Hesiod's Boeotian origin and later reports that remark that the monster sat on Mt Phikion outside Thebes, it would appear that Phix was a local Boeotian form of her name. According to her usual legend, she would set a riddle for passers-by and would kill them if they were unable to solve it, but was fated to meet her own death if anyone should provide the correct solution. There is reason to suppose, however, that she may simply have carried away young Thebans without posing any question in the earliest tradition. Sophocles is the first author to state unequivocally that she posed a riddle (although this already seems to be indicated in a brief fragment from Pindar).[92] Since it is characteristic of local monsters of this kind to appear on the scene without need for explanation, it is hardly surprising that there was no settled tradition on why the Sphinx should have arrived to plague Thebes. Some mythographers, as we have seen, connected her arrival with Laios' abduction of Chrysippos (see p. 307); in that case she was sent by Hera, but there was also an account in which she was sent by Dionysos for some unstated reason (perhaps because Pentheus had opposed his rites).[93]

When the Sphinx proceeded to kill one Theban after another, including the king's son Haimon in some accounts,[94] Kreon finally grew so desperate that he offered the kingdom and the hand of the former queen, Iokaste, to anyone who could rid the city of this terror. Either in the hope of winning this reward, or by chance while he was seeking a new home in exile, Oedipus now arrived at Thebes and provided the correct answer to the riddle of the Sphinx. This riddle, which has been recorded in comparable forms in many parts of the world, asked what single being is four-footed,

Figure 9.1   Oedipus and the Sphinx. Red-figure kylix c. 470 BC, attributed to the
Oedipus painter. The Vatican Collection: Museo Gregoriano Etrusco.

two-footed and three-footed. In its traditional form, as recorded in some hexameter
verses which probably originated in Attic tragedy (or possibly early epic), it ran as
follows:

> There is a being on earth that is four-footed, two-footed and three-footed, yet
> has a single voice; and of all beings that move on the ground or through the
> air or sea, it alone changes its form; and when it moves with the support of
> the most feet, then is the speed of its limbs at the weakest.[95]

Oedipus inferred that the riddle refers to man, who crawls on all fours as an infant, walks upright on two legs when grown up, and employs a stick as a third foot in old age. When her secret was revealed to all and sundry by the newcomer, the Sphinx took her own life by hurling herself from the Theban acropolis or from a cliff outside the city, or else surrendered herself to Oedipus to be killed.[96]

The unholy marriage of Oedipus and his downfall

In the account familiar from tragedy and the later tradition, Oedipus claimed IOKASTE, the wife of the late king, along with the kingdom as his reward for ridding Thebes of the Sphinx, and lived with her for a long period, fathering two daughters by her, Antigone and Ismene, and two quarrelsome sons, Polyneikes and Eteokles; but when the truth about his birth and his father's death finally came to be revealed, Iokaste hanged herself, and Oedipus blinded himself and then abidcated the throne to depart into exile.[97] Early epic accounts seem to have followed a different pattern, however, in which Oedipus continued to rule at Thebes after the revelations (here made quite soon after his accession) and subsequently married a second wife who became the mother of his children. Odysseus refers to his continuing rule in the *Odyssey* when describing how he saw the dead mother of Oedipus in Hades:

> I saw the mother of Oidipodes, the beautiful Epikaste, who did a dreadful deed in the ignorance of her mind by marrying her own son, who wedded her after killing his father; but the gods soon made these things known to men. But he, through the cruel counsels of the gods, reigned on over the Kadmeians in lovely Thebes suffering woes, while she went down to the house of Hades, the mighty keeper of the gates, fastening the deadly noose to the roof of the lofty hall in the stress of her grief; but to him she left behind many sorrows, all that a mother's Erinyes (Furies) can bring to pass.[98]

The *Iliad* reports, furthermore, that funeral games were held for Oedipus at Thebes after he had fallen (apparently in battle),[99] which would indicate that he was an honoured ruler at the time of his death. Since Oedipus continued to rule at Thebes, the sorrows that are ascribed to him in the *Odyssey* could hardly be related to any blinding or exile as in the later tradition; one should perhaps suppose that the poet was referring above all to the hostility that arose between Oedipus and his sons, which is known to have been a central feature of his story in early epic (see below). He would doubtless have been troubled by regret and conscience too. By saying that the gods soon (*aphar*) made his transgression known,[100] Homer certainly seems to indicate that this must have happened fairly swiftly before Oedipus would have had time to father several children by the incestuous marriage. In the *Oedipodeia*, the relevant epic in the Theban cycle, Oedipus took a second wife after the revelations, marrying Euryganeia, daughter of Hyperphas, who bore him the four children who are borne to him by Iokaste in tragic and later sources; this may well have been the accepted tradition in early epic.[101]

Aeschylus' *Seven against Thebes* is the earliest surviving source for the story that Oedipus fathered his four children by his own mother, and that he blinded himself after discovering that he had killed his father and married his mother.[102] This was the third play in a trilogy first produced in 467 BC, of which the preceding *Laios* and *Oedipus* (which would have given a full account of the hero's career) are now lost; it is not known whether Oedipus went into exile in Aeschylus' version (most likely not). The dominant account of the fall of Oedipus was established once and for all in a tragedy that was composed half a century or more later, Sophocles' *Oedipus the King*, which related the story as follows.

After Oedipus had reigned at Thebes as a highly respected sovereign for many years, the city was struck by a terrible plague, and he dispatched Kreon to Delphi to enquire about a cure; and when the oracle declared that the epidemic would be brought to an end if the murderer of Laios were killed or at least expelled, the king set to work to discover who this might be. He publicly cursed the guilty man, and proclaimed that anyone who could help to identify him should step forward, and ordered furthermore that no one should offer him shelter or have anything to do with him, whoever he might be.[103] When he then interrogated Teiresias, the seer tried to keep silent initially, but indicated under pressure that Oedipus himself was the man who was polluting the land, and that he was therefore searching for himself. At this point, however, his words made no impression on Oedipus, who simply accused him of having accepted bribes from Kreon to jeopardize his position.[104] On hearing of this, Kreon came to the palace to protest, and became embroiled in a bitter argument with the king; but Iokaste persuaded them to separate after overhearing their raised voices, and questioned Oedipus about the cause of the quarrel after Kreon had left. When she was told that Teiresias had accused her husband of having committed the murder, she tried to reassure him by arguing that prophecies are not to be trusted, at least to judge by the oracle that had been delivered to Laios about his son (whom she naturally supposed to be dead), and by asserting furthermore that Oedipus could hardly have been responsible for the death of Laios, since he had been killed abroad by brigands at a place where three roads ran together. Far from being reassured, however, Oedipus was alarmed by what she said about the crossroads, for he himself had once killed an aged man at a crossroads. Beginning to suspect for the first time that there might be something in the seer's words, he questioned Iokaste further, only to find that his fears were confirmed. On learning that she had been informed of the details of the incident by an attendant of Laios who had escaped and was now living in the countryside outside the city, Oedipus ordered that he should be fetched.[105]

While this was being arranged, a messenger arrived from Corinth to report that the citizens had invited Oedipus to rule over them as the successor of his putative father, Polybos, who had died of sickness and old age during his absence. If Polybos had really been his father, this meant that Oedipus could not have been guilty of the death of his father, and he initially found some relief in that thought; but it so happened that the messenger was the shepherd who had first brought him to Polybos as a baby after receiving him from the Theban shepherd who had been sent to expose him; and when this was revealed by the Corinthian, Iokaste realized who her husband must be, and went off into the palace on her own to kill herself.[106] It happened that the attendant of Laios who had been summoned by the king was the very person who had taken him out for exposure, and when he confirmed the truth of the

Corinthian's words on his arrival, Oedipus was at last compelled to recognize the truth about his origins and about his subsequent life. He rushed into the palace to discover that Iokaste had hanged herself; and tearing the brooches from her clothing, one in each hand, he gouged out his eyes with the brooch-pins.[107]

There were inevitably tragic and later accounts that differed from that of Sophocles. In Euripides' *Phoenician Women*, for instance, Iokaste is still alive at the time of the first Theban War, and finally kills herself after her two sons have killed themselves in the course of that conflict.[108] Although little has survived of the same author's *Oedipus*, it is reported that Oedipus was blinded by the servants of Laios in that play, apparently after it was discovered that he had killed Laios but before it became known that he was the son of the former king (for he is referred to the son of Polybos in a fragment preserved in this connection).[109] Hyginus records a version in which Oedipus' foster-mother Periboia came to Thebes after the death of he husband and revealed that Oedipus had been no more than an adoptive son; and when the man who had exposed him then recognized from the scars on his feet and ankles that he was the son of Laios, he blinded himself with the brooches from his mother's dress as in Sophocles' account, and departed into exile with his daughter Antigone.[110]

A rather different account of Oedipus' downfall which may perhaps be of early origin is recorded in the scholia to Euripides' *Phoenician Women*; it is ascribed to Peisandros, here apparently the Hellenistic mythographer of that name rather than the epic poet. After killing Laios and his attendants at the Cleft Way as in the usual story, Oedipus buried them at once in their clothing, removing Laios' sword and belt (*zōstēr*, warrior's belt) to keep them for his own use. When Iokaste had become his wife, he happened to pass through the same area with her after performing some sacrifices on Mt Kithairon, and he told her of everything that had happened there, pointing to the relevant spot and showing her the belt. Although Iokaste realized from what he said that he must have been the man who had killed her former husband, she kept quiet for the moment in spite of her distress, for she was not yet aware of the worst of the matter, that her husband was also her son. This was revealed at a later time when an aged horse-breeder arrived at Thebes to seek a reward for having rescued the young Oedipus many years before; he explained that he had discovered the exposed child and had brought him to Merope, queen of Sicyon, producing his swaddling-clothes as proof together with the pins that had been driven through his ankles. Iokaste killed herself after hearing this, and Oedipus blinded himself; but he subsequently took a new wife, Euryganeia, who bore him his four children.[111] Since the revelation occurred before Iokaste had had time to bear any children to Oedipus, who fathered his children by his second marriage, and since the narrative itself moreover seems ill-suited to a tragedy, some have argued that this account may have originated in early epic.

The death of Oedipus and his final resting-place

There were three traditions about the final resting-place of Oedipus. In early epic accounts in which he remained at Thebes after his origins were revealed, he apparently received a splendid funeral at Thebes, as is indicated in the *Iliad* and was doubtless also the case in the Hesiodic *Catalogue*;[112] while in Sophocles' *Oedipus at Kolonos* and the standard later tradition, he died in exile and was buried at Kolonos just outside Athens, where a heroic shrine was erected to him in historical times; and there was also a further tradition that claimed that he was buried at the Boeotian town of Eteonos. The familiar story that he met his death at Kolonos after long wanderings with his daughter Antigone first appears in the last decade of the fifth century in Sophocles' *Oedipus at Kolonos* (or perhaps slightly earlier in Euripides' *Phoenician Women*, if the relevant passage is not part of a later addition). But it seems likely that Sophocles was appealing to an existing tradition (even if it was not a particularly old one) when he placed Oedipus' death at Kolonos, especially since the story had some basis in cult; thus in 411 BC, when the Athenians defeated some Thebans in a cavalry engagement near Kolonos, they believed that they had benefited from the protection of the deified Oedipus.[113]

The plot of Sophocles' *Oedipus at Kolonos* turns on three oracles. Oedipus has received an oracle telling him that he will at last come to rest when he finds shelter in a sanctuary of the Semnai (Awful Goddesses, i.e. Erinyes, Furies); Kreon, who is now ruling at Thebes after having expelled Oedipus, has learned from the Delphic oracle that Oedipus must be buried at Thebes if the city is to be secure, while Athens will prevail over Thebes if he is buried in Attica; and third, Oedipus' son Polyneikes has been told that he will prevail in his conflict with his brother Eteokles if he has his father's support. The play begins as Oedipus arrives at Kolonos with his daughter Antigone and sits down on a rock in the sanctuary of the Eumenides (Kindly Ones, i.e. Erinyes). Although he is warned by a local man that this is forbidden ground, he recognizes that he has found the place foretold in the oracle and is determined not to move.[114] His other daughter, Ismene, arrives soon afterwards to tell him that Eteokles has driven Polyneikes into exile, and that Kreon will be coming to fetch Oedipus back to Thebes for the reasons indicated in the above-mentioned oracle.[115] In response to a summons from the elders of Kolonos, Theseus, the king of Athens, then appears on the scene, and responds sympathetically to Oedipus' appeals, offering him sanctuary as requested.[116] Kreon appears next with a group of followers, and initially assumes a conciliatory tone in the hope of persuading Oedipus to return with him voluntarily; but he soon resorts to force when Oedipus greets him with scorn, first arresting the daughters of Oedipus with the help of his guards and then approaching Oedipus himself. Theseus is alerted, however, by the loud protests of the elders of Kolonos (who form the chorus) and comes to the rescue of his guests.[117] Oedipus' final visitor is his son Polyneikes, who comes to ask for his blessing before attacking Eteokles at Thebes; but Oedipus blames his sons for having failed to save him from being exiled, and so curses Polyneikes instead, praying that his attack may fail and that he and his brother may kill one another in the fighting (as will duly occur).[118] On hearing three peals of thunder, Oedipus recognizes that the time has come for him to die. He tells Theseus not to disclose the place of his death, and to transmit the secret only within the royal line, saying that his tomb will protect Athens against the Thebans if his instructions are followed. Now striding forth confidently without need of a guide, Oedipus sets off toward the appointed place accompanied by his daughters and Theseus.[119] A messenger reveals something of the mysterious events that followed, reporting that Oedipus was summoned by a divine voice as he was saying farewell to his daughters, and that he then withdrew to a place apart and vanished from human sight in some wondrous manner that was known to Theseus alone.[120]

In a rather different account, perhaps also originating in tragedy, Oedipus came to the hill of Hippios at Kolonos after being expelled from Thebes by Kreon, and sat down as a suppliant in the temple of Demeter and Athena Poliouchos. Kreon tried to remove him by force, but Theseus came to his aid; and when he was dying of old age, he asked Theseus to ensure that no Theban should be shown the site of his grave.[121] For what it is worth, Pausanias was told at Kolonos that the bones of Theseus had been brought from Thebes; it is just possible that this represents an earlier stage in the development of his Athenian legend.[122]

In connection with the tradition that represented him as having been buried at Eteonos, it was said that his friends had wanted to bury him at Thebes, but took him to an obscure place called Keos in some other part of Boeotia when this was forbidden to them. Since the local people blamed his presence for troubles that afflicted them thereafter, his friends subsequently removed his remains to Eteonos on the slopes of Mt Kithairon. They reburied him there at dead of night without realizing that they were in the precinct of Demeter; and when the people of Eteonos came to know of this, they sought the advice of the oracle of Apollo, which instructed them not to move this suppliant of the goddess. The relevant tomb could be recognized by an inscription.[123]

THE THEBAN WARS AND THEIR AFTERMATH

Polyneikes, son of Oedipus, quarrels with his brother Eteokles and departs to Argos

POLYNEIKES and ETEOKLES, the two sons of Oedipus, quarrelled over the succession after the exile or death of their father (or when he became too old to rule, or when they were due to take over from Kreon who had been ruling as regent until they came of age). The resulting conflict proved to be disastrous for both of them, for they were destined to kill one another when Polyneikes tried to settle the matter by marching against Thebes with foreign allies from Argos. The quarrel also brought disaster to Thebes itself; for although it remained unconquered during this first Theban War, the sons of the defeated Argive leaders launched a second expedition ten years later and captured the city, which never recovered its former strength and glory. The first expedition was known as that of the Seven because its leader appointed seven of the bravest participants to serve as champions, and the second as that of the Epigonoi (i.e. the after-born or successors).

Although disputes could easily arise between rival heirs in the absence of any strict rules of primogeniture, the fundamental cause of the quarrel between Eteokles and Polyneikes was usually said to have been a curse that was uttered against them by their father. In the *Thebais*, indeed, in the epic cycle, Oedipus cursed his sons twice over, on the first occasion because they had angered him by serving him at a silver table that had belonged to Kadmos and by passing wine to him in a golden cup of the same origin, even though he had expressly ordered them not to do so (presumably because these heirlooms reminded him of the crime that he had committed against his father). So he prayed that they should not divide their patrimony in friendship, but that war and hatred should always be their lot; and when they angered him once again by sending him a haunch of meat as his portion at a sacrifice rather than the more honourable shoulder-piece (whether by negligence or design), he cursed them yet more grievously by praying that they should die by one another's hand.[124] In tragedy and later sources, other explanations are offered for his cursing of his sons. Thus in Sophocles' *Oedipus at Kolonos*, as we have seen, he cursed them to mutual destruction for not having lifted a hand to help him when he had been expelled from Thebes by Kreon; or in other accounts, he cursed them for having shut him up in a dungeon after his unwitting transgressions had been revealed.[125]

The stories that were put forward to explain how the feud between the brothers initially developed fall into three main patterns. In an account ascribed to Hellanicus, Eteokles allowed Polyneikes to choose whether he preferred to become the new king of Thebes or to take what he wanted from the family treasures and settle elsewhere. He chose to take the two divine heirlooms, the necklace and robe of Harmonia, but later broke the agreement by trying to seize the Theban throne in addition.[126] In a comparable account by the early lyric poet Stesichorus, the mother of the two princes tried to arrange a just settlement through a division of the inheritance, proposing that one of them should depart with his father's flocks and gold while the other remained behind to rule at Thebes; so they cast lots, and when that of Polyneikes came out first, he departed with the possessions in accordance with the terms of the draw.[127] Here again we may suppose that Polyneikes was to blame for the subsequent war; and since his name means 'Much Strife' while that of his brother means 'True Glory', it is reasonable to assume that he was originally thought to have been the guilty party. In the second main version of the story, as ascribed to Pherecydes, Eteokles expelled his brother from Thebes by force, and Polyneikes therefore had some justification in resorting to force on his own account.[128] Or in a third version, which first appears in Euripides' *Phoenician Women*, the two brothers agreed to rule in alternate years, but Eteokles refused to surrender the throne to Polyneikes after occupying it for the first year, giving him ample reason to feel aggrieved. This was the account that was generally favoured in the later tradition.[129]

Whatever the exact circumstances of his exile, Polyneikes travelled across the Isthmus of Corinth to the city of Argos, where he married a daughter of the king and gained support from him for an expedition against his native city. Euripides provides the earliest surviving account of the events that led up to his marriage. After reaching Argos at night, he sought shelter in the porch of the palace, but soon quarrelled and came to blows with another man who arrived there with the same intent, namely TYDEUS, son of Oineus, a violent Aetolian prince who had been exiled from his homeland for murder (see p. 418). The noise was sufficient to awaken the king, ADRASTOS, son of Talaos, who hurried down to investigate. On observing the ferocious brawl, he was reminded of a mysterious oracle that he had received from Apollo ordering him to marry his daughters to a lion and a boar; since the two men resembled wild animals fighting over a den, he welcomed them into his palace in spite of the unfortunate circumstances of their meeting, and offered his daughter ARGEIA to Polyneikes and his other daughter, Deipyle, to Tydeus.[130] He promised to restore them to their native lands furthermore, beginning with Polyneikes.[131] Some later authors explained his interpretation of the oracle in other ways, saying that he recognized the two men as the lion and boar because Polyneikes had a lionskin on his shoulders and Tydeus a boar's hide, or because they had images of the foreparts of such animals on their shields (referring to the Sphinx and Calydonian boar respectively).[132]

Pausanias records an account of Polyneikes' exile and marriage that follows a quite different pattern. Polyneikes departed into exile initially while Oedipus was still on the throne, in the hope that this would enable him to escape his father's curses, and he married Argeia at this time; but Eteokles sent for him after the death of Oedipus and he came back to Thebes (presumably with his wife). The two brothers quarrelled, however, and Polyneikes went into exile for a second time, and now asked his father-in-law to help him to seize power at Thebes.[133] This account may quite possibly have been derived from early epic. It is likely in any case that Argeia was married to Polyneikes before the death of Oedipus in the Hesiodic *Catalogue*, since she is reported to have attended the funeral of Oedipus,[134] and it is hard to imagine why she should have done so if she had not married into the family.

Adrastos appoints seven champions for an expedition against Thebes; Amphiaraos and Eriphyle

Adrastos lost no time in gathering together a sizeable army to attack Thebes. In tragedy and the later tradition at least, he appointed seven champions to lead the assault, one for each of the seven gates in the walls of the city. It is not known whether these champions, who were known as the Seven against Thebes, already figured in early epic; Pindar may have been following the epic tradition in stating that the Argive dead were burned on seven funeral pyres,[135] but this does not necessarily imply that there were seven champions (especially if it is remembered that two of the usual champions, Amphiaraos and Kapaneus, could not have been cremated, for reasons that will become apparent presently).

Most sources agree on the names of at least six of the Seven.[136] Three of the most important of them belonged to Argive royal lines, namely **Adrastos** himself, who was descended from Bias, **Amphiaraos**, son of Oikles, who was descended from Melampous, and **Kapaneus**, son of Hipponoos, who belonged to the old Inachid ruling line as a descendant of Proitos. To these we can add the two outsiders **Polyneikes** and **Tydeus**, and also **Parthenopaios**, who was usually regarded as a son of Atalanta from Arcadia (but sometimes as a son of Talaos and brother of Adrastos). As for the remaining champion, he was variously named as **Mekisteus**, son of Talaos, **Eteoklos**, son of Iphis, or **Hippomedon**, son of Aristomachos; but these figures, all of them minor members of Argive royal lines, were so colourless as to be practically interchangeable. If any of the usual champions were omitted for some reason, more than one of these lesser figures could be included in the list. Thus in Aeschylus' *Seven against Thebes*, in which Adrastos does not include himself among the champions (see p. 321), both Eteoklos and Hippomedon are numbered among the Seven; or additional Argives could be included from among the lesser men if Polyneikes and Tydeus were excluded as foreigners.

AMPHIARAOS, the most formidable of the men who were selected as champions by Adrastos, was a gifted seer like his forebear Melampous and realized that the expedition was doomed to disaster. Foreknowing that none of the leaders would return alive apart from Adrastos, he initially refused to take part and tried to discourage the others. Anxious to find a solution to this difficulty, Polyneikes sought the advice of a prominent Argive, Iphis, son of Alektor (see p. 334), who told him that the seer could be forced to take part if his wife ERIPHYLE desired it; for Amphiaraos had once quarrelled with Adrastos over the kingdom, even driving him into exile for a time (see p. 332), and when the pair had finally settled their differences, Adrastos had given his sister Eriphyle to Amphiaraos on the sworn agreement that they should accept her decision if they should ever quarrel in the future. So

Polyneikes approached her in secret and promised her a splendid treasure, the divine necklace of Harmonia, if she would order her husband to march off against Thebes as Adrastos wished. In one version at least, Amphiaraos had foreseen trouble from this quarter and had specifically forbidden her to accept any gift from Polyneikes, but the temptation proved irresistible nevertheless. Eriphyle repaid the bribe by sending her husband to his death, so becoming a byword for treachery. Setting off under compulsion, and knowing that Eriphyle had allowed herself to be corrupted, Amphiaraos ordered his son Alkmaion (and his other son Amphilochos too in one version) to put her to death when he grew up, and to mount a second expedition against Thebes at some future time.[137]

The *Iliad* reports that Tydeus and Polyneikes visited Mycenae before the war in the hope of enlisting further allies; but although the Mycenaeans initially agreed to provide a force of troops, Zeus deterred them by sending bad omens.[138]

The death of Opheltes and embassy of Tydeus

As Adrastos and his army were marching toward the Isthmus, they passed through Nemea in the northern Argolid, where they became involved in a strange incident that led to the founding of the Nemean Games. The city was ruled at that time by Lykourgos, son of Pheres, an immigrant from Thessaly (see p. 426), who had appointed HYPSIPYLE, the former queen of Lemnos, to act as nursemaid to his infant son OPHELTES. As we will see, the Lemnian women had conspired together to kill all their menfolk, but Hypsipyle had broken the agreement by sparing her aged father Thoas (see p. 384); and when the other women had discovered this, they had sold her into slavery. Or in another version, she had escaped abroad after her action had been discovered, but had then been captured by pirates who had sold her to Lykourgos.[139] Adrastos and his companions now encountered her in Nemea and asked her to show them the way to a spring, for they were thirsty after their long journey (or else needed water for a sacrifice). So she placed the infant Opheltes on a bed of wild parsley and led them to the water. Although an oracle had warned that Opheltes should never be placed on the ground until he could walk, she thought that he would be safe because he would not actually be in contact with the ground. On returning from the spring, however, she found that the child had been killed by a snake. Adrastos and his followers killed the snake, and interceded with Lykourgos on Hypsipyle's behalf; and they then gave little Opheltes a magnificent funeral, renaming him Archemoros (Beginning of Doom) because Amphiaraos declared that his death was an evil sign that indicated that many members of the army would lose their lives in the forthcoming conflict. They also held funeral games in honour of the dead child, so founding the Nemean Games, at which the judges wore dark clothing as a sign of mourning and the victors were awarded a crown of wild parsley. As for Hypsipyle, she was finally rescued from her captivity by Euneos and Thoas, the two sons whom she had borne to Jason.[140]

Before launching his assault against Thebes, Adrastos sent Tydeus ahead to the city to see whether the dispute could be settled in Polyneikes' favour by diplomatic means. According to the *Iliad*, Tydeus set off after the army had passed some distance on its way and had reached the thickly reeded Asopos (presumably the river of that name in southern Boeotia). Apollodorus states that he set off from Kithairon, in much the same area, while Diodorus offers a different version in which Adrastos sent him from Argos before the start of the expedition. As the story is recounted in the *Iliad*, Tydeus found the Kadmeians (i.e. Thebans) feasting in the palace of Eteokles on his arrival, and challenged them all to contests, doubtless in wrestling or the like, which he won easily with a little help from Athena. Angered by the humiliation, the Thebans arranged for fifty young men to ambush him during his return journey, but he killed all of them with the sole exception of Maion, son of Haimon and grandson of Kreon, whom he spared in response to signs from the gods. As in the case of the similar embassy before the Trojan War (see p. 454), the mission failed in its main purpose.[141]

The fighting at Thebes and fate of the Seven

Although we have almost no direct information on how the fighting at Thebes was described in the early epic tradition, there seems to have been general agreement from an early period on the fate of the main Argive champions.[142] After an initial

Figure 9.2 Tydeus devours Melanippos' brains. Terracotta relief from the pediment of Temple A at Pyrgi. Etruscan, c. 460 BC.

Figure 9.3   Descent of Amphiaraos. Etruscan Urn, Volterra. Photo: Richard Stoneman.

confrontation in which the Thebans were driven back into their city, the attackers tried to storm the walls but were driven back in their turn. The major casualty during the assault was the impiously arrogant **Kapaneus**, who boasted that he would enter and set fire to the city whether Zeus wished it or not, provoking that god to strike him with a thunderbolt while he was scaling the walls. According to Apollodorus,[143] this incident marked a turning-point, for it caused the other Argives to flee back from the city walls. Either during the attack on the walls or during a pause in the fighting after the attackers fell back, **Polyneikes** and Eteokles confronted one another in single combat and killed one another.[144] As the battle proceeded in front of the city, **Tydeus** was fatally wounded by Melanippos, son of Astakos, a descendant of one of the Spartoi (Sown Men, who were supposed to have founded the military caste at Thebes, see p. 296). Tydeus was a favourite of Athena, who planned to confer immortality on him; but Amphiaraos hated him for his violent ways and for having helped to instigate the war, and was determined to frustrate the goddess's intent. So he cut off the head of Melanippos and tossed it to Tydeus in the expectation of a savage reaction; and when Tydeus cracked it open to gulp down the brains of his killer, Athena was so revolted that she withheld the magical potion that she had intended to apply to him. Melanippos was commonly said to have been killed by Amphiaraos (although an interpolation in Apollodorus' text suggests that Tydeus had managed to kill him after being wounded by him).[145] **Parthenopaios** was killed by Periklymenos, son of Poseidon and Chloris, daughter of Teiresias,[146] who went on to pursue **Amphiaraos** from the battlefield, and would have struck him in the back with his spear if Zeus had not intervened by opening up a chasm in the ground with a thunderbolt, so enabling the seer to disappear beneath the earth together with his chariot and charioteer. This latter episode is already described by Pindar; and it is reported elsewhere that the charioteer of Amphiaraos was a certain Baton who was a kinsman of his.[147] Amphiaraos vanished from human sight, either at Knopia, a place near Thebes on the road to Potniai, or further away at Harma (Chariot) between Thebes and the east coast, or at Oropos on the frontier between Boeotia and Attica. He delivered oracles during his posthumous existence, principally at Oropos but also at Knopia (hence the traditions that located his disappearance at these places).[148] Of all the Argive champions, **Adrastos** alone escaped, thanks to the speed of his wondrous horse Areion, which was a child of Poseidon by Demeter Erinys (see p. 101).[149] No picturesque stories are associated with the deaths of the minor champions; according to Apollodorus, **Eteoklos** and **Hippomedon** were killed by Leades and Ismaros respectively, two brothers of the Melanippos who is mentioned above as the killer of Tydeus.[150]

Aeschylus presents an idiosyncratic account of the conflict in his *Seven against Thebes*. In this tragedy, each of the seven champions from the Argive force is said to have confronted a Theban defender at each of the seven gates, in accordance with the following arrangement:

Gate	Assailant	Defender
Proitides	Tydeus	Melanippos, son of Astakos
Elektrai	Kapaneus	Polyphontes
Neistai	Eteoklos	Megareus, son of Kreon
Onkaiai	Hippomedon	Hyperbios, son of Oinops
Borrhaiai	Parthenopaios	Aktor, son of Oinops
Homoloides	Amphiaraos	Lasthenes
Hypsistai	Polyneikes	Eteokles

With the exception of Eteokles, Melanippos and Megareus, the defenders are otherwise unknown, and some of them may have been invented by Aeschylus himself. Towards the end of the play, a messenger reports that all has gone well for the Thebans at six of the gates, but that the king of Thebes and his brother have killed one another at the seventh gate;[151] this would mean, of course, that the outcome was settled by a series of single combats at the individual gates before there could be occasion for any subsequent fighting in front of the city. To maintain a consistent pattern, Aeschylus departs from the usual tradition by excluding Adrastos, as a known survivor, from his list of champions. It will be noted, furthermore, that except in the case of the opponents of Polyneikes and Tydeus, the defenders who kill the champions are not the men who are usually said to have killed them.

For a tale from Euripides in which Menoikeus, son of Kreon, is said to have sacrificed himself to ensure victory for Thebes, see p. 330.

Kreon tries to forbid the burial of the Argive dead

After the death of the two sons of Oedipus, KREON took power at Thebes once again, either as king in his own right or as regent for Laodamas, the infant son of Eteokles. He ordered that the Theban dead should be buried with all honour, especially Eteokles, but that bodies of the attackers should be left to rot, a decree that offended not only against the common feelings of humanity, but also against the gods above and below, since the latter were defrauded of their due and the former polluted by the corpses that were left in their realm.[152] There is no indication that this story of the prohibition was known before the fifth century BC (although it should be remembered that we have very little early evidence on anything connected with the war). When the fateful decree first appears in Attic tragedy, it has two notable consequences: Kreon's niece Antigone tries to bury her brother Polyneikes, setting in course a train of events that brings disaster to the Theban royal family, and Adrastos enlists the aid of Theseus and the Athenians to force the Thebans to allow the burial of the Argive dead. Polyneikes was finally buried at Thebes, alongside his brother in some accounts,[153] while the bodies of the other champions (apart from Amphiaraos of course) were taken off to Attica to be buried at Eleusis.[154] Pindar is doubtless drawing on the early epic tradition when he speaks of seven funeral pyres burning near Thebes itself.[155]

The decree forbidding the burial of the Argive dead is first attested for the *Eleusinians* of Aeschylus, a lost tragedy dating to the end of the first quarter of the fifth century. In this play, Theseus helped Adrastos to recover the bodies of his comrades by negotiating a settlement, evidently with the threat of force, rather than by defeating the Thebans in battle as in the usual account.[156] Pausanias reports that the Thebans themselves preferred this version of the story,[157] as is wholly understandable; some said that this was the first truce ever to be arranged for the burial of the dead.[158] The title of Aeschylus' play suggests that the chorus would have been made up of citizens of Eleusis, the town where the Argive dead would have been laid to rest. When the theme is taken up again in Euripides' *Suppliants*, a play written half a century later, the chorus is made up of the mothers of the Argive dead, who accompany Adrastos to Athens and appeal as suppliants to Aithra, the mother of Theseus, at the shrine of Demeter at Eleusis. On arriving to investigate, Theseus responds sympathetically to the entreaties of Adrastos and the women of the chorus, who are now supported by Aithra, and agrees to take up their cause. Ignoring a Theban herald who asks him to expel Adrastos and warns him not to set foot on Theban soil, Theseus collects an army together to attack Thebes, defeats Kreon and the Thebans, and takes the dead back to give them an honourable burial. Since Kapaneus was killed by a thunderbolt from Zeus, his corpse is marked off from the others as sacred and burned on a separate funeral-pyre;[159] as it is burning, his wife Euadne throws herself on to it to join him in death,[160] an act very reminiscent of Hindu *sati*, but without parallel in Greek mythology. It is a happy thought of various latish authors to make the suppliants take refuge at the altar of Mercy (Eleos) in Athens rather than at Eleusis.[161]

The mythology of Antigone

The standard version of the story of ANTIGONE was established by Sophocles in his play of that name. Although the king has forbidden the burial of Polyneikes on pain of death, his sister Antigone, as his nearest surviving relative, is determined to bury him nonetheless, and the play begins as she vainly attempts to persuade ISMENE, her more cautious sister, to join her in the enterprise.[162] So Antigone was obliged to take action on her own, and granted her brother a formal burial at least by scattering some dust over his corpse. The dust was soon noticed by Kreon's guards, who brushed it away and lay in wait nearby; and when Antigone returned to replace it and to pour funeral-libations, they captured her and hauled her in front of Kreon.[163] She defended her actions with stubborn courage, arguing that the king had abused his authority and that the unwritten and unfailing laws of the gods took precedence over his arbitrary decree; but her defiance merely served to antagonize him, and he resolved that she should be walled up alive in a tomb.[164] When Ismene was then brought in front of him, she was so moved by the plight of her sister that she asked to share in her guilt and punishment, but Antigone protested that she had no right to make any such claim since she had failed to take action when the moment had demanded.[165] Kreon's son HAIMON, who was betrothed to Antigone, arrived after the two girls were led away, and tried to persuade his father to show mercy to his fiancée, warning him that the Thebans sympathized with her and were saying that she deserved to be honoured rather than killed. But Kreon refused to listen and ordered that the sentence should be put into effect.[166] He was finally obliged to relent, however, when the seer Teiresias revealed that the gods had been offended by his prohibition of the burial, and were therefore rejecting all Theban sacrifices and prayers;[167] but his change of heart came too late since Antigone had already hanged herself in her sepulchre. As the audience subsequently learns from a messenger, Kreon entered the vault to find that she was hanging from a linen noose, while Haimon, who had entered just before, was embracing her corpse and bewailing her fate. When Kreon called out to him, Haimon drew his sword and tried to strike his father with it, but missed him and then committed suicide by driving it into his own body. On hearing this news from the messenger, Eurydike, the wife of Kreon, retired into the palace to kill herself in her turn; and Kreon is left to contemplate his guilt as the play draws to a close.[168]

Little is known of the prior mythology of Antigone; indeed, there is no record even of her name until the fifth century BC. She first appears in a passage from Pherecydes, who mentions her along with her usual brothers and sisters as one of the children who were borne to Oedipus by his second wife Euryganeia;[169] in the tragic and later tradition, of course, they are regarded as children of Iokaste. In the present text of Aeschylus' *Seven against Thebes*, Antigone and Ismene are introduced into the final section of the play, in which they lament the death of their brothers until they are interrupted by a herald, who arrives to announce that the ruling body of the city has forbidden the burial of Polyneikes; Antigone then declares openly that she will see to his burial, to the approval of the chorus of Theban women, who offer to form the funeral cortege for the brothers.[170] If this scene formed part of the original play, it would have been written some twenty-five years before Sophocles treated the same theme in the *Antigone*. There is good reason to suppose, however, that the end of Aeschylus' play was altered at a later date, perhaps in the final decade of the fifth century, well after the production of the *Antigone*. The laments uttered by the two sisters prior to the arrival of the herald may originally have been shared out between the two half-choruses. The account of the interdiction and Antigone's defiance of it in the final scene with the herald differs in important respects from that offered by Sophocles. The edict forbidding the burial has been issued by the deputies of the people (*probouloi*) rather than by Kreon;[171] no penalty is announced for disobedience; and it is indicated that Antigone will give her brother a proper burial with the help of the other Theban women rather than a token burial on her own in secret.[172] It is quite possible that this comes closer to the original story than does the starker version in Sophocles' play, who heightens the dramatic tension by presenting Antigone as a solitary heroine who engages in a battle of wills with the king.

Ion of Chios, a poet of the fifth century BC, is reported to have written in a dithyramb that Antigone and Ismene were burned to death in the temple of Hera by Laodamas, son of Eteokles.[173] Although we have no record of how they had offended him, they had presumably fled to the temple for sanctuary, obliging him to resort to this act of sacrilege if he was to cause their death. It is at least possible that they had angered him by burying Polyneikes against his orders.

To return to the usual story in which Antigone is arraigned before Kreon, there are versions in which she is saved from death by her fiancé Haimon. Hyginus records a version of this kind in which Antigone removed Polyneikes' body under cover of darkness with the help of his wife Argeia and placed it on the funeral-pyre of Eteokles. She was captured by the guards, although her accomplice managed to escape, and brought in front of Kreon, who handed her over to Haimon to be put to death; but Haimon, who was betrothed to her, as in Sophocles' version, loved her too much to make more than a pretence of obeying, and secretly hid her away with some shepherds. While she was in hiding, she bore Haimon a son, here unnamed, who visited Thebes when he grew up to take part in some games. Since the descendants of the Spartoi could be identified by a distinctive birthmark (shaped like a lance), Kreon realized who he must be and ordered his execution. The king remained obdurate even when Herakles (who spent his earlier years in Thebes as a subject of Kreon) begged him to show mercy; and Haimon was so distressed that he took his own life after first killing his secret wife Antigone.[174] Although some have argued that this account was largely based on the lost *Antigone* of Euripides (in which Antigone is known to have married Haimon after her capture and to have borne him a son called Maion), it seems more likely that it is a composite version drawn from a variety of sources. What little is left of Euripides' plot suggests that a happy ending was somehow achieved, perhaps with Haimon being allowed to marry Antigone through the intervention of Dionysos, who is addressed by somebody in terms of zealous adoration in a surviving fragment.[175]

As we have seen above, Haimon and his son Maion were already known in early epic as a victim of the Sphinx and an opponent of Tydeus respectively (see pp. 309 and 319); but these traditions are inconsistent with those that present Haimon as the fiancé or secret lover of Antigone, since he would have been killed before her birth or at least have belonged to an earlier generation. Sophocles is the first author to present him as being betrothed to Antigone,[176] and it is quite possible that he invented the idea, so preparing the way for Euripides to make a further alteration in the tradition by presenting Maion as his son by Antigone; although Maion would certainly not have been the product of any secret union in the early epic tradition, we have no record of the name of his original mother.

Pausanias mentions that there was a place near Thebes called 'Antigone's Pull' (*Syrma Antigonēs*); according to the local tradition, it was called by that name because Antigone had tried to carry Polyneikes' body from there, but had found it too heavy to lift and had therefore pulled it along the ground to place it on Eteokles' pyre.[177] According to another local tradition, Maion buried Tydeus beside the road from Thebes to Chalkis after the defeat of the Seven[178] (evidently giving him a proper burial because Tydeus had spared his life previously, as was well known from the *Iliad*, see p. 319).

We may conclude with a mysterious early account of the death of Ismene. The elegiac poet Mimnermus (second half of the seventh century BC) is reported to have stated that she was killed by Tydeus at the instigation of Athena while she was having intercourse with a certain Theoklymenos. There is otherwise no record of a hero of this name at Thebes. When the incident is portrayed, however, on a Corinthian black-figure amphora of c.560 BC (Louvre

E640), the naked figure which is shown fleeing as Tydeus threatens Ismene with a sword is named as Periklymenos instead; and since Periklymenos was mentioned in the *Thebais* as the killer of Parthenopaios (one of the Seven, see p. 320), it is reasonable to assume that the Theoklymenos in the report above can be identified with this Theban hero.[179] Tydeus might have been in a position to kill Ismene while he was visiting Thebes as an ambassador, but we have no way of telling why Athena should have wanted him to do so, or why she should have chosen him in particular for this task. Pherecydes also states that Ismene was killed by Tydeus, at a spring that bore her name.[180]

The Epigonoi capture Thebes under the leadership of Alkmaion

Ten years after the expedition of the Seven, the sons of the fallen champions launched a second expedition against Thebes to avenge the fate of their fathers. The force was commanded by ALKMAION, son of Amphiaraos, who had been ordered by his father to attack Thebes when he came of age; and the attackers were destined to succeed on this occasion just as their fathers had been destined to fail.[181] The leading warriors were known as the EPIGONOI (i.e. the Afterborn or Younger Generation; the Greek term lacks the pejorative associations of its English derivative 'epigone').

As in the case of the Seven, the various catalogues of the Epigonoi are not entirely consistent.[182] Since most authors agreed on the identities of six of the Seven, we will begin with the sons of these. **Alkmaion** takes the place of his father Amphiaraos on this second expedition, often in the company of his younger brother **Amphilochos**. Adrastos accompanies the expedition, but is now too old to fight as one of the leading warriors; he is replaced in this respect by his son **Aigialeus**, who will be the only leader to die on this successful expedition, just as his father was the only champion to return from defeat on the first occasion. Polyneikes is replaced by his son **Thersandros** (and sometimes by a lesser son also, a certain Timeas or Adrastos). Thersandros will become the new king of Thebes after the city is captured. Tydeus is replaced by his son **Diomedes**, Kapaneus by **Sthenelos**, and Parthenopaios by **Promachos** (or else a son named Stratolaos, or Therimenes, or Biantes). The last member of the Seven was variously named as Mekisteus, Eteoklos or Hippomedon, and sons of these – **Euryalos**, **Polydoros** and **Maion** respectively – may sometimes be found accordingly among the Epigonoi. The number of the Epigonoi was not limited to seven as in the case of the champions on the first expedition; most catalogues list eight or more, largely because two sons of Amphiaraos or of Polyneikes were often said to have joined the Epigonoi.

It was perhaps inevitable that some authors should have recycled the story of Eriphyle's treachery (see p. 318) by suggesting that Thersandros, son of Polyneikes, bribed her to persuade her sons to join the Epigonoi by offering her the robe of Harmonia, just as Polyneikes had bribed her to force her husband to join the Seven by offering her the necklace of Harmonia. This was not a happy inspiration, however, since her sons had no reason to fear disaster as their father had, and she was not in a position to compel them in any case as she had been with their father. Apollodorus offers some sort of explanation, saying that her persuasions were needed because Alkmaion was reluctant to march off before he had punished her for her betrayal of Amphiaraos. It will be remembered that Amphiaraos had ordered Alkmaion to avenge him. In Diodorus' account, Alkmaion is said to have consulted the Delphic oracle about the campaign and the punishment of his mother, and was told that he should join the campaign and also take action against his mother, all the more so because she had now accepted the second bribe to endanger his own life.[183]

Very little is recorded of the campaign of the Epigonoi, which was described in a poem in the epic cycle. Pindar reports that Amphiaraos delivered a prophecy from his grave when they arrived at Thebes, foretelling that Alkmaion would enter the city first of all carrying a shield showing an image of a dragon, and that the omens were more favourable for Adrastos than they had been on the previous expedition, except with regard to his own family (for his son was destined to be the only victim among the Argive leaders).[184] In Apollodorus' account, which is probably based on the early epic tradition, the Epigonoi ravaged the villages around Thebes to provoke the Thebans to venture out of their city, and then defeated them in battle, presumably at some site near the city. Although LAODAMAS, son of Eteokles, the king and commander of the Thebans, killed Aigialeus, the son of Adrastos, he was soon killed in his turn by Alkmaion, and the Thebans were so dismayed by his death that they lost courage and took refuge behind their city walls. Realizing that the city was doomed, the seer Teiresias advised them to send a herald to the enemy to distract them with talk of a settlement while the citizens made a secret departure by night. As soon as the Argives realized that the Thebans had fled, they entered the city, plundered it, and pulled down the walls. In accordance with a previous vow, they sent the finest of the spoils to Delphi to be dedicated to Apollo (see further on p. 331).[185] According to Herodotus, the Theban exiles settled far away in Hestiaiotis, the north-western region of Thessaly, displacing the Dorians who had previously lived there; the historian may well have drawn this information from the early epic account in the *Epigonoi* (which he was certainly acquainted with, as we know from a passing allusion in another context).[186]

Pausanias offers a different account of the conflict, saying that the Thebans established a base about eight miles north-east of their city at Glisas, and were defeated in a battle nearby. Laodamas killed Aigialeus as above, but survived in this version to lead the defeated troops back into Thebes. The supposed tomb of the Argive dead could be seen at Glisas; Promachos, son of Parthenopaios, is mentioned as having been included among the fallen. Laodamas fled from Thebes under cover of nightfall with the citizens who chose to accompany him, and settled in Illyria (in the north-west adjoining the Adriatic).[187] To reconcile this account with the one above in which the Theban emigrants were said to have settled in Thessaly, it was suggested that some of the Thebans were unwilling to follow Laodamas all the way to Illyria, and therefore turned aside to settle in Thessaly; this tale also provided an explanation for the name of one of the gates of Thebes, for it was said that this last group were subsequently invited home, and that the gate through which they entered was named the Homoloidian Gate after Homole, the place of their exile in Thessaly.[188] This second account of the war and its aftermath was probably of later origin than the preceding version. Although it is not impossible that the battle was set at Glisas in early epic, this seems unlikely in view of town's position, for it lay well out of the way of any army approaching Thebes from the south; Hellanicus in the fifth century BC is the first author to name it as the battle-site.[189]

The Epigonoi entered Thebes unopposed after it had been deserted by most of its citizens, and installed Thersandros, the son of Polyneikes, as its ruler.[190] The conquerors were said to have pulled down the walls, and the city ceased to be of any great importance in mythical history thenceforth. The new king and his descendants will be considered below (see pp. 328ff). As the Argive army was marching home to Argos, Adrastos died on the way at Megara of old age and sorrow at the death of his son. His tomb could be seen in the city (although he also had heroic shrines in other places), and his son Aigialeus was buried nearby, at Pagai in the Megarid.[191]

The later history of Alkmaion

After arriving back in Argos, ALKMAION exacted vengeance against his mother Eriphyle for having caused the death of his father a decade before (see p. 318), by putting her to death, taking this action on his own or in conjunction with his brother Amphilochos. Although he had acquired the approval of Apollo at Delphi beforehand (either before or after the war), he was persecuted and sent mad nevertheless by his mother's Erinyes (Furies), just as Orestes was supposed to have been after killing his mother Klytaimnestra (see pp. 511ff).[192] When first overcome by madness, Alkmaion fled to his grandfather Oikles in Arcadia, and then onward to Psophis in the same province, where he was purified by the local ruler, Phegeus. The king offered him his daughter Arsinoe as a wife, and he started a new life with her in her homeland, giving her the necklace and robe of Harmonia as wedding-gifts. He was still polluted, however, in spite of the purification that he had received, and the land became barren on account of his presence. An oracle advised him to search for a land on which the sun had not yet shone at the time when he had killed his mother;[193] and his search took him across the Isthmus to the Greek mainland. After spending some time with Oineus at Calydon, he travelled further north into Epirus and visited the springs of the great river Acheloos, where he received purification from the god of the river. He finally discovered the land that the oracle had spoken of when he arrived at the mouth of the Acheloos at the entrance to the Corinthian Gulf; for new land had been laid down there by silt from the river since the time of his mother's death. He made this his new home, marrying Kallirhoe, a daughter of the river-god. When she subsequently asked to be given the necklace and robe of Harmonia, threatening to leave him if she failed to acquire them, he returned to Psophis and tricked Phegeus into handing them over, by claiming that the Delphic oracle had advised him that he should dedicate them at Delphi if he was to be cured of his madness. After his departure, however, a servant of his told Phegeus that he was really taking the treasures to his new wife. So the king ordered his two sons, Pronoos and Agenor, to lay an ambush for Alkmaion and put him to death. When their sister Arsinoe reproached them afterwards for having murdered her former husband, they took her to Tegea in south-eastern Arcadia and handed her over to the ruler, Agapenor, as a slave-woman, telling him that she herself had committed the murder.

On learning of Alkmaion's fate, his new wife Kallirhoe appealed to Zeus (who had become her lover) to cause her two young sons, AKARNAN and AMPHO-TEROS, to grow to maturity immediately to enable them to avenge their father's murder. Her request was duly granted, and the two young men (as they had now become) set off at once for Arcadia. They happened to call in at the palace of Agapenor while the sons of Phegeus were still there after bringing their sister, and they took advantage of this opportunity to kill them; and they then travelled on to Psophis to kill Phegeus, the instigator of the murder, along with his wife. Although they were pursued afterwards as far as Tegea, they were saved by the intervention of the Tegeans and some Argives, and hurried back to their mother to report their success. At the order of Acheloos, they dedicated the robe and necklace of Harmonia to Apollo at Delphi. Akarnan was the eponym of Acarnania, the westernmost province of Central Greece; he and his brother were said to have colonized the area with settlers assembled in Epirus. Their new home lay close to their birthplace, for the Acheloos ran to the sea along the border between Acarnania and Aetolia, the adjoining province to the east.[194]

Thersandros, king of Thebes, and his descendants

THERSANDROS, son of Polyneikes, had become the new ruler of Thebes in the mean time, ten years after his father had been killed while trying to seize the throne from Eteokles. Since Thersandros was of Kadmeian descent like the ousted king, Laodamas, son of Eteokles, the city continued to be ruled by the old royal family in spite of its fall, even if it was not the centre of power that it had once been. Demonassa, daughter of Teiresias, the wife of Thersandros, bore him a son and heir who was named TEISAMENOS (Avenger) in commemoration of his father's achievement in avenging the defeat and death of Polyneikes.[195] After ruling uneventfully for some years, Thersandros set out for Troy as the leader of the Boeotian contingent; but he never arrived there because he was killed on the way by Telephos, king of Mysia, when the Greeks attacked his land in the belief that it was Troy (see p. 446). Since Teisamenos was not yet of fighting age, the Thebans chose Peneleos, son of Hippalkimos (a descendant of Boiotos, son of Poseidon, the eponym of Boeotia) as their new leader.[196]

Although Thersandros is never mentioned in the Homeric epics, he must have been an ancient figure since the story of his death was recounted in the *Cypria*, an early epic in the Trojan cycle.[197] The Catalogue of Ships in the *Iliad* names Peneleos and Leitos, son of Elektryon, another descendant of Boiotos, as the leaders of the Boeotians (along with three obscure heroes, Arkesilaos, Prothoenor and Klonios, who are all killed in the fighting and were probably invented by Homer himself). The most striking feature of this passage in the *Iliad* is the fact that Thebes is not singled out from the other Boeotian towns as a place of any special significance; indeed there is no mention of Thebes as such, but only of Hypothebai (i.e. Lower Thebes), apparently a settlement that had grown up around the ruined and abandoned city.[198] Setting aside the obviously fabulous features in the story of the Theban wars, the legend may well have had some basis in historical fact, in so far as it reflected a serious decline in the city's fortunes at the end of the Mycenaean period.

When Peneleos was killed toward the end of the Trojan War by Eurypylos, the last major ally of the Trojans (see p. 472), Teisamenos was old enough to take over as leader. He returned home safely to Thebes to rule as his father's successor; but his son Autesion was troubled by ancient family curses and finally went abroad on the advice of the Delphic oracle, accompanying the Heraklids and Dorians to the Peloponnese. On his departure, the Thebans offered the throne to Peneleos' grandson Damasichthon, and they were then ruled by him and his heirs until the monarchy was abolished in the time of his grandson.[199]

The exiled Autesion had two notable children, Argeia and Theras, who rose to importance in their new homeland in the Peloponnese. Argeia married one of the Heraklid leaders, Aristodemos, who fathered the first Heraklid kings of Sparta by her, or else came to rule there himself (see further on p. 291). Since Aristodemos died while his twin sons were still very young in either case, their uncle Theras ruled the kingdom as regent while they were growing up; and after delivering the throne to them, he sailed abroad to establish a royal line on the island of Thera (see further on p. 571).

Teiresias, the great seer of Thebes, and his daughter Manto

Before departing from Thebes, we must consider the career of the great Theban seer TEIRESIAS, whose life was thought to have spanned most of the earlier history of the city from the reign of Pentheus until the arrival of the Epigonoi. His fame is as old as Homer, who reports that Persephone granted him the special privilege of retaining his wits in Hades, while other dead mortals flit around as empty shades.[200] He was of good Theban birth as a descendant of Oudaios, one of the men who had sprung from the dragon's teeth; his father was a certain Eueres and his mother a nymph called Chariklo. He lived a prodigious while, seven generations according to the Hesiodic *Melampodeia*,[201] and he was famous on two accounts, for his deeds as a seer, and for having turned into a woman and back into a man.[202] His sex-changes resulted from encounters with snakes. According to a version ascribed to Hesiod (presumably from the *Melampodeia*, a poem concerned with seers), he once saw a pair of snakes mating on Mt Kyllene in Arcadia, and was transformed into a woman when he struck and wounded them; but when he saw the same snakes mating on a second occasion, he was changed back into a man. Ovid states that he remained a woman for seven years until he saw the same snakes mating again, and struck them again when he saw them (as he is also reported to have done in other sources, and may already have been the case in the full Hesiodic account). He either struck the snakes with his staff or trampled on them.[203] In another version, he was turned into a woman when he saw two snakes coupling and killed the female, and was turned back into a man when he subsequently killed a male snake in the same circumstances.[204] There was disagreement on whether the incident occurred on Mt Kithairon in his Boeotian homeland or on Kyllene in Arcadia.[205]

In the Hesiodic account, he came to acquire his prophetic powers as a result of his experiences as a woman. For when Zeus and Hera were once arguing as to whether men or women gain more pleasure from sexual intercourse, they decided to refer the matter to the arbitration of Teiresias, who was alone in a position to judge from personal experience; and he responded that if the pleasure may be judged on a scale of ten, a man enjoys one part only while a woman enjoys all ten. Or in a secondary version, he is reported to have said that a man enjoys one part and a woman nine, as if there were ten units of pleasure to be shared out between them.[206]

Hera was angered by his reply, presumably because she thought it shaming for women, and reacted by turning him blind; but Zeus, who was evidently pleased to have found his arguments confirmed, compensated him by granting him prophetic powers and an extended life-span.[207]

Apollodorus remarks that conflicting explanations were offered for the blindness of Teiresias, for some also said that he was blinded by the gods for betraying their secrets to mortals (which would imply that he already possessed his prophetic powers at the time), while Pherecydes said that he was blinded by Athena because he saw her naked (in unstated circumstances). The goddess covered his eyes with her hands to render him sightless; and when his mother Chariklo, who was presumably present because she was bathing with Athena, asked her to restore his sight, she was unable to do so, but compensated him instead by enabling him to understand the language of birds (i.e. granting him divinatory powers, cf. p. 426), and by giving him a cornel-wood staff to enable him to walk like those who can see.[208] Callimachus recounts the story at some length in his fifth *Hymn*, the *Bath of Pallas*, reporting that the incident occurred as Athena was bathing during the midday heat in Hippocrene (the Horse's Spring) on Mt Helikon in Boeotia. She was accompanied by a single companion, the nymph Chariklo, who was a particular friend of hers. When the young Teiresias, who was out hunting on the mountain with his dogs, happened to come to the spring to quench his thirst, he saw Athena naked and was told by her that he would be deprived of his eyesight forever. Chariklo cried out in reproach and distress, asking if this was what was meant by the friendship of a goddess; but Athena assured her that she was not to blame for her son's blindness since the laws of Kronos (i.e. divine law) ordained that the punishment must follow from the offence. Although she therefore had no power to alter Teiresias' fate in this regard, she told Chariklo to cease from her laments because she would confer benefits on him that would far outweigh his loss, by granting him prophetic powers, and a long life, and unimpaired wits after his death.[209] While recounting this story, Callimachus refers to the comparable story of Aktaion, who suffered an even worse punishment after seeing Artemis naked (see p. 298);[210] it is likely that one of these stories inspired the development of the other, but we cannot tell for sure which was of earlier origin.

In Attic tragedy and the later tradition (and doubtless in early epic too, although we have no definite evidence on the matter), Teiresias was said to have performed valuable services for Thebes and the Theban kings at various stages in the troubled history of the city. When Thebes was about to be attacked by the Seven, for instance, he revealed that there was only one salvation for the city, since the blood-guilt for the sacred dragon (see p. 296) still weighed heavily on it; to atone for its death and finally allay the anger of Ares, it was necessary that a descendant of the Spartoi who was still a virgin should sacrifice his own life at the spot where the dragon had been killed. MENOIKEUS, son of Kreon, who alone answered to these specifications, resolved to take this action for the sake of the city in spite of his father's opposition, and stabbed himself accordingly on the city walls, ensuring that he would fall into the former lair of the dragon below. This legend and indeed Menoikeus himself first appear in the *Phoenician Women* of Euripides.[211] Teiresias plays a central role in three other surviving plays from the same period. In Euripides' *Bacchae*, he vainly attempts to persuade Pentheus to stop opposing Dionysos and his cult;[212] in Sophocles' *Oedipus the King*, as we have seen, he reluctantly reveals that Oedipus himself is to blame for the plague that has fallen on Thebes; and in Sophocles' *Antigone*, he warns Kreon that the gods have been angered by his decree forbidding the burial of Polyneikes and by his treatment of Antigone. In the dramatic context, the seer tends to be greeted with disbelief or scorn when he first offers his advice or revelations. It is recorded elsewhere, among other things, that he advised Laios to appease Hera for having abducted the young Chrysippos; that he told Amphitryon that Zeus had assumed his form to sleep with his wife (see p. 247), and that he revealed the destiny that awaited Herakles after the infant hero first demonstrated his prowess by strangling two snakes (see p. 249).

Teiresias met his long-delayed death when the glory of his city was brought to an end by the victory of the Epigonoi. As he was fleeing the area along with most of the other citizens, he stopped to drink at the spring of Tilphousa (see p. 144) in western Boeotia, and expired as his was doing so, apparently because of the chill of the water. His tomb could be seen beside the spring.[213] He had a daughter MANTO (Divineress) who was captured at Thebes by the Epigonoi and sent to Delphi along with other plunder, animate and inanimate, as an offering to Apollo; for they had vowed to dedicate the finest of the spoils to the god if they conquered the city.[214] Some said that Teiresias was captured too and sent off to Delphi along with his daughter, but died on the way at Tilphousa.[215]

Apollo was able to make good use of Manto by sending her over to Klaros, near Kolophon on the west coast of Asia Minor, to found the celebrated oracle of Apollo Klarios. In the earliest version of the story, he instructed her to marry whomever she first met on emerging from his oracle at Delphi, and this turned out to be a Mycenaean called Rhakios, who took her across the Aegean to the site of Klaros (a journey that would have been difficult for a woman on her own). After her arrival, she wept at the sad fate of her ravaged city, hence the name of Klaros (here interpreted as being derived from *klaein*, to weep). A spring was formed from her tears, presumably the sacred spring from which the prophet of the oracle used to drink before delivering his prophecies.[216] In another version of the story, Rhakios was a Cretan who had already established himself in the region of Kolophon with a group of settlers from his native island. The Delphic oracle ordered Manto to cross over the Aegean along with some other captives from Thebes; and when they arrived in Asia, they were captured by some of the Cretan settlers and taken to Rhakios, who asked Manto to become his wife and invited the other Thebans to become citizens of his colony.[217] Manto bore him a son, MOPSOS, who became a celebrated seer like his mother and grandfather, and served as the prophet of Klarian Apollo; for his main stories, see p. 488.

In a lost play by Euripides, *Alkmaion in Corinth*, Alkmaion was said to have fathered two children by Manto, a son Amphilochos and a daughter Tisiphone. He entrusted them to Kreon, king of Corinth, to be reared, but Tisiphone grew up to be so beautiful that the king's wife began to imagine that her husband might fall in love with her, and sold her into slavery for fear of being displaced. As chance would have it, she was purchased by Alkmaion, who kept her as a maidservant without realizing that she was his daughter. The truth finally emerged, however, when he returned to Corinth to recover his two children. Since this story conflicts with Manto's usual legend, and there is no previous record of Tisiphone or the present Amphilochos (who is evidently a doublet of Amphilochos, son of Amphiaraos, see p. 325), there is good reason to suppose that this story was invented by Euripides himself.[218]

331

The implications of the Theban Wars for the dynastic history of the Argolid

At the time of the Theban wars, which took place a generation or so before the Trojan War, the Argolid was no longer under common rule, but had come to be divided into two separate sections for reasons that were considered in Chapter 7 (see pp. 237ff). The north-western section, which was ruled from Mycenae, had fallen under the control of Atreus' branch of the Pelopid family, while the other section of the province, whose main city was Argos, was still under the control of the old Argive ruling family and the royal lines established by Bias and Melampous (see p. 429 for the origin of the latter). Although Adrastos tried to enlist the Mycenaeans for the expedition of the Seven (see p. 318), the Argive cities under Pelopid rule took no part in either of the Theban wars and were unaffected by their outcome; but the dynastic history of the other section of the Argolid was greatly affected by the two wars, since many leading members of its ruling families were killed in them or as a consequence of them.

It will be remembered that the three ruling lines in this section of the Argolid were a branch of the old Inachid line, as descended from Proitos, and two newer lines founded by Bias and Melampous, two brothers from outside who won shares of Proitos' kingdom. The two latter families are particularly prominent in the mythology of the Theban wars. Adrastos, a grandson of Bias, and Amphiaraos, a great-grandson of Melampous, were the foremost Argive leaders in the expedition of the Seven (see Tables 14 and 13); but Proitos' Inachid line was also represented, in the person of Kapaneus and Eteoklos (see Table 5). Although ADRASTOS, son of Talaos, who ruled from his palace in the city of Argos, was not the only king in the land, he was apparently acknowledged as the overlord of all the non-Pelopid lands of the Argolid at the outset of the Theban wars; his status in that regard may be compared to that of his grandson Diomedes at the time of the Trojan War. His authority had been painfully acquired, however, since he and his family, the Biantids, had previously met with defeat in a power-struggle with Amphiaraos, who had been supported by his own family and also by the Proitids. Adrastos had been forced into exile as a consequence, and had sought refuge in the city of Sicyon to the west of Corinth. His Sicyonian connections were certainly very ancient since the *Iliad* refers to him as a former king of the city.[219] According to one tradition, he chose it as his sanctuary because his mother was a daughter of Polybos, king of Sicyon, and he inherited the throne after the death of the king as his closest male descendant; or else he married a daughter of Polybos after his arrival and came to inherit the throne because the king had no sons of his own.[220] Amphiaraos held power in Argos in the mean time, but eventually decided to negotiate a settlement with Adrastos for unrecorded reasons. So Adrastos was able to return home, and established a dominant position in the land (whether immediately or by degrees). To seal his reconciliation with Amphiaraos, he offered his sister Eriphyle to him as a wife; and in the hope of securing their new-found friendship, the two brothers-in-law swore to accept Eriphyle's decision if they should ever have any serious disagreement in the future (for she could be expected to be fair-minded as the sister of the one and wife of the other).[221] Although this may have seemed an excellent idea at the time, it would bring nothing but disaster as we have seen (p. 317) because Eriphyle would allow herself to be bribed into imposing a decision that was detrimental to her husband and indeed to Adrastos too.

Amphiaraos was a great-grandson of **Melampous** and the only son of his father **Oikles**[222] (who has no myths of his own); he took part in the expedition of the Seven as the only member of his line who was available to do so. Although he could foresee by his own prophetic powers that he would not return, Eriphyle forced him to march off with Adrastos. His two sons, **Alkmaion** and **Amphilochos**, survived the second Theban war, but were not destined to play any significant part in Theban affairs. Alkmaion, who would otherwise have inherited his father's position, was obliged to depart into exile after killing his mother to avenge his father's fate (see pp. 327ff); and he was killed before the Trojan War in circumstances already described. His two sons, **Akarnan** and **Amphoteros**, were born abroad, and remained abroad in Acarnania (see p. 328). His brother Amphilochos seems to have lived in Argos after returning from the war, though not as a figure of any prominence, and later took part in the Trojan War, again in no prominent capacity. He had inherited his father's prophetic powers, and joined together with another seer to found an oracle in Asia Minor after the war, returning to Argos for a brief visit only (see p. 489). Since he left no children, this Melampodid line in Argos died out; see Table 13.

Adrastos, a son of **Talaos** and grandson of **Bias**,[223] led the expedition of the Seven and was accompanied on it by his brother **Mekisteus**, who was killed at Thebes; Parthenopaios, another of the Seven, was sometimes classed as a further brother of his (see p. 317). He also had a brother **Pronax** who met his death before the war.[224] After surviving the first war with the aid of his divine horse Areion, Adrastos marched against Thebes for a second time with the Epigonoi, although he was now too old to fight in battle. His only son **Aigialeus** and his nephew **Euryalos**, the son of the above-mentioned Mekisteus, represented the Biantid family as leading warriors on this occasion. Since Aigialeus was killed in battle (see p. 326) and his grief-stricken father died shortly afterwards on the way home, Adrastos' throne passed through the female line to **Diomedes** after the war. Diomedes, who had also marched with the Epigonoi, was the only son of Tydeus, a member of the Aetolian royal family who had married a daughter of Adrastos after being exiled from his native land (see p. 316). Tydeus was dead by this time, having been killed at Thebes as one of the Seven. As a great warrior who had succeeded to Adrastos' position as overlord of the non-Pelopid lands of the Argolid, Diomedes commanded the men of Argos, Tiryns and the eastern Argolid at the Trojan War. He was assisted by two subordinate leaders, Euryalos, son of Mekisteus, from the junior branch of this Biantid line, and Sthenelos, son of Kapaneus, from the old Argive ruling line.[225]

In Pausanias' account of the legendary history of Argos, Adrastos is said to have had an heir in the male line too, a grandson **Kyanippos** who was fathered by Aigialeus before his early death. It is explained with some plausibility that he was too young to succeed to the throne after the death of Adrastos or to fight at Troy, and that his family was therefore represented at Troy by Diomedes and Euryalos as in the epic tradition.[226] Only in very late sources is it suggested that he fought at Troy and entered the city as one of the warriors in the Wooden Horse.[227] His later career will be considered below.

The old Argive royal line was represented among the Seven by **Kapaneus**, son of Hipponoos, a descendant of Proitos in the third or fourth generation,[228] and **Eteoklos**, son of Iphis, a descendant of Proitos in the fifth generation; see Table 5. It will be noted that these genealogies are not properly synchronized with those of the Biantids and Melampodids. Since **Hipponoos**, the father of Kapaneus, lived abroad as king of Olenos in Achaea, **Iphis**, the father of Eteoklos and father-in-law of Kapaneus, was the leading member of the Proitid line within the Argolid in the period preceding the Theban wars. He was fated to suffer a triple bereavement as a result of the first war, since he was not only deprived of his son Eteoklos (who was killed in the fighting) and his son-in-law Kapaneus (who was struck by a thunderbolt, see p. 320), but also lost his daughter **Euadne** when she jumped on to the funeral pyre of her husband Tydeus (see p. 322).[229] The latter story first appears in Euripides' *Suppliants*, in which Iphis vainly attempts to persuade her from following that course, and laments afterwards that nothing but desolation awaits him in his old age, for there will be no one left to greet him either in his own house or in that of his son-in-law.[230] Kapaneus left a son, **Sthenelos**, who marched against Thebes as one of the Epigonoi, and inherited the throne of Iphis when that king died at some stage before the Trojan War.

Diomedes was a hero of the very first rank who was celebrated for the part that he played in the Trojan War; see further on pp. 461ff. In contrast to Diomedes himself, who is prominent in the earlier books of the *Iliad*, dominating the fighting while Achilles is absent from the battlefield, EURYALOS appears on two occasions only after being initially mentioned as a lieutenant of Diomedes, first in a short battle-scene in which he kills two minor Trojans, and second when he is ignominiously defeated by Epeios in a boxing-match during the funeral games for Achilles.[231] In Polygnotos' mural of the sack of Troy, which would have been based on the epic tradition for the most part, Euryalos was shown among the injured with wounds to the head and wrist.[232] This would suggest that he was thought to have returned home alive; and his supposed grave could be seen correspondingly at Argos.[233]

STHENELOS, the other lieutenant of Diomedes, appears much more frequently in the *Iliad* than Euryalos, but only in a supporting role as the charioteer and closest comrade of Diomedes. The two had already fought at one another's side as Epigonoi. There is a memorable passage in the *Iliad* in which Agamemnon tries to spur on Diomedes by accusing him of being a worse fighter than his father, prompting Sthenelos to reply on his behalf that this can hardly be true since the Epigonoi captured Thebes, and with a lesser army too, after their fathers had perished in the attempt.[234] It was generally accepted that Sthenelos returned home to Argos after the war (even if Lycophron states that he was buried at Kolophon in Asia Minor).[235] According to a local tradition at Argos, he brought a notable trophy back to the city, for he was awarded the effigy of Zeus Herkeios that had stood in the court-yard of Priam's palace at Troy, and deposited it in the temple of Larisan Zeus on the acropolis at Argos, where it could be seen by visitors in historical times.[236]

Although Diomedes also returned safely to Argos, and apparently continued to rule there in the early tradition, it was commonly agreed from the Hellenistic period onward that he was forced into exile on his arrival and settled in Italy; this came about because his wife Aigialeia had been seduced by Kometes, a son of Sthenelos, who had then plotted to kill her husband (see further on p. 487). Since Diomedes apparently had no children by Aigialeia, his family played no further part in the affairs of the Argolid. As for Kometes and Aigialeia, nothing at all is recorded of their subsequent life (as is by no means surprising, since the story of their love affair would simply have been invented to provide an explanation for the exile of Diomedes). According to Pausanias' account of the local history, **Sthenelos** ruled after his return as king in the Proitid line, while **Kyanippos** (a late-invented son of Aigialeus and grandson of Adrastos, see p. 333) inherited the position that had been occupied by the Biantid king Adrastos and his successor Diomedes. Sthenelos was succeeded by his son **Kylarabos** (or Kylarabes, or Kylasabos), who also inherited the Biantid share of the kingdom; Kyanippos died without an heir; and when Kylarabos himself died without an heir, the kingdom passed to **Orestes**, son of Agamemnon, the Pelopid king of Mycenae, and the whole of the Argolid was thus united under Pelopid rule.[237] The grave of Kylarabos could be seen along with that of his father Sthenelos at the Kylarabis, a gymnasium in Argos that bore his name.[238]

CHAPTER TEN

LEGENDS OF CRETE AND ATHENS

—— ·•· ——

MINOS, THESEUS AND THE MINOTAUR

Of the three main branches of the Inachid family, only the smallest remains to be considered, the branch that was established by Europa on Crete after she was abducted to that island by Zeus. As was explained in Chapter 7, the early Argive, Theban and Cretan royal lines were all descended from Io, an Argive princess who settled in Egypt, through one or other of her two great-grandsons, Belos, king of Egypt, or Agenor, king of Phoenicia (see pp. 231ff). Europa and her brother Kadmos, the founder of the Theban royal line, were children of the latter. As we saw at the beginning of the previous chapter, the abduction of Europa led to the scattering of Agenor's family since he sent his sons in search of her and they remained abroad after failing to find her. Unbeknown to them all, Zeus had taken her across the sea to Crete, where he had fathered a family of sons by her. Her line in Crete is much shorter than those of Kadmos in Thebes or Danaos in Argos (even if some mythographers tried to remove the chronological inconsistency, see below), and it is also of lesser significance overall, although it includes a few figures of high note, above all the great Minos.

As anyone who has even a passing acquaintance with the myth of the Minotaur will be aware, the mythical history of Crete in the age of Minos was closely intertwined with that of Athens. Daidalos, an exile from Athens, helped Pasiphae to conceive the Minotaur and built the labyrinth as a home for it; by sailing against Athens during the reign of Aigeus, Minos forced the Athenians to send a regular tribute of young people as food for the Minotaur; and Theseus, the son and heir of Aigeus, eventually killed the Minotaur with the aid of advice from Daidalos, so setting in course the train of events that would lead to the death of Minos himself. In view of the important connections between Athens and Crete during the only period of mythical history in which either place is truly prominent, it will be convenient to consider the mythology of Athens along with that of Crete in the present chapter, interweaving the story of Theseus with that of Minos and his family in the first part of the chapter. We will return to the Athenian royal family in the second part, to trace the rest of its history from the beginning to its conclusion after the Trojan War.

The genealogies of this Cretan branch of the Inachid family are not properly synchronized with those of the Argive and Theban branches since Minos lived only two generations before the Trojan War while Kadmos and Danaos lived at least seven generations before it. The Cretans were commanded at Troy by Minos' grandson Idomoneus; and correspondingly, Theseus and his father Aigeus, the Athenian adversaries of Minos, belonged to the generations that lived immediately before the Trojan War. To remove the resulting chronological inconsistencies, some mythographers tried to lengthen the Cretan line by claiming that the Minos who was a son of Europa was the grandfather of the famous Minos through a son called Lykastos (the eponym of a Cretan city of that name).[1]

Zeus abducts Europa to Crete and fathers three sons by her

In the earliest surviving account of the abduction of EUROPA, as ascribed to Hesiod (i.e. the author of the *Catalogue*) and Bacchylides, Zeus fell in love with her when he saw her gathering flowers with her attendant maidens in a meadow in Phoenicia, and turned himself into a bull to carry her away. After beguiling her by breathing a crocus from his mouth, he took her on to his back and carried her through the sea to Crete, where he reverted to his proper form and took her as his mistress.[2] Later authors have nothing essential to add even if they are able to provide a variety of picturesque details. According to the Hellenistic poet Moschus, who supplies the most elaborate account, the bull was yellow with a circle of white on its forehead, and it emitted a divine fragrance that drowned out the scent of the flower-strewn meadow; and after winning Europa's confidence by its gentle and flirtatious behaviour and its melodious lowings, it knelt down to entice her on to its back. Or in the broadly similar account by Ovid, it was as white as the undriven snow. Some authors followed the early Argive mythographer Acusilaus in regarding it as an ordinary bull that was sent by Zeus or the gods; in that case, the Cretan bull that was later captured by Herakles could be identified with it (see p. 261).[3]

Zeus fathered three important sons by Europa in her new homeland, Minos, Rhadamanthys and Sarpedon. He gave her some marvellous gifts, a necklace from the workshop of Hephaistos (sometimes identified with the necklace of Harmonia, see p. 297), a huge man of bronze called Talos, who guarded the coasts of the island until he was killed by Medeia (see p. 396), and an infallible hunting-dog and hunting-spear (which were later taken to Attica by Prokris, see p. 372).[4] When the time came for him to take leave of her, he arranged for her to marry ASTERIOS (or Asterion), king of Crete, who adopted her divinely begotten sons and fathered no further children by her. According to Diodorus, this Asterios was a son of Tektamos and grandson of Doros who had established himself as king of the island after sailing over from Central Greece with some Aeolian and Pelasgian followers.[5]

Minos, Pasiphae and the origin of the Minotaur

After the death of their adoptive father MINOS and Sarpedon fought for the throne, and Minos gained the upper hand, driving Sarpedon and his followers into exile.[6] Or in another account, the two brothers fell out with one another because both of them fell in love with the same boy, Miletos, son of Apollo; and Minos was so angry when Miletos showed a preference for Sarpedon that he expelled the two of them from the island.[7] The mythology of Sarpedon and Miletos will be considered in greater detail later in the chapter (see pp. 349ff), as will the mythology of Rhadamanthys, the other brother of Minos (see p. 351). We will concentrate for the present on the reign of Minos and the story of the Minotaur.

Minos married PASIPHAE, a daughter of the sun-god Helios, who bore him four sons, Katreus, Deukalion, Androgeos and Glaukos, and several daughters including Ariadne and Phaidra.[8] He also fathered various illegitimate children by local nymphs, so angering Pasiphae by his many infidelities that she finally put a spell on him, causing him to ejaculate snakes, scorpions and millipedes whenever he slept with another woman; but he was eventually cured of this inconvenient affliction by another mistress, the Athenian heroine Prokris (see p. 372).[9] For his unsuccessful pursuit of the nymph Britomartis, see p. 191. In the political sphere, he was noted for two things above all, his wisdom as a lawmaker and his power as the founder of a great maritime empire. As the first ruler to recognize the potentialities of sea-power, he used his navy to extend his rule to most of the Aegean islands; Greek authors of the classical and Hellenistic periods liked to imagine that his empire was comparable to that of Athens in the age of Perikles.[10] He was also regarded as the framer of the Cretan constitution, which was highly admired in antiquity; in this field of his activity, he benefited from the advice of Zeus, visiting his father at his sacred cave on Mt Ida every nine years to consult him on his lawmaking.[11] As has already been mentioned (see p. 122), Minos was so famed for his justice on earth that he was chosen to become one of the judges of the dead during his posthumous life in Hades. There was a dissenting tradition, however, especially fostered at Athens (a land oppressed by him in myth), that represented him as having been a brutal tyrant. His name has been associated with the distinctive 'Minoan' civilization of Crete ever since that name was attached to it by Sir Arthur Evans at the beginning of the last century (but it is safer to put this out of one's mind when considering his ancient myths).

Most of the main legends of Minos were connected in one way or another with the story of the MINOTAUR. This monster came to be born to his wife Pasiphae in the following circumstances. To demonstrate to the Cretans that his claim to the throne was approved by the gods, Minos prayed to Poseidon to send a bull up from the sea, promising to sacrifice it to him on its arrival; but he was so impressed by its beauty when it appeared that he mixed it into his own herds, substituting another at the sacrifice. Or in a rather different version, he used to sacrifice the finest bull that was born in his herds each year as an offering to Poseidon, but when a beast of wholly exceptional beauty was born one year, he kept it for himself and sacrificed another instead. In either case, Poseidon was so angry not to receive the proper bull that he turned it wild and caused Pasiphae to conceive an unnatural passion for it.[12] Now it happened that DAIDALOS, the finest of all craftsmen, was in Crete at the time after fleeing his native Athens to escape prosecution for murder (see below). So Pasiphae confided her secret to him, and he enabled her to gratify her desire by constructing a wooden cow with an ox-hide covering, and telling her to crouch down inside it in the presence of the bull. As the product of her intercourse with the bull, she gave birth to a monster with the head and tail of a bull and the body of a man.[13] It was usually known as the Minotaur (*Minotauros*, i.e. bull of

Figure 10.1   Pasiphae nurses the infant Minotaur. Interior of an Etruscan canteen. 340–320 BC. Cliché Bibliothèque Nationale de France, Paris.

Minos), although some mythographers report that it was properly named Asterios or Asterion after Minos' adoptive father.[14] At the request of Minos, Daidalos constructed a huge covered maze, the Labyrinth, to serve as its home and prison.[15]

Daidalos had left Athens because he had murdered his nephew. For he had taken his nephew Talos (or Kalos, or Perdix) as his apprentice, but had grown increasingly jealous when the youth turned out to be so ingenious that he had threatened to overshadow his master. For Talos proceeded to invent all kinds of wonderful devices including the potter's wheel and an instrument for inscribing circles; and when he happened to see a snake's jawbone with its neat row of jagged teeth (or else the backbone of a fish), he was inspired to invent the first saw. This last feat overstrained the jealousy of Daidalos, who murdered him by hurling him down from the Acropolis. When his corpse was discovered on the ground below, Daidalos was arraigned for murder at the court of the Areiopagos (see p. 366); but he escaped the inevitable penalty by stealing away to Crete.[16] The mythographers contrived a royal pedigree for Daidalos by fitting him into the royal family as a grandson or great-grandson of Erechtheus, king of Athens, through his father Eupalamos or Metion.[17]

Minos attacks Athens and Megara, and forces the Athenians to send consignments of young people as food for the Minotaur

The Minotaur was fed on youths and maidens who were sent over from Athens at regular intervals ever since the Athenians were first obliged to compensate Minos for the death of his son ANDROGEOS. As one of the finest athletes of the age, Androgeos had travelled to Athens to compete in the Panathenaic Games and had met his death afterwards in disputed circumstances. It was commonly agreed that he aroused resentment by carrying off the victory in every event; and in one account, his jealous rivals ambushed and killed him as he was setting off for Thebes to compete in the funeral games for Laios.[18] Or else Aigeus, the king of Athens, sent him out to confront the ferocious bull of Marathon (see p. 344) for reasons of state, because he feared that the young Cretan was conspiring with some enemies of his, the sons of Pallas (see pp. 356–7).[19] When Minos heard of his son's fate, he made immediate preparations for a war against Athens. The news was brought to him as he was offering a sacrifice to the Charites (Graces) on Paros; since he stopped the flute-music and threw the garland from his head but went on to complete the sacrifice, such sacrifices were performed on the island without flutes or garlands ever afterwards.[20]

Before launching his main attack against Athens, Minos laid siege to neighbouring Megara. The city had close connections with Athens at that time because it was under the rule of NISOS, son of Pandion, a brother of the king of Athens; and some sources claim that Minos had special cause for hostility because Megarian athletes had joined together with Athenians to murder his son.[21] Nisos proved to be a troublesome opponent because he had a purple hair (or lock of hair) on his head which rendered him invulnerable or guaranteed the safety of his city as long as it remained in place; but the problem was resolved when his daughter SKYLLA fell in love with Minos after catching sight of him from the ramparts, and pulled the magical hair from her father's head while he was asleep.[22] Or according to Aeschylus, Minos bribed her to take this action by offering her necklaces of Cretan gold.[23] If she had hoped to win the love of Minos by helping him to capture the city, she was soon undeceived, for he was so appalled by her unfilial act of treachery that he tied her to the stern of his ship and dragged her through the sea until she drowned; or else he ordered that she should be thrown from his ship, and she was washed ashore on Cape Skyllaia in the Argolid.[24]

The legend of Skylla became very popular in Hellenistic and Roman times, and many different accounts are preserved of the story of her death. Most authors agree that she was transformed into a mythical bird, the *kiris* (or *ciris* in Latin form); and it could be explained that this was an appropriate form for her because she had 'cut off (*keirō* in Greek) her father's magical hair. In Parthenius' Hellenistic version, she was turned into this mysterious bird as she was being dragged through the sea behind Minos' ship.[25] Subsequent accounts often add that she was persecuted in her new life by her father, who was transformed into a fierce sea-eagle.[26] In Ovid's version, in which Minos simply abandoned her rather than towing her behind his ship, she leapt into the sea and clung to his departing ship, but let go in terror when she saw her father hovering above in eagle-form, and turned into a *ciris* as she fell.[27] A long and elaborate narrative combining material from different versions may be found in the pseudo-Vergilian *Ciris*. Hyginus departs from the usual pattern by stating that Skylla was transformed into a fish called the *ciris*, which is attacked with great savagery by the sea-eagle;[28] since there is mention in Greek literature of a fish called the *kiris*,[29] it would seem that this is a genuine variant (as opposed to an error, as is common enough in Hyginus). For another tale in which a maiden came to a bad end after removing a magical hair from the head of her father, see p. 247.

Athens was able to offer more effective resistance, and the war dragged on until Minos eventually lost patience and prayed for the assistance of his father Zeus, who responded by afflicting the Athenians with a famine and a plague. After attempting to free themselves from their troubles by means of human sacrifices (see further on p. 370), the Athenians consulted the Delphic oracle, which advised them to compensate Minos by offering him whatever reparation he might demand. As the terms of the resulting settlement, Minos ordered that they should send seven youths and seven maidens to Crete every nine years (or every year) to serve as food for the Minotaur for as long as the monster should live.[30]

This tribute continued to be sent until Theseus, the son and successor of Aigeus, was sent as one of the youths in the tribute and killed the Minotaur in its lair. Before following the story to its conclusion and considering how the triumph of Theseus became the indirect cause of the death of Minos, we must examine the origins and earlier life of this greatest of Athenian heroes.

The birth of Theseus and his adventures on the road to Athens

Although AIGEUS, king of Athens, married twice over after ascending to the throne, taking Meta, daughter of Hoples, as his first wife, and Chalkiope, daughter of Rhexenor, as his second, he failed to father any children by either marriage and came to feel increasingly vulnerable without an heir to support and succeed him. When he consulted the Delphic oracle about the matter, he received an enigmatic response advising him 'not to untie the mouth of the wineskin until he arrived at the heights of Athens'. In terms of some fairly obvious symbolism, this meant that he should not have intercourse with any woman until he reached his wife in Athens, evidently because this would result in the conception of a son. Aigeus was mystified, however, and travelled out of his way during his return journey to seek the advice of PITTHEUS, son of Pelops, the king of Troizen, who was renowned for his wisdom. Although Pittheus recognized the meaning of the oracle at once, he kept it to himself because he wanted to ensure that his daughter AITHRA would bear the child to Aigeus (for the first and perhaps only son of the king of Athens would surely be destined for a glorious future). So he plied his guest with wine at a banquet on the evening of his arrival, and then introduced Aithra into his bed.

When Aigeus woke up on the following morning and realized what he had done, he told Aithra that she should bring up their son if she should bear one, but keep his origin a secret. He then placed a sword and some sandals under a large rock nearby, and instructed Aithra to take their son to the rock when he grew up, saying that if he were able to roll it aside, he should recover the hidden objects and take them to Athens as tokens of his identity.[31]

So runs the common story, but there was also a tradition that claimed that Theseus was really a son of Poseidon. According to the local legend at Troizen Athena sent a dream to Aithra one night ordering her to cross over to the little island of Sphairia just off the coast to pour a libation to Sphairos (a former chariot-driver of Pelops who was buried on the island); and while she was there, Poseidon caught her by surprise and had intercourse with her, causing her to conceive Theseus. As a result of this incident, she founded a shrine on the island to Athene Apatouria (Deceitful Athene) and changed its name to Hiera (Holy Island).[32] To reconcile the conflicting traditions about Theseus' birth, some mythographers suggested that Aithra slept with Aigeus and Poseidon on the same night.[33]

Aithra duly gave birth to a son who was brought up at the Troizenian court under the name of THESEUS. Only a single story is recorded of his childhood in Troizen. Herakles called in one day and left his lionskin on the ground while he was dining with Pittheus; and when Theseus (who was now seven) and his young friends caught sight of the skin, they all ran away in terror with the sole exception of Theseus, who seized an axe and attacked it in the belief that it was a living lion.[34] When he came of age, he rolled the rock aside with ease to recover his father's tokens, and made preparations for his journey to Athens. Since Troizen lay on the eastern coast of the Argolid, facing Athens from the opposite side of the Saronic Gulf, he could either travel by a direct sea-route or else follow the coastal path that led northwards round to Isthmus of Corinth. He opted for the longer land-route in the face of every warning because it provided more prospect for adventure.[35] His expectations were more than fulfilled, for he was waylaid by a succession of colourful villains and established his heroic credentials by performing a cycle of five or six exploits.[36]

The earliest literary reference to this cycle of heroic deeds is to be found in an ode of Bacchylides written in the first half of the fifth century BC, which lists all of the deeds described below except for the first, his slaying of the Club-man Periphetes at Epidaurus.[37] The cycle is regularly portrayed on Attic vases; the artistic evidence indicates that it must have been familiar (without the Club-man as yet) by the final decade of the sixth century, after having presumably been established in an epic poem composed in the latter part of that century. Although Diodorus is the first author to refer explicitly to Theseus' confrontation with the Club-man, Euripides already mentions that Theseus used a club from Epidaurus, which would imply that the tragedian knew of the episode;[38] and the visual record confirms that the story was probably in circulation by the fifth century.

On reaching Epidaurus further up the eastern coast of the Argolid, Theseus was confronted by **Periphetes**, otherwise known as Korynetes (the Club-man), who carried a bronze or iron club because he was weak on his feet, and used it to cudgel passing strangers to death. He is often described as a son of Hephaistos, evidently because of his lameness. When assaulted by this brute, Theseus wrested the club from his grip and killed him with it. The ancient mythographers state that Theseus adopted the club for his own use (although it is not really a special attribute of his in the same way as the club of Herakles).[39]

When Theseus reached the Isthmus of Corinth, he was confronted by **Sinis**, otherwise known as Pityokamptes (the Pine-bender), a savage son of Poseidon (or Polypemon) who made use of pine-trees to cause the death of travellers. In one version, he would bend two pine-trees to the ground, fasten his victim to them, and then let go of them, causing his victim to be torn in half as the trees sprung upwards.[40] Or in another version, he would compel his victim to help him to bend a single pine-tree to the ground and then suddenly let go, causing the unfortunate traveller to be tossed into the air and killed.[41] Theseus turned his own method against him, causing him to be killed as he had formerly killed others. His daughter Perigune hid herself in a bed of wild asparagus, but Theseus sought her out and seduced her, fathering a son Melanippos (a minor Attic hero who had a shrine at Athens).[42]

As Theseus was proceeding up the Isthmus, he killed the **sow of Krommyon**, a ferocious beast that had long been a menace to travellers. It was named Phaia (the Grey) after the old woman who had reared it. In vase-paintings, Theseus is usually shown confronting the beast with his sword as the old woman (who is named only once, as Kromyo) urges it forward with her outstretched arm or arms.

At the Skeironian Cliffs in Megara, the province adjoining Attica to the west, Theseus encountered **Skeiron**, a villain who forced passers-by to wash his feet and kicked them over the cliffs as they were doing so, propelling them into the sea below to fall prey to a giant turtle. Theseus bent down as if in obedience to his command, but seized him by his feet and hurled him into the sea, where he was eaten by the turtle.

The Megarians refused to accept that Skeiron was a rogue of such a kind. According to the local tradition as recorded by Pausanias, he was of royal descent as a great-grandson of the primordial king Lelex, and he married the daughter of Pandion (an exiled king of Athens who came to rule at Megara, see p. 374). After the death of Pandion, he quarrelled over the succession with Nisos, a son of the dead king, and the matter was referred for arbitration to Aiakos (the righteous king of Aegina, see p. 531). Aiakos decided that Nisos should become king of Megara and Skeiron its polemarch (military commander).[43] While acting in this function, Skeiron not only suppressed brigandage but constructed the main thoroughfare through the Isthmus, the Skeironian Way, which led through the rough countryside to the south-west of the city of Megara; Herodotus remarks that when the Greeks set out to fortify the Isthmus against the Persians, the first action that they undertook was to block this path.[44] The Megarians claimed that the wife of Aiakos, who was called Endeis, was a daughter of Skeiron (rather than of Cheiron as in the original tradition), and argued that the pious Aiakos would hardly have agreed to the alliance if Skeiron had really been such a villain as the other Greeks pretended. Although they were willing to accept that he had been killed by Theseus, they claimed that he had met his death in honourable circumstances when Theseus, as king of Athens, was seizing Eleusis from the Megarians who then controlled it.[45]

As Theseus was passing through Attica, he was confronted by **Kerkyon**, king of Eleusis, a son of Poseidon (or Hephaistos, or Branchos), who used to force passing strangers to wrestle with him and killed them in the ring. But the young hero killed him in his turn by raising him up into the air and dashing him to the ground. Kerkyon's wrestling-ground could be seen in historical times beside the road that led from Megara to Eleusis. As this story might suggest, Theseus was reputed to have been a very fine wrestler or even the man who had first established wrestling as an art rather than an exercise in brute strength.[46]

This Eleusinian Kerkyon was sometimes identified with Kerkyon, son of Agamedes, an Arcadian from Stymphalos; for the circumstances of his arrival in that case, see p. 559.

Kerkyon had a daughter ALOPE who bore HIPPOTHOON, the eponym of one of the Kleisthenian tribes of Athens, to Poseidon.[47] She gave her new-born child to her nurse to be exposed, but it was suckled by a mare and rescued by a shepherd. When a fellow shepherd asked to rear the child, the man who had found it passed it on to him but kept the fine clothing in which it had been wrapped. A quarrel arose as a consequence since the second shepherd wanted the clothes as proof that the child had been free-born, and the two of them referred the matter to the king for arbitration. On seeing the royal garments, Kerkyon forced the truth out of Alope's nurse, and ordered that his daughter should be killed and the child exposed once again. It was suckled by a mare, however, as on the first occasion and then discovered by the shepherds, who suspected that the child must be under divine protection; and Alope for her part was transformed by Poseidon into the spring of that name near Eleusis. After Kerkyon was killed by Theseus, Hippothoon (who was grown up by now) asked to inherit his grandfather's kingdom, and Theseus was happy to grant his request on learning that he was a son of Poseidon like himself.[48]

At Erineos, no great distance from Athens, Theseus encountered the villain who is commemorated in proverb for his 'Procrustean bed'. The Greeks knew him variously as **Prokroustes** (Hammerer), Damastes and Polypemon. He owned a house by the roadside that contained two special beds, one short and the other long, and he used to lure travellers to their destruction by inviting them to enjoy his hospitality. For if they were short, he would demonstrate his hospitality by laying them on the long bed and hammering out their legs until they fitted it; or if they were tall, he would lay them on the short bed and cut off the parts of their body that projected beyond it. Or in another version of the story, he had a single bed and would adapt his visitors to fit it by pruning their bodies or hammering them out as the occasion demanded.[49] Theseus meted out the same treatment to him and reached Athens without further incident.

Theseus is acknowledged as heir to the Athenian throne, and sets off for Crete with the tribute

Theseus was faced with perils of a more insidious nature on his arrival, for Medeia had married Aigeus after parting from Jason and had borne him a son Medos (see p. 400) and was prepared to plot the death of Theseus to protect her position and the prospects of her son. Realizing who he was before he was able to prove his identity to his father, she persuaded Aigeus that the newly arrived stranger was conspiring to seize the throne; and the king reacted by sending him to confront the savage bull of Marathon (usually identified with the Cretan bull that had been sent mad by

Poseidon, see p. 338, and had later been brought to the mainland by Herakles, see p. 261). After travelling to its haunts in north-eastern Attica, Theseus subdued it to his will without suffering any harm and drove it to back to Athens, where he or the king offered it in sacrifice to Apollo. Theseus was said to have stayed with an old woman called Hekale while performing this exploit. Medeia adopted a new plan after this setback, by mixing a poisoned draught and arranging that Aigeus should serve it to Theseus at a banquet; but Aigeus noticed at the very last moment that the young man was wearing the sword that he had placed under the rock at Troizen, and knocked the wine-cup out of his hands to prevent the poison from reaching his lips. Medeia's schemes were thus exposed, and Aigeus (or Theseus) drove her out of the kingdom along with her son (see further on p. 400). Theseus for his part received public acknowledgement from his father and was recognized thenceforth as the legitimate heir to the throne. There was a version of this legend in which the attempted poisoning was Medeia's only scheme, and Theseus set out against the bull of his own accord to court the favour of the Athenians.[50]

While Theseus was travelling across Attica to confront the bull, he was caught by a storm and was granted shelter and hospitality by an old woman called HEKALE, who lived in the deme (parish) of that name between Athens and Marathon. As he was setting out on the following morning, she vowed to offer a sacrifice to Zeus if he returned safely from his encounter with the bull. He discovered on his return, however, that she had died in the meantime, and he acknowledged her kindness by ordering that she should be honoured at the annual local festival of Zeus Hekaleios. She was also called Hekaline in that connection, supposedly because Theseus had addressed her by this pet name during his stay. This aetiological legend was recounted at some length by Callimachus in a miniature epic, the *Hekale*, which is preserved only in fragmentary form.[51]

When the third tribute of youths and maidens was due to be sent to Crete as food for the Minotaur, Theseus volunteered to be included in it in the hope that he would be able kill the monster and so relieve Athens from the tribute; or else he was simply chosen by lot along with the other young people.[52] Or in yet another version, Minos used to sail to Athens to pick out the victims himself, and he selected Theseus as his first choice on the present occasion.[53] In connection with the usual story in which the tribute was conveyed in an Athenian ship, it was said that it was fitted with black sails on account of its gloomy mission, and that Aigeus ordered Theseus to raise white sails as a sign of his safe return if he should come back unscathed.[54]

A memorable story of fairly ancient origin is recounted in connection with Theseus' voyage to Crete; it presupposes that Minos sailed to Athens to collect the tribute, and that Theseus was a son of Poseidon as in the Troizenian tradition (see p. 342). When Minos, who was noted for his amorous disposition, took a fancy to one of the girls in the tribute (a certain Eriboia) and began to caress her cheeks, Theseus ordered him to desist; and to justify this intervention against a son of Zeus, he proclaimed that he too was of semi-divine origin as a son of Poseidon, the great god of the seas. After first praying to Zeus to send a lightning-bolt as proof of his own birth, Minos removed a golden ring from his finger and hurled it into the sea, challenging Theseus to fetch it back again if he was really a son of Poseidon.

So Theseus jumped from the stern of the ship, trusting in his father to ensure his safety. Some dolphins swam up to him and carried him down to his father's palace in the depths of the sea, where Amphitrite, the consort of Poseidon, presented him with a purple robe and a golden crown that she had received from Aphrodite on the day of her wedding (and presumably also ensured that he gained possession of the ring of Minos, even though this is not explicitly stated in our source).[55] Or in another account, Thetis gave him a crown while the Nereids brought him the ring.[56] Poseidon can be seen receiving him in person in some Attic vase-paintings. When he rose up from the sea with the divine gifts and the ring, Minos was put to shame and the young Athenians rejoiced.

Theseus kills the Minotaur with help from Ariadne, but abandons her during the return voyage

After his arrival in Crete, Theseus received invaluable assistance from one of the king's daughters, ARIADNE, who fell in love with him and consulted the builder of the labyrinth on his behalf. Daidalos told her that Theseus would be able to find his way out again if he attached the end of a ball of thread to the door as he entered the maze, unwound the thread as he advanced through the passageways, and rewound it to trace his way back after his confrontation with the Minotaur. So she brought this advice and the necessary ball of thread to Theseus, who promised to repay her by taking her back to Athens as his wife.[57] Or in a less familiar version, she already

Figure 10.2 Theseus and Ariadne. © R. Sheridan/Ancient Art & Architecture Collection.

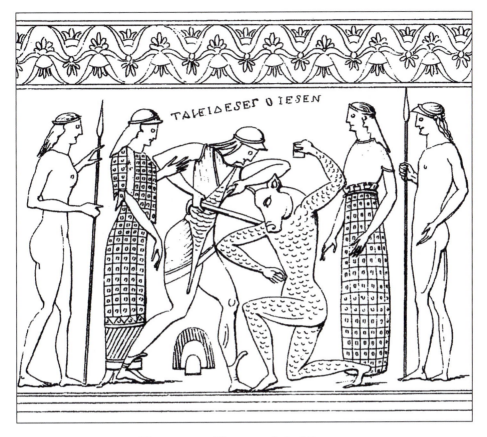

Figure 10.3   Theseus and the Minotaur.

possessed an object that could ensure his salvation, for Dionysos had previously seduced her by giving her a wonderful jewelled crown made by Hephaistos that shone in the dark; so she gave this crown to her prospective husband, who used it to light his way through the murk of the labyrinth.[58]

On encountering the Minotaur at the heart of the labyrinth, Theseus confronted and killed it, with a sword in most accounts. Vase-painters give freer rein to their imagination, however, and also show him attacking the monster with a spear, or club, or stone, or even his bare fists. After escaping from the maze by use of the ball of thread (or the crown), he hurried down to the harbour with Ariadne and the young Athenians from the tribute, and knocked holes into the bottoms of the Cretan ships to prevent any danger of pursuit before sailing off into the night.[59]

During the voyage north, Theseus called in at the island of Naxos (or Dia), where he abandoned Ariadne. An early tradition suggested that he did so deliberately because he was in love with another woman, namely Aigle, a daughter of the Phocian hero Panopeus;[60] but it was commonly agreed in the later tradition that he was obliged to leave Ariadne behind because Dionysos wanted her as his wife. Athena appeared to him for that reason while he was asleep on the shore and ordered him to sail home without Ariadne; or else Hermes ordered him to do so;[61] or Dionysos simply carried the girl away while he was lying asleep.[62] She met with a happy fate in any case since Dionysos not only made her his consort but also proved to be a devoted and more or less faithful husband (see p. 179). The *Odyssey* offers an exceptional version of Ariadne's story in which Artemis shot her on Dia in response to evidence laid against her by Dionysos;[63] the story that lay behind this brief and surprising report seems to have been forgotten at an early period.

After calling in at Delos, where the youths from the tribute first performed the crane-dance, a serpentine dance that imitated the windings of the labyrinth,[64] Theseus and his companions finally arrived within sight of Attica. In the exultation of the moment or because he was still grieving over the loss of Ariadne, Theseus forgot to raise white sails on the ship to show his father that he was safe; and when Aigeus saw the black sails from his vantage-point on the Acropolis or Cape Sounion at the southern tip of Attica, he hurled himself down to his death. Some claimed that the Aegean Sea was named after him because he threw himself into it on this occasion. After landing at Phaleron, the old harbour of Athens, Theseus became aware of the tragic consequence of his oversight and ascended to the city in mourning rather than in triumph, as the new king of Athens.[65] We will consider the course of his reign after first completing our survey of Cretan myth.

The flight of Daidalos and Ikaros, and death of Minos

On discovering that Daidalos had provided invaluable advice to Theseus, Minos ordered that he should be arrested and imprisoned in the labyrinth along with his son IKAROS, who had been borne to him by a slave-girl in the palace. Or in another account, Minos took this action after discovering (rather belatedly it would seem) that Daidalos had enabled Pasiphae to conceive the Minotaur by building the wooden cow for her. Daidalos was far too clever to submit to incarceration without devising a means of escape, and set to work to make pairs of wings for himself and his son, constructing them from bird's feathers and wax. Before flying off, he warned his son not to soar too high, for the wax would then be melted by the sun, nor to descend too low, for the wings would then be damaged by moisture from the sea; but Ikaros was so exhilarated by the flight that he soared higher and higher until his wings eventually melted and he plunged to his death in the sea below. He fell into the south-eastern region of the Aegean that was known as the Ikarian Sea ever afterwards. Herakles, who was serving Omphale in Asia Minor at the time, found his body on an island off the coast and buried him there, naming the island Ikaria in his memory. Or else his father saw to his burial. Daidalos flew with greater prudence and made his way safely to Sicily, where he was offered refuge by Kokalos, the king of Kamikos in the west of the island.[66]

After learning that Daidalos had escaped, Minos set out to track him down and travelled far and wide in the course of his search. Wherever he went, he would produce a spiral seashell and promise a handsome reward to anyone who could draw a thread through it; for he was convinced that no one other than Daidalos had the ingenuity to perform such a delicate feat. When he eventually arrived at Kamikos and made his usual challenge, Kokalos took the shell from him and secretly gave it to Daidalos, who was keeping out of sight; and Daidalos achieved the feat just as Minos had supposed he would, by boring a small hole at the top of the shell, attaching a thread to an ant, and causing the ant to crawl through the shell until it emerged at the mouth. On receiving the shell with the thread drawn through it, Minos realized that Daidalos was somewhere close by, and demanded that he should be surrendered to him. Kokalos assured him that this would be done and invited him to enjoy his hospitality in the meantime; but while Minos was taking his bath, the king's daughters caused his death by pouring boiling water (or molten pitch) over him. Some said that Daidalos arranged the murder by fitting a special pipe into the ceiling above the bath.[67]

THE BROTHERS AND DESCENDANTS OF MINOS

Sarpedon and Miletos in Asia Minor

Before passing on to the children and descendants of Minos, we must consider the myths of his two brothers, Sarpedon and Rhadamanthys. As has been briefly mentioned, SARPEDON quarrelled with his brother over the succession (or a love affair) soon after the death of their adoptive father Asterion, and was driven into exile on the Asian mainland. After coming ashore there, he established himself as the king of Lycia, the westernmost province on the southern coast of Asia Minor.

Lycia was of more importance in Greek myth than one might suppose, partly because the Lycians commanded by Sarpedon and Glaukos are presented in the *Iliad* as the most significant foreign allies of the Trojans, and partly because a king of the land, Iobates, plays a central part in the interrelated legends of Proitos, king of Argos (see p. 237), and the Corinthian hero Bellerophon (see p. 433). In the *Iliad*, as opposed to the standard later tradition, the Sarpedon who fought at Troy is neither a brother of Minos nor even of Cretan descent, but a son of Zeus by Laodameia, the daughter of Bellerophon[68] (who had married a Lycian princess after surviving various ordeals that had been set for him by her father Iobates); and correspondingly, when Homer has occasion to refer to the love affair between Europa and Zeus elsewhere in the poem, he names Minos and Rhadamanthys alone as the offspring of their liaison.[69] In the sixth book of the epic, Diomedes encounters Glaukos, the cousin of Sarpedon, in battle, and is so impressed by his valour that he enquires about his ancestry, prompting him to give a full account of his family history, from which we can reconstruct a family tree for the descendants of Bellerophon as shown in Table 4.

Glaukos mentions[70] that his uncle Isandros had been killed by Ares as he was fighting against the Solymoi (a fierce neighbouring people who had previously been worsted by Bellerophon, see p. 434) and that his aunt Laodameia had been killed in anger by Artemis for some unexplained reason. After listening to Glaukos, Diomedes tells him that their two families are bound by ties of friendship because his grandfather Oineus had once entertained Bellerophon at his palace in Aetolia, and he therefore proposes that the two of them should not merely refrain from fighting one another but should exchange their armour as a token of friendship.[71] Since Diomedes was wearing ordinary bronze armour and Glaukos magnificent golden armour which was worth a hundred oxen, Homer is moved to remark that Zeus must have robbed Glaukos of his wits, and a phrase from this passage, 'gold for bronze', was adopted as a favourite proverb for an unequal bargain.[72]

The Homeric account of Sarpedon's origins is displaced in the later tradition by the familiar account that makes him a son of Zeus and Europa from Crete. This genealogy first appears in the Hesiodic *Catalogue* and Herodotus' *Histories*.[73] It by no means clear why such a change should have been regarded as desirable (although it has been suggested that the new genealogy may have been introduced to provide Sarpedon with a more favourable ancestry, since Sisyphos was a notorious rogue and his descendants tended to come to a bad end). Cretans figure regularly in foundation myths for places in Asia Minor in any case, since the Cretans were thought to be a very ancient people and their island was appropriately situated in relation to Asia. Chronological difficulties are raised, however, if Homer's Sarpedon is classed as a son of Minos, since this would mean that he must have been born two generations before the Trojan War (see p. 337). The Hesiodic *Catalogue* resolved the problem by suggesting that Zeus granted him the exceptional privilege of living for longer than an ordinary mortal (probably for three generations, as stated by Apollodorus, although there is a gap in the Hesiodic fragment at the relevant point).[74] Some later authors preferred to reconcile this later genealogy with the Homeric one by positing that there were two Sarpedons, the one who was born to Europa in Crete and a grandson of the same name who commanded the Lycians at Troy; in that case, the Cretan Sarpedon fathered a son in Lycia called Euandros, who married Deidameia, daughter of Bellerophon, and fathered the Homeric Sarpedon by her.[75]

Although the surviving fragments of the Hesiodic *Catalogue* fail to explain why Sarpedon should have left his native Crete, Herodotus explains his departure by a power-struggle in which he was expelled by the victorious Minos. According to Herodotus, the followers of Sarpedon who helped him to establish himself in Asia Minor were known as the Termiloi (apparently a name that the Lycians applied to themselves), but the people of the kingdom subsequently came to call themselves Lycians when Lykos, a son of Pandion II, king of Athens, arrived to live among them after being driven from Attica by his brother Aigeus (see p. 374).[76] In a later account of Sarpedon's expulsion, as has been mentioned, he is said to have quarrelled with Minos over the love of a boy called MILETOS. As the story is recounted by Apollodorus, this boy was a son of Apollo by a certain Areia, daughter of Kleochos, and Minos expelled him along with Sarpedon out of jealousy because he preferred the latter; Miletos founded the city of Miletos in Caria after his arrival in Asia Minor, while Sarpedon won a kingdom for himself further to the south in Lycia by joining with Kilix (the eponym of Cilicia, see p. 294) in a war against the Lycians.[77] This story was apparently of relatively late origin since Miletos was not founded by a Miletos from Crete in the earliest surviving foundation-myth, as recorded by Ephorus (a historian of the fourth century BC), but rather by Sarpedon himself, who named the new city after the city of Miletos in Crete.[78]

A Miletos is first named as the eponymous founder of Miletos in a tale ascribed to Aristikritos, a Milesian author who probably lived in the third century BC. Areia, daughter of Kleochos, bore Miletos to Apollo in Crete as in Apollodorus' account, and hid him in a yew-tree (*milax*) after his birth; but he was recovered by his grandfather Kleochos, who named him Miletos after his hiding-place. The surviving report is vague about the circumstances of his exile, merely stating that he was obliged to go abroad because he aroused the resentment of Minos; the story may well have followed the same course as in Apollodorus' version (or else Minos suspected that Miletos was plotting against him as in an account by Ovid, who describes Miletos as a son of Apollo by a certain Deione). He travelled first to the island of Samos, where he founded the Samian Miletos, and then to the Asian mainland, where he founded the far greater Carian Miletos.[79] In a somewhat later account ascribed to Nicander (second century), Miletos becomes a member of the Cretan royal family; he was borne to Apollo as usual, by Akakallis, daughter of Minos, who exposed him in the woods for fear of her father's anger. He was suckled by some she-wolves, however, at the will of Apollo, until he was recovered and reared by some herdsmen (see also on p. 597). When he grew up to become a handsome young man, Minos conceived a passion for him and planned to force him to his will, but he set off by night for Caria on the advice of Sarpedon, and founded the city of Miletos.[80]

Miletos married a local woman who bore him two children, a son KAUNOS, who was the eponym of the city of that name in southern Caria, and a daughter BYBLIS, who was associated with a Milesian spring called the Tears of Byblis. The pair became famous in the later tradition for the story of Byblis' incestuous love for her brother. In one account, she finally confessed her love to him and made advances to him, causing him such a shock that he left Miletos forever and founded the city of Kaunos as his new home. Finding that she was unable to quell her passion for her absent brother, Byblis hanged herself, and a spring arose afterwards from her tears.[81] Or in a rather different version, she tried to conceal her passion, but it proved too much for her, and she tried to commit suicide by hurling herself from a neighbouring mountain; but the local nymphs took pity on her and transformed her into a hamadryad nymph (see p. 210), and she lived among them thereafter as their friend and companion. The name of the spring is mentioned here, but it is not stated that it was formed from her tears.[82] In Ovid's version, which is exceptional in suggesting that she was actually transformed into the spring, she went mad with grief when her advances were rejected by her brother, and wandered through the surrounding lands in a state of distraction until she finally lay down in exhaustion and wept without cease, dissolving into her own tears to form a spring.[83]

Rhadamanthys, brother of Minos

RHADAMANTHYS, the other brother of Minos (or his only brother in earliest tradition), remained with him in Crete, unlike Sarpedon, for some years at least. He was no less renowned than Minos himself for his justice and his wisdom as a lawmaker, and was said to have established the principle that a person who inflicts a wrong should be repaid in exact proportion (*ius talionis*).[84] As we have already seen (see p. 250), the young Herakles saved himself from a charge of murder by appealing to another law of his that justified retaliation against violence initiated by another. Since he was credited with similar activities as a lawmaker and judge to those of his brother, the mythographers tried to distinguish their spheres of activity in various ways. According to some accounts, Minos reigned as king and established the laws and constitution of Crete while Rhadamanthys served under him as a judge and as guardian of the principles that were laid down by him.[85] Or else Minos ruled and legislated in Crete while Rhadamanthys performed a corresponding function in the smaller islands to the north and some coastal districts of

Asia Minor. It was explained in that case that the islanders had been so impressed by his reputation for justice that they had delivered themselves into his hands of their own free will;[86] or else Minos had grown so jealous of his fame that he had tried to marginalize him by sending him to rule the remoter parts of his empire.[87]

Rhadamanthys also had Boeotian connections, for he was said to have left Crete at some stage to marry Alkmene, the mother of Herakles, after the death of her first husband Amphitryon. The couple were supposed to have lived at Okaleia in western Boeotia. Some claimed that Rhadamanthys instructed the young Herakles in archery or even brought him up (although Amphitryon was generally thought to have survived until Herakles was grown up). Since Apollodorus indicates that he fled to his new homeland as an exile, there must presumably have been some story that explained the reason for his flight, but the surviving literature is not helpful on the matter (even if one source suggests that he fled after killing a brother of his, in accordance with a standard motif).[88]

An alternative tradition stated that Rhadamanthys married Alkmene posthumously in the Isles of the Blessed (a home for the privileged dead, see p. 116); for when she died of old age at Thebes, Zeus ordered Hermes to steal her from her coffin and carry her across the sea to the Isles to become the bride of Rhadamanthys (who was evidently already there). Hermes substituted a stone for her in her coffin, which became so heavy as a consequence that her sons found it too heavy to carry on her funeral-day and opened it up. On discovering the mysterious stone, they set it up in a sacred grove at Thebes, near the site of Alkmene's heroic shrine. Although recounted as part of a narrative ascribed to Pherecydes, one may suspect that this aetiological tale was of Hellenistic origin.[89] The tradition of the posthumous marriage may be quite ancient however. The story of the petrifaction of Alkmene's corpse could be cited to explain why she had no grave at Thebes.[90]

The *Odyssey* alludes to a tale in which the Phaeacians conveyed Rhadamanthys across the sea to Euboea to meet Tityos for some unstated reason.[91]

Rhadamanthys was granted an honoured status in the afterlife in accordance with his high virtues. Homer mentions in the *Odyssey* that he lives in the Elysian plain, though without explaining why; and Pindar places him in the Isles of the Blessed (which comes to much the same), where he assists Kronos as a counsellor, continuing to exercise his wisdom and justice in this more exalted setting.[92] Or in the usual tradition from the time of Plato onwards, he was appointed to be one of the judges in the Underworld along with his brother Minos (see p. 122).[93]

The children of Minos and Pasiphae, and the legend of Glaukos

Minos and Pasiphae had four daughters in the usual account, Ariadne, Phaidra, Akakallis and Xenodike, and four sons, Katreus, Deukalion, Androgeos, and Glaukos.[94] **Ariadne**, as we have just seen (p. 347), eloped with Theseus, but was left behind by him on Naxos to become the consort of Dionysos (who rendered her immortal in some accounts). In spite of the humiliations that Theseus had imposed on Crete and its royal family, Deukalion, son of Minos, offered **Phaidra** to him as a wife, evidently as a diplomatic move; the marriage ended in tragedy when she fell in love with her stepson Hippolytos (see p. 358). **Akakallis** (or Akalle) is a curious figure who originated as a minor goddess. She was remembered in Cretan legend as a heroine who had borne various eponyms and city-founders to Apollo and Hermes.

She bore Naxos, for instance, to Apollo, and Kydon, the eponym of the Cretan city of that name, to Hermes.[95] As was noted above, she was also the mother of Miletos in one version of his story, though apparently not the earliest. According to Apollonius, Minos became so angry with her after she had once become pregnant by Apollo that he drove her out, causing her to settle in Libya, where she gave birth to Garamas, the eponym of a Libyan people called the Garamantes; a son of his killed one of the Argonauts during their visit to Africa (see p. 395).[96] Nothing is recorded of the life of **Xenodike**, another heroine who is mentioned as a daughter of Minos.[97]

Two of the sons of Minos never rose to power in Crete, **Androgeos** because he died early while visiting Attica as an athlete (see p. 340), and **Glaukos** because he was the last-born. As the eldest son, **Katreus** succeeded to the throne after the death of Minos, and he was succeeded in his turn by his brother **Deukalion** after he and his only son died in quick succession in tragic circumstances. Deukalion was the father of Idomoneus, who was ruler of the Cretans at the time of the Trojan War and led the Cretan contingent to Troy. Before tracing the history of the ruling line, we must consider the single myth that is recorded for the young Glaukos.

During his early childhood, GLAUKOS fell into a large jar of honey while chasing a mouse (or while playing with a ball), and was drowned. Mystified by his disappearance, Minos searched everywhere for him and finally called together the finest seers of the age to advise him on the best course of action. He was told by the Kouretes (see p. 219, or by Apollo) that Glaukos would be found by the man who could find the best image to describe a marvellous cow in the king's possession, which changed colour every four hours (or twice a day) from white to red and then to black. So Minos put this question to the diviners, and Polyidos, a Corinthian seer who was descended from Melampous (see p. 430), replied most appropriately that the cow resembled a blackberry (or mulberry), which changes colour in that sequence as it ripens. Polyidos set to work immediately to apply his skills to discover the location of the child; and when he saw an owl putting birds to flight above the cellar in which Glaukos had met his accident, he recognized this as a sign and searched the cellar until he found the child. Minos was not satisfied with a corpse, however, and ordered that Polyidos should be shut in with the dead child until he discovered a way to bring him back to life again. When a snake happened to approach the child's body, Polyidos threw a stone at it and killed it, thinking that he would be in even worse trouble if any harm came to the body. This action proved to be his salvation, since another snake crept up to its dead companion and brought it back to life again by applying a special herb to it; and when Polyidos imitated the snake by applying the herb to the body of Glaukos, the young prince was duly returned to life. Before allowing the seer to sail home with his reward, Minos demanded that he should teach Glaukos to become a seer like himself. So Polyidos instructed him under constraint; but as he was about to sail away, he told Glaukos to spit into his mouth, and on doing so the child forgot all that he had learned.[98]

Katreus and his children; Idomoneus and Meriones

KATREUS, the eldest son and successor of Minos, had four children, a son Althaimenes and three daughters, Apemosyne, Aerope and Klymene.[99] When he once consulted an oracle about how his life would end, he was told that he would die at the hand of one of his children; and even though he tried to keep the prophecy secret, his son ALTHAIMENES came to hear of it and sailed away to Rhodes to avoid any danger of fulfilling it. Or in another account, Althaimenes took this action because he himself had been warned by an oracle that he was fated to kill his father.[100] One of his sisters, Apemosyne, accompanied him into exile. After arriving on Rhodes, he climbed Mt Atabyrion, the tallest peak on the island, and surveyed the surrounding area, looking at all the other islands in the neighbourhood. On catching sight of Crete in the far distance, he began to think of his ancestral gods, and decided to raise a shrine to Zeus on this Rhodian mountain.[101] Such was the legend that was offered to explain the origin of the cult of Atabyrian Zeus, which was indeed very ancient, perhaps ultimately of Phoenician origin.

Flight alone would not suffice to save Althaimenes from shedding the blood of his father; and before doing so, he would cause the death of his sister APEMOSYNE too. Hermes happened to conceive a passion for Apemosyne, but was unable to catch her however hard he tried because she could run so much faster than he could; so he resorted to a ruse instead, by spreading some freshly cut hides across her path and so causing her to slip to the ground as she was returning from a spring. He then proceeded to rape her (an uncharacteristic action for Hermes, who is normally a kindly god). When she told her brother what had happened, he refused to believe her, thinking that she was trying to conceal a liaison with a mortal lover, and kicked her so violently that she was killed.[102] Some time later, Katreus came to feel that he was now too old to rule in Crete, and sailed to Rhodes to recall his long-lost son. When he and his companions landed, however, in a remote part of the island, the local people mistook them for pirates and pelted them with stones. Although Katreus tried to explain his purpose, his words were drowned out by the barking of the dogs; and when Althaimenes arrived on the scene in response to the commotion, he killed his father with a throw of his spear without realizing who he was. On discovering afterwards that he had killed his father just as the oracle had predicted, he prayed to the gods to be removed from the earth, and was swallowed up in a chasm; or he simply died of a broken heart.[103]

Althaimenes first appears in Hellenistic sources; it would seem that he was a hero of Rhodian origin who was attached to the Cretan royal line by the Rhodians. According to an alternative tradition, he was of Heraklid birth as a descendant of Temenos (the first Heraklid king of Argos, see p. 291) in the third generation. In that case, he left the Peloponnese with a force of Dorians and Pelasgians after quarrelling with his elder brother, and was advised by an oracle to proceed toward Zeus and Helios (the Sun) to ask them for a land to colonize. So he called in first at Crete, which was the birthplace of Zeus, and left some followers there before travelling on to Rhodes, the island of Helios (see p. 43), where he defeated the Carian inhabitants and founded the three Dorian cities of Lindos, Ialysos and Kameiros.[104] This was said to have occurred at the same period as the Ionian settlement of Asia Minor (see p. 408), well after the Trojan War; but according to the usual and earlier tradition, the three cities were founded before the war by the Heraklid Tlepolemos (see p. 293).

After learning from the above-mentioned oracle that he would be killed by one of his children, Katreus had come to fear that his daughters KLYMENE and AEROPE might present a danger to him, and had therefore handed them over to the seafarer Nauplios to be sold abroad. Nauplios treated them more generously, however, as in the similar story of Auge (see p. 543), by offering Aerope to Pleisthenes, king of Mycenae, as a wife and taking Klymene as his own wife.[105] Or according to a conflicting tale from a lost play by Euripides, Katreus asked Nauplios to drown Aerope at sea after discovering that she had been seduced by a slave, but Nauplios took her to Pleisthenes instead.[106] Although there was disagreement on whether she married Atreus or Pleisthenes (an obscure figure who was sometimes interposed into the Mycenaean king-list between Atreus and Agamemnon, see p. 508), she became the mother of Agamemnon and Menelaos in either case. It so happens that Nauplios is said to have delivered her to Pleisthenes in surviving accounts of that story. She was best remembered for the legend that presented her as betraying her husband Atreus after engaging in a love affair with his brother Thyestes (see p. 506). As for Klymene, she bore two or more sons to Nauplios, including the prince of inventors Palamedes (see p. 236).

DEUKALION, son of Minos, the successor of Katreus, has no proper myths of his own; at the most, he is said to have re-established good relations with Theseus and Athens by offering his sister Phaidra to him as a wife (see p. 358). His son and successor IDOMONEUS, who was generally thought to have been the last descendant of Europa to rule in Crete, led a large contingent of Cretans to the Trojan War in eighty ships.[107] He would have been the first Greek ruler to realize that such a war might be in prospect since Menelaos was staying in Crete when he learned of the abduction of Helen (see pp. 445–6).[108] Idomoneus is commended in the *Iliad* as one of the most valiant of the Greek warriors, even though he was older than most of his comrades and his hair was flecked with grey.[109] He was numbered among the warriors who put themselves forward to fight in single combat with Hektor, and he dominated the fighting for a time while the Greeks were under desperate pressure by their ships.[110] It is stated in the *Odyssey* that he returned home safely, and there is no suggestion as yet that he met with any trouble on his arrival.[111] In the later tradition, however, he is said to have been forced into exile. There are two main accounts of how this came about. In one, Idomoneus had entrusted his kingdom to a certain Leukos, son of Talos, whom he had rescued from exposure; but Leukos took advantage of his benefactor's absence to kill his wife and children and then seize power as a tyrant, and he became sufficiently powerful to be able to drive Idomoneus into exile on his return.[112] Or in another account preserved in Latin sources, Idomoneus was struck by a violent storm during his return voyage and vowed to sacrifice whomever he first encountered after making a safe landfall in Crete; but this turned out to be his own son (or daughter), and he was driven out by the Cretans when he tried to fulfil his vow. Or he actually completed the sacrifice, and was driven out by his people when his action provoked a plague.[113] After his departure, he settled at Sallentium on the heel of Italy; Vergil mentions his presence there without explaining the reason for his exile.[114]

MERIONES, the Cretan who served as second-in-command to Idomoneus at Troy, was the son of a certain Molos, who was either an illegitimate son of Deukalion or a further son of Minos.[115] He appears quite frequently in the *Iliad* as a valiant warrior; he joins with his commander in offering to oppose Hektor in single combat, fights bravely in the battle around the Greek ships, wounding Deiphobos and killing others, and helps Menelaos to recover the body of Patroklos.[116] He is likely to be most familiar, however, as the possessor of a remarkable leather helmet which was armoured with rows of shining boar's tusks; since helmets of this Mycenaean design would have been obsolete long before Homer's time, the relevant passage in the *Iliad* is often quoted to show how extremely ancient material could be preserved in oral epic. Meriones lends the helmet to Odysseus when he sets off on his night reconnaissance in the tenth book of the poem.[117] Meriones is mentioned among the warriors in the Wooden Horse,[118] and he apparently returned safely to Crete in the early and local tradition (even if some late sources claim that he ended up in Sicily or Paphlagonia).[119] Diodorus reports that he shared a tomb with Idomoneus at Knossos, and that the Cretans honoured the pair in hero-cult and used to invoke their aid in time of war.[120] On witnessing a strange festival in Crete in which the image of a headless man was exhibited, Plutarch was told that the effigy represented Meriones' father Molos, who had been discovered without a head after he had tried to rape a nymph.[121]

THESEUS, KING OF ATHENS

Theseus becomes king, and abducts an Amazon, provoking an Amazon invasion

We must now return to THESEUS to consider the course of his later life after his return from Crete. He ascended to the throne immediately after his arrival as a result of the suicide of his father (see p. 348), and proceeded to institute various political reforms. It was claimed above all that he achieved the unification ('synoecism', *synoikismos*) of Attica by uniting the various independent communities of the land (twelve in number according to tradition) into a single state ruled from Athens.[122] Thucydides already describes how he was supposed to have abolished the councils and magistracies of the individual settlements to create a single assembly and seat of government in the capital city.[123] In reality, of course, this would have been a gradual process. Since Athens was noted in classical times for its large population of resident aliens or 'metics' (*meroikoi*), who made an invaluable contribution to the economic and cultural life of the city, this feature of the state was also attributed to the foresight of Theseus, who was said to have laid the ground for it by first encouraging the settlement of resident foreigners. To commemorate his two main achievements, he founded the annual festivals of the Synoikia and Metoikia. Another of his innovations was supposed to have been the introduction of the first Athenian coinage; the coins were said to have been stamped with the image of an ox rather than of an owl as in later times. A convenient though by no means complete account of the innovations and reforms (even extending to the introduction of a form of democracy!) can be found in Plutarch's life of Theseus; most of this pseudo-historical material was of Hellenistic origin.[124]

Theseus was faced with a revolt at some point from PALLAS, son of Pandion, a younger brother of Aigeus, and his fifty sons, the Pallantidai. Pallas laid claim to the throne on the allegation that the true father of Aigeus had not been Pandion, king of Athens, but rather a certain Skyrios (presumably the eponym of the island of Skyros, where Theseus was supposed to have owned ancestral properties, see p. 362). There was disagreement as to whether Pallas launched his revolt in the present period immediately after Theseus' ascent to the throne, or later when Theseus was married to Phaidra, or earlier when Theseus first arrived in Athens.[125] In the fullest account, as recorded by Plutarch, Pallas divided his force, marching openly against Athens from Sphettos with part of it while the other part lay hidden at Gargettos on the other side of the city, so as to be able to launch a surprise attack from the rear; but a herald called Leos betrayed the plan to Theseus, who was thus able to slaughter the concealed troops in a surprise attack of his own. On hearing of their fate, the other contingent scattered and the revolt petered out. The episode is first attested in a passing allusion by Euripides, who remarks that Theseus once went to Troizen in the company of Phaidra to be purified after slaughtering the Pallantidai.[126] An Athenian tradition stated that Theseus was tried for murder at the court of the Delphinion, but was acquitted on a plea of justified killing.[127]

As his first foreign adventure after his rise to power, Theseus sailed to the land of the Amazons in the north-eastern corner of Asia Minor and abducted an Amazon to make her his wife or concubine. She is usually named as ANTIOPE, or occasionally as Hippolyte or Melanippe.[128] In one version of the legend, Theseus sailed to the region as an ally of Herakles when the hero was sent to fetch the belt of the Amazon queen Hippolyte (see p. 263), and Antiope was awarded to him by Herakles as a reward for his valiant assistance.[129] Or Herakles was vainly attempting to capture the Amazon city of Themiscyra by siege, Antiope fell in love with Theseus and betrayed the city so as to be able to join him.[130] On chronological grounds, however, most mythographers favoured the alternative tradition in which Theseus led an expedition of his own to the area at a later period than that of Herakles.[131] Very little is recorded from the early tradition about this enterprise. Pindar remarks that Theseus was accompanied by his friend Peirithoos (see below), who is also shown among his allies on Attic vase-paintings, and Pherecydes is reported to have written that Theseus seized the Amazon with the help of his charioteer Phorbas.[132] He can be seen taking her to his chariot or carrying her off in it in vase-paintings from the latter part of the sixth century BC onwards. Plutarch cites a version in which the Amazons were more friendly than they are usually represented as being and sent an Amazon to Theseus' ship with gifts; but the hero took advantage of the situation to abduct her, by inviting her on to his ship and then immediately sailing off.[133] Theseus brought an Amazon back to Athens with him in any case, where she seems to have lived quite happily with him, bearing him a son Hippolytos.

The Amazons were greatly angered by the abduction of their sister-Amazon, as is natural, and ventured into Greece for the first time in their history to exact vengeance against Theseus. According to Hellanicus, they travelled by way of the northern shores of the Black Sea, crossing over the Cimmerian Bosporos (i.e. the Straits of Azov, between Asia and the Crimea) while it was frozen over in winter.[134] On arriving at Athens, they set up camp at a place known as the Amazeion, which was apparently situated on the slopes of the Areiopagos; according to Aeschylus, the Areiopagos (Hill of Ares, see p. 365) first came to be known as such because they offered sacrifices to their main god Ares on it during their stay.[135] Antiope had no wish to be taken home in the usual tradition, and joined battle at Theseus' side until she was killed by an Amazon called Molpadia. When the warrior-women were finally defeated, the survivors fled to neighbouring Megara and beyond, hence (so it was claimed) the Amazon graves that could be seen in various parts of Greece. Plutarch's life of Theseus provides a detailed account of the battle, and also refers to accounts in which Theseus' wife arranged a peace-treaty after the war had dragged on for three months, or secretly arranged for the wounded Amazons to be nursed at Chalcis in Euboea. The tomb of Antiope could be seen at Athens in historical times, as could that of the Amazon who had killed her.[136]

The tragedy of Phaidra and Hippolytos

It was convenient that Antiope should be removed from the scene since Theseus was said to have married the Cretan princess PHAIDRA at some point,[137] either as his second wife or as his only legitimate wife if the Amazon had merely been his concubine. There was also an account, however, apparently originating in early epic, in which Antiope was still alive at the time of the wedding; for Plutarch cites the author of the *Theseis* as stating that she and some fellow Amazons attacked Theseus after the marriage but were killed by Herakles.[138] Apollodorus records a similar story in which the previous wife of Theseus and some other Amazons tried to break into the wedding-feast fully armed with the intention of killing the guests; but Theseus' men managed to close the doors, and she was intercepted and killed outside.[139] Phaidra was offered to Theseus by her brother Deukalion, who was now king of Crete, apparently as a diplomatic measure to ease the bad relations that had prevailed between Crete and Athens since the murder of Androgeos. Theseus fathered two sons by her, Akamas and Demophon, and adopted them as his heirs, sending his previous son Hippolytos away to his grandfather Pittheus in Troizen.[140]

Since Pittheus had no sons of his own, HIPPOLYTOS could have expected to succeed him as king of Troizen, but he was destined to meet an early death instead as a result of the machinations of his stepmother. For Phaidra conceived a desperate passion for him, and was so mortified when he rejected her that she made false allegations against him, telling Theseus that had tried to rape or seduce her. Taking her at her word, Theseus cursed him to Poseidon, who sent a bull from the sea to frighten his horses as he was driving his chariot along the shore at Troizen, causing him to be thrown out and killed. On hearing of his fate, Phaidra was overcome by remorse and hanged herself.[141] Such was the original version of the story, so far as we can tell; but Phaidra is portrayed more sympathetically in Euripides' surviving *Hippolytos* (his second play on the theme).

In this play, Hippolytos is presented as a chaste and austere huntsman who is a devotee of the virgin goddess Artemis. He has scorned the cult and works of Aphrodite, by contrast, provoking the goddess of love to create trouble for him by causing Phaidra to fall helplessly in love with him. Phaidra is ashamed of her semi-incestuous passion in this account, and struggles in vain to subdue it, even trying to find a release in death by refusing her food; but her practically minded nurse worms the secret out of her, and then approaches Hippolytos on her behalf without her knowledge. The young Hippolytos, who is portrayed as an unimaginative and self-righteous young man, is thoroughly shocked and responds with a long diatribe on the vileness of women; and when Phaidra hears of this, she fears that Hippolytos will denounce her and takes her own life, leaving a note accusing him of rape (partly out of anger, and partly to ensure that her reputation and the prospects of her sons will be salvaged). On reading the letter, Theseus curses Hippolytos to his father Poseidon (who had previously promised him the fulfilment of three curses), and scornfully brushes aside his son's protestations of innocence. Poseidon causes Hippolytos to be fatally injured at Troizen in the manner described above, and his fellow hunters carry him home to his father in the final scene of the play; having learned the truth from Artemis just before, when the situation was already past mending, Theseus begs his son's forgiveness and is reconciled with him before he expires.[142]

Hippolytos was accorded divine honours at Troizen at a shrine that had supposedly been founded by Diomedes. The maidens of the city used to visit his shrine before their marriage to dedicate a lock of their hair to him (a practice foretold by Artemis at the end of Euripides' *Hippolytos*).[143] When Pausanias visited the region, he found that the Troizenians refused to show his grave or acknowledge the usual story of his death (officially at least), claiming instead that he had been raised to the heavens to become the constellation of the Charioteer (Auriga).[144] The standard death-story was firmly established in the local folklore nonetheless, for his grave could in fact be seen there, as could the old twisted olive-tree on which his reins had become entangled before he was thrown from his chariot.[145] Visitors could also see a myrtle-tree that grew with perforated leaves because Phaidra had mutilated them in her frustration as she was spying on Hippolytos while he was taking exercise nearby.[146]

An early tradition which can be traced back to the *Naupactia*, a lost epic composed in the sixth century BC or thereabouts, suggested that Asklepios restored Hippolytos to life again after his unfortunate death, presumably because he considered that his fate had been undeserved.[147] This story inspired the development of a curious Italian appendix to the legend of Hippolytos in which he was said to have been transferred to Latium to become a cultic associate of Diana, an ancient Italian goddess who was identified with Artemis. Her most venerable cultic centre was her sacred grove at Aricia, which was situated beneath the Alban Mount about seventeen miles south-east of Rome; it lay in a wooded hollow by a still lake, the Lacus Nemorensis (Lake of Nemi), which was also known by the more poetic name of Diana's Mirror. Diana shared the grove with two interesting lesser deities, the spring-goddess Egeria, who also had a cult at Rome and was supposed to have acted as adviser to Romulus' successor Numa Pompilius, and an obscure minor god of aged appearance called VIRBIUS. Now it was a rule of the grove that horses were strictly excluded from it; and to account for the origin of this rule along with the origin of Virbius himself, the following supplement was added to the legend of Hippolytos. After he was revived by Asklepios (with the help of the healing-god Paian in this account from Ovid) Diana/Artemis enshrouded him in a deep mist because she knew that the lord of the Underworld disapproved of the revival of mortals. To ensure his future safety, she then transformed his appearance to make him look older, conferred a new name on him (which would have been desirable in any case since his old one would have reminded him of horses, *hippoi*), and spirited him away to her grove at Aricia to live there under her protection as a minor god. Since he had been dragged to his death by horses, he wanted to have nothing more to do with them and they were banned from the grove from that time onwards; and it could be explained that he was now called Virbius because he had been 'a man twice over' (a Latin etymology, *vir bis*!).[148]

Theseus and Peirithoos abduct Helen, and try to abduct Persephone from the Underworld

Theseus was accompanied on his later adventures (including his journey to the land of the Amazons in some accounts) by his friend PEIRITHOOS, who was a Lapith chieftain from northern Thessaly. Plutarch provides a rather facile story to explain how the pair came to form their partnership. To test whether Theseus was really as strong and brave as his reputation suggested, Peirithoos drove some of his cattle away from the plain of Marathon in northern Attica and turned to confront him when he arrived in pursuit. Each was so impressed by the courage and bearing of the other that they refrained from fighting, and Peirithoos reached his hand out to Theseus and declared that he was ready to submit to any penalty that he proposed; but Theseus asked to become his friend instead, and they spent much of their time together from that moment onward.[149] When Peirithoos married the Lapith princess Hippodameia, Theseus visited him in his northern homeland to attend the wedding and fought at his side in the ensuing conflict between the Lapiths and the Centaurs (see further on p. 555); and the two friends went off together to take part in the hunt for the Calydonian boar and (in some accounts) the voyage of the Argonauts.[150] But their most remarkable enterprise was the final one in which they set out to abduct the daughters of Zeus, including the queen of the Underworld, as new brides after the death of their wives.

They began by seizing Helen from Sparta. This is a very ancient legend which must already have been known to Homer in some form, since he mentions in the *Iliad* that Theseus' mother Aithra (who was captured when Helen was recovered from Attica, see below) was present at Troy as a servant of Helen.[151] Alcman and Stesichorus are reported to have written about the episode.[152] Although Helen was presumably of marriageable age in the original version, this would have come to seem implausible when rational and consistent chronologies were developed for this period of mythical history, and mythographers from Hellanicus onwards suggest accordingly that she was still a young girl aged seven, or ten, or twelve or the like.[153] In Diodorus' account of the story, Peirithoos visited Theseus after the death of Hippodameia, and proposed the abduction after learning that his friend too had lost his wife; and after seizing Helen, who was only ten but already surpassed all other women in beauty, they cast lots for her on the agreement that the one who gained her would help his friend to gain whatever bride he chose, whatever peril that might entail. So when Peirithoos lost and declared that he wanted to seize Persephone from the Underworld, Theseus was obliged to assist him. Plutarch offers a similar version, reporting that the pair captured Helen as she was dancing in the temple of Artemis Orthia at Sparta, and were pursued as far as Tegea in southern Arcadia.[154] Or else each hero made his own choice of bride, Theseus choosing Helen first of all.[155] According to Hellanicus, they thought that they deserved to marry daughters of Zeus because Peirithoos was a son of Zeus and Theseus a son of Poseidon.[156] Hyginus records a strange version in which Zeus observed their daring abduction of Helen and then appeared to them in a dream to recommend that they should ask Hades to hand over Persephone as a bride for Peirithoos.[157]

Before setting off for the Underworld, Theseus took Helen to Aphidnai in north-eastern Attica and entrusted her to the care of Aphidnos, the eponymous ruler of the town, telling him to keep her there under the strictest secrecy; and he summoned his mother Aithra from Troizen to act as her companion. The secret was betrayed or leaked out, however, and the two brothers of Helen, the Dioskouroi, invaded Attica during Theseus' absence and attacked Aphidnai. They soon seized the town and recovered their sister, and also took Aithra home with them to Sparta, where she was obliged to serve Helen as a maid. While they were in Attica, they exacted vengeance against Theseus by transferring the throne to Menestheus, son of Peteos, a member of another branch of the Athenian royal family. Akamas and Demophon, the two sons of Theseus, fled to Euboea to take refuge with Elephenor, king of the Abantes; see pp. 375–6 for their subsequent history.[158]

Two main stories were developed to explain how the Dioskouroi came to discover where Helen was being hidden. According to Herodotus, they terrorized the people of Athens by burning their villages until the men of Dekaleia, or perhaps Dekalos himself, agreed to guide them to Helen's hiding-place; and for that reason, the Spartans granted special privileges to the Dekaleians ever afterwards and left their town unharmed whenever they invaded Attica[159] Dekaleia, which lay in north-central Attica, was used by the Spartans as a forward base during the Peloponnesian War. According to another account, the secret was betrayed by Akademos, the eponym of the Academy (Akadameia), a sacred grove on the outskirts of Athens which is best remembered as the site of Plato's school (hence modern 'academies').[160] According to an eccentric tale from Stesichorus, Theseus fathered a child, Iphigeneia, by Helen, who gave birth to her in the Argolid while travelling home and handed her over to Klytaimnestra (who was of course her true mother in the usual tradition).[161]

After descending below at the bottomless cave at Tainaron in the southern Peloponnese, Theseus and Peirithoos somehow persuaded the infernal ferryman Charon to convey them across the boundary-river (see p. 113) into the realm of Hades. Two surviving lines from the early epic account in the *Minyas* indicate that they had to wait by the river-bank for a time until Charon's boat returned to its moorings.[162] It would seem that they approached Hades openly to ask him to release Persephone rather than attempting to abduct her by stealth, but very little is recorded of this aspect of the adventure in surviving sources. Another epic fragment gives an impression of the sort of reasoning that they might have employed, stating that Peirithoos believed that he had a better claim to Persephone because he was a child of Zeus like herself while Hades was merely her uncle![163] It was crazy, of course, to suppose that Hades would surrender his wife to a mortal on this or any other ground, and he proceeded to imprison them in his underground kingdom. According to Apollodorus, he made a show of friendliness, inviting the two of them to sit down as if they were about to enjoy his hospitality; but when they did so, they found that their flesh became attached to the seat, the 'Chair of Forgetfulness' (*thronos Lēthēs*), and that they were also bound down by coils of snakes in addition.[164] The epic poet Panyasis already stated that their flesh became attached to the rock that they were sitting on, and we read elsewhere that they were held down by chains or coils of serpents.[165]

Although both were probably detained forever in the original story, it came to be believed that Herakles released one or both of them when he descended to the Underworld to fetch Kerberos (as his penultimate or final labour, see p. 268). In the usual account, the great hero was able to pull Theseus up from his seat, but not Peirithoos since he carried the greater guilt as the one who had proposed the abduction of Persephone. In Apollodorus' narrative, the earth shook in warning when Herakles extended his hand to Peirithoos.[166] There are conflicting accounts, however, in which Peirithoos was rescued also or neither was released.[167]

The exile and death of Theseus

On arriving home from Hades, Theseus discovered that Menestheus had seized power with the help of the Dioskouroi and was now firmly in control. So he had to seek a new home and sailed to Skyros, an island in the Aegean to the east of Euboea, because he owned ancestral lands there; or else he arrived there by accident after being blown off course as he was trying to travel to the court of his father-in-law Deukalion in Crete.[168] Although Lykomedes, the king of the island, pretended to be happy to receive him, he set to work to contrive his death because he feared that his own position might be threatened if such a great hero should be present in the land, or because he wanted to perform a favour for Menestheus. He achieved his aim by taking Theseus up to the highest point on the island on the pretext of showing him his estates and then pushing him over a cliff. Or in a more banal account that absolves Lykomedes from any blame, Theseus simply slipped and fell as he was taking his after-dinner walk. His season of glory had passed in any case; Plutarch remarks that his death attracted little attention at the time.[169]

Menestheus continued to rule at Athens until he left to fight at Troy as leader of the Athenian contingent.[170] Since he was either killed in the fighting or decided to settle abroad afterwards, one or both of the sons of Theseus were able to recover their father's kingdom after the war (see p. 375).

Theseus brought posthumous aid to the Athenians at the battle of Marathon, marching ahead of them in full armour as they advanced against the Persians.[171] After the Persian Wars, the Delphic oracle ordered that his bones should be fetched home to Athens; and when Cimon, a prominent Athenian statesman and general, captured Skyros in 475 BC, he was thus very eager to locate the hero's burial-place. One day, when he noticed that an eagle had landed on what appeared to be a burial-mound and was pecking at it with its beak and tearing at it with its talons, he concluded that this must be a sign and ordered his followers to dig at that spot. When they did so, they found the coffin of a man of enormous size (as the heroes of old were supposed to have been) with a bronze spear and a sword lying beside it. Thinking that these must surely be the remains and arms of Theseus, Cimon brought them back to Athens to the great enthusiasm of the people, and the exiled hero was received back into his city.[172]

In some celebrated stories from Attic tragedy, Theseus is presented as a noble ruler who came to the aid of heroes and heroines from other cycles of myth when they fell victim to misfortune and injustice. He granted sanctuary to the blind and exiled Oedipus at Kolonos just outside Athens, saving him and his daughter from being hauled back to Thebes by Kreon (see p. 314); at the urging of Adrastos, he forced Kreon, king of Thebes, to consent to the burial of the Argive dead after the expedition of the Seven (see p. 322); and he granted refuge to the Heraklids at Athens after the death of their father and helped them to defeat their persecutor, Eurystheus (see p. 287).

THE ATHENIAN ROYAL FAMILY

Athenian legends and the Athenian king-list

We must now complete our survey of Athenian myth by tracing the mythical history of Attica from the ages that preceded the birth of Theseus to those that followed his death. Although Attica had a hero of the very first rank in Theseus, and also produced a few lesser figures such as Daidalos, Kephalos or Menestheus who played a role in major episodes from saga, the province was of surprisingly limited significance in early heroic myth. If due exception is made for the stories that have already been covered in this chapter, most of the legends of Attica and the Athenian royal family can be assigned to the category of local myth, either as tales from folklore or as antiquarian legends that were devised to account for the origin of local cults, institutions and other peculiarities. Even if Attic legends of this kind were probably of no greater interest or number than those of many another province, the cultural and political prominence of Athens from the time of the Persian Wars onwards, and also the eloquence of its writers, ensured that they came to be better known than many of their equivalents in other lands. The legends of the province also attracted special interest from the mythographers. Hellanicus made a particular study of them in the fifth century BC, and authors of the Hellenistic period followed his lead by developing a special branch of literature, Atthidography, that was devoted to the antiquities of the land. For reasons such as these, this largely provincial body of legend established a firm foothold in the canon of panhellenic myth (as is attested by the full treatment of it in Apollodorus' handbook).

The Attic king-list was a highly artificial creation that did not finally acquire its definitive form, as shown in Table 19, until as late as the third century BC. In the time of Herodotus, it would seem that only four kings were recognized as having reigned before Theseus, firstly Kekrops and Erechtheus/Erichthonios, the earthborn first rulers of the land, and then Pandion and Aigeus, the two predecessors of Theseus. But since Kekrops and Erichthonios were supposed to have lived at the very beginning of history (like Pelasgos in Arcadia or Deukalion in Central Greece) while Theseus and his immediate predecessors must have lived in the period directly preceding the Trojan War, the mythographers were obliged to add several new names to the list if it was to be synchronized with comparable lines in other places (such as Argos or Thebes). This was achieved in two ways. In the first place, additional earthborn rulers, Kranaos and Amphiktyon (who were already known as early Athenians but not as kings), were inserted between Kekrops and Erichthonios at the head of the list; and second, some kings who were already included in the list were reduplicated. A second Kekrops and a second Pandion were thus introduced, while Erechtheus/Erichthonios (who was originally the same person under two different names, see below) was divided into two separate individuals, the earthborn Erichthonios and his grandson Erechtheus, son of Pandion. By this process, the following king-list was developed: Kekrops I – Kranaos – Amphiktyon – Erichthonios – Pandion I – Erechtheus – Kekrops II – Pandion II – Aigeus – Theseus. Since the early kings of Athens not only originated in cult rather than in heroic myth but were also reduplicated in many cases, it is hardly surprising that most of them should be insubstantial figures with few proper myths. As a further step in the systematization of Attic myth, mythographers allocated floating stories associated with other heroes or heroines to a specific point in time, usually by attaching the relevant hero or heroine to the royal line as a child or descendant of a particular king.

Kekrops, the earthborn first king of Athens, and his children

The Athenians commonly supposed that their earliest king was KEKROPS, who had sprung from the earth and bore the marks of his chthonic origin in his twofold form, for he had a serpent's tail in place of human legs.[173] The autochthony of Kekrops and Erichthonios (and of Kranaos and Amphiktyon too in the fully developed king-list) reflected the proud claim of the Athenians to be an 'autochthonous' or indigenous people who had inhabited their land from very ancient times, and provided a mythical confirmation for that claim; as it happens, this cherished belief of theirs was not wholly unfounded, for the Athenians had inhabited their own land for longer than most of their neighbours, and certainly for longer than the Dorians in the Peloponnese. Since the Athenians were also distinguished by the special relationship that they enjoyed with Athena, the guardian-goddess of their city and land, it was assumed that the goddess must have established herself as the patroness of the land in the time of its first king, so ensuring that the city acquired its proper identity at the very beginning of its history (just as the Argives assumed that Hera had established herself as the great goddess of their land in the time of their first king, Phoroneus, see p. 227). As has been recounted in connection with the mythology of Poseidon, Athena won her position in the city by defeating Poseidon in a contest for the land (see p. 102); and Kekrops played a crucial part in determining the outcome in most accounts, whether by acting as arbitrator (on his own or in conjunction with Kranaos), or by bearing witness before the twelve gods that Athena had laid claim to the land by planting the first olive-tree there.[174] This is the only myth from the early tradition in which Kekrops is assigned any active role; he was a venerable ancestor, a sort of Adam, rather than a subject of legend.

When the Atthidographers of the Hellenistic period set out to develop a coherent account of the growth of civilization in Athens, they came to describe Kekrops as a primordial culture-hero who had introduced the first elements of civilization to Attica (or indeed to the human race) and had founded some of the most ancient cults of the land, much as Phoroneus was supposed to have done in Argos, or Pelasgos in Arcadia. Among other innovations, he was said to have introduced the first laws, the building of cities, the practice of burying the dead, the use of animal-skins for clothing, and even the art of writing[175] (although Kadmos, see p. 298, and Palamedes were more favoured candidates for that particular honour). The best-known story of this kind, the one that presents him as the inventor of monogamous marriage, was apparently devised to provide a rationalistic (if far-fetched) explanation for the origin of the idea of his hybrid form; for Clearchus of Soloi (third century BC) claimed that he had come to be credited with this form because he had tried to abolish promiscuity in favour of a permanent union between men and women in which the contrasting natures of each would be united into one.[176] In the religious realm, Kekrops was said to have founded the cult of Zeus Hypatos (the Highest) on the Acropolis, which could be thought to be very ancient because the god was honoured with offerings of honey-cakes rather than with blood-sacrifices, and to have established the cult and festival of the pre-Olympian deity Kronos.[177] In poetic parlance, the Athenians could be called Kekropians (Kekropiai or Kekropidai) after their first king, and Athens the city of Kekrops.

Instead of taking a local nymph as his wife as did many primordial rulers, Kekrops married Aglauros, the daughter of a certain Aktaios (or Aktaion); some antiquarians claimed that this Aktaios (Coast-man) had in fact preceded him as the first king of Athens, which had originally been named Akte after him. Aglauros (or Agraulos) bore three notable daughters, HERSE, PANDROSOS and AGLAUROS (or Agraulos), to her semi-serpentine husband, and also a son of lesser interest called Erysichthon.[178]

The three girls, the Kekropides or Aglaurides, were best remembered for the part that they played in the story of Erichthonios. When this strangely conceived child was brought to birth by Gaia (see p. 184 for the story of his origin), she handed him over to Athena, who shut him up in a chest and entrusted him to the daughters of Kekrops, strictly ordering them not to open it. Needless to say, the temptation was irresistible, and one or more of the sisters peered into the chest, with disastrous consequences. Although the basic story is always much the same, it is recorded in all manner of different versions. In the earliest surviving account in Euripides' *Ion*, the three sisters opened the chest to discover that Athena had place two guardian-snakes in it along with the child, and they met a bloody death afterwards on some rocks, presumably after jumping down from the Acropolis in terror or madness as in some later accounts. It is usually suggested in subsequent sources that one or two of the sisters alone peeped into the chest and so incurred this fate. According to Apollodorus, the chest was entrusted to Pandrosos, but her two sisters opened it and were killed by the guardian-snake that was coiled around the child. These were the erring sisters in Pausanias' version also (although we are told here that the chest was entrusted to all three of them); or in an account by the early Hellenistic mythographer Amelesagoras, the offence was committed by Aglauros and Pandrosos, or in Ovid's version, by Aglauros alone. If Athena was planning to make the child immortal, as Apollodorus alone reports, the girls may have frustrated her plan.[179]

Whatever part they may have played in this joint myth, all three sisters were said to have embarked on love affairs with gods which resulted in the birth of various minor children. According to a fairly old tradition, Aglauros bore a daughter ALKIPPE to Ares, the god of war. This Alkippe appears together with her father in a legend that was devised to account for the origin of the Areiopagos, an ancient high court at Athens that tried crimes involving bloodshed. When a brutal son of Poseidon called Halirrhothios (Sea-foam) tried to rape Alkippe, Ares caught him in the act and killed him, much to the anger of Poseidon, who prosecuted the war-god for murder in a trial judged by the twelve gods (i.e. the other major Olympian gods). In the course of the trial, which was held on a hill to the west of the Acropolis that was known thenceforth as the Areiopagos (Hill of Ares), Ares persuaded the court that he had been justified in killing a man who was trying to rape a close relation of his (as would have been acceptable in classical Athens if the rapist were killed immediately after being caught *in flagrante*).[180] In the three subsequent trials that were held on the Areiopagos in mythical times, Kephalos was condemned to exile for accidentally killing his wife (see p. 372), Daidalos was condemned to death *in absentia* for murdering his nephew (see p. 340), and, most famously of all, Orestes was tried there for killing his mother in the first case to be judged by a jury of Athenian citizens (see p. 511).

Other tales told of liaisons between daughters of Kekrops and the god Hermes. Pandrosos (or one or other of her sisters) bore him a son Keryx (Herald), who was of some local importance as the mythical ancestor of the Eleusinian family of the Kerykes, which provided the heralds who presided at the Eleusinian Mysteries.[181] This at least was the belief of the Kerykes themselves, since some claimed that Keryx had been a son of Eumolpos (a figure who was closely associated with Eleusis and the mysteries, see p. 370).[182] Herse was also seduced by Hermes and bore him a son called Kephalos, who grew up to be so beautiful that he was abducted by Eos, goddess of the dawn (see p. 47).[183] This Kephalos should properly be distinguished from the Kephalos who married Prokris, a later princess of Athens, but the two were sometimes confused, as we will see (p. 372). The traditional story of a liaison between Hermes and Herse inspired the development of a tale of sisterly jealousy that is recounted by Ovid in the *Metamorphoses*. On seeing the lovely Herse among the maidens who were carrying the sacred objects to the temple of Athena during the great festival of the Panathenaia, Hermes fell desperately in love with her; and when he tried to find her at her home afterwards, he encountered her sister Aglauros, who offered to help him if he would reward her with a fortune in gold. Athena was angry with Aglauros, however, for having opened the chest that contained Erichthonios, and she was therefore determined that the girl should not win the favour of Hermes and a fortune in gold besides. So she incited Envy (Invidia in Ovid's Latin) to frustrate her plan by causing her to become jealous of her sister for having gained the love of a god. Overcome by this new-found jealousy, Aglauros was no longer willing to assist Hermes when he arrived to court her sister, but seated herself in front of the door of Herse's bedroom to prevent him from entering. When she persisted in her action in spite of his appeals, retorting that she would remain exactly where she was, he said 'Granted!' and turned her to stone, opening up the door with a wave of his wand. The stone was as dark as Aglauros' thoughts. This tale was apparently of Hellenistic origin, at least in its original form, since a papyrus from Herculaneum has revealed an earlier version, probably by Callimachus, in which Pandrosos was turned to stone.[184]

ERYSICHTHON, the only son of Kekrops, was a minor culture-hero who was associated primarily with Prasiai on the east coast of Attica; he was said to have died there while still young and childless as he was returning from the holy island of Delos with a statue of Eileithuia, goddess of Childbirth. Of the three ancient wooden images (*xoana*) of the goddess that could be seen at her temple at Athens, one was identified as the image that Erysichthon had brought from Delos, while the other two were supposed to have been brought from Crete several generations later by Phaidra (the Cretan princess who married Theseus). Erysichthon's tomb could be seen at Prasiai, where his corpse was said to have been buried after his ship had arrived in port.[185]

Three further earthborn kings, Kranaos, Amphiktyon and Erichthonios

As was noted above, two minor heroes, Kranaos and Amphiktyon, were inserted into the king-list as successors of Kekrops. The earthborn KRANAOS ruled at the time of the great flood and was thus a contemporary of Deukalion, who even sought refuge with him in one account; he named the land of Attica after his daughter Atthis, who was borne to him along with two other daughters by his Spartan wife Pedias.[186] He was eventually driven out by AMHIKTYON, who was earthborn like himself (or was sometimes identified with Amphiktyon, son of Deukalion, whose proper home was Thermopylae, see p. 404). This was an act of treachery in one account because Amphiktyon was married to the king's daughter Atthis (although this conflicts with another tradition in which Kranaos named the land after Atthis when she died young as an unmarried maiden). There is nothing of interest to report of Amphiktyon except that Dionysos was supposed to have visited him in Athens and taught him how to mix water into wine in the proper proportion (for it was the Greek custom to water wine before serving it).[187]

After twelve years, Amphiktyon was expelled in his turn by yet another earth-born hero, ERICHTHONIOS.[188] In contrast to local autochthones like Kekrops and Pelasgos who sprang from the earth without need of a father, Erichthonios was conceived by Gaia (Earth) to a specific divine father, Hephaistos; for Gaia was fertilized by semen that was emitted by him as he was trying to make love to Athena, as described in Chapter 5 (see p. 184). Since Athena was not only involved in the incident that led to Erichthonios' conception, but also received him from Gaia imme-diately after his birth and reared him herself on the Acropolis (after briefly entrusting him to the daughters of Kekrops), she came as close to being a mother to him as was possible for a virgin goddess. The special relationship that she had established with Athens in the time of Kekrops was thus deepened; and the strange birth-legend also explained how the city came to be placed under the joint patronage of Athena and Hephaistos, as two deities who presided over the handicrafts that were so essential to the city's prosperity.

In the Hellenistic and later tradition, a clear distinction was drawn between Erichthonios, the marvellous child who was born from the earth and reared by Athena, and Erechtheus, who was remembered in more adult roles as a leader in war and paterfamilias and was honoured in cult on the Acropolis in close connection with Poseidon. It is generally believed, however, that this distinction with the accom-panying division of roles was first established by the mythographers for chronological reasons, and that the two figures were originally a single person under alternative names. The most telling evidence in this regard is the fact that Homer and Herodotus apply the name Erechtheus to the earthborn hero; Homer refers in the *Iliad* to 'great-hearted Erechtheus, who was reared of old by Athena, daughter of Zeus, when the grain-giving ploughland brought him to birth', and Herodotus refers similarly to Erechtheus as earthborn.[189] There is no unequivocal evidence for the name Erichthonios until it appears in the visual arts and tragedy in the second half of the fifth century BC (although it is reported without direct citation that Pindar and the author of the *Danais*, an early epic of uncertain date, applied the name to the earthborn child).[190] It seems altogether probable in any case that the longer name was of later origin, especially in view of the fact that Erechtheus/Erichthonios was known as Erechtheus in connection with his cult on the Acropolis. After the dividing of the inheritance, only a single notable deed was assigned to Erichthonios as an adult, namely the founding of the Panathenaia, the principal festival of Athena at Athens; since he was identified as the nursling who had been reared by Athena, it is understandable that this particular action should have been credited to him rather than to Erechtheus. Since games were held in connection with the festival, it was further suggested that he invented the four-horse chariot and used to compete as a chariot-driver in the games; an astral myth adds that Zeus was so impressed by his initiative in imitating the sun-god Helios (who travelled across the sky in a chariot of this kind, see p. 43) that he raised him to the heavens to become the constellation of the Charioteer (Auriga). It is no surprise to discover that his wife bore the same name, Praxithea, as the wife of Erechtheus; described as a naiad nymph, she bore him a single son, Pandion, who succeeded him as king of Athens.[191]

Pandion and his daughters Prokne and Philomela

PANDION I married his maternal aunt Zeuxippe, who bore him two sons, Erechtheus and Boutes, and two daughters, Prokne and Philomela.[192] Two famous stories were set in his reign, the legend of Ikarios which told how wine was introduced into Attica (see p. 176), and the grisly legend of TEREUS, king of Thrace, who married a daughter of Pandion and later raped and mutilated her sister. Pandion invited the assistance of Tereus when he became embroiled in a border-dispute with Labdakos, king of Thebes; and after bringing the war to a successful conclusion with his aid of his Thracian ally, he expressed his gratitude by offering him his elder daughter PROKNE as a wife. So Tereus took her away to his northern homeland, where she bore him a son, Itys. All went well until Prokne began to feel lonely and asked her husband to travel to Athens to fetch her sister PHILOMELA for a visit. As he was coming back with Philomela, he conceived a violent lust for her and raped her; and to conceal his crime, he cut out her tongue and hid her away in a remote spot, telling Prokne that she had died during the journey. But Philomela wove an account of her sufferings into a tapestry and sent it to her sister, who fetched her home and proceeded to exact a grim revenge on Tereus. Slaughtering Itys, the only child of their union, she boiled his flesh, and served it as a meal to her unknowing husband. She then took flight with Philomela, heading southward. As soon as Tereus discovered the true nature of the meal, he hastily seized an axe and chased after the two sisters, finally catching up with them at Daulis (an ancient town in Central Greece to the east of Delphi). They prayed for help to the gods, who took pity on them and transformed the pursuer and pursued alike into birds, turning Prokne into a nightingale, Philomela into a swallow and Tereus into a hoopoe (or hawk).[193]

Although the transformations follow this pattern in all Greek sources, some Latin sources alter it by presenting Prokne as the swallow and Philomela as the nightingale;[194] and it so happens that this secondary version is the one that was transmitted into the Renaissance tradition, hence the use of Philomela (or Philomel, Philomèle etc.) as a poetic name for a nightingale. The original version is clearly preferable, however, since it explains why the nightingale sings so mournfully (she is lamenting her child) and why the swallow chatters inarticulately (she has no tongue, but persists in trying to tell her story). In some late sources, the murdered Itys is said to have been transformed into a bird also, namely a pheasant (*fasanus*).[195] According to Ovid at least, Pandion died of grief after learning of the fate of his daughters.[196] Although Tereus is always regarded as a Thracian, he is sometimes said to have ruled at Daulis; or according to a Megarian tradition, he ruled at Pagai in the Megarid, and committed suicide in Megara after the two sisters escaped into neighbouring Attica.[197] He is described as a son of Ares,[198] as is fitting in view of his violent nature and the Thracian connections of the war-god.

Erechtheus and his war against Eumolpos and the Eleusinians

After Pandion's death, his twin sons divided the inheritance between them, ERECHTHEUS taking the throne, and BOUTES the priesthood of Athena and Poseidon (two deities who had a joint cult in the Erechtheion).[199] Boutes was the eponymous ancestor of the Boutadai and Eteoboutadai, the families that provided the priestesses for the cult of Athena Polias; he had a heroic shrine of his own in the Erechtheion.[200] Erechtheus married Praxithea, daughter of Phrasimos, a grand-daughter of the Attic river-god Kephisos. She bore him four daughters, Prokris, Oreithuia, Kreousa, and Chthonia, and various sons including a second Kekrops, who became the next king of Athens, and Metion, whose sons later seized power for a time by expelling Erechtheus' grandson. The ever-ingenious Daidalos, whose exploits have already been considered, was often classed as a grandson of Erechtheus, either through Metion or through another son of his called Eupalamos (i.e. Handyman, the Ingenious).[201]

The most notable event in the reign of Erechtheus was a war between Athens and the town of Eleusis about twelve miles to the north-west; the legend of this conflict served to explain how Eleusis, with its famous mystery-cult (which had supposedly been founded by Demeter herself, see p. 128), came to be absorbed into the Athenian state. The legend first appears in the remains of a lost play by Euripides, the *Erechtheus*. When the war broke out, the Eleusinians summoned the aid of EUMOLPOS, son of Poseidon, who marched to their assistance with a large force of Thracians. In the face of this threat, Erechtheus consulted the Delphic oracle, which declared that the Athenians would prevail if the king sacrificed one of his daughters; and when he duly slaughtered his youngest daughter, sometimes named as Chthonia, his surviving daughters committed suicide because all of them had sworn beforehand to share the fate of the chosen victim.[202] There were also accounts in which Erechtheus slaughtered more than one of his daughters.[203] Although he proceeded to defeat the enemy in accordance with the oracle, killing Eumolpos in battle, Poseidon was so angered by the death of his son that he killed Erechtheus in his turn or asked Zeus to kill him with a thunderbolt; according to Euripides, Poseidon struck the ground with his trident after the battle, causing the king to be swallowed up in a chasm.[204] After suffering this defeat, the Eleusinians made peace with the Athenians on the agreement that their city would be subject to Athens from that time onwards but that they would continue to administer the mysteries independently.[205] In historical times, sacrifices were offered to Erechtheus as a hero at the altar of Poseidon in the Erechtheion.[206]

Since Eumolpos was the eponymous ancestor of the Eumolpidai, the family that provided the priests who officiated at the Eleusinian Mysteries, he could hardly have been a foreigner from Thrace in the original tradition. The *Homeric Hymn to Demeter*, which is our earliest source for him, includes him among the Eleusinian princes who were instructed by Demeter in her mysteries.[207] He was presented as a Thracian, however, in Euripides' *Erechtheus*, apparently as a son of Poseidon by Chione, a daughter of Boreas, the North Wind, whose home lay in Thrace (see p. 48).[208] Since Chione's mother Oreithuia was a daughter of Erechtheus who had been abducted from Athens by Boreas (see below), Eumolpos was of partly Athenian descent in this account in spite of his Thracian birth. For his subsequent history, we have to rely on Apollodorus' narrative, which may well have been based (directly or indirectly) on information provided in Euripides' play. After bearing Eumolpos to Poseidon, Chione threw him into the sea for fear of her father's anger, but he was rescued by Poseidon, who entrusted him to his daughter Benthesikyme to be reared in Ethiopia. When he grew up, Benthesikyme's husband (whose name is lost owing to a corruption in the text) offered one of his daughters to him as a wife, but later sent him into exile when he tried to rape her sister. Although he found sanctuary in the land of his birth with Tegyrios, king of Thrace, and his son Ismaros married the daughter of Tegyrios, he was forced into exile once again when he was caught plotting against him. He went to Eleusis and established friendly relations with the Eleusinians, but was called back by Tegyrios when Ismaros subsequently died, and later succeeded to the throne. Since he was now a powerful ruler, the Eleusinians naturally turned to him when they became embroiled in a war with their more powerful neighbour.[209] Some authors, including Isocrates, suggest that Eumolpos was hoping to seize Athens for himself, laying claim to it on the ground that it properly belonged to his father Poseidon rather than to Athena (i.e. because he thought that Athena had been wrongly adjudged the winner when the two gods had competed for the land, seen p. 102).[210]

There was also a version of the legend in which Eumolpos was not killed by Erechtheus but survived to return to Eleusis, where he presided over the mysteries; in that case, his son Immarados (who can be equated with Ismaros) was the victim of Erechtheus.[211] Eumolpos is quite often described as the founder of the Eleusinian Mysteries in later sources[212] (although some mythographers claimed that there were two figures of that name, the one who founded the mysteries and the one who made war against Athens at a later period[213]). It was sometimes said that the Athenians invited Ion to act as their military commander during their war against Eumolpos.

The above-mentioned story of the death of the daughters of Erechtheus provided a mythical explanation for the origin of the HYAKINTHIDES, a group of heroines or minor goddesses who were honoured in Attic cult. There was an alternative story in which the Hyakinthides were said to have originated as the four daughters of a Spartan called Hyakinthos (not to be confused with the celebrated favourite of Apollo) who had settled in Attica; for when Attica had been struck by a famine and plague during the war with Minos (see p. 341), the Athenians had slaughtered the daughters of Hyakinthos on the grave of Geraistos the Kyklops (otherwise unknown) in obedience to an ancient oracle. On this occasion, as we have seen, the sacrifice failed to achieve its purpose.[214] It could be explained in this story that the Hyakinthides were known by that name because they had been the daughters of Hyakinthos. In the other story in which they had originated as the daughters of

Erechtheus, it was explained that they had come to be known as the Hyakinthides because they had died on a hill called Hyakinthos.[215] If all the daughters of Erechtheus met their death in the above circumstances, this story is not easily reconciled with the forthcoming traditions in which the daughters of Erechtheus are said to have contracted splendid marriages.

The daughters of Erechtheus, and the legend of Kephalos and Prokris

Two of the daughters of Erechtheus led unexceptional lives, CHTHONIA marrying her uncle Boutes,[216] and KREOUSA marrying Xouthos, son of Hellen, to become the mother of Ion and Achaios (see p. 406). Euripides provides Kreousa with a more eventful history in his unconventional account in the *Ion* however, by suggesting that she bore Ion to Apollo before her marriage, abandoned him in a cave under the Acropolis, and later came close to murdering him when Xouthos adopted him at the order of the Delphic oracle (see further on pp. 407–8).

OREITHUIA was carried away by Boreas, the North Wind, while she was playing by the banks of the Ilissos just outside Athens; the pretty and secluded site of the incident is described in Plato's *Phaedrus*. There were also accounts in which she was seized from the Acropolis or Aeiopagos. As Plato remarks, the myth could easily be rationalized if it was imagined that she had been blown from a height by a gust of wind. Boreas carried her north to his chilly home in Thrace, where she bore him twin sons, Zetes and Kalais, known as the Boreads (Boreadai), and also two daughters, Chione (Snow-woman), who bore Eumolpos to Poseidon (see above), and Kleopatra, who became the first wife of the Thracian seer Phineus (see p. 386).[217] The Boreads were winged beings who could fly through the air like their divine father; for the famous myth of their pursuit of the Harpies, see p. 387. The Athenians were proud to have a special relationship with Boreas, who was supposed to have come to their aid in more than one moment of peril. When they were under threat from the Persian fleet in 480 BC, an oracle advised them to 'call on the aid of their son-in-law'; and since Boreas had taken an Athenian princess as his wife, they offered sacrifices to him and his consort. He duly responded by blowing up a savage storm which destroyed a great many Persian ships as they were lying in an exposed position off southern Thessaly. A comparable stroke of good fortune twelve years earlier when the fleet of Darios was struck by a storm off Athos was also attributed to the good services of the wind-god.[218] Stories of this kind doubtless contributed to the popularity of the local legend of Oreithuia's abduction, which is depicted very frequently and often very strikingly in Athenian vase-paintings.

PROKRIS, the remaining daughter of Erechtheus, married KEPHALOS, a son of Deion (or Deioneus), son of Aiolos (see p. 435), from Central Greece, and lived with him in the country outside Athens. There are several conflicting accounts of their troubled marriage. In the earliest surviving narrative by Pherecydes, Kephalos subjected her to a bizarre test soon after their wedding by abandoning her for eight years and then returning in disguise to see whether he could seduce her by offering her some finery; but although she yielded to the temptation, the two of them patched up their differences and resumed their married life. She later came to suspect that he was seeing another woman because he was absent so much of the time on hunting-trips. When she questioned a servant on the matter, he confirmed her suspicions by telling her that he had seen his master on a hilltop calling out repeatedly, 'Come here, Nephele!' Supposing that he had been summoning a woman called Nephele (Cloud), even though he had really been calling for shade from the sun, Prokris concealed herself on the same hill to spy on his actions; and when he called out once again just as the servant had described, she jumped up and ran to confront him, giving him such a start that he hurled his spear by force of instinct and killed her.[219]

In subsequent accounts, Prokris is often said to have left home for a time after her husband caught her committing an infidelity or trapped her into doing so. According to Apollodorus, a certain Pteleon won his way into her bed by offering her a golden crown, and she sought refuge with Minos in Crete after her husband found out. Minos fell in love with her and was eager to seduce her; but his wife Pasiphae had become so exasperated by his infidelities that she had put a spell on him, causing him to ejaculate wild beasts (snakes, scorpions and millipedes according to another source) if he ever slept with another woman, with fatal effect on her. In return for two precious gifts, however, a swift dog and a marvellous hunting-spear that always hit its mark, Prokris found a cure for his malady by giving him a wonderful potion containing the 'Kirkaian root', and then went to bed with him. Fearing the jealousy of Pasiphae, she returned to Athens afterwards, taking the gifts with her, and reached an accommodation with her husband. She liked to go hunting with him, for she was as fond of hunting as he was; and as she was pursuing some game through the thicket one day, Kephalos hurled his javelin (presumably the unfailing one from Crete) without realizing that it was her, and struck her dead. He was tried for murder as a consequence at the court of the Areiopagos, and was condemned to perpetual exile (rather than to death as would have been the case if the killing had been deliberate). He chose to settle at Thebes.[220] Or in an account from a poem in the epic cycle, he went to Thebes to be purified after committing the involuntary killing, and was thus available to allow the wonderful dog from Crete to be used against the Teumessian fox (see p. 246).[221] This would suggest that the tale of Prokris' journey to Crete may have been quite ancient; it may be significant that a Prokris should be mentioned by Homer in the company of Phaidra and Ariadne (both daughters of Minos) among the women who were seen by Odysseus in the Underworld.[222] Prokris' death-story first appears in the visual arts in the second half of the fifth century BC.

A further complication was introduced into the story if the present Kephalos is identified with the Kephalos who was abducted by Eos (properly a wholly different person, a son of Hermes and Herse, see p. 366, rather than a son of Deion). It seems likely that this was an innovation introduced by Nicander. We may start with the familiar account in Ovid's *Metamorphoses* before passing on to that recorded by Antoninus, which probably follows Nicander more closely (although no source is indicated). The dawn-goddess abducted Kephalos two months after his marriage, so Ovid relates, but he yearned so passionately for his wife that the goddess soon lost patience with him and sent him back to her. In her anger at being scorned, however, Eos encouraged him to doubt the fidelity of his wife, and transformed his appearance to enable him to test her in the guise of a stranger. By promising her a fortune in return for her favours, he brought her to the point of yielding and then revealed his true identity. Overcome by shame, and feeling resentment at the male sex on account of his underhand behaviour, she left home in shame to wander the hills as a huntress. Finding that he was tormented by love in her absence, he finally sought a reconciliation, confessing that he too might have yielded to such a temptation. So she returned to him, bringing two marvellous gifts, a swift-running dog and a wonderful spear that she had received from Artemis. Rather as in the story from Pherecydes above, she was later told that Kephalos was in the habit of calling out for Aura while out hunting, and inferred from this that he was meeting with a nymph of that name (although he was really calling for a cooling breeze, as *aura* can mean in both Greek and Latin). So she hid herself in the hunting-field to spy on him, and when he heard her in the undergrowth, he hurled his unerring spear in that direction in the belief that a wild animal was hiding there.[223]

Antoninus' account follows a similar course initially, except that Kephalos asked one of his friends to test the virtue of his wife after his temporary abduction. After refusing a first offer of gold, she agreed to sleep with the stranger when he doubled the bribe, and was duly caught by her husband when she arrived for the assignation. She abandoned him in shame and sought refuge with Minos in Crete. As in Apollodorus' version above, she won his favour by helping him to overcome his strange sexual problem; but in this account, he was distressed by it because it was preventing him from fathering children by his wife (rather than from sleeping with other women). Prokris contrived a mechanical solution by inserting a goat's bladder into a woman's vagina and causing him to discharge the snakes, scorpions and millipedes into it before he had intercourse with his wife. On finding that he was able to father children by her as a consequence, he rewarded Prokris by giving her the infallible dog and hunting-spear. She now returned to Attica and put Kephalos himself to the test. Cutting her hair short and changing into male clothing, she approached him in the guise of a young man and showed him the wonderful dog and spear; and he coveted them so greatly that he agreed to submit to the stranger in homosexual intercourse as the price for acquiring them. Prokris then revealed her true identity and accused him of having committed an even worse fault than her own. Antoninus concludes by telling how the dog was used against the Teumessian fox without making any reference to the death of Prokris.[224]

We may conclude with a related account offered by Hyginus. Eos accosted Kephalos while he was out hunting one morning, but he rejected her, saying that he had sworn to remain faithful to his wife. So the goddess transformed his appearance and gave him some beautiful gifts to enable him to test whether his wife was as faithful as he was. Prokris was caught out in the usual way and fled to Crete, where she sought to join the hunting-party of Artemis; but she was turned away because the goddess accepted virgins alone as her companions. On hearing Prokris' story, however, Artemis felt sorry for her, and gave her the unfailing dog and spear and sent her off to test Kephalos. She achieved this in the same way as in the preceding version. The couple resumed their married life now that the wrongs were balanced out, and all might have been well if Prokris had not feared that her husband might be meeting Eos in secret. As she was spying on him from some bushes at daybreak one morning, he saw them stirring and killed her unknowingly by hurling his unfailing javelin.[225]

The last kings of Athens

To return to the highly artificial history of the Athenian succession that was developed by the Atthidographers, Erechtheus was succeeded by his son KEKROPS II, who either inherited the throne as the eldest son or was awarded it through the arbitration of Xouthos, son of Hellen (see p. 406).[226] This second Kekrops, a nonentity who was invented for chronological reasons, was succeeded by his son, PANDION II, who was soon forced into exile by his cousins the sons of Metion. He sought refuge with Pylas, the king of the neighbouring province of Megara, who offered him his daughter, Pylia, as a wife. When Pylas himself was later obliged to depart into exile after killing his uncle, he transferred the kingdom to his Athenian son-in-law. While in Megara, Pandion fathered four sons, Aigeus, Pallas, Nisos and Lykos, who reconquered Athens after his death and banished the usurpers. Although the four brothers agreed to divide the kingdom, AIGEUS held all the power, to the increasing discontent of PALLAS, who later mounted a revolt with the aid of his fifty sons, but was defeated by Theseus (see pp. 356–7).[227] LYKOS, who was credited with prophetic powers, was the eponymous ancestor of the Lykomides, an important priestly clan at Athens; he was finally expelled by Aigeus and either settled in Messenia with Aphareus (see p. 422), whom he instructed in the mysteries of Demeter and Persephone, or else in Lycia in Asia Minor, hence the name of that land (see p. 350).[228] NISOS was usually said to have ruled in Megara as his father's successor;[229] he was betrayed by his daughter Skylla when Minos attacked Megara and Athens (see p. 340).

The adventures of Aigeus and Theseus, as described above, finally take us into the realm of major heroic myth. For reasons that have already been considered, Theseus was displaced towards the end of his life by MENESTHEUS, son of Peteos, who could claim to rule with some legitimacy since he was descended from Erechtheus through a side-branch of the Athenian royal family. Since Theseus was absent in the Underworld when Menestheus seized power, his two sons, Demophon and Akamas, had to see to their own safety and sought refuge in Euboea with Elephenor, king of the Abantes. Menestheus is an ancient figure who appears in the *Iliad* as the leader of the Athenian contingent at Troy, and is listed among the suitors of Helen in the Hesiodic *Catalogue*.[230] Although Homer remarks that nobody could equal him, and Nestor alone could rival him, in the marshalling of chariots and fighting men, he is by no means prominent in the *Iliad*, making only a few brief appearances in the battle-scenes.[231] Either because he was killed in the fighting at Troy or because he settled on Melos or in Italy or even Iberia afterwards, he failed to return home after the war, leaving the way open for one or both of the sons of Theseus to recover their ancestral throne.[232]

Theseus died in exile before the Trojan War soon after his escape from the Underworld (see p. 362). Although his sons DEMOPHON and AKAMAS are never mentioned in the Homeric epics, it is known that they appeared in two later epics in the Trojan cycle, the *Little Iliad* and the *Sack of Troy*, which told how they recovered their grandmother Aithra at the end of the war. According to the standard later tradition, they sailed to Troy towards the end of the war for that specific purpose. As was explained above, Aithra had been captured by the Dioskouroi when they came to Attica to recover Helen after she was abducted by Theseus (see p. 361), and had been obliged to serve Helen as a maidservant thereafter, initially at Sparta and later at Troy. When Troy finally fell to the Greeks, her grandsons sought her out in the city or discovered her among the captives in the Greek camp, and asked Agamemnon to allow them to take her home to Athens.[233] There was disagreement as to whether both came to rule at Athens or – as was more commonly credited – one alone did; it was generally explained in the post-classical tradition that one or other of them lost his life after becoming entangled with a Thracian princess on the way home.

This princess was PHYLLIS, the daughter of the king of the Bisaltians (or Edonians) of south-western Thrace. In Apollodorus' account, she fell in love with Demophon when he called in at her land, and her father gave her to him as a wife with the kingdom as a dowry. He wanted to sail to his own land after a while, however, and set off on his way in spite of her pleadings, fending her off by swearing that he would return to her in due course. She accompanied him to the shore at Nine Ways and gave him a casket, telling him that it contained an object sacred to Mother Rhea, and that he was not to open it unless he had abandoned all hope of returning to her. When the appointed time for his return passed by, Phyllis cursed him and killed herself; and when her faithless husband, who had settled in Cyprus for some reason, opened the casket, he was overcome by a sudden terror and leapt on to his horse and galloped away, riding at such reckless speed that he was thrown off and fell on to his sword.[234] Akamas sometimes replaces Demophon in other accounts of this story; it is indeed likely that he was the original husband of Phyllis, since he is mentioned in this role before his brother and had early connections with Thrace. Aeschines, an Athenian orator of the fourth century BC, states that he received the town of Nine Ways (Ennea Hodoi) as his dowry.[235] This was the original name of Amphipolis, a town on the Thracian coast that was seized and colonized by the Athenians in 437 BC; some claimed that it had been called Nine Ways because Phyllis ran down to the shore at that spot nine times on the day on which her husband was due to return.[236] A lost account by Callimachus seems to have helped to establish the popularity of the tale.[237]

The name of Phyllis (which was in fact derived from the name of a district in Thrace) bears a resemblance to the Greek word for leaves, and her legend was thus adapted to explain why leaves were known as *phylla*. The trees that sprang up by Phyllis' tomb used to weep for her each year on the anniversary of her death by shedding their leaves, which came to be named after her as a consequence;[238] or after her suicide, Phyllis was transformed into an almond-tree which had no leaves initially, but brought them forth for the first time when her deceiver (Demophon in this case) embraced the trunk of the tree after making a belated return.[239]

According to a tale of Hellenistic origin, Akamas fathered a child by LAODIKE, an unmarried daughter of Priam, when he travelled to Troy with Diomedes just before the war to try to negotiate the return of Helen. After falling desperately in love with him, Laodike arranged for him to be invited to a banquet at Dardanos, a town in the Troad, and slipped into his bed afterwards, pretending to be one of Priam's concubines. She bore him a son, MOUNITOS, who was brought up by his great-grandmother Aithra. Mounitos was united with his father after the fall of Troy and set off for Athens with him, but died of a snake-bite during a hunting-trip when they called in at Thrace on the way. For the more conventional mythology of Laodike, see p. 480.[240]

There was a tradition that suggested that Demophon and Akamas served at Troy with Elephenor and his Euboeans, presumably after setting out with them at the beginning of the conflict.[241]

If Demophon came to rule at Athens, he was succeeded by son Oxyntes and thence his grandson THYMOITES, who was the last descendant of Erichthonios and Theseus to rule at Athens.[242] During the reign of Thymoites, a war broke out between Attica and Boeotia, and the Boeotians proposed that the outcome should be determined by single combat between the kings of the two lands; but Thymoites, who was none too brave, was unwilling to take the risk, and offered to surrender the throne to anyone who was willing to fight the duel on his behalf. The challenge was taken up by MELANTHOS, a descendant of Neleus who had been expelled from Pylos by the Heraklids along with the rest of his family (see p. 290 for the circumstances) and had been advised by oracles to settle at Athens. He won the fight by means of a ruse. For as he was drawing close to Xanthios (or Xanthos), the king of Boeotia, he accused him of having cheated by bringing a second; and when the king looked back in astonishment to see if anyone was really following him, Melanthos hurled his spear at him and struck him dead. It was claimed that the Athenians celebrated their victory by founding their annual festival of the Apatouria, which could thus be said to recall his deception (*apatē*) in its name.[243] A secondary version removes the deception by alleging that Melanthos called out to his opponent because he saw a phantom walking behind him. Or according to a wholly different tradition, he seized power at Athens by killing Thymoites.[244]

Melanthos was succeeded by his son KODROS, who was usually thought to have been the last king of Athens. During his reign, Aletes, the first Heraklid ruler of Corinth (see p. 290), marched against the city with a Dorian army after receiving an oracle that promised him victory if the Athenian king were not harmed. Kodros came to hear of the oracle, however, and sacrificed his own life for the sake of his city by entering the enemy camp disguised as a woodcutter and provoking one of the troops to kill him. As soon as the Dorians discovered his true identity, they abandoned all hope of victory and withdrew; and the Athenians decided to have no more kings after Kodros as a tribute to his incomparable patriotism. So his son Medon became the first archon (senior magistrate) of Athens, or at least a ruler with restricted powers.[245] For Medon's quarrel with his brother Neileus, and the Ionian migration to Asia Minor that resulted from it, see p. 409.

CHAPTER ELEVEN

JASON AND THE
ARGONAUTS

—— .•. ——

Apart from the Theban Wars, which have been considered in connection with the history of the Inachids, there were two other great adventures in the period before the Trojan War that drew leading heroes from different parts of Greece, namely the voyage of the Argonauts and the hunt for the Calydonian boar. The fathers of many Homeric warriors can be found among the heroes who took part in these two enterprises, which can be traced to a slightly earlier period than the Theban Wars and involved a much wider range of participants. If the Theban Wars broke out as the result of a conflict within the Inachid family, these other adventures were connected with the Deukalionids, the next great family that we will have to consider, for they were conducted under Deukalionid leadership in response to difficulties that had arisen in different branches of that family. Although the early epic accounts of the Argonautic expedition have been lost as in the case of the Theban Wars (and also the boar-hunt), we know far more about it than about the other episodes, largely because an epic from the Hellenistic era, the *Argonautica* of Apollonius of Rhodes, has survived in full along with scholia (ancient explanatory notes) that provide invaluable information on the earlier tradition and Argonautic lore in general. Since the history of the Deukalionids is exceptionally complicated and the mythology of the Argonauts is so rich and of such wide interest, it will be best to single out the latter for separate treatment in the present chapter before we pass on to trace the full history of the Deukalionids in the next chapter.

The origin of the golden fleece

The myth of the Argonauts told how Jason, son of Aison, set off with a crew of fifty heroes to fetch a golden fleece from Colchis at the eastern end of the Black Sea at the order of his uncle, Pelias, king of Iolkos. Before passing on to the expedition itself, we must consider the origin and nature of the object of Jason's quest, and the motives of Pelias in sending him off on this perilous enterprise.

The golden fleece had come from a wondrous ram that had carried a young Boeotian prince, PHRIXOS, to safety in Colchis after his stepmother had plotted to cause his death. His father ATHAMAS, whom we have already encountered as a foster-parent of the infant Dionysos (see p. 172), was famed for his tangled marital affairs, which will be discussed further in the next chapter (see pp. 420ff.). According to the usual tradition, he first married NEPHELE (Cloud, apparently a minor goddess), who bore him two children, Phrixos and Helle; but he later put her aside (or was deserted by her) and remarried, taking INO, a daughter of Kadmos, king of Thebes, as his new wife. As is the manner of stepmothers in folklore, Ino resented the children whom he had fathered by his previous wife, and hated them indeed so very greatly that she set out to contrive their death. On the pretence no doubt that it would serve as a helpful charm, she persuaded the women of the land to roast the coming year's seed-corn over fire in secret from the men; and when the grain failed to germinate as a result of this treatment, Athamas reacted as she had foreseen by sending an envoy (or envoys) to Delphi to seek the advice of the oracle. Intercepting the envoy (or envoys) on the way, she bribed him (or them) to report to the king that the oracle had revealed that the famine would be brought to an end if Phrixos (and his sister Helle too in some accounts) were sacrificed to Zeus. Although Athamas was naturally reluctant to order the death of his son, he finally agreed to do so at the insistence of his people; or in another version, Phrixos resolved the matter on his behalf by volunteering to be sacrificed for the common good. As he was being brought to the altar, however, his mother Nephele intervened by bringing or sending a golden-fleeced ram which carried him to safety on its back. This was a marvellous beast that had been given to her by Hermes and was able to fly through the sky.[1] It took Helle in addition to her brother whether or not she was due to be sacrificed, soaring up into the air with them and heading for the east. As it was approaching Asia, however, Helle lost her grip and fell into the narrow straits that separate Europe from Asia, which were therefore known as the Hellespont (Sea of Helle) from that time onwards.[2] Phrixos for his part was carried ever further until the ram alighted in the land of Colchis at the eastern end of the Black Sea. In gratitude for his deliverance, he sacrificed the ram to Zeus Phyxios (God of Escape), and then presented its golden fleece to the local ruler, AIETES.[3]

Aietes was a son of Helios (the Sun) by the Okeanid Perse or Perseis, and a brother of the enchantress Kirke.[4] Although he was a cold-hearted despot who was not usually friendly to strangers, he was impressed by the wonderful gift of the fleece and welcomed Phrixos to his court, offering him his daughter Chalkiope (or Iophossa) as a wife. Phrixos fathered four sons by her, Argos, Melas, Phrontis and Kytisoros,[5] and lived without further adventure in Colchis until he died of old age.[6] In the Argonautic epic of Apollonius, as we will see, his sons set off for Greece when they were old enough in the hope of recovering their grandfather's inheritance, but were shipwrecked on an island in the Black Sea, where they remained until Jason picked them up and brought them back to Colchis.[7] Since Aietes had been warned by his divine father to beware of treachery from within his own family, he was highly suspicious when he saw them arriving in the company of strangers, and this was one of the reasons why he bore such malice against the Argonauts.[8] He was noted for his harsh and distrustful nature in any case; according to Apollonius, indeed, he would never have accepted Phrixos into his court in the first place if Hermes had not come to warn him that this was the will of Zeus.[9]

The king dedicated the golden fleece to Ares, suspending it on an oak-tree in the grove of Ares near his city of Aia, where it was guarded by an unsleeping dragon.[10]

Or in other accounts, Phrixos hung it up in the temple of Ares in the city,[11] or it was kept in the palace of Aietes,[12] or deposited on the island of Aia in the river Phasis.[13] The ram itself flew up to the heavens, or was transferred there by Nephele, to become the constellation of the Ram (Aries); since the ram had been deprived of its gleaming coat, this constellation, the first in the zodiac, is extremely faint.[14]

This story of the origin of the fleece varies to a greater or lesser extent in different versions. In one account of the events in Boeotia, for instance, the envoy who brought the false message to Athamas felt such pity for Phrixos when he saw him being led out to sacrifice that he betrayed Ino's plot to the king at the last moment. On learning of his wife's treachery, Athamas ordered that she and her son Melikertes should be put to death; but Dionysos, who owed a debt to Ino for having nursed him during his infancy, saved her by casting a mist around her.[15] In what was apparently a continuation of the same story, Dionysos sent Phrixos and Helle mad, but they were rescued as usual by their mother Nephele, who brought the golden-fleeced ram to them as they were wandering through a forest in a state of frenzy.[16] In another version of the myth, Phrixos and Helle were hurled into the sea instead of being taken to an altar, but were saved by the ram in much the same manner as usual.[17] There are also versions in which Zeus sent the ram to prevent the unholy sacrifice from being fulfilled,[18] or the ram spoke to Phrixos and Helle in a human voice to warn them that they were due to be sacrificed and told them to climb on to its back.[19] Rationalistic versions explain that the ram was really a ship which had a ram as its figure-head,[20] or a man called Krios (Ram) who was the steward of Athamas or childhood attendant (*paidagōgos*) of Phrixos.[21] Helle was sometimes said to have been rescued by Poseidon after falling into the Hellespont; in that case she bore him a son nearby named variously as Edonos (the eponym of the Edones of Thrace), or Paion (the eponym of Paionia, a region in northern Macedonia; but see also p. 412), or the giant Almops (the eponym of an district in Macedonia).[22]

Hyginus recounts a rather foolish tale, doubtless of Hellenistic origin, that was devised to explain the origin of the golden-fleeced ram. A certain THEOPHANE, daughter of Bisaltes (or perhaps simply a Bisaltian of Thrace in the original account), aroused the love of Poseidon, who carried her off to the island of Crumissa (*sic*, of unknown location). When her suitors subsequently sailed off to recover her, Poseidon turned himself into a ram, his mistress into a beautiful ewe, and the people of the island into cattle. On finding that the island was deserted, the suitors began to kill the newly transformed islanders for food, provoking Poseidon to turn them into wolves; and Poseidon then mated with Theophane in animal-form, causing her to conceive the marvellous ram.[23] Ovid seems to have been acquainted with this story in some form at least, for he mentions in passing that Poseidon once 'deceived Bisaltis with a ram'.[24] According to Apollonius, the ram had golden fleece because Hermes (who was often said to have given the beast to Nephele) had turned it to gold.[25]

Although Apollonius states that Phrixos died of old age, another account suggests that Aietes eventually killed him after receiving prophetic warning that he should fear death at the hand of a foreigner descended from Aiolos.[26] After being shipwrecked and rescued by the Argonauts when they first tried to sail to Greece, the sons of Phrixos reached their ancestral homeland by accompanying the Argonauts on their return voyage.[27] It is reported in one tradition that Argos, son of Phrixos, married Perimele, daughter of Admetos, to become the father of Magnes,[28] the eponym of Magnesia (but see also p. 436). If this Argos is identified as the Argos who built the *Argo*, as in Pherecydes' account[29] though not in most others (see p. 382), he must obviously have been in Greece before the Argonauts sailed. Herodotus may be consulted for a legend in which Kytisoros, another son of Phrixos, rescued his grandfather Athamas when the citizens of Alos in Thessalian Achaea were about to sacrifice him as a scapegoat.[30]

How Jason came to be sent on his quest

Phrixos' adventure with the ram would provide the Argonauts with a suitable object for their quest. To understand why Pelias, king of Iolkos, should have asked his nephew Jason to undertake the perilous mission of fetching the golden fleece from Colchis, it is necessary to consider the earlier history of Iolkos and its ruling family. This Thessalian city, which lay near the coast at the head of the Gulf of Pagasai, was founded by **Kretheus**, a son of Aiolos and great-grandson of Deukalion (see further on p. 425). Kretheus married his niece **Tyro** and fathered three sons by her including **Aison**, who might have expected to succeed him in normal circumstances as the eldest; but it happened that Tyro had borne twin sons to Poseidon before her marriage, and one of these, **Pelias**, succeeded to the Iolkian throne instead, excluding Aison and his son **Jason** from the inheritance.[31]

PELIAS came to be born and rose to power in the following circumstances. When Zeus destroyed Salmoneus along with his entire city (see p. 422), he spared his young daughter TYRO and entrusted her to the care of Kretheus in Thessaly; and after arriving in her new homeland, Tyro conceived a passion for a local river-god, Enipeus, and used to linger by his waters, telling him of her love. Her behaviour attracted the attention of a much greater god, Poseidon, who seduced her in the guise of Enipeus and had intercourse with her by the river-bank, causing a huge wave to arch overhead to conceal them from sight. As the product of this union, she bore him twin sons, Pelias and Neleus.[32] According to the earliest account in the *Odyssey*, from which the preceding description of the episode is taken, Poseidon ordered her to rear the children herself; but in the standard later tradition, she was said to have exposed them at birth. They were rescued by some countrymen, as heroic children always are in such circumstances, in this case by some horse-breeders, who gave Pelias his name because a horse had kicked him in the face just before, leaving a black-and-blue (*pelion*) mark.[33] Some said that they were suckled by animals until they were discovered, Pelias by a mare and Neleus by a bitch.[34] Sophocles seems to have offered a rather different account in his lost *Tyro*, saying that the twins were set afloat in a container of some kind (*skaphē*) on the river, much like Romulus and Remus at Rome (see p. 596).[35] When the twins grew up, they rediscovered their mother and rescued her from her stepmother Sidero (Iron-woman), who had been cruelly mistreating her in the mean time. Although Sidero is sometimes described as the second wife of Tyro's father Salmoneus,[36] it would make more sense to assume that she was the first wife of Kretheus, during the period while he was still acting as guardian to Tyro before taking her as his wife. Pelias killed Sidero in any case, and in circumstances that would have a bearing on the story of the Argonauts; for he slaughtered her at an altar of Hera after she had taken sanctuary there, and compounded the fault by ceasing to honour Hera thereafter.[37] Hera hated him as a consequence and did her best to help Jason and the Argonauts; and in one early version of the story, as we will see, she even contrived that Pelias should send Jason on his mission in the first place because she knew that this would ultimately cause Pelias' own destruction.

The two brothers quarrelled after a time, and Pelias drove Neleus out of Thessaly, causing him to seek refuge in Messenia (see p. 424).[38] He remained at Iolkos for his own part, where he would have enjoyed an honoured position as stepson of the founder after his mother's marriage to Kretheus; and he succeeded to the throne after the death of Kretheus even though the king had fathered sons of his own by Tyro. The fact that Pelias came to rule the city instead of Aison, the eldest son of Kretheus, need not necessarily imply that he seized the throne illegitimately, for sons who are borne to gods by the wives of kings in legend can be regarded as legitimate heirs of those kings; and in one early version of Pelias' legend at least, Aison and Jason laid no claim to his throne, and Hera contrived that he should send Jason for the fleece for reasons of her own. We will begin with this version, as known primarily from a surviving passage from Pherecydes and the corresponding narrative of Apollodorus (which seems to be based on that of Pherecydes). Pelias reigned as Kretheus' successor in Jason's home-city of Iolkos, but Jason preferred to live outside in the country because he had a passion for agriculture. There is no reason to suppose that he feared for his safety as in the other main version of the story in which (as we will see) his parents sent him into the country at birth as a protective measure. When he returned to Iolkos to have his fateful meeting with Pelias, it was to attend a sacrifice in response to a general summons from the king rather than with the intention of taking any action against him. For when Pelias was once intending to offer a sacrifice to Poseidon by the sea-shore, he summoned all the citizens to attend, including Jason, who received the message as he was ploughing his fields beside the river Anauros. He took off his sandals to cross the river, but forgot to put his left sandal on again when he arrived at the opposite bank side (or else lost it in the current). Now Pelias had once received an oracle warning him to beware of the man with a single sandal; and when he saw Jason arrive at the ceremony with one foot bare, he called the prophecy to mind and was thoroughly alarmed. So he invited Jason to the palace on the following day and asked him what he would do if he had been told by an oracle that he would be murdered by one of his fellow-citizens. At the inspiration of Hera, who had long hated Pelias for reasons already explained, Jason immediately replied that he would send him to fetch the golden fleece; for the goddess put this thought into his mind because she knew that if he were sent on that mission, he would return with the Colchian enchantress Medeia who would cause the death of Pelias (see p. 397). Pelias assumed, however, that such a quest would bring death to anyone who attempted it, and sent Jason on his way without hesitation.[39]

In the most familiar form of the legend, Pelias was a brutal tyrant who first robbed Aison of his rightful throne and later tried to cause the death of Jason when he arrived to reclaim it; we will follow the earliest surviving account in Pindar's fourth Pythian Ode. To ensure that the new-born Jason would be safe from Pelias, his parents pretended that he had died at birth and sent him away in secret at night while making a show of lamentation, wrapping the infant in purple robes as befitted a royal prince. They entrusted him to the care of the Centaur Cheiron, who lived in a cave on Mt Pelion to the east. We should doubtless assume that Jason was reared by Cheiron in the preceding version too. Jason remained in hiding in the country, unknown to Pelias or anyone outside his family circle, until he was twenty years old, when he returned to Iolkos to demand the throne from Pelias. Now Pelias had received two oracles, one telling him that death would come to him from a descendant of Aiolos, and the other warning him to beware of the man who would come down from the mountains wearing only a single sandal; so when Jason, who was a great-grandson of Aiolos, appeared in the city wearing a single sandal and demanded the throne, Pelias realized that he would have to contrive his removal and destruction. Pretending that he was willing to surrender the throne, he asked Jason to perform a special favour for him before taking over the kingdom; for he claimed that Phrixos had appeared to him in a dream to ask that the golden fleece should be fetched home to Greece, and this was a task that was better suited to a young man like Jason than an old man like himself. Jason readily agreed to undertake the mission on his behalf, giving him reason to suppose that he had saved himself from the threatened danger.[40]

Jason's missing sandal is not explained by the river-crossing in Pindar's version; it would seem that he was deliberately wearing a sandal on one foot only in accordance with a practice that was sometimes adopted by Greek warriors (for this could make it easier for them to gain a firm foothold on slippery ground).

There is a reference in the *Theogony* to 'the many grievous labours' that were imposed on the son of Aison by Pelias (in the concluding section of the poem, however, which was added after Hesiod's time); although Pelias is described as violent and overbearing, nothing is stated on his motive in imposing these labours.[41] Since Mimnermus (late seventh century BC) refers in similar terms to the grievous task that was set for Jason by the brutal (*hybristēs*) Pelias,[42] it seems to have been agreed from early times that Pelias was a man of violent character.

It is suggested in some accounts that Aison succeeded his father Kretheus as king of Iolkos but died prematurely, bequeathing the kingdom to Pelias on the understanding that he would rule as regent until Jason came of age; but when Jason returned from the country as a young man, Pelias sent him off to fetch the fleece as usual to save himself from having to hand over the throne (or because an oracle had warned him to beware of the one-sandalled man).[43]

Apollonius is very brisk in his account of the origin of Jason's quest, merely stating that he came to attend Pelias' sacrifice, losing one of his sandals in the river Anauros on the way, and was sent off on his voyage because the king had been warned by an oracle to beware of the man with one sandal.[44] It is reported elsewhere in the poem that Hera had a special fondness for Jason as the result of an encounter by the Anauros; for she had once sat down by the river in the guise of an old woman to test human righteousness, and Jason had felt compassion for her as he was returning from a hunting-trip and had carried her through the water on his shoulders.[45]

Jason prepared for his mission by organizing the construction of the greatest ship that had ever been built, the *Argo*, and by summoning leading heroes from all parts of Greece to accompany him on the voyage. The '*Argo* which is famous to all (*pasimelousa*)', as Homer already calls her,[46] was said to have been the first large seagoing ship (although the ship that carried the fifty Danaids to Argos, see p. 233, would in fact have been built at an earlier stage in mythical history). She was usually pictured as a fifty-oared ship (*pentēkontoros*), hence the usual number of her crew, who were known as the Argonauts (*Argonautai*, i.e. sailors of the *Argo*). Using timber cut on Mt Pelion nearby,[47] Argos, son of Arestor (or of Polybos or Phrixos) built her at Pagasai, the port of Iolkos, under the guidance of Athena. As a finishing touch, the goddess fitted an oracular timber into her bow; taken from the sacred oak at the oracle of Zeus at Dodona, it was endowed with the power of speech (see p. 394).[48] Ancient authors explain that the ship was called the *Argo* because she was so swift (*argos*, doubtless the true origin of the name) or in honour of her builder Argos.[49]

The myth of the Argonauts was extremely ancient and underwent many changes in the course of time. It seems likely that Jason would have been accompanied by a crew of Minyans (legendary inhabitants of his own region) in the earliest tradition, and that the voyage of the Argonauts would have taken them into a purely mythical realm at the eastern edges of the earth. As time progressed, however, and the Greeks became better acquainted with the lands and seas to the east of them, the geography became less fanciful, and Colchis, a real land at the eastern end of the Black Sea, replaced the mythical land of Aia as the destination of Jason's quest; and in due course, the adventure was developed into a panhellenic enterprise involving heroes from far beyond Jason's home in north-eastern Greece.

To recruit worthy companions to sail with him in the *Argo*, Jason sent messengers to every corner of Greece to summon fifty of the foremost heroes of the age. These would have been men who reached their maturity a generation or so before the Trojan War, and many were fathers of great warriors who fought at Troy. As is commonly the case with collaborative enterprises in legend, no two lists are in full agreement on the names of the participants; since the Argonauts generally acted as a collective body (in surviving accounts at least) and few were remembered for any individual exploits, plausible names from the appropriate era could be suggested almost at will by poets and mythographers. The earliest useful information is provided by Pindar, who identifies ten Argonauts in addition to Jason himself and the seer Mopsos, evidently choosing from those who had been fathered by gods, namely Herakles, the two Dioskouroi, Zetes and Kalais (the Boreads, the twin sons of Boreas, god of the north wind), Euphemos and Periklymenos (two sons of Poseidon from the Peloponnese), Orpheus, and two heroes of lesser note, Echion and Eurytos, who were twin sons of Hermes from Alope in Thessaly.[50] Although fuller lists would surely have been provided in early epic, and are reported to have been provided in lost plays by Aeschylus and Sophocles, the earliest catalogue to survive is that offered at the beginning of Apollonius' Argonautic epic, which lists fifty-five Argonauts.[51] The catalogues offered by subsequent authors seem to be largely derived from this with varying degrees of alteration, with the exception of that of Apollodorus, which was plainly of separate origin.[52] From among the heroes who are to be found in every catalogue and are not already named by Pindar, the following may be picked out as being most worthy of note: Admetos, Akastos, son of Pelias, the Arcadian Ankaios (see p. 544), the Samian Ankaios (see p. 573), Hylas (a favourite of Herakles, see below), Idas and Lynkeus, the seer Idmon, Iphiklos, son of Phylakos, Kepheus, son of Aleos, Meleagros, Menoitios, Polyphemos, son of Elatos, the helmsman Tiphys, and Telamon.

The outward voyage of the Argonauts

The Argonauts sailed to Colchis by way of the Hellespont and the southern shores of the Black Sea; accounts of their return journey were more varied. We will take

Apollonius' Hellenistic epic as our guide for the outward journey, noting each successive landfall.[53]

(*i*) After setting off from Pagasai and rounding Cape Sepias, they stopped at Aphetai for two days before continuing on their way (an idea that arose because the name of the place might suggest in Greek that it is a starting-point). Herakles was sometimes said to have been left behind there (see below).[54] (*ii*) They then skirted northern Thessaly and the Chalkidike before sailing east across the open sea to Lemnos, where they made their longest halt. There were no men on the island at the time because they had all been killed by the women. For not long before, Aphrodite had afflicted the women with an evil smell to punish them for having neglected her cult, causing them to become so repulsive to their husbands that they had driven them from their beds and replaced them with captive women from Thrace; and the Lemnian women had been so enraged by this treatment that they had conspired together to murder every man on the island in a single night. One woman alone had broken the agreement, HYPSIPYLE, the daughter of the king and present queen of the island, who had saved her aged father Thoas by secretly sending him out to sea in a chest (or putting him on a ship, or hiding him away in the palace). On seeing the *Argo* approaching their shore, the women armed themselves and poured down to the beach, fearing that they were under attack from the Thracians; but the Argonauts sent their herald Aithalides to Hypsipyle to assure her that they had no hostile intentions. So she convened an assembly, and the women agreed to invite the Argonauts into their homes; for they realized that they would need male protectors or at least male children to guard them from attack and provide for them in their old age. Believing that the women were in difficulties because their menfolk had settled abroad in Thrace, the Argonauts were happy to oblige them and lived with them for a year, fathering many children. Jason stayed at the palace with Hypsipyle, who bore him two sons, Thoas (or Nebrophonos) and Euneos. As time progressed, however, and the Argonauts constantly postponed their departure from one day to another, Herakles, who had remained behind on the ship, finally lost patience and urged his comrades to continue on their way.[55]

(*iii*) On the advice of Orpheus, they first rowed northward to the island of Samothrace to be initiated into the mysteries of the gods of Samothrace (see p. 220), who protected sailors against the perils of the sea.[56] This is of course a comparatively late episode. (*iv*) After this detour, they entered the Straits of the Hellespont (Dardanelles) to make their way through to the Black Sea. They made their first landfall at Kyzikos on the Asian shore of the Propontis (Sea of Marmora), where they enjoyed the hospitality of KYZIKOS, king of the Doliones. As they were climbing a neighbouring mountain on the next morning to survey their route, the *Argo* was attacked by the Gegeneis (Earthborn), a race of six-armed giants who lived on the mountain; but Herakles, who had stayed on the ship with some of the younger heroes, kept them at bay with his arrows, bringing many of them to the ground, until the rest of the crew returned to complete the slaughter. By a stroke of ill-fortune, the Argonauts were caught by adverse winds on the night after their departure and were driven back to their starting-point; and when they jumped ashore in the dark without realizing where they were, their former hosts mistook them for enemies from Euboea and engaged them in battle. Many of the Doliones perished in the fighting, including Kyzikos, who was killed unknowingly by Jason. In the light of dawn, however, both sides discovered their tragic and irremediable error, and joined together to mourn the death of the king.[57]

(*v*) Further along the southern shore of the Propontis, the Argonauts called in at the land of the Mysians. While preparations were being made for a feast on that evening, Herakles wandered off into a forest to find some wood for a new oar, having broken his original oar by rowing it with excessive force. On seeing a pine-tree that would suit the purpose, he knocked it with his club to free it from the ground and then pulled it up roots and all. He had been accompanied on the expedition by a young favourite of his, HYLAS, son of Theiodamas or Keux, who also wandered off on his own to fetch some water from a spring. He was destined never to return, for the nymph of the spring was so enchanted by his youthful beauty that she pulled him into the water to keep him for herself. Or in Theocritus' account, he was seized by three such nymphs as he leant over the pool to fill his jar. His cries were heard by one Argonaut alone, Polyphemos, son of Elatos, a Thessalian Lapith, who warned Herakles that something had happened to his favourite; but although the two of them searched all night, they were unable to find any trace of him. Their comrades sailed off at dawn without realizing that anything was amiss, and travelled some distance before discovering that the crew was incomplete. A fierce quarrel broke out as a consequence, but the recriminations were soon brought to a halt by the appearance of the sea-god Glaukos (see p. 221), who rose up from the waves alongside the ship and announced that Herakles was fated to continue his labours and Polyphemos was fated to found the Mysian city of Kios, while Hylas had become the husband of the water-nymph who had seized him.[58]

According to Apollonius, Telamon tried to persuade the Argonauts to sail back to pick up Herakles, but he was successfully opposed by Zetes and Kalais, the sons of Boreas. They paid a heavy price for their words, for when Herakles later encountered them on Tenos as they were returning from the funeral-games for Pelias, he killed them and buried them on the island, marking their burial-mound with a pair of columns. It was said that one of these columns would move in response to the blowing of the North Wind (Boreas).[59] In some accounts, however, the Boreads are said to have met their death during their pursuit of the Harpies (see p. 387).

The legend of Hylas was rooted in local Mysian lore. As Apollonius remarks, the people of the area used to conduct a ritual search for him, supposedly in fulfilment of an oath that their ancestors had sworn to Herakles.[60] The people would roam through the mountains in a frenzy calling out for him at his festival each year, and sacrifices used to be offered to him at the spring which he was supposed to have visited, where the priest would call his name three times. He presumably originated as a minor god who disappeared and was then reborn with the vegetation each year. 'Shouting for Hylas' was a proverbial phrase for a futile enterprise.[61] According to Nicander, the nymphs transformed Hylas into an echo for fear that Herakles would find him among them, hence the echoes that would greet the ritual cries of the priest.[62]

Herakles was a comparatively late addition to the crew of the *Argo*. Even when he was included among the Argonauts, he was rarely said to have travelled the whole way, for no exploits were recorded for him in connection with the winning of the fleece, and he would have tended to overshadow the traditional leader. Some claimed that he was left behind at the very beginning because he was clumsy at rowing and broke the oars,[63] or because the

oracular timber on the *Argo* announced that he was too heavy for the ship or too far superior to the rest of the crew;[64] or else he was left behind by accident as he was fetching water
at Aphetai on the Thessalian coast.[65] It could easily be explained on the other hand that he
never joined the expedition in the first place because he was occupied with his labours or
serving his sentence as a slave of Omphale (see p. 274).[66] Only in some novelistic accounts
from the Hellenistic period was Herakles said to have sailed all the way to Colchis and even
to have been the leader of the expedition.[67]

(*vi*) Before leaving the Propontis, the Argonauts called in at the land of the
Bebrycians (Bebrykes), who lived in the region of Chalkedon near the southern
entrance to the Bosporos. Their ruler AMYKOS, a son of Poseidon by the Bithynian
nymph Melia, was a violent ruffian who forced passing strangers to box with him
and killed them in the ring. On this occasion, however, the finest of all boxers,
Polydeukes (one of the Dioskouroi, see p. 526), was present to respond to the challenge and stepped forward with alacrity. So the two pugilists wrapped thongs of
leather around their hands in accordance with ancient practice, and then exchanged
punches until Polydeukes shattered the king's skull with a blow above the ear. The
Bebrycians, who evidently had no sporting instincts, broke into the ring with their
clubs and spears, but were routed by the Argonauts after a brisk fight.[68]

(*vii*) As the Argonauts were making their way into the Bosporos, a huge wave
towered over their ship and threatened to overwhelm them, but they were steered
to safety by their helmsman Tiphys and moored on the European shore of the strait.
The surrounding area was ruled by the Thracian seer PHINEUS, who was not only
blind but was in great misery because he was being persecuted by the Harpies.
Apollonius explains his fate by saying that he had been granted prophetic powers
by Apollo but had misused his gift to foretell the plans of Zeus to mortals in
unerring detail, provoking that god to deprive him of his sight and send the Harpies
against him. These loathsome creatures, here imagined as being like carrion-birds
with women's heads, had brought him close to starvation, for they would swoop
down to steal most of his food whenever he tried to eat, and would impart a revolting
stench to the little that they left behind.[69]

In the many conflicting accounts of the legend of Phineus, all kinds of explanations are
offered for his blindness and (where relevant) his persecution by the Harpies. In two different
accounts from the Hesiodic corpus, he was blinded 'because he revealed the route to Phrixos'
(presumably the route to Colchis), or because he chose long life at the expense of his sight
in unexplained circumstances.[70] Or in an account which first appears in Hellenistic times,
he was blinded by Poseidon for telling the sons of Phrixos how to find their way to Greece;[71]
or he chose to surrender his sight when the gods offered him a choice of two options, saying
that he could either become a blind seer or else be healthy though short-lived without
prophetic powers.[72] It is possible that the latter story is a more complete version of the
second of the two Hesiodic accounts mentioned above.

According to another group of stories, Phineus' troubles arose because he or his second wife
mistreated the sons whom he had fathered by his first marriage. Sophocles wrote at least two
plays on this matter, but our information on them is very incomplete. In a full narrative
recorded by the Hellenistic mythographer Asclepiades, Phineus first married Kleopatra, a
daughter of Boreas, and then a certain Eurytie, who laid false accusations (doubtless of seduction) against the sons of his previous wife. So he handed them over to her to be killed, much

to the anger of Zeus, who offered him a choice between blindness and death. In opting for blindness, he incautiously stated that he no longer wanted to see the sun, and so offended the sun-god Helios, who responded by sending the Harpies against him; but he was finally delivered from them by the Boreads after the arrival of the Argonauts, as in Apollonius' account (see below).[73] There are various other accounts in which Phineus' second wife, who is also named as Idaia or Eidothea, accused her stepsons of trying to rape or seduce her, and so prompted Phineus to blind or kill them, or to hand them over to her to be blinded and imprisoned or put to death. Apollodorus alludes to a version in which Boreas (properly the Boreads?) and the Argonauts punished Phineus in some unspecified way for having blinded his sons in these circumstances.[74] Or in an account recorded by Diodorus, the Argonauts found that Phineus had imprisoned his two sons in a vault, where they were subjected to constant scourgings. Although Phineus tried to justify the punishment by the gravity of the charge that had been laid against them, the young men were set free by the Boreads (who were brothers of their mother Kleopatra); and when Phineus then joined battle with the Argonauts, he was killed by Herakles along with many others.[75]

For the nature and origin of the Harpies (Harpuiai, i.e. Snatchers), see p. 57.

To return to Apollonius' narrative, Phineus told the Argonauts that an oracle had declared that he would be delivered from the Harpies by two of their number, Zetes and Kalais, the twin sons of Boreas, who were brothers of his wife; and as soon as he had assured them that they would not incur the anger of the gods by doing so, the Boreads readily agreed to come to his aid. Or in another version, Phineus established a deal with the Argonauts by promising to use his prophetic powers to advise them on their journey if they would rid him of the Harpies.[76] The Boreads lay in wait as some food was spread out to draw down the Harpies, and raised their swords and chased them through the air as soon as they arrived; for the brothers were winged and could fly swiftly through the sky, as might be expected of sons of a wind-god. They pursued the Harpies as far as the Strophades, some small islands to the west of the Peloponnese, where they would have killed them if Iris (the goddess of the rainbow and a divine messenger, see p. 57) had not appeared and ordered them to desist. Explaining that it was not lawful for them to attack the Harpies with their swords since they were agents of Zeus, she promised that they would never trouble Phineus again in the future, and they duly returned to their den in Crete.[77] Apollonius claims that the islands had formerly been known as the Plotai or Floating Islands, but were now renamed the Strophadai or Islands of Turning because the Boreads had turned back (*hupestrephon*) there.[78] According to a rather different version recorded by Apollodorus, the Harpies were fated to die at the hands of the Boreads, while the Boreads were fated to die if they ever failed to catch their prey; and since the Harpies died of exhaustion during the pursuit, one dropping into a Peloponnesian river and the other onto the Strophades (here wrongly identified with the Echinadian Islands), the pursuers died along with the pursued.[79] There are also versions in which the Boreads finally caught up with the Harpies and killed them.[80]

Once the Harpies were dead or gone, Phineus provided the Argonauts with invaluable information about the future course of their voyage, advising them above all on how to survive the most immediate danger that awaited them, the Symplegades or Clashing Rocks. These were two huge rocks that stood at the northern end of the Bosporos and used to crash together with immense force, crushing anything that was caught between them. As they were drawing close to the rocks – so Phineus advised – they should let loose a dove and cause it to fly between them; if it were crushed by them, they should turn back, taking this as an evil sign from the gods, but if it should pass through safely, they should follow after it, rowing as hard as they possibly could.[81] After the dove was sent forth by the Argonaut Euphemos, it made a safe passage, losing only the very tip of its tail-feathers as the rocks crashed together; and the Argonauts rowed into the gap with all speed as soon as the rocks began to separate. With a little help from Athena, they fared as well as the dove, suffering only a little damage to the stern-ornaments of their ship.[82]

The Symplegades or 'Clashing Rocks' and the Planktai or 'Wandering Rocks' were mythical hazards of a comparable nature which were presumably doublets. In the *Odyssey*, Kirke is said to have warned Odysseus that the returning *Argo* was the only ship that had ever sailed safely past the Planktai.[83] Although Kirke's account is far from clear, it would appear that ships were driven against the Planktai by waves and blasts of fire; there is certainly no suggestion that they were supposed to crash together. Pindar is the first author to report explicitly that the Argonauts had to pass through 'living' rocks that crashed together; he indicates that they had to confront this danger during their outward journey, as is mentioned by Euripides in the *Medeia*.[84] Euripides refers to the rocks as the Symplegades, while Simonides apparently called them the Synormades (which means much the same) in a somewhat earlier account;[85] they could also be called the Plegades, Syndromades and the like. Another name, as applied to them in the *Argonautica*, is the Kyaneai (Dark Blue Rocks).[86] Herodotus mentions that the Persian king Darios visited the Kyaneai somewhere near the northern entrance of the Bosporos, and identifies these rocks with the wandering (*planktai*) rocks of Greek legend.[87] They came to be distinguished, however, from the Homeric Planktai for two good reasons. These clashing rocks were traversed by the Argonauts during their outward journey rather than during their return journey as Homer states of the Planktai; and like the neighbouring perils on Odysseus' route, the Planktai came to be located in the seas around Italy (even if they would originally have lain in a purely mythical realm). Apollonius classes the Clashing Rocks and Wandering Rocks as separate perils accordingly, presenting the Argonauts as encountering the latter at a later time during their return journey (see p. 395).[88]

Since there were no moving rocks on the trade-route to the Black Sea in classical times, they must have become fixed at some point if they had ever existed. Pindar remarks that the passage of the Argonauts caused the 'living' rocks to 'die'; and Apollodorus explains that they were fated to stand still if anyone should ever pass safely through them in a ship.[89]

Phineus was sometimes said to have lived on the Thracian coast of the Black Sea at Salmydessos or elsewhere; but if it is supposed the Clashing Rocks were located at the entrance to the Black Sea, it is obviously preferable that he should have lived on the Thracian coast of the Bosporos as in Apollonius' account.[90]

The Argonauts now sailed along the northern coast of Asia Minor until they reached Colchis at the far end of the Black Sea. (*viii*) They landed next at the desert island of Thynias, where Apollo manifested himself to them as he was travelling north from Lycia to the land of the Hyperboreans. On the advice of Orpheus, they raised an altar in his honour, offered sacrifices on it, and dedicated the island to him.[91] (*ix*) When they called in at the land of the Mariandynians further along the coast (in the area in which the Greeks would later found the city of Herakleia Pontica), they received a friendly welcome from the king, Lykos, son of Daskylos, because he was grateful to them for having subdued Amykos and the Bebrycians, who were old enemies of his. In the course of their visit, however, they lost two important members of the crew, the helmsman Tiphys, who died of an illness, and the seer Idmon, who was killed by a wild boar while out hunting. Ankaios, a son of Poseidon from Samos (see p. 573, not to be confused with his Arcadian namesake), volunteered to take over as helmsman, while the Lapith seer Mopsos (a son of Ampyx, not to be confused with the more famous son of Manto) took the place of Idmon.[92]

(*x*) As they were continuing on their way, they passed the tomb of Sthenelos, son of Aktor, a hero who had accompanied Herakles on his expedition to the land of the Amazons and had died there from an arrow-wound during the return voyage. Since he desired to gaze on heroes like himself, if only for a moment, Persephone allowed his ghost to rise up to witness their passing; and they called in at the shore on the advice of their new seer to propitiate him with libations and sacrifices.[93] (*xi*) They landed next at the site of the future city of Sinope (just to the east of the northernmost projection on the coast), at the spot where Zeus had been fooled by Sinope, daughter of Asopos, after he had abducted her to that far-off region (see pp. 536–7).[94] (*xii*) On meeting with rough seas near the mouth of the river Thermodon, they beached the *Argo* there for a while, but were wise enough to hurry on as soon as they could to avoid any danger of a confrontation with the warlike Amazons who inhabited the area.[95] (*xiii*) In the last stages of the journey, the Argonauts called in at the island of Ares, which was inhabited by the fearsome birds of Ares which could shoot out their feathers like arrows. On the advice of an Arcadian called Amphidamas, who had seen Herakles use a bronze rattle to put the Stymphalian birds to flight (see p. 260), the Argonauts frightened the birds off by shouting loudly and striking their shields. Phineus had ordered them to visit the island because he knew that they would find some useful helpers there, namely the sons of Phrixos, who had been shipwrecked in the area as they were trying to sail from Colchis to Greece (see p. 378). Jason was happy to take them on board, knowing that they would be able to offer invaluable advice on affairs in Colchis.[96] After skirting the rest of the coast of Asia Minor, the Argonauts arrived at the mouth of the Phasis, the great river that ran through Aietes' kingdom of Colchis.

How Jason gained the golden fleece

As they rowed up the river, they could see Aietes' city of Aia and the towering mountains of the Caucasus on their left, and the plain of Ares and sacred grove of Ares on their right. The golden fleece was suspended from an oak in the grove.[97] After bringing the ship to anchor in a shaded backwater, Jason slept on it overnight with his comrades and set off for the palace on the following morning accompanied by Telamon, Augeias and the sons of Phrixos. Although Aietes was highly suspicious, imagining that they were plotting to seize his throne, he entertained them with due ceremony and decided to test Jason's mettle by offering to hand over the fleece if he could perform two formidable tasks in a single day. In the first place, he must yoke two fire-breathing bronze-hooved bulls to a plough and then plough the intractable meadow of Ares with them; and after achieving this, he must sow the field with teeth from a dragon and then kill all the armed warriors who would spring up from them. The bull had been presented to the king by Hephaistos, while the teeth had come from the Theban dragon that had been killed by Kadmos several generations earlier (for Athena had kept some of its teeth and had passed them on to Aietes).[98]

The Argonauts were filled with gloom when Jason reported back to them since the tasks seemed to lie beyond the capacity of any mortal. Although Peleus, Telamon, Idas, the Dioskouroi and even the youthful Meleagros volunteered to attempt them nonetheless, Argos, son of Phrixos, urged a more cautious approach, suggesting that he should ask his mother (a daughter of Aietes, see p. 378) to enlist the help of her sister MEDEIA, who was a priestess of Hekate and adept in magical arts and enchantments; and when this suggestion was confirmed by an omen, it won the approval of everyone apart from Idas.[99] Now Hera was eager that Jason should succeed in his mission for reasons mentioned above, and she had therefore already taken measures to ensure that Medeia should fall in love with him; for she had approached Aphrodite to ask her to bring this about through the agency of her son Eros.[100] Under the sway of the passion thus aroused, Medeia readily agreed to help Jason when Argos' mother Chalkiope asked her to do so, and arranged to meet him in secret at dawn at the temple of Hekate outside the city.[101] She provided him with a magical ointment to render him invulnerable to injury and flame, saying that it would protect him for a day if he rubbed it on to his body, shield and weapons; and she also advised him on how to defeat the men who would spring up from the dragon's teeth, telling him to throw a stone into their midst from a concealed position to provoke them to fight among themselves before he launched his own attack. Jason responded by promising to take her home with him as his wife.[102]

After making a sacrifice to Hekate during the following night, Jason applied the ointment as Medeia had advised and set off at daybreak to accomplish the tasks.

Figure 11.1 Jason disgorged by a dragon.
Drawing after a red-figure cup by Duris, c. 470 BC.

Figure 11.2 Medeia helps Jason seize the Golden Fleece, second century AD.
© R. Sheridan/Ancient Art & Architecture Collection.

When the fire-breathing bulls rushed forth from their hidden lair, he fended them off with his shield as the flame gushed harmlessly around him, and then forced them to their knees to submit them to the yoke; and goading them forward with the tip of his spear, he compelled them to plough the meadow of Ares, sowing the dragon's teeth as he passed. The task was competed by mid-afternoon, and the armed warriors began to spring up from the furrows shortly afterwards. Putting his trust in Medeia's advice, he raised a boulder from the ground and hurled it among them without revealing himself; and they duly attacked one another and fought until only a few were left alive, at which point he rushed forward and finished them off with little difficulty. Aietes was so enraged at his triumph that he strode back to the city without saying a word. He had never had any intention of surrendering the fleece, and now gathered his main advisers together to plot the destruction of his unwelcome visitors.[103] His schemes were foiled by Medeia, however, who stole away from the palace during the night and warned the Argonauts to make a quick departure.

Before the sun rose into the sky, she guided the ship to the grove of Ares and led Jason to the fleece. She lulled the guardian-dragon to sleep by chanting incantations and sprinkling a magical potion into its eyes, so making it possible for Jason to snatch the fleece without suffering any danger.[104] In this version by Apollonius (which may have been based on a similar account by Antimachus of Colophon, a poet of the fifth century BC[105]), Jason's theft of the fleece hardly ranks as a heroic exploit; but in the earlier tradition, as attested by Pindar and Pherecydes, Jason confronted and killed the dragon (doubtless with his sword) in the true manner of a monster-slaying hero.[106] In a striking variant which is known only from visual images (the earliest dating to the first quarter of the fifth century BC), Jason apparently slew the dragon from inside after being swallowed by it. Euripides' *Medeia* seems to be exceptional in suggesting that Medeia took over the hero's role by killing the dragon herself.[107]

In an early epic account from the *Naupaktia*, Aietes invited the Argonauts to a feast at the palace (evidently after Jason had fulfilled his tasks) with the intention of killing them when they fell asleep afterwards; but Aphrodite distracted him at the critical time by inspiring him with a sudden lust for his wife Eurylyte, and the Argonauts took to flight during his absence on the advice of the seer Idmon. Hearing the clatter of their feet as they were leaving, Medeia rushed after them with the golden fleece and sailed away with them. Jason had presumably brought the fleece to the palace after killing the dragon (or it may perhaps have been kept there).[108]

The return voyage of the Argonauts

The object of the journey was now accomplished, and the Argonauts could begin their return. Although it was commonly agreed that the Argonauts sailed out to Colchis by way of the Hellespont, Bosporos and Black Sea, accounts of their return journey were far more varied. The proposed itineraries can be divided into four main categories.

(*i*) It could simply be imagined that they retraced the route of their outward journey, sailing west across the Black Sea and then back to the Aegean by way of the Bosporos and Hellespont; but although they are occasionally stated to have followed this course in tragedy and later sources,[109] most authors favoured a more adventurous itinerary.

(*ii*) In some accounts from the earlier tradition, the Argonauts rowed eastwards up the Phasis to the encircling Ocean and then passed southward around it until they arrived at the east coast of Africa. Dragging the *Argo* ashore there, they hauled or carried it overland in a westerly or north-westerly direction, either to Lake Tritonis in Libya (which was supposed to have an outlet that opened into the Mediterranean, see p. 396) or to the Nile. After reaching the Mediterranean, they were able to make their way home by a known route. This version can be traced back to the Hesiodic *Catalogue*; Pindar remarks that the Argonauts carried their ship through the wilds of Africa for twelve days.[110]

(*iii*) Timagetos, a geographer of the fourth century BC, proposed a westerly route in which the Argonauts sailed back across the Black Sea, rowed up the Istros (Danube) and then made their way to the western Mediterranean by passing down a branch of the river that supposedly led into the Tyrrhenian Sea. They were then able to make their way home by sailing around the southern coasts of Italy and Greece.[111] Apollonius, whose surviving account will be summarized below, offers a related but rather more complicated version in which the side-branch of the Istros took the Argonauts to the head of the Adriatic; from there they rowed up the Eridanos (Po) and passed through to the western Mediterranean by way of the Rhone, which is here described as a branch of the same river (along with a third branch which led to the northern seas). Some authors tried to remove the geographical implausibilities from Timagetos' version by suggesting that the Argonauts rowed to the head-waters of the Istros and then carried the *Argo* overland (across the Alps!) until they arrived at a suitable southward-flowing stream.[112]

(*iv*) Inspired by the northern explorations of the Greek seafarer Pytheas of Massalia (Marseilles), the early Hellenistic historian Timaeus of Tauromenium (died c. 260 BC) proposed a northerly route. Finding that they were unable to escape through the Bosporos because it was blocked by the Colchians, the Argonauts sailed across to the north-eastern corner of the Black Sea to leave it through the Tanais (Don). After rowing up to its source, they hauled the *Argo* overland until they found another river that issued into the outer Ocean in the north. By sailing anti-clockwise around that Ocean, always keeping the mainland to their left, they found their way to the region of Gadeira (Cadiz) and entered the Mediterranean through the Straits of Gibraltar.[113]

On discovering that the Argonauts had fled with his daughter and the golden fleece, Aietes hastily assembled a large force of Colchians to hunt them down. He either led the pursuit himself or placed the fleet under the command of his son APSYRTOS (or Absyrtos). Since Apsyrtos was considered to have been no more than an infant at this time in the early tradition, he originally appeared in quite another role. In the earliest recorded account of his story by Pherecydes, Medeia seized him from his cot and brought him to the *Argo* at the bidding of Jason; and when the Argonauts came under pursuit, they slaughtered the child, chopped him up, and threw his remains into the river (presumably the Phasis).[114] Although the surviving summary offers no explanation, they evidently adopted this brutal measure to cause Aietes to fall behind as he delayed to recover the remains of his child; this is explicitly stated by Apollodorus, whose account was apparently derived from a different source since it varies in some of its details. For according to his narrative, Medeia killed and dismembered the child herself, and the incident must have occurred rather later at the opposite end of the Black Sea since Aietes is said to have buried the child at Tomoi, a town on the Thracian coast whose name could be interpreted as meaning 'Pieces' or 'Slices'.[115] In some versions from tragedy, on the other hand, Apsyrtos was killed in the palace at Colchis before the Argonauts departed.[116]

Apollonius offered a wholly different account of his fate as we will see, presenting him as a fully-grown man who led the Colchian pursuit on his father's behalf until he was treacherously murdered through the machinations of his sister.

For a full and detailed account of the return journey of the Argonauts, we must turn once again to Apollonius.[117] After leaving the river Phasis, they sailed westward across the Black Sea, stopping off at the mouth of the river Halys about half-way down the northern coast of Asia Minor to offer a sacrifice to Hekate. Remembering that the seer Phineus had advised them to choose a different route on their return, they discussed the matter during this halt and agreed to a suggestion from Argos, son of Phrixos, who proposed that they should sail up the Istros (Danube) and then down to the Adriatic through a side-branch of the river. A large Colchian fleet had set out in the mean time under the command of Apsyrtos; after crossing the Black Sea without finding any sign of the Argonauts, the fleet separated into two sections, one passing out through the Bosporos while the other headed for the Istros. Although Hera laid down a trail of heavenly light to guide the Argonauts to the river, the latter section of the Colchian fleet (which was led by Apsyrtos) entered it ahead of them by passing through its southernmost mouth. As a consequence, the Colchians were able to reach the (imaginary) Adriatic mouth of the river ahead of the *Argo* and so block the ship's escape.[118] They offered generous terms to the Argonauts, promising to let them depart with the fleece if Medeia were put ashore to allow her fate to be decided by arbitration; but Medeia had no intention of submitting to any such process and plotted the death of Apsyrtos to ensure that she would not be detained. By encouraging her brother to believe that she would help him to regain the fleece, she lured him to a secret meeting on the island in the river-mouth where she was supposed to be put ashore; and when he arrived at the appointed meeting-place at the temple of Artemis, Jason, who had been waiting in ambush nearby, caught him by surprise and murdered him. As a pre-arranged signal, Medeia raised a torch to the Argonauts, who massacred the crew of Apsyrtos' ship in a surprise attack and then rowed through to the open sea with Jason and Medeia. To save them from being pursued, Hera deterred the surviving Colchians by sending terrible lightning-flashes.[119]

After the Argonauts had passed some way down the Adriatic, Hera sent storm-winds to carry them back again, for Zeus had been angered by the treacherous murder of Apsyrtos and therefore had other plans for them. The speaking timber on the *Argo* (see pp. 382–3) warned them of his displeasure, and announced that they would not escape the sea and its dangers unless the murderers were purged of their blood-guilt by the enchantress Kirke (who was Medeia's aunt).[120] Since Kirke's island lay off the west coast of Italy, the Argonauts travelled to the western Mediterranean by the implausible route mentioned above, namely by passing up the Eridanos (Po) and then down the Rhone, here regarded as a branch of the same river. While doing so, they passed the spot at which Phaethon had plunged to his death (see p. 45). After making their way back into the Mediterranean, they called in at the Stoichades (Îles d'Hyères, to the west of Toulon) and then at Aithalia (Elba), where they wiped the sweat from their skin with pebbles from the shore; as a result, the beach has been covered ever since with pebbles that resemble scrapings from human skin. When they finally arrived at Kirke's island, Jason and Medeia seated themselves as suppliants in her halls, and she performed the rites that were necessary to purify them from the murder.[121]

The next stage of the voyage took the Argonauts around the southern tip of Italy to the island of Alkinoos, king of the Phaeacians, whose realm is here identified with the island of Corcyra (Corfu) off north-western Greece. On the way, they were confronted by some of the dangers that would later threaten Odysseus when he passed through the same seas after the Trojan War. As they were sailing past the island of the Sirens – enchanting singers who lured sailors to their death through the beauty of their song (see p. 496) – Orpheus drowned out their voices by strumming a loud and rapid melody on his lyre. One member of the crew, however, a certain Boutes, son of Teleon from Athens, heard enough of their song to feel impelled to jump overboard and swim towards them; but Aphrodite snatched him up from the sea and carried him away to Cape Lilybaeum at the western tip of Sicily (where she was said to have taken him as her lover, and to have borne him a son, Eryx, see p. 266).[122] During the most dangerous section of the voyage at the Straits of Messina, the Argonauts benefited from the unseen help of Thetis and her fellow-Nereids, who guided them between Skylla and Charybdis (see p. 496), and then through the Planktai (Wandering Rocks, see p. 388), propelling the ship from one sister to another as though it were a ball. After escaping these perils and skirting the meadows of Thrinacia where the daughters of Helios herded the cattle and sheep of the Sun, they sailed swiftly across the Ionian Sea to the island of Alkinoos.[123]

On the very day of their arrival, the Colchians who had sailed out through the Bosporos also arrived at the island and demanded that Alkinoos should surrender Medeia, threatening him with war if he refused. Medeia approached Arete, the queen of the Phaeacians, and appealed to her as a suppliant, arousing such pity in her that she begged her husband to resist the Colchian demands. When Alkinoos replied that he would not separate Medeia from Jason if she were married to him, but would feel obliged to return her to her father if she were still a virgin, Arete sent a secret message to Jason to inform him of the decision. So he married Medeia without delay, and the couple spent their wedding-night in the sacred cave of Makris, lying together on the golden fleece. Makris, the former owner of the cave, was a daughter of Aristaios who had been expelled from her native Euboea by Hera for having tended the infant Dionysos. On hearing Alkinoos' judgement on the following day, the Colchians accepted it without attempting to fulfil their threats, and asked to be allowed to remain among the Phaeacians since they were afraid to return to Aietes without Medeia.[124]

After leaving the island on the seventh day, the Greeks set off to sail around the southern tip of the Peloponnese, but were blown off course by a violent storm which carried them south for nine days and nights until the *Argo* was finally cast ashore on the desert coast of Libya. On the advice of the guardian-nymphs of the land, they hoisted the ship on to their shoulders and carried it overland for twelve days and nights until they arrived at Lake Tritonis. They lost two of their companions in the area before proceeding on their way, for Kanthos, son of Abas, was killed by Kaphauros (a local herdsman who was descended from Minos, see p. 353) while trying to rustle his sheep, and the seer Mopsos died from a snake-bite. Poisonous snakes had abounded in Libya ever since they had first sprung up from the blood that had dripped from the Gorgon's head as Perseus was flying over the land (see p. 240). After launching the ship on to the waters of the lake, the Argonauts searched in vain for an outlet to the sea. Orpheus proposed that they should set a tripod on the shore as an offering to the local gods for their safe return; and when they did so, Triton, the god of the lake, appeared to them in the guise of a young man and directed them on their way. He also gave Euphemos the clod of earth from which the island of Thera would subsequently grow (see p. 397 and 571). On reaching the open sea, they sailed east along the African coast and then north toward Crete.[125]

While searching for fresh water in the neighbourhood of the Tritonian lake (which was presumably salty), the Argonauts came across the nymphs of the Hesperides and asked them where they could find some water. Now it happened that Herakles had arrived there the previous day to steal some of the apples of the Hesperides (see p. 272), and the nymphs were therefore able to point them to a spring that the hero had created nearby with a stamp of his foot. As a result of this sequence of events, Herakles saved the lives of his former comrades even though he had been separated from them long before. The Argonaut Lynkeus, who had exceptional powers of sight, thought that he could just see the hero disappearing into the distance, rather as someone at the beginning of the month might see or suppose that he sees the moon through a bank of cloud.[126]

On arriving at Crete, the Argonauts found that the island was guarded by TALOS, a huge man of bronze who had been constructed by Hephaistos and had been presented to Minos by his creator (or to Europa by Zeus) to fulfil this function. He was also described, rather less appropriately, as the last survivor of the bronze race (even though the members of that race were not literally made of bronze in the Hesiod's myth of the races, see p. 70).[127] He used to keep watch by running round the island three times a day, and would repel unwelcome visitors by hurling rocks at their ships;[128] it was also claimed that he used to destroy his adversaries by burning them up, either by heating himself in a fire and then enfolding them in a deadly embrace, or by simply hurling them into a fire.[129] He was vulnerable, however, at the ankle since the single vein that ran through his body was covered by a thin membrane alone at that point and his life-fluid (*ichor*) would run out if it were punctured.[130] Or else the vein had a stopper at the ankle in the form of a bronze nail, which could be pulled out with similar effect.[131] Although he tried to repel the *Argo* in his usual manner as it approached the shores of Crete, Medeia was able to take advantage of this weakness of his to bring about his death. After first invoking the Keres (Death-spirits) against him, she so confused him by casting the evil eye on him and sending phantoms against him that he cut his ankle on a rock as he was trying to heave up a boulder, and he expired as his life-fluid gushed out like molten lead.[132] Or in an earlier form of the story, she gained access to him by promising to make him immortal and then caused his death by pulling the nail from his ankle. There was also a further version in which the Argonaut Poias, the father of the great archer Philoktetes, killed him by shooting an arrow into his ankle.[133] When he was safely dead, the Argonauts landed to draw water and rested on the island overnight.[134]

As the Argonauts were sailing north toward the scattering of islands in the southern Aegean, they were engulfed by a night of such impenetrable darkness that it seemed to have risen up from the Underworld. Finding that he was unable to make out a course, Jason prayed for help to Apollo, who revealed (*anephēne*) the little island of Anaphe with a flash of his golden bow. So the Argonauts sheltered on the island for the night, founding a sanctuary there to Apollo.[135] In response to a prophetic dream, Euphemos hurled the clod of earth that he had received from Triton into the sea nearby on the following morning, and the island of Thera grew up from it (see p. 571). The Argonauts continued northward through the Aegean islands, stopping briefly at Aegina, and then passed through the straits between Euboea and Central Greece to reach their home-port in Thessaly.[136]

Jason and Medeia in Greece

After arriving in Iolkos, Jason delivered the golden fleece to Pelias to prove that he had fulfilled his task, and then set out to sea in the *Argo* with his comrades for one last time, taking the ship to the Isthmus of Corinth to dedicate it to Poseidon, the great god of the sea.[137] On his return, he schemed with Medeia to contrive the death of the king.

Although it was generally agreed in the classical and later tradition that Medeia used her special skills to cause his death, there is no definite evidence for this from before the mid-sixth century BC. As has been mentioned, Pherecydes recorded a version of the myth, presumably of fairly ancient origin, in which Hera caused Jason to be sent for the fleece because she knew that Medeia would come back with him and cause the death of Pelias (see p. 381); but this cannot have been the only early version, since a tradition from the archaic period suggested that Jason and the Argonauts attended the funeral games for Pelias,[138] which would have been out of the question if Jason had connived in his death. There is no sign of any such thing in the relevant passage in the *Theogony*, even if Pelias is described as violent and overbearing; for we are merely told that Jason brought the daughter of Aietes back with him in his ship, and that she bore him a son Medeios who was brought up in the mountains by Cheiron (i.e. on Mt Pelion, not far from Iolkos). One may suspect that Jason settled down with Medeia at Iolkos under the rule of Pelias in the earliest version of the story. This son Medeios is also known to have been mentioned by Cinaethon, an early Spartan epic poet (who gave him a sister called Eriopis), but he disappears from sight thereafter; he was probably the eponym of the Medes, serving the function that was assigned to Medos, the son of Medeia and Aigeus (see below), in the subsequent tradition.[139]

In the usual account, Medeia ingratiated herself with the daughters of Pelias in order to work his destruction. She told them that she would be able to rejuvenate their aged father by means of her potions and spells; and as proof of her powers, she killed and dismembered an old ram, and then brought it back to life again as a young lamb by boiling its remains in a cauldron together with magical herbs. Greatly impressed by this demonstration, the princesses chopped up their father and put his remains into the cauldron; but on this occasion Medeia omitted to add the necessary herbs and Pelias regained neither his youth nor his life.[140] In the original tradition, Medeia would have been perfectly capable of rejuvenating Pelias if she had wanted to. Some surviving verses from the *Returns*, an early epic in the Trojan cycle, tell how she turned Jason's father Aison into a young man in the bloom of his youth by brewing up herbs in her golden cauldrons; and it was sometimes even suggested that she rejuvenated Jason himself.[141] In rationalized accounts of her deception of the princesses, however, from the time of Euripides onwards, it is explained that she resorted to trickery to achieve her end, usually by substituting a new sheep for the dead one.[142]

Having no wish to remain in Iolkos after this gruesome vengeance had been exacted, Jason consigned the kingdom to Akastos, the son and heir of Pelias, and sailed away with Medeia to start a new life abroad.[143] Or in another account, Akastos drove Jason and Medeia out of the land after learning of his father's fate.[144]

Aison was already dead in most accounts by the time of his son's return. According to Apollodorus, Pelias decided to kill Aison when he became convinced that Jason would never return; but Aison asked to take his own life, and committed suicide by drinking bull's blood (which was thought to be dangerous because it would coagulate in the drinker's throat). Aison's wife, Perimede, cursed Pelias for causing the death of her husband and hanged herself, leaving an infant son Promachos, who was killed in his turn by the king. Or in the slightly different account by Diodorus, Pelias ordered Aison to commit suicide, and his wife (here called Amphinome) stabbed herself afterwards.[145] These events could be presented as providing an added motive for the revenge of Jason and Medeia.

In the visual arts and literary accounts, the number of the daughters of Pelias (the Peliades) varies from two to five. Apollodorus lists four, Alkestis, Pelopia, Peisidike and Hippothoe, and Hyginus adds a fifth, Medousa.[146] Alkestis was famous in her own right as the noble-minded wife of Admetos (see p. 151); some said that she was marked out from her sisters as the only one who refused to lay hands on her father.[147] As soon as the true effects of their action became clear, the Peliades fled into exile (or were expelled by their brother Akastos). According to an Arcadian tradition, they settled at Mantineia, where their supposed graves could be seen in historical times; or in another account, Jason found good husbands for them abroad.[148] Akastos was best remembered otherwise for the part that he played in the legend of Peleus (see pp. 533–4).

After their departure from Iolkos, Jason and Medeia settled in Corinth (except in an early epic account that took them to Corcyra[149]). In the standard later version of their Corinthian legend, as inspired by Euripides' *Medeia*, they lived there content-edly for some years until Kreon, the king of Corinth (not to be confused with his Theban namesake), offered his daughter Glauke to Jason as a wife. Placing social and political advantage ahead of ties of loyalty and gratitude, Jason agreed to accept her, much to the anger and distress of Medeia, who begged him to reconsider. When her pleas fell on deaf ears, however, she plotted a gruesome revenge. After rubbing a noxious potion into a fine robe and tiara, she told her two young sons to take them to the palace as gifts for the bride; and when the princess put them on, they burst into flames, causing her to be burnt to death, as was her father too when he rushed to her rescue. As her final act of vengeance against her husband, Medeia murdered their two children before taking flight to Athens; she escaped there on a chariot drawn by winged dragons which was provided for the purpose by her grand-father Helios.[150]

Figure 11.3   Medeia kills her children. © R. Sheridan/Ancient Art & Architecture Collection.

A local tradition at Corinth claimed that Mermeros and Pheres, the two sons of Jason and Medeia, were stoned to death by the Corinthians themselves for having brought the deadly gifts to the princess. The spirits of the dead children avenged their undeserved fate by visiting death on the infants of Corinth until the citizens, on the advice of an oracle, appeased them by offering annual sacrifices to them and by raising an altar to Phobos (Fear). The sacrifices were continued until the city was razed by the Romans in 146 BC.[151] Or in another account, Medeia killed Kreon with some of her potions and then fled to Athens, setting her sons on the altar of Hera Akraia because they were too young to accompany her. She assumed that Jason would come to their rescue, but some associates of Kreon put them to death and spread the rumour that she had not only killed Kreon but her own children too.[152]

According to a wholly different account offered by the Corinthian epic poet Eumelos, the Corinthians invited Medeia to their city to become their queen since the land had been granted to her father by Helios long before and the throne had fallen vacant in the mean time (see further on p. 432). Medeia ruled there in conjunction with Jason until he discovered that she had caused the death of all of their children at birth, having buried each of them in turn in the sanctuary of Hera in the hope of rendering them immortal. When he abandoned her as a consequence, sailing back to Iolkos, Medeia decided to leave also and transferred the throne to Sisyphos (who was more commonly regarded as the founder of the city, see p. 430).[153]

Or in a story from a Hellenistic source, the Corinthians came to reject Medeia's rule because she was a foreigner and a sorceress, and killed her fourteen children, seven boys and seven girls, even though they had sought sanctuary at the altar of Hera. The gods sent a plague to punish the Corinthians for this grave act of sacrilege, and the citizens of high birth were obliged to expiate for the crime thereafter by dedicating seven boys and seven girls each year to perform certain rites in the temple of Hera.[154] As with the other local story mentioned above, this is an aetiological legend that was devised to provide an explanation for a cultic practice.

On arriving in Athens, Medeia won the favour of the ruler, Aigeus, by curing him of his infertility. He asked her to become his wife and she bore him a son, Medos, who was destined to give his name to Media and the Medes. When Theseus subsequently arrived, however, to claim his birthright as the firstborn son of Aigeus, Medeia was expelled along with her child for attempting to plot his death (see further on p. 344).[155] In one account, she returned home to Colchis to find that Aietes had been deposed by his brother Perses, and she killed the usurper to restore her father to the throne.[156] Or else her son Medos did so, and then advanced to the south-east with an army of Colchians to establish a kingdom of his own, conquering the lands to the south of the Caspian Sea that would be known as Media thereafter.[157] Or in another account, Aigeus granted Medeia an escort to take her wherever she wished, and she travelled first to Phoenicia and then into the interior of Asia, where she married an illustrious local ruler. She bore Medos to this king rather than to Aigeus as in the usual tradition; and Medos gave his name to the people of the land when he succeeded to the throne.[158]

In contrast to his wife, Jason had no significant adventures after the end of their marriage; only the manner of his death remains to be considered. In Euripides' *Medeia*, he is told by Medeia that he will meet with a shabby death when struck by a falling timber from the *Argo*; and some claimed that she herself contrived such a death for him by persuading him to sleep under the rotting poop of the ship.[159] Or else he committed suicide in his distress at the loss of his children;[160] or he was killed along with his prospective bride and father-in-law in the fire at the palace in Corinth.[161]

It may be said that Jason's star declines in the classical and later tradition as that of Medeia rises, for she comes to be portrayed as an increasingly strong-minded and imposing figure (if not exactly an admirable one) while Jason comes to be shown as irresolute by comparison and even mean-minded. Euripides' portrayal of the couple in his *Medeia* seems to have played a major part in encouraging this trend. In the early epic tradition, however, Jason would doubtless have been a hero of unimpeachable valour who could rank with other great monster-slaying heroes such as Perseus, Theseus or Bellerophon.

CHAPTER TWELVE

THE HISTORY OF
THE DEUKALIONID FAMILY

—— ·◆· ——

The two greatest families in Greek heroic mythology were the Inachids, who
originated in Argos, and the Deukalionids, who originated in Central Greece and
spread to other areas of the Greek mainland and also to the western Peloponnese.
After having devoted the preceding chapter to the greatest adventure associated with
this second family, Jason's quest for the golden fleece, we must now go on to trace
its full history from the time of its founding. **Deukalion**, son of Prometheus, the
founder of the family, and his wife **Pyrrha**, who was the daughter of the first woman
Pandora, were the central figures in the myth that was devised to account for the
origin of the people of Eastern Locris in east-central Greece. After surviving a great
primordial flood that inundated much of Greece (or the whole of it or indeed the
whole world in accounts from the later tradition), Deukalion and Pyrrha created a
new race of people in Locris by tossing stones over their shoulders; and they also
produced various children by natural process, including **Hellen**, the eponym of the
Greek people, the Hellenes. Hellen was in his turn the father or grandfather of Aiolos,
Doros, Achaios and Ion, the eponyms of the four main divisions of the Greek people,
the Aeolians, Dorians, Achaeans and Ionians. None of these were of any significance
as heroes of legend (apart from Ion to some limited extent). All the main heroes and
heroines of the family were descended from **Aiolos** alone through his many sons and
daughters; the history of the Deukalionids is largely the history of the Aiolids.

Aiolos, who would have lived in Central Greece near the lands of Deukalion, had
seven sons and five daughters who scattered to different parts of Greece. As might
be imagined from this, the present family is more complicated in its structure and
history than the family of the Inachids, in which there were only three main lines
located in places of the first importance. Not only did the Deukalionids come to
establish ruling lines in a greater variety of places of variable significance, but each
of these ruling lines tended to be prominent in mythical history for only a generation or two (in marked contrast to the Inachid lines in Argos and Thebes). Even
if some of the forthcoming material is therefore bound to be of relatively limited
interest, it will be worthwhile nonetheless to review the history of the family in a
full and systematic manner rather than merely pick out a few of the more notable
heroes and myths. In doing so, we will follow the practice of the ancient mythographers by considering each of the children of Aiolos and their respective descendants

in turn, beginning with his daughters (pp. 409ff) and then passing on to his sons (pp. 420ff).

The ruling lines founded by these sons and daughters of Aiolos were located in three main areas, in southern Thessaly in the lands adjoining the Gulf of Pagasai, in Aetolia in the south-western reaches of the mainland, and in the western Peloponnese. The principal Deukalionid kingdoms may thus be pictured as lying on a semicircle centred on the family's area of origin, extending from Thessaly in the north-east through Aetolia and then across the Gulf of Corinth to Elis and Messenia. Some lines were established elsewhere, however, in Central Greece and at Corinth and on the Aegean island of Seriphos.

The *Aetolian* royal family was descended from Kalyke, one of the daughters of Aiolos, as was the less important *Eleian* royal line also. Calydon, the chief city of Aetolia, was famous in myth as the home of **Oineus** and his son **Meleagros**, who led many of the foremost heroes of Greece in the hunt for the Calydonian boar (see pp. 414ff), the second of the great panhellenic adventures associated with this family. All the other main branches of the family were descended from sons of Aiolos. As we saw in the last chapter, **Kretheus** founded a *Thessalian* branch that was important for its association with the Argonautic saga. We will consider other aspects of the Thessalian mythology of Kretheus' family in the present chapter (pp. 425ff), and also another interesting Thessalian line that was founded in Phylake by a son of another of the sons of Aiolos (p. 435). One of the sons of Kretheus, **Amythaon**, crossed over to *Messenia* in the south-western corner of the Peloponnese, where he founded a family of diviners and Peloponnesian rulers that included the great seer **Melampous** among its members (pp. 426ff). Amythaon lived as a guest of his half-brother **Neleus** in sandy Pylos, which was celebrated in myth as the home of **Nestor**, the long-lived youngest son of Neleus (pp. 424–5ff). Neleus had established his kingdom on coastal lands in Messenia that were granted to him by **Perieres**, son of Aiolos, who had founded a Messenian ruling line that was destined to die out relatively early, leaving the Neleids in control of the land (pp. 422ff). Mention should also be made of the *Corinthian* line that was founded by **Sisyphos**, son of Aiolos, a cunning trickster who was the grandfather of a great hero of more conventional kind, the monster-slayer **Bellerophon**. We have already encountered **Athamas**, a much-married *Boeotian* member of the family (see further on pp. 420ff); and many other notable heroes and heroines from these and other areas will be found among the descendants of Deukalion and Aiolos.

DEUKALION AND HIS IMMEDIATE FAMILY

Deukalion and Pyrrha survive the great flood

DEUKALION, the first man of Central Greece and a survivor of the great flood, was a son of Prometheus. According to quite early reports, his mother was an Okeanid called Hesione[1] (even if one might have supposed that he would be immortal if both of his parents were divine). He married his cousin PYRRHA, who was the daughter of Epimetheus, the foolish brother of Prometheus, by the first woman, Pandora.[2] Since Pandora was a creation of the gods (see p. 93), Pyrrha was the first woman to be born on the earth by natural process. Deukalion and Pyrrha were associated primarily with the region of Locris in east-central Greece.

When the myth of the great flood was introduced from the Near East, Noah's role (or something like it) was assigned to Deukalion as a hero from the suitably remote past. The earliest full account to survive in any Greek source is that provided by Apollodorus, which runs as follows. In response to a warning from his father Prometheus, who knew that Zeus was planning to send a flood to destroy the race of bronze, Deukalion constructed a large chest, loaded it with provisions, and climbed into it with his wife. Zeus duly proceeded to pour heavy rain from the sky, causing most of Greece to be submerged and every human being to be destroyed apart from a few who found refuge on the highest mountains; but Deukalion and Pyrrha floated safely in their chest for nine days and nights, eventually drifting ashore on Mt Parnassos. After the rains ceased, Deukalion climbed out and offered a sacrifice to Zeus Phyxios (of Escape). When Zeus now sent Hermes to him to offer him the choice of whatever he most desired, he asked to be provided with a new race of people. He was told that this would come to pass if he and his wife picked up some stones and threw them over their shoulders; and when they did so, the stones thrown by Deukalion turned into men and those thrown by Pyrrha turned into women.[3]

Pindar is the first author to refer directly to the flood, telling how the mighty waters overflooded the dark earth until they suddenly ebbed away through the devices of Zeus; Deukalion and Pyrrha descended from Mt Parnassos afterwards to settle at Opous in Eastern Locris, where they brought new people into being by the means just described.[4] The stone-throwing is mentioned in a Hesiodic fragment, which states that the people who were brought into being in this way were the Leleges (i.e. the aboriginal inhabitants of Eastern Locris).[5] As Pindar indicates, this part of the story was inspired by an etymological fancy, since the Greek word *laas*, meaning a stone, is deceptively similar to the word *laos*, meaning people. Although Deukalion was thought to have ruled in Locris in the earliest tradition, authors from the Hellenistic period often describe him as a Thessalian, and report accordingly that he was the king of Phthia or indeed of Thessaly as a whole.[6] Hellanicus states correspondingly that he was washed ashore on Othrys, a mountain in southern Thessaly, rather than on Parnassos in Central Greece.[7] Athenian tradition claimed that he took refuge at Athens at the time of the flood, and even that he was buried there in a tumulus near the sanctuary of Olympian Zeus, which he was supposed to have founded.[8] As to the cause of the flood, Apollodorus states, as we have seen, that Zeus sent it to destroy the people of that era, as identified with the vicious bronze race in Hesiod's myth of the races (although the people of that race perished through their own violence in Hesiod's account, see p. 70); while others suggest that Zeus sent the flood to punish human iniquity, which is not so very different, or to avenge the crime of Lykaon or of his sons (see p. 538).[9]

As originally conceived in Greek myth, the great flood was a local affair which affected mainland Greece alone; and correspondingly, the stone-throwing was not designed to explain how all or much of the world came to be repopulated, but to account for the origin of a special people in Greece, the Leleges of Eastern Locris.

In Roman accounts, however, the flood is transformed into a universal deluge that covered the entire world, leaving only a few mountain-tops (or Parnassos alone) still exposed. According to Ovid, Zeus was so shocked by the crime of Lykaon and human iniquity in general that he decided to eliminate the present race to replace it with a new one. Although he initially intended to achieve this by hurling thunderbolts at every part of the earth, he feared that he might set fire to the heavens if he adopted that course, and resorted to the use of water instead. The Nereids were soon amazed to see groves and towns beneath the sea, and dolphins took possession of the woods and knocked against the tops of oak-trees, and birds dropped into the sea in exhaustion for want of anywhere to settle. Everyone drowned or died of starvation until no mortal was left alive apart from Deukalion and Pyrrha, who sailed through the waters in a little boat until they ran ashore on Parnassos; and Zeus was contented that they should survive because he knew of their virtue and piety. So he drove away the storm-clouds with the help of the North Wind, while Poseidon settled the waves with his trident and called on Triton to blow his conch-shell horn to recall the waters to their proper courses. On seeing that they were all alone in the world, Deukalion and Pyrrha sought an oracle from Themis, who instructed them to throw the bones of their great mother over their shoulders. Although they were initially mystified by this reply, Deukalion came to recognize that it referred to the stones in the body of Mother Earth, and the couple duly set to work to bring a new race of mortals into being.[10]

Hellen and the eponyms of the four main divisions of the Hellenic people

Deukalion and Pyrrha had one notable son, Hellen, and various other children too in differing accounts;[11] two of the latter, Protogeneia and Amphiktyon may be singled out for mention. PROTOGENEIA, the first woman to be fathered by a mortal, was seduced by Zeus and bore him a son, Aethlios, whom we will encounter below as the first king of Elis and father of Endymion (see p. 411).[12] AMPHIKTYON was the eponymous founder of an important religious association, the Amphictyonic League. The common sanctuaries of the league were the temple of Apollo at Delphi and temple of Demeter Ampktionis at Anthela near Thermopylae; Herodotus mentions that Amphiktyon had a shrine at the latter temple. In reality, of course, the name of this and other such associations (*amphiktyoneiai*) indicated that they were formed from 'dwellers around' or neighbours (*amphiktyones*). Lokros, the eponym of Deukalion's home-province of Locris, was said to have been a grandson or great-grandson of Amphiktyon. Through confusion with the present Amphiktyon, who would have ruled at Thermopylae, the primordial king of Athens of the same name (see p. 367) was sometimes described as a son of Deukalion.[13]

HELLEN was the eponym of the Greek people, the Hellenes, and the ancestor of all the main lines in the family through children borne to him by his wife, the nymph Orseis.

The Hellenes, whose name came to be applied to the Greek people as a whole, were originally a particular tribe of Greeks who lived in southern Thessaly. They still appear as such in the

Iliad, which names them among the men who were led to Troy by Achilles (who came from Phthia in the same region);[14] although Homer uses the word 'Panhellenes' as a general term on one occasion,[15] he commonly refers to the Greeks as Achaeans, Argives or Danaans. The Hellenes (in the broad sense of the word) were named Graeci in Latin, after the Graikoi, a Hellenic people who lived to the west of the Homeric Hellenes. Graikos, the eponym of the Graikoi, appears in the Hesiodic *Catalogue* as a son of Zeus by a further daughter of Deukalion called Pandora.[16]

The Hellenes considered that their race could be divided into four main groups, the Aeolians, Dorians, Achaeans and Ionians, as distinguished by differences of dialect, history, distribution, institutions, and so on; and this idea could be expressed in genealogical terms by making Hellen, the eponym of the Hellenic race, the father or grandfather of the eponyms of the above groups. It was stated accordingly that he fathered three sons, **Aiolos**, **Doros** and Xouthos, and that Xouthos became the father of **Achaios** and **Ion**.[17] The latter pair were separated off from Aiolos and Doros as members of a subsequent generation because the Achaeans and Ionians were thought to be more closely related to one another than to the Aeolians and Dorians.

It was of course appreciated that the different tribal groups had not always lived in the same regions, and that the pattern of distribution in classical times was the outcome of a long and complicated process of migration. We are to imagine that Hellen lived in the district of Phthiotis in southern Thessaly, the home of the Hellenes in the *Iliad*, and that he was succeeded there by Aiolos, whose children and descendants would scatter to various parts of the mainland and Peloponnese. Doros would have settled in the small province of Doris in Central Greece, which was regarded as the ancestral homeland of the Dorians (unless we are to imagine that he lived in northern Thessaly, which was sometimes thought to have been the earliest home of his people); and Xouthos was said to have departed to Athens, the most important of the Ionian cities, where he married an Athenian princess and fathered Ion and Achaios.

Doros, Ion and Achaios would have been eponyms and little more in the earliest accounts of the Deukalionid family; not only would they have had no legends, but they would also have been of scant significance genealogically since Aiolos, through his many sons and daughters, was presented as the progenitor of all the main lines in the family. DOROS had a single son, AIGIMIOS, whose mythology has already been considered in connection with Herakles (see p. 282). As was recounted in Chapter 8, close and enduring relations were established between his family and that of Herakles when the great hero assisted him to victory in a war against the Lapiths while the Dorians were living in the north; and when the Heraklids subsequently invaded the Peloponnese to reclaim their ancestral rights in the area, the Dorians accompanied them as allies and settled there under their rule. Although not particularly ancient in its fully developed form, this legend of the return of the Heraklids provided a mythical explanation for the Dorian migration to the Peloponnese (and also a justification since the Dorians, as a people of northern origin, could have had no claim of their own to lands in the Peloponnese). Aigimios had two sons, Dymas and Pamphylos, who were the eponyms of two of the Dorian tribes, the Dymanes and Pamphyloi; Hyllos, son of Herakles, who became an adoptive son of Aigimios, was the eponym of the third tribe, the Hylleis. It is reported that Dymas and Pamphylos, the two sons of Aigimios, joined the Heraklids in their final invasion of the Peloponnese (even if this seems implausible chronologically) but were killed in the battle in which the Heraklids established the victory.[18]

Achaios and Ion and their descendants

The Hesiodic *Catalogue* seems to have dismissed the family of XOUTHOS in five lines, merely stating that he married Kreousa, daughter of Erechtheus, who bore Ion and Achaios to him, and also a daughter Diomede[19] (who married her cousin Deion, see p. 435). In the course of time, however, various stories were developed about Xouthos and his sons and descendants, and also a legendary account of the Ionian settlement of Asia Minor. Although most of these tales are of relatively late origin and of artificial character, they are of sufficient interest to be worth examining in a brief excursus.

Xouthos was born in Thessaly, as were all the sons of Hellen, but he fell out with his brothers, who accused him of having stolen from their joint inheritance, and was driven into exile in Athens; or else he was obliged to settle abroad because Hellen bequeathed his throne to his eldest son Aiolos, ordering his other sons to seek their fortune elsewhere. After winning an honoured position in his new home-land by helping the Athenians in a war against the Euboeans, he married an Athenian princess, Kreousa, daughter of Erechtheus, who bore him two sons, Ion and Achaios, the eponyms of the Ionians and Achaeans.[20] When Erechtheus died, Xouthos was asked to arbitrate on the succession, and awarded the throne to the king's eldest son Kekrops (the second Athenian king of that name, see p. 374), so angering the other princes that they drove him out of the land. So he and his two sons travelled to Aigialos (i.e. the Coast-land), the coastal province of the northern Peloponnese that would later be known as Achaea.[21]

Two parts of Greece were known as Achaea (Achaia) in classical times, the coastal region of the Peloponnese between Sikyon and Elis, and a region of south-eastern Thessaly (Phthiotian Achaea). According to Pausanias' account of the history of Xouthos' family, ACHAIOS gave his name directly to the Thessalian Achaea and only indirectly to the Peloponnesian Achaea. For he decided to leave Aigialos after the death of his father, in order to travel to Thessaly to recover the inheritance that his father had lost after falling out with his brothers; and he conquered much of south-eastern Thessaly with the help of followers from Aigialos and Athens, and founded a ruling line in his newly won kingdom, naming it Achaea after himself.[22] After his departure from the Peloponnese, Aigialos fell under the control of his brother Ion, and it continued to be ruled by descendants of Ion as an Ionian kingdom until it was eventually conquered by some 'Achaeans' in circumstances that must now be explained.

Archandros and Architeles, two of the sons of Achaios, decided to leave Thessalian Achaea to make their home in the Peloponnese, where they married two daughters of Danaos, king of Argos; and since they came to rule over Argos and Sparta, the people there came to be known as Achaeans. It hardly needs saying that this part of the story is an arbitrary invention that has nothing to do with the ancient traditions of either place. When Teisamenos, the last Pelopid king of Argos and Sparta, was expelled by the Heraklids and their Dorian allies several generations later (see p. 290), he led his 'Achaean' followers north to Aigialos, and tried to reach a peaceful settlement with the descendants of Ion who ruled the land. The Ionian princes resorted to war, however, fearing that Teisamenos would be chosen as supreme ruler on account of his splendid ancestry and fine character if the two populations were allowed to mix. Although Teisamenos himself was killed in the subsequent fighting, his Achaeans defeated the Ionians and forced them out of the land. So Aigialos fell under Achaean control and came to be known as Achaea, while the Ionians left to settle at Athens, where they were assured of a friendly welcome because Ion had performed valuable services for the Athenians in earlier times (see below).[23] There was also an account in which Achaios established himself in Aigialos after being exiled from his birthplace of Athens for an accidental killing, and so gave his name to the Peloponnesian Achaea in his own lifetime.[24]

When Achaios departed for Thessaly, ION remained in Aigialos as we have seen, and raised an army to make war on Selinous, the current ruler of the land. In the face of this threat the king decided to seek a compromise by offering his daughter, Helike, to Ion and proposing to make him his heir (for he had no son of his own). On ascending to the throne, Ion named his people the Ionians after himself and founded the city of Helike in the name of his wife.[25]

By virtue of his birth as the son of an Athenian princess, Ion was linked from the beginning to Athens, which liked to regard itself as the mother-city of the Ionians; and a still closer connection was established through various stories that presented him as having commanded the Athenians in war, or even as having become their king. In a continuation of the preceding narrative from Pausanias, it is stated that the Athenians invited Ion back at some stage to command them in a war against the Eleusinians, and that he died there and was buried at Potamoi in southern Attica, where his tomb could be seen in historical times.[26] The war in question was the one in which Eumolpos led the Eleusinians against Athens (during the reign of Erechtheus in the standard version, see p. 369). Or in another account, in which Ion's father Xouthos was not expelled from Athens, Ion led the Athenians to victory in the war before ever leaving the land, and won such credit with the citizens that they chose him as their king and named themselves Ionians after him; and Athens prospered under his rule and sent out colonies to Aigialos. Or he was simply elected to become king on account of his personal qualities after the death of his grandfather Erechtheus.[27] It should be noted, however, that there is no proper place for him in the succession, and that his name is not to be found in the standard king-list (see p. 364). Herodotus remarks that the four tribes of early Athens (prior to the reforms of Kleisthenes) were named after Ion's four sons, Geleon, Aigikores, Argades and Hoples.[28]

In a surviving play, the *Ion*, Euripides offers a distinctive account of Ion's story, presenting him as a son of Apollo who had ruled at Athens as the successor of his adoptive father Xouthos. In this version, Kreousa was raped by Apollo in a cave under the Acropolis before her marriage to Xouthos, and exposed the resulting child in the cave at birth, keeping the whole matter secret from her father in accordance with the god's instructions. Although she naturally supposed that the infant would die, Hermes recovered him at Apollo's request and carried him away to Delphi, where he was reared as a temple-servant at the shrine of Apollo.[29] In the mean time, Kreousa married Xouthos, who had fought as an ally of her father Erechtheus and came to succeed him as king of Athens. As the years passed by, Kreousa failed to produce any children, and the couple eventually travelled to Delphi to consult the oracle of Apollo.[30] Xouthos was told that the first person whom he met on going (*iōn*) out of the temple should be accepted by him as his son; and when this turned out to be the young temple-servant, Xouthos duly claimed him as his son, naming him Ion in reference to the circumstances of their meeting. He assumed that this must be a child whom he had fathered during Bacchic revels at Delphi before his marriage to Kreousa.[31] Having no idea that her own child had survived, Kreousa naturally assumed the same, and tried to kill Ion with some poisoned wine out of jealousy. Before he could drink it, however, he was alerted by a bad omen and poured it on to the ground, and when a dove suddenly died after sipping the spilt fluid, he came to realize that somebody had been plotting his death.[32] After forcing the truth out of a servant, Ion set out to kill Kreousa, but was prevented by the intervention of Apollo's priestess from Delphi. When she revealed his true origin by producing the cradle in which he had been exposed by Kreousa, a reconciliation was established between the mother and son; and Athena then appeared and ordered Kreousa to take Ion home with her, and to allow Xouthos to continue to believe that Ion was his own son.[33] The goddess declared that Xouthos himself would father two children by Kreousa, Achaios and Doros (!), and that Ion would later succeed to the throne and father four sons who would give their names to the tribes of Athens (see above); these would in turn father sons who take part in the colonization of the Cyclades and the coast of Asia Minor.[34] The preceding story, which may have been largely invented by Euripides himself (unless the lost *Kreousa* of Sophocles contained something similar), conflicted too sharply with the usual traditions about Ion and the Athenian succession to be accepted as anything more than a fiction.

The legendary account of the Ionian settlement of the west coast of Asia Minor was set at a very late stage in the mythical history of Greece, two generations after the Heraklids made their final return to the Peloponnese. At that period, many of the descendants of the Ionians who had been expelled from Achaea were said to have set out from Athens with Athenian and Pylian allies to found a new Ionian realm on the opposite shore of the Aegean. To understand the circumstances of this migration, it is necessary to consider how the return of the Heraklids (see pp. 286ff) affected events in Pylos and Athens. When the Heraklids established themselves in Peloponnese, they laid claim to Pylos, the Messenian city that had been the centre of power of Neleus and Nestor (see p. 290), on the ground that Herakles had settled the succession there, leaving the city in trust for his descendants (see p. 286); so the Neleids were obliged to leave, and most of them went to Athens. The most notable of these Neleid emigrants was Melanthos, who won the throne of Athens (see p. 376), and Alkmaion, the mythical founder of the noble family of the Alkmaionidai (see pp. 424–5).[35] The ruler who welcomed the Ionians to Athens was therefore not of native Athenian stock, but a Neleid, Melanthos. Settlers left Athens for Asia Minor two generations later as the result of a dispute within

Melanthios' family. For after the death of his son and successor Kodros, two of his grandsons, Medon and Neleus, quarrelled over the succession because Neleus was unwilling to accept the authority of his elder brother since he was lame in one foot; and when the Delphic oracle was consulted on the matter, it awarded the kingdom to Medon and instructed Neleus and the other sons of Kodros to colonize Asia Minor with any Athenians who cared to accompany them.[36]

Along with some contingents from other parts of Greece, the younger sons of Kodros set off accordingly with a mixed force in which Ionians predominated. On arriving at the central region of the west coast of Asia Minor, the emigrants divided into separate groups to found the twelve main cities of the area, which was known as Ionia from that time forth. Some of these cities had independent foundation-myths of their own which had to be reconciled with this story. It was said, for instance, that Miletos had been founded long before by a young man from Crete called Miletos (see p. 350), but was now resettled by Neleus and a party of the newcomers, who killed all the male inhabitants (apart from those who fled) and married their wives and daughters.[37] It is interesting to compare this legendary account of the Ionian migration with that of the Dorian migration into the Peloponnese (see pp. 286ff, a myth of far greater significance). A notable feature of both legends is the fact that the leaders are of different stock from most of their followers. As Pausanias remarks,[38] a similar pattern can be observed in other legends of the kind, for Iolaos, an Inachid of Argive descent, was said to have led Thespian and Athenian colonists to Sardinia (see p. 251), while Theras, who was of Theban descent, led Spartans and Minyans to Thera (see p. 571).

THE DAUGHTERS OF AIOLOS AND THEIR DESCENDANTS

Aiolos and his four lesser daughters

AIOLOS, the eponym of the Aeolians, married Enarete, daughter of Deimachos, who bore him a large family of seven sons and five daughters.[39] Many important figures from early heroic myth, associated for the most part with Thessaly, Central Greece and the western Peloponnese, can be found among his descendants. We will consider each of his children and their respective lines in succession, starting with his daughters. Aiolos himself is little more than a cipher.

Aiolos, son of Deukalion, should be distinguished from the Aiolos who is keeper of the winds in the *Odyssey* (see p. 493), even if the two are occasionally confused in ancient sources. Although essentially an eponym and genealogical link rather than a hero of myth, the present Aiolos does make an appearance in one interesting mythical tale as the seducer of HIPPE (or Hippo), the daughter of the Centaur Cheiron. It should be remembered in this connection that the daughters or wives of Centaurs were fully human in form. In the best-preserved version of her tale, from the astronomical literature, Hippe fled into the mountains in shame after becoming pregnant by Aiolos; and when her father arrived in search of her as she was about to give birth to her child, she prayed to the gods to make her unrecognizable by changing her form. So she was transformed into a horse (as seems fitting enough for the child of a Centaur); and she was then transferred to the sky by Artemis on account of her piety to become the constellation of the Horse (now known as Pegasus).[40] Hippe bore Aiolos a daughter, Melanippe, who appeared in two plays by Euripides; in a fragment from one of these plays, Melanippe declares that her mother was turned into a horse by Zeus for relieving mortals from pain by means of charms.[41] Or she was transformed for using her divinatory powers to reveal the secrets of the gods to mortals.[42] Or in yet another account, as ascribed to Callimachus, she was transformed by Artemis because she had ceased to honour the goddess and attend the hunt (presumably staying away from her because she had become pregnant).[43] Aiolos would doubtless have come across Hippe while hunting on Mt Pelion.

Of the five daughters of Aiolos, one, Alkyone, was remembered as the heroine of a transformation myth, while the other four are of genealogical significance alone. From that point of view, Kalyke was by far the most significant, for she was not only the ancestor of the Aetolian royal family, which produced such notable heroes as Oineus and Meleagros, but also of the Eleian royal line. We will follow the history of her family in some detail after briefly considering her sisters and their respective families.

(*i*) ALKYONE married Keux, a son of Heosphoros (the Morning Star). This Keux should be distinguished from the one who received Herakles at Trachis (see p. 282), even if they were sometimes confused in antiquity. He and his wife met an early death because they used to call one another Zeus and Hera, so angering the real Zeus that he transformed them into two different kinds of bird, Alkyone into a halcyon and Keux into a sea-bird of uncertain identity, the *keux*.[44] Or in another version, Keux was drowned in a shipwreck, and Alkyone mourned for him without cease or even jumped into the sea in her sorrow, awakening the pity of the gods, who transformed her and her dead husband into halcyons.[45] The halcyon was a mythical sea-bird which nested by the sea, or indeed on the sea, during the 'halcyon days' of winter. It was said that Zeus created this calm, lasting a week or a fortnight, because he had felt sorry at seeing the offspring of the transformed Alkyone being carried away by the waves; or in Ovid's version, in which Alkyone's father is identified with the Aiolos who was keeper of the winds, Aiolos restrains the wind for a week each year to provide a smooth sea for his grandchildren.[46]

(*ii*) PEISIDIKE married MYRMIDON, the eponym of the Myrmidons, a warlike people of southern Thessaly who would later be ruled by Peleus and were commanded at Troy by his son Achilles. The couple had two sons, AKTOR and a certain Antiphos of whom nothing is recorded.[47] Aktor succeeded his father as ruler of the Myrmidons in Phthia, and was succeeded in turn by his son EURYTION, who received Peleus into his kingdom[48] in circumstances that will be explained in a later chapter (see p. 533).

(*iii*) KANAKE bore a number of children to Poseidon, including Aloeus, the putative father of the gigantic Aloadai (who launched an assault against heaven, see p. 91), and Triopas or Triopes, the father of Erysichthon (see p. 133).[49]

(*iv*) PERIMELE bore two children to the Aetolian river-god Acheloos, a certain Orestes (not the famous one) and Hippodamas, whose daughter Euryte became the mother of Oineus (see p. 413).[50]

Endymion and his family in Elis

(v) To proceed to the main Aiolid line on the female side, KALYKE married Aethlios, the first king of Elis, to found the Eleian royal family, and also, through a side-branch, the Aetolian royal family (which was of far greater importance in myth). Aethlios was a fairly close relation of hers as a son of Zeus by Protogeneia, daughter of Deukalion. She bore him a single son, ENDYMION, who succeeded him as king of Elis, the north-western province of the Peloponnese.[51] Or in a rather different account, Endymion was born to Aethlios and Kalyke in Thessaly, and led some Aeolian followers to the Peloponnese to establish himself as the first king of Elis.[52]

Endymion is of interest in two respects, both for the romantic stories that told of his relationship with the moon-goddess Selene and his eternal sleep, and for the part that he played in the dynastic affairs of Elis. Although it was generally agreed that he was an attractive young man who aroused the love of Selene and that he sank into an everlasting sleep for one reason or another, the tradition of these matters is inconsistent and poorly attested. According to one account, Zeus offered him the choice of whatever he desired at the urging of Selene after she fell in love with him, and he asked to sleep forever so as to be exempted from the ravages of age and from death itself in its usual form;[53] or else Zeus allowed him to choose the time and manner of his passing, and he fell asleep forever at a moment selected by himself;[54] or since legend related that Selene used to visit him while he was asleep, it came to be suggested that she herself had put him to sleep so as to be able to visit him at will and steal kisses from him.[55] A wholly different story recounted that he was admitted into the company of the gods and fell in love with Hera, to the understandable annoyance of Zeus, who put an end to the matter by condemning him to eternal sleep; or in a variant that was doubtless inspired by the corresponding legend of Ixion (see p. 554), Zeus fooled him into making love with a cloud-image of Hera and cast him into Hades for his pains.[56]

Selene was so entranced by the beauty of Endymion that she used to make regular visits to him at night, whether to make love with him (before the time of his eternal sleep), or simply to gaze at him as he lay asleep.[57] There was a tradition that claimed that the site of his everlasting sleep and of his admirer's visits was a cave in Asia Minor, on Mt Latmos to the south-east of Miletos. Some explained accordingly that he eventually left Elis to settle on Latmos, where his grave could be seen in historical times; but the Eleians claimed that his grave was located in their own territory at Olympia, near the starting-point for the foot-race in the Olympian Games.[58] If he had fallen asleep forever, of course, he would have had no grave at all. There was a tradition in Elis that Selene bore fifty daughters to him.[59]

Aitolos and his descendants in Aetolia

By his earthly wife, who was either a naiad nymph or an ordinary mortal of varying name, Endymion fathered three sons, Paion, Epeios and AITOLOS, and also a daughter, Eurykyde, who bore Eleios, the eponym of the land, to Poseidon. To determine the succession, Endymion ordered his sons to race for the throne at Olympia, and the victory was won by Epeios. Although Aitolos was content to remain in Elis under his brother's rule, Paion was so angered by his defeat that he went as far away as possible, settling in the region of northern Macedonia that would be known as Paionia ever afterwards (but see also p. 379). Aitolos ruled in Elis for a time after the death of Epeios, but eventually had to depart into exile after committing an accidental killing; for while he was attending the funeral games of the early Arcadian ruler Azan (see p. 549), he ran over a certain Apis, son of Phoroneus or Iason of Pallantion, in his chariot.[60]

The throne of Elis passed to Eleios, the eponym of the land, a son of Poseidon by Eurykyde, daughter of Endymion. Pausanias may be consulted for an account of the subsequent history of the family.[61] Putting aside the interesting body of legend associated with the Olympian Games, there are only two stories of any real interest in the legendary history of Elis, that of the conflict between Herakles and Augeias, king of Elis (see pp. 260 and 277) and that of the accession of Oxylos (a descendant of Aitolos who gained the throne by acting as a guide to the Heraklids, see p. 289). Although Aigeus was usually regarded as a son of the sun-god Helios, he is fitted into the Eleian royal line through a neat rationalization in Pausanias' account, for it is explained that he was really a son of the above-mentioned Eleios, and that the idea of his divine birth arose because the name of Eleios sounds quite similar to that of Helios.[62]

Aitolos left the Peloponnese to settle in the south-western corner of the mainland, in the area that faced his former home of Elis from the other side of the Corinthian Gulf. Although the current rulers of the land, three obscure sons of Apollo called Doros, Laodokos and Polypoites, offered him a friendly welcome, he killed them nevertheless to seize power in his own right, and killed or subjugated the original inhabitants of the land, the Kouretes (not to be confused with the daimones of the same name who guarded the infant Zeus). He named his kingdom Aetolia after himself.[63]

By his wife Pronoe, Aitolos fathered two sons, **Pleuron** and **Kalydon**, who gave their names to Pleuron and Calydon, the two main cities of the land. Pleuron's son **Agenor** married Kalydon's daughter **Epikaste**, who bore him two children, **Porthaon** and **Demodike** (or Demonike). Porthaon married Euryte daughter of Hippodamas (see p. 410) and fathered a number of sons by her, including **Oineus**, who was destined to become the greatest of the mythical kings of Calydon.[64] For the structure of the family, see Table 10. All the major myths of Aetolia, including the panhellenic adventure of the hunt for the Calydonian boar, are set in the reign of Oineus and are connected with him and his immediate family.

Of the lesser sons of Porthaon, only Agrios (the Wild) is of any real interest; he won the throne for a time when his sons deposed the aged Oineus (see p. 419), and he was the father of the brutish Thersites.[65]

According to Hesiodic *Catalogue*, Porthaon also fathered three daughters by another wife, Laothoe, daughter of Hypereis, namely Eurythemiste, who became the wife of Thestios, Sterope, who bore the Sirens to the river-god Acheloos, and Stratonike, who was carried away by Apollo to become the wife of Melaneus.[66] This Melaneus had been fathered by Apollo on a nymph called Pronoe; he was a superb archer, as befitted a son of Apollo, and founded a notable family of archers through his son Eurytos, whose feud with Herakles has already been described (see pp. 273 and 283).

DEMODIKE, the above-mentioned sister of Porthaon, is of importance from a genealogical point of view. Although she was courted by many mortals on account of her exceptional beauty, and was promised magnificent gifts, she yielded to none of them and bore four children to the god Ares instead, two of whom, Thestios and Euenos, are of significance as the fathers of some very notable daughters.[67] THESTIOS, king of Pleuron, sometimes also described as a son of Agenor,[68] was second only to Oineus as one of the most powerful rulers in Aetolia. By a wife who is variously named, he fathered three noteworthy daughters, Leda, Althaia and Hypermnestra, and also some sons, the **Thestiadai**, who joined the hunt for the Calydonian boar and provoked a conflict with Meleagros afterwards by disputing the allocation of the spoils (see p. 417).[69] **Leda** married Tyndareos, king of Sparta, and bore various children of the first importance either to him or to Zeus, including Helen, Klytaimnestra and the Dioskouroi (see p. 525); **Althaia**, as we will see shortly, married Oineus and played a central part in the story of her son Meleagros; and **Hypermnestra** married an Argive ruler, Oikles, to become the mother of the seer Amphiaraos. Thestios makes no personal appearance in myth except in the tale that suggests that he offered refuge to Tyndareos and Ikarios after they were expelled from Sparta by Hippokoon (see p. 525).

Thestios' brother EUENOS, the eponym of the river of that name in eastern Aetolia, was a minor Aetolian ruler who is remembered solely as the father of **Marpessa**, a maiden of rare beauty who was courted at the same time by Apollo and the Messenian prince Idas.[70] For the story of how she was abducted by Idas, with fatal consequences for her father, and then rejected Apollo in favour of her mortal suitor, see p. 153.

Oineus and his family at Calydon

OINEUS, king of Calydon, married ALTHAIA, daughter of Thestios, who bore him several sons including Meleagros and Toxeus, and two noteworthy daughters, Deianeira, whom we have already encountered as the second wife of Herakles (see p. 279), and Gorge, who married Andraimon, the successor of Oineus.[71] As we will see (p. 417), all the other daughters of Oineus were said to have been transformed into birds as they were mourning for Meleagros after his premature death. Meleagros had an elder brother TOXEUS (Bowman) who was killed by his own father, so Apollodorus tells us, 'because he jumped over the ditch (*taphros*)'.[72] This is an intriguing story because it can be interpreted as providing a parallel for the Roman myth of the death of Remus, who was killed for jumping over the walls of Rome while they were in the course of construction (see p. 599); but it is impossible to draw any definite conclusion from Apollodorus' brief remark. Meleagros survived to become the great hero of the family in any case, even if he too was destined to die prematurely. It was sometimes suggested that he was really a son of Ares, evidently in view of his martial prowess.[73] The other sons of Oineus are empty names apart from Agelaos, who is mentioned by Bacchylides as a victim of the Calydonian boar;[74] none were available in any case to protect Oineus during the troubles of his old age or to inherit the throne from him.

In view of the meaning of Oineus' name (Wine-man), it is hardly surprising that there should have been tales that linked him to Dionysos and the introduction of wine. Apollodorus remarks that he was the first mortal to receive a vine from Dionysos,[75] and Hyginus provides a tale to explain how this came about. While staying with Oineus as a guest, Dionysos fell in love with the wife of his host; and when Oineus noticed this, he was considerate enough to remove himself from the scene by pretending that he had to perform some sacred rites outside the city. So Dionysos went to bed with Althaia, causing her to conceive Deianeira; and he rewarded Oineus for his indulgent hospitality by giving him a vine-cutting and instructing him in the cultivation of vines, and by decreeing that wine (*oinos* in Greek) should be named after him.[76] Or according to another tale, a certain Staphylos, who worked for Oineus as a herdsman, noticed that one of his goats liked to eat the fruit of an unfamiliar plant (i.e. a vine) and skipped around in a friskier fashion afterwards. On receiving some of the fruit from his herdsman, Oineus prepared a new drink from it and offered some to Dionysos, who proceeded to instruct him in the cultivation of vines, decreeing that the drink should be named after him and that its source (i.e. *staphyloi*, bunches of grapes) should be named after Staphylos.[77]

The early historian and geographer Hecataeus offers a wholly different account of the origin of the cultivation of grapes, providing Oineus with a different genealogy at the same time. In very early times, a son of Deukalion called Orestheus travelled to Aetolia to establish a kingdom there. When a dog happened to give birth to a plant-stem, he ordered that it should be buried in the ground; and a vine sprang up from it yielding a profusion of grapes. In commemoration of this incident, he named his son Phytios (he who causes to grow), and Phytios subsequently named his own son Oineus after the vines (*oinai*, an old-fashioned name for vines, which were usually called *ampeloi* in later times). Aitolos, the eponym of the land, was a child of Oineus rather than of Endymion in this account.[78]

In his surviving myths at least, Oineus is not presented as a warlike figure, but as a gracious ruler who was always ready to offer hospitality and refuge to strangers from abroad. The *Iliad* reports that he once entertained Bellerophon at his home for twenty days and exchanged splendid gifts with him;[79] he offered refuge to Alkmaion for a time when that hero was being persecuted by the Furies (see p. 327), and to the young Agamemnon and Menelaos after the murder of their father (see p. 508); and Herakles stayed with him for some years after marrying his daughter Deianeira, until an unfortunate accident caused the hero to seek a new home (see p. 280).

Meleagros and the hunt for the Calydonian boar

A most remarkable event occurred soon after the birth of MELEAGROS (Meleager in Latin); for either on the day of his birth or seven days afterwards (i.e. at the time when a Greek child would normally be given its name), the Moirai (Fates) appeared to his mother Althaia and revealed that her son's life would come to an end when a log that was burning in the hearth was fully consumed. In the relatively elaborate account by Hyginus, one of the sisters declared that Meleagros would be noble-hearted, and another that he would be brave, but the third sister Atropos (who was the one who the cut the thread of life to bring people's lives to an end) looked toward a brand that was burning in hearth and said, 'He will live as long as that brand remains unconsumed'. However the warning was delivered, Althaia

Figure 12.1 Meleagros and other participants in the hunt for the Calydonian boar (upper band). Detail from the François Vase, Attic black-figure volute krater from Chiusi, c. 570 BC. Photo: Richard Stoneman.

leapt up from her bed in response and removed the log to a place of safety, shutting it up in a chest in most accounts. It appears that she kept the matter secret from everyone else, including her son. According to Apollodorus at least, Meleagros was invulnerable as long as the log was kept safe.[80]

Before taking the lead in the greatest adventure in Aetolian legend, Meleagros sailed with the Argonauts,[81] and won a victory with his javelin at the funeral games for Pelias.[82] His name appears in all surviving catalogues of the Argonauts; since he was little more than an adolescent at the time, Oineus arranged for him to be accompanied by his maternal uncle Iphiklos, and also another uncle, Laokoon (a half-brother of the king). Maternal uncles often played a role in the initiation of young men. Meleagros comes out well in Apollonius' *Argonautica*, killing two of the enemy during the battle with the Doliones (see p. 384), and even offering, young as he was, to perform the tasks that were set as a condition for the removing of the fleece (although they would ultimately be performed by Jason); the poet remarks that none of the Argonauts was superior to him save Herakles alone.[83]

Meleagros was best remembered as the young man who had led many of the foremost heroes of Greece in the hunt for the Calydonian boar, and had perished soon after he had killed the beast as the result of a quarrel over the allocation of the trophies. The great hunt had come to be convened in the following circumstances. When Oineus was once offering the first-fruits of his harvest (or simply a general sacrifice) to all the gods one year, he happened to forget Artemis, who was so angry that she sent a boar of unparalleled size and ferocity against the land; and it uprooted the crops, destroyed the livestock and killed anyone who was unfortunate enough to encounter it.[84] Although Oineus tried to appease the goddess with sacrifices of goats and red-backed oxen, her anger persisted,[85] and he summoned leading heroes from far and wide to hunt the boar, promising its hide as a prize of honour to the one who killed it.[86] Since the king was now too old to venture into the field himself, Meleagros took command of the assembled force. Among the heroes who responded to the challenge were Jason and a number of former Argonauts, Theseus and his friend Peirithoos, Peleus and his brother Telamon, Ankaios and Kepheus from Arcadia, Idas and Lynkeus from Messenia, the Dioskouroi from Sparta, and Admetos and Eurytion from Thessaly. The hunt took place after the voyage of the Argonauts but before the Theban War; if Amphiaraos joined the hunt, as he did in one account, he was the only boar-hunter who went on to march against Thebes. In addition to all these heroes, a notable heroine, Atalanta, arrived from Arcadia to attend the hunt, and played a leading part in it in most accounts. Apollodorus and Hyginus provide useful catalogues of the hunters, as does Ovid in his *Metamorphoses*.[87]

Although the tale of the boar-hunt and the conflict that arose from it was almost as famous as the tale of the Argonauts, it so happens that no very important account of it has survived. For the course of the hunt itself, Apollodorus and Ovid should be consulted first of all, together with the earlier though less complete account in Bacchylides' fifth Ode.[88] When the boar-hunters set off on their mission after nine days of feasting, Kepheus, Ankaios and some of the other men were reluctant to take to the field in the company of a woman, but Meleagros insisted that Atalanta should be allowed to come. As it turned out, she proved to be a more valiant and effective hunter than any of the men, apart from Meleagros himself. According to Bacchylides, the hunt lasted for six days and the main victims of the boar were Ankaios (a redoubtable Arcadian who wore a bearskin and carried a double-headed axe, see p. 544) and Meleagros' favourite brother Agelaos. Others who are named as victims in later sources are Ainesimos, who was a son of Hippokoon from Sparta, and a certain Hyleus[89] (and even, rather absurdly, Ixion and Telamon[90]). Many more were wounded, and some were killed accidentally by fellow-hunters, notably Eurytion, king of Phthia, who died at the hand of Peleus (see p. 533). Ovid mentions that dogs and hunting-nets were employed, as would be expected; the dogs can be seen much earlier in vase-paintings, which sometimes even attribute names to individual hounds.

It was generally agreed that the boar was killed by Meleagros after first being wounded by Atalanta. According to Apollodorus, Atalanta landed the initial blow by shooting an arrow into its back, and Amphiaraos then proceeded to shoot it in the eye, leaving it for Meleagros to deal the death-blow by stabbing it in the side; or in Ovid's account, Atalanta shot it beneath the ear, and Meleagros finished it off by hurling a spear into its back and driving another spear through its shoulders.[91] The Hellenistic poet Lycophron departs from the usual pattern by suggesting that Ankaios killed the boar after being fatally wounded by it.[92]

The death of Meleagros

The story might well have ended happily at this point if Meleagros, as the slayer of the beast, had chosen to keep the prize of honour for himself; but he decided to award the hide and tusks to Atalanta instead, either out of admiration for her valour and skill[93] or because he had fallen in love with her.[94] By making this gesture, he inadvertently provoked a quarrel with his maternal uncles, the sons of Thestios, who protested that the prize should go to them by right of birth rather than to a woman and a foreigner if their nephew chose not to take it. When they advanced from words to action by seizing the hide from Atalanta, Meleagros flew into a rage and killed them, and so incurred his own destruction; for his mother Althaia was so furious to hear that he had killed her brothers that she rekindled the log on which his life depended, and he expired as soon as it was burnt away.[95] His sisters wept for him so inconsolably that Artemis took pity on them and transformed them into guinea-fowl (*meleagrides*). Deianeira and Gorge were left unchanged, however, at the request of Dionysos, and so survived to marry Herakles and Andraimon respectively as ancient tradition demanded.[96]

In some accounts, including the earliest in the *Iliad*, the quarrel between Meleagros and his uncles developed into a full-scale war. There is no mention of Atalanta in Homer's version, or of the folk-tale motif of the log. We are told, without further detail, that Artemis provoked a dispute between the Aetolians (i.e. Calydonians) and the Kouretes over the head and shaggy hide of the dead boar, and that all went badly for the Kouretes as long as Meleagros remained in the fray; but when his mother cursed him for killing one of her brothers (or some of her brothers, for the text is ambiguous), he withdrew from the fighting in anger, and the Kouretes gained the advantage and launched a threatening assault against Calydon. As the Kouretes pressed the city ever harder, the holiest priests were sent to Meleagros by the elders to entreat him to return to the fighting and to offer him gifts if he would do so; and he was then visited in succession by his father, and his sisters, and Althaia herself, and his dearest comrades, but he remained obdurate until his wife Kleopatra reminded him of the miseries of death and enslavement that awaited the inhabitants of a fallen city. So he rejoined the fighting and won the day for his people.[97] His defeated opponents, the Kouretes, may presumably be identified as the people of Pleuron, the city that was ruled by Thestios and his family.

Although Homer does not state explicitly that Meleagros was killed in the conflict, we are perhaps meant to infer this from Althaia's curse; for we are told that she beat the earth with her hands, calling on Hades and Persephone to cause his death, and, ominously, that the 'Erinys who walks in darkness, and has no pity in her heart, heard her from Erebos'.[98] If the story is viewed in its context in the epic, it is understandable that Homer should have been vague on the matter since Phoinix recounts the story as a paradigm while trying to persuade Achilles to return to the fighting at Troy (after he has withdrawn as the result of a dispute with Agamemnon, see p. 463). According to a fragment from the Hesiodic *Catalogue*, Apollo shot Meleagros as he was fighting against the Kouretes outside Pleuron; and Meleagros is reported to have suffered the same fate in an early epic called the *Minyas*.[99] Apollo was presumably acting on behalf of his sister Artemis. It seems likely that the rest of the story in these two poems would have followed much the same course as in the *Iliad*, but this cannot be known for certain. Apollodorus offers an account of the Homeric version of the myth as an alternative after first recounting the standard later version. War broke out between the Kouretes and the Calydonians, so he tells us, when the sons of Thestios laid claim to the hide on the ground that one of them, Iphiklos by name, had been the first to hit the boar (a detail not derived from the *Iliad*). After sallying out against the Kouretes, Meleagros killed some sons of Thestios, and his mother cursed him for it, causing him such anger that he stayed in his home thereafter. He finally emerged, however, in response to the supplications of his wife, and killed the surviving sons of Thestios before meeting his own death in the fighting.[100]

Meleagros was married to Kleopatra, the daughter of Idas and Marpessa; Apollodorus reports that she hanged herself after his death.[101] In the *Cypria*, an early epic in the Trojan cycle, Protesilaos was said to have been married to Polydora, a presumably legitimate daughter of Meleagros[102] (rather than to Laodameia as in subsequent tradition, see p. 450); but there is otherwise no mention of any children from the marriage. Parthenopaios, one of the Seven against Thebes, was sometimes described as a son of Meleagros by Atalanta.[103]

One should not necessarily assume that Homer was unacquainted with the tale of the magical brand just because he omits it from his account of the story of Meleagros. Fairytale motifs of this kind, some surely of great antiquity, appear with special frequently in the mythology of the Deukalionids; and it is quite possible that the tale of the brand was already familiar in Homer's time but was ignored by him as being out of place in high epic. The early Attic tragedian Phrynichos is the first author who is definitely known to have written about it.[104]

The later life of Oineus, and his successors at Calydon

After the death of Althaia, who hanged or stabbed herself in remorse after the death of her son,[105] Oineus married Periboia, daughter of Hipponoos, who was descended from the old Inachid ruling family of Argos. She bore Oineus a single son only in the usual tradition, but a very notable one, TYDEUS, who was one of the Seven against Thebes (see p. 317).[106] An alternative tradition which first appears in the Hellenistic period suggests that Oineus fathered Tydeus by one of his own daughters, Gorge, after Zeus had inspired him with an incestuous passion for her for some unstated reason.[107] Tydeus grew up to become a promising young man, but was soon obliged to depart into exile after killing one or more of his relations. According to the Hesiodic *Catalogue*, he slew his paternal uncles because they were plotting against his father; or else he killed some cousins of his, the sons of Melas or Agrios, for similar reasons. Or in another set of accounts, he accidentally killed a brother of his, usually named as Olenias or Melanippos.[108] He sought refuge at Argos, where the king, Adrastos, not only offered him hospitality but also gave his daughter Deipyle to him as a wife (see p. 316 for the circumstances). Adrastos promised to restore him to his original homeland, but Tydeus was killed at Thebes (see p. 320) before the promise could be put into effect. He left a son, Diomedes, who was destined to become a hero of even greater stature than himself. When Adrastos died after having lost his only son in the second Theban War, Diomedes inherited his kingdom as his grandson in the female line (see p. 333), and he subsequently commanded the men of Argos, Tiryns and the eastern Argolid at Troy.

All manner of tales were recounted to explain how Oineus came to acquire his second wife Periboia. Her father Hipponoos, who was also the father of Kapaneus, ruled at Olenos in Achaea. According to the Hesiodic *Catalogue*, he discovered that Periboia had been seduced by Hippostratos, son of Amarynkeus, a member of the Eleian royal family, and sent her away to Oineus to be put to death (evidently because he lived at a suitably remote distance); but Oineus chose to take her as his wife instead. Or in the *Thebais*, a poem in the epic cycle, Oineus won her as a prize of war after attacking her father's city.[109] Or when she became pregnant and told her father that Ares was to blame, he sent her away to Oineus to be killed (presumably because he thought that she was trying to cover up a love affair with a mortal), and the bereaved king married her as usual. Or Hipponoos discovered that she had been seduced by Oineus himself, and sent her away with him on learning that she was pregnant.[110]

When Oineus grew too old to retain proper control of his kingdom, some nephews of his, the sons of Agrios, revolted against him to place their father on the throne; and they not only robbed him of his birthright but imprisoned him and cruelly mistreated him. He found a saviour, however, in his grandson Diomedes, who rushed to his rescue together with Alkmaion (a great Argive hero who became the leader of the Epigonoi, see p. 325). The two of them stole into Aetolia and killed all the sons of Agrios apart from two alone, Thersites and Onchestos, who had escaped to the Peloponnese beforehand. Realizing that Oineus was no longer capable of ruling in security, Diomedes transferred his kingdom to his son-in-law Andraimon and took him away to the Peloponnese.[111] In one version of the story, Oineus arrived safely in Argos, where he was tended by Diomedes until he died; or else he was murdered on the way by the two surviving sons of Agrios, who ambushed him in Arcadia at a place known as the Hearth of Telephos. For the subsequent career of Thersites, which was equally disreputable, see pp. 466–7; nothing further is recorded of his brother Onchestos. As for Oineus, he was buried in the western Argolid whatever the circumstances of his death, at the city of Oinoe, hence its name.[112] In another account of these events, Diomedes expelled Agrios (or killed him and his sons) after the Trojan War with the aid of Sthenelos, son of Kapaneus, and restored Oineus to the throne;[113] but this is implausible in terms of any rational chronology. Oineus was proverbial for the misfortunes of his old age.[114]

Nothing is recorded of the birth and origin of ANDRAIMON, who succeeded to the Calydonian throne because he was married to Oineus' daughter Gorge. He was also associated with Amphissa, the main city of Western Locris; indeed, he was supposed to have been buried there in a joint tomb with his wife.[115] His son THOAS appears in the *Iliad* as the leader of the Aetolian contingent at Troy.[116] Although mentioned occasionally in the epic as a respected chieftain, he does not stand out as a hero of individual character or achievement. In the *Little Iliad*, a later epic in the Trojan cycle, he inflicted wounds on Odysseus to make him unrecognizable when he made his secret incursion into Troy in the closing stages of the war (see p. 472); and he is listed among the warriors who hid in the Wooden Horse.[117] He probably resumed power in Calydon after the war in the early tradition, although he was sometimes said to have settled abroad in Italy.[118] According to the local tradition at Amphissa, the bronze temple-statue of Athena in her sanctuary on the acropolis had been brought back from Troy by Thoas as part of the spoils of the war.[119] Apollodorus records a curious tale in which Odysseus is said to have taken refuge with Thoas after being exiled from his homeland for killing Penelope's suitors, and to have married an unnamed daughter of the king, who bore him a son called Leontophonos.[120] Haimon, the son and successor of Thoas, was the father of Oxylos,[121] who acted as guide to the Heraklids during their final invasion of the Peloponnese (see p. 289). As a reward for his services, Oxylos asked to be granted the throne of Elis, which had been ruled by his ancestors many generations earlier before the departure of Aitolos.

THE SONS OF AIOLOS AND THEIR DESCENDANTS

The sons of Aiolos and their families will be considered in the following order: (1) Athamas, (2) Salmoneus, (3) Perieres, (4) Kretheus, (5) Sisyphos, (6) Deion, and (7) Magnes.

We have already encountered the Boeotian ruler **Athamas** in connection with the rearing of Dionysos (see p. 172) and the origin of the golden fleece (see p. 377); he was of significance for the stories that were told of him and his immediate family rather than as the founder of a dynasty. **Salmoneus** established a kingdom in the north-western Peloponnese, but soon provoked the destruction of his household and city by his impious behaviour; his daughter Tyro, the only member of his family to survive, became the wife of his brother Kretheus, who had remained in Thessaly. **Perieres** emigrated to the Peloponnese like Salmoneus, but settled further south in Messenia, where he founded an early ruling line. **Kretheus** was the founder of Iolkos in Thessaly; since we have already considered the careers of his son Aison and grandson Jason in connection with the Argonautic expedition, we will concentrate here on the other branches of his family that were descended from his son Pheres, who founded Pherai to the west of Iolkos, and his son Amythaon, who emigrated to Messenia and founded an important family of seers and Argive rulers. **Sisyphos** was the cunning founder of the early Corinthian royal line. And finally, there were two brothers of lesser importance, **Deion**, who was associated with Phocis in Central Greece, and **Magnes**, who was the eponym of Magnesia on the Thessalian coast, and the father of Diktys and Polydektes, who have been mentioned for the part that they played in the legend of Perseus.

Athamas and his wives

ATHAMAS was a Boeotian king who was remembered for the misfortunes of his family life and for the part that he played in the rearing of Dionysos. He was some-times said to have ruled at Orchomenos in north-western Boeotia, or else at Thebes (although there is no proper place for him in the succession).[122] There were many divergent accounts of his marriages and of the conflicts that arose from them. According to the standard tradition, however, as has been recounted in connection with the golden fleece, he first married a minor goddess, NEPHELE (Cloud), who bore him two children, Phrixos and Helle, but he later put her aside to marry a Theban princess, Ino, daughter of Kadmos, who bore him two further children, Learchos and Melikertes. Ino was jealous of her stepchildren, as we have seen, and would have caused their death (or at least the death of Phrixos) if Nephele had not arranged for them to be carried away from Greece on a golden ram (see p. 378).[123] In a variation on the standard account, Athamas married Ino first, but subsequently put her aside at the order of Hera to marry Nephele; he continued to see Ino in secret, however, and when Nephele eventually discovered this and abandoned him, Ino recovered her former position and then plotted the death of Nephele's children in the same way as in the usual story.[124]

Athamas was later deprived of his other children too in tragic circumstances. In one account, he came to discover that Ino had plotted the death of his previous children, and was so angry that he killed Learchos, the elder of the two sons whom she had borne to him, and chased after Ino herself, causing her to jump into the sea in terror with her infant son Melikertes in her arms.[125] In the more favoured version, however, Hera caused the death of the two children by sending Ino and Athamas mad, to punish them for having reared Dionysos, an illegitimate child of Zeus (see p. 172). In his frenzy, Athamas hunted Learchos down and shot him in the belief that he was a deer, while Ino threw Melikertes into a cauldron of boiling water and then jumped into the sea with him.[126] Or in Ovid's version, Athamas tracked down Ino and her two children in the belief that she was a lioness with two cubs, and snatched Learchos from her arms and hurled him through the air, causing him to smash his head against a rock. Now utterly distraught, Ino rushed away with Melikertes in her arms, howling like a wild beast, and hurled herself into the sea.[127] Dionysos (or in Ovid's account, Aphrodite) took pity on Ino and turned her into a minor sea-goddess, Leukothea (the White Goddess), whom we shall encounter again as the saviour of Odysseus (see pp. 497–8). Melikertes was also deified, under the name of Palaimon.[128]

After these events, Athamas was banished from his kingdom and set off to seek a new home. When he consulted the oracle at Delphi, he was advised to settle at a place where he was offered hospitality by wild animals. As he was passing through Thessaly after lengthy wanderings, he ran across some wolves which were sharing out the remains of a dead sheep; and when they fled at the sight of him, leaving their food behind, he recognized that the oracle had been fulfilled. So he made his home in that region, which was known as the Athamantian Plain from that time onward. He now married yet again, taking THEMISTO, a daughter of the Thessalian hero Hypseus, as his third wife. Of the four sons of this marriage, only Schoineus is worthy of mention, as the father of Atalanta in the Boeotian tradition (see p. 546).[129]

Some sources suggest that Athamas married Themisto while he was still in Boeotia. In Pherecydes' account of his marital affairs, she apparently took the place of Ino as the wicked stepmother who plotted the death of Nephele's children.[130] Or in a tale recorded by Hyginus, Athamas married Ino first of all, fathering Learchos and Melikertes by her as usual, but formed a union with Themisto when Ino disappeared in mysterious circumstances. He later discovered, however, that Ino was not dead as he had supposed, but had simply left home to participate in Bacchic revels on Mt Parnassos, and he brought her back into the house under a concealed identity, pretending to Themisto that she was merely a maidservant. Themisto, who assumes the role of the wicked stepmother in this version, wanted to kill her predecessor's children, and confided her plans to the supposed maidservant, telling her to dress the prospective victims in black and the new children in white to ensure that there would be no mistake. But Ino dressed Themisto's children in black clothes to ensure that they would be killed instead; and when Themisto discovered what she had done, she took her own life.[131]

A combined version is also recorded in which Athamas first married Nephele, and then Themisto, and finally Ino. Nephele and Ino bore their usual children to him, while Themisto bore him two sons called Sphinkios and Orchomenos. After being displaced by Ino, Themisto hid in the palace with the intention of killing Ino's children; but she killed her own children instead because the nurse had put the wrong clothes on them, and committed suicide as a consequence.[132]

The impious Salmoneus and his destruction

SALMONEUS settled in Elis in the north-western Peloponnese, where he founded a city beside the river Alpheios, naming it Salmone after himself. He doomed himself to an early death, however, by usurping the prerogatives of Zeus. Not only did he call himself Zeus and demand that he should receive the sacrifices that had formerly been offered to the king of the gods, but imitated his thunder by dragging bronze kettles and animal hides behind his chariot, and imitated his lightning by hurling blazing torches up into the sky. Zeus punished his impertinence by striking him with a genuine thunderbolt, and proceeded to destroy his entire city along with its inhabitants (presumably because they had acceded to the will of Salmoneus by honouring him as Zeus).[133] It has long been suspected that this legend contains a recollection of weather-magic, in which the actions here ascribed to insane presumption would have been performed to induce rain-storms through sympathetic magic.

During his short life, Salmoneus married Alkidike, daughter of Aleos, who bore him a daughter of considerable importance, TYRO.[134] As we have seen in the preceding chapter (see p. 380), she was entrusted to her uncle Kretheus after her father's death, and bore some notable sons to him and to the god Poseidon. According to the Hesiodic *Catalogue*, Zeus spared Tyro alone when he destroyed the city of Salmoneus because she had constantly rebuked her father for putting himself on a level with the gods.[135]

The families of Perieres and Neleus in Messenia

PERIERES emigrated to the Peloponnese like his brother Salmoneus, settling in Messenia in the south-west. He established himself as the ruler of the land and married Gorgophone, a daughter of Perseus, whose name (Gorgon-slayer) referred to that hero's greatest exploit. She bore him two sons, Aphareus and Leukippos, who inherited the kingdom after his death.[136] Although they were ostensibly joint rulers, APHAREUS held most of the power. He married Arene, a daughter of Oibalos, king of Sparta, and fathered twin sons, Idas and Lynkeus, who are the first

Figure 12.2   Idas and Lynkeus with the Dioskouroi, stealing cattle. Relief from the
Siphnian treasury, Delphi.

members of the line to have any proper myths.[137] Arene was the eponym of an old
Messenian town which is mentioned in the *Iliad* as lying within Nestor's domain.[138]

   Although IDAS and LYNKEUS, who were known jointly as the Apharetidai (Sons
of Aphareus), usually acted in conjunction, Idas performed one notable exploit of
his own when he abducted Marpessa from her native Aetolia and won her as his
wife in the face of competition from Apollo (see p. 153). There is a reference to
this legend in the *Iliad*, which describes Idas as the mightiest man of his time.[139]
Marpessa bore him a single child, Kleopatra, who became the wife of Meleagros (see
p. 418).[140] His brother Lynkeus was proverbial for the exceptional and indeed
magical keenness of his eyesight,[141] which he used to good effect in the brothers'
greatest adventure (see p. 528); no individual exploits are recorded for him, and he
apparently never married. It was naturally assumed the brothers participated in the
main adventures of their time by sailing with the Argonauts and joining the hunt
for the Calydonian boar;[142] but they were remembered above all for their conflict
with their Spartan neighbours, the Dioskouroi, which proved fatal to both sets of
twins (see pp. 527ff).

Hyginus records an eccentric tale that suggests that Idas crossed over to Asia Minor at some
stage and tried to rob Teuthras, king of Mysia, of his throne. Teuthras called on the aid of
Telephos, who had crossed over to Asia Minor in search of his mother Auge (see p. 543),
and Telephos defeated Idas in battle with the help of Parthenopaios (whose presence is left
unexplained).[143]

LEUKIPPOS, who ruled alongside Aphareus in Messenia, had two daughters, HILAEIRA and PHOIBE (the Leukippides),[144] who were abducted to Sparta by the Dioskouroi; in some but not all accounts, this was the incident that provoked the confrontation between the Apharetidai and the Dioskouroi, since the girls were already betrothed to their Messenian cousins (see p. 527).

According to a Peloponnesian tradition, Apollo fathered the great healer Asklepios by ARSINOE, a further daughter of Leukippos, rather than by Koronis in Thessaly as was commonly believed (see p. 149).[145] Pausanias reports that an Arcadian once enquired about the matter at Delphi, and was told on the authority of Apollo himself that the Thessalian tradition was correct.[146] The Messenians liked to believe nonetheless that part of their land had once been ruled by Asklepios, and later by his sons Machaon and Podaleirios, whose supposed tombs could be seen in that land at Gerenia and Pharai respectively.[147]

When NELEUS was expelled from Thessaly by his brother Pelias (see p. 380), he sought refuge in Messenia and received a friendly welcome from Aphareus, who offered him a strip of land on the coast. Through his mother Tyro (who had borne him and his twin brother to Poseidon, see p. 380), he was of course of Aiolid descent like his host. Among the towns that he came to rule as a result of Aphareus' generosity was Pylos – the 'sandy Pylos' familiar from Homer – where he settled and built his palace. He married Chloris, a daughter of Amphion, king of Orchomenos, who bore twelve mighty sons to him, including the shape-shifter Periklymenos and Nestor as the youngest; but Neleus later brought disaster on himself and his family by offending Herakles, who mounted an expedition against Pylos and killed him and all of sons apart from Nestor, who was still below military age (see further on p. 278). In the course of his reign, Neleus welcomed his cousin Amythaon, son of Kretheus, to his city of Pylos (see p. 426); for the story of how Amythaon's son Melampous won Neleus' only daughter, Pero, as a wife for his brother Bias, see pp. 426–7.[148]

NESTOR proved to be more fortunate than his father, for he not only survived into old age but added greatly to his inheritance. As will be apparent from the preceding account, Idas and Lynkeus were the only male descendants of Perieres in the second generation; and when they met an early death before the Trojan War as a result of their quarrel with the Dioskouroi, the lands that had belonged to Perieres and his descendants passed into the possession of Nestor.[149] Accompanied by two of his sons, Antilochos and Thrasymedes, Nestor led the men of Pylos and other Messenian towns to Troy,[150] and returned home safely afterwards. Antilochos was killed towards the end of the war while rescuing his father from Memnon, a foreign ally of the Trojans (see p. 468). The third book of the *Odyssey* describes how Nestor received Telemachos, the young son of Odysseus, at the Pylian court shortly after the war. For his characterization in the *Iliad*, see p. 460. In the time of his great-grandchildren, his entire family was expelled from Messenia by the Heraklids (see p. 290); but this calamity did not cause the final eclipse of the Neleid family, since one of the exiles, Melanthos, won the throne of Athens (see p. 376), and Neleids were said to have led the Ionians in their settlement of the coast of Asia Minor (in legend at least, see p. 409). The great Athenian family of the Alkmaionidai

(Alcmaeonids), of which Kleisthenes and Perikles were noted members, was supposed to have been founded by a Neleid exile, Alkmaion, son of Sillos, a great-grandson of Neleus.[151]

To summarize, Perieres established an Aiolid line in Messenia which ruled the entire province until his son Aphareus granted a share of the coast-land to Neleus, son of Poseidon and Tyro, who was also of Aiolid descent; and since Leukippos, the other son of Perieres, had no male children and the sons of Aphareus died prematurely, the whole of the province fell under the control of the Neleid family when it was headed by Nestor, son of Neleus.

It should be remarked that there were conflicting accounts of the birth and origin of Perieres, since he was sometimes inserted into the Spartan royal line;[152] but the genealogical questions associated with this matter are too complicated and recondite to be worth examining here.

There is also record of a wholly different royal family that is said to have ruled Messenia in very early times before the arrival of Perieres. This line was founded as a result of the ambition of MESSENE, daughter of Triopas, an Argive princess who married the younger son of Lelex, the earthborn first king of Sparta; for when the throne passed to Myles, the elder son of Lelex, she urged her husband Polykaon to establish a kingdom of his own in the fertile lands to the west. So he settled there with some Spartan and Argive followers, and named the land Messenia after his wife.[153] There was a temple of Messene in the city of that name[154] (which was founded as the capital of the land after it was freed from the Spartans in the fourth century BC), and images of her can be seen on Messenian coins. She was evidently a figure of fairly late invention; after searching vainly for information about her family history in early epic, Pausanias concluded that her line must have died out before Perieres arrived there several generations later.[155]

Kretheus and his sons

KRETHEUS was the founder of the Thessalian city of Iolkos, which was best known for its association with the Argonauts. He married Tyro, the daughter of his brother Salmoneus, after initially acting as her guardian, and fathered three sons by her, Aison, Pheres and Amythaon.[156]

Although AISON would have succeeded to the Iolkian throne in normal circumstances, his mother had previously borne twin sons to Poseidon, and one of these, Pelias, became king of Iolkos instead (whether legitimately or by usurpation). Aison remained in or near Iolkos, but sent his son Jason (properly Iason) into the country to be reared by the Centaur Cheiron. The subsequent history of this branch of the family and the career of Pelias have already been considered in connection with the Argonauts. When Jason returned to Iolkos after fetching the golden fleece, he brought the sorceress Medeia, who contrived the death of Pelias; but Jason and Medeia chose to leave afterwards (or were driven out), and the throne passed to Akastos, the son of Pelias (see p. 398). As for Aison, who is a comparatively colourless figure, Pelias was usually said to have killed him while Jason was away with the Argonauts (see p. 398).

Aison's brother PHERES founded the Thessalian city of Pherai, which lay to the west of Iolkos. He married Periklymene, daughter of Minyas, who bore him two sons, Admetos and Lykourgos. ADMETOS succeeded to his father's kingdom, which was famous for its rich flocks of sheep, and married ALKESTIS, the eldest daughter of Pelias.[157] The myths of this celebrated couple have already been recounted in connection with Apollo (see pp. 151–2). Their son EUMELOS (rich in flocks) commanded the men of Pherai, Iolkos and the neighbouring towns during the Trojan War; his magnificent horses, which had been bred by Apollo, were the fastest at Troy after the divine horses of Achilles.[158] LYKOURGOS, the younger son of Pheres, departed to the north-western corner of the Argolid to become the king of Nemea. He was best remembered as the father of Opheltes, who was killed by a snake while Adrastos and his followers were passing through Nemea on the way to Thebes (see p. 318); as we have seen, this legend explained the origin of the Nemean Games, one of the four great athletic festivals of ancient Greece. The supposed tomb of Lykourgos could be seen at Nemea in historical times.[159]

Unlike his two brothers, AMYTHAON, the last of these sons of Kretheus, chose to leave his native Thessaly, and settled with his half-brother Neleus at Pylos in Messenia. He married Eidomene, a daughter of Pheres, and founded a notable family of seers and wise heroes.[160] The Hesiodic *Catalogue* characterizes the Amythaontids by stating that they were distinguished by their intelligence (*nous*), just as the Aiakides (the family of Achilles and Aias, see pp. 350ff) were distinguished by their strength, and the Atreids (the family of Agamemnon and Menelaos) by their wealth.[161] As is not uncommon with the founders of great mythical families, Amythaon has no stories of his own; at the most, Pindar reports that he visited Iolkos to be present when Jason came to demand the throne from Pelias.[162]

How Melampous gained his prophetic powers and won a bride for his brother Bias

Amythaon had two sons, MELAMPOUS and BIAS, who eventually settled in the Argolid, founding new royal lines there. Melampous became the finest seer of his age, moreover, and founded a branch of the family that would produce many other notable seers. He acquired his prophetic powers during his earlier years in the following manner. While he was living in the country outside Pylos, his servants killed some snakes which had made their home in an oak-tree outside his house; and on learning of this, he gathered some wood to cremate the dead reptiles and took care of their young. When the latter were fully grown, they came up to Melampous while he was asleep one night and licked his ears with their tongues, giving him the power to understand the speech of birds and other animals. He woke up in a fright, but discovered at once that he could interpret the cries of the birds in the sky above him; and from that time onwards, he was able to foretell the future to his fellow mortals.[163] Or in a slightly different account, a snake crept forward and killed a servant as Melampous was attending a sacrifice at the court of a certain Polyphates; and when the king killed the snake in its turn, Melampous buried it and took care of its young, with the same consequences as above.[164] Melampous also acquired divinatory skills of a more technical kind by learning how to interpret the entrails of sacrificial animals, and profited too from an encounter with Apollo, the god of prophecy, beside the river Alpheios.[165]

The interpretation of the flights, cries and other actions of birds played an important part in technical (as opposed to inspired) divination; in the tale above, which presents the seer as learning the language of birds in a literal sense and so acquiring hidden knowledge from them, we can recognize a mythical expression of this. As uncanny beasts that creep into crevices of the earth, it is understandable that snakes should have been associated with divination and prophecy. They appear in a variety of contexts in tales of the mythical diviners. In one account at least, Kassandra and her brother Helenos acquired their prophetic powers in the same way as Melampous, when snakes licked their ears while they were lying overnight in the shrine of Thymbraian Apollo at Troy (see p. 154).[166] The seer Polyidos learned how revive the dead Glaukos by observing the actions of a snake (see p. 353); the seer Teiresias underwent his changes of sex as a result of meetings with snakes (see p. 329); and Iamos, the founder of a clan of seers at Olympia, was fed by snakes when he was exposed as an infant (see p. 548).

Melampous used his special powers to procure a wife for his brother Bias, and later to win kingdoms in Argos for Bias and himself. Bias fell in love with Pero, the only daughter of Neleus, who had so many suitors that her father exploited the matter to his own advantage by promising to give her to the one who brought him the cattle of PHYLAKOS (a son of the Aiolid Deion who lived at Phylake in Thessaly, see p. 435). Knowing that this would be a hazardous task because the cattle were guarded by a fierce dog which neither man nor beast could approach, Bias sought the assistance of Melampous, who agreed to perform the task on his behalf. Before setting off, the seer predicted that he would be caught in the act as he tried to steal the cattle, but that he would gain possession of them nonetheless after suffering a year's imprisonment. He was arrested just as he had foretold, and when the year had almost passed, he heard some wood-worms talking together in the roof of his cell; when one of them asked how much of the roof-beam had been eaten away, others replied that very little was left. He hastily informed his jailers, asking them to remove him to another cell; and as soon as they had done so, the roof of his former cell collapsed. On learning of these events, Phylakos realized that his prisoner must be gifted with exceptional powers. So he offered him his freedom and the cattle besides if he could find a cure for his son IPHIKLOS, who was afflicted with impotence. For one day, as he had been gelding some rams, Phylakos had seen his son misbehaving in some unspecified way and had chased after him with the bloodied knife in his hand, causing him such a fright that he had become impotent. Melampous soon discovered the cause of the impotence from a vulture, which told him that he could achieve a cure if he scraped some rust from the knife into some water and gave it to the young man to drink for ten days. The vulture informed him, furthermore, that Phylakos had thrust the knife into the bark of a sacred oak-tree (or a wild pear-tree), and that the bark had grown over it since. Melampous sought out the knife and worked a cure in accordance with the vulture's advice; and Phylakos gave him the cattle as he had promised. After driving them south to Pylos, the seer handed them over to Neleus, who then allowed Bias to marry his daughter.[167] For the further history of the family of Phylakos, see p. 435.

How Melampous won kingdoms for himself and Bias in the Argolid; the Melampodid seers

After remaining in Pylos for a while, Melampous won kingdoms in the Argolid for his brother and himself by delivering the daughters of Proitos, king of Tiryns, from an attack of madness, or by delivering the women of Argos from a general outbreak of madness (or, in a combined version, by curing the princesses and the other women too). There can be few episodes in Greek myth in which the tradition is more complex and inconsistent. To start with Pherecydes' version, which was probably quite ancient, Hera afflicted the daughters of Proitos with madness because they had mocked the poverty of her Argive temple, saying that their father's palace was more splendid by far. After their madness had endured for ten years, Proitos sought the help of Melampous, promising him a share of the kingdom and one of the maidens as a wife if he could effect a cure; and the seer achieved it by appeasing Hera with supplications and sacrifices.[168] Although there is no mention of Bias in the surviving summary, it is likely enough that Melampous shared his prize with him as in the standard tradition. The lyric poet Bacchylides (died mid-fifth century BC) offers a similar account of the origin of the girls' madness, but says that Proitos contrived a cure through his own initiative by vowing a sacrifice of fifty red-haired cattle to Artemis, who then interceded with Hera to secure the removal of the madness.[169] In yet another account from the earlier tradition, in this case from the Hesiodic *Catalogue*, Dionysos inflicted the madness on the princesses to punish them for rejecting his rites, and Melampous worked the cure, winning a share of the land for his brother too. Although the details have been lost, the girls behaved in a wanton manner during their madness (perhaps by wandering around wholly or partially unclothed as in some vase-paintings), and their bodies were covered with scabs, and their hair dropped out.[170]

Herodotus offers a wholly different version of the story, stating that the Argives fetched Melampous from Pylos when the women of the land were once afflicted by a general outbreak of madness; but when he demanded half of the land as his fee for the cure, they regarded the claim as outrageous and dispensed with his services. Later, however, when still more of the women caught the disease, they approached him once again, saying that they were willing to accept his terms. Now that the situation had altered in his favour, he demanded even more from them, refusing to act until they agreed to give Bias a share of the kingdom also. Herodotus does not say who was ruling in Argos at the time, nor does he explain the cause of the madness.[171] According to Diodorus, there was an outbreak of madness of this kind during the reign of Proitos' grandson, Anaxagoras, son of Megapenthes; and it was inflicted by Dionysos and cured by Melampous, who received two-thirds of the kingdom as his reward and shared it with Bias. Pausanias also places the incident in the reign of Anaxagoras.[172] In all likelihood, there were two separate madness-legends, one in which the daughters of Proitos were sent mad by Hera and another in which the women of Argos were sent mad by Dionysos (apparently at a somewhat later period); and if that is so, Melampous would presumably have been associated with one story alone in the first place, perhaps the latter.

We may conclude with Apollodorus' account of the legend, which is clearly a composite version. When the daughters of Proitos were driven mad, either by Hera or by Dionysos (for both possibilities are indicated), they roamed through Arcadia and the rest of the Peloponnese in a state of complete abandon. Although Melampous offered to cure them in return for a third of the kingdom, Proitos considered this to be exorbitant and refused to pay; but when the other women went mad also, abandoning their homes and even killing their own children, Proitos agreed to pay the stipulated fee. Melampous now asked for more, however, demanding a third of the kingdom for Bias too. As soon as his terms were accepted, Melampous set off with the most vigorous of the young men of Argos to drive the women out of the wilds with shouts and ecstatic dancing. One of the three daughters of Proitos died in the course of the proceedings, but the others were purified and cured along with the rest of the women.[173] Two other scraps of information are worth recording. The early Argive mythographer Acusilaus states that the daughters of Proitos were sent mad by Hera because they disparaged the wooden cultic image (*xoanon*) of the goddess; and Vergil mentions that they believed themselves to be cows during their madness, a detail which may be of early origin.[174]

Although Proitos had only two daughters named Lysippe and Iphianassa in the account ascribed to Pherecydes, Apollodorus adds a third named Iphinoe (probably in accord with the Hesiodic *Catalogue*), and most other sources agree that there were three even if there is less agreement about their names. Apollodorus reports that Melampous married Iphianassa (as does Pherecydes) while Iphinoe died in the chase and Lysippe became the wife of Bias. The latter marriage is of little significance, however, since Bias' children and heirs are always said to have been borne to him by Pero. In Diodorus' account, in which Melampous is said to have won his bride by curing the women of Argos during the reign of Anaxagoras, he married Iphianeira, a daughter of Megapenthes and sister of Anaxagoras.[175]

The royal lines founded by Melampous and Bias were destined to play a prominent role in the subsequent history of the land, providing most of the Argive leaders during the Theban Wars; Adrastos, for instance, was descended from Bias, and Amphiaraos from Melampous. This aspect of the mythology of the Amythaontids has been considered above in connection with the mythical history of Thebes (see pp. 316ff and 332ff).

Melampous' branch of the family was also noted for the many seers who were born from it. This is already indicated in the *Odyssey*, which provides the greater part of the family tree in Table 13[176] (in which later additions are marked in italics). We have encountered Amphiaraos, the elder (or eldest) son of Oikles, and his son Alkmaion, as leading warriors in the Theban Wars. There were two important seers in this line (which was descended from Antiphates, son of Melampous), **Amphiaraos** himself, who delivered oracles at his shrine at Oropos during his posthumous existence (see p. 321), and his son **Amphilochos**, who was the joint founder of an oracle at Mallos in Asia Minor (see p. 489).

According to the *Odyssey*,[177] Mantios, the younger son of Melampous, had two sons, **Polypheides**, who was granted the gift of prophecy by Apollo, and Kleitos, who was abducted by Eos (Dawn) on account of his exceptional beauty. Polypheides settled at Hyperesia in Achaea, where he delivered prophecies to all comers and fathered a son, **Theoklymenos**, who was no less gifted as a seer. After killing one of his relations, Theoklymenos fled from his birthplace for fear of being killed in a vendetta, and sought refuge at Pylos on the Messenian coast, where he met Telemachos, the son of Odysseus, who was about to sail home after visiting Nestor and Menelaos. Fearing that he was still being pursued for the murder, Theoklymenos asked to accompany Telemachos to Ithaca; and he was able to repay him soon after their arrival by interpreting a striking omen for him. For when a hawk flew by on the right (i.e. the side of good omen) with a dove in its talons, and plucked out the dove's feathers so that they fell to the ground between Telemachos and his ship, Theoklymenos interpreted this as meaning that his host's family would maintain its supremacy on Ithaca.[178] He later told Penelope, furthermore, that this indicated that Odysseus was already in the land, plotting evil for her suitors.[179] While he was at the palace shortly before the massacre of the suitors, he foresaw their death through a sinister vision; for the meat that they were eating seemed to be spattered with blood, as did the walls and ceiling of the room, and the heads and limbs of the suitors seemed to be shrouded in night, and the porch and courtyard of the palace seemed to be thronged with ghosts.[180] This is a passage of particular interest because divination is practised through purely technical means elsewhere in the Homeric epics, by the interpretation of bird-flights and the like. Inspired divination can otherwise be recognized only in a single passage in the *Iliad*, in which the seer Helenos apprehends a plan that the gods have decided upon in their consultations.[181]

The most notable diviner in the family after Melampous himself and Amphiaraos was **Polyeidos** (or Polyeides), son of Koiranos, who is first mentioned in the *Iliad* as a rich and noble Corinthian seer;[182] he was descended either from Mantios, son of Melampous, or from a further son of Melampous called Abas.[183] His most famous myth, which tells how he found a lost Cretan prince, Glaukos, and brought him back to life again, has been recounted in connection with the family of Minos (see p. 353); his other stories are set in Corinth or the neighbouring region. In a tale recorded by Pindar, he advised the Corinthian hero Bellerophon on how to gain divine help in taming the winged horse Pegasos (see p. 434); and according to a local tradition at Megara, he once travelled there to purify Alkathoos after he had accidentally killed his son Kallipolis (see p. 567).[184] When Iphitos, son of Eurytos, was travelling from city to city in search of his stolen horses (see p. 273), he met Polyeidos, who vainly urged him not to take his search to Tiryns, where he was destined to be murdered by Herakles.[185] The *Iliad* mentions the seer in connection with his son Euchenor, who was shot by Paris during the Trojan War. When Polyeidos had told him before the war that he would either die of a grievous illness in his own halls or be killed by the Trojans among the Greek ships, Euchenor had preferred the prospect of the latter death to that of a hateful sickness, reckoning that this would also save him from having to pay compensation to Agamemnon, the overlord of Corinth, for not joining him on the expedition.[186]

The Klytidai, a clan of seers at Olympia, claimed to be descended from Melampous through a certain **Klytios**, who was a son of Alkmaion by his first wife, Arsinoe, daughter of Phegeus. Since Alkmaion was murdered by the sons of Phegeus (see p. 327), it could easily be explained that Klytios had left Arcadia to settle at Olympia because he had been unwilling to live at his grandfather's court in the presence of his father's murderers.[187]

Sisyphos, king of Corinth, and his son Glaukos

SISYPHOS was the founder of the Deukalionid ruling family at Corinth. Homer alludes to him in the *Iliad* as the most cunning of men who lived at that city of Ephyre 'in a corner of horse-breeding Argos'.[188] Although it is far from certain that this was the same place as Corinth, the two cities were commonly identified in the subsequent tradition, and the myths of the Sisyphids were annexed to Corinth even if they did not originally belong to the city. The main features of the family history were established at an early date, for Homer already describes Sisyphos as a son of Aiolos and as the grandfather of the great Bellerophon through his son Glaukos. His craftiness remained the defining aspect of his character in the later tradition, in which he is generally portrayed as an appealing rogue. As we have already seen (p. 117), he was subjected to unending torment in the Underworld, either for having betrayed a secret of Zeus or for having cheated death when he died on the first occasion. The following story lay behind both explanations. When Zeus abducted Aigina, a daughter of the river-god Asopos, from her birthplace in the northern Peloponnese (see p. 530), he took her through the territory of Sisyphos, who informed her father about the matter in return for the creation of a spring on Corinthian acropolis. Zeus was so angry that he sent Thanatos (Death personified) to haul him down to the Underworld; but Sisyphos contrived to tie up Thanatos, so making it impossible for anyone else to die until Ares finally set him free and delivered Sisyphos to him. This was not the end of the matter, however, since Sisyphos had another trick in hand. Before departing, he told his wife not to perform the proper funeral rites for him; and on arriving below, he complained of this to Hades and Persephone, and asked to be allowed to make a brief visit to the upper world to remind his wife of her duties. After making his escape by this means, he simply remained at Corinth until he died for a second time, of old age.[189]

Although this story of his double death was by far his most famous myth, there were also tales that brought him into contact with two other masters of deception and trickery, Odysseus and the greatest of all thieves, Autolykos (who was the maternal grandfather of Odysseus). Sisyphos once engaged in a contest of wits with Autolykos, whose father Hermes, the patron god of thievery, had granted him the power to escape detection when he stole and to alter the appearance of what he had stolen. He was thus able to alter the colour and markings of cattle, for instance, or to give them horns or remove their horns; and he once made use of his skills to steal large numbers of cattle from the herds of Sisyphos. Although Sisyphos was convinced that Autolykos was stealing from him since his own herds were diminishing as those of Autolykos increased, he was unable to prove it because the appearance of his cattle had been altered. So he set a trap for the thief by marking the hooves of his cattle with his name or the inscription 'Autolykos stole me'; and when Autolykos repeated his depredations, he followed him to his home on Mt Parnassos, identified the stolen cattle from the tell-tale inscriptions, and reclaimed all that had been taken from him. It is claimed in this tale that Sisyphos fathered the wily Odysseus during his visit, for he secretly seduced Autolykos' daughter Antikleia, causing her to become pregnant with Odysseus, who was reared by her husband Laertes as his own son after her marriage.[190]

Nothing is reported of Sisyphos' activities as a ruler except that he was supposed to have founded the Isthmian Games in honour of Melikertes (see p. 421) after the boy's body was put ashore on the Isthmus of Corinth by a dolphin.[191]

According to the standard tradition, Corinth/Ephyre was founded by Sisyphos and ruled by his family thereafter until it was seized by the Heraklid Aletes (see p. 290); but the Corinthian epic poet Eumelos offered a wholly different account of the city's earlier history, suggesting that the territory of Corinth was initially awarded to Aietes by his father, the sun-god Helios, and was subsequently ruled by his daughter Medeia. According to Eumelos, Helios assigned the Ephyraean land (i.e. the region of Corinth) to Aietes, and the adjoining Asopian land (i.e. the region of Sicyon to the west) to another son of his, Aloeus. Aietes left for Colchis, however, where he would later be visited by Jason and the Argonauts (see p. 389), and entrusted his Ephyraean patrimony to a certain Bounos, son of Hermes. After the death of Bounos, both territories fell under the control of Epopeus, son of Aloeus, who bequeathed them to his son Marathon. To escape his father's violence and lawlessness, Marathon took refuge in Attica (hence the name of the village of Marathon in the north-east), only making a brief visit to his original homeland after his father's death to divide it between his two sons Korinthos and Sikyon, who gave their names to the territories that they came to rule. When Korinthos subsequently died without a male heir, the Corinthians invited Medeia, the daughter of Aietes, to become their queen, and she ruled there for a time in conjunction with her husband Jason. As she gave birth to each of her children, she hid them away in the sanctuary of Hera in the hope of making them immortal, but they died in every case, and Jason was so appalled when he finally learned of this that he sailed away to Iolkos. After being abandoned by her husband, Medeia decided to leave also, and transferred the kingdom to Sisyphos (who was thus the first ruler in a new Aiolid line in this account rather than the city's founder).[192]

In the account familiar from Euripides, Jason and Medeia lived at Corinth as guests of the city's ruler, Kreon (see p. 398), whose commonplace name (which simply means 'Ruler') would suggest that he was first invented for the sake of this story. He could doubtless have been inserted into the Sisyphid line at some point; according to the Euripidean scholia, he was the son of a certain Lykaithos who ascended to the throne after the departure of Bellerophon (presumably as a member of the same family, although this is not stated).[193]

The Corinthians liked to believe that Korinthos, the eponym of their city, had been a son of Zeus, but this was apparently regarded as something of a joke by the other Greeks, and the very expression 'Korinthos, son of Zeus' became a proverbial phrase for a piece of tiresome nonsense.[194] The name of the city was prehellenic (as in the case of other names such as Hyakinthos that have the same suffix).

Sisyphos married Merope, daughter of Atlas, who bore him a son and heir, GLAUKOS,[195] and perhaps other children too. Glaukos was famous for the remarkable manner of his death, for it was said that he was torn apart by his own chariot-horses. He had fed them on human flesh in the hope of making them dangerous in battle, but he was obliged to feed them on dull vegetarian food while attending the funeral games for Pelias, and they satisfied their craving for red meat by devouring Glaukos himself.[196] Or in other accounts, Aphrodite sent them mad to punish Glaukos for scorning her rites, or because she was angry with him because he had prevented his horses from mating in the hope of making them swifter;[197] or the animals were driven into a homicidal frenzy after eating a special grass at Potniai in Boeotia that had a maddening effect on horses[198] (or because they had drunk water from a well there that had the same effect[199]). After suffering this terrible death, Glaukos became a malicious ghost, the TARAXIPPOS or 'Horse-scarer', who was supposed to cause panic among the chariot-horses during races at the Isthmian Games (which were held near Corinth).[200]

There was less agreement about the origin of the more famous Taraxippos who haunted the race-course at Olympia. Some stories traced its origin to the chariot-races in which the local hero Oinomaos used to compete with his daughter's suitors (see p. 503); perhaps it was the angry ghost of Myrtilos, who had been killed by Pelops after helping him to victory in the race, or Oinomaos himself, who had been killed during his race with Pelops, or one of the suitors who had been killed by Oinomaos during previous races.[201] If a race-course was troubled by a Taraxippos, it would be wise for the charioteers to appease him with prayers and sacrifices before setting out on their races.

The adventures of Bellerophon in Argos and Lycia

Glaukos married Eurymede or Eurynome, daughter of Nisos, who bore him a son of far greater stature than himself, the monster-slaying hero BELLEROPHON (or Bellerophontes).[202] There was also a tradition that suggested that Poseidon was the true father of Bellerophon, as is stated in the Hesiodic *Catalogue* and indicated by Pindar.[203]

According to the relevant fragment from the *Catalogue*, Sisyphos initially chose Mestra, the shape-shifting daughter of Erysichthon, as a wife for Glaukos, paying valuable bride-gifts for her, but she soon fled back to her father's house. Since there are large gaps in the papyrus, we cannot tell whether she made use of her special powers to do so (as when she fled from her masters to gain money for her father, see p. 133). Although Sisyphos was understandably aggrieved, Zeus had other plans for her, having no wish that she should bear an ordinary human family; and she was carried off by Poseidon to the island of Cos, where she bore him two sons. So Sisyphos was obliged to choose another bride for his son, a 'daughter of Pandionides' (presumably his usual wife as named above, who was a granddaughter of Pandion, king of Athens). Even if the marriage endured on this occasion, it was Zeus's will that Glaukos should father no children even by this wife, and his putative son Bellerophon was fathered by Poseidon instead.[204]

While still a young man, Bellerophon had to leave Corinth forever as the result of an accidental killing. His victim is variously named, some suggesting, for instance, that he killed a certain Belleros (since his name could be interpreted as meaning 'Belleros-slayer') or else a brother of variable name.[205] Bellerophon sought refuge in the Argolid with Proitos, king of Tiryns, who purified him and welcomed him to his court; but trouble arose when the king's wife, who is generally named as Stheneboia (but is called Anteia in the *Iliad*) conceived a passion for the handsome stranger and pressed him to meet her in secret. For when she found herself rejected, her desire turned to fury and she told her husband that Bellerophon had tried to rape or seduce her. Although Proitos fully believed her, he was reluctant to take direct action against a guest whom he had purified, and sent him off to his father-in-law Iobates, the king of Lycia in Asia Minor, with a sealed tablet or letter asking that he should be put of death.

As Homer tells the story, the king of Lycia (here unnamed) entertained him on his arrival for nine days, slaughtering nine cows, and questioned him at dawn on the tenth day, asking to see the message that he had brought. After learning of Proitos' wish, he ordered Bellerophon to kill the CHIMAIRA, a fire-breathing monster which was thought to be unconquerable. Homer describes it as being like a lion in front, a dragon behind, and a goat (*chimaira*, hence its name) in the middle; in subsequent depictions, it resembles a lion in its basic form, but has a snake in place of a tail, and a goat's head projecting from the middle of its back. Bellerophon proceeded to kill it, trusting in signs from the gods. The king then contrived two further ordeals for him, by sending him out against the Solymoi, a bellicose people of the area, and the Amazons, female warriors who were a match for any man; but he returned safe in each case after slaughtering the enemy, and the king subjected him to a final ordeal by picking out a chosen band of warriors from throughout his land. When Bellerophon killed them without exception, the king realized that he must be the intrepid offspring of some god and offered him his daughter Philonoe (or Antikleia) in marriage along with a share of the kingdom.[206] Bellerophon fathered three children by his Lycian wife, namely a daughter Laodameia, who bore Sarpedon to Zeus, and two sons, Hippolochos, who became the father of Glaukos (Sarpedon's second in command at Troy), and Isandros, who met an early death; for further consideration of this family, see pp. 349–50. Things turned out badly for Bellerophon in the end, so Homer tells us, for he came to be hated by all the gods for some unspecified reason, 'and he went wandering alone over the Aleian plain [i.e. Plain of Wandering], eating his heart out, shunning the paths of men'.[207]

In all subsequent accounts, Bellerophon is said to have ridden out against the Chimaira on the back of the winged horse Pegasos, which was a son of Poseidon by the Gorgon Medusa (see p. 60 for the circumstances of his birth). According to Pindar, he had initially found Pegasos hard to tame and had consulted the seer Polyeidos (see p. 430), who told him to sleep overnight in the shrine of Athena in Corinth. The goddess appeared to him in his sleep and told him to accept a bridle from her for use on Pegasos, and to sacrifice a white bull to his father Poseidon, as tamer of horses. He woke up to find a wonderful golden-banded bridle lying beside him, and employed it to good effect (see also p. 183).[208] Or in another version, Athena tamed Pegasos on the hero's behalf by placing a bit in his mouth;[209] or else Bellerophon captured him as he was drinking at the spring of Peirene at Corinth, or received him as a gift from his father Poseidon.[210] However he came to possess him, he made good use of him to defeat his enemies by riding out against them from above.

According to a tale from a lost play by Euripides, the *Stheneboia*, Bellerophon returned to Tiryns after surviving his ordeals and wreaked revenge on Stheneboia with the help of his flying horse; for he persuaded her to ride up into the sky with him, and pushed her off while they were high over the Aegean near Melos.[211] His sad predicament at the end of his life, as described in the *Iliad*, is explained in some late sources as a fate that he had incurred by attempting to fly up to Olympos on the back of Pegasos. For Zeus had been so angered by his presumption that he had sent a gadfly against the horse, causing Bellerophon to be thrown to the ground in Lycia, where he wandered around in misery ever afterwards.[212] Or in another version, he became giddy with fear on looking downwards and fell to his death.[213] As for Pegasos, he continued on his way, and Zeus granted him an honoured position in the heavens as the constellation of the Horse (now known correspondingly as Pegasus).[214]

Since Bellerophon was never able to return to Corinth, the throne passed out of Glaukos' line to a certain Thoas, who is said to have been a grandson of Sisyphos through a son of his called Ornytion or Ornytios; and the city was then ruled by Thoas and his descendants for three generations until one of the Heraklids, Aletes, conquered it with a Dorian army (see p. 290).[215] Ornytion had a further son, Phokos, who settled at Phocis in Central Greece (see p. 565).

Two lesser Aiolids, Deion and Magnes, and their families

DEION (or Deioneus), who has no myths of his own, ruled the province of Phocis in Central Greece. He married Diomede, daughter of Xouthos, who bore him a number of children including Kephalos, whose stormy marriage with Prokris in Attica was considered in Chapter 10 (see pp. 371ff), and PHYLAKOS, the eponymous founder of Phylake in southern Thessaly.[216] Lying to the south-west of Iolkos and Pherai, Phylake ranked with Achilles' home-town of Phthia in mythical history as one of the two main cities of Phthiotis, the south-eastern region of Thessaly. Phylakos married Klymene, daughter of Minyas, who bore him two children, a son IPHIKLOS and a daughter Alkimede, who married Aison to become the mother of Jason.[217] As was recounted earlier in the chapter, Phylakos imprisoned the seer Melampous for trying to steal his cattle, but later released him to enable him to find a cure for the impotence that he had unwittingly induced in his son Iphiklos (see further on p. 427). Iphiklos was duly cured and married a certain Astyoche who bore him two sons of note, PROTESILAOS, who was the first of the Greeks to leap ashore at Troy and the first to be killed (see further on p. 450), and PODARKES, who commanded the men of Phylake and neighbouring cities in the Trojan War after the death of his brother.[218] In late epic, Podarkes was said to have fallen to the Amazon Penthesileia in the last stages of the war;[219] he was named Podarkes or 'Swift-foot' in commemoration of his father's most remarkable capacity, his prodigious swiftness of foot. For it was said that Iphiklos could outpace the wind, and that he could run so swiftly over standing corn that the ears had no time to bend or break, or so swiftly over the sea that he never sank beneath the surface.[220] This is mentioned in a fragment from the Hesiodic *Catalogue*, and was certainly a very ancient feature of the tradition since Homer refers to Iphiklos as a particularly fast runner and knows that his son was called 'Swift-foot'.[221] Some claimed that he won the foot-race at the funeral games for Pelias.[222]

Deion also had two daughters, Asterodeia and Philonis, who remained in their native land of Phocis. Asterodeia married Phokos, son of Aiakos,[223] who was one of the two eponyms of the land along with Phokos, son of Ornytion; for the part that these two eponyms were supposed to have played in the history of Phocis, and for the twin sons who were born to the former by Asterodeia, see p. 565. Philonis also produced two sons in one birth, but in very different circumstances. She was so beautiful that she attracted the desire of two gods at once, Apollo and Hermes, who both slept with her on the same day; and she conceived the mythical musician Philammon to Apollo, and the master-thief Autolykos (see p. 431) to Hermes.[224] Both of her sons spent their lives on Parnassos, the mountain that dominated their grandfather's realm. Philammon fathered Thamyris, an even greater musician than himself, on a Parnassian nymph called Argiope. She gave birth to her child in Thrace (where he would later engage in his celebrated contest with the Muses, see p. 206) because Philammon refused to take her into his home.[225] If this story shows him in a rather bad light, he met a noble death while trying to prevent the Phlegyans from plundering Delphi (see p. 560).[226] Pherecydes is exceptional in suggesting that he rather than Orpheus was the singer who accompanied the Argonauts.[227]

In Apollodorus' account, the remaining son of Aiolos was MAGNES, the eponym of Magnesia, the coastal district of northern Thessaly; he married a naiad nymph and fathered two sons, Polydektes and Diktys, who settled on the island of Seriphos and played an important role in story of Perseus (see pp. 239ff).[228] In the Hesiodic *Catalogue*, however, Magnes was of different birth as a son of Zeus by Thuia daughter of Deukalion, and was the brother of Makedon, the eponym of Macedonia.[229] Although the name of the seventh son of Aiolos has not been preserved in the surviving fragments of the *Catalogue*, it has been plausibly suggested that he may have been Minyas (the eponym of the Minyans, see p. 558).

CHAPTER THIRTEEN

THE TROJAN
WAR

— .•. —

THE ORIGIN OF THE WAR AND THE
GREEK CROSSING

Zeus lays plans for a great war

The culminating event of the mythical history of Greece was the great war in
which Agamemnon, king of Mycenae, and Menelaos, king of Sparta, led a great
army against Troy, a rich and powerful city in the north-western corner of Asia
Minor, and finally conquered it after besieging it for ten years. The conflict was
provoked by the abduction of Helen, the wife of Menelaos, who was carried off to
Asia by Paris, the son of Priam, king of Troy; and this episode was itself an element
in a divine plan that had been devised to rid the earth of an excess of human beings.
For Gaia (Earth) had complained to Zeus that she was overburdened by all the mortals
who were swarming over her surface and were not only far too numerous but impious
besides; and after relieving the problem to some extent by inciting the Theban Wars,
Zeus had planned to cause even greater carnage by means of thunderbolts and floods.
But Momos, the personification of fault-finding (see p. 26), criticized his plans and
proposed a subtler course of action, suggesting that a destructive war should be
provoked between Europe and Asia by indirect means. As the first two steps towards
this end, she said that the goddess Thetis should be married to a mortal and that Zeus
should father a daughter of surpassing beauty. So Zeus fathered Helen, and Thetis
was married to Peleus at a magnificent wedding that was attended by the gods (see
p. 54). During the wedding-feast, Eris, the personification of Strife (see p. 30),
provoked a furious quarrel between Hera, Athena and Aphrodite by hurling an apple
in front of them marked with the inscription 'to the most beautiful'; and Zeus then
instructed the divine messenger Hermes to escort the three goddesses to Mt Ida in
the land of Troy to be judged for their beauty by Paris. When Aphrodite persuaded
Paris to award her the victory by promising that she would help him to marry Helen,
a daughter of Zeus who was the most beautiful woman in the world, the projected
conflict between Greece and Asia became inevitable; for the Trojan prince would have
to seize her from her legitimate husband in Greece if he were to make her his wife.
This would be a hazardous action because her husband Menelaos was not only a man

of some eminence as king of Sparta, but was also the brother of Agamemnon, the most powerful ruler in Greece; and most importantly of all, the many suitors of Helen had bound themselves by oath to come to the aid of her chosen husband if she should ever be taken from him (see p. 440). It was therefore by no means difficult for Menelaos to raise a large force of allies to sail against Troy to recover his wife, so bringing the divine plan to its fulfilment. Such is the earliest surviving account of the origin of the war, as was presented in the *Cypria*, the first epic in the Trojan cycle.[1] It was also suggested that Zeus contrived the abduction of Helen to ensure that his daughter would be famous ever afterwards for having been the cause of the mightiest war in history; or else he provoked the war simply to bring everlasting glory to the men of the heroic age.[2]

The birth and early life of Helen, and her marriage to Menelaos

HELEN of Sparta and Troy was no ordinary woman but a daughter of Zeus whose beauty was tinged with more than a trace of the divine. Her putative father was Tyndareos, the last Atlantid king of Sparta, whose wife LEDA bore various children either to him or to Zeus.[3] Tyndareos' branch of the Atlantid family, which formed the original ruling line in Sparta, will be examined in full in a later chapter (see pp. 524ff); for the present it will be sufficient to note that Leda bore three daughters to her husband, including Klytaimnestra, who became the wife of Agamemnon and was also the mother of Kastor and Polydeukes, the Dioskouroi, who were fathered either by Zeus or Tyndareos (or one by each) according to differing accounts. Although the Dioskouroi were great heroes, by far the greatest in the early Spartan line, they were able neither to fight at Troy nor to succeed to the Spartan throne because they met a premature death shortly before the Trojan War (see pp. 526ff for the circumstances). As a consequence, Tyndareos adopted his son-in-law Menelaos, the husband of Helen, as his successor. It was universally agreed that Helen was not in fact a true daughter of Tyndareos, but a child of Zeus; but strangely enough, there was disagreement about the identity of her mother (even if it was always accepted that she was reared by Leda at Sparta).

In the earliest recorded tradition, Zeus fathered Helen by the minor goddess NEMESIS (the personification of Retribution, see p. 26), and Leda was no more than her foster-mother. The circumstances of her conception were described in the *Cypria*, which told how Nemesis fled by land and water in the hope of escaping the embraces of Zeus, now turning into a fish to speed through the seas and encircling Ocean, and now assuming the forms of all manner of dreadful beasts as she was fleeing overland; but when she finally turned into a goose, Zeus assumed the same form and mated with her, causing her to conceive Helen, who was born from an egg.[4] The goose-mating was said to have occurred at Rhamnous, a coastal town in the north-eastern corner of Attica which contained a sanctuary of Nemesis.[5] In some later accounts, Zeus or both partners mated in swan-form.[6] The *Cypria* would presumably have reported that the resulting egg was transferred to Leda in some way after it was laid by Nemesis; later sources state either that it was brought to

Leda by a shepherd who discovered it in a grove in Attica, or that it was dropped into her lap by Hermes (doubtless at the order of Zeus).[7]

The competing tradition that made Helen a true daughter of Leda was as old if not older, for Helen states in the *Iliad* that she and the Dioskouroi shared the same mother (evidently Leda, who is always the mother of the Dioskouroi and is named as such in the *Odyssey*).[8] Euripides' *Helen*, a play first produced in 412 BC, and works of art from the latter part of the fifth century provide the earliest evidence for the familiar account of Helen's origin in which Zeus fathered her by mating with Leda in the form of a swan. Leda herself was in her ordinary human form; although the idea of the god's transformation was evidently inspired by the legend of his bird-mating with Nemesis, there could be no question of Leda, as a mere mortal, transforming herself as Nemesis was supposed to have done. According to Euripides, Zeus assumed the form of a swan in order to put a seduction-ruse into action; for he caused an eagle to chase him through the air while he was in that form, and then sought shelter in Leda's lap[9] (much as in the myth in which he was said to have seduced Hera by settling in her lap as a storm-tossed cuckoo, see p. 137). Leda laid an egg as a result of this encounter, just as Nemesis was supposed to have done; it could be seen in later times in the temple of the Leukippides in Sparta, hanging from the roof on ribbons.[10] Some claimed that the Dioskouroi were born from the same egg or a similar one.[11]

Helen's childhood was brutally interrupted when she was abducted by Theseus and Peirithoos while she was still below marriageable age, perhaps as young as eight or ten; but Theseus was unable to hide her away until he could marry her, as he had intended, because the Dioskouroi discovered her hiding-place and recovered her while he was absent on another adventure (see further on p. 361). While doing so, they captured Aithra, the mother of Theseus, who had been looking after Helen on her son's behalf; and she was obliged to serve Helen thereafter as an attendant, first at Sparta and later at Troy. Since Aithra is mentioned in this role in the *Iliad*, the story of this first abduction of Helen must have been familiar by Homer's time, even if the poet makes no explicit mention of it.[12]

When Helen reached maturity, she was courted with due formality by most of the principal rulers and heroes of Greece, including MENELAOS, son of Atreus, who had no kingdom of his own as yet but had long enjoyed the favour of Tyndareos (see p. 508). He could also count on the support of his brother Agamemnon, the rich and powerful king of Mycenae. It should be remembered that Agamemnon himself and the great hero Achilles, who might otherwise have been formidable contenders, were not in a position to compete for Helen's hand because the former was already married to Klytaimnestra, the half-sister of Helen, and the latter was too young. According to the early account in the Hesiodic *Catalogue*, in so far as it is known from quite extensive fragments, the suitors conducted their courtship at a distance (initially at any rate) by sending heralds to Sparta with all kinds of valuable gifts. The Dioskouroi seem to have played a central role both in dealing with the envoys and in determining the outcome. They finally chose in favour of Menelaos, even though they had been planning to award Helen to another suitor (whose name is not preserved) until Agamemnon intervened on his brother's behalf.

Since Agamemnon was not only rich enough to offer precious gifts but also a son-in-law of Tyndareos, it is understandable that his intervention should have proved decisive. The poet explicitly states that Menelaos was chosen because he offered the greatest gifts (evidently with the help of his brother). We are told that Odysseus knew in his heart that Menelaos was bound to win because he was the richest in possessions and was forever sending messages to the Dioskouroi.[13] In the standard later tradition, the suitors gathered at Sparta and the decision was made by Tyndareos;[14] or in another version, he allowed Helen herself to choose in accordance with her heart's desire.[15]

According to a tradition that was already known to Stesichorus and the author of the Hesiodic *Catalogue*, Tyndareos feared that the rejected suitors might cause trouble when he revealed his choice, and he therefore demanded that they should all swear beforehand that they would come to the aid of the chosen suitor if he should be threatened with violence or robbed of his wife. In one account, this measure was suggested to him by the cunning Odysseus, who was aware of Tyndareos' worries and offered to provide a solution if the king would do him a favour in return, by helping him to win Penelope as his wife; for Tyndareos was in a position to assist him in this matter since Penelope was a daughter of his brother Ikarios (see p. 525).[16] According to local tradition, the oaths were taken at a place known as the Horse's Grave (*Hippou Mnēmē*), which lay by the river Eurotas not far to the north of Sparta; for it was said that Tyndareos sacrificed a horse there, told the suitors to stand on pieces of its flesh as they swore their oaths, and then buried its remains at the spot.[17] These oaths would be of greater significance than Tyndareos could ever have imagined, since they would oblige many of the foremost heroes of Greece to fight on behalf of Menelaos at Troy after Helen was abducted by Paris.

As the story of the oath would imply, most of the Greek leaders at Troy were reckoned to have been suitors of Helen. Apollodorus and Hyginus provide catalogues of the suitors,[18] evidently based for the most part on the muster-list in the second book of the *Iliad*. The following suitors are named in the surviving fragments of the Hesiodic *Catalogue*: Menelaos, the Telamonian Aias, the two sons of Amphiaraos (i.e. Alkmaion and Amphilochos), Elephenor of Euboea, Idomeneus of Crete, Patroklos and Iphiklos from Thessaly, Thoas from Aetolia, and Odysseus. All of these are listed as Greek leaders in the *Iliad* except for the sons of Amphiaraos (one of whom, Alkmaion, died before the outbreak of the war). Since Apollodorus excludes Patroklos and Idomeneus from his list, it is unlikely that he based it on the *Catalogue*. The author of that poem tried as best he could to relate the manners of courtship of the individual suitors to their known characters and circumstances. Aias, for instance, who possessed little of his own but was brave with his spear, promised to provide suitable bride-gifts and wondrous deeds too by robbing sheep and cattle from his neighbours.[19] Odysseus, on the other hand, had such a shrewd idea of his prospects that he spared himself the expense of sending any presents at all.[20]

After her marriage to Menelaos, Helen lived a luxurious and uneventful life at the Spartan court for some years, bearing a single child, Hermione, to her husband, who succeeded Tyndareos as king at some stage. Hermione is described in the *Odyssey* as 'having the beauty of golden Aphrodite'; she is said to have been nine years old when Paris arrived to disturb the tranquillity of the court.[21]

Although Hermione is the only child of Helen and Menelaos in the Homeric epics, the couple are sometimes credited with a son too, Nikostratos (Victorious Army), whose name would suggest that he was born after the Trojan War. Or else Nikostratos was an illegitimate son of Menelaos by a slave girl, as in the case of Megapenthes, who was fathered by the king shortly after the abduction of Helen, hence his name (Great Sorrow).[22] Megapenthes is mentioned along with Hermione in the *Odyssey*; for when Telemachos visits the Spartan court after the Trojan War, he finds that the marriages of both are being celebrated there, since Menelaos is sending Hermione to Neoptolemos (see p. 490) and bringing a Spartan maiden to his own home as a bride for Megapenthes.[23] Since it was commonly agreed that Menelaos bequeathed his throne to his nephew Orestes (see p. 514), it seems to have been assumed that he had no male descendant to succeed him at the time of his death. A Rhodian tale claimed nonetheless that Megapenthes and Nikostratos banded together after his death to drive Helen into exile, causing her to sail away to Rhodes, where she hoped to take refuge with Polyxo, the queen of the island, who was of Argive birth. As misfortune would have it, Polyxo blamed Helen for the death of her husband Tlepolemos at Troy (see p. 293), and exacted her revenge by inciting some of her maids to dress like Furies and hang Helen from a tree. This legend explained the origin of the Rhodian cult of Helene Dendritis (of the tree).[24]

The birth and early life of Paris, and his judgement of the three goddesses

Troy was ruled at this period by PRIAM (properly Priamos), son of Laomedon, who was now quite old and lived in his splendid palace in Ilion (the city of Troy) with his family all around him. The *Iliad* credits him with fifty sons, nineteen of whom were borne to him by his wife HEKABE (or Hecuba in Latin form), and with many female children too, including twelve married daughters who lived with him in the palace; his sons slept with their wives in fifty adjoining chambers of polished stone, while the above-mentioned daughters slept with their husbands in twelve chambers on the opposite side of the courtyard.[25] As these arrangements would suggest, the royal family dominated the life of the city and the fighting in wartime in a manner that was foreign to the Greeks. Priam's family will be examined further below (pp. 451ff) along with the main noble families; for the time being, we will concentrate on PARIS, who was marked out for a special destiny that would set him apart from his many brothers.

Just before Paris was due to be born, his mother Hekabe was disturbed by a sinister dream in which she saw herself giving birth to a flaming torch that burned down the city (and perhaps the forests of Mt Ida too); or in the earliest surviving account by Pindar, she imagined that she gave birth to a fire-breathing hundred-handed Erinys (Fury) that hurled the entire city to the ground. After consulting with the diviners, who could hardly have found it difficult to interpret this particular dream, Priam ordered that his forthcoming child should be exposed at birth to ensure that he could never bring any harm to the city; but although the new-born Paris was duly abandoned on Mt Ida, he was rescued by a shepherd (or shepherds) and reared in the hills in rural isolation.[26] According to a tradition first reported by the Hellenistic poet Lycophron, the exposed infant was suckled by a she-bear for several days until he was recovered by the shepherd.[27]

In another account of the events surrounding the birth of Paris, Priam consulted a local oracle about his kingdom shortly after Paris was born, and was ordered to kill the woman who had just given birth along with her child. Now it happened that Killa, a sister of Hekabe, who was married to a Trojan elder called Thymoites, had given birth to a child at the very same time as the result of a secret liaison with Priam; and Priam killed Killa and her son Mounippos rather than Hekabe and Paris. Or in a rather different version, Priam received corresponding advice from Aisakos (a son of his who was gifted with prophetic powers, see p. 453), and Mounippos was a legitimate son of Thymoites.[28]

The abandoned child was named Paris by his rescuer and grew up to become a sturdy young man. Ancient authors often refer to him by an alternative name of Alexandros (Alexander), effectively meaning warrior; some claimed that this title was conferred on him during his early years in the country because he was so brave in 'repelling' robbers and 'defending' the livestock (in accordance with meanings of the Greek verb *alexō*).[29] One day, after he had come of age, a favourite bull of his was seized by some servants of Priam; for the king – who naturally supposed that his exposed son was dead – had decided to hold some games in memory of his long-lost son, and had sent some men out into the country to fetch a suitable prize. On seeing them leading his bull away, Paris ran after them to demand an explanation,

Figure 13.1 *The Judgement of Paris*, by Peter Paul Rubens.
Courtesy of The National Gallery, London.

and was told about the games. So he went to Troy to win his bull back again and was victorious in every event, defeating every rival including his own brothers. One of the princes, Deiphobos, was so angry at being defeated by an apparent commoner that he drew his sword against him, causing him to take refuge at the altar of Zeus Herkeios; but his true identity was soon revealed by his prophetic sister Kassandra, and Priam then acknowledged him as his son and invited him to assume his rightful position as a member of the royal family.[30]

Even if Paris was now welcomed back into the family as though his mother's ill-omened dream were no longer of significance, the divine plan that would cause him to bring disaster to Troy (see p. 437) was still underway; and it was set in full course when Hermes brought Hera, Athena and Aphrodite to him on Mt Ida to be judged for their beauty. This contest is known to have been described in the introductory section of the *Cypria*, although the surviving summary offers little detail, merely reporting that Paris judged in favour of Aphrodite because she won him over by promising Helen to him as a wife; we are not told whether the other two goddesses also offered inducements. A fragment from the poem describes how Aphrodite prepared herself for the contest, by clothing herself in perfumed garments dyed with flowers of the spring which had been made for her by the Charites and Horai (Graces and Seasons), and by weaving sweet-smelling garlands of flowers with the help of her attendants. As the legend is usually recounted in tragedy and later sources, quite possibly on the basis of epic accounts, each of the goddesses offered a bribe to Paris, Hera promising him royal sway, Athena success in war, and Aphrodite the loveliest of women as a wife. If it is kept in mind that the goddesses are (so to speak) incorporated in their own gifts, Hera representing royalty, Athena conquest and Aphrodite delight of love, this may surely be recognized as a literary handling of that old problem, so familiar in folklore, 'Which good thing is the best?', all the more so when it is remembered that the goods thus offered held a very high place in the popular Greek table of values. By his response to the goddesses' inducements, Paris makes a choice between different forms of life and exposes himself to judgement by the choice that he makes. By deciding in favour of Aphrodite, he earned the undying hatred of the other goddesses; and by then proceeding to abduct Helen from Sparta with her help, he would incur the vengeance of Menelaos and the Greeks in general. As we have seen, Menelaos could call on the support of all the former suitors of Helen in these circumstances, and the Trojan War would therefore be set in train, and the plan of Zeus fulfilled.[31]

There is only a single direct reference to the judgement of Paris in the *Iliad*, even if a number of passages relating to Hera, Athena and Aphrodite can be best interpreted in the light of that legend. After making it clear throughout the poem that Hera and Athena were exceptionally hostile to Troy, Homer offers an explanation for their attitude in the final book. The question arises in connection with Achilles' mistreatment of Hektor's corpse (see p. 465). The gods finally became so disgusted by the Greek hero's behaviour that they wanted to send Hermes to steal Hektor's body away from him, a plan that was approved by all of them apart from Hera, Poseidon and Athena, who persisted in the hatred that they had long felt for sacred Ilion and for Priam and his people 'because of the blind folly (*atē*) of Alexandros (Paris), who had scorned the goddesses (i.e. Hera and Athena) when they had come to his steading, and gave his preference to the one who offered him grievous lust' (ἥ οἱ πόρε μαχλοσύνην ἀλεγεινήν;

obviously Aphrodite).[32] This may be expressed in a rather obscure manner, but there is no reason to suppose that it refers to anything other than the familiar tale of the judgement of Paris, especially when it is remembered that Hera and Athena support the Greeks throughout the *Iliad* while Aphrodite supports the Trojans and maintains a special association with Paris and Helen.

Paris sails to Greece to abduct Helen

Paris now prepared to sail off to Greece to win Helen as his wife. On the advice of Aphrodite, he arranged for some ships to be built for him by Phereklos son of Tekton (whose subsequent death at the hand of the Cretan hero Meriones is described in the *Iliad*).[33] He received ample warning about the consequences of the enterprise before he set sail for Troy. According to the *Cypria*, two notable seers from his own family, his brother Helenos and his sister Kassandra, foretold what would happen if he went ahead;[34] and a tradition that first appears in the fifth century BC suggests that he received similar warnings from his own wife; for he was already married to a prophetic nymph called Oinone, who told him that he would bring disaster on himself and his city too.[35] He set out to sea nevertheless together with Aineias, who accompanied him at the order of Aphrodite.

The predicament of OINONE was particularly sad because she knew from the beginning that the love of Paris would bring her nothing but unhappiness. He met her while he was still living out on Mt Ida with the shepherds; she was a daughter of Kebren, the god of a local river. When Paris assured her of his love and swore that he would never abandon her, she was able to tell him through her own prophetic arts (which she had acquired from the gods or from Rhea specifically) that even if he loved her immeasurably at the moment, the time would come when he would desert her to abduct a woman from Europe. As he was about to set off, she told him that he would suffer a grave wound in the conflict that would be provoked by his forthcoming action, and that she alone would be able to cure him; or she simply told him to come to her if he should suffer a wound. When he was indeed afflicted by a serious arrow-wound in the last stages of the war (see p. 471), he called Oinone's words to mind and sent a messenger to Mt Ida to summon her help; but she was now so embittered that she refused to come, saying that Paris should turn to Helen instead. On seeing his dead body afterwards, however, she was overcome by remorse and killed herself. Or in a slightly different version, she thought again after first refusing to help him and arrived with healing drugs, only to find that he had died in the mean time.[36]

According to Hellanicus, Oinone and Paris had a son called KORYTHOS, who went to Troy to take part in the fighting and fell in love with Helen; she treated him kindly enough because he was exceptionally handsome, until Paris came to hear of his visits and killed him. Or in another account, Oinone sent him to Helen to stir up trouble, hoping that Helen would find him attractive and Paris would feel jealous as a consequence. The plan worked all too well, though not in a way that she would have wished, for Paris suspected the worst when he saw the two of them sitting together in Helen's bedroom one day, and killed Korythos in the heat of the moment. This gave Oinone an added reason for refusing to heal Paris when he was subsequently wounded.[37]

When Paris arrived in Laconia, he was entertained initially by the Dioskouroi, and then travelled on to Sparta, where he received generous hospitality from Menelaos and Helen. After nine days, however, Menelaos had to sail away to Crete to attend the funeral of Katreus, the former king of the island (who was his maternal grandfather, see p. 355); so he entrusted his guests to the care of Helen, telling her to provide them with whatever they asked. Paris took advantage of his absence to pay court to Helen, an endeavour that proved none too difficult in view of his own physical attractions and the aid that he received from Aphrodite. As soon as she was willing to consent, he eloped with her by night, loading much of her husband's treasure on to his ship before they sailed.[38] They consummated their union before leaving in the *Cypria*, while the *Iliad* states that they did so after their departure on an island of uncertain location called Kranae[39] (Rocky Island, later identified with the isle of Helene off the southern tip of Attica, or with Cythera, or a small island off the Laconian coast near Gythion[40]). Presumably in her function as the protector of marriage, Hera sent storm-winds against the eloping couple, causing them to be carried to Sidon in Phoenicia. The *Iliad* alludes to their visit, mentioning that Paris bought some finely embroidered robes there, and it would appear that he even conquered the city in the *Cypria*. After a brief delay (or after waiting in the area for some time to avoid pursuit), Paris and Helen completed their voyage and arrived at Troy, where they formalized their union with due ceremony.[41]

Stesichorus, a poet of the sixth century BC, recounted two versions of Helen's story, first offering the usual version in which she helped to provoke the Trojan War by eloping with Paris, and then writing a Palinode, or poem of recantation, in which he provided a wholly different tale, apparently of his own invention, to vindicate Helen's honour. Legend claimed that she had struck him blind for insulting her in the first poem, and he had then composed the recantation in order to regain his sight (see further on p. 583). According to the Palinode (of which very little has survived), Helen neither embarked with Paris on his ship nor arrived at Troy, but apparently remained in Sparta for the duration of the war while a phantom (*eidōlon*) of her accompanied Paris to Troy.[42] A similar story is recounted in a surviving play by Euripides, the *Helen*, in which Hera is said to have created the phantom in her anger at having been passed over in the judgement of Paris. This phantom was abducted to Troy by Paris, while the true Helen was conveyed to Egypt by Hermes, and lived there at the royal court until the end of the war; when Menelaos was shipwrecked in Egypt while sailing home with the phantom Helen after the war, the phantom disappeared and the true Helen took her place. According to Euripides, Helen was in danger of being held back in Egypt because the original ruler, Proteus, had died during the time of the war and had been succeeded by his vicious son Theoklymenos, who wanted to force Helen to marry him, and killed every Greek who ventured into his realm; but Helen managed to deceive him with the help of his noble-minded sister, the priestess Theonoe. Euripides states similarly in the *Elektra* that Zeus sent a phantom of Helen to Troy while the true Helen stayed in Egypt with Proteus.[43]

Herodotus claimed to have heard from the priests of Egypt that Paris had been driven to Egypt by a gale after sailing off with Helen, and that Proteus had taken Helen and the stolen treasure away from him because he disapproved of his immoral behaviour. This is a rationalistic version without the phantom Helen; for we are told that the Greeks made war on Troy believing that Helen must be there, even though the Trojans assured them that she and the treasure had been detained in Egypt; and when it was discovered after the fall of Troy that there was indeed no sign of her in the city, the Greeks realized that the Trojans had been telling the truth, and Menelaos sailed off to Egypt to recover Helen from Proteus.[44]

Menelaos and Agamemnon mount an expedition against Troy, but make a false start

Menelaos was informed of his wife's abduction by the goddess Iris (who often acted as a divine messenger, see pp. 56–7), and hurried back to Greece to consult with his brother Agamemnon about raising an army to recover Helen from Troy.[45] Since all the former suitors of Helen were bound by oath to support her husband in such circumstances (see p. 440), most of the leading rulers and heroes of Greece would be obliged to fight as his allies. In the *Cypria*, Menelaos (and possibly Agamemnon too) travelled through Greece with Nestor to recruit chieftains for the expedition. Or else Agamemnon simply sent heralds to advise the former suitors of their obligations.[46] Of the many suitors, Odysseus alone attempted to avoid the summons (see p. 459). Others agreed to take part of their own free will, most notably Achilles, who had been a child at the time of Helen's marriage, but was now invited to take part because he was a young warrior of exceptional promise.

After the necessary arrangements had been made, the Greek chieftains and their followers assembled at Aulis, a town on the east coast of Boeotia, to prepare for the voyage across the Aegean to Troy. A comprehensive and very ancient catalogue of the leaders, which also provides invaluable information about their places of origin and relative power, can be found in the second book of the *Iliad* (lines 494–759); some of the more prominent heroes will be discussed below (pp. 455ff). While at Aulis, the Greeks witnessed a portent that was interpreted for them by the seer Kalchas. A snake crept from beneath the altar during a sacrifice to Apollo and climbed into a tree which held a nest containing eight sparrow-chicks; it devoured the chicks, and also the mother-bird as she fluttered around in response to their cries, but was then turned to stone by Zeus. As Kalchas revealed, this meant that the Greeks would spend nine years fighting at Troy before the city finally fell to them in the tenth year.[47]

When the Greeks first set out for Troy, they were so ignorant of the geography of the area that they landed in the neighbouring territory of Mysia and ravaged it in the belief that it was Troy. On discovering that his kingdom was under attack, TELEPHOS, son of Herakles and Auge (see p. 543), the ruler of the Mysians, hastily assembled an army and pursued the Greeks back to their ships, killing many of them, including Thersandros, son of Polyneikes, the leader of the Boeotian contingent (see p. 328). Achilles finally put him to flight, however, and wounded him severely in the thigh when he tripped over a vine-branch. Pindar mentions that Achilles stained the vine-clad plain of Mysia with his blood; and some claimed that the accident was provoked by Dionysos because Telephos had failed to pay him due honour.[48]

Having no quarrel with the Mysians, the Greeks re-embarked and sailed off in search of Troy, but the fleet was soon struck by a violent storm that scattered the ships, and they made their way back to their separate homelands as best they could. Since ten years would pass before they would make their second crossing, this false start meant that Troy would not fall until twenty years after they had first assembled.[49] This story of the delay was certainly of early origin since it was recounted in the *Cypria*, and it may already have been known to Homer, for Helen remarks in the *Iliad* at one point that it is twenty years since she left home.[50]

During the period between the two sailings, Telephos became increasingly troubled by the state of his wound, which stubbornly refused to heal, and he eventually decided to travel to Greece to consult the Delphic oracle. On being advised that the inflictor of the wound should become its healer, he set off to find Achilles, who was now in Argos (for the Greek forces had gathered there before proceeding to Aulis for the second sailing). In a famous scene from the lost *Telephos* of Euripides, Telephos appeared among the Greeks dressed in rags like a beggar, and subsequently seized Orestes, the infant son of Agamemnon, from his cot and threatened to kill him if help were refused to him. Although Achilles protested that he knew nothing of medicine, Odysseus explained that the oracle had not been referring to Achilles himself when it had spoken of the 'inflictor' of the wound, but rather to the spear that had actually inflicted the wound. This suggestion turned out to be correct, for when Achilles scraped some rust from his Pelian spear into some water and applied it to the wound, Telephos was immediately cured. The cure was achieved by a form of sympathetic magic, as in the story of Iphiklos (see p. 427). Telephos repaid the favour by guiding the Greeks across the Aegean when they set out for Troy.[51]

The Greeks make a successful crossing after the sacrifice of Iphigeneia

As the Greek force was preparing to sail from Aulis for a second time, the fleet was detained in port as the result of an act of impiety committed by Agamemnon. According to the *Cypria*, he shot a stag while hunting in the area and was then foolish enough to boast that he was a finer hunter than Artemis herself. When the goddess punished his presumption by sending adverse winds (or imposing a dead calm) to prevent the fleet from sailing, the seer Kalchas revealed that Agamemnon was to blame, and declared that Artemis would not be appeased until one of his unmarried daughters was offered in sacrifice to her. So his daughter IPHIGENEIA was summoned from Mycenae on the pretence that she was to be married to Achilles, and was then brought to sacrifice; but at the last moment, Artemis substituted a stag for her on the altar, and transferred her to the land of the Taurians (the Crimea) to become a goddess.[52] Or in a version which first appears in Euripides' *Iphigeneia in Tauris*, Artemis installed Iphigeneia as her mortal priestess in the land of the Taurians (from where she was subsequently recovered by her brother Orestes); or in the simplest version, as found in Pindar and Aeschylus, she was indeed killed at the altar. Artemis abandoned her wrath in any case and withdrew the adverse winds (or the windstill) to allow the Greek fleet to proceed on its way.[53]

The mythology of Iphigeneia, which is of concern to us here only in relation to the sailing of the fleet, will be considered further in the next chapter in connection with the history of her family (see pp. 512ff). Although the early epic account of the cause of Artemis' anger remained the standard one, there were other versions also. According to Euripides in the *Iphigeneia in Tauris*, the goddess demanded the sacrifice as reparation for a broken vow. For Agamemnon had made a vow many years before in which he had undertaken to offer her the finest thing born in that year; but when his lovely daughter Iphigeneia had been born, he had failed to sacrifice her in accordance with his vow.[54] Or in a version recorded by

Figure 13.2 Iphigeneia is transformed into a deer. Apulian red-figure volute krater.
© The British Museum.

Apollodorus, the offence had dated back to the previous generation; for Agamemnon's father Atreus had vowed to Artemis that he would offer her the finest lamb born in his flocks, but had failed to sacrifice a golden-fleeced lamb (see p. 506) when it had appeared.[55] Or Artemis was angered because Menelaos had shot a deer that was sacred to her.[56]

Agamemnon was certainly placed in a terrible predicament by Artemis' demand; although Aeschylus and Sophocles also wrote plays on this tempting subject, only Euripides' *Iphigeneia in Aulis* has survived. Achilles tries to save Iphigeneia in that play after discovering that she has been summoned on the pretence of being married to him, but the situation is finally resolved by the maiden herself, who agrees to be sacrificed for the common good.

After making a safe passage across the Aegean, the Greeks called in at the island of Tenedos just off the coast of the Troad. Although the ruler of the island, TENES (or Tennes), tried to keep them away by pelting them with stones, they landed nonetheless, and Achilles killed Tenes with a sword-thrust to the breast.[57] Or in a version that is less creditable to the Greek hero, he killed Tenes when the king intervened to stop him from raping his sister Hemithea.[58]

Tenes had become embittered and hostile to strangers as a result of his unfortunate earlier history. He was a son of Kyknos, son of Poseidon (possibly to be identified

448

with the Kyknos mentioned below, p. 451), who ruled at Kolonai on the mainland and had fathered Tenes by his first wife, Prokleia, daughter of Laomedon. After the death of Prokleia, Kyknos had married a second wife, Philonome, who had conceived a passion for her stepson and had made amorous advances to him; but her love turned to rancour when she found herself rejected, and she exacted revenge on him by telling her husband that he had tried to seduce her. Kyknos believed her and became even more convinced when she persuaded a flautist, Eumolpos, to bear false witness to her claim. So Kyknos locked Tenes into a chest along with his sister Hemithea, who had spoken in support of him, and launched it into the sea. After it was washed ashore on Tenedos (then known as Leukophrys), Tenes was invited to become the ruler of the island, and renamed it after himself. When Kyknos eventually discovered that his wife had deceived him, he exacted a pitiless revenge by burying her alive and stoning Eumolpos to death. He then sailed off to Tenedos to seek his son's forgiveness; but when he moored his ship and tried to speak, Tenes was too embittered even to listen and severed his mooring-ropes with an axe.[59]

There was a tradition that Apollo was the true father of Tenes, and that Thetis had foreseen that her son Achilles would meet an early death at the hand of Apollo if he killed a son of that god; so she arranged that he should be accompanied by a servant called MNEMON (Unforgetting), whose duty it was to keep him ever mindful of this danger. But Mnemon forgot to warn him about Tenes, and Achilles was so angry to learn of his negligence that he thrust a spear through his chest.[60] As we shall see (p. 468), Apollo was said to have killed Achilles (or to have helped Paris to kill him) in front of the walls of Troy.

PHILOKTETES, son of Poias, a great archer from southern Thessaly who was the current owner of the bow of Herakles (see p. 285), was marooned by his comrades in course of the sea-crossing. According to the *Cypria*, he was bitten by a snake while he was feasting on Tenedos with his fellow-warriors, and was then abandoned by them on Lemnos (some thirty miles to the west) because of the stench of his wound.[61] Sophocles offers a rather different account in his *Philoktetes*, indicating that the hero was bitten at a place called Chryse by a snake that was guarding the roof-less shrine of the goddess Chryse.[62] Euripides apparently said much the same in the prologue of his lost play of the same name, stating that Philoktetes was bitten as he was guiding his comrades to the altar of Chryse to offer a sacrifice.[63] The place in question should doubtless be distinguished from the Chryse that is mentioned in the *Iliad* as the home of the priest Chryses; Pausanias reports that it was an island – evidently a very small one – that lay close to Lemnos until it was submerged beneath the sea (presumably as the result of a seismic disturbance).[64] Some later sources suggest that Philoktetes suffered his wound at a shrine of Chryse on Lemnos itself.[65] In Hyginus' version, Hera is said to have sent the snake against him on Lemnos because she was angry with him for having helped Herakles by kindling his funeral-pyre; or according to another suggestion, Chryse was an amorous nymph who incited the snake to bite Philoktetes when he spurned her advances.[66] Whatever the exact circumstances of the wounding, his comrades were so disturbed by the smell of his festering wound, and perhaps also by his ill-omened cries of pain, that they abandoned him to his fate. By shooting wild birds with his bow, he survived in isolation on Lemnos for almost ten years until he was finally rescued and brought to Troy, where he was healed at last by a son of Asklepios (see p. 471).[67] His predicament is vividly portrayed in Sophocles' *Philoktetes*, which tells how Odysseus and Neoptolemos came to recover him; Lemnos is presented as an uninhabited island in this connection[68] (although this conflicts with other aspects of its mythology, most notably in relation to the visit of the Argonauts, p. 384).

In a wholly different account of the wounding of Philoktetes from Latin sources, Herakles had made him swear never to reveal the resting-place of his mortal remains, and had given him his poisoned arrows by way of a reward. After learning from an oracle that they would need the arrows during the Trojan War, the other Greeks had later questioned Philoktetes about Herakles; and when he had finally told them that the hero was dead, they had insisted that he should show them where the hero was buried. Wanting to preserve his oath in a formal sense at least, he had said nothing but had indicated the hero's burial-place with a stamp of his foot. He paid for his transgression nonetheless, for one of the poisoned arrows fell from his quiver during the journey to Troy and inflicted an apparently incurable wound on his foot. So his comrades abandoned him as in the usual story, after first seizing the remaining arrows.[69]

The Greek landing at Troy

On seeing the invasion-force sailing in from the sea, the Trojans attempted to prevent the Greeks from landing by pelting their ships with stones. The first Greek warrior to leap ashore was PROTESILAOS, son of Iphiklos, who commanded the men from Phylake (see p. 435) and the neighbouring cities of southern Thessaly. The main features of his story are already noted in the *Iliad*, which mentions that he was killed by a Dardanian warrior as soon as he landed, leaving a grieving wife in Phylake and a half-completed house (for he was newly married). Subsequent sources from the *Cypria* onward identify his killer as Hektor, doubtless because it seemed appropriate that the first enemy should be killed by the greatest of the defending warriors. According to a tradition which is first reported by Apollodorus (but may well have been quite ancient), the first man ashore was fated to be the first to die, and Achilles held back because he had been warned of this by Thetis.[70] Or else this was commonly known, and Protesilaos showed exceptional courage by leaping ashore when everyone else was holding back.[71]

The unfortunate young wife of Protesilaos was LAODAMEIA, a daughter of Akastos, king of Iolkos (except in the *Cypria*, in which she was named as Polydore, daughter of Meleagros).[72] The earliest record of her legend is contained in what we can piece together of the lost *Protesilaos* of Euripides. In that tragedy, Protesilaos was said to have left for the war after he had been married to Laodameia for only a single day; and after his death, he prayed to the gods of the Underworld to be allowed to return to her for an additional day. His wish was granted, but Laodameia apparently took her own life when he had to depart.[73] In another account, the dead Protesilaos was brought to her after she herself had prayed to the gods to be allowed to meet him for three hours, but she died of a broken heart after Hermes took him away again.[74] Or else she made a bronze image of him to console herself after he was taken back to Hades; and when a servant happened to see her embracing the statue while peeping through a crack in the door, he supposed that she had a lover and informed her father Akastos. On bursting into the room, however, he saw that it was merely a statue, and tried to relieve her of her torment by having it burned. But this only served to increase her distress, and she jumped on to the pyre with it and was burned to death.[75] In yet another account, she fashioned such an image and consorted with it as though it were her husband, arousing the pity of the gods, who arranged for Hermes to bring Protesilaos up from Hades for a reunion. Supposing that he had returned safely against all expectation, she was overjoyed to see him, and was so distressed when he was taken away again that she took her own life.[76]

After the death of Protesilaos, Achilles jumped ashore at the head of his Thessalian followers, the Myrmidons, and confronted KYKNOS, son of Poseidon, the most formidable of the many warriors who were opposing the Greek landing. It is quite possible that this Kyknos may be identified with the Kyknos who was the father of Tenes (see p. 448), although this is never stated. He was especially dangerous because his divine father had rendered him invulnerable (in the strict sense, i.e. immune to piercing wounds); his name means 'Swan' in Greek, and it would seem that he was suitably pale or perhaps an albino, since the Hesiodic *Catalogue* refers to his 'white head' and Hellanicus stated that he was white-skinned from birth.[77] Another tale suggests that he was tended by swans as an infant.[78] Although the *Cypria* is known to have recounted the story of his death, a passing allusion by Aristotle provides the earliest evidence for his invulnerability (unless this can already be inferred from a fragment of Sophocles' *Poimenes*).[79] Pindar mentions that Achilles killed him without offering any details. Apollodorus reports, perhaps in accordance with an early tradition, that Achilles caused his death by hurling a stone at his head.[80] Or in Ovid's fuller narrative, Achilles lost his temper after finding that his spear and sword made no impression on the body of Kyknos, and battered the face of the invulnerable hero with the hilt of his sword. As Kyknos was retreating from this onslaught, his withdrawal was blocked by a large boulder, and Achilles took advantage of this to dash him to the ground. Achilles then kneeled down on him, crushing his ribs with his shield, and killed him at last by throttling him with the leather strap of his helmet. Ovid concludes by saying that Kyknos was turned into a swan by his father Poseidon, but this was doubtless a Hellenistic innovation (if not a detail invented by Ovid himself).[81]

The Trojans were so dismayed by the death of Kyknos that they retreated towards the safety of their city, and all the remaining Greeks now jumped out of their ships and pursued the fleeing enemy across the plain, covering it with dead bodies. As a result of these events, the invaders established a firm grounding on the plain and penned the Trojans behind their city walls. The long siege commenced.[82]

LEADING FIGURES IN THE CONFLICT

Priam and the Trojan royal family

At this point, we must turn aside to say something about the leading figures on either side of the conflict. On the Trojan side, the many sons of Priam were most prominent in battle and in the life of the city; Priam himself was too old to take part in the fighting, although he continued to be the fount of all authority at Troy. The *Iliad* refers to twenty-two of his sons by name, and later sources add many further names to the list (whether from the early tradition or as products of later invention); the majority of them have no definite stories, or simply appear for a moment in an epic battle-scene before they are killed or captured by a Greek opponent. Although Priam complains in the *Iliad* that he has been robbed of most of his sons, he mentions the names of only two who were killed in the earlier years of the conflict, namely **Mestor**, whose legend has been lost, and **Troilos**,[83] who was killed at an early point by Achilles when he was little more than a child (see p. 462). Troilos is most familiar nowadays for the medieval tale of his love for Cressida. **Lykaon** was another Priamid who was surprised by Achilles outside the city walls at an early stage in the war; Achilles spared his life, however, preferring to sell him into slavery abroad, but proved to be less forbearing when he encountered him in battle for a second time after he had been ransomed (see p. 462). By virtue of his role as the prime defender of Troy in the *Iliad*, **Hektor** stands out from the other Priamids as the greatest warrior among them and as a hero of distinctive and rounded character; in the latter respect, only **Paris** (who was no mean warrior in spite of his effeminate airs) is remotely comparable. Hektor is portrayed in the *Iliad* not only as a brave and chivalrous warrior who was surpassed by Achilles alone, but also as an affectionate husband and father. He was married to Andromache, whose father Eetion and seven brothers had been killed by Achilles during his sack of their city, Hypoplakian Thebes;[84] the famous passage in the *Iliad* in which Hektor meets her on the ramparts before setting out for battle is one of the most moving sections of the poem (as was felt in classical Greece also, to judge by a remark in Plato's *Ion*[85]). Their infant son Astyanax (who is present at this meeting and is much alarmed by the nodding plume of Hektor's helmet) was destined to meet a gruesome death during the sack of Troy (see p. 477). **Deiphobos** and **Helenos**, who make occasional appearances in the *Iliad* as notable sons of Priam, rose to their greatest prominence at the very end of the war. They competed for the hand of Helen after the death of Paris, and Helenos was so upset when she was awarded to his brother that he withdrew from the city to live on Mt Ida, where he was subsequently captured by Odysseus; for Helenos was a seer, and Odysseus had been advised by the Greek seer Kalchas that he could reveal some conditions that would need to be fulfilled if Troy were to be taken (see pp. 471–2). Deiphobos lost Helen and his life also to Menelaos during the night of the sack (see pp. 476–7), while Helenos, who had assured his own survival by the information that he had revealed to the Greeks, accompanied Achilles' son Neoptolemos to Epirus (see p. 490). The Benjamin of the family, **Polydoros**, appears in the *Iliad* as the youngest and dearest son of Priam who enters battle against his father's order and is soon killed by Achilles.[86] According to a conflicting tale which first appears in tragedy, Priam tried to secure him from danger by sending him away to Polymestor, a Thracian son-in-law of his, along with a quantity of treasure; but when the fortunes of war turned against the Trojans, Polymestor murdered Polydoros to steal the treasure (see p. 479).

The daughters of Priam will be considered below in connection with the fall of Troy (see pp. 479–80). Although three brothers of Priam appear in the *Iliad* among the elders who meet on the ramparts,[87] it was generally agreed in the later tradition that all the sons of Laomedon apart from Priam were killed when Troy was stormed by Herakles (see p. 276).

As a child by his first wife Arisbe (or a nymph called Alexirrhoe), Priam had a son AISAKOS who possessed prophetic powers and was finally turned into a bird. Apollodorus states that he married Asterope, a daughter of the river Kebren, and mourned for her so grievously after her death that he was turned into a bird (of an unspecified kind).[88] Or in Ovid's account, he fell in love with Hesperia, daughter of Kebren, after encountering her by her father's waters; but when he chased after her with amorous intent, she stepped on a poisonous snake and was killed. He was so tormented by remorse that he hurled himself into the sea, and so aroused the pity of the sea-goddess Tethys, who transformed him into a bird, apparently a diver (*mergus*). He was by no means happy to have been rescued, however, and dived repeatedly into the sea in his new form in the hope of ending his life, and grew ever thinner, hence the form and habits of the diver.[89] Some said that it was he who interpreted Hekabe's dream before the birth of Paris (see p. 442).[90]

AINEIAS, the son of Anchises and Aphrodite (see pp. 200–1 for the story of his birth), was the leading representative of the junior branch of the Trojan royal family, which was descended from Assarakos, the younger brother of Priam's grandfather Ilos (see p. 522). He grew up on Mt Ida outside the city, where he had an unfortunate encounter with Achilles early in the war (see p. 462). His branch of the family had been cast into the shade by the senior branch that ruled from the city, and the *Iliad* presents him as feeling some resentment at his position, especially when he considers that Priam is failing to pay him the honour that he deserves. He helps to defend Troy to the best of his power nonetheless, commanding his Dardanians as a separate contingent with Antilochos and Akamas, two sons of Antenor (see below), as his lieutenants.[91] Although a warrior of standing, he is by no means overwhelming in battle; indeed, he only survives his moments of greatest peril because gods come to his aid, as when Aphrodite and Apollo save him from Diomedes, and Poseidon from Achilles.[92] Poseidon explains to the other gods on the latter occasion that he is fated to survive because he and his descendants are destined to rule over the Trojans after the destruction of Priam's line.[93] A far grander destiny was assigned to him in the later tradition, as we will see in Chapter 17.

Some noble families at Troy, and the failure of the Greek embassy

Herodotus was inclined to accept that Helen had been in Egypt during the war (see p. 445) because he was unable to believe that the Trojans would have refused to surrender her if they had been able to, whether Paris wished it or not; but that would have spoiled the story of course, and there is no suggestion in mythical accounts that real pressure was ever exerted on Paris to propitiate the Greeks by handing her over. In a memorable scene in the *Iliad*, the Trojan elders see Helen walking towards them while they are sitting together on the ramparts one day, and remark that it is no shame (*ou nemesis*) that the Trojans and Greeks should have suffered such woes for such a woman, who looks wondrously like an immortal goddess; and if they add nonetheless that they wish that she would go away and cease to be a curse to them and their children, this is merely a wish rather than the expression of an active desire.[94] The matter was settled definitively, for good or ill, when the Greeks sent envoys to Troy at the very beginning of the war (just after they landed, or else just before while the fleet was at Tenedos). The delegation was headed by Menelaos and Odysseus, who declared that there would be no need for a war if Helen were surrendered along with the treasures that had been stolen by Paris.

In so far as it is possible to talk of a 'peace party' and 'war party' at Troy, these were headed by Antenor and Antimachos respectively, the senior members of two noble families at Troy. The two Greek ambassadors received hospitality from ANTENOR, a wise elder who was married to THEANO, the Trojan priestess of Athena. Believing with some justification that the Greek demands were legitimate, Antenor argued to the Trojans at their assembly that they should yield on the points in question, for it could bring them no good to fight a war for a dishonourable cause; but ANTIMACHOS turned the audience against him, even going so far as to urge that the Greek ambassadors should be killed on the spot. Such is the story recorded in the *Iliad*; and later sources add that it was only through the intervention of Antenor that the two Greeks escaped with their lives.[95] Homer attributes mercenary motives to Antimachos, saying that he always took the lead in opposing the return of Helen because Paris provided him with handsome gifts of gold; but his ignoble behaviour brought nothing but pain to him in the long run, since Agamemnon inflicted a brutal death on his two sons, Peisandros and Hippolochos, after encountering them on the battlefield, rejecting any thought of a ransom in view of the conduct of their father.[96] The Greeks were so impressed by Antenor's behaviour, on the other hand, that they hung a panther-skin on the door of his house during the sack of Troy to indicate that his family and possessions were not to be touched.[97]

If Antenor was motivated by considerations of justice in the earlier tradition, some late accounts place a wholly different interpretation on his actions, presenting him as a traitor who conspired with the Greeks for purely selfish reasons, and even suggesting that he and his wife betrayed the city to them by opening the city gates and the trap-door of the Wooden Horse, or by helping them to steal the Palladion (a talisman that protected the city).[98]

Antenor had a number of sons, including AGENOR, who had his moment of glory when he dared to make a stand against Achilles at the height of his advance while all the other Trojans were in full flight, desperately seeking the safety of the city walls. Agenor struck first with a throw of his spear, but to no effect since it bounced off Achilles' leg-armour, and he would doubtless have been killed in the Greek hero's counter-attack if Apollo had not wrapped him in a cloud of mist and spirited him away; Apollo then assumed his guise to lure Achilles away while the rest of the Trojans were making their escape, leaving Hektor alone to confront him.[99] Agenor was finally killed by Neoptolemos, the son of Achilles, during the sack of the city.[100]

Apart from the families of Antenor and Antimachos, only one other noble family, that of the Panthoids, was of any real significance. Its senior member PANTHOOS, who is mentioned among the Trojan elders who met on the ramparts, had three sons, Polydamas (or Poulydamas in epic parlance), Euphorbos and Hyperenor. POLYDAMAS was born on the same night as Hektor, and was as renowned for his wisdom as Hektor was for his martial prowess.[101] He offers shrewd advice to Hektor on four occasions in the *Iliad*, but Hektor is not always patient enough to accept it. When Polydamas urges that the Trojans should withdraw to the city after Achilles' return to battle, Hektor brings disaster on himself and many of his comrades by his disdainful response.[102] Hektor comes to appreciate that he has ample reason to be reproached for this, and his fear of Polydamas' scorn is one of the main factors that impel him to remain outside the city to confront Achilles on his own.[103] EUPHORBOS, the other main son of Panthoos, inflicted the first wound on Patroklos before Hektor delivered the death-blow; but he was killed soon afterwards by Menelaos while trying to avenge the death of his brother Hyperenor.[104] The shield that Menelaos had supposedly taken from Euphorbos on that occasion could be seen at the Heraion at Mycenae, or at Branchidai in Asia Minor according to another claim.[105] The sage Pythagoras, who believed in the transmigration of the soul, claimed to have been Euphorbos in one of his previous lives; and he was said to have authenticated the claim by identifying the shield of Euphorbos in the temple of Apollo at Branchidai.[106]

The three greatest foreign allies of the Trojans – Penthesileia, Memnon and Eurypylos – arrived towards the end of the war after the period covered in the *Iliad* (see pp. 466ff). A list of their other main allies can be found at the end of the second book of the *Iliad*.[107]

The Atreids and the greater and lesser Aias

Of the many Greek leaders, a few deserve special mention. In Homer and the later tradition alike, AGAMEMNON, the brother of the wronged Menelaos, appears as a man who owes his great prestige to his high position as king of Mycenae rather than to any outstanding personal merits of his own, even though he is brave and effective enough as a warrior. He lacks a sure touch in dealing with his fellow-leaders, who, it should be remembered, are not formally subject to his orders; for he tends to act in an abrupt and high-handed manner, and is yet not sufficiently resolute to provide a proper lead in the face of misfortune, tending to fall into despondency when the army is threatened with a serious reverse. These features of his character are central to the plot of the *Iliad* as we shall see. MENELAOS is somewhat eclipsed by his more eminent brother, and in Homer's portrait at least is a man of less distinctive character; as a warrior, he is not in the very first rank, although efficient; Achilles, Agamemnon, Aias, Diomedes and, in the other camp, Hektor, outclass him. He is a noble figure nonetheless in the early tradition; and the hostile portrayals of him in Attic tragedy, which are coloured by anti-Spartan sentiment, should not be taken as representative. The two brothers are often referred to as the Atreidai (i.e. sons of Atreus); they belonged to the Pelopid family, which had originated in Asia Minor but had come to rule at Mycenae and Sparta by the time of the Trojan War, replacing the original ruling families. The bloody history of the family, which was notorious for its internal feuds, will be traced in full in the next chapter.

The most formidable warriors on the Greek side were Achilles and the greater or Telamonian AIAS (or AJAX in Latin form). Aias was the only legitimate son of Telamon, who had been the main ally of Herakles during the first Greek war against Troy (see p. 276); as the commander of a relatively small contingent that he had brought from his native Salamis in twelve ships,[108] Aias owed his predominance to his personal qualities alone. In contrast to most heroes of the first rank, who are expected to be accomplished as well as brave, he is slow-witted and a poor speaker in Homer's portrait, but he possesses a certain bluff common sense, is straightforward, loyal and utterly dependable, and his courage is unshakeable. Known as the 'bulwark of the Achaeans', he is tall, thick-set and immensely strong, and he defends himself with a towering shield of Mycenaean design, which is formed from seven layers of bull's hide under an outer layer of bronze.[109] He is as handy at wielding large stones as more conventional weapons, and is especially effective when the situation seems to be most hopeless. With his courage go self-will and pride, the latter finally causing his ruin when the arms of the dead Achilles are awarded to Odysseus rather than to himself (see p. 470). He often fights in the company of his half-brother Teukros, who is a skilled archer, and of his namesake, the lesser Aias, son of Oileus, who led a sizeable contingent of troops from his native Locris in Central Greece. As swift-moving light-armed warriors, both could take shelter behind Aias and his mighty shield and emerge into the open as circumstances demanded.[110]

Of opposite nature in many ways to the greater Aias, the lesser or Locrian Aias is lightly built and fights as a light-armed skirmisher accordingly, wearing only a linen corselet for protection, and relying on his speed and skill as a spearsman rather than any exceptional strength. Though a splendid fighter in his fashion, he is a man of unappealing character who is vicious, quarrelsome and impious, and he is disliked accordingly by the other warriors. This is illustrated in the *Iliad* by the manner in which he interacts with his comrades at the funeral-games for Achilles; he abuses Idomeneus in a most insulting manner, provoking that hero to retort that he is the meanest of all the Greeks in everything apart from abuse; and his other comrades are happy to laugh at him shortly afterwards during the foot-race when Athena causes him to slip headfirst into some cow-dung to prevent him from defeating Odysseus.[111] He was apparently far more prominent in the later epics in the Trojan cycle. As we will see, he committed a brutal act of sacrilege during the sack of Troy (see p. 478), so angering Athena that she imperilled many of his comrades during their return voyage and caused his own death (see pp. 482ff).

The earlier life of Achilles and his recruitment

Pre-eminent among the Greeks at Troy, greater even than Aias as a warrior and greater than him in other respects, is ACHILLES (properly Achilleus or Achileus), the son of Peleus, king of Phthia in southern Thessaly. Partly of divine descent through his mother, the Nereid Thetis, he is the strongest, swiftest, handsomest and most valiant warrior in the army. His troops, the Myrmidons (and also the Thessalian Hellenes and Achaeans), who had accompanied him to Troy in fifty ships, provide him with a worthy command.[112] Although he and the Telamonian Aias are unrelated as yet in the *Iliad*, the pair came to be classed together as cousins, as grandsons of Aiakos, king of Aegina, and members of a common branch of the Asopid family (see pp. 529ff). His family background will be considered in that connection; for the circumstances of his birth, and his mother's early abandonment of him, see also pp. 54–5.

According to a story that first appears in Roman sources, his mother rendered him invulnerable soon after his birth by dipping him into the waters of the Styx,

Figure 13.3 Thetis makes Achilles invulnerable by dipping him in the River Styx. Marble. Thomas Banks (1735–1805), Victoria and Albert Museum.

one of the rivers of the Underworld.[113] He was not wholly protected, however, since she was gripping him by one of his ankles and that part of his body never came into contact with the water; it was thus possible for him to suffer a wound in the ankle, as was agreed to have been the cause of his death (see p. 468). A tradition of earlier origin claimed a similar invulnerability for Aias; for it was said that Herakles wrapped the baby Aias in his impenetrable lionskin (from the invulnerable Nemean lion, see p. 256) and prayed to his father Zeus to make him invulnerable likewise. Once again, however, the protection was incomplete, since Herakles' quiver was lying in the lionskin and prevented Aias' ribs from coming into contact with the skin; and it was thus possible for him to kill himself by falling on his sword, as he was traditionally supposed to have done (see p. 471). Although the story is first recorded in this form in Lycophron and his scholia, a fragment from Aeschylus already refers to the partial invulnerability of Aias, and Pindar mentions (apparently in accordance with a Hesiodic account) that Herakles prayed before the birth of Aias that Telamon should have a son who would share the quality of the lionskin.[114] This theme of a conditional invulnerability or immortality appears with some regularity in Greek myth; it could be said that such stories merely serve to emphasize the limitations of the mortal condition.

After being abandoned by his divine wife, who did not care to live with a mortal, Peleus entrusted the young Achilles to the Centaur Cheiron to be reared on Mt Pelion. To ensure that Achilles would come to share in the strength and courage of the most fearless of wild beasts, Cheiron fed him on the flesh and viscera of boars and lions and the marrows of bears; and the young hero developed his valour and martial skills by hunting savage lions and boars in the wild hill-country around Cheiron's cave. He also learned to move with exceptional speed by running down stags without the help of dogs. Cheiron educated him, furthermore, in the arts of war and the more peaceful skills of medicine (as mentioned in the *Iliad*) and music.[115] Homer adds that he spent part of his childhood with Phoinix, son of Amyntor, the king of the Dolopians, who instructed him in the art of public speaking and other practical matters.[116]

Phoinix had become a vassal of Achilles' father in the following circumstances. Amyntor, the father of Phoenix, had upset his wife by neglecting her in favour of a concubine, and she had persuaded her son to seduce the girl in the hope that experience of the love of a younger man would turn her against her aged lover. Amyntor had cursed his son to the Erinyes (Furies) on hearing of this, praying that he should be childless (as would indeed be the case); and Phoinix had left home as a consequence, and had sought the help of Peleus, who had installed him as king of the Dolopians (Dolopes) in a territory adjoining his own.[117] In some post-Homeric accounts, Phoinix is said to have been blinded by his father but cured afterwards by Cheiron.[118] Amyntor ruled either at Eleon, a town in Boeotia, or at Ormenion under Mt Pelion in Thessaly; for his confrontation with Herakles as king of Ormenion, see p. 283.

Achilles finally returned to his father's court as a highly accomplished young man, and it was from there that Nestor and Odysseus recruited him for the Trojan War in the earliest account in the *Iliad*.[119] In the standard later tradition, however, Thetis was said to have hidden him away on Scyros, an island to the east of Euboea, because she knew that he was fated to meet a premature death if he took part in the war. Or else Peleus took him to the island. He was left under the care of its ruler, Lykomedes, and lived among the maidens of the court in female disguise.[120] When rumours about his hiding-place eventually seeped out, Odysseus travelled to Skyros to investigate, either on his own or with Diomedes. To trick the young hero into betraying himself, Odysseus presented some fine clothing and trinkets to the women and girls of the court, mixing a few weapons among them, and Achilles duly revealed his true sex by reaching out for the weapons.[121] Or in a more elaborate account, Odysseus placed some women's goods in the forecourt of the palace along with a shield and a spear, and then arranged for a trumpet to be sounded to the accompaniment of shouts and the clashing of arms; imagining that the palace was under attack, Achilles immediately stripped off his women' clothing and seized the shield and spear.[122] After his identity was discovered by such means, he willingly agreed to depart for the war.

While Achilles was hiding among the maidens of the palace, he embarked on a love affair with DEIDAMEIA, a daughter of the king, causing her to become pregnant with a son, Neoptolemos (also known as Pyrrhos), who would become a great warrior like his father and fight at Troy in the last stages of the war (see p. 472).[123] This feature of the legend of Achilles was certainly very ancient, for the *Iliad* already mentions that he had a son on Skyros and the *Cypria* told of his love for Deidameia. In the latter epic, however, he met her at a slightly later time than in the story above and in different circumstances, when he happened to call in at Scyros as he was sailing home after the first crossing ended in misfortune (see p. 446 for the circumstances).[124]

Odysseus and Palamedes

ODYSSEUS was a hero of idiosyncratic character who relied as much on ingenuity, or even sheer unscrupulousness, to win his ends as on his undoubted valour and resource. He was the king of rocky Ithaca, an island off the west coast of Central Greece, and the husband of the faithful Penelope and father of Telemachos, who was still a child when the war broke out. During the war, he was prominent in every episode that required quick wits; in battle he was formidable but not one of the very foremost champions; when lots are cast in the *Iliad* to see who shall fight Hektor, for instance, the Greeks pray that the lot may fall upon the greater Aias, Diomedes or Agamemnon (Achilles being absent) rather than on Odysseus, although he has volunteered.[125] Besides giving helpful and shrewd advice on many occasions, it is he who volunteers, among others, to go with Diomedes on the perilous night-expedition in the tenth book of the epic, and is chosen by Diomedes 'because he can use his wits exceedingly well'.[126] He and Diomedes are often represented as acting in conjunction, both in the *Iliad* and in the subsequent tradition. Their greatest joint enterprise was the theft of the Palladion in the last stages of the war (see p. 472).

After Homer, the character of Odysseus suffers a remarkable degeneration. In the *Odyssey*, he is at times unscrupulous; but from the cyclic epics onward, and especially in Attic tragedy, he is often presented as a thoroughly villainous double-dealer. His conduct toward PALAMEDES was particularly vile, all the more so because he involved Diomedes in his foul dealing. Palamedes, the eldest son of Nauplios (see pp. 235–6), was quite as clever as Odysseus himself, and was credited with all manner of inventions, ranging from dice and draughts to measures and weights; above all, he was often said to have devised all or part of the Greek alphabet.[127] When Menelaos and Nestor (or the two Atreids) travelled to Ithaca to recruit Odysseus for the Trojan War, Palamedes accompanied them and incurred the undying enmity of Odysseus by exposing him when he feigned madness in the hope of avoiding the war. For although he was bound by oath to take part as a former suitor of Helen, he was by no means eager to do so (perhaps because he had received an oracle warning him that he would return alone after twenty years[128]). So he yoked two ill-assorted beasts together, an ox and a horse or ass, to plough his fields, and also sowed the furrows with salt instead of grain in some accounts. Palamedes saw through his pretence, however, and placed his infant son in front of the plough to show that he was quite sane enough to avoid him, or else threatened the child with a sword to show that Odysseus was sane enough to rush to his rescue.[129] Odysseus was embittered against Palamedes from that time forth, and became all the more so when Palamedes won great popularity among the troops for his useful and diverting inventions; and he therefore contrived his death during the early years of the siege of Troy. In the earliest version in the *Cypria*, he and Diomedes drowned him while he was out fishing.[130] Or he forged a letter under the name of Priam promising Palamedes a large sum of gold for betraying his fellow Greeks, and ensured that the message would be discovered on the body of a murdered prisoner. When it was subsequently read out in front of Agamemnon and the other leaders, they agreed that Palamedes' tent should be searched, and discovered quantities of gold that had been hidden there beforehand by Odysseus; and Palamedes was condemned accordingly and stoned to death.[131]

There was also an account in which Odysseus, Agamemnon and Diomedes plotted together to cause the death of Palamedes (by much the same means as in the preceding story) because they were jealous of the popularity that he had gained with the troops.[132] Or in a late account, Odysseus and Diomedes told Palamedes that some treasure had been hidden in a well and hurled stones down on him after he descended to look for it.[133]

This murder, however contrived, would have fateful consequences, since Nauplios, the father of Palamedes, would later avenge it by luring many Greeks to their death as they were sailing home from Troy (see p. 485). In a lost play by Euripides, Oiax, a son of Nauplios who was also serving at Troy, informed his father of the murder by inscribing the story on oar-blades and tossing them into the sea (rather like a message in a bottle), a splendidly impractical means of communication which is mocked by Aristophanes in the *Thesmophoriazusae*.[134]

Nestor and Diomedes

If NESTOR is one of the best-known characters in the mythology of the Trojan War, this is largely because of the affectionate and yet humorous portrayal of him in the *Iliad*. As the only surviving son of Neleus (for all the rest had all been killed by Herakles, see p. 278), he was the king of sandy Pylos on the western coast of the Peloponnese. See p. 424 for his family background. Since he was much older than the other leaders, over sixty at the period covered in the *Iliad*,[135] he was unable to achieve as much as he might have wished in the field, but he was highly valued nonetheless for his wise counsels and long-winded but engaging reminiscences. He always shows himself as a peace-maker when the younger leaders quarrel in the *Iliad*, and in the first part of the epic, his advice is Agamemnon's chief guide; but after he fails in his scheme to bring about a reconciliation between Agamemnon and Achilles by sending a delegation to the latter (see p. 463), he slips somewhat into the background, his place being taken in large measure by Diomedes, who has an old head on young shoulders.

Nestor was accompanied to the war by two of his sons, his eldest son Antilochos, who became a close friend of Achilles, and also Thrasymedes. Antilochos was destined to be killed toward the end of the war while rescuing his father from death (see p. 468). Nestor arrived home safely, however, along with Thrasymedes, and both appear in the *Odyssey* in scenes set after the war. He welcomes Telemachos, the young son of Odysseus, to his court in the third book of that epic, in which he is shown as enjoying a dignified old age. He is much the same as ever, still full of good advice and old stories, and has only a single serious regret, that he has lost his eldest son.

From among the other leading warriors, DIOMEDES in particular deserves to be singled out. Of Aetolian descent as the son of Tydeus, Polyneikes' old comrade during the Theban War (see p. 418), he had married a daughter of Adrastos, king of Argos, and had inherited the kingdom of his father-in-law (see p. 333 for the circumstances). He was therefore a powerful ruler of comparable rank to Agamemnon, and led a large force of troops to Troy from Argos, Tiryns and the eastern Argolid, with Sthenelos and Euryalos (see p. 334) as his lieutenants.[136] He is prominent throughout the *Iliad*, both for his valour and also, especially from the tenth book onward, for his frank and judicious advice to Agamemnon. Like his father before him, he is particularly favoured by Athena, who inspires him to dominate the fighting in the fifth book of the epic, and even to confront deities. Although he is shot in the shoulder by Pandaros, he kills him soon afterwards and then knocks Aineias to the ground by striking him on the hip with a stone; and when Aphrodite comes to the aid of Aineias (who is her son), he stabs her in the wrist with his spear, causing her to flee up to Olympos to seek a cure for the pain.[137] Shortly afterwards, when he attacks Aineias again, who is now protected by Apollo, the god pushes him back three times and finally warns him not to measure himself against the immortal gods.[138] He subsequently wounds Ares in the belly all the same, with some help from Athena, causing him to scream as loudly as nine or ten thousand men and flee up to Olympos for relief (see p. 168).[139] Although Diomedes is undoubtedly a hero of the highest rank, he is nevertheless a rather colourless figure who lacks the individual character of an Achilles, Aias or Odysseus. He returned home safely to Argos after the fall of Troy. In the post-epic tradition, however, he was greeted with fresh trouble at home, for his wife had deserted him for another man at the incitement of Aphrodite, and he was driven into exile in southern Italy (see further on pp. 483 and 487).

Pindar states that Athena turned Diomedes into an immortal god; and according to the relevant scholia, the poet Ibycus said the same, adding that he married Hermione and lived with the Dioskouroi during his new existence. As was remarked above, Diomedes' father Tydeus had been a favourite of Athena, and she had intended to confer immortality on him until she was deterred at the last moment (see p. 320 for the circumstances); and according to Pherecydes, Tydeus prayed before dying that she should confer this benefit on his son instead.[140] He was worshipped as a god in some places in southern Italy, notably Metapontum and Thurii.[141] His shield could be seen in the temple of Athena in Argos, and the people of that city also liked to believe that he had deposited the Palladion with them[142] (although this particular relic was claimed by many other places, including Sparta and Rome).

THE COURSE OF THE WAR AND THE SACK OF TROY

The earlier years of the war

For the first nine years of the war, the Trojans avoided direct contact with the enemy, preferring to shelter behind their city walls in the hope that the Greeks would eventually become exhausted by the siege. This calculation was not altogether unsound, since the invaders often ran short of food and became demoralized by the stalemate; according to the *Cypria*, indeed, they might have sailed home at one point if Achilles had not restrained them.[143] To raise the spirits of the troops and to deprive the Trojans of supplies and support, the Greeks conducted raids against settlements in the area and also against islands and cities further down the coast, ranging as far south as Clazomenae and Colophon in some accounts.[144] Although Priam's stronghold itself, heavily garrisoned as it was and defended by a considerable force of Trojan and allied troops, was impregnable to the rudimentary siege-operations of the period, the Greek campaign of attrition started to wear down the king's resources and made it impossible for him to replenish them by trade.

Achilles took the lead in the Greek raids, and also rustled the cattle of Aineias on Mt Ida[145] and caught two sons of Priam outside the city walls. He captured LYKAON as he was cutting fig-wood for chariot-rails in his father's orchard at night, but spared his life on that occasion, choosing instead to sell him into slavery on Lemnos, where he was purchased by a son of Jason (apparently Euneos; see p. 384 for the circumstances of his birth). He was eventually ransomed, however, and spent eleven days with his friends before entering battle on the twelfth (for we are now in the period covered by the *Iliad*, after direct hostilities had resumed); and when he had the misfortune to encounter Achilles for a second time, he was slaughtered without mercy, plead though he might.[146] In what is perhaps the most famous episode from the early years of the war, Achilles ambushed another son of Priam, TROILOS, when he ventured out of the city with his sister Polyxena to fetch water from a fountain-house. As can be seen in vase-paintings of the incident, Troilos was very young, hardly more than a child. Although his death is mentioned by Priam in the *Iliad*,[147] no details are offered there or in any other pre-Hellenistic source, and we have to rely on visual images to gain an idea of how the story would have been told in the earliest tradition. On the François vase, which can be dated to about 570 BC, Achilles can be seen pursuing the beardless Troilos as he tries to escape on his horse, and a woman, almost certainly Polyxena as in other images of the kind, is shown running away ahead of them. Or on other vases, Achilles drags Troilos from his horse by his hair, or kills him at an altar. In a later version of this myth, as first recorded by Lycophron, Achilles conceived a passion for Troilos and pursued him with amorous intent, causing him to take sanctuary in the shrine of Thymbraian Apollo. On finding that he could neither win the youth over nor persuade him to leave the shrine, Achilles lost his temper and decapitated him at the altar.[148] Other reports from the later tradition explain his murder of the helpless youth by saying that a prophecy had declared that Troy would be impregnable if he survived to the age of twenty, or that his death was one of the preconditions for the fall of the city.[149] As a fiction of medieval origin, the story of his romance with Cressida lies beyond the scope of the present work.[150]

The events of the Iliad

The events narrated in the *Iliad* are set in the tenth and final year of the war. By contrast to the other epics in the Trojan cycle, which were composed somewhat later (even if most of their content would probably have been familiar to Homer), the

Figure 13.4   Achilles and Aias playing draughts. Drawing after a vase-painting.

Iliad has a very limited time-scale, and the bulk of the poem is devoted to four crucial days in the fighting. It is announced at the beginning of the poem that its theme will be the anger of Achilles, as provoked by a quarrel between him and the leader of the expedition, Agamemnon, who offended his pride by depriving him of his concubine and valued war-prize, BRISEIS. Agamemnon had been awarded a similar war-prize, a captive woman called CHRYSEIS, but her father Chryses, who was a priest of Apollo, had come to the Greek camp to request her ransom; and when Agamemnon had sent him away under threat of violence, he had prayed for vengeance to Apollo, who had proceeded to shoot arrows into the Greek camp to cause a plague. When the seer Kalchas had explained the cause of the disease, stating that it could be brought to an end only if Chryseis were returned to her father without demand of a ransom, Agamemnon had reluctantly agreed to surrender her; but he had insisted on being compensated for his loss, and had reacted to some critical comments from Achilles by telling him to hand over Briseis for that purpose. Now Achilles was greatly attached to her, and would have regarded this as an unacceptable slight to his honour in any case. So he withdrew his allegiance from Agamemnon and stayed away from the fighting, taking his Myrmidon followers and friend Patroklos with him.[151] When deprived in this way of their foremost champion, the Greeks at last became vulnerable to Trojan attack; and although they managed to hold their ground for a time while Diomedes was dominating the field, they were soon driven back to their camp by the shore, and were obliged to fortify it with a ditch and a wall.[152] The Trojans were then able to camp out on the plain for the first time since the Greek landing, their watch-fires shining out like countless stars on a clear windless night.[153]

At the urging of Nestor and the other leaders, Agamemnon now agreed to seek a reconciliation with Achilles, and sent Phoinix, Odysseus and the Telamonian Aias to him as envoys to promise him the return of Briseis and valuable compensation besides, including marriage to a daughter of Agamemnon and seven cities as her dowry if the war should be brought to a successful conclusion. Each of the envoys pressed him to accept these terms, Odysseus speaking first and then old Phoinix, who was able to appeal to him in more personal terms because he had known him since his childhood, having acted as his tutor for a period. He failed to sway the embittered Achilles, however, and the last speaker, Aias, was not much more success-ful, even though his inarticulate appeal proved to be more effective than the eloquent speeches of his companions. Achilles would promise no more than to reconsider his position if the enemy should break through to the Greek camp and begin to set fire to the ships. He definitely put himself in the wrong by rejecting these princely overtures; and there is thus a certain poetic justice in the heavy misfortune that befell him afterwards when he lost his closest friend.[154]

On the following day, the Greeks conducted a successful counter-attack with Agamemnon at the forefront, almost driving the Trojans back into their city; but the Greek fortunes turned as Agamemnon, Diomedes and Odysseus were succes-sively wounded; and when Hektor then returned to the fighting (for Zeus had warned him to stay away as long as Agamemnon was in the field), the tide of the battle was soon reversed and the Greeks were driven back towards their ships.[155] Attacking the Greek wall with several columns at once, Hektor broached the gate with a huge stone and led the Trojans through to the ships in the face of determined opposi-tion from Aias.[156] When they were almost in a position to set fire to the ships, and had actually kindled the stern of one of them, Achilles yielded to the pleas of his favourite retainer PATROKLOS, who had witnessed the disaster, and allowed him to borrow his armour and enter battle at the head of the Myrmidons. Supposing that they were under attack from Achilles himself, the Trojans retreated in disorder, suffering many losses as Patroklos pursued them almost up to the city walls. By taking the pursuit this far, he was disobeying the orders of Achilles, who had told him to come back safely after driving the enemy from the ships; and he was killed under the walls owing to the intervention of Apollo, who knocked his helmet and armour from his body, leaving him dazed and exposed. Euphorbos, son of Panthoos, took advantage of the situation to wound him in the back with his spear, and Hektor finished him off with a spear-thrust to the belly.[157]

During the ensuing struggle for the body of Patroklos, Menelaos killed Euphorbos, but was pressed back by the Trojans under the leadership of Hektor, who then stripped Achilles' armour from the corpse; the Greeks finally managed to recover the corpse, however, and carried it back toward the ships with the Trojans in close pursuit. On hearing of his friend's death, Achilles lamented so bitterly that his mother Thetis rose up from the sea with her sister-Nereids to investigate. He told her that he was determined to avenge the death of Patroklos by killing Hektor, even though he was warned by her that he would be fated to meet his own death soon afterwards. After she left to fetch him a new set of armour from Hephaistos, he took some immediate action on the advice of the divine messenger Iris, by advancing to the trench that protected the camp and giving three mighty shouts to cast fear into the Trojans. On hearing him, they fell back in alarm, giving the Greeks an opportunity to remove the corpse of Patroklos from the field.[158] After receiving his new armour from Thetis early on the following morning, Achilles summoned an assembly to settle his differences with Agamemnon. He formally renounced his anger, while Agamemnon offered a rather grudging apology and offered to pay due compensation.

After returning to battle, Achilles soon routed the Trojans, slaughtering many of them with great brutality and angering the river-god Skamandros by choking his waters with corpses (see p. 42). He might even have forced his way into the city if Apollo had not intervened, first by inciting Agenor to make a stand and then by luring Achilles away in the guise of Agenor (see p. 454). All the Trojan warriors were able to escape back into the city as a consequence, leaving Hektor alone to confront Achilles outside the city walls. On seeing Achilles advancing toward him like a war-god, Hektor lost his nerve and took to flight; but after he had been pursued three times around the walls, Athena appeared to him in the guise of his brother Deiphobos to trick him into making a stand. He was fatally wounded in the ensuing duel with a spear-wound to the neck. Although he pleaded with Achilles to allow his body to be ransomed to his parents for an honourable burial, Achilles threaded leather thongs through his ankles after his death, attached the corpse to his chariot, and dragged it past the city in full sight of the Trojans and then down to the Greek camp.[159] After the funeral of Patroklos and the splendid funeral-games that followed,[160] Achilles continued to brood over Patroklos' death and to mistreat Hektor's corpse for eleven days, until the gods finally intervened. Thetis was dispatched to her son to order him to accept a ransom for Hektor's body, while Iris visited Priam to order him to bring a ransom to Achilles. So Priam made a secret visit to the Greek camp at night under the guidance of Hermes, and appealed as a suppliant to Achilles, who was at last moved to pity and joined with the old man in lamenting the sorrows of the war. Achilles sent him away with his son's body on the following morning, and the poem ends with Hektor's funeral.[161]

Three foreign allies of the Trojans: Rhesos, Penthesileia and Memnon

The Greeks were never entirely able to sever the communications between the Trojans and their numerous allies in Thrace and Asia. These allies can be divided into two main groups, those who are listed in the catalogue of Trojan forces at the end of the second book of the *Iliad*[162] (most of whom were apparently present from the early years of the war), and the handful of allies of more exotic character who arrived in the last stages of the war. Few significant heroes are to be found among the allies of the first group; only Sarpedon and Glaukos, from Lycia in the south-western corner of Asia Minor (see pp. 349–50), are of any real importance. Sarpedon was the most prominent victim of Patroklos; after his death, Zeus ordered Hypnos and Thanatos (Sleep and Death) to carry his body home to Lycia (see p. 30). The first of the more exotic allies was the Thracian king Rhesos, whose arrival and speedy death are described in the *Iliad*; the adventures of the others – the Amazon Penthesileia, the Ethiopian Memnon, and Eurypylos, son of Telephos – were recounted in the next two epics in the Trojan cycle, the *Aithiopis* and the *Little Iliad*. These latter figures were warriors of the highest stature who were capable of presenting a genuine threat to the Greeks. They might have remained as familiar as Hektor if we still possessed the early epics that commemorated their exploits; a late epic account of the last stages of the war can be found in the *Posthomerica* of Quintus of Smyrna, a poem composed in the fourth century AD.[163]

By calling RHESOS a son of the Thracian king Eioneus, Homer differs from later authors, who generally state that he was borne to the Thracian river-god Strymon by one or other of the Muses.[164] In the Homeric account, he arrived at Troy with some Thracian followers on the night before the Trojan attack on the Greek ships, and camped some distance away from the main Greek force. His horses were whiter than snow and swifter than the wind, his chariot was fashioned from gold and silver, and his magnificent golden armour seemed more suitable for a god than a mortal. During his first night at Troy, which was fated to be his last, Odysseus and Diomedes happened to creep out as scouts to check on what the enemy were doing; and they ran across Dolon, a none too heroic Trojan who had set out on a comparable mission. Dolon was dressed in a wolf's skin, and had undertaken the mission after Hektor had promised to give him the chariot and divine horses of Achilles. Overcome with terror, he soon informed his captors about the dispositions of the Trojans and about their new ally in particular; but it brought him no benefit since Diomedes cut off his head all the same. As a result of this stroke of fortune, the two Greeks were able to catch the Thracians in their sleep. Diomedes put Rhesos and twelve of his companions to the sword while Odysseus seized the snow-white horses.[165] Later sources cite prophecies to justify this nocturnal slaughter. According to the *Rhesos*, a surviving play on the episode which is dubiously ascribed to Euripides, Athena had revealed that no Greek would be able to withstand Rhesos if he should live through the night; or in another account, an oracle had revealed that Troy would be impregnable if Rhesos' horses grazed on the plain or drank from the Skamandros.[166] In a version ascribed to Pindar, Hera and Athena advised the night-raid after Rhesos had fought against the Greeks for a day, inflicting great damage on them.[167]

When the fortunes of the Trojans were at a low ebb after the death of Hektor, a force of Amazons arrived at Troy under the leadership of PENTHESILEIA, who was a daughter of the war-god Ares by Otrere, queen of the Amazons. She had come to seek purification from Priam after accidentally killing a relative, or else to seek glory in battle since it was a law of the Amazons that they must do so if they were to be allowed to consort with men.[168] She fought bravely, killing many of the Greeks, including Machaon, son of Asklepios, until she was finally killed in her turn by Achilles, who admired her prowess and mourned for her after her death. Her legend was recounted in the *Aithiopis*, the next epic in the Trojan cycle after the *Iliad*, as was the legend of Memnon, king of the Ethiopians.[169] Although this epic would presumably have been very different in tone from the *Iliad*, allowing freer rein to the fantastical, the Homeric epic does refer to the Amazons on two occasions, as former adversaries of Bellerophon (see p. 434) and of Priam (who had helped to defeat them in his younger days when they had invaded neighbouring Phrygia).[170]

Achilles' sympathy with the dead Amazon was greeted with scorn by the brutish THERSITES, who made fun of him, saying that he had fallen in love with her. He also mutilated her corpse in some accounts, by gouging out one or both of her eyes with the point of his spear. Achilles lost his temper and killed him with a blow to the face; and since the slaying caused dissension in the Greek camp, he sailed away to Lesbos afterwards to be purified. The rites were performed by Odysseus after

Figure 13.5 The dying Memnon is borne away by his mother, Eos (Dawn).
Red-figure cup by Douris. Musée du Louvre.

Achilles had first offered sacrifices to Apollo, Artemis and Leto. This purification from the *Aithiopis* is the first to be attested in Greek literature (for there is no mention of this procedure in the Homeric epics).[171]

We first encountered Thersites as a member of the Aetolian royal family who joined together with his brothers, the sons of Agrios, to depose and maltreat Oineus, the king of Calydon, their aged uncle; unlike most of his brothers, he escaped the retribution that he richly deserved (see p. 419). In the *Iliad*, however, he is presented as a man of low birth, a foul-tongued troublemaker who likes to abuse his betters and is the ugliest of all the men who went to Troy. When he reviles the kings in his usual manner at the great assembly that is convened after the withdrawal of Achilles, he is soon silenced by Odysseus, who exposes him to general ridicule by beating him on the back and shoulders with his golden sceptre.[172] Although the surviving summary of the *Aithiopis* says nothing about his origins, it is unlikely that he was a mere commoner (let alone the uncouth figure portrayed in the *Iliad*) if his killing provoked serious discord among the other Greeks; it may even be the case that Diomedes (who was a grandson of Oineus and thus a kinsman of Thersites) already took the lead in objecting to Achilles' action as in the late epic of Quintus of Smyrna.[173] Since Homer describes him as being lame and generally misshapen, a tale was invented in later times to account for his condition; for it was claimed that while he was participating in the hunt for the Calydonian boar, he deserted his position in terror, to the great anger of Meleagros, the leader of the hunt, who responded by throwing (or chasing) him over a cliff.[174]

Soon after the death of Penthesileia, MEMNON, son of Eos (Dawn) and Tithonos, arrived at Troy with a force of Ethiopians. Although his people, the Aithiopes or 'Burnt-faces', came to be identified with the black Africans who lived in the lands to the south of Egypt, they were originally a purely mythical people who lived near the sunrise at the edges of the earth; and Memnon's kingdom was usually located in the east accordingly, whether in a mythical region beyond the known world or in Syria or Persia. It was often said that he came from Susa, the old administrative capital of Persia.[175] Some later authors, writing when the Ethiopians had come to be associated primarily with Africa, suggest that Memnon had led his Ethiopians out of their original homeland in Africa to win a kingdom in Asia.[176] Memnon was the last and perhaps the most formidable of the opponents of Achilles, whom he resembled in some notable respects, for he too was a son of a goddess who owned divine armour that had been fashioned by Hephaistos. After killing many adversaries in battle, he speared Antilochos, son of Nestor, who sacrificed his own life to rescue his father; for Nestor's chariot had become immobilized after one of his horses had been struck by an arrow shot by Paris, and he had appealed to his son to save him from Memnon, who was plying his spear nearby. Now Antilochos was a close friend of Achilles, indeed his very closest since the death of Patroklos; and just as the great hero had avenged the death of Patroklos, he now set out to avenge the death of Antilochos by killing Memnon. After Memnon was duly slain, his divine mother appealed to Zeus to grant him immortality.[177]

According to local tradition, Memnon was buried in the Troad beside a stream called the Asopos; in Quintus' late epic, the dawn breezes are said to have joined together at the bidding of Eos to carry his corpse to that spot.[178] A legend reminiscent of that of the birds of Diomedes (see p. 487) related that his Ethiopian comrades were transformed into some remarkable birds, the Memnonides, who commemorated their master's death on its anniversary each year by fighting a battle above his tomb.[179] Or in Ovid's version of the tale (which is the earliest to survive although there is reason to suppose that the legend itself is quite old), Zeus caused the birds to spring from the ashes on Memnon's tomb in response to the pleas of Eos, who begged him to soothe her distress by granting some exceptional honour to her dead son.[180] A late tradition suggests that the morning dew is formed from the tears that Eos continues to shed for Memnon. These tales conflict with the earliest account in the *Aithiopis* in which Zeus granted him immortality at his mother's request.[181]

The death of Achilles and suicide of Aias

After killing Memnon, Achilles pursued the Trojans back across the plain and might have forced his way into the city if he had not been shot in the ankle by Paris, or by Apollo, or by both together. A late tradition suggested that he was invulnerable except at the ankle (see p. 457). During the struggle that ensued for his body and divine armour, Aias managed to hoist the corpse onto his shoulders, and then carried it back to the Greek ships while Odysseus fought off the Trojans from behind.[182] The *Odyssey* provides an account of his magnificent funeral, reporting that he was mourned for seventeen days and nights by his comrades and by Thetis too, along with her Nereid sisters from beneath the sea and the nine Muses, who led the dirges. After his body was consumed by the flames of his funeral-pyre, his comrades gathered

Figure 13.6   The voting over the arms of Achilles. Red-figure vase by Douris. Kunsthistorisches Museum, Vienna 3695.

his remains and mixed them with those of Patroklos in a golden urn that had been fashioned by Hephaistos; and they raised a huge burial-mound over their remains and those of Antilochos, so that it was visible as a landmark from far out at sea.[183]

In the Homeric view, Achilles departed to the Underworld in the usual way, where he would subsequently be encountered by Odysseus as a king among the shades. In the *Aithiopis*, however, Thetis snatched him away from his funeral-pyre and conveyed him to Leuke (the White Island), a posthumous home for favoured heroes and heroines on the earth's surface (much like Elysion, see p. 116);[184] and in the subsequent tradition, it was generally accepted that he was granted immortality, either on Leuke (which came to be identified with an island in the Black Sea) or in Elysion. He was often said to have contracted a posthumous marriage, usually with Medeia or Helen, but sometimes with Iphigeneia or Polyxena.[185]

After the funeral of Achilles, splendid games were held in his honour, and his divine arms and armour were offered as a prize to the Greek warrior who was adjudged to be the bravest. According to the *Odyssey*, Thetis set up the contest, and it was judged by Athena and 'the sons of the Trojans' (i.e. the Trojan captives), who caused great anger to the Telamonian Aias by passing him over in favour of Odysseus.[186] Or in the curious version attested for the *Little Iliad*, a non-Homeric epic in the Trojan cycle, some men were sent out to eavesdrop under the walls of Troy in accordance with a suggestion from Nestor, and they heard two girls arguing about the relative merits of Aias and Odysseus; when one asserted that Aias was the braver because he had carried Achilles' body from the battlefield while Odysseus had been unwilling to do so, the other retorted (at the inspiration of Athena, who specially favoured Odysseus) that even a woman could carry such a load once it was on her shoulders, but she would not have the nerve to fight off the enemy (as Odysseus had done while he was covering

469

Figure 13.7 Aias' suicide. Attic cup, Brygos painter.
Metropolitan Museum, New York L 69–11.

Aias' retreat).[187] In some later accounts, the Greek warriors decided the issue themselves through a ballot.[188] By whatever process, Odysseus was selected to receive the prize of honour, to the anger and astonishment of Aias, who was unable to believe even for a moment that Odysseus might be the better man. To judge by the surviving literature, indeed, Aias really deserved to win the contest if sheer steadfastness and courage were to be the criterion. In connection with his meeting with Aias in the Underworld, where he saw him standing apart from all the other ghosts, still consumed with anger at his defeat, Odysseus remarks in the *Odyssey* that he came to wish that he had never won, and concedes that Aias was unsurpassed in his martial prowess by any of the Greeks apart from Achilles himself.[189]

Aias committed suicide soon after he met with this humiliation in the contest for the arms. Although the Homeric epics have nothing definite to say about his death, except that it followed from his defeat,[190] the surviving summary of the *Little Iliad* states that he went mad after losing the contest, and destroyed the livestock of his comrades and then killed himself. For the earliest full account of these events, we have to rely on Sophocles' *Aias* (although Pindar already notes that Aias killed himself by falling on his sword in the dead of night). According to Sophocles, Aias had planned to avenge his ill-deserved defeat by attacking the Greek leaders while they were asleep at night, but Athena frustrated his intent by sending him mad, and he therefore killed their cattle and sheep instead. When he recovered his wits and discovered what he had done, he was so ashamed that he resolved to commit suicide, ignoring the pleas of his concubine Tekmessa.[191] As the artistic evidence makes clear, it was agreed from an early period that he fixed his sword into the earth and fell on it; a tradition suggested that he was vulnerable only at the point where the sword transfixed him, at his chest or collar-bone, see p. 457. In the *Little Iliad*, Agamemnon refused him a proper heroic funeral by cremation, ordering that he should be interred in a coffin instead;[192] or in Sophocles' version, Menelaos and Agamemnon proposed that his corpse should be left in the open as prey for scavengers until Odysseus persuaded Agamemnon to allow his burial.[193] As his child by Tekmessa, Aias left a son called Eurysakes (Broad Shield, so named after the towering shield of his father, see p. 456), who now fell under the care of Aias' half-brother Teukros.[194]

Preconditions for the fall of Troy; Philoktetes shoots Paris, Neoptolemos kills Eurypylos, and Odysseus steals the Palladion

During the next stage of the conflict, the Greeks took three important steps to advance the prospect of final victory. They fetched their long-abandoned comrade Philoktetes, who proceeded to kill Paris with the bow of Herakles; they fetched Achilles' young son Neoptolemos, who would make a crucial contribution to the subsequent fighting, helping to fill the gap that had been left by the death of his father; and Odysseus stole into Troy to steal its protective talisman, the Palladion (an ancient image of Athena, see p. 523). These measures were revealed by a prophecy (or prophecies) as actions that needed to be taken as preconditions for the fall of the city. In the early epic account in the *Little Iliad*, Odysseus mounted an ambush to capture HELENOS, a son of Priam who was a gifted seer; and Helenos revealed, doubtless under pressure, that Philoktetes should be fetched from Lemnos (where he had been marooned on account of a wound sustained during the outward journey, see p. 449). After being healed of his wound by Machaon, son of Asklepios, Philoktetes engaged in single combat with Paris and shot him dead. Menelaos, who had ample reason to hate him, mutilated his corpse, but it was eventually recovered by the Trojans for burial. The Greeks then took the two further actions mentioned above, of fetching Neoptolemos and seizing the Palladion, quite possibly as further measures that were advised by the captured Helenos (although nothing is explicitly stated on the matter in the surviving testimonies in the *Little Iliad*).[195] Apollodorus offers a rather different account of these events, in which Helenos remained within the city until after the death of Paris, and it was the Greek seer Kalchas who advised that Philoktetes should be fetched. This led to the death of Paris as in the *Little Iliad*, and Helenos then competed with his brother Deiphobos for the hand of Helen. Helenos was so aggrieved when she was awarded to his brother that he left the city to live on Mt Ida; and it was at this stage that Odysseus captured him, on the advice of Kalchas. Helenos now revealed further measures that should be taken if Troy was to fall, namely that they should fetch Neoptolemos, seize the Palladion and send for the bones of Pelops.[196]

The latter condition for the fall of Troy is first mentioned by Lycophron in the Hellenistic period; the bones were said to have been buried at Letrina, near Olympia in Elis.[197] It is not clear why their presence should have affected the fate of Troy (although the Asiatic origin of Pelops, see p. 502, may have something to do with the matter). According to a tale recorded by Pausanias, a shoulder-bone alone was fetched, and it was subsequently lost during the return voyage when the ship that was carrying it was wrecked in a great storm off Euboea (evidently that sent by Athena, see p. 485). Many years later, a fisherman from the Euboean city of Eretrea caught the bone in his nets, and was so amazed by its size that he travelled to Delphi to consult the oracle about it. Eleian envoys happened to be there at the time, seeking a cure for a plague; and they were advised to restore the shoulder-bone to its proper home, while the fisherman was advised to hand it over to them. The Eleians rewarded its finder (who was named Damarmenos) by appointing him and his descendants to be the guardians of the bone.[198]

When Neoptolemos arrived in the Troad after being fetched by Odysseus from his birthplace of Scyros (see p. 458), he took the lead in defeating the last major ally of the Trojans, EURYPYLOS, son of Telephos. It is fitting that his opponent in the last heroic duel of the war should be the son of a hero who had tangled with his father Achilles when the Greeks had first set foot on Asian soil (see p. 446). According to the early mythographer Acusilaus, who may have drawn this detail from the *Little Iliad*, Eurypylos had been held back in his native Mysia by his mother Astyoche until Priam had bribed her to change her mind by sending her a wonderful golden vine.[199] It is reported elsewhere that this marvel had been fashioned by Hephaistos, and had been presented to one of Priam's predecessors – either Tros or Laomedon – by Zeus as compensation for the abduction of Ganymedes (see p. 522).[200] Although the *Odyssey* mentions in passing that Eurypylos and his comrades met their death 'on account of a woman's gifts',[201] we cannot be sure that Homer had the same story in mind. Some mythographers explained that Priam persuaded Eurypylos to come by promising him one of his daughters as a wife.[202] After arriving with a force of troops from Mysia, which lay in an adjoining region of Asia Minor, he fought valiantly, killing many Greeks, including Machaon, son of Asklepios, and the Boeotian leader Peneleos (see p. 328); but he proved to be no match for Neoptolemos, who demonstrated his heroic prowess by cutting him down in battle.[203]

After the death of Eurypylos, Odysseus entered Troy surreptitiously to steal the city's protective talisman. In the early epic account in the *Little Iliad*, he made two secret incursions, first entering the city in beggar's disguise to spy out the ground, and then returning with Diomedes to steal the Palladion. Although he was seen and recognized by Helen during his first incursion, she did not betray him but engaged in a treacherous conversation instead, discussing plans for the taking of the city; it would seem that she had become discontented with her predicament at Troy.[204] This encounter is already mentioned in the *Iliad*, in which Helen herself tells Telemachos how she had recognized his father in the city, and had taken him home and bathed him. After she had sworn not to betray him, he had revealed all that the Greeks were intending. He had put many Trojans to the sword before leaving, causing the women of the city to lament, but Helen had rejoiced in her heart, for her thoughts had turned to her homeland and she now regretted that Aphrodite had beguiled her into abandoning her husband and child.[205] In

Apollodorus' account, Odysseus is said to have made only a single incursion. After creeping up to the city by night with Diomedes, he disguised himself as a beggar and made his way in while his comrade waited outside. Although he was recognized by Helen, she helped in the theft of the Palladion, and he then took it back to the Greek ships with the help of Diomedes.[206] Some claimed that Odysseus and Diomedes stole into the city through a sewer;[207] and there is artistic evidence for a version in which they seized the statue jointly.

In a version which portrays Odysseus in a very poor light, Diomedes climbed into Troy to seize the Palladion, and Odysseus tried to kill him during the return journey to steal the statue and the glory for himself; but as he was raising his sword to strike, Diomedes was alerted by a glint of moonlight from the blade (or by the shadow of the blade), and forced Odysseus to walk in front of him for the rest of the way. This story was cited in explanation of the proverbial expression 'Diomedeian compulsion' (*Diomēdeios anankē*), a phrase which is said to have originated in the *Little Iliad*. Although some such incident was presumably described in the epic, the circumstances must have been rather different since the Palladion had been stolen from Troy by Odysseus rather than Diomedes, in accordance with what would become the standard account in the subsequent tradition.[208]

The stratagem of the Wooden Horse; the ruse of Sinon and fate of Laokoon

Finding that the city still seemed as impregnable as ever in spite of these various measures, the Greeks adopted a new approach by attempting a ruse rather than relying on the open use of force as hitherto. For at the suggestion of Athena (or of that most ingenious of mortals Odysseus), they constructed a huge wooden horse with a hollow interior to serve as a hiding-place for a concealed force of troops. A cleverly disguised trap-door was set in its side to enable them to enter and leave. Epeios, son of Panopeus, a hero from Phocis (see pp. 465–6), built it with the assistance of Athena, using timber from the forests of Mt Ida. When the Horse was completed, a picked band of troops was stationed inside under the command of Odysseus, and the rest of the Greeks set fire to their camp and sailed out to sea as if they had decided to abandon the siege. Estimates of the number of the troops in the Horse vary from twelve to fifty or a hundred. They were intended to act as an advance guard who would open the city gates to the main force if the Trojans dragged the Horse into the city. The Greek fleet was waiting off the coast at Tenedos in the mean time, watching out for the fire-signal that would call the ships back.[209]

On the morning after the Greeks had put their plan into effect, the Trojans saw the Wooden Horse standing all alone on the deserted plain and went out to investigate. In the earliest account in the *Odyssey*, they dragged it into the city and then argued about the best course of action, some proposing that they should break it open, others that they should haul it to the top of a cliff and throw it over, and others again that they should leave it where it was as an offering to the gods. They finally sealed their own fate by deciding to adopt the latter course.[210] It is reported elsewhere that the Greeks encouraged the Trojans to regard the Horse as a sacred object by marking it with an inscription which stated that it was a thank-offering to Athena for their safe return.[211] The story of the Wooden Horse was apparently

Figure 13.8 The Wooden Horse. Drawing after an archaic vase.

recounted in much the same way in two other epics in the Trojan cycle, the *Little Iliad* and the *Sack of Troy*; in the former poem, the Trojans demolished part of the city wall to allow for the entry of the huge object.[212] Homer adds a peculiar detail to the story, stating that Helen walked around the Horse calling out to the men inside in perfect imitation of the voices of their wives; but although Menelaos and Diomedes were tempted to respond, they were restrained by Odysseus, who also placed his hand over the mouth of a certain Antiklos (who is otherwise unknown) to prevent him from speaking aloud. Such is the strange tale recounted in the *Odyssey* by Menelaos, who accounts for his wife's caprice by saying that it must have been inspired by some god who favoured the Trojans.[213]

When compared to these early accounts of the stratagem of the Horse, the versions offered in the *Aeneid* and late Greek epic are significantly different in two main respects. In the first place, the Trojans are far more suspicious of the Horse and therefore argue about what they should do with it while it is still in its original position; and second, the Greeks appreciate that the Trojans will be suspicious and therefore arrange for SINON, a cousin of Odysseus, to be captured by them in circumstances that will enable him to convince them that the Horse presents no danger and should be taken into the city. Sinon already appears in early epic, but only as the man who is left behind to light the beacon-signal to recall the Greek fleet at the appropriate moment. Instead of hiding himself, however, in these later accounts, he ensures that he is found by the Trojans, and then sets out to win their trust by leading them to believe that he is a deserter who has reason to hate his fellow Greeks.

In Vergil's narrative, the Trojans conduct a heated debate in front of the Horse before Sinon appears on the scene, some arguing that they should haul it into the city, while others urge that they should beware of any gift from the Greeks and should therefore destroy it, or at least break it open to see whether anything is hidden inside.

Laokoon, a Trojan priest, takes the lead in advancing the latter view, and almost proves his point by thrusting his spear into the side of the Horse, causing it to echo within; but at that very moment, Sinon, who has been captured in accordance with the Greek plan, is brought forward for questioning. He claims to have been on bad terms with the other Greeks ever since he had vowed to avenge the unjust killing of Palamedes (see p. 460), and alleges that Odysseus had plotted his destruction by persuading the seer Kalchas to declare that he should be sacrificed to ensure the safe departure of the Greek fleet; and as soon as the Trojans are convinced by his story and are ready to believe that he hates his former comrades, they listen trustingly to what he has to say about the Wooden Horse. He tells them that the Greeks built the Horse on the advice of Kalchas to expiate for their sacrilege in having stolen Athena's cultic image, the Palladion; and if the Trojans should harm this sacred object, they would be sure to suffer a terrible destruction, but they could expect a splendid destiny on the other hand if they were to bring it into their city. So they resolve to do so, and feel that their decision is confirmed when Laokoon and his two sons are killed shortly afterwards by two snakes which swim over from Tenedos; for they interpret this as indicating that the gods are angry with him for having desecrated the sacred object. When the Horse is inside the walls, the prophetess Kassandra adds her own warnings, but to no effect since she is fated always to be disbelieved (see p. 154). Sinon adopted hardier means to win the trust of the Trojans in the Greek epic of Quintus of Smyrna, by keeping silent for a considerable time as they tortured him and cut off his ears and nose, and so giving them cause to believe that they had forced the truth out of him. Or in another late epic by Tryphiodorus, Sinon mutilates himself to make his story seem more credible.[214]

Widely differing accounts are offered of the fate of LAOKOON and its significance. In the early epic version from the *Sack of Troy*, he met his death after the Trojans had brought the Horse into their city. As they were feasting in the happy belief that the war had ended to their advantage, two snakes appeared and destroyed Laokoon along with one of his two sons; and Aineias and his followers regarded this as a portent and withdrew to Mt Ida outside the city.[215] The meaning of the sign is not hard to make out: the death of Laokoon indicates the impending fall of the city, while the death of his son (evidently the eldest although this is not stated in the surviving summary) points to the destruction of Priam's senior branch of the ruling family. So by withdrawing, Aineias, as the main representative of the junior branch, will survive to take over. In Vergil's account by contrast, the snakes seem to act by divine will to ensure that Laokoon's warnings about the Horse will be discounted; in Quintus' epic, in which the episode serves a similar function, it is explicitly stated that Athena sent the snakes with this intent (after first making Laokoon blind). Both of Laokoon's sons are killed in these accounts.[216] According to Apollodorus, the snakes were sent by Apollo 'as a sign' when the Horse was already in the city; they swam over the sea from some neighbouring islands and devoured the sons of Laokoon. This accords with a poorly attested version from Sophocles in which the sons alone were killed (a matter of uncertain significance). Since the relevant section of Apollodorus' text is preserved only in summary form, it is not clear what Apollo was trying to indicate, or whether anyone took any action as a result; in Sophocles' version, Aineias' father interpreted the episode as a sign, and Aineias was therefore encouraged to leave the city before its fall, much as in early epic.[217] The snakes were usually said to have come from some islands of uncertain identity, the Kalydnai; Bacchylides already said as much, adding rather unexpectedly that they turned into human form on their arrival.[218]

In versions of a wholly different kind first recorded in Roman mythographical sources, the snakes were sent by Apollo to punish Laokoon for behaving in a manner inappropriate to a priest, whether by having intercourse with his wife in front of the divine images in the precinct of Apollo, or by marrying and fathering children against the will of Apollo.[219] Although Laokoon was primarily the priest of Thymbraian Apollo, some authors, including Vergil and the Hellenistic poet Euphorion, state that he was chosen by lot to become the priest of Poseidon at some stage (for the original priest had been stoned to death by the Trojans for failing to offer the proper sacrifices to avert the Greek landing).[220] For what it is worth, Laokoon is described in late sources as a son of Aineias' grandfather Kapys or of the Trojan elder Antenor.[221]

The sack of Troy

In the depth of the night, while the Trojans were asleep after celebrating their apparent victory, the Greeks put their plan into effect. Sinon lit a beacon-fire in the city (or on the tomb of Achilles by the shore) to recall the fleet from Tenedos and guide it on its way;[222] and the warriors who had been waiting inside the Wooden Horse opened the trap-door and slipped down to the ground on ladders or a rope.[223] Or in Vergil's account, which portrays the events of the night through Aineias' eyes and often departs from the early epic tradition, Helen recalled the fleet by raising a torch from the citadel; and as the fleet was sailing over from Tenedos, a fire-signal was lit on the king's ship as a cue to Sinon, who then removed some planks from the Wooden Horse to release the warriors from their confinement.[224] Whatever the exact course of the preceding events, the warriors from the Horse killed the sentries and anyone who might have raised the alarm, and then opened the city gates to admit the main force (if this was necessary, for in some accounts, as mentioned above, the walls had already been breached by the Trojans to allow for the entry of the Horse). All the Greek troops were now able to join together to slaughter the unsuspecting Trojans.

No full early account has survived of the course of events on the night of the sack, even if continuous narratives from a later period can be found in book 2 of the *Aeneid* and book 13 of Quintus' *Posthomerica*. We will concentrate on the fates of the most prominent Trojans, as these would have been presented in the early epic tradition in particular. Pausanias' description of Polygnotos' great mural of the sack of Troy, which was painted in the mid-fifth century BC, may be consulted for further information on how prominent individuals from both sides would have fared on that night in early accounts.[225]

In the standard account from the *Sack of Troy* in the epic cycle, Neoptolemos forced his way into the palace and killed **Priam** with his lance as the king was seeking sanctuary at the altar of Zeus Herkeios in the central courtyard.[226] The *Little Iliad* presented the episode somewhat differently, suggesting that Neoptolemos dragged him away from the altar and killed him at the doorway of the palace.[227] There are also later accounts in which the young hero decapitated him or hauled him out of the city to slaughter him on the grave of Achilles;[228] and in Vergil's portrayal, he killed a surviving son of his, Polites, in front of him before putting him to the sword.[229] Menelaos made for the house of **Deiphobos** to recover his errant wife **Helen**. According to the *Odyssey*, he was accompanied by Odysseus, who became engaged in a desperate fight there but won in the end with the help of Athena; but our summary of the *Sack of Troy* makes no mention of Odysseus in this connection, merely stating that Menelaos found Helen and took her back to the ship after killing Deiphobos.[230] In the *Little Iliad*, he had apparently planned to kill her, but cast his sword away after catching a glimpse of naked breasts; or in another version, the sight of her divine beauty deterred the Greek troops from stoning her as they had planned, or from putting her to the sword.[231] In the *Aeneid*, Aineias saw her hiding in the temple of Hestia (Vesta in Latin form) and would have killed her if his divine mother Aphrodite (Venus), who was also Helen's protectress, had not prevented him.[232] Theseus' mother **Aithra**, who had been obliged to attend Helen as a maidservant (see p. 361), was discovered among the captives after the sack by Demophon and Akamas, the two sons of Theseus, who were allowed to take her away after Agamemnon had gained Helen's consent (see also on p. 375).[233] **Andromache**, the widow of Hektor, was seized by Neoptolemos along with her infant son **Astyanax**. Some surviving lines from the *Little Iliad* describe how Neoptolemos took her down to the Greek ships, but snatched the young Astyanax from his nurse, and then grasped him by the feet and flung him down from a tower. In the *Sack of Troy*, by contrast, Odysseus caused his death by hurling him from the city walls;[234] or in some later accounts, the Greeks, with some encouragement from Odysseus, resolved at a meeting after the fall of the city that Astyanax should be put to death.[235] Vase-painters often depict his murder in conjunction with that of Priam. This was a rational if ruthless measure since it eliminated the only member of the Trojan royal family who might be likely to seek revenge in the future. Andromache was assigned to Neoptolemos after the sack and accompanied him to Epirus as his concubine (see p. 489).

Hekabe, the wife of Priam, was seized and taken down to the ships, as were her daughters; of these, only **Kassandra** has a notable story associated with her capture.

Figure 13.9   Return of Helen to Menelaos. Red-figure skyphos, Boston MFA 13. 186.

According to the *Sack of Troy* in the epic cycle, she claimed sanctuary by clinging to a cultic image of Athena, but the lesser Aias dragged her away by force, pulling the statue from its position as he did so. His fellow warriors were so appalled by his behaviour that they would have stoned him if he had not taken refuge at the altar of Athena, presumably in the very same temple where he had committed his act of sacrilege.[236] Athena exacted a terrible vengeance as we will see (pp. 482ff), causing the death not only of Aias but of many of his comrades too as they were sailing home to Greece; these events were described in the next epic in the Trojan cycle, the *Returns*. Later authors heightened the story of Aias' sacrilege by saying that he raped Kassandra under the statue of the goddess. It is quite possible that this was already stated by Alcaeus (born in the latter part of seventh century BC) but the relevant verb is unfortunately missing from the papyrus.[237] The evidence from the visual arts would suggest in any case that the story was familiar by the sixth century. The first author to speak unequivocally of a rape is Lycophron, who adds that the statue raised its eyes upward in disgust.[238]

Something must now be said about the main survivors among the Trojan men. Of the sons of Priam, **Helenos** was already in the Greek camp, having betrayed preconditions for the fall of Troy under a greater or lesser degree of compulsion (see p. 471); he would accompany Neoptolemos to Epirus after the war (see p. 490). In the post-epic tradition at least, Priam had sent his youngest son **Polydoros** abroad in the hope of ensuring his safety, but to no effect since he was murdered by his host (see below). **Aineias**, who belonged to another branch of the family, escaped during the turmoil with his aged father **Anchises** on his back (see p. 585), if he had not already withdrawn from the city shortly before (see p. 475). The Trojan nobleman **Antenor** was spared along with his family because he had supported the Greek ambassadors when they had proposed a peaceful settlement at the outbreak of the war (see p. 454).

The fate of the Trojan women

After massacring the men of military age, as was the usual practice after the forcible seizure of a city, the Greeks put Troy (or what remained of it) to the torch and went down to their camp by the ships to share out the spoils. The story now focuses on the sad fate of the captive women, in particular those who belonged to the immediate family of Priam.[239] **Hekabe** (Hecuba), the main wife of Priam, stands out prominently in all versions of the Troy-saga as a majestic but most unhappy figure who was fated to see her sons killed one after another, and her husband cut down in the courtyard of his own palace. Nothing is known of how she fared after the fall of the city in early epic; although it is commonly stated in the later tradition that she was allotted to Odysseus, there is no indication of that in the *Odyssey* or in the surviving testimonies on the *Sack of Troy*. She was usually said to have died soon afterwards, and in most remarkable circumstances too, for she was transformed into a dog by the shores of the Hellespont (or as she was being carried over its waters in a ship), met a swift death thereafter, and was buried at Kynossema (Bitch's Grave) near the entrance to the Hellespont on its European shore.[240] In Euripides'

Hecuba, which is the earliest securely datable source for the transformation, it is fore-told that Hekabe will never reach Greece, for she will change into a fiery-eyed dog on the ship that will carry her away, and then climb up its mast and fall to her death in the sea, to be buried at Kynossema.[241] It is clear from the allusive manner in which Hekabe's fate is described that this must already have been a familiar tale. In subsequent accounts, Hekabe is said to have been transformed after leaping into the sea in her anguish at the fate of her homeland,[242] or as she was being stoned by the Greeks in response to curses that she had uttered against them[243] (or by the Thracians because she had blinded their king Polymestor,[244] see below). Some said that she became a ghost-hound that disturbed the lands around the Hellespont with its howling, or that she became the hound of Hekate.[245] In some rationalized accounts, by contrast, she was simply stoned like a dog without undergoing a trans-formation.[246] The early lyric poet Stesichorus offers an exceptional account of her fate by stating that Apollo transferred her to Lycia after the war.[247]

In Euripides' *Hecuba*, Odysseus is said to have taken Hekabe across the Hellespont to the Thracian Chersonnese, where her attendants discovered the body of her young son POLY-DOROS on the shore.[248] This Polydoros, who was her last-born son, had been entrusted to POLYMESTOR, king of Thrace, by Priam, who had also given Polymestor a quantity of gold to ensure the continuance of his line if Troy should fall;[249] so Hekabe realized that Polymestor must have killed her son to steal the gold for himself. With the permission of Agamemnon, she invited Polymestor and his sons to visit her, and induced them to enter her tent without protection by promising to reveal where the ancestral treasures of Priam had been hidden; and she then blinded Polymestor and murdered his sons with the assistance of her women.[250] At the end of the play, Polymestor discloses the above-mentioned prophecy about Hekabe's fate, and Agamemnon orders that their blinded king should be marooned on a desert island. Both in this play and in his *Trojan Women*, Euripides paints a poignant picture of the aftermath of the fall of Troy and of the predicament of the female captives.

The daughters of Priam and Hekabe met with varying fates. Their prophetic daughter **Kassandra**, who had already suffered at the hands of the lesser Aias during the night of the sack, was awarded to Agamemnon as a war-prize and subsequently murdered in Argos by his wife Klytaimnestra (see p. 508).[251] According to a story that was already recounted in the *Sack of Troy*, **Polyxena** was slaughtered on the grave of Achilles. Later sources explain that the ghost of Achilles demanded that she should be offered to him as his share of the spoils (or as his bride in death), and state that the sacrifice was performed by the hero's son, Neoptolemos. Although Sophocles' play on the matter, the *Polyxena*, has been lost, a full surviving account of this disturbing episode may be found in the first part of Euripides' *Hecuba*. The idea that the sacrifice was a sort of forced marriage first appears in the Hellenistic period, in Lycophron. Seneca states more explicitly that Achilles wanted Polyxena as his posthumous wife in the Elysian Fields.[252]

Revisionist mythographers have much to say about Polyxena. Philostratus suggests that she accompanied Priam when he visited the Greek camp to seek the return of Hektor's body, and fell in love with Achilles at that time; and after his death, she stole out of the city and stabbed herself on his grave so as to become his posthumous bride.[253] Or in accounts from

Latin sources, Achilles saw her during a pause in the fighting and incurred his own death by seeking to marry her, for Paris and Deiphobos took advantage of the negotiations to murder him in the shrine of Thymbraian Apollo just outside the city.[254]

Although it is not clear why the *Cypria* should have had anything to say about the matter, it apparently offered an account of Polyxena's fate that differed from that in the *Sack of Troy*, stating that she was fatally wounded by Odysseus and Diomedes during the capture of the city and was buried by Neoptolemos afterwards.[255]

According to a tale first reported by Lycophron, another daughter of Priam, **Laodike**, was swallowed up in a chasm in the earth near the tomb of her ancestor Ilos. Quintus explains in his late epic that she prayed to the gods to meet with this fate so as to be spared the indignity of enslavement.[256] The *Iliad* refers to her as the most beautiful of the daughters of Priam, and mentions that she was married to Helikaon, son of Antenor. It is quite possible that her connection with the family of Antenor saved her from enslavement in early epic, especially since Odysseus saved her husband during the sack in the *Little Iliad*.[257] For a Hellenistic love-story that claimed that she had previously borne a son to Akamas, son of Theseus, see p. 376. In all but the earliest traditions, Aineias was said to have been married to **Kreousa**, daughter of Priam. Polygnotos portrayed her among the Trojan captives in his painting of the sack,[258] while subsequent literary accounts disagree on whether she escaped with her husband or was left behind. In the best-known version in the *Aeneid*, Aineias was distressed to find that she had become separated from him as they were fleeing from the burning city, and went back to look for her; but her ghost appeared to him to tell him that she had been held back by the Mother of the Gods, and that it was the will of the gods that he should travel abroad without her.[259] Or according to Lycophron, the Greeks allowed him to depart and to select something to take with him, and he chose to take his father and household gods rather than his wife, children and property; or else he escaped during the sack with his wife and children too.[260]

CHAPTER FOURTEEN

THE RETURNS OF THE GREEKS AND THE HISTORY OF THE PELOPIDS

——— ·•· ———

THE RETURN JOURNEYS OF THE GREEKS

The stories of the return journeys (*nostoi*) of the Greeks were recounted in a special epic in the Trojan cycle, the *Nostoi* or *'Returns'*. A central theme of this epic was the wrath of Athena, which was provoked by an act of sacrilege committed at her shrine by the lesser Aias during the sack of Troy (see pp. 477–8), and was directed not only against him but also against the Greeks in general for having failed to punish him. The goddess sowed discord in the Greek camp, causing Agamemnon and Menelaos to quarrel and so return home separately with different sections of the army; and she then sent a fearsome storm against Agamemnon's section of the fleet. Some heroes were driven far off course, some were killed, while a few avoided the perils of the sea altogether by travelling away by land. The varying itineraries and fates of the returning Greeks will form the subject of the first half of the present chapter. Four heroes in particular have interesting stories associated with their returns. Odysseus wandered far abroad into strange realms and distant seas, as recounted in the second of the Homeric epics, while Neoptolemos, the son of the dead Achilles, travelled overland on the advice of his divine grandmother and settled in Epirus, on the north-western fringes of Greece, with Hektor's widow as his concubine and Helen's daughter as his wife. Agamemnon for his part made a safe sea-crossing but was murdered by his wife (or her lover) on arriving home in Argos, while his brother Menelaos delayed for several years in Egypt after being driven out far off course by a storm, and therefore did not set foot in the Peloponnese until after Agamemnon's murder had been avenged by his son Orestes. As it happens, this cycle of intrafamilial conflict and vengeance was nothing exceptional in the history of Agamemnon's family, the Pelopids. Since the main myths of the Pelopids fall equally on either side of the Trojan War, we will devote the second half of the chapter to the bloody history of the family, tracing its earlier history before returning to consider the murder of Agamemnon and all that followed from it.

Athena's wrath at the sacrilege of the lesser Aias, and its implications for the Greek returns

Of all the deeds that were committed by the Greeks during the sack of Troy, none was considered more shameful than the lesser Aias' act of sacrilege in seizing Kassandra from her place of sanctuary in the temple of Athena, and even raping her by the altar in some accounts. In the earliest recorded version, from the *Sack of Troy* in the epic cycle, he dragged her away as she was trying to cling to the cultic image of the goddess, and his fellow Greeks were so appalled by his behaviour that they would have stoned him if he had not taken refuge at the altar of Athena (apparently the one that he had violated!). The summary of this lost epic concludes with the ominous statement that the goddess planned to bring disaster to the Greeks on the high seas, presumably because they had failed to avenge the sacrilege.[1] The resulting theme of the wrath of Athena is already in evidence in Nestor's account of the Greek returns in the *Odyssey*, and it was central to the plot of the *Returns* as has been noted. As it happens, neither the *Odyssey* nor the surviving testimonies on the *Returns* make any explicit mention of the cause of the goddess's anger, but it can be assumed that Aias' sacrilege was to blame, as was certainly indicated in the *Sack of Troy* and commonly accepted in the subsequent tradition.

The returns of the Greeks were disrupted in a number of ways as a direct or indirect result of the goddess' rancour. Even before the Greek force was ready to depart, she incited its two main leaders to quarrel over the best course of action, Agamemnon arguing that they should delay their departure until they had taken measures to appease the goddess, while his brother Menelaos urged that they should depart immediately. The fleet was divided as a consequence, for Menelaos and those who shared his opinion, including Nestor and Diomedes, set off in advance of Agamemnon and the rest of the army. When Agamemnon subsequently led the others out to sea after offering sacrifices to Athena, he soon had reason to suppose that the mind of the goddess had not yet been softened, for the fleet was struck by a violent storm in which the lesser Aias, who had caused the trouble in the first place, met a well-deserved death. Agamemnon escaped, however, and arrived home safely, as did Nestor and Diomedes after setting off previously with Menelaos. Special fates were reserved for Menelaos and Odysseus, whose returns were delayed for a number of years as they wandered in foreign parts.

Thus far the *Returns* was in agreement with the *Odyssey*, but it went beyond the earlier epic by offering an account of two overland journeys, the first within Asia Minor by the seer Kalchas and some companions, and the second by Neoptolemos, who travelled by land to northern Greece with Helenos and others. The *Odyssey* makes no mention of the former journey, and makes only a brief reference to the travels of Neoptolemos, saying that he arrived back safely with the Myrmidons, presumably after making a sea-crossing to his father's land in Thessaly (although this is not explicitly stated). His divine grandmother Thetis advised him to travel overland in the *Returns*, evidently because she was aware that the fleet would be endangered as a result of Athena's anger.[2]

Menelaos and Agamemnon quarrel at the incitation of Athena, and depart separately with different sections of the army

Since little is recorded of the *Returns* beyond a brief outline of its plot, we will begin by examining in further detail what Nestor and Menelaos have to say about the returns of the Greeks in the *Odyssey*, and then consider how the story of the great storm was developed in the subsequent tradition. When Telemachos, the son of Odysseus, visits Nestor and Menelaos in the *Odyssey* to seek news of his long-absent father, they have much of interest to say about their own return voyages and the fate of their comrades. Nestor tells him that Zeus had planned a dismal return for the Greeks because not all of them had behaved wisely or righteously (presumably during the sack of the city), and many of them had come to grief accordingly through the wrath of Athena. The goddess had started the mischief by inciting Agamemnon and Menelaos to quarrel immediately after the fall of Troy. The two leaders summoned a meeting of the troops to put forward their opposing views, Menelaos arguing that they should make an immediate departure, and Agamemnon that they should delay until they had offered splendid sacrifices to Athena (little realizing that she would not be appeased by them, for the mind of a god is not turned in a moment). The meeting was an ill-ordered and ill-tempered affair, held at sunset when the troops were befuddled with wine; and no common decision was reached at it since neither brother was able to convince more than part of the audience. So Menelaos sailed away on the following morning with half of the Greek force while the other troops remained behind with Agamemnon.[3]

Soon after their departure, Menelaos and those who had sailed with him stopped off at the island of Tenedos to offer sacrifices for their safe return. Further dissension arose at this point, and some followed the lead of Odysseus by turning their ships around and heading back towards Troy. Nothing more is revealed about the progress of this group of ships until we learn from Odysseus' own narrative later in the epic that he was blown to Thrace with twelve ships (see p. 492). Nestor and Diomedes headed for home in accordance with the original plan, initially sailing south down the Asian coast; and they were closely followed by Menelaos, who caught up with them at Lesbos. They then sailed directly across the Aegean to Euboea, stopping off at its southern tip to offer sacrifices to Poseidon for their safe passage. Diomedes arrived home safely in Argos on the fourth day of the voyage, while Nestor continued on his way around the southern tip of the Peloponnese, benefiting from favourable winds until he reached his city of Pylos on the west coast.[4]

Menelaos is driven to Egypt and remains in the area for eight years

Menelaos parted from the others soon after leaving Euboea, for his steersman Phrontis suddenly died as the fleet was approaching the southern tip of Attica, and he was therefore obliged to call in at the coast to bury him. When he resumed the voyage, he was struck by a violent storm off Cape Malea at the south-eastern corner of the Peloponnese, and his squadron of ships was split into two. Although some of his ships were wrecked on Crete, Menelaos himself was driven all the way to Egypt with the five surviving ships, and remained in that region for eight years, amassing quantities of treasure.[5] As he recounts to Telemachos in the *Odyssey*, he had a curious adventure when he finally decided to sail home to Sparta. As he was trying to set out to sea, he was becalmed for twenty days at Pharos, a small island off the Nile delta, until he and his men ran out of supplies and were reduced to catching fish, the very last resort for a Greek warrior. In the end, however, the sea-nymph Eidothea took pity on him and told him to lie in wait for her father Proteus, the old man of the sea, who would be able to provide the advice that he needed. She guided him and three of his companions to the cave in which Proteus used to take his noon-tide siesta among his herds of seals; and she disguised them by wrapping them in freshly cut seal-skins, placing a dab of ambrosia under their noses to counteract the vile stench. They were thus able to catch Proteus by surprise, and they kept a firm grip on him even though he tried to escape by constantly changing his shape, turning first into a lion and then into a snake, a leopard, a boar, and running water and a towering tree. When finally compelled to speak, he revealed that Menelaos and his followers had been held back because they had failed to offer the proper sacrifices to Zeus and the other gods before setting out to sea, and recommended that they should return to the Nile to rectify the omission. He was also able to tell Menelaos about the fates of Agamemnon, Aias and Odysseus, as we will see shortly. On receiving the offerings that were due to them, the gods granted a fair wind to Menelaos to carry him swiftly home; and he arrived to learn that the murder of Agamemnon had just been avenged by his son Orestes.[6]

Although we are told that Menelaos lingered in foreign parts for almost as long as Odysseus, wandering through Cyprus and Phoenicia and visiting the Ethiopians and Libyans and other peoples of strange speech, Homer has no specific adventures to report for him until the time of his departure; these long years are essentially a blank.[7] The tale of his wanderings was evidently invented (quite possibly by Homer himself) for a single purpose, to keep him out of the way until the cycle of vengeance had been completed within his brother's family; for it would otherwise have been hard to explain why Menelaos himself should have failed to take any action over the murder of his brother and the usurpation of the Mycenaean throne.

It hardly needs saying that Menelaos was accompanied on his travels by Helen, his newly recovered wife. The *Odyssey* refers to various gifts that were received by her during her stay in Egypt, notably some wonder-working drugs and a silver work-basket that ran on wheels.[8] As has been mentioned (see p. 445), there were unorthodox versions of her legend in which she remained in Egypt during the war while a phantom of her accompanied Paris to Troy; in that case, Menelaos was reunited with the true Helen when he visited Egypt after the war, recovering her from Proteus, king of Egypt, or from his violent son and successor Theoklymenos.[9]

According to a Hellenistic legend, the helmsman of Menelaos during the voyage to Egypt was a certain KANOPOS (or Kanobos), who was appointed to this post after the death of Phrontis (see above); he was the eponym of the city of the same name at the Kanopic mouth of the Nile. While he was in Egypt, Theonoe, the daughter of the king, conceived an un-requited passion for him; and when he died from a snake-bite at the mouth of the Nile as he and his comrades were preparing to sail home, Menelaos and Helen had him buried at the site of the city that bore his name.[10] The name Kanopos was also conferred on a brilliant star in the southern sky (alpha Carinae), which was not visible from the Greek mainland but would rise above the horizon as ships sailed south to Egypt; there was apparently an astral myth in which Kanopos was raised to the sky to become this star after his death.[11]

Agamemnon's section of the fleet is struck by a great storm; the death of the lesser Aias; Nauplios the wrecker

Although Menelaos and Nestor could obviously have had no direct knowledge of how Agamemnon's section of the fleet had fared at sea, Menelaos was able to report the essentials to Telemachos because he had questioned Proteus about the matter. The old man of the sea, who was something of a seer like other sea-gods of his kind, had declared that only two of the Greek chieftains had perished since leaving Troy, the lesser Aias out at sea and Agamemnon in his homeland; for Aias had been shipwrecked and killed by Poseidon, and Agamemnon had been murdered as soon as he had arrived in the Argolid. With regard to Aias, Proteus had explained that Poseidon had driven him on to the Gyraian Rocks (of uncertain location, see below), but had saved him from the sea afterwards; he would therefore have survived if he had not foolishly boasted that he had escaped against the will of the gods, gravely angering Poseidon, who had reached for his trident and had split the rock on which he was standing, causing him to be thrown into the sea and drowned.[12] As for Agamemnon, he had escaped the dangers of the sea through the protection of Hera, but had been murdered by his wife's lover, Aigisthos, after setting foot on his native soil.[13] Proteus also revealed that Odysseus was still alive, even though he had lost all his companions, and was detained for the present on the island of Kalypso (see p. 497).[14] Nestor for his part was able to inform Telemachos that he had heard news of the safe returns of Neoptolemos, Philoktetes and Idomoneus (all of whom had apparently sailed with Agamemnon).[15]

It is not clear from the *Odyssey* whether all the Greeks who had sailed off with Agamemnon were imperilled by a great storm, as was certainly the case in the *Returns*. In the latter epic, the ghost of Achilles appeared to Agamemnon and the others as they were sailing away from Troy, and tried to hold the fleet back by fore-telling what would befall them (evidently a storm that would be sent against them as a result of the anger of Athena). The storm descended on them at the Kapherides Rocks, causing the death of the lesser Aias. This bare outline is all that is recorded in the surviving summary of the poem.[16] The rocks were located at Cape Kaphareus at the southern tip of Euboea (the long island that skirts the east coast of Central Greece). According to subsequent sources, the seafarer Nauplios, who had been embittered against the Greeks ever since his son Palamedes had been unjustly killed at Troy (see pp. 459–60), took advantage of the storm to lure many ships to their destruction. He achieved this by lighting beacon-fires on the headland, causing the sailors to steer towards them in the belief that they were being guided to a safe haven, and so run ashore on the rocks. Cape Kaphareus was notorious as a hazard to shipping in any case, as is witnessed in its later name of Xylophagos, 'Eater of Timber'.[17] Although Sophocles and Euripides are the earliest authors who are definitely known to have referred to Nauplios' activities as a wrecker, it is at least possible that he already figured in that role in the *Returns*, since the epic is known to have referred to him in some context, and it located the storm at the appropriate place.[18]

The location of the Gyraian Rocks, where the lesser Aias is said to have met his death in the *Odyssey*,[19] was disputed in later tradition, for some authors placed them at Cape Kaphareus in Euboea while others claimed that they lay further south in one of the smaller islands, either Mykonos or Tenos. Later accounts of the progress of the storm and destruction vary accordingly, since Aias would have been killed in the course of the general disaster if he died off Euboea, but must have been killed before or after the mass of the fleet was most gravely imperilled if he died further south among the smaller Aegean islands. Hyginus brings all the events together, stating that the gods sent a storm against the Greeks at the Kapharean Rocks because they had despoiled the shrines of the gods, and that Aias was struck dead there by Athena in the course of the storm.[20] Apollodorus recounts on the other hand that Zeus sent the storm at the request of Athena while the fleet was off Tenos in the southern Aegean; and although Aias perished at that point after his ship was destroyed by a thunderbolt, the rest of the fleet was driven on towards Euboea, where many ships were lured on to Cape Kaphareus by a false beacon kindled by Nauplios.[21] There were also versions that reversed this order of events by stating that the storm struck the fleet off Euboea, causing the usual destruction, while Aias was killed somewhat later after being driven southward to the islands.[22]

Athena was often said to have hurled a thunderbolt at Aias or his ship, or at the Greek ships in general, even though this was not a customary weapon of hers; she borrowed it for the specific purpose from her father Zeus.[23] According to Apollodorus, Aias escaped on to a rock after his ship was shattered by the thunderbolt, but proceeded to boast about his good fortune (much as in the *Odyssey*), saying that he had survived against the will of Athena. Poseidon was so angered by his presumption that he split the rock with his trident, causing him to be propelled into the sea and drowned; and his body was cast ashore on Mykonos, where it was discovered and buried by Thetis.[24] Or in a slightly different account, it was washed ashore and buried by the goddess on the neighbouring island of Delos (which was normally too holy for human burials).[25] The malevolent activities of Nauplios figure in most narratives; Hyginus even suggests that he killed the survivors who managed to swim to the shore.[26] Awkward though this subject may seem for a dramatist, Sophocles portrayed the revenge of Nauplios in a lost play called *Nauplios the Fire-Kindler* (*Nauplios Pyrkaios*).

Even though many ships were supposed to have been wrecked as a result of the storm and also (in the post-epic tradition at least) of the treachery of Nauplios, the victims are anonymous almost without exception. The only hero of any significance to be named as having been killed off Euboea is Meges, son of Phyleus, a grandson of Augeias who led the men of Doulichion and the Echinadian Islands to Troy. In addition to Meges, who makes a few minor appearances in the *Iliad*, two lesser victims are sometimes cited from among the leaders who are listed in the second book of the epic, namely Gouneus from Epirus and Prothoos from Magnesia (although they both settled in Libya in another account).[27] It would seem that the myth of the great storm was elaborated at a relatively late period when it was already firmly established that most of the major heroes had arrived home safely.

In the early epic tradition, the returning heroes would doubtless have resumed their normal lives after arriving home from the war; with the exception of Odysseus and Menelaos, indeed, none of the chieftains were even said to have been driven far off course on the way. There are nevertheless many aetiological legends of younger origin in which greater and lesser heroes alike are said to have gone abroad to found new cities in distant parts, either because they were blown off course while trying to sail home or because they met with trouble on arriving home. Although any detailed consideration of mythology of this kind would take us far out of our way, it may be worthwhile to consider by way of example how Diomedes and Philoktetes, two notable heroes who are stated to have made a safe return in the *Odyssey*,[28] came to end up in Italy in Hellenistic and later accounts.

To explain why Diomedes should have met with trouble when he arrived home in Argos, some authors added an epilogue to the well-known story in the *Iliad* in which he is said to have wounded Aphrodite in battle at Troy (see p. 461);[29] for it was suggested that the goddess of love exacted revenge on him by inciting his wife Aigialeia to commit adultery with other men, and finally to desert him for Kometes, son of Sthenelos (a minor member of the Argive royal family, see p. 334). The guilty couple tried to kill Diomedes on his return, much as in the more ancient myth of Agamemnon and Klytaimnestra; but he escaped by taking sanctuary at the altar of Athena (or Hera) and then fleeing abroad to Italy.[30] In another version of the story, the embittered Nauplios sailed to Argos to turn Aigialeia against her husband. He was sometimes said to have also incited the infidelity of Klytaimnestra and to have persuaded the wife of Idomeneus to take a lover; the surviving sources fail to explain how he set about this delicate task.[31]

When Diomedes arrived in Apulia in south-east Italy, the local ruler Daunus (Daunos or Daunios in Greek) offered him his daughter and a share of the kingdom if he would help him in a war against the neighbouring Messapians (Calabrians).[32] Various towns were said to have been founded in the region by Diomedes thereafter, including Canusium, Sipontum and Argyripa (Arpi, supposedly called Argos Hippion, i.e. Argos of the Horses, at the time of its founding).[33] He offers some personal reflections on his past experiences in the *Aeneid* when some Italian envoys visit him at Argyripa in the vain hope of enlisting his support against Aeneas.[34] The most memorable feature of his Italian legend is the lore associated with the birds of Diomedes. The island of Diomedeia off the Apulian coast, where the hero was supposedly buried, was said to be inhabited by some remarkable birds which were friendly to Greek visitors but would attack any foreigner who set foot on the island; they tended the tomb of Diomedes, furthermore, by sprinkling it with fresh water every day. Although it was agreed that these birds were the transformed companions of Diomedes (or the descendants of them), divergent accounts were offered of the circumstances of their transformation. In a Hellenistic version recorded by Antoninus (probably from Nicander), they were transformed at the will of Zeus, who took pity on them after they were murdered by some Illyrians who coveted their land. This would explain why they were so hostile to foreigners.[35] Or in some Latin accounts, the transformation was a punishment imposed by Aphrodite, either because their leader had wounded her long ago or because some of them had abused her for having persecuted him afterwards.[36] Or else they were transformed, presumably by some god in pity, after they were shipwrecked on the island and Diomedes was treacherously killed there by Aineias.[37] Or they were transformed by Athena after Diomedes was treacherously killed by Daunus or a son of his.[38]

The great archer Philoktetes also acquired an Italian legend. Although Sophocles still indicates a happy return for him in the *Philoktetes*,[39] which was first performed in 409 BC, he is said to have been diverted to lower Italy in subsequent sources, either because he was blown off course during his return voyage or because he was greeted with a revolt when he arrived home in southern Thessaly.[40] He was credited with having founded four towns in his new homeland in the toe of Italy, namely Petilia, Krimissa, Makalla and Chone,[41] all of them thoroughly insignificant places (as is characteristic of the foundations that were ascribed to Greek heroes in the Italian west, see p. 580). Now that his wanderings were over and done with, he raised a temple to Apollo Aleios (the Wanderer) at Krimissa and hung his great bow in it as a dedication to the god; or in other accounts, he dedicated his bow in the sanctuary of Apollo at Thurii or at Makalla (from where it was later taken to Kroton).[42] Other relics of the kind could be seen in that part of the world; at the little town of Lageria, for instance, between Thurii and Metapontum, visitors could see the tools that had been used by Epeios (its supposed founder) when constructing the Wooden Horse.[43] Another notable hero who was transferred to the Italian west in the later tradition was Idomoneus, king of Crete; but the tales that were invented to account for his exile (see p. 355) are more interesting than anything that is recorded of his subsequent life.

The adventures of Kalchas and other Greeks who travelled overland within Asia Minor

We must now consider the adventures of some heroes who travelled away by land after the fall of Troy. Two groups are mentioned as having done so in the *Returns*, firstly the seer Kalchas and some companions who travelled south in Asia Minor, and then Neoptolemos and his party who set off by land for north-western Greece.

KALCHAS and some of his comrades left their ships at Troy and made their way to the city of Kolophon, about half-way down the coast, setting off just before the departure of Agamemnon. According to our summary of the *Returns*, he was accompanied by Leonteus and Polypoites[44] (who had been the leaders of the Lapiths during the war, see p. 556); and some later sources add the names of Podaleirios, son of Asklepios, and Amphilochos, son of Amphiaraos.[45] It was said that they decided to make this land journey either because their ships were no longer seaworthy or because Kalchas could foretell by his own divinatory powers that danger awaited the fleet at sea.[46] After arriving in Kolophon, Kalchas and his companions were entertained by another celebrated seer, MOPSOS, who was a grandson of the great Theban seer Teiresias (see p. 331). Before long, however, the two seers quarrelled over the art of divination and challenged one another to a contest, a risky enterprise for Kalchas because he had been warned by an oracle that he would die if he ever met a better diviner than himself. In Apollodorus' account of the story, Kalchas started the contest by posing a question to Mopsos, who was asked to say how many figs were growing on a fig-tree nearby. He replied that there were ten thousand, or a bushel by volume with a single fig left over, which turned out to be correct; but when Mopsos then asked Kalchas to tell him how many piglets a certain sow was carrying, Kalchas replied incorrectly that there were eight, and Mopsos was able to correct him in advance by foretelling that the sow would give birth to nine piglets, all of them male, at the sixth hour on the following day. Kalchas was so distraught when this turned out to be correct that he died or took his own life.[47]

This is apparently a composite version put together from two earlier accounts in which Kalchas posed a single question to Mopsos; a similar pattern can be observed in the account offered by the Hellenistic poet Lycophron. In a Hesiodic account, probably from the *Melampodeia*, Kalchas died after Mopsos was found to have given the correct answer to the question of the figs;[48] while in another early version ascribed to Pherecydes, Kalchas died after Mopsos replied correctly to the question about the piglets (in this case by saying that the sow would give birth to three piglets, one of them female).[49]

According to a wholly different account, a rivalry developed between Kalchas and Mopsos over the possession of the oracle of Apollo at Klaros (near Kolophon, see p. 331), and matters came to a head when Mopsos predicted defeat for Amphimachos, king of Lydia, in a forth-coming war, while Kalchas urged the king on with a prediction of victory. When the king was then defeated, Mopsos came to be honoured all the more highly and Kalchas committed suicide.[50] Proclus' summary of the *Returns* states, rather surprisingly, that Teiresias died at Kolophon and was buried there by Kalchas' party (but Teiresias' name may well have been substituted for that of Kalchas by error).[51]

After the death of Kalchas, his companions dispersed in various directions. Polypoites and Leonteus travelled eastward to settle in the land of the Medes, or else returned to Troy and sailed home to Thessaly.[52] Podaleirios visited the Delphic oracle to ask where he should settle, and was advised to make his home in a place where he would suffer no harm if the sky fell in; and he therefore settled at Syreon in the Carian Chersonnese, a place that was encircled by tall mountains on every side.[53] And finally, AMPHILOCHOS, who was a seer like so many descendants of Melampous (see p. 429), joined together with Mopsos to found a joint oracle at Mallos in Cilicia, in the south-eastern corner of Asia Minor. Although Amphilochos decided to sail home after a time, the situation there proved unsatisfactory and he returned to Mallos a year later to reclaim his original position; but he found that Mopsos was unwilling to accept him back, and each caused the death of the other when they tried to settle the matter by single combat. They worked together happily enough during their posthumous existence nonetheless, continuing to deliver prophecies at their joint oracle, which was highly regarded in Hellenistic times.[54] Another tradition suggested that Amphilochos founded Amphilochian Argos after the Trojan War, a city on the Ambracian Gulf in southern Epirus.[55]

Neoptolemos travels overland to Epirus with Helenos and Andromache; his marriage and early death

NEOPTOLEMOS, the young son of Achilles, was usually said to have avoided the dangers of the sea-crossing. According to the *Returns*, he travelled overland on the advice of his grandmother Thetis, crossing over to northern Greece by way of Thrace; he encountered Odysseus in south-western Thrace in the course of his journey, at the coastal town of Maroneia (see p. 489), and buried his father's aged tutor Phoinix when he died on the way. Instead of travelling to his father's homeland in Thessaly (which he had never seen because he had been reared on Skyros, the home-island of his mother, see p. 458), he settled in the north-west in the land of the Molossians in Epirus.[56] Apollodorus adds two further details which may well have come from the early epic tradition, stating that Neoptolemos sailed with Agamemnon's section of the fleet as far as Tenedos, but delayed on the island at the urging of Thetis when the others resumed their voyage, and waited there for two days before continuing his journey by the land-route; in this account, furthermore, as in most others, he was accompanied by two notable Trojans, namely Andromache, the widow of Hektor, who had been assigned to him during the division of the spoils, and the seer Helenos, a son of Priam who had fallen out with his fellow Trojans (see p. 471).[57] Although most post-Homeric sources accept that he settled in Epirus, he is occasionally said to have travelled part or all of the way by sea, either sailing across to Thessaly, where he burned his ships on the advice of Thetis before proceeding overland to Epirus,[58] or else wandering far off course to Epirus as he was attempting to sail to his birthplace on Skyros.[59]

By defeating the local people in battle, Neoptolemos won a kingdom for himself in Epirus, and settled there with Andromache as his concubine; she bore him a son, Molossos, who later succeeded to the throne and gave his name to his subjects, the Molossians.[60] Although Neoptolemos also had a legitimate wife, Hermione, the daughter of Menelaos and Helen, it was commonly agreed that she bore him no children. According to the *Odyssey*, Menelaos had promised her to him at Troy, and sent her to him in the city of the Myrmidons (i.e. Phthia, the home of Peleus and Achilles in Thessaly) after returning from the war;[61] but she was usually thought to have lived with him in Epirus in the subsequent tradition. In many accounts from the classical period onwards, she had already been given or promised to Orestes while Menelaos was away at Troy, and conflict thus arose between Orestes and Neoptolemos when the latter claimed his bride after the end of the war (see further on pp. 514–5).

Neoptolemos' grandfather Peleus was still alive at the end of the Trojan War. The Homeric epics indicate that the aged king of Phthia was in a sadly vulnerable position while his only son Achilles was away at Troy,[62] and some later sources claim that Akastos or the sons of Akastos expelled him from his kingdom after the death of Achilles. Akastos and his family certainly had good reason to hate him since he had sacked their city of Iolkos (see p. 534 for the circumstances). In one account, Peleus tried to find his way to Neoptolemos after he was expelled by Archandros and Architeles, the two sons of Akastos, but was driven by a storm to the island of Kos, where he was sheltered by a certain Molos until his death.[63] Our summary of the *Returns* states without further explanation that Neoptolemos was acknowledged by his grandfather after reaching the land of the Molossians; we should perhaps assume that Peleus travelled there to seek his grandson after being expelled from his kingdom.

A late source, Dictys, provides an interesting narrative which may have originated in tragedy, saying that Neoptolemos sailed over from Molossia to help his grandfather after hearing of his expulsion, and found him hiding in a cave on the Sepiades, a group of islands to the west of southern Thessaly. Neoptolemos ambushed and killed the sons of Akastos, here named Menalippos and Pleisthenes, when they visited the islands on a hunting-trip; and he then lured Akastos to the cave by disguising himself as a Trojan captive and telling him that Neoptolemos was lying there unguarded. Thetis intervened, however, to prevent Neoptolemos from killing Akastos; and after this narrow escape, Akastos agreed to surrender all claim to the kingdom of Peleus. So Neoptolemos went off to reclaim it in the company of his father and grandmother Thetis.[64] It was not often suggested that Neoptolemos himself came to rule in Phthia.[65] In some accounts, as we will see (p. 534), Peleus killed Akastos before the Trojan War while sacking his city of Iolkos.

Although varying accounts were offered of the precise course of events, it was commonly agreed that Neoptolemos met a violent death at Delphi before many years had passed. Three main versions of his death-story can be distinguished, stating either that he was killed in a quarrel over the sacrifices, or that he provoked his own death by demanding reparation from Apollo for the death of his father, or that Orestes murdered him or arranged his murder because he was angry at having lost Hermione to him.

(*i*) According to Pindar, Neoptolemos visited Delphi to dedicate some of the finest of the Trojan spoils to Apollo, but became embroiled in a quarrel over the meat from the sacrifices and met his death as a consequence. As the scholia explain, he objected to the traditional practice by which the temple attendants kept most of the meat for themselves.[66] The Delphian who killed him was sometimes said to have been a certain Machaireus (Knife-man), son of Daïtes (Divider or Apportioner), whose name refers to the special knife or *machaira* that the priests would use to divide the meat. Such a knife would have been well-fitted to serve as a murder-weapon if a dispute over the meat had turned violent; Pindar mentions that Neoptolemos was killed with a *machaira* (and may perhaps have intended that his audience should recall the name of the killer from this).[67] In a somewhat different account from another poem, Pindar states that Apollo had planned an early death for Neoptolemos because of the manner in which he had killed Priam (i.e. at an altar of Zeus, see p. 476), and therefore slew him in his sacred precinct while he was quarrelling with the temple attendants.[68] According to Pherecydes, Neoptolemos visited Delphi to consult the oracle about his childless marriage, but was moved to anger when he saw the Delphians removing meat from the sanctuary and tried to take it away from them; although the surviving quotation goes on to state that the hero killed himself with a *machaira*, the text is surely corrupt, and we can safely assume that he would have been killed by a Delphian as usual.[69]

(*ii*) Some accounts claim that Neoptolemos went to Delphi to seek reparation from Apollo for having killed or helped to kill his father Achilles at Troy (see p. 468 for the circumstances). When he proceeded to plunder the temple or even set fire to it, he was killed by the temple attendants, or by Machaireus specifically, or by Apollo himself.[70]

(*iii*) In other accounts, Orestes killed Neoptolemos at Delphi, or at least arranged for him to be killed there because he was angry at having lost his wife Hermione to him (see pp. 514–15 for the circumstances). This version first appears in Euripides' *Andromache*, and it is quite possible that Euripides was responsible for its invention; it was probably not very old in any case.[71] In this play, incidentally, Hermione had not previously been married to Orestes although she had been promised to him; see p. 515 for a summary of the plot and for other accounts.

Neoptolemos was honoured in hero-cult at his Delphian tomb, which could be seen in the precinct of Apollo if one turned to the left after leaving the temple. Pindar indicates that his death was divinely ordained because he was destined to watch over the ceremonies at the shrine. He was supposed to have come to the assistance of the Delphians when they were attacked by the Gauls in 279 BC.[72]

THE WANDERINGS OF ODYSSEUS AND HIS LATER LIFE

Odysseus wanders through distant seas for ten years

Odysseus was driven far off course and wandered the seas for ten years before finally rejoining his wife Penelope in his native Ithaca; we will follow his adventures as they are described in the *Odyssey*, marking each successive landfall. (*i*) According to Nestor's account of the Greek returns in the *Odyssey*, Odysseus initially set off with Menelaos' section of the fleet, but parted with it as a result of unspecified disagreements when it called in at the island of Tenedos nearby (see p. 483), and headed back towards Troy with his followers.[73] (*ii*) Odysseus mentions nothing of this in his own narrative, merely stating that the wind bore him from Troy to Ismaros, a town of the CICONIANS (Kikones) in south-western Thrace. At the outset, he had twelve ships under his command. He launched a frankly piratical raid on Ismaros, and captured the women of the city and quantities of treasure; but when his men insisted on delaying to feast and drink, the Ciconians of the surrounding area gathered to make a counter-attack, and expelled the Greeks, causing many losses.[74] During the sack of the city, Odysseus protected MARON, son of Euanthos, the local priest of Apollo, along with his wife and child; and Maron repaid him by giving him some treasure and twelve jars of sweet wine,[75] which would prove invaluable, as we will see shortly, when his own life came under threat from the Kyklops Polyphemos. (*iii*) After leaving the land of the Ciconians, Odysseus and his followers were driven southwards for two days and nights to Cape Malea at the south-eastern tip of the Peloponnese; and as they were trying to sail round the cape to make for Ithaca (off the west coast of mainland Greece), they were caught by the savage North Wind and were driven across the sea for nine days and nights to the land of the LOTOS-EATERS. As with all the places visited by Odysseus during his more distant wanderings, their land is located in a purely mythical realm in Homer's account, even if later tradition placed it on the Libyan coast.[76] When Odysseus sent some of his men to investigate, the Lotos-eaters received them graciously and offered them some of their lotos-fruit, which caused those who ate it to forget their homecoming and friends and to desire nothing more than to sit there chewing the honey-sweet fruit. On discovering what had happened to them, Odysseus dragged them back to their ships by force and made a hasty departure.[77]

(*iv*) From there he sailed on to the land of the KYKLOPES, who were a race of giants with a single eye in the middle of their forehead. Leaving the other ships and their crews at an uninhabited island not far off the coast, he went exploring with his own crew, entered the deserted cave of a Kyklops called POLYPHEMOS, and gazed at the many crates of cheese and pens crowded with lambs and kids that filled the cave. Against all the advice of his comrades, who urged him to steal some provisions and hurry away, Odysseus insisted that they should wait until the owner returned, for he was curious to see what he was like and hoped to receive gifts of hospitality. After driving his flocks into the cave, Polyphemos blocked up the entrance with a huge rock; and on discovering the strangers, he demonstrated his notion of hospitality by dashing out the brains of two of them and eating their flesh

Figure 14.1   Odysseus tied to the belly of a ram. Bronze group,
sixth century BC. Delphi Museum.

for his supper. In the morning, he breakfasted in the same way and then drove his
flocks to pasture, pushing the rock back afterwards to leave the men imprisoned.
Odysseus now had time to devise a means of vengeance. To kill the giant as he
slept would achieve nothing, for he and his comrades would be unable to shift the
rock; so he sharpened a stake and hardened its end in the fire to procure a weapon
for use against the Kyklops, and on that evening, when Polyphemos had supped on
two more of his men, gave him a draught of some very powerful wine that he had
received from Maron at Ismaros. Having made him very drunk by this means, he
and his men heated the end of the stake and used it to gouge out the single eye of
their jailer. Polyphemos cried out to his fellow Kyklopes, who lived on the heights
around, and they came rushing from every side to investigate. Odysseus had prepared
for this eventuality, however, by telling Polyphemos that his name was Nobody
(*Outis*); so when the Kyklopes asked him what the trouble was, and he replied from
inside that 'Nobody' was attacking him, they went away again, supposing that he
must simply be ill if nobody was causing him any harm. In the morning, when
Polyphemos opened the cave to let out his sheep and goats, Odysseus and his men
escaped with them, each of the men tied to the underside of a ram, and Odysseus
clinging to the belly of the largest ram of all.[78] While sailing off in his ship,
Odysseus taunted the Kyklops in the heedlessness of his triumph, and revealed his
true name. Polyphemos responded by hurling two huge stones at the ship, which
narrowly escaped destruction, and then praying to his father Poseidon to take action
against the newly identified Odysseus. He prayed that Odysseus should never reach
home, or if he was fated to do so, that he should arrive home late after losing all
his comrades and find trouble awaiting him in his house.[79]

(*v*) After his encounter with the Kyklopes, Odysseus made a happier landfall at
Aiolia, the island of AIOLOS, ruler of the winds, who entertained him and his men
without stint for a full month. Each of the six sons of Aiolos was married to one
of his six daughters, and all of them lived together at the palace with their father

493

and mother, feasting continually day after day. His kingdom is a purely mythical place in the *Odyssey*, a floating island surrounded by cliffs of unyielding bronze; but it came to be suggested in the later tradition that he lived on one of the Aeolian (Lipari) Islands to the north of Sicily. He finally helped Odysseus on his way by enclosing all but one of the winds in a leather bag and attaching it to his ship, so that only the gentle west wind was left to blow him safely home. When Ithaca came within sight and there seemed no further occasion for worry, Odysseus fell asleep after his long exertions at the helm, and his men took advantage of this to investigate the contents of the bag, supposing that it contained gifts of silver and gold that he was intending to keep for himself; but as soon as they opened it up, the winds rushed out and blew them straight back to their starting-point. Aiolos turned Odysseus away without further help, saying that it would be wrong for him to offer assistance to a man who was evidently hated by the gods.[80]

(*vi*) After six days on the high seas, the voyagers reached the land of the LAISTRY-GONIANS (Laistrygones), a race of cannibal giants. When three of the crew were sent ashore to investigate, they ran across the daughter of the king as she was fetching water, and she took them to the palace; the queen, who was as large as a mountain, summoned her husband Antiphates, who seized one of the men for his supper while the others fled to the ships. Alerted by the shouts of Antiphates, the other Laistrygonians hurried to the cliffs around the harbour, sank the ships below by hurling huge boulders at them, and then speared the crewmen like fish to provide themselves with fresh meat. Odysseus and his crew alone survived because their ship was moored outside the harbour entrance.[81]

(*vii*) Odysseus' next port of call was the mythical island of Aiaie, the home of the enchantress KIRKE (Circe), who was a daughter of Helios by the Okeanid Perse (or Perseis) and the sister of Aietes.[82] Observing a column of smoke arising from Kirke's house in the forested interior, Odysseus divided his forces into two and sent one group to investigate under the command of his brother-in-law Eurylochos. On arriving at the house in the forest, they encountered lions and wolves outside which fawned on them, standing on their hind legs and wagging their tails rather than attacking them as might be expected; for these were human beings whom Kirke had transformed by means of her enchantments. Kirke seemed most friendly and invited them to drink some barley-mixture, but it contained some drugs that transformed them into pigs, although they retained their human intelligence. Eurylochos had remained outside, however, suspecting a trap, and he rushed back to Odysseus to report what had happened. As Odysseus was hurrying to the rescue, he ran across Hermes, who gave him a herb called moly to serve as a counter-charm. He was thus unaffected by Kirke's drugs, and she was so dismayed when he proceeded to threaten her with his sword that she proposed that they should settle their differences by going to bed together. She then swore not to harm him and agreed to return his comrades to their original form. In the later tradition, Kirke was said to have borne children to Odysseus, namely Telegonos (see below), Latinos and Agrios.[83] When his comrades began to grow impatient after a year on the island, he asked Kirke to allow them to continue on their way, and was alarmed to be told that he must first visit the Underworld to seek a prophecy from the ghost of Teiresias.[84]

Figure 14.2   Odysseus, tied to the mast, listens to the Sirens' song.
Red-figure stamnos from Vulci. BM 1843.11.3–31.

(*viii*) In accordance with Kirke's instructions, he sailed across the outer Ocean to a
land of gloom in the furthermost west, and arrived safely at the boundaries of Hades
(see p. 109). After pouring some blood into a trench to allow the shades to drink from
it to revive their wits, he was able to speak to many of them, including his mother
Antikleia, who had died (or perhaps killed herself) during his absence; she was
able to tell him about the state of affairs at home and about the sorrows of his ageing
father Laertes.[85] Teiresias prophesied that he would reach home in spite of the antagonism of Poseidon (who had been angered by the blinding of Polyphemos), but
warned that he would lose his comrades and ship if they harmed the cattle of Helios
on the way (see below); and he also told him that he could expect trouble at home,
since his halls were thronged with suitors who were courting his wife and wasting
his property. After killing the suitors, he should travel abroad to the mainland
(so Teiresias advised), and proceed inland with an oar until he met people who knew
nothing of the sea and mistook the oar for a winnowing-fan. He should then fix the
oar into the ground and make his peace with Poseidon by sacrificing a ram, bull and
boar to him. In the end, after all his troubles, he could expect to meet a peaceful death
among his own people in his prosperous old age.[86] Other aspects of Odysseus' visit
to the Underworld are discussed in connection with the mythology of that realm in
Chapter 4.

(*ix*) After returning to Kirke's island, Odysseus set off on his journey home, and soon had to confront some fearsome perils, forearmed with advice from Kirke.[87] He had to find his way past the SIRENS (Seirenes) first of all, female daimones who sang so enchantingly that passing sailors were lured to their island, where they apparently wasted away because they could turn their attention to nothing other than the sweet singing. Homer describes them as sitting in a meadow surrounded by the mouldering bodies of their victims. Odysseus ordered his men to stop their ears with wax, and had himself bound to the mast, giving strict orders that he should be tied all the tighter if he tried to break loose; and he was thus able to enjoy the song and yet live to tell the tale.[88]

Since nothing is stated about the outward appearance of the Sirens in the *Odyssey*, Homer may have imagined them as being like human women in form. In the subsequent literature, however, and in the visual arts from the time of the earliest representations in the sixth century BC, they are commonly pictured as Harpy-like creatures with the body of a bird and head of a woman. There are generally three of them, though only two in the *Odyssey*, and they are usually said to have been children of the river-god Acheloos by one or other of the Muses.[89]

According to a tradition that first appears in Apollonius' *Argonautica*, they had once been servants or companions of the young Persephone.[90] Transformation myths were devised in this connection to explain their peculiar form. Ovid states that they were originally human in form, but prayed to be furnished with wings while they were searching for the abducted Persephone, to enable them to extend their search over the seas also.[91] Or in Hyginus' version, this was apparently a punishment that was imposed on them by Demeter because they had failed to come to the aid of Persephone.[92] There was also a wholly different story in which they were transformed by Aphrodite because they had scorned the joys of love.[93]

The Hellenistic poet Lycophron is the first to report that they were fated to hurl themselves into the sea if anyone should survive after hearing their singing, as did Odysseus.[94] Local traditions in western Italy claimed that their bodies were washed ashore on different parts of the coast from Naples southwards.[95] The Siren Parthenope, who was supposedly washed ashore at Naples, had a most interesting cult there and an annual festival in which she was honoured with torch-races.[96]

See p. 395 for the Argonauts' encounter with the Sirens, which is set at an earlier period in mythical history. There is also a strange story in which Hera persuaded them to engage in a singing-contest with the Muses (see p. 207), who celebrated their victory by plucking out the Sirens' feathers to make crowns for themselves.[97]

Odysseus had learned from Kirke that he would have to choose between two possible routes after passing the Sirens, for he could either face the hazard of the Planktai (Wandering Rocks) or try to make a safe passage through the narrow straits between the monstrous SKYLLA and the whirlpool CHARYBDIS; but since Kirke had warned him that only a single ship, the *Argo*, had ever survived the Planktai, and then only with the help of the Nereids (see p. 395), he was bound to select the latter route.[98] Preferring to lose a few of his men to Skylla than to face the risk of having his ship sucked into the whirlpool crew and all, Odysseus steered closer to Skylla than to Charybdis. The six-headed monster, who lived in a cave in the side of a cliff, duly reached out to snatch away six men, but the rest of the crew survived unscathed.[99]

In Homer's description, Skylla had twelve legs and six long necks, each ending in a frightful head with three rows of teeth; the lower part of her body was concealed inside her cave, but she would reach out with her necks to seize dolphins or seals, or sailors from passing ships.[100] Later tradition suggested that she lived in a cave in the Straits of Messina, the narrow channel that separates Italy from Sicily, although rationalizers were eager to explain away this sailor's yarn by alleging that a whirlpool, rock or other natural danger of the area lay behind it.[101] She is usually depicted in works of art with a woman's upper body and head, and a lower body formed from one or two fish-tails or dragon-tails, and often with the fore-parts of one or more dogs springing from her hips. Late authors explain her monstrous form through transformation stories. On learning that Poseidon had embarked on a love affair with Skylla (here described as a daughter of Phorkys), his wife Amphitrite sprinkled magic herbs into her bathing-place, causing her to be transformed from a beautiful nymph into a many-headed monster.[102] Or in Ovid's version, the sea-god Glaukos fell in love with Skylla, and sought the help of the enchantress Kirke when she failed to respond; but Kirke herself promptly fell in love with Glaukos, and was so jealous when he reaffirmed his love for Skylla that she transformed her into a monster by sprinkling her bathing-place with herbs and chanting magical spells.[103]

(x) The voyagers arrived next at the island of THRINACIA (Thrinakie), where the cattle and sheep of the sun-god Helios were pastured under the care of his daughters Phaethousa and Lampetie. Having received warnings on the matter from both Teiresias and Kirke, Odysseus made his men swear that they would on no account slaughter any of the god's cattle or sheep; but when they ran short of food after being held back on the island for a full month by adverse winds, they killed some of the cattle without the knowledge of their leader, while he was in another part of the island praying to the gods for help. Lampetie reported the theft to her father Helios, who complained in his turn to Zeus; and Zeus struck Odysseus' ship with a thunderbolt as it was sailing away from the island, causing the entire crew to be killed apart from Odysseus himself.[104]

(xi) While making his way to safety as best he could on a raft constructed from the wreckage, Odysseus was almost sucked into Charybdis, but survived to be washed ashore on the island of KALYPSO nine days afterwards.[105] Kalypso, who is described as a daughter of Atlas, was a minor goddess who lived all on her own on the island of Ogygia. She was delighted by the handsome stranger and detained him on her island as her lover for seven long years; but although she offered to make him immortal and ageless, he yearned for his wife and his native land and grew ever more sorrowful. Athena finally intervened with the gods on his behalf, prompting Zeus to send Hermes to Kalypso to order his release. She consented, though with a heavy heart, and helped him on his way by furnishing him with tools and materials to enable him to build a large boat.[106]

(xii) Odysseus sailed over the sea for nineteen days until he came within sight of Scherie, the land of the PHAEACIANS (Phaiakes), on the eighteenth; but before he could draw into the coast, his enemy Poseidon, who had been away feasting with the Ethiopians, caught sight of his boat and realized that the gods must have acted to help him. So the god set to work to reverse his good fortune, by raising a mighty storm to wreck his boat (see further on p. 100). His plight was observed, however, by the sea-goddess Leukothea (formerly Ino, see p. 421), who felt pity for him and lent him her divine veil (*krēdemnon*), telling him that he would be saved from drowning if he tied it around his chest. After two days and nights in the water, he managed to crawl ashore by the mouth of a river in Scherie, weakened and exhausted but alive. As soon as he had dropped the veil back into the water to allow Leukothea to recover it, he lay down under some bushes nearby and fell asleep.[107]

On the next morning, NAUSIKAA, the daughter of ALKINOOS, king of the Phaeacians, came to the river-mouth with her maids to wash the clothes of the household. Odysseus was awakened by them as they were playing a ball-game afterwards, and emerged from the bushes to investigate, naked and salt-streaked, hastily breaking off a leafy branch to hold in front of him. Nausikaa stood to face him as all her maidens fled, and responded sympathetically when he explained his troubles and asked for help. After providing him with clothes and refreshment, she guided him to the city and advised that he should appeal as a suppliant to her mother ARETE, who was greatly honoured by the king and the people alike.[108] The king and queen welcomed him into their palace, and at a great banquet on the following day, the whole company listened with hushed interest as Odysseus recounted the story of his adventures; we learn most of what we know about his wanderings from his own narrative on this occasion.[109] After loading a ship with magnificent gifts and offering appropriate sacrifices, Alkinoos sent Odysseus on his way on the following evening. As the magical ship sped through the sea on its overnight journey to Ithaca, flying faster than the swiftest of birds, Odysseus slept on a rug on the deck; and he was still fast asleep when the sailors laid him ashore at the end of the journey, placing his gifts under an olive-tree nearby. When he woke up to find himself alone on the shore, he did not appreciate that he was home after his long years of wandering until he was assured of the fact by his protectress Athena.[110] Poseidon had to content himself with turning the Phaeacian ship to stone on its return, as a hint (which was duly taken) that the Phaeacians should never provide passage to mortals in such a way in the future.[111]

Odysseus exacts vengeance on the suitors after arriving home in Ithaca, and is reunited with his wife Penelope

To protect Odysseus while he made preparations for his revenge against the suitors, Athena altered his appearance to cause him to be mistaken for an old beggar, and told him to take shelter with his faithful swineherd Eumaios as she travelled over to the Peloponnese to summon his son Telemachos (who had been visiting Nestor and Menelaos to seek news of him).[112] Odysseus revealed his true identity to Telemachos on his arrival, though not yet to Eumaios, and the three of them walked to the palace on the following morning. Although the disguised king received a touching welcome from his old hound Argos, the suitors mistook him for a beggar as would be expected, and their leader, Antinoos, treated him with great brutality, hurling a stool at him and setting up a fight between him and the beggar Iros. After the suitors had taken their fill of food and drink in the evening, however, they went to their homes for the night at the urging of Telemachos, giving him and his father an opportunity to prepare for the forthcoming conflict by removing all the arms and armour from the hall and locking them away in a store-room.[113]

Figure 14.3   Penelope at her loom with Telemachos. Red-figure skyphos. Chiusi, Museo Nazionale; mus nat 1831.

By pretending that he was a brother of Idomeneus, king of Crete, and that he had entertained Odysseus on his home island shortly after the war, the disguised Odysseus won the sympathy of Penelope, who was now at her wit's end. For she had tried to put the suitors off by telling them that she would be unable to remarry until she had woven a shroud in preparation for the death of her father-in-law Laertes, and then extending the task by unravelling each day's work during the following night; but the stratagem had finally been betrayed by one of her maids, and she had now reached the end of the work. She disclosed that she was intending to announce on the next morning that she would marry the suitor who could string her husband's bow (a formidable weapon which would require immense strength to draw), and then shoot an arrow through a row of double-headed axes.[114] While the suitors were attempting this feat on the next morning, Odysseus withdrew for a while to reveal his identity to Eumaios and the cowherd Philoitios, and returned to the hall with them as the contest was drawing to an unsuccessful conclusion. Now that it had become clear that none of the suitors would be able to fulfil the demanded terms, the disguised Odysseus asked, in an apparently ingenuous fashion, to be allowed to try his hand. The objections of the suitors were brushed aside by Penelope, who thought it shameful that a stranger should be treated with discourtesy, and also by Telemachos, who was aware of his father's plan.

Penelope left the hall at the stranger's request before he set to work. He strung the bow without difficulty, performed the prescribed feat, and then shot Antinoos, the arrogant ringleader of the suitors, through the throat. The other suitors quaked with fear when he now revealed his true identity; and in the furious struggle that followed, he killed them one and all with the help of his son and his two faithful servants, and also of Athena who intervened on occasion to deflect the spears of the suitors.[115] Odysseus and his helpers then completed the task by hanging twelve disloyal servant-maids who had consorted with the suitors, and killing the goatherd Melanthios, who had helped the suitors during the fight by bringing arms from the store-room.[116] Eurykleia, an old servant-woman who had recognized the disguised Odysseus from a scar, now awakened Penelope to tell her that her husband had come back and had rid her of the suitors; and the reunited couple spent the night together on their remarkable marriage-bed, which had been constructed by Odysseus long before around the trunk of a living olive-tree.[117] Odysseus made himself known to his father Laertes on the next day, and the blood-feud that was initiated by the dead suitors was swiftly brought to an end through the intervention of Athena.[118]

Posthomeric accounts of the later life of Odysseus

Odysseus is re-established in his kingdom under auspicious circumstances at the end of the *Odyssey*, and we assume that he will live there happily ever afterwards, reunited with his faithful wife; but his story was developed further in the last epic in the Trojan cycle and in the subsequent tradition. The epic in question, the *Telegonia*, which was named after Telegonos, a son who was borne to Odysseus by Kirke, was an eccentric poem which took him abroad for further adventures and provided him with an exotic death on his return. It will be remembered that when Odysseus met Teiresias during his visit to the Underworld in the *Odyssey*, the seer instructed him to visit the mainland after killing the suitors to offer sacrifices to Poseidon; although this is plainly envisaged as a temporary visit in the Homeric account, the author of the *Telegonia* took up the story and expanded it to introduce Odysseus into a long-lasting foreign entanglement. For when he arrived in the land of the Thesprotians in north-western Greece to offer the sacrifices, the queen of the Thesprotians, Kallidike, urged him to stay and offered him the throne. So he remained and married her (apparently forgetting Penelope!), and fathered a son Polypoites by her; and he defeated a neighbouring people, the Brygoi, when they attacked the kingdom, even though they gained an initial victory owing to the support of the war-god Ares.[119]

After the death of Kallidike, Odysseus transferred his Thesprotian kingdom to Polypoites and returned to Ithaca. While he had been living with Kirke long before, she had conceived a son, TELEGONOS, to him, who had been growing up on her remote island in the mean time. On learning from his mother that he was a son of Odysseus, Telegonos decided to sail off in search of him, and arrived on the coast of Ithaca by sheer chance soon after his father had returned from Thesprotia. Having no idea where he was, he proceeded to ravage the island (or simply to plunder some cattle); and when Odysseus rushed to the defence of his kingdom and property, Telegonos inflicted a fatal wound on him without realizing who he was.[120] Telegonos wielded a most unusual weapon, a spear tipped with the needle from a sting-ray, which had been made for him by Hephaistos at the request of Kirke, using a stingray that had been caught by the sea-god Phorkys.[121] This account of the death of Odysseus seems to have been inspired by some words of Teiresias in the *Odyssey*, in which the seer predicts that death will come to him *ex halos*[122] (which could mean 'out of the sea', although it evidently means 'away from the sea' in the original context). When Telegonos discovered the identity of his victim, he was overcome by grief and sailed back to Kirke's island with his father's corpse, also bringing Penelope and Telemachos. The *Telegonia* descended into utter absurdity at this point (if it had not done so already) by concluding with a pair of weddings in which Telegonos married Penelope, his father's widow, while Kirke married Telemachos, the son of her former lover. We know from the surviving summary of the epic that Kirke conferred immortality on Telegonos, Telemachos and Penelope; and according to a further report that was probably also derived from the poem, she transferred Telegonos and Penelope to the Isles of the Blessed.[123]

Many unorthodox accounts of the final years and ultimate fate of Odysseus and Penelope are recorded from the later tradition. For a representative sample, we may turn to three stories cited by Apollodorus as variants after his summary of the events of the *Telegonia*. Odysseus sent Penelope away to her father because she had been seduced by the chief suitor Antinoos, and she bore Pan to Hermes in Arcadia on the way; or Odysseus killed her because she had been seduced by Amphinomos (another of her suitors, who is presented in the *Odyssey* as being more civilized and scrupulous than his fellows); or Odysseus was sentenced to exile for having killed the suitors, and sought refuge at the court of Thoas in Aetolia (see pp. 419–20), where he married the king's daughter and fathered a son by her.[124] Tales of this kind are really of little interest except as curiosities; it is surely better to leave Odysseus and Penelope as Homer leaves them at the end of the *Odyssey*, living peacefully together in Ithaca after a sufficiency of adventures and misadventures.

THE HISTORY OF THE PELOPIDS

While Agamemnon was away at Troy, his wife Klytaimnestra (Clytemnestra) took his cousin Aigisthos as her lover, and the two of them joined together to contrive the murder of the king on his return. As sons of Atreus and Thyestes respectively, Agamemnon and Aigisthos belonged to two different branches of the Pelopid family, which had been divided by mutual hatred ever since Atreus and Thyestes had first begun to compete by fair means or foul for the throne of Mycenae, which had been under Inachid rule until that time. The Pelopids were latecomers not only to Mycenae and the Argolid but even to the Peloponnese itself since Pelops, the father of Thyestes and Atreus, had been the first member of the family to establish himself in Greece. For he had been born far away in Asia Minor, where his father Tantalos had ruled over a corner of Lydia. Before considering Agamemnon's return and the death that awaited him in his homeland, we will trace the notoriously violent history of his family from the very beginning.

Tantalos of Lydia and his children

Pelops, the founder of the Pelopid family in Greece, was the eponym of the Peloponnese (the name of which is thus interpreted as meaning the island – i.e. peninsula – of Pelops). He ruled at Pisa in the north-western Peloponnese while his most important sons, Agamemnon and Menelaos, rose to power in Mycenae and Sparta, which had previously been ruled by Inachid (see p. 243) and Atlantid lines (see p. 524) respectively. If Pelopid rule in these centres was late established, it was also relatively short-lasting, since the return of the Heraklids fifty (or a hundred) years after the Trojan War marked the end of the family's power in the peninsula (see p. 290).

Although it may be conjectured that Pelops originated as the eponym of a Peloponnesian people of related name, presumably the Pelopes,[125] he was already regarded as an immigrant from the east in the early archaic tradition, as a son of TANTALOS, who ruled the lands around Mt Sipylos in Lydia. According to the standard tradition as first recorded by Euripides, Tantalos was a son of Zeus, and his mother is reported to have been a certain Plouto (Wealth), which seems appropriate enough for a man who was proverbial for his riches.[126] In addition to enjoying exceptional worldly wealth, he benefited from the special favour of the gods, who allowed him to mix with them on familiar terms and share in their feasts; but as we have already seen, his good fortune tempted him to presumption, and he was condemned to everlasting torment for abusing his privileges. For the different accounts of his crime, and the nature of his posthumous punishment, see pp. 117–18. He had a daughter, Niobe, who married Amphion, king of Thebes, but returned to her Asian homeland to die (see pp. 157 and 306), and two sons, the great Pelops and his far less famous brother Broteas, who remained in Asia Minor.[127]

Tantalos was sometimes credited with a further son, Daskylos, who ruled over the Mariandynians in Bithynia on the north coast of Asia Minor. Lykos, the son and successor of Daskylos, offered a friendly welcome to the Argonauts when they called in at his land during their voyage to Colchis (see p. 389). According to Apollonius, he told them how Herakles had visited his father while travelling through Asia to fetch the belt of the Amazon queen Hippolyte, and had helped him to subdue some neighbouring peoples; or in another account, Herakles performed such services for Lykos himself. Although Apollonius says nothing about the origin of this ruling line, his ancient commentators report that Daskylos was classed as a son of Tantalos in the writings of Herodorus and Nymphis (late fifth century and third century BC respectively), two authors from Herakleia Pontica, a Greek colony founded in that area in the sixth century BC.[128]

In addition to the legends already considered in which Tantalos is said to have been punished in the Underworld for a crime committed against the gods, a further tale of crime and punishment is recorded for him that differs from all the others. One of the shrines of Zeus on Crete was guarded by a golden dog, a wonderful automaton which had been fashioned by Hephaistos; and this dog was once stolen by a certain Pandareos, son of Merops, a citizen of Miletos in Asia Minor (or of the Cretan city of that name), who took it across to the Asian mainland and entrusted it to Tantalos for safe-keeping. When Hermes came to seek it out at the bidding of Zeus, Tantalos swore by Zeus and the other gods that he knew nothing of the missing dog; but Hermes discovered it in his home nonetheless, and Zeus piled Mt Sipylos on top of him to punish him for his perjury.[129] As the author of the theft, Pandareos tried to escape punishment by fleeing to Athens and thence to Sicily, together with his wife Harmothoe and his three unmarried daughters; but his flight was observed by Zeus, who killed him along with his wife and delivered his daughters to the Harpies.[130] Or in another version recorded in Antoninus' anthology of transformation myths, Zeus punished Pandareos by turning him to stone. Although it is stated here that Tantalos swore his false oath to Pandareos when he arrived to reclaim the dog, one may suspect that this is simply an error, especially since Zeus is said to have punished him for his perjury in the usual way. According to this author, Rhea had originally stationed the dog to guard the she-goat that suckled the infant Zeus at his sacred cave on Crete, and Zeus had later appointed it to be the guardian of the cave.[131]

Very little is recorded of BROTEAS, son of Tantalos. An ancient image of the Mother of the Gods on the side of Mt Sipylos (which still survives and was actually of Hittite origin) was identified in the local tradition as the work of Broteas. Apollodorus' account of his death is preserved only in a rather poor summary, which states that he failed to honour Artemis and claimed that even fire could not harm him, and went mad as a consequence, presumably at the will of the goddess, and hurled himself into a fire. It is not known whether he lived long enough to succeed to his father's throne.[132]

In one of the various accounts of his crime, Tantalos is said to have killed his other son, PELOPS, while he was still a boy, and to have served his flesh as a meal to the gods to test their omniscience. They recognized the true nature of the meal, however, and soon pieced him together and brought him back to life again, achieving this in some accounts by boiling his remains in a cauldron.[133] Demeter alone ate some of the unholy meal, consuming one of his shoulders while she was distracted by her grief after the loss of her daughter Persephone; but she compensated him by providing him with a new shoulder of ivory (or else the gods provided the shoulder, or Hermes did so at the order of Zeus).[134] He was now more beautiful than ever, and grew up into such a handsome youth that Poseidon fell in love with him and carried him off to Olympos for a while.[135]

Pelops wins a bride and kingdom in the Peloponnese

After he was brought down to earth again, his thoughts turned to marriage, and he decided to seek the hand of HIPPODAMEIA, the daughter of OINOMAOS, king of Pisa (in the region of Olympia in the western Peloponnese). He knew that this would be a perilous enterprise because her father forced all her suitors to compete with him in a chariot-race on the following terms. The challenger would take her into his chariot and set off in advance of Oinomaos, who would delay until he had sacrificed a lamb to Zeus; if he caught up with the suitor (as was likely because his father Ares had provided him with a team of immortal horses), he would kill him by thrusting a spear into his back; but if the suitor should happen to escape, he could take Hippodameia as his wife. Twelve or more adventurers had died in this way before the arrival of Pelops; but Pelops had an advantage over his predecessors since he could call on the help of his divine admirer Poseidon, who gave him a golden chariot drawn by winged horses (or else a winged chariot).[136] Although this would doubtless have sufficed to ensure his victory in the original story, an act of treachery on the part of Oinomaos' charioteer becomes the deciding factor in the standard later tradition. Pelops corrupted this charioteer, MYRTILOS, son of Hermes, by promising him a share of the kingdom or a night with Hippodameia;[137] or else Hippodameia persuaded him to act on her behalf after falling in love with her new suitor.[138] Myrtilos sabotaged his master's chariot by failing to insert the linchpins into the wheel-axles (or by replacing the linchpins with waxen dummies), causing the king to be thrown to the ground and killed when he set off in pursuit of Pelops.[139] As so often in stories of this kind, Myrtilos gained no advantage from his treachery, for Pelops killed him in his turn soon afterwards, either to save himself from having to pay the promised reward,[140] or because Myrtilos tried to rape or merely kiss Hippodameia, or because she falsely accused him of trying to do so.[141] Some said that Oinomaos had cursed Myrtilos for his perfidy before succumbing to his wounds, praying that he should perish at the hand of Pelops. By pushing him out of his chariot as he was driving it through the sky, Pelops caused him to plunge to his death in the sea below, in the area of the south-western Aegean that was known as the Myrtoan Sea ever afterwards. While falling through the air, Myrtilos cursed the house of his murderer, a curse that was destined to be fulfilled in ample measure.[142]

It was generally agreed that the violent and brutal Oinomaos was a son of the war-god Ares; in the local tradition, his mother was Harpina, daughter of Asopos, the eponym of a minor town of that name near Olympia;[143] but some authors, apparently following the Hesiodic *Catalogue*, preferred to regard him as an Atlantid, identifying his mother as Sterope (or Asterope), daughter of Atlas (see p. 519).[144] The mythographers offered two explanations for his brutal treatment of his daughter's suitors, some saying that he was in love with her himself, and others that he had learned from an oracle that he was fated to die at the hand of his son-in-law.[145] In some accounts, he cut off the heads of the dead suitors and nailed them to his house, or fixed them to the pillars of the local temple of Ares or Poseidon.[146] He had another daughter, Alkippe, who bore Marpessa to Euenos (see p. 413), and a son, Leukippos, who angered Apollo by courting Daphne (see p. 155). Pausanias may be consulted for the local traditions that connected Oinomaos and Pelops with topographical features at Olympia.[147]

As a result of these events, Pelops won not only his favoured bride but her father's kingdom in addition. He married Hippodameia as soon as he had been purified by Hephaistos. Since he was supposed to have given his name to the entire Peloponnese, it was doubtless often assumed that he extended his power far beyond the bounds of Pisa, as in the account of Apollodorus, renaming the peninsula after himself after conquering much or all of it;[148] but this idea cannot easily be reconciled with the usual traditions regarding the early history of the other main regions of the Peloponnese. If it is indeed the case that Pelops was originally the eponym of a people called the Pelopes, these would presumably have been associated with a wider area of the Peloponnese than the little territory of Pisa alone.

The children of Pelops and Hippodameia, and exile of Atreus and Thyestes

Plutarch once wrote that Pelops was the most powerful king in the Peloponnese not so much by virtue of his possessions as of the number of his children, for he married his daughters to men of standing and established many of his sons as rulers of Peloponnesian cities.[149] Pindar already credits him with six sons, and many more are added to the list in later sources.[150] Most are mere eponyms, however, without any stories, and only four can be said to be of any real significance in heroic legend, namely **Atreus** and **Thyestes**,[151] whose myths will be considered presently, and **Pittheus**,[152] who became the ruler of Troizen in the Argolid and contrived that his daughter Aithra should become the mother of Theseus (see p. 341), and lastly **Alkathoos**,[153] who was a major figure in Megarian legend (see p. 567). To these **Kopreus**, the herald of Eurystheus (see p. 257), might be added if he was indeed a son of Pelops as some late sources suggest.[154] Most of the other sons of Pelops were brought into being to serve as the eponyms of various places in the Peloponnese; for who could be a better father for eponyms of Peloponnesian cities than the man who gave his name to the peninsula itself? Amongst others, we find **Troizen** (who accompanied Pittheus to Troizen),[155] **Epidauros**,[156] **Kleonymos** (the eponym of Kleonai in Argolid),[157] **Kynosuras**, and **Letreus**[158] (the eponym of Letrinai in Elis). Pelops also had three daughters, **Astydameia**, **Nikippe** and **Lysippe**, who married three sons of Perseus – Alkaios, Sthenelos and Elektryon respectively – in the western Argolid,[159] helping to prepare the way for the subsequent arrival of Atreus and Thyestes.

In addition to his children by Hippodameia, Pelops had another son, CHRYSIPPOS, who was either an illegitimate child by a local nymph or a son whom he had fathered by a previous marriage.[160] He favoured Chrysippos above his other children, to such an extent that they came to imagine that he might bequeath the throne to him. So with some encouragement from their mother, Atreus and Thyestes eventually murdered him and threw his body down a well. Pelops came to learn of their crime, however, and expelled them from his kingdom; and he uttered a terrible curse against them, praying that they and their descendants should perish in mutual strife. He also vented his fury on Hippodameia in some accounts, causing her to kill herself or to flee to Midea in the Argolid.[161] For a conflicting account of the death of Chrysippos, see p. 505.

In historical times, Pelops was honoured as a divine hero at his supposed burial-place at Olympia. The magistrates used to offer an annual sacrifice of a black ram at his heroic shrine, which was said to have been founded by Herakles.[162] The Pisaians and Eleians disputed the control of Olympia and of its great festival until the district of Pisa (which was apparently ruled from a city of that name in early times) was overrun by the Eleians, probably in the sixth century BC. The only other mythical ruler to be recorded for it apart from Oinomaos and Pelops is its eponymous founder PISOS, a son of Perieres, who had settled there after leaving his father's kingdom of Messenia to the south.[163]

Atreus competes with Thyestes for the Mycenaean throne, and serves his children to him as a meal

After leaving the land of their birth, ATREUS and THYESTES settled in the Argolid. Some mythographers explained that they came to that area because Sthenelos, son of Perseus, invited them to rule Midea as his vassals after seizing power at Mycenae (see p. 245), or because Sthenelos' son Eurystheus entrusted Mycenae to Atreus (who was a maternal uncle of his) when he set off to wage war against the Heraklids (see p. 287).[164] The two brothers later became embroiled in a savage and mutually destructive power-struggle as a result of their father's curse (or that of Myrtilos, see above, or both curses). The trouble began when the Mycenaeans received an oracle ordering them to choose a Pelopid as their ruler after the death of Eurystheus, the last Inachid ruler, who was killed along with his sons while he was trying to eliminate the Heraklids. For Atreus and Thyestes were equally anxious to win the throne of this wealthy and powerful city, and the ensuing contest degenerated into an unscrupulous and bloody feud.[165] They could prove their claim most effectively by demonstrating that a portent from the gods favoured one or the other of them, and Atreus was convinced that he had the advantage because a wonderful golden lamb had been born into his flocks. Hermes had sent the lamb in one account, knowing that it would become a cause of contention, because he wanted to take vengeance on the family of Pelops for the murder of his son Myrtilos (see p. 503).[166] Or else it had been sent by Artemis after Atreus had made her a vow undertaking to offer her in sacrifice the finest beast born in his flocks; but the golden lamb had been so beautiful that he had risked her anger by breaking his vow, and had throttled it instead to put it (or strictly speaking, its fleece) into a chest.[167] For whatever reason, the golden lamb proved to be no blessing for Atreus, for his wife Aerope was seduced by Thyestes and secretly stole it to advance her lover's cause. When the Mycenaean succession was being discussed soon afterwards at a meeting of the citizens, Thyestes proposed accordingly that the throne should pass to the one who possessed the golden lamb, and Atreus willingly agreed to these terms, supposing that he could produce the lamb; but it was his brother who stepped forward with it and was acclaimed as king of Mycenae.[168]

This was not the end of the matter, however, since Thyestes had angered the gods by his manipulation of the portent, and Zeus sent Hermes to Atreus to tell him that his claim to the throne would be confirmed by a far more impressive portent than that of the lamb; for on a forthcoming day, the sun would reverse its usual course by rising in the west and setting in the east (or reverse its course forever by rising in the east for the first time, instead of in the west as previously). So Atreus persuaded his brother to promise that he would surrender the throne if this unparalleled event should occur; or he simply announced that the portent of the lamb would shortly be annulled by a far greater portent. In the face of this sign of divine displeasure, Thyestes was obliged to abdicate in favour of Atreus, who banished him from the land.[169]

When Atreus later discovered that his wife had committed adultery with his brother and had stolen the lamb for him, he drowned her and lured Thyestes back to Mycenae on the pretence of seeking a reconciliation. He then exacted a terrible revenge on him by killing his sons, boiling their flesh, and serving it up to him as a meal. Thyestes ate it without hesitation since the heads, hands and feet had been removed to disguise the true nature of the feast; but as soon as he had swallowed it down, Atreus produced the severed extremities to show him what he had eaten, and sent him into exile once again.[170] Thyestes lost three sons as a result of his brother's action, Aglaos, Orchomenos and Kallileon (or Kaleos);[171] or in some Latin accounts, he lost two sons named Tantalos and Pleisthenes.[172] It was sometimes suggested that the sun reversed its course in horror at the cannibal meal rather than as a portent during the dispute over the succession.[173]

Aigisthos kills Atreus to place his father Thyestes on the throne

At the outset of his second period of exile, Thyestes slept with his own daughter PELOPIA, and fathered a new son by her, AIGISTHOS, who would finally avenge him by killing Atreus, and so restore him to the Mycenaean throne. In one account, he slept with his daughter knowingly on the advice of an oracle, which had told him that she would bear him a son who would exact the vengeance that he desired; or in another version, as recounted below, he raped her without recognizing her while she was participating in nocturnal rites.[174] Aeschylus' *Agamemnon* offers a very different account of Aigisthos' origin, stating that he was a legitimate child of Thyestes who escaped the fate of his brothers because he was still a baby in swaddling-clothes at the time. He is described as the thirteenth child in the play as we have it (but it is surely probable that there is a corruption in the text).[175] Whatever the exact circumstances of his origin, he was destined to bring disaster on the opposing branch of the family, first by killing Atreus to put his father on the throne, and subsequently (after Thyestes was displaced by Atreus' son Agamemnon) by seducing the wife of Agamemnon and conspiring in his death.

Hyginus offers an elaborate account of the events that led up to the death of Atreus, in what is apparently a composite version based on tragic plots. After inadvertently eating his children, Thyestes fled to the court of Thesprotos (the eponym of the Thesprotians) in Epirus, and then travelled on to Sicyon, where his daughter Pelopia was staying at the time. He happened to arrive on a night on which sacrifices were being offered to Artemis, and hid himself in a grove for fear of profaning the rites. The dancers were being led by Pelopia, who stained her robes with blood from the sacrifices and went down to a stream to wash; and as she was doing so, Thyestes jumped out of the bushes with his head veiled and raped her. Although neither was aware of the other's identity, Pelopia secured some evidence for the future by seizing her assailant's sword and hiding it away. Back in the Argolid, Mycenae was afflicted by barrenness as a result of the crime of Atreus, and the king was advised by an oracle to fetch his brother back. Knowing that Thyestes had sought refuge with Thesprotos, Atreus travelled to Epirus to seek him out, but found no sign of him because he had departed abroad to his grandfather's homeland in Asia Minor. Atreus did catch sight of Pelopia, however, at the court of Thesprotos, and he asked to marry her in the belief that she was a daughter of the king. After arriving at Mycenae, she gave birth to her incestuously conceived son, and exposed him; but some shepherds suckled him at the teats of a goat (*aiga* in Greek, hence his name of Aigisthos) until he was recovered at the order of Atreus, who brought him up as his own son. Some time later, Agamemnon and Menelaos caught Thyestes at Delphi and brought him back to Mycenae. Atreus threw him into prison and ordered Aigisthos (who was grown up by this time) to kill him. Thyestes recognized Aigisthos' sword as the one that had been seized from him during the rape at Sicyon, and asked him where it had come from; and when the young man replied that his mother had given it to him, Thyestes asked that she should be fetched. She told him that she had seized it during the rape, and then picked it up as if to examine it and plunged it into her breast (for she had evidently realized as a result of the preceding conversation that the rapist had been her father). Pulling the blood-stained sword out of her body, Aigisthos took it away and showed it to Atreus to make him believe that he had killed Thyestes in accordance with his order; and when Atreus was subsequently offering a sacrifice on the shore (presumably in thanksgiving for the death of his brother), Aigisthos took advantage of this opportunity to kill him, and restored the throne to Thyestes.[176]

Agamemnon and Menelaos survive to expel Thyestes

Atreus left two young sons, AGAMEMNON and MENELAOS, who were smuggled abroad to neighbouring Sicyon by their nurse after their father's murder. The king of Sicyon sent them on to the court of Oineus in Calydon (presumably because he thought that they would be safer if they were sent further away); and Tyndareos encountered them there, evidently during the period of his Aetolian exile (see p. 525), and brought them back to the Peloponnese when he returned home to Sparta. As soon as they were old enough, the two brothers travelled to Mycenae to recover their father's kingdom. When Thyestes sought sanctuary at the altar of Hera, they allowed him to leave under safe conduct in return for an oath in which he swore to settle on the island of Cythera (off the south-eastern tip of the Peloponnese). Agamemnon took over the throne as the elder brother, and married Klytaimnestra (Clytemnestra in Latin form), one of the daughters of Tyndareos.[177] They had a single son, Orestes, and (in the usual tradition) three daughters, Iphigeneia, Elektra and Chrysothemis. Menelaos, as we have seen (pp. 439ff), stayed at Sparta with Tyndareos, marrying his putative daughter Helen and eventually succeeding to the throne.

Agamemnon and Menelaos are sometimes described as sons of PLEISTHENES, son of Atreus, rather than as sons of Atreus himself.[178] It is stated in this connection that Atreus was married to his niece Kleola or Kleolla, a daughter of Dias, son of Pelops, while Pleisthenes was married to Aerope; or else the pattern is inverted and Atreus is said to have married Aerope as usual while Pleisthenes married Kleola.[179] This makes little difference since Pleisthenes is a shadowy figure who is said to have died prematurely, leaving his sons to be reared by Atreus.[180]

Aerope was a daughter of Katreus, king of Crete; for the circumstances of her marriage to Atreus (or Pleisthenes), see p. 355.

According to a passage in the *Iliad*, Agamemnon owned a sceptre of Hephaistos' workmanship which had been handed down within the family ever since Zeus had presented it to Pelops; for Pelops had given it to his son Atreus, who had bequeathed it to his brother Thyestes, who had left it to his nephew Agamemnon. This would suggest, in marked contrast to later accounts, that power was transferred peacefully from one member of the family to the next.[181]

Aigisthos and Klytaimnestra plot the death of Agamemnon

After Helen was abducted to Troy by Paris, Menelaos sought the help of his powerful brother at Mycenae, and the two of them assembled a large force of allies to launch an expedition against Troy, as recounted in the preceding chapter. Aigisthos set to work to avenge his father's expulsion during their absence, by seducing Agamemnon's wife KLYTAIMNESTRA and seizing power at Mycenae; and since he and Klytaimnestra could not allow the king to survive after he returned from the war, Agamemnon's fate was sealed. The events that led up to the death of Agamemnon are described in the following manner in the *Odyssey*. Although Agamemnon had ordered one of his servants (an *aoidos*, minstrel or bard) to watch over Klytaimnestra, and the gods sent Hermes to Aigisthos to warn him not to court her or kill her husband, Aigisthos marooned the minstrel on a desert island and soon persuaded Klytaimnestra to yield to him, paying no heed to the bidding of the gods. He then took her into his own house, in an unspecified corner of the Argolid, and assumed control of her husband's kingdom.[182] To ensure that he would not be caught by surprise when Agamemnon finally returned, he posted a watchman by the shore and promised him a reward of two talents of gold for news of the king's arrival; and when Agamemnon landed in the Argolid a year afterwards, weeping for joy at his supposed deliverance, the watchman rushed to inform his master. Picking out twenty of his best men, Aigisthos prepared an ambush in his house, and then drove down to the shore in his chariot to invite Agamemnon to a banquet. After the festivities, he felled his unsuspecting guest like an ox at the corn-crib; and his followers then crept out of their hiding-place to attack Agamemnon's companions, and exchanged blows with them until not a man was left alive from either party. As Agamemnon lay dying on the floor, Klytaimnestra emerged to kill Kassandra, a captive whom he had brought from Troy as a prize of war (see p. 479). Klytaimnestra would have been obliged to keep out of sight until that time because she had no proper occasion to be in the house of Aigisthos. There is no indication in Homer's account that she had any personal grievance against her husband; Aigisthos murdered Agamemnon out of simple necessity to preserve his ill-gotten power, and Klytaimnestra connived in the murder out of loyalty to her lover.[183]

In the later tradition from the classical period onwards, the Homeric account of the murder of Agamemnon was largely eclipsed by the very different version that was developed in Aeschylus' *Agamemnon*, a great tragedy that gives an unexpected depth to what was originally a simple tale of ambition, adultery and betrayal. Klytaimnestra now becomes the dominant partner in the intrigue. It is she who takes the precautions against Agamemnon's return, appointing a look-out to watch for a beacon-fire announcing the fall of Troy; and she receives the returning conqueror with deceptive enthusiasm at his own palace while Aigisthos remains out of sight. After persuading Agamemnon to enter the palace over a path spread with purple robes, and thus to commit an act of arrogance that is designed to provoke the gods, she incapacitates him in his bath by throwing some clothing around him, and then strikes him down with three blows (presumably sword-blows, although this is not stated). The horror of the murder is in no way diminished by the fact that it takes place off-stage, and that the audience learns of it from Agamemnon's cries and from Klytaimnestra's exultant account when she reappears afterwards. Kassandra is also killed by her, as in Homer's version. Aigisthos finally emerges from his hiding-place after the deeds have been committed and rejoices over the destruction of the house of Atreus. Although Agamemnon must necessarily be killed if the usurper is to maintain his position, just as in the earlier tradition, Klytaimnestra's action is now also motivated by revenge, for she has hated her husband ever since he ordered the sacrifice of their daughter Iphigeneia before the war (see p. 447).[184]

Orestes avenges the murder of Agamemnon with the support of his sister Elektra

ORESTES, the only son of Agamemnon, who was still a child at the time of his father's murder, survived this moment of peril because he was smuggled away by his nurse Arsinoe or Laodameia, or by his father's herald Talthybios; or in other versions, he was sent away by his sister Elektra, or had been sent away beforehand by his mother.[185] He was reared in exile by his maternal uncle Strophios, the king of Krisa near Delphi (see p. 566), who brought him up with his own son Pylades.[186] The two boys established a close friendship, and Pylades accompanied Orestes when he finally returned to Mycenae to avenge his father's murder. Our earliest source for the latter story, the *Odyssey*, mentions that Orestes returned home as soon as he was old enough, arriving eight years after Agamemnon's death, and avenged his father by killing Aigisthos in his turn; and since the epic also reports that Orestes 'held a funeral feast for the Argives over his hateful mother and the craven Aigisthos', we should probably assume that he killed Klytaimnestra too. The Hesiodic *Catalogue* is the first source to state explicitly that he committed matricide, by killing 'his overweening mother with the pitiless bronze'; and Stesichorus indicates at much the same period that he was pursued by the Erinyes (Furies) for doing so.[187]

The tale of Orestes' revenge takes the following form in the first full account in Aeschylus' *Libation-bearers* (*Choephoroi*). After learning from Apollo at Delphi that he must kill those who had been responsible for his father's murder or else suffer grievously himself, he made his way to Mycenae together with Pylades. While visiting his father's grave after his arrival to dedicate a lock of his hair, he encountered his sister Elektra, who arrived at the grave with a group of slave-women to pour libations at the order of her mother. As Elektra explained to her brother, Klytaimnestra had been troubled by a sinister dream in which she had fancied that she gave birth to a snake (evidently signifying Orestes) which bit her, drawing blood, when she tried to suckle it, and she had therefore ordered that libations should be offered in the hope of averting the portended danger. After approaching Agamemnon's grave with his sister to call on the aid of his father's spirit, Orestes gained entrance to the palace for Pylades and himself by pretending to Klytaimnestra (who naturally failed to recognize him) that he was a stranger from Central Greece who had been asked to report the death of Orestes. Once they were inside, Orestes killed Aigisthos, who had been summoned to hear the news, and then turned his sword against Klytaimnestra too, even though she tried to deter him by baring her breast and begging him not to kill the mother who had suckled him.[188]

Sophocles and Euripides later wrote tragedies on the same theme in which Orestes' sister plays a fuller and more aggressive role. Sophocles' *Elektra* portrays her as having been present when Orestes' childhood attendant (*paidagōgos*) arrived at the palace to allege that Orestes had been killed in a chariot-race, a false report at which she was as much dismayed as her mother was relieved. Now believing that her brother was no longer alive to avenge the murder of Agamemnon, Elektra planned to kill Klytaimnestra and Aigisthos herself, but was unable to persuade her more cautious sister Chrysothemis (who is rather like Ismene in the *Antigone*, see p. 322) to assist her in the enterprise. Orestes and Pylades were already in Mycenae, however, and they soon arrived at the palace, where Orestes made himself known to Elektra, who waited outside to watch out for Aigisthos while her brother killed Klytaimnestra inside. When Aigisthos appeared, Elektra lured him inside by telling him that he would be able to see the body of Orestes, but the corpse that was revealed to him was that of Klytaimnestra, and he was killed in his turn by Orestes.[189] In Euripides' idiosyncratic play of the same title, Aigisthos had forced Elektra to marry a poor farmer to make it impossible for any son of hers to be able to claim the throne (although her husband, who was a man of fine character, had refused to consummate the marriage out of respect for her feelings). She had naturally become embittered, and when Orestes arrived at the farm-house with his friend, she eagerly assisted him in plotting the death of Aigisthos and Klytaimnestra; and in the case of the latter she even played a direct part in the execution of the murder, exhorting her weaker-minded brother when he hesitated, and putting her hand to the sword as he plunged it in. In this version, Orestes committed the murders outside the palace where nobody would be available to protect the victims, killing Aigisthos in the meadows while he was offering a sacrifice to the nymphs, and then killing Klytaimnestra in the farm-house after she had been summoned there on the pretence that Elektra had given birth to a son.[190]

Orestes is persecuted by the Erinyes

After killing his mother, Orestes was persecuted and driven mad by the Erinyes (Furies), female spirits of vengeance who were especially ruthless in punishing offences committed by one member of a family against another (see p. 38). This was commonly agreed in the post-Homeric tradition at least, for there is no mention of any such trouble in the *Odyssey*, which presents Orestes' actions as exemplary and concentrates on the killing of Aigisthos, never stating directly that he also killed his mother. Athena urges Telemachos, the son of Odysseus, to take similar action against the rapacious young men when have invaded the house of his absent father, pointing to the fame that noble Orestes has won for killing his father's murderer.[191] Klytaimnestra is of interest to Homer primarily as a counter-example to Penelope, the faithful wife of Odysseus; we should doubtless assume that Orestes, as the only surviving male member of the household, would have been fully justified in taking action against her. The earliest literary evidence for his persecution by the Erinyes is contained in a report on a lost poem by Stesichorus, the *Oresteia*, in which Apollo gave him a bow to defend himself against the Erinyes.[192] They come to the fore in the last two plays of Aeschylus' Oresteia trilogy. At the end of the *Libation-bearers*, soon after Orestes has killed his mother, he exclaims in horror that his mother's Erinyes have appeared to him, saying that they are hunting him down and that he must now pass on;[193] and they form the chorus of the final play in the trilogy, the *Eumenides*. At the beginning of that play, we find that Orestes has fled to Delphi to seek the help of Apollo, who had ordered him to commit the murder in the first place. Apollo promises him his protection, but tells him to travel on to Athens and submit himself to Athena.[194] Stirred on by the ghost of Klytaimnestra, the Erinyes follow him to Athens, where both they and Orestes agree to accept the justice of Athena. The goddess decides the case shall be judged by a panel of twelve Athenian citizens at the court of the Areiopagos,[195] so setting a precedent for trial by jury. Apollo himself appears as the advocate of Orestes; the Erinyes plead their own cause with terrible eloquence; and when the votes of the jury are equally divided, Athena as president of the court uses her casting-vote to acquit Orestes,[196] so establishing that an acquittal should be registered if the votes should ever be equal in the future (as was the practice at Athens). To appease the Erinyes, Athena offers them a home in her city of Athens, proposing that they should be worshipped henceforth at the foot of the Acropolis under the new name of the Eumenides or 'the Kindly Goddesses'.[197]

The preceding tale was obviously invented at Athens, whether by Aeschylus himself or some earlier author; but there were also competing traditions in which Orestes was said to have won deliverance from the Erinyes in various parts of the Peloponnese. According to a quite early tale recorded by Pherecydes, he fled to Oresthasion in south-eastern Arcadia, where he sought sanctuary in the temple of Artemis, seating himself as a suppliant on the altar of the goddess. When the Erinyes approached him for the kill, she drove them away accordingly, and the city was renamed Oresteion in commemoration of the incident.[198] Or in another Arcadian legend set near the site of Megalopolis, the Erinyes manifested themselves in order to drive him mad, appearing to him as wholly black; but when he bit off one of the fingers of his left hand in his frenzy, they suddenly seemed to turn white, and he regained sufficient composure to avert their wrath by burning sacrifices to them. The Erinyes had a local sanctuary at Ale (Cure), the place where this was supposed to have happened.[199] Or according to the Troizenian tradition, Orestes was purified from the taint of matricide by nine men of Troizen while seated on a sacred stone outside the temple of Artemis Lykeia; or he was cured of his madness while sitting on a comparable stone near Gythion in Laconia.[200] Or he turned the pitiless Erinyes into the kindly Eumenides by sacrificing a black sheep to them at the Achaean town of Keryneia, which contained a sanctuary of the Erinyes that had supposedly been founded by Orestes.[201]

According to some Hellenistic and later sources, Orestes was arraigned for murder by mortal accusers and then tried in accordance with conventional procedure. In one such version, Klytaimnestra and Aigisthos had left a child called Erigone, who prosecuted Orestes at the Areiopagos, either on her own or in conjunction with her grandfather Tyndareos; and she was so distressed by his subsequent acquittal that she hanged herself.[202] Or else Orestes was prosecuted at the same court by Perileos (or Perilaos), son of Ikarios, a cousin of Klytaimnestra, since Tyndareos was no longer alive to institute proceedings;[203] or Tyndareos himself charged Orestes with murder at Mycenae, but the citizens allowed him to depart into exile out of respect for his father.[204]

Orestes recovers his sister Iphigeneia from the land of the Taurians

According to a further tale which first appears in Euripides' *Iphigeneia in Tauris*, Orestes discovered from Apollo at Delphi that he would not be fully delivered from the Erinyes until he had fetched an ancient statue of Artemis from the land of the Taurians (the Crimea).[205] Although he was unaware of it as yet, his sister IPHIGENEIA was serving there as the priestess of Taurian Artemis; for the goddess had spirited her away to the land of the Taurians when her father had brought her to sacrifice at Aulis.[206] As was described in the preceding chapter, Agamemnon offended Artemis while the Greek army was making preparations for the voyage to Troy at Aulis in Boeotia, and it was revealed by a seer that the goddess would continue to hold the fleet in port until Agamemnon made amends by bringing one of his daughters to sacrifice (see further on p. 447). Three differing accounts were offered of her fate after she was laid on the altar. In those accounts in which she was said to have been killed or, at the opposite extreme, to have been rescued by Artemis and rendered immortal, her earthly life came to an end at that point. In this version from Euripides, however, she is said to have been rescued by Artemis and transferred abroad as a mortal, and she can therefore re-enter the common history of the Pelopids when she is recovered from her exile by her brother.

In the versions in which Iphigeneia is rescued, Artemis substitutes a deer (or some other animal) for her at the altar. She is already associated with the land of the Taurians in the earliest surviving account from the *Cypria*, but as a goddess rather than priestess; although the summary of the epic offers no detail on the matter, merely stating that the goddess 'transported her to the Taurians and made her immortal', she was presumably turned into the Taurian maiden goddess who was equated with Artemis (and was served by Iphigeneia in Euripides' account); Herodotus mentions at one point that the Taurian goddess was identified with Iphigeneia.[207] In another early account from the Hesiodic *Catalogue* (in which this daughter of Agamemnon is called Iphimede), Artemis saved her by placing a phantom (*eidōlon*) of her on the altar, and rubbed her with ambrosia to make her immortal as Artemis Einodia ('of the wayside'); since Einodia was a title of Hekate, and the early lyric poet Stesichorus is said to have stated that Iphigeneia was turned into that goddess, this may have meant that she became Hekate, an infernal double of Artemis.[208] In a Hellenistic account ascribed to Nicander, Artemis is said to have rendered her immortal under the title of Orsilochia, which is reported to have been a title of Artemis in the Tauric Chersonese. Nicander suggests that Artemis substituted a bull (*tauros*) for her at the altar, and that she named the people of her new homeland the Taurians (*Tauroi* in Greek) in commemoration of the fact.[209]

As priestess of Taurian Artemis, Iphigeneia was obliged to preside over the bloody local rites in which any male foreigner who set foot in the land would be sacrificed to the goddess. So when Orestes and his companion Pylades were captured soon after their arrival, Thoas, the king of the Taurians, ordered that they should be taken to Iphigeneia to be slaughtered in the customary manner. On learning that the pair had come from Argos, Iphigeneia offered to release one of them if he would take a message home; and when she explained who she was and asked that her brother should be informed of her predicament, Orestes realized that she must be his sister, whom he had considered to be dead. After sharing in the joy of their reunion and exchanging news, Iphigeneia set to work to contrive their escape. She told Thoas that the captives were polluted because they had killed their mother, and said that they would have to be purified in the sea along with the statue (which had been polluted by their presence) before they could be brought to sacrifice; and she added that the king himself should remain in the temple during their absence to purify it, and that the local people should be ordered to stay indoors to avoid any danger of pollution. On arriving at the shore at the lonely spot where Orestes' ship had been secretly moored, Iphigeneia told the guards to keep at a distance while she performed the purifications, and was thus able to escape out to sea unhindered with the prisoners and the statue. Athena manifests herself to Thoas at the end of the play to order him to make no attempt at pursuit, and she reveals that the fugitives will arrive safely in Attica, and that Orestes will dedicate the statue at Halai while Iphigeneia will become the priestess of Artemis at Brauron.[210] In connection with the cult of Artemis Tauropolis at Halai, which was supposed to have been founded by Orestes, the priest used to graze a man's throat with a sword in a rite imitative of the human sacrifice that had once been performed by Iphigeneia, but would restrict himself to drawing a single drop of blood.[211]

According to Attic tradition, Iphigeneia served Artemis at Brauron, a town on the east coast of Attica, until the end of her days, and was buried there after her death (although other places, including Megara, also claimed to have her tomb). She received cultic honours as a heroine at her Attic tomb, and it is reported that the clothing of women who died in childbirth (a function that was of special concern to her mistress Artemis) would be dedicated to her.[212] The statue that had supposedly been stolen from the land of the Taurians by herself and her brother could be seen at Brauron in historical times; but as in the case of the Trojan Palladion, a variety of places claimed to possess it. The Spartans alleged, for instance, that Orestes had brought it to their city when he became king there, and identified it with their ancient image of Artemis Orthia; or in an Italian version of the legend, Orestes was said to have deposited it at Aricia in Latium.[213]

Hyginus records a tale in which Aigisthos is said to have had a son called ALETES, who seized power at Mycenae during Orestes' absence when a messenger falsely reported that he and his companion had been sacrificed to Taurian Artemis. Elektra decided to travel to Delphi to question the oracle about her brother's fate, and happened to arrive there just as Orestes and Iphigeneia were calling in after their escape from the land of the Taurians. When the messenger who had previously brought the false message told Elektra that Iphigeneia had killed her brother (as she might well have done as the priestess of Taurian Artemis), she seized a firebrand from the altar and would have killed Iphigeneia if Orestes himself had not intervened. After recognizing each other's identity, Orestes and Elektra travelled to Mycenae, where Orestes killed Aletes, and would also have killed Erigone, the other child of Aigisthos and Klytaimnestra, if Artemis had not rescued her and installed her in Attica as one of her priestesses.[214]

The marriage and death of Orestes, and the truncated reign of his son Teisamenos

By killing Aigisthos and recovering his paternal inheritance, Orestes gained control of Mycenae and the section of the Argolid that was ruled from it; and according to Pausanias' account of the local history of the area, the rest of the Argolid fell under his control also when Kylarabos, son of Sthenelos, who had become the sole ruler of the other lands of the Argolid (see p. 335), died without leaving any children. And he finally inherited Sparta, the other main Pelopid kingdom, when his uncle Menelaos died without an heir.[215]

From the classical period onwards, it was generally accepted that Orestes married HERMIONE, the only daughter of Helen and Menelaos, who bore him his son and heir Teisamenos (i.e. Avenger, so named because Orestes had avenged the murder of Agamemnon). It was accepted at the same time, however, that Hermione was also married to Neoptolemos at some stage. According to the *Odyssey*, Menelaos promised her to Neoptolemos at Troy, and fulfilled his promise after the war by sending her away to him (see p. 490); it would seem that he was her only husband in the original tradition.[216] The earliest known source for her marriage to Orestes is a lost play by Sophocles called the *Hermione*, which suggested that Menelaos had promised her to Neoptolemos without realizing that his father-in-law Tyndareos had given her to Orestes at Sparta during his absence. Menelaos took her away from her husband after the war to deliver her to Neoptolemos in accordance with his promise; but when Neoptolemos was killed at Delphi soon afterwards while trying to exact reparation from Apollo for the death of his father (see p. 491), Hermione was able to resume her marriage to Orestes, and bore him his son.[217] In other accounts, Neoptolemos asserted his claim to her by seizing her from Orestes, who retaliated by ambushing him at Delphi or arranging for him to be murdered there (see p. 491).

In Euripides' *Andromache*, the only surviving play on the theme, we are told that Hermione married Neoptolemos as her first husband and went to live with him in his grandfather's kingdom in southern Thessaly. Because the marriage proved to be childless, she grew increasingly jealous of her husband's concubine Andromache, who had borne him a son (here unnamed, usually Molossos, see p. 490), and even imagined that Andromache was using magic to render her barren. So while Neoptolemos was absent on a trip to Delphi, she and her father Menelaos (who had come from Sparta for that purpose) set out to kill Andromache and her son, causing her to send her son away and take refuge at the shrine of Thetis; but Menelaos gained hold of her son and prised her away from her place of sanctuary by threatening to kill him. He and his daughter would then have killed Andromache and her son alike if Peleus, the grandfather of Neoptolemos, had not made an opportune appearance and rescued them. Menelaos then made a hasty departure, leaving Hermione to worry about the reaction of Neoptolemos when he returned to hear of the plot. Orestes, who had been betrothed to her previously, happened to call in at this time as he was travelling north to consult the oracle at Dodona; and on learning of her predicament, he offered to take her away with him, explaining that he had already taken measures to ensure that Neoptolemos would be killed at Delphi. For he hated Neoptolemos for having taken Hermione as his wife when he himself was betrothed to her. As might be gathered from this summary, Hermione is not an appealing character in this play and her father is utterly contemptible.[218]

It is generally agreed in subsequent sources that Hermione bore no children to Neoptolemos during their brief marriage. Orestes for his part was said to have fathered an illegitimate son by his half-sister Erigone, namely Penthilos, who founded colonies on Lesbos and the adjoining mainland, and was the mythical ancestor of the Lesbian noble family of the Penthilidai.

Orestes lived to an advanced age, seventy or even ninety in some accounts, until he finally died from a snake-bite at Oresteion in Arcadia.[219] According to Pausanias, the Delphic oracle had instructed him to leave Mycenae to settle in Arcadia when it was under the rule of Aipytos, son of Hippothoon (see p. 549).[220] Tradition claimed that he was initially buried in or near Tegea in southern Arcadia, but was later reburied at Sparta, where his bones could be seen in historical times.[221]

Herodotus tells how this reburial was supposed to have come about in the sixth century BC. After repeatedly failing to conquer the city of Tegea, the Spartans sought the advice of the Delphic oracle, which told them that they would be victorious if the bones of Orestes were brought home to Sparta; and when they consulted the oracle once again after failing to find the bones, it declared that the bones were lying in a place where two winds blew under strong constraint, and where blow was struck on blow and woe on woe. The meaning of the oracle remained a mystery until a Spartan agent called Lichas happened to call in at a smithy in Tegea while some iron was being hammered out. When the smith remarked to him that he had discovered a huge coffin, ten feet long, while digging a well in the courtyard outside, Lichas reflected on the work that was being carried out in front of him, and suddenly realized that the oracle must have been referring to a smithy, and that the remains in the coffin would therefore be those of Orestes. For the 'winds' mentioned in the oracle were the blasts of air that issued from the bellows of the forge, and the 'blows' were those of the hammer on the anvil, and the 'woes' were those that would be inflicted by the iron that was being hammered out (evidently to make weapons of war). So Lichas arranged for the bones to be transferred to Sparta, and Tegea fell under the sway of Sparta soon afterwards just as the oracle had predicted.[222]

TEISAMENOS, the son of Orestes, was the last Pelopid to hold power at Argos and Sparta. He reigned as his father's successor until he was displaced by the Heraklids (see p. 290), who either killed him in battle or forced him into exile by defeating him in battle. In the latter case, he withdrew to Achaea in the northern Peloponnese with his sons and followers, but was killed soon afterwards when he became embroiled in a war with the rulers of the land; his followers were victorious, however, and the land was ruled by his sons and descendants thereafter (see further on p. 407). According to Achaean tradition, he was buried at the Achaean city of Helike until the Spartans took his bones home to Sparta at the order of the Delphic oracle.[223]

CHAPTER FIFTEEN

THE ATLANTIDS, THE ASOPIDS AND THE ARCADIAN ROYAL FAMILY

—— ·◆· ——

Three major heroic families remain to be considered, the Atlantids, who were descended from the seven daughters of Atlas, the Asopids, who were descended from the many daughters of the Peloponnesian river-god Asopos, and finally the Arcadian royal family. As in the case of the Pelopids, the first two families are of especial interest in relation to the origin and ancestral background of leading figures in the Trojan War. The family of Helen at Sparta and the family of Priam and Paris at Troy were brought together into the same genealogical system as two different branches of the Atlantid family (along with the Pelopids indeed, through a female line); and in the posthomeric tradition at least, the two greatest warriors in the Greek expeditionary force, Achilles and Aias (Ajax), were bracketed together as cousins of common Asopid descent. Both families were quite extensive, however, and will be considered in their full extent. The daughters of Atlas are also of some interest in their own right in their common nature as the Pleiades. The Arcadian royal family, which was descended from Pelasgos, the earthborn first man of that mountainous region, was rather similar in character to the Athenian royal family in so far as few of its members played any major role in heroic saga and it was primarily associated with a distinctive body of local legend.

THE ATLANTIDS

Atlas and his seven daughters, the Pleiades

Atlas, a son of the Titan Iapetos (see p. 49), managed to father a sizeable family even though he had to hold up the heavens; for his wife Pleione, daughter of Okeanos, bore him seven notable daughters, who were of twofold significance. Under their collective name of the Pleiades, they were identified with the seven stars of the splendid star-cluster of that name in the constellation of the Bull; and under their individual names, they were of genealogical importance as the founders of the various branches of one of the great families of heroic mythology, the family of the Atlantids. All but one of them bore children to major gods; and one, Maia, even became the mother of an Olympian god. Although we will be concerned primarily with the heroic lines that they founded through their various liaisons, we will begin with the myths that were associated with them in their other nature as star-maidens.

In ancient and modern folklore alike, stars gathered together in conspicuous clusters are commonly identified either as maidens or as animals of one kind or another. Both ideas came to be applied to the stars of the Pleiades in ancient times, for the Greeks liked to believe that they were the daughters of Atlas (a notion already attested in Hesiod's *Works and Days*[1]), while the Romans called them the Septentriones, that is to say the seven plough-oxen. The ancient Greek name for the star-cluster came to be applied to the daughters of Atlas when they were identified with the stars; and the traditional name of their mother, Pleione, was also secondary to that of the star-cluster, for it was plainly devised to enable the name of the Pleiades to be interpreted as a matronymic. The astral myths of the Pleiades fall into two groups, some explaining how the daughters of Atlas (who are regarded as a group of maidens in this connection) came to be transferred to the heavens, and others explaining why one of the Pleiades shines less brightly than the others.

Since the constellation of Orion rises as the Pleiades set, Orion seems to pursue them across the sky. It was explained accordingly that Orion had once encountered them as they were passing through Boeotia (his original homeland, see p. 561) with their mother Pleione, and had pursued them all in the hope of raping Pleione; but when the chase had continued for five (or seven) years, Zeus took pity on the maidens and transferred them to the heavens, where the pursuit is represented in the stars.[2] Or in a somewhat different version, when Orion set out to rape the maidens themselves, causing them to pray to the gods for help, Zeus saved them by turning them into doves (*peleiades*) and removing them to the stars.[3]

A wholly different story was devised to provide a joint explanation for the origin of the Pleiades and of the Hyades, another star-cluster in Taurus made up of five stars that outline the face of the Bull. It is suggested in this connection that the Pleiades were not the only children of Atlas, but were members of a larger family along with five other sisters and a brother called HYAS. When Hyas was killed by a lion (or snake, or boar) during a hunting-trip in Libya, five of his sisters were so overwhelmed by their grief that they soon died of a broken heart, arousing the pity of Zeus, who placed them in the sky as the Hyades; and when the seven remaining sisters also died after a lapse of time, Zeus transferred them to the same region of the sky as the Pleiades. The Hyades were named after their brother because they had shown the greatest grief for him, and the other sisters were called the Pleiades because there were more (*pleious*) of them.[4]

According to a another suggestion, as recorded in some stray verses from Aeschylus, Zeus transferred the seven daughters of Atlas to the sky because he pitied them for the sorrow that they felt for their father (who had to perform the painful duty of holding up the sky);[5] or according to the Hellenistic poetess Moiro, the Pleiades had been doves during their earthly life, and had earned the gratitude of Zeus by bringing ambrosia to him from the streams of Ocean when he was an infant.[6] Stories like these could be made up almost at will.

Although tradition stated that there were seven stars in the Pleiades, this was a merely conventional number since more stars can be distinguished and six are brighter than all the rest. To explain why one of the seven stars should be less radiant, it was suggested that the Pleiad Merope hides her light because she is ashamed at having been the only sister to have married a mortal (i.e. Sisyphos, see below).[7] Or else another of the sisters, Elektra, was so distressed to behold the destruction of Troy (which was ruled by descendants of hers, see below) that she covered her face and has been barely visible ever since; or else she abandoned her sisters altogether to become a comet, an idea inspired by the thought that the tail of a comet (i.e. long-haired star, *astēr komētēs*) resembles the loosened hair of a woman in mourning.[8]

To pass on to the second aspect of the mythology of the daughters of Atlas, their genealogical function as founders of heroic families or mothers of notable children, two of them were founders of major families whose histories have yet to be traced, namely **Elektra** as the progenitor of the Trojan royal line, and **Taygete** as the progenitor of the early Spartan royal line. Another sister, **Alkyone**, is also of some significance in heroic genealogy as the ancestor of some important figures in Theban myth and also of the main Euboean royal line. We will start, however, with the other sisters who will require briefer consideration. Through **Sterope** and **Merope**, two heroic families that have already been discussed, the Pelopids and the Corinthian royal family, were provided with an Atlantid genealogy through the female line; **Maia** was the mother of Hermes; and **Kelaino** had no child of any significance.[9]

Maia and her divine son, and the three lesser Atlantid families

(*i*) An exceptional destiny was reserved for MAIA, who became the mother of an Olympian god. She lived a secluded life in a cave on Mt Kyllene in Arcadia, where Zeus visited her secretly at night and fathered the god Hermes by her. Since Hermes was a precocious infant who set off to steal the cattle of Apollo on the first day of his life and left home forever on the second, Maia had little opportunity to devote any motherly care to him.[10] According to her only other legend, Zeus asked her to rear another Arcadian child of his, Arkas, after the premature death of his mother Kallisto (see p. 541). Maia would doubtless have been something more than an ordinary mortal in the earliest tradition; the *Homeric Hymn to Hermes* refers to her as a nymph. The *Odyssey* mentions her as the mother of Hermes without saying anything about her origin.[11]

(*ii*) If the highest destiny was reserved for Maia, the lowest was reserved for MEROPE, who was the only sister to enter into a union with a mortal; for she became the wife of Sisyphos, the founder of the early Corinthian royal line (see p. 430).[12] She was the mother of Glaukos and grandmother of the great Bellerophon.

(*iii*) According to one tradition at least, STEROPE (or Asterope), bore Oinomaos, king of Pisa, to the war-god Ares.[13] As we have already seen (pp. 503–4), Oinomaos was the father-in-law of Pelops, who established himself in the Peloponnese by winning his daughter Hippodameia along with his kingdom in a deadly bridal-contest. Through his children by Hippodameia, Pelops founded the important family of the Pelopids, which included Agamemnon and Menelaos among its members. By classing Oinomaos as a son of Sterope, the framers of the Atlantid genealogies drew the Pelopids into the same genealogical system as the Spartan and

Trojan royal families, the other families that played the leading role in the events that led up to the Trojan War. Since the local tradition in Oinomaos' native area claimed that his mother was a local eponym called Harpina (see p. 504), Sterope sometimes came to be described as his wife rather than as his mother.[14] He was said to have been a son of Ares in either case, as was appropriate for such a notoriously brutal man.

(*iv*) KELAINO aroused the desire of Poseidon and bore him an obscure son called Lykos, of whom nothing is recorded beyond the fact that his father transferred him to the Isles of the Blessed and rendered him immortal.[15]

Eurypylos, a primordial king of Cyrene in North Africa, was sometimes said to have been a further product of this liaison.[16] He was reigning at the time when Apollo brought the nymph Kyrene to the area (see p. 152); and since he had promised to surrender the kingdom to anyone who could kill a savage lion that was bringing terror to the land, he handed it over to Kyrene after she achieved that feat.[17] It may be remembered that Apollo had fallen in love with her after seeing her wrestling with a lion in her native Thessaly. According to Pindar, the Libyan god Triton assumed the form of Eurypylos when he manifested himself to the Argonauts (see p. 396).[18]

(*v*) ALKYONE became a mistress of Poseidon like Kelaino and bore him twin sons called Hyrieus and Hyperes. HYRIEUS was the eponymous founder of the city of Hyria in eastern Boeotia. He married a nymph called Klonia and fathered two notable sons by her, Lykos and Nykteus, who settled at Thebes and gained considerable influence and power there as was described in Chapter 9 (see pp. 302ff); Antiope, the daughter of Nykteus, was the mother of Zethos and Amphion, who ruled Thebes for a period (see p. 305).[19] According to a conflicting tradition that presents Hyrieus as being childless and indeed wifeless, three visiting gods provided him with a son, Orion, by most unconventional means (see p. 561). The mythical builders Trophonios and Agamedes constructed a treasure-house for him at Hyria, and were caught out by him when they tried to steal from it afterwards (see p. 559).

HYPERES, the other son (or other main son) of Alkyone, was the progenitor of the most important ruling family in Euboea. His daughter ARETHOUSA had intercourse with Poseidon beside the Euripos, the narrow straits that separate Boeotia from the island of Euboea, and bore him a son ABAS, who was the eponymous first ruler of the Abantes of Euboea.[20] These are mentioned in the *Iliad* as the people who were commanded at Troy by Abas' grandson Elephenor, a race of swift-running warriors who wore their hair long and were always eager to rend the chest-armour of their adversaries with their ash-shafted spears.[21] Abas was succeeded by his son CHALKODON, who was said to have been killed in battle by Amphitryon when he led an army across to Boeotia to try to exact a tribute from the Thebans; his tomb could be seen at Teumessos in Boeotia, beside the road that led from Thebes to the shortest crossing to Euboea opposite Chalkis.[22] According to the *Iliad*, ELEPHENOR, the leader of the Euboeans at Troy, was killed in battle by Agenor, a son of the Trojan nobleman Antenor.[23] Before setting off to the war, he offered refuge to Akamas and Demophon, the two sons of Theseus, after their father's throne was seized by Menestheus (see p. 361). Euboea was rarely of much significance in heroic myth. Io was said to have called in at the island during her wanderings as a cow (see p. 231); Herakles fought his final campaign there (see p. 283); and Nauplios lit false beacons at the southern end of the island to lure many of the returning Greeks to their destruction after the Trojan War (see p. 485).

Alkyone was sometimes credited with some lesser children in addition to Hyrieus and Hyperes, namely Anthas, who is mentioned as the eponymous founder of Anthedon in Boeotia and of Antheia in Achaea,[24] and a daughter Aithousa, who bore Eleuther, the eponymous founder of Eleutherai, to Apollo.[25]

The history of the Trojan royal family

(*vi*) The Trojan royal family was descended from ELEKTRA through her son DARDANOS. She bore him to Zeus along with another son, Iasion (or Eetion), on the island of Samothrace in the north-eastern corner of the Aegean.[26] When Iasion (or Eetion) grew up, Zeus struck him with a thunderbolt for presuming to engage in a love affair with the goddess Demeter, or for committing some act of sacrilege against her (see further on p. 132). In his sorrow at his brother's fate, Dardanos decided to leave the island of his birth to settle on the mainland nearby. Since boats had not yet been invented, he improvised a means of transport by setting out to sea on inflated hides or a raft.[27] An alternative tradition suggested that he had to take to the sea to escape the great flood.[28] He drifted across to the closest point on the Asian coast, at the Troad in the north-western corner of Asia Minor. The region was under the rule of the native-born first king of the land, TEUKROS, who offered a friendly welcome to the newcomer, granting his daughter Bateia to him as a wife along with a share of the kingdom. Teukros was a son of Skamandros, the god of the main river of the Troad (see p. 42), who had fathered him by a nymph of Mt Ida.[29]

According to an alternative account which became popular in Hellenistic and later times, Teukros was himself of Greek origin as an immigrant from Crete. In that case, he had crossed over to Asia with his father Skamandros and some Cretan followers; and since an oracle had advised them to settle where they were attacked during the night by 'the earthborn', they settled in the Troad after discovering that mice had gnawed at their bow-strings and the leather of their weapons as they were camping there overnight. Teukros had then named the main river of the area after his father. This story provided an explanation for the origin of the local cult of Apollo Smintheus (of the mice); the *Iliad* already mentions that the god was honoured under that title at a shrine on Tenedos just of the coast of the Troad.[30] There was also an Athenian tradition that suggested that Teukros had emigrated from Attica.[31]

As regards the geography of the land, Troy (Troia in Greek) is properly the name of the territory, while Ilion (Ilium in Latinized form) is the name of its main city; but the name Troy may also be applied in a looser sense to the city, in both ancient and modern usage. The Troad (Troas) is an alternative name for the region of Troy.

Since Teukros had no male children, Dardanos inherited the entire territory after his death, and named it Dardania after himself. He founded a settlement on Mt Ida, the mountain range to the east of the Trojan plain. Although the *Iliad* credits him with only a single son, ERICHTHONIOS, later sources from the Hesiodic

Catalogue onwards often add a second son, Ilos (an insignificant doublet of the Ilos who was the eponymous founder of Ilion, see below).[32] After succeeding to the throne, Erichthonios moved down from the hill-country to the Trojan plain, where – so the *Iliad* tells us – he pastured three thousand mares in the marshlands and became the wealthiest of mortals.[33] He married Astyoche, a daughter of Simoeis (the god of the second main river of the Troad), and fathered a single son by her, TROS, the eponym of the land of Troy. Tros succeeded his father as king and married Kallirhoe, daughter of Skamandros, who bore him three sons, Ilos, Assarakos and Ganymedes.[34]

GANYMEDES spent little time in his native land since he was soon abducted to Olympos on account of his beauty to serve as a cupbearer to Zeus and the other gods. His fate is mentioned in the *Iliad*, which states that the gods snatched him away to live in their company as the wine-pourer of Zeus because he was exceptionally beautiful, the most beautiful of all mortal men.[35] Or according to another early source, the *Homeric Hymn to Aphrodite*, Zeus caused him to be swept up to heaven by a whirlwind, to the great distress of his father, who had no idea where he had been taken. Zeus took pity on Tros, however, and not only sent Hermes to tell him that Ganymedes would be living among the gods as an immortal, but presented him with some divine horses to compensate him for his loss.[36] These horses later became a source of trouble, as was so often the case with divine gifts, when Herakles sought to acquire them (see p. 275). Another tradition suggested that Zeus presented a golden vine to Tros (or to his grandson Laomedon) as compensation for Ganymedes (see p. 472).[37]

In what has come to be the most familiar account of the abduction, Zeus sent an eagle (his special bird) to carry off Ganymedes, or else transformed himself into an eagle for that purpose.[38] This idea first surfaces in Hellenistic times; in the earliest artistic representations on red-figure vases, Zeus is shown performing the abduction in his usual form. Although it is stated from the beginning that Ganymedes was raised up to heaven because of his beauty, there is no indication that Zeus was thought to have become his lover in the earliest tradition. From the classical period onwards, however, it seems to have been commonly assumed that Zeus abducted him or arranged his abduction with this end in view, as is first indicated by Theognis and Pindar.[39] It may be noted in this connection that the word catamite (*catamitus* in the original Latin) was derived from a Latin form of Ganymedes' name.

ILOS, the eldest of the three sons of Tros, succeeded to the throne and founded the city of Ilion (often loosely called Troy), which became the seat of rule of the kings of Troy from that time forth. The remaining brother, ASSARAKOS, founded the junior branch of the royal family, which was based outside the city on Mt Ida. Kapys, the son of Assarakos, was the father of Anchises, who aroused the love of Aphrodite and fathered the great Aineias by her (see p. 200).[40]

According to a story that was apparently modelled on the Theban foundation legend, Ilos chose the site of his city by taking a cow as his guide. For he visited neighbouring Phrygia at some point in his reign and won the wrestling contest in some games that were held there by the king; and in addition to the ordinary prize of fifty youths and fifty girls, the king gave him a dappled cow at the bidding of an oracle, and told him to found a city wherever it first lay down. So he followed the cow until it sank to the ground on the hill of Phrygian Ate, an eminence on the Trojan plain, and chose that as the site of his new city of Ilion.[41] Or in a somewhat different version, Apollo granted an oracle to Ilos himself, telling him to found the city where he saw one of his cattle fall to the ground as he was driving the herd to neighbouring Mysia.[42] After observing the appointed sign, he prayed to Zeus for confirmation; and when he emerged from his tent on the following morning, he found that a wooden effigy (*xoanon*) of Pallas Athene had fallen from the sky during the night and was lying on the ground outside.[43] This statue, which was known as the Palladion (i.e. effigy of Pallas Athene; Palladium in Latin form), would serve as a protective talisman for Ilion; Ilos raised a magnificent temple to Athena to house it, where it remained until Odysseus stole it in the last stages of the Trojan War to deprive the Trojans of its protective power (see p. 472). The tomb of Ilos is mentioned in the *Iliad* as a landmark on the Trojan plain.[44]

Ilos and his wife Eurydike, daughter of Adrastos, had a single son LAOMEDON, who succeeded to the throne.[45] Laomedon had a large family of sons and daughters of whom three alone need concern us, Tithonos, Priam and Hesione. Tithonos was famous as the lover of the dawn-goddess Eos (see p. 47), and as the father of Memnon (see p. 468); we will return to the other two in connection with the downfall of their father. Laomedon was a powerful but heedlessly arrogant ruler who brought disaster on himself and his people by two dishonourable acts of ingratitude, first toward Apollo and Poseidon and then toward Herakles. The two gods were once obliged to serve him as labourers for a year as a penalty for having rebelled against Zeus; or else they submitted themselves to him of their own accord to test whether he was really as presumptuous as he was reputed to be. While they were with him, they fortified Ilion with massive walls on the agreement that they would receive a fee for their work; but when the work was completed, Laomedon not only refused to pay them but treated them in a most insulting manner, threatening to sell them into slavery and cut off their ears. To punish the king for his duplicity, Apollo sent a plague while Poseidon sent a flood and a fearsome sea-monster to prey on the inhabitants of the land.[46] The arrival of this monster set in course the train of events that would lead Laomedon to commit his second act of ingratitude. The Trojans learned from oracles that they would be delivered from the monster if the king would expose his daughter HESIONE to it; so he fastened her to some rocks by the sea-shore, where Herakles happened to catch sight of her as he was sailing past Troy on his way to the land of the Amazons (or was sailing to Colchis with the Argonauts). As has already been recounted, he promised to save Hesione in return for the divine horses that had been presented to Tros as compensation for the loss of Ganymedes; but when he tried to claim his reward after fulfilling the task, Laomedon refused to hand over the horses (or tried to substitute mortal ones). So he returned at a later date with a sizeable force of allies and sacked Ilion for the first time in its history, killing Laomedon and all his sons apart from the youngest, PRIAM (see further on p. 276). He offered Hesione to Telamon, king of Salamis, who had fought as his ally, and allowed her to choose whomever she wished from among the captives. She released her only surviving brother, ransoming him with her veil; he was originally called Podarkes, but was now given his familiar name of Priam because she 'purchased' him in this way (as though his name were derived from *priamai*, to buy).[47] For a more detailed account of Herakles' adventures at Troy, see pp. 275–6.

Priam succeeded to the throne and continued to rule at Troy until the city was burned down and he himself was killed at the end of the Trojan War; something has already been said about him and his large family in connection with the culminating episode in the history of Troy (see especially pp. 451ff and 474ff). Owing to Homer's fine portrait of him, in which he is presented as a noble and sympathetic character, it is possible to imagine him as a living individual, in contrast to his predecessors. He makes his most telling appearances in book 3 of the *Iliad*, as he talks to Helen and the Trojan elders on the ramparts of the city, and in the final book, when he visits Achilles to seek the return of Hektor's body.[48]

The early Spartan royal family

(*vii*) The Spartan royal family was descended from the Atlantid **Taygete**, who bore LAKEDAIMON, the eponym of the Peloponnesian province of that name, to her divine lover Zeus.[49]

The south-eastern province of the Peloponnese, which adjoined Arcadia and the Argolid to the north and Messenia to the west, was known to the Greeks as *Lakedaimōn*, as was its main city also. *Sparta* was an alternative name for the city, with poetic and patriotic overtones. The name Sparta has also come to be applied in a looser sense to the territory as a whole. *Laconia* (or Laconica, cf. *gē Lakonikē* in Greek) was a Latin name for Lakedaimon.

Taygete was the eponym of Taygetos, the towering mountain range that divides Laconia from Messenia. The only proper myth recorded for her, the tale recounted in Chapter 8 in which she was said to have dedicated the Cerynitian hind to Artemis after the goddess saved her from being raped by Zeus (see p. 260), does not accord well with the usual tradition that makes her the founder of a royal line through a son borne to Zeus. Her son LAKEDAIMON married Sparta, the eponym of the main city of the land, who was a daughter of Eurotas, the eponym of the main river of the land, and a granddaughter (or great-granddaughter) of Lelex, the earthborn first ruler of the land. Lakedaimon and Sparta had a daughter Eurydike, who became the wife of Akrisios, king of Argos (see p. 238), and a son Amyklas, who was the eponymous founder of Amyklai, an ancient town on the Eurotas about three miles south-east of Sparta. Amyklas was succeeded by his son Kynortas or Kynortes (either directly or after the death of an elder brother Argalos). Hyakinthos, the short-lived Laconian favourite of Apollo (see p. 155), is the only early member of the family to be of any real interest as a mythological figure; having originated in prehellenic cult rather than in heroic mythology, he was inserted into the royal line as a son of Amyklas, doubtless because Amyklai was his most important cultic centre.[50]

Kynortas was succeeded by his son Oibalos, another nonentity like himself; and with the sons of Oibalos, we at last enter the realm of major heroic myth. Oibalos had three sons, his presumptive heir TYNDAREOS (whom we have already encountered as the protector of the young Agamemnon and Menelaos, see p. 508, and as the putative father of Helen, see p. 438), and Hippokoon and Ikarios. HIPPOKOON, who was of illegitimate birth in some accounts, had a large family of twelve or twenty sons, and seized the throne with their support, driving Tyndareos into exile.[51] In one version of the legend, he expelled Ikarios along with his brother, and the two of them sought refuge at the court of Thestios (see p. 413) at Pleuron in Aetolia. They repaid their host by assisting him in a border war and so helping him to extend his power into neighbouring Acarnania (where Ikarios settled as a local ruler according to one tradition).[52] Or in another account, Ikarios helped Hippokoon to expel Tyndareos and remained with him in Sparta afterwards; in that case, Tyndareos lived closer to home during the period of his exile, seeking refuge at Pellana in Laconia or with Aphareus, king of Messenia.[53] Hippokoon and his sons finally provoked their own downfall by angering Herakles, who mounted an expedition against Sparta and killed every one of them (see further on pp. 278–9). Tyndareos was then recalled by the victorious hero; and Ikarios was usually said to have lived with him at Sparta after he regained his rightful throne.

To start with the younger brother, IKARIOS married a nymph called Periboia (or a woman otherwise named), who bore him various children of whom PEN-ELOPE, the future wife of Odysseus, was by far the most important.[54] It is no surprise to discover that the most memorable myths of Ikarios should be connected with Penelope and her marriage. In one account, as we have seen, Tyndareos interceded with Ikarios on Odysseus' behalf in return for advice on how to avoid trouble from Helen's suitors (see p. 440); or else Odysseus' father Laertes interceded on his son's behalf;[55] but a more picturesque legend suggested that Ikarios arranged a bridal-race for Penelope's suitors in the streets of Sparta, hence the name of one such street Aphetais (Leaving-Street), which was where the defeated suitors were left behind by the victorious Odysseus.[56] According to another local tale, which was put forward to explain the origin of a statue of Aidos (Shame or Modesty personified) on the road north from Sparta, Ikarios was distressed to think that his beloved daughter would be living far away from him on Ithaca, and tried to pursuade Odysseus to settle down in Laconia; and when Odysseus proved unwilling, he begged Penelope to remain with him, even following after her in his chariot when she set off for Ithaca with her husband. Odysseus finally lost patience and told Penelope that she must either accompany him of her own free will or agree to return home with her father. Hesitating to speak aloud, she covered her face with her veil, and Ikarios divined her meaning and allowed her to pass on her way; and he commemorated the incident by raising a statue to Aidos at the spot.[57]

TYNDAREOS married LEDA, a daughter of his former host Thestios, and came to preside over a mixed family consisting partly of his own children and partly of children who were fathered by Zeus on his wife. **Helen**, as we have seen (p. 438), was either one of Leda's children by Zeus or else her adoptive child as the daughter of Zeus and Nemesis. Leda also bore three legitimate daughters to her husband, namely **Klytaimnestra** (Clytemnestra in Latin), who became the wife of Agamemnon, and **Timandra**, who married Echemos (an Arcadian king who was best remembered for having delayed the return of the Heraklids, see p. 288), and **Phylonoe**, of whom nothing is recorded beyond the fact that she was rendered immortal by Artemis.[58]

There was disagreement about the origin of **Kastor** and **Polydeukes** (Pollux in Latin), the two sons of Leda. The *Odyssey* suggests that both were children of Zeus, while the Hesiodic *Catalogue* describes them as sons of Tyndareos;[59] but according to Pindar and the standard later tradition, they were of mixed paternity since Leda conceived Kastor to Tyndareos and Polydeukes to Zeus on the same night.[60] The twins were known as the Dioskouroi (Sons of Zeus, Dioscuri in Latin form) irrespectively throughout antiquity.

According to a tale which can be traced back to Stesichorus, Tyndareos once offended Aphrodite by forgetting her when he was offering sacrifices to all the gods, and she reacted by causing his daughters (i.e. Klytaimnestra, Timandra and his putative daughter Helen) to abandon their husbands for other men. So Helen eloped with Paris, Klytaimnestra embarked on a love affair with Aigisthos with fatal effect for her husband (see p. 508), and Timandra abandoned Echemos for Phyleus (presumably the son of Augeias of that name, see p. 261).[61]

When Helen grew up to become the most beautiful woman in Greece, she attracted suitors from all parts of the Greek world. Through a process of selection that has already been described (see p. 439), Tyndareos (or his sons, or Helen herself) chose Menelaos, son of Atreus, as her husband. Menelaos, who was of Pelopid descent, had no kingdom of his own, but benefited from the support of his brother Agamemnon, the rich and powerful king of Mycenae. He was already living in Sparta for reasons explained on pp. 507–8, and now settled down at the court of Tyndareos with his bride. When the early death of the Dioskouroi (who were killed before the Trojan War, see below) deprived the king of his only male heirs, he adopted his son-in-law Menelaos as his successor, and the crown passed out of the Atlantid line. The kingdom remained under Pelopid rule for two generations thereafter, passing to Menelaos' nephew Orestes, who thus came to rule over Sparta as well as his native Argolid (see p. 514), and thence to Teisamenos, son of Orestes. Teisamenos was finally displaced by the Heraklids (see p. 516), who could lay claim to Sparta on the ground that Herakles had placed Tyndareos on the throne as a result of his campaign against Hippokoon. In one account, indeed, Herakles explicitly told Tyndareos that the kingdom was to be held in trust for his descendants.

The Dioskouroi, and their conflict with the sons of Aphareus

From this branch of the Atlantid family, only the DIOSKOUROI remain to be considered. Inseparable from the time of their birth, they grew up to become two of the greatest heroes in Greece during the period immediately preceding the Trojan War; but as the result of a quarrel with some Messenian cousins, they were killed before they could ascend to the Spartan throne or fight at Troy. Kastor was particularly noted for his horsemanship and Polydeukes for his prowess as a boxer.[62] Along with most of the main heroes of their generation, they sailed with the Argonauts and joined the hunt for the Calydonian boar; in the course of the former adventure, Polydeukes applied his boxing skills to kill the murderous pugilist Amykos (see p. 386).[63] A reference to Polydeukes in a partially preserved poem by Alcman suggests that there was also an early tradition in which the Dioskouroi aided Herakles in his campaign against Hippokoon.[64] As well as appearing in a supporting role in these joint adventures, the twins played a leading role in three legends of their own: they rescued the young Helen from Attica after she was abducted from Sparta by Theseus (see p. 361), they abducted Hilaeira and Phoibe, two Messenian princesses, and they became embroiled in a fatal conflict with Idas and Lynkeus, two Messenian princes.

IDAS and LYNKEUS, known jointly as the Apharetidai, were the two sons of Aphareus, who was ruling Messenia at this time in conjunction with his brother Leukippos (see p. 422). In what was probably the earliest version of the story, they quarrelled with the Dioskouroi as the result of a disagreement over some cattle. According to the full account recorded by Apollodorus, the two sets of brothers had joined together to rustle some cattle from Arcadia, and the trouble began when the spoils were entrusted to Idas for division. For he cut a cow into four and proposed that half of the spoils should go to the one who ate his portion first, and the rest to the one who ate his portion second; and he then devoured his own portion and that of his brother too before anyone else had a chance. He claimed all of the cattle as a result of this ruse and drove them away to Messenia with the help of his brother. The Dioskouroi were unwilling to be deprived of their proper share through sharp practice of this kind and hurried off in pursuit. On arriving in Messenia, they seized all the cattle that had been stolen from Arcadia along with many others, and set an ambush for Idas and Lynkeus; for the conclusion of the story, see below.[65] Some such tale was already recounted in the first epic in the Trojan cycle, the *Cypria*. The surviving summary is not very informative, however, merely stating that a fight broke out when the Dioskouroi were caught in the act as they were stealing some cattle from Idas and Lynkeus.[66] Pindar agrees that the quarrel arose over cattle, but reports nothing further.[67] Although it is quite possible that the early epic version is preserved in Apollodorus' fanciful tale of Idas' deception and its aftermath, we cannot be sure about the matter.

In another version of the story, the trouble arose because the Dioskouroi abducted HILAEIRA and PHOIBE, the daughters of Leukippos, two Messenian princesses who were betrothed to Idas and Lynkeus. Some accounts even suggest that the Dioskouroi were invited to the wedding-feast when the sisters were due to marry Idas and Lynkeus, and took advantage of the occasion to carry them off for themselves.[68] Or in Theocritus' account, Idas and Lynkeus pursued and confronted the Dioskouroi after they had abducted their brides, and Lynkeus accused the twins of having bribed Leukippos to hand over his daughters, even though they had been promised to Idas and himself, by offering him gifts of cattle and mules.[69] The story varies to differing extents in other versions. There is a composite version, for instance, in which Idas and Lynkeus reproached the Dioskouroi for not having paid a bride-price to Leukippos for his daughters, and the twins then proceeded to remedy the fault by driving off some cattle that belonged to the father of their accusers, so provoking the fatal conflict between the two pairs of brothers.[70]

Although the surviving literary accounts are of Hellenistic and later origin, the story of the abduction was clearly familiar by the sixth century BC, for it was depicted on the Amyklaian throne[71] and other works of art from that period; but even if the abduction itself figured in early epic, it may not have carried the same implications in the early tradition, since we cannot be sure that Idas (whose marriage to Marpessa is mentioned in the *Iliad*, see p. 153) and his brother were originally thought to have been betrothed to the maidens. Polydeukes took Phoibe as his wife and Kastor took Hilaeira; although some sources report a son for each marriage, there is disagreement on their names and none are of any significance.[72] Under their joint name of the Leukippides, Hilaeira and Phoibe were honoured as minor goddesses at their sanctuary in Sparta, where they were served by virgin priestesses who were known as Leukippides like themselves.[73]

Although the different accounts of the confrontation between the two sets of brothers vary considerably in their details, it was commonly agreed that Kastor and the two sons of Aphareus were killed and that Polydeukes was removed from the company of mortals. Pindar and Apollodorus provide similar narratives which were probably based on the early epic account in the *Cypria*. When the Dioskouroi tried to lay an ambush for the sons of Aphareus in Messenia, they were foiled by the superhuman eyesight of Lynkeus, who climbed the heights of Taygetos between Laconia and Messenia to survey the entire Peloponnese. He finally observed that the twins were hiding in Messenia inside a hollow oak-tree, apparently making use of his magical vision to see through its trunk. This feature of the story (which is mentioned by Pindar though not by Apollodorus) is already recorded in some surviving verses from the *Cypria*. After rushing down to the tree with his brother, Idas inflicted a fatal wound on Kastor, but the two brothers were then put to flight by Polydeukes, who pursued them to the burial-place of their father Aphareus. Although they tried to repel him by uprooting their father's gravestone and hurling it at his chest, he contrived to press forward and killed Lynkeus with his spear; and Zeus then came to his assistance by striking Idas with a thunderbolt.[74]

Polydeukes is regarded as a son of Zeus in this story while Kastor is a wholly mortal son of Tyndareos. In Pindar's account, Polydeukes returned to his fallen brother to find that he was on the point of death, and prayed to Zeus to be allowed to die with him; but Zeus responded by offering him two choices, saying that he could either enjoy full immortality on Olympos in accordance with his divine parentage, or else share his immortality with his brother, so that each of them would spend half of their time in the Underworld and the other half with the gods on Olympos. Polydeukes chose the latter alternative without a moment's hesitation. Or in Apollodorus' narrative, in which Kastor had met an immediate death at the hand of Idas, Polydeukes was brought to the ground by a stone that was hurled by Lynkeus just before he was killed by him. Zeus carried Polydeukes up to heaven after killing Idas with the thunderbolt, but he refused to accept immortality while his brother Kastor lay dead. So Zeus allowed him to share his immortality with his brother by arranging that both of them should live among the gods and among mortals (i.e. in Hades) on alternate days. These events took place just before the Greek forces assembled for the Trojan War; according to the *Cypria*, the Dioskouroi entertained Paris when he first arrived in Laconia, and became embroiled in this conflict with Idas and Lynkeus shortly afterwards, around the time of Helen's abduction.[75] This would explain, of course, why they were unable to prevent Paris from escaping with her.

Some authors alter the preceding pattern by suggesting that Kastor was killed by Lynkeus rather than by Idas, or that Idas was killed by Polydeukes rather than by Zeus, but this makes little practical difference.[76] In the version recorded by Hyginus, Idas and Lynkeus took up their arms to try to recover the daughters of Leukippos after they were abducted by the Dioskouroi. After Lynkeus was killed by Kastor in the ensuing fight, Idas put all other thoughts aside to attend to the burial of his brother; but this merely provided an occasion for further confrontation since Kastor intervened to prevent him from raising a monument to Lynkeus, saying that he had met with a thoroughly ignominious defeat. Idas was so angry that he thrust his sword into Kastor's thigh, inflicting a fatal wound; or in another version recorded in the same source, he killed Kastor by pushing the monument over to crush him under it. On hearing of Kastor's fate, Polydeukes rushed to the site, killed Idas in single combat, and then prayed that he should be allowed to share his own immortality with his brother.[77] Or in an exceptional account by Theocritus in which both of the Dioskouroi survive, Kastor proposed that he and Lynkeus, as the two younger brothers, should settle the quarrel by single combat so as to avoid unnecessary bloodshed. When Lynkeus lost two of his fingers in the fray and dropped his sword, he ran off towards his brother, who was lying by the tomb of Aphareus; but Kastor sped after him and transfixed him with his sword. Idas leapt up in response, seizing that memorial-stone from his father's tomb, and would have hurled it at his brother's killer if Zeus had not prevented him by striking him dead with a thunderbolt. So Kastor survived, as did Polydeukes, who had been no more than a spectator.[78] For the other major story associated with Idas, see pp. 153–4.

It was inevitably suggested in astral mythology that the Dioskouroi were raised to the heavens to become the constellation of the Twins (Gemini); Zeus brought this about because he wanted to commemorate their brotherly devotion.[79] They were honoured as gods, particularly in their native Sparta, and became increasingly popular throughout the Greek world as protectors who could be appealed to in times of danger, especially at sea. In the latter connection, they were sometimes identified with the Kabeiroi or gods of Samothrace (see p. 220). They manifested themselves in St Elmo's fire, an electrical discharge that plays around the masts of ships during thunderstorms; as the early lyric poet Alcaeus expresses the matter, they run up the mastheads shining bright from afar, bringing light to the black ship in the night of affliction.[80] The cult of the Dioskouroi was introduced to Rome at a relatively early period; according to Roman tradition, a temple was raised to them in the Forum in 484 BC in fulfilment of a vow that had been made by Aulus Postumius at the battle of Lake Regillus. It was claimed, indeed, that the Twins had appeared in person at the battle (c. 496), helping the Romans to victory against the Latins by leading them in a cavalry charge.[81] Kastor overshadowed his brother for some reason at Rome, where the twins were quite often referred to as the Castores.

THE ASOPIDS

The Asopid family was formed from the descendants of the Peloponnesian river-god ASOPOS, whose waters flowed to the sea on the northern coast of the peninsula to the west of Corinth. Asopos and his wife Metope, a daughter of the river Ladon, had many daughters who were abducted by Zeus and other gods to many different parts of the Greek world, where they founded local lines through children borne to their abductors or simply served as local eponyms. Although the family was quite large overall, it is primarily of interest for the single branch of it that produced Achilles and the greater Aias (Ajax). As the bravest and mightiest of the Greek warriors at Troy, Achilles and Aias form a natural pair in much the same way as Agamemnon and Menelaos; and it was doubtless for that reason that they came to be classed as cousins, even though there is no suggestion in the *Iliad* that they were related in any way, and it might be supposed in any case that they were originally unrelated because they were connected with widely separate areas. When described as cousins, they were said to have been grandsons of Aiakos, king of Aegina, and great-grandsons of the Asopid Aigina, who was abducted to the island of that name by Zeus. It was explained that their fathers Telamon and Peleus had been expelled from Aegina for committing a murder within the family, and had settled in different areas, Peleus in Thessaly in the north and Telamon at Salamis off the coast of Attica, hence the widely separate birthplaces of Aias and Achilles. See Table 18. Formally at least, the genealogy of Achilles remains consistent from the time of the *Iliad*, which traces his ancestry to Peleus, Aiakos and Zeus;[82] but it seems likely that Peleus and Aiakos were originally of Thessalian birth, and that Aiakos was first transferred to Aegina when the common Asopid genealogy was devised for Aias and Achilles. The myth of the abduction of Aigina, as developed in that connection, then provided the model for numerous other stories in which daughters of Asopos were said to have been carried abroad by one god or another. A sizeable family came to be built up in this manner in the course of time, even if most of its added members were arbitrarily invented eponyms of little general interest. We will concentrate on Aigina's branch of the family initially and primarily, before casting a brief glance at the secondary branches.

Aigina, daughter of Asopos, and her son Aiakos

Zeus fell in love with AIGINA after seeing her by her father's streams in the land of Sicyon in the northern Peloponnese, and carried her off, taking her eastward past Corinth and across the sea to an island in the Saronic Gulf between Argos and Attica. On discovering that she had vanished, her father Asopos set off in search of her, and visited Corinth first to question its ruler, Sisyphos, who could see for miles around from his towering citadel of Akrokorinthos. As it happened, the abduction had indeed been observed by Sisyphos, who betrayed the secret to the river-god in return for the creation of a spring on his acropolis. This turned out to be a dubious bargain, however, since Zeus could hardly allow such an indiscretion to go unpunished (see further on p. 431). Nor did Asopos gain any advantage from the information, for when he tried to recover his daughter, Zeus hurled thunderbolts at him to force him to return to his streams. As a consequence, so we are told, coals could be collected from the Asopos from that time onward (although there is apparently no sign of them nowadays).[83]

On arriving at Aegina, which had been known as Oinone or Oinopia until that time, Zeus settled Aigina there as his mistress and renamed the island in her honour.

She bore him a single son, AIAKOS, who grew up to become the first king of Aegina.[84] He had no one to rule over initially, either because the island had been uninhabited before the arrival of his mother, or because Hera had caused the death of the original population after learning that her husband had embarked on a love affair with Aegina. In the latter case, the goddess achieved her aim by sending a terrible plague or by sending a snake to poison the water-supplies.[85] Aiakos prayed to his father to send him some people to relieve his loneliness and provide him with subjects to rule over, and Zeus granted his wish by transforming the local ants (*myrmēkes*) into human beings. This story was devised to account for the name and origin of the Myrmidons, the Thessalian people who were ruled by his son Peleus and commanded by Achilles at Troy; we are to understand that Peleus took some of the Aiginetan 'ant-people' away with him when he departed into exile.[86]

Aiakos was a man of incomparable piety and righteousness. When the whole of Greece was afflicted by a famine as a result of the murder of Stymphalos (see p. 549) or else of Androgeos (see p. 340), an oracle declared that Aiakos alone would be capable of delivering the land from its barrenness if he were to offer prayers to the gods (or to Zeus specifically) on behalf of all the Greeks.[87] And whenever disputes arose, Aiakos could be relied upon as a just arbitrator, as when he arbitrated between Skeiron and Nisos over the Megarian succession (see p. 343).[88] It was even claimed that he arbitrated in disputes between the gods,[89] even if no specific examples of his activities in this regard have been preserved. His exceptional virtues were duly acknowledged after his death when he was appointed to be one of the judges of the dead or else the gate-keeper of Hades (see p. 122).[90]

Peleus and Telamon are exiled from Aegina for killing their half-brother Phokos

For all his high principles, Aiakos mismanaged his family affairs and became estranged from his sons. He married Endeis, daughter of Cheiron (or Skeiron), who bore him his two legitimate children, PELEUS and TELAMON; but he also fathered a son out of wedlock by the Nereid Psamathe.[91] On finding herself accosted by a mortal, the sea-nymph tried to escape his embrace by turning herself into a seal (*phōkē*), but he kept a firm hold on her and caused her to conceive a son, PHOKOS, whom he reared as a member of his family.[92] He was especially fond of Phokos and showed him such favour that his wife and legitimate sons grew increasingly resentful, until Peleus and Telamon eventually banded together to murder the intruder with the encouragement of their mother. Although accounts differ on whether Peleus or Telamon delivered the fatal blow or both did so jointly, it was generally agreed that they conspired together to cause his death. According to the usual tradition, one or the other killed Phokos by hurling a discus at his head while the three of them were exercising together. Other versions of the legend in which they were said to have killed him because they were jealous of his athletic prowess or simply by accident were plainly of secondary origin. Whatever the exact course of events, Aiakos sent Peleus and Telamon into exile on hearing of the death of Phokos, and never allowed them to set foot on Aegina again.[93]

As has been mentioned, Achilles states in the *Iliad* that he is the son of Peleus and grandson of Aiakos, son of Zeus; but the Homeric epics are less informative about Aias, reporting nothing about the descent of his father Telamon. It is never suggested in any way that Achilles and Aias are related; and although the title of Aiakides (son or descendant of Aiakos) is applied quite frequently to Achilles and Peleus,[94] it is never applied to Aias or his half-brother Teukros. There is thus every reason to suppose that Aias and Achilles and their respective fathers had not yet been brought together into a common family. It is impossible to tell exactly when the linkage was established. Pindar is the first author to state explicitly that Telamon was a son of Aiakos (even if some surviving lines from an early epic, the *Alkmaionis*, already imply that Telamon and Peleus were brothers by saying that they joined together to murder Phokos).[95] Although Homer mentions that Achilles' grandfather Aiakos was a son of Zeus like the Aiginetan of the later tradition, the mother of this Aiakos is left unnamed; as was noted above, Peleus and Aiakos were probably regarded as being purely Thessalian at this stage. If that is correct, the mother of Aiakos may possibly have been a daughter of the Thessalian Asopos, which flowed into the Malian Gulf in the very region of Peleus' kingdom.[96]

According to a local tradition at Aegina, Telamon once sailed back to the island in the vain hope of persuading his father to allow him back, but Aiakos refused to allow him even to set foot on the shore, and he was therefore obliged to pile up a mound in the sea so as to speak from there (hence a feature of the local topography).[97] Another local tradition, also recorded by Pausanias, suggested that Aiakos had surrounded the island with reefs below the waterline to protect it from its enemies[98] (although one might have thought that he would have asked his father to arrange such a matter). According to a legend recounted by Pindar, Apollo and Poseidon summoned the help of Aiakos when they were building the walls of Troy (see p. 523); for as a scholion explains, the city would surely have been impregnable if its walls had been of wholly divine construction. After the walls were completed, three snakes tried to leap on to the ramparts, but two of them fell back and died while only one succeeded; and Apollo interpreted this omen by declaring that Troy would be seized at Aiakos' section of the wall. His descendants would play a part, furthermore, in its capture on two occasions.[99]

Along with a Corinthian hero of the same name, Phokos was one of the eponyms of the province of Phocis in Central Greece, which he was said to have visited for a period before his death (see further on p. 565). According to Pindar and some later sources, Menoitios, the father of Achilles' friend Patroklos, was a son of Aigina by her second marriage to Aktor, son of Myrmidon; the Hesiodic *Catalogue* is exceptional in suggesting that Menoitios was a fourth son of Aiakos.[100]

Telamon becomes king of Salamis, and fathers Aias and Teukros

Telamon remained near his birthplace, settling on the island of Salamis not far to the north, just off the coast of Attica. Salamis was then under the rule of another Asopid called Kychreus, who was a son of Poseidon by Salamis, daughter of Asopos (see p. 535), and was therefore related to Telamon; having no sons of his own, he offered his daughter Glauke to his Aeginetan relation and adopted him as his heir. Telamon duly succeeded his father-in-law but remarried at some stage, taking Periboia (or Eriboia), a daughter of Alkathoos, king of Megara, as his new wife; and it was by her that he fathered his only legitimate son, the mighty AIAS (or Ajax in Latin).[101]

As Pindar relates, Herakles called in at Salamis to recruit Telamon for his campaign against Troy, and prayed to his father Zeus to ask that his host should be granted a brave and hardy son; and when Zeus sent an eagle as a sign of his assent, Herakles told Telamon that he would father a son of such a character, and that he should name him Aias after the eagle (*aietos*).[102] As befitted the father of such a hero, Telamon was one of the greatest warriors of his own generation. He sailed with the Argonauts, joined the hunt for the Calydonian boar[103] and, in some accounts at least, accompanied Herakles to the land of the Amazons (see p. 263); but he was best remembered for having been the foremost ally of Herakles during the first sack of Troy (see further on p. 276). As a reward for his assistance on that occasion, Herakles offered him Hesione, the daughter of Laomedon, the defeated king, as a concubine; and she bore him another worthy son, TEUKROS, who accompanied Aias on the second and greatest of the Greek expeditions against Troy. After performing valiant service at Troy, Aias committed suicide in the closing stages of the war (see pp. 469ff for the circumstances), and Teukros was banished by Telamon when he arrived home without him (see p. 577). Eurysakes, a son whom Aias had fathered by his concubine Tekmessa at Troy, was thus destined to become the successor of Telamon at Salamis.[104] The Athenians claimed that he and his brother Philaios ceded the island to Athens and settled in Attica.[105]

Peleus in Thessaly; his divine marriage and son Achilles

Peleus travelled much further from his original home than his brother, making his way to Phthia in southern Thessaly, where he was purified by Eurytion (or Eurytos), the ruler of the land. The Phthian ruling line had been founded by Eurytion's grandfather, Myrmidon, son of Zeus and Eurymedousa, who was the eponym of the local people, the Myrmidons; Myrmidon had married Peisidike, one of the daughters of Aiolos (see p. 410), who had borne him two sons including Aktor, the father of Eurytion. An alternative tradition suggested that Peleus was received at Phthia by Aktor himself. Since Eurytion had no male heir, he invited Peleus to settle in his kingdom, offering him his daughter Antigone as a wife along with a third of the land; Antigone bore him a single child, a daughter called Polydora.[106] The *Iliad* already refers to Polydora as a daughter of Peleus, mentioning that she married Boros, son of Perieres, but bore a son Menesthios to a local river-god Spercheios; this Menesthios later became one of Achilles' lieutenants at Troy.[107] The story of Peleus' marriage to Antigone and purification by Eurytion probably goes back to early epic since it was known to Pherecydes.[108] Events followed much the same course in the alternative version in which Peleus was received by Aktor, son of Myrmidon; in that case, he married a daughter of Aktor who is named either as Polymele or Eurydike.[109]

Along with other leading heroes of the age, Peleus and his host were invited to Aetolia to take part in the hunt for the Calydonian boar; and as Peleus was aiming a spear at the boar, he accidentally killed Eurytion instead, and was therefore obliged to depart into exile once again. He sought refuge in a more northerly region of Thessaly, at Iolkos, where he was purified by Akastos, the son and successor of Pelias.[110] During his stay at the Iolkian court (or perhaps during an earlier visit, since the games in question should properly have taken place before the boar-hunt), he competed in the splendid funeral games that were held by Akastos after the death of his father. Attic vase-painters liked to show Peleus wrestling with the great heroine Atalanta, contrasting his dark body with the paler body of his female opponent. He was said to have been defeated by her. Or else he competed against Hippalkimos, one of the many sons of Pelops, with greater success, or wrestled with Jason.[111]

Matters took a turn for the worse when Astydameia (or Hippolyte), the wife of Akastos, fell in love with Peleus and tried to lure him to a secret meeting; for she was so angered by his refusal that she told her husband that he had tried to rape or seduce her. As is usual in stories of this kind (see for instance p. 538), Akastos believed her allegations but was unwilling to take action against a guest. So he invited Peleus to join him on a hunting-trip on Mt Pelion with the intention of exposing him to danger. Peleus met with excellent fortune in the chase itself, defeating his companions in a hunting-contest by killing more beasts than they could. They tried to cheat by stealing some of his prey, but he had taken the precaution of cutting out the tongues of his victims and was able to expose the fraud by producing them from his knapsack. When he fell asleep after his exertions, Akastos abandoned him on the mountainside, removing his sword to leave him exposed without defence to the Centaurs and savage beasts that roamed the slopes. His sword was, incidentally, a divine weapon that had been made for him by Hephaistos; Akastos hid it under a pile of dung. As Peleus was searching for it after he awoke, he was seized by a band of Centaurs and would surely have been killed by them if the noble Centaur Cheiron had not come to his rescue. Cheiron also helped him further by recovering his sword.[112] In another version of the legend, the gods so admired Peleus' virtue in resisting the advances of Astydameia that they sent him the divine sword on this occasion, telling Hermes to take it to him to enable him to fight off the Centaurs (or simply wild beasts, *thēria*) who were threatening his life.[113] There was also a version in which Akastos told Peleus that he was intending to abandon him, saying that this was an ordeal that would reveal whether or not he was guilty of the rape.[114]

Peleus was sometimes said to have returned to Iolkos to exact revenge. According to Pindar, he seized the city on his own without the aid of an army.[115] Or in Apollodorus' account, which was probably based on that of Pherecydes, he raised an army for the purpose at a later period, enlisting the aid of Jason and the Dioskouroi; and after killing Astydameia, he dismembered her body and led the army into the city through her remains.[116] Some said that he killed Akastos too. A version of this story was apparently recounted in the Hesiodic *Catalogue*, for a surviving fragment reports that he brought quantities of Iolkian treasure to Phthia (evidently after sacking the city).[117] Or according to other accounts, Akastos and his family remained in power in Iolkos, and he or his sons later harried or expelled Peleus when the aged king was unable to defend himself after his son Achilles had gone away to Troy (see further on p. 490).

During the next period of his life, Peleus returned to Phthia to take over the kingdom of his dead father-in-law and married the goddess Thetis. This would imply that his first wife, Antigone, must have died at some stage; Apollodorus explains this very neatly by saying that Astydameia had provoked her to commit suicide as a further act of revenge against Peleus, by sending her a message claiming that he was intending to put her aside to marry Akastos' daughter Sterope.[118]

For the circumstances of Peleus' marriage to Thetis and the brief and unhappy course of their union, see pp. 52ff. In the usual account, she bore him a single son, ACHILLES (properly Achilleus), before abandoning him to return to the company of her sister-Nereids in the sea; for unlike Harmonia, the goddess who married Kadmos at Thebes, she thought it an insufferable indignity to be yoked to a mortal.[119] In some accounts, however, Achilles was not the first and only child of the marriage, for she had borne previous children to Peleus but had caused their deaths by trying to find out whether they were immortal (see p. 55).[120] After Peleus was deserted by her, he entrusted the young Achilles to the care of his former benefactor, the Centaur Cheiron, who brought him up on Mt Pelion. The childhood and education of Achilles have already been considered in connection with the Trojan War (see pp. 456ff). Peleus lived to a great age; for some stories that were recounted about his later life and final fate, see p. 490.

Lesser Asopids

The rest of the Asopid family need not detain us for long. The next branch to be added after that of Aigina was doubtless the branch associated with Salamis, the only other island of any significance in the Saronic Gulf. SALAMIS, daughter of Asopos, was abducted to the island by Poseidon, where she bore him a son, KYCHREUS, who became the island's first ruler. He won the throne – or merely great glory – by killing an enormous snake that had been devastating the land.[121] Or according to a conflicting tradition, he reared the snake, which was eventually driven out by a certain Eurylochos and went to Eleusis on the mainland nearby, where it became an attendant of Demeter.[122] Kychreus was supposed to have manifested himself to the Athenians at the battle of Salamis in the form of a snake that appeared in their ships.[123] As we have just seen, Kychreus welcomed the exiled Telamon to his island, giving him his daughter Glauke and accepting him as his successor because he had no sons of his own. Pherecydes offered an account, however, in which Telamon was the grandson of Kychreus, as the son of Glauke and a certain Aktaios (probably to be distinguished from the father-in-law of Kekrops);[124] and this doubtless reflects the older tradition in which Telamon was of native Salaminian origin.

Another island that came to be credited with an Asopid eponym was Corcyra (Kerkyra, modern Corfu) in the Ionian Sea off north-western Greece. Corcyra acquired its most important mythical associations at second hand because it came to be identified with the Homeric island of the Phaeacians (Phaiakes), which was visited by Odysseus (see p. 497) and was also introduced into Argonautic myth (see p. 395). In the *Odyssey*, the Phaeacians are an exotic people who have close relations with the gods, and their island of Scherie lies far beyond the everyday world in the furthermost reaches of the sea, so far away that mortal visitors are virtually unknown. In view of the nature of his land and people, Alkinoos, the king of the Phaeacians, could hardly be provided with a conventional heroic genealogy in the Homeric account. We are told in the *Odyssey* that he was a son of Nausithoos (Swift sailor), who had led the Phaeacians to their distant land to save them from being plundered by the Kyklopes,[125] and he was married to Arete (Virtue), who was apparently his sister in the original text of the poem.[126] A passage which was probably added after the time of Homer makes her his niece, explaining that Nausithoos was a son of Poseidon by Periboia, the eldest daughter of Eurymedon, king of the Giants, and Arete was the daughter of another son of Nausithoos, a certain Alexenor who was shot down in his halls by Apollo while still newly married.[127] This is, of course, sheer fancy, on a level with Plato's genealogies for the kings of Atlantis. Subsequently, however, when Alkinoos' land came to be identified with a real place just off the coast of Greece, he and his family were drawn into the heroic genealogies as Asopids. According to the usual later tradition, KERKYRA, daughter of Asopos, was abducted by Poseidon to the island that was named after her, where she bore him a son, Phaiax, who gave his name to the Phaeacians (now identified as the primordial inhabitants of Corcyra). Alkinoos is now described as a son of this Phaiax, as is his wife Arete, who is his sister as in the original Homeric account.[128] Although Hellanicus is our earliest definite source for this Asopid line, it is quite possible that it was already to be found in the Hesiodic *Catalogue*, for it is known that the poem referred to the family relationships of Alkinoos (which it would hardly have done if he had not been given a proper heroic genealogy).[129] Since Corcyra was a Corinthian colony, it is tempting to suppose that the myth of Kerkyra was developed at Corinth in imitation of the similar stories that were told about Aigina and Salamis nearby. When composing his Argonautic epic, Apollonius seems to have been troubled by the discrepancy between the Homeric and later genealogies of Alkinoos, for he states that Nausithoos was Alkinoos' predecessor as king of the Phaeacians on Corcyra, while Kerkyra was abducted by Poseidon to Black Corcyra instead, an insignificant island further up the Adriatic.[130]

Further Asopids were added as time progressed until Asopos came to be credited with a large family of twelve or twenty daughters. Diodorus lists twelve, adding the following to those already mentioned: *Peirene*, the eponym of the spring of that name at Corinth, *Kleone*, the eponym of Kleonai in the Argolid, *Thebe*, the eponym of Thebes (sometimes regarded as the wife of Amphion, see p. 306), *Tanagra*, the eponym of Tanagra in Boeotia, *Thespeia*, the eponym of Thespiai to the west of Thebes, *Ornia*, the eponym of Orneai in the Argolid, *Chalkis*, the eponym of the Euboean city of that name, *Asopis* (otherwise unknown) and *Sinope* (see below).[131] Another Asopid of note is *Harpina*, who was the mother of Oinomaos in the tradition of his native Elis (see p. 504).[132]

Of these, only Peirene and Sinope are of any real interest in their own right. PEIRENE (who is also described as a daughter of the river-god Acheloos or of Oibalos, king of Sparta) was loved by Poseidon and bore him two sons, Leches and Kenchrias, who were the eponyms of Lecheia and Kenchreai, the two harbours of Corinth on the western and eastern shore of the Isthmus respectively.[133] According to a local tale recorded by Pausanias, which follows a standard pattern and was doubtless of fairly late origin, Peirene wept so bitterly for Kenchrias after he was killed by Artemis that she turned into the famous Corinthian spring that bore her name.[134] The remains of an impressive fountain-house can still be seen at the site. As the eponym of the Greek colony of Sinope on the north coast of Asia Minor, SINOPE was the Asopid who was carried furthest abroad. Zeus abducted her to the site of the future city (a trading-port that is best remembered as the birthplace of Diogenes the Cynic) and tried to win her over by promising to give her whatever she most desired; but she proved to be too clever for him, for she told him that what she most desired was to remain a virgin. She subsequently worked the same trick on Apollo and the local river-god Halys. Or in another version, she was abducted to the area by Apollo, and bore him a son, Syros, who gave his name to the Syrians who lived in the hinterland.[135]

The first woman to be mentioned as a daughter of Asopos is Antiope, who is named as such in the *Odyssey*;[136] but as we have seen (see p. 303), she was given a wholly different genealogy in the later tradition. She would surely have been a child of the Asopos that flowed through southern Boeotia rather than of the Peloponnesian Asopos, as would (strictly speaking) other Boeotian eponyms like Thebe, Plataia (see p. 138) and Tanagra. The mythographers seem to have been unconcerned about this distinction, however, since all the daughters of Asopos are generally treated as sisters; this tendency is already apparent in the works of Pindar and Bacchylides, who both describe Aigina (who was specifically connected with the Peloponnesian Asopos) and the Boeotian eponym Thebe as daughters of the same father.[137]

THE ARCADIAN ROYAL FAMILY

Pelasgos, the earthborn first king of Arcadia

In much the same way as the Athenians, the Arcadians cherished the partially justified belief that they were an indigenous (or 'autochthonous') people who had inhabited their land from the earliest times with little admixture from outside. They liked to claim, indeed, that they were the most ancient inhabitants of Greece, a race of 'pre-Selenians' who had lived in their rugged home in the heart of the Peloponnese even before the moon (*selēnē*) first rose into the sky.[138] Their ancestral hero and first king was PELASGOS, who was born from the earth at the beginning of history, as early as Deukalion or earlier still, and may even have been the first man of all. Although Pausanias is inclined to doubt that he was really the first man in Arcadia (for how could he have had anyone to rule over in that case?), he quotes some lines from the early epic poet Asios which express the idea that he was the ancestor of the human race: 'the black earth brought forth god-like Pelasgos in the mountains with their high-foliaged trees so that a mortal race might come to be'.[139] He was the eponym of the Pelasgians, the people who were supposed to have been the aboriginal (i.e. prehellenic) inhabitants of Greece; in terms of Arcadian myth, he was said to have given his name to the people of the land, who retained it until his great-grandson Arkas renamed them as Arcadians after himself.[140] Like Kekrops at Athens, he was more a local Adam than a subject for legend, although he came to be credited with various achievements as a culture-hero in the later tradition.

Pausanias records a rather artificial scheme in which Pelasgos is said to have introduced the first rudiments of civilization into Arcadia, leaving scope for his successors to improve on his innovations and so raise the Arcadians to a fully human way of life. So Pelasgos first invented huts and sheepskin tunics to protect his people from the elements, leaving it for Lykaon and Arkas to show them how to build towns and weave clothes from wool; and likewise, Pelasgos taught the Arcadians to feed on acorns rather than leaves, grasses and roots which might turn out to be poisonous, leaving it for Arkas to introduce bread and the cultivation of grain.[141] Acorns remained a part of the diet of the Arcadians until a relatively late period, hence the title of 'acorn-eaters' that was traditionally applied to them.

As has already been noted, the Argives tried to annex Pelasgos to their own royal line by describing him as a son of Niobe, daughter of Phoroneus (see p. 230).[142] The Pelasgos who received Demeter at Argos in early times (see p. 129) and was buried there in the sanctuary of Pelasgian Demeter[143] was either identified with this primordial Pelasgos or else regarded as being of somewhat later birth as an early member of the Argive royal line (as a son of Triopas or Agenor).[144] In Aeschylus' *Suppliants*, Argos is under the rule of Pelasgos, son of Palaichthon, at the time of Danaos' arrival. The earthborn Palaichthon ('long in the land', i.e. 'indigenous inhabitant'), whose name appears in no other source, seems to have been an arbitrarily invented figure.[145] A Pelasgos (or perhaps more than one) also appears in Thessalian genealogies as the father of various local eponyms; since the area around Larissa in central Thessaly was known as Pelasgiotis, it is no surprise that this Pelasgos should sometimes be described as a son of the city-eponym Larissa, either by Poseidon or Haimon.[146]

Lykaon and his fifty sons

Pelasgos married the mountain-nymph Kyllene (or the Okeanid Meliboia, or a certain Deianeira), who bore him a single son, his heir and successor LYKAON.[147] As might be inferred from his name, Lykaon was especially associated with Mt Lykaion in south-western Arcadia. He was the mythical founder of the ancient cult of Zeus Lykaios, which was celebrated in a dramatic setting on the highest peak of the mountain; in front of the altar, which consisted of a mound of earth, there stood two pillars with gilded eagles on top of them facing toward the rising sun. Lykaon was also said to have founded Lykosura below, reputedly the oldest town in the world, and the Lykaian Games, which were held in conjunction with the festival of Lykaian Zeus and were reputed to be the oldest of their kind.[148] The cult of Zeus on the mountain, which was highly respected throughout Greece, was particularly important in Arcadia itself because it provided a focus of unity for the people of the land, who lived in widely scattered communities.

Lykaon fathered fifty sons by many different women, and also a notable daughter, Kallisto, who became the mother of the eponym of the land. As can be seen from the catalogue of names preserved by Apollodorus, most of the sons of Lykaon were eponyms of Arcadian towns.[149] Since all of them (or all apart from one, who was childless) died early at the hand of Zeus, none survived to found families of their own, and all subsequent members of the Arcadian royal family were thus descended from Kallisto through her son Arkas. The fall of the house of Lykaon was provoked by a gruesome act of sacrilege, when the king or his sons attempted to feed human flesh to Zeus. Although Lykaon himself was almost certainly the original transgressor, the crime is more commonly assigned to his sons, apparently because authors of later ages found it hard to believe that the pious founder of the main cult of Zeus in Arcadia could have been guilty of such an act. Apollodorus explains accordingly that the sons of Lykaon exceeded all others in arrogance and impiety, and demonstrated this to the full when Zeus visited them in the guise of a poor traveller to test whether they were really as bad as their reputation suggested. They invited him into the palace to enjoy their hospitality, but mixed the guts of a slaughtered child into the meat from the sacrifices, and served this unholy mixture to him as a meal. Appalled by their action (which was carried out at the instigation of the eldest brother Mainalos), Zeus overturned the table and struck them dead with thunderbolts along with their father, sparing only the youngest brother, Nyktimos, because Ge (Earth) interceded on his behalf.[150]

NYKTIMOS survived to inherit the throne in this version, and it is stated likewise in Pausanias' pseudo-historical account of the earliest developments in Arcadia that he was Lykaon's successor. It makes little difference, however, whether he became king or not, since it was agreed that he had no children and was thus succeeded by Arkas. Pausanias explains that Nyktimos took precedence over his brothers because he was the eldest (for there could be no question of Zeus destroying the family in this rationalized narrative), while Apollodorus states that he was the youngest of the brothers, as seems fitting in the mythical context since he could be said to have been spared because he was too young to take part in the crime.[151] If Zeus' confrontation with the sons of Lykaon was placed in Trapezous in south-western Arcadia (as in many accounts, including that of Apollodorus), it could be explained that the town had come to be called by that name because Zeus had overturned the table (*trapeza*) there.[152] The gesture is a stock motif in stories of this kind, for it symbolizes the breaking off of direct contact between gods and mortals. Apollodorus mentions that some people explained the origin of the great flood (see p. 403) by saying that it was occasioned by the impieties of the sons of Lykaon.

It is suggested in another version that Zeus once visited Lykaon as a guest (for the gods would sometimes mingle directly with mortals in the very earliest times), and the sons of the king mixed human flesh into the food to test whether or not he was truly a god.[153] They killed their youngest brother Nyktimos for the purpose in one account.[154] Mention should also be made of a partially rationalized version offered by Nicolaus of Damascus (a historian who once served as tutor to the children of Antony and Cleopatra). To ensure that his people would behave righteously, Lykaon told them that Zeus visited the land regularly in disguise to test their ways; and when the king offered up a sacrifice one day, claiming that he was expecting a visit from the god, his sons killed a child and mixed his flesh into the meat from the sacrifices to test whether he was telling the truth (for Zeus would be sure to recognize what they had done if he was really due to make a visit). A fierce storm then erupted with much lightning, apparently at the will of Zeus, and the murderers of the child were killed without exception.[155]

In other accounts, Lykaon himself put Zeus to the test by serving him a meal containing human flesh while the god was visiting him as a guest. The king procured the flesh by killing his grandson Arkas (who was subsequently revived by the gods), or his son Nyktimos, or a Molossian hostage. As it happens, this is the only version to be credited to a pre-Hellenistic source, since it was recounted somewhere in the Hesiodic corpus that Lykaon was so angered by Zeus' seduction of his daughter Kallisto (see below) that he cut up a child, apparently Arkas, and served his remains to the god as a meal. It seems that Zeus responded by overturning the table and transforming Lykaon into a wolf. Zeus punishes Lykaon in the same manner in the well-known account in Ovid's *Metamorphoses*, when the king serves human flesh to him to test his divinity; Ovid was bound to choose this version to accord with the theme of the poem since it is the only one that involves a transformation.[156] Pausanias was told in Arcadia that Lykaon was turned into a wolf (*lykos*) because he sacrificed a human child on the altar of Zeus Lykaios; and the Arcadians linked this story to a strange werewolf superstition that came to be associated with the cult of Zeus Lykaios.[157] For ever since the time of Lykaon, so it was said, one of the men who participated in the annual sacrifice on Mt Lykaion would turn into a wolf after tasting the sacrificial meat, which was reputed to contain human flesh. The wolf-men who were thus created were not obliged to remain in that form forever, for they would return to their original form after nine years if they abstained from human flesh in the mean time. If they tasted it even once, on the other hand, there could be no possible escape for them.[158] It is tempting to suppose that the local legend about Lykaon's child-sacrifice represents the original story from which all subsequent variants took their start; but Pausanias collected the story at such a late period (the second century AD) that we cannot be sure that it was genuinely ancient rather than a product of antiquarian invention.

Kallisto and Arkas

KALLISTO, the daughter of Lykaon, left home to roam the mountains of Arcadia as a virgin hunting-companion of Artemis; but she attracted the roving eye of Zeus, who raped or seduced her, causing her to become pregnant with a male child, Arkas. Although this proved disastrous to Kallisto herself, who was transformed into a bear as a consequence, it at least ensured that Lykaon had an heir to succeed him after losing his sons. Arkas ascended to the throne either immediately after the death of his grandfather, or after the intervening reign of Nyktimos in accounts in which that son of Lykaon escaped the fate of his brothers.

Kallisto would have had no connection with Lykaon in the earliest tradition. It seems likely that she originated as a hypostasis of Artemis (who had a cult as Artemis Kalliste, 'the most beautiful', in Arcadia), and then came to be regarded as one of the companion-nymphs of the goddess. Hesiod is reported to have classed her as a nymph, presumably in the *Catalogue* (as against the *Astronomy*, which apparently described her as a daughter of Lykaon).[159] According to Apollodorus, the early Corinthian epic poet Eumelos already called her a daughter of Lykaon, while the epic poet Asios described her as a daughter of Nykteus, and Pherecydes as a daughter of an obscure Arcadian called Keteus (probably to be regarded as a son of Lykaon in this connection).[160] By classifying her as a daughter of Lykaon, mythographers could construct a unified family tree for the Arcadian royal family in which every line could be traced back to Lykaon and Pelasgos (see Table 20; the details of the scheme can vary); but it is obvious enough that the genealogies for Arkas' branch of the family were of separate origin from those associated with Lykaon, for the former relate to eastern Arcadia alone while the sons of Lykaon served as eponyms for towns in every part of the land.

Although it was generally agreed that Kallisto was raped or seduced by Zeus while she was a companion of Artemis, and that she was transformed into a bear (*arktos*) thereafter and gave birth to her son Arkas while in that form, the story was recounted in all manner of different versions. All of them can be assigned, however, to one of two main categories.

(i) In the simpler versions of the story, Kallisto was transformed as a result of Hera's jealousy and was shot dead by Artemis while she was pregnant with Arkas. Some said that Zeus turned her into a bear after raping her in the hope of confusing his jealous wife, who had seen him pursuing Kallisto into a forest and tried to catch him in the act; on finding a bear in the place of the girl whom she had expected, however, Hera soon worked out what had happened, and provoked Artemis to shoot the bear by pointing it out to her as prey while she was out hunting. After Kallisto was killed in this way, Zeus rescued her child, apparently by snatching him from her womb (as Apollo did with Asklepios, see p. 149), and entrusted him to Maia, another Arcadian mistress of his (see p. 161), to be reared in her cave on Mt Kyllene.[161] Or in other accounts, Hera turned Kallisto into a bear as a punishment after catching her with Zeus, and Artemis then shot her in her bear-form, either knowingly as a favour to Hera or unknowingly when she happened to run across the bear during a hunting-trip. Zeus saw to the rescue of his son as usual; it is recorded in one such version that he sent Hermes to recover the child from her body.[162]

(ii) In the more elaborate versions of her legend, Kallisto gave birth to her son in the wilds after the full term of her pregnancy, and survived for long enough in bear-form to be hunted by Arkas when he grew up. As an easily accessible example of such a version, we may first turn to Ovid's narrative in the *Metamorphoses*. When Zeus once happened to catch sight of Kallisto lying on her own in the grass, he assumed the form of Artemis to approach her and then proceeded to rape her in spite of her determined resistance. On a sultry day nine months afterwards, Artemis invited her attendants to bathe with her after the hunt and noticed that Kallisto was pregnant when she was obliged to undress. So the goddess expelled her from her company, and she gave birth to her child shortly afterwards. Now Hera had known all along that she had attracted the desire of Zeus, and the birth of the child added a further sting to her resentment, provoking her to take action against the girl at last by transforming her into a bear. Kallisto roamed the countryside in that form for fifteen years until her son ran across her one day while he was out hunting. Having no reason to suspect that she was his mother, he would have transfixed her with his hunting-spear if Zeus had not saved him from matricide by removing him and his mother to the heavens, to become the neighbouring constellations of the Great Bear and Bootes (the Herdsman, also known in Greek as Arktophylax or the Bear-guard).[163]

In accounts from the astronomical literature, Artemis herself is said to have worked the transformation after noticing that Kallisto was pregnant, and she gave birth to her child while in bear-form. Although there would presumably have been versions which concluded in much the same way as Ovid's, with her simply being hunted by her son when he grew up, the surviving accounts are more complicated and apparently rather garbled. We are told in one such account that the transformed Kallisto was captured in the mountains by some goatherds, who handed her over to Lykaon along with her child. Some time later, she happened to wander into the precinct of Lykaian Zeus, which was forbidden ground to any mortal under pain of death; and her son chased after her along with some other Arcadians and would have killed her if Zeus, calling to mind their former relationship, had not snatched them away and transferred them to the stars. Or in a slightly different account,

Zeus snatched them away when both of them came under threat from the Arcadians.[164] Certain features of this narrative seem distinctly odd. It would surely not have been unlawful, for instance, for animals to stray on to the sacred precinct; and while herdsmen regularly come to the rescue of abandoned infants in myth, the capture of bears seems to lie outside their province. Although the question is too complicated to be worth examining further here, there is good reason to suppose that the story has become distorted, and the surviving accounts should therefore be treated with some caution.

In a further version recorded in the astronomical literature, Lykaon slaughtered Arkas while he was still young and served his flesh to Zeus because he was angry with the god for having seduced his daughter (or because he wanted to test whether his visitor was really a god). Zeus was so appalled that he overturned the table and transformed Lykaon into a wolf; and he then reassembled the dead child and entrusted him to a herdsman to be reared in the country. When Arkas was somewhat older, he encountered his bear-mother while hunting in the woods and pursued her without realizing who she was. He happened to chase her on to the precinct of Lykaian Zeus, and Zeus removed the pair of them to the stars to save them from the anger of the Arcadians.[165]

Amphion, an early Hellenistic comic poet, developed a humorous version of Kallisto's story in which Zeus assumed the form of Artemis to approach and seduce her. He deceived her so thoroughly that when Artemis subsequently questioned her about her pregnancy, she naively protested that the goddess herself was to blame. Artemis was thoroughly annoyed by her reply, as is understandable, and transformed her into a bear. Amphion's account of the seduction appealed to Ovid, as we have seen; but in his narrative, Kallisto recognized the nature of Zeus' deception at the last moment, as one would expect, and resisted him as best she could.[166]

After ascending to the throne, ARKAS gave his name to the land and also to his people, who had been known as Pelasgians hitherto. In Pausanias' account of the earliest history of Arcadia, he is said to have improved on the innovations of Pelasgos by showing his people how to weave cloth from wool and make bread from grain, and so saving them from having to dress in sheepskins and feed on acorns as previously; he was able to instruct them in these matters because an obscure hero called Adristos had taught him the art of spinning and Triptolemos (an Eleusinian associate of Demeter, see p. 131) had instructed him in the cultivation of grain while spreading Demeter's gift of corn.[167] Whether by a local nymph called Erato or Chrysopeleia (see p. 211) or by an ordinary human wife, Leaneira, daughter of Amyklas, or Meganeira, daughter of Krokon, Arkas fathered two sons, Apheidas and Elatos, and in some accounts a further son of lesser importance called Azan.[168]

Apheidas and his descendants at Tegea, including Auge and Ankaios

The kingdom was divided between the sons of Arkas after their father's death, Apheidas receiving the district of Tegea in the south-east, and Elatos the lands around Mt Kyllene in the north-east. Both founded extensive lines. If Azan is included among the brothers, he inherited the district of Azania in the north of the province (but his line died out after one generation in any case, see p. 549).[169] As might already be inferred from the nature of this partition, the Arkasid genealogies and the associated family history do not cover the whole of Arcadia, but only the eastern regions of the province. It has been suggested accordingly that this genealogical system was not of native origin, but was devised in Argos, and thus presents a limited picture of Arcadia as viewed from its eastern neighbour. Although a scheme of inheritance was eventually devised in which descendants of Arkas from both main branches of the family were presented as ruling the whole of Arcadia (or the greater part of it) in ordered succession, the resulting pseudo-history is too artificial to be worth tracing here; Pausanias may be consulted on the matter. We will simply pick out some of the more interesting heroes and heroines, most of them from Apheidas' Tegean portion of the land. It is by no means surprising that Tegea should be more prominent than any other Arcadian city in myth, since it was not only the most important city in the province (until the foundation of Megalopolis in the fourth century BC), but was also more exposed to the outside world than any other, lying as it did in the south-eastern plain rather than in the mountains, and on the main route between Argos and Sparta.

Apheidas, who has no myths of his own, had a single son, ALEOS, who succeeded him as king of Tegea (or first founded the city in the lands that he inherited). Aleos founded the Tegean cult of Athena Alea[170] and appointed his daughter AUGE to serve as the virgin priestess of the goddess. While Herakles was returning from his campaign against Hippokoon at Sparta (see p. 279), he passed through Tegea and raped the princess without realizing who she was, causing her to become pregnant with a son, TELEPHOS. After giving birth to her child, Auge tried to hide him away in the precinct of Athena Alea; but the land was struck by a famine and plague as a result of the sacrilege, and when oracles explained that the precinct had been profaned, the king searched it and discovered the infant. He ordered that it should be exposed on Mt Parthenion, and handed his daughter over to the seafarer Nauplios to be sold in a foreign land. Nauplios treated her more generously, however, by offering her in marriage to Teuthras, the wealthy king of Mysia in Asia Minor; and fate also smiled on her son, for he was suckled by a doe in the wilds until some shepherds came to his rescue. The mythographers could explain his name by a characteristically tortured etymology, saying that he was called Telephos because he had been suckled at the teat (*thēlē*) of a deer (*elaphos*). When he was grown up, he travelled to Delphi to question the oracle about his birth, and was advised to cross over to Mysia, where he was reunited with his mother. Having no children of his own, Teuthras adopted Telephos as his son and heir, and he succeeded to the throne shortly before the Trojan War.[171] For the story of how he was wounded by Achilles when the Greek army attacked his kingdom, see p. 446.

The legend of Auge is recorded in a number of different forms. In another account, Aleos noticed that she had become pregnant, and refused to believe her when she told him that she had been raped by Herakles. Imagining that the trouble had really arisen because she had engaged in an illicit love affair, he handed her over to Nauplios, asking that she should be taken out to sea to be drowned. She gave birth to her child on Mt Parthenion during the journey to the coast and hid him away in some bushes. Nauplios took him to his home-city, the port of Nauplia or Nauplion in the Argolid, where he passed her on to some Carian travellers who were setting out for Asia Minor. Her story ended happily as a consequence, for they entrusted her to Teuthras after arriving home in Asia. Her abandoned child was suckled by a doe as usual until he was discovered by some herdsmen, who took him to their master, a local ruler called Korythos. He was raised by Korythos and eventually rediscovered his mother in the way described above.[172] Or in a simpler version of the story, Auge took him with her after giving birth to him on Mt Parthenion, and Nauplios sold the pair of them to Teuthras, who took Auge as his wife and adopted her son.[173]

In yet another version, Aleos packed Auge and her son into a chest and launched it into the sea after discovering that she had given birth to the child as a result of a secret love affair with Herakles; but they were washed safely ashore in Asia Minor, where Auge became the wife of Teuthras as usual.[174] The earliest surviving account in a papyrus fragment from the Hesiodic *Catalogue* follows an entirely different pattern, stating that Teuthras took Auge into his palace and reared her as his daughter at the will of the gods, and that Herakles seduced her in Asia as he was travelling to Troy to claim the horses of Laomedon. It is indicated that Auge was of Arcadian birth as in the subsequent tradition.[175]

Aleos had two sons, Lykourgos and Kepheus, who were both said to have ruled at Tegea at some stage.[176] LYKOURGOS is mentioned in the *Iliad* for his feat in having killed Areithoos the Mace-man (Korynetes, a title shared by an opponent of Theseus, see p. 342), a formidable warrior who used to smash his way through the enemy ranks with an iron mace. Relying on guile rather than brute force, Lykourgos caught him on a narrow path where he had no room to swing his mace, and felled him with a spear-thrust to the midriff.[177] Lykourgos was the father of Ankaios and grandfather of Atalanta, two Arcadians of valiant and distinctive character whose adventures took them outside their native province.

ANKAIOS was a brawny hero who used to wear a bear-skin and wielded a double-headed axe. He first left Arcadia to sail with the Argonauts. According to Apollonius' account, Kepheus and Amphidamas, the two younger brothers of Lykourgos, set off to join the Argonauts but Lykourgos himself had to remain behind to look after his ageing father Aleos and sent his son Ankaios instead. To explain why Ankaios came to adopt his uncouth weapon and garb (which may be compared to the club and lionskin of Herakles), Apollonius states that Aleos tried to keep him at home also by hiding his arms and armour in the recesses of the palace, and he was therefore obliged to make use of the axe and bear-skin as the best available substitutes.[178] On account of his massive strength, he was assigned to the same rowing-bench as Herakles; and when a pair of oxen were due to be sacrificed to Apollo before the start of the voyage, Ankaios felled one of them with a single blow of his axe while Herakles felled the other with a blow of his club. Ankaios is otherwise mentioned for the part that he played in the battle between the Argonauts and Bebrycians (see p. 386), in which he deployed his axe to good effect.[179] He was best remembered, however, for having met with a glorious death during a subsequent adventure, the hunt for the Calydonian boar; for as the hunters were approaching the beast to make the kill, it gored Ankaios in the thigh, inflicting a fatal wound on him (see p. 416).[180] There is good reason to suppose that this tale goes back to early epic; in a scene from the hunt on the François Krater (c. 570 BC), Ankaios can be seen lying beneath the boar as Meleagros and Peleus confront it with their spears. Ankaios was reputed to have shown such bravery in continuing to stand up to the beast in spite of his grievous wound that the Tegeans honoured him as one of their greatest heroes. When the temple of Athena Alea was rebuilt in the fourth century BC, the architect and sculptor Skopas portrayed the incident in a sculpture on the pediment, which showed the wounded Ankaios being held up by his brother Epochos as his axe dropped from his grasp.[181]

Ankaios left a son, AGAPENOR, who was king of Tegea at the time of the Trojan War. The *Iliad* states that he led the men of Arcadia to Troy in sixty ships, which were provided for them by Agamemnon because they had nothing to do with seafaring (as is natural for inhabitants of a landlocked territory). According to the Hellenistic and later tradition, Agapenor was driven off course to Cyprus while sailing home after the war, and decided to make his home there, founding Paphos (i.e. the port of New Paphos) on the west coast.[182] Before his departure to Troy, the sons of Alkmaion killed their father's murderers at his palace at Tegea (see p. 328).

The legend of Atalanta in Arcadia and Boeotia

Two separate provinces, Arcadia and Boeotia, claimed to have produced an Amazonian heroine of the name of ATALANTA. The Arcadian Atalanta was descended from Lykourgos through a further son of his, Iasos (or Iasios, or Iasion), while the Boeotian Atalanta was a daughter of Schoineus, son of Athamas, the eponym of the Boeotian town of Schoinos.[183] It is difficult to tell whether these were originally separate figures, or whether alternative traditions came to be developed about a single Atalanta in the different regions. As far as can be judged from the surviving evidence, the Atalanta who attended the Calydonian boar-hunt (see p. 416) and was exposed at birth by her father (see below) was always regarded as an Arcadian, while the legend of Atalanta's bridal-races was primarily associated with the Boeotian heroine of that name. So it is certainly possible that there were two Atalantas of separate origin; but even if this was the case, the two came to be confused or identified from quite an early period, and it will therefore be convenient to treat the Arcadian and Boeotian as a single person, taking due note of any regional distinctions.

When Atalanta was born in Arcadia, her father Iasos ordered that she should be exposed in the wilds because he wanted male children alone. After she was abandoned on Mt Parthenion, however, she was suckled by a she-wolf that had lost its cubs and was eventually rescued by some passing hunters. They brought her up in the mountains and she chose to remain there when she grew up, living a hardy life as a virgin huntress with a cave for a home. When two drunken Centaurs called Rhoikos and Hylaios once approached her cave at night with the intention of raping her, she was alerted by the sight of their torches and shot them dead with two successive arrows.[184] She demonstrated similar valour and skill when she subsequently ventured abroad, showing that she could match herself against any male hero. Although Diodorus and Apollodorus list her among the Argonauts,[185] it is most unlikely that she would have been included in their number in the early tradition. Apollonius explains that she asked to join the expedition, but that Jason – who had met her in Arcadia and had received a spear from her as a gift – was unwilling to take her because he feared that other members of the crew might fall in love with her and quarrel.[186] During the period between the voyage of the Argonauts and the hunt for the Calydonian boar, Atalanta travelled to Iolkos to compete in the funeral games for Pelias and defeated Peleus in the wrestling (see p. 534).[187] She played a prominent part in the great boar-hunt, as has already been described, and it was agreed that she performed her greatest heroic exploits on that occasion. She inflicted the first wound on the boar in the usual account, and Meleagros, the leader of the hunt, was so impressed by her bravery that he awarded her the prize of honour even though he killed the boar himself.[188] She brought the spoils home with her, and the most durable of them, the huge tusks of the boar, could be seen in Tegea accordingly until they were plundered by Augustus.[189]

When Atalanta's father eventually insisted that she should settle down and marry, she tried to escape marriage by forcing her suitors to compete with her in a race at the risk of their lives. If she had been exposed at birth, as in her Arcadian legend, it is of course hard to see how her parents could have had any occasion or motive to put pressure on her to marry (even if Apollodorus cobbles an account together by saying that she was reunited with her parents after her foreign adventures, and that her father then urged her to marry[190]). It is likely that this legend of the bridal-races was originally developed in connection with a Boeotian Atalanta who was reared at home. The theme is first attested in some fragments from the Hesiodic *Catalogue* in which Schoineus, the Boeotian father of Atalanta, announces the conditions of the contest to the assembled suitors.[191] In contrast to the more usual pattern in which the father of the bride competes against her suitors (as in the case of Oinomaos and Hippodameia, see p. 503), Atalanta confronted her suitors in person in order to rid herself of them. According to Apollodorus, she marked out a course for a foot-race, knocking a stake into the ground half-way along it; and she told her suitors to set off from that point, saying that she would chase after them from the starting-point fully armed. If she caught up with any suitor within the limits of the course, he would pay with his life, for she would thrust her spear into his back; but he would be able to claim her as his wife if he should reach the end of the course ahead of her.[192] After she had outrun and killed a number of her suitors, a young man eventually escaped her with the benefit of some aid from Aphrodite. According to the Boeotian tradition, the successful suitor was HIPPO-MENES, a son of Megareus, king of Onchestos (a city in southern Boeotia); or in the Arcadian tradition, he was MEILANION (or Melanion), son of Amphidamas, who was a cousin of Lykourgos and thus, a cousin of Atalanta.[193]

The successful suitor, whether Hippomenes or Meilanion, contrived his victory by praying for the assistance of Aphrodite, who could be expected to sympathize with him as the goddess of love. She provided him with some golden apples (or three such apples specifically) and told him to throw them down one after another during the race and so cause Atalanta to be left behind as she delayed to pick them up.[194] It was sometimes said that these apples came from the Hesperides like those fetched by Herakles (see p. 269); or in Ovid's account, the goddess brought them from her sacred grove at Tamasus in Cyprus, which contained an apple tree with golden leaves and branches.[195] There are traces of an alternative tradition in which Meilanion won the favour of Atalanta by helping her in various ways during her hunting-trips.[196]

It was often said that Atalanta and her husband were transformed into lions soon after their marriage. The story can be traced back to the fourth century BC but was probably rather older. According to the earliest complete account in Ovid's *Metamorphoses*, Hippomenes angered Aphrodite by failing to thank her for having provided him with the golden apples. So she incited the couple to make love in a cave that was sacred to the Mother of the Gods (here identified with Cybele) while they were travelling home; and the Mother punished them for the sacrilege by turning them into lions. Or in another version which was probably of earlier origin, the couple suffered this punishment because they desecrated a precinct of Zeus by making love in it while they were out hunting.[197] Some Latin sources add that they were never able to make love again after their transformation because lions and lionesses never mate with one another (for the bizarre idea had arisen that lions do not mate among themselves but only with leopards).[198] Parthenopaios (the Maiden-born, one of the Seven against Thebes, see p. 317) was often said to have been Atalanta's son, whether by her husband Meilanion or by Meleagros or Ares.[199]

Kepheus and Echemos of Tegea

KEPHEUS, son of Aleos, the most significant brother of Lykourgos, was also said to have ruled at Tegea at some stage. Like his father before him, he was supposed to have founded one of the ancient sanctuaries of Athena in the city, in his case that of Athena Polias (Guardian of the City). If that was the case, it is fitting that the goddess should have helped him to protect the city by giving him a lock of the Gorgon's hair which would render it impregnable;[200] she can be seen presenting it to him on Tegean coins. Since he had no fewer than twenty sons, Herakles sought his help when he was setting out to confront Hippokoon, king of Sparta, who had twelve or twenty sons of military age; Kepheus and his sons duly helped the hero to victory (see p. 279), but at the expense of their own lives (or of the lives of all but three of them).[201] The story of the Gorgon's hair is recorded in a second version in connection with this legend, for it is said that Kepheus was reluctant to leave his city undefended until Herakles provided a lock of the Gorgon's hair as a protection; he had received the lock from Athena in a bronze jar and now entrusted it to Kepheus' daughter Sterope, telling her that any attacking army would be put to flight if she held it up from the city-walls three times, taking care to avert her own gaze.[202] It would seem that the lock would cast terror into all who beheld it even if it would not suffice to turn them to stone as would the complete head of the Gorgon.

Another noteworthy hero in this branch of the family was ECHEMOS, son of Aeropos, a later king of Tegea who was a grandson or great-grandson of Kepheus. He was famous for having killed Hyllos, son of Herakles, in single combat at the Isthmus of Corinth, and so having prevented the Heraklids from invading the Peloponnese at their first (or second) attempt; see further on p. 288. By virtue of this great service that their king was supposed to have performed for the Peloponnesians in legendary times, the Tegeans used to claim the privilege of holding one of the wings whenever they served in Peloponnesian armies.[203] According to Pindar, Echemos had previously carried off a notable victory in the sporting field by winning the wrestling-contest at the first Olympian Games.[204] He married Timandra, a sister of Klytaimnestra, who proved to be as faithless as the other daughters of Thestios (see p. 526).[205]

The descendants of Elatos and Azan in northern Arcadia

We must now pass on to the other main branch of Arkas' family, which was descended from his son ELATOS (see p. 542). It was far less important than Apheidas' branch, at least from a panhellenic perspective, as is understandable since Elatos inherited lands that were wilder and more isolated than those around Tegea, in the craggy north-eastern corner of Arcadia around Mt Kyllene.[206] This Elatos should properly be distinguished from the Lapith chieftain of the same name who was the father of Kaineus and Ischys (see p. 556), even if Ischys was sometimes regarded as a son of his from Arcadia.[207] He has no myths apart from a story that claims that he finally wandered off to Central Greece to become the founder of Elateia in Phocis.[208] Of the various sons who were ascribed to him, two alone need concern us, Aipytos, who makes some appearance in early literature, and Stymphalos, who was the ancestor of all the main heroes in this line.

The tomb of AIPYTOS under Mt Kyllene is mentioned in the *Iliad* as an Arcadian landmark.[209] Pausanias approached the site with special interest because of its Homeric associations, but was clearly disappointed by what he found, a mound of no great size surrounded by a stone platform. He explains that Aipytos died from a snake-bite while he was out hunting on Mt Sepia (Viper, apparently a shoulder of Kyllene), and was buried there by his hunting-companions because they found it impracticable to carry his body home.[210] Pindar refers to him in connection with the birth of IAMOS, the mythical ancestor of the Iamidai, a family of seers at Olympia. After bearing a daughter Euadne to Poseidon, the Laconian nymph Pitane (the eponym of a hamlet of the same name near Sparta) entrusted her to Aipytos to be reared; and when Euadne grew up, she was seduced in her turn by Apollo and conceived a son to him. Although she tried to conceal her pregnancy, her guardian did not fail to observe it, and he hurried off to Delphi to seek the advice of the oracle. Euadne gave birth to her child while Aipytos was away and exposed him in the countryside, though with a heavy heart; but two snakes saved his life at the will of the gods by feeding him on honey. Aipytos had discovered from the oracle in the mean time that the child was a son of Apollo, and that he was destined to be a great seer who would found an unfailing line of prophets. So his mother was able to recover him, and she named him Iamos because he had been lying in a bed of wild pansies (*ia*, evidently *viola tricolor* in this case since the poet indicates that their flowers were yellow and purple).[211]

According to Pindar, Aipytos reigned at Phaisane on the river Alpheios in south-eastern Arcadia. After growing up in his household, Iamos stepped into the river when he came of age and prayed to his grandfather Poseidon and father Apollo, beseeching them to grant him the splendid destiny that had been foretold for him. The voice of his father spoke out in response and guided him to Olympia, where the god conferred the gift of prophecy on him. When Herakles subsequently founded the Olympian games, Iamos delivered prophecies at the altar of Zeus, as did his descendants, the Iamidai, in future times.[212] The Iamidai exercised their art by reading signs from the hides of the sacrificial animals that were burnt at the altar.

STYMPHALOS, the second of these sons of Elatos, was the eponymous founder of the city of Stymphalos below Mt Kyllene;[213] the neighbouring Stymphalian Lake was celebrated in myth as the site of one of the labours of Herakles, who cleared away vast flocks of birds that once infested its banks (see p. 260). During the reign of Stymphalos, Pelops set out to conquer Arcadia, but pretended to make friends with Stymphalos on finding that he was unable to defeat him, and then treacherously murdered him and scattered his remains. The whole of Greece was afflicted by a terrible famine as a result of this crime until the pious Aiakos interceded with the gods through his prayers (see p. 531).[214] In some accounts at least, Stymphalos was the father of the mythical builder Agamedes (see p. 558). Two of his more distant descendants are worthy of mention. AIPYTOS, son of Hippothoos, who ruled in Arcadia after the Trojan War,[215] met a remarkable death as the result of an act of impiety. This occurred at Mantineia in eastern Arcadia where the great builders Trophonios and Agamedes (see pp. 558ff) had raised a wooden temple to Poseidon, and had spread a woollen thread across its entrance to indicate that no mortal was allowed to set foot in it. Aipytos ignored the prohibition, however, and cut the thread to enter the temple. As he was doing so, waves broke over his eyes to strike him blind, and he dropped dead within a short time.[216] KYPSELOS, the son and successor of Aipytos, was ruling in Arcadia when the Heraklids and Dorians seized control of the main kingdoms of the Peloponnese. On discovering that one of the Heraklid leaders, Kresphontes, was still unmarried, Kypselos offered his daughter Merope to him as a wife, rightly calculating that he could secure the independence of his kingdom through the resulting marriage-alliance.[217] Kresphontes became king of Messenia and fathered several children by Merope, naming the youngest Aipytos after his wife's grandfather; and when he was subsequently murdered by a usurper, Kypselos harboured Aipytos in Arcadia until he was old enough to avenge the murder and recover his rightful throne (see further on p. 292)

AZAN, the eponym of the district of Azania in northern Arcadia, was sometimes named as a third son of Arkas; his only son Kleitor, who left no heir, was the eponymous founder of Kleitor, the main city of Azania.[218] When Azan went to Olenos on the north coast of the Peloponnese to marry Hippolyte, the daughter of its ruler Dexamenos, a Centaur called Eurytion tried to rape his bride (much as in the more famous story of Hippodameia in Thessaly, see p. 555), but was killed by Herakles who happened to be present as a guest.[219] The games that were celebrated after Azan's death were said to have been the first funeral-games ever to be held;[220] for a significant incident that occurred during these games, see p. 412.

CHAPTER SIXTEEN

LEGENDS OF
GREEK LANDS

—— ·◆· ——

Every part of Greece had its local legends, as did the Greek islands too and the Greek colonies overseas. Many of the most important of these have already been considered, either in connection with the mythical history of major centres such as Thebes and Athens or as we were tracing the tangled histories of the great families of heroic mythology; but there remain many more, some relating to major figures such as Orpheus and Orion who did not belong to any of the great families, and others that never came to be of more than regional significance, and others again that happened to become famous beyond their regional bounds because they were taken up by some notable poet or were especially attractive in themselves. The present chapter will offer a selection of the more interesting of these remaining stories and bodies of myth, particularly the older ones involving mythical figures of venerable origin. We will approach them on a regional basis, starting at the northern fringes of the Greek world and then passing southwards through Thessaly and Central Greece, before finally venturing overseas to the Aegean islands and further abroad.

Orpheus and Harpalyke, two notable Thracians

Although not strictly a part of Greece, Thrace was of some importance in Greek myth as the home of a variety of gods and heroes who were mostly of a violent disposition; the war-god Ares had his home there, as did Boreas, the wild North Wind, and such heroes as Lykourgos, who persecuted the young Dionysos and his nurses (see p. 173), and Diomedes, who fed his horses on human flesh (see p. 262), and Tereus, who raped his sister-in-law and cut out her tongue (see p. 368). Some Thracians were remembered for something other than their brutality, however, such as Rhesos, a colourful but short-lived ally of the Trojans (see p. 466), and the musician Thamyris (see p. 206), and the mythical singer ORPHEUS, who remains to be discussed.

It will not be necessary for us to devote any consideration to the wider and thornier problems that arise in connection with this mysterious figure, who was the apocryphal author of theogonies (see p. 24) and other writings on religious matters, and was thus associated with distinctive 'Orphic' teachings; for we are concerned with him solely as a mythical hero who lived a generation before the Trojan War and met an early death after trying to rescue his wife from the Underworld.

Figure 16.1   Sculptural Group of a Seated Poet and Two Sirens, by an unknown artist.
Courtesy the J. Paul Getty Museum.

Orpheus was usually said to have been fathered by the Thracian king Oiagros on
one of the Muses, generally Kalliope.[1] He was a devoted follower of Dionysos, as
befitted a good Thracian, and adept in magic and all manner of wisdom (the later
the account the more varied his accomplishments); but he was above all a wonderful
singer and musician, so very wonderful that the birds and beasts, and even inanimate rocks and trees, would follow him in enchantment as he sang to his lyre, and
rivers would halt in their courses at the sound of his melodies. The power that he
exercised over animals is first mentioned by Simonides, who states that birds would
hover overhead and fishes leap clear out of the water in response to his music.[2] His
instrument was the lyre (*kithara* or *phorminx*), Apollo's chosen vehicle, and it was
sometimes said that Apollo himself gave him his lyre or taught him his musical
skills.[3] While sailing with Jason and the Argonauts, he saved his comrades from
death by outsinging the Sirens (see p. 395).

Orpheus loved and married a dryad nymph called EURYDIKE, but their union was brief because she soon died from a snake-bite. According to Vergil, this came about when the rustic deity Aristaios tried to rape her and she trod on a poisonous snake as she was fleeing from him (see p. 153); or in Ovid's version, the accident occurred as she was roaming the meadows with her fellow nymphs shortly after her wedding (which had been attended by sinister omens). Orpheus was grief-stricken in any case, and resolved to make his way down into the Underworld in the hope of recovering her. He turned his incomparable singing to good advantage during this perilous enterprise, exploiting it to charm Kerberos into allowing him into the world of the dead and then to soften the heart of grim Hades himself. The Roman poets embroider on this theme at will, suggesting that the shades of the dead were entranced by his singing, and that the great sinners who suffer torment below were moved to pause from their futile labours, and that the eagle stopped pecking at the liver of Tantalos, and that Ixion's wheel stopped in its flight, and that the pitiless Furies wept for the first time in their lives. It was perhaps because of the thrill of his music that Hades and Persephone allowed him to lead his wife out of the land of the dead, laying down only a single condition, that he should never look back at her until he arrived in the world above. As they were approaching the light of day, however, he was unable to restrain himself from looking back to check that Eurydike was following him, and she disappeared at that instant and was lost to him forever.[4]

Some version of this story was known to Euripides (and probably to Aeschylus too),[5] but we have to wait until the Roman period for any full account of it. Moschus, a bucolic poet of the second century BC, is the first author to mention that Orpheus' wife was called Eurydike; a somewhat earlier poet, Hermesianax, names her as Agriope instead, but this name appears nowhere else.[6] In view of the lack of early evidence, it is difficult to tell whether the story was very ancient; there is no sign of it in the visual arts until the Hellenistic period (even if the death of Orpheus, which is not necessarily connected with the fate of Eurydike, is shown on fifth century vase-paintings). Orpheus was portrayed with his lyre in Polygnotos' great mural of the Underworld (second half of the fifth century), but Eurydike was apparently not included, and there is nothing to indicate that Orpheus was not a mere shade like his neighbours.[7]

In his despondency at having lost all hope of recovering his wife, Orpheus withdrew into an embittered solitude and shunned the company of women; or he even came to hate the entire female sex. In the account of his death that has become familiar through Ovid and Vergil, the women of Thrace took offence at his scorn and attacked him when they caught sight of him one day while they were roaming the hills as Bacchants; under the influence of their religious frenzy, they assaulted him ever more violently and finally tore him to pieces.[8] Or in a rather different version, he provoked the women to this extreme action by redirecting his affections from women to men, and so introducing homosexuality into the land for the first time. It is reported in this connection that he engaged in a love affair with Kalais, one of the twin sons of Boreas (the North Wind, whose home lay in Thrace, see p. 48); since Kalais had sailed with Orpheus as an Argonaut and was a Thracian like himself, he was an obvious candidate for this role.[9]

In some other accounts of the killing of Orpheus, the women of Thrace came to resent him for reasons that were unconnected with his reaction to the loss of Eurydike, either because he had refused to admit women into mystery cults that he had founded, or because he had drawn their menfolk away from them through the enchantment of his music.[10] The earliest known account is one that is supposed to have been offered in the lost *Bassarids* of Aeschylus (if it is indeed the case that the whole of the following narrative was derived from that play). Our report states, rather mysteriously, that Orpheus ceased to honour Dionysos after his visit to the Underworld because of what he had seen there, and came to honour the sun-god Helios instead as the greatest of the gods, equating him with Apollo. He used to climb Pangaion, a lofty mountain in southern Thrace, before sunrise every morning to ensure that he would always be the first to behold the object of his worship. Dionysos grew so angry at his behaviour, however, that he caused his death by sending the Bassarids (i.e. Maenads, Bacchants) against him.[11] There are also exceptional accounts in which Zeus struck him with a thunderbolt because he had been revealing divine secrets in the mysteries that he had founded, or Aphrodite incited the women against him because his mother Kalliope had judged that Adonis, a young favourite of the goddess, should spend half the year away from her with Persephone (see p. 199).[12]

All kinds of details and additional stories attached themselves to this legend of the death of Orpheus. Just as the whole of nature had been moved by Orpheus' music during his lifetime, the whole of nature, animate and inanimate alike, sorrowed for him at his death; the local nymphs wept for him, the trees shed their leaves, the rivers swelled with their own tears, and even the flinty rocks wept at his passing.[13] The husbands of the Thracian women were so angered by their murder of Orpheus that they inflicted pin-wounds on them as a punishment and sign of infamy, so initiating the custom in Thrace by which all women were tattooed.[14] The head of Orpheus, which was flung into the river Hebros, floated out to sea and was eventually washed ashore on Lesbos, an island renowned for its lyric poets.[15] His lyre was transferred to the heavens by the Muses, or by Zeus at the request of the Muses, to become the constellation of the Lyre (Lyra); or else it drifted to Lesbos and was buried on the shore with the head of Orpheus, or was dedicated in a temple of Apollo on the island.[16] In a story connected with the latter tradition, Neanthes, a son of the tyrant Pittakos, was said to have stolen it from the temple to play on it by night, and to have paid by his impiety by being torn apart by dogs.[17]

Another Thracian who is worthy of mention is the Amazonian heroine HARPA-LYKE. Vergil, whose portrait of Camilla seems to have been partially inspired by her legend, refers to her in the *Aeneid* as a Thracian who could outrun horses and even the swift-flowing Hebros (the greatest river in Thrace).[18] She was the daughter of a local ruler called Harpalykos, who suckled her at the teats of cows and mares after the death of her mother, and later trained her in the arts of war in the hope of making her his successor. While travelling home to Greece after the Trojan War, Neoptolemos, the son of Achilles, attacked the kingdom and inflicted a grave wound on Harpalykos in the course of the fighting; but he was saved by his martial daughter, who launched a counterattack and put the enemy to flight. Or according to another tale of the kind, she raised a force to rescue her aged father after he was seized by the Getai, a fierce people of northern Thrace. In the end, however, his plans for his daughter came to nothing, since he was killed by his subjects in a revolt and Harpalyke withdrew to the woods in sorrow. She supported herself by cattle-raiding until some herdsmen attacked her in her woodland lair and killed her.[19]

The Lapiths and Centaurs of northern Thessaly

The great province of Thessaly in the north-east of the Greek mainland was exceptionally rich in myth. Many of the leading heroes and heroines of the southern half of the province were of Deukalionid birth and have thus been considered in Chapters 11 and 12. The most important of the Thessalian cities under Deukalionid rule was Iolkos at the head of the Gulf of Pagasai, the city from which Pelias sent Jason and the Argonauts off on their quest. Peleus and Achilles, who were of different descent as Asopids (see pp. 530ff), lived further to the south in Phthia. The only major body of Thessalian myth that remains to be discussed is that associated with the LAPITHS (Lapithai), a warlike people of northern Thessaly who were best remembered for their conflict with the Centaurs.

It would be futile to attempt to construct a coherent history of the Lapith race; although about seventy heroes and heroines are named as Lapiths in one source or another, the individuals in question are clearly of disparate origin, and the Lapith genealogies were never properly systematized by the Greek mythographers. We will therefore concentrate on the families that produced the Lapiths who were most important in myth, the two families that were descended from Ixion and Elatos.

IXION, whose own parentage was a matter of dispute, has already been mentioned among the dead sinners who suffered everlasting torment in the afterlife (see p. 118). He started his career in appropriate fashion with a cynical murder. For when he was seeking to marry Dia, daughter of Deioneus (or Eioneus), son of Magnes, he promised her father that he would pay him a large bride-price in return for her hand; but he laid a deadly trap for him when he invited him to fetch it after the wedding. For he dug a large pit, filled it with blazing coals, and then covered it over with a network of twigs and a sprinkling of earth to ensure that Deioneus would fall into it and be burned to death. Since a crime of this heinous nature, which came very close to murdering a blood-relative, had never been committed by anyone before, Ixion could find no one to purify him, man or god, until Zeus finally took pity on him.[20] Zeus not only purified him from his crime but also invited him up to Olympos to share the life of the gods; and by way of gratitude, he set out to seduce Hera, the wife of his benefactor. Hera complained to her husband, who tested the truth of her accusation by fashioning a cloud-image of her and laying it in Ixion's bed. He proceeded to have intercourse with the cloud-Hera, causing it to conceive a child, KENTAUROS, who would subsequently bring the race of Centaurs into being by mating with wild mares on Mt Pelion. Zeus punished Ixion for his treachery by tying him to a wheel and causing him to be whirled forever through the sky above (or through the air of the Underworld in the later tradition). Some authors describe this as a flaming wheel, or claim that Ixion was bound to it by coils of snakes; see also on p. 118.[21] His hybrid descendants thrived, however, and turned out to be as rough and impious as their progenitor. The Centaurs (Kentauroi, a name of uncertain origin) were part man and part horse as everyone knows, being pictured either as a complete man with the chest and hind-quarters of a horse springing from the small of his back, or else as a horse with the torso of a man springing from its body where its equine neck and head would otherwise be; the former is the older representation.

Female Centaurs were a late invention; as in the case of semi-animal nature-spirits such Satyrs and Tritons, it was imagined that Centaurs had nymphs as their wives and daughters. Diodorus mentions an alternative genealogy for Kentauros, the father of the Centaurs, in which he was a son of Stilbe,[22] a daughter of the Thessalian river-god Peneios, who bore him to Apollo along with Lapithes, the eponym of the Lapiths. Cheiron and Pholos were of nobler character than the other Centaurs and were thus said to be of higher birth, being respectively the son of Kronos and Philyra (see p. 73) and a son of Seilenos by a Melian nymph.[23]

As the offspring of his marriage to Dia, Ixion fathered the great Lapith chieftain PEIRITHOOS, whom we have already encountered as the ever-faithful companion of Theseus (see p. 360). Or according to the *Iliad*, Zeus fathered him on the wife of Ixion (here unnamed). The foreign adventures of Peirithoos have already been described in connection with Theseus, including the incursion that he made into the Underworld with his friend in the hope of winning Persephone as his bride. This ill-advised enterprise was usually said to have been his last, since Hades kept him imprisoned forever in the world below. When he first sought to marry, he contented himself with a mortal bride, a certain HIPPODAMEIA (variously described as a daughter of Boutes, Adrastos or Atrax;[24] not to be confused with the daughter of Oinomaos in any case). In addition to the most prominent Thessalians and his Athenian friend, he invited the Centaurs to his wedding-feast, as was proper since they were not only his neighbours but also his relations. They drank far too much wine, however, in accordance with their unbridled nature, and began to molest the female guests; or they even tried to rape the bride when she was brought into the hall. Their outrageous behaviour provoked a furious struggle in which Peirithoos and the Lapiths subdued them with the help of Theseus. Although this was the end of the matter in one version of the story, it was commonly believed that the Centaurs gathered their forces after this initial confrontation, and engaged in a full-scale war with the Lapiths until they were defeated by them and expelled from Thessaly. Theseus continued to fight in support of the Lapiths; or in a rather different account in which he had not attended the wedding, he travelled to Thessaly for the specific purpose of helping in the war after it had commenced. The Centaurs sought a new home in Arcadia, another wild mountainous region, where they remained until they were foolish enough to provoke a fight with Herakles (see p. 259).[25]

The legend of the conflict between the Lapiths and the Centaurs was a very ancient story that was known to Homer. The aged Nestor remarks in the *Iliad* that the mightiest warriors whom he had ever seen or ever expected to see were Peirithoos, Dryas, Kaineus, Exadios and Polyphemos (all Lapiths) and their ally Theseus,

Figure 16.2 Kaineus battered into the ground by Centaurs.
Bronze relief from Olympia, c. 650 BC.

who had fought and destroyed the mighty beasts (*phēres*) of the mountains; and the *Odyssey* reveals something about the origin of the hostilities, if the same episode is envisaged, as seems probable. As the Centaur Eurytion was once being entertained in the halls of Peirithoos, so the latter epic reports, he became drunk and misbehaved in some unspecified way toward his Lapith hosts, who dragged him outside and cut off his ears and nostrils, hence the feud between Centaurs and men.[26]

Hippodameia apparently bore a single child alone to Peirithoos, his son and heir POLYPOITES. The *Iliad* states that he was conceived (or possibly born, the Greek is ambiguous) on the day on which Peirithoos took vengeance on the 'shaggy beasts' and drove them out of Pelion. Together with Leonteus, son of Koronos (see below), Polypoites was joint leader of the Lapith contingent at Troy.[27] Although both survived the war, there was disagreement on whether they returned home afterwards or remained in Asia, settling in the land of the Medes (see p. 489).

To pass on to the second of our Lapith families, ELATOS, a Lapith chieftain who ruled at Larissa, fathered three children of far greater significance than himself, Polyphemos, Ischys and Kaineus.[28] After helping to defeat the Centaurs, POLYPHEMOS joined the Argonauts, but was accidentally left behind in Mysia during the outward journey while he was helping Herakles to search for his lost favourite Hylas (see further on p. 385). He was the mythical founder of the city of Kios in that region. According to Apollonius, he tried to rejoin the Argonauts after establishing the city, but died on the way in the land of the Chalybes, toward the eastern end of the northern coast of Asia Minor.[29] His brother ISCHYS courted or married Koronis, a Thessalian mistress of Apollo, while she was pregnant with a child by the god, and so brought disaster on himself and his beloved (see further on p. 149).

The most remarkable of these children of Elatos was KAINEUS, who was originally born as a girl called KAINIS. While still quite young, Kainis was raped by Poseidon, who tried to make some sort of reparation by offering her the choice of whatever she desired. To ensure that she could never be subjected to such treatment again, she asked to be transformed into a man, and an invulnerable man besides. So Kainis became Kaineus, a warrior of rare strength who soon established himself as a local chieftain.[30] In the arrogance of his power, however, he became brutal and impious. He fixed his own spear into the earth in the market-place of his city and ordered his people to honour it as a god (a tale which may have been suggested by some local aniconic cult); or in a slightly different version, he refused to offer prayer or sacrifice to the gods but paid honour to his spear instead.[31] Zeus was appalled by his presumption and arranged for him to be killed during the war between the Lapiths and the Centaurs. Since swords, spears and other piercing weapons could inflict no harm on the invulnerable hero, the Centaurs hammered him into the ground with tree-trunks or boulders, or both together. According to Ovid alone, he now underwent a further and more thoroughgoing transformation, for a yellow bird of a kind never seen before (a phoenix?) flew up into the air at the place where he had been buried under the earth.[32]

Kaineus left a son, KORONOS, who sailed with the Argonauts and was later killed by Herakles while he was leading the Lapiths in a war against the Dorians (see p. 282).[33] Koronos' son LEONTEUS has already been mentioned as the joint commander of the Lapith forces at Troy. In some accounts, the member of the family who joined the Argonauts was not Koronos himself but a son of his who was named Kaineus after his grandfather.[34]

While we are in northern Greece, some mention should be made of the region of Epirus (Epeiros, i.e. the Mainland) on the western coast. Great heroes such as Herakles (see p. 280) and Alkmaion (see p. 327) occasionally ventured into it; and according to tales from post-Homeric epics from the Trojan cycle, Neoptolemos settled there after the Trojan War (see p. 490) and Odysseus spent part of his later life there (see p. 500). The ancient oracle of Zeus at Dodona, at which the will of the god was interpreted from the rustlings of a sacred oak and other natural signs, lay in the mountainous centre of the province; it was said that a dove had flown from Thebes in Egypt long ago, and had settled on the oak and had spoken out in a human voice to order the foundation of the oracle.[35] Epirus had at least one memorable character of its own in the bogeyman ECHETOS, a mythical king of Epirus who was proverbial for his brutality. In two passages in the *Odyssey*, Antinoos, the most prominent of Penelope's suitors, tries to force his will on the beggar Iros and the disguised Odysseus by threatening to send them to Echetos 'the bane of all mortals, who will cut off your nose and ears with the pitiless bronze, and will rip off your genitals and give them raw as a meal to the dogs'. Later sources record a single tale about him, namely that when he discovered that his daughter Amphissa or Metope had been seduced by a certain Aichmodikos, he blinded her by thrusting spikes of bronze into her eyes, and then threw her into a dungeon and forced her to mill grains of bronze (as though to make flour for bread, a futile task comparable to those inflicted on the great sinners in Hades). In one account, he is said to have told her that she would recover her sight if she fulfilled the task.[36]

The Minyans of Orchomenos; the master-builders Trophonios and Agamedes

Boeotia, the province of Central Greece adjoining Attica to the north, ranked with the Argolid as an important centre for early heroic myth. In the mythology of Boeotia as in most of its history, Thebes was very much the dominant city, and most of the main legends of the land have therefore been recounted in Chapter 9 in connection with the mythical history of that city. The city of Orchomenos in the north-west, which controlled the fertile lowlands around the Copaic Lake, would have been a place of comparable significance in the Mycenaean period; it was proverbial for its wealth, which is compared to that of Egyptian Thebes in the *Iliad*.[37] Its star declined, however, and its mythical record is disappointingly thin. In the Homeric epics and Greek tradition generally, it was regarded as the main home of the Minyans, an ancient people who were also associated with Iolkos in Thessaly. MINYAS, the eponym of the Minyans, was thought to have been an early ruler of Orchomenos. It was naturally assumed that he must have been extremely rich, and a Mycenaean beehive tomb in the city was identified as his treasure-house; Pausanias brackets it with the walls of Tiryns (also of Mycenaean origin) as a Greek monument which bears comparison with the pyramids of Egypt.[38] For the story of the Minyades, three daughters of Minyas who scorned the rites of Dionysos when they were first introduced to Orchomenos, see p. 174. Minyas was credited with various other children, including Orchomenos, the eponym of the city, and Elara, the mother of the gigantic Tityos (see p. 147), and Klymene, the wife of Phylakos and maternal grandmother of Jason.

The first Orchomenian ruler to play a role of any significance in mythical history is ERGINOS, son of Klymenos, who imposed a tribute on the Thebans after his father was killed by a man of that city; as has already been recounted, Herakles freed the Thebans from this tribute in his first campaign, leading them to victory against the Minyans and killing Erginos (see p. 252).[39] Some claimed that Herakles greatly reduced the wealth and power of Orchomenos at that time, whether by inflicting a crushing defeat on the Orchomenians and razing their city, or by redirecting the river Kephisos to flood the plains to the east of the city, and so creating or extending the great Copaic Lake which covered so much of northern Boeotia.[40] An elaborate but highly artificial account of the dynastic history of Orchomenos, up to the reign of Erginos and beyond, can be found in Pausanias.[41]

According to one tradition at least, TROPHONIOS and AGAMEDES, the famous mythical builders and architects, were born at Orchomenos as sons of Erginos;[42] and it is certainly the case that they were primarily associated with Boeotia and Central Greece (although various buildings in the Peloponnese came to be attributed to them, and Agamedes was of Arcadian birth in one account, see p. 549). Some of their buildings were imaginary structures which were the mythical precursors of buildings of ordinary human workmanship on the same site, as was the case with their wooden temple of Poseidon at Mantineia[43] (see p. 549) or their stone temple of Apollo at Delphi. The latter temple was said to have been the fourth of a series of five, as the successor to a temple of bronze which had been built there by Hephaistos (see p. 167) and the predecessor of the historical temple.[44] Other buildings which were described as their work were Mycenaean structures whose original purpose had long been forgotten, such as the 'house of Amphitryon' at Thebes or the 'treasure-house of Hyrieus' at Hyria in eastern Boeotia.[45] In one tradition, the two brothers died together in the happiest of circumstances after building the above-mentioned temple at Delphi; for when they prayed to Apollo for a reward, asking to be granted whatever is best for man, the god indicated that this would come to them in three (or seven) days, and on that day they were granted a sudden and painless death.[46] Or in a less creditable tale, they came to a bad end when they tried to steal from the treasure-house of Hyrieus. By leaving a stone loose during the construction of the building, they had ensured that they would be able to creep into it afterwards to plunder the treasures; but when the king noticed that his treasure was diminishing even though the locks and seals remained untouched, he laid a trap inside, and Agamedes was snared in it. Fearing that his brother might be compelled to name his accomplice, Trophonios cut off his head, leaving Hyrieus with an anonymous corpse.[47] He then fled, and was usually said to have been swallowed up by the earth at Lebadeia in western Boeotia, where his celebrated oracle was located in historical times.[48]

In another version of the treasure-house story, Agamedes was ensnared as he and his brother were stealing from the treasure-house of Augeias at Elis. The snare had been set by the king on the advice of the ingenious Daidalos. Trophonios fled to Lebadeia as in the other version, while Kerkyon, son of Agamedes, who had also participated in the crime, fled to Athens (see p. 344).[49] Herodotus recounts a very similar story about two brothers who had been stealing from the treasure-house of Rhampsinitos, king of Egypt.[50]

The story in which the builder-heroes were granted an easy death by Apollo may well have been inspired by the well-known Argive legend of KLEOBIS and BITON, which told of the death of two young men who were sons of a priestess of Hera at Argos. When they were once planning to drive her to the festival of the goddess in an ox-cart, the oxen happened to be late in returning from the fields; and since time was running short, the two brothers harnessed themselves to the cart instead and dragged their mother for forty-five stades (over five and a half miles) to the temple of Hera. Their mother was so proud of their action and the acclaim that they won by it that she addressed a special prayer to Hera, asking that they should be granted the greatest blessing that mortals can receive; and the goddess rewarded them by granting them a peaceful death on that very day, as they were sleeping after the sacrifices and feasting. Herodotus remarks encouragingly that this was a god-given proof of how much better it is to be dead than alive; the captured Seilenos said much the same to Midas when the king sought to benefit from his wisdom (see p. 213).[51]

The oracle of Trophonios at Lebadeia was supposed to have been discovered in the following way. When Boeotia had once suffered a drought for two years, the cities of the land sent some ambassadors to Delphi to consult the oracle, which ordered them to go to Lebadeia to seek a cure from Trophonios. Although they could find no sign of an oracle when they first arrived there, the oldest of the envoys, a certain Saon, caught sight of a swarm of bees and followed them until they disappeared into a cleft in the earth. This proved to be the site of the oracle of Trophonios, and Saon was instructed in its rites and procedures by the dead hero himself.[52] Those who wanted to consult Trophonios would descend on their own into a kiln-shaped chasm in the earth, and lie down at the bottom, pushing their feet into a narrow opening between the wall and the floor; they would then be drawn through the opening, as if caught up by the current of a rushing river, and would be returned in the same way after receiving a revelation from the hero. The experience was so terrifying that people who visited Trophonios were said to be incapable of laughing for some time afterwards, or even for the rest of their life according to popular lore.[53]

Phlegyas and the Phlegyans

Another remarkable figure who was associated with north-western Boeotia (and also southern Thessaly in some accounts) was PHLEGYAS, the eponymous king of a violent people, the Phlegyans (Phlegyai), who were notorious for having raided the sanctuary of Apollo at Delphi. They were evidently a byword for bellicosity from an early period, since the *Iliad* remarks that the war-god Ares and his son Phobos (Fear) used to venture out of their Thracian homeland to join them in battle.[54] Later sources report that they lived as outlaws, preying on neighbouring peoples and paying no regard to the gods.[55] Their raid on Delphi was supposed to have been the ultimate outrage that caused their downfall. According to Pausanias' account of the story, they were successful at the time, killing Philammon (see p. 435) and a picked force of Argives who tried to defend the sacred place, but were punished for their sacrilege afterwards by Apollo himself, who destroyed all but a few of them by means of earthquakes, lightning-strokes and plague.[56] In Latin sources, the attack is turned into an individual enterprise by Phlegyas, who is said to have attempted to burn Apollo's temple to avenge the death of his daughter Koronis (an unfaithful mistress of Apollo whose death had been ordered by the god, see p. 149). Apollo shot him dead, however, and sent him down to Hades where he suffered due punishment.[57] According to the *Aeneid*, a rock hangs over him forever threatening to fall down on him (a motif borrowed from the early mythology of Tantalos, see p. 117), and he cries out through the infernal gloom, warning others to learn from his sufferings by holding to justice and respecting the gods. He is regularly mentioned in Roman literature thereafter as a sinner who was subjected to posthumous punishment alongside Sisyphos, Tantalos and their like;[58] although he is never mentioned in this connection in surviving Greek sources, one may suspect that this fate was first assigned to him in Hellenistic literature.

Phlegyas is described as a son of Ares, either by Dotis, whose name associates her with the Dotian Fields in Thessaly, or by Chryse, a member of the Orchomenian royal family.[59] As the former genealogy would indicate, Phlegyas was sometimes regarded as a Thessalian, particularly in his role as the father of Koronis, the Thessalian mother of Asklepios.[60] Other reports make him the father of Ixion or a brother of Gyrton,[61] allying him to the Lapiths of Thessaly (none too appropriately, for the Lapiths were a heroic people of very different character to the brigandly Phlegyans). The legends of the Phlegyans tend to locate them in Central Greece, however, in the area to the west of the Copaic Lake. The *Homeric Hymn to Apollo* refers to them accordingly as an overbearing and impious people who lived in a town set in a beautiful glade near the Kephisian (i.e. Copaic) Lake; the place in question may be Phlegya, a town near Orchomenos of which Phlegyas could be

regarded as the eponym.[62] In Pausanias' late and artificial account of the Orchomenian succession, Phlegyas is fitted into the royal line, though not without some
awkwardness;[63] or in some accounts the Phlegyans are shifted further west to the
Phocian city of Daulis, evidently because of its proximity to Delphi.[64] According
to Pherecydes, Zethos and Amphion fortified Thebes to protect it against the
Phlegyans, who seized it nonetheless after the death of the two brothers (see further
on p. 306).[65] Apollodorus refers to a tradition in which Phlegyas was killed by
Lykos and Nykteus (in unstated circumstances, before the pair settled in Thebes
see p. 302).[66]

The life and death of the great hunter Orion

ORION was primarily associated with eastern Boeotia, even if his most striking
stories are set in the Greek islands. He appears in the Homeric epics in two guises,
as a mighty hunter of long ago who continues his favourite activity during his
posthumous existence in the Underworld, and as the heavenly hunter who strides
through the sky above as the constellation Orion.[67] As a ghost in Hades, he is
observed by Odysseus as he rounds up game in the fields of asphodel with a bronze
club in his hand; and as a figure in the sky, he is followed by his hunting-dog (in
the form of Sirius, the brightest star in the sky),[68] and causes anxiety to the (Great)
Bear, who keeps a weather eye on him from her station by the northern pole of the
sky.[69] Although of gigantic size, even bigger than the Aloadai (see p. 91), he is not
yet the uncouth being of the later tradition, for Homer describes him as the most
handsome of mortals; and we are told in the *Odyssey* that the ever-susceptible Eos
(Dawn) fell in love with him and carried him off, causing resentment among the
gods, who incited Artemis to shoot him.[70] Though evidently a major hero in early
times, as is amply attested by these allusions in Homer and by the very fact that a
splendid constellation was named after him, it would appear that he came to seem
excessively crude and primitive as time progressed, for he was eclipsed by heroes
like Perseus and Herakles and sank into relative obscurity. As a consequence, the
picture that is presented of him in the surviving literature is both skewed and
incomplete; since the richest material is provided by astronomical sources, which
are concerned above all to explain how he came to be transferred to the sky, we
have many accounts of his death (generally of late origin) but little record of his
earlier life and Boeotian legends.

  There are two conflicting accounts of his birth. According to Pherecydes and
Hesiod (in the *Astronomy* or possibly the *Catalogue*), he was fathered by Poseidon on
Euryale, a daughter of Minos,[71] and was thus born in Crete (which was a favourite
location for stories of his death). Or in another account, which first appears in
Hellenistic times, he was born from the earth in Boeotia in most extraordinary
circumstances. When Hyrieus, the eponymous founder of Hyria in eastern Boeotia
(see p. 520), was once entertaining Zeus, Poseidon and Hermes at his home, they
rewarded him for his gracious hospitality by allowing him to choose what he most
desired; and being childless and indeed unmarried, he asked to be granted a son.
So they emitted some semen (or else urinated) into the hide of an ox that he had
sacrificed to them, and ordered that it should be buried in the earth for ten (lunar)

months; and a child duly emerged from the ground at the end of that period. He was called Ourion initially on account of his origin (the Greek verb *ourein* could refer both to urination and the ejaculation of semen), but his name was later short-ened to Orion for reasons of delicacy.[72] Apollodorus presumably had this story in mind when writing that Orion was earthborn.[73] In the usual tradition, as we have seen (p. 520), Hyrieus was said to have fathered sons of his own through a marriage to a nymph. Orion seems to have been more closely associated with Tanagra than with Hyria. His tomb could be seen in that town in south-eastern Boeotia, which is mentioned accordingly as having been his home; indeed, a scholiast reports that 'most people say that Orion was a Tanagran'.[74] The Tanagran poetess Corinna mentions him several times in the scanty remains of her verse, referring to him as the lord of Boeotia, and Euphorion states that Hemera (Day, here to be identified with Eos) took him from Tanagra when she carried him away.[75] Although most of the astral myths relating to his death are set in the Greek islands, the myth of his pursuit of the daughters of Atlas (which explained how they came to be transferred to the sky as the Pleiades, see p. 518) was set in Boeotia.[76]

Another Boeotian tale, which was recounted in a lost poem by Corinna, tells of two daugh-ters of Orion, Metioche and Menippe, known as the Koronides. They were reared in Boeotia after the death of their father and sacrificed their lives to save their homeland from a plague. For when an oracle revealed that the infernal gods who had inflicted the plague would be appeased if two maidens offered themselves up to them in sacrifice, the daughters of Orion cried out three times to the gods below that they were offering themselves as willing victims and cut their throats with the shuttles from their looms. Feeling pity for the two maidens, Hades and Persephone caused their bodies to disappear and two comets to rise up into the sky in place of them. They were honoured as the Koronides thereafter at Orchomenos, where the young people would bring them expiatory offerings of honey each year.[77]

Orion married a woman called Side who also belongs to Boeotia; her name corres-ponds to the Boeotian term for a pomegranate, and she was regarded as the eponym of the Boeotian town of Sidai. She was consigned to the Underworld by Hera while still quite young for having dared to claim that she rivalled the goddess in beauty.[78] It may be relevant to the origin of this myth that the pomegranate had Underworld associations, as we saw in connection with Persephone (see p. 128). After the prema-ture death of Side, Orion crossed over to Chios to seek the hand of Merope, daughter of Oinopion. This Oinopion (Wine-face) was a son of Dionysos and Ariadne who had left Naxos, the island of his birth, to become the ruler of Chios, an island that was renowned for the quality of its wine. It was said that the arts of viniculture and wine-making were introduced to the island by Oinopion, who had learned them from Dionysos himself; and the Chians liked to claim accordingly that they had been the first people in the world to make red wine.[79] Although Orion tried to win the favour of his prospective father-in-law by clearing the island of wild beasts, Oinopion was reluctant to give his daughter to such an uncouth being and constantly deferred the wedding. Orion grew increasingly impatient and finally broke into Merope's room one night while he was drunk and raped her. On learning of this outrage, Oinopion blinded him as he was lying asleep afterwards, and cast him out on the shore (or drove him out of the island).

Figure 16.3 *Blind Orion searching for the Rising Sun*, by Nicolas Poussin (1594–1665). Courtesy of The Metropolitan Museum of Art, New York.

Unable to know where he was heading or indeed where he should try to go, Orion wandered helplessly around the Aegean; he could roam without restriction because he was gifted with the power of being able to walk over the sea (or at least wade through it), a power that he had doubtless acquired from his father Poseidon. He eventually happened to find himself on the island of Lemnos, where Hephaistos had his forge; and the divine blacksmith took pity on him and offered him his assistant, Kedalion, as a guide. So Orion hoisted Kedalion on to his shoulders and headed east towards the sunrise in accordance with Kedalion's directions, until he was able to find a cure for his blindness by turning his face towards the rays of the rising sun. Or else he was healed by the sun-god Helios himself. Although he hurried back to Chios to exact revenge for his blinding, Oinopion escaped him by hiding in an underground chamber which had been prepared for him by his people (or by Hephaistos at the order of Poseidon).[80]

The conflicting tales about Orion's death are generally set on one or other of the Greek islands. This is already the case in the Homeric account mentioned above, in which Artemis shot him on Ortygia (often identified with Delos in later sources) after Eos had abducted him to that island. Artemis took this action because the gods disapproved of love affairs between goddesses and mortal men; or in a later variation, she killed Orion on Delos for trying to rape Oupis, one of the Hyperborean maidens who brought offerings to the island after the birth of Apollo and Artemis (see p. 190).[81] Or in a version which first appears in Callimachus, Orion incurred this fate by attempting to court or rape Artemis herself.[82] A wholly different story in which Orion was killed by a giant scorpion is most generally favoured in the astronomical literature of the Hellenistic and Roman periods. As with the myth of his pursuit of the Pleiades, this is a true astral myth that was directly inspired by a feature of the night sky, for the constellation of the Scorpion rises as Orion sets and therefore seems to pursue Orion through the heavens. In the standard version derived from Eratosthenes, Orion once boasted that he would kill every beast on the earth as he was hunting on Crete with Artemis and Leto, causing such anger to Gaia (Earth) that she sent forth a huge scorpion to cause his death. At the request of his divine hunting-companions, Zeus transferred him to the heavens, placing the scorpion in an adjoining region of the sky.[83]

In Aratus' version (which is described by him as an old story), Orion angered Artemis by laying hands on her robe as he was clearing Chios of its wild beasts, and she responded by causing the neighbouring hills to break open and the scorpion to emerge for the attack.[84] Or in a later variant, he angered Artemis by disparaging her hunting-skills, provoking her to ask Gaia to send the scorpion against him;[85] or in the very odd version in Ovid's *Fasti*, Gaia sent the scorpion against Leto for some unstated reason, and Orion was killed by it when he stepped in its path to protect the goddess.[86]

Istros, a pupil of Callimachus, devised a deliberately perverse account in which Artemis – who was a resolute virgin in her normal mythology – fell in love with Orion and agreed to marry him. Her brother Apollo was thoroughly dismayed, but she paid no heed to his objections; so one day, when he saw the head of Orion bobbing in the waves as he was swimming far out at sea, he bet his sister that she would be unable to hit the distant speck with one of her arrows. Since she valued nothing more highly than her reputation as an archer, she rose to the challenge and shot an arrow straight through Orion's head without realizing what it was. When his body was subsequently washed ashore, she was grief-stricken and transferred her dead suitor to the stars.[87]

Three lesser provinces: Locris, Doris and Phocis

The province of Locris in Central Greece fell into two separate parts, Eastern (or Opuntian) Locris, which lay on the Euboean Straits to the north of Boeotia and Phocis, and Western or Ozolian Locris, which lay to the south-west on the Corinthian Gulf and was separated from the other Locris by the province of Phocis. In the very earliest times, Opous, the main city of Eastern Locris, was the home of Deukalion and Pyrrha, who settled there after the great flood (see p. 403); and it later fell under the rule of LOKROS, son of Physkos, a descendant of Deukalion in the third or fourth generation. This Lokros was said to have given his name to both Eastern and Western Locris under the following circumstances. As the king of the Leleges, the descendants of the people who had sprung up from the stones that were flung by Deukalion and Pyrrha (see p. 403), Lokros ruled initially at Opous (which had yet to acquire its name), and named his people the Locrians after himself. During the period of his rule, Zeus abducted Protogeneia, a daughter of Opous, king of the Epeians in Elis, from her home in the Peloponnese and slept with her on Mt Mainalos in Arcadia, causing her to conceive a son. Knowing that Lokros was wifeless and childless, Zeus arranged for her to marry him afterwards, and Lokros adopted her son at birth, naming him Opous after his grandfather. The king was delighted with the child and gave him a city and people to govern when he grew up; and the main city of the land was named Opous in his honour.[88]

To account for the name and origin of Western or Ozolian Locris, it was explained that Lokros eventually quarrelled with his adoptive son, and decided to transfer the throne to him and found a new Locris elsewhere. When he consulted the Delphic oracle about the enterprise, he was advised to establish his seat of rule at the place where he was bitten by a wooden dog; and as he was continuing west through Central Greece from Delphi, he pricked his foot on a dog-rose in the lands to the west of Mt Parnassos, and recognized that he should settle there in accordance with the words of the oracle.[89] The most notable hero of the Locrians was Aias, son of Oileus, who commanded the Locrian contingent at Troy (see p. 456 etc.); known as the lesser or Locrian Aias to distinguish him from his greater namesake, Aias, son of Telamon, he was said to have been born at Naryx, a coastal city of Western Locris, as a descendant of Lokros in the sixth generation.[90]

Various tales were offered to explain why the Western Locrians were called Ozolians. According to one, a bitch once gave birth to a piece of wood instead of a puppy while the land was under the rule of a certain Orestheus, son of Deukalion; and when Orestheus planted this piece of wood into the ground, a vine grew up from it, and the people of the area were named Ozolians after the shoots (*ozoi*) of this precious plant. This account of the origin of the vine is already recounted by Hecataeus, though without the present aetiology; Hecataeus states that Orestheus founded his kingdom in Aetolia (see p. 414).[91] The name *Ozolioi* is in fact suggestive of smelliness; Strabo points to the sulphur-springs of the area.[92] Or if a myth is desired in this connection, some explained that the Centaur Nessos escaped to this area after he was fatally wounded by Herakles (see p. 281), and when he died there, his corpse rotted away unburied, imparting an unpleasant smell to the air which has never disappeared, hence the name of the Ozolians. Or according to another suggestion, the autochthonous first inhabitants of the land wore uncured hides as a protection against the cold and therefore acquired an unpleasant smell.[93]

The province of Phocis to the west of Boeotia was of little significance in myth except as the region that harboured Delphi. It had two eponyms, both named PHOKOS, the one a grandson of Sisyphos from Corinth and the other a son of Aiakos from Aegina.[94] The Corinthian was said to have arrived in the province first, and to have settled at Tithorea in the north with Antiope as his wife (see further on p. 305).[95] Schedios and Epistrophos, who are mentioned in the *Iliad* as the leaders of the Phocian contingent at Troy,[96] were descended from this Phokos. The son of Aiakos arrived from Aegina a generation later and lived in Phocis for a while before he returned home to be murdered by his half-brothers (see p. 532). He married Asterodeia (or Asteria, or Asteropeia), a daughter of the Aiolid Deion (see p. 435), who was ruler of part of Phocis at least at that time. She bore him twin sons, KRISOS and PANOPEUS, who quarrelled even while they were still in their mother's womb (just like Proitos and Akrisios in Argos).[97] They were the eponymous founders of Krisa and Panopea, two towns on opposite sides of Phocis to the south of Tithorea; it was explained that their father had lived in this southern part of the land and had given his name to it, while the other Phokos, who had settled further north, had given his name to the northern part of the land.[98] Krisos was the father of STROPHIOS, who became a brother-in-law of Agamemnon by marrying his sister Anaxibia.[99] After the murder of Agamemnon, Strophios provided refuge to his son Orestes at Krisa, bringing him up together with his own son Pylades; and since the two boys became close friends, Pylades accompanied Orestes when he returned to the Peloponnese to avenge his father's murder (see pp. 510–11). Pylades married Orestes' sister Elektra, who bore two sons of no particular note, Strophios and Medon (or Medeon). Panopeus, the other son of the Aiginetan Phokos, was the father of EPEIOS,[100] who fought at Troy but was more skilled as a craftsman than a warrior, and helped his comrades to victory by building the Wooden Horse (see p. 473).

Phocis was fringed on part of its western border by the little province of Doris, which was thought to have been the ancestral home of the Dorians. It was also associated with another people, the Dryopians (Dryopes), who were said to have lived there until Herakles drove them out (see p. 281), so leaving the land free for the Dorians, who had previously lived further north in Thessaly.[101] This at least was the story that had developed by the classical period to reconcile the conflicting accounts of the early history of the area (see p. 282). The Dorians were later supposed to have entered the Peloponnese as allies of the Heraklids (see p. 287), abandoning their home in Central Greece.

The local legends of Megara

The legends of Megara, Attica's neighbour to the west at the head of the Isthmus of Corinth, are rarely of more than local significance, even if the city became involved in Minos' war against Athens (see p. 340) and one of its subsequent rulers, Alkathoos, is a figure of some interest. The first ruler of the city was supposed to have been a certain KAR, who was a son of Phoroneus, the first king of Argos; he was the eponym of the Megarian acropolis, which was known as Karia. Rather than accept that their city had been named after Megareus, a man of foreign origin (see below), the Megarians preferred to argue that it had acquired its name at the very beginning when Kar had founded the Megaron (hall, i.e. temple) of Demeter on the acropolis.[102]

According to the local tradition as reported by Pausanias, Megara was ruled by descendants of Kar for twelve generations until the throne was seized by a newcomer from Egypt, Lelex, son of Poseidon and Libye, who gave his name to his subjects; since the name in question, Leleges, was a vague term that was applied to the aboriginal inhabitants of various parts of Greece, it is no surprise that primordial rulers or heroes called Lelex should recorded for a number of places, including Sparta (see p. 524). Lelex was succeeded by his son Kleson and then his grandson Pylas, who offered refuge to Pandion II, king of Athens, during his exile (see p. 374). When Pylas subsequently killed his uncle Bias, he transferred the throne to Pandion, who had married his daughter Pylia, and departed into exile in the Peloponnese, where he was said to have founded sandy Pylos, Nestor's city in Messenia, and also the city of the same name in Elis. Pandion died in Megara, where his heroic shrine could be seen in historical times, and was succeeded by his son Nisos, who remained in Megara when Aigeus and the other sons of Pandion returned to Athens to recover their father's kingdom (see p. 374).[103]

As described in Chapter 10, Minos was supposed to have attacked Megara while it was under the rule of Nisos, son of Pandion. According to the tradition that was accepted elsewhere in Greece, the city fell to Minos as the result of an act of treachery by the king's daughter Skylla (see p. 340); and it was further accepted that MEGAREUS, a son of Poseidon from Onchestos in Boeotia, had arrived to fight as an ally of Nisos, but was killed in battle and buried in the city, which came to be known as Megara from that time onward (instead of Nisa as previously).[104] Pausanias reports, however, that the Megarians themselves refused to countenance any of this. As already mentioned, they claimed that Megara had already been known as such long before the arrival of Megareus; and they were unwilling even to discuss the idea that their city had suffered a humiliating defeat during the reign of Nisos. They disagreed accordingly about Megareus, claiming that he had settled in Megara as a subject of Nisos after marrying his daughter Iphinoe, and that he had later succeeded to the throne, apparently after his father-in-law had died a natural death.[105]

Even though Megareus married the king's daughter and became the ruler of the land in the local tradition, his life ended in tragedy because his elder son, Timalkos, was killed by Theseus when he accompanied the Dioskouroi into Attica to recover Helen (see p. 361; Theseus was generally said to have been absent at the time), and his younger son, Euippos, fell victim to the savage lion of Kithairon.[106] This lion was killed by Herakles in the usual tradition (see p. 251), but the Megarians linked its death to the fate of this prince of theirs, saying that Megareus had offered his daughter Euaichme and the succession to anyone who could kill the lion that had caused the death of his son. On hearing that this valuable reward was on offer, ALKATHOOS, a son of Pelops who had been banished from his homeland because he had been involved in the murder of Chrysippos (see p. 505), killed the lion and cut off its tongue as evidence; and when he arrived in Megara to find that others were also claiming to have killed the lion, he was thus able to win the throne for himself by producing the tongue from his knapsack.[107]

Alkathoos was said to have established the Megarian temple of Apollo Graios and Artemis Agrotera in gratitude for his success in the lion-hunt, and also to have fortified the western acropolis, which was named after him. Apollo assisted him in the latter enterprise, laying his lyre (*kithara*) on a particular stone while he was doing so; and for that reason, the stone made a sound like the twang of a lyre-string if anyone tossed a pebble at it in later times.[108] Alkathoos lost his sons before his own death as had Megareus before him, for his elder son, Ischepolis, was killed by the Calydonian boar, and his other son, Kallipolis, perished in the most tragic of circumstances when he arrived in Megara with the news. For Alkathoos happened to be offering a sacrifice to Apollo and Kallipolis scattered the fire-wood from the altar in his haste, causing his father to believe that he had committed a sacrilege; and in his anger, Alkathoos struck him a fatal blow on the head with a log from the altar before he could speak.[109] The heroic shrine of Alkathoos, which was later used as a state archive, could be seen at the foot of the western acropolis.[110]

The myths of Corinth, Megara's neighbour to the north, have already been discussed in connection with its Deukalionid ruling family (see p. 430). Within the Peloponnese to the west of Corinth lay the city of Sicyon, which had been founded from Argos. Two of its mythical rulers make significant appearances in heroic myth, firstly Epopeus, who provoked an attack from Thebes by harbouring and marrying the fugitive Antiope (see p. 303), and secondly Polybos, who reared Oedipus as his adoptive son a generation or so later (see p. 308), and offered a home to Adrastos when he was exiled from Argos (see p. 332). Pausanias provides a complicated and artificial account of the Sicyonian succession from the time of the city's foundation.[111]

Three romantic legends from Patrai

There is little left to report of the old heroic legends of the Peloponnese, which have been examined in connection with the Inachids, Deukalionids and Atlantids. While we are in this area, however, it would be a shame to pass over some romantic legends that were collected by Pausanias at Patrai on the northern coast.

Not far from Patrai, near the mouth of the river Selemnos, there was once a town called Argyra (although it was no more than a ruin by Pausanias' time). According to local legend, a handsome shepherd boy called SELEMNOS had once lived in that area, and had attracted the love of a sea-nymph called ARGYRA, who used to emerge from the sea to consort with him; but she ceased to visit him when his beauty began to fade, and he died of a broken heart. Aphrodite, as the goddess who presided over love, took pity on him and transformed him into the river Selemnos; and when he continued to yearn for Argyra even in his new form, she granted him the additional favour of causing him to forget his love. Ever afterwards, so it was claimed, the river would confer the same favour on anyone who bathed in it, causing men and women alike to forget their passions. Pausanias, who rarely makes any personal observations, feels impelled to remark that if this is really the case, the waters of the Selemnos are of greater worth than a large amount of money.[112]

At Patrai itself, there was a sanctuary of Artemis Triklaria at which human sacrifices were said to have been offered in early times. According to the temple legend, a maiden called KOMAITHO had once served as a priestess in the temple long before the Trojan War, and had fallen in love with a young man called MELANIPPOS; but their parents had refused to allow them to marry, and they had consummated their passion in secret, making love inside the temple on more than one occasion. In her anger at the sacrilege, Artemis afflicted the land with famine and disease; and when the local people sought the advice of the Delphic oracle, they were told not only that the guilty couple should be offered in sacrifice to Artemis, but also that the most attractive youth and maiden in the area should be offered up to her likewise in each successive year. The oracle indicated that the Patraians would be relieved of this painful duty when a foreign king arrived in their land with a foreign deity, an event that finally occurred in the following circumstances just after the Trojan War. During the division of the spoils after the sack of Troy, EURYPYLOS, son of Euaimon, a Thessalian ruler, was given a most precious object, a chest containing a statue of Dionysos which had been fashioned by Hephaistos; this statue had been passed down in the Trojan royal family ever since it had been presented to the first king, Dardanos, by his father Zeus. Since Kassandra had put a curse on any Greek who found the statue, Eurypylos was driven mad when he opened the chest to look at it. He was sufficiently lucid at times, however, to be able to consult the Delphic oracle, which told him to settle in a land where he found a people offering a strange sacrifice and to install the chest there for worship. When his ship was then blown to the northern coast of the Peloponnese in the region of Patrai, he stepped ashore there and saw a maiden and youth being led to the altar of Artemis for that year's sacrifice. He realized at once that this must be the sacrifice that the oracle had meant; and on seeing this foreign king in their land, the Patraians recalled the oracle that they had received long before and checked whether he had a god inside the chest, as was indeed the case. So Eurypylos was delivered from his madness and the people of Patrai from their human sacrifices. In historical times, they offered sacrifice to Eurypylos every year in connection with their festival of Dionysos.[113]

Patrai was a place of no great importance until Augustus planted a colony there after defeating Marcus Antonius. Among some plunder from Aetolia that was deposited at the city by the emperor, there was an ancient statue of Dionysos from Calydon which thus came to be housed in the Patraian temple of Calydonian Dionysos; the following tale, which is set in its place of origin on the mainland opposite, was recounted in connection with it. A Calydonian priest of Dionysos called KORESOS had fallen in love with a maiden called KALLIRHOE, but the more he pressed himself on her the less she liked him. Finding that all his pleas and promises made no impression on her, he prayed to the cultic image (apparently for vengeance rather than assistance), and Dionysos responded by afflicting the Calydonians with a madness that caused many of them to die insane. When they sought the advice of the oracle of Zeus at Dodona, they were told that Dionysos was to blame, and that his anger would not be allayed until Koresos had sacrificed a human victim to him, either Kallirhoe or someone who volunteered to take her place. As Kallirhoe was being brought to the altar, Koresos found that his love for her outweighed his meaner feelings of resentment, and sacrificed himself to the god in place of her as a willing substitute. On seeing him lying dead at her feet, Kallirhoe felt pity for him and remorse at the way that she had treated him, and killed herself in her turn, cutting her throat by a local spring that was known by her name ever afterwards.[114]

Anios of Delos and his wonder-working daughters; Akontios and Kydippe; Kyparissos

We must now travel further abroad to consider some of the more interesting myths of the Greek islands. At the time of the Trojan War, the holy island of Delos was home to a picturesque family consisting of the priest-king ANIOS and his three daughters, Oino, Spermo and Elais, who could draw wine (*oinos*), grain (cf. *sperma*, a seed) and olive-oil (*elaion*) from the ground at will. These remarkable maidens were known collectively as the OINOTROPHOI (Wine-growers).[115] Anios was a son of Apollo, who had seduced his mother RHOIO (Pomegranate-woman), daughter of Staphylos (Grape-cluster-man, a son of Dionysos) in the land of her birth on the Carian coast of Asia Minor. Her father refused to believe her when she told him that a god had made her pregnant, and locked her up in a chest and set her adrift in the sea (a familiar motif in Greek myth, as we have seen with Danae and Auge). She was washed ashore on Delos, where she gave birth to her child and placed him on Apollo's altar, praying to the god to save him if he recognized him as his son. Anios was duly reared and befriended by his divine father, who instructed him in the arts of divination.[116] It was said that his mother named him Anios because of all the distress (*ania*) that she had suffered on his account.[117] In another version of her story, she was washed ashore on Euboea (where she subsequently married a certain Zarex), and her son was transferred to Delos after his birth by Apollo.[118]

Anios grew up to become a celebrated seer and priest of Apollo, and ruled over the holy island. He married a certain Dorippe and fathered the above-mentioned daughters, who acquired their special powers through the grace of Dionysos.[119] A variety of tales are recorded in which the Greek army is said to have sought (or been offered) the services of the Oinotrophoi just before the Trojan War or after its outbreak. In one account, the Greek force called in at Delos on its way to Troy; and since Anios was aware that the gods had revealed that Troy would remain unconquered for ten years, he vainly attempted to persuade the Greeks to remain with him for the following nine years, promising that his daughters would be able the furnish them with the necessary provisions. This story may already have appeared in the *Cypria*.[120] Or when the Greeks ran short of food during the long siege of Troy, Agamemnon sent Palamedes to Delos to fetch the Oinotrophoi; or in a version attributed to Simonides, Menelaos and Odysseus sailed to Delos at some stage with many followers for that purpose.[121] Ovid offers an account in which Agamemnon seized the Oinotrophoi, here four in number, by force of arms, and ordered them to feed the Greek fleet; but they all escaped, two of them fleeing to Euboea and the others to Andros, which was ruled by a son of Anios. When the Greeks sailed to Andros and forced the king to surrender the latter pair, they prayed for help to Dionysos, who transformed them into snow-white doves.[122] Only in some late Latin accounts are the Oinotrophoi said to have came to Aulis (where the army first assembled) to provide the Greeks with provisions for their voyage and campaign.[123] Ovid and Vergil both say that Aeneas and his followers called in at Delos on their way to Italy, and received a friendly welcome from Anios (see p. 588).[124]

The legend of Anios and his wonder-working daughters is so quaint as to suggest that it may have been of popular origin; from Keos, to the south-east of the tip of Attica, comes a pretty romance which is more of a literary product, at least in the form in which it has come down to us. AKONTIOS, a young Kean from a respectable but relatively poor family, fell in love with a higher-born Naxian (or Athenian) named KYDIPPE when he happened to meet her at a festival on Delos. After following her to the temple of Artemis, he threw an apple in front of her inscribed with the words, 'I swear by Artemis to marry none but Akontios'. Kydippe picked it up (apples were a very common love-gift but it seems that she did not realize this) and innocently read the message, speaking the words aloud as readers commonly did in ancient times. By so doing, she bound herself to Akontios by a solemn oath. When her father subsequently tried to marry her to the man of his choice, she suffered a mysterious illness and he was obliged to postpone the marriage; and after being forced to do so on two further occasions, he sought the advice of the Delphic oracle, which revealed that Artemis was making his daughter ill to prevent her from breaking her oath. So he agreed that she should marry Akontios, whose scheme was thus brought to fulfilment.[125]

Keos is also the location of the story of KYPARISSOS, at least in the best-known account of it by Ovid. Kyparissos was a young favourite of Apollo who was turned into a cypress-tree in the following circumstances. A tame stag lived on the island in his time, a splendid beast which was sacred to the nymphs and wholly without fear; and although it was friendly to everyone, Kyparissos was especially fond of it and used to lead it to new pastures and refreshing springs, and would wreathe its horns with garlands and even ride on its back, guiding it with scarlet reins. One day, however, while it was resting under the shade of some trees in the midday heat, Kyparissos happened to throw his hunting-spear in that direction and accidentally killed it. In the intensity of his grief, he resolved to join it in death, even though Apollo urged him to show a proper sense of proportion. As he was wasting away in his sorrow, he prayed to the gods to be allowed to mourn forever, and was transformed into a cypress, a tree associated with mourning and graveyards.[126] In another account, Kyparissos was a young Cretan who fled from his homeland to escape the advances of Apollo (or Zephyros), and was transformed into a cypress-tree on Mt Kasion in Syria. This version of his story, which was presumably of Hellenistic origin, seems to have been modelled on the famous legend of Apollo and Daphne (see p. 155), which is also set in Syria in one version.[127]

The legendary history of Thera; Merops of Kos; Ankaios of Samos

Stony Seriphos further to the south was famous in myth for its association with Perseus (see pp. 239ff); and on the southern bounds of the archipelago lay Anaphe, which was revealed to the night-bound Argonauts by Apollo (see p. 397), and Thera, which grew from a clod of earth which was thrown into the sea by the Argonaut Euphemos (see p. 397). The myths of this latter island will merit further attention.

Thera (also known as Santorini in modern times) is formed from the remains of an ancient volcano which exploded in a massive eruption in about 1400 BC. Cyrene, the most important Greek colony in Africa, was founded from it in the middle of the seventh century BC. According to legend, Kadmos visited it during his fruitless search for Europa (see p. 295), and installed some of his Phoenician followers on the island as settlers under the leadership of a kinsman of his, a certain Membliaros.[128] It was said that the island was known as Kalliste (the Most Beautiful) in these early times. It continued to be ruled by descendants of Membliaros until THERAS, son of Autesion, who was a descendant of Kadmos, arrived there eight generations later and claimed the throne by virtue of his descent. His father Autesion had been heir to the throne at Thebes, but had left the city to accompany the Heraklids to the Peloponnese, and Theras spent much of his earlier life in Sparta as a consequence (see p. 329). His sister Argeia married Aristodemos, one of the Heraklid leaders, and bore him twin sons, Prokles and Eurysthenes, who became the first Heraklid kings of Sparta (see p. 290 for the circumstances); and since they were infants when the kingdom was allocated to them, Theras ruled on their behalf as regent until they came of age. After enjoying this taste of power, he was reluctant to live in Sparta as a subordinate when the twins took over the throne, and therefore decided to sail away to claim Kalliste as a kingdom of his own. The inhabitants readily accepted him as their ruler, and he renamed the island after himself.[129]

Theras was accompanied to his new home by some Dorian followers from Sparta (for Thera had a Dorian population in classical times) and also some descendants of the Argonauts. It will be remembered that the island was supposed to have grown from a clod of earth that the Argonaut Euphemos had received from the god of Lake Tritonis in Libya (see p. 396). Euphemos had thrown the clod into the sea at the proper site in response to a prophetic dream, which had revealed that the new island would provide a home for his descendants;[130] and this was duly brought to pass in the time of Theras as a result of the following circumstances. When the Argonauts had called in at Lemnos during their outward journey, many of them had fathered children by the women of the island, who had previously slaughtered their menfolk (see p. 384); and the descendants of these children were later expelled from Lemnos and settled in Laconia, where they married local women. They behaved with such arrogance, however, that their hosts turned against them, and some of them, including descendants of Euphemos, were therefore happy to sail away with Theras when he invited them to accompany him. This was a significant feature of the legend because it enabled a link to be established between the origins of Thera and the founding of Cyrene from the island in historical times; for it was claimed that Battos, who led a party of Theraeans and Cretans to found this important colony in North Africa, was a remote descendant (supposedly in the seventeenth generation) of the Euphemos who had received the marvellous clod of earth from Triton in North Africa.[131] A circle was thus completed, and the establishment of the colony in Africa was legitimized in mythical terms. Cyrene was ruled by descendants of Battos until the middle of the fifth century BC; it was supposed to have been named after a Thessalian nymph who had been abducted to its site in early times by Apollo (see p. 152). It may be noted that this account of the mythical history of Thera is marred by a serious chronological inconsistency, since Kadmos could not possibly have visited it if it was first formed in the time of the Argonauts, who must have lived several generations later by any reckoning.

The most important heroic myths of Rhodes, the island of the Sun (see p. 43), have been covered already in connection with the Cretan royal family (see p. 354) and the Heraklids (see p. 293). The island of Cos, further up the coast of Asia Minor, was visited by Herakles while he was sailing home after his attack on Troy (see p. 276). It was ruled in the very earliest times by an earthborn king called MEROPS, who was finally transformed into an eagle. In the version from the astronomical literature, this came about after his much-loved wife, the nymph Echemeia (or Ethemeia), offended Artemis by ceasing to honour her and was shot dead by her. Merops missed her so greatly that he wanted to kill himself, but Hera (presumably as the goddess who presided over married love) took pity on him and transferred him to the heavens. Before doing so, she turned him into an eagle, thinking that he would continue to grieve for his wife if he retained his human form and memory, and he is therefore represented in the sky as the constellation of the Eagle (Aquila).[132] In another version, the goddess Rhea, who had formerly been received by Merops as a guest, took pity on him in the same circumstances and transformed him into an eagle, here an earthly eagle which became the special bird of Zeus.[133] Since

Merops lived at the beginning of history, there is nothing surprising in the notion that he should have mixed with the gods on familiar terms (as did Lykaon, for instance, or Tantalos in Asia Minor nearby). It is reasonable to assume that this was the earlier version of the story, before it was altered to provide a constellation myth. Merops was the eponym of the Meropes, the primordial inhabitants of the island; it is said that the island was named Meropia until Merops renamed it after his daughter Kos.[134] There was an early epic entitled the *Meropis*, but nothing is known of its contents.

The island of Samos further up the coast had a memorable hero in ANKAIOS, who not only sailed with the Argonauts like his Arcadian namesake (see p. 383), but was also killed by a boar just like him. A son of Zeus or Poseidon by Astypalaia (the eponym of an island of the same name to the west of Cos), Ankaios ruled over the Leleges, the aboriginal inhabitants of Samos. He was skilled in the arts of seamanship, as befits an islander, and volunteered to become the steersman of the *Argo* after the original helmsman, Tiphys, died on the outward journey (see p. 389). When he arrived home from his adventures, he turned his attention to agriculture and planted many vines, but was warned by a seer that he would meet his death before he could drink from their fruit. Since all seemed well with him when the crop was ripe, he pressed some grapes and summoned the seer to rebuke him for his incompetence. 'I'm still alive', he said, 'and the fruit is ripe, and I'm just about to drink; look, you can see the wine in the cup'. In no way disconcerted, the seer replied, 'There's many a slip between the cup and the lip'; and at that very moment, a man ran up to warn Ankaios that a wild boar was ravaging his vineyard. So he put the cup aside to confront the beast, and was killed by it before he could raise the cup to his lips.[135] Hence the famous proverb, which was transmitted into English through the Latin version in Erasmus' anthology of ancient adages.

Kinyras, Pygmalion and the legends of Cyprus

Cyprus attracted settlers from Greece and the Levant alike from the late Bronze Age onwards, and was thus significant as a point of contact between Greek and Near Eastern culture. It was a principal centre for the cult of Aphrodite, hence the goddess's title of the Cyprian (Kypris or Kypria). The most notable Cypriot in Greek heroic legend was KINYRAS, the mythical founder of the cult of Aphrodite–Astarte at Paphos on the west coast of the island (where the goddess was supposed to have come ashore after she was born among the waves). He originated as the eponym and mythical ancestor of the clan of priests who presided over this cult, the Kinyridai, whose name was derived from a Semitic expression meaning 'sons of the lyre'. He is first mentioned in the *Iliad*, which reports that he sent a magnificent breastplate to Agamemnon as a gift of friendship after learning that the Greeks were mounting an expedition against Troy; this was an exotic piece of metal-work of Near Eastern design, ornamented with ten bands of dark blue enamel (*kyanos*) and twelve of gold and twenty of tin, and with enamelled snakes reaching up to the neck, three on each side.[136] Later authors elaborate on this Homeric story by suggesting that the Greeks tried to enlist Kinyras as an ally. According to Apollodorus, Menelaos visited him on Cyprus for that purpose in the company of Odysseus and the herald Talthybios, and met with apparent success, for Kinyras not only presented the breastplate as a gift for Agamemnon but promised to send a large force of troops in fifty ships; but when the time came for him to fulfil his oath, he did so in a purely formal manner alone by sending a single proper ship out to sea with forty-nine ships of clay, crewed with men of clay, which soon foundered in the waves.[137] Or in another account, Palamedes was sent to enlist the aid of Kinyras, but secretly advised him to have nothing to do with the war; so although Palamedes announced on his return that Kinyras would send a hundred ships, none ever appeared.[138]

There was no settled tradition on the birth and origin of Kinyras. He was born on Cyprus in some accounts, usually as a son of Paphos, the eponym of the Cypriot city of that name; or else he was born in Cilicia, the province of Asia Minor facing Cyprus to the north, as a son of Sandakos (a descendant of Kephalos and Eos), and emigrated to Cyprus with a group of followers to found the city of Paphos.[139] He married a certain Kenchreis, who bore him a notable daughter, Myrrha (or Smyrna); for the story of how Myrrha deceived her father into sleeping with her and conceived Adonis to him, see p. 198.[140] Or else he married Metharme, daughter of Pygmalion, and fathered Adonis by her as a legitimate child along with various other children.[141] Kinyras killed himself in one account after discovering that he had slept with his own daughter; or else he reigned in prosperity to an extraordinary age; or he was put to death by Apollo after being defeated by him in a musical contest.[142]

In connection with the latter story, it was said that his daughters threw themselves into the sea in sorrow at his death and were turned into halcyons (a mythical bird, see p. 410).[143] According to another tale, which presumably refers to the temple-prostitution that was practised in connection with the cult of Aphrodite-Astarte, Aphrodite forced them to sleep with strangers as a punishment after they had offended her in some unspecified manner.[144] Ovid records a comparable tale in which some Cypriot women called the Propoitides denied the divinity of Aphrodite, so angering her that she caused them to become the first women to lose their good name by prostituting themselves in public.[145]

Another Cypriot tale mentioned by Ovid is that of the Kerastai (Cerastae in Latin form) or Horned Men, a race of men with horns on their foreheads who caused distress to the tender-hearted Aphrodite by offering human sacrifices to Zeus. She even thought of abandoning her Cypriot shrines, but the sight of their horns inspired her with a better idea and she settled the matter in another way by transforming them into bulls.[146] Ovid also makes a passing allusion to the daughters of Kinyras, remarking that they were transformed into the steps of a temple (though without explaining why).[147]

Few stories from Greek myth are more familiar than that of **PYGMALION**, the king of Cyprus who fell in love with a statue of his own creation. Having long remained a bachelor because of the dubious morals of the women around him, Pygmalion carved an ivory image of a woman of perfect beauty and conceived an ever-deepening passion for it. He kissed and embraced it, presented gifts to it as though it were alive, and adorned it with robes and fine jewellery, and laid it out on a couch strewn with purple cloth; and when the day arrived for the feast of Aphrodite, he offered rich sacrifices to the goddess and prayed to be granted a wife like the ivory maiden, not quite daring to say that the statue itself was the object of his desire. But the goddess divined his hidden thoughts and brought the statue

Figure 16.4 Pygmalion and Galatea (oil on canvas) by Jean Léon Gérôme (1824–1904). Whitford and Hughes, London, UK/Bridgeman Art Library.

to life. Such is the story recounted by Ovid, who adds that Pygmalion fathered Paphos, the mother of Kinyras, by his newly created wife; although the woman has come to be known as Galatea, no ancient author ascribes any name to her. There is also some record of an earlier Greek version in which Pygmalion fell in love with an ivory image of Aphrodite, here not of his own creation, and treated it much as if it were alive, taking it to bed and embracing it. To this extent at least, the story resembles that in which Laodameia consorted with a statue of her dead husband (see p. 450); there is no suggestion in the surviving sources that Aphrodite brought the statue to life in this account.[148]

It was perhaps inevitable that Salamis, the principal Greek city on Cyprus, should have been assigned a mythical founder from the island of that name off the coast

Figure 16.5   *The Last Watch of Hero*, by Frederick Lord Leighton (1830–1896).
© Manchester Art Gallery.

of Attica. It was explained that Teukros, the illegitimate son of Telamon, king of Salamis (see p. 276), was banished by his father when he returned from the Trojan War without his half-brother Aias (who had committed suicide, see p. 471). His position as a king on Cyprus is first mentioned by Pindar, and the reason for his exile is first indicated in Euripides' *Helen*, in which Teukros himself makes an appearance and tells how he was banished by his father, and then settled on Cyprus on the advice of an oracle from Apollo.[149] Later sources add nothing essential to this story, although some mythographers explained that Telamon had particular cause for anger because Teukros failed to bring the ashes of Aias and arrived without his son and concubine (who had sailed on another ship).[150] According to Vergil, Teukros established himself on Cyprus with the aid of Belos, the father of Dido.[151] He married one of the daughters of Kinyras, or else a granddaughter of his, Eune, daughter of Kypros; the Teukridai, the traditional rulers of Cypriot Salamis, claimed to be his descendants.[152] Other notable Greeks who were said to have travelled to Cyprus after the Trojan War were Agapenor, king of Arcadia (see p. 545), and Akamas, son of Theseus (see p. 375).

Three love-stories from Asia Minor and beyond

HERO and LEANDROS (or Leander in Latin) were two ill-starred lovers who lived on either side of the narrow straits of the Hellespont (Dardanelles). Leandros, who lived at Abydos on the Asian shore, fell in love with Hero, a young priestess of Aphrodite, after meeting her at a festival of the goddess in her home-town of Sestos on the opposite shore. He used to swim across the straits at night to visit her in secret, guided on his way by a lamp that she shone from her tower by the shore; but one night, when he rashly attempted to make the crossing even though a fierce storm was blowing, Hero's guiding flame was extinguished by the wind, and he soon lost his bearings and was swept to his death by the dangerous current. When Hero looked down from her tower on the following morning and saw his corpse at the water's edge, she hurled herself down so as to be united with him in death. This legend, which was apparently of Hellenistic origin, first appears in Vergil and Ovid and is recounted in full in an epyllion (miniature epic) by Musaeus, probably dating to the fifth century AD. It has remained popular ever since; the Elizabethan rendering by Marlowe and Chapman is finer than any version that has survived from the ancient world.[153]

The legend of PHILEMON and BAUCIS, which is also set in Asia Minor and was apparently based on Phrygian traditions, is a love-story too in its very different way. As Zeus and Hermes were once travelling through Phrygia in human disguise and looking for somewhere to rest, they were turned away from countless homes until Philemon and Baucis, a poor and aged peasant couple, welcomed them into their lowly cottage. As the pair were providing their guests with such food and drink as their means allowed, they noticed that the mixing-bowl that they were using for the wine filled itself of its own accord as often as it was drained, and inferred from this that their visitors must be gods. Although they were then eager to kill their only goose in honour of their divine guests, the two gods prevented them and told them that they were planning to punish the people all around, but that the old pair would escape if they climbed to the top of the mountain that rose up behind their cottage. On reaching the top, the couple looked back and saw that the gods had flooded the countryside below to punish the local people for their hard-heartedness, leaving only their own cottage unaffected. As they watched in amazement, their cottage was then transformed into a splendid temple with a floor and columns of marble and a roof of gold. When the gods promised to grant them whatever they most desired, they asked to serve as their priest and priestess in the newly created temple, and to die at the same instant so that neither would be left alone. After a long and happy old age, they died together as they had asked, and were transformed into two trees, an oak and a lime, which grew from a single trunk.[154] Goethe was greatly struck by this story and adapted it to his own purposes in the final book of his *Faust*.

The ill-starred lovers PYRAMOS and THISBE appear in two legends of a very different nature. The less familiar story connects them with a river and a spring, the river Pyramos, which flowed to the sea in Cilicia in the south-eastern corner of Asia Minor, and the spring of Thisbe, which issued into the sea nearby (or perhaps into the mouth of the river itself). Long ago, so it was said, there had been two lovers called Pyramos and Thisbe whose passion had ended in tragedy, for Thisbe had committed suicide after becoming pregnant and Pyramos had followed her example after learning of her fate; but the gods had taken pity on them and had transformed them into the above-mentioned river and spring, to enable them to associate intimately in their new form by mingling their waters (just as Alpheios was supposed to mingle his waters with those of Arethousa, see p. 42).[155]

Ovid's Babylonian love-tragedy of Pyramos and Thisbe, which is acted out by Peter Quince and his company in a *Midsummer Night's Dream*, follows quite another course. Although the names of the lovers must have been transferred from one story to the other, it is not certain which was the older (even if one may suspect that the preceding story was). Ovid's hero and heroine lived further to the east in any case, having grown up in adjoining houses in Babylon. When their youthful passion turned to love and they sought to marry, their parents ordered them to stop associating with one another, and they were reduced to communicating through a chink in the wall that separated their two houses. They finally arranged to steal away at night to meet outside the city by the tomb of a certain Ninus, where they could lie beneath a mulberry-tree that stood beside a cool spring. Thisbe arrived first but was soon scared away when a lioness came down to the spring to quench its thirst after a kill. The veil that she had been wearing to conceal her features slipped from her shoulders as she fled; and the lion caught sight of it on the ground and ripped it to pieces with its blood-stained jaws. When Pyramos arrived and saw the bloodied fabric lying there with the lion's footprints all around, he naturally assumed that his beloved had been devoured and killed himself with his sword. Thisbe returned as soon as she dared for fear of disappointing her lover, but found him dead on the ground and killed herself in her turn. After Pyramos had stabbed himself and pulled the sword from his wound, a stream of blood had gushed out to spatter the fruit on the mulberry-tree above and to sink into its roots, causing the fruit (which had formerly been white) to turn red; and in response to Thisbe's dying prayer, the gods ordained that the ripe fruit of the mulberry should always be a mournful red in commemoration of the lovers' fate.[156]

Strange folk in far places

Strange distorted and monstrous folk were reputed to live at the fringes of the known world. The elder Pliny (first century AD) provides a useful catalogue of these monstrous races,[157] which later found their way into medieval lore; the majority of them, and certainly the most imaginative, had been introduced into the Greek tradition by Ctesias and authors of the Hellenistic period who compiled fanciful accounts of the marvels of the east. Ctesias of Cnidos worked as a physician at the Persian court at the end of the fifth century BC and wrote a book called the *Indika* on his return, which was full of tall tales and helped to establish the enduring notion that India was a land of wonders. Among the folk who were described in the book were the Dogheads (Kynokephaloi, or Cynocephali in Latin form), people with dog's heads who lived in the mountains of India and communicated by barking rather than through articulate speech; and the Shadefeet (Skiapodes), who could hop along quite briskly on their single leg when necessity demanded, but preferred to spend their time lying on their backs using their single large foot as a parasol; and another race of people had ears that reached down to their shoulders, and were born with white hair that turned dark with age. These latter folk reappear in exaggerated form in the medieval tradition as the Panotii (All-ears), people whose ears were so large that they could use them as blankets.

If monstrous races such as these were of comparatively late invention, others of a less extreme nature, the Pygmies and Arimaspians, can be traced back to the archaic era. The diminutive PYGMIES (Pygmaioi) lived somewhere in Africa. Their small stature is indicated in their name, which refers to a Greek unit of measurement, the *pygmē* (fist), corresponding to the distance between a man's elbow and knuckles. They are first mentioned in a simile in the *Iliad*, in which the cries of advancing Trojan warriors are compared to those uttered by cranes as they set off to escape the winter 'and fly with much clamour to the Ocean's streams, bringing death and slaughter to the Pygmy men'.[158] Whether this idea of battles between the cranes and Pygmies (who would have been of much the same size) was drawn from current folklore or was simply a passing fancy of Homer's, it certainly became a central and enduring feature of Pygmy lore. In vase-paintings and other images from the sixth century BC onwards, the Pygmies are often shown fighting against the cranes with clubs, lances and other weapons, or riding against them on goats or rams. They are usually portrayed in a comical manner as plump little figures with outsized genitals. A transformation myth was devised in Hellenistic times to account for the feud between the Pygmies and the cranes. It was explained that there had once been a Pygmy woman called Oinoe (or Gerana) who had failed to honour Artemis and Hera and had therefore been turned into a crane by way of punishment; and when she had then irritated the Pygmies by fluttering around their town in search of her much-missed infant son Mopsos, they had taken up their clubs to drive her out, hence the state of war that has existed between the cranes and Pygmies ever since.[159]

Most authors from Herodotus onwards regarded the Pygmies as an African people;[160] whether reports about the real people who have come to be known by that name ever reached the Greeks by way of Egypt is now impossible to tell. In the only other myth recorded for them, the Pygmies make a none too serious entry into heroic mythology as adversaries of Herakles, who tangled with them as he was travelling through North Africa on his way to the Hesperides. When he sank into an exhausted sleep after his wrestling-match with Antaios (see p. 270), the Pygmies tried to tie him down, much as the Lilliputians did with Gulliver but with less success, for Herakles released himself with no great difficulty and bundled the little men into his lionskin to take them home to Greece as a curiosity.[161]

The one-eyed ARIMASPIANS lived on the opposite side of the world in the far north. They too engaged in regular hostilities with some animal neighbours, in this case the fabulous GRIFFINS (*grypes*), monsters of Near Eastern design with the body of a lion and the head and wings of an eagle. The trouble arose because the Arimaspians were constantly trying to steal from large hoards of gold which were jealously guarded by the Griffins. This story was related in an early hexameter poem, the *Arimaspea*, probably dating to the seventh century BC, which told how its reputed author, Aristeas of Proconnesos, was supposed to have travelled to the far north while possessed by Apollo. He eventually found himself among the Issedones, who lived quite close to the Hyperboreans (a mythical people who lived at the northern edges of the earth, see p. 148); and it was from these Issedones that he learned about the Arimaspians and Griffins, who inhabited the stretch of land that lay between his hosts and the Hyperboreans. Although Herodotus reports the story (along with many other ethnographic curiosities), he is inclined to believe that the Arimaspians really had two eyes just like everyone else.[162]

Some foundation-myths from the Italian west

Although there were many foundation-myths that ascribed the founding of cities in southern Italy and Sicily to heroes from Greek legend, most are of little general interest, partly because they are late and arbitrary and are rarely accompanied by memorable stories, and partly because most of them relate to insignificant places. Since the Greeks who lived in the main colonies of the west were well aware that their cities had been founded from specific regions of the motherland in historical times, it is understandable that foundation-myths for this area should be concerned with obscure places (often not even Greek) or with the mythical prehistory of Greek or Hellenized cities from the time before the Greeks truly arrived.

Most of the foundations in the first category are credited to heroes of the Trojan War who were said (in the later tradition at least) to have wandered west for various reasons after their return, as in the case of Idomoneus (see p. 355) and Diomedes and Philoktetes (see p. 487). As we have seen, Diomedes was said to have founded a number of towns in Apulia, a part of Italy that contained no Greek colonies at all, even if it had come to be extensively Hellenized by the period at which these myths were devised. For an example of a story from the second category, relating to the mythical prehistory of Greek colonies, we may turn to Croton, a prosperous city in toe of Italy (which was colonized by Achaeans from the Peloponnese at the end of the eighth century BC).

As Herakles was travelling through Italy with the cattle of Geryon after his excursion to Sicily (see p. 265), he arrived at the site of the future city of Croton, where he was entertained by the local ruler, Kroton, son of Phaiax (a brother of Alkinoos from Phaeacia); but during the time of his visit, a certain Lakinios (or Lakinos) tried to steal some of his cattle, provoking a confrontation in which Herakles accidentally killed his host. By way of atonement, he built a tomb for him and offered him a splendid funeral, foretelling that a famous city would be founded there long afterwards under Kroton's name.[163] An almost identical tale was told of Epizephyrean Locri (founded from Locris at much the same period) further down the coast, where the hero was said to have killed the city's eponym, Lokros, son of Phaiax, while trying to prevent an adventurer, Latinos, from stealing his cattle; in this case, Herakles himself was said to have ordered the founding of the colony at a later period after he had become a god on Olympos, indicating his will through an oracle.[164] Myths of a rather different kind ascribed a Greek (or Trojan) pedigree to the original inhabitants of cities or areas that were later settled by Greeks or came under Greek influence. According to a relatively early story of this kind, as attested by Herodotus, the Iapygians and Messapians of Apulia were descended from Cretans who had been driven ashore there after travelling to Sicily to avenge the death of Minos (who was supposed to have been murdered in Sicily, see p. 349).[165] Far more interesting, however, are the legends that tell of the early history of Segesta (Egesta or Aigesta in Greek), an important Hellenized city of non-Greek origin in north-western Sicily.

When Aeneas called in at Sicily on his return from Carthage, he was supposed to have left some of his Trojan followers behind to found the city under the leadership of its eponym, AIGESTES (or Acestes in Latin), a son of the local river-god Krimisos. The story is told by Vergil in the fifth book of the *Aeneid*; in one account, some Greeks who had accompanied Philoktetes to the west participated in its foundation.[166] Aigestes had offered a friendly welcome to Aeneas because he was himself the son of a Trojan mother, who had arrived in Sicily in the following circumstances. When Poseidon had sent a sea-monster against Troy during the reign of Laomedon (see p. 523), an oracle from Apollo had ordered that maidens of noble birth should be exposed to it, prompting many Trojan noblemen to send their daughters abroad; among them was a certain Hippotes or Hippostratos, who sent his daughter Egesta (or Segesta) to Sicily, where the river-god Krimisos had intercourse with her in the form of a bear or a dog and so caused her to conceive Aigestes.[167] Or in a somewhat different version, a certain Phoinodamas urged his fellow Trojans to expose Laomedon's daughter Hesione to the monster, so angering the king that he delivered the three daughters of Phoinodamas to some sailors, telling them to expose the girls on Sicily as prey to wild beasts; but they were saved through the will of Aphrodite, and Krimisos fathered Aigestes by one of them by having intercourse with her in the form of a dog.[168]

To pass forward to historical times, a memorable and romantic story was recounted in connection with the founding of Tarentum (or Taras under its Greek name), a Greek colony on the heel of Italy which was founded at the end of the eighth century BC by some emigrants from Sparta known as the Partheniai. According to the present story, the Partheniai were led by a Spartan called PHALANTHOS, who received an oracle at Delphi before his departure telling him that he would win a land and city for himself when rain fell on him from a clear sky. Although he met with some success in battle after his arrival in Italy, he failed to capture any city or territory and grew increasingly despondent, suspecting that the god at Delphi had set an impossible condition for his success. One day, however, as he was lying with his head in his wife's lap to enable her to pick the lice from his hair, he felt her tears pattering down on him as she wept at the failure of his hopes; and since her name was Aithra (which means Clear Sky in Greek), he suddenly realized that her tears must be the 'rain' that the oracle had referred to. So he returned to battle with renewed confidence, to such effect that he captured Tarentum from its native inhabitants on the very next night and founded a Greek city there.[169]

Arion and the dolphin; two ghost-stories from Greek colonies in Italy

Many of the Greek cities of Italy and Sicily grew wealthy and were able to support a flourishing cultural life. Among the artists and writers who sought to benefit from their patronage was ARION of Methymna, a lyric poet of the seventh century BC, who was born on Lesbos but spent most of his life at the court of Periandros (Periander), the ruthless but cultivated tyrant of Corinth. At one time, so the story goes, Arion made a tour of Sicily and Italy, amassing a considerable profit from his recitations, until he finally set off for Greece in a Corinthian ship that was sailing out of Tarentum. When it reached the open sea, he came to realize that the sailors were plotting to throw him overboard in order to steal his money. After vainly urging them to accept his money in return for his life, he asked them to permit him to give a last recital on the deck in his magnificent singing-robes, saying that he would then take his own life by leaping into the sea. As soon as he fell into the water, however, he was rescued by a dolphin which had been attracted by the sound of his music; and it took him on its back and carried him to Greece, putting him ashore at Cape Tainaron at the southern tip of the Peloponnese. He hurried back to Corinth and told the whole story to Periandros, who was reluctant to believe him until he could interrogate the crew of the ship. When they claimed on their arrival that they had left Arion safe and sound at Tarentum, the poet suddenly revealed himself wearing the robes that he had donned for his farewell recital. Their lies were thus exposed in a most dramatic fashion, and Periandros sentenced them to death.[170]

Such is the standard version of the story as recounted by Herodotus. Later authors adapted it to explain the origin of the constellation of the Dolphin (Delphinus), saying that Apollo, the divine patron of poets, rewarded the dolphin for its rescue of Arion by transferring it to the stars.[171] Visitors to Tainaron could see a bronze statue of a man on a dolphin that had supposedly been dedicated by Arion.[172] Ancient writers have much to say about dolphins, which were known to be friendly to human beings and were reputed to be fond of music. Some dolphin stories were legendary like that of Arion or a tale recorded for Enalos, one of the legendary first colonists of Lesbos (the Penthilidai, p. 515); after a girl whom he loved was hurled into the sea in obedience to an oracle, Enalos tried to kill himself by throwing himself into the sea after her, but he and his beloved were both rescued by dolphins that carried them to the shore.[173] Other stories were based on fact, as in the case of Pliny's sad tale of the dolphin of Hippo Diarrhytus (an African coastal town not far from Carthage) which proved too friendly for its own good. For by allowing people to stroke it and feed it, and even to ride on its back, it attracted so many visitors to the town that the citizens, who were obliged to entertain visitors of high rank who came to see it, finally killed it because they could no longer afford the expense.[174]

Our last two legends are in effect ghost-stories, for both tell how people from the historical era were supposed to have come into contact, violent and otherwise, with dead figures from the mythical past; the stories are connected with cities on either side of the toe of Italy, one with Epizephyrean Locri on the east coast and the other with Temesa on the west.

Believing that their colony had been founded from Naryx in Eastern Locris, the birthplace of the Locrian Aias, a violent hero of the Trojan War (see p. 456), the men of Epizephyrean Locri used to leave an empty space in their battle-line in the hope that their ancestral hero would come to their assistance. One day (so the story goes), as they were fighting against an army from Croton, a Crotoniate called AUTOLEON (or Leonymos) tried to rush through the empty space to attack the enemy line from the rear, but was severely wounded in the thigh (or chest) by the long-dead Aias. When the festering wound failed to heal, he consulted an oracle (or the Delphic oracle specifically), which advised him to seek a cure from Aias himself on Leuke (the White Island), an island in the Black Sea which was the posthumous home of Achilles and other great heroes of the Trojan War (see p. 116). On arriving at the island, he offered sacrifice to these inhabitants and above all to Aias, who duly healed him of his wound. Now Helen was living there too, as the posthumous consort of Achilles, and she took advantage of Autoleon's visit to ask him to take a message to the poet Stesichorus, who lived in Sicily no great distance from Autoleon's home-town. For she had blinded Stesichorus for insulting her in one of his poems, and she now wanted him to know that he would recover his sight if he composed a recantation. It was as a consequence of this message, so the story claims, that Stesichorus wrote his famous Palinode, or poem of recantation, in which he asserted that the Helen who had eloped with Paris was a mere phantom rather than the heroine herself (see further on p. 445). By virtue of this connection, it can be inferred that these events must have taken place in the first half of the sixth century BC.[175]

The little town of Temesa, which was founded from Croton, was troubled during much of its earlier history by an aggressive ghost, the so-called HERO OF TEMESA. The problem began when Odysseus and his followers called in at the town in the course of their wanderings, and one of them, a certain Polites (who is mentioned in the *Odyssey* as a victim of Kirke's enchantments) got drunk and raped a local girl; for the inhabitants responded by stoning him to death, and his angry spirit subjected them to a reign of terror by way of revenge, committing murders and attacking old and young alike. Although the Temesians were initially inclined to abandon their town and leave Italy altogether, the Delphic oracle advised them to appease their tormentor by honouring him as a hero, and building him a shrine and presenting the most beautiful of their maidens to him each year as a bride in death. This proved effective, and the latter custom was maintained (so the story claims) until a famous boxer called Euthymos (a historical figure who won an Olympian victory in the fifth century BC) happened to visit Temesa when the Hero of Temesa was just about to receive one of his brides. Feeling pity for her at first, and then falling in love with her, he offered to save her if she would marry him afterwards. So he lay in wait at the shrine in place of her, and when the Hero arrived for his victim, gave him such a drubbing that he fled the land and plunged beneath the waves, never to return. Or in another account, Euthymos fought with the Hero because he had been exacting a tribute from the local people, and forced him to repay all the money with interest. The shrine of Polites could still be seen at Temesa in Roman times.[176]

CHAPTER SEVENTEEN

AENEAS, ROMULUS
AND THE ORIGINS
OF ROME

——— ·◆· ———

Many of the legends of early Rome were modelled more or less directly on older stories from Greece, and the same is also true of the relatively few original myths that came to be developed about the Roman gods (mainly by Ovid in the surviving literature); but even if the associated bodies of legend were partly of a hybrid nature as a consequence, they belong to the Roman tradition rather than the Greek and must be interpreted in relation to Roman concerns, and therefore lie beyond the scope of a survey of Greek myth. Of rather greater relevance to our concerns, perhaps, are Roman aetiological tales that added a Roman extension to Greek myth by bringing Greek heroes in person to Rome or Latium. We have had occasion to refer to the remarkable appendix to the legend of Hippolytos, son of Theseus, in which he was said to have been transferred to Latium after his death and revival to become a cultic associate of Diana, the local equivalent of his patron goddess Artemis, at her sacred grove at Aricia (see p. 359). To explain another feature of the grove, it was also suggested that Orestes deposited the statue of Taurian Artemis there after stealing it from its original home with help of his sister Iphigeneia (see p. 514). Herakles, who was honoured in Roman cult as Hercules, might be very naturally imagined as having visited the site of Rome as he was travelling through Italy with the cattle of Geryon. Roman authors took advantage of this possibility to propose not only that his most ancient cult had come to be founded there as a consequence, but also that he had modified certain native rites involving human sacrifice (so providing an explanation, for instance, for a ritual practice in which straw puppets were cast into the Tiber from a Roman bridge). As we saw in connection with the former story, the site of the future city was said to have been ruled at this time by a Greek, Evander (see p. 266), who had left his native city of Pallantion in Arcadia to settle on the Palatine hill. By far the most important legend of this kind, however, and one that cannot possibly be passed over without a proper examination, is that in which AINEIAS, a Trojan hero from Greek myth, was said to have travelled to Latium after the fall of Troy and to have come to be connected, however distantly, with the origins of Rome itself.

Greek legends that associated Aineias with the founding of Rome, and their chronological implausibility

Aineias was the leading member of the junior branch of the Trojan royal family at the time of the great war between Greece and Troy (see p. 453); he had been borne to Anchises, a great-grandson of Tros, by the goddess Aphrodite (see pp. 200–1 for the circumstances of his conception). In his original Greek legend, he was marked out from other male members of the royal family not so much by his personal qualities as by the fact that he was destined to survive; for someone needed to be available to rule the Trojans after the fall of Troy and the destruction of Priam's senior branch of the family. In one of the battle-scenes in the *Iliad*, the great god Poseidon, who is normally no friend of the Trojans, rescues Aineias from danger for that very reason, stating that it is ordained that he shall survive so that the race of Dardanos (the founder of the Trojan royal line) shall not perish in its entirety;[1] and the same conclusion can be drawn from an episode in the *Sack of Troy*, a lost epic in the Trojan cycle, in which Aineias and his followers withdraw from Troy before its fall in response to a portent (see p. 475).[2] In the *Homeric Hymn to Aphrodite*, which tells how Aphrodite came to bear Aineias to Anchises (see p. 200), the goddess prophesies correspondingly to Anchises that his son and descendants will reign among the Trojans.[3] In the usual tradition from the classical period onwards, Aineias was still in Troy on the night of the sack, as in Vergil's account in the *Aeneid*, but escaped through the carnage with his aged father on his back, taking the household gods with him. Authors from Xenophon onwards report that the Greeks allowed him safe passage because they so admired his piety in trying to save his father and household gods.[4] This Greek tradition about his conduct on that fateful night provided the basis for the Roman characterization of the just and dutiful Aeneas.

If Aineias survived the war, he was available to be transferred abroad as the mythical tradition evolved. Largely to explain the origin of local cults or dedications, or of place-names that seemed to have some connection with Aineias, it came to be suggested that he had settled in neighbouring Thrace or in a variety of places in Greece itself. The stories that presently concern us, however, are those that take him further abroad to Italy, and connect him in one way or another with the founding of Rome.

Much as one would like to be able to trace how the Italian legend of Aineias first developed in the Greek tradition, the surviving evidence is so inadequate that this is hardly possible. Inscriptions on the *Tabula Iliaca Capitolina*, an Italian limestone relief dating from about 15 BC, seem to suggest that Stesichorus, a Greek-Sicilian poet of the sixth century BC, already presented Aineias as sailing off to Hesperia (i.e. the Italian West);[5] but it has been convincingly argued on a variety of grounds that we cannot rely on this monument for reliable information on what Stesichorus may have said about Aineias. It has been observed, furthermore, that if Stesichorus had really presented Aineias as sailing to Italy, Dionysius of Halicarnassus, who was well acquainted with his work, could hardly have failed to mention it in his detailed survey of Aineias's Italian legend. Dionysius is our source for the next earliest report, for he cites the mythographer Hellanicus (fifth century BC) as having written that Aineias sailed to Italy with Odysseus and became the founder of Rome;

he named it after one of the Trojan women who had accompanied him, a certain Rhome, who had grown weary of their long wanderings and had brought them to an end in Latium by inciting the other women to set fire to the Trojan ships.[6] Once again, alas, there is ample reason to doubt the reliability of the attribution, both on internal grounds and because Dionysius also ascribes a conflicting story to Hellanicus in which Aineias settles closer to home at Pallene on the northern shores of the Aegean.[7]

Whatever the true origin of the story above in which Aineias founded Rome and named it after Rhome, it is characteristic of the facile pseudo-legends that were invented by Greek authors to account for the origin of Rome (as of other foreign cities). Some thirty stories of the kind are recorded from the Hellenistic and early Roman period, not all involving Aineias. To Greeks who were versed in the legendary lore of their own land, it seemed self-evident that just as Corinth was named after Korinthos, or Chaironeia after Chairon, or Cyrene after a nymph called Kyrene, so Rome must have been named after someone called Rhome or Rhomos or the like.[8] As the next stage in the process, it was necessary that some kind of pedigree or origin should be ascribed to the chosen eponym, and that appropriate circumstances should be imagined for the founding of the city that was supposedly named after that person. For a far-off place like Rome, no detail was required in the latter connection, and certainly none that demanded any knowledge of the local traditions and topography. In foundation-stories of this nature in which Rhome is selected as the eponym, she is usually linked to Aineias in one way or another, whether as a companion of his as above, or as his wife, or as the wife or daughter of his son Askanios. In that case, the city could be said to have been founded by Aineias or Askanios and named in her honour.[9] There are also accounts, however, in which she has nothing to do with Aineias, being described, for instance, as a captive who had been brought from Troy by Greek warriors, or as a daughter of Euandros (an Arcadian hero who was supposed to have established himself on the site of Rome).[10] Similar considerations apply to the male eponym Rhomos, who may either be connected with Aineias as a son or grandson of his or else be given an entirely different pedigree, as a son of Odysseus and Kirke, for instance, or of Emathion.[11] When Rhomos is the eponym, he founds the city himself.

It would be pointless to attempt to trace all the permutations. A certain Romanos, son of Odysseus and Kirke, is also mentioned as the eponymous founder, as is Romis, tyrant of the Latins, who drove the Etruscans from the area to found the new city.[12] As the latter example would indicate, the founder or eponym may be given a native pedigree. There are versions, for example, in which Rhome and Rhomos are described as children of Italos, the eponym of Italy, or the city is said to have been of Etruscan foundation.[13] Or else it was founded by some Pelasgians (aboriginals) who named it Rome in commemoration of their military strength (*rhōmē*, a purely Greek etymology).[14] But that is quite enough of this nonsense.

Most of these Greek accounts of the founding of Rome are either anonymous or are ascribed to obscure writers who are hard to date. If it is accepted that the account ascribed to Hellanicus is of doubtful origin, the earliest datable version is one that is recorded for the minor historian Callias, who would have been writing around 300 BC (see p. 602).

Although the Romans came to accept that Aineias and his Trojans had some connection with the origins of their city, the idea that it was actually founded by Aineias (or an immediate descendant or associate of his) was a purely Greek idea which never seems to have been taken very seriously at Rome itself. In the surviving Roman literature, no author apart from the historian Sallust ever refers to Aineias as founder.[15] It has been argued, to be sure, that the Romans did regard him as their founder in early times, adopting him as such under Etruscan influence before putting him aside for Romulus, but this is a hazardous speculation in the absence of any definite evidence from the city itself, whether literary or archaeological. The Romans developed a foundation myth of their own in any case, in which the founding was ascribed to Romulus, a Latin prince from Alba Longa. It is generally believed nowadays that this was a legend of indigenous origin and respectable antiquity, perhaps dating back to the sixth century BC; and it is known for certain that the story was well-established by the end of the fourth century (see p. 602). In contrast to the Greek stories mentioned above, which would never have been more than rudimentary, this Roman legend was rich in content and grew ever more so, making extensive reference to the local topography and traditions, and embracing many local aetiologies. It overshadowed all other stories of the kind, leaving them as no more than historical curiosities; for not only was it bound to impose itself at the expense of arbitrarily invented foreign stories, but chronological researches showed ever more clearly that Rome could not possibly have been founded by Aineias or a near contemporary of his as most Greek stories suggested.

On any rational chronology, Rome must have been founded considerably later than the period immediately following the fall of Troy (i.e. the closing stages of the era of legend in Greece). The historian Timaeus (died c. 260 BC), a Greek-Sicilian who had a good knowledge of the local traditions in Italy, dated the founding of Rome to 814 BC, while Roman antiquaries during the following two centuries came to favour a somewhat later date, finally accepting Varro's estimate of 754/3 BC as canonic. By any calculation, the heroes of Trojan legend must have lived in a remoter antiquity than this. According to the most widely accepted chronology, as developed by Eratosthenes of Alexandria in the third century BC, Troy fell in 1184 BC (towards the end of the Mycenaean period in our reckoning, which seems appropriate enough). If a connection was to be established between Aineias and the founding of Rome, this meant that there was a gap of at least four centuries to be filled between the time of his arrival in Italy and the actual foundation of the city.

In what came to be accepted as the standard Roman account, the founder Romulus (who would originally have had no connection whatever with Aineias or Troy) was considered to be a fairly distant descendant of Aineias who founded Rome many generations after his Trojan forebear had emigrated to that area. After arriving in Latium, the territory on the east coast of Italy in which Rome would later be located, Aineias (or Aeneas in Latin) established himself there with his Trojan followers after some initial conflict with the native Italians. Not far from the coast near the site of his first landing, he founded the city of **Lavinium** as his new home and centre of rule. His son and successor Askanios (or Ascanius in Latin) did not remain at Lavinium, however, but ventured further inland to found **Alba Longa**, about twelve miles south-east of the site of Rome. Descendants of Aeneas ruled Alba for some twelve generations thereafter until Romulus was born into the family under perilous circumstances while his father was temporarily excluded from his rightful throne. Romulus survived nonetheless to found the city of **Rome**, peopling it initially with settlers from Alba.

Aeneas' travels and arrival in Latium as described by Vergil

The Roman legend of Aeneas may be approached most conveniently through the *Aeneid*, which tells how he wandered to the west after the destruction of Troy and established himself in Latium. We may call him Aeneas henceforth in accordance with Latin usage, and follow the same procedure when referring to other figures from Greek legend who appear in the story.

After the fall of Troy, Aeneas and other Trojan survivors constructed a fleet of ships and sailed off to seek a new home. Although Aeneas initially wanted to settle nearby on the southern coast of Thrace, Polydorus, a son of Priam who had been treacherously murdered there (see p. 479), spoke up from his grave to warn him to forsake that savage land. So he sailed southward, calling in next at the holy island of Delos, where he received a friendly welcome from the priest-king Anius (see p. 569). When Aeneas entered the temple of Apollo to pray for guidance, a supernatural voice ordered him and his followers to seek out the land of their ancestors, declaring that his descendants were destined to rule the world from it. On being reminded by his father Anchises that Troy had originally been settled from Crete by Teucer (Teukros, see p. 521), he led his fellow Trojans to that island and proceeded to found a city there, but the newcomers were soon afflicted by a famine and a plague. The significance of this was revealed when the family gods of Aeneas appeared to him in a dream one night and told him that Delian Apollo had not intended him to settle in Crete but rather in Italy, for that had been the original homeland of his ancestor Dardanus, the founder of the Trojan royal line. Although Dardanus was supposed to have crossed over from Samothrace in the Greek tradition (see p. 521), Vergil is referring to an Etrusco-Roman story in which he was presented as having come from Corythus in Etruria (apparently Tarquinii, though often identified with Cortona).[16]

As the Trojans were sailing west from Crete, they were caught by a storm and driven in a north-westerly direction around the Peloponnese to the little islands of the Strophades, where they were confronted by the Harpies, fierce bird-like creatures with women's faces (see p. 57), who pillaged and fouled their food much as in the legend of Phineus (see p. 386). When these pests were finally driven off, their leader, Celaeno, cast fear into the Trojans by telling them that Apollo had revealed that hunger would drive them to 'eat their tables' before they would be able to found their Italian city. The meaning of these enigmatic words will become apparent shortly.[17] The wanderers called in next at Epirus in north-western Greece, where they found that Helenus, a son of Priam, was now ruling the kingdom that had been established there by Neoptolemus (see further on pp. 489–90), and was married to Hector's widow Andromache. He had assuaged his nostalgia for his homeland by building an imitation of the Trojan citadel and by naming features of the landscape after corresponding features at Troy. Through his powers as a seer, he was able to advise Aeneas about his forthcoming journey, telling him above all that he should found his new city where he saw a huge white sow lying on the ground suckling thirty piglets. While making his way to that place, which would be located somewhere on the far coast of Italy, he should visit the Sibyl of Cumae, who would be able to reveal more about the ordeals that awaited him in Italy.[18]

Aeneas and his followers then sailed around the foot of Italy and the southern shores of Sicily, narrowly avoiding the whirlpool Charybdis and observing Polyphemus and other Cyclopes from afar (for it was supposed in the later tradition that the Homeric Kyklopes had lived in Sicily). When the voyagers arrived at Drepanum on the western corner of Sicily, they received a hospitable reception from a local ruler called Acestes, who was of Trojan descent through his mother (see p. 581). The aged Anchises died soon afterwards and was buried there.[19] Aeneas set sail for western Italy in the following year, but the goddess Juno (the Roman equivalent of Hera), who had long hated the Trojans, persuaded Aeolus, the ruler of the winds, to unleash a violent storm in the hope of wrecking the fleet; but though some of the ships were destroyed, Neptune calmed the storm, and Aeneas made for the nearest shore with the seven surviving vessels, making a safe landfall on the African coast near Carthage. The newly established city was ruled by its founder, Dido, a Phoenician princess from Tyre, who welcomed the seafarers to her city and fell desperately in love with Aeneas at the incitation of Venus. On finding himself alone with her when the two of them entered the same cave to escape a thunderstorm while out hunting, he embarked on a love affair with her; but after he had tarried with her for some months, Jupiter sent Mercury (the Roman equivalent of Hermes) to him to recall him to his appointed task. He responded to the call of duty and prepared to set off, ignoring the pleas of Dido, who killed herself with his sword after his departure.[20]

After arriving back in Sicily, Aeneas held funeral games in honour of his father on the anniversary of his death. The Trojan women, who had grown tired of their endless wanderings, set fire to the ships at the incitation of Juno while the games were under way; but Aeneas prayed for the assistance of Jupiter, who sent a rainstorm to douse the flames, and all but four of the ships were saved. Leaving his older and weaker followers behind to found the city of Acesta (i.e. Segesta) under the leadership of Acestes, Aeneas now set out for Italy once again.[21] In accordance with the advice that he had received from Helenus, he called in first at Cumae, just to the north of the Bay of Naples, where the Cumaean Sibyl delivered prophecies to him about his future adventures in Latium; and in response to his urgent request, she agreed to guide him down to the Underworld for a reunion with his dead father. His journey through the different regions of the Underworld has already been described (see pp. 123ff). At the end of it, his father was able to encourage him by offering him a preview of the glorious destiny of his family and of Rome.[22] After he escaped back into the upper world, he and his followers sailed up the coast to the mouth of the Tiber and landed in Latium. As they were eating an improvised meal in the open air nearby, seated on the grass and using flat cakes of bread as platters, they felt so hungry that they finished off by eating the platters themselves, causing the son of Aeneas to joke that they were even devouring their tables; and on hearing his words, Aeneas suddenly realized that the Harpy's prophecy had been fulfilled and that they had therefore discovered their new homeland. And before long, he found the sow and thirty piglets that had been foretold by Helenus as indicating the site of his new home-city of Lavinium.[23]

Since Latinus, the aged king of Latium, had been advised by an oracle to marry his daughter Lavinia to a foreigner, he welcomed the envoys of Aeneas and let them know that he was willing to accept him as a friend and quite possibly as his son-in-law also. Before matters could be taken any further, however, Juno intervened once again by sending the Fury Allecto to the area to stir up trouble against the Trojans. Allecto inspired a fierce hatred for them in Amata, the wife of Latinus, and likewise in Turnus, prince of the Rutulians, who had been the favoured suitor of Lavinia up until that time; and when the Fury then incited Ascanius, the son of Aeneas, to shoot a pet stag that belonged to the royal family, open warfare ensued. Aeneas found himself confronted by a confederation of the Latins, the Rutulians, and the followers of Mezentius, a tyrannous Etruscan ruler who had been exiled from his native city of Caere.[24] He acquired some allies of his own, however, including Tarchon, an Etruscan king who had learned from a diviner that he would defeat his enemy Mezentius if he took a foreigner as his leader, and Evander, the ruler of the present inhabitants of the site of Rome. Since Evander was too old to fight on his own account, he provided a force of cavalry under the command of his son Pallas. Latinus stood apart from the conflict. After fierce fighting and various shifts of fortune, Aeneas defeated his opponents, sealing his victory by killing Turnus in single combat (the culminating episode that marks the end of the *Aeneid*). He then proceeded to marry Latinus' daughter after making peace on terms that were very favourable to the conquered Latins, who were to retain their names and customs but to accept the gods and sacred rites that Aeneas had brought to their land.

Latinus, the eponym of Latium and the Latins, is a fairly ancient figure who is first mentioned at the end of Hesiod's *Theogony* (in a section of the poem that was probably added in the sixth century BC); he is there described as a son of Odysseus and Kirke 'who ruled over the famous Tyrrhenians (i.e. Etruscans) very far off in a nook of the holy islands'.[25] The author's knowledge of the geography of the west was evidently very deficient. Latinus was also described as a son of Telemachos and Kirke[26] or else given a native pedigree as a son of Faunus, a rustic godling who was equated with the Greek Pan; according to the *Aeneid*, Latinus fathered him by a Laurentine water-nymph called Marica.[27] A further tradition suggested that Hercules fathered him by the wife or daughter of Faunus (presumably meaning Fauna in either case).[28]

Since the story of Aeneas' conflict with the Italians had no foundation either in history or in any old tradition, different authors could remodel it to suit themselves, and the role of Latinus varies accordingly. In Cato's version, Latinus granted a friendly reception to the Trojans, allocating land to them and offering his daughter Lavinia to Aeneas; but when the Trojans subsequently broke faith with him by raiding the Latin territories, Latinus made war on them, forming an alliance for that purpose with Turnus, lord of the Rutulians, who bore a grudge against Aeneas for having married Lavinia; and Latinus and Turnus were both killed in the ensuing conflict.[29] Or in Dionysius' account, Latinus was fighting a war against the Rutulians at the time of the Trojans' arrival but broke it off to march against the foreigners. On the night before he was due to engage them in battle, however, both he and Aeneas were visited in their sleep by gods who instructed them to reach a peaceful settlement. So Latinus granted territory to the Trojans, who now became his allies and helped him to defeat the Rutulians.[30] Vergil departs from the earlier tradition by presenting Latinus as an old man who takes no part in the fighting.

Although the *Aeneid* ends with Aeneas's victory over his Italian foes, the destiny that lies in wait for him and his descendants is not merely presupposed but is explicitly foretold within the poem. It is indicated that he will found his city of Lavinium in accordance with the sign foretold for him by Helenus; and shortly before he discovers the sow and thirty piglets, the god of the river Tiber explains to him that the sign means that his son Ascanius will found Alba thirty years after the founding of Lavinium.[31] While Aeneas is making his visit to the Underworld, furthermore, his dead father Anchises offers him a vision of the future of his family and of Rome by telling him of the destinies that await various souls who are due to be reborn into earthly bodies.[32] Anchises points first to Silvius, the posthumous son of Aeneas who will found the line of kings that will rule in Alba Longa;[33] and he then identifies a few of these kings by name before pointing to Romulus as the divinely fathered member of the family who will found Rome itself.[34] The pageant continues with the legendary kings of Rome and a selection of its foremost men down to Julius Caesar and Augustus; as we will see, the Julians claimed to be descended from Aeneas.

Aeneas' city of Lavinium, and his death and apotheosis

Lavinium was an old Latin city that lay near the coast about seventeen miles south of Rome, at the site of the modern Pratica di Mare; Aeneas was said to have named it after his second wife Lavinia. Although the city's Trojan legend was presumably quite ancient, nothing is known for certain about its time of origin. The Greek-Sicilian historian Timaeus, who visited Lavinium in the first half of the third century BC to investigate its antiquities, provides the earliest definite evidence for Aeneas' connection with the town. It had become accepted by that time that Aeneas had not only founded the city itself but had deposited his household gods there to found its 'Trojan' cult of the Penates; Timaeus was shown the earthenware pots in which he was supposed to have transported them from Troy.[35] Knowledge of him must have reached the area considerably earlier, whether by way of Etruria, where he was well known by the end of the sixth century BC, or of the Greek colonies in the south; but archaeological investigations have failed to provide any unequivocal early evidence for his presence in Lavinium. After first stepping ashore in Latium, Aeneas and his followers were said to have camped at a place called Troia, which lay a few miles down the coast between Lavinium and Ardea.[36] If the place had acquired its name before the legend of Aeneas had become established in the area, as is certainly possible from a linguistic point of view, its presence may have suggested or at least encouraged the idea that Aeneas had settled in the vicinity.

In the *Aeneid*, as we have seen, Aeneas was told by the seer Helenus that he should found his city at the place where he found a large white sow with thirty young. Or in the accounts offered by Dionysius and Diodorus,[37] which seem to reflect the influence of Greek tales of animal-guides (as in the Theban foundation legend, see

p. 295), Aeneas was advised by an oracle that a four-footed animal would lead him to the site of his city; and when a pregnant white sow escaped as he was bringing it to sacrifice after his landing and then fled to a certain hill where it gave birth to thirty young, he called the oracle to mind and resolved to found his city there. In what was perhaps the earliest form of the myth, the thirty piglets symbolized the thirty cities that would subsequently form the Latin League;[38] but the number was more commonly thought to have a chronological significance. In the version ascribed to the Roman historian Fabius Pictor (writing in about 200 BC or slightly earlier), Aeneas received a vision in his sleep that ordered him to delay the founding of his city for thirty years in accordance with the number of the piglets.[39] Or in the *Aeneid*, the god of the Tiber appeared to him in his sleep on the night before he saw the portent, and explained that it indicated that he should found Lavinium at that site while his son Ascanius should found Alba thirty years later.[40] In that case, it could be said that Alba was named after the white (*alba*) sow.[41] Whether or not the story of the sow originated as a genuine local legend, it certainly came to be accepted at Lavinium as a highly valued feature of the city's foundation legend. The antiquarian Varro, writing in the first century BC, reports that there were not only statues of the sow and its young in the town but that the corpse of the sow itself could be seen there, pickled in brine.[42]

The grave and shrine of Aeneas could be seen near Lavinium beside a local stream, the Numicus or Numicius. He was honoured there as a minor deity under the name of Aeneas Indiges, having displaced the former occupant of the shrine, who had been called Pater Indiges or the like. According to Dionysius, there was a mound of no great size surrounded by a handsome and neatly ordered grove of trees, and the shrine was marked with the following inscription: 'to the father and god of the locality, who presides over the waters of the river Numicius'.[43] It was said that Aeneas had disappeared into the waters of the stream, evidently because his shrine was set on its bank; or in rationalistic accounts, it could be explained that he had simply been carried away by the stream after being killed in battle beside it. A fourth-century BC shrine set in a tumulus near Lavinium has sometimes been identified with the shrine of Aeneas, but this is highly questionable, especially since the excavated site is not situated near a stream. Although Aeneas was not honoured as a hero or god in Roman cult, the Augustan poets tell of his apotheosis. In the *Aeneid*, Jupiter announces to his mother Venus (the Roman goddess equated with Aphrodite) that he is destined to be raised up to the heavens as a god; and in Ovid's *Metamorphoses*, Venus prepares for his apotheosis by asking the god of the Numicius to wash every mortal element out of his corpse.[44]

There were long-established cultic connections between Rome and Lavinium. In accordance with a practice which may well have been inaugurated when the Romans first gained control over Lavinium, a party of senior magistrates and priests would travel from Rome each year to perform various traditional rites in the town, above all to offer sacrifices to Vesta and the Penates.[45] Vesta was the goddess of the hearth, the Italian equivalent of Hestia (see p. 139), while the Penates were deities who had originated as guardian-spirits of the store-room (*penus*). They and the goddess were honoured both in domestic cult as protectors of the household in accordance with their original nature, and in public cult as deities of wider importance who watched over the city and state. Now the Romans believed that their state Penates, the *Penates publici*, had come from Lavinium, and that they could be identified with the Trojan gods who had been established there by Aeneas. There may have been a measure of truth in this, to the extent that the state cult of the Penates may have been introduced from Lavinium or at least reorganized in connection with the Lavinian cult.

Ascanius, son of Aeneas, and the founding of Alba Longa

The founding of Alba Longa marks the next stage in the legend. In contrast to Lavinium, Alba had once been a powerful place, and it was believed that Rome and various other Latin cities had been founded from it. Since Roman tradition stated accordingly that the founder Romulus was of Alban descent, any linkage with Aeneas and the Trojans had to be established by way of Alba, by making Romulus and his Alban forebears descendants of Aeneas. Through the harmonization of Greek, Roman and Lavinate traditions, the canonic pattern was thus established in which Aeneas founded Lavinium while his son ASCANIUS founded Alba and his descendant Romulus founded Rome. It is not necessary to assume that Alba Longa (which was destroyed by the Romans at quite an early period) ever had a Trojan legend of its own in the same way as Lavinium. If Alban families at Rome such as the Julii and Cloelii claimed Trojan descent, it is surely more probable that this was a late development inspired by antiquarian lore than an ancient claim rooted in Alban tradition.

Ascanius (as Askanios was known in Latin) was taken over from the Greek tradition. Although Homer makes no mention of him or indeed of any son of Aineias (referring only to an Askanios who was a Bithynian ally of the Trojans[46]), it is reasonable to assume that he was named in early epic as Aineias' heir. Aineias certainly had such an heir in the early tradition since the *Homeric Hymn to Aphrodite* presents the goddess as telling Anchises that his son (i.e. Aineias) and descendants will rule among the Trojans;[47] and Askanios is the name that is invariably given to this son of Aineias from the classical period onwards. When it came to be imagined that Aineias had settled abroad after the fall of Troy rather than staying to rule in the Troad, Askanios was naturally said to have accompanied him, and he was thus available to become the founder of Alba in Italian legend. In the usual tradition, as would be expected, Aeneas was said to have fathered Askanios by his Trojan wife, who was originally known as Eurydike, but later as Kreousa (or Creusa in Latin, as in the *Aeneid*).

Various explanations were put forward to account for Ascanius' action in leaving Lavinium to found a new city. In the version favoured by Vergil and Dionysius, he founded Alba thirty years after the founding of Lavinium because his father had received a prophecy revealing that the portent of the sow and piglets indicated that he should do so.[48] Or according to another tradition, he decided to leave Lavinium when trouble arose between him and his father's Italian widow. For Lavinia, who was pregnant at the time of her husband's death, fled into the woods for fear of her stepson's jealousy, and gave birth to her child there, who was known as Silvius ('he of the woods') as a consequence; and since Ascanius met with hostility from the people of Lavinium as a result of the queen's plight, he invited her back to take over the throne and went off to found a new city of his own.[49]

Livy records a divergent account in which Ascanius was born in Italy as Aeneas' son by Lavinia and Silvius was a son of Ascanius. In this version, Ascanius was too young to take power at the time of his father's death, and Lavinia ruled on his behalf as regent until he came of age; and when he eventually departed to found the new settlement at Alba, he restored Lavinium to the capable charge of his mother.[50] To understand the likely origin of this unorthodox version, it is necessary to consider a further aspect of Ascanius' Italian legend. Julius Caesar belonged to the gens Julia, a family of Alban origin, as did Augustus through his mother's line and by adoption; and this family claimed descent from Ascanius by equating him with Iulus, the legendary founder of their line. It was explained in this connection that Ascanius had been called Ilus (i.e. man of Ilion or Troy) during his Trojan years, and that this alternative name of his was altered slightly to Iulus in his new homeland. Now if Aeneas fathered Ascanius by his Italian wife rather than by his first wife at Troy, Ascanius could not be identified with Iulus in this way; so it would seem that this was an anti-Julian version that was developed to exclude the identification.

Since Ascanius might have been expected to take his household gods with him, a story was devised to explain why the 'Trojan' cult of the Penates remained in Lavinium. Although Ascanius ordered that a special temple should be constructed for them at Alba and proceeded to install them there, they fled back to their previous home of their own accord during the night; for it was discovered on the following morning that they had disappeared (even though the doors of the temple had been kept shut, and its walls and roof remained intact), and it was soon reported from Lavinium that they were standing once again on their original pedestals. After they ran back to their original home for a second time, they were allowed to remain there, and six hundred men were sent back with their families to attend to their cult.[51] There is otherwise nothing to report about the founding of Alba or indeed about Ascanius' reign as a whole.

The Albam dynasty of the Silvii

Even if Ascanius was the founder of Alba Longa, he was not the founder of its ruling dynasty since the throne passed to his half-brother SILVIUS after his death.[52] Such an account may have been preferred because Silvius was born to an Italian mother, and the Alban kings and latterly Romulus could be regarded as being equally of Latin and Trojan origin if he had been the founder of the line. It was explained that he succeeded to the throne because Ascanius had no children of his own; or else Ascanius did have a son called Iulus (or Iulius) who tried to claim the throne after his death, but the Albans elected Silvius instead, preferring to appoint Iulus to priestly authority.[53]

From the time of Silvius onwards, the throne passed peacefully from father to son until Numitor, the grandfather of Romulus, was forcibly excluded by his younger brother, and the sequence of events that would lead to the founding of Rome was thus set in train. For reasons already indicated, most antiquarians came to believe that more than four centuries must have elapsed between the arrival of Aeneas and the founding of Rome, and a long line of Alban kings was therefore fabricated to fill the gap. Although the surviving catalogues differ from one another to some extent, all agree that Romulus was separated from Aeneas by some fifteen generations. Nothing is known for certain about the source of the original king-list, but it is reasonable to assume that it was compiled around the third century BC rather than much earlier or later. In Livy's account, the following kings are said to have ruled after Silvius: Aeneas Silvius, Latinus Silvius, Alba, Atys, Capys, Capetus, Tiberinus, Agrippa, Romulus Silvius, Aventinus, and Proca, the father of Numitor.[54] Such a list could hardly be anything other than highly artificial, and it will be apparent at first sight that most of these names were either recycled from elsewhere in the tradition, as in the case of the first two, or else invented as eponyms of suitable places or geographical features, as in the case of Alba and Tiberinus.

The other main lists are provided by Diodorus (7.5.10–11), Ovid (*Metamorphoses* 14.610–21, *Fasti* 42–52) and Dionysius of Halicarnassus (1.71.3). **Aeneas Silvius**, **Latinus Silvius** and **Romulus Silvius** are shadows of their more famous namesakes. It is reported that Romulus Silvius provoked the anger of Jupiter by imitating his thunder and lightning, and was struck dead by a thunderbolt;[55] but this is simply a reworking of the Greek myth of Salmoneus (see p. 422). His house was supposed to have been submerged below the Alban Lake, where its remains could be seen in historical times. The names of Atys and Capys were also recycled from the earlier tradition. **Atys** shares his name (which is related to that of the Phrygian god Attis) with several members of the early Lydian royal family mentioned by Herodotus.[56] The Epitus who takes the place of Atys in some lists has a name of Homeric origin, derived from a passage in the *Iliad* which states that a certain Epytos was the herald of Aineias' father.[57] The name of **Capys** is based on that of Kapys, son of Assarakos, the grandfather of Aineias, who is also mention in the *Iliad*.[58] In an Italian context, his name is suggestive of Capua; the *Aeneid* states accordingly that it was founded by a Capys who accompanied Aeneas from Troy, while another account suggests that it was founded by Rhomos who named it after Aeneas' grandfather.[59] It is harder to say why Capys' successor should have been called **Capetus**; the only Kapetos recorded in Greek mythology is thoroughly obscure, appearing in a list of the suitors of Hippodameia who were killed by her father Oinomaos.[60] **Agrippa** would have been classed as an Alban king long before the time of Augustus' famous minister M. Vipsanius Agrippa; his name was presumably suggested by that of a legendary figure from the earlier history of Rome, Menenius Agrippa, who was supposed to have played a prominent part in the events that led to the appointment of the first tribune of the plebeians.[61] **Alba** was obviously named after the city while **Tiberinus** was invented to serve as the eponym of the Tiber; a facile story explains that the river was known as the Albula until it was renamed in honour of Tiberinus after he was drowned while leading an army across it (or was swept away by it after being killed in battle beside it).[62] **Aventinus** was the eponym of the Aventine hill at Rome. As the father of Numitor and Amulius, **Proca** would presumably have appeared in the Roman foundation-myth before the invention of the dynasty of the Silvii. His name, which can be related to the Latin word *procer*, means chieftain or prince.

The birth, exposure and earlier life of Romulus and Remus

PROCA, king of Alba, who reigned some twelve generations after the city was founded by Ascanius, had two sons of contrasting nature, the noble-minded NUMITOR and the vicious AMULIUS. Although Numitor should have succeeded to the throne as the elder brother, Amulius drove him out and then murdered his sons to reinforce his position.[63] He also seized the daughter of Numitor, who was known either as RHEA SILVIA or as ILIA, and forced her to become a Vestal Virgin, ostensibly as an honour but in reality to prevent her from marrying and bearing children who might present a danger to him. His precautions proved ineffective, however, in the face of divine intervention. It was a duty of the priestesses of Vesta, at Alba as at Rome, to fetch pure spring-water for use in the cult of the goddess; and while the daughter of Numitor was visiting the grove of Mars (the god of war) for this purpose one day, the god caught her by surprise and raped her, causing her to conceive twin sons, ROMULUS and REMUS.[64] Her uncle responded to this unwelcome development with his customary ruthlessness, ordering that she should be imprisoned or killed after the birth of her children[65] and that the new-born infants should be hurled into the Tiber. His plans were destined to be foiled once again, however, because the river happened to be in flood at the time. In one version of the story, the king's servants set the children afloat in a basket or other small vessel, but the overbrimming waters cast them safely ashore under the Palatine hill at the site of Rome.[66] Or fearing to approach the raging waters, the men left the basket on the ground near the river-bank, and it was subsequently washed away by the rising waters and carried gently downstream to the site of Rome.[67] Or the men simply deposited the children at the edge of the flood-waters at the site of Rome itself.[68] By whatever course of events, the twins ended up at a point on the river-bank that was marked by an ancient tree, the Ruminalis fig-tree (*ficus Ruminalis*).

Having supposedly stood at the site since before the city's foundation, the Ruminalis fig-tree could still be seen in the age of Augustus, although it was apparently in poor shape by then. It was associated with a minor goddess called Rumina. According to the Roman antiquarians, her name was derived from the word *ruma* or *rumis*, a Latin term for the female breast, and she was a deity who presided over the suckling of children. If that is the case, it is understandable that milk-offerings should have been made to her, and that her tree should have been a fig-tree, which could be connected with breast-feeding and fertility on account of its milky sap. Although it has been questioned whether the tree originally had anything to do with Rumina, and indeed whether the traditional explanation of her name and nature is correct, we can assume that the tree was introduced into the legend of the twins (who were supposed to have been suckled beneath it) because it was regarded as being connected with suckling. Since the name of the tree bears some resemblance to that of Romulus, some ancient authors, including Livy, claimed that it had been named after him, having originally been known as the *ficus Romularis*. There was another such tree at the Comitium (assembly-place) adjoining the Forum.

A she-wolf heard the abandoned infants crying as it was coming down to the river to drink, and suckled them until they were discovered and rescued by their own kind.[69] Wolves were specially associated with Mars, the father of the twins; and some authors stressed this connection by adding that a woodpecker, the bird of

Mars, tended them also by bringing them food in its beak.[70] The fact that the Ruminalis fig-tree was located near the grotto of the Lupercal, which had a name suggestive of wolves (*lupi*), may have influenced the development of this part of the legend.

Although exposed infants are regularly suckled by animals in Greek legend, there is no record in early legend of any hero being suckled by a she-wolf. According to a Hellenistic tale ascribed to Nicander (second century BC), Miletos, the founder of the Ionian city of that name, was tended by wolves at the will of his father Apollo after he was exposed by his mother of Crete. Since the legend of Miletos followed other patterns in the previous tradition (see pp. 350–1), it seems altogether likely that this version involving the wolves was invented by Nicander himself, perhaps with the Roman legend in mind.[71] The only other Greek tale of the kind is presented as a Greek parallel for the legend of Romulus and Remus in the pseudo-Plutarchean *Greek and Roman Parallel Stories*. An Arcadian nymph called Phylonome once bore twin sons to Ares (the Greek equivalent of Mars) and exposed them in the river Erymanthos for fear of her father's anger; but they were cast ashore safely on the river-bank and suckled by a she-wolf until they were rescued by the shepherd Tyliphos, who reared them as his own children under the names Lykastos and Parrhasios; and in due time they established themselves as the rulers of Arcadia. Ascribed to an evidently fictitious author, Zopyros of Byzantium, this is not really a parallel at all, but an apocryphal myth that was fabricated by the author on the basis of the Roman story.[72]

The twins were eventually discovered by FAUSTULUS, the chief herdsman of Amulius, who took them home and entrusted them to the care of his wife ACCA LARENTIA. Or else some local shepherds stumbled across them and passed them on to Faustulus.[73] The name of the charitable Faustulus is derived from the Latin word *faustus*, meaning lucky or auspicious; he was a bringer of good fortune. The twins were reared by him and his wife in rural isolation, and supported themselves by their own labours when they grew up, working with the local herdsmen and building huts for themselves as shelter. A thatched hut that was supposedly of their construction, the *casa Romuli* or 'hut of Romulus', could be seen on the Palatine hill in historical times near the steps of Cacus; and there was another hut of the kind on the Capitoline hill.[74] As befitted youths of royal descent, the twins showed themselves to be more enterprising than their fellow herdsmen, and became their acknowledged leaders; it was said that they helped them to fight back against cattle-rustlers, or acted rather in the manner of Robin Hood, plundering from the local brigands and sharing the proceeds with their rustic friends. One may suspect that they would have engaged in cattle-rustling on their own account in the earliest tradition.[75]

The twins finally discovered their true identity after Remus happened to be delivered into the hands of their exiled grandfather Numitor. They and their friends lived on the Palatine hill, while the herdsmen of Numitor pastured their cattle on the neighbouring Aventine; and the two different groups were constantly quarrelling over grazing-rights and other matters. One day, after the feud had turned violent, the herdsmen of Numitor captured Remus in an ambush while his brother and friends were attending a sacrifice (or taking part in the disorderly festival of the Lupercalia), and hauled him in front of their master on a charge of cattle-theft.

Or else they took him to Amulius, who handed him over to his brother for judgement. On hearing of Remus' plight, Faustulus told Romulus all that he knew or had guessed about the origin of the two brothers and their royal birth; and fortified by this knowledge, Romulus hurried off to Numitor to intercede on his brother's behalf. Numitor had already inferred from Remus' noble appearance and conduct that he might be something more than an ordinary herdsman, and had therefore been making enquiries of his own. So when Romulus arrived, he ordered the release of Remus (if he had not already done so) and acknowledged the young men as his grandsons. The three of them then conspired together to avenge the wrongs that had been inflicted on them by Amulius. With the help of their rustic friends, who stole into Alba by separate routes beforehand, Romulus and Remus caught Amulius by surprise in the palace and killed him; and Numitor summoned a meeting of the citizens to reveal the crimes of the usurper and reclaim his rightful throne. Different accounts of the story vary considerably in their details; Livy offers a version, for instance, in which Remus was delivered to Numitor under false charges by some local brigands who had been robbed by him and his brother; and the recognition-scene in which Numitor becomes acquainted with his grandchildren was sometimes greatly elaborated under the influence of comparable scenes from Greek tragedy. But the general pattern is always much the same.[76]

The twins set off to found Rome; the contest of the auguries, and the death of Remus

Instead of remaining in Alba under their grandfather's rule, Romulus and Remus decided to found a city of their own by the Tiber in the area where they had been washed ashore and had passed their happy earlier years. Numitor approved of their plan (or even suggested it in one account) and assigned followers and land to them for their new colony.[77] The twins soon quarrelled, however, either about the site of the city since Romulus wanted to establish it on the Palatine while Remus favoured the Aventine, or else about the throne since each of them wanted to become its ruler and give his name to it, as Rome or Remora. They agreed to refer their dispute to the arbitration of the gods by seeking an omen from bird-flights, a favourite form of divination in ancient Italy. So Romulus took the Palatine hill as his viewing-station while Remus went off to the Aventine a short way to the south. Although it was commonly agreed that Romulus claimed victory after observing a flight of twelve vultures (one of the most important augural birds), the course of the story varies in its different versions. In the earliest surviving account from some lines of verse quoted from Ennius, Remus apparently saw no birds at all (even if the passage breaks off too early for this to be entirely certain).[78] In other accounts, Remus saw six vultures before Romulus saw his twelve, and the significance of the omens was thus more disputable since they could be interpreted as favouring Romulus on grounds of number or Remus on grounds of priority. According to Livy, a fight broke out between the supporters of each brother and Remus was killed in the fray.[79] It was more generally believed, however, that Romulus was adjudged the victor and Remus met his death slightly later in other circumstances.

To mark out the bounds (*pomerium*) of the new city, Romulus yoked a bull and cow together and ploughed a furrow around the base of the Palatine hill; and after sacrificing the plough-cattle and other victims, he set his followers to work to raise a defensive wall along the line of the furrow and to build the city itself. While the wall was in the course of construction, Remus, who was still aggrieved at having been defeated in the contest over the auguries, mocked his brother by jumping over the half-completed ramparts and so committing a deliberately inauspicious act. Or else he did so with a more positive intent, to show the inadequacy of the fortifications. Romulus was furious in any case and killed him in a fit of anger, cursing anyone who should dare to cross over the walls in the future to suffer a comparable fate.[80]

There are two surviving myths from the Greek tradition that bear some resemblance to the Roman story. An obscure Boeotian ruler called Poimandros, who was the eponymous founder of Poimandria (near Tanagra or perhaps to be identified with it), was said to have killed his son Ephippos for jumping over a defensive ditch that he had set around his city.[81] Or in a somewhat different version, he killed his son (here named as Leukippos) with a stone by accident when aiming at a builder who had disparaged the ditch and jumped over it.[82] In the other story of the kind, of which the barest outline is preserved, Oineus was said to have killed his son Toxeus for 'jumping over the ditch' at his city of Calydon (see p. 413).[83] These legends – or the first at least since so little is known of the second – seem to carry the same moral as that of Remus, namely that anyone who violates the defensive circle commits an ill-omened act that deserves drastic punishment, irrespective of ties of kinship. Anyone who crossed over the Roman walls in historical times was in fact liable to a death penalty. It should also be remembered in this connection that the Romans and Etruscans (unlike the Greeks) regarded city-walls as sacred. There is no reason to suppose that the legend of the death of Remus was modelled on stories from Greece; it was known to Ennius and was probably a central feature of the foundation legend from early times. Romulus' act of fratricide, justified though it may have been from a certain point of view, evidently came to be felt as something of an embarrassment, since many accounts stress that he felt grave remorse afterwards or even absolved him from the murder altogether. In Ovid's version in the *Fasti*, for instance, a certain Celer who took the lead during the building work was charged by Romulus to kill anyone who dared to jump over the walls; and when Remus, who had not heard of his brother's order, cast scorn on them and jumped over them to prove their inadequacy, Celer struck him dead with a shovel.[84]

How Romulus acquired people for his new city; his conflict with the Sabines, and death and apotheosis

Being now the sole and undisputed sovereign of the little community, Romulus set out to procure more citizens by opening a sanctuary or *asylum* (from Greek *asylon* – the name and institution alike are Greek, with no close equivalent in Italy) on the Capitoline hill, in the dip between its two summits; and landless men and outcasts, and runaway slaves and criminals, duly flocked to it from the lands all around.[85] The future of the city was not yet assured, however, since women were also required but the neighbouring peoples rejected all proposals of intermarriage, partly because they feared that Rome might grow too powerful, and partly because of the dubious origins of many of its citizens. So Romulus resorted to trickery.

He invited men from the surrounding territories, particularly the Sabines, to attend the Roman festival of the Consualia with their wives and children, announcing that there would be splendid sacrifices and public games and shows; and in response to a prearranged signal, the young men of Rome rushed into the crowd during the festivities and carried off all the unmarried girls. The episode has come to be known as the rape (i.e. abduction) of the Sabine women. After the other visitors had fled, Romulus tried to reassure the captives, promising them that they would be treated with proper respect if they were married to Roman citizens; and they eventually became reconciled to their lot. Some authors agree with Livy in stating that thirty girls were seized, while others suggest that there were many more, over five hundred.[86]

Even if the abducted maidens came to accept their fate, their relations were less philosophical and roused their cities to war. Although the smaller states were easily defeated, the Sabines, under their king TITUS TATIUS, presented more of a threat. They marched against Rome and seized the Capitol as a result of the treachery of TARPEIA, the daughter of the citadel's commander, who opened the gates to them in secret because she coveted their gold armbands. In return for her help, they had promised to give her 'what they were wearing on their left arms'; but they fulfilled their promise in a wholly different manner from what she had been expecting, by crushing her to death under their shields (for they also carried those on their left arms).[87] As in similar Greek stories of filial treachery (see pp. 247 and 340), the Sabines were so shocked by Tarpeia's behaviour (even though they had benefited from it) that they preferred to kill her rather than to reward her for it. After this initial success, the Sabines were able to use the Capitol as a base to attack the main Roman force on the Palatine. The opposing armies clashed on low ground between the two hills, on the site of the Forum, then a marshy and undrained strip of land. A hard-fought battle ensued in which the Romans finally began to win the upper hand; but as the two armies were preparing for the final confrontation, the abducted women, many of them mothers by this time and carrying their infants in their arms, rushed in between the Romans and Sabines and appealed to them to make peace, protesting that they would rather die than lose their husbands on the one hand or their fathers on the other. This appeal had the desired effect, and the two leaders stepped forward to make terms. They not only agreed to a truce but also resolved that their two peoples should be united into a single nation under their joint rule. Romulus remained on the Palatine with the original settlers while Titus Tatius and his Sabines settled on the Capitol and Quirinal.[88] This completes the cycle of legend that began with Romulus' establishment of the asylum; as a consequence of the war, Rome acquired further citizens, and the arrival of the Sabines serves to account for a strong Sabine element in the population. The ensuing period of dual kingship in which Titus Tatius was supposed to have ruled alongside Romulus could serve as a precedent for the dual consulship of the republican era.

This shadowy colleague of Romulus, who never found his way into the canonic list of the Roman kings, was probably a figure of relatively late invention. He was said to have given his name to one of the three early Roman tribes, the Titii or Titienses, and to have founded one of the minor priestly colleges at Rome, the Sodales Titii, whose function is unknown. Before many years had passed, he provoked his own death through an act of injustice, leaving Romulus to rule on his own once again. For when some ambassadors from Lavinium were once subjected to an assault at Rome, and their fellow townsmen demanded compensation, Titus Tatius refused to pay it because the men who had perpetrated the violence were relations of his; and when he subsequently visited Lavinium to perform an annual sacrifice (see p. 592), the townsmen rioted and murdered him.[89]

Putting aside a mass of other material, pseudo-historical and aetiological, we may conclude with the story of Romulus' death. As he was reviewing his troops one day on the Campus Martius (Field of Mars) just outside the city, a violent thunderstorm broke out and he was enveloped in a cloud so thick that he was completely hidden from view; and when the storm cleared, he was nowhere to be seen, and no trace of him could ever be found. As the Romans were arguing about the meaning of this mysterious event, a certain Julius Proculus, a farmer of Alba Longa, came to the Forum to report that the glorified Romulus had appeared to him and had told him that he had become the god Quirinus, and that Rome was destined to become the capital of the world.[90] After having once been one of the highest gods at Rome, as is indicated by the fact that his *flamen* (special priest) ranked with those of Iuppiter and Mars as one of the *flamines maiores*, Quirinus seems to have suffered something of an eclipse; Romulus was presumably identified with him because he was a god with martial associations who was thought to bear some resemblance to Mars (whatever his original nature). If the historians were happy to allow the exact nature of Romulus' departure to remain a mystery, a poet such as Ovid could describe how his father Mars had descended from heaven in his blood-stained chariot to sweep him away to his new home among the gods.[91] Since this story of the founder's apotheosis was clearly Greek-inspired, and there is no evidence of an early cult of Romulus at Rome, it is doubtless a relatively late feature of the foundation legend, originating in the second or third century BC.

Rationalistic accounts are also recorded in which Romulus is said to have been secretly assassinated. In one such version, the patricians conspired against him because they considered that he was no longer ruling like a king but was exercising his power in an arbitrary and tyrannical fashion. So they joined together to murder him in the Senate-house, and then cut his body into small pieces and carried them away under their clothing to bury them in secret.[92] The earliest evidence for such a story is provided by an anecdote from Plutarch which would suggest that it was familiar by 67 BC; for during the controversy over the Lex Gabinia of that year, which granted exceptional powers to Pompey, one of the consuls is supposed to have cried out that Pompey would meet with the same fate as Romulus if he set out to imitate him.[93] In another story of the same kind, some newly enrolled citizens who had a grievance against Romulus took advantage of the above-mentioned storm on the Campus Martius to do away with him while he was hidden from view.[94]

An important matter that remains to be considered is the question of the origin of the legend of Romulus and Remus. Was this a genuine product of the Roman imagination, perhaps even originating in folklore? And is it possible to draw any conclusion about its time of origin? The tale of exposure and wondrous deliverance of the twins certainly follows a pattern that is very familiar in Greek myth, in which a hero is conceived to a god by an unmarried girl who is isolated from ordinary family life in some way, and is exposed at birth but saved by the attentions of an animal, which suckles the child until he is discovered by a shepherd or herdsman; the countryman then rears him in pastoral seclusion until he emerges to fulfil some exceptional destiny. Twins figure, moreover, in some Greek myths of this kind, such as that of Pelias and Neleus (see p. 380). If the story of the exposure and rescue of Romulus and Remus was not of native origin, it would surely have been no difficult matter for some Greek or Roman author to invent it through imitation of famous Greek stories such as these; and precisely because the parallels are so striking, and for a variety of other reasons too, most classical scholars were once inclined to believe that it was a literary fabrication of relatively late origin. Tales of the exposure and rescue of royal children, however, are by no means confined to Greek myth, but accord with a widespread pattern which is attested in the traditions of other Indo-European peoples and far beyond. So there is nothing inherently implausible in the notion that the Romulus-legend may have been developed at Rome independently of Greek influence, perhaps even as a folk-tale. Partly as the result of the admission of a wider range of comparative evidence, but above all as the result of a reassessment of relevant aspects of the Greek and Roman tradition, there has been a marked shift in the consensus in recent decades, and most authorities are now inclined to accept that the legend of Romulus and Remus was a fairly ancient story of indigenous origin.

Although there is no positive evidence to show exactly when the legend of the exposure of Romulus and Remus was first developed, we can at least be sure that it was familiar at Rome by the end of the fourth century BC. Livy reports that two Roman magistrates (curule aediles), Cnaeus Ogulnius and Quintus Ogulnius, raised a statue of the wolf and twins near the Ruminalis fig-tree in 296 BC, paying for it with fines that they had collected from usurers;[95] and some thirty years later, probably in 266 BC, this group of the wolf and twins was shown on the earliest silver coinage minted at Rome. This would suggest that the story was not only well-established by this period, but had acquired an accepted status at Rome as the standard foundation-legend. Since the minor historian Callias, who worked at the court of Agathocles of Syracuse (died 289 BC), is the earliest datable Greek author known to have referred to Romulus in connection with the founding of Rome,[96] the evidence from Greek literature takes us no further back. If it is indeed the case that the legend of Romulus and Remus was of native invention, it is reasonable to assume nonetheless that the basic story was quite old, perhaps dating back to the early sixth century BC.

NOTES

—— •◆• ——

The forthcoming references are intended above all to indicate the main ancient sources for mythical narratives and mythological information in the preceding text; references to secondary sources have been kept to a minimum. Except in the case of myths that are recorded in very few accounts or only a single account, the references to ancient accounts of mythical narratives are not exhaustive; although more sources, especially from the Latin literature, could often have been cited, it can be more confusing than helpful to pile up references to obscure, repetitive or misleading accounts from the later record. Special attention is paid to the pre-Hellenistic tradition, and a special effort has been made to include accounts that are easily accessible in English translation (even if this is not possible in every case). For readers who wish to seek more detailed information on early sources, Timothy Gantz's *Early Greek Myth* (see the Bibliographical Note) can be recommended; and in the footnotes to his Loeb edition of Apollodorus' *Library* (Harvard, first published in 1921), Sir James Frazer provides useful lists of references to sources of every period for most important myths.

Conventional abbreviations are generally used for authors and their works. For Greek authors, these usually accord with those listed at the front of the Greek lexicon of Liddell and Scott; but longer forms have sometimes been used to make them more immediately intelligible to the general reader, and the names of works of literature are sometimes cited in English translation for the same reason. Some of the abbreviations that will be most frequently encountered are listed below; for further information on these and other authors and their works, please see the little dictionary of literary sources for Greek myth in Chapter 1.

Ael.	Aelian (*V.H.* = *Varia Historia*, i.e. *Historical Miscellany*)
Aesch.	Aeschylus
Ant. Lib.	Antoninus Liberalis
Apollod.	Apollodorus (i.e. the *Library*; Epit. = Epitome, referring to the latter part of the work which is preserved only in epitomized form)
A.R.	Apollonius of Rhodes, *Argonautica*
Arist.	Aristophanes
Athen.	Athenaeus

Bacch.	Bacchylides
Call.	Callimachus
D.H.	Dionysius of Halicarnassus (*Ant. Rom.* = *Roman Antiquities*)
D.S.	Diodorus of Sicily
Eur.	Euripides
Hdt.	Herodotus
Hes.	Hesiod (*Theog.* = *Theogony*; *W.D.* = *Works and Days*; *Cat.* = the pseudo-Hesiodic *Catalogue of Women*)
Hom.	Homer (*Il.* = *Iliad*; *Od.* = *Odyssey*)
Hom. Hymn	*Homeric Hymn*
Hyg.	Hyginus (*Fab.* = *Fabulae*, i.e. *Mythical Tales*; *Astr.* = *Astronomia*)
Lucian	*D. D.* = (*Dialogues of the Gods; D. M.* = *Dialogues of the Dead*)
Lyc.	Lycophron
Ov.	Ovid (*Met.* = *Metamorphoses*)
Paus.	Pausanias
Pi.	Pindar (*Ol.* = *Olympian Ode, Pyth.* = *Pythian Ode, Nem.* = *Nemean Ode, Isth.* = *Isthmian Ode*)
Pl.	Plato
Plut.	Plutarch (*Thes.* = *Life of Theseus*)
Serv.	Servius
Simon.	Simonides
Stes.	Stesichorus
Verg.	Vergil (*Aen.* = *Aeneid*; *Ecl.* = *Eclogue*; *Georg.* = *Georgic*)

Fragments from *early epic* (apart from Hesiodic fragments) are cited from *Epicorum Graecorum Fragmenta*, ed. M. Davies (Göttingen, 1988). These are indicated by the inclusion of the name 'Davies' after the reference.

Fragments from early *lyric poetry* are cited from *Poetae Melici Graeci* (*PMG*), ed. D.L. Page (Oxford, 1962); the excellent new volumes of *Greek Lyric* in the Loeb series (ed. D.A. Campbell, 5 vols, 1982 onward), which provide parallel translations of the fragments, generally follow the same numbering. Fragments from *elegy and iambus* are cited from *Iambi et Elegi Graeci*, ed. M.L. West (Oxford 1971). Fragments from *early mythographers* such as Pherecydes and Hellanicus are cited from the first volume of *Die Fragmente der griechischen Historiker*, ed. F. Jacoby (Leiden, 1923). References from this source are given as follows, Pher. 3F22 (for instance) or Hellanic. 4F85, in which the first number is the one assigned to the author and the second number refers to the relevant fragment. Some fragments from the works of minor historians are cited from later volumes of this great work. References are otherwise to standard collections of fragments that will be familiar to classical scholars, e.g. that of Merkelbach and West for Hesiodic fragments (Oxford, 1967), or those of Nauck or Radt for fragments from tragedy.

It is worth noting that in the classical field, for good practical reasons, the term 'fragment' is applied not only to surviving passages from lost works but also to reports on the contents of those works (although these are strictly testimonies rather than fragments).

NOTES

2   THE BEGINNINGS OF THINGS

1   Bronze, Hom. *Il.* 17.425, cf. *Od.* 3.2; iron, *Od.* 15.329.

2   As the Aloadai proposed to do, Hom. *Od.* 11.315–16 (see further on p. 91).

3   Hes. *Theog.* 620–3, cf. Hom. *Il.* 8.478–81.

4   See Aesch. *Prom. Bound* 788ff.

5   Hes. *Theog.* 116.

6   Ibid. 696–700.

7   Ibid. 807–14.

8   Ibid. 116–22.

9   Ibid. 123.

10 Cf. Pl. *Symp.* 195bc, Acus. 2F6; as demiurgic force, Pherecydes of Syros 7A11, B13 DK, the Orphic theogonies, etc.

11 Hes. *Theog.* 720–5.

12 Hom. *Il.* 8.13–16.

13 Pl. *Gorg.* 523b, *Phdo.* 113e; cf. Eur. *Orest.* 264–5 (Orestes fears that he may be consigned to Tartaros) and from later times, Verg. *Aen.* 6.542ff.

14 Hes. *Theog.* 821–2, Apollod. 2.1.2, Soph. *Oed. Col.* 1574 respectively.

15 Hes. *Theog.* 123.

16 Ibid. 124–5.

17 Ibid. 126–32.

18 Orphica fr. 28 Kern, Mousaios 2B14 DK, Epimenides 3B5 DK.

19 Arist. *Birds* 693–702.

20 Orphica fr. 54 Kern.

21 See for instance Aristotle's discussion of the different views of the earlier philosophers on the first principle, *Metaphysics* 1.3.

22 Ov. *Met.* 1.5–31.

23 Cornutus 85; empty space, Aristotle *Physics* 4.1, 208b31.

24 Ps.Cyprian *Genesis* 3 (vol. 2, p. 283 Hertel).

25 Hom. *Il.* 14.256–61 (261 quoted).

26 Hes. *Theog.* 224.

27 E.g. Hom. *Il.* 8.488, Eur. *Orest.* 175ff.

28 Westermann Mythographi, p.379, Narrat. 54.

29 Paus. 1.40.5

30 Hes. *Theog.* 211–25.

31 *Cypria* fr. 1 Davies.

32 Aesop fable 124 Chambry, cf. Babrius 59, Lucian *D.D.* 28.2, *Nigrinus* 32.

33 Aristotle *Parts of Animals* 3.2.

34 Aristid. *Orat.* 28.136.

35 Hes. *Theog.* 217and 903 respectively.

36 Pi. *Ol.* 1.26–7.

37 Aesch. *Eum.* 723–8.

38 Apollod. 1.6.2, 1.6.3.

39 Hom. *Il.* 24.49, 24.209–10 (cf. 20.127–8), *Od.* 7.197–8.

40 Hes. *Theog.* 905, *Shield* 258–60, Apollod. 1.3.1, etc.

41 Seneca *Apocol.* 4 (thread turned to gold as Nero's fate is being spun), Stat. *Theb.* 8.59, *iterataque pensa Sororum* (on Eurydike being restored to Orpheus).

42 Isidorus *Etymologiae* 8.11.93, cf. Anthol. Latin. 792 Riese (*tres sunt fatales quae ducunt fila sorores;/ Clotho baiulat, Lachesis trahit, Atropos occat*).

43 Ps.Aristotle *On the Universe* 7.401b18ff.

44 Pl. *Rep.* 617cd, 620de.

45 Hyg. *Fab.* 277.

46 Hes. *Theog.* 215–6 (Hesperides), 334–5 (snake), Eur. *Hippol.* 742–3, *Madness of Herakles* 394–9, A.R. 4.1396–9 (snake first named as Ladon) with schol. Ibid., Apollod. 2.5.11, etc.

47 Pher. 3F16.

48 A.R. 4.1427–8, Apollod. 2.5.11, Hes. fr. 360 (*dub.*).

49 Hes. *Theog.* 758–61.

50 Ibid. 762–6.

51 Hom. *Il.* 16.666–83.

52 Hom. *Il.* 14.229–91.

53 Licymnius 771 *PMG*, Diogenian. 4.60.

54 Ov. *Met.* 11.592ff, cf. Stat. *Theb.* 10.76ff.

55 Pher. 3F119.

56 Eur. *Alc.* 1139–42.

57 Proclus on *Cypria*.

58 Hom. *Il.* 11.3–14.

59 Hes. *Theog.* 226–32.

60 Hom. *Il.* 19.91–4, cf. Pl. *Symp.* 195de.

61 Hom. *Il.* 19.95–131.

62 Apollod. 3.12.3.

63 Hes. *W.D.* 802–4.

64 Eustath. on *Il.* 18.476 (= Alcman 61).

65 Paus. 1.22.3 and 3.11.9 respectively.

66 Hom. *Il.* 3.103–7, cf. 19.258–60 (Earth invoked as witness for oath, along with Zeus, Helios and the Erinyes).

67 *Hom. Hymn* 30 *to Earth the Mother of All*, 1–10.

68 Hes. *Theog.* 132–88.

69 See e.g. P. Grimal (ed.), *Larousse World Mythology*, 1965, p.35 (Egyptian), 493 (Maori).

70 Hes. *Theog.* 453ff.

71 H.G. Güterloch, *Kumarbi*, Zurich 1946.

72 See e.g. P. Grimal (ed.) *Larousse World Mythology*, 1965, 73–6, Hesiod *Theogony*, ed. M.L. West, 1966, 20–1.

73 See M.L. West l.c. 22–7.

74 Hes. *Theog.* 424, 486.

75 Hes. *Theog.* 207–10; the meaning of the first etymology is uncertain, see West on 209.

76 Olympiodorus. on Plato's *Phaedrus*, p.41 Westerink (= Orph. Fr. 220 Kern); allusion in Pl. *Laws* 701c and probable allusion in Pi.fr 133 (requital for Persephone's ancient grief).

77 Hes. *Theog.* 133–8.

78 Hom. *Il.* 8.478–81, 14.203–4 and 274, 15.224–5; banished gods named as Titans, 14.279.

79 Hom. *Il.* 8.479.

80 Hes. *Theog.* 337ff, Hom. *Il.* 21.195–7.

81 Hom. *Il.* 14.201.

82 Hes. *Theog.* 389–98.

83 Apollod. 1.1.4.

84 Helios as son of Hyperion, Hom. *Od.* 12.176, *Hom. Hymn. Demeter* 26, 74; Hyperion as title of Helios, Hom. *Il.* 8.480, *Hom. Hymn. Apollo* 369.

85 Apollod. 1.1.3.

86 Hes. *Theog.* 182–7.

87 Hom. *Il.* 9.447–57 and 9.571–2.

88 Hom. *Od.* 2.132–6, 11.277–80.

89 *Thebais* fr. 2 Davies.

90 Hom. *Il.* 19.259–60 (cf. 3.278–9, where not explicitly named).

91 Hes. *W.D.* 802–4.

92 Hom. *Od.* 17.475.

93 Hom. *Il.* 19.418.

94 Heraclitus 22B94 DK.

95 Aesch. *Eum.* 51ff.

96 E.g. Apollod. 1.1.4; all three names can be found in the *Aeneid*, 7.324, 6.571, 12.846 respectively.

97 Aesch. *Eum.* 416, cf. Lyc. 437, Serv. *Aen.* 7.327; Soph. *Oed. Col.* 40, 106.

98 Hes. *Theog.* 133.

99 Hom. *Il.* 14.197–204; Pher. 3F18a.

100 Aesch. *Prom. Bound* 286ff.

101 Hyg. *Astr.* 2.1.

102 Hes. *Theog.* 337–70; Okeanids look after young, 347.

103 Hom. *Od.* 7.245; Hes. *Theog.* 359, 1017–18.

104 Hes. *Theog.* 361.

105 *Hom. Hymn. Demeter* 417–24.

106 Apollod. 1.4.5, Hes. *Theog.* 243.

107 E.g. D.S. 5.23.3, Hyg. *Fab.* 154; already implied Eur. *Hippol.* 735–41.

108 Hdt. 3.115.

109 Aratus 360.

110 Ov. *Met.* 8.576–89.

111 Ibid. 8.590–610.

112 Moschus 6, Verg. *Aen.* 3.694–6; early allusions, Ibycus 42, Pi. *Nem.* 1.1–2.

113 Ov. *Met.* 5.572–641.

114 Paus. 5.7.2–3.

115 Hom. *Il.* 22.147–52 (two springs), 20.73–4 (two names).

116 Ibid. 21.130–2.

117 Ibid. 21.209–382.

118 E.g. Apollod. 3.12.1–2.

119 Dyes sheep, Aristotle *H.A.* 3.12, 519a16, Ael. *N.A.* 8.21; three goddesses dye hair in it, schol. *Il.* 21.1, or Aphrodite alone Eustath.Hom.1197.

120 Hes. *Theog.* 371–4.

121 Pi. *Ol.* 7.54–76.

122 Eur. *Phaethon* fr. 781.10–12 Nauck, cf. Eratosth. 24 (citing Aeschylus, but the part of the story in which the two gods are identified may have been drawn from elsewhere). For the radiance of Apollo, e.g. *Hom. Hymn. Apollo* 440–7.

123 E.g. *Hom. Hymn* 31 to *Helios* (across sky on chariot etc.), Eur. *Ion* 82 (four-horse chariot), 122 (wings), Ov. *Met.* 2.153–4 and Hyg. *Fab.* 183 (names of horses), Eur. fr. 779.8 Nauck (riding on horseback).

124 Hom. *Il.* 8.485 (plunges into Ocean), Aesch. fr. 186 Nauck (washes self and horses in western sea after journey); for the cup of the sun, see Athen. 11.469d ff, citing a string of poets from Stesichorus (= 185) and Mimnermus (= 12) onward.

125 Hom. *Od.* 12.127–41, 260–425.

126 Ibid. 8.267–71, *Hom. Hymn. Demeter* 62–81.

127 Theoc. 25.118–37.

128 Hes. *Theog.* 956–7, Hom. *Od.* 10.136–9; Pasiphae as legitimate daughter of Helios, e.g. Apollod. 1.9.1.

129 Hom. *Od.* 12.132–3.

130 Eur. fr. 771 Nauck, Ov. *Met.* 1.750ff.

131 Hes. fr 311 (= Hyg. *Fab.* 154).

132 Ov. *Met.* 1.750–2.324, cf. Eur. *Phaethon* frr., Lucret. 5.396–405, Hyg. *Fab.* 154.

133 Hyg. *Fab.* 152A.

134 Ibid. 154, Eur. *Hippol.* 737–41 (allusion), A.R. 4.603–11 (trees as source of amber), D.S. 5.23.3–4, Ov. *Met.* 2.340–66.

135 Hyg. *Fab.* 152A.

136 Ibid. 154, Ov. *Met.* 2.367–80, Verg. *Aen.* 10.189–93.

137 Claudian 6.173ff, Serv. *Aen.* 10.189.

138 Ov. *Met.* 4.190–270, Westermann, anon., p. 348.

139 The artistic record is more helpful on these matters than the literary record, but see for instance Pi. *Ol.* 3.19–20, Ov. *Fast.* 4.374, Serv. *Aen.* 5.721.

140 *Hom. Hymn 32 to Selene* (bore Pandeia to Zeus, 14–16).

141 Verg. *Georg.* 3.191–3, with Serv. ad loc. referring to Nicander.

142 *Hom. Hymn. Hermes* 99–100.

143 *Hom. Hymn 21 to Helios* 4–7.

144 Eur. *Phoen.* 175 with schol., schol. Arat. 445.

145 Alcman 57.

146 Aesch. fr. 170 Nauck.

147 Theoc. 2.10–11 etc.

148 E.g. Hom. *Od.* 2.1 and *Il.* 19.1 respectively.

149 Hom. *Il.* 11.1–2, *Od.* 5.1–2.

150 Hom. *Il.* 20.236–7, Apollod. 3.12.3, schol. *Il.* 11.5.

151 *Hom. Hymn. Aphrodite* 218–38; allusions in Sappho 58, Mimn. 4.

152 Hellanic. 4F140, schol. Lyc. 18, Serv. *Georg.* 3.328.

153 Hom. *Il.* 3.150–3.

154 Schol. *Il.* 11.1.

155 Hes. *Theog.* 984–5.

156 Hom. *Od.* 5.121–4.

157 Ibid. 15.249–51.

158 Hes. *Theog.* 986–91.

159 Apollod. 1.4.4.

160 Hes. *Theog.* 378–82.

161 Apollod. 1.7.4 and schol. *Il.* 10.267 respectively.

162 Hom. *Il.* 23.193–218.

163 Aiolos, Hom. *Od.* 10.21.8.

164 Hes. *Theog.* 375–7.

165 Ibid. 383–5.

166 Ibid. 386–403.

167 Ibid. 782–806.

168 Ibid. 377, 404–12.

169 Ibid. 507–12.

170 Ibid. 514–16.

171 Apollod. 1.2.3.

172 E.g. Hyg. *Fab.* 150.

173 Hes. *Theog.* 517–20, Hom. *Od.* 1.52–4.

174 Paus. 5.11.5, 5.18.4.

175 Hdt. 4.184.

176 Hes. *Theog.* 233–9.

177 Ibid. 234–6.

178 Nereus as old man of sea, Hom. *Od.* 24.58, cf. *Il.* 1.358, 18.36 etc.; Proteus, *Od.* 4.365; Phorkys, *Od.* 13.96, 345.

179 Pher. 3F16, Apollod. 2.5.11.

180 Panyasis fr. 7A Davies (from Athen. 11.469d).

181 Horace *Ode* 1.15.

182 Ael. *N.A.* 14.28, Lucian *Tragodop.* 87.

183 Hes. *Theog.* 240–64.

184 Hom. *Il.* 18.36–8, 49–50 (with father in cave under sea), Hdt. 7.191 (Persians offer sacrifice to them), Eur. *Ion* 1078–86 (out of sea to dance), *Iph. Taur.* 427–9, *Iph. Aul.* 1054–7; Ov. *Met.* 2.11–14 (habits as portrayed in imaginary work of art); Theoc. 7.59–60 (with halcyons in waves).

185 Hes. *Theog.* 243–64, cf. Hom. *Il.* 18.38–49, Apollod. 1.2.7, Hyg. *Fab.* praef.

186 Hom. *Il.* 18.65ff, *Od.* 24.47ff, A.R. 4.843ff, 930ff.

187 Pi. *Isth.* 8.28–48, cf. Apollod. 3.13.5 (with variants).

188 Pi. *Nem.* 5.34–7.

189 Aesch. *Prom. Bound* 209–10.

190 Ibid. 755–70, 944ff, cf. Apollod. 3.13.5, Hyg. *Fab.* 54, *Astr.* 15.

191 Aesch. fr. 306 Radt. With schol. Pi. *Isth.* 8.56b and Serv. *Ecl.* 6.42.

192 *Cypria* fr. 2 Davies, Hes. *Theog.* fr 210, cf. schol. A.R. 4.790 (combined version in which Zeus persists nonetheless until he receives the prophecy from Themis), Apollod. 3.13.5; Hom. *Il.* 24.59–60 (Thetis reared by Hera).

193 Pi. *Nem.* 4.62–8 and schol., 3.35–6 and schol., Soph. fr. 561 Nauck, Eur. fr. 1093 Nauck, Apollod. 3.13.5.

194 Paus. 5.18.5.

195 Hdt. 7.191, Eur. *Androm.* 1265–8.

196 Schol. A.R. 1.582, schol. Lyc. 175.

197 E.g. Apollod. 3.13.5, schol. Lyc. 178.

198 Ov. *Met.* 11.235–406.

199 Pi. *Pyth.* 3.87ff, Apollod. 3.13.4, etc.

200 Hom. *Il.* 24.59–63.

201 Pi. *Pyth.* 3.88–95.

202 Hes. fr. 300.

203 Lyc. 177–90.

204 A.R. 4.866–79, Apollod. 3.13.6, schol. Lyc. 178.

205 Philoxenus *Kyklops* frr. 815–24 *PMG*.

206 Theoc. 11.11ff.

207 Ov. *Met.* 13.750–897, cf. Sil. Ital. 14.221ff, Serv. *Ecl.* 7.37, 9.39.

208 Et. Magn. s.v. Galatia (citing Timaeus), D.S. 5.24.

209 Parthen. *Narrat.* 30, Et. Magn. s.v. Keltoi.

210 Ael. *N.A.* 14.28.

211 Hes. *Theog.* 265–9.

212 Call. *Hymn* 4.228–39.

213 For Zeus, Hom. *Il.* 2.786ff, 8.397ff, 11.185ff, 15.143ff, 24.74ff, 143ff; for Hera, 18.166ff; summons winds, 23.198ff, also acts on own initiative, 3.121ff, 5.353ff; golden-winged, 8.398, 11.185.

214 Proclus on *Cypria*; for other early appearances, see *Hom. Hymn. Demeter* 314ff, *Hom. Hymn. Apollo* 102ff.

215 A.R. 2.284–300.

216 Hes. *Theog.* 782ff.

217 Alcaeus 327.

218 Cited by Athenaeus, 14.645b.

219 Hom. *Od.* 1.241–3.

220 Ibid. 14.371.

221 Ibid. 20.63–78.

222 Hes. *Theog.* 267, cf. Apollod. 1.9.21 (gives variants); Kelaino added, e.g. Verg. *Aen.* 3.211, Hyg. *Fab.* 14.

223 A.R. 2.188–93, cf. Apollod. 1.9.21, Hyg. *Fab.* 14, 18.

224 Aesch. *Eum* 50–1.

225 Verg. *Aen.* 3.210–62.

226 Hom. *Il.* 16.148–51.

227 Suid. s.v. Kyllaros citing Stesichorus; Schol. *Il.* 23.346, Q.S. 4.569–70.

228 Hes. *Theog.* 270–336.

229 Ibid. 270–1.

230 Ibid. 273, cf. Pher. 3F11 and Apollod. 2.4.2 (Deino added), Heraclit. *de Incred.* 13 (Perso).

231 Pher. 3F11.

232 Aesch. *Phorkides* frr., cf. *Prom. Bound* 792–800 (single eye and tooth, live near Gorgons).

233 Hes. *Theog.* 274–8.

234 *Cypria* fr. 26 Davies.

235 E.g. Pher. 3F11, Apollod. 2.4.2, schol. Pi. *Pyth.* 10.72b.

236 Aesch. *Prom. Bound* 788ff.

237 Hes. *Theog.* 276–7, cf. Pher. 3F11 (Hermes and Athena point her out to Perseus as the only mortal *Gorgon*), Apollod. 2.4.2.

238 Hes. *Theog.* 276–83.

239 Ibid. 283, 287–8.

240 Hom. *Il.* 5,738–42, 11.32–7.

241 Pher. 3F11, Apollod. 2.4.3.

242 Hom. *Il.* 11.36–7.

243 Eur. *Ion* 987–96.

244 Ov. *Met.* 4.790–803.

245 Apollod. 2.4.3.

246 Eur. *Ion* 999–1005.

247 Paus. 2.21.6.

248 Hes. *Theog.* 287–8.

249 E.g. Stes. 186 (six-armed, six-legged, and winged), Aesch. *Ag.* 870 and Eur. *Madness of Herakles* 423–4 (triple-bodied), Apollod. 2.5.10 (three bodies joined together at waist).

250 Hdt. 4.8, Str. 3.2.11, 3.5.4, Apollod. 2.5.10, Pliny *N.H.* 4.120.

251 Hecat. 1F26.

252 Hes. *Theog.* 295–305.

253 Apollod. 2.1.2.

254 Hes. *Theog.* 306–18.

255 Fifty heads, Hes. *Theog.* 312, Simon. 569; a hundred, Pi. fr. 249a SM, Horace *Ode* 2.13.34; nine, Alcaeus 443.

256 Soph. *Trach.* 1098, Eur. *Madness of Herakles*, 611, Apollod. 2.5.2, Verg. *Aen.* 6.417–18, Hyg. *Fab.* 15. etc.

257 Hom. *Il.* 8.367–8, *Od.* 11.623–6.

258 Hes. *Theog.* 313–15.

259 Ibid. 319–25, cf. Homer's description in *Il.* 6.179–82, and Apollod. 2.3.1.

260 Hes. *Theog.* 326–32.

261 Pi. *Isth.* 6.47–8, Bacch. 13.46–54.

262 Hes. *Theog.* 333–6; first called Ladon, A.R. 4.1396; hundred-headed according to Pher. 3F16b, cf. Apollod. 2.5.11.

263 Hom. *Od.* 1.70–3.

264 By Hekate, e.g. Acus. 2F42, A.R. 4.828–9; by Krataiis, Apollod. *Epit.* 7.20.

265 Lyc. 44–8 and schol.

3   THE RISE OF ZEUS AND REVOLTS AGAINST HIS RULE

1 Aphrodite can only be regarded as one of the younger Olympian deities if she was the daughter of Zeus and Dione; if she was born from the sea-foam that surrounded the severed genitals of Ouranos, as in Hesiod's account (see p. 67), she was born at an earlier period than any other Olympian deity (not that it makes any practical difference).

2 Hes. *Theog.* 132–53.

3 Ibid. 138–46.

4 First in Call. *Hymn* 3.46ff, cf. Verg. *Aen.* 8.416ff.

5 E.g. Apollod. 3.10.4; already in Hesiodic Catalogue, see frr. 52 and 54.

6 Pi. fr. 266 SM.

7 Eratosth. 39, Hyg. *Astr.* 2.39.

8 Paus. 2.2.2.

9 Hellanic. 4F88, schol. Aristid. 52.10, p.408 Dindorf.

10 Polyphemos' single eye, Hom. *Od.* 9.382ff etc., his parentage, 1.68–72, 9.528–9; Homer says nothing about the appearance or birth of the Kyklopes in his general account of them, 9.105–15, or subsequently.

11 E.g. Paus. 2.16.4, 2.25.7, 7.25.3, Apollod. 2.2.1.

12 Hes. *Theog.* 147–53; called Hekatoncheires, Palaeph. 19, Apollod. 1.1.1.

13 Hom. *Il.* 1.402.

14 Hes. *Theog.* 817–19.

15 Hom. *Il.* 1.396–406.

16 Ibid. 1.403–4.

17 *Titanomachia* fr. 3 Davies.

18 Paus. 2.1.6.

19 Solinus 11.16.

20 Hes. *Theog.* 154–200.

21 Ibid. 453–67.

22 Ibid. 468–91.

23 Ibid. 492–506.

24 Ibid. 617–735.

25 Apollod. 1.1.1–1.2.1.

26 Pi. *Pyth.* 4.289–91, Aesch. frr. 190–3 Radt.

27 Hes. *W.D.* 109–120, cf. Ov. *Met.* 1.89–112.

28 Hes. *W.D.* 109–201, cf. Aratus 100–36, Ov. *Met.* 1.89–150.

29 Silver race, Hes. *W.D.* 121–42.

30 Hes. *W.D.* 143–55.

31 Ibid. 156–73.

32 Ibid. 174–201.
33 Pi. *Ol.* 2.70–7.
34 Hes. *W.D.* 169–169e.
35 Plut. *Moralia* 419e–420a.
36 Verg. *Aen.* 8.319ff, 355–8; see also D.H. *Ant. Rom.* 1.34.5, 1.36.1 (Golden Age in Italy under Kronos), Euhemerus 63F16.
37 Paus. 1.18.7, schol. Pi. *Ol.* 5.10.
38 Paus. 8.36.2–3.
39 E.g. D.S. 5.66.1, the house of Rhea at Knossos.
40 *Hom. Hymn. Demeter* 441–70.
41 Bacch fr. 42 SM.
42 Prob. *Georg* 3.92–4.
43 A.R. 2.1231–41.
44 Hyg. *Fab.* 138.
45 Hes. *Theog.* 1001–2, Pi. *Pyth.* 6.22, cf. Pher. 3F50.
46 Hom. *Il.* 15.307–10, 2.447–9 respectively.
47 Hom. *Il.* 17.593–6, 4.164–8.
48 Athena, Hom. *Il.* 2.456–52, 5.733–42, 18.203–6, 21.400–2; Apollo, 15.229–30 with 318–22, and 24.18–21.
49 Hes. fr. 343.
50 Hes. *Theog.* 477–84.
51 Dikte and Ida cited as alternative locations, Call. *Hymn* 1.4–6; Ida the earlier, e.g. Pi. *Ol.* 5.40–1, Dikte first in Call. l.c., A.R. 1.509 and 1130, Arat. 33 (where erroneously placed near Ida).
52 E.g. Musaeus 2B8 DK (from Eratosth. 13), Ov. *Fast.* 5.111–21, Hyg. *Fab.* 139.
53 Call. *Hymn* 1.46–9 (suckled by milk of goat Amaltheia), Apollod. 1.1.6–7 (Adrasteia and Ida, daughters of Melisseus, fed Zeus on milk of Amaltheia), Hyg. *Astr.* 2.13 (similar, but daughters of Mellisseus not named); cf. A.R. 3.132–6 (Adrasteia nurse of Zeus, made beautiful ball for him), D.S. 5.70.3 (nymphs not named), schol. *Od.* 5.272 and schol. Arat. 46 (Helike and Kynosura).
54 E.g. Athen. 375f, 491a.
55 Call. *Hymn* 1.51–3 (earliest surviving source), D.S. 5.65.4, Apollod. 1.1.7, Lucretius 2.633–9, Ovid *Fasti* 4.207–10 (here with Corybantes, see p. 219). See also Epimenides 3B22, Eur. fr. 472 Nauck, Corinna 654.12–16.
56 Hyg. *Fab.* 139.
57 Ant. Lib. 19.
58 Eratosth. 13, Hyg. *Astr.* 2.13.
59 Schol. Arat. 46.
60 Eratosth. 30, Hyg. *Astr.* 2.16.
61 Paus. 8.38.2–3, 8.41.2.
62 Paus. 4.33.1.
63 Hom. *Il.* 15.187–93, cf. Apollod. 1.2.1.
64 Hom. *Il.* 14.313–28.
65 Hes. *Theog.* 886–900, cf. Apollod. 1.3.6.
66 Hes. fr. 343.
67 Hes. *Theog.* 901–6.
68 Pi. fr. 30 SM.
69 Proclus on *Cypria*, *Hom. Hymn* 23 to Kronos 2–3.
70 On succession at Delphi, e.g. Aesch. *Eum.* 1–8, Paus. 10.5.3.
71 Hom. *Il.* 15.87–9, 20.4–6, *Od.* 2.68–9.

72 Hes. *Theog.* 907–11.
73 Ibid. 912–14.
74 Ibid. 915–17.
75 Ibid. 918–20.
76 Ibid. 921–3.
77 Hom. *Il.* 14.293–6.
78 Hes. *Theog.* 922–9.
79 Hom. *Od.* 8.312 (Hephaistos indicates that he has *two* parents) with *Il.* 1.577–9, 14.338.
80 Hom. *Il.* 4.2–3, 5.905, 5.722; Apollod. 1.3.5 notes that the Homeric account differs from that of Hesiod.
81 Paus. 6.20.2–6.
82 E.g. Hom. *Il.* 11.270, Paus. 1.44.3 (sanctuary of Eileithuiai at Megara).
83 Hes. *Theog.* 353, 17.
84 Hom. *Il.* 5.370–4.
85 *Hom. Hymn. Apollo* 93.
86 Str. 7.7.12.
87 Pher. 3F90, Apollod. 1.1.3.
88 Pi. *Ol.* 10.49, Hdt. 2.7, 6.108, Thuc. 6.54.
89 E.g. schol. A.R. 2.533.
90 Schol. Pi. *Ol.* 5.10a (= Herodorus 31F34a).
91 Hom. *Il.* 5.339–42.
92 Ibid. 8.19–27.
93 Ibid. 1.396–405.
94 Hes. *Theog.* 823–35.
95 Ant. Lib. 28, citing Nicander.
96 Apollod. 1.6.3.
97 Hes. *Theog.* 836–68.
98 Ibid. 869–80.
99 Apollod. 1.6.1–3.
100 *Hom. Hymn. Apollo* 305–55, cf. Stes. 239 for circumstances of birth.
101 Schol. *Il.* 2.783.
102 Apollod. 1.6.3.
103 Pi. fr 91 SM.
104 Ant. Lib. 28, citing Nicander, cf. Ov. *Met.* 5.318–31.
105 Hom. *Il.* 15.237, Arist. *Birds* 516.
106 Hdt. 2.156.
107 Ov. *Met.* 5. 329.
108 Hyg. *Astr.* 2.28.
109 Hom. *Il.* 2.781–3.
110 Hes. *Theog.* 304.
111 See West on *Theog.* l.c.
112 Pi. *Pyth.* 8.16, *Pyth.* 1.16–17, cf. Aesch. *Prom. Bound* 351–2.
113 J.B. Pritchard (ed.), *Ancient Near Eastern Texts*, Princeton 1955, 125–6.
114 Pi. *Pyth.* 1.19–29, Aesch. *Prom. Bound* 363–7.
115 Pher. 3F54.
116 Hes. *Theog.* 180–6.
117 Claudian *Gigantomachy* 6–14.
118 Hes. *Theog.* 954.
119 Hom. *Od.* 10.119–20, 7.201–6, 7.58–60 respectively.
120 Schol. *Il.* 14.295 (= Euphorion fr. 99 Powell).

121 Xenophanes 21B1.19–24.
122 Pi. *Nem.* 1.67–9, *Pyth.* 8.12–13, Hes. fr. 43a.63–5.
123 E.g. Paus. 8.29.1, D.S. 4.21.5–7 (cf. 5.71.4) respectively.
124 Apollod. 1.6.1.
125 Schol. Pi. *Nem.* 1.101.
126 Pi. *Pyth.* 8.12–13, Arist. *Birds* 1249–52.
127 Apollod. 1.6.1.
128 Schol. Pi. *Isth.* 6.47.
129 Pi. *Isth.* 6.31–5, *Nem.* 4.25–30.
130 Schol. Pi. *Nem.* 4.43.
131 Apollod. 1.6.2.
132 A.R. 3.1225–7, Claudian *Gigantomachy* 85–91.
133 Euripides mentions that Enkelados fell to Athena, *Madness of Herakles* 906–9. The Sicilian location may have been introduced by Callimachus, see fr. 1 and schol. Pi. *Pyth.* 4.11.
134 Aesch. *Seven* 424, cf. *Ag.* 692 (Zephyros).
135 Snake-legged, Apollod. 1.6.1 (a late feature of his account), Ov. *Met.* 1.184, Claudian *Gigantomachy* 80–1; Paus. 8.29.3 regards the notion as absurd.
136 Apollod. 1.6.1, 3.
137 Hes. *Theog.* 820–3.
138 Hom. *Od.* 11.305–8, Hes. fr. 19.
139 Apollod. 1.7.4.
140 Schol. A.R. 1.482, citing Eratosthenes.
141 Hom. *Od.* 11.306–20.
142 Apollod. 1.7.4, Hyg. *Fab.* 28.
143 Apollod. 1.7.4, schol. *Il.* 5.385, schol. Pi. *Pyth.* 4.156a.
144 Pi. *Pyth.* 4.88–9.
145 Hyg. *Fab.* 28; Verg. *Aen.* 6.582 indicates that they were punished in Tartarus, but gives no details.
146 Hom. *Il.* 5.385–91.
147 Schol. *Il.* 5.385.
148 Paus. 9.29.1–2.
149 D.S. 5.50.6–55.2, cf. Parthen. 19.
150 Paus. 9.22.5, Serv. *Aen.* 3.578 respectively.
151 Paus. 10.28.4.
152 Hes. *Theog.* 535–60.
153 Ibid. 561–612.
154 Ibid. 521–31.
155 Hes. *W.D.* 42–58.
156 Ibid. 59–82.
157 Ibid. 83–9.
158 Hes. *Theog.* 511–14.
159 Hes. *W.D.* 90–105.
160 Hom. *Il.* 24.525–33.
161 Aesch. *Prom. Bound* 1–87.
162 Ibid. 7–11, 107–13.
163 Ibid. 197–241.
164 Ibid. 441–506.
165 Ibid. 907–19, with 209–13, 515–25; the secret is obscurely indicated rather than directly stated.

166 Ibid. 944–1093.

167 Aesch. *Prom. Unbound*, frr; in Caucasus, fr 199 Radt (from Str. 4.1.7), tormented there by eagle, fr. 193 (see Cic. *Tusc.* 2.22–5), chorus of Titans, fr. 190.

168 Apollod. 1.7.1, 2.5.11, D.S. 4.15.2, Hyg. *Astr.* 2.15, etc.

169 Hes. fr. 2.

170 Aesch. *Prom. Bound* 560, Acus. 2F34.

171 Philemon 89, Horace *Ode* 1.16.13–16, Apollod. 1.7.1, Hyg. *Fab.* 142.

172 Paus. 10.4.3.

173 Paus. 1.30.2, schol. Soph. *Oed. Col.* 55.

4   THE BROTHERS AND SISTERS OF ZEUS

1 Hom. *Il.* 13.21–2.

2 Hdt. 7.129.

3 Pi. *Isth.* 8.34, Aesch. *Prom. Bound* 924–5.

4 Hom. *Il.* 13.17–30.

5 *Hom. Hymn 22 to Poseidon* 1–5.

6 Hom. *Il.* 7.445, 13.43.

7 Hom. *Od.* 5.291–8.

8 Hdt. 7.192.

9 Thuc. 1.128.

10 Xen. *Hell.* 4.7.4, Paus. 3.11.9.

11 *Hom. Hymn 22 to Poseidon* 5.

12 *Hom. Hymn. Apollo* 230–38. The nature and purpose of the rite is disputed; it seems unlikely that the damaged chariot would have been dedicated to the god and left in the grove.

13 Paus. 8.25.4–7; cf. Apollod. 3.6.8 (Demeter mated with him in the form of an Erinys).

14 Paus. 8.25.10; schol. *Il.* 15.639 and 23.346 (Kopreus).

15 Schol. *Il.* 23.346 and 347 respectively.

16 Paus. 8.42.1–4.

17 Paus. 8.8.1–2.

18 Schol. Pi. *Pyth.* 4.138 (both Thessalian versions), schol. Stat. *Theb.* 4.43 (blow of trident, Areion too).

19 Serv. *Georg.*1.12, Tzetz. Lyc. 766 (at Kolonos, also called Skeironites).

20 Apollod. 3.14.1, cf. Hyg. *Fab.* 164 (Zeus sends Hermes to restrain Poseidon); Paus. 1.26.6 (mark of trident and sea of Erechtheion).

21 Verg. *Georg.* 1.12–14 with Servius on 1.12, Vat. Myth. 1.2.

22 Ov. *Met.* 6.72–82.

23 Hyg. *Fab.* 164 (Zeus), Xen. *Mem.* 3.5.10 (Kekrops), Apollod. 3.14.1 (Kekrops and Kranaos, or Erysichthon, as variants).

24 Varro in Augustine *City of God* 18.9.

25 Paus. 1.26.6, Hdt. 8.55.

26 Paus. 2.15.5.

27 Paus. 2.22.5.

28 Plut. *Moralia* 741a.

29 Paus. 2.30.6.

30 Paus. 2.32.7.

31 Paus. 2.1.6.

32 Hom. *Il.* 21.441–57. Apollo was a firm supporter of the Trojans however.

33 Hom. *Il.* 7.445–53.

34 Ibid. books 13–14; warned off by Zeus, 15.185ff.

35 Hom. *Od.* 1.19–21 and 68ff, 5.286ff, etc.

36 Ibid. 13.128ff.

37 Nereid, Hes. *Theog.* 243; consort of Poseidon, ibid. 931–4, Pi. *Ol.* 6.104–5, Bacch. 17.109–11; presented as mother of Nereids, Mel. adesp. 21; she is mentioned as a great goddess of the seas on four occasions in the *Odyssey*, 3.91, 5.421–2, 12.60, 12.97.

38 Schol. *Od.* 3.91.

39 Eratosth. 31, Hyg. *Astr.* 2.17.

40 Hes. *Theog.* 930–3.

41 Apollod. 3.15.4 and 1.4.5 respectively.

42 Ibid. 3.15.4.

43 Hdt. 4.179, Pi. *Pyth.* 4.28ff (Triton not named).

44 Verg. *Aen.* 6.171–4.

45 Hyg. *Astr.* 2.23.

46 Paus. 9.21.1.

47 Paus. 9.20.4; on Tritons, see also Ael. *V.H.* 13.21, Pliny *N.H.* 36.4, 7.

48 E.g. Pl. *Gorg.* 493b, *Crat.* 403a.

49 See e.g. the testament of Theophrastus in Diogenes Laertius 5.51.

50 Paus. 6.25.2.

51 Str. 8.344, Paus. 2.35.5 (Klymenos).

52 Seneca *Herc. Fur.* 724–5.

53 Hom. *Od.* 11.9.ff.

54 Ibid. 24.1–14.

55 Hom. *Il.* 23.99–101, 16.855–7, 22.361–3.

56 Hom. *Od.* 10.501–15, 11.13–22.

57 Ibid. 11.23ff.

58 Hom. *Od.* 11.508–40, 572–5.

59 Hom. *Il.* 23.71–4 (unnamed boundary-river), 8.369 (Styx), cf. Verg. *Aen.* 6.384ff; Acheron first as boundary-river in Alcaeus 38, cf. Sappho 95 (implied), Aesch. *Seven* 854–60, Paus. 10.28.1, etc.

60 Hom. *Od.* 10.513–4.

61 E.g. Pl. *Rep.* 10.621c, Verg. *Aen.* 6.714–15.

62 E.g. Eur. *Alcest.* 443.

63 Hes. *Theog.* 783–92.

64 Hdt. 6.74.

65 Paus. 8.18.4–6.

66 Thesprotian Acheron, Hdt. 5.92, Paus. 1.17.5 (also mentions the Thesprotian Kokytos), 9.30.3 (oracle of dead by it at Aornos), Plut.*Cimon* 6 (at Acheron near Heracleia); Acheron in Elis, Str. 8.344.

67 Theogn. 705–6, Arist. *Frogs* 186.

68 Pl. *Rep.* 621a.

69 Ed. G. Pugliese Carratelli, *Parola del Passato*, 154–5, 1974, pp. 10–11; English translation in W. Burkert, *Greek Religion*, Cambridge, Mass., 1985, p. 293.

70 Paus. 9.39.4.

71 Gates of Hades, Hom. *Il.* 5.644–6, cf. 23.71, Hes. *Theog.* 773; Hades as warder of gates, Hom. *Il.* 8.367, 13.415.

72 E.g. Hom. *Il.* 22.52, *Od.* 24.204.

73 Hes. *Theog.* 767–73.

74 Hom. *Od.* 24.11–14.

75   Aesch. *Libation-Bearers* 622, cf. Soph. *Ajax* 831–4, Eur. *Alc.* 743–4.

76   Hom. *Il.* 23.100.

77   Ibid. 22.362–3, *Od.* 11.222.

78   Hom. *Il.* 23.71–4.

79   Hom. *Od.* 11.51–80.

80   *Minyas* fr. 1 Davies (from Paus. 10.28.1).

81   *Hom. Hymn. Demeter* 334ff.

82   And perhaps Athena too if she actually accompanied Herakles when she helped him to fetch Kerberos, Hom. *Od.* 11.623–6.

83   Arist. *Frogs* 180–270, Verg. *Aen.* 6.295–38, Lucian *D.M.* 4, 10, 22.

84   Serv. *Aen.* 6.392.

85   As witless, e.g. Hom. *Od.* 10.492–5, 11.476; examples of spontaneous action, *Il.* 23.72–3, *Od.* 11.36–50.

86   Aesch. *Suppl.* 231, Pi.*Ol.* 2.59.

87   Hom. *Od.* 11.568–71.

88   Hom. *Il.* 19.259–60, cf. 3.278–9.

89   Hom. *Od.* 4.561–9 (564–8 quoted).

90   Pi. *Ol.* 2.75–7, cf. Hes. *W.D.* 169ad.

91   Pi. *Ol.* 2.78–9 (Peleus, Kadmos, Achilles), Ibycus 291 (Achilles and Medeia), 294 (Diomedes), Eur. *Bacch.* 1338–9 (Kadmos and Harmonia), Ant. Lib. 33 (Alkmene).

92   Pi. *Ol.* 2.70–4, fr. 129 SM.

93   Ibid. 2.63–5.

94   Achilles on Leuke, Proclus on Aethiopis, Pi. *Nem.* 4.49, Eur. *Iph. Taur.* 436–8, Apollod.Epit. 5.5; Leonymos (see p. 583) sees heroes of the Trojan War on island, Paus. 3.19.12; further lore in Philostr. *Her.* 20.32–40.

95   Verg. *Aen.* 6.542, 744.

96   Hom. *Od.* 11.575–81, cf. Apollod. 1.4.1, Verg. *Aen.* 6.595–600.

97   Hom. *Od.* 11. 582–92, cf. Apollod. *Epit.* 1.24.

98   Hom. *Od.* 11. 593–600; had escaped death on first occasion, Pher. 3F119; had informed on Zeus, Apollod. 1.9.3, Paus. 2.5.1.

99   *Returns* fr. 9 Davies (from Athen. 281b); cf. Alcman 79, Pi. *Ol.* 1.55–8, Pher. 3F38; 'stone of Tantalos' as proverbial phrase, Archil. 91, Pi. *Isth.* 8.10.

100   Paus. 10.31.2 (in Polygnotos' painting), Apollod. *Epit.* 2.1, Hyg. *Fab.* 82.

101   Pi. *Ol.* 1.25–7, 35–51, cf. Apollod. *Epit.* 2.3 (vague), Hyg. *Fab.* 83, schol. Lyc. 152.

102   Pi. *Ol.* 1.52–64, schol. Eur. *Orest.* 10.

103   Eur. *Orest.* 7–10, Ov. *Met.* 6.213, Seneca *Thyest.* 90.

104   Schol. *Il.* 20.234 citing Mnaseas, schol. Pi. *Ol.* 1.97 respectively.

105   A.R. 3.61–3, Verg. *Georg.* 3.37–9, Verg. *Aen.* 6.601.

106   *Minyas* fr. 4 Davies (from Paus. 9.5.4).

107   Verg. *Aen.* 6.585–6.

108   Ibid. 6.618–20, Val. Flacc. 2.192–4.

109   Verg. *Aen.* 6.582.

110   Ps.Pl. *Axiochos* 371e.

111   Paus. 10.31.

112   Paus. 10.29.2, Cratinus fr. 348 Kock, D.S. 1.97.2, Plut. *Moralia* 473c.

113   Pl. *Gorg.* 523be, cf. Eur. *Orest.* 265, ps.Pl. *Axiochos* 371e, Verg. *Aen.* 6.577ff.

114   Hom. *Od.* 11.489–91.

115   Pi. *Ol.* 2.56ff.

116   Pl. *Apol.* 41a, *Gorg.* 523e–524a.

117   Pl. *Apol.* 41a.

118   Pl. *Gorg.*524a, Verg. *Aen.* 6.430–3, 564–9.

119   Arist. *Frogs* 465ff, Apollod. 3.12.6, Lucian *D.M.* 20.1.

120   Hom. *Od.* 4.563–4, Pi. *Ol.* 2.75.

121   Pl. *Rep.* 363d, *Phdo. 69c*, Diog. Laert. 6.39, Plut. fr. 178, Aristid. *Or.* 22.10; cf. Arist. *Frogs* 145ff, 273ff.

122   Ps.Pl. *Axiochos* 372a.

123   Lucian *D.M.* 30.1.

124   Pl. *Rep.* 330de.

125   Democritus 68B297 DK, cf. ibid.199.

126   Paus. 10.28.4.

127   Ibid.

128   Arist. *Frogs* 288–96.

129   Verg. *Aen.* 6.133–48 with Servius schol.

130   Ibid. 264–382.

131   Ibid. 383–547.

132   Ibid. 624.

133   Ibid. 548–627.

134   Ibid. 628–78.

135   Hom. *Il.* 5.395–8; he went up to Olympos to be healed by Paian in any case, ibid. 399–402.

136   Serv. *Ecl.* 7.61.

137   Hom. *Il.* 9.454–7.

138   *Hom. Hymn. Demeter* 1–94.

139   Baubo, Clem. Alex. *Protrep.* 2.20.

140   *Hom. Hymn. Demeter* 93–300.

141   Half the year in each realm, e.g. Ov. *Met.* 5.564–67, Hyg. *Fab.* 146.

142   *Hom. Hymn. Demeter* 301–489. For the myth as a whole, see also Apollod. 1.5.1–3, D.S. 5.4–5, Ov. *Met.* 5.345–571, *Fasti* 4.417–620.

143   Ov. *Met.* 5.538–50.

144   Apollod. 1.5.3, 2.5.12.

145   Trampled by Demeter, Oppian *On Hunting* 3.486ff; transformed by Persephone, Str. 8.3.14, Ov. *Met.* 10.728–30, Photius s.v. Mintha.

146   E.g. Isocr. 28.28, Xen. *Hell.* 6.3.6.

147   Ant. Lib. 24, Ov. *Met.* 5.446–61, cf. Nic. *Ther.* 486ff.

148   *Hom. Hymn. Demeter* 207–11.

149   Paus. 1.37.1–2.

150   Conon 15.

151   Paus. 2.36.7.

152   Paus. 1.14.2.

153   Paus. 1.13.7, cf. Plut. *Pyrrhus* 34.

154   E.g. D.S. 5.4.2.

155   Ov. *Met.* 5.409–37.

156   Cicero *Against Varro* 2.4.106; Persephone abducted near Henna, Ov. *Met.* 5.385ff, D.S. 5.3.2–3.

157   *Hom. Hymn. Demeter* 401.

158   Hom. *Od.* 11. 46–7, 225–7, 385–6, 633–5.

159   Ibid. 10.491–5.

160   E.g. Theognis 702–4, D.S. 4.26.1, Moschus 3.123–4 respectively.

161   *Hom. Hymn. Demeter* 153, 474.

162 For alternatives, see e.g. Paus. 1.14.2, Apollod. 1.5.2, Serv. *Georg.* 1.19, 1.163; identified with child nursed by Demeter, Ov. *Fast.* 4.507ff, Hyg. *Fab.* 147; for Rarian Meadow, see Paus. 1.38.6.

163 Apollod. 1.5.2, Ov. *Met.* 5.642–7, D.H. *Ant. Rom.* 1.12.

164 Ov. *Met.* 5.648–61.

165 Hyg. *Astr.* 2.14.

166 Paus. 7.18.2.

167 Hom. *Od.* 5.125–8.

168 Hes. *Theog.* 969–74.

169 Apollod. 3.12.1, D.H. *Ant. Rom.* 1.61.4; desecration of cultic image, Hellanic. 4F23, Conon 21; grey hairs, Ov. *Met.* 9.422.

170 Hes. *Theog.* 971, cf. D.S. 5.77.1.

171 Hellanic. 4F23, Apollod. 3.12.1, D.S. 5.48.2 (eccentric account of Iasion's legend in 5.48–9), Ov. *Am.* 3.10.25; son of Katreus, son of Minos, schol. *Od.* 5.25, cf. schol. Theoc 3.50.

172 Hellanic 4F23, Hes. fr. 177.8–12.

173 Hyg. *Astr.* 2.4.

174 Call. *Hymn* 6.22–115.

175 Lyc. 1391–6 with scholia.

176 Erysichthon called Aithon, Hes. fr. 43a.2–7; Mestra uses her powers to secure food for him, first Palaeph. 23, Lyc. l.c.

177 Ov. *Met.* 8.738–878.

178 Hyg. *Astr.* 2.14; Triopas also committed the sacrilege in D.S. 5.61.

179 D.S. 3.64.1, schol. Arist., vol. 3 p.648 Dindorf, Suidas s.v iacchos.

180 Arist. *Frogs* 324ff, 397ff.

181 Hdt. 8.65.

182 Hom. *Il.* 4.8, Hes. *Theog.* 12, cf. *Phoronis* fr. 3 Davies; Pi. *Nem.* 10.2

183 Paus. 2.38.2.

184 Paus. 8.22.2

185 D.S. 5.72.4.

186 Hom. *Il.* 14.346–41.

187 Varro in Lactant. *Div. Inst.* 1.17.8, cf. Augustine *City of God* 6.7.

188 Athen. 15.672cd.

189 Paus. 7.4.4.

190 Schol. *Il.* 1.609.

191 Hom. *Il.* 14.295–6.

192 Call. fr. 75.4–5, schol. *Il.* 14.296.

193 Euboea sacred to Hera, schol. A.R. 4.1138; reared there by Makris, schol. *Il.* 2.535.

194 Steph. Byz. s.v. Karystos, Dirphys and Elymnia.

195 Schol. Theoc. 15.64, Paus. 2.36.2.

196 Paus. 2.17.4.

197 Plut. *In Euseb.* 3.1.6 (= *On the Plataian Daidalia* fr. 3; see Loeb Plutarch vol. 7 p.44).

198 Paus. 9.3.3–4.

199 Paus. 9.3.1–2.

200 Plut. l.c.

201 Hom. *Il.* 14.153ff.

202 Hom. *Il.* 15.18–28; cf. 14.253–6, 18.117–19, 19.96ff.

203 Transformation of Antigone, Ov. *Met.* 6.93–5, cf. Serv. *Aen.* 1.27, Lactant. *Narrat.* 6.1; latter version, Vat. Myth. 1.79.

204 Hes. *Theog.* 454, *Hom. Hymn. Aphrodite* 22–3.

205 See e.g. *Hom. Hymn* 29 *to Hestia* 1–6, Pi .*Nem.* 11.1–9, Arist. *Birds*, 865–7.
206 Arist. *Wasps* 846, Zenob. 1.40, Hesych. s.v. *aph' Hestias*.
207 Aristotle *Meteorology* 2.9.6.
208 Pl. *Phdr.* 246e–247a.
209 Hes. *W.D.* 733–4.
210 *Hom. Hymn. Aphrodite* 22–32.
211 Schol. Arist. *Wasps* 846.

5   THE YOUNGER OLYMPIAN GODS AND GODDESSES

1 Hom. *Il.* 4.100–3.
2 Hdt. 1.173.
3 Hes. *Theog.* 918–20, *Hom. Hymn. Apollo* 14–15.
4 *Hom. Hymn. Apollo* 115–32.
5 Ibid. 214–76.
6 Ibid. 277–387.
7 Ibid. 388–546.
8 Ibid. 363–74.
9 Athen. 701c citing Clearchus, Apollod. 1.4.1, Ov. *Met.* 1.438–47, etc.; Delphyne, A.R. 2.706, male form Delphynes, schol. ibid. citing Callimachus.
10 Eur. *Iph. Taur.* 1234–58, Athen. 701c.
11 Hyg. *Fab.* 140.
12 Aesch. *Eum.* 1–8.
13 For the Stepteria, Plut. *Moralia* 293c, 418ab, 1136b, Ael. *V.H.* 3.1, Str. 9.3.12.
14 Str. 9.3.10, Pollux 4.84.
15 Plut. *Moralia* 409ef, schol. Pi. *Pyth.* 4.6.
16 Plut. 409ef, Str. 9.419 respectively.
17 For the alleged vapour, e.g. Str. 9.3.5, Pliny *N.H.* 2.208; see also D.S. 16.26.1–3 for a quaint tale that links the discovery of the oracle to the vapour (some goats and their goatherd came within range of the vapour and experienced its divinely maddening effects; and when news of the matter was noised abroad, it was agreed that this must be an oracle of Earth).
18 It is in this connection that she is first mentioned by the philosopher Heraclitus, 22B92 DK.
19 Heracleides Ponticus in Clem. Alex. *Strom.* 1.108 (Hellespontine and Erythraean Sibyls), Varro in Lactant. *Div. Inst.* 1.6 (Hellespontine and Marpessan), Paus. 10.12.1–4 (competing claims of Marpessos and Erythrai for the early Sibyl Herophile, who later came to Delphi).
20 Varro l.c., also Suid. s.v. Sibylla (with another catalogue).
21 Hom. *Od.* 11.576, Hes. fr. 78.
22 Pher. 3F55.
23 Hom. *Od.* 11.580–1; burial-place, Paus. 10.4.4.
24 Pher. 3F56, Pi. *Pyth.* 4.90–2 (mentions Artemis only), A.R. 1.759–62 (Apollo alone), Apollod. 1.4.1, Paus. 3.18.15 (on Amyklaian throne).
25 Schol. A.R. 1.181 and Hyg. *Fab.* 55 respectively.
26 Athen 307c.
27 A.R. 4.611–18; cf. Eratosth. 29, Hyg. *Astr.* 2.15 (after shooting the Kyklopes, Apollo hid the arrow in the land of the Hyperboreans).
28 Pi. *Pyth.* 10.29–36.

29 Hdt. 4.32–5.

30 Hes. *Theog.* 59, cf. Pi. *Pyth.* 3.34 (she lived by the lake).

31 This account, Acus. 2F17.

32 Main narrative, Pi. *Pyth.* 3.25–46; *Hom. Hymn. Apollo* 209–10 (Apollo and Ischys competed for the daughter of Azan, presumably to be identified with Koronis), *Hom. Hymn* 16 *to Asklepios* (merely that Koronis bore Asklepios to Apollo on the Dorian plain); Paus. 2.26.5 (Hermes recovered child from pyre).

33 Crow first mentioned, Hes. *Theog.* 60, cf. Pher. 3F2, Ov. *Met.* 2.596–632, etc.

34 Artemon 569F5 (transformation first mentioned); Ant. Lib. 20.7, Apollod. 3.10.3, Ov. *Met.* 2.631–2, Hyg. *Fab.* 202, *Astr.* 2.40.

35 Schol. Pi. *Pyth.* 3.59 and Hyg. *Fab.* 202 respectively.

36 Hes. fr. 50, Apollod. 3.10.3 (cited as variant), Paus. 2.26.6, 4.3.2.

37 Paus. 2.26.4.

38 Pi. *Pyth.* 3.45–53, Apollod. 3.10.3.

39 E.g. Hyg. *Fab.* 14 and 173 respectively.

40 Hom. *Il.* 729–33 (skilled healers, leaders of a Thessalian contingent), 11.833–6 (best healers), etc.

41 E.g. Apollod. *Epit.* 5.8 (Podaleirios), Proclus on *Little Iliad* (Machaon).

42 Arist. *Wealth* 701–2 with schol. 701, Paus. 2.11.6–7, Suid. s.v Epione.

43 Pi. *Pyth.* 3.54–8 (revived unnamed person for pay), Apollod. 3.10.3–4 (includes interpolation giving alternative names from different sources for the person revived), Hyg. *Astr.* 2.14 (revived Hippolytos), D.S. 4.71.1–3 (revived so many that Hades complained).

44 Apollod. 3.10.4, cf. Eur. *Alcest.* 1–10; the story was recounted in the Hesiodic *Catalogue*, see frr. 54–6.

45 Apollod. 3.10.4, a detail apparently recorded in the *Catalogue* (see Hes. fr. 54b with 54a.11–12 and 56) and by Acusilaus (2F19).

46 Pher. 3F35 (also that Asklepios was condemned to serve Admetos for a year).

47 Apollod. 3.10.4, cf. Call. *Hymn* 2.47–54.

48 Apollod. 1.9.15, Hyg. *Fab.* 50, 51, schol. Eur.*Alcest.* 254.

49 Apollod. 1.9.15, Aesch. *Eum.* 723–8.

50 Pl. *Symp.* 179b, Apollod. 1.9.15 (mentioned as variant), cf. Hyg. *Fab.* 251, Lucian *de Luctu* 5.

51 Eur. *Alcest.* 476–567.

52 Ibid. 805–60 (Herakles discovers the truth and resolves to rescue Alkestis), 1098ff (restores her to Admetos).

53 Phrynichos fr. 3 Snell. Thanatos appears in person at the beginning of Euripides' *Alcestis*, 24–76; Herakles explains that he has fought with him to recover Alkestis, ibid. 1140–2.

54 Pi. *Pyth.* 9.4–70; Kyrene's story was apparently recounted in the Hesiodic *Catalogue*, see frr. 215–16, but virtually nothing has survived.

55 A.R. 2.500–15.

56 D.S. 4.81.2–3.

57 See e.g. Nonnus 5.229ff.

58 See e.g. D.S. 4.82, Paus. 10.17.3.

59 Verg. *Georg.* 4.281–558.

60 Hom. *Il.* 9.555–64.

61 Schol. *Il.* 9.557, citing Simonides (= 563 *PMG*), Apollod. 1.7.8–9.

62 Schol. *Il.* 9.557; see also Bacch. fr.20 (Euenos roofed Poseidon's temple with the skulls of Marpessa's suitors).

63 Aesch. *Ag.* 1202–12, cf. Apollod. 3.12.5.

64 Pi. *Paean* 8a, cf. *Pyth.* 11.33 (*mantis*); Proclus on *Cypria*.

65 Schol. *Il.* 7.44. In Hyg. *Fab.* 93 the two versions are run together.

66 Ov. *Met.* 14.130ff.

67 Petronius *Satyricon* 48.8.

68 Parthen. *Narrat.*15, cf. Paus. 8.20 (Daphne here a daughter of Ladon; ends with death of Leukippos without mention of Daphne's transformation), Prob. *Ecl.* 3.62.

69 Ov. *Met.* 1.452–567; also a daughter of Peneios in Hyg. *Fab.* 203; laurel from Tempe, Call. fr. 194.

70 Schol. Lyc. 6, Liban. *Narrat.* 11.

71 Hes. *Theog.* 171; Eur. *Helen* 1469–74, Ov. *Met.* 10.162–219.

72 Zephyros as rival, Palaeph. 46, Lucian *D.D.* 14, cf. Paus. 3.19.4–5; Boreas as rival, Serv. *Ecl.* 3.63, Vat. Myth. 2.181.

73 From blood, Ov. *Met.* 10.196–216, Philostr. *Imag.* 1.34; from ashes, Philargyrius on *Ecl.* 3.63; full transformation, Servius on *Ecl.* 3.63.

74 Paus. 1.19.3–4.

75 Hom. *Il.* 24.599–617, Apollod. 3.5.6, D.S. 4.74.3, Ov. *Met.* 6.146–312; see also p. 306 and note.

76 Paus. 1.21.4, 8.2.5,7.

77 Hdt. 7.26 (skin at Kelainai, flayed by Apollo), Xen. *Anab.* 1.2.8 (skin, defeated in contest, no details); full narrative, Apollod. 1.4.2, Hyg. *Fab.* 165, cf. D.S. 3.59.2–5.

78 From his blood, Palaeph. 48, Hyg. *Fab.* 165, Vat. Myth. 1.15, etc.; from tears shed for him, Ov. *Met.* 6.383–400, cf. Vat. Myth. 1.15.

79 Ov. *Met.* 11.146–93.

80 Hyg. *Fab.* 191, Vat. Myth. 1.90.

81 Et. Magn s.v. Hermaion.

82 Hom. *Od.* 5.43ff, *Il.* 24.322ff respectively.

83 Hes. *Theog.* 938–19 (daughter of Atlas), *Hom. Hymn. Hermes* 1–16 (nymph), Apollod. 3.10.1–2.

84 *Hom. Hymn. Hermes* 17–18.

85 Ibid. 20–67.

86 Ibid. 68–86.

87 Ant. Lib. 23.3 and Apollod. 3.10.2 respectively.

88 *Hom. Hymn. Hermes* 87–93.

89 Ibid. 94–153.

90 Ibid. 154–83.

91 Ibid. 184–234.

92 Ibid. 235–396.

93 Ibid. 397–506.

94 Ibid. 507–80.

95 Ibid. 552–63.

96 Pher. 3F49.

97 Alcaeus 308.

98 Apollod. 3.10.2. In the *Hom. Hymn. Hermes*, 51, Hermes strings the lyre with sheep-gut.

99 Ant. Lib. 23.

100 Ov. *Met.* 2.676–707.

101 D.S. 4.6.5.

102 Ov. *Met.* 4.285–388; on pool, Str. 14.2.16.

103 Schol. Lyc. 1176.

104 Hom. *Il.* 1.577–9 and 14.338 with *Od.* 8.312.

105 Hes. *Theog.* 927–9, Apollod. 1.3.5 (also noting Homeric version), cf. the humorous treatment of the matter in Lucian *de Sacrificiis* 6.

106 Hom. *Il.* 18.395–405, cf. *Hom. Hymn. Apollo* 317–21 (tended by Thetis and her sisters).

107 Hom. *Il.* 1.590–4; Apollod. and Lucian ll.cc. both assume that he was lamed by the fall.

108 Paus. 1.20.2, Lib. *Narrat.* 30, Hyg. *Fab.* 166; for early records of the story, Alcaeus 349, Pi. fr. 283 SM.

109 Hom. *Il.* 1.597–600.

110 See esp. Hom. *Il.* 18.368–477.

111 Eratosth. 32 (Hes. fr. 148a). Forge on Lemnos, Cic. *N.D.* 3.22, schol. *Il.* 14.231.

112 Call. *Hymn* 4.141–7. Hephaestus is addressed as lord of Etna in Eur. *Cycl.* 599.

113 Thuc. 3.88 (reputed to be at Hiera in the Aeolian Islands); Call. *Hymn* 3.46–50 (at isle of Lipara), cf. A.R. 4.760–2 with schol. 761, Theoc. 2.133–4; Verg. *Aen.* 8.414–54 (Lipara, linked to Etna by an underground cavern and galleries).

114 Call. *Hymn* 3.46–60, cf. Verg. l.c.

115 His own house, Hom. *Il.* 18.369ff, houses for other gods, 1.605–8, cf. A.R. 3.36–8 (palace of Aphrodite).

116 Hom. *Il.* 20.10–12.

117 Ibid. 14.166–8, 338–9.

118 Paus. 10.5.5, Pi. *Paean* 11.

119 Hom. *Il.* 18.417–21 and 373–9 respectively.

120 Hom. *Od.* 7.91–4.

121 Hom. *Il.* 18.468ff, 8.194–5, 2.100–1 respectively.

122 Mimn. 12.

123 Hes. *Theog.* 945–6, Hom. *Il.* 18.382–3; cf. Hom. *Od.* 8.266ff, in which he is married to Aphrodite.

124 A.R. 1.202–6.

125 Paus. 2.31.4–5, Plut. *de Mus.* 5.

126 Hom. *Il.* 5.855–98.

127 Hom. *Il.* 13.301, *Od.* 8.361; cf. Hdt. 5.7, Soph. *Antig.* 969–70, Call. *Hymn* 4.63–5, etc.

128 Hom. *Il.* 5.855–67.

129 Ibid. 21.391–414.

130 Ibid. 5.840–5.

131 Hes. *Shield* 357–67, 424–66.

132 Hom. *Il.* 5.384–91.

133 Ibid. 5.333 and 592–3; as mother or daughter of Ares, schol. *Il.* 5.337, Cornutus 21; her statue in temple of Ares at Athens, Paus. 1.8.5.

134 Enyalios as title of Ares, Hom. *Il.* 13.518–22, 17.210–11, 20.69, Hes. *Shield* 371, A.R. 3.322 etc.; as separate deity, Alcman 44 (Alcman sometimes treated him as a separate deity and sometimes identified him with Ares), Arist. *Peace* 459, D.H. *Ant. Rom.* 3.48, schol. *Il.* 17.211; puppies sacrificed to him, Paus. 3.14.9.

135 Hom. *Il.* 4.440–1, cf. 5.518, 20.47–51; 11.3–14, 73–4, incites strife of war at bidding of Zeus; mentioned 18.535.

136 Hom. *Il.* 4.440, 15.119–20; 13.299 (Phobos a son of Ares), Hes. *Theog.* 933–6 (Deimos and Phobos his sons by Aphrodite); Hes. *Shield* 463–6 (D. and P. his charioteers); cult of Phobos at Sparta, Plut. *Cleomenes* 8–9.

137 Kydoimos and Ker, Hom. *Il.* 18.535–40, cf. Hes. *Shield* 156–60. For Kydoimos, see also *Il.* 5.591–3, Q.S. 1.307–11.

138 Hes. *Theog.* 933–7.

139 Simon. 575, Cic. *N.D.* 3.22, etc.

140 See e.g. the discussion and references in W. Burkert, *Greek Religion*, Cambridge, Mass., 1985, p.162.

141 Ov. *Met.* 3.259–298, cf. D.S. 3.64.3–4, Apollod. 3.4.3 (similar though less detailed); but in D.S. 4.2.1–3 Semele makes the fateful request on her own initiative. From the earlier tradition, see Eur. *Bacch.* 1–9 (Hera to blame for Semele's fate, no details).

142 Hyg. *Fab.* 167, 179.

143 Hom. *Il.* 14.325 (Semele bore Dionysos to Zeus), Hes. *Theog.* 941–3 (likewise, and that mother and child divinized), *Hom. Hymn* 1 *to Dionysos* (Zeus brought him to birth, but account lost; the epithet *eiraphiotes* as applied to Dionysos in lines 2, 17 and 20 is significant in this regard if it means 'insewn'); Pi. *Ol.* 2.25–6 (first states that Semele killed by thunderbolt), cf. Eur. *Bacch.* 6ff; full story of birth of D., D.S. 3.64.3–5 (cf. 4.2.3), Apollod. 3.4.3, Ov. *Met.* 3.298–315.

144 *Hom. Hymn* 1 *to Dionysos* 1–8, *Hom. Hymn* 26 *to Dionysos* 1–6.

145 E.g. D.S. 4.2.3.

146 Hom. *Il.* 6.132–3.

147 Hesych. s.v. Nysa.

148 Ov. *Met.* 7.294–6.

149 Pher. 3F90, Apollod. 3.4.3.

150 Paus. 3.24.3–4.

151 Hom. *Il.* 6.130–40.

152 Apollod. 3.5.1.

153 Soph. *Antig.* 955–6, Str. 10.3.16, Apollod. 3.5.1, etc.

154 Hyg. *Fab.* 132; self-mutilation also in Serv. *Aen.* 3.14, Vat. Myth. 1.122.

155 Hyg. *Fab.* 242.

156 Soph. *Antig.* 955–65.

157 Eumelus *Europeia* fr. 1 Davies.

158 Stes. 234.

159 Eur. *Bacch.* 23–42.

160 Ibid. 215–58.

161 Ibid. 576–970.

162 Ibid. 971–1215.

163 Ibid. 1280–1392. On this myth, see also Apollod. 3.5.2, Ov. *Met.* 3.511–733, Hyg. *Fab.* 184.

164 Ant. Lib. 10; on death of Hippasos, see also Plut. *Quaest. Graec.* 38.

165 Ael. *V.H.* 3.42.

166 Ov. *Met.* 3.1–41, 389–415.

167 Suid. s.v. Melanaigis.

168 Ov. *Met.* 3.559–60, 4.607–14.

169 Schol. *Il.* 1.59.

170 Paus. 2.20.3, 2.22.1.

171 Augustine *City of God* 18.12 and schol. *Il.* 14.319 respectively.

172 Paus. 2.23.8.

173 He is 'many-named', Soph. *Antig.* 1115; some samples of his many names are given by Ov. *Met.* 4.11ff.

174 Euripides' *Bacchae* and its commentators (especially E.R. Dodds) are very informative on these matters.

175 Both versions in Hyg. *Astr.* 2.4.

176 Apollod. 3.14.7, Hyg. *Fab.* 130, *Astr.* 2.4, schol. *Il.* 22.29, Prob. *Georg.* 2.385.

177 Hyg. ll.cc., Serv. *Georg.* 2.389.

178 Hyg. *Astr.* 2.4.
179 Ibid. and *Fab.* 230 (the suggestion that Canicula can be identified with Procyon, i.e. the constellation of the Lesser Dog, is erroneous; it is really the dog-star, Greek Seirios).
180 *Hom. Hymn 7 to Dionysos* 2–6.
181 Ibid. 6–57.
182 Ov. *Met.* 3.582–3, 687–91, cf. Hyg. *Fab.* 134, Serv. *Aen.* 4.469.
183 Apollod. 3.5.3; Naxos as destination, Ov. *Met.* 3.636ff, Hyg. *Fab.* 134, Vat. Myth. 1.122 and generally in later sources.
184 Apollod. 3.5.3, cf. Ov. *Met.* 3.658–69, Hyg. *Fab.* 134, Nonnus 45.105ff, etc.
185 Hyg. *Astr.* 2.17.
186 Nonnus *D.*, cf. Eur. *Bacch.* 13ff, D.S. 3.37.3–6, Paus. 10.29.2.
187 Hes. *Theog.* 947–9.
188 Children listed in late sources only, notably Apollod. *Epit.* 1.9 (Thoas, Staphylos, Oinopion and Peparethos), schol. A.R. 3.997 (Oinopion, Thoas, Staphylos, Latramys, Euanthes, Tauropolis). There was an alternative tradition in which Oinopion and Staphylos were children of Theseus and Ariadne, Ion of Chios 204 (as cited in Plut. *Thes.* 20).
189 Ov. *Fast.* 3.409ff, Nonnus 10.175ff.
190 Hyg. *Fab.* 129, cf. Apollod. 1.8.1.
191 Ov. *Met.* 6.125.
192 Nonnus 15.169–16.405.
193 *Hom. Hymn 28 to Athena*, cf. Stes. 233.
194 Pi. *Ol.* 7.35–8 (Hephaistos), Eur. *Ion* 452–7 (Prometheus), Apollod. 1.3.6 (Hephaistos or Prometheus), Lucian *D.D.* 8 (Hephaistos), schol. Pi. *Ol.* 7.66 (Palamaon or Hermes).
195 Aesch. *Eum.* 292–3, Eur. *Ion* 872, cf. Apollod. 1.3.6 (born by river Triton) and 3.2.3 (reared by god Triton), schol. A.R. 1.109.
196 Paus. 9.33.5 and 8.26.6 respectively.
197 Pi. *Ol.* 7.39–53, D.S. 5.56.5–7.
198 Hom. *Il.* 8.373.
199 Maiden, Str. 17.816; brandishing, schol. *Il.* 1.200, Vat. Myth. 1.124, etc. Other explanations of a less plausible nature were also offered.
200 Philodem. *de Piet.* p. 6 Gomperz.
201 Apollod. 3.12.3.
202 Apollod. 1.6.2, schol. Lyc. 355; hence her title of Pallas, schol. *Il.* 1.200, Vat. Myth. 1.124.
203 Pi. *Ol.* 13.63–86.
204 Paus. 2.21.3.
205 Pi. *Pyth.* 12.6–12.
206 Apollod. 1.4.2, Hyg. *Fab.* 145 (Hera and Aphrodite made fun of her, and she understood the reason when she viewed her reflection in a spring as she played); cf. Melanippides 758, Palaeph. 47, Ov. *Fast.* 6.697.
207 Hom. *Il.* 9.389–90, *Od.* 7.110, 20.72.
208 Hom. *Il.* 5.733–5, 14.178–9, cf. A.R. 1.721ff (Jason's cloak).
209 Ov. *Met.* 6.1–145; allusion in Verg. *Georg.* 4.246.
210 Eratosth. 13, Hyg. *Astr.* 2.13, both citing Euripides.
211 Hyg. *Fab.* 166.
212 Apollod. 3.14.6.
213 As stated in Hyg. *Fab.* 166; the preceding etymology is merely implied.
214 E.g. Apollod. 3.14.6; see further in Chapter 10.
215 Hom. *Il.* 21.471.

216 *Hom. Hymn. Aphrodite* 15–20.
217 Hom. *Od.* 6.102–8, translated on p. 188.
218 Aesch. *Ag.* 140–3.
219 Schol. *Il.* 20.67.
220 Plut. *Moralia* 659a.
221 Hes. fr. 23b.
222 Aesch. *Suppl.* 676, cf. Eur. *Phoen.* 108–10.
223 Hom. *Il.* 21.470.
224 Ibid. 21.471–96.
225 Hom. *Od.* 6.102–8.
226 Ibid. 11.321–5, 5.121–4.
227 Ibid. 11.171–3, 15.478–9.
228 Hom. *Il.* 6.205.
229 *Hom. Hymn. Apollo* 25–90.
230 Ibid. 91–119; Artemis on Ortygia, 14–18. See also the shorter accounts of the birth of the twins in Theognis 5–10 and Pi. *Paean* 12.
231 Call. *Hymn* 4.55–227.
232 Apollod. 1.4.1; on Artemis as midwife of Apollo, cf. Serv. *Aen.* 3.73, Vat. Myth. 1.37 (which says that this is why the virgin goddess is invoked by women in childbirth).
233 Hyg. *Fab.* 140, cf. Serv. *Aen.* 3.73 (Hera incites Python to pursue the pregnant Leto).
234 Pi. *Paean* 7b.43–52, Call. *Hymn* 4.35–40, Apollod. 1.4.1 (Asterie then turned herself into a quail), Hyg. *Fab.* 53 (transformed by Zeus), Serv. *Aen.* 3.73.
235 Ant. Lib. 35.
236 Ov. *Met.* 6.317–81.
237 Hdt. 4.33–5.
238 Call. *Hymn* 4.291–9; for Hekaerge, cf. Paus. 5.7.8.
239 Paus. 10.23.3.
240 Aristotle *History of Animals* 6.35, schol. A.R. 2.124.
241 E.g. Paus. 2.7.7.
242 E.g. Apollod. 3.8.2, Ov. *Met.* 2.401–95; full references will be given in connection with the main discussion in Chapter 15.
243 Hom. *Od.* 11.326 and schol. (citing Pherecydes = 3F170).
244 Call. fr. 569.
245 Eur. *Helen* 381–3.
246 Call. *Hymn* 3.189–200, cf. Paus. 2.30.3, D.S. 5.76.3–4 (rejects usual story, claims that Britomartis was called Diktynna because she invented hunting-nets), ps.Verg. *Ciris* 284ff, schol. Eur. *Hippol.* 146.
247 Call. *Hymn* 3.220–3.
248 Ant. Lib. 40.
249 Paus. 8.27.17.
250 Ant. Lib. 17.
251 Paus. 6.22.8–10.
252 Hyg. *Fab.* 200, Ov. *Met.* 11.291–345.
253 Hes. *Theog.* 404–12.
254 Ibid. 411–52.
255 *Hom. Hymn. Demeter* 24–5, 52–9, 438–40.
256 E.g. Eur. *Helen* 569–70, *Ion* 1048–50, Soph. fr. 492 Nauck, Arist. fr. 500, 501 Kock.
257 See e.g. Arist. *Wealth* 595 with schol. 594.
258 Eur. *Med.* 395ff, cf. A.R. 3.251–2, 477–80, 528–30, etc.; Theoc. 2.10–16.
259 Hes. *Theog.* 188–202, Hom. *Il.* 5.370–1 with 3.374.

260 Kypris, Hom. *Il.* 5.330, 422, etc.; her sanctuary at Paphos in Cyprus, Hom. *Od.* 8.362–3, *Hom. Hymn. Aphrodite* 58–9.

261 Hes. *Theog.* 192–3; sanctuary, Hdt. 1.105, Paus. 3.23.1.

262 Pl. *Symp.* 180de, Xen. *Symp.* 8.9.

263 Paus. 1.22.3.

264 Theoc. *Epigram* 13, Paus. 9.16.2.

265 Pi. fr. 107 (Bowra).

266 Hes. *Theog.* 120–2 (in cosmogony), 201–2 (with Aphrodite).

267 Simon. 575.

268 Sappho 130, 47, 188, Ibycus 287.

269 Eur. *Med.* 530–1, cf. *Iph. Aul.* 544ff.

270 Paus. 9.27.1.

271 A.R. 3.83–166 (Aphrodite bribes him to take action), 275–98 (he shoots an arrow into Medeia).

272 Ov. *Met.* 1.452–77.

273 Apuleius *Golden Ass* 4.28–6.26.

274 Hes. *Theog.* 201–2, 62–5.

275 Aesch. *Suppl.* 1035–43; Arist. *Peace* 456, Lucian *D.D.* 20.16, *Anth. Pal.* 12.157, etc.

276 Paus. 1.30.1.

277 Paus. 6.23.3,5.

278 Ezekiel 8.14, *et ecce ibi mulieres sedebant plangentes Adonidem*; the Pentateuch and the Authorized Version keep the name Thamouz/Tammuz as in the Hebrew text.

279 Apollod. 3.14.4, Ov. *Met.* 10.298–514, schol. Lyc. 829, Serv. *Ecl.* 10.18, etc.; much of this may go back to Panyasis, see fr. 22 Davies. See also Hyg. *Fab.* 58 (somewhat different).

280 Ant. Lib. 34.

281 Hes. fr. 139, Ov. *Met.* 10.322, Hyg. *Fab.* 58, schol. *Il.* 5.385.

282 E.g. Hyg. *Fab.* 58, schol. Lyc. 829.

283 Ov. *Met.* 10.469–502.

284 Hes. fr. 139.

285 Apollod. 3.14.4.

286 Both variants in schol. Lyc. 831; see also Serv. *Aen.* 5.72, *Ecl.* 10.18, schol. Theoc. 1.3 and 47.

287 Apollod. 3.14.4, cf. Eur. *Hippol.* 1420–2 (probable allusion).

288 Hyg. *Astr.* 2.6.

289 Ov. *Met.* 10.535–727.

290 Ov. *Met.* 10.728–39.

291 Bion 1 (Lament for Adonis), 64–7, schol. Lyc. 831, Serv. *Ecl.* 10.18 respectively.

292 Sappho 140a; Bion 1.

293 Rites of Adonis, see e.g. Plut. *Nicias* 13 (regarding an event set in 415 BC), Arist. *Lysistr.* 388ff (refers to same event); gardens of Adonis, Hesych. and Suid. s.v *Adonidos kepoi* (and paroemiographers on the same), Pl. *Phdr.* 276b, Theophrastus *History of Plants* 6.7.3.

294 Hom. *Il.* 20.230–41.

295 Thus *Hom. Hymn. Aphrodite* 45ff.

296 Ibid. 58–171.

297 Ibid. 172–290.

298 Soph. fr. 373 Radt, Hyg. *Fab.* 94 (boasted to companions over wine), Verg. *Aen.* 2.648–9 with Servius ad loc.

299 Hom. *Od.* 8.266–366.

300 Pi. *Pyth.* 4.87–8, Aesch. *Suppl.* 664–5 (her *eunator*).

301 Paus. 2.25.1.

302 Paus. 3.17.5.

303 Hes. *Theog.* 933–7 (together with Panic and Fear, see p. 169, who are very much their father's children).

304 Ael. *V.H.* 12.18 (states that executed for adultery), Palaeph. 49, Serv. *Aen.* 3.279.

305 Athen. 2.69d, citing Cratinus (= fr. 370 *PCG*), cf. Ael. l.c.

306 Str. 10.2.9 (quoting Menander = fr. 285 K.), Suid. s.v. Sappho (second notice).

307 Ov. *Her.* 15.

6 LESSER DEITIES AND NATURE-SPIRITS

1 Hes. *Theog.* 52–5, 915–17, cf. Alcman 8.9–10, *Hom. Hymn. Hermes* 429, Apollod. 1.3.1, etc.

2 D.S. 4.7.1, citing Alcman (= 67 *PMG*) and others unnamed.

3 Paus. 9.29.2, citing Mimnermus (= 13 West), schol. A.R. 3.1.

4 Hes. *Theog.* 22–34.

5 Ibid. 36–52.

6 Hom. *Il.* 1.1 ('Sing, goddess, of the wrath of Peleus' son Achilles'), and 2.484–93.

7 Hom. *Il.* 2.485–6.

8 Hes. *Theog.* 75–9, 916–17.

9 Hom. *Od.* 24.60.

10 Hes. *Theog.* 68.

11 For such differentiations, see e.g. schol. A.R. 3.1, *Anth. Pal.* 9, 504 and 505, *Anth. Latin.* 88 and 664, D.S. 4.7.3–4.

12 Hom. *Il.* 2.491, 484; Hes. *Theog.* 1–23.

13 Hes. *W.D.* 1, *Theog.* 53–5 (born in Pieria), cf. *Theog.* 25, 36ff on Olympian Muses.

14 Solon 1.2, Hes. *Shield* 206.

15 Paus. 9.29.2 (Helikonian Muses), Plut. *Symp.* 9.14 (Sicyonian; and also referring to three Delphian Muses named Nete, Mese and Hypate); on this question, see also e.g. D.S. 4.7.2, Arnob. *Adv. Nat.* 3.47, Serv.*Aen.* 1.12.

16 Hom. *Il.* 2.594–600 (599–600 quoted).

17 Asclep. 12F10. For the earlier tradition, see also Hes. fr. 65 (Thamyris blinded in Dotian Fields), *Minyas* fr. 4 Davies (T. pays the penalty in Hades for his boast; from Paus. 4.33.7), Eur. *Rhes.* 923–5 (blinded).

18 Apollod. 1.3.3.

19 Pollux 4.141.

20 Ant. Lib. 9, following Nicander.

21 Ov. *Met.* 5.294–317, 662–78.

22 Paus. 9.34.2, Steph.Byz. s.v. Aptera (contest took place at Aptera in Crete).

23 All mentioned as children of Muses in Apollod. 1.3.2–4.

24 Ov. *Met.* 5.273–92.

25 Hes. *Theog.* 907–11, Apollod. 1.3.1.

26 Hom. *Il.* 5.338, *Od.* 8.359–66.

27 *Hom. Hymn* 5 *to Aphrodite* 58–63.

28 Hes. *Theog.* 60–5.

29 Sappho 53 (invoked on their own), 103, 128 (with Muses); Pi.*Ol.* 14.1–17, 9.26–8, *Nem.* 4.6–8, 9.53–5, *Pyth.* 6.1–3, 9.89–90, etc.; cf. Bacch. 19.1–6, Eur. *Madness of Herakles* 673–5.

30 Hes. *Theog.* 909.

31 Pi. *Ol.* 14.8–9.

32 E.g. *Hom. Hymn. Apollo* 186–96, Theogn. 15–18.

33 Paus. 9.35.1.

34 Hes. *Theog.* 945–6, Hom. *Il.* 14.264–8.

35 Paus. 9.38.1; the Charites of Orchomenos are invoked in Pi. *Ol.* 14.

36 Hes. *Theog.* 901–3; on their civic role, see also Pi. *Ol.* 13.6–8.

37 Paus. 9.35.1.

38 *Hom. Hymn 6 to Aphrodite* 1–15, cf. *Cypria* fr. 4 Davies (garments made for Aphrodite by Horai and Charites), Hes. *W.D.* 73–5 (adorning of newly created Pandora).

39 Hom. *Il.* 5.749–51, 8.393–5.

40 Hom. *Il.* 6.420, *Od.* 13.356, etc.

41 Hom. *Od.* 13.355–60, 17.239–46, 9.154–5. See also ibid. 13.102ff for the sacred cave of the nymphs by the shore at Ithaca.

42 Hom. *Il.* 20.7–9.

43 Hes. fr. 304.

44 *Hom. Hymn. Aphrodite* 257–72.

45 Schol. Lyc. 480; cf. Eumelus fr. 11 Davies as reported in Apollod. 3.9.1 (that Arkas fathered his two sons by the nymph Chrysopeleia).

46 Schol. A.R. 2.477.

47 A.R. 2.462–79.

48 D.S. 4.84.2–4, Ael. *V.H.* 10.18.

49 Ov. *Met.* 4.276–7, Serv. *Ecl.* 5.20.

50 Theoc. 1.64ff.

51 Hes. fr. 10a.17–19.

52 Pi. fr. 143 Bowra.

53 Arist. Fr.44 Rose (from Plut. *Moralia* 115de), cf. Cic. *Tusc.* 1.48; caught in the 'Gardens of Midas' in Macedonia, Hdt. 8.138; Midas caught 'the Satyr' at a spring in Phrygia by mixing wine into it Xen. *Anab.* 1.2.13; in Theopompus 115F75c (as cited in Ael. *V.H.* 3.18), Midas delivers a moral lecture to Midas by telling him of the contrasting ways of life of some imaginary peoples in an imaginary geographical setting.

54 Paus. 6.24.8 and 1.23.6 respectively.

55 Ov. *Met.* 11.85–145.

56 Theoc. 1.15–18.

57 See e.g. Paus. 10.23.5–6 (description of Panic terror in war), Polyaen. *Strateg.* 1.2 (Pan as general and tactical innovator).

58 Shepherd-god, lover of music, *Hom. Hymn 19 to Pan* 1-.26; Pan *philochoros*, Aesch. *Pers.* 448; his skill on the 'pan-pipes', Theoc. 1.2–3, Verg. *Ecl.* 4.56–9, etc.

59 E.g. Cornutus 67.

60 Pl. *Crat.* 408b, *Hom. Hymn. Pan* 47.

61 *Hom. Hymn. Pan* 27–47.

62 Hdt. 2.145, cf. Apollod. *Epit.* 7.38, Hyg. *Fab.* 224, Lucian *D.D.* 22.2.

63 E.g. Hecat. 1F371, Theoc. *Syrinx* 1ff, schol. Lyc. 772 respectively.

64 Apollod. 1.4.1, Ael. *N.A.* 6.42 respectively.

65 Ov. *Met.* 1.689–712, cf. Westermann anon. p.347; rationalized version, Longus 2.34, Achilles Tatius 8.6 (set near Ephesus with local aetiology).

66 Nonnus 42.258ff (simpler version), Liban. *Narrat.* 27 and 28 (version involving Boreas); allusions to the story in Theoc. *Syrinx* 4, Propertius 1.18.20, Lucian *D.D.* 22.4, etc. Pan's pine-crown, Lucretius 4.584–5.

67 *Daphnis and Chloe* 3.23; allusions to Pan's love for Echo in Theoc. *Syrinx* 5, Moschus 5.1–4.

68 Ov. *Met.* 3.341–510.

69 Conon 24 and Serv. *Ecl.* 2.47 respectively.

70 Paus. 9.31.6.

71 Hdt. 6.105, Paus. 1.28.4.

72 Plut. *Moralia* 419b.

73 Paus. 7.17.5, Arnob. *Adv. Nat.* 5.5–7.

74 Sallustius *On Gods and Universe* 4, cf. Ov. *Fasti* 4.223ff.

75 D.S. 3.58–9.

76 Hes. fr. 10a.17–19.

77 Call. *Hymn* 1.51–3, Eur. *Bacch.* 120ff, cf. Apollod. 1.1.6–7, D.S. 5.65.4.

78 For translation and discussion, see W.K.C. Guthrie, *The Greeks and their Gods*, London, 1950, 46ff.

79 Pher. 3F48 (children of Apollo and Rhytia), Apollod. 1.3.4 (of Apollo and the Muse Thalia), Str. 10.3.19 (various).

80 Pl. *Laws* 790c–791a.

81 Eur. *Bacch.* 120–34.

82 Diogenes Laertius 6.59.

83 Pher. 3F48, Acus. 2F40.

84 Paus. 9.25.6, with evidence from the visual arts and votive inscriptions (referring to Kabeiro and *pais*, i.e. child or son).

85 Schol. A.R. 1.917.

86 Anonymus Ambrosianus *De. Re. Metr.* 2.6 (in *Analecta Studemundi* 1, p. 224).

87 A.R. 1.1129–31 with schol.

88 D.S. 5.64.3; five of each sex, Soph. fr. 366 Radt, Str. 10.3.22.

89 D.S. 5.64.3, Pher. 3F47.

90 *Phoronis* fr. 2 Davies, cf. Hes. fr. 282 (discovered metal-working in Crete), Str. 10.3.22.

91 D.S. 17.7.5.

92 Ov. *Met.* 4.281–2, Soph. fr 365 Radt.

93 D.S. 5.64.6–7, Paus. 8.31.3.

94 Suid. s.v. Telchines.

95 D.S. 5.55.3.

96 Call. *Hymn* 4.30–1 and Str. 14.2.7 respectively.

97 D.S. 5.55.3.

98 Str. 14.2.7, Zenob. 5.41.

99 Call. fr. 75.64–9, Ov. *Met.* 7.365–7, Serv. *Aen.* 4.377, schol. Stat. *Theb.* 2.274.

100 D.S. 5.55.1.

101 Ov. *Met.* 13.917–65, Paus. 9.22.5, schol. Lyc. 754, schol. Eur. *Orest.* 364.

102 Aesch. *Glaukos Pontios*, fr. 25–9 Radt.

103 A.R. 1.1310–28.

104 Eur. *Orest.* 362–9.

105 Schol. A.R. 1.932; for Hellespontine traditions regarding his birth, see also schol. Theoc. 1.81, Tzetz. Lyc. 831.

106 Ov. *Fasti* 1.391–440.

107 Ibid. *Fasti* 6.319–48.

108 Ov. *Met.* 9.340–7.

109 Hyg. *Astr.* 2.23.

110 Asclep. 12F6, Suid, s.v. Thamyris, schol. Eur. *Rhes.* 342, etc.

111 E.g. Seneca *Medea* 110ff, Serv. *Aen.* 4.127 (Dionysos and Aphrodite).

112 E.g. Serv. *Aen.* 1.651, Eustath. on *Il.* 18.493, Serv. *Aen.* 4.127 respectively.

113 Schol. *Il.* 18.493, Vat. Myth. 1.74.

114 Apollod. 3.10.3, citing 'the Orphics'.

115 Ant. Lib. 23, Serv. *Ecl.* 8.30, Suid. s.v. Thamyris, Athen. 603d respectively.

116 Hyg. *Fab.* 273.

117 Plut. *Moralia* 357ff.

118 Ov. *Met.* 1.149–50, Juvenal 6.19–20.

119 Aratus 100–36.

120 Ibid. 98–9.

121 Stat. *Theb.* 4.514–15.

122 Lactant. on ibid. 516.

7 THE EARLY HISTORY OF THE INACHIDS

1 Apollod. 2.1.1; Hyg. *Fab.* 143 (Argia).

2 *Phoronis* fr.1 Davies, cf. Acus. 2F23.

3 Paus. 2.15.5.

4 Hyg. *Fab.* 143.

5 Paus. 2.15.5.

6 Paus. 2.19.5, schol. Soph. *El.* 4.

7 Apollod. 2.1.1, Paus. 2.22.1, schol. Eur. *Orest.* 932 respectively.

8 Apollod. 2.1.1, Paus. 2.22.6 (grove).

9 Hes. fr. 124, Acus. 2F26 (both from Apollod. 2.1.3).

10 E.g. Apollod. 2.1.2–3, Paus. 2.16.1.

11 Apollod. 2.1.3 (ascribed to 'many of the tragedians'), Aesch. *Prom. Bound* 590, Hdt. 1.1, Ov. *Met.* 1.584, etc.

12 Apollod. 2.1.1–3.

13 Aesch. *Suppl.* 291–305.

14 Apollod. 2.1.3.

15 Ov. *Met.* 1.668–721.

16 As stated in Hes. fr. 126, Apollod. 2.1.3.

17 Pher. 3F66, Hes. fr. 294 from *Aigimios*. Argos earthborn, Acus. 2F27 (from Apollod. l.c.), Aesch. *Suppl.* 305, *Prom. Bound* 567; son of Arestor, also Hes. fr. 246, schol. Eur. *Phoen.* 1116; son of Agenor, Apollod. l.c.; son of Peiranthos, Hyg. *Fab.* 145.

18 Soph. *Inachos* fr. 281 Radt, schol. Eur. *Phoen.* 1116.

19 Apollod. 2.1.2.

20 Moschus 2.55–60, Ov. *Met.* 1.720–3, Vat. Myth. 1.18 respectively.

21 A.R. 1.111–12, 324–5.

22 Apollod. 2.1.1–3.

23 Acus. 2F24 (see Paus. 2.16.3).

24 Paus. 2.17.5, Euseb. 3.8.1.

25 Aesch. *Prom. Bound.* 640–86; Zeus touches her in Egypt and Epaphos is thus born there, ibid. 847–51.

26 Ov. *Met.* 1.568ff; writes with hoof in dust, 649–50.

27 Hes. fr. 296 (Euboea named after cow), Str. 10.1.3 (named after her because she gave birth to Epaphos in cave there), Et. Magn. s.v. Euboia and Steph. Byz. s.v. Argoura (both quoted under Hes. fr. 296).

28 Apollod. 2.1.3, cf. Aesch. *Suppl.* 540–73; etymology for Ionian Gulf, Apollod. l.c., Aesch. *Prom. Bound* 840–1.

29 Aesch. *Prom. Bound* 786–815; Apollod. l.c. also refers to Io's passage through the 'Cimmerian land'.

30 Apollod. 2.1.3; on the touch of Zeus, Aesch. *Suppl.* 311–14, 584–9, *Prom. Bound* 847–51, Moschus 2.50–2.

31 Identified with Isis, Call. *Epigr.* 57 (first mention), Apollod. 2.1.3, Ov. *Met.* 1.747, Hyg. *Fab.* 145 (Zeus made her a goddess of the Egyptians called Isis), Lucian *D.D.* 3, etc. The Greeks also identified Isis with Demeter as Apollodorus remarks, cf. Hdt. 2.59, 156. Epaphos identified with Apis, Hdt. 2.153, 3.27.

32 Apollod. 2.1.3.

33 Pi. *Nem.* 10.5, Hyg. *Fab.* 149, 275, cf. Aesch. *Prom. Bound* 810–15 (the 'distant colony' here is evidently Memphis).

34 Memphis, Apollod. 2.1.4, schol. Lyc. 894; Kassiepeia, Hyg. *Fab.* 149.

35 Apollod. 2.1.4, cf. Aesch. *Suppl.* 314–16, Pi. *Pyth.* 4.14–15.

36 Apollod. 2.1.4, cf. Hes. frr. 137–8 (Belos and Agenor mentioned, but no surviving record of parentage), Aesch. *Suppl.* 317 (Belos as son of Libye), Moschus 2.38–40 (Libye seduced by Poseidon).

37 See e.g. Apollod. 3.1.1. with 3.4.1.

38 Apollod. 2.1.4, cf. Aesch. *Suppl.* 315–23.

39 They were described as such by Euripides, for instance, according to Apollod. l.c.

40 Hes. fr. 137 (cited by Str., 1.2.34, who ascribes the same to Stesichorus).

41 Apollod. 2.1.4, *Danais* fr. 1 Davies. Aigyptos could fear for his own part that Danaos would become too powerful through marriage-alliances if he married his daughters elsewhere, cf. Serv. *Aen.* 10.497.

42 Apollod. 2.1.4 (ship described as first of kind), cf. Aesch. *Prom. Bound* 853–6, Hyg. *Fab.* 168.

43 Schol. *Il.* 1.42, schol. Eur. *Orest.* 872, schol. Stat. *Theb.* 2.222.

44 Apollod. 2.1.4, Hdt. 2.182, Call. fr. 100, D.S. 5.58.1, Str. 14.2.8, 11.

45 Paus. 2.19.3 (wolf story), 2.16.1 (descent of Gelanor), Apollod. 2.1.4 (merely that Gelanor surrendered the kingdom to Danaos).

46 Apollod. 2.1.5, cf. Aesch. *Prom. Bound* 859–69, Hyg. *Fab.* 168.

47 Apollod. 2.1.5.

48 Pi. *Pyth.* 9.111–16.

49 Paus. 3.12.2.

50 Ps.Pl. *Axiochos* 371e (probably first century BC) is our first literary source for the Danaids as water-carriers, but they already appear as such in southern Italian vase-paintings of the fourth century BC; also in Ovid *Ibis* 177–8, 355–6, Horace *Ode* 3.11.22–32, Lucian *D.M.* 8, etc.

51 Paus. 2.24.3.

52 Zenob. 4.86.

53 Tzetz. *Chil.* 2.254–7.

54 Apollod. 2.1.5.

55 Schol. Eur. *Orest.* 872 citing Phrynichos (= fr.1 Snell), Paus. 7.21.6.

56 Apollod. 2.1.4, Hyg. *Fab.* 169.

57 Hyg. *Fab.* 169A. On this episode, see also Aesch. frr. 128–33 Mette, Propertius 2.26.45–50, Lucian *D.M.* 8.

58 Paus. 2.37.5.

59 Hes. fr. 128, Call. fr. 65, 66, Str. 8.6.8, schol. Eur. *Phoen.* 188.

60 Pher. 3F4, Apollod. 2.1.4; as founder of Nauplion, Paus. 2.38.2.

61 A.R. 1.133–8.

62 Apollod. 2.1.5, citing *Returns* (= fr. 1 Davies) and the tragic poets.

63 Apollod. 2.1.5 etc.

64 Ibid., schol. Eur. *Hec.* 886 respectively; or because of her desire for children according to Aesch. *Prom. Bound* 865–7. See also Pi. *Nem.* 1.6 (Hypermnestra alone kept sword in scabbard) and Horace's fine lines in *Ode* 3.11.33–52 (which suggest that she will be parted from Lynkeus forever, cf. Ov. *Heroides* 14).

65 Paus. 2.25.4.

66 Apollod. 2.1.5 (imprisoned by Danaos), Paus. 2.19.6 (trial, statue), 2.20.5 (site of trial), 2.21.1 (sanctuary).

67 Apollod. 2.1.5.

68 Schol. Eur. *Hec.* 886, Serv. *Aen.* 10.497, cf. Archil. 305.

69 Apollod. 2.2.1, Paus. 2.16.1.

70 Hyg. *Fab.* 170.

71 *Pp. Oxy.* 10.1241 Col. IV l. 13–14, Serv. *Aen.* 3.286, Apollod. 2.2.1 respectively.

72 Paus. 2.20.4, 2.21.2.

73 Apollod. 2.2.1, cf. Hes. fr. 129, Bacch. 11.65–9.

74 Schol. *Il.* 2.536, schol. Pi. *Pyth.* 8.73, Steph. Byz. s.v. Abantis.

75 Apollod. 2.2.1; cf. the similar tradition about Krisos and Panopeus, p. 565, and the Hebrew story of Jacob and Esau, *Genesis* 25.22–3.

76 Paus. 2.25.6, Hesych. s.v. Daulis.

77 Apollod. 2.2.1.

78 Hom. *Il.* 6.160ff.

79 Bacch. 11.64–72. On this conflict, see also schol. Eur. *Orest.* 965.

80 Apollod. 2.2.2, cf. Hes. fr. 129.24 for names of daughters; there are two Proitides only, Lysippe and Iphianassa, in Pher. 3F114, and their names vary to differing extents in other sources.

81 See e.g. Apollod. 2.2.2, Hdt. 9.34.

82 Eustath. Hom. p. 1480.4.

83 Apollod. 2.4.1, Pher. 3F10. Pherecydes seems to have been Apollodorus' main source for his account of the life of Perseus.

84 Horace *Ode* 3.16.1–4, Ov. *Met.* 4.697–8.

85 First Pi. *Pyth.* 12.17–18, Pher. 3F10, Soph. *Antig.* 944–50; possibly in Hes. fr. 135, but the papyrus is too poorly preserved for it to be possible to tell whether the 'golden' in line 5 has anything to do with a shower of gold.

86 Apollod. 2.4.1, Pher. 3F10, schol. *Il.* 14.319; the main features of the story already in Hes. fr. 135.

87 Pi. fr. 284 SM (in schol. *Il.* cit.); cited as variant in Apollod. 2.4.1.

88 Simon. 543.

89 Apollod. 2.4.1, Pher. 3F10; descent of Diktys and brother, Apollod. 1.9.6, Hes. fr. 8; alternative genealogy, Pher. 3F4.

90 Apollod. 2.4.2, Pher. 3F11; allusion to *eranos*, Pi. *Pyth.* 12.14–15.

91 Although Apollodorus' language is somewhat ambiguous, we should surely understand that Polydektes refuses to *take* the contribution from Perseus, rather than that he fails to *get* it; this is made absolutely clear by Pherecydes, who was probably Apollodorus' source at this point. Pherecydes also indicates that each guest was expected to contribute a single horse; Apollodorus' reference to 'horses' in connection with Perseus is probably an error.

92 Pher. 3F11, Apollod. 2.4.2–3, cf. Hes. *Shield* 216–37, Ov. *Met.* 4.770–86; decapitation of Medusa and birth of her two children in Hes. *Theog.* 278–83.

93 See Hyg. *Astr.* 2.12 and Eratosth. 22 along with other material cited under Aesch. fr. 262 Radt.

94　Apollod. 2.4.3 (gains marriage-promise from Kepheus), Eur. *Andromeda*, fr. 132 Nauck
　　(from Andromeda herself); full narrative Ov. *Met.* 4.665–764; Eratosth. 15 and 17,
　　Hyg. *Astr.* 2.9 and 11 (exposure of Andromeda in Euripides' play), Eratosth. 16 and
　　36, Hyg. *Astr.* 2.10 (Kassiepeia had claimed to rival the Nereids in beauty in Sophocles'
　　Andromeda), Hyg. *Fab.* 64 (K. claimed that A.'s beauty surpassed that of Nereids),
　　schol. Lyc. 836 (Perseus turned monster to stone).

95　As can be inferred from the fragments of Euripides' *Andromeda*.

96　Apollod. 2.4.3, Hyg. *Fab.* 64 (Agenor).

97　Ov. *Met.* 5.1–47.

98　Apollod. 2.4.3 with 2.4.5 (Perses); on Perses, see also Hdt. 7.61, Hellanic. 4F59.

99　Polyidos 837 *PMG*, Ov. *Met.* 4.631–62.

100　A.R. 4.1504–17, Ov. *Met.* 4.617–20.

101　Apollod. 2.4.3, Pher. 3F11; cf. Pi. *Pyth.* 10.46–8 and 12.12 (turned islanders to stone,
　　without further details).

102　Ov. *Met.* 5.242–9, Serv. *Aen.* 6.289.

103　Apollod. 2.4.3, Pher. 3F11.

104　Pi. *Pyth.* 12.14–15.

105　Hyg. *Fab.* 63.

106　Pher. 3F12, Paus. 2.16.2.

107　Apollod. 2.4.4 (it is possible, however, that this is simply a careless summary of
　　Pherecydes' version).

108　Apollod. 2.4.4, schol. A.R. 4.1091 (*hērōon*); or Clem. Alex. *Protrep.* 3.45, buried in
　　temple of Athena on acropolis of city.

109　Apollod. 2.4.4, Paus. 2.16.3.

110　Both etymologies in Paus. 2.16.3; the first also in Hecat. 1F22, Steph. Byz. s.v.
　　Mykenai.

111　Paus. 2.16.5.

112　Paus. 2.16.4, cf. Pi. fr. 169 SM; Pher. 3F12 states, rather surprisingly, that he had
　　brought them over from Seriphos with him.

113　Apollod. 2.4.5; cf. Hes. fr. 135 (poorly preserved, but probably Sthenelos, Alkaios and
　　Elektryon as three sons), Herodorus 31F15 (Mestor added).

114　Paus. 2.21.8 (first to remarry).

115　Apollod. 2.4.5 (genealogies), 2.4.6 (sons of Pterelaos arrive to claim land).

116　Herodorus 31F15.

117　Apollod. 2.4.6, Tzetz. Lyc. 932 (probably following Apollod.); cf. Pher. 3F13b, A.R.
　　1.747–51 (allusion to fight as portrayed on cloak of Jason) with schol. 747.

118　Apollod. 2.4.6; Elektryon killed in anger, Hes. *Shield* 11–12, 80–3, cf. schol. *Il.* 4.323
　　(killed as a result of disagreement over cattle).

8　THE LIFE OF HERAKLES AND RETURN
OF THE HERAKLIDS

1　Apollod. 2.4.6, Pher. 3F13.

2　Apollod. 2.4.6–7, cf. Ant. Lib. 41.8–10 (very similar), Paus. 9.19.1, Ov. *Met.*
　　7.762–93. The story of the fox goes back to the epic cycle, fr. incerti loci 1 Davies.

3　Eratosth. 33, Hyg. *Astr.* 2.35.

4　Apollod. 2.4.7.

5　Ibid., Tzetz. Lyc. 932. Komaitho fell in love with Kephalos, schol. Lyc. 934, Tzetz. l.c.

6   Hes. *Shield* 27–56, D.S. 4.9.1–3, Apollod. 2.4.8, Hyg. *Fab.* 29. Cup and lengthening of night first in Pher. 3F13.

7   Hom. *Il.* 19.95–125.

8   Ov. *Met.* 9.281–323.

9   Ant. Lib. 29.

10   Paus. 9.11.2.

11   Pi. *Nem.* 1.33–72, Theoc. 24.1–102, Apollod. 2.4.8, D.S. 4.10.1; eight months, Apollod. l.c., ten months, Theoc. 24.1, new-born, Plautus *Amphitryo* 1123ff.

12   Pher. 3F69 (from Apollod. 2.4.8).

13   Eratosth. 44, Lyc. 1327–8 with scholia; other versions, D.S. 4.9.6, Paus. 9.25.2.

14   Apollod. 2.4.9, cf. Theoc. 24.103–29.

15   Apollod. 2.4.9, D.S. 3.67.2, Ael. *V.H.* 3.32 (kills Linos with plectrum).

16   Paus. 1.43.7, Conon 19; see also Paus. 2.19.7.

17   Paus. 9.29.3.

18   Apollod. 2.4.10.

19   Paus. 9.27.5; seven nights, Herodorus 31F20.

20   D.S. 4.29.3.

21   Apollod. 2.7.6, D.S. 4.29–30.

22   Apollod. 2.4.10.

23   Paus. 1.41.4.

24   Apollod. 2.4.11, Paus. 9.37.2.

25   D.S. 4.10.3–5.

26   Pher. 3F14, Apollod. 2.4.12.

27   D.S. 4.11.1.

28   Nic. Damasc. 90F13.

29   Paus. 9.11.1.

30   Hom. *Od.* 11.269–70.

31   Stes. 58 (see Paus. 9.11.1).

32   Pi. *Isth.* 4.61–6.

33   Apollod. 2.4.11.

34   Ibid. 2.4.12.

35   Nic. Damasc. 90F13.

36   D.S. 4.10.6–11.2.

37   Ael. *V.H.* 2.32; Apollod. 2.4.12 (the Pythia changed his name from Alkeides).

38   D.S. 4.10.1.

39   Hom. *Od.* 11.622, cf. *Il.* 8.363, 19.132–3.

40   D.S. 4.11.3–26.4, Apollod. 2.5.1–12.

41   Apollod. 2.4.12 with 2.5.11.

42   Ibid. 2.4.11.

43   Eur. *Madness of Herakles* 38ff and passim.

44   Paus. 9.17.2, 9.19.3.

45   Hes. *Theog.* 326–32.

46   Epimenides 3B2 DK, cf. Herodorus 31F4 and 21 (from moon, beings born there are fifteen times bigger than on earth), Euphorion fr. 84 Powell (cited Plut. *Moralia* 677a; lion son of Selene), Hyg. *Fab.* 30 (nourished by Moon in a two-mouthed cave), Steph. Byz. s.v. Apesas.

47   Apollod. 2.5.1, D.S. 4.11.3–4; cf. Eratosth. 12 (killed by strangulation, as already described by Pisander = fr. 2A Davies).

48   Theoc. 25.204–71.

49   Ibid. 25.272–9.

50 Apollod. 2.5.1.

51 Ibid.; Hom. *Il.* 15.639–40 (that Kopreus took messages from Eurystheus to Herakles).

52 Cf. Stes. 229 (from Athen 12.152 f., indicating that Stesichorus was the first poet to represent him in the guise of a bandit with a club, lionskin and bow), Pisander T1 and fr. 1 Davies (club and lionskin, latter from Str. 15.1.9).

53 Pi. *Isth.* 6.47–8, Bacch. 13.46–54.

54 Apollod. 2.4.10.

55 Ibid. 2.4.11, Paus. 2.31.13 respectively.

56 Theoc. 25.207–10.

57 A.R. 1.1196 (bronze-tipped), Peisandros 16F4 (bronze); D.S. 4.14.3 (received club from Hephaistos).

58 Apollod. 2.4.11, D.S. 4.14.3 respectively.

59 Apollod. 2.5.1, Call. frr. 54–9 (see also *Suppl. Hell.* pp. 110ff), schol. Stat. *Theb.* 4.160.

60 Eratosth. 12, Hyg. *Astr.* 2.24.

61 Hes. *Theog.* 313–8.

62 E.g. Alcaeus 443 and Apollod. 2.5.2 (nine), Simon. 569 (fifty), D.S. 4.11.5 (a hundred).

63 E.g. Apollod. 2.5.2; earliest references Eur. *Madness of Herakles* 1274, Palaeph. 38.

64 Apollod. 2.4.2, D.S. 4.11.5–6, cf. Soph. *Trach.* 573–4, Eur. *Madness of Herakles*, 419–22, Paus. 2.37.4, Ov. *Met.* 9.69–76.

65 Hellanic. 4F103, Herodorus 31F23; the proverbial phrase was already known to Archilochus, fr. 259 West.

66 Eratosth. 11, Hyg. *Astr.* 2.23.

67 Apollod. 2.5.4, D.S. 4.12.1–2; earliest references Hecat. 1F6, Soph. *Trach.* 1097.

68 Apollod. 2.5.4, D.S. 4.12.3–8 (Dionysos left the wine-jar); early references in Stes. 181 (Pholos served wine to Herakles in a huge bowl), Soph. *Trach.* 1095–6 (Herakles defeated the Centaurs).

69 Apollod. 2.5.5, D.S. 4.33.1 respectively.

70 Apollod. 2.5.3.

71 D.S. 4.13.1.

72 Pi. *Ol.* 3.28–32.

73 Schol. Pi. *Ol.*3.53.

74 Call. *Hymn* 3.98–109.

75 Eur. *Madness of Herakles*, 375–9, D.S. 4.13.1.

76 Apollod. 2.5.6 (receives castanets from Athena), cf. Pher. 3F72; rationalistic accounts in which Herakles made them himself, Hellanic. 4F104b, D.S. 4.13.2; Pisander fr. 5 Davies (from Paus. 8.22.4, Herakles did not kill the birds).

77 A.R. 2.1030ff; Hyg. *Fab.* 30 (Stymphalian birds shoot out feathers), schol. A.R. 2.382 (the birds took refuge on isle of Ares after chased away by Herakles), Serv. *Aen.* 8.299.

78 Paus. 8.22.4–6.

79 Best account Apollod. 2.5.5; D.S. 4.13.3 (diverted Alpheios), Apollod. l.c. (Peneios and Alpheios), Paus. 5.1.9–10 (Manios); see also Pi. *Ol.* 10.29–30, Theoc. 25.7–152, schol. *Il.* 2.629 and 11.700 (Phyleus as arbiter, judges against Augeias); Hom. *Il.* 2.628–30 (reference to exile of Phyleus).

80 Ael. *V.H.* 1.24.

81 Paus. 5.5.4.

82 Acus. 2F29 (from Apollod. 2.5.7).

83 Apollod. 2.5.7, D.S. 4.13.4; Paus. 1.27.9 (origin of bull of Marathon).

84 E.g. Verg. *Aen.* 8.293–5 and Vat. Myth. 1.47 respectively.

85 Hyg. *Fab.* 30.

86 Pi. fr. 169a SM, Eur. *Alc.* 482–98, *Madness of Herakles* 380–5.

87 D.S. 4.15.3–4.
88 Apollod. 2.5.8, Hellanic. 4F105 (Abderos torn part by horses of Diomedes).
89 Apollod. 2.5.8, D.S. 4.15.4.
90 Ov. *Met.* 9.196, Hyg. *Fab.* 30.
91 Apollod. 2.5.9.
92 Eur. *Madness of Herakles* 408–18; cf. Eur. *Ion* 1143–5.
93 A.R. 2.966–9.
94 Pi. *Nem.* 3.38–9 with schol. 64, fr. 172 SM, Hellanic. 4F106, D.S. 4.16 (full narrative), schol. A.R. 2.778, 780.
95 Apollod. 2.5.9.
96 Pher. 3F18, Apollod. 2.5.10.
97 Pisander fr. 6 Davies, Panyasis fr. 7a Davies respectively.
98 Pher. 3F18.
99 Apollod. 2.5.10; cf. from early tradition Hes. *Theog.* 287–94, 982–3, Stes. 186.
100 Str. 3.5.5.
101 D.S. 4.18.4–5 (both possibilities), cf. Pliny *N.H.* 3.4, Eur. *Madness of Herakles* 235ff (opened straits). Early reference to raising of pillars, Pi. *Nem.* 3.21–6.
102 Ael. *V.H.* 5.3 (Arist. Fr. 678 Rose), Euphorion fr. 166 Powell, Parthenius fr.31.
103 Str. 3.5.3–5.
104 Str. 4.1.7, D.H. *Ant. Rom.* 1.41.3, Hyg. *Astr.* 2.6. The episode was mentioned in the *Prometheus Unbound*, Aesch. fr. 199 Radt.
105 D.S. 4.21–4.
106 Ps.Arist. *Mirab.* 97.
107 Hellanic. 4F111, Apollod. 2.5.10, cf. Varro *Re. Rust.* 2.1.9, Aulus Gellius 11.1.2.
108 Apollod. 2.5.10.
109 D.S. 4.23.2–3, Paus. 3.16.4–5; on Dorieus, see also Hdt. 5.42–8.
110 Livy 1.7.3–15, Propertius 4.9, Verg. *Aen.* 8.190–279, Ov. *Fast.* 1.543–84, D.H. *Ant. Rom.* 1.39; on Caca, Serv. *Aen.* 8.190.
111 D.H. 1.40.3–5.
112 Apollod. 2.5.10.
113 Hdt. 4.8–10.
114 Hom. *Il.* 8.367–8, Hom. *Od.* 11.623–6.
115 Eur. *Madness of Herakles* 23, Apollod. 2.5.12 etc.
116 Serv. *Aen.* 6.392, Vat. Myth. 2.150.
117 Bacch. 5.56–175, cf. Pi. fr. 249a SM.
118 Apollod. 2.5.12.
119 Ibid.
120 Schol. *Il.* 5.395.
121 D.S. 4.26.1.
122 Respectively Apollod. 2.5.12 (cf. Paus. 2.31.2), Paus. 2.35.7, schol. A.R. 2.354 citing Herodorus (= 31F31) and Euphorion (= fr. 37 Powell).
123 Schol. A.R. 2.354.
124 Hesych. s.v. *eleutheron hydōr*; on the waters, Athen. 123bc, Paus. 2.17.1.
125 Ov. *Met.* 10.65–7.
126 Apollod. 2.5.12 (adopted by Pylios, initiated by Eumolpos), Plut. *Thes.* 33 (Pylios), D.S. 4.25.1 (initiated by Mousaios), 4.14.3 (Demeter founds Lesser Mysteries).
127 First in A.R. 4.1396.
128 Apollod. 2.5.11 (cf. Odysseus' interrogation of the shape-shifting Proteus, Hom. *Od.* 4.454ff).
129 Pher. 3F17, Apollod. 2.5.11.

130 Apollod. 2.5.11, D.S. 4.17.4, Pi. *Isth.* 4.52–4.

131 Ov. *Met.* 9. 183–4, *Ibis* 393–5.

132 Apollod. 2.5.11, Lucan 4.593–653.

133 Ov. *Met.* 9.183–4.

134 Pi. *Pyth.* 9.106, Pher. 3F75, 76.

135 Plut. *Sertorius* 9, Str. 17.3.8.

136 Apollod. 2.5.11, cf. Pher. 3F17, D.S. 4.18.1, 4.27.3.

137 Apollod. 2.5.11.

138 Isocr. *Busiris* 15; Hdt. 2.45 already casts scorn on the story, saying that it reflects Greek ignorance of the character and customs of the Egyptians.

139 Pher. 3F17.

140 D.S. 4.27.3.

141 Apollod. 2.5.11.

142 Ibid., Pher. 3F17, D.S. 4.15.2.

143 Apollod. 2.5.4.

144 Aesch. *Prom. Bound* 1026–9.

145 Apollod. 2.5.11, Pher. 3F17.

146 Panyasis fr. 10 Davies, Soph. *Trach.* 1090–1, 1099–1100, Eur. *Madness of Herakles* 394–9, A.R. 4.1393–1405.

147 Eratosth. 4, Hyg. *Astr.* 2.6.

148 Apollod. 2.5.11.

149 Ibid. 2.6.1, D.S. 4.31.1.

150 Apollod. 2.6.1, cf. Herodorus 31F37, D.S. 4.31.1–2.

151 Respectively D.S. 4.31.1–2, Apollod. 2.6.2, schol. *Od.* 21.22. Apollodorus is exceptional in referring to cattle rather than horses.

152 D.S. 4.31.2, cf. Soph. *Trach.* 269–73, schol. *Od.* 21.22 (= Pher. 3F82b, but doubtful); see Hom. *Od.* 21.22–30 for an early account of the murder of Iphitos.

153 Apollod. 2.6.2.

154 Ibid., D.S. 4.31.4–5.

155 Apollod. 2.6.2, Paus. 10.13.4, Plut. *Moralia* 557c; first definite literary reference, Cicero *N.D.* 3.16.42, possible early reference, Pi. *Ol.* 9.32–3.

156 Pher. 3F82b (sold by Hermes for three talents), Apollod. 2.6.2 (Eurytos refuses money); cf. Soph. *Trach.* 247–52 (sold into slavery for a year), D.S. 4.31.5–7 (sold by friend abroad, compensation paid to sons of Iphitos), Hyg. *Fab.* 32 (sold).

157 Paus. 10.13.4.

158 Paus. 3.21.8.

159 E.g. Ov. *Heroides* 9.55ff, Lucian *D.D.* 13.2, Plut. *Quaest.Gr.* 45.

160 Athen 415bc, schol.Theoc. 10.41, Pollux *Onomast.* 4.54.

161 Serv. *Ecl.* 8.68.

162 Apollod. 2.6.2–3, D.S. 4.31.7 (killed Syleus with own hoe).

163 Eur. *Syleus* frr. (687–94 Nauck).

164 Conon 17.

165 Apollod. 2.6.3, D.S. 4.31.7 (no details); Zenob. 5.10, Apostol. 11.19; petrifaction, Pher. 3F77, Suda s.v. Kerkopes.

166 D.S. 4.31.7, Hyg. *Astr.* 2.14 respectively.

167 D.S. 4.33.2, 4.34.1, Paus. 8.14.1–3.

168 Apollod. 2.5.9, cf. Hom. *Il.* 5.648–51, Hellanic. 4F26b (substitution).

169 D.S. 4.42.

170 Hom. *Il.* 5.638–42.

171 D.S. 4.32.3–4.

172 Apollod. 2.6.4, Hellanic. 4F109 (Alexikakos).
173 Apollod. 2.6.4, cf. Soph. *Ajax* 434–6, 1299–1303, Hyg. *Fab.* 89.
174 Apollod. 3.12.7.
175 Ibid. 2.7.1; early references to episode, Hom. *Il.* 14.250–61, 15.24–30, Pi. *Nem.* 4.26 and *Isth.* 6.31–2, Pher. 3F78.
176 Hom. *Il.* 2.676–9, Pher. 3F78 (Thessalos fathered on Chalkiope).
177 Plut. *Quaest. Gr.* 58.
178 E.g. Apollod. 2.7.2, schol. *Il.* 23.638, 641.
179 Hes. fr. 17, Apollod. 2.7.2.
180 Hom. *Il.* 11.750–2, 23.638–42.
181 Ibycus 285.
182 Pi. *Ol.* 10.31–4, Pher. 3F79, D.S. 4.33.1, Paus. 5.2.1, 8.14.9.
183 Apollod. 2.7.2.
184 Pi. *Ol.* 10.24–30, Pher. 3F79, D.S. 4.33.3, Apollod. 2.7.2.
185 Paus. 5.2.1–2.
186 Apollod. 2.7.2, cf. Pi. *Ol.* 10.34–8 (city destroyed), D.S. 4.33.4, Paus. 5.3.1 (different version in which Augeias is spared).
187 Schol. *Il.* 11.690 and Isocr. 6.19 respectively.
188 Hom. *Il.* 11.688–92.
189 Hes. fr. 33a.12–19, A.R. 156–60; sometimes described as a son of Poseidon, e.g. schol. *Il.* 2.336.
190 Hes. fr. 33b, Apollod. 2.7.3.
191 Schol. A.R. 1.156, Ov. *Met.* 12.555–72, Hyg. *Fab.* 10 respectively.
192 Hes. fr. 33a, Apollod. 2.7.3, Paus. 3.26.8 (Nestor at Gerenia; Gerenios is an epithet of Nestor in the *Iliad*, e.g. 9.162).
193 Hom. *Il.* 5.395–7 (disputed passage about Herakles' wounding of Hades) with schol. ibid. 398–402 (to Olympos to be healed); Pi. *Ol.* 9.29–35 with schol. 43, 44a; Apollod. 2.7.3 (Hades wounded while assisting Pylians); Paus. 6.25.2–3 (Herakles assisting Eleian Pylians).
194 Hes. *Shield* 357–67, Panyasis fr.6 Davies.
195 Apollod. 2.7.3, Paus. 3.15.3 respectively.
196 Apollod. 2.7.3, Paus. 3.15.4.
197 Pi. *Ol.* 10.65–6.
198 Apollod. 2.7.3.
199 Ibid. (Kepheus and sons and Iphikles killed), D.S. 4.33.5–6 (three sons of Kepheus survive).
200 Paus. 3.15.5, 3.19.7, Sosibius 595F13.
201 Apollod. 2.7.3.
202 D.S. 4.34.1.
203 Soph. *Trach.* 6–26, Apollod. 2.7.5, Ov. *Met.* 9.1–88; see also Archil. 286 (lost poem that told how Herakles courted Deianeira and fought the tauriform Acheloos).
204 Apollod. 2.7.5, Pi. fr. 249a SM.
205 Origin of horn, Zenob. 2.48; early references to it, Anacreon 361, Pher. 3F42; Amaltheia as goat itself, Call. *Hymn* 1.47–8 with schol.
206 Ov. *Fasti* 5.111–28, Hyg. *Fab.* 31; for rationalizations, see D.S. 4.35.4.
207 Ov. *Met.* 9.85–8.
208 Their children, e.g. Hes. fr. 25.17–19, D.S. 4.37.1–2, Paus. 1.32.5 (Makaria).
209 Apollod. 2.7.6, D.S. 4.36.1 (king here named Phyleus).
210 Apollod. 2.7.6, D.S. 4.36.2–3, cf. Hellanic. 4F2 and Herodorus 31F3 (both in Athen. 410f–411a), Paus. 2.13.8 (disliked something that the boy gave him to drink), schol. A.R. 1.1212 (used water from foot-bath).

211 Soph. *Trach.* 555–77, Apollod. 2.7.6, D.S. 4.36.3–5, Hyg. *Fab.* 34; early references, Archil. 286–9, Bacch. 16.31–5 (baneful gift from Nessos).

212 Schol. A.R. 1.1212.

213 Apollod. 2.7.7.

214 D.S. 4.37.1, with Paus. 4.34.9; Dryopians in Messenia, Paus. 4.8.3.

215 Paus. 4.34.10.

216 D.S. 4.37.2, Hdt. 7.90, 8.46.

217 Hdt. 8.31 (Doris formerly Dryopis), 8.43 (Dryopians expelled from Doris by Herakles), 1.56 (Dorians migrated from Thessaly to Dryopis/Doris and finally to Peloponnese).

218 Apollod. 2.7.7.

219 Ibid., D.S. 4.36.5, Paus. 1.32.5.

220 Hes. *Shield* 253–6.

221 Apollod. 2.7.7, D.S. 4.37.2–4.

222 Schol. Pi. *Ol.* 2.147 and Stes. 207 respectively.

223 Hes. *Shield* 57–67.

224 Ibid. 68ff (stirred up by Apollo), 367–422 (the fight).

225 Ibid. 424–66.

226 Ibid. 472–80.

227 Apollod. 2.7.7.

228 Ibid. 2.5.11, Hyg. *Fab.* 31.

229 Stes. 207.

230 D.S. 4.37.4, Apollod. 2.7.7; Str. 9.5.18 (on Ormenion).

231 *Oichalia Halosis* fr. 2 Davies (see Paus. 4.2.3 and Str. 9.5.17), Soph. *Trach.* 74.

232 Apollod. 2.7.7., D.S. 4.37.5, cf. Hes. fr. 26.28–33, Soph. *Trach.* 351ff.

233 Hyg. *Fab.* 35.

234 Schol. *Il.* 1.52.

235 Apollod. 2.7.7, D.S. 4.38.1–2, cf. Hes. fr. 25.20–5 (Deianeira gives poisoned robe to Lichas, and its deadly effect), Ov. *Met.* 9.136ff.

236 Soph. *Trach.* 232ff. Deianeira asks Lichas to take the robe to Herakles, 600ff; its effects reported to her, 750ff.

237 Soph. *Trach.* 38–40.

238 Bacch. 16.13–35.

239 Soph. *Trach.* 772–82, Apollod. 2.7.7.

240 Ov. *Met.* 9.211–29, cf. Hyg. *Fab.* 36 (rock appeared in sea at place where he fell).

241 Str. 9.4.4.

242 Apollod. 2.7.7, D.S. 4.38.3, Soph. *Trach.* 930–1 (Deianeira stabbed herself), 971ff (Herakles' arrival in Trachis), Paus. 2.23.5 (her tomb near Trachis or at Argos).

243 Apollod. 2.7.7.

244 Soph. *Trach.* 1157ff, cf. Aesch. fr.73b Radt.

245 D.S. 4.38.3–4.

246 Poias lights pyre, Apollod. 2.7.7; Philoktetes does so, D.S. 4.38.4, Ov. *Met.* 9.233ff, Seneca *Herc. Oet.* 1485–7, Hyg. *Fab.* 36 etc.

247 Hom. *Il.* 18.117–19.

248 Hom. *Od.* 11.601–27; interpolation 602–4.

249 Hes. *Theog.* 949–55.

250 Apollod. 2.7.7, Ov. *Met.* 9. 271–2.

251 Lucian *Hermotimus* 7, Ov. *Met.* 9.250–5, 262–72, Seneca *Herc. Oet.* 965–71, cf. Theoc. 24.82–3, Call. *Hymn* 4.159.

252 D.S. 4.38.4–5.

253 Hom. *Od.* 11.602–4, Hes. *Theog.* 949–55 (but see pp. 285–6 on the late origin of these passages); Hes. fr. 25.26–33, Pi. *Nem.* 1.69–72, 10.17–18, *Isthm.* 4.55–60, Eur. *Heraclidae* 910–18, Ov. *Met.* 9.242ff, Apollod. 2.7.7.

254 Apollod. 2.7.7.

255 D.S. 4.39.2, schol. Lyc. 39.

256 Apollod. 2.8.1, D.S. 4.57.2–4, Paus. 1.32.5; cf. Hecat. 1F30.

257 Apollod. 2.8.1, D.S. 4.57.4, Paus. 1.32.5; received by Demophon, Ant. Lib. 33, Eur. *Heraclidae* 1–249.

258 Eur. *Heraclidae* 403–9 (maiden of noble birth to be sacrificed), 474ff (Makaria offers herself; it should be mentioned, however, that she is not directly named in the text); Paus. 1.32.5 (child of Herakles to offer self, spring of Makaria at Marathon); Zenob. 2.61 (Makaria in proverbial phrase).

259 Apollod. 2.8.1, cf. D.S. 4.57.6 (without mention of Alkmene).

260 Eur. *Heraclidae* 844ff (prays to be rejuvenated, 740–7; this is granted, 796); that killed by Iolaos, cf. Pi.*Pyth.* 9.79–81, Paus. 1.44.14 (buried in Megarid), Str. 8.6.19 (head and body buried separately).

261 Schol. Pi. *Pyth.* 9.137.

262 Hdt. 9.26, cf. D.S. 4.58.1–5 (Heraklids must withdraw for fifty years).

263 Apollod. 2.8.2 (the text is slightly defective since there is a short gap and it is erroneously stated that the sons of 'Kleolaos', i.e. Kleodaios, rather than of Aristodemos consulted the Delphic oracle after the death of Aristomachos); to be supplemented by Euseb. *Praep. Evang.* 5.20.

264 It was claimed that Naupaktos had been given that name because Temenos had 'built ships' (*naus epexato*) there, Apollod. 2.8.2, cf. Paus. 10.38.5, Str. 9.4.7.

265 Apollod. 2.8.3, Paus. 3.13.4 (indicates that this is an aetiological legend explaining the origin of the cult of Apollo Karneios), Conon 26.1.

266 Apollod. 2.8.3, Paus. 5.3.5–6 (driving one-eyed mule, specifies crossing-point), Str. 8.3.33.

267 Apollod. 2.8.3 (Teisamenos killed), Paus. 7.1.3 (Teisamenos escaped north).

268 Paus. 5.3.6, Str. 8.3.33 (= Ephorus 70F115); for the story of how he seized the city of Elis, and his rule there, see Paus. 5.4.1–4, 6.23.8, Polyaen. *Strateg.* 5.48.

269 Paus. 2.4.3–4, cf. Conon 26.2 (here Aletes drove out the Sisyphid kings).

270 Paus. 2.6.4. The rise to power of Phalkes, Aletes and Oxylos is noted by Ephorus 70F18b (from Str. 8.8.5) along with other dynastic changes associated with return of the Heraklids.

271 Apollod. 2.8.3, two latter versions, Paus. 3.1.6. For names of Medon and Strophios, Paus. 2.16.5.

272 Apollod. 2.8.4, Polyaen. *Strateg.* 1.6 (clearer account).

273 Paus. 4.3.4–5.

274 Hdt. 6.52.

275 Paus. 3.16.6.

276 Hdt. 6.52.

277 Hyg. *Fab.* 137, Eur. *Merope* frr., cf. Apollod. 2.8.5 (son of dead king here called Aipytos).

278 Paus. 4.3.6–8, 8.5.7.

279 Paus. 4.3.8.

280 Apollod. 2.8.5; Hyrnethos' tomb in Argos, Paus. 2.23.3.

281 Paus. 2.19.1 (Keisos becomes king), 2.26.2 (Deiphontes in Eidauros; see also 2.28.3 for the story of the death of Hyrnetho at Epidauros).

282 Paus. 2.19.2.

283 Hyg. *Fab.* 219.

284 Hdt. 8.137–8 (a good story); D.S. 7.15 and 17.
285 Hom. *Il.* 2.658–60 (Astyocheia), Apollod. 2.7.6 (Astyoche), Pi. *Ol.* 7.23–4 (Astydameia) with schol. 42 citing Hesiod (= fr. 232) and Simonides (= 554 *PMG*).
286 Hom. *Il.* 2.653–70.
287 Pi. *Ol.* 7.27–38.
288 Schol. *Il.* 2.662, Apollod. 2.8.2 respectively.
289 Apollod. 2.8.2, D.S. 4.58.4–7 respectively. Diodorus states unhelpfully that Tlepolemos killed Likymnios 'in a quarrel over certain matters'; on this, see also schol. Pi. *Ol.* 7.49a, 54.
290 Pi. *Ol.* 7.31ff.
291 D.S. 4.58.8, already indicated in Hom. *Il.* 2.656.
292 Hom. *Il.* 2.667–70, 653–4, and 5.627–59 respectively.

9   THE MYTHICAL HISTORY OF THEBES

1   Apollod. 3.1.1; Agenor's wife as Argiope, Pher. 3F21, Hyg. *Fab.* 6.
2   For the dispersion of Agenor's family, see Apollod. 3.1.1.
3   Kilix becomes eponym of Cilicia, Hdt. 7.91, Apollod. 3.1.1, Hyg. *Fab.* 178; Phoinix in Phoenicia, Apollod. l.c., in Africa, Hyg. l.c.
4   Hdt. 6.46–7 (here a son of Phoinix); for his connection with the island of Thasos, also Conon 37.1, Apollod. 3.1.1 (poorly expressed if properly preserved), Paus. 5.25.12, Steph.Byz. s.v. Thasos, etc.
5   Apollod. 3.4.1.
6   Hom. *Il.* 14.321–2, Hes. fr. 140, 141.7–8; Phoinix as son of Agenor and father of Phineus, Hes. fr. 138.
7   As children of Agenor, Hdt. 4.147, Apollod. 3.4.1, Hyg. *Fab.* 178 and most Hellenistic and later sources; as children of Phoinix, Hellanic. 4F51, Conon 32.
8   Son of Phoinix, Hdt. 6.47; of Agenor, Paus. 5.25.12; of Poseidon or Kilix, Apollod. 3.1.1 (citing Pherecydes for latter parentage = 3F87).
9   Hellanic. 4F51, Apollod. 3.4.1, Ov. *Met.* 3.8–25.
10 Schol. Eur. *Phoen.* 638 (cites supposed oracle), Paus. 9.12.1, Hyg. *Fab.* 178.
11 Sacrifices to Athena, Hellanic. 4F51, Apollod. 3.4.1, schol. Eur. *Phoen.* 1062; to Earth, schol. Eur. *Phoen* 638.
12 Hellanic. 4F51 (said to be son of Ares), Apollod. 3.4.1 (some say he was the son of Ares); schol. Soph. *Antig.* 126 (son of Erinys Tilphousa); Eur. *Phoen.* 931 (earthborn).
13 By unspecified means, Hellanic. 4F51, Apollod. 3.4.1; with sword, Pher. 3F88; with stone, Hellanic. 4F96, cf. Eur. *Phoen.* 657–65, Ov. *Met.* 3.50–94 (with stone and javelin).
14 Hellanic. 4F51, Apollod. 3.4.1, Eur. *Phoen.* 666–75, 818–21.
15 Pher. 3F22.
16 Ibid., Hellanic. 4F1, and likewise in later sources, e.g. Apollod. 3.4.1, Paus. 9.5.1.
17 Hellanic. 4F51 (a year), Apollod. 3.4.2 (a great year; it is erroneously stated that he underwent this servitude to atone for the slaughter of the Sown Men, see p. 296).
18 Sown by Athena, Stesichorus 195; at the order of Ares, Pher. 3F22, Hellanic. 4F1; by Ares, Eur. *Madness of Herakles* 252–3.
19 Hellanic. 4F1.
20 Ibid. 4F51.
21 Pher. 3F22, cf. Apollod. 1.9.23 (Aietes received half of them from Athena).
22 Apollod. 3.4.1.
23 Ibid. 3.4.2, Pi. *Pyth.* 3.86ff, Theognis 15–18 (Muses and Graces sing), Paus. 9.12.3 (site on acropolis where Muses sang).

24 Hellanic. 4F98 (necklace from Aphrodite, robe from Athena), D.S. 4.66.3 (both from Aphrodite), schol. Pi. *Pyth.* 3.167a (necklace from Aphrodite), Apollod. 3.4.2 (both from Kadmos, who had acquired them from Hephaistos), Pher. 3F89 (from Apollod. l.c., Kadmos acquired necklace from Europa), etc.

25 Pi. *Pyth.* 3.80–106.

26 Paus. 9.12.3.

27 Schol. Eur. *Phoen.* 7 citing Ephorus and Demagoras, D.S. 5.48.2–49.2.

28 Paus. 9.8.3.

29 Hdt. 5.59 (introduced by Kadmos and his companions), D.S. 3.67.1 (by Kadmos); Stes. 213 (invented by Palamedes), Aesch. *Prom. Bound.* 460–1 (by Prometheus), Tac. *Ab. Exc.* 11.14 (by Kekrops), Photius s.v. Phoinike (by Aktaion), etc.

30 Hes. *Theog.* 975–8, Apollod. 3.4.2, D.S. 4.2.1.

31 Schol. Eur. *Phoen.* 8.

32 Ov. *Met.* 3.138–252; cf. Call. *Hymn* 5.107–18, Apollod. 3.4.4, Hyg. *Fab.* 181.

33 Paus. 9.2.3.

34 Hyg. *Fab.* 180, Stat. *Theb.* 3.210ff, Fulgentius 3.3.

35 D.S. 4.81.4.

36 Acus. 2F33, Hes. fr. 217A.

37 Paus. 9.2.3 (= Stes. 236).

38 Eur. *Bacch.* 337–40, cf. D.S. 4.81.4.

39 Lists of dogs, Ov. *Met.* 3.206–32, Hyg. *Fab.* 181, Coll. Alex. 71–2; see also the verses quoted in Apollod. 3.4.4. Their grief, Hes. fr. 217A bis, Apollod. l.c.; sent mad by Artemis, Apollod. l.c., Paus. 9.2.3 (with rationalization).

40 Paus. 1.44.8.

41 Apollod. 3.5.4.

42 Ov. *Met.* 4.563ff.

43 Passes throne to Polydoros, Paus. 9.5.1; transfers throne to Pentheus initially, Eur. *Bacch.* 43–4, 212–13.

44 Steph. Byz. s.v. Bouthoe.

45 Apollod. 3.5.4.

46 Hyg. *Fab.* 184, 240, 254.

47 Apollod. 3.5.4, Steph. Byz. s.v. Illyria.

48 Pi. *Ol.* 2.78; Hom. *Od.* 4.561–9 (on Menelaos).

49 Schol. Pi. *Pyth.* 3.153b.

50 Nic. *Ther.* 607–8 (live as snakes in Illyria), Eur. *Bacch.* 1331–2 (transformation), 1338–9 (Ares transfers them to Isles of Blessed), cf. Apollod. 3.5.4.

51 Hyg. *Fab.* 6.

52 Ov. *Met.* 4.569–603.

53 Eur. *Bacch.* 1330ff; Kadmos' response to prophecy, 1352ff; cf. Hdt. 9.43 (Enchelean attack on Delphi).

54 Hes. *Theog.* 978, Hdt. 5.59, Eur. *Phoen.* 7–9.

55 Apollod. 3.5.5–7, Paus. 9.5.1–5.

56 Apollod. 3.5.5.

57 Hom. *Od.* 11.260, Asius fr. 1 Davies (quoted in Paus. 2.6.2).

58 Eur. *Antiope*, fr. 180 Nauck, Hes. fr. 81 (reared at Hyria).

59 Proclus on *Cypria*.

60 Apollod. 3.5.5, Hyg. *Fab.* 8 (ascribed to *Antiope* of Euripides), schol. A.R. 4.1090 (Zeus raped Antiope in form of Satyr).

61 Paus. 2.6.1–2.

62 Hyg. *Fab.* 8, cf. Apollod. 3.5.5 (very brief).

63 Hyg. *Fab.* 7.

64 Asius fr. 1 Davies.

65 Eur. *Bacch.* 519ff.

66 Thrown into spring, Apollod. 3.5.5, Nic. Damasc. 90F7; eponym of stream, Paus. 9.25.3; body turned into stream, Hyg. *Fab.* 7, blood turned into stream, Vat. Myth. 1.96.

67 Paus. 9.17.3–4.

68 E.g. Apollod. 3.5.5, Paus. 9.5.3 (built lower city), D.S. 19.53.5.

69 Eur. *Antiope* frr. in Page *SLP* 68.86–9, Apollod. 3.5.5, Palaeph. 41 (citing 'Hesiod' for use of lyre in wall-building, = fr. 182), A.R. 1.735–41, Paus. 9.5.4 (includes reference to *Europeia* = Eumelus *Europeia* fr.3 Davies); Pher. 3F41a (had acquired lyre from Muses).

70 Eur. *Antiope*, frr 183–8 Nauck, Pl. *Gorg.* 485e, 506b.

71 Hom. *Od.* 11.260–5, Pher. 3F41.

72 Hom. *Il.* 24.602–17, D.S. 4.74.3, Apollod. 3.5.6, Ov. *Met.* 6.146–312, Hyg. *Fab.* 9. See also p. 157 and notes.

73 Apollod. 3.5.6, Ov. *Met.* 6.271–2, and Hyg. *Fab.* 9 respectively.

74 Apollod. 3.5.6, cf. Paus. 9.5.3. Thebe was also said to have been a mistress of Zeus, Paus. 5.22.6, citing Pindar, cf. Pi. *Isthm.* 8.17–20 and schol.

75 Hom. *Od.* 19.518–23, Pher. 3F124; death of Zethos, Paus. 9.5.5.

76 Telesilla 721 *PMG*, Paus. 2.21.10.

77 Paus. 5.16.4.

78 Hom. *Od.* 11.281–91, Hes. fr. 33a.6–7.

79 Apollod. 3.5.5 (abduction alone mentioned), Peisandros 16F10 (adds that Chrysippos killed himself), Athen. 602f–603a (taken to Thebes).

80 Schol. Eur. *Phoen.* 66, Peisandros 16F10 respectively.

81 Hyg. *Fab.* 85; it is stated in this account that Laios abducted Chrysippos from the Nemean Games. In the revisionist account in Dositheos 54F1 (see Plut. *Moralia* 313c), Pelops finally condones the love affair because Laios says that he is in love with the boy, and Chrysippos is killed by his mother while he is lying at Laios' side.

82 Apollod. 3.5.7 (both variants), Hom. *Od.* 11.271 (Epikaste).

83 Soph. *Oed. King.* 711ff, 1017ff, Apollod. 3.5.7; cf. Eur. *Phoen.* 12–31 (exposed, and then recovered by servants of Polybos).

84 Schol. Eur. *Phoen.* 26, 28, Hyg. *Fab.* 66.

85 E.g. Peisandros 16F10.8, schol. Eur. *Phoen.* 26, cf. schol. *Od.* 11.271.

86 Paus. 2.6.3.

87 Merope, Soph. *Oed. King* 775; Periboia, Apollod. 3.5.7, Hyg. *Fab.* 66; Medusa or Antiochis, schol. Soph. *Oed. King* 775, citing Pherecydes (= 3F93) for former.

88 E.g. Eur. *Phoen.* 29–31, Apollod. 3.5.7.

89 Soph. *Oed. King* 729–813, cf. Apollod. 3.5.7.

90 Eur. *Phoen.* 32–45, cf. D.S. 4.64.2, Hyg. *Fab.* 67.

91 Paus. 10.5.2.

92 Phix, Hes. *Theog.* 326 with schol.; her riddle first mentioned in Soph. *Oed. King* 130–1, 393–4, or in Pi. fr. 177d SM if the unnamed riddler is the Sphinx; Eur. *Phoen.* 45–9, 806–11, 1026–31, Asclep. 12F7b, D.S. 4.64.3, Apollod. 3.5.8, Hyg. *Fab.* 67.

93 Hera, Peisandros 16F10, Apollod. 3.5.8 (without explanation); Dionysos, schol. Eur. *Phoen.* 1031, citing Euripides (= fr. 178 Nauck).

94 Haimon killed, *Oedipodeia* fr. 1 Davies, Peisandros 16F10, Apollod. 3.5.8.

95 Asclep. 12F7a (quoted in Athen. 456b); for riddle, see also Apollod. 3.5.8, D.S. 4.64.3–4 (very concise version).

96   Killed herself, e.g. Palaeph. 4, Apollod. 3.5.8, D.S. 4.64.4; killed by Oedipus, e.g.
     Eur. *Phoen.* 1507, schol. ibid. 26. Mode of death not stated in Soph. *Oed. King.*

97   Soph. *Oed. King* and standard later tradition, e.g. Apollod. 3.5.8, Hyg. *Fab.* 67.

98   Hom. *Od.* 11.271–80.

99   Hom. *Il.* 23.679–80.

100 Hom. *Od.* 11.274.

101 *Oedipodeia*, fr. 2 Davies (see Paus. 9.5.5).

102 Aesch. *Seven* 752–7, 783–4.

103 Soph. *Oed. King* 1–281.

104 Ibid. 282–462.

105 Ibid. 513–862.

106 Ibid. 924–1085.

107 Ibid. 1110–1530.

108 Eur. *Phoen.* 1427ff.

109 Eur. *Oed.* fr. 541 Nauck.

110 Hyg. *Fab.* 67.

111 Peisandros 16F10 (= schol. Eur. *Phoen.* 1760).

112 Hom. *Il.* 23.679–80, Hes. fr. 192, 193.

113 Soph. *Oed. Col.* 1457ff, Eur. *Phoen.* 1703–9; Paus. 1.30.4 (heroic shrine).

114 Soph. *Oed. Col.* 1–309.

115 Ibid. 310–460.

116 Ibid. 549–667.

117 Ibid. 720–1043.

118 Ibid. 1249–1446.

119 Ibid. 1457–1555.

120 Ibid. 1579–1666.

121 Schol. *Od.* 11.271.

122 Paus. 1.28.7.

123 Schol. Soph. *Oed. Col.* 91.

124 *Thebais* frr. 2 and 3 Davies.

125 Soph. *Oed. Col.* 421ff, Eur. *Phoen.* 63–8 respectively.

126 Hellanic. 4F98.

127 Stes. 222b (Pap. Lille 76).

128 Pher. 3F96.

129 Eur. *Phoen.* 69–80, cf. Apollod. 3.6.1, D.S. 4.65.1; Hyg. *Fab.* 67 states that Oedipus
     ordered the alternation.

130 Eur. *Phoen.* 408–29, *Suppl.* 132–50.

131 Eur. *Phoen.* 427–9, Apollod. 3.6.1.

132 Hyg. *Fab.* 69, Apollod. 3.6.1. respectively.

133 Paus. 9.5.6.

134 Hes. fr. 192.

135 Pi. *Nem.* 9.24, *Ol.* 6.15.

136 For records of their names, see Aesch. *Seven* 375ff, Soph. *Oed. Col.* 1313ff, Eur. *Suppl.*
     861ff, *Phoen.* 1090ff, D.S. 4.65.7, Apollod. 3.6.3, Paus. 10.10.2, Hyg. *Fab.* 70.

137 Apollod. 3.6.2, cf. Asclep. 12F29, D.S. 4.65.5–6; Hyg. *Fab.* 73 (Adrastos made the
     necklace and offered it to Eriphyle); earlier allusions to Eriphyle's treacherous accep-
     tance of a bribe, Hom. *Od.* 11.326–7, 15.244–7, Soph. *El.* 837–9; Paus. 5.17.7–8
     (episode portrayed on chest of Kypselos), ibid. 9.41.2 (tradition about necklace).

138 Hom. *Il.* 4.376–81.

139 Apollod. 3.6.4 and Hyg. *Fab.* 15 respectively.

140 Apollod. 3.6.4, Hyg. *Fab.* 74, Hypoth. Pi. *Nem.* Odes; remains of Eur. *Hypsipyle*, ed. G.W. Bond, Oxford, 1963; earliest references to fate of Opheltes/Archemoros, Simon. 553, Bacch. 9.10–20; tomb of Opheltes, Paus. 2.15.3.

141 Hom. *Il.* 4.382–400, 5.802–8, Apollod. 3.6.5, cf. D.S. 4.65.4.

142 For a useful summary of the course of events, see Apollod. 3.6.7–8.

143 Aesch. *Seven* 423–46, Eur. *Phoen.* 1172–86, *Suppl.* 496–9, Apollod. 3.6.7.

144 Aesch. *Seven* 807–19, Eur. *Phoen.* 1356–1424, Apollod. 3.6.8.

145 Pher. 3F97, Apollod. 3.6.8; *Bacch.* 41 (Athena planned to confer immortality on Tydeus), schol. Pi. *Nem.* 10.12 (she made his son Diomedes immortal instead, as the dying hero requests in Pherecydes' account).

146 *Thebais* fr. 4 Davies (see Paus. 9.18.4, also citing a local tradition in which Parthenopaios was killed by a certain Asphodikos), Eur. *Phoen.* 1157–62, Apollod. 3.6.8 citing Euripides (mentions variant in which killed by Amphidikos, son of Astakos).

147 Pi. *Nem.* 9.24–7, 10.8–9, Eur. *Suppl.* 925–7, Apollod. 3.6.8; Paus. 5.17.8 (Baton on chest of Kypselos), 2.23.2 and 10.10.2 (on Baton).

148 Paus. 1.34.1–2 (Oropos), 1.34.2 and 9.19.4 (Harma); 9.8.2 (Knopia); see also Str. 9.2.10 (oracle moved from Knopia to Oropos).

149 *Thebais* fr. 6A Davies (see Paus. 8.25.8; line on Areion quoted), Apollod. 3.6.8, Hyg. *Fab.* 70.

150 Apollod. 3.6.8.

151 Aesch. *Seven* 792–819.

152 E.g. Apollod. 3.7.1 (Kreon succeeds as king, forbids burial), Paus. 9.5.6 (as regent for Laodamas).

153 Aesch. *Seven* 914, 1002–4, cf. schol. Pi. *Ol.*6.22, together at family burial-place. Paus. 9.18.3, near Proitian Gates, where honoured in hero-cult; when offerings were burned to them, so it was claimed, the flames and even the smoke would divide into two, cf. Hyg. *Fab.* 68.

154 Where their supposed graves could be seen in historical times, Paus. 1.39.2; see also Hdt. 9.27, Plut. *Thes.* 29.

155 Pi. *Ol.* 6.15, *Nem.* 9.22–4.

156 As reported in Plut. *Thes.* 29.

157 Paus. 1.39.2.

158 Plut. *Thes.* 29.

159 Eur. *Suppl.* 934–7, 980–1.

160 Eur. *Suppl.* 990–1107, Apollod. 3.7.1, Hyg. *Fab.* 243.

161 Apollod. 3.7.1, Stat. *Theb.* 12.481ff.

162 Soph. *Antig.* 1–99.

163 Ibid. 162–445.

164 Ibid. 446–525 with 773–80 (Antigone's sentence).

165 Ibid. 526–81.

166 Ibid. 626–780.

167 Ibid. 928–1114.

168 Ibid. 1155–1358.

169 Pher. 3F95.

170 Aesch. *Seven* 1005–77.

171 Ibid. 1006.

172 Ibid. 1067ff.

173 Ion of Chios 740 *PMG.*

174 Hyg. *Fab.* 72.

175 Eur. *Antig.* frr; address to Dionysos, fr. 177 Nauck.

176 Soph. *Antig.* 568ff, 626ff.

177 Paus. 9.25.2.

178 Paus. 9.18.2.

179 Mimnermus 21; Periklymenos as killer of Parthenopaios, *Thebais* fr. 4 Davies, as son of Poseidon, Eur. *Phoen.* 1156–7 etc.

180 Pher. 3F95.

181 Apollod. 3.7.2; Homer alludes to the expedition and its success, *Il.* 4.405–9.

182 Apollod. 3.7.2, Paus. 2.20.4 and 10.10.2, Hyg. *Fab.* 71, schol. *Il.* 4.404.

183 Apollod. 3.7.2, D.S. 4.66.3.

184 Pi. *Pyth.* 8.39–56.

185 Apollod. 3.7.3–4, cf. D.S. 4.66.3–5.

186 Hdt. 1.56; allusion to *Epigonoi*, ibid. 4.32.

187 Paus. 9.5.7, 9.8.3, 9.9.2, 9.19.2; Hdt. 5.61 (Thebans settled in land of Encheleis in Illyria).

188 Paus. 9.8.3.

189 Hellanic. 4F100.

190 Apollod. 3.7.4 (Epigonoi enter city, nothing stated on the succession), Paus. 9.5.7 (Thersandros becomes king).

191 Paus. 1.43.1 (Adrastos), 1.44.7 (Aigialeus).

192 Asclep. 12F29, D.S. 4.65.7, 4.66.2–3, Apollod. 3.7.5, Hyg. *Fab.* 73.

193 The best source for this oracle is Thuc. 2.102, cf. Paus. 8.24.8; the text of our main narrative, Apollod. l.c., is imperfectly preserved at the relevant point.

194 For the whole preceding story, Apollod. 3.7.5–7; cf. Paus. 8.24.8–10 (sons of Phegeus here called Temenos and Axion), Ov. *Met.* 9.407–17.

195 Paus. 9.5.7–8, 3.15.8.

196 Paus. 9. 5.8.

197 Proclus on *Cypria*.

198 Hom. *Il.* 2.494–510.

199 Paus. 9.5.8.

200 Hom. *Od.* 10.490–5.

201 Tzetz. Lyc. 682, citing Hesiodic verses (= fr. 276); Tzetzes remarks that others said that Teiresias lived for nine generations.

202 Apollod. 3.6.7, citing Hesiod (under fr. 275 with relevant texts).

203 Ov. *Met.* 3.324–31, cf. Hyg. *Fab.* 75 (trampling mentioned as alternative), Vat. Myth. 1.16.

204 Schol. *Od.* 10.494, Eustath. on *Od.* 10.492; Phlegon 257F36 (wounds one of them on second occasion on advice of an oracle from Apollo).

205 E.g. Kithairon in schol. *Od.* 10.494, Kyllene more often, e.g. Apollod. 3.6.7, Phlegon l.c.

206 This version in Apollod. only, doubtless through misinterpretation of the relevant lines of the *Melampoeia* (as cited in schol. Lyc. 683 and, in a slightly different form, in an interpolation in Apollodorus' text).

207 Apollod. 3.6.7, Phlegon l.c., Hyg. *Fab.* 75, schol. Lyc. 683 (all quoted under Hes. fr. 275).

208 Apollod. 3.6.7, citing Pherecydes (= 3F92).

209 Call. *Hymn* 5.57–130.

210 Ibid. 5.107–16, cf. Ov. *Met.* 3.131ff.

211 Eur. *Phoen.* 834ff; parting speech of Menoikeus, 987–1018, Kreon laments his death, 1310–21. Cf. Apollod. 3.6.7, Hyg. *Fab.* 68.

212 Eur. *Bacch.* 266ff, cf. Ov. *Met.* 3.511ff.

213 Apollod. 3.7.3, cf. D.S. 4.67.1.
214 *Epigonoi* fr. 3 Davies, Apollod. 3.7.4, cf. D.S. 4.66.5–6 (here called Daphne).
215 Paus. 9.33.1 (also mentions that his tomb could be seen beside the spring).
216 *Epigonoi* fr. 3 Davies.
217 Paus. 7.3.1.
218 Apollod. 3.7.7.
219 Hom. *Il.* 2.572.
220 Pi. *Nem.* 9.13–15 (flight from Argos) with schol. 20 and 30; Hdt. 5.67 (inherited Sicyonian throne as grandson of Polybos), Paus. 2.6.3 (as son-in-law of Polybos).
221 Apollod. 3.6.2, D.S. 4.65.6, schol. Pi. *Nem.* 9.30.
222 For the descent of Amphiaraos, see Hom. *Od.* 15.225–44, D.S. 4.68.4–5.
223 E.g. Apollod. 1.9.13.
224 Schol. Pi. *Nem.* 9.30.
225 Hom. *Il.* 2.559–68.
226 Paus. 2.30.9, 2.18.4.
227 Tryphiodorus 159, Tzetz. *Posthom.* 643.
228 For descent of Kapaneus, see schol. *Il.* 2.564, schol. Eur. *Phoen.* 181, (Hipponoos–Anaxagoras–Megapenthes–Proitos), schol. Pi. *Nem* 9.30 (Hipponoos here son of Megapenthes).
229 Eur. *Suppl.* 981ff, Apollod. 3.7.1.
230 Eur. *Suppl.* 1072ff.
231 Hom. *Il.* 6.20–8, 23.677–99.
232 Paus. 10.25.2.
233 ps.Arist. *Peplos* 35.
234 Hom. *Il.* 4.403–10.
235 Lyc. 424–34.
236 Paus. 2.24.4–5.
237 Paus. 2.18.4–5.
238 Paus. 2.22.9–10.

10   LEGENDS OF CRETE AND ATHENS

1 D.S. 4.60.3, Steph. Byz. s.v. Lykastos.
2 Schol. *Il.* 12.92 citing Hesiod (= fr. 171) and Bacchylides (= fr.105).
3 Moschus 2, Ov. *Met.* 2.836–75; genuine bull, Acus. 2F29, D.S. 5.78.1.
4 Children, Hes. fr. 141, Apollod. 3.1.1, D.S. 4.60.3, etc.; the necklace, Hes. fr. 141, Pher. 3F89; bronze man, A.R. 4.1643–4; dog and spear, Eratosth. 33, Hyg. *Astr.* 2.35.
5 Passed on to Asterion, schol. *Il.* 12.292, Apollod. 3.1.2, D.S. 4.60.3; origin of Asterion/Asterios, D.S. 4.60.2.
6 Hdt. 1.173.
7 Apollod. 3.1.2.
8 Ibid.; Ariadne and Deukalion mentioned as children of Minos in Hom. *Od.* 11.321–2, *Il.* 13.451.
9 Apollod. 3.5.1, Ant. Lib. 41.
10 The supposed sea-empire of Minos, e.g. Thuc. 1.4.1, Hdt. 1.171, Aristotle *Politics* 2.10 (1271b 33–40), Str. 1.3.2, D.S. 5.78.3, 84.1.
11 Visits to Zeus, Pl. *Laws* 624b, ps.Pl. *Minos* 319bc, D.S. 5.78.3; the idea was apparently inspired by Hom. *Od.* 19.178–9.

12 Apollod. 3.1.3–4 (bull sent up from sea), D.S. 4.77.2–4 (latter version); see also Hes. fr. 145 (very incomplete, but bull apparently sent up from sea and became father of Minotaur), Eur. *Cretans* frr. 81–2 Austin, Hyg. *Fab.* 40. For another account of why the bull was sent, see Paus. 1.27.9.

13 Apollod. 3.1.4, Palaeph. 2 (first mention of wooden cow), D.S. 4.77.1,3, Ov. *Met.* 8.131–3, 9.736–40, cf. Hyg. *Fab.* 40 (Pasiphae inspired with the aberrant desire by Aphrodite for neglecting her cult).

14 E.g. Apollod. 3.1.4.

15 Apollod. 3.1.4, D.S. 4.77.4 etc.; labyrinth first mentioned as home of Minotaur, Philochorus 328F17, Call. *Hymn* 4.311.

16 Murder of Talos and exile, D.S. 4.76.4–7, Apollod. 3.15.8; cf. Paus. 1.21.5 (Kalos as victim), Soph. fr. 323 Radt and Hyg. *Fab.* 39 (Perdix), Ov. *Met.* 8.236–59 (Perdix transformed into a partridge, *perdix*, afterwards).

17 Son of Metion, Pher. 3F146, D.S. 4.76.1; son of Eupalamos, Bacch. 26.5–7, Apollod. 3.15.9.

18 Apollod. 3.15.7.

19 D.S. 4.60.4–5.

20 Apollod. 3.15.7.

21 Serv. *Aen.* 6.14, schol. Stat. *Achill.* 192.

22 Apollod. 3.15.8, Paus. 1.19.5, Ov. *Met.* 8.6–94, Hyg. *Fab.* 198; c.f Call. fr. 288 (allusion only).

23 Aesch. *Libation-Bearers* 614–22.

24 Apollod. 3.15.8, Paus. 2.34.7 respectively.

25 Schol. Dionys. *Per.* 420 citing Parthenius.

26 Indicated Dionys. *Av.* 2.15, Verg. *Georg.* 1.406–9; full treatment ps.Verg. *Ciris*.

27 Ov. *Met.* 8.95–151.

28 Hyg. *Fab.* 198, Serv. *Aen.* 6.286.

29 Opp. *Hal.* 1.129, 3.187.

30 Apollod. 3.15.8, cf. D.S. 4.61.1–3, Plut. *Thes.* 15.

31 Apollod. 3.15.6–7, Plut. *Thes.* 3; cf. Eur. *Med.* 663–86, *Suppl.* 1–7.

32 Paus. 2.33.1.

33 Apollod. 3.15.6–7, Hyg. *Fab.* 37.

34 Paus. 1.27.8; on childhood of Theseus, see also Plut. *Thes.* 4–5.

35 Plut. *Thes.* 6; Paus. 2.32.7 ('Theseus' Rock' near Hermione).

36 For the cycle as a whole, see Apollod. 3.15.6–7, Epit. 1.1–4, D.S. 4.59.2–5, Plut. *Thes.* 8–11, Ov. *Met.* 7.435–47 (brief summary), Hyg. *Fab.* 38.

37 Bacch. 18.16–30.

38 D.S. 4.59.2, Eur. *Suppl.* 714–15.

39 For this and each of the following exploits, see the sources cited in n. 36.

40 This version in D.S. 4.59.3, Paus. 2.1.4.

41 E.g. Apollod. 3.16.2, Hyg. *Fab.* 38.

42 Plut. *Thes.* 8, Paus. 10.25.2.

43 Paus. 1.39.5.

44 Construction of road, Paus. 1.44.10; blocked during Persian War, Hdt. 8.71.

45 Plut. *Thes.* 10.

46 Paus. 1.39.3.

47 Hellanic. 4F43, Paus. 1.5.2.

48 Hyg. *Fab.* 187.

49 For this less common account, D.S. 4.59.5, schol. Eur. *Hippol.* 977.

50 Apollod. *Epit.* 1.5–6; Medeia attempted poisoning only, Plut. *Thes.* 12; on poison, cf. Call. fr. 232–3, Ov. *Met.* 7.404–19.

51 Plut. *Thes.* 14 (following Philochorus = 328F109), Call. *Hekale* frr.

52 Volunteered, Apollod. *Epit.* 1.7, Plut. *Thes.* 17, Hyg. *Fab.* 41; by lot, Pher 3F148.

53 Hellanic. 4F164 (cited as variant by Plut. l.c.).

54 Apollod. *Epit.* 1.7–8, Plut. *Thes.* 17, D.S. 4.61.4; scarlet sails to be raised as signal, Simon. 550.

55 Bacch. 17, cf. Paus. 1.17.3.

56 Hyg. *Astr.* 2.5.

57 Pher 3F148, D.S. 4.61.4 (vague), Apollod. *Epit.* 1.8, Hyg. *Fab.* 42, schol. *Il.* 18.590.

58 Eratosth. 5, Hyg. *Astr.* 2.5.

59 Apollod. *Epit.* 1.9, schol. *Il.* 18.590; sabotaged Cretan ships, Pher. 3F150.

60 Hes. fr. 147, 298; cf. Hyg. *Fab.* 43 (abandons her because he fears disapproval if he brings her to Athens).

61 E.g. Pher. 3F148, Serv. *Georg.* 1.222 respectively.

62 D.S. 4.61.5, Apollod. *Epit.* 1.9; for other variants, see Plut. *Thes.* 20.

63 Hom. *Od.* 11.321–5.

64 Plut. *Thes.* 21.

65 Ibid. 22 (fullest), D.S. 4.61.6–7, Apollod. *Epit.* 1.10, Paus. 1.22.5; hence the name of the Aegean Sea, Hyg. *Fab.* 43, Serv. *Aen.* 3.74.

66 Apollod. *Epit.* 1.12–13, Str. 14.1.19, D.S. 4.77.5–9 (with rationalized alternative), Paus. 9.11.3 (rationalized), Ov. *Met.* 8.183–235, Hyg. *Fab.* 40.

67 Apollod. *Epit.* 1.14–15, D.S. 4.79.1–3 (without shell story), schol. Pi. *Nem.* 4.95a (pipe through ceiling), Zenob. 4.92 (pitch); Hdt. 7.170 (Minos died in Sicily while seeking Daidalos), Soph. *Kamikoi*, fr. 324 Radt (mention of shell).

68 Hom. *Il.* 6.191–9.

69 Ibid. 14.321–2.

70 Ibid. 6.150ff.

71 Ibid. 6.215–31.

72 Ibid. 6.233–6.

73 Hdt. 1.173, Hes. fr. 141.

74 Hes. fr. 141.20–1, Apollod. *Epit.* 3.1.2.

75 D.S. 5.79.3.

76 Hdt. 1.172.

77 Apollod. 3.1.2.

78 Ephoros 70F127 (= Str. 14.1.6).

79 Aritokritos 493F3; for Ovid's account, see *Met.* 9.442–8.

80 Ant. Lib. 30.

81 Conon 2.

82 Ant. Lib. 30.

83 Ov. *Met.* 9.451–665.

84 Aristotle *Nic. Eth.* 5.5 (1132b25).

85 Plut. *Thes.* 16, cf. Pl. *Laws* 624a–625b, ps.Pl. *Minos* 318d, 320bc.

86 D.S. 5.79.1; cf. Apollod. 3.1.2 (Rhadamanthys laid down laws for the islanders).

87 D.S. 5.84.2–3.

88 Apollod. 2.4.11, 3.1.2; schol. Lyc. 50 (left Crete after killing brother).

89 Ant. Lib. 33 (citing Pherecydes = 3F84).

90 Paus. 9.16.4.

91 Hom. *Od.* 7.321–4.

92 Ibid. 4.563–4, Pi. *Ol.* 2.75, *Pyth.* 2.73.

93 Pl. *Apol.* 41a, Gorg. 523e, D.S. 5.79.2, etc.

94 Apollod. 3.1.2.

95 Schol. A.R. 4.1492; mother of Miletos, Ant. Lib. 30.

96 A.R. 4.1485–97.

97 Hyg. *Astr.* 2.34.

98 Apollod. 3.2.1–2, with Hyg. *Fab.* 136 (explains nature of wondrous cow and mentions omen of owl and bees); cf. Aesch. fr. 116 Radt (cow), Palaeph. 26 (story of snakes). This was the subject of Aeschylus' *Kressai*, Sophocles' *Manteis*, and Euripides' *Polyidos*.

99 Apollod. 3.2.1.

100 Former version, Apollod. 3.2.1; latter, D.S. 5.59.1–2.

101 Apollod. 3.2.1, D.S. 5.59.2.

102 Ibid. 3.2.1.

103 Ibid. 3.2.2, D.S. 5.59.3–4.

104 Conon 47, cf. Str. 10.4.15.

105 Apollod. 3.2.2.

106 Schol. Soph. *Ajax* 1297 citing Eur. *Kressai*.

107 Hom. *Il.* 2.645–52.

108 Proclus on *Cypria*, Apollod. *Epit.* 3.3.

109 Commended by Agamemnon, Hom. *Il.* 4.256–64, grey hairs, 13.361–2.

110 Hom. *Il.* 7.165, 13.361ff.

111 Hom. *Od.* 3.191–2.

112 Apollod. *Epit.* 6.10, schol. Lyc. 1093; variant, schol. Lyc. 1223.

113 Serv. *Aen.* 3.121, 12.320, Vat. Myth. 1.195, 2.210.

114 Verg. *Aen.* 3.400–1.

115 Son of Molos, Hom. *Il.* 10.269–70; Molos brother of Deukalion, D.S. 5.79.4, illegitimate son of Deukalion, Apollod. 3.3.1.

116 See Hom. *Il.* 7.165–6, 13 passim, 17.715ff.

117 Hom. *Il.* 10.261–71.

118 Q.S. 12.720.

119 Grave in Crete, D.S. 5.79.4; see also ps.Aristotle *Peplos* 15. Sicily, Plut. *Marc.* 20, Paphlagonia, Steph. Byz. s.v. Kressa.

120 D.S. 5.79.4.

121 Plut. *Moralia* 417e.

122 Isocrates *Helen* 35, D.S. 4.61.8–9, Plut. *Thes.* 24.

123 Thuc. 2.15.

124 Plut. *Thes.* 23–5.

125 Apollod. *Epit.* 1.11, Plut. *Thes.* 13, Eur. *Hippol.* 34–7 (cf. Paus. 1.22.2) respectively.

126 Plut. *Thes.* 13, cf. Philochorus 328F108 (schol. Eur. *Hippol.* 35); earliest reference Eur. l.c.

127 Paus. 1.28.10, Pollux 8.119.

128 Apollod. *Epit.* 1.16 (mentioning Melanippe and Hippolyte as variants, citing Simonides for the latter, cf. Isocrates *Panathenaicus* 193), cf. Plut. *Thes.* 26.

129 Plut. *Thes.* 26 (citing Philochorus = 328F110), Hyg. *Fab.* 30.

130 Paus. 1.2.1.

131 'Most authorities, including Pherecydes (= 3F151), Hellanicus (= 4F156) and Herodorus (= 31F26), tell us that Theseus made an expedition of his own there after the time of Herakles', Plut. *Thes.* 26.

132 Peirithoos, Pi. fr. 175 and vase-paintings; Phorbas, Pher. 3F152.

133 Plut. *Thes.* 26 citing Bion.

134 Hellanic. 4F167.

135 Aesch. *Eum.* 685–90; On the Amazoneion, D.S. 4.28.2, cf. Apollod. *Epit.* 1.16 (camped by the Areiopagos).

136 Full account with variants in Plut. *Thes.* 27; see also D.S. 4.28.3–4, Paus. 1.2.1 (tombs of Antiope and Molpadia), 1.41.7 (Amazons flee to Megara).

137 E.g. Apollod. *Epit.* 1.17. Phaidra is mentioned among the celebrated women in the Underworld in Hom. *Od.* 11.321.

138 Plut. *Thes.* 28 citing the *Theseis* (= fr. 1 Davies).

139 Apollod. *Epit.* 1.17.

140 D.S. 4.62.1, Apollod. *Epit.* 1.17–18.

141 Eur. *Hippol.* I frr., and hypothes. *Hippol.* II (brief remarks on the contrast between the two plays), cf. Asclepiades 12F28 (a version of this kind, perhaps based on *Hippol.* I), Seneca *Phaedra*.

142 Eur. *Hippol.* (II, the surviving play).

143 Eur. *Hippol.* 1423–7.

144 All in Paus. 2.32.1.

145 Paus. 2.32.9.

146 Paus. 2.32.3.

147 *Naupactia* fr. 10C Davies (from Apollod. 3.10.3).

148 Ov. *Met.* 15.487–546.

149 Plut. *Thes.* 30.

150 As boar-hunters, Plut. *Thes.* 29, Apollod. 1.8.2, Ov. *Met.* 8.303; as Argonauts, Hyg. *Fab.* 14 (as against A.R. 1.101–4).

151 Hom. *Il.* 3.143–4.

152 Alcman 21 (one source Paus. 1.41.5), Stesichorus 191 (see p. 361 and note).

153 Hellanic. 4F168b (seven), D.S. 4.63.2 (ten), Apollod. *Epit.* 1.23 (twelve).

154 D.S. 4.63.1–4, Plut. *Thes.* 31.

155 Apollod. *Epit.* 1.23, schol. A.R. 1.100.

156 Hellanic. 4F134.

157 Hyg. *Fab.* 79.

158 Plut. *Thes.* 31–4, D.S. 4.63.3.5, Apollod. *Epit.* 1.23–4 (suggests, perhaps mistakenly, that the Dioskouroi captured Athens), Paus. 1.17.6.

159 Hdt. 9.73.

160 Plut. *Thes.* 32.

161 Stesichorus 191 (as reported in Paus. 2.22.7).

162 *Minyas* fr. 1 Davies (cited in Paus. 10.28.1).

163 Hes. fr. 280.

164 Apollod. *Epit.* 1.24.

165 Panyassis fr. 9 Davies (as reported in Paus. 10.29.2), cf. Apollod. *Epit.* 1.24 (held down by snakes also), Vat. Myth. 1,48 (chained down), Horace *Odes* 3.4.78–80 (Peirithoos still chained), 4.7.27–8 ('Lethaean bonds').

166 Apollod. 2.15.2, cf. Eur. *Madness of Herakles* 1169–70 (earliest reference to rescue of Theseus), schol. A.R. 1.101.

167 E.g. D.S. 4.26.1 and Hyg. *Fab.* 79 (both released); D.S. 4.63.4 (some say neither released), cf. Verg, *Aen.* 610 with 617–18.

168 Plut. *Thes.* 35 and Paus. 1.17.6. respectively.

169 Plut. *Thes.* 35 (both versions), Apollod. *Epit.* 1.24 (Lykomedes cast him into an abyss), Paus. 1.17.6 (Lykomedes plotted his death because of his high reputation), Lyc. 1324–6 with schol. 1326.

170 Plut. *Thes.* 35; as Athenian leader at Troy, Hom. *Il.* 2.546–56.

171 Plut. *Thes.* 35, Paus. 1.15.4.

172 Plut. *Thes.* 36.

173 Apollod. 3.14.1; his double form, Eur. *Ion* 1163–4, Arist. *Wasps* 438 with schol.

174 Kekrops as judge, Xen. *Mem.* 3.5.10, Call. fr. 194.66–8; as witness, Call. fr. 260.25–6, Apollod. 3.14.1; Kekrops and Kranaos as judges, Apollod. l.c.

175 Respectively Pliny *N.H.* 7.194, Cicero *On Laws* 2.63, Philochorus 328F98, Tacitus *Annals* 11.14. On this matter in general, see Philochorus F94–8 with Jacoby's notes.

176 Clearchus fr. 63 Wehrli; later Justin 2.6.7, Suidas s.v Kekrops.

177 Paus. 8.2.3 (Zeus Hypatos), 1.26.6 (bloodless sacrifices), Philochorus 328F97 (Kronia).

178 Apollod. 3.14.2 (mother and daughter named as Agraulos), Paus. 1.2.6. Aglauros the usual form, first Eur. *Ion* 23, 496. Aktaios as first king of Athens. Paus. l.c., cf. Str. 397, Steph. Byz. s.v Akte.

179 Eur. *Ion* 20–24, 267–74, Apollod. 3.14.6, Paus. 1.18.2, Amelasagoras 330F1, Ov. *Met.* 2.552–61; see also Euphorion fr. 9 Powell, Hyg. *Fab.* 166, *Astr.* 2.13.

180 Hellanic. 4F38, Apollod. 3.14.2, Paus. 1.21.7; Euripides alludes to the tale in *Electra* 1258–63, *Iph. Taur.* 945–6.

181 Son of Aglauros, Paus. 1.38.3; of Pandrosos, Androtion 324F1; of Herse, *Inscriptiones Graecae* 14.1389.

182 Paus. 1.38.3.

183 Apollod. 3.14.3; Hes. *Theog.* 986–91 refers to his connection with Eos without saying anything about his birth.

184 Ov. *Met.* 2.708–832, *P. Herc.* 243II.

185 Died young and childless, Apollod. 3.14.2, Paus. 1.2.6; Paus. 1.31.2 (death and tomb), 1.18.5 (statue from Delos), Athen. 9, 392d (= Phanodemos 325F2, on mission to Delos).

186 Apollod. 3.14.5, Paus. 1.2.6, Marmor Parium 239A 2,4 Jac. (received Deukalion).

187 Apollod. 3.14.6, Paus. 1.2.6.

188 Apollod. 3.14.6, Paus. 1.2.6.

189 Hom. *Il.* 2.547–8, Hdt. 8.55.

190 Harpocrat. s.v. Autochthones, 'Pindar and the author of the *Danais* say that Erichthionios appeared from the earth' (= Pi. fr. 253 Snell, *Danais* fr. 2 Davies). Clear distinction between the earthborn Erichthonios and the later Erechtheus in Eur. *Ion* 8–26. The name Erichthonios first on a hydria dated to c. 440–30 BC, Berlin F2537.

191 Founder of Panathenaia, Hellanic. 4F39 (earliest mention), Apollod. 3.14.6; invented chariot, became constellation, Eratosth. 13, Hyg. *Astr.* 2.13.

192 Apollod. 3.14.8.

193 Ibid., cf. Conon 31, Ov. *Met.* 6.424–674; early indications, Hes. *W.D.* 568 and Sappho 135 (swallow called Pandionis), Aesch. *Suppl.* 58–67 (wife of Tereus killed own child, now pursued as nightingale by hawk, cf. Hyg. *Fab.* 45 in which Tereus became hawk), Soph. *Tereus* frr. 581–95 Radt (apparently much as in later vulgate).

194 Hyg. *Fab.* 45, Serv. *Ecl.* 6.78, Vat. Myth. 1.4.

195 Serv. *Ecl.* 6.78, Vat. Myth. 1.4.

196 Ov. *Met.* 6.675–6.

197 Thuc. 2.29, Paus. 1.41.8.

198 Apollod. 3.14.8, Hyg. *Fab.* 45.

199 Apollod. 3.15.1.

200 Harpocration s.v. Boutes, Paus. 1.26.6 (altar).

201 Apollod. 3.15.1; descent of Daidalos from Erechtheus ibid. 3.15.8 (Eupalamos – Metion – Erechtheus), D.S. 4.76.1 (Metion – Eupalamos – Erechtheus), Pher. 3F146 (Metion – Erechtheus).

202 Apollod. 3.15.4, much as in Eur. *Erechtheus*, see fr. 360 Nauck (one of three daughters must be killed) and frr. 50 and 65 Austin (daughters swear to kill themselves along with chosen victim, honoured as Hyakinthides); cf. Hyg. *Fab.* 46 (curious version in which Poseidon orders the sacrifice after Erechtheus has killed Eumolpos).

203 Eur. *Ion* 275–80 (killed all but the youngest, Kreousa), Demosthenes 60.27.

204 Apollod. 3.15.4, Hyg. *Fab.* 46, Eur. *Ion* 281–2 (cf. *Erechtheus* fr. 65 Austin) respectively.

205 Paus. 13.8.3.

206 Paus. 1.26.6.

207 *Hom. Hymn. Demeter* 154, 475.

208 See Lycurgus *Against Leocrates* 98–100.

209 Apollod. 3.15.4.

210 Isocrates *Panathenaicus* 193, Hyg. *Fab.* 46.

211 Paus. 1.38.3, 2.14.2.

212 E.g. Plut. *Moralia* 607b, Lucian *Demonax* 34.

213 Schol. Soph. *Oed. Col.* 1053.

214 Apollod. 3.15.8, cf. Hyg. *Fab.* 238 (a Spartan called Hyakinthos killed his daughter Antheis on behalf of the Athenians).

215 Phanodemus 325F4.

216 Apollod. 3.5.1.

217 Abduction first mentioned, Simon. 534, cf. Pausanias. 5.19.1 (on chest of Kypselos); Acus. 2F30 (from Acropolis), Pl. *Phdr.* 229be, Apollod. 3.15.2, schol. A.R. 1.211.

218 Hdt. 7.188–9 (both incidents), Paus. 1.19.6; cf. Ael. *V.H.* 12.61 for a comparable story associated with Thurii.

219 Pher. 3F34.

220 Apollod. 3.15.1; fled to Thebes, Paus. 1.37.4.

221 Fr.ep.incerti loci 1 Davies.

222 Hom. *Od.* 11.321.

223 Ov. *Met.* 7.670–862.

224 Ant. Lib. 41.

225 Hyg. *Fab.* 189.

226 Apollod. 3.15.5, cf. Paus. 7.1.2 (Xouthos arbitrated).

227 Apollod. 3.15.5–6, Paus. 1.5.3, 1.39.4; on exile of king of Megara in Peloponnese, Paus. 4.36.1, 6.22.5.

228 Exile in Messenia, Paus. 4.1.6–7, 4.2.6; in Lycia, Hdt. 1.173, Paus. 1.19.4, Steph. Byz. s.v Lykia; his prophecies, Paus. 10.12.6.

229 E.g. Paus. 1.39.4.

230 Hom. *Il.* 2.546–56; Hes. fr. 200, cf. Apollod. 3.10.8.

231 Hom. *Il.* 2.553–5; 4.327–8, 13.331ff, 13.195–6, 689–90.

232 E.g. Plut. *Thes.* 35 (died at Troy), Tzetz. Lyc. 911 (went to Melos).

233 *Little Iliad* fr. 23 Davies, *Sack of Troy* fr. 4 Davies; Apollod. *Epit.* 5.22, Q.S. 13.496–543.

234 Apollod. *Epit.* 6.16–17.

235 Aeschines 2.13; cf. schol. Lyc. 495 (much as Apollod. except that Akamas takes the place of Demophon), Lucian *On Dancing* 40.

236 Hyg. *Fab.* 59.

237 Call. fr. 556. The story was familiar to the Roman poets, see e.g. Ov. *Rem. Am.* 591–608, *Heroides* 2, ps.Verg. *Culex* 131ff.

238 Hyg. *Fab.* 59.

239 Serv. *Ecl.* 5.10.

240 Parthenius 16, schol. Lyc. 495 citing Euphorion; cf. Lyc. 494–503.

241 Plut. *Thes.* 35, Athen. 96d.

242 Paus. 2.18.7.

243 Hellanic. 4F125, Harpocrates s.v Apatouria.

244 Conon 29.

245 Conon 26, cf. Hellanic. 4F125 (similar except that Aletes is not named), Pl. *Symp.* 208d (brief allusion), Paus. 1.19.6 (location of incident).

11   JASON AND THE ARGONAUTS

1 Apollod. 1.9.1, schol. *Il.* 7.86, Tzetz. Lyc. 22; Phrixos volunteers to be sacrificed, Pher. 3F98, Hyg.*Fab.* 2; ram first mentioned, Hes. fr. 68, Pher. 3F99.

2 Apollod. 1.9.1, Aesch. *Pers.* 70 (Hellespont etymology), Hdt. 7.58 (Helle's tomb by Hellespont), A.R. 1.256–7 (allusion).

3 Apollod. 1.9.1, early reference in Hes. fr. 299.

4 Hes. *Theog.* 956–7, Hom. *Od.* 10.136–9, Apollod. 1.9.1.

5 Apollod. 1.9.1, A.R. 2.1140–56; wife as Iophossa, Hes. fr. 255, Acus. 2F38.

6 A.R. 2.1150–1.

7 A.R. 2.1093ff.

8 A.R. 3.594–604.

9 A.R. 3.584–8.

10 Apollod. 1.9.1 and 24, A.R. 4.99–144; cf. Pi. *Pyth.* 4.244–6 (in a thicket, guarded by a dragon). The fleece is often shown on a tree in works of art.

11 Hyg. *Fab.* 3, cf. *Astr.* 2.20, Serv. *Georg.* 2.140; Hellanic. 4F129 (lies in temple of Zeus).

12 Hes. fr. 299, *Naupactia* fr. 8 Davies.

13 Pher. 3F100.

14 Eratosth. 19, Hyg. *Astr.* 2.20.

15 Hyg. *Fab.* 2.

16 Beginning of Hyg. *Fab.* 3.

17 Schol. Hes. *Theog.* 993a.

18 Paus. 9.34.4, cf. A.R. 2.1179–82.

19 Palaeph. 30, schol. *Il.* 7.86, cf. A.R. 1.763–4, Hecat. 1F17 (ram tells Phrixos to take courage after Helle has fallen off).

20 D.S. 4.47.4, schol. A.R. 1.256.

21 Palaeph. 30 (steward sends Phrixos to safety); Dionysius Scytobrachion in schol. A.R. 1.256, 2.1144, 4.176, D.S. 4.46.5–6 (*paidagōgos* Krios takes him away to save him from Ino's plot, and is flayed when they are captured by Aietes).

22 Hyg. *Astr.* 2.20 (Paian, Edonos), Steph. Byz. s.v. Almopia (Almops) and Edonos.

23 Hyg. *Fab.* 188.

24 Ov. *Met.* 6.117.

25 A.R. 2.1144–5.

26 A.R. 2.1151 and Hyg. *Fab.* 3 respectively.

27 A.R. 4.22, 735–6.

28 Ant. Lib. 23.

29 Pher. 3F106.

30 Hdt. 7.197.

31 Apollod. 1.9.8 and 11, cf. Hom. *Od.* 11.235–59 (on Tyro's children).

32 Apollod. 1.9.8, Hom. *Od.* 11.238–54 (mating with Enipeus), Hes. fr. 30.24–35.

33 Apollod. 1.9.8.

34 Schol. *Il.* 10.334, cf. Ael. *V.H.* 12.42.

35 See Aristotle *Poetics* 16, 1454b25.

36 E.g. D.S. 4.68.2.

37 Both faults in Apollod. 1.9.8.

38 The parting of the brothers, Apollod. 1.9.9–10, D.S. 4.68.3, Paus. 4.2.5, cf. Hom. *Od.* 11.256–7.

39 Pher. 3F105, Apollod. 1.9.16.

40 Pi. *Pyth.* 4.71–168.

41 Hes. *Theog.* 992–6.

42 Mimn. 11.

43 Schol. *Od.* 12.69, schol. *Theog.* 993.

44 A.R. 1.5–17, cf. Hyg. *Fab.* 12.

45 A.R. 3.66–75, cf. Hyg. *Fab.* 13.

46 Hom. *Od.* 12.70.

47 Eur. *Med.* 1–4, A.R. 1.386, 525 (Pelian Argo).

48 Apollod. 1.9.16, Aesch. *Argo* fr. 20 Radt, Antimachus fr. 58, A.R. 1.524–7, Lyc. 1319–21.

49 Both explanations of name in D.S. 4.41.3. For Argos and the building of the Argo, see also A.R. 1.18–19, 111–14, 722–4, schol. A.R. 1.4, Eratosth. 35, Hyg. *Astr.* 2.37, *Fab.* 14.

50 Pi. *Pyth.* 4.171–83.

51 A.R. 1.20–233; cf. Hyg. *Fab.* 14, *Orphic Argonautica* 119–231, Val. Flacc. 1.350–486.

52 Apollod. 1.9.16.

53 A.R. 1.559–2.1285; for a summary with some material from other sources, see Apollod. 1.9.17–23.

54 A.R. 1.559–608.

55 A.R. 1.609–913, Apollod. 1.9.17; earlier references to killing of Lemnian men, Pi. *Pyth.* 4.252 (ibid. 253–4, Argonauts compete in games there and sleep with women, on return voyage), Aesch. *Libation-Bearers* 631–6, Hdt. 6.138, schol. A.R. 1.769 on Aeschylus' *Hypsipyle* and Sophocles' *Lemniai*; Hom. *Il.* 7.467–9 (Euneos as son of Jason and Hypsipyle).

56 A.R. 1.910–21. Scenes from the visit would have been presented in Aeschylus' *Kabeiroi* (in which Jason and his comrades appeared in a drunken state, Athen. 10.428f).

57 A.R. 1.922–1152, Apollod. 1.9.18, Hyg. *Fab.* 16.

58 A.R. 1.1177–1357, Apollod. 1.9.19, Theoc. 13, Ant. Lib. 26 citing Nicander (Hylas here a son of Keux).

59 A.R. 1.1289–1308.

60 A.R. 1.1349–57.

61 Zenob. 6.21 (follows Apollodorus for the Hylas story).

62 Ant. Lib. 26 and schol. A.R. 1.1236.

63 schol. Pi. *Pyth.* 4.303b.

64 Apollod. 1.9.19 citing Pherecydes (= 3F11a), Aristotle *Politics* 3, 1284a16.

65 Hes. fr. 263 (for marriage of Keux), Hdt. 7.193.

66 With Omphale, Herodorus 31F41, Ephorus 70F14.

67 Apollod. 1.9.19 citing Demaratus (to Colchis) and Dionysius Scytobrachion (as leader); cf. Str. 12.4.3, Theoc. 13.74–6 (to Colchis on foot after left behind in Mysia).

68 A.R. 1.1358–2.162, Apollod. 1.9.20, Theoc. 22.27–134; the episode was portrayed in a Satyr-play by Sophocles, the *Amykos*, frr. 111–12 Radt, and a comedy by Epicharmus, frr. 6–8 Kaibel.

69 A.R. 2.164–233.

70 Hes. frr. 254 and 157 respectively.

71 Apollod. 1.9.21 (cited as variant), Istros 334F67.

72 Et. Gen. s.v. *opizesthai* (cited under Hes. fr. 157).

73 Asclep. 12F31.

74 Apollod. 1.9.21.

75 D.S. 4.43.3–44.4.

76 This variant Apollod. 1.9.21.

77 A.R. 2.234–300; ibid. 434, Harpies went to Mt Dikte in Crete, cf. *Naupactia* fr. 3A Davies (to Mt Arginous in Crete).

78 A.R. 2.295–7, cf. Hes. fr. 156.

79 Apollod. 1.9.21 (it can be inferred that the Boreads must have died too although this is not explicitly stated).

80 E.g. Ibycus 292, Aesch. fr. 260 Radt.

81 A.R. 2.309ff.

82 A.R. 2.549–609, cf. Apollod. 1.9.22.

83 Hom. *Od.* 12.59–72.

84 Pi. *Pyth.* 4.207–11, Eur. *Med.* 1–2.

85 Simon. 546.

86 A.R. 2.318.

87 Hdt. 4.85.

88 A.R. 4.922ff.

89 Pi. *Pyth.* 4.209–11.

90 At Salmydessos, e.g. Soph. *Antig.* 966ff, Apollod. 1.9.21. See also schol. A.R. 2.177.

91 A.R. 2.669–719.

92 A.R. 2.720–898, Apollod. 1.9.23; on death of Idmon and Tiphys, cf. Herodorus 31F50–1, 54 (Idmon died during return voyage), Nymphis 432F15, 16.

93 A.R. 2.911–29.

94 A.R. 2.946–61.

95 A.R. 2.962–1000.

96 A.R. 2.1030–1225; Phrixos advised them to travel there, ibid. 384–9. The birds that shoot out their feathers already in Eur. fr. 838 Nauck.

97 A.R. 2.1241–1280.

98 A.R. 2.1281–5, 3.167–3438, cf. Apollod. 1.9.23; Pher. 3F22a (on origin of dragon's teeth), 3F112 (bulls fire-breathing and bronze-hooved).

99 A.R. 3.472–575.

100 A.R. 3.6–166, 275–98.

101 A.R. 3.609–739.

102 A.R. 3.1025–1130, cf. Pi. *Pyth.* 4.220–3, Ov. *Met.* 7.74–99.

103 A.R. 3.1163–1407; on fulfilment of tasks, cf. Pi. *Pyth.* 4.224–41, Apollod. 1.9.23, Ov. *Met.* 7.100–48.

104 A.R. 4.6–211, cf. Apollod. 1.9.23.

105 Schol. A.R. 4.156.

106 Pi. *Pyth.* 4.241–50, Pher. 3F31 (in schol. A.R. cit.).

107 Eur. *Med.* 480–2.

108 *Naupactia* frr. 6–7 Davies; Herodorus apparently offered a similar account, 31F53.

109 Soph. fr. 547 Radt, implied in Eur. *Med.* 1262–4, Herodorus 31F10.

110 Hes. fr. 241, Pi. *Pyth.* 4.19–39, 251–62, Hecat. 1F18.

111 Schol. A.R. 4.262b, 291b, citing Timagetos.

112 Apollonius' account, 4.595ff; rationalized accounts, Pliny *N.H.* 3.22, Zosimos *Histories* 5.29.2–3.

113 D.S. 4.56.3 (= Timaeus 566F85).

114 Pher. 3F32.

115 Apollod. 1.9.24.

116 Soph. fr. 343 Radt, Eur. *Med.* 1334–5, cf. Call. fr. 8.

117 A.R. 4.212–1781, cf. Apollod. 1.9.24–6 (omitting visit to Africa).

118 A.R. 4.212–337.

119 A.R. 4.338–510. For another account of the murder of Apsyrtos set at a later stage in the voyage, see Hyg. *Fab.* 23.

120 A.R. 4.552–95.

121 A.R. 4.596–752.

122 Sirens, A.R. 4.894–921; Aphrodite bore Eryx to Boutes, Hyg. *Fab.* 260.

123 A.R. 4.885–997.

124 A.R. 4.998–1222.

125 A.R. 4.1223–1637; on Triton episode, cf. Hdt. 4.179, Pi. *Pyth.* 428–37.

126 A.R. 4.1393–1484.

127 A.R. 4.1638–44 (given to Europa by Zeus), Simon. 568 (given to Minos by Hephaistos), Apollod. 1.9.26 (gives Simonides' story and, as variants, that Talos was a member of the bronze race or was formed like a bull).

128 Apollod. 1.9.26, A.R. 4.1644.

129 Schol. Pl. *Rep.* 337a, Zenob. 5.85, Eustath. on *Od.* 20.302.

130 A.R. 4.1645–8.

131 Apollod. 1.9.26.

132 A.R. 4.1659–81.

133 Both variants in Apollod. 1.9.26.

134 A.R. 4.1689–93.

135 A.R. 4.1694–1730.

136 A.R. 4. 1731–81.

137 Apollod. 1.9.26.

138 Paus. 5.17.9–10 (Jason and various Argonauts at games on chest of Kypselos).

139 Hes. *Theog.* 992–1002, Cinaethon fr. 2 Davies (from Paus. 2.3.7).

140 Apollod. 1.9.27, Ov. *Met.* 7.297–349, Paus. 8.11.2–3; the story can be traced back to the last quarter of the sixth century BC in vase-paintings.

141 Aison in *Returns* fr.6 Davies, Ov. *Met.* 7.176–293; Jason in Simon. 548, Pher. 3F113, Lyc. 1315 with schol.

142 Euripides in Nauck 2 550f, D.S. 4.51–2 following Dionysius Scytobrachion.

143 Hyg. *Fab.* 24 (because Akastos had been a fellow-Argonaut), D.S. 4.53.1.

144 Apollod. 1.9.27.

145 Ibid., D.S. 4.50.1–2, cf. Val. Flacc 1.693–826 (both parents drink bull's blood).

146 Apollod. 1.9.27, Hyg. *Fab.* 24.

147 D.S. 4.52.2.

148 Paus. 8.11.3; married abroad, D.S. 4.53.1–2.

149 *Naupactia* fr. 9 Davies (from Paus. 2.3.7).

150 Eur. *Med.*, cf. Apollod. 1.9.28, D.S. 4.54, Hyg. *Fab.* 25, Ov. *Met.* 7.394–9.

151 Paus. 2.3.6.

152 Schol. Eur. *Med.* 264.

153 Eumelus fr. 3A Davies (from Paus. 2.3.8).

154 Schol. Eur. *Med.* 264 citing Parmeniskos.

155 See e.g. Apollod. *Epit.* 1.5–6, Plut. *Thes.* 12.

156 Apollod. 1.9.28.

157 D.S. 4.56.1, cf. the elaborate version in Hyg. *Fab.* 27.

158 D.S. 4.55.6–7.
159 Eur. *Med.* 1386–8 and schol.
160 D.S. 4.55.1, schol. Eur. *Med.* 1387.
161 Hyg. *Fab.* 25.

12   THE HISTORY OF THE DEUKALIONID FAMILY

1   Aesch. *Prom. Bound* 560, Acus. 2F34.
2   Apollod. 1.7.2.
3   Ibid.
4   Pi. *Ol.* 9.41–56.
5   Hes. fr. 234 (from Str. 7.7.2); the stone-throwing is also mentioned in Acus. 2F35.
6   Hellanic. 4F6 (king of Thessaly), Apollod. 1.7.2 (king of Phthia), Conon 27 (Phthiotis).
7   Hellanic. 4F117.
8   Marmor Parium 239A4 Jac., Paus. 1.18.8 (burial).
9   Apollod. 1.7.2, schol.Stat. *Theb.* 3.560, Apollod. 3.8.2 respectively.
10 Ov. *Met.* 1.163–415. See also Horace *Ode* 1.2.5–12, Manil. 4.831–3, Lucan 5.75–6, Hyg. *Fab.* 152 for universal flood, and Prob. *Georg.* 1.60–3, schol. Hor. *Ode* 1.2.9 for oracle.
11 Apollod. 1.7.2; cf. Hes. fr. frr. 5–7 (two daughters, Pandora, who bore Graikos to Zeus, and Thuia, who bore Magnes and Makedon to Zeus), Pher. 3F23 (Protogeneia first attested as daughter of Deukalion), Hecat. 1F13 (different account of the family); Zeus true father of Hellen, Conon 27.1, Apollod. l.c., schol. *Od.* 10.2.
12 Apollod. 1.7.2, Paus. 5.1.3.
13 Hdt. 7.200, Paus. 10.8.1–2, D.H. *Ant. Rom.* 4.25.3–4; identified with Athenian Amphiktyon, e.g. Apollod. 1.7.2.
14 Hom. *Il.* 2.681–5.
15 Ibid. 2.530.
16 Hes. fr. 5.
17 Apollod. 1.7.3, cf. Hes. fr. 9, 10a.20–3.
18 Death of sons of Aigimios, Apollod. 2.8.3.
19 Hes. fr. 10a.20–4.
20 Str. 8.7.1 (Hellen sends younger sons abroad), Paus. 7.1.2 (Xouthos driven out by brothers on accusation of stealing); marriage of X. and children, Hes. fr. 10a.20–4, Eur. *Ion* 57–64, 294–8 (Kreousa assigned to him for help in Euboean war), Conon 27, Apollod. 1.7.3, etc.
21 Paus. 7.1.2.
22 Ibid.
23 Paus. 7.1.3–4.
24 Conon 27.
25 Paus. 7.1.2.
26 Paus. 7.1.2 and 1.31.2.
27 Str. 8.7.1 and Conon 27 respectively.
28 Hdt. 5.65.
29 Eur. *Ion* 1–56.
30 Ibid. 57–66.
31 Ibid 510–65.
32 Ibid. 988–1208 (Kreousa's plot and its failure).

33 Ibid 1208–1622.

34 Ibid. 1574–94.

35 See e.g. Paus. 2.18.6–7.

36 Paus. 7.2.1–2; Neleus as founder of twelve cities of Ionia, first Hellanic. 4F48, 125.

37 Paus. 7.2.3.

38 Ibid. 7.2.2

39 Apollod. 1.7.3.

40 Eratosth. 18, Hyg. *Astr.* 2.18.

41 Page *GLP* III, no. 14.

42 Hyg. *Astr.* 2.18, cf. Ov. *Met.* 2.633–75 (in which she is transformed, presumably at the will of Zeus, after revealing the fates of Asklepios and Cheiron).

43 Call. fr. 569 (from Hyg. l.c.).

44 Apollod. 1.7.4, cf. Hes. fr. 15,16, schol. *Il.* 9.562.

45 Prob. *Georg.* 1.399 citing Nicander, cf. Ov. *Met.* 11.410–750 (Alkyone here described as a daughter of Aiolos, ruler of the winds), Hyg. *Fab.* 65.

46 Schol. *Il.* 9.562, Ovid l.c.

47 Apollod. 1.7.3, cf. Hes. fr. 10a.99–101.

48 Apollod. 3.13.1, cf. Pher. 3F1b.

49 Apollod. 1.7.4.

50 Ibid. 1.7.3, cf. Hes. fr. 10a.34–5.

51 Hes. fr. 10a.58–62 (parentage of Endymion), Paus. 5.1.3 (Aethlios first king of Elis, his wife not named).

52 Apollod. 1.7.6.

53 Zenob. 3.76, cf. Apollod. 1.7.6.

54 Schol. A.R. 4.57.

55 Cic. *Tusc.* 1.92.

56 Both in schol. A.R. 4.57.

57 Sappho 199, A.R. 4.57–8, Lucian *D.D.* 19.

58 A.R. 4.57–8, Str. 14.1.8 (grave on Latmos), Paus. 6.20.9 (grave in Elis), Paus. 5.1.5 (conflicting traditions, story of his move).

59 Paus. 5.1.4.

60 Paus. 5.1.4–8; Apollod. 1.7.6 (that he killed Jason).

61 Paus. 5.1.8–5.5.1.

62 Paus. 5.1.8–9.

63 Apollod. 1.7.6, cf. Paus. 5.1.8, Conon 14.

64 Apollod. 1.7.7, 10, cf. Hes. fr. 10a.63ff.

65 Hes. fr. 10a.50–2, Apollod. 1.7.10 on parentage; Apollod. 1.8.6, schol. *Il.* 2.212, father of Thersites.

66 Hes. fr. 26.

67 Hes. fr. 22 (courted by many), Apollod. 1.7.7 (children by Ares).

68 Paus. 3.13.8, citing Asius (= fr. 6 Davies).

69 Apollod. 1.7.10, Hes. fr. 23a.

70 Hom. *Il.* 9.556–60, Apollod. 1.7.8; see pp. 153–4 and notes.

71 Apollod. 1.8.1–2, Hes. fr. 25.10–19.

72 Apollod. 1.8.1.

73 E.g. Plut. *Moralia* 312a, Apollod. 1.8.2.

74 Bacch. 5.115–20.

75 Apollod. 1.8.1.

76 Hyg. *Fab.* 129.

77 Serv. *Georg.* 1.9, cf. Vat. Myth. 1.87 (herdsman here called Ovista).

78 Hecat. 1F15.

79 Hom. *Il.* 6.216–21.

80 Hyg. *Fab.* 171 (on day of birth), Apollod. 1.8.2 (when seven days old), D.S. 4.34.6 (Moirai appear in a dream), Ov. *Met.* 8.541ff; earliest sources for fateful log, Phrynichos *Pleuroniai* cited Paus. 10.31.2, Bacch. 5.140–4, Aesch. *Libation-Bearers* 602–12.

81 A.R. 1.190–201, Apollod. 1.9.16.

82 Stes. 179, Simon. 564, Hyg. *Fab.* 273.

83 A.R. 1.196–7.

84 Hom. *Il.* 9.533–42, Apollod. 1.8.2, D.S. 4.34.2–3, Ov. *Met.* 8.271–99; Athen. 9.402a (boar white), Str. 8.6.22 (born of son of Krommyon).

85 Bacch. 5.97–110.

86 E.g. Apollod. 1.8.2; half of kingdom too in Vat. Myth. 2.144.

87 Apollod. 1.8.2, Hyg. *Fab.* 173, Ov. *Met.* 8.299–317.

88 Apollod. 1.8.2, Ov. *Met.* 8.329–424, Bacch. 5.111–20; earliest source, Hom. *Il.* 9.538–46.

89 Bacch. 5.115–20 (Ankaios and Agelaos), Apollod. 1.8.2 (Hyleus and Ankaios), Ov. *Met.* 8.362–4 (Ainesimos); for death of Ankaios, see Ov. *Met.* 8.391–402, Paus. 8.45.2.

90 Stat. *Theb.* 2.469–73.

91 Apollod. 1.8.2, Ov. *Met.* 8.380–2 and 414–19.

92 Lyc. 491–3.

93 E.g. Ov. *Met.* 8.386–7, Hyg. *Fab.* 174.

94 E.g. Ov. *Heroides* 4.99–100, D.S. 4.34.4.

95 Apollod. 1.8.2–3, Ov. *Met.* 8.425–525, Hyg. *Fab.* 174.

96 Ant. Lib. 2 (following Nicander), Apollod. 1.8.3, Ov. *Met.* 8.533–46, Ael. *N.A.* 4.42, Hyg. *Fab.* 174.

97 Hom. *Il.* 9.529–98.

98 Ibid. 9.571–2.

99 Hes. fr. 25.10–13, *Minyas* fr. 3 Davies (from Paus. 10.31.2).

100 Apollod. 1.8.3.

101 Hom. *Il.* 9.556–8, Apollod. 1.8.3, Paus. 4.2.7.

102 *Cypria* fr. 18 Davies (from Paus. 4.2.7).

103 Hyg. *Fab.* 70, Vat. Myth. 1.174.

104 Cited in Paus. 10.31.2.

105 E.g. D.S. 4.34.7, Apollod. 1.8.3.

106 Apollod. 1.8.4–5.

107 Peisandros 16F1.

108 Hes. fr. 10a.55–57, Pher. 3F122; see also Apollod. l.c., Hyg. *Fab.* 69, schol. Stat. *Theb.* 2.113 etc.

109 Hes. fr. 12, *Thebais* fr. 8 Davies (both from Apollod. 1.8.4).

110 D.S. 4.35.1–2, Apollod. 1.8.4.

111 Apollod. 1.8.6.

112 Ibid. (killed on way), Paus. 2.25.2.

113 Hyg. *Fab.* 175, cf. Ant. Lib. 37 (Sthenelos not mentioned).

114 Athen. 6.223d.

115 Paus. 10.38.3.

116 Hom. *Il.* 2.638–44.

117 *Little Iliad* fr. 8 Davies; Verg. *Aen.* 2.262.

118 E.g. Lyc. 1013ff.

119 Paus. 10.38.3.

120 Apollod. *Epit.* 7.40.

121 Paus. 5.3.6.
122 Orchomenos, Hellanic. 4F126, Paus. 9.34.5; Thebes, schol. *Il.* 7.86 citing Philostephanos; Apollod. 1.9.1, simply called king of Boeotia.
123 E.g. Apollod. 1.9.1.
124 Schol. *Il.* 7.86.
125 Ibid., Paus. 1.44.11.
126 Apollod. 1.9.2 and 3.4.3; Paus. 1.44.11 alludes to this version too; cf. Eur. *Med.* 1286–92 (Ino jumps into sea with both children), schol. and Tzetz. Lyc. 229.
127 Ov. *Met.* 4.415–542.
128 Apollod. 3.4.3, Ov. *Met.* 4.531–42; for various traditions about Leukothea and Melikertes, Paus. 1.42.8, 1.44.11, 4.34.4, schol. Lyc. 107, 229.
129 Apollod. 1.9.2; schol. A.R. 2.514 (plain named after him because he settled there after expelled from kingdom).
130 Pher. 3F98.
131 Hyg. *Fab.* 4 (supposedly following Euripides).
132 Hyg. *Fab.* 1.
133 Hes. fr. 30.1–23, Apollod. 1.9.7; cf. Soph. fr. 10c. Radt and Eur. fr. 14 Nauck (imitation of thunder and lightning respectively), Verg. *Aen.* 6.585–94.
134 Apollod. 1.9.8, cf. Hes. fr. 30.25.
135 Hes. fr. 30.24–30.
136 Apollod. 1.9.5, Paus. 4.2.2–4.
137 Paus. 4.2.4–5.
138 Hom. *Il.* 2.591.
139 Ibid. 9.557–60.
140 Ibid. 9.553–7, Paus. 4.2.7; see also Apollod. 1.8.3 (hanged herself after Meleagros's death).
141 Pi. *Nem.* 10.61–2, Apollod. 3.10.3, Paus. 4.2.7.
142 E.g. A.R. 1.151–5 (and passim) and Apollod. 1.8.2 respectively.
143 Hyg. *Fab.* 100.
144 Apollod. 3.10.3; see also Paus. 3.16.1 (daughters of Apollo in *Cypria* = fr. 9 Davies).
145 Apollod. 3.10.3, Hes. fr. 50, schol. Pi. *Pyth.* 3.14 (also quoting two Hesiodic lines included under previous).
146 Paus. 2.26.6.
147 Paus. 4.3.1–2, 3.26.9.
148 Hom. *Od.* 11.281–7, Hes. fr. 33a, Apollod. 1.9.9, Paus. 4.2.5, 4.36.1.
149 Paus. 4.3.1.
150 Nestor and his contingent, Hom. *Il.* 2.591–602; Antilochos, 5.565ff etc.; Thrasymedes, 9.81 etc.
151 Paus. 2.18.6–7 (expulsion of Neleids, two noble families at Athens descended from them).
152 As son of Kynortes, son of Amyklas, Apollod. 3.10.3, citing Stesichorus (= 227 *PMG*).
153 Paus. 4.1.1–2.
154 Paus. 4.31.11.
155 Paus. 4.2.1–2.
156 Apollod. 1.9.11, Hes. fr. 38.
157 Apollod. 1.9.14–15.
158 Hom. *Il.* 2.763–7; in chariot-race at funeral games for Patroklos, 23.287–565.
159 Apollod. 1.9.14; Paus. 2.15.3 (grave).
160 Apollod. 1.9.11.
161 Hes. fr. 203.

162 Pi. *Pyth.* 4.124–6.

163 Apollod. 1.9.11.

164 Schol. A.R. 1.118.

165 Apollod. 1.9.11.

166 Schol. *Il.* 2.744.

167 Apollod. 1.9.12, Pher. 3F33; cf. Hom. *Od.* 11.281–97, 15.222–38, Hes. fr. 37.1–8 (reference to story), fr. 272 (healing of Iphiklos).

168 Pher. 3F114; cf. Acus. 2F28 (from Apollod. 2.2.2), girls had scorned statue of the goddess.

169 Bacch. 11. 40–57, 82–109.

170 Hes. fr. 129–33.

171 Hdt. 9.34.

172 D.S. 4.68.4–5, cf. Paus. 2.18.4 (cause of madness not specified).

173 Apollod. 2.2.2.

174 Acus.2F28, Verg. *Ecl.* 6.48–51.

175 Apollod. 2.2.2, cf. Pher. 3F114 (Lysippe and Iphianassa only, latter married Melampous), Ael. *V.H.* 3.42 (Elege and Kelaine), Serv. *Ecl.* 6.45 (Lysippe, Iphinoe, Kyrianassa); D.S. 4.68.5 (Melampous married Iphianeira, daughter of Megapenthes).

176 Hom. *Od.* 15.225–56.

177 Ibid. 15.249ff.

178 Ibid. 15.525–34.

179 Ibid. 17.151–61.

180 Ibid. 20. 350–7.

181 Hom. *Il.* 7.44–53.

182 Ibid. 13.663–4.

183 Paus. 1.34.5, Pher. 3F115a.

184 Pi. *Ol.* 13.74ff, Paus. 1.43.5.

185 Pher. 3F82b.

186 Hom. *Il.* 13.660–72.

187 Paus. 6.17.6.

188 Hom. *Il.* 6.152–4, Apollod. 1.9.3.

189 Pher. 3F119, cf. Apollod. 3.12.6 (passing reference only); earliest allusions to episode, Alcaeus 38, Theognis 702–12; Paus. 2.5.1 (bribed with offer of spring).

190 Hyg. *Fab.* 201, schol. Lyc. 344; on Autolykos' powers, see also Hes. fr. 67.

191 Paus. 2.1.3, cf. Apollod. 3.4.3.

192 Eumelos frr. 3A and 5 Davies (from Paus. 2.3.8 and 2.1.1).

193 Schol. Eur. *Med.* 20.

194 Paus. 2.1.1, Pi. *Nem.* 7.104–5 with schol. 155, Pl. *Euthyd.* 292e.

195 Hom. *Il.* 6.154–5 (wife not named), Asclep. 12F1, Apollod. 1.9.3.

196 Asclep. 12F1 (perhaps following the lost *Glaukos Potnieus* of Aeschylus), cf. Hyg. *Fab.* 250 (devoured at funeral games for Pelias, no details), Paus. 6.20.19.

197 Verg. *Georg.* 3.266–8 with Serv. on 268.

198 Schol. Eur. *Orest.* 318, Et. Magn. s.v Potniades, Pliny *N.H* 25.94.

199 Serv. *Aen.* 268; on the well, see Paus. 9.8.1.

200 Paus. 6.20.19.

201 Paus. 6.20.15–18 (offering other suggestions too).

202 Apollod. 1.9.3 (Eurymede), Hyg. *Fab.* 157 (Eurynome), cf. Hom. *Il.* 6.154 (Bellerophon, son of Glaukos).

203 Hes. fr. 43a. 71–83, Pi. *Ol.* 13.66–69.

204 Hes. fr. 43a 2–83.

205 E.g. schol. *Il.* 6.155, Apollod. 2.3.1 respectively.
206 Hom. *Il.* 6.155–95, cf. Apollod. 2.3.1–2, Hyg. *Fab.* 57. Bellerophon's wife unnamed in *Il.*, Philonoe in Apollod., Antikleia in schol. Pi. *Ol.* 13.120, Kassandra in schol. *Il.* 6.155. On Chimaira, see also Hes. *Theog.* 319–25, on B's Lycian ordeals, Pi. *Ol.* 13.83–90.
207 Hom. *Il.* 6.195–206.
208 Pi. *Ol.* 13.63–90.
209 Paus. 2.4.1.
210 Str. 8.6.21 and schol. *Il.* 6.155 respectively.
211 Hypoth. Eur. *Stheneboia* (Nauck pp. 567–8).
212 Schol. *Il.* 6.155, schol. Lyc. 17, schol. *Od.* 13.130c.
213 Hyg. *Astr.* 2.18.
214 Ibid., cf. Eratosth. 18.
215 Paus. 2.4.3.
216 Apollod. 1.9.4; Phylakos as founder of Phylake, Steph. Byz. s.v. Phylake, schol. *Il.* 2.69.
217 Schol. A.R. 1.45; already mentioned as father of Iphiklos, Hom. *Il.* 2.705, 13.698; as father of Alkimede, Pher. 3F104, A.R. 1.45–7.
218 Hom. *Il.* 2.695–710; Hes. fr. 199 differs from other sources by describing Protesilaos as a son of Aktor, son of Deion.
219 Q.S. 1.235ff, 814ff.
220 Over corn, Hes. fr. 62, over sea, schol. A.R. 1.45 citing Demaratos.
221 Nestor considers it a feat to have once beaten him in a foot-race, Hom. *Il.* 23.636; Podarkes his son, 2.704–5.
222 Paus. 5.17.10 (as depicted on chest of Kypselos).
223 Schol. Lyc. 939, cf. Hes. fr. 58.8–9; Asterodeia is the only daughter mentioned by Apollod. 1.9.4.
224 Hes. fr. 64, Pher. 3F120; cf. Hyg. *Fab.* 200 (reports that the same tale was told of Chione, daughter of Daidalion, cf. Ov. *Met.* 11.301ff).
225 Paus. 4.33.3, cf. Conon 7 (somewhat different, the nymph leaves in shame at having become pregnant); on parentage of Thamyris, also Apollod. 1.3.3, schol. *Il.* 2.595.
226 Paus. 9.36.2.
227 Pher. 3F26.
228 Apollod. 1.9.6.
229 Hes. fr. 7.

13   THE TROJAN WAR

1 Proclus on *Cypria* with fr. 1 Davies, schol. Eur. *Orest.* 1641.
2 Apollod. *Epit.* 3.1–2.
3 See e.g. Apollod. 3.10.6–7.
4 *Cypria* fr 7 Davies (from Athen. 8.334b–d).
5 Eratosth. 25; shrine, Paus. 1.33.2.
6 Zeus as swan, Apollod. 3.10.7, both as swans, Eratosth. 25.
7 Apollod. 3.10.7 and Hyg. *Astr.* 2.8 respectively.
8 Hom. *Il.* 3.236–8, *Od.* 11.298–300.
9 Eur. *Helen* 16–22; cf. Hyg. *Astr.* 2.8, Zeus adopts similar ruse to seduce Nemesis.
10 Paus. 3.16.1.
11 Lyc. 505–7, schol. *Od.* 11.298, Vat. Myth. 1.78, 1.204.
12 On all of this, see pp. 360–1 and notes.

13 Hes. frr. 196–204.

14 Apollod. 3.10.8–9.

15 Eur. *Iph. Aul.* 66–71, Hyg. *Fab.* 78.

16 Stes. 190, Hes. fr. 204.78–86, Eur. *Iph. Aul.* 51–65, Apollod. 3.10.9 (suggested by Odysseus).

17 Paus. 3.20.9.

18 Apollod. 3.10.8, Hyg. *Fab.* 81.

19 Hes. fr. 204.44–51.

20 Hes. fr. 198.4–6.

21 Hom. *Od.* 4.12–14; Apollod. *Epit.* 3.3 (nine when abandoned).

22 Hes. fr. 175, Apollod. 3.11.1; Paus. 2.18.5 (Nikostratos illegitimate like Megapenthes).

23 Hom. *Od.* 4.1–19.

24 Paus. 3.19.9–10.

25 Hom. *Il.* 6.242–50, 24.494–7.

26 Pi. *Paean* 8a, Apollod. 3.12.5, Hyg. *Fab.* 91 (serpents issue from firebrand), schol. Lyc. 86 (forests on Ida burned too).

27 Lyc. 138 with schol., Ael. *V.H.* 12.42, Apollod. 3.12.5 (for five days).

28 Lyc. 319–22 with schol. 319 schol. Lyc. 224 (Thymoites true father of child), Serv. *Aen.* 2.32.

29 E.g. Apollod. 3.12.5.

30 Hyg. *Fab.* 91.

31 Proclus on *Cypria*, *Cypria* fr.5, 6 Davies; Eur. *Troad.* 923–37, *Androm.* 274–92, *Iph. Aul.* 1283–1309, *Helen* 23–30; Isocr. *Helen* 41–4; Apollod. *Epit.* 3.2; Hyg. *Fab.* 92; Lucian *D.D.* 20.

32 Hom. *Il.* 24.25–30 (quotation 28–30).

33 Hom. *Il.* 5.59–68 (built Paris' ships, 62–3), Apollod. *Epit.* 3.2.

34 Proclus on *Cypria*.

35 E.g. Apollod. 3.12.6.

36 Parthen. *Narrat.* 4 (= Hegesianax 45F2), Conon 23; Apollod. 3.12.6 (brings remedies too late); on Paris and Oinone, see also Lyc. 57–68, Ov. *Heroides* 5, Q.S. 10.259–331 (refuses help), 411–89 (throws herself on to his pyre).

37 Hellanic. 4F29 (= Parthen. *Narrat.* 34), Conon 23.

38 Proclus on *Cypria*, Apollod. *Epit.* 3.3.

39 Hom. *Il.* 3.443–5.

40 E.g. Str. 9.1.22, Eustath. Hom. 433.21, Paus. 3.22.1 respectively.

41 Proclus on *Cypria*, Apollod. *Epit.* 3.3–4, Hom. *Il.* 6.288–92.

42 Stes. 192; for legend of poet's blinding and recantation, Pl. *Phdr.* 243a–b (with quotation from palinode), Isocr. *Helen* 64, Horace *Epode* 17.38–45; phantom Helen, Pl. *Rep.* 586c. See also p. 583 and note.

43 Eur. *Helen*, Eur. *Electra* 1280–2, cf. Apollod. *Epit.* 3.5.

44 Hdt. 2.112–20, with general discussion of question.

45 Proclus on *Cypria*, Apollod. *Epit.* 3.6.

46 Proclus on *Cypria*, cf. Apollod. *Epit.* 3.6 (heralds sent out).

47 Hom. *Il.* 2.299–330, Proclus on *Cypria*, Apollod. *Epit.* 3.15, Ov. *Met.* 12.11–23.

48 Proclus on *Cypria*, Pi. *Isth.* 8.48–51, Apollod. *Epit.* 3.17, schol. *Il.* 1.59.

49 Proclus on *Cypria*, Apollod. *Epit.* 3.18.

50 Hom. *Il.* 24.765–6.

51 Apollod. *Epit.* 3.19–20, Hyg. *Fab.* 101 (fuller narrative), Propertius 2.1.63–4 (mode of cure first recorded); Eur. *Telephos* ffr, scene from that play mocked in Arist. *Acharn.* 430ff.

52 Proclus on *Cypria*.
53 Eur. *Iph. Taur.* 1–30, etc.; Pi. *Pyth.* 11.22–3, Aesch. *Ag.* 228ff; see also Soph. *Electra* 563–76, Apollod. *Epit.* 3.21–2, Hyg. *Fab.* 98, Ov. *Met.* 12.24–38.
54 Eur. *Iph. Taur.* 20–4.
55 Apollod. *Epit.* 3.21–2, 2.10.
56 Serv. *Aen.* 2.116, cf. Hyg. *Fab.* 98.
57 Apollod. *Epit.* 3.26; Proclus on *Cypria* merely states that the Greeks sailed to Tenedos.
58 Plut. *Quaest. Gr.* 28.
59 Apollod. *Epit.* 3.23–5, Paus. 10.14.2; cf. Lyc. 232–9 with schol. 232, Conon 28, D.S. 5.83, schol. *Il.* 1.38.
60 Lyc. 240–2 with school.; on mother's warning, cf. Plut. *Quaest. Gr.* 28, Apollod. *Epit.* 3.26.
61 Proclus on *Cypria*.
62 Soph. *Philoct.* 263–70, 1326–8.
63 Euripides' *Philoktetes* as reported in Dio Chrysostom *Or.* 59.
64 Paus. 8.33.4; Homeric Chryse, *Il.* 1.37, 100. See also Appian *Mithridat.* 77.
65 Schol. *Il.* 2.722, schol. Soph. *Philoct.* 194.
66 Hyg. 102; rejected Chryse's advances, schol. Lyc. 911, schol. Soph. *Philoct.* 194.
67 Apollod. *Epit.* 3.27; ill-omened cries. Soph. *Philoct.* 8–11, 1032–4; how he fed himself on island, ibid. 164–7, 287–92, 706–11.
68 Lemnos uninhabited, Soph. *Philoct.* 2.
69 Serv. *Aen.* 3.402, Vat. Myth. 1.59.
70 Killed by Dardanian, Hom. *Il.* 2.695–702; killed by Hektor, Proclus on *Cypria*, Soph. *Poimenes* fr. 455 Nauck, Apollod. *Epit.* 3.29–30. See also Lyc. 526–33 with scholia.
71 Hyg. *Fab.* 103.
72 *Cypria* fr. 18 Davies (from Paus. 4.2.7).
73 Report on Euripides' *Protesilaos*, Nauck p. 563 (from a scholion to Aristides, vol. 3, p. 671 Dindorf).
74 Hyg. *Fab.* 103.
75 Ibid. 104.
76 Apollod. *Epit.* 3.30. From the Roman literature, see also Ov. *Heroides* 13 (a letter written by Laodameia).
77 Hes. fr. 237, Hellanic. 4F148.
78 Athen. 393b.
79 Proclus on *Cypria*, Arist. *Rhetoric* 2.24, 1396b 16–18, Soph. *Poimenes* fr. 500 Radt.
80 Pi. *Ol.* 2.82, *Isth.* 5.39, Apollod. *Epit.* 3.31.
81 Ov. *Met.* 12.70–140.
82 Proclus on *Cypria*, Apollod. *Epit.* 3.31.
83 Hom. *Il.* 24.255–7.
84 Ibid. 6. 414–27.
85 Ibid. 6.392–496; Pl. *Ion* 535b.
86 Hom. *Il.* 20.407–18.
87 Ibid. 3.147 with 20.237–8.
88 Apollod. 3.12.5.
89 Ov. *Met.* 11.749–95.
90 Apollod. 3.12.5, cf. Lyc. 224–7.
91 Hom. *Il.* 2.819–23.
92 Ibid. 5.311ff, 20.309ff.
93 Ibid. 20.300–8.

94 Hom. *Il.* 3.146ff.

95 Ibid. 3.203–24, 11.138–42, schol. *Il.* 3.205–6, Proclus on *Cypria* (embassy sent after landing), Bacch 15, Hdt. 2.118 (with unconventional matter), Apollod. *Epit.* 3.28–29 (sent before landing).

96 Hom. *Il.* 11.122–47.

97 Str. 13.1.53 citing Sophocles, Paus. 10.27.2 (in Polygnotos' painting of the sack of Troy), schol. *Il.* 3.205–6.

98 D.H. *Ant. Rom.* 1.46, Serv. *Aen.* 2.15, schol. Lyc. 340; Tzetz. Lyc. 658 (Palladion).

99 Hom. *Il.* 21.544–611.

100 *Little Iliad* fr. 18 Davies (from Paus. 10.27.1), cf. Q.S. 13.213–17.

101 Hom. *Il.* 18.251–2.

102 Ibid. 18.249–313. For other occasions on which he advises Hektor, see *Il.* 12.59ff, 12.209ff, 13.725ff.

103 Hom. *Il.* 22.99ff.

104 Ibid. 16.805–17, 17.1–60.

105 Paus. 2.17.3.

106 Diogenes Laertius 8.4–5.

107 Hom. *Il.* 2.824–77.

108 Ibid. 2.557–8.

109 Ibid. 7.219–67.

110 On Teukros, see e.g. Hom. *Il.* 8.266–72; on the Locrian Aias, 13.701–8, 14.520–3.

111 At games, Hom. *Il.* 23.473ff; corselet, speed and skill with spear, ibid. 2.527–30.

112 Hom. *Il.* 2.681–5.

113 Statius *Achill.* 1.269–70, Serv. *Aen.* 6.57.

114 Lyc. 455–61 with scholia; Aesch. fr. 83 Radt (vulnerable only in armpit); Pi. *Isth.* 6.42–9, Hes. fr. 250.

115 Hom. *Il.* 11.831–2 (healing skills), Pi. *Nem.* 3.43–53 (hunting exploits), Apollod. 3.13.6 (diet), Statius *Achill.* 2.381ff (education, diet).

116 Hom. *Il.* 9.432ff.

117 Ibid. 9.447–84 with schol. 448.

118 Apollod. 3.13.8, cf. Lyc. 421–3; Phoinix already blinded in Eur. *Phoinix*, hence the allusion in Arist. *Acharn.* 421.

119 Hom. *Il.* 11.765–90.

120 Apollod. 3.13.8; Paus. 1.22.6 (Achilles shown among girls on Skyros in a painting by Polygnotos, fifth century BC, earliest definite evidence for story).

121 Ov. *Met.* 13.162–70, schol. *Il.* 19.326, schol. Lyc. 277.

122 Hyg. *Fab.* 96; cf. Apollod. 3.13.8 (discovered by blowing of trumpet).

123 Apollod. 3.13.8 etc; on his love for Deidameia, see also Bion 2.

124 Hom. *Il.* 19.326–7, Proclus on *Cypria*, with fr.16 Davies.

125 Hom. *Il.* 7.161–80.

126 Ibid. 10.247.

127 See e.g. Gorgias *Palamedes* 30, schol. Eur. *Orest.* 432, Soph. fr. 429, 432 Radt; Serv. *Aen.* 2.81 (draughts as diversion for troops).

128 Hyg. *Fab.* 95.

129 Proclus on *Cypria* (child seized 'for punishment' at suggestion of Palamedes), Apollod. *Epit.* 3.7 (Palamedes threatens child with sword); Odysseus yokes horse and ox, Hyg. *Fab.* 95, yokes ass and ox, schol. Lyc. 384, yokes two different animals and sows salt, Serv. *Aen.* 2.81, Vat. Myth. 1.35; Palamedes places child in front of plough, Hyg. l.c., Serv. l.c., schol. Lyc. 815.

130 *Cypria* fr. 20 Davies (from Paus. 10.31.1).

131 Hyg. *Fab.* 105, cf. Apollod. *Epit.* 3.8, Vat. Myth. 1.35.

132 Schol. Eur. *Orest.* 432.

133 Dictys 2.15.

134 See Arist. *Thesm.* 768ff with schol. 771.

135 He has seen two generations of men pass away by the time of the war, Hom. *Il.* 1.250.

136 Hom. *Il.* 2.559–68.

137 Ibid. 5.297–367.

138 Ibid. 5.431–42.

139 Ibid. 5.825–67.

140 Pi. *Nem.* 10.7 with schol. 12, Pher. 3F97.

141 Schol. Pi. *Nem.* 10.12.

142 Call. *Hymn* 5.35 with schol., Paus. 2.23.5.

143 Incident mentioned in Proclus on *Cypria*; on the miseries suffered by the troops, Aesch. *Ag.* 558–72; see also the comments of Thucydides, 1.11.

144 Hom. *Il.* 9.128–30 (sack of Lesbos), 2.690–3 (Lyrnessos and Hypoplakian Thebes), Proclus on *Cypria* (Lyrnessos, Pedasos and many neighbouring cities), Apollod. *Epit.* 3.32–3 (Clazomenae, Smyrna, Colophon, etc.), schol. *Il.* 6.35. Eustath. on *Il.* 2.690.

145 Hom. *Il.* 20.89–94, 187–90, Proclus on *Cypria*, Apollod. *Epit.* 3.32.

146 Hom. *Il.* 21.34–135, 23.740–7; Proclus on *Cypria* (Patroklos took Lykaon to Lemnos).

147 Hom. *Il.* 24.257, cf. Proclus on *Cypria* ('Achilles kills Troilos'), Ibycus 282a.41–5 (beauty of T.), schol.*Il.* 24.257 citing Sophocles (T. ambushed while exercising horses near Thymbraion); see also Apollod. *Epit.* 3.32 (A. ambushed T. and slaughtered him in the sanctuary of Thymbraian Apollo).

148 Lyc. 307–13 with schol. 307.

149 Vat. Myth. 1.210 and Plaut. *Bacchides* 953–5 respectively.

150 It first appears in the *Roman de Troie* of Benoit de Sainte-More (12th century); Chaucer followed the version in Boccaccio's *Il Filostrato*.

151 Hom. *Il.* Book 1.

152 Ibid. Book 5 (Diomedes dominates)–7 (434ff, Greeks make ditch and wall).

153 Ibid. Book 8.

154 Ibid. Book 9.

155 Ibid. Book 11.

156 Ibid. Books 12–15.

157 Ibid. Book 16.

158 Ibid. Books 17–18.

159 Ibid. Books 19–22; death and defilement of Hektor in 22.

160 Ibid. Book 23.

161 Ibid. Book 24.

162 Ibid. 2.819ff.

163 A translation is conveniently available in the Loeb series, as also of the shorter *Capture of Troy* by Tryphiodorus.

164 Hom. *Il.* 10.435, as against Eur. *Rhes.* 387–8, Apollod. 1.3.4.

165 Hom. *Il.* 10.423–514.

166 Eur. *Rhes.* 600ff, schol. *Il.* 10.435, Verg. *Aen.* 469–73 with Servius on 469.

167 Pi. fr. 262 SM in schol. *Il.* cit.

168 Q.S. 1.18ff (accidentally killed sister Hippolyte while aiming spear at a boar), cf. D.S. 2.46.5 (killed relative), Apollod. *Epit.* 5.1 (killed Hippolyte; in 5.2, this Hippolyte is wrongly identified with the Amazon abducted by Theseus, an absurdity in chronological terms); Hellanic. 4F149 (Amazon came to win glory).

169 Proclus on *Aethiopis*, cf. Apollod. *Epit.* 5.1, Q.S. Book 1.

170 Hom. *Il.* 6.186, 3.184–9.

171 Proclus on *Aethiopis*, Apollod. *Epit.* 5.1, Lyc. 999–1001 with schol. (Thersites gouged out eye), Q.S. 1.718–81, schol. Soph. *Philoct.* 445, Eustath. on *Il.* 2.219.

172 Hom .*Il.* 2.211–77.

173 Q.S. 1.766ff.

174 Hom. *Il.* 2.216–9 (deformed state), Pher. 3F123 (thrown over cliff), schol. *Il.* 2.212 citing Euphorion (chased over cliff).

175 E.g. Hdt. 5.54 (Susa as city of Memnon), D.S. 2.22 following Ctesias (Susa); cf. Str. 15.3.2 (also citing Simonides = 539 *PMG*, for burial in Syria).

176 E.g. Paus. 1.42.2.

177 Proclus on *Aethiopis*, Hom. *Od.* 4.187–8 (Antilochos killed by Memnon), 11.522 (Memnon mentioned), Pi. *Pyth.* 6.28–42 (Priam saved from Memnon), Apollod. *Epit.* 5.3, Q.S. 2.

178 Q.S. 2.549ff.

179 Q.S. 2.642–50, Serv. *Aen.* 1.751, Dionys. *Av.* 1.8.

180 Ov. *Met.* 13.576–622.

181 Ov. *Met.* 13.621–2, Serv. *Aen.* 1.489.

182 Proclus on *Aethiopis* (killed by Paris and Apollo), cf. Hom. *Il.* 19.416–17 (fated to be killed by a god and a mortal), 22.358–60 (by Paris and Apollo at Scaean Gate), Apollod. *Epit.* 5.3–4; Apollo alone, Hyg. *Fab.* 107, Q.S. 3.26–66; Paris alone mentioned, Eur. *Androm.* 655, *Hecuba.* 387–8; Apollo guides hand of Paris, Verg. *Aen.* 6.56–8.

183 Hom. *Od.* 24.43–94, cf. Q.S. 3.380–787.

184 Hom. *Od.* 11.467ff, Proclus on *Aethiopis*.

185 To Medeia, Apollod. *Epit.* 5.5, A.R. 4.811–15 with schol. 814 citing Ibycus (291 *PMG*) as first to offer story; to Iphigeneia, schol. *Il.* 19.326, Ant. Lib. 27 (Iphigeneia as Orsilochia); to Polyxena, Seneca *Troad.* 954.

186 Hom. *Od.* 11.544–56, with schol. 547 (Trojan captives), cf. Q.S. 5.157ff.

187 *Little Iliad* fr. 2A Davies.

188 Pi. *Nem.* 8.26–7, cf. 7.23–30.

189 Hom. *Od.* 11.548–63.

190 Ibid. 11.548–9.

191 Proclus on *Little Iliad*, Pi. *Isth.* 4.35–6, Soph. *Ajax*, Apollod. *Epit.* 5.6–7, cf. Q.S. 5.

192 *Little Iliad* fr 3 Davies, cf. Apollod. *Epit.* 5.7.

193 Soph. *Ajax* 1047–1373.

194 Soph. *Ajax* 530ff, 982ff, Q.S. 5.521ff.

195 Proclus on *Little Iliad*.

196 Apollod. *Epit.* 5.8–10.

197 See Lyc. 52–6 with schol. 52.

198 Paus. 5.13.4–6.

199 Acus. 2F40.

200 Schol. *Od.* 11.521; on origin of vine, *Little Iliad* fr. 7 Davies (from Paus. 3.26.9; presumably mentioned because Priam offered it to Eurypylos' mother in epic), Apollod. *Epit.* 5.12 (no details), Q.S. 8.128ff.

201 Hom. *Od.* 11.520–1.

202 Schol. *Od.* 11.521.

203 Hom. *Od.* 11.506–22, Proclus on *Little Iliad* with fr. 7 Davies (from Paus. 3.26.9), Apollod. *Epit.* 5.12 (no details), Q.S. 8.128ff.

204 Proclus on *Little Iliad* with fr. 8 Davies.

205 Hom. *Od.* 4.242–58.

206 Apollod. *Epit.* 5.13.

207 Soph. fr. 367 Radt, Serv. *Aen.* 2.166.

208 Conon 34, Zenob s.v., Serv. *Aen.* 2.166; *Little Iliad* fr. 9 Davies.

209 Hom. *Od.* 8.492–5 (made by Epeios with Athena's help), *Little Iliad* fr. 9 Davies (made by Epeios on advice of Athena), Apollod. *Epit.* 5.14 (at suggestion of Athena), Q.S. 12.21ff; lists of men in horse, Q.S. 12.314–30 (names thirty, says that more), Tzetz. *Posthomerica* 641–50 (twenty-three), Eustath. on *Od.* 11.522 (names twelve, reports that a hundred in Stesichorus). Apollod. l.c. states that there were fifty men, or a thousand (surely a textual error) according to the *Little Iliad*.

210 Hom. *Od.* 8.492–520.

211 Apollod. *Epit.* 5.15.

212 Proclus on *Little Iliad* and *Sack of Troy*, c.f. Apollod. *Epit.* 5.16–18.

213 Hom. *Od.* 4.271–89, cf. Tryph. 463–90. See also *Od.* 11.523–32 on the fears of the warriors as they entered the Horse.

214 Verg. *Aen.* 2.1–249, Q.S. 12.218ff (capture and torture of Sinon, 360–422), Tryph. 227ff.

215 Proclus on *Sack of Troy*.

216 Q.S. 12.444ff, blinds him, 395ff; for the death of Laokoon and his sons in Verg. *Aen.*, see 2.199–33.

217 Apollod. *Epit.* 5.18, Soph. fr. 373 Radt.

218 Bacch. fr. 9 SM, cf. schol. Lyc. 347 (from Kalydnai).

219 Serv. *Aen.* 2.201 and Hyg. *Fab.* 135 respectively.

220 Verg. *Aen.* 2.201, with Servius ad loc. citing Euphorion.

221 Hyg. *Fab.* 135 (corrected from Acoetes) and Tzetz. Lyc. 347 respectively.

222 *Little Iliad* fr. 11 Davies (at midnight, as the clear moon was rising), Proclus on *Sack of Troy* (lit fire-signal after entering the city by a pretence), Apollod. *Epit.* 5.19 and Tryph. 510–11 (on tomb of Achilles), Q.S. 13.21–9.

223 E.g. Apollod. *Epit.* 5.20 (on rope after first to leave, Echion, son of Portheus, was killed when jumping), Verg. *Aen.* 2.262 (rope), Q.S. 13.306–60 (on ladder constructed by Epeios).

224 Verg. *Aen.* 6.515–19 (Helen's signal), 2.254–9 (Sinon).

225 Paus. 10.25–27.

226 Proclus on *Sack of Troy*, Eur. *Hecuba* 22–4, *Troades* 16–17, 481–4, Apollod. *Epit.* 6.21, Paus. 4.17.4.

227 *Little Iliad* fr. 11A Davies.

228 Decapitated, Verg. *Aen.* 2.557 with Servius on ibid. 506–7 and 557, Q.S. 13.220–50; on grave of Achilles, Serv. *Aen.* 557.

229 Verg. *Aen.* 2.526–58; cf. Q.S. 13.214 (Neoptolemos kills Polites when attacked by him in the course of the fighting).

230 D.S. 8.517–20, Proclus on *Sack of Troy*, Apollod. *Epit.* 5.22, Q.S. 13.354ff.

231 *Little Iliad* fr. 19 Davies and Stes. 201 respectively. See also Eur. *Androm.* 627–31 for former story, with schol. ibid. 628 (ascribing it to Ibycus also).

232 Verg. *Aen.* 2.567–93.

233 *Little Iliad* fr. 23 Davies (from Paus. 10.25.2), Proclus on *Sack of Troy* with fr. 4 Davies, Apollod. *Epit.* 5.22.

234 *Little Iliad* fr. 20 Davies, Proclus on *Sack of Troy* with fr. 3 Davies.

235 Eur. *Troad.* 719–39, 433–5. On the fate of Astyanax, see also Eur. *Androm.* 8–11, Apollod. *Epit.* 5.23, Q.S. 13.252–7 (killed by Greeks on night of sack); allusion to possible fate, Hom. *Il.* 24.734–5.

236 Proclus on *Sack of Troy*, cf. Paus. 5.19.5 (as depicted on chest of Kypselos).

237 Alcaeus 262.

238 Lyc. 357–64, Apollod. *Epit.* 5.22, Q.S. 13.420–9; Vergil, *Aen.* 2.402–6, makes no mention of the rape.

239 See e.g. Eur. *Troad.*, Apollod. *Epit.* 5.23.

240 On tomb, Str. 13.1.28, D.S. 13.40.

241 Eur. *Hecuba.* 1260–75.

242 Nicander fr. 62.

243 Lyc. 330–4, 1174–88 with scholia, Vat. Myth. 3.9.8.

244 Ov. *Met.* 13.565–71, Vat. Myth. 2.209.

245 Anon. lyric. fr. 965 *PMG*, Lyc. 1176 respectively.

246 E.g. schol. Lyc. 315.

247 Stes. 198.

248 Eur. *Hec.* 678ff, body brought to Hekabe.

249 Ibid. 1ff.

250 Hekabe's confrontation with Polymestor and sons, Eur. *Hec.* 953ff.

251 Already in Hom. *Od.* 11.421–2.

252 Proclus on *Sack of Troy*, Eur. *Hec.* 35–44 (ghost of Achilles demands her sacrifice if Greeks are to sail), 93–5, cf. 107–15, 309–10 (as his share of the spoils), 534–8, Lyc. 323–9 (his bride in death), Ov. *Met.* 13.439ff, Seneca *Troad.* 938–44, 1118–64, Q.S. 14.214ff.

253 Philostr. *Her.* 20.18; *Vit. Apoll.* 4.16.4.

254 Hyg. *Fab.* 110; the story is developed at length in Dictys 3–5.

255 *Cypria* fr. 27 Davies.

256 Lyc. 314–18, 496–8, Apollod. *Epit.* 5.23, Q.S. 13.544–51, Tryph. 660–3.

257 Hom. *Il.* 3.121–4, *Little Iliad* fr. 13 Davies (from Paus. 10.26.2).

258 Paus. 10.26.1.

259 Verg. *Aen.* 2.735–94.

260 Lyc. 1263–9 and D.H. *Ant. Rom.* 1.46.2–4 respectively.

14   THE RETURNS OF THE GREEKS AND THE HISTORY OF THE PELOPIDS

1 Proclus on *Sack of Troy*.

2 Proclus on *Returns*; divergent account of Neoptolemos' return in Hom. *Od.* 3.188–9.

3 Hom. *Od.* 3.130–58.

4 Ibid. 3.159–83.

5 Ibid. 3.276–312; cf. Proclus on *Cypria* (arrives at Egypt with five ships, the others having been destroyed at sea).

6 Hom. *Od.* 4.351–586.

7 Ibid. 4.78–90.

8 Ibid. 4.227–32, 125–32.

9 E.g. Apollod. *Epit.* 6.29, Eur. *Helen* respectively.

10 Conon 8.

11 Schol. Aratus 351 (star rises as ships sail south), Str. 1.1.6 (recently named); there was probably a catasterism in the lost *Kanobos* of Apollonius of Rhodes.

12 Hom. *Od.* 4.491–511.

13 Ibid. 4.512–37.

14 Ibid. 4.555–60.

15 Ibid. 3.186–92.

16 Proclus on *Returns*.

17 Mentioned as more recent name in Apollod. *Epit.* 6.11.

18 First references to Nauplios' activities, Eur. *Helen* 766–7 (shipwrecks, beacon lit by Nauplios in Euboea), 1126–31 (many lured on to rocks at Cape Kaphareus); this was the subject of the *Nauplios Pyrkaios* (Nauplios the Fire-Kindler) of Sophocles, but almost nothing is recorded of the play; Nauplios is mentioned in *Returns* fr. 1 Davies (from Apollod. 2.1.5, that his wife was called Philyra).

19 Hom. *Od.* 4.500.

20 Hyg. *Fab.* 116, cf. Q.S. 14.419ff.

21 Apollod. *Epit.* 6.5–11.

22 Schol. *Il.* 13.66, cf. Lyc. 373–402.

23 Borrows Zeus' lightning to use it against the Greek ships, Eur. *Troad.* 78–81, Verg. *Aen.* 1.39–45, Q.S. 14.443–540, kills Aias with thunderbolt, Apollod. *Epit.* 6.6, Hyg. *Fab.* 116.

24 Apollod. *Epit.* 6.6.

25 Lyc. 398–402 with schol. 402, schol. *Il.* 13.166.

26 Hyg. *Fab.* 166.

27 Meges and Prothoos, Tzetz. Lyc. 902 (citing 'Apollodorus and the rest' = Apollod. *Epit.* 6.15a); Gouneus, ps.Arist. *Peplos* 25. Cf. schol. Lyc. 899 (Gouneus and Prothoos in Libya), Tzetz. Lyc. l.c (Gouneus to Libya).

28 Hom. *Od.* 3.180–1 and 190 respectively.

29 Hom. *Il.* 5.330–41.

30 Lyc. 612–16 with schol. 592, 610, schol. *Il.* 5.412, Eustath. on ibid.

31 Apollod. *Epit.* 6.9–10.

32 Ant. Lib. 37.2–3, Ov. *Met.* 14.457–8, 510–11, Pliny *N.H.* 3.103, Serv. *Aen.* 8.9.

33 Str. 6.3.9, schol. Lyc. 592 (Argyrippa with etymology).

34 Verg. *Aen.* 11.252ff.

35 Ant. Lib. 37.

36 Verg. *Aen.* 11.271–7 and Ov. *Met.* 14.484–509 respectively.

37 Ps.Arist. *Mirab.* 79.

38 Schol. Lyc. 592. Lycophron 596–611 describes the behaviour of the birds without explaining the circumstances of the transformation; see also ps.Arist. *Mirab.* 79, Str. 6.3.9, Pliny *N.H.* 10.126, Ael. *N.A.* 1.1.

39 Soph. *Philoct.* 1421–30 (the divine Herakles foretells his fortunate future to him).

40 Tzetz. Lyc. 911, Str. 6.1.3 respectively.

41 Str. 6.1.3 and Lyc. 911–27 with scholia.

42 Tzetz. Lyc. 911, Justin 20.1.16, ps.Arist. *Mirab.* 107 respectively.

43 Ps.Arist. *Mirab.* 108.

44 Proclus on *Returns*.

45 Apollod. *Epit.* 6.2, schol. Lyc. 427.

46 Schol. *Il.* 2.315, Q.S. 14.360–3 respectively.

47 Apollod. *Epit.* 6.3–4; cf. Lyc. 426–30 (similar, but answers not specified), schol. Lyc. 427 (both questions posed by Mopsos; latter reply, ten piglets of which one male).

48 Hes. fr. 278 (see Str. 14.1.27).

49 Pher. 3F142 (from Str. l.c.); three piglets (or properly ten?) of which one female.

50 Conon fr. 6. For a wholly different account of the death of Kalchas, see Serv. *Ecl.* 6.72.

51 Proclus on *Returns*.

52 Ps.Arist. *Peplos* 27; Tzetz. Lyc. 980, 1047.

53 Apollod. *Epit.* 6.18; settled at Syrnos in Caria, Paus. 3.26.10, Steph. Byz. s.v. Syrna.

54 Lyc. 438–42 with schol. 440, Str. 14.5.16; cf. Apollod. *Epit.* 6.19 (Amphilochos, son of Alkmaion, see p. 331, as opposed to the son of Amphiaraos, is here described as Mopsos' partner in the duel, probably by error).

55 Thuc. 2.68.

56 Proclus on *Returns*.

57 Apollod. *Epit.* 6.5 and 12; Proclus cites the *Sack of Troy* as mentioning that Neoptolemos took Andromache as his prize. According to Serv. *Aen.* 2.166, cf. Paus. 1.11.1, Neoptolemos made this journey on the advice of Helenos.

58 Schol. *Od.* 3.188, Eustath on 3.189.

59 Pi. *Nem.* 7.36–7.

60 Apollod. *Epit.* 6.12–13, schol. *Od.* 3.188.

61 Hom. *Od.* 4.5–9.

62 E.g. Hom. *Il.* 24.488–9, *Od.*11.494–7.

63 Schol. Eur. *Trojan Women* 1128; in the play itself, 1126–9, Peleus is said to have been expelled by Akastos himself. It has been suggested that Kos may be a mistake for Ikos, which is mentioned as the burial-place of Peleus in Anth. Pal. 7.2.

64 Dictys 6.7–9.

65 As in Apollod. *Epit.* 6.13 (succeeded to kingdom after his grandfather was expelled by the sons of Akastos and died). He presumably came to rule in Phthia in the earliest tradition, although the *Odyssey* mentions nothing more than his safe return and his subsequent presence in Phthia, 3.186–9, 4.5–9.

66 Pi. *Nem.* 7.40–3 with schol. ibid. 62.

67 Asclep. 12F15 (in schol. cit.) states that almost all the poets agree that Machaireus was the killer, and names his father as Daïtes. Machaireus also appears as the killer on other versions of the story, e.g. Apollod. *Epit.* 6.14. Killed with *machaira*, Pi. *Nem.* 7.42.

68 Pi. *Paean* 6.117ff.

69 Pher. 3F64a.

70 Str. 9.3.9, Apollod. *Epit.* 6.14, Eustath. on *Od.* 4.4. Tried to plunder Delphi, Paus. 10.7.1, schol. Pi.*Nem.* 7.58.

71 Eur. *Androm.* 1085–1165; killed by Orestes himself, Verg. *Aen.* 3.330–2, Apollod. *Epit.* 6.14, Hyg. *Fab.* 123.

72 Pi. *Nem.* 7.44–8 and schol. ibid. 62, Paus. 10.24.5 (site of grave), 10.23.3 (helped against Gauls).

73 Hom. *Od.* 3.155–65.

74 Ibid. 9.39–66.

75 Ibid. 9.196–205.

76 Hdt. 4.177, Pliny *N.H.* 5.28.

77 Hom. *Od.* 9.67–104.

78 Ibid. 9.105–465.

79 Ibid. 9.456–535.

80 Ibid. 10.1–76.

81 Ibid. 10.77–132.

82 Ibid. 10.133–9, cf. Hes. *Theog.* 956–7 (mother named as Perseis).

83 Hes. *Theog.* 1011–16 (in a post-Hesiodic section of the poem); Telegonos, also Proclus on *Telegonia*.

84 Hom. *Od.* 10.140–498.

85 Ibid. 11; Antikleia, ibid. 152–224.

86 Ibid. 11.100–37.

87 Kirke's advice, Hom. *Od.* 12.37–141.

88 Hom. *Od.* 12.166–200.

89 See e.g. Apollod. 1.7.10, *Epit.* 7.18–19, A.R. 4.891–902, Lyc. 712–13 with schol., Hyg. *Fab.* 125.

90 A.R. 4.896–8.

91 Ov. *Met.* 5.552–67, Vat. Myth. 1.186.

92 Hyg. *Fab.* 141.

93 Schol. *Od.* 12.39.

94 Lyc. 712–16, cf. Apollod. *Epit.* 7.19, Hyg. *Fab.* 125, 141.

95 Lyc. 717–27 with scholia, ps.Arist. *Mirab.* 103.

96 Lyc. 717, 732–7 with scholia.

97 Paus. 9.34.2, schol. Lyc. 653.

98 Hom. *Od.* 12.55 (Kirke on Planktai).

99 Ibid. 12.234–59.

100 Ibid. 12.83–100, cf. Hyg. *Fab.* 199.

101 E.g. Sallust *Hist.* 4.27, Serv. *Aen.* 3.420, schol. Lyc. 46; cf. Palaeph. 20 (Skylla originally the name of a pirate ship).

102 Ps.Verg. *Ciris* 70–6, schol. Lyc. 46.

103 Ov. *Met.* 12.83–100, cf. Hyg. *Fab.* 1999; see also Athen. 7.297b. Serv. *Ecl.* 6.74 gives both versions.

104 Hom. *Od.* 12.260–425.

105 Ibid. 12.426–50.

106 Ibid. 5.1–261.

107 Ibid. 5.262–493.

108 Ibid. Book 6.

109 Odysseus among the Phaeacians, Hom. *Od.* 7–8; he recounts his adventures to them, ibid. 9–12.

110 Hom. *Od.* 13.1–249.

111 Ibid. 13.146–84.

112 Ibid. 13.392–438.

113 Ibid. 17–18.

114 Ibid. 19; Penelope's tapestry, ibid. 138–58.

115 Ibid. 21–22.389.

116 Ibid. 22.417–77.

117 Ibid. Book 23.

118 Ibid. 24.205–548.

119 Proclus on *Telegonia*, Apollod. *Epit.* 7.34–5.

120 Proclus on *Telegonia*, Apollod. *Epit.* 7.35–6, Hyg. *Fab.* 127.

121 Schol. *Od.* 11.134.

122 Hom. *Od.* 11.134.

123 Proclus on *Telegonia*, Apollod. *Epit.* 7.37, cf. Hyg. *Fab.* 127 (states that Telemachos and Penelope travelled to Kirke's island at the order of Athena, who also proposed the marriages).

124 Apollod. *Epit.* 7.38–40.

125 This can be no more than a theory, however, since there is no surviving record of a people of that name.

126 First named as a son of Zeus, Eur. *Orestes* 5; mother as Plouto, schol. ibid. 4, Paus. 2.22.4; lived at Sipylos, Pi. *Ol.* 1.35–7, Pher. 3F38 and generally in the subsequent tradition.

127 Pelops is already named as a son of Tantalos in *Cypria* fr. 13 Davies; Niobe is connected with Sipylos in Hom. *Il.* 24.605–17, but is not identified as a daughter of Tantalos, as is agreed in subsequent sources from Hes. fr. 183 onwards; on Broteas, see n.132.

128 A.R. 2.751–95 with schol. 752 citing Herodorus and Nymphis, Apollod. 2.5.9.

129 Schol. *Od.* 19.518.

130 Schol. *Od.* 20.66.

131 Ant. Lib. 36.

132 Image on mountain, Paus. 3.22.4; his death, Apollod. *Epit.* 2.2 (it is clear from the context that this must be the son of Tantalos even if he is not explicitly named as such). Ovid *Ibis* 517–18 also refers to a Broteas (identified by the scholia as a son of Zeus, or a son of Hephaistos and Athena) who burned himself to death on a pyre.

133 Pi. *Ol.* 1.35–53 (story mentioned but rejected, cf. Eur. *Iph. Taur.* 386–91), Bacchylides fr. 42 SM (Rhea cured Pelops by putting him into a cauldron), Apollod. *Epit.* 2.3, schol. Lyc. 152, Serv. *Georg.* 3.7 etc.

134 Pi. *Ol.* 1.26–7 (alludes to ivory shoulder), Lyc. 152–5 (first mentions that Demeter ate shoulder), schol. ibid. 152 (distracted by loss of daughter), Ov. *Met.* 6.404–11 (ivory shoulder), Hyg. *Fab.* 83 (Demeter fitted it), schol. Pi. *Ol.* 1.40 (Hermes did so at bidding of Zeus).

135 Pi. *Ol.* 1.40–5, Lyc. 156–7, Apollod. *Epit.* 2.3.

136 Pi. *Ol.* 1.67–88 (chariot with winged horses from Poseidon, apparently won without help from Myrtilos); full account of race, D.S. 4.73, Apollod. *Epit.* 2.3–5; suitors previously killed, Hes. fr. 259, Paus. 6.21.9–11, schol. Pi. *Ol.* 1.127.

137 E.g. Hyg. *Fab.* 84 and Paus. 8.14.11 respectively.

138 Apollod. *Epit.* 2.7, schol. A.R. 1.752.

139 Apollod. *Epit.* (left out axle-pins), Pher. 3F37a (substituted waxen dummies); schol. A.R. 1.752, schol. Lyc. 157 (both versions).

140 Hyg. *Fab.* 84, Paus. 8.14.11.

141 Apollod. *Epit.* 2.8, Pher. 3F37, schol. *Il.* 2.104 respectively; see also Eur. *Orest.* 988–96 with schol. 990.

142 Apollod. *Epit.* 2.7, schol. Lyc. 157.

143 Paus. 5.22.6.

144 E.g. Hellanic. 4F19a, Eratosth. 23; alternatively, Sterope was the wife of Oinomaos, Apollod. 3.10.1.

145 E.g. Apollod. *Epit.* 2.4 (both variants), Lucian *Charid.* 19 (former), schol. A.R. 1.752 (latter).

146 Apollod. *Epit.* 2.5, Hyg. *Fab.* 84.

147 Paus. Bks. 5–6.

148 Apollod. *Epit.* 2.9, cf. Thuc. 1.9.

149 Plut. *Thes.* 3.

150 Pi. *Ol.* 1.89 (unnamed, three lists in schol. 144); thirteen lists in schol. Eur. *Orest.* 4.

151 These were doubtless regarded as sons of Pelops by Homer's time, see *Il.* 2.105–6.

152 First described as a son of Pelops in tragedy, Eur. *Med.* 683–4, *Heraclidae*, 207; for his arrival in Troizen, Paus. 2.30.8.

153 First as a son of Pelops in Theognis 773–4; his arrival in Megara, Paus. 1.41.4.

154 Apollod. 2.5.1, schol. *Il.* 15.639; he is already mentioned by Homer, *Il.* 15.639–40.

155 Paus. 2.30.8, schol. *Il.* 2.561, Steph. Byz. s.v. Troizen.

156 Paus. 2.26.3.

157 Pher. 3F20, cf. Acus. 2F3; otherwise Kleon or Kleonos, schol. Eur. *Orest.* 4, or Kleone, daughter of Pelops, Paus. 2.15.1.

158 Schol. Eur. *Orest.* 5 and Paus. 6.22.8 respectively.

159 Hes. fr. 190.

160 Schol. Eur. *Orest.* 5, schol. Pi. *Ol.* 1.144; Hellanic. 4F157 (by previous wife).

161 Hellanic. 4F157, schol. Eur. *Orest.* 4 (similar accounts, the former specifying the nature of the curse, and the latter that the corpse was thrown into a well); Paus. 6.20.7 (Hippodameia exiled), Dositheos 54F1 (Hippodameia committed the murder). See also Thuc. 1.9, Pl. *Crat.* 395b.

162 Paus. 5.13.1–3, Pi. *Ol.* 1.90–6 with schol.

163 Paus. 6.22.1–2; 5.17.9 (Pisos shown on chest of Kypselos).

164 Apollod. 2.4.6, Thuc. 1.9 respectively.

165 For a convenient summary of the ensuing events, see Apollod. *Epit.* 2.10ff.

166 Schol. Eur. *Orest.* 995, 998.

167 Apollod. *Epit.* 2.10, schol. *Il.* 2.105, cf. Pher. 3F133.

168 Apollod. *Epit.* 2.11, schol. Eur. *Orest.* 811, schol. *Il.* 2.105.

169 Eur. *Orest.* 1001–6 (sun reverses course temporarily to travel east), Eur. *Electra* 699–736 and Pl. *Statesman* 268e–269a (sun reverses course forever to establish present pattern), Eur. *Iph. Taur.* 812–16 (allusion to change of course); Zeus sends Hermes to Atreus beforehand, Apollod. *Epit.* 2.11–12, schol. Eur. *Orest.* 811, schol. *Il.* 2.105; rationalized, Str. 1.2.15 cf. Eur. fr. 861 Nauck.

170 Apollod. *Epit.* 2.13, cf. Aesch. *Ag.* 1590–1602, Paus. 2.18.2, Hyg. *Fab.* 88, Seneca *Thyestes* 682ff.

171 Apollod. *Epit.* 2.13, schol. Eur. *Orest.* 4.

172 Hyg. *Fab.* 88, 246, cf. Seneca *Thyestes* 218ff (these the only sons named although it is stated that there were three).

173 Ov. *Tristia* 2.391–2, Seneca *Thyestes* 776ff, Martial 1.45.1–2, Hyg. *Fab.* 88, 258; apparently already in Sophocles, see Anth. Pal. 9.98.

174 On advice of oracle, Apollod. *Epit.* 2.14 (daughter unnamed), Hyg. *Fab.* 87, schol. Eur. *Orest.* 15; in ignorance, Hyg. *Fab.* 88, as summarized in following paragraph.

175 Aesch. *Ag.* 1604–6.

176 Hyg. *Fab.* 88.

177 Tzetz. *Chiliades* 1.456–65 (as inserted into gap in Apollod. *Epit.* 2.15).

178 Hes. fr. 194, 195.

179 Aerope seems to be the mother of Menelaos in the papyrus fragment in Hes. fr. 195, even if Tzetzes (under fr. 194) quotes 'Hesiod' as saying that Menelaos and Agamemnon were children of Pleisthenes and Kleolla. According to Apollod. 3.2.2, Nauplios married Aerope to Pleisthenes, who fathered A. and M. by her (a story probably derived from Euripides, see schol. Soph. *Ajax* 1297).

180 Schol. *Il.* 2.249.

181 Hom. *Il.* 2.100–8.

182 Hom. *Od.* 1.35–43 (Aigisthos warned by Hermes), Hom. *Od.* 3.263–75 (maroons minstrel, seduces Klytaimnestra).

183 Hom. *Od.* 4.513–37, 11.409–34; see also 3.234–5, 4.91–2, 24.96–7, 24.199–200 (passages indicating that Klytaimnestra shared in the guilt of the murder); cf. Proclus on *Returns* (merely that Agamemnon murdered by K. and A.).

184 Aesch. *Ag.* (watchman, 1ff; trampling of purple, 905–74; the murder as heard by the chorus from outside, 1343ff; Kassandra's account of it, 1372ff; as avenging sacrifice of Iphigeneia, 1412ff; Aigisthos' speech after the murder, 1577ff).

185 Taken away by nurse, Pi. *Pyth.* 11.16–18, with schol. 25b citing Pherecydes (= 3F144) and Herodorus (= 31F11); by Talthybios, Dictys 6.2; saved by Elektra, Soph. *El.* 11–14, 1110–11, 1349–50, Apollod. *Epit.* 6.24, Hyg. *Fab.* 117; sent away by mother, Aesch. *Ag.* 877ff.

186 Pi. *Pyth.* 11.34–6, Soph. *El.* 15–16 (best of friends with Pylades), *Iph. Taur.* 916–19 (Strophios married to a daughter of Atreus), Paus. 2.29.4 (married to Anaxibia, sister of Agamemnon, citing Asius = fr. 5 Davies), Apollod. *Epit.* 6.24.

187 Hom. *Od.* 3.306–12, Proclus on *Returns* (vengeance of Orestes and Pylades, no details), Hes. fr. 23a.28–30, Stes. 217, Pi. *Pyth.* 11.36–7.

188 Aesch. *Libation-Bearers* (Klytaimnestra's dream, 523–33, cf. dream in Stes. 219, Soph. *El.* 417–25; Orestes final confrontation with his mother, 829ff).

189 Soph. *Elektra* (*paidagōgos* comes to palace, 660ff; Elektra seeks help of Chrysothemis in killing Aigisthos, 938ff; Orestes and Pylades arrive, 1098ff; killing of Klytaimnestra, 1367ff, of A., 1442ff).

190 Eur. *Elektra* (E. married to farmer, 19ff; killing of Aigisthos described, 774ff; of Klytaimnestra, 1201ff).

191 Hom. *Od.* 1.293–300; see also 1.39–44, 3.303–12, 4.546–7, 11.461.

192 Stesichorus 217.

193 Aesch. *Libation-Bearers* 1048–64.

194 Aesch. *Eum.* 64ff.

195 Ibid. 470ff.

196 Ibid. 734ff.

197 Ibid. 804ff.

198 Pher. 3F135.

199 Paus. 8.34.2–3.

200 Paus. 2.31.7,11 and 3.22.1 respectively.

201 Schol. Soph. *Oed. Col.* 42 (sacrifice), Paus. 7.25.4 (sanctuary).

202 Apollod. *Epit.* 6.25, Marmor Parium 239F25, Et. Magn. s.v. Aiora (acted with Tyndareos, hanged herself afterwards), Dictys 6.4 (hanged herself).

203 Paus. 8.34.4.

204 Hyg. *Fab.* 119; mentioned as variant without any details in Apollod. *Epit.* 6.25.

205 Eur. *Iph. Taur.* 77–91.

206 Ibid. 1ff.

207 Proclus on *Cypria*, Hdt. 4.103.

208 Hes. fr. 23a.17–26, 23b (see Paus. 1.43.1), Stesichorus 215.

209 Ant. Lib. 27, following Nicander.

210 Eur. *Iph. Taur.* (recognition scene, 769ff; I.'s plan for escape, 1029ff; Athena's revelations, 1435ff).

211 Eur. *Iph. Taur.* 1458–61.

212 Ibid. 1462–7.

213 At Brauron, Paus. 1.23.9, 1.33.1; at Sparta, Paus. 3.16.7; at Aricia, Serv. *Aen.* 2.116, 6.136.

214 Hyg. *Fab.* 122.

215 Paus. 2.18.4–5.

216 Hom. *Od.* 4.5–9.

217 Soph. *Hermione* as reported in schol. *Od.* 4.4 and Eustath. on ibid.

218 Paus. 2.18.5, reporting Cinaethon (= fr. 4 Davies), 3.2.1 (Penthilos on Lesbos), Str. 13.1.3.

219 Asclepiades 12F25 (seventy at time), Apollod. *Epit.* 6.28; Vell. Pat. 1.1.3 (died at ninety, place not stated).

220 Paus. 8.5.4.

221 Paus. 8.54.4.

222 Hdt. 1.67–8, cf. Paus. 3.3.6.

223 Apollod. 2.8.3 (killed in battle), Paus. 7.1.3 (expelled and killed later in Achaea).

15 THE ATLANTIDS, THE ASOPIDS AND THE ARCADIAN ROYAL FAMILY

1   Hes. *W.D.* 383.
2   Hyg. *Astr.* 2.21 (seven years), schol. Pi. *Nem.* 2.16 (five years), schol. A.R. 3.225.
3   Schol. Arat. 254, schol. *Il.* 18.486.
4   Hyg. *Fab.* 192, cf. Hyg. *Astr.* 2.21, schol. *Il.* 18.486.
5   Aesch. fr. 312 Nauck.
6   See Athen. 491b.
7   Hyg. *Astr.* 2.21, Eratosth. 23, Ov. *Fasti* 4.175–6, Serv. *Georg.* 1.138.
8   Ovid *Fasti* 4.177–8, schol. Arat. 257, Q.S. 13.551–61; as comet, Hyg. *Fab.* 192, Hyg. *Astr.* 2.21, schol. *Il.* 18.486.
9   For the family of Atlas and Pleione, Hes. fr. 169, Hellanic. 4F19, Apollod. 3.10.1.
10   *Hom. Hymn 4 to Hermes* 1–12, *Hom. Hymn 18 to Hermes* 1–9, Apollod. 3.10.2.
11   *Hom. Hymn 4 to Hermes* 4, Hom. *Od.* 14.435; Maia reared Arkas, Apollod. 3.8.2.
12   Hellanic. 4F19a, Apollod. 3.10.1; Merope first named as his wife, Pher. 3F119 (her descent unstated).
13   Hellanic. 4F19a.
14   Apollod. 3.10.1, Paus. 5.10.6; Harpina as the mother of Oinomaos, Paus. 5.22.6.
15   Hellanic. 4F19b, Apollod. 3.10.1.
16   Schol. Pi. *Pyth.* 4.57, Tzetz. Lyc. 886.
17   Schol. A.R. 2.498.
18   Pi. *Pyth.* 4.33.
19   Apollod. 3.10.1.
20   Hes. fr. 188A.
21   Hom. *Il.* 2.536–45.
22   Paus. 9.19.3, cf. 8.15.6, 9.17.2.
23   Hom. *Il.* 4.457–72.
24   Steph. Byz. s.v. Anthedon, Paus. 9.22.5.
25   Paus. 9.20.2, Steph. Byz. s.v. Eleutherai.
26   Conon 21, Apollod. 3.12.1, cf. Hellanic. 4F23 (her children Dardanos, Eetion and Harmonia). Elektra was apparently the mother of Dardanos and Eetion in the Hesiodic *Cataogue*, fr. 177, although the relevant papyrus is full of gaps.
27   Conon 21, Apollod. 3.12.1.
28   Lyc. 72–8 with schol. 73.
29   Hellanic. 4F24, D.S. 4.75.1, Apollod. 3.12.1.
30   Lyc. 1302–8 with scholia, Serv. *Aen.* 3.108; Apollo Smintheus, Hom. *Il.* 1.38–9.
31   D.H. *Ant. Rom.* 1.61.
32   Hom. *Il.* 20.215–20, Hes. fr. 177.13–15, Apollod. 3.12.1–2.
33   Hom. *Il.* 20.220–2.
34   Hom. *Il.* 20.219–33, D.S. 4.75.2–3, Apollod. 3.12.2.
35   Hom. *Il.* 20.232–5.
36   *Hom. Hymn. Aphrodite* 202–17.
37   Schol. *Od.* 11.521.
38   Sent eagle, Eratosth. 30, Pliny *N.H.* 34.79, Apollod. 3.12.2; turned himself into eagle, Ov. *Met.* 10.155–6, Lucian *D.D.* 10.
39   Theognis 1345–8, Pi. *Ol.* 1.40–5, Pl. *Phdr.* 255c.
40   Hom. *Il.* 20.239–40, Apollod. 3.12.2, etc.
41   Apollod. 3.12.3.
42   Schol. Lyc. 29.

43 Apollod. 3.12.3.

44 Hom. *Il.* 11.371–2 etc.

45 Apollod. 3.12.3, cf. Hom. *Il.* 20.236.

46 Hom. *Il.* 7.452–3, 21.441–57, Apollod. 2.5.9.

47 On these events, see e.g. Apollod. 2.5.9 with 2.6.4; fuller references will be found under the full discussion in Chapter 8.

48 Hom. *Il.* 3.146ff, 24.159ff.

49 Apollod. 3.10.3, Paus. 3.1.2.

50 Apollod. 3.10.3, Paus. 3.1.1–4; almost nothing has survived from the relevant sections of the Hesiodic *Catalogue*, see fr. 129.10–12 (reference to Eurydike, daughter of Lakedaimon, who married Akrisios, cf. Apollod. l.c.), fr. 171 (very patchy, but apparently refers to Hyakinthos as a son of Amyklas).

51 Apollod. 3.10.4–5.

52 Ibid., Str. 10.2.24.

53 Paus. 3.1.4, schol. Eur. *Orest.* 457.

54 Apollod. 3.10.5–6, cf. Pher. 3F128, schol. *Od.* 4.797.

55 Pher. 3F129.

56 Paus. 3.12.1.

57 Paus. 3.20.10–11.

58 Apollod. 3.10.6–7, Hes. fr. 23a (three daughters of Tyndareos and Leda).

59 Hom. *Od.* 11.298–300 (cf. *Hom. Hymn.*17 and 33.1–5), Hes. fr. 24.

60 Pi. *Nem.* 10.80–2, Apollod. 3.10.7.

61 Schol. Eur. *Orest.* 249, quoting Stesichorus (= 223 *PMG*) and referring to 'Hesiod' also (= fr. 176).

62 Hom. *Il.* 3.237, *Od.* 11.300, Apollod. 3.11.2.

63 Boar-hunt, Apollod. 1.8.2, Ov. *Met.* 8.301–2; Argonauts, A.R. 1.146–50, Apollod. 1.9.16; Polydeukes kills Amykos, A.R. 2.1–97.

64 Alcman 1.1ff.

65 Apollod. 3.11.2.

66 Proclus on *Cypria*.

67 Pi. *Nem.* 10.60.

68 Schol. *Il.* 3.243, schol. Pi. *Nem.* 10.112.

69 Theoc. 22.137–70.

70 Schol. Lyc. 547. On this episode, see also Lyc. 535–49 and schol. 538.

71 Paus. 3.18.11.

72 Apollod. 3.11.2.

73 Paus. 3.16.1.

74 Pi. *Nem.* 10.55–90, Apollod. 3.11.2; cf. Proclus on *Cypria* with frr. 6 (Kastor mortal) and 13 Davies (Lynkeus sees Dioskouroi hiding in oak).

75 Proclus on *Cypria*.

76 E.g. Ov. *Fasti* 5.709–10, Hyg. *Fab.* 80 respectively.

77 Hyg. *Fab.* 80.

78 Theoc. 22.171ff.

79 Eratosth. 10, Hyg. *Astr.* 2.22.

80 Alcaeus 34.

81 Cic. *N.D.* 2.2.6, 3.5.11, D.H. *Ant. Rom.* 6.13.

82 Hom. *Il.* 21.188–9.

83 Apollod. 3.12.6; that Asopos bribed Sisyphos with offer of spring, Paus. 2.5.1. See also Pi. *Isth.* 8.17–23 and *Paean* 6.134–40 (both referring to the abduction without details), Pher. 3F119 (S. told Asopos that Zeus had abducted Aigina), Call. *Hymn* 4.78 (Asopos struck by thunderbolt).

84   Pi. *Nem.* 8.6–8 with 13, *Isth.* 8.16–24, D.S. 4.72.5, Apollod. 3.12.6, Paus. 2.29.2.

85   Ov. *Met.* 7.520ff (plague), Hyg. *Fab.* 52 (snake).

86   Hes. fr. 205, Apollod. 3.12.6, Str. 8.6.16, Ov. *Met.* 7.614–60, Hyg. *Fab.* 52; cf. Serv. *Aen.* 4.402 (transformation story set in Peleus' Thessaly).

87   Apollod. 3.12.6, cf. D.S. 4.6.1–2 (drought caused by murder of Androgeos), Isocr. *Evagoras* 14–15 and Paus. 2.29.6 (cause not stated).

88   Paus. 1.39.5.

89   Pi. *Isth.* 8.23–4.

90   As judge, Pl. *Gorg,.* 524a, Ov. *Met.* 13.25, etc.; as doorkeeper, Arist. *Frogs* 465ff, keeper of keys, Apollod. 3.12.6.

91   Apollod. 3.12.6, Paus. 2.29.7, cf. Bacch 13.96–9 (two sons by Endeis), Pi. *Nem.* 5.8–13; Phokos as son by Psamathe, already Hes. *Theog.* 1003–5.

92   Apollod. 3.12.6, schol. Eur. *Androm.* 687.

93   Apollod. 3.12.6 (Telamon kills Phokos), *Alcmaeonis* fr. 1 Davies (Telamon strikes with discus, Peleus kills with axe), Paus. 2.29.7 (Peleus kills), D.S. 4.72.6 (Peleus kills accidentally).

94   Hom. *Il.* 21.188–9 (Achilles on own descent); Peleus as Aiakides, *Il.* 16.15, 18.433; Achilles as Aiakides, 2.874–5, 11.805 and often.

95   Pi. *Isth.* 6.19–27, *Alcmaeonis* fr. 1 Davies.

96   On this Thessalian Asopos, Hdt. 7.199.

97   Paus. 2.29.7.

98   Paus. 2.29.5.

99   Pi. *Ol.* 8.30–52.

100 Pi. *Ol.* 9.69–70, Hes. fr. 212a.

101 Apollod. 3.12.7, D.S. 4.72.7.

102 Pi. *Isth.* 6.35–54, cf. Hes. fr. 250.

103 E.g. A.R. 1.90–3 and Apollod. 1.8.2 respectively.

104 Serv. *Aen.* 1.619 (Teukros banished, Tekmessa and Eurysakes arrive on later ship), Justin 44.3 (Eurysakes turns Teukros away when he tries to return later).

105 Plut. *Solon* 10.

106 Apollod. 3.13.1, cf. Ant. Lib. 38 (received by Eurytion, son of Iros), D.S. 4.72.6 (received by Aktor, who leaves the kingdom to him because he has no heir).

107 Hom. *Il.* 16.173–8.

108 Pher. 3F1b, 61b.

109 Tzetz. Lyc. 175 (Polymele), schol. *Il.* 16.175 (Eurydike).

110 Apollod. 3.13.2, 1.8.2, Ant. Lib. 38.

111 Apollod. 3.9.2; cf. Hyg. *Fab.* 273 (Peleus victor in wrestling), Paus. 5.17.10 (was shown wrestling against Jason on chest of Kypselos).

112 Apollod. 3.13.3, cf. Hes. fr. 208, 209 (Akastos hides Peleus' sword in the hope that he will be killed by Centaurs), Pi. *Nem.* 4.54–61, 5.26–34.

113 Schol. Pi. *Nem.* 4.92a, schol. Ar. *Clouds* 1063, schol. A.R. 1.224.

114 Schol. A.R. 1.224.

115 Pi. *Nem.* 3.33–4.

116 Apollod. 3.13.7, cf. Pher. 3F62, schol. A.R. 1.224 (killed Akastos).

117 Hes. fr. 211.

118 Apollod. 3.13.3–5.

119 A.R. 4.869–79 with schol. 869, Apollod. 3.13.6.

120 Lyc. 177–9 with schol. (six killed in fire), schol. A.R. 4.816 (many), cf. Hes. fr. 300 (into cauldron of water).

121 D.S. 4.72.3–4, cf. Apollod. 3.12.7.

122 Hes. fr. 226.

123 Paus. 1.36.1.

124 Pher. 3F60.

125 Hom. *Od.* 8.564–5, 6.3–10.

126 Ibid. 7.54–5.

127 Ibid. 7.56–68.

128 Hellanic. 4F77 with D.S. 4.72.3.

129 Hes. fr. 222.

130 A.R. 4.539–51, 566–71.

131 D.S. 4.72.1–5.

132 Paus. 5.22.6.

133 Paus. 2.2.3.

134 Paus. 2.2.3.

135 A.R. 2.946–54, with schol. 953 (latter version).

136 Hom. *Od.* 11.2660.

137 Pi. *Isth.* 8.17–24, Bacch. 9.39–56.

138 A.R. 4.263–5 with schol. 264 (citing Aristotle = fr.549 Rose, and other authors).

139 Paus. 8.1.4, citing Asius (= fr. 8 Davies); Pelasgos as earthborn, also Apollod. 2.1.1 and 3.8.1 citing Hesiod (= fr. 160), and Str. 5.2.4 citing Ephorus (= 70F113) and quoting Hesiodic verses (= fr. 161).

140 Paus. 8.4.1.

141 Paus. 8.1.5–6.

142 Acus. 2F25.

143 Paus. 1.14.2, 2.22.2 respectively.

144 Son of Triopas, schol. Eur. *Orest.* 920; of Agenor, Hyg. *Fab.* 124.

145 Aesch. *Suppl.* 234ff (king first appears), 250–1 (as son of earthborn Palaichthon), etc.

146 D.H. *Ant. Rom.* 1.17, schol. *Il.* 2.681; for children, D.H. l.c., Steph. Byz. s.v. Kranon and Dotion.

147 Apollod. 3.8.1., schol. Eur. *Orest.* 1645, cf. Hyg. *Fab.* 161 (Lykaon son of Pelasgos).

148 Paus. 8.2.1, cf. schol. Eur. *Orest.* 1648 (named Zeus as Lykaios, founded games); on Mt Lykaon, see Paus. 8.38, gilded eagles, 8.38.7.

149 Apollod. 3.8.1; for a different catalogue, see Paus. 8.3.1–5.

150 Apollod. 3.8.1.

151 Paus. 8.3.1, Apollod. 3.8.1.

152 Apollod. 3.81, Eratosth. 8, schol. Lyc. 481; otherwise named after its founder Trapezous, son of Lykaon, Paus. 8.3.2, Steph. Byz. s.v. Trapezous.

153 Hyg. *Fab.* 176.

154 Schol. Lyc. 481.

155 Nic. Damasc. 90F38.

156 Eratosth. 8, citing Hesiod = fr. 163 (serves Arkas to Zeus, to avenge seduction of Kallisto), Tzetz. Lyc. 482 (serves Nyktimos), Ov. *Met.* 1.218–39 (serves Molossian hostage, to test divinity of Zeus).

157 Paus. 8.2.3.

158 Paus. 8.2.6, cf. Pl. *Rep.* 565d and Pliny *N.H.* 8.81.

159 As nymph, Apollod. 3.8.2 citing Hesiod (= fr. 163); as daughter of Lykaon, Eratosth. 1, citing Hesiod (possibly the *Astronomy* if the report can be relied upon).

160 Eumelus fr. 10 Davies, Asius fr. 9 Davies, Pher. 3F157 (all in Apollod. 3.8.2).

161 Apollod. 3.8.2, cf. the similar version cited in Hyg. *Astr.* 2.1.

162 Artemis kills her unknowingly, Call. fr. 362, Hyg. *Astr.* 2.1; kills her knowingly, e.g. Paus. 8.3.6.

163 Ov. *Met.* 2.401–530; although Ovid does not name the constellations here, he does so in the *Fasti* in connection with the rising of Bootes, 2.189–92.
164 Eratosth. 1, Hyg. *Astr.* 2.1.
165 Eratosth. 8, Hyg. *Astr.* 2.4.
166 Amphis fr. 47 (as reported in Hyg. *str.* 2.1 etc.), Ov. *Met.* 2.425–7.
167 Paus. 8.4.1.
168 Apollod. 3.9.1, Paus. 4.1.2 (Includes Azan).
169 Paus. 4.1.3–4.
170 Athene Alea, Paus. 8.4.8; Aleos as founder of Tegea, 8.45.1.
171 Apollod. 2.7.4, 3.9.1.
172 D.S. 4.33.7–12.
173 Alcidamas *Odyss.* 14–16.
174 Paus. 8.4.9, cf. Str. 13.1.69 (that mother and child put into chest in unnamed play by Euripides).
175 Hes. fr. 165; see also Hyg. *Fab.* 99, 100 for stories in which Auge is the adopted daughter of Teuthras.
176 Apollod. 3.9.1, Paus. 8.4.8 (Amphidamas also as son; otherwise son of Lykourgos, e.g. Apollod. 3.9.3).
177 Hom. *Il.* 7.137–47, cf. Paus. 8.4.10, 8.11.4 (tomb of Areithoos by narrow road).
178 A.R. 1.167–71.
179 A.R. 1.397–8, 425–30; on Bebrycians, ibid. 2.118ff.
180 Ovid provides the fullest account, *Met.* 8.390–402; cf. Bacch. 5.115–17, Apollod. 1.8.2. Lyc. 486–93 even suggests that the wounded Ankaios killed the boar.
181 Paus. 8.45.2, 7.
182 Hom. *Il.* 2.609–14, Paus. 8.5.2.
183 E.g. Apollod. 3.9.2.
184 Apollod. 3.9.2; more detailed account of confrontation with Centaurs in Ael. *V.H.* 13.1.
185 D.S. 4.48.5, Apollod. 1.19.6.
186 A.R. 1.769–73.
187 Apollod. 3.9.2, 3.13.3.
188 E.g. Apollod. 1.8.2, Ov. *Met.* 8.380ff.
189 Paus. 8.46.1.
190 Apollod. 3.9.2.
191 Hes. fr. 75.
192 Apollod. 3.9.2.
193 E.g. Apollod. 3.9.2.
194 Hes. frr. 74 and 76 (Hippomenes), Apollod. 3.9.2 (Melanion), Ov. *Met.* 10.560–680 (Hippomenes), Hyg. *Fab.* 185 (Hippomenes).
195 Hesperides, Serv. *Aen.* 3.113; Tamasus, Ov. *Met.* 10.644–51.
196 Ov. *A.A.* 2.185–92, cf. Xen. *On Hunting* 1.7.
197 Ov. *Met.* 10.681–704, cf. Serv. *Aen.* 3.113; in shrine of Zeus, Apollod. 3.9.2, Hyg. *Fab.* 185. Story first mentioned in Palaeph. 13.
198 Hyg. *Fab.* 185, Serv. *Aen.* 3.113.
199 E.g. Hellanic. 4F99 (by Melanion), Hyg. *Fab.* 99 (by Meleagros), Apollod. 3.9.2 (by Ares or Melanion).
200 Paus. 8.47.6.
201 Apollod. 2.7.3, cf. D.S. 4.33.6 (three sons survive).
202 Apollod. 2.7.3.
203 Hdt. 9.26.
204 Pi. *Ol.* 10.66.

205 Apollod. 3.10.6, Hes. frr. 23a.31–5 (bore him a son Laodokos), 176 (deserted him for Phyleus).
206 Paus. 8.4.4.
207 An Ischys is thus mentioned by Paus. l.c. among the children of the Arcadian Elatos.
208 Paus. 8.4.4.
209 Hom. *Il.* 2.603–4.
210 Paus. 8.16.2–3.
211 Pi. *Ol.* 6.27–57.
212 Pi. *Ol.* 6.57–71; Phaisane ibid. 34.
213 Paus. 8.4.6.
214 Apollod. 3.12.6.
215 Paus. 8.5.4.
216 Paus. 8.5.5, 8.10.2–3.
217 Paus. 8.5.6.
218 Paus. 8.4.4–5.
219 D.S. 4.37.1.
220 Paus. 8.4.5.

16   LEGENDS OF GREEK LANDS

1 Pl. *Symp.* 179d, A.R. 1.23–5, Apollod. 1.3.2, etc.; son of Apollo, e.g. Asclepiades 12F6.
2 Simonides 567, Aesch. *Ag.* 1629–30, Eur. *Iph. Aul.* 1211–14, *Bacch.* 560–4, A.R. 1.26–31, D.S. 4.25.2.
3 Eratosth. 24, schol. Arat. 269, Vat. Myth. 2.44.
4 Conon 45.2, Apollod. 1.3.2, Ov. *Met.* 10.1–85, Verg. *Georg.* 454–503, ps.Verg. *Culex* 268–95.
5 See Eur. *Alc.* 357–62, Eratosth. 24 referring to Aeschylus.
6 Moschus 3.124, Hermesianax fr. 7 Powell.
7 Paus. 10.30.2.
8 Ov. *Met.* 11.1–66, Verg. *Georg.* 4.520–7.
9 Phanocles fr. 1 Powell, cf. Hyg. *Astr.* 2.7 (some say that torn apart because introduced love of young boys).
10 Conon 45.4, Paus. 9.30.3 respectively.
11 Eratosth. 24.
12 Paus. 9.30.3, Hyg. *Astr.* 2.7 respectively.
13 Ov. *Met.* 11.44–9.
14 Phanocles fr.1 Powell, Plut. *Moralia* 557e; contrasting account in *Anth. Pal.* 7.10.
15 Hyg. *Astr.* 2.7, Ov. *Met.* 11.50–60, Aristides 24.
16 To heavens, Eratosth. 24, Hyg. *Astr.* 2.7; to Lesbos, Ov. *Met.* 11.50–55, Philostr. *Her.* 10.6, Phanocles fr. 1.19 (buried with head), Lucian *Adv. Indoc.* 11 (placed in temple).
17 Lucian. *Adv. Indoc.* 12.
18 Verg. *Aen.* 1.316–17.
19 Hyg. *Fab.* 193; rescues father from Getae, Serv. *Aen.* 1.317.
20 D.S. 4.69.3–4, schol. A.R. 3.62, schol. Pi. *Pyth.* 2.40b; early allusions, Aesch. *Eum.* 718 (committed first murder), Pi. *Pyth.* 2.31–2 (similar).
21 Pi. *Pyth.* 2.21–48, cf. D.S. 4.69.4–5, Apollod. *Epit.* 1.20, Lucian *D.D.* 6; Hyg. *Fab.* 62 (bound to wheel by Hermes), schol. Eur. *Phoen.* 1185 (fiery wheel), Verg. *Georg.* 3.37–9 (snakes on wheel); suffers punishment in Underworld, A.R. 3.61–2 and usually thereafter, e.g. Verg. l.c. and *Aen.* 6.601.

22 D.S. 4.69.1–2.
23 Apollod. 1.2.4 (cf. Hes. *Theog.* 1001–2, Cheiron Philyrides), 2.5.4 respectively.
24 E.g. D.S. 4.70.3, Hyg. *Fab.* 33, Ovid *Heroides* 17.248 respectively.
25 War between Lapiths and Centaurs, D.S. 4.70.3–4, Plut. *Thes.* 30, Ov. *Met.* 12.210–535; Centaurs try to rape bride, conflict apparently settled in battle immediately, Apollod. *Epit.* 1.21; Theseus arrives after start of conflict, Herodorus 31F27 (from Plut. l.c.), cf. Isoc. *Helen* 26; alternative account in which war starts because Centaurs demand share of kingdom, D.S. 4.70.2.
26 Hom. *Il.* 1.262–72, cf. 2.741–4; *Od.* 21.295–304.
27 Hom. *Il.* 2.738–47.
28 Father of Kaineus and Polyphemos, Hyg. *Fab.* 14, schol. A.R. 1.40; father of Ischys, Pi. *Pyth.* 3.31. with schol. 55.
29 A.R. 4.1470–9.
30 Apollod. *Epit.* 1.22 (very brief), Ov. *Met.* 12.189–207; early references to change of sex, Hes. fr. 87, Acus. 2F22 (here called Kaine as girl).
31 Acus. 2F22 (cf. schol.*Il.* 1.264) and schol. A.R. 1.57 respectively.
32 Acus 2F22, A.R. 1.59–64, Apollod. *Epit.* 1.22, Ov. *Met.* 12.459–535.
33 As Argonaut, A.R. 1.57–8; war with Dorians, D.S. 4.37.3, Apollod. 2.7.7.
34 Apollod. 1.9.16.
35 Hdt. 2.55–7.
36 Hom. *Od.* 18.83–7, 21.306–9, schol. *Od.* 18.86, A.R. 4.1092–5.
37 Hom. *Il.* 9.379–84.
38 Paus. 9.36.3.
39 Apollod. 2.4.11, Paus. 9.37.2.
40 D.S. 4.10.5 (Herakles razes Orchomenos), Paus. 9.38.5 (floods plain).
41 Paus. 9.34.5–37.3.
42 Paus. 9.37.2–3.
43 Paus. 8.10.2.
44 *Hom. Hymn. Apollo* 296–7, Paus. 10.5.5.
45 Paus. 9.11.1 and 9.37.3 respectively.
46 Plut. *Moralia* 109a (citing Pindar), ps.Pl. *Axiochos* 367c, Cic. *Tusc.* 1.47.
47 Paus. 9.37.3.
48 As in Paus. l.c.
49 Schol. Arist. *Clouds* 508.
50 Hdt. 2.121.
51 Hdt. 1.31, Cic. *Tusc.* 1.47 (specifies that their mother was a priestess of Hera); see Paus. 2.19.4 for another story about Biton.
52 Paus. 9.40.1.
53 Paus. 9.39.4, Lucian *D.M.* 3.2.
54 Hom. *Il.* 13.298–302.
55 E.g. *Hom. Hymn. Apollo* 278–80, schol. *Il.* 13.301.
56 Paus. 9.36.1–2.
57 Serv. *Aen.* 6.618, schol. Stat. *Theb.* 1.713.
58 Verg. *Aen.* 6.616–20, cf. Stat. *Theb.* 1.712ff, Val. Flacc. 2.192ff.
59 Apollod. 3. 5. 5, Paus. 9.36.1 respectively.
60 Koronis as daughter of Phlegyas, Hes. fr. 60, Apollod. 3.10.3 etc.; she lived by the Boibian Lake in the Dotian Fields, Hes. fr. 59, cf. Pi. *Pyth.* 3.34, *Hom. Hymn* 16 to *Asklepios* 2–3, hence Dotis as a name for the mother of Phlegyas.
61 E.g. schol. A.R. 3.62 (citing Euripides = fr. 424 Nauck), Steph. Byz. s.v. Gyrton respectively. Gyrton was the city of Ixion and Peirithoos; the Phlegyans were sometimes identified with the Gyrtonians, e.g. schol. *Il.* 13.301, 302.

62   *Hom. Hymn. Apollo* 278–80; on Phlegya, Steph. Byz. s.v. Phlegya.
63   Paus. 9.36.1.
64   Schol. *Il.* 13.302.
65   Pher. 3F41.
66   Apollod. 3.5.5.
67   Hom. *Od.* 11.572–5, *Il.* 18.486.
68   Hom. *Il.* 22.26–30.
69   Hom. *Il.* 18.487–8, *Od.* 5.273–4.
70   Hom. *Od.* 11.308–10, 5.121–4.
71   Hes. fr. 148a (= Eratosth. 32), Pher. 3F52.
72   Ov. *Fasti* 5.493–536, Hyg. *Fab.* 195, *Astr.* 2.34, schol. *Il.* 18.486, schol. *Od.* 5.121; first mentioned Palaeph. 51.
73   Apollod. 1.4.3.
74   Schol. Nic. *Ther.* 15; tomb, Paus. 9.20.3.
75   Corinna 654.38, 655.14, 662, 673, Euphorion fr. 103 Powell.
76   Schol. Arat. 254, schol. A.R. 3.225–70.
77   Ant. Lib. 25, cf. Ov. *Met.* 13.685–99.
78   Apollod. 1.4.3, Ovid *Art of Love* 1.731 (only other reference to Side), Athen. 650f (on Sidai).
79   Schol. A.R. 3.997 (birth), D.S. 5.79.1 (learned art of wine-making from Dionysos), Athen. 26b (red wine on Chios).
80   Eratosth. 32 (ascribed to Hes. = fr. 148a), Parthen. 20 (events on Chios only, daughter of Oinopion called Hairo), Apollod. 1.4.3, Hyg. *Astr.* 2.34, Lucian *Dom.* 28–9 (guided by Kedalion, cured by Helios).
81   Apollod. 1.4.5, schol. *Od.* 5.121.
82   Hyg. *Astr.* 2.34 citing Call. (= fr. 570), Horace *Ode* 3.4.70–2.
83   Eratosth. 32, Hyg. *Astr.* 2.26; cf. Nic. *Ther.* 15 (Artemis and Leto send scorpion against him for some reason).
84   Aratus 634–46, cf. Eratosth. 7, schol. *Il.* 18.486 citing Euphorion (= fr. 101 Powell), Palaeph. 51.
85   Schol. German. Arat. 63–4.
86   Ov. *Fasti* 5.537–44.
87   Hyg. *Astr.* 2.3 citing Istros (= Istros 334F64).
88   Pi. *Ol.* 9.40–68; descent of Lokros, Hecat. 1F16 with Steph. Byz. s.v. Physkos.
89   Plut. *Quaest. Gr.* 15, Eustath. On *Il.* 2.531.
90   From Naryx, Str. 9.425, cf. Ov. *Met.* 14.468; descent from Lokros, Eustath. On *Il.* 2.531.
91   Hecat. 1F15, Paus. 10.38.1.
92   Str. 9.4.8.
93   Paus. 10.38.1 for both suggestions.
94   Paus. 2.29.2–3, 10.1.1.
95   Paus. 10.32.6–7, 9.17.3–4 (joint grave of Phokos and Antiope).
96   Hom. *Il.* 2.517–26.
97   Hes. fr. 58 (wife Asterodia, sons quarrelled in womb), Paus. 2.29.4 (citing Asius = fr. 4 Davies, on name of sons), Lyc. 939 and schol.
98   Paus. 2.29.2–3.
99   Paus. 2.29.4.
100 Paus. 2.29.4; as builder of Wooden Horse, Hom. *Od.* 8.492–5.
101 See Hdt. 1.56, 8.31 and 8.43.
102 Paus. 1,39.4, 1.40.5 (Karia and Demeter's Megaron), 1.44.9, Steph. Byz. s.v. Karia.

103 Paus. 1.39.5, 1.42.8 (Kleson), 1.44.5 (parentage of Lelex).

104 Paus. 1.39.5.

105 Paus. 1.39.5 with 1.41.4 (Megareus as king; the course of the succession as proposed in 1.41.5 represents Pausanias' own conjecture rather than a reported tradition).

106 Paus. 1.41.4.

107 Paus. 1.41.4, with schol. A.R. 1.517 (story of tongues); Pi. *Isth.* 8.67, *Nem.* 5.45–6 with schol. 84, games of Alkathoia held at Megara in commemoration of his exploit.

108 Paus. 1.42.1, Ov. *Met.* 8.14–19.

109 Paus. 1.42.7.

110 Paus. 1.43.4.

111 Paus. 2.5.5–6.4.

112 Paus. 7.23.1–2.

113 Paus. 7.19.1–3; Eurypylos, Hom. *Il.* 2.734–7 and passim.

114 Paus. 7.21.1.

115 Apollod. *Epit.* 3.10.

116 D.S. 5.62.1–2.

117 Schol. Lyc. 570.

118 Schol. Lyc. 580.

119 Schol. Lyc. 570, Apollod. *Epit.* 3.10 (wife of Anios not named).

120 Lyc. 569–83 with schol. 570 (quoting Pherecydes = 3F140, and claiming that some such story was recounted in the *Cypria* = fr. 19 Davies).

121 Schol. Lyc. 581, schol. *Od.* 6.164 respectively.

122 Ov. *Met.* 13.632–74.

123 Dictys 1.23, Serv. *Aen.* 3.80.

124 Verg. *Aen.* 3.78–124, Ov. *Met.* 13.631ff.

125 Call. frr. 67–75, Aristaenetus Ep. 1.10, Ovid *Heroides* 20, 21.

126 Ov. *Met.* 10.106–42.

127 Serv. *Aen.* 3.680; Syrian location also in Philostr. *V.A.* 1.16.

128 Hdt. 4.147.

129 Hdt. 4.142–50, Paus. 3.1.5–8, 4.3.4.

130 A.R. 4.1747–54.

131 Hdt. 4.145–59, Pi. *Pyth.* 4.4–65, schol. A.R. 4.1764.

132 Hyg. *Astr.* 2.16.

133 Schol. *Il.* 24.293.

134 Steph. Byz. s.v. Merops and Kos.

135 A.R. 2.854–95; Schol. A.R. 1.188, schol. Lyc. 488.

136 Hom. *Il.* 11.19–40.

137 Apollod. *Epit.* 3.9, Eustath. On *Il.* 11.20.

138 Alcidamas *Odyss.* 20–21.

139 E.g. schol. Pi. *Pyth.* 2.27, Apollod. 3.14.3 respectively.

140 Ov. *Met.* 10.298ff, Hyg. *Fab.* 58.

141 Apollod. 3.14.3.

142 Hyg. *Fab.* 242, Pliny *N.H.* 7.49, Eustath. on *Il.* 11.20 respectively.

143 Eustath. l.c.

144 Apollod. 3.14.3.

145 Ov. *Met.* 10.238–42.

146 Ibid. 10.222–37.

147 Ibid. 6.98–100.

148 Ibid. 10.243–97; other version Clem. Alex. *Protr.* pp. 17,31ff, Arnob. *Adv. Nat.* 6.22.

149 Pi. *Nem.* 4.46, Eur. *Helen* 87–104; cf. Soph. *Ajax* 1008–20 (Teukros suspects that his father will banish him).

150 Serv. *Aen.* 1.619.

151 Verg. *Aen.* 1.619–22 with Servius on 621.

152 Paus. 1.3.2 and 2.29.4, cf. Isocr. *Evagoras* 18–19; Eune as wife, schol. Lyc. 450.

153 Musaeus *Hero and Leander*; Verg. *Georg.* 3.258–63, Ov. *Heroides* 18,19.

154 Ov. *Met.* 8.618–724.

155 A. Westermann *Mythographoi: Scriptores Poeticae Historiae Graecae*, Brunswick, 1843, p. 324.

156 Ov. *Met.* 4.55–166.

157 Pliny *N.H.* 7.1–32.

158 Hom. *Il.* 3.3–7.

159 Ant. Lib. 16, Athen. 9.393e–f, Ael. *N.A.* 15.29; allusion in Ov. *Met.* 6.90–2.

160 Hdt. 2.32, cf. Hes. fr. 150.9–19, Arist. *H.A.* 8.12.

161 Philostr. *Imag.* 2.22, Ammianus 22.12.4.

162 Aristeas fr. 4A Davies (from Str. 1.2.10, Pliny *N.H.* 7.10 and Paus. 1.24.6), Hdt. 3.116, 4.13, 4.27, Aesch. *Prom. Bound* 803–6.

163 D.S. 4.24.7, Serv. *Aen.* 3.552; see also Ov. *Met.* 15.12–59 (the city's foundation legend; mentions Herakles' visit to the site, but not the Lakinios episode).

164 Conon 3 (Latinos in MSS, sometimes amended to Lakinos).

165 Hdt. 7.170, cf. Conon 25, Str. 6.3.6.

166 Verg. *Aen.* 5.700ff; companions of Philoktetes, Str. 6.1.3.

167 Serv. *Aen.* 1.550.

168 Schol. Lyc. 952. For a rationalized version of the myth, see D.H. *Ant. Rom.* 1.52.

169 Paus. 10.10.3.

170 Hdt. 1.23–4.

171 Hyg. *Fab.* 194, *Astr.* 2.17, Serv. *Ecl.* 8.55, cf. Ov. *Fast.* 2.81ff.

172 Hdt. 1.24, Paus. 3.25.7.

173 Athen. 11.446c–d, Plut. *Moralia* 163c, 984d.

174 Pliny *N.H.* 9.8–26.

175 Conon 18, Paus. 3.19.11–13.

176 Paus. 6.6.8–10, cf. Call. frr. 98–9, Ael. *V.H.* 8.18 (Hero exacted a tribute, Euthymos forced him to repay it with interest), Str. 6.1.5 (temple of Polites at Temesa).

17 AENEAS, ROMULUS AND THE ORIGINS OF ROME

1 Hom. *Il.* 20.287–309.

2 Proclus on *Cypria*.

3 *Hom. Hymn. Aphrodite* 196–8.

4 Xen. *On Hunting* 1.15, cf. Apollod. *Epit.* 5.21.

5 Stes. 205.

6 Hellanic. 4F84 (= D.H. *Ant. Rom.* 1.72.1–2)

7 Hellanic. 4F31 (see D.H. *Ant. Rom.* 1.47.1–6).

8 See e.g. Plut. *Rom.* 2, D.H. *Ant. Rom.* 1.72.1.

9 See e.g. D.H. *Ant. Rom.* 1.72.5 (by Aineias), 1.72.6 (by Askanios), Plut. *Rom.* 2.1.

10 Both in Serv. *Aen.* 1.273 (former from Herakleides Lembos, cf. Fest. p. 329 L.)

11 See e.g. D.H. *Ant. Rom.* 1.72, Plut. *Rom.* 2.1.

12 Plut. *Rom.* 2.1.

13 D.H. *Ant. Rom.* 1.72.6.

14 Plut. *Rom.* 1.1.

15 Sallust *Cat.* 6.1.2.

16 Verg. *Aen.* 3.1–191.

17 Ibid. 192–267.

18 Ibid. 268–505.

19 Ibid. 506–715.

20 Ibid. Books. 1 and 4.

21 Ibid. Book 5.

22 Ibid. Book 6.

23 Ibid. 7.1–36, 107–29.

24 Ibid. 7.148ff; oracle granted to Latinus on marriage of daughter, 7.81–101. The succeeding events take us to the end of the epic.

25 Hes. *Theog.* 1011–16.

26 Hyg. *Fab.* 127.

27 Verg. *Aen.* 7.47–9.

28 D.H. *Ant. Rom.* 1.43.1, Justin 43.1.

29 Cato *Origines* frr. 8–12.

30 D.H. *Ant. Rom.* 1.57-2-59.1.

31 Verg. *Aen.* 3.388–93, 8.31–85.

32 Ibid. 6.703ff.

33 Ibid. 6.760–6.

34 Ibid. 6.767–87.

35 D.H. *Ant. Rom.* 1.67.4 (= Timaeus 566F59).

36 Cato *Origines* fr. 4, Livy 1.1.3, D.H. *Ant. Rom.* 1.53.3, Serv. *Aen.* 1.5, 7.158.

37 D.S. 7.5.4–5 (citing Fabius Pictor), D.H. *Ant. Rom.* 1.56.

38 Lyc. 1253–60, Pliny *N.H.* 3.69.

39 D.S. 7.5.5.

40 Verg. *Aen.* 8.42–8.

41 D.S. 7.5.6.

42 Varro *Res Rust.* 2.4.18.

43 D.H. *Ant. Rom.* 1.64.5.

44 Livy 1.2.6 (does not commit himself on whether deified), Serv. *Aen.* 1.259 (some say that fell into river, Ovid that carried up to heaven), Ov. *Met.* 14.581–608 (turned into a god), Verg. *Aen.* 1.295–6, 12.794–5 (this foretold); D.H. *Ant. Rom.* 1.64 (with rationalistic explanation), Fest. 94 L.

45 Serv. *Aen.* 2.296, 3.12, 8.664, Val. Max. 1.6.7, Macrob. *Sat.* 3.4.11.

46 Hom. *Il.* 2.862–3.

47 *Hom. Hymn. Aphrodite* 191–201.

48 Verg. *Aen.* 8.47–9, D.H. *Ant. Rom.* 1.66.

49 Serv. *Aen.* 6.760.

50 Livy 1.3.6.

51 D.H. *Ant. Rom.* 1.67, Val. Max. 1.87.

52 Cato fr.13, D.H. *Ant. Rom.* 1.70; and in all catalogues of Alban kings (see p. 595).

53 Ascanius childless, Serv. *Aen.* 6.760; Silvius chosen instead of Iulus, D.H. *Ant. Rom.* 1.70.3, D.S. 7.5.8.

54 Livy 1.3.6–9.

55 D.H. *Ant. Rom.* 1.71.3, D.S. 7.5.11 (here as Aramulius Silvius); cf. Livy 1.3.9, Ov. *Met.* 14.617–18.

56 Hdt. 1.7, 1.34 etc.

57 Hom. *Il.* 17.323–5.

58 Ibid. 20.239.

59 Verg. *Aen.* 10.145, this Capys also mentioned 1.183, 9.576; Romus named city after old Capys, D.H. *Ant. Rom.* 1.73.3.

60 Paus. 6.21.10.
61 See Livy 2.32.
62 D.S. 7.5.10, D.H. *Ant. Rom.* 1.71.2, Serv. *Aen.* 8.72 and 330.
63 Livy 1.3.4, D.H. *Ant. Rom.* 1.71.4, Plut. *Rom.* 3, Justin 34.2, Serv. *Aen.* 6.777.
64 Livy 1.3.11–4.2, D.H. *Ant. Rom.* 1.77, Plut. *Rom.* 3, Justin 34.2.
65 E.g. schol. Hor. *Ode* 1.2.18 (citing Ennius), Serv. *Aen.* 1.273, Justin 34.2, Conon 48.
66 D.H. *Ant. Rom.* 1.79.6–8.
67 Plut. *Rom.* 3.
68 Livy 1.4.4–5.
69 Livy 1.4.5–6, Ov. *Fast.* 2.413–22, D.H. *Ant. Rom.* 1.76.6–8, Plut. *Rom.* 3.
70 Plut. *Rom.* 3, Serv. *Aen.* 1.273.
71 Ant. Lib. 30.
72 Ps.Plut. *Parallel Tales* 36.
73 Full narrative, D.H. *Ant. Rom.* 1.79.6–9; cf. Varro *de Re Rust.* 2.1.9, Livy 1.4.6–7, Plut. *Rom.* 6, Florus 1.1.3.
74 D.H. *Ant. Rom.* 1.79.10–11, Plut. *Rom.* 10, Livy 1.4.5.
75 Livy 1.4.8–9, Plut. *Rom.* 6.
76 D.H. *Ant. Rom.* 1.79.12–83.2, Plut. *Rom.* 7–10, Livy 1.5.6, Justin 43.2–3.
77 E.g. D.H. *Ant. Rom.* 1.85.1–4, Livy 1.6.
78 Ennius *Annals* 80ff.
79 Livy 1.7, cf. Serv. *Aen.* 1.273, Florus 1.1. For another version involving an initial deception on the part of Romulus, see Plut. *Rom.* 1.9, D.H. *Ant. Rom.* 1.86.3–4.
80 Livy 1.7 (cited as commoner version), Ennius *Annals* 94–6, D.H. *Ant. Rom.* 1.87.4, Plut. *Rom.* 10 (but ditch instead of wall), Florus 1.1.8.
81 Suppl. Hell. 715.
82 Plut. *Moralia* 299c.
83 Apollod. 1.8.1, cf. allusion in Suppl. Hell. 715.
84 Ov. *Fast.* 4.835–56.
85 Calpurnius Piso fr. 4P. (earliest mention), Livy 1.8.5, D.H. *Ant. Rom.* 2.15, Plut. *Rom.* 9.3.
86 Livy 1.9, D.H. *Ant. Rom.* 2.30, Plut. *Rom.* 14, Serv. *Aen.* 8.635; Fabius Pictor 809F5, Ennius *Scen.* 370, *Ann.* 98.
87 Livy 1.11.7–8, D.H. *Ant. Rom.* 2.38–40, Val. Max. 9.6.1, Festus 496 L, Propertius 4.4.
88 Livy 1.12–13, D.H. *Ant. Rom.* 2.41–6, Plut. *Rom.* 18–20.
89 Livy 1.14.1–3, D.H. *Ant. Rom.* 2.51–2, Plut. *Rom.* 23.1–2.
90 Livy 1.16, cf. Ov. *Fast.* 2.475–510, D.H. *Ant. Rom.* 2.56.2 with 2.63.3–4, Plut. *Rom.* 27.3 and 28.
91 Ov. *Met.* 14.805–28, cf. Ennius *Ann.* 65–6.
92 D.H. *Ant. Rom.* 2.56.3–4, cf. Livy 1.16.4.
93 Plut. *Pompey* 25.
94 D.H. *Ant. Rom.* 2.26.5.
95 Livy 10.32.12.
96 As cited in D.H. *Ant. Rom.* 1.72.5 (= Callias 564F5).

BIBLIOGRAPHICAL
NOTE

—— ·•· ——

Three good dictionaries of classical mythology are currently available in English. The oldest is that of Pierre Grimal, which was first published in Paris in 1951; it has been issued in two English editions, as *The Dictionary of Classical Mythology* (Blackwell, Oxford, 1986, a full translation with references to ancient sources) and as *The Penguin Dictionary of Classical Mythology* (1991, abridged with some alterations, without references). It is useful and generally reliable, if perhaps somewhat dull. An edition of Edward Tripp's *Meridian Handbook of Classical Mythology* has recently been published in Britain as *Collins Dictionary of Classical Mythology* (2002). It concentrates for the most part on myths from the more accessible sources and main ancient anthologies, but is broader in its range of reference than the other two dictionaries in some other respects, for it includes entries on peoples, places and authors. Readers who have no special knowledge of the ancient world may find it particularly helpful for that reason. Jenny March's *Cassell Dictionary of Classical Mythology* (London, 1998) is scholarly and accessible, a model of its kind; it is both enjoyable to dip into and useful as work of reference. Various other dictionaries have been published. William Smith's *Dictionary of Greek and Roman Biography* (3 vols, London, 1844) is an old war-horse that deserves an honourable mention; and Richard Stoneman's little dictionary, *Greek Mythology* (London, 1991) departs from the common pattern by including entries on post-classical legend and folklore. We must next turn to two authors who have produced well-known surveys of Greek myth in two volumes. Carl Kerényi's *Gods of the Greeks* (London, 1951) and *Heroes of the Greek* (London, 1974) are works of strong individual character founded on an exhaustive knowledge of the ancient sources. Robert Graves's Penguin guide, *The Greek Myths* (first published in 1955), makes attractive reading and conveys much solid information, but should be approached with extreme caution nonetheless. Although Graves was certainly well acquainted with the relevant ancient sources, he tended to run together material of diverse origin and value when constructing his summaries of the various bodies of myth, and the resulting narratives are by no means free of eccentric errors and arbitrary fancies. As for the explanatory notes, they are either the greatest single contribution that has ever been made to the interpretation of Greek myth or else a farrago of cranky nonsense; I fear that it would be impossible to find any classical scholar who would agree with the former diagnosis.

To proceed to works of a more academic character, Timothy Gantz's *Early Greek Myth: A Guide to the Literary and Artistic Sources* (Baltimore and London, one volume in cloth, 1993, two volumes in paperback, 1996) can be recommended unreservedly as a comprehensive guide to the early mythical tradition; anyone who wants to trace the early development of Greek myths in the original sources will find it invaluable. Although it concentrates on archaic myth in particular, as the title would suggest, it takes due account of the standard later tradition as reported by authors such as Apollodorus and Hyginus; the artistic record is primarily referred to in so far as it provides the earliest evidence for myths or for specific variants or motifs. Full and detailed information on the ancient artistic representations of myths and figures from myth can be found in the magnificent volumes of the *Lexicon Iconographicum Mythologiae Classicae* (1981 onward). The various publications of Karl Schefold (some of which have been translated into English, see below) can also be very helpful in this regard. The other main reference works on Greek myth are German works of long standing. An exhaustive analysis of the entire corpus of Greek heroic mythology is provided by Carl Robert in *Die griechische Heldensage* (3 vols, Berlin, 1920–6; = *Griechische Mythologie* 2, and originally undertaken as a revision of the work of that title by Ludwig Preller). Alas, it has no index. The most comprehensive articles on individual figures from Greek mythology are to be found in two German encyclopaedias, Roscher's Lexicon, which is devoted exclusively to classical mythology, and the great *Realencyclopädie*, which is a general encyclopaedia of classical civilization. The former (W.H. Roscher (ed.), *Ausführliches Lexikon der griechischen und römischen Mythologie*) was published in six volumes with four supplements at Leipzig from 1884 to 1937. The articles tended to get longer and more detailed as the work progressed. Although the interpretations (especially in the earlier volumes) often appeal to outdated theories of nature-symbolism, the articles provide very useful and often very thorough surveys of the mythological traditions associated with major and minor figures from classical myth and legend. The corresponding articles in the eighty volumes of 'Pauly–Wissowa' (*Paulys Realencyclopädie der classischen Altertumswissenschaft*, Stuttgart, 1894–1963) naturally show some variation in their comprehensiveness and quality, but this is generally one of the richest resources available to the mythologist. The abridged version, *Der Kleine Pauly*, edited in five volumes by W. Sontheimer and K. Ziegler (Stuttgart, 1964), can also be very helpful, especially in hunting references.

There is no end to the number of books that have been written on Greek mythology. As two introductory work of rather different kinds, I would recommend Fritz Graf, *Greek Mythology: An Introduction* (Baltimore, 1993) and G.S. Kirk *The Nature of Greek Myth* (Penguin, Harmondsworth, 1974). I have otherwise picked out a small selection of books in the hope of providing profitable suggestions for further reading, especially to those who have no special knowledge of the field.

Bremmer, J. (ed.), *Interpretations of Greek Mythology*, London, 1987
Bremmer, J. and Horsfall, N.M., *Roman Myth and Mythography*, London, 1987
Burkert, W., *Structure and History in Greek Mythology and Ritual*, Berkeley, 1979
—— *Greek Religion*, Cambridge, Mass., 1985
Buxton, R.C.A., *Imaginary Greece: The Contexts of Mythology*, Cambridge, 1994

Buxton, R.C.A. (ed.), *From Myth to Reason?*, Oxford, 1999

Carpenter, T.H., *Art and Myth in Ancient Greece*, London, 1991

Dalley, S., *Myths from Mesopotamia*, Oxford, 1989

Détienne, M., *The Gardens of Adonis*, Hassocks, 1977

—— *The Creation of Mythology*, Chicago, 1986

Détienne, M. and Vernant, J.-P., *Cunning Intelligence in Greek Culture and Society*, Hassocks, 1978

Dodds, E.R., *The Greeks and the Irrational*, Berkeley, 1951

Dowden, K., *Death and the Maiden: Girl's Initiation Rites in Greek Mythology*, London, 1989

—— *The Uses of Greek Mythology*, London, 1992

Edmunds, L., *Approaches to Greek Myth*, Baltimore/London, 1990

Forbes-Irving, P., *Metamorphosis in Greek Myth*, Oxford, 1990

Guthrie, W.K.C., *The Greeks and their Gods*, London, 1950

Kirk, G.S., *Myth: Its Meaning and Functions in Ancient and Other Cultures*, Cambridge, 1970

Lefkowitz, M.L., *Women in Greek Myth*, London, 1986

Lloyd-Jones, H., *The Justice of Zeus*, Berkeley, 1971

Lyons, D., *Gender and Immortality: Heroines in Ancient Greek Myth and Cult*, Princeton, 1997

March, J.H., *The Creative Poet: Studies on the Treatment of Myth in Greek Poetry*, London, 1987

Nilsson, M.P., *The Mycenaean Origin of Greek Mythology*, Berkeley, 1932

Otto, W.F., *The Homeric Gods*, London, 1956

Schefold, K., *Myth and Legend in Early Greek Art*, London, 1966

—— *Gods and Heroes in Late Archaic Greek Art*, London, 1992

Sourvinou-Inwood, C., *'Reading' Greek Death*, Oxford 1995

Sissa, Giulia, *The Daily Life of the Greek Gods*, Stanford, 2000

Vernant, J.P., *Myth and Society in Ancient Greece*, Hassocks, 1980

—— *Myth and Thought among the Greeks*, London, 1992

—— *Mortals and Immortals: Collected Essays*, London, 1991

Vernant, J.-P., and Vidal-Naquet, P., *Myth and Tragedy in Ancient Greece*, New York, 1988

Veyne, P., *Did the Greeks Believe in their Myths?*, Chicago, 1986

West, M.L., *The Hesiodic Catalogue of Women*, Oxford, 1965 [on the structure and origins of the heroic genealogies]

—— *The East Face of Helicon*, Oxford, 1997 [on Eastern influences on Greek myth]

GENEALOGICAL
TABLES

———— •◆• ————

Table 1   The first gods and the origins of the Olympians

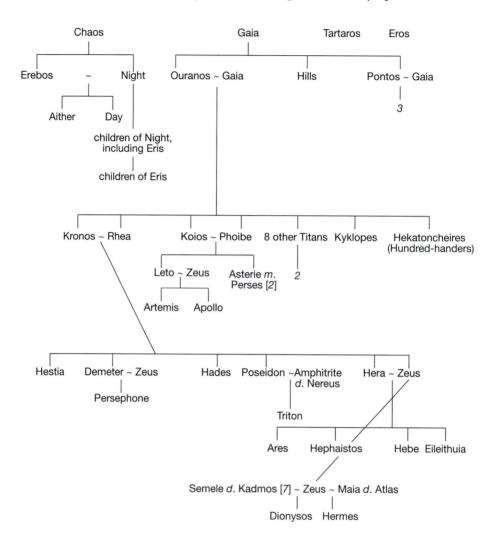

Table 2 Descendants of the Titans

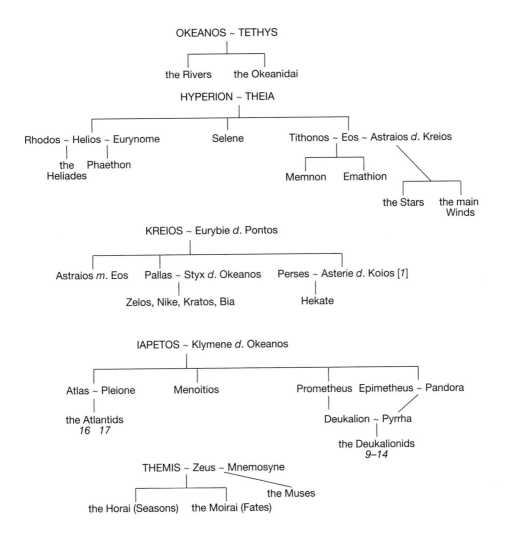

Table 3 The descendants of Pontos and Gaia

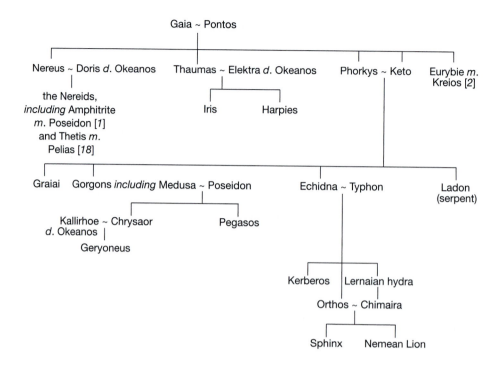

Table 4   Inachids 1: The early Inachids in Argos and Egypt

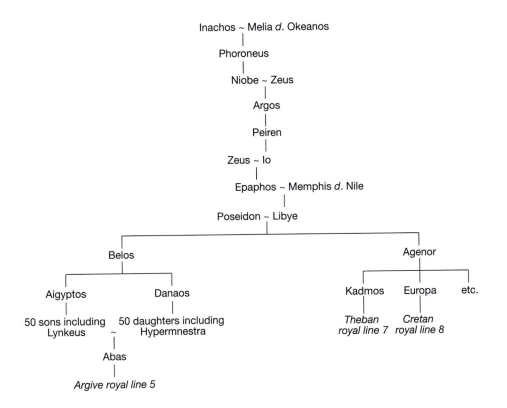

Table 5   Inachids 2: The descendants of Danaos in the Argolid

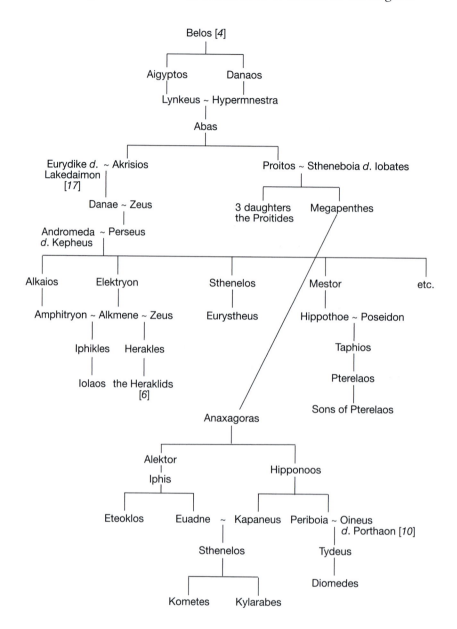

Table 6   Inachids 3: The Heraklids

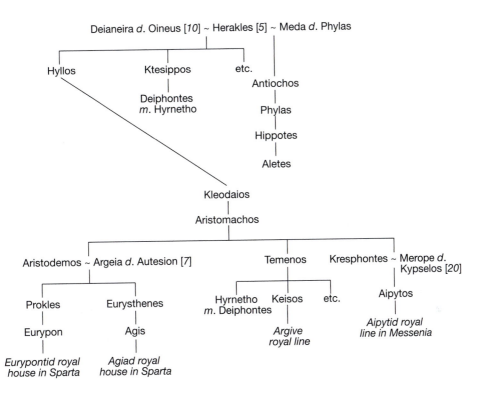

Table 7   Inachids 4: The descendants of Kadmos at Thebes

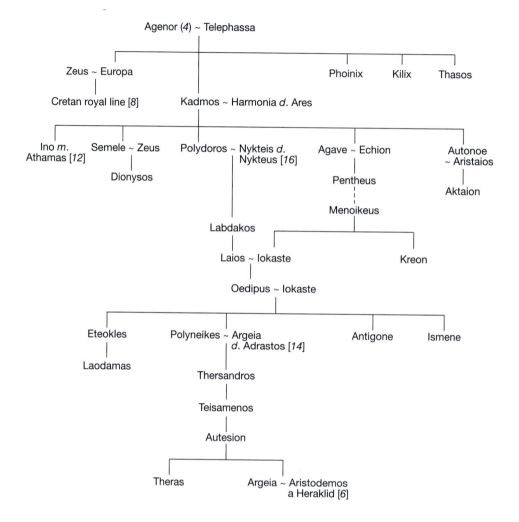

Table 8   Inachids 5: The descendants of Europa in Crete

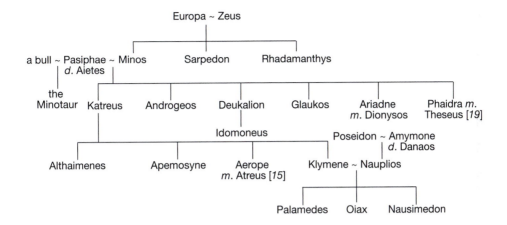

Table 9 Deukalionids 1: The early Deukalionids

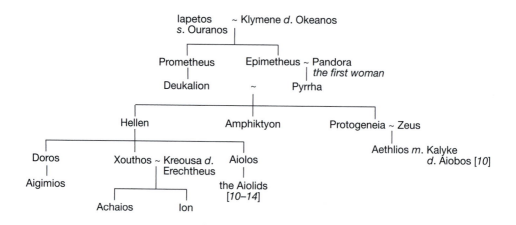

Table 10   Deukalionids 2: The Aetolian royal family

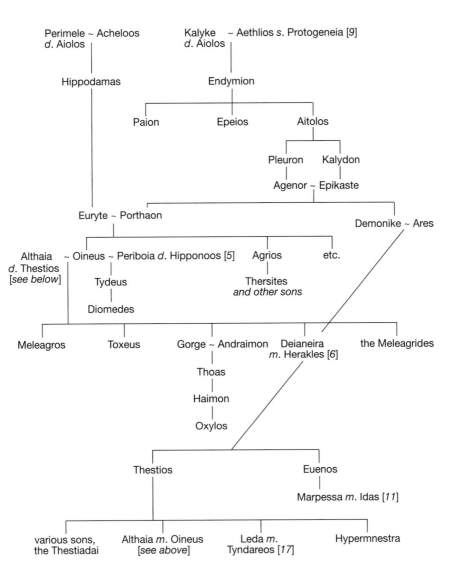

Table 11 Deukalionids 3: Descendants of Aiolos in Messenia and Thessaly

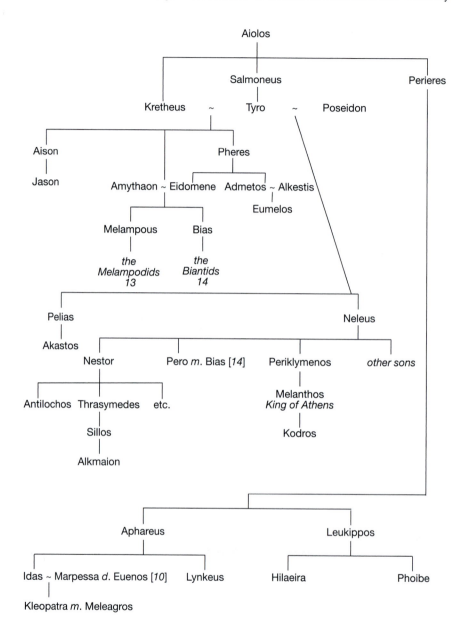

Table 12   Deukalionids 4: Further descendants of Aiolos

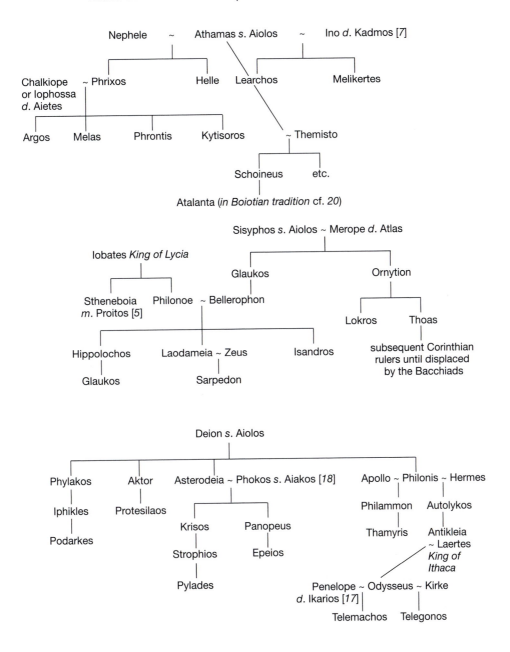

Table 13 Deukalionids 5: The descendants of Melampous

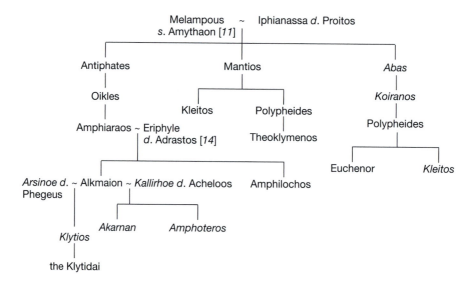

Note: The names marked in italics are those not mentioned by Homer, see pp. 429–30.

Table 14 Deukalionids 6: The descendants of Bias

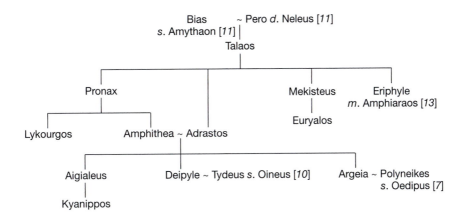

Table 15   The Pelopids

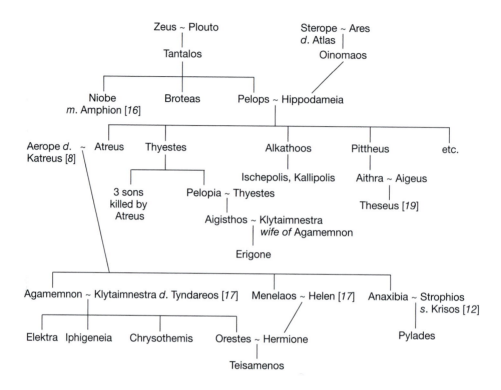

Table 16   Atlantids 1: The Trojan royal family and the descendants of Alkyone

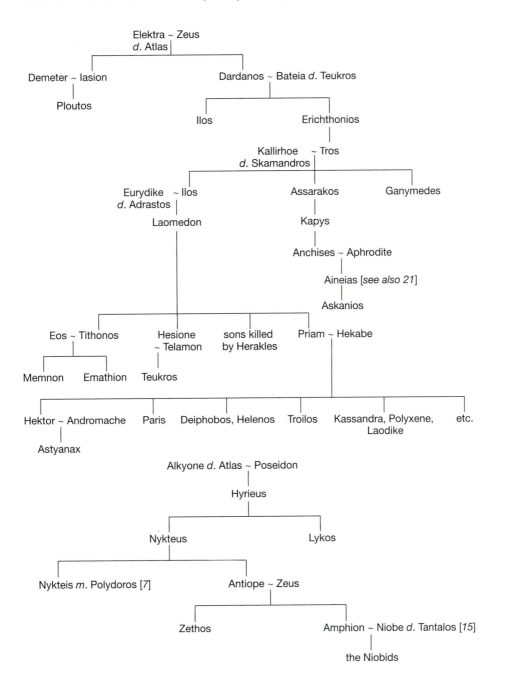

Table 17   Atlantids 2: The early Spartan royal family

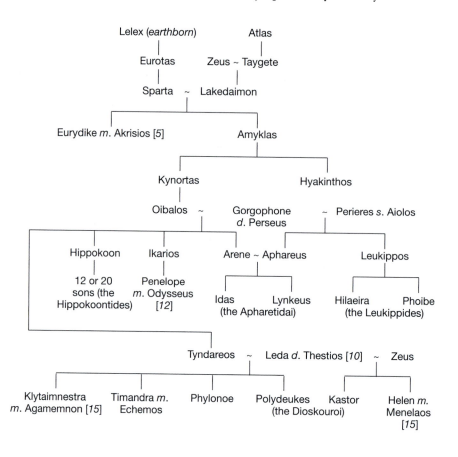

Table 18   The Asopids

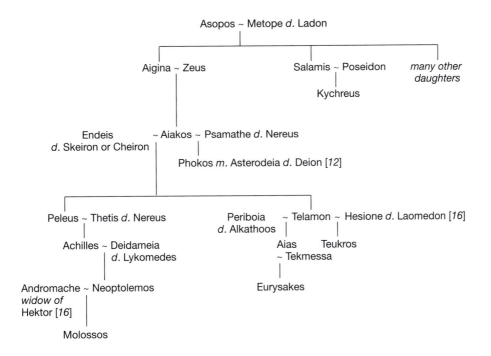

Table 19 The kings of Athens

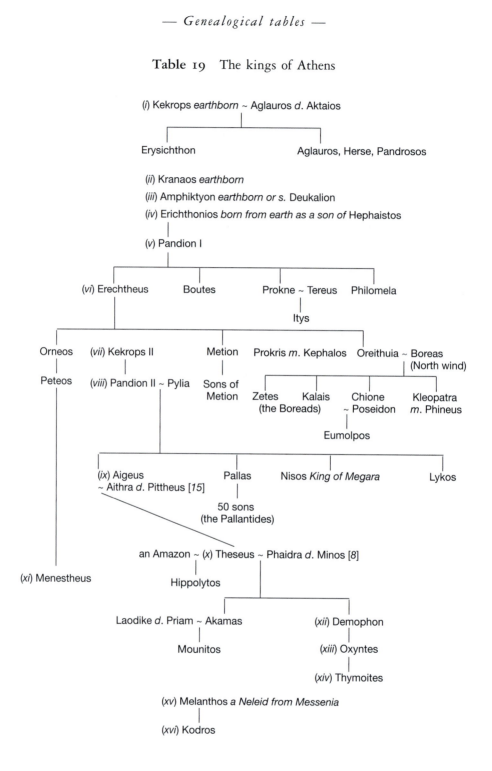

(*i*) Kekrops *earthborn* ~ Aglauros *d.* Aktaios

Erysichthon

Aglauros, Herse, Pandrosos

(*ii*) Kranaos *earthborn*

(*iii*) Amphiktyon *earthborn or s.* Deukalion

(*iv*) Erichthonios *born from earth as a son of* Hephaistos

(*v*) Pandion I

(*vi*) Erechtheus   Boutes   Prokne ~ Tereus   Philomela

Itys

Orneos   (*vii*) Kekrops II   Metion   Prokris *m.* Kephalos   Oreithuia ~ Boreas

Peteos   (*viii*) Pandion II ~ Pylia   Sons of Metion   Zetes   Kalais   Chione   Kleopatra

(the Boreads)   ~ Poseidon   *m.* Phineus

(North wind)

Eumolpos

(*ix*) Aigeus   Pallas   Nisos *King of Megara*   Lykos

~ Aithra *d.* Pittheus [15]

50 sons

(the Pallantides)

an Amazon ~ (*x*) Theseus ~ Phaidra *d.* Minos [8]

(*xi*) Menestheus   Hippolytos

Laodike *d.* Priam ~ Akamas   (*xii*) Demophon

Mounitos   (*xiii*) Oxyntes

(*xiv*) Thymoites

(*xv*) Melanthos *a Neleid from Messenia*

(*xvi*) Kodros

Table 20 The Arcadian royal family

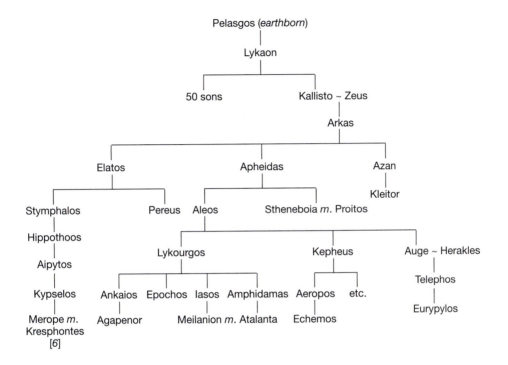

Table 21   The Trojan ancestry of Romulus

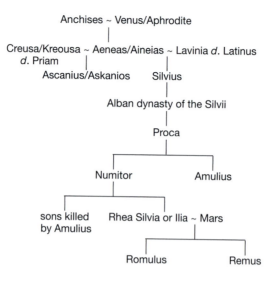

INDEXES

——— •◆• ———

The names of characters from Greek myth are almost always given in their original Greek form. Although the Latinized forms may be more familiar to many readers, no confusion need arise if the following distinctions are kept in mind:

- The Greek consonant kappa (representing a *k* or hard *c*) is transliterated as a *k* rather than as a *c* as in Latin usage. 'Kyklopes' and 'Kanake' will thus be found rather than 'Cyclopes' and 'Canace'.
- The Greek diphthongs *ai* and *oi* (pronounced as in 'aisle' and 'coin') are not transliterated into *ae* and *oe* as in Latin usage. 'Aithra' and 'Oineus' will thus be found rather than 'Aethra' and 'Oeneus'.
- The Greek diphthongs – or strictly speaking, digraphs – *ei* and *ou* (pronounced roughly as in 'feint' and 'boule' in classical Attic) are not transliterated into long *i* and *u* as in Latin usage. 'Teiresias' will thus be found rather than 'Tiresias', and 'Boutes' rather than 'Butes'.
- The final *–os* often found in men's names, e.g. Kadmos and Anios, is not represented as *–us* as in Latin usage.

For everyday purposes and in ordinary conversation, it is neither customary nor desirable for English speakers to attempt to pronounce Greek names exactly as they would have been pronounced in classical Athens. If a semi-Anglicized pronunciation is adopted, Greek names can easily be pronounced without grave distortion if a few basic rules are observed.

Consonants: The Greek consonant chi is transliterated as *ch*; it represents an aspirated *k* (much as can be heard in the English word 'cat' when it is emphatically enunciated). In Greek names, it may be pronounced as a *k*, as when we speak of Achilles. It should certainly not be pronounced as in 'chess'. The Greek *g* (gamma) is properly a hard *g* as in 'game'.

Vowels: There are no mute vowels in Greek words. In particular, a final *-e* and the *e* in final *–es* should always be sounded as a long *e*, as when we speak of Aphrodite and Socrates. In Greek, *ae*, *oe* and *oo* (as found, for instance, in the names of Pasiphae, Kallirhoe and Acheloos) are never diphthongs, and each vowel should be sounded separately. In names, *ai* will usually be a diphthong; as such (e.g. in the names of Aigyptos and Andraimon), it may be pronounced as in 'high'. The diphthong *eu* may be pronounced as in 'euphony', and *au* as in 'how'; the pronunciations of other diphthongs are indicated just above in the notes on Greek and Latin forms.

MAIN INDEX

———— •◆• ————

THE GREAT OLYMPIAN GODS

————— •◆• —————

APHRODITE

I Her birth 67, 80, 194–5; her nature and origin 195–6; her associates Eros, Himeros, Pothos and Peitho 196–8; her love for Adonis 198–200; how she seduced Anchises to father Aineias 200–1; her husband, lovers and children 201–2; her image in works of art 202–3.

II She distracts *Aietes* to enable the Argonauts to flee 392; aids the suitor of *Atalanta* 546–7, causes the destruction of Atalanta and her husband 547; rescues the Argonaut *Boutes* from the sea and transfers him to Sicily 395; is wounded in battle by *Diomedes* 461, and punishes him by causing his wife to be unfaithful 487; causes *Eos* to be constantly falling in love 48; causes the death of *Glaukos* of Corinth by sending his horses mad 432; gives a gift to *Harmonia* at her wedding 297; mother of *Hermaphroditos* 164; causes the ruin of *Hippolytos* by causing his stepmother Phaidra to fall in love with him 358–9; abducts *Kephalos*, son of Eos, to make him her temple-servant 47; transforms *Kerastai* (Cerastae) of Cyprus into bulls 574; causes the daughters of *Kinyras* to become prostitutes 574; afflicts the *Lemnian women* with an evil smell 384; arranges for *Medeia* to fall in love with Jason 197, 390; inspires *Myrrha* with an incestuous love for her father 198; reared by *Nereus* 51; her love for *Nerites* 56; incites women of Thrace against *Orpheus* 553; fosters the daughters

of *Pandareos* 57; confers grace and allure on *Pandora* 95; selected by *Paris* in his judgement of the three goddesses 447, and helps him to win the love of Helen 445; rejuvenates *Phaon* 202; becomes the mother of *Priapos* 222; brings a statue to life as a bride for *Pygmalion* 574–5; transforms *Selemnos* into a river 568; transforms the *Sirens* into their monstrous form 496; punishes *Tyndareos* by causing his daughters to be faithless 526.

APOLLO

I His birth 188–9; his nature, name and origins 142–4; he establishes his oracle at Delphi 144–6; he kills Tityos for molesting his mother 147–8; his association with the Hyperboreans 148–9; he engages in a love affair with Koronis, avenges her infidelity and rescues their unborn son, the healing-god Asklepios 149–51; he is enslaved to Admetos for killing the Kyklopes and helps him in various ways 151–2; he abducts Kyrene and fathers the rustic god Aristaios 152–3; he meets with frustration or unhappiness in love 153–6; he joins with his sister Artemis in killing the Niobids and engages in a musical contest with Marsyas 157–8.

II He kills *Achilles* or helps Paris to kill him 468; saves *Agenor* from Achilles and assumes his form 455; helps *Alkathoos* to fortify the acropolis at Megara 567; agrees that *Alkmaion* should kill his mother 327; kills the *Aloadai* 91; fathers *Anios* and instructs him in divination 569–70; he pursues *Daphne*, but she escapes through a transformation 155; kills *Eurytos* 250; shoots the Giant *Ephialtes* 90; provides musical accompaniment at the wedding of *Harmonia* 297; transfers *Hekabe* to Lycia 479; identified with Helios 43; arms *Herakles* with a bow 257, fights with him for the Delphian tripod 273, is confronted by him at Pylos 278; tracks down the infant *Hermes* to recover his stolen cattle 162; courts *Hestia* 140; loves *Hyakinthos* but accidentally kills him 155–6; rapes Kreousa to father *Ion* 407–8; fathers *Iamos* and instructs him in prophecy 548–9; reveals Anaphe to *Jason* and the Argonauts 397; grants prophetic powers to *Kassandra* in return for her favours but condemns her to be disbelieved when she refuses to yield to him 154; causes the destruction of the grave of *Kyknos* 283; his love for *Kyparissos* 571; helps to build the wall of Troy for *Laomedon*, but sends a plague when his fee is withheld 523; avenges the death of his son *Linos* 250; he competes with Idas for *Marpessa*, but she rejects him when Zeus grants her the choice 154; instructs *Melampous* in prophecy 426; shoots *Meleagros* 417; fathers *Melaneus* 412; causes the death of *Neoptolemos* at Delphi 491; leader of the *Muses* 207; agrees that *Orestes* should kill his mother 510 and advises him when he is persecuted by the Erinyes 511; helps to bring about the birth of *Orion* 561, contrives his destruction 564; gives *Orpheus* a lyre and instructs him in music 551; causes the destruction of *Patroklos* 464; fathers *Philammon* 435; punishes *Phlegyas* and the Phlegyans for attacking Delphi 560; tricked by *Sinope* 537; punishes the spring-nymph *Telphousa* for deceiving him 144; flees from *Typhon* 85.

ARES

I His birth 79; his nature and associates 168–70; becomes husband or lover of Aphrodite 201–2, their children 169.

II He causes the death of *Adonis* 199; *Aietes* dedicates the golden fleece to him 378–9, Aietes receives dragon's teeth from him 296; he fathers *Alkippe* by Aglauros 365; is imprisoned in a jar by the *Aloadai* 92; fathers children by *Demodike* 413; is wounded by *Diomedes* 461, and complains to Zeus 168; helps in the defeat of the *Giants* 90; kills *Halirrhothios* for raping his daughter Alkippe and is prosecuted for murder at the Areiopagos 365–6; *Hephaistos* traps him in adultery with Aphrodite 201; is wounded by *Herakles* at Pylos 278; suffers humiliation when he fights Herakles to avenge the death of his son Kyknos 282; is angered when *Kadmos* kills his Theban dragon 295–6, but is subsequently reconciled with him 297 and finally transfers him and his wife to the Isles of the Blessed 300; was perhaps the true father of *Meleagros* 413; *Menoikeus* kills himself to allay his anger over the death of the Theban dragon 330; gives a golden chariot and winged horses to his son *Oinomaos* 503; frees *Thanatos* (Death) after he is tied up by Sisyphos 431.

ARTEMIS

I Her birth 188–9; her nature and origin 186–8; her early deeds and her relationship with her companions 190–2; tales of vengeance 192.

II Punishes *Admetos* for failing to sacrifice to her 151; sends a boar against *Adonis* 199; inflicts a grisly death on *Aktaion* for seeing her naked 299; causes the death of the *Aloadai* for making advances to her and Hera 92; helps *Arethousa* to escape the advances of the river-god Alpheios 42; kills *Ariadne* on behalf of Dionysos 348; sends a golden lamb into the flocks of *Atreus* 506; kills *Bouphagos* 192; *Broteas* sinks into madness after failing to honour her 503; the travails of her companion *Britomartis* 191–2; the *Cerynitian hind* is dedicated to her by Taygete 260, she threatens to remove it from Herakles 259; kills *Chione* for an impertinence 192; identified with *Diana* 193; helps in the defeat of the *Giants* 90; transforms *Hippe* for ceasing to honour her and hunt with her 191, 410; *Hippolytos* honours her at the expense of Aphrodite 358–9, Artemis/Diana asks Asklepios to revive the dead Hippolytos and transfers him to Italy 359; *Iphigeneia* is brought to sacrifice to appease her anger 447–8, but is saved by her and transferred abroad 447, 512–13; punishes her companion *Kallisto* after she becomes pregnant by Zeus 191, 540–1; kills *Kenchrias* 536; kills *Koronis* on behalf of Apollo 149; shoots *Maira* for ceasing to accompany her in the hunt after becoming pregnant 191; transforms the sisters of *Meleagros* into birds 417; joins with Apollo in killing the *Niobids* 157; sends the Calydonian boar to punish *Oineus* for failing to sacrifice to her 516; causes the death of her hunting-companion *Orion* 563–4; confers immortality on *Phylonoe* 525; helps *Prokris* 373; identified with *Selene* 46; turns *Siproites* into a woman 192; saves *Taygete* from being raped 260; kills *Tityos* 148; flees from *Typhon* 85.

ATHENA

I   She is born from the head of Zeus after he has swallowed her mother Metis 77–8, 181; her nature, origin and functions 180–1, 182–4; her special relationship with Athens and her Athenian foster-son Erichthonios 184–6.

II   Judges or interferes in the contest between *Aias*, son of Telamon, and Odysseus for the arms of Achilles 469, and sends Aias mad afterwards 471; causes the humiliation of the lesser *Aias* at the funeral games for Achilles 456, is angered by his sacrilegious behaviour during the sack of Troy 478, 481–2, and therefore causes the Greek leaders to quarrel 482–3 and a storm to be sent against the returning fleet 485–6; gives dragon's teeth to Aietes 296, 390; uses the *aigis* 74, 182; enters into a weaving-contest with *Arachne* and transforms her into a spider 184; guides Argos in the construction of the *Argo* 382; gives

Gorgon's blood to *Asklepios* to enable him to heal and revive people 61; helps *Bellerophon* to tame Pegasos 183, 434; purifies the *Danaids* 234; aids *Diomedes* in battle at Troy 461; gives *Erichthonios* a phial of Gorgon's blood 61; helps in the defeat of the *Giants* 90; gives *Harmonia* a robe at her wedding 297; tricks *Hektor* into a fatal confrontation with Achilles 465; rewards the *Heliadai* for being the first to pay honour to her 182; saves *Herakles* from killing his father 253, provides him with a bird-scarer 260, assists him in the Underworld 268, fetches him to assist in fighting the Giants 277, helps him in battle at Pylos 278, helps him to defeat Ares 283; incites Tydeus to kill *Ismene* 324–5; helps *Kadmos* by sowing dragon's teeth 296; punishes the daughters of *Kekrops* for opening the chest in which Erichthonios had been placed by her 365; gives *Kepheus* a lock of the Gorgon's hair to protect his city 547; she invents the flute and discards it, but it is recovered by *Marsyas* 157, 183; transforms *Medusa* into a monster 61; in fable of *Momos* 27; helps *Odysseus* during his return voyage and after his arrival in Ithaca 497–500; presides at the trial of *Orestes* and acquits him with her casting vote 511; creates the palladion in commemoration of *Pallas* after accidentally killing her 183; teaches handicrafts to the daughters of *Pandareos* 57; adorns and teaches *Pandora* 93, 95; is judged for her beauty by *Paris* 443; guides *Perseus* to the Graiai and helps him to acquire the Gorgon's head 239–40, receives the head from him after his return 242; competes with *Poseidon* for possession of Attica 102–3, and of Troizen 103; blinds *Teiresias* for seeing her naked, but compensates him by granting him the gift of prophecy 330; urges *Telemachos* to take action against Penelope's suitors 511; tells *Theseus* to leave Ariadne on Naxos for Dionysos 347; reared by *Triton* 182; plans to confer immortality on the dying *Tydeus*, but is deterred 320; recovers the heart

of *Zagreus* 35; plots a revolt against
Zeus 67, 88.

DEMETER

I Born as a child of Kronos and Rhea 67;
is swallowed at birth by Kronos but later
vomited up again 68; becomes a wife or
mistress of Zeus and bears Persephone to
him 78; seeks to recover Persephone after
she is abducted by Hades 125–8 and
agrees to share her with Hades 128; stays
at Eleusis and reveals her mysteries
127–8; sends Triptolemos to spread her
gift of grain 131–3; her love affair with
Iasion, who fathers Ploutos by her 132.

II She transforms *Askalabos* into a gecko
129; punishes *Askalaphos* for revealing
that Persephone has eaten in the
Underworld 129; punishes *Charnabon* for
plotting the destruction of Triptolemos
132; reveals her mysteries in Argos after
Chrysanthis, the wife of the king, reveals
that Persephone had been abducted there
129; is interrupted when she tries to
confer immortality on the infant
Demophoon 128; afflicts *Erysichthon* (or
Triopas) with insatiable hunger to punish
him for desecrating her grove 133;
founds rites to purify *Herakles* before he
is initiated at Eleusis 269; receives a
snake as her attendant after it has been
reared by *Kychreus* on Salamis 535;
transforms *Minthe* into a herb 129;
absent-mindedly eats a shoulder of *Pelops*
503; gives the first fig-tree to *Phytalos*
129; transforms negligent companions of
Persephone into Sirens 496; her part in the
myth of *Zagreus* 35.

DIONYSOS

I His birth 170–1; his childhood and
nurses 171–2; he exacts vengeance on
mortals who reject him and his rites
173–5; his rites and attendants 175–6; he
grants the gift of wine to Ikarios in Attica
with unfortunate consequences for him
and his daughter Erigone 176–7; some
pirates come to a bad end when they try
to abduct him 177–9; his expedition to
India 179; his wife and loves 179–80.

II He punishes *Akrisios* 175; his love for
Ampelos 179; teaches *Amphiktyon* to water
wine 367; grants special powers to the
daughters of *Anios* 570; drives *Antiope*
mad 304; takes *Ariadne* as his wife 179,
347–8; afflicts the daughters of *Eleuther*
with madness 175; helps in the defeat of
the *Giants* 90; persuades *Hephaistos* to
return to Olympos 166; is tended as an
infant by *Ino and Athamas* 172, 421;
afflicts the Calydonians with madness to
punish the sacrilege of *Koresos and
Kallirhoe* 569; sends *Lykourgos* mad and
causes his death as punishment for
persecuting him and his nurses 173; is
tended as an infant by *Makris* 395;
grants *Midas* the power to turn things to
gold 214; is tended as an infant by the
nymphs of Nysa 172; punishes the
Minyades for rejecting his rites 174;
instructs *Oineus* in the cultivation of vines
after sleeping with his wife Althaia to
father Deianeira 413–14; provokes the
death of *Orpheus* 553; contrives the death
of *Pentheus* to punish him for scorning his
rites 173–4; is repelled by *Perseus* when
he attacks Argos with the Sea-women
175; competes with *Poseidon* for
possession of Naxos 503; fathers *Priapos*
222; afflicts the daughters of *Proitos* or
the Argive women with madness 174–5,
428–9; attended by *Satyrs and Seilenoi*
175, 212; punishes *Telephos* for neglecting
his cult 446; protects Tanagran women
from a *Triton* 106; his unconventional
mythology in the myth of *Zagreus* 35.

HEPHAISTOS

I His birth 79, 165; his nature and origin
164–6; he is thrown down from Olympos
by Hera or Zeus and brought back again
by Dionysos 165–6; his achievements as
a craftsman 166–7; his marriage and
children 166–7.

II He makes armour for *Achilles* 464;
provides *Aietes* with bronze-footed bulls
167, 390; traps *Aphrodite* in bed with
Ares 201; makes an early temple of
Apollo at Delphi 167; makes a crown that
Dionysos passes on to *Ariadne* 347; helps

to bring *Athena* to birth from the head of
Zeus 181; brings about the birth of an
earthborn son *Erichthonios* while trying to
make love to Athena 184–5; helps in the
defeat of the *Giants* 90; made a bird-
scarer used by *Herakles* 260; made the
necklace of *Harmonia* 297; made the
golden cup that enabled *Helios* to travel
back to the east on the Ocean 44; made
the weapon that caused the death of
Odysseus 500; makes an underground
horse for *Oinopion* 563; provides the
blinded *Orion* with a guide 563; made
the golden dog that was stolen by
Pandareos 502; fashions *Pandora* from
moistened earth 93–6; makes a sword for
Peleus 534; made a sceptre which was
passed down in the family of *Pelops* 508;
chains *Prometheus* to a rock 95; forces
Skamandros to return to his courses 43;
makes the bronze man *Talos* to guard the
shores of Crete 396; flees from *Typhon* 85;
identified with *Volcanus* 167.

HERA

I   Born as child of Kronos and Rhea 67; is
swallowed at birth by Kronos but later
vomited up again 68; marries Zeus and
bears Ares, Hebe and Eileithuia to him
78–9; bears Hephaistos as another child
by Zeus or as a fatherless child 79; her
nature as the goddess of marriage 134–5;
local traditions relating to her marriage
or first union with Zeus 135–8; myths of
revenge 138–9.

II She causes the death of the Aeginetans in
anger at Zeus' love affair with *Aigina*
531; molested by one of the *Aloadai* 92;
transforms *Antigone*, daughter of
Laomedon 139; helps the *Argonauts*
during their return voyage 394; deprives
Echo of the power of independent speech
217; molested by a *Giant* 89, raped by a
Giant 88; throws her deformed son
Hephaistos down from Olympos 165–6;
delays the birth of *Herakles* to ensure that
Eurystheus becomes king of Mycenae
instead of him 247–8, persecutes
Herakles 249, 252, 254, 264, 267, 276,
wounded by him at Pylos 278, finally

reconciled with him 286; sends *Ino and
Athamas* mad for rearing Dionysos 172,
421; persuades *Hypnos* to lull Zeus to
sleep 30; places the transformed *Io* under
guard 228–9, sends a gadfly after her,
causing her to wander to Egypt 229–31,
incites the Kouretes to abduct her son
Epaphos 232; *Iris* is often presented as
her special messenger 57; *Ixion* comes to
a bad end after attempting to seduce her
554; *Jason* wins her favour by an act of
benevolence 382, she contrives that
Pelias sends him to fetch the golden
fleece 381, arranges that Medeia shall fall
in love with him 390; grants an easeful
death to *Kleobis and Biton* 559; rears the
Lernaian hydra to be a danger to Herakles
63, sends a crab to assist it against
Herakles 258; transforms *Kallisto* to cause
her death after she becomes pregnant by
Zeus 541; tries to prevent *Leto* from
giving birth to her children 189; expels
Makris from Euboea for rearing Dionysos
395; transfers *Merops* to the heavens as an
eagle 572; persuades the *Muses* to
compete with the Sirens in a singing-
contest 207; rears the *Nemean lion* to be a
danger to Herakles 64, 256; *Okeanos and
Tethys* rear her under the Ocean 40;
confers benefits on the daughters of
Pandareos 57; is judged for her beauty by
Paris 443, sends storm-winds against his
ship 445; sends a snake against *Philoktetes*
449; competes with *Poseidon* for
possession of Argos 103; causes *Priapos* to
be born deformed 222; afflicts the
daughters of *Proitos* with madness 428–9;
contrives the destruction of *Semele* to put
an end to her love affair with Zeus
170–1; sends *Side*, wife of Orion, to the
Underworld 562; sends the *Sphinx*
against Thebes 307, 309; blinds *Teiresias*
329–30; brings *Typhon* to birth as a
fatherless child 84; incites the Titans to
attack *Zagreus* 35; plots a revolt against
Zeus 67, 82.

HERMES

I   His birth 161, 519; his nature, functions
and origin 158–61; he rustles the cattle

of Apollo as a new-born child, but is
soon reconciled with him and is allotted
his functions by Zeus 161–3.

II Warns *Aigisthos* not to court
Klytaimnestra or harm Agamemnon 508;
transfers *Alkmene* to the Isles of the
Blessed 352; gives a lyre to *Amphion* 305;
rapes *Apemosyne* on Rhodes 354; rescues
Ares after he is imprisoned by the
Alaoadai 92; kills *Argos Panoptes* to steal
the transformed Io 229; takes the infant
Arkas to Maia to be reared 541; recovers
the unborn *Asklepios* from his mother's
body 149; sends a golden lamb into the
flocks of *Atreus* 506, visits him to tell
him that the gods support his claim to
the Mycenaean throne 506; bribes *Battos*
not to reveal that he has stolen the cattle
of Apollo and punishes him for his
subsequent perfidy 163; purifies the
Danaids 234; raises *Daphnis* to heaven
211; is sent to *Deukalion* after the great
flood to offer him the choice of what he
most desires 403; conveys the infant
Dionysos to Ino and Athamas 172; is sent
to *Hades* to ask him to release Persephone
128; conveys *Helen* to Egypt 445;
deceives Hera into suckling the infant
Herakles 249, arms him with a sword
257, helps him in the Underworld 268,
sells him at auction to Omphale 274;
father of *Hermaphroditos* 164; seduces
Herse and turns her sister Aglauros to
stone 366; transfers the infant *Ion* to
Delphi 408; tends to displace *Iris* as
messenger of the gods 56–7; identified
with *Mercurius* 164; gives *Odysseus* a herb
to render him invulnerable to Kirke's
spells 494 and is sent to Kalypso to order
her to allow him to return home 497;
plays a part in bringing *Orion* to birth
561; father of *Pan* 215, 501; recovers a
golden dog stolen by *Pandareos* 502;
confers speech and guile on *Pandora* 95;
brings Hera, Athena and Aphrodite to
Mt Ida to be judged by *Paris* 443; brings
a sword to *Peleus* to enable him to defend
himself in the wilds 534; guides the dead
suitors of *Penelope* to the Underworld
112; helps *Perseus* to acquire the Gorgon's

head 239–40, 242; visits *Philemon and
Baucis* 577; sleeps with *Philonis* 435;
provides a marvellous ram for the rescue
of *Phrixos* 378; guides *Priam* to the
Greek camp to see Achilles 158, 465; is
sent by Zeus to interrogate *Prometheus* 96;
restores *Protesilaos* temporarily to the
world of the living 450–1; learns
divinatory arts from the *Thriai* 162; is
sent to compensate *Tros* for the abduction
of Ganymedes 522; recovers Zeus's
tendons after they are removed by *Typhon*
84, flees from Typhon 85.

POSEIDON

I Born as child of Kronos and Rhea 67; is
swallowed at birth by Kronos but later
vomited up again 68; receives the seas as
his special domain when he divides the
universe with Zeus and Hades 76, 98; his
nature as the lord of the seas and of the
earthquake 98–100; as god of horses
101–2; myths in which he competes with
other deities for possession of Greek
lands 102–4; he marries Amphitrite and
fathers Triton and other children by her
104–7; his other children by mortal
mothers 107.

II He causes the death of the lesser *Aias*
485–6; protects *Aineias* 585; sleeps with
Iphimedeia to father the *Aloadai* 91;
rescues *Amymone* from a Satyr and fathers
Nauplios by her 235; fathers the divine
horse *Areion* by mating with Demeter in
animal form 101; prosecutes *Ares* for
killing his son Halirrhothios 365;
competes with *Athena* for possession of
Attica 102–3, of Troizen 103; perhaps
the true father of *Bellerophon* 433, gives
Pegasos to him 434; hides *Centaurs* under
a mountain 259; competes with *Dionysos*
for Naxos 103; causes the death of
Erechtheus for killing his son Eumolpos
369–70; fathers *Eumolpos* by Chione and
rescues him after she throws him into the
sea 370; helps in the defeat of the *Giants*
90; competes with *Helios* for Corinth
103; rescues *Helle* from the Hellespont
and fathers a son by her 379; competes
with *Hera* for Argos 103; wounded by

to fall to the earth when he tries to fly up to heaven on Pegasos 434; his part in the origin of the *cornucopia* or horn of Amaltheia 280; approaches *Danae* in the form of a shower of gold to father Perseus 238; orders the purification of the Danaids 234; causes a great flood in the age of *Deukalion* 403–4; brings *Dionysos* to birth from his thigh after the death of his mother Semele 171; punishes *Endymion* for trying to seduce Hera 411; abducts *Europa* to Crete and fathers Minos and other children by her 337; takes *Ganymedes* up to heaven and becomes his lover 522; fathers *Helen* by mating with Nemesis or Leda in bird form 438–9; ensures that *Helios* gains his special domain 43; throws *Hephaistos* down from Olympos 166; Hera tricks him into granting *Herakles* a lesser inheritance than he had intended 248, he separates Herakles and Apollo when they fight over the Delphian tripod 273, he raises Herakles to heaven 286; fathers *Hermes* by Maia 161, 519, adjudicates when Apollo accuses him of having stolen his cattle 162, grants Hermes his functions 162; allows *Hestia* to remain a virgin and grants her special privileges 140; transforms *Hippe* 410; seduces *Io*, transforms her into a cow and tries to steal the cow from Hera 228–9, fathers Epaphos by her 230–1; strikes *Iasion* with a thunderbolt for engaging in a love affair with Demeter 132, 521; punishes *Ixion* for trying to seduce Hera 118, 554; grants Harmonia to *Kadmos* as a wife 297, sends them to Elysion 300; causes the destruction of *Kaineus* as punishment for his impiety 557; rapes or seduces *Kallisto* to father Arkas 540, turns her into a bear 541, transfers her and her son to the heavens 542; strikes *Kapaneus* with a thunderbolt to punish him for his

impious boasting 320; destroys the family of *Lykaon* 539–40, turns Lykaon into a wolf 540, 542; in fable of *Momos* 27; separates Apollo and Idas when they quarrel over *Marpessa*, and allows her to choose between them 154; strikes *Menoitios* with a thunderbolt 49; advises his son *Minos* on law-making 338, helps him to impose his will on the Athenians 341; takes *Niobe*, daughter of Phoroneus, as his mistress, fathering Argos as his first mortal child 228; turns *Niobe*, daughter of Tantalos, to stone to relieve her sorrow 157, 306; inspires *Oineus* with an incestuous passion for his daughter 418; accidentally causes the death of *Pallas* while she is fighting with Athena 183; consents to Hades' abduction of *Persephone* 127, asks him to return her to the upper world 128, arranges a compromise 128; strikes *Phaethon* with a thunderbolt when he is unable to control the chariot of the Sun 45; visits *Philemon and Baucis* and grants them special privileges 577–8; transfers the *Pleiades* to the heavens 518; allows his son *Polydeukes* to share his immortality with his half-brother Kastor 528; destroys *Salmoneus* and his city as punishment for his impious behaviour 422; grants his son *Sarpedon* an abnormally long life 350; engages in a love affair with *Semele*, but inadvertently causes her death 170–1; abducts *Sinope* 537; punishes *Sisyphos* for revealing his abduction of Aigina 117, 431, 530; adopts the children of *Styx* and orders that divine oaths should be sworn by her waters 49; grants prophetic powers to *Teiresias* 330; transfers the *Teumessian fox* and its pursuer to the heavens 247; courts *Thetis* but marries her to a mortal when warned off by Themis 52; fathers *Zagreus* by Persephone 35.

SELECTIVE GEOGRAPHICAL
INDEX

——— ·◆· ———